EDGE OF ETERNITY

"[FOLLETT] IS A COMMANDING STORYTELLER
WHO HAS TAKEN ON AN IMPOSSIBLY LARGE
TASK AND ACCOMPLISHED IT WITH PASSION,
INTELLIGENCE, AND SKILL."
—*The Washington Post*

"CHARACTERS SO VIVID IT IS
EASY TO KEEP THEM ALIVE IN OUR MIND."
—*The Huffington Post*

"COMPULSIVELY READABLE."
—*The Seattle Times*

"MESMERIZING."
—*Publishers Weekly* (starred review)

PRAISE FOR THE NOVELS OF KEN FOLLETT

Edge of Eternity

"[Follett] is a commanding storyteller who has taken on an impossibly large task and accomplished it with passion, intelligence, and skill. Like its predecessors, *Edge of Eternity* is a solid, rigorously researched work of popular fiction. It's an honest entertainment that brings back vivid, sometimes painful, memories of the not-too-distant past."
— *The Washington Post*

"*Edge of Eternity* is as compulsively readable a mighty page-turner as its two predecessors." — *The Seattle Times*

"Hugely ambitious, the trilogy serves as a massive history lesson as well as an example of good old-fashioned story-telling." — *New York Daily News*

"Follett never forgets he is telling a story. The historical events are the backdrop but the characters are the focal point. Good storytellers know this, and Follett is an excellent one." — *The Huffington Post*

"Mesmerizing . . . flowing with spicy, expertly paced melodrama, character-rich exploits, familial histrionics, and international intrigue." — *Publishers Weekly* (starred review)

"Worth the wait. . . . Once again, Follett has written pitch-perfect popular fiction that readers will devour."
— *Library Journal* (starred review)

"A glorious conclusion to a remarkable trilogy that is wonderful, exhilarating reading for all ages. Fine, fine historical fiction." — Historical Novel Society

"Follett does an outstanding job of interweaving and personalizing complicated narratives set on a multicultural stage."
— *Booklist*

"Follett . . . knows how to turn in a robust yarn without too much slack . . . a well-written entertainment."
— *Kirkus Reviews*

Winter of the World

"This book is truly epic. . . . The reader will probably wish there were a thousand more pages." — *The Huffington Post*

"Some of the biggest-picture fiction being written today."
— *The Seattle Times*

"Follett's real gifts are those of a natural storyteller: swift, cinematic pacing, the ability to juggle multiple narratives coherently, and an eye for the telling detail . . . a consistently compelling portrait of a world in crisis."
— *The Washington Post*

"Gripping . . . powerful."   — *The New York Times*

"Masterfully sweeping stories . . . political intrigue, amorous episodes, suspense, and drama. History comes to life."
— *The Louisville Courier-Journal*

"[Follett] is so good at plotting a story, even one that takes on such a complex topic as the World War II era. That's what makes *Winter of the World* so hard to put down. You want to know what happens next." — The Associated Press

"An entertaining historical soap opera." — *Kirkus Reviews*

"The man tells a story so well. . . . Follett can make things glow with some beautifully written episodes. . . . If you read Volume I, you'll have to read Volume II. And once you read Volume II, you'll be committed to reading Volume III. See you in a couple of years."   — *St. Louis Post-Dispatch*

"Clips along at a brisk pace. . . . He knows how to keep the pages turning and how to make the reader feel a kinship with the characters' struggles. . . . No matter the ultimate destination, readers can expect to savor the journey — and agonize while waiting for the final book to arrive."
— *The Christian Science Monitor*

Fall of Giants

"Follett is masterly in conveying so much drama and historical information so vividly . . . grippingly told."
— *The New York Times Book Review*

"*Fall of Giants*: Follett at his finest. . . sweeping epic that will thrill his fans for hours on end."   — *The Huffington Post*

"Follett conjures the winds of war." — *The Washington Post*

"Tantalizing."   — *Newsday*

"A good read. . . . It's a book that will suck you in, consume you for days or weeks, depending upon how quick a reader you are, then let you out the other side both entertained and educated. That's quite the feat."   — *USA Today*

"Follett apparently intends to give readers the sweeping history of that century in the form of a novel that follows five families — one American, two British, one German, and one Russian. That's a big job. But *Fall of Giants* suggests that Follett is up to the task."   — *St. Louis Post-Dispatch*

"Follett entwines fiction and factual events well. . . . This is a dark novel, motivated by an unsparing view of human nature and a clear-eyed scrutiny of an ideal peace. It is not the least of Follett's feats that the reader finishes this near thousand-page book intrigued and wanting more."
— *Chicago Sun-Times*

"Follett once again creates a world at once familiar and fantastic. . . . A guiltless pleasure, the book is impossible to put down. . . . Empires fall. Heroes rise. Love conquers. After going through a war with these characters, you're left hoping that Follett gets moving with the next giant installment."
— *Time Out*

"*Fall of Giants* grand in scope, scale, and story."
— The Associated Press

"Suspenseful, tightly constructed, sharply characterized, plot-driven."   — *The Seattle Times*

PENGUIN BOOKS

EDGE OF ETERNITY

Ken Follett burst into the book world with *Eye of the Needle*, an award-winning thriller and international bestseller. After several more successful thrillers, he surprised everyone with *The Pillars of the Earth* and its long-awaited sequel, *World Without End*, a national and international bestseller. Follett's new, magnificent historical epic, the Century Trilogy, opened with *Fall of Giants*, followed by *Winter of the World*, both #1 *New York Times* bestsellers. He lives in England with his wife, Barbara.

CONNECT ONLINE
ken-follett.com

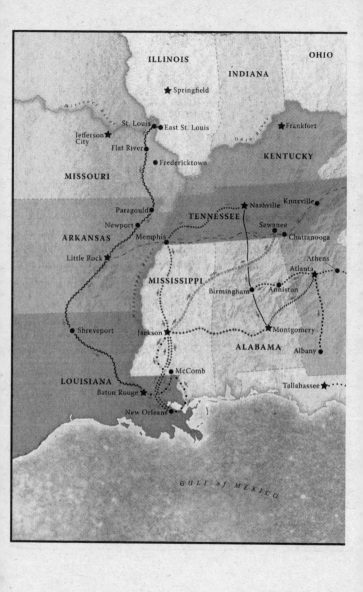

EDGE OF ETERNITY

Book Three of The Century Trilogy

Freedom Rides 1961

••••••••	Original CORE Freedom Ride, May 4–17
————	Nashville Movement Freedom Ride, May 17–21
▲▲▲▲▲▲	Mississippi Freedom Rides, May 24–August
∿∿∿∿∿	Connecticut Freedom Ride, May 24–25
• • • • •	Interfaith Freedom Ride, June 13–16
•—•—•—	Organized Labor/Professional Freedom Ride, June 13–16
∿∿∿∿∿	Missouri to Louisiana CORE Freedom Ride, July 8–15
— — —	New Jersey to Arkansas CORE Freedom Ride, July 13–24
▥▥▥▥▥	Monroe Freedom Ride, August
◦◦◦◦◦◦◦	Prayer Pilgrimage Freedom Ride, September
▲▼▲▼▲▼	Albany Freedom Rides, November–December
◦•◦•◦•◦	McComb Freedom Rides, November–December
••••••••	Route 40 Campaign, November–December

KEN FOLLETT

EDGE

of

ETERNITY

PENGUIN BOOKS

PENGUIN BOOKS
An imprint of Penguin Random House LLC
375 Hudson Street
New York, New York 10014
penguin.com

Published by Signet, an imprint of New American Library,
a division of Penguin Group (USA) LLC 2015
Originally published in a Dutton edition 2014
Published in Penguin Books 2016

ISBN 9780451474025 (mass market pbk.)

Printed in the United States of America
10 9 8 7 6 5 4 3 2 1

Cover design: Richard Hasselberger
Cover photos: *Apollo 11* spaceship lifting off © Morse / Getty Images; White House © Steve Allen / Getty Images; Capt. Donald R. Brown dashes from helicopter © Horst Faas / AP Photo

To all the freedom fighters,
especially Barbara

Cast of Characters

American

DEWAR FAMILY

Cameron Dewar
Ursula "Beep" Dewar, his sister
Woody Dewar, his father
Bella Dewar, his mother

PESHKOV-JAKES FAMILY

George Jakes
Jacky Jakes, his mother
Greg Peshkov, his father
Lev Peshkov, his grandfather
Marga, his grandmother

MARQUAND FAMILY

Verena Marquand
Percy Marquand, her father
Babe Lee, her mother

CIA

Florence Geary
Tony Savino
Tim Tedder, semiretired
Keith Dorset

OTHERS

Maria Summers
Joseph Hugo, FBI
Larry Mawhinney, Pentagon

Nelly Fordham, old flame of Greg Peshkov
Dennis Wilson, aide to Bobby Kennedy
Skip Dickerson, aide to Lyndon Johnson
Leopold "Lee" Montgomery, reporter
Herb Gould, television journalist on *This Day*
Suzy Cannon, gossip reporter
Frank Lindeman, television network owner

REAL HISTORICAL CHARACTERS

John F. Kennedy, thirty-fifth U.S. president
Jackie, his wife
Bobby Kennedy, his brother
Dave Powers, assistant to President Kennedy
Pierre Salinger, President Kennedy's press officer
Rev. Dr. Martin Luther King Jr., president of the
    Southern Christian Leadership Conference
Lyndon B. Johnson, thirty-sixth U.S. president
Richard Nixon, thirty-seventh U.S. president
Jimmy Carter, thirty-ninth U.S. president
Ronald Reagan, fortieth U.S. president
George H. W. Bush, forty-first U.S. president

British

LECKWITH-WILLIAMS FAMILY

Dave Williams
Evie Williams, his sister
Daisy Williams, his mother
Lloyd Williams, M.P., his father
Eth Leckwith, Dave's grandmother

MURRAY FAMILY

Jasper Murray
Anna Murray, his sister
Eva Murray, his mother

MUSICIANS IN THE GUARDSMEN AND PLUM NELLIE

Lenny, Dave Williams's cousin
Lew, drummer
Buzz, bass player
Geoffrey, lead guitarist

OTHERS

Earl Fitzherbert, called Fitz
Sam Cakebread, friend of Jasper Murray
Byron Chesterfield (real name Brian Chesnowitz),
    music agent
Hank Remington (real name Harry Riley), pop star
Eric Chapman, record company executive

German

FRANCK FAMILY

Rebecca Hoffmann
Carla Franck, Rebecca's adoptive mother
Werner Franck, Rebecca's adoptive father
Walli Franck, son of Carla
Lili Franck, daughter of Werner and Carla
Maud von Ulrich, née Fitzherbert, Carla's mother
Hans Hoffmann, Rebecca's husband

OTHERS

Bernd Held, schoolteacher
Karolin Koontz, folksinger
Odo Vossler, clergyman

REAL HISTORICAL PEOPLE

Walter Ulbricht, first secretary of the Socialist Unity
    Party (Communist)
Erich Honecker, Ulbricht's successor
Egon Krenz, successor to Honecker

Polish

Stanislaw "Staz" Pawlak, army officer
Lidka, girlfriend of Cam Dewar
Danuta Gorski, Solidarity activist

REAL HISTORICAL PEOPLE

Anna Walentynowicz, crane driver
Lech Wałęsa, leader of the trade union Solidarity
General Jaruzelski, prime minister

Russian

DVORKIN-PESHKOV FAMILY

Tanya Dvorkin, journalist
Dimka Dvorkin, Kremlin aide, Tanya's twin brother
Anya Dvorkin, their mother
Grigori Peshkov, their grandfather
Katerina Peshkov, their grandmother
Vladimir, always called Volodya, their uncle
Zoya, Volodya's wife
Nina, Dimka's girlfriend

OTHERS

Daniil Antonov, features editor at TASS
Pyotr Opotkin, features editor in chief
Vasili Yenkov, dissident
Natalya Smotrov, official in the Foreign Ministry
Nik Smotrov, Natalya's husband
Yevgeny Filipov, aide to Defense Minister Rodion
    Malinovsky
Vera Pletner, Dimka's secretary
Valentin, Dimka's friend
Marshal Mikhail Pushnoy

REAL HISTORICAL CHARACTERS

Nikita Sergeyevitch Khrushchev, first secretary of the
    Communist Party of the Soviet Union

Andrei Gromyko, foreign minister under Khrushchev
Rodion Malinovsky, defense minister under Khrushchev
Alexei Kosygin, chairman of the Council of Ministers
Leonid Brezhnev, Khrushchev's successor
Yuri Andropov, successor to Brezhnev
Konstantin Chernenko, successor to Andropov
Mikhail Gorbachev, successor to Chernenko

Other Nations

Paz Oliva, Cuban general
Frederik Bíró, Hungarian politician
Enok Andersen, Danish accountant

The Families at the Beginning of
Edge of Eternity

Ma Peshkov

Grigori = Katerina ≠ Lev   Marga ≠ Lev = Olga

Ilya Dvorkin = Anya   Zoya = Volodya   Greg ≠ Jacky   Lloyd = Daisy = Boy
                                                    Jakes Williams ¦ Fitzherbert

Dimka Tanya   Kotya Galina   George   Evie Dave

8th Earl Fitzherbert

Walter = Lady Maud   Bea = Fitz ≠ Ethel Williams

Eric Carla = Werner   Boy Fitzherbert   Lloyd Williams = Daisy

Rebecca Walli Lili   Evie Dave
(adopted) (father unknown)

Dai Williams = Cara

Fitz ≠ Ethel = Bernie   Mildred = Billy

Lloyd = Daisy   Millie = Abie Avery   Enid Lillian

Evie   Dave   Lenny

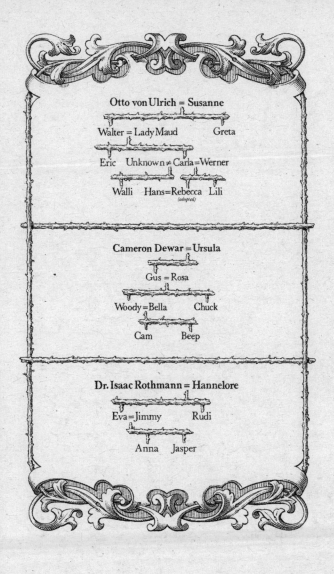

Otto von Ulrich = Susanne

Walter = Lady Maud   Greta

Eric   Unknown ≠ Carla = Werner

Walli   Hans = Rebecca   Lili
(adopted)

Cameron Dewar = Ursula

Gus = Rosa

Woody = Bella   Chuck

Cam   Beep

Dr. Isaac Rothmann = Hannelore

Eva = Jimmy   Rudi

Anna   Jasper

PART ONE

WALL

1961

Rebecca Hoffmann was summoned by the secret police on a rainy Monday in 1961.

It began as an ordinary morning. Her husband drove her to work in his tan Trabant 500. The graceful old streets of central Berlin still had gaps from wartime bombing, except where new concrete buildings stood up like ill-matched false teeth. Hans was thinking about his job as he drove. "The courts serve the judges, the lawyers, the police, the government—everyone except the victims of crime," he said. "This is to be expected in Western capitalist countries, but under Communism the courts ought surely to serve the people. My colleagues don't seem to realize that." Hans worked for the Ministry of Justice.

"We've been married almost a year, and I've known you for two, but I've never met one of your colleagues," Rebecca said.

"They would bore you," he said immediately. "They're all lawyers."

"Any women among them?"

"No. Not in my section, anyway." Hans's job was administration: appointing judges, scheduling trials, managing courthouses.

"I'd like to meet them, all the same."

Hans was a strong man who had learned to rein himself in. Watching him, Rebecca saw in his eyes a familiar flash of anger at her insistence. He controlled it by an effort of will.

"I'll arrange something," he said. "Perhaps we'll all go to a bar one evening."

Hans had been the first man Rebecca met who matched up to her father. He was confident and authoritative, but he always listened to her. He had a good job—not many people had a car of their own in East Germany—and men who worked in the government were usually hard-line Communists, but Hans, surprisingly, shared Rebecca's political skepticism. Like her father he was tall, handsome, and well dressed. He was the man she had been waiting for.

Only once during their courtship had she doubted him, briefly. They had been in a minor car crash. It had been wholly the fault of the other driver, who had come out of a side street without stopping. Such things happened every day, but Hans had been mad with rage. Although the damage to the two cars was minimal, he had called the police, shown them his Ministry of Justice identity card, and had the other driver arrested for dangerous driving and taken off to jail.

Afterward he had apologized to Rebecca for losing his temper. She had been scared by his vindictiveness, and had come close to ending their relationship. But he had explained that he had not been his normal self, due to pressure at work, and she had believed him. Her faith had been justified: he had never done such a thing again.

When they had been dating for a year, and sleeping together most weekends for six months, Rebecca wondered why he did not ask her to marry him. They were not kids: she had then been twenty-eight, he thirty-three. So she had proposed to him. He had been startled, but said yes.

Now he pulled up outside her school. It was a modern building, and well equipped: the Communists were serious about education. Outside the gates, five or six older boys were standing under a tree, smoking cigarettes. Ignoring their stares, Rebecca kissed Hans on the lips. Then she got out.

The boys greeted her politely, but she felt their yearning adolescent eyes on her figure as she splashed through the puddles in the school yard.

Rebecca came from a political family. Her grandfather had been a Social Democrat member of the Reichstag, the national parliament, until Hitler came to power. Her mother had been a city councilor, also for the Social Democrats, during East Berlin's brief postwar period of democracy. But East Germany was a Communist tyranny now, and Rebecca saw no point in engaging in politics. So she channeled her idealism into teaching, and hoped that the next generation would be less dogmatic, more compassionate, smarter.

In the staff room she checked the emergency timetable on the notice board. Most of her classes were doubled today, two groups of pupils crammed into one room. Her subject was Russian, but she also had to teach an English class. She did not speak English, though she had picked up a smattering from her British grandmother, Maud, still feisty at seventy.

This was the second time Rebecca had been asked to teach an English class, and she began to think about a text. The first time, she had used a leaflet handed out to American soldiers, telling them how to get on with Germans: the pupils had found it hilarious, and they had learned a lot too. Today perhaps she would write on the blackboard the words of a song they knew, such as "The Twist"—played all the time on American Forces Network radio—and get them to translate it into German. It would not be a conventional lesson, but it was the best she could do.

The school was desperately short of teachers because half the staff had emigrated to West Germany, where salaries were three hundred marks a month higher and people were free. The story was the same in most schools in East Germany. And it was not just teachers. Doctors could double their earnings by moving west. Rebecca's mother, Carla, was head of nursing at a large East Berlin hospital, and she was tearing her hair out at the scarcity of both nurses and doctors. The story was the same in industry and even the armed forces. It was a national crisis.

As Rebecca was scribbling the lyrics of "The Twist" in a notebook, trying to remember the line about "my little sis," the deputy head came into the staff room. Bernd Held was probably Rebecca's best friend outside her family. He was a slim, dark-haired man of forty, with a livid scar across his forehead where a shard of flying shrapnel had struck him while he was defending the Seelow Heights in the last days of the war. He taught physics, but he shared Rebecca's interest in Russian literature, and they ate their lunchtime sandwiches together a couple of times a week. "Listen, everybody," Bernd said. "Bad news, I'm afraid. Anselm has left us."

There was a murmur of surprise. Anselm Weber was the head teacher. He was a loyal Communist—heads had to be. But it seemed his principles had been overcome by the appeal of West German prosperity and liberty.

Bernd went on: "I will be taking his place until a new head can be appointed." Rebecca and every other teacher in the school knew that Bernd himself should have got the job, if ability had been what counted; but Bernd was ruled out because he would not join the Socialist Unity Party, the SED—the Communist Party in all but name.

For the same reason, Rebecca would never be a head teacher. Anselm had pleaded with her to join the party, but it was out of the question. For her it would be like checking herself into a lunatic asylum and pretending all the other inmates were sane.

As Bernd detailed the emergency arrangements, Rebecca wondered when the school would get its new head. A year from now? How long would this crisis go on? No one knew.

Before the first lesson she glanced into her pigeonhole, but it was empty. The mail had not yet arrived. Perhaps the postman had gone to West Germany, too.

The letter that would turn her life upside down was still on its way.

She taught her first class, discussing the Russian poem "The Bronze Horseman" with a large group seventeen and eighteen years old. This was a lesson she had given every year since she started teaching. As always, she guided the pupils to the orthodox Soviet analysis, explaining that the conflict between personal interest and public duty was resolved, by Pushkin, in favor of the public.

At lunchtime she took her sandwich to the head's office and sat down across the big desk from Bernd. She looked at the shelf of cheap pottery busts: Marx, Lenin, and East German Communist leader Walter Ulbricht. Bernd followed her gaze and smiled. "Anselm is a sly one," he said. "For years he pretended to be a true believer, and now—zoom, he's off."

"Aren't you tempted to leave?" Rebecca asked Bernd. "You're divorced, no children—you have no ties."

He looked around, as if wondering whether someone might be listening; then he shrugged. "I've thought about it—who hasn't?" he said. "How about you? Your father works in West Berlin anyway, doesn't he?"

"Yes. He has a factory making television sets. But my mother is determined to stay in the East. She says we must solve our problems, not run away from them."

"I've met her. She's a tiger."

"That's the truth. And the house we live in has been in her family for generations."

"What about your husband?"

"He's dedicated to his job."

"So I don't have to worry about losing you. Good."

Rebecca said: "Bernd—" Then she hesitated.

"Spit it out."

"Can I ask you a personal question?"

"Of course."

"You left your wife because she was having an affair."

Bernd stiffened, but he answered: "That's right."

"How did you find out?"

Bernd winced, as if at a sudden pain.

"Do you mind me asking?" Rebecca said anxiously. "Is it too personal?"

"I don't mind telling *you*," he said. "I confronted her, and she admitted it."

"But what made you suspicious?"

"A lot of little things—"

Rebecca interrupted him. "The phone rings, you pick it up, there's a silence for a few seconds, then the person at the other end hangs up."

He nodded.

She went on: "Your spouse tears a note up small and flushes the shreds down the toilet. At the weekend he's called to an unexpected meeting. In the evening he spends two hours writing something he won't show you."

"Oh, dear," said Bernd sadly. "You're talking about Hans."

"He's got a lover, hasn't he?" She put down her sandwich: she had no appetite. "Tell me honestly what you think."

"I'm so sorry."

Bernd had kissed her once, four months ago, on the last day of the autumn term. They had been saying good-bye, and wishing one another a happy Christmas, and he had lightly grasped her arm, and bent his head, and kissed her lips. She had asked him not to do it again, ever, and said she would still like to be his friend; and when they had returned to school in January both had pretended it had never happened. He had even told her, a few weeks later, that he had a date with a widow his own age.

Rebecca did not want to encourage hopeless aspirations, but Bernd was the only person she could talk to, except for her family, and she did not want to worry them, not yet. "I was so sure that Hans loved me," she said, and tears came to her eyes. "And I love him."

"Perhaps he does love you. Some men just can't resist temptation."

Rebecca did not know whether Hans found their sex life satisfactory. He never complained, but they made love only about once a week, which she believed to be infrequent for newlyweds. "All I want is a family of my own, just like my mother's, in which everyone is loved and supported and protected," she said. "I thought I could have that with Hans."

"Perhaps you still can," said Bernd. "An affair isn't necessarily the end of the marriage."

"In the first year?"

"It's bad, I agree."

"What should I do?"

"You must ask him about it. He may admit it, he may deny it; but he'll know that you know."

"And then what?"

"What do you want? Would you divorce him?"

She shook her head. "I would never leave. Marriage is a promise. You can't keep a promise only when it suits you. You have to keep it against your inclination. That's what it means."

"I did the opposite. You must disapprove of me."

"I don't judge you or anyone else. I'm just talking about myself. I love my husband and I want him to be faithful."

Bernd's smile was admiring but regretful. "I hope you get your wish."

"You're a good friend."

The bell rang for the first lesson of the afternoon. Rebecca stood up and put her sandwich back in its paper wrapping. She was not going to eat it, now or later, but she had a horror of throwing food away, like most people who had lived through the war. She touched her damp eyes with a handkerchief. "Thank you for listening," she said.

"I wasn't much comfort."

"Yes, you were." She went out.

As she approached the classroom for the English lesson, she realized she had not worked out the lyrics to "The Twist." However, she had been a teacher long enough to improvise. "Who's heard a record called 'The Twist'?" she asked loudly as she walked through the door.

They all had.

She went to the blackboard and picked up a stub of chalk. "What are the words?"

They all began to shout at once.

On the board she wrote: "Come on, baby, let's do the Twist." Then she said: "What's that in German?"

For a while she forgot about her troubles.

She found the letter in her pigeonhole at the midafternoon break. She carried it with her into the staff room and made a cup of instant coffee before opening it. When she read it she dropped her coffee.

The single sheet of paper was headed: "Ministry for State Security." This was the official name for the secret police: the unofficial name was the Stasi. The letter came from a Sergeant Scholz, and it ordered her to present herself at his headquarters office for questioning.

Rebecca mopped up her spilled drink, apologized to her colleagues, pretended nothing was wrong, and went to the ladies' room, where she locked herself in a cubicle. She needed to think before confiding in anyone.

Everyone in East Germany knew about these letters, and everyone dreaded receiving one. It meant she had done something wrong—perhaps something trivial, but it had come to the attention of the watchers. She knew, from what other people said, that there was no point protesting innocence. The police attitude would be that she must be guilty of something, or why would they be questioning her? To suggest they might have made a mistake was to insult their competence, which was another crime.

Looking again, she saw that her appointment was for five this afternoon.

What had she done? Her family was deeply suspect, of course. Her father, Werner, was a capitalist, with a factory that the East German government could not touch because it was in West Berlin. Her mother, Carla, was a well-known Social Democrat. Her grandmother Maud was the sister of an English earl.

However, the authorities had not bothered the family for a couple of years, and Rebecca had imagined that her marriage to an official in the Justice Ministry might have gained them a ticket of respectability. Obviously not.

Had she committed any crimes? She owned a copy of George Orwell's anti-Communist allegory *Animal Farm,* which was illegal. Her kid brother, Walli, who was fifteen, played the guitar and sang American protest songs such as "This Land Is Your Land." Rebecca sometimes went to West Berlin to see exhibitions of abstract painting. Communists were as conservative about art as Victorian matrons.

Washing her hands, she glanced in the mirror. She did not *look* scared. She had a straight nose and a strong chin and intense brown eyes. Her unruly dark hair was sharply pulled back. She was tall and statuesque, and some people found her intimidating. She could face a classroom full of boisterous eighteen-year-olds and silence them with a word.

But she *was* scared. What frightened her was the knowledge that the Stasi could do anything. There were no real restraints on them: complaining about them was a crime in itself. And that reminded her of the Red Army at the end of the war. The Soviet soldiers had been free to rob, rape, and murder Germans, and they had used their freedom in an orgy of unspeakable barbarism.

Rebecca's last class of the day was on the construction of the passive voice in Russian grammar, and it was a shambles, easily the worst lesson she had given since she qualified as a teacher. The pupils could not fail to know that something was wrong and, touchingly, they gave her an easy ride, even making helpful suggestions when she found herself lost for the right word. With their indulgence she got through it.

When school ended, Bernd was closeted in the head's office with officials from the Education Ministry, presumably discussing how to keep the school open with half the staff gone. Rebecca did not want to go to Stasi headquarters without telling anyone, just in case they decided to keep her there, so she wrote him a note telling him of the summons.

Then she caught a bus through the wet streets to Normannen Strasse in the suburb of Lichtenberg.

The Stasi headquarters there was an ugly new office block. It was not finished, and there were bulldozers in the car park and scaffolding at one end. It showed a grim face in the rain, and would not look much more cheerful in sunshine.

When she went through the door she wondered if she would ever come out.

She crossed the vast atrium, presented her letter at a reception desk, and was escorted upstairs in an elevator. Her fear rose with the lift. She emerged into a corridor painted a nightmarish shade of mustard yellow. She was shown into a small, bare room with a plastic-topped table and two uncomfortable chairs made of metal tubing. There was a pungent smell of paint. Her escort left.

She sat alone for five minutes, shaking. She wished she smoked: it might steady her. She struggled not to cry.

Sergeant Scholz came in. He was a little younger than Rebecca—about twenty-five, she guessed. He carried a thin file. He sat down, cleared his throat, opened the file, and frowned. Rebecca thought he was trying to seem important, and she wondered whether this was his first interrogation.

"You are a teacher at Friedrich Engels Polytechnic Secondary School," he said.

"Yes."

"Where do you live?"

She answered him, but she was puzzled. Did the secret police not know her address? That might explain why the letter had come to her at school rather than at home.

She had to give the names and ages of her parents and grandparents. "You're lying to me!" Scholz said triumphantly. "You say your mother is thirty-nine and you are twenty-nine. How could she have given birth to you when she was ten years old?"

"I'm adopted," Rebecca said, relieved to be able to give an innocent explanation. "My real parents were killed at the end of the war, when our house suffered a direct hit."

She had been thirteen. Red Army shells were falling and the city was in ruins and she was alone, bewildered, terrified. A plump adolescent, she had been singled out for rape by a group of soldiers. She had been saved by Carla, who had offered herself instead. Nevertheless that terrifying experience had left Rebecca hesitant and nervous about sex. If Hans was dissatisfied, she felt sure it must be her fault.

She shuddered and tried to put the memory away. "Carla Franck saved me from . . ." Just in time, Rebecca stopped herself. The Communists denied that Red Army soldiers had committed rape, even though every woman who had been in East Germany in 1945 knew the horrible truth. "Carla saved me," she said, skipping the contentious details. "Later, she and Werner legally adopted me."

Scholz was writing everything down. There could not be much in that file, Rebecca thought. But there must be something. If he knew little about her family, what was it that had attracted his interest?

"You are an English teacher," he said.

"No, I'm not. I teach Russian."

"You are lying again."

"I'm not lying, and I have not lied previously," she said crisply. She was surprised to find herself speaking to him in this challenging way. She was no longer as frightened as she had been. Perhaps this was foolhardy. He may be young and inexperienced, she told herself, but he still has the power to ruin my life. "My degree is in Russian language and literature," she went on, and she tried a friendly smile. "I'm head of the department of Russian at my school. But half our teachers have gone to the West, and we have to improvise. So, in the past week, I have given two English lessons."

"So, I was right! And in your lessons you poison the children's minds with American propaganda."

"Oh, hell," she groaned. "Is this about the advice to American soldiers?"

He read from a sheet of notes. "It says here: 'Bear in mind that there is no freedom of speech in East Germany.' Is that not American propaganda?"

"I explained to the pupils that Americans have a naïve pre-Marxist concept of freedom," she said. "I suppose your informant failed to mention that." She wondered who the snitch was. It must have been a pupil, or perhaps a parent who had been told about the lesson. The Stasi had more spies than the Nazis.

"It also says: 'When in East Berlin, do not ask police officers for directions. Unlike American policemen, they are not there to help you.' What do you say to that?"

"Isn't it true?" Rebecca said. "When you were a teenager, did you ever ask a Vopo to tell you the way to a U-Bahn station?" The Vopos were the *Volkspolizei*, the East German police.

"Couldn't you find something more appropriate for teaching children?"

"Why don't you come to our school and give an English lesson?"

"I don't speak English!"

"Nor do I!" Rebecca shouted. She immediately regretted raising her voice. But Scholz was not angry. In fact he seemed a little cowed. He was definitely inexperienced. But she should not get careless. "Nor do I," she said more quietly. "So I'm making it up as I go along, and using whatever English-language materials come to hand." It was time for some phony humility, she thought. "I've obviously made a mistake, and I'm very sorry, Sergeant."

"You seem like an intelligent woman," he said.

She narrowed her eyes. Was this a trap? "Thank you for the compliment," she said neutrally.

"We need intelligent people, especially women."

Rebecca was mystified. "What for?"

"To keep their eyes open, see what's happening, let us know when things are going wrong."

Rebecca was flabbergasted. After a moment she said incredulously: "Are you asking me to be a Stasi informant?"

"It's important, public-spirited work," he said. "And vital in schools, where young people's attitudes are formed."

"I see that." What Rebecca saw was that this young secret policeman had blundered. He had checked her out at her place of work, but he knew nothing about her notorious family. If Scholz had looked into Rebecca's background he would never have approached her.

She could imagine how it had happened. "Hoffmann" was one of the commonest surnames, and "Rebecca" was not unusual. A raw beginner could easily make the mistake of investigating the wrong Rebecca Hoffmann.

He went on: "But the people who do this work must be completely honest and trustworthy."

That was so paradoxical that she almost laughed. "Honest and trustworthy?" she repeated. "To spy on your friends?"

"Absolutely." He seemed unaware of the irony. "And there are advantages." He lowered his voice. "You would become one of us."

"I don't know what to say."

"You don't have to decide now. Go home and think about it. But don't discuss it with anyone. It must be secret, obviously."

"Obviously." She was beginning to feel relieved. Scholz would soon find out that she was unsuitable for his purpose, and he would withdraw his proposal. But at that point he could hardly go back to pretending that she was a propagandist for capitalist imperialism. Perhaps she might come out of this unscathed.

Scholz stood up, and Rebecca followed suit. Was it possible that her visit to Stasi headquarters could end so well? It seemed too good to be true.

He held the door for her politely, then escorted her along the yellow corridor. A group of five or six Stasi men stood near the elevator doors, talking animatedly. One was startlingly familiar: a tall, broad-shouldered man with a slight stoop, wearing a light gray flannel suit that Rebecca knew well. She stared at him uncomprehendingly as she walked up to the elevator.

It was her husband, Hans.

Why was he here? Her first frightened thought was that he, too, was under interrogation. But a moment later she realized, from the way they were all standing, that he was not being treated as a suspect.

What, then? Her heart pounded with fear, but what was she afraid of?

Perhaps his job at the Ministry of Justice brought him here from time to time, she thought. Then she heard one of the other men say to him: "But, with all due respect, Lieutenant . . ." She did not hear the rest of the sentence. Lieutenant? Civil servants did not hold military ranks—unless they were in the police . . .

Then Hans saw Rebecca.

She watched the emotions cross his face: men were easy

to read. At first he had the baffled frown of one who sees a familiar sight in an alien context, such as a turnip in a library. Then his eyes widened in shock as he accepted the reality of what he was seeing, and his mouth opened a fraction. But it was the next expression that struck her hardest: his cheeks darkened with shame and his eyes shifted away from her in an unmistakable look of guilt.

Rebecca was silent for a long moment, trying to take this in. Still not understanding what she was seeing, she said: "Good afternoon, *Lieutenant* Hoffmann."

Scholz looked puzzled and scared. "Do you know the lieutenant?"

"Quite well," she said, struggling to keep her composure as a dreadful suspicion began to dawn on her. "I'm beginning to wonder whether he has had me under surveillance for some time." But it was not possible—was it?

"Really?" said Scholz, stupidly.

Rebecca stared hard at Hans, watching for his reaction to her surmise, hoping he would laugh it off and immediately come out with the true, innocent explanation. His mouth was open, as if he were about to speak, but she could see that he was not intending to tell the truth: instead, she thought, he had the look of a man desperately trying to think of a story and failing to come up with something that would meet all the facts.

Scholz was on the brink of tears. "I didn't know!"

Still watching Hans, Rebecca said: "I am Hans's wife."

Hans's face changed again, and as guilt turned to anger his face became a mask of fury. He spoke at last, but not to Rebecca. "Shut your mouth, Scholz," he said.

Then she knew, and her world crashed around her.

Scholz was too astonished to heed Hans's warning. He said to Rebecca: "You're *that* Frau Hoffmann?"

Hans moved with the speed of rage. He lashed out with a meaty right fist and punched Scholz in the face. The young man staggered back, lips bleeding. "You fucking fool," Hans said. "You've just undone two years of painstaking undercover work."

Rebecca muttered to herself: "The funny phone calls, the sudden meetings, the ripped-up notes ..." Hans did not have a lover.

It was worse than that.

She was in a daze, but she knew this was the moment to find out the truth, while everyone was off balance, before they began to tell lies and concoct cover stories. With an effort she stayed focused. She said coolly: "Did you marry me just to spy on me, Hans?"

He stared at her without answering.

Scholz turned and staggered away along the corridor. Hans said: "Go after him." The elevator came and Rebecca stepped in just as Hans called out: "Arrest the fool and throw him in a cell." He turned to speak to Rebecca, but the elevator doors closed and she pressed the button for the ground floor.

She could hardly see through her tears as she crossed the atrium. No one spoke to her: doubtless it was commonplace to see people weeping here. She found her way across the rain-swept car park to the bus stop.

Her marriage was a sham. She could hardly take it in. She had slept with Hans, loved him, and married him, and all the time he had been deceiving her. Infidelity might be considered a temporary lapse, but Hans had been false to her from the start. He must have begun dating her in order to spy on her.

No doubt he had never intended actually to marry her. Originally, he had probably intended no more than a flirtation as a way of getting inside the house. The deception had worked too well. It must have come as a shock to him when she proposed marriage. Maybe he had been forced to make a decision: refuse her, and abandon the surveillance, or marry her and continue it. His bosses might even have ordered him to accept her. How could she have been so completely deceived?

A bus pulled up and she jumped on. She walked with lowered gaze to a seat near the back and covered her face with her hands.

She thought about their courtship. When she had raised the issues that had got in the way of her previous relationships—her feminism, her anti-Communism, her closeness to Carla—he had given all the right answers. She had believed that he and she were like-minded, almost miraculously so. It had never occurred to her that he was putting on an act.

The bus crawled through the landscape of old rubble and new concrete toward the central district of Mitte. Rebecca tried to think about her future but she could not. All she could do was run over the past in her mind. She remembered their wedding day, the honeymoon, and their year of marriage, seeing it all now as a play in which Hans had been performing. He had stolen two years from her, and it made her so angry that she stopped crying.

She recalled the evening when she had proposed. They had been strolling in the People's Park at Friedrichshain, and they had stopped in front of the old Fairy Tale Fountain to look at the carved stone turtles. She had worn a navy blue dress, her best color. Hans had had a new tweed jacket: he had managed to find good clothes even though East Germany was a fashion desert. With his arm around her, Rebecca had felt safe, protected, cherished. She wanted one man, forever, and he was the man. "Let's get married, Hans," she had said with a smile, and he had kissed her and replied: "What a wonderful idea."

I was a fool, she thought furiously, a stupid fool.

One thing was explained. Hans had not wanted to have children yet. He had said he wanted to get another promotion and a home of their own, first. He had not mentioned this before the wedding, and Rebecca had been surprised, given their ages: she was now twenty-nine and he thirty-four. Now she knew the real reason.

By the time she got off the bus she was in a rage. She walked quickly through the wind and rain to the tall old town house where she lived. From the hall she could see, through the open door of the front room, her mother deep in conversation with Heinrich von Kessel, who had been a Social Democrat city councilor with her after the war. Rebecca walked quickly past without speaking. Her twelve-year-old sister, Lili, was doing homework at the kitchen table. She could hear the grand piano in the drawing room: her brother, Walli, was playing a blues. Rebecca went upstairs to the two rooms she and Hans shared.

The first thing she saw when she walked into the room was Hans's model. He had been working on this throughout their year of marriage. He was making a scale model of the Brandenburg Gate out of matchsticks and glue. Everyone he knew had to save their spent matches. The model was almost done, and stood on the small table in the middle of the room. He had made the central arch and its wings, and was working on the quadriga, the four-horse chariot on the top, which was much more difficult.

He must have been bored, Rebecca thought bitterly. No doubt the project was a way of passing the evenings he was obliged to spend with a woman he did not love. Their marriage was like the model, a flimsy copy of the real thing.

She went to the window and stared out at the rain. After a minute, a tan Trabant 500 pulled up at the curb, and Hans got out.

How dared he come here now?

Rebecca flung open the window, heedless of the rain blowing in, and yelled: "Go away!"

He stopped on the wet sidewalk and looked up.

Rebecca's eye lit on a pair of his shoes on the floor beside her. They had been handmade by an old shoemaker Hans had found. She picked one up and threw it at him. It was a good shot and, although he dodged, it hit the top of his head.

"You mad cow!" he yelled.

Walli and Lili came into the room. They stood in the doorway, staring at their grown-up sister as if she had become a different person, which she probably had.

"You got married on the orders of the Stasi!" Rebecca shouted out of the window. "Which of us is mad?" She threw the other shoe and missed.

Lili said in awestruck tones: "What are you doing?"

Walli grinned and said: "This is crazy, man."

Outside, two passersby stopped to watch, and a neighbor appeared on a doorstep, gazing in fascination. Hans glared at them. He was proud, and it was agony for him to be made a fool of in public.

Rebecca looked around for something else to throw at him, and her gaze fell on the matchstick model of the Brandenburg Gate.

It stood on a plywood board. She picked it up. It was heavy, but she could manage.

Walli said: "Oh, wow."

Rebecca carried the model to the window.

Hans shouted: "Don't you dare! That belongs to me!"

She rested the plywood base on the windowsill. "You ruined my life, you Stasi bully!" she shouted.

One of the women bystanders laughed, a scornful, jeering cackle that rang out over the sound of the rain. Hans flushed with rage and looked around, trying to identify its source, but he could not. To be laughed at was the worst form of torture for him.

He roared: "Put that model back, you bitch! I worked on it for a year!"

"That's how long I worked on our marriage," Rebecca replied, and she lifted the model.

Hans yelled: "I'm ordering you!"

Rebecca heaved the model through the window and let it go.

It turned over in midair, so that the board was uppermost and the quadriga below. It seemed to take a long time to drop, and Rebecca felt suspended in a moment of time. Then it hit the paved front yard with a sound like paper being crumpled. The model exploded and the matchsticks scatted outward in a spray, then came down on the wet stones and stuck, forming a sunburst of destruction. The board lay flat, everything on it crushed to nothing.

Hans stared at it for a long moment, his mouth open in shock.

He recovered himself and pointed a finger up at Rebecca. "You listen to me," he said, and his voice was so cold that suddenly she felt afraid. "You'll regret this, I tell you," he said. "You and your family. You'll regret it for the rest of your lives. And that's a promise."

Then he got back into his car and drove away.

CHAPTER TWO

For breakfast, George Jakes's mother made him blueberry pancakes and bacon with grits on the side. "If I eat all this I'll have to wrestle heavyweight," he said. George weighed a hundred and seventy pounds and had been the welterweight star of the Harvard wrestling team.

"Eat hearty, and give up that wrestling," she said. "I didn't raise you to be a dumb jock." She sat opposite him at the kitchen table and poured cornflakes into a dish.

George was not dumb, and she knew it. He was about to graduate from Harvard Law School. He had finished his final exams, and was as sure as he could be that he had passed. Now he was here at his mother's modest suburban home in Prince George's County, Maryland, outside Washington, DC. "I want to stay fit," he said. "Maybe I'll coach a high school wrestling team."

"Now that would be worth doing."

He looked at her fondly. Jacky Jakes had once been pretty, he knew: he had seen photographs of her as a teenager, when she had aspired to be a movie star. She still looked young: she had the kind of dark-chocolate-colored skin that did not wrinkle. "Good black don't crack," the Negro women said. But the wide mouth that smiled so broadly in those old photos was now turned down at the corners in an expression of grim determination. She had never become an actress. Perhaps she had never had a chance: the few roles for Negro women generally went to light-skinned beauties. Anyway, her career had ended before it began when, at the age of sixteen, she had become pregnant with George. She had gained that careworn face raising him alone for the first six years of his life, working as a waitress and living in a tiny house at the back of Union Station, and drilling him in the need for hard work and education and respectability.

He said: "I love you, Mom, but I'm still going on the Freedom Ride."

She pressed her lips together disapprovingly. "You're twenty-five years old," she said. "You please yourself."

"No, I don't. Every important decision I've ever made, I've discussed with you. I probably always will."

"You don't do what I say."

"Not always. But you're still the smartest person I've ever met, and that includes everyone at Harvard."

"Now you're just buttering me up," she said, but she was pleased, he could tell.

"Mom, the Supreme Court has ruled that segregation on interstate buses and bus stations is unconstitutional—but those Southerners just defy the law. We have to do something!"

"How do you think it's going to help, this bus ride?"

"We're going to board here in Washington and travel south. We'll sit at the front, use the whites-only waiting rooms, and ask to be served in the whites-only diners; and when people object we're going to tell them that the law is on our side, and they are the criminals and troublemakers."

"Son, I know you're *right*. You don't have to tell me that. I understand the Constitution. But what do you think will happen?"

"I guess we'll get arrested sooner or later. Then there'll be a trial, and we'll argue our case in front of the world."

She shook her head. "I sure hope you get off that easy."

"What do you mean?"

"You grew up privileged," she said. "At least, you did after your white father came back into our lives when you were six years old. You don't know what the world is like for most colored folk."

"I wish you wouldn't say that." George was stung: he got this accusation from black activists, and it annoyed him. "Having a rich white grandfather pay for my education doesn't make me blind. I know what goes on."

"Then maybe you know that getting arrested might be the least bad thing that could happen to you. What if things get rough?"

George knew she was right. The Freedom Riders might be risking worse than jail. But he wanted to reassure his mother. "I've had lessons in passive resistance," he said. All those chosen for the Freedom Ride were experienced civil rights activists, and they had been put through a special training program that included role-playing exercises. "A white man pretending to be a redneck called me nigger, pushed and shoved me, and dragged me out of the room by my heels—and I let him, even though I could have thrown him out the window with one arm."

"Who was he?"

"A civil rights campaigner."

"Not the real thing."

"Of course not. He was acting a part."

"Okay," she said, and he knew from her tone that she meant the opposite.

"It's going to be all right, Mom."

"I'm not saying any more. Are you going to eat those pancakes?"

"Look at me," George said. "Mohair suit, narrow tie, hair close-cropped, and shoes shined so bright I could use the toe caps for a shaving mirror." He usually dressed smartly anyway, but the Riders had been instructed to look ultra-respectable.

"You look fine, except for that cauliflower ear." George's right ear was deformed from wrestling.

"Who would want to hurt such a nice colored boy?"

"You have no idea," she said with sudden anger. "Those Southern whites, they—" To his dismay, tears came to her eyes. "Oh, God, I'm just so afraid they'll kill you."

He reached across the table and took her hand. "I'll be careful, Mom, I promise."

She dried her eyes on her apron. George ate some bacon, to please her, but he had little appetite. He was more anxious than he pretended. His mother was not exaggerating. Some civil rights activists had argued against the Freedom Ride idea on the grounds that it would provoke violence.

"You're going to be a long time on that bus," she said.

"Thirteen days, here to New Orleans. We're stopping every night for meetings and rallies."

"What have you got to read?"

"The autobiography of Mahatma Gandhi." George felt he ought to know more about Gandhi, whose philosophy had inspired the civil rights movement's nonviolent protest tactics.

She took a book from on top of the refrigerator. "You might find this a little more entertaining. It's a bestseller."

They had always shared books. Her father had been a literature professor at a Negro college, and she had been a reader from childhood. When George was a boy he and his mother had read the Bobbsey Twins and the Hardy Boys together, even though all the heroes were white. Now they regularly passed each other books they had enjoyed. He looked at the volume in his hand. Its transparent plastic cover told him it was borrowed from the local public library. "*To Kill a Mockingbird,*" he read. "This just won a Pulitzer Prize, didn't it?"

"And it's set in Alabama, where you're going."

"Thanks."

A few minutes later he kissed his mother good-bye, left the house with a small suitcase in his hand, and caught a bus to Washington. He got off at the downtown Greyhound station. A small group of civil rights activists had gathered in the coffee shop. George knew some of them from the training sessions. They were a mixture of black and white, male and female, old and young. As well as a dozen or so Riders, there were some organizers from the Congress of Racial Equality, a couple of journalists from the Negro press, and a few supporters. CORE had decided to split the group in two, and half would leave from the Trailways bus station across the street. There were no placards and no television cameras: it was all reassuringly low-key.

George greeted Joseph Hugo, a fellow law student, a white guy with prominent blue eyes. Together they had organized a boycott of the Woolworth's lunch counter in Cambridge, Massachusetts. Woolworth's was integrated in most states but segregated in the South, like the bus service. But Joe had a way of disappearing just before a confrontation, and George had him pegged as a well-meaning coward. "Are you coming with us, Joe?" he asked, trying to keep the skepticism out of his voice.

Joe shook his head. "I just came by to say good luck." He smoked long mentholated cigarettes with white filter tips, and he was twitchily tapping one on the edge of a tin ashtray.

"Pity. You're from the South, aren't you?"

"Birmingham, Alabama."

"They're going to call us outside agitators. It would have been useful to have a Southerner on the bus to prove them wrong."

"I can't. I have stuff to do."

George did not press Joe. He was scared enough himself. If he started to discuss the dangers he might talk himself out of going. He looked around the group. He was pleased to see John Lewis, a quietly impressive theology student who was a founding member of the Student Nonviolent Coordinating Committee, the most radical of the civil rights groups.

Their leader called for attention and began a short statement to the press. While he was speaking George saw, slipping into the coffee shop, a tall white man of forty in a crumpled linen suit. He was handsome though heavy, his face showing the flush of a drinker. He looked like a bus passenger, and no one paid him any attention. He sat next to George and, putting one arm around his shoulders, gave him a brief hug.

This was Senator Greg Peshkov, George's father.

Their relationship was an open secret, known to Washington insiders but never publicly acknowledged. Greg was not the only politician to have such a secret. Senator Strom Thurmond had paid for the college education of a daughter of his family's maid: the girl was rumored to be his child—which did not stop Thurmond being a rabid segregationist. When Greg had appeared, a total stranger to his six-year-old son, he had asked George to call him Uncle Greg, and they had never found a better euphemism.

Greg was selfish and unreliable but, in his own way, he cared for George. As a teenager George had gone through a long phase of anger with his father, but then he had come to accept him for what he was, figuring that half a father was better than none.

"George," Greg said now in a low voice, "I'm worried."

"You and Mom too."

"What did she say?"

"She thinks those Southern racists are going to kill us all."

"I don't think that'll happen, but you could lose your job."

"Has Mr. Renshaw said something?"

"Heck, no, he doesn't know anything about this, yet. But he'll find out soon enough if you get arrested."

Renshaw, who was from Buffalo, was a childhood friend of Greg's, and senior partner in a prestigious Washington law firm, Fawcett Renshaw. Last summer Greg had got George a vacation job as a law clerk at the firm and, as they both had hoped, the temporary post had led to the offer of a full-time job after graduation. It was a coup: George would be the first Negro to work there as anything other than a cleaner.

George said with a touch of irritation: "The Freedom Riders are not lawbreakers. We're trying to get the law enforced. The segregationists are the criminals. I would have expected a lawyer such as Renshaw to understand that."

"He understands it. But all the same he can't hire a man who has been in trouble with the police. Believe me, it would be the same if you were white."

"But we're on the side of the law!"

"Life is unfair. Student days are over—welcome to the real world."

The leader called out: "Everybody, get your tickets and check your bags, please."

George stood up.

Greg said: "I can't talk you out of this, can I?"

He looked so forlorn that George longed to be able to give in, but he could not. "No, I've made up my mind," he said.

"Then please just try to be careful."

George was touched. "I'm lucky to have people who worry about me," he said. "I know that."

Greg squeezed his arm and left quietly.

George stood in line with the others at the window and bought a ticket to New Orleans. He walked to the blue-and-gray bus and handed over his bag to be loaded in the luggage compartment. Painted on the side of the bus were a large greyhound and the slogan: IT'S SUCH A COMFORT TO TAKE THE BUS . . . AND LEAVE THE DRIVING TO US. George got on board.

An organizer directed him to a seat near the front. Others were told to sit in interracial pairs. The driver paid no attention to the Riders, and the regular passengers seemed no more than mildly curious. George opened the book his mother had given him and read the first line.

A moment later the organizer directed one of the women to sit next to George. He nodded to her, pleased. He had met her a couple of times before and liked her. Her name was Maria Summers. She was demurely dressed in a pale gray cotton frock with a high neckline and a full skirt. She had skin the deep, dark color of George's mother's, a cute flat nose, and lips that made him think about kissing. He knew she was at the University of Chicago Law School, and like him was about to graduate, so they were probably the same age. He guessed she was not only smart but determined: she would have to be, to get into Chicago Law with two strikes against her, being both female and black.

He closed his book as the driver started the engine and pulled away. Maria looked down and said: "*To Kill a Mockingbird.* I was in Montgomery, Alabama, last summer."

Montgomery was the state capital. "What were you doing there?" George said.

"My father's a lawyer, and he had a client who sued the state. I was working for Daddy during the vacation."

"Did you win?"

"No. But don't let me keep you from reading."

"Are you kidding? I can read anytime. How often does a guy on a bus have a girl as pretty as you sit down next to him?"

"Oh, my," she said. "Someone warned me you were a smooth talker."

"I'll tell you my secret, if you want."

"Okay, what is it?"

"I'm sincere."

She laughed.

He said: "But please don't spread that around. It would spoil my reputation."

The bus crossed the Potomac and headed into Virginia on Route 1. "You're in the South, now, George," said Maria. "Are you scared yet?"

"You bet I am."

"Me, too."

The highway was a straight, narrow slash across miles of spring green forest. They passed through small towns where the men had so little to do that they stopped to watch the bus go by. George did not look out of the window much. He learned that Maria had been brought up in a strict church-going family, her grandfather a preacher. George said he went to church mainly to please his mother, and Maria confessed that she was the same. They talked all the way to Fredericksburg, fifty miles along the route.

The Riders went quiet as the bus entered the small historic town, where white supremacy still reigned. The Greyhound terminal was between two red-brick churches with white doors, but Christianity was not necessarily a good indication in the South. As the bus came to a halt, George saw the restrooms, and was surprised that there were no signs over the doors saying WHITES ONLY and COLORED ONLY.

The passengers got off the bus and stood blinking in the sunshine. Looking more closely, George saw light-colored patches over the toilet doors, and deduced that the segregation signs had been removed recently.

The Riders put their plan into operation anyway. First, a white organizer went into the scruffy restroom at the back, clearly intended for Negroes. He came out unharmed, but that was the easier part. George had already volunteered to be the black person who defied the rules. "Here goes," he said to Maria, and he walked into the clean, freshly painted restroom that had undoubtedly just had its WHITES ONLY sign removed.

There was a young white man inside, combing his pompadour. He glanced at George in the mirror, but said nothing. George was too scared to pee, but he could not just walk out again, so he washed his hands. The young man left and an older man came in and entered a cubicle. George dried his hands on the roller towel. Then there was nothing else to do, so he went out.

The others were waiting. He shrugged and said: "Nothing. Nobody tried to stop me—no one said anything."

Maria said: "I asked for a Coke at the counter and the waitress sold me one. I think someone here has decided to avoid trouble."

"Is this how it's going to be, all the way to New Orleans?" said George. "Will they just act as if nothing has happened? Then, when we've gone, impose segregation again? That would kind of cut the ground from under our feet!"

"Don't worry," said Maria. "I've met the people who run Alabama. Believe me, they're not that smart."

CHAPTER THREE

Walli Franck was playing the piano in the upstairs drawing room. The instrument was a full-size Steinway grand, and Walli's father kept it tuned for Grandma Maud to play. Walli was remembering the riff to Elvis Presley's record "A Mess of Blues." It was in the key of C, which made it easier.

His grandmother sat reading the obituaries in the *Berliner Zeitung*. She was seventy, a slim, straight figure in a dark blue cashmere dress. "You can play that sort of thing well," she said without looking up from the paper. "You've got my ear, as well as my green eyes. Your grandfather Walter, after whom you were named, never could play ragtime, rest his soul. I tried to teach him, but it was hopeless."

"You played ragtime?" Walli was surprised. "I've never heard you do anything but classical music."

"Ragtime saved us from starving when your mother was a baby. After the First World War, I played in a club called Nachtleben right here in Berlin. I was paid billions of marks a night, which was barely enough to buy bread; but sometimes I'd get tips in foreign currency, and we could live well for a week on two dollars."

"Wow." Walli could not imagine his silver-haired grandmother playing the piano for tips in a nightclub.

Walli's sister came into the room. Lili was almost three years younger, and these days he was not sure how to treat her. For as long as he could remember she had been a pain in the neck, like a younger boy but sillier. However, lately she had become more sensible and, to complicate matters, some of her friends had breasts.

He turned from the piano and picked up his guitar. He had bought it a year ago in a pawnshop in West Berlin. It had probably been pledged by an American soldier against a loan that was never repaid. The brand name was Martin and, although it had been cheap, it seemed to Walli a very good instrument. He guessed that neither the pawnbroker nor the soldier had realized its worth.

"Listen to this," he said to Lili, and he began to sing a Bahamian tune called "All My Trials" with lyrics in English. He had heard it on Western radio stations: it was popular with American folk groups. The minor chords made it a melancholy song, and he was pleased with the plaintive fingerpicking accompaniment he had devised.

When he had finished, Grandma Maud looked over the top of the newspaper and said in English: "Your accent is perfectly dreadful, Walli, dear."

"Sorry."

She reverted to German. "But you sing nicely."

"Thank you." Walli turned to Lili. "What do you think of the song?"

"It's a bit dreary," she said. "Maybe I'll like it more when I've heard it a few times."

"That's no good," he said. "I want to play it tonight at the Minnesänger." This was a folk club just off the Kurfürstendamm in West Berlin. The name meant "troubadour."

Lili was impressed. "You're playing at the Minnesänger?"

"It's a special night. They're having a contest. Anybody can play. The winner gets a chance of a regular gig."

"I didn't know clubs did that."

"They don't usually. This is a one-off."

Grandma Maud said: "Don't you have to be older to go to such a place?"

"Yes, but I've got in before."

Lili said: "Walli looks older than he is."

"Hmm."

Lili said to Walli: "You've never sung in public. Are you nervous?"

"You bet."

"You should play something more cheerful."

"I guess you're right."

"How about 'This Land Is Your Land'? I love that one."

Walli played it, and Lili sang along.

While they were singing, their older sister, Rebecca, came in. Walli adored Rebecca. After the war, when their parents had been desperately working all hours to feed the family, Rebecca had often been left in charge of Walli and Lili. She was like a second mother, but not so strict.

And she had such guts! He had watched with awe as she threw her husband's matchstick model out of the window. Walli had never liked Hans, and was secretly glad to see him go.

All the neighbors were talking about how Rebecca had unknowingly married a Stasi officer. It had given Walli status in school: no one had previously imagined there was anything special about the Francks. Girls especially were fascinated by the thought that everything said and done in his house had been reported to the police for almost a year.

Even though Rebecca was his sister, Walli could see that she was gorgeous. She had a fabulous figure and a lovely face that showed both kindness and strength. But now he noticed that she looked as if someone had died. He stopped playing and said: "What's the matter?"

"I've been fired," she said.

Grandma Maud put down the newspaper.

"That's crazy!" Walli said. "The boys in your school say you're their best teacher!"

"I know."

"Why did they sack you?"

"I think it was Hans's revenge."

Walli recalled Hans's reaction when he had seen his model smashed, thousands of little matchsticks scattered across the wet pavement. "You'll regret this," Hans had yelled, looking up through the rain. Walli had regarded that as bluster, but a moment's thought would have told him that an agent of the secret police had the power to carry out such a threat. "You and your family," Hans had screamed, and Walli was included in the curse. He shivered.

Grandma Maud said: "Aren't they desperate for teachers?"

"Bernd Held is frantic," Rebecca said. "But he was given orders from above."

Lili said: "What will you do?"

"Get another job. It shouldn't be difficult. Bernd has given me a glowing reference. And every school in East Germany is short of teachers, because so many have moved to the West."

"You should move west," said Lili.

"We should all move west," said Walli.

"Mother won't, you know that," said Rebecca. "She says we must solve our problems, not run away from them."

Walli's father came in, dressed in a dark blue suit with a waistcoat, old-fashioned but elegant. Grandma Maud said: "Good evening, Werner, dear. Rebecca needs a drink. She's been fired." Grandma often suggested that someone needed a drink. Then she would have one, too.

"I know about Rebecca," Father said shortly. "I've talked to her."

He was in a bad mood: he had to be, to speak ungraciously to his mother-in-law, whom he loved and admired. Walli wondered what had happened to upset the old man.

He soon found out.

"Come into my study, Walli," said Father. "I want a word." He went through the double doors into the smaller drawing room, which he used as his home office. Walli followed him. Father sat behind the desk. Walli knew he was to remain standing. "We had a conversation a month ago about smoking," Father said.

Walli immediately felt guilty. He had started smoking to look older, but he had grown to like it, and now it was a habit.

"You promised to give it up," his father said.

In Walli's opinion it was none of his father's business whether he smoked or not.

"Did you give it up?"

"Yes," Walli lied.

"Don't you know that it smells?"

"I suppose I do."

"I could smell it on you as soon as I walked into the drawing room."

Now Walli felt a fool. He had been caught out in a childish lie. This did not make him feel any more friendly toward his father.

"So I know you haven't given it up."

"Why did you ask me the question, then?" Walli hated the petulant note he heard in his own voice.

"I was hoping you'd tell the truth."

"You were hoping to catch me out."

"Believe that if you wish. I suppose you've got a pack in your pocket now."

"Yes."

"Put it on my desk."

Walli took the pack from his trouser pocket and angrily threw it onto the desk. His father picked up the pack and casually tossed it into a drawer. They were Lucky Strikes, not the inferior East German brand called f6, and it was almost a full packet, too.

"You'll stay in every evening for a month," his father said. "At least you won't be visiting bars where people play the banjo and smoke all the time."

Panic made Walli's stomach cramp. He struggled to remain calm and reasonable. "It's not a banjo—it's a guitar. And I can't possibly stay in for a month."

"Don't be ridiculous. You'll do as I say."

"All right," Walli said desperately. "But not starting tonight."

"Starting now."

"But I have to go to the Minnesänger club tonight."

"That's just the kind of place I want you to keep away from."

The old man was impossible! "I'll stay in every night for a month from tomorrow, okay?"

"Your quarantine will not be adjusted to suit your plans. That would defeat the purpose. It is intended to inconvenience you."

In this mood Father could not be shaken from his resolution, but Walli was mad with frustration, and he tried anyway. "You don't understand! Tonight I'm entering a contest at the Minnesänger—it's a unique opportunity."

"I'm not postponing your punishment to permit you to play the banjo!"

"It's a guitar, you stupid old fool! A guitar!" Walli stormed out.

The three women in the next room had obviously heard everything, and they stared at him. Rebecca said: "Oh, Walli . . ."

He picked up his guitar and left the room.

Until he got downstairs he had no plan, just rage; but when he saw the front door he knew what to do. With his guitar in his hand he walked out of the house and slammed the door so hard the house shook.

An upstairs window was thrown up and he heard his father shout: "Come back, do you hear me? Come back this minute, or you'll be in even worse trouble."

Walli walked on.

At first he was just angry, but after a while he felt exhilarated. He had defied his father and even called him a stupid old fool! He headed west, walking with a jaunty step. But soon his euphoria faded and he began to wonder what the consequences would be. His father did not take disobedience lightly. He commanded his children and his employees, and he expected them to comply. But what would he do? For two or three years now Walli had been too big to be spanked. Today Father had tried to keep him in the house as if it were a jail, but that had failed. Sometimes Father threatened to take him out of school and make him work in the business, but Walli considered that an empty threat: his father would not be comfortable with a resentful adolescent roaming around his precious factory. All the same, Walli had a feeling the old man would think of something.

The street he was on passed from East Berlin to West Berlin at a crossroads. Lounging on the corner, smoking, were three Vopos, East German cops. They had the right to challenge anyone crossing the invisible border. They could not possibly speak to everyone, because so many thousands of people went over every day, including many *Grenzgänger*, East Berliners who worked in the West for higher wages paid in valuable deutschmarks. Walli's father was a *Grenzgänger*, though he worked for profits, not wages. Walli himself crossed over at least once a week, usually to go with his friends to West Berlin cinemas, which showed sexy, violent American films that were more exciting than the preachy fables in Communist movie houses.

In practice the Vopos stopped anyone who caught their eye. Entire families crossing together, parents and children, were almost certain to be challenged on suspicion of trying to leave the East permanently, especially if they had luggage. The other types the Vopos liked to harass were adolescents, particularly those wearing Western fashions. Many East Berlin boys belonged to antiestablishment gangs: the Texas Gang, the Jeans Gang, the Elvis Presley Appreciation Society, and others. They hated the police and the police hated them.

Walli was wearing plain black pants, a white T-shirt, and a tan Windbreaker. He looked cool, he thought, a little like James Dean, but not a gang member. However, the guitar might get him noticed. It was the ultimate symbol of what they called "American unculture"—even worse than a Superman comic.

He crossed the road, careful not to look at the Vopos. Out of the corner of his eye he thought he saw one staring at him. But nothing was said, and he passed without stopping into the free world.

He caught a tram along the south side of the park to the Ku'damm. The best thing about West Berlin, he thought, was that *all* the girls wore stockings.

He made his way to the Minnesänger club, a cellar in a side street off the Ku'damm where they sold weak beer and frankfurter sausages. He was early, but the place was already filling up. Walli spoke to the club's young owner, Danni Hausmann, and put his name down on the list of competitors. He bought a beer without being questioned about his age. There were lots of boys like himself carrying guitars, almost as many girls, and a few older people.

An hour later the contest began. Each act did two songs. Some of the competitors were hopeless beginners strumming simple chords but, to Walli's consternation, several guitarists were more accomplished than he. Most looked like the American artists whose material they copied. Three men dressed like the Kingston Trio sang "Tom Dooley," and a girl with long black hair and a guitar sang "The House of the Rising Sun" just like Joan Baez, and got loud applause and cheers.

An older couple in corduroys got up and did a song about farming called "Im Märzen der Bauer" to the accompaniment of a piano-accordion. It was folk music, but not the kind this audience wanted. They got an ironic cheer, but they were out-of-date.

While Walli was waiting his turn, getting impatient, he was approached by a pretty girl. This happened to him a lot.

He thought he had a peculiar face, with high cheekbones and almond eyes, as if he might be half Japanese; but many girls thought he was dishy. The girl introduced herself as Karolin. She looked a year or two older than Walli. She had long, straight fair hair parted in the middle, framing an oval face. At first he thought she was like all the other folkie girls, but she had a big wide smile that made his heart misfire. She said: "I was going to enter this contest with my brother playing guitar, but he's let me down—I don't suppose you'd care to team up with me?"

Walli's first impulse was to refuse. He had a repertoire of songs and none were duets. But Karolin was enchanting, and he wanted a reason to continue to talk to her. "We'd have to rehearse," he said doubtfully.

"We could step outside. What songs were you thinking of?"

"I was going to do 'All My Trials,' then 'This Land Is Your Land.'"

"How about 'Noch Einen Tanz'?"

It was not part of Walli's repertoire, but he knew the tune and it was easy to play. "I never thought of doing a comic song," he said.

"The audience would love it. You could sing the man's part, where he tells her to go home to her sick husband. Then I'd sing, 'Just one more dance,' and we could do the last line together."

"Let's try it."

They went outside. It was early summer, and still light. They sat on a doorstep and tried out the song. They sounded good together, and Walli improvised a harmony on the last line.

Karolin had a pure contralto voice that he thought could sound thrilling, and he suggested that their second number could be a sad song, for contrast. She rejected "All My Trials" as too depressing, but she liked "Nobody's Fault but Mine," a slow spiritual. When they ran through it, the hairs stood up on the back of Walli's neck.

An American soldier entering the club smiled at them and said in English: "My God, it's the Bobbsey Twins."

Karolin laughed and said to Walli: "I guess we do look alike—fair hair and green eyes. Who are the Bobbsey Twins?"

Walli had not noticed the color of her eyes, and he was

flattered that she was aware of his. "I've never heard of them," he said.

"All the same, it sounds like a good name for a duo. Like the Everly Brothers."

"Do we need a name?"

"We do if we win."

"Okay. Let's go back in. It must be almost our turn."

"One more thing," she said. "When we do 'Noch Einen Tanz,' we should look at one another now and again, and smile."

"Okay."

"Almost as if we're boyfriend and girlfriend, you know? It will look good onstage."

"Sure." It would not be difficult to smile at Karolin as if she were his girlfriend.

Back inside, a blond girl was strumming a guitar and singing "Freight Train." She was not as beautiful as Karolin, but she was pretty in a more obvious way. Next, a virtuoso guitarist played a complicated fingerpicking blues. Then Danni Hausmann called Walli's name.

He felt tense as he faced the audience. Most of the guitarists had fancy leather straps, but Walli had never bothered to get one, and his instrument was held around his neck by a piece of string. Now, suddenly, he wished he had a strap.

Karolin said: "Good evening, we're the Bobbsey Twins."

Walli played a chord and began to sing, and found he no longer cared about a strap. The song was a waltz, and he strummed it jauntily. Karolin pretended to be a wanton strumpet, and Walli responded by becoming a stiff Prussian lieutenant.

The audience laughed.

Something happened to Walli then. There were only a hundred or so people in the place, and the sound they made was no more than an appreciative collective chuckle, but it gave him a feeling that he had not experienced before, a feeling a bit like the kick from the first puff of a cigarette.

They laughed several more times, and at the end of the song they applauded loudly.

Walli liked that even better.

"They love us!" Karolin said in an excited whisper.

Walli began to play "Nobody's Fault but Mine," plucking the steel strings with his fingernails to sharpen the drama of the plangent sevenths, and the crowd went quiet. Karolin changed and became a fallen woman in despair. Walli watched the audience. No one was talking. One woman had tears in her eyes, and he wondered if she had lived through what Karolin was singing about.

Their hushed concentration was even better than the laughter.

At the end they cheered and called for more.

The rule was two numbers each, so Walli and Karolin came down off the stage, ignoring the cries for an encore, but Hausmann told them to go back. They had not rehearsed a third song, and they looked at one another in panic. Then Walli said: "Do you know 'This Land Is Your Land'?" and Karolin nodded.

The audience joined in, which made Karolin sing louder, and Walli was surprised by the power of her voice. He sang a high harmony, and their two voices soared above the sound of the crowd.

When finally they left the stage he felt exhilarated. Karolin's eyes were shining. "We were really good!" she said. "You're better than my brother."

Walli said: "Have you got any cigarettes?"

They sat through another hour of the contest, smoking. "I think we were the best," Walli said.

Karolin was more cautious. "They liked the blond girl who sang 'Freight Train,'" she said.

At last the result was announced.

The Bobbsey Twins came second.

The winner was the Joan Baez look-alike.

Walli was angry. "She could hardly play!" he said.

Karolin was more philosophical. "People love Joan Baez."

The club began to empty, and Walli and Karolin headed for the door. Walli felt dejected. As they were leaving, Danni Hausmann stopped them. He was in his early twenties, and dressed in modern casual clothes, a black roll-neck sweater and jeans. "Could you two do half an hour next Monday?" he said.

Walli was too surprised to reply, but Karolin quickly said: "Sure!"

"But the Joan Baez imitator won," said Walli, then he thought: Why am I arguing?

Danni said: "You two seem to have the range to keep an audience happy for more than one or two numbers. Have you got enough songs for a set?"

Once again Walli hesitated, and again Karolin jumped in. "We will by Monday," she said.

Walli remembered that his father planned to imprison him in the house for a month of evenings, but he decided not to mention that.

"Thanks," said Danni. "You get the early slot, eight thirty. Be here by seven thirty."

They were elated as they walked out into the lamplit street. Walli had no idea what he would do about his father, but he felt optimistic that everything would work out.

It turned out that Karolin, too, lived in East Berlin. They caught a bus and began to talk about which numbers they would do next week. There were lots of folk songs they both knew.

They got off the bus and headed into the park. Karolin frowned and said: "The guy behind."

Walli looked back. There was a man in a cap thirty or forty yards behind them, smoking as he walked. "What about him?"

"Wasn't he in the Minnesänger?"

The man did not meet Walli's eye, even though Walli stared at him. "I don't think so," said Walli. "Do you like the Everly Brothers?"

"Yes!"

As they walked, Walli started to play "All I Have to Do Is Dream," strumming the guitar that hung around his neck on its string. Karolin joined in eagerly. They sang together as they crossed the park. He played the Chuck Berry hit "Back in the USA."

They were belting out the refrain, "I'm so glad I'm living in the USA," when Karolin halted suddenly and said: "Hush!" Walli realized they had reached the border, and saw three Vopos under a streetlight glaring at them malevolently.

He shut up immediately, and hoped they had stopped soon enough.

One of the cops was a sergeant, and he looked past Walli.

Walli glanced back and saw the man in the cap give a curt nod. The sergeant took a step toward Walli and Karolin and said: "Papers." The man in the cap spoke into a walkie-talkie.

Walli frowned. It seemed Karolin had been right, and they had been followed.

It occurred to him that Hans might be behind this.

Could he possibly be so petty and vengeful?

Yes, he could.

The sergeant looked at Walli's identity card and said: "You're only fifteen. You shouldn't be out this late."

Walli bit his tongue. There was no point in arguing with them.

The sergeant looked at Karolin's card and said: "You're seventeen! What are you doing with this child?"

This made Walli recall the row with his father, and he said angrily: "I'm not a child."

The sergeant ignored him. "You could go out with me," he said to Karolin. "I'm a real man." The other two Vopos laughed appreciatively.

Karolin said nothing, but the sergeant persisted. "How about it?" he said.

"You must be out of your mind," Karolin said quietly.

The man was stung. "Now that's just rude," he said.

Walli had noticed this about some men. If a girl gave them the brush-off they became indignant, but any other response was taken as encouragement. What were women supposed to do?

Karolin said: "Give me back my card, please."

The sergeant said: "Are you a virgin?"

Karolin blushed.

Once again the other two cops sniggered.

"They ought to put that on women's identity cards," said the man. "Virgin, or not."

"Knock it off," Walli said.

"I'm gentle with virgins."

Walli was boiling. "That uniform doesn't give you the right to pester girls!"

"Oh, doesn't it?" The sergeant did not give back their identity cards.

A tan Trabant 500 pulled up and Hans Hoffmann got

out. Walli began to feel frightened. How could he be in this much trouble? All he had done was sing in the park.

Hans approached and said: "Show me that thing you have around your neck."

Walli summoned up the nerve to say: "Why?"

"Because I suspect it is being used to smuggle capitalist-imperialist propaganda into the German Democratic Republic. Give it here."

The guitar was so precious that Walli still did not comply, scared as he was. "What if I don't?" he said. "Will I be arrested?"

The sergeant rubbed the knuckles of his right hand with the palm of his left.

Hans said: "Yes, eventually."

Walli ran out of courage. He pulled the string over his head and gave Hans the guitar.

Hans held the guitar as if to play it, hit the strings, and sang in English: "You ain't nothing but a hound dog." The Vopos laughed hysterically.

Even the cops listened to pop radio, it seemed.

Hans pushed his hand under the strings and tried to feel inside the sound hole.

Walli said: "Be careful!"

The top E string broke with a ping.

"It's a delicate musical instrument!" Walli said despairingly.

Hans's reach was constrained by the strings. He said: "Anyone got a knife?"

The sergeant put his hand inside his jacket and pulled out a knife with a wide blade—not part of his standard-issue gear, Walli felt sure.

Hans tried to cut the strings with the blade, but they were tougher than he thought. He managed to snap the B and the G, but could not saw through the thicker ones.

"There's nothing inside," Walli said pleadingly. "You can tell by the weight."

Hans looked at him, smiled, then brought the knife down hard, point first, on the soundboard near the bridge.

The blade went straight through the wood, and Walli cried out in pain.

Pleased by this response, Hans repeated the action,

smashing holes in the guitar. With the surface weakened, the tension in the strings pulled the bridge and the wood surrounding it away from the body of the instrument. He prized away the rest of it, revealing the inside like an empty coffin.

"No propaganda," he said. "Congratulations—you are innocent." He handed Walli the wrecked guitar, and Walli took it.

The sergeant handed back their identity cards with a grin.

Karolin took Walli's arm and drew him away. "Come on," she said in a low voice. "Let's get out of here."

Walli let her lead him. He could hardly see where he was going. He could not stop crying.

CHAPTER FOUR

George Jakes boarded a Greyhound bus in Atlanta, Georgia, on Sunday, May 14, 1961. It was Mother's Day.

He was scared.

Maria Summers sat next to him. They always sat together. It had become a regular thing: everyone assumed that the empty seat next to George was reserved for Maria.

To hide his nervousness, he made conversation with Maria. "So, what did you think of Martin Luther King?"

King was head of the Southern Christian Leadership Conference, one of the more important civil rights groups. They had met him last night at a dinner in one of Atlanta's black-owned restaurants.

"He's an amazing man," said Maria.

George was not so sure. "He said wonderful things about the Freedom Riders, but he's not here on the bus with us."

"Put yourself in his place," Maria said reasonably. "He's the leader of a different civil rights group. A general can't become a foot soldier in someone else's regiment."

George had not looked at it that way. Maria was very smart.

George was half in love with her. He was desperate for an opportunity to be alone with her, but the people in whose homes the Riders stayed were solid, respectable black citizens, many of them devout Christians, who would not have allowed their guest rooms to be used for smooching. And Maria, alluring though she was, did nothing more than sit next to George and talk to him and laugh at his wisecracks. She never did the little physical things that said a woman wanted to be more than friends: she did not touch his arm, or take his hand getting off the bus, or press close to him in a crowd. She did not flirt. She might even be a virgin at twenty-five.

"You talked to King for a long time," he said.

"If he wasn't a preacher, I'd say he was coming on to me," she said.

George was not sure how to respond to that. It would be no surprise to him if a preacher made a pass at a girl as enchanting as Maria. But she was naïve about men, he thought. "I talked to King a bit."

"What did he say to you?"

George hesitated. It was King's words that had scared George. He decided to tell Maria anyway: she had a right to know. "He says we're not going to make it through Alabama."

Maria blanched. "Did he really say that?"

"He said exactly that."

Now they were both scared.

The Greyhound pulled out of the bus station.

For the first few days George had feared that the Freedom Ride would be too peaceful. Regular bus passengers did not react to the black people sitting in the wrong seats, and sometimes joined in their songs. Nothing had happened when the Riders defied WHITES ONLY and COLORED notices in bus stations. Some towns had even painted over the signs. George feared the segregationists had devised the perfect strategy. There was no trouble and no publicity, and colored Riders were served politely in the white restaurants. Every evening they got off the buses and attended meetings unmolested, usually in churches, then stayed overnight with sympathizers. But George felt sure that as they left each town the signs would be restored, and segregation would return; and the Freedom Ride would have been a waste of time.

The irony was striking. For as long as he could remember, George had been wounded and infuriated by the repeated message, sometimes implicit but often spoken aloud, that he was inferior. It made no difference that he was smarter than 99 percent of white Americans. Nor that he was hardworking, polite, and well dressed. He was looked down upon by ugly white people too stupid or too lazy to do anything harder than pour drinks or pump gas. He could not walk into a department store, sit down in a restaurant, or apply for a job without wondering whether he would be ignored, asked to leave, or rejected because of his color. It made him burn with resentment. But now, paradoxically, he was disappointed that it was not happening.

Meanwhile the White House dithered. On the third day of the Ride the attorney general, Robert Kennedy, had made a speech at the University of Georgia promising to enforce civil rights in the South. Then, three days later, his brother the president had backtracked, withdrawing support from two civil rights bills.

Was this how the segregationists would win? George had wondered. By avoiding confrontation, then carrying on as usual?

It was not. Peace had lasted just four days.

On the fifth day of the Ride one of their number had been jailed for insisting on his right to a shoeshine.

Violence had broken out on the sixth.

The victim had been John Lewis, the theology student. He had been attacked by thugs in a white restroom in Rock Hill, South Carolina. Lewis had allowed himself to be punched and kicked without retaliation. George had not seen the incident, which was probably a good thing, for he was not sure he could have matched Lewis's Gandhian self-restraint.

George had read short reports of the violence in the next day's papers, but he was disappointed to see the story overshadowed by the rocket flight of Alan Shepard, the first American in space. Who cares? George thought sourly. The Soviet cosmonaut Yuri Gagarin had been the first man in space, less than a month ago. The Russians beat us to it. A white American can orbit the earth, but a black American can't enter a restroom.

Then, in Atlanta, the Riders had been cheered by a welcoming crowd as they got off the bus, and George's spirits had lifted again.

But that was Georgia, and now they were headed for Alabama.

"Why did King say we're not going to make it through Alabama?" Maria asked.

"There's a rumor the Ku Klux Klan are planning something in Birmingham," George said grimly. "Apparently the FBI knows all about it but they haven't done anything to stop it."

"And the local police?"

"The police are *in* the damn Klan."

"What about those two?" With a jerk of her head Maria indicated the seats across the aisle and a row back.

George looked over his shoulder at two burly white men sitting together. "What about them?"

"Don't you smell cop?"

He saw what she meant. "Do you think they're FBI?"

"Their clothes are too cheap for the Bureau. My guess is they're Alabama Highway Patrol, undercover."

George was impressed. "How did you get to be so smart?"

"My mother made me eat my vegetables. And my father's a lawyer in Chicago, the gangster capital of the USA."

"So what do you think those two are doing?"

"I'm not sure, but I don't think they're here to defend our civil rights. Do you?"

George glanced out of the window and saw a sign that read ENTERING ALABAMA. He checked his wristwatch. It was one P.M. The sun was shining out of a blue sky. It's a beautiful day to die, he thought.

Maria wanted to work in politics or public service. "Protesters can have a big impact, but in the end it's governments that reshape the world," she said. George thought about that, wondering whether he agreed. Maria had applied for a job in the White House press office, and had been called for an interview, but she had not got the job. "They don't hire many black lawyers in Washington," she had said ruefully to George. "I'll probably stay in Chicago and join my father's law firm."

Across the aisle from George was a middle-aged white woman in a coat and hat, holding on her lap a large white plastic handbag. George smiled at her and said: "Lovely weather for a bus ride."

"I'm going to visit my daughter in Birmingham," she said, though he had not asked.

"That's nice. I'm George Jakes."

"Cora Jones. Mrs. Jones. My daughter's baby is due in a week."

"Her first?"

"Third."

"Well, you seem too young to be a grandmother, if you don't mind my saying so."

She purred a little. "I'm forty-nine years old."

"I would never have guessed that!"

A Greyhound coming in the opposite direction flashed its lights, and the Riders' bus slowed to a halt. A white man came to the driver's window and George heard him say: "There's a crowd gathered at the bus station in Anniston." The driver said something in reply that George could not hear. "Just be careful," said the man at the window.

The bus pulled away.

"What does that mean, a crowd?" said Maria anxiously. "It could be twenty people or a thousand. They could be a welcoming committee or an angry mob. Why didn't he tell us more?"

George guessed her irritation masked fear.

He recalled his mother's words: "I'm just so afraid they'll kill you." Some people in the movement said they were ready to die in the cause of freedom. George was not sure he was willing to be a martyr. There were too many other things he wanted to do, like maybe sleep with Maria.

A minute later they entered Anniston, a small town like any other in the South: low buildings, streets in a grid, dusty and hot. The roadside was lined with people as if for a parade. Many were dressed up, the women in hats, the children scrubbed, no doubt having been to church. "What are they expecting to see, people with horns?" George said. "Here we are, folks, real Northern Negroes, wearing shoes and all." He spoke as if addressing them, although only Maria could hear. "We've come to take away your guns and teach you Communism. Where do the white girls go swimming?"

Maria giggled. "If they could hear you, they wouldn't know you were joking."

He wasn't really joking; it was more like whistling past the graveyard. He was trying to ignore the spasm of fear in his guts.

The bus turned into the station, which was strangely deserted. The buildings looked shut up and locked. To George it felt creepy.

The driver opened the door of the bus.

George did not see where the mob came from. Suddenly they were all around the bus. They were white men, some in work clothes, others in Sunday suits. They carried baseball bats, metal pipes, and lengths of iron chain. And they were screaming. Most of it was inchoate, but George heard some words of hate, including *Sieg heil!*

George stood up, his first impulse to close the bus door; but the two men Maria had identified as state troopers were faster, and they slammed it shut. Perhaps they are here to defend us, George thought; or maybe they're just defending themselves.

He looked through the windows all around him. There were no police outside. How could the local police not know that an armed mob had gathered at the bus station? They had to be in collusion with the Klan. No surprise there.

A second later the men attacked the bus with their weapons. There was a frightening cacophony as chains and crowbars dented the bodywork. Glass shattered, and Mrs. Jones screamed. The driver started the bus, but one of the mob lay down in front of it. George thought the driver might just roll over the man, but he stopped.

A rock came through the window, smashing it, and George felt a sharp pain in his cheek like a bee sting. He had been hit by a flying shard. Maria was sitting by a window: she was in danger. George grabbed her arm, pulling her toward him. "Kneel down in the aisle!" he shouted.

A grinning man wearing knuckle-dusters put his fist through the window next to Mrs. Jones. "Get down here with me!" Maria shouted, and she pulled Mrs. Jones down next to her and wrapped her arms protectively around the older woman.

The yelling got louder. "Communists!" they screamed. "Cowards!"

Maria said: "Duck, George!"

George could not bring himself to cower before these hooligans.

Suddenly the noise diminished. The banging on the bus sides stopped and there was no more breaking glass. George spotted a police officer.

About time, he thought.

The cop was swinging a nightstick but talking amiably to the grinning man with the knuckle-dusters.

Then George saw three more cops. They had calmed the crowd but, to George's indignation, they were doing no more. They acted as if no crime had been committed. They chatted casually to the rioters, who seemed to be their friends.

The two highway patrolmen were sitting back in their seats, looking bewildered. George guessed their assignment was to spy on the Riders, and they had not reckoned on becoming victims of mob violence. They had been forced to join the Riders' side in self-defense. They might learn to see things from a new point of view.

The bus moved. George saw, through the windshield, that a cop was urging men out of the way and another was waving the driver forward. Outside the station, a patrol car moved in front of the bus and led it onto the road out of town.

George began to feel better. "I think we got away," he said.

Maria got to her feet, apparently unhurt. She took the handkerchief out of the breast pocket of George's suit coat and mopped his face gently. The white cotton came away red with blood. "It's a nasty little gash," she said.

"I'll live."

"You won't be so pretty, though."

"I'm pretty?"

"You used to be, but now . . ."

The moment of normality did not last. George glanced behind and saw a long line of pickup trucks and cars following the bus. They seemed to be full of shouting men. He groaned. "We didn't get away," he said.

Maria said: "Back in Washington, before we got on the bus, you were talking to a young white guy."

"Joseph Hugo," George said. "He's at Harvard Law. Why?"

"I thought I saw him in the mob back there."

"Joseph Hugo? No. He's on our side. You must be mistaken." But Hugo was from Alabama, George recalled.

Maria said: "He had bulging blue eyes."

"If he's with the mob, that would mean that all this time he's been pretending to support civil rights . . . while spying on us. He can't be a snitch."

"Can't he?"

George looked behind again.

The police escort turned back at the city line, but the other vehicles did not.

The men in the cars were shrieking so loud they could be heard over the sound of all the engines.

Beyond the suburbs, on a long, lonely stretch of Highway 202, two cars overtook the bus, then slowed down, forcing the driver to brake. He tried to pass, but they swerved from side to side, blocking his way.

Cora Jones was white-faced and shaking, and she clutched her plastic handbag like a life preserver. George said: "I'm sorry we got you into this, Mrs. Jones."

"So am I," she replied.

The cars ahead pulled aside at last and the bus passed them. But the ordeal was not ended: the convoy was still behind. Then George heard a familiar popping sound. When the bus began to weave all over the road he realized it was a burst tire. The driver slowed to a halt near a roadside grocery store. George read the name: Forsyth & Son.

The driver jumped out. George heard him say: "*Two* flats?" Then he went into the store, presumably to phone for help.

George was as tense as a bowstring. One flat tire was just a puncture; two was an ambush.

Sure enough, the cars in the convoy were stopping and a dozen white men in their Sunday suits were piling out, yelling curses and waving their weapons, savages on the warpath. George's stomach cramped again as he saw them running toward the bus, ugly faces twisted with hatred, and he knew why his mother's eyes had filled with tears when she talked about Southern whites.

At the head of the pack was an adolescent boy who raised a crowbar and gleefully smashed a window.

The next man tried to enter the bus. One of the two burly white passengers stood at the top of the steps and drew a revolver, confirming Maria's theory that they were state troopers in plain clothes. The intruder backed off and the trooper locked the door.

George feared that might be a mistake. What if the Riders needed to get out in a hurry?

The men outside began to rock the bus, as if trying to turn it over, all the while yelling: "Kill the niggers! Kill the niggers!" Women passengers were screaming. Maria clung to George in a way that might have pleased him if he had not been in fear of his life.

Outside, he saw two uniformed patrolmen arrive, and his hopes lifted; but, to his fury, they did nothing to restrain the mob. He looked at the two plainclothesmen on the bus: they looked foolish and scared. Obviously the uniformed men did not know about their undercover colleagues. The Alabama Highway Patrol was evidently disorganized as well as racist.

George cast around desperately for something he could do to protect Maria and himself. Get out of the bus and run? Lie down on the floor? Grab a gun from a state trooper and shoot some white men? Every possibility seemed even worse than doing nothing.

He stared in fury at the two highway patrolmen outside, watching as if nothing wrong was happening. They were cops, for Christ's sake! What did they think they were doing? If they would not enforce the law, what right did they have to wear that uniform?

Then he saw Joseph Hugo. There was no possibility of mistake: George knew well those bulging blue eyes. Hugo approached a patrolman and spoke to him, then the two of them laughed.

He was a snitch.

If I get out of here alive, George thought, that creep is going to be sorry.

The men outside shouted at the Riders to get off. George heard: "Come out here and get what's coming to you, nigger lovers!" That made him think he was safer on the bus.

But not for long.

One of the mob had returned to his car and opened the trunk, and now the man came running toward the bus with something burning in his hands. He hurled a blazing bundle through a smashed window. Seconds later the bundle exploded in gray smoke. But the weapon was not just a smoke bomb. It set fire to the upholstery, and in moments thick black fumes began to choke the passengers. A woman screamed: "Is there any air up front?"

From outside, George heard: "Burn the niggers! Fry them!"

Everyone tried to get out of the door. The aisle was jammed with gasping people. Some were pressing forward, but there seemed to be a blockage. George yelled: "Get off the bus! Everybody get off!"

From the front, someone shouted back: "The door won't open!"

George recalled that the state trooper with the gun had locked the door to keep the mob out. "We'll have to jump out the windows!" he yelled. "Come on!"

He stood on a seat and kicked most of the remaining glass out of the window. Then he pulled off his suit coat and draped it over the sill, to provide some protection from the jagged shards still remaining stuck in the window frame.

Maria was coughing helplessly. George said: "I'll go first and catch you as you jump." Grasping the back of the seat for balance, he stood on the sill, bent double, and jumped. He heard his shirt tear on a snag, but felt no pain, and concluded that he had escaped injury. He landed on the roadside grass. The mob had backed off from the burning bus in fear. George turned and held his arms up to Maria. "Climb through, like I did!" he shouted.

Her pumps were flimsy compared with his toe-capped oxfords, and he was glad he had sacrificed his jacket when he saw her small feet on the sill. She was shorter than he, but her womanly figure made her wider. He winced when her hip brushed a shard of glass as she squeezed through, but it did not tear the fabric of her dress, and a moment later she fell into his arms.

He held her easily. She was not heavy, and he was in good shape. He set her on her feet, but she dropped to her knees, gasping for air.

He glanced around. The thugs were still keeping their distance. He looked inside the bus. Cora Jones was standing in the aisle, coughing, turning round and round, too shocked and bewildered to save herself. "Cora, come here!" he yelled. She heard her name and looked at him. "Come through the window, like we did!" he shouted. "I'll help you!" She seemed to understand. With difficulty, she stood on the seat, still clutching her handbag. She hesitated, look-ing at the jagged bits of glass all around the window frame; but she had on a thick coat, and she seemed to decide a cut was a better risk than choking to death. She put one foot on the sill. George reached through the window, grabbed her arm, and pulled. She tore her coat but did no harm to her-self, and he lifted her down. She staggered away, calling for water.

"We have to get away from the bus!" he yelled to Maria. "The fuel tank might explode." But Maria was so racked by coughing that she seemed helpless to move. He put one arm around her back and the other behind her knees and picked her up. He carried her toward the grocery store and set her down when he thought they were at a safe distance.

He looked back and saw that the bus was now emptying rapidly. The door had at last been opened, and people were stumbling through as well as jumping from the windows.

The flames grew. As the last passengers got out, the in-side of the vehicle became a furnace. George heard a man shout something about the fuel tank, and the mob took up the cry, shouting: "She's gonna blow! She's gonna blow!" Everyone scattered in fear, getting farther away. Then there was a deep thump and a sudden fierce gout of flame, and the vehicle rocked with the explosion.

George was pretty sure no one was left inside, and he thought: At least no one is dead—yet.

The detonation seemed to have sated the mob's hunger for violence. They stood around, watching the bus burn.

A small crowd of what appeared to be local people had gathered outside the grocery store, many cheering the mob; but now a young girl came out of the building with a pail of water and some plastic cups. She gave a drink to Mrs. Jones, then came to Maria, who gratefully downed a cup of water and asked for another.

A young white man approached with a look of concern. He had a face like a rodent, forehead and chin angling back from a sharp nose and buck teeth, red-brown hair slicked back with pomade. "How are you doing, darling?" he said to Maria. But he was concealing something, and as Maria started to reply he raised a crowbar high in the air and brought it down, aiming at the top of her head. George flung out an arm to protect her, and the bar came down hard on his left forearm. The pain was agonizing, and he roared. The man lifted the crowbar again. Despite his arm George lunged forward, leading with his right shoulder, and barged into the man so hard that he went flying.

George turned back to Maria and saw three more of the mob running at him, evidently bent on revenging their rat-like friend. George had been premature in thinking the segregationists had had their fill of violence.

He was used to combat. He had been on the Harvard wrestling team as an undergraduate, and had coached the team while getting his law degree. But this was not going to be a fair fight with rules. And he had only one working arm.

On the other hand, he had gone to grade school in a Washington slum, and he knew about fighting dirty.

They were coming at him three abreast, so he moved sideways. This not only took them away from Maria, but turned them so that they were now advancing in single file.

The first man swung an iron chain at him wildly.

George danced back, and the chain missed him. The momentum of the swing threw the man off balance. As he staggered, George kicked his legs from under him, and he crashed to the ground. He lost hold of his chain.

The second man stumbled over the first. George stepped forward, turned his back, and hit the man in the face with his right elbow, hoping to dislocate his jaw. The man gave a strangled scream and fell down, dropping his tire iron.

The third man stopped, suddenly scared. George stepped toward him and punched him in the face with all his might. George's fist caught the man full on the nose. Bones crunched and blood spurted, and the man screamed in agony. It was the most satisfying blow George had ever struck in his life. To hell with Gandhi, he thought.

Two shots rang out. Everyone stopped what they were doing and looked toward the noise. One of the uniformed state troopers was holding a revolver high in the air. "Okay, boys, you've had your fun," he said. "Let's move out."

George was furious. Fun? The cop had been a witness to attempted murder, and he called it fun? George was beginning to see that a police uniform did not mean much in Alabama.

The mob returned to their cars. George noticed angrily

that none of the four police officers troubled to write down any license plates. Nor did they take any names, though they probably knew everyone anyway.

Joseph Hugo had vanished.

There was another explosion in the wreckage of the bus, and George guessed there must be a second fuel tank; but at this point no one was near enough to be in danger. The fire then seemed to burn itself out.

Several people lay on the ground, many still gasping for breath after inhaling smoke. Others were bleeding from various injuries. Some were Riders, some regular passengers, black and white. George himself was clutching his left arm with his right hand, holding it against his side, trying to keep it motionless because every movement was excruciatingly painful. The four men he had tangled with were helping one another limp back to their cars.

He managed to walk to where the patrolmen stood. "We need an ambulance," he said. "Maybe two."

The younger of the two uniformed men glared at him. "What did you say?"

"These people need medical attention," George said. "Call an ambulance!"

The man looked furious, and George realized he had made the mistake of telling a white man what to do. But the older patrolman said to his colleague: "Leave it, leave it." Then he said to George: "Ambulance is on its way, boy."

A few minutes later, an ambulance the size of a small bus arrived, and the Riders began to help each other aboard. But when George and Maria approached, the driver said: "Not you."

George stared at him in disbelief. "What?"

"This here's a white folks' ambulance," the driver said. "It ain't for nigras."

"The hell you say."

"Don't you sass me, boy."

A white Rider who was already on board came back out. "You have to take everyone to the hospital," he said to the driver. "Black and white."

"This ain't a nigra ambulance," the driver said stubbornly.

"Well, we're not going without our friends." With that the white Riders began to leave the ambulance one by one.

The driver was taken aback. He would look foolish, George guessed, if he returned from the scene with no patients.

The older patrolman came over and said: "Better take 'em, Roy."

"If you say so," said the driver.

George and Maria boarded the ambulance.

As they drove away, George looked back at the bus. Nothing remained but a drift of smoke and a blackened hulk, with a row of scorched roof struts sticking up like the ribs of a martyr burned at the stake.

CHAPTER FIVE

Tanya Dvorkin left Yakutsk, Siberia—the coldest city in the world—after an early breakfast. She flew to Moscow, a distance of a little over three thousand miles, in a Tupolev Tu-16 of the Red Air Force. The cabin was configured for half a dozen military men, and the designer had not wasted time thinking of their comfort: the seats were made of pierced aluminum and there was no soundproofing. The journey took eight hours with one refueling stop. Because Moscow was six hours behind Yakutsk, Tanya arrived in time for another breakfast.

It was summer in Moscow, and she carried her heavy coat and fur hat. She took a taxi to Government House, the apartment building for Moscow's privileged elite. She shared a flat with her mother, Anya, and her twin brother, Dmitri, always called Dimka. It was a big place, with three bedrooms, though Mother said it was spacious only by Soviet standards: the Berlin apartment she had lived in as a child, when Grandfather Grigori had been a diplomat, had been much more grand.

This morning the place was silent and empty: Mother and Dimka had both left for work already. Their coats were hanging in the hall, on nails knocked in by Tanya's father a quarter of a century ago: Dimka's black raincoat and Mother's brown tweed, left at home in the warm weather. Tanya hung up her own coat beside them and put her suitcase in her bedroom. She had not expected them to be in, but all the same she felt a twinge of regret that Mother was not here to make her tea, nor Dimka to listen to her adventures in Siberia. She thought of going to see her grandparents Grigori and Katerina Peshkov, who lived on another floor in the same building, but decided she did not really have the time.

She showered and changed her clothes, then took a bus to the headquarters of TASS, the Soviet news agency. She was one of more than a thousand reporters working for the agency, but not many were flown around in air force jets. She was a rising star, able to produce lively and interesting articles that appealed to young people but nevertheless adhered to the party line. It was a mixed blessing: she was often given difficult high-profile assignments.

In the canteen she had a bowl of buckwheat kasha with sour cream, then she went to the features department, where she worked. Although she was a star, she did not yet merit an office of her own. She greeted her colleagues, then sat at a desk, put paper and carbons into a typewriter, and began to write.

The flight had been too bumpy even to make notes, but she had planned her articles in her head, and now she was able to write fluently, referring occasionally to her notebook for details. Her brief was to encourage young Soviet families to migrate to Siberia to work in the boom industries of mining and drilling: not an easy task. The prison camps provided plenty of unskilled labor, but the region needed geologists, engineers, surveyors, architects, chemists, and managers. However, Tanya in her article ignored the men and wrote about their wives. She began with an attractive young mother called Klara who had talked with enthusiasm and humor about coping with life at sub-zero temperatures.

Halfway through the morning Tanya's editor, Daniil Antonov, picked up the sheets of paper from her tray and began to read. He was a small man with a gentle manner that was unusual in the world of journalism. "This is great," he said after a while. "When can I have the rest?"

"I'm typing as fast as I can."

He lingered. "While you were in Siberia, did you hear anything about Ustin Bodian?" Bodian was an opera singer who had been caught smuggling in two copies of *Doctor*

Zhivago he had obtained while singing in Italy. He was now in a labor camp.

Tanya's heart raced guiltily. Did Daniil suspect her? He was unusually intuitive for a man. "No," she lied. "Why do you ask? Have you heard something?"

"Nothing." Daniil returned to his desk.

Tanya had almost finished the third article when Pyotr Opotkin stopped beside her desk and began to read her copy with a cigarette dangling from his lips. A stout man with bad skin, Opotkin was editor in chief for features. Unlike Daniil he was not a trained journalist but a commissar, a political appointee. His job was to make sure features did not violate Kremlin guidelines, and his only qualification for the job was rigid orthodoxy.

He read Tanya's first few pages and said: "I told you not to write about the weather." He came from a village north of Moscow and still had the north-Russian accent.

Tanya sighed. "Pyotr, the series is about Siberia. People already know it's cold there. Nobody would be fooled."

"But this is *all* about the weather."

"It's about how a resourceful young woman from Moscow is raising her family in challenging conditions—and having a great adventure."

Daniil joined the conversation. "She's right, Pyotr," he said. "If we avoid all mention of the cold, people will know the article is shit, and they won't believe a word of it."

"I don't like it," Opotkin said stubbornly.

"You have to admit," Daniil persisted, "Tanya makes it sound exciting."

Opotkin looked thoughtful. "Maybe you're right," he said, and dropped the copy back into the tray. "I'm having a party at my house on Saturday night," he said to Tanya. "My daughter graduated college. I was wondering if you and your brother would like to come?"

Opotkin was an unsuccessful social climber who gave agonizingly boring parties. Tanya knew she could speak for her brother. "I'd love to, and I'm sure Dimka would too, but it's our mother's birthday. I'm so sorry."

Opotkin looked offended. "Too bad," he said, and walked on.

When he was out of earshot Daniil said: "It's not your mother's birthday, is it?"

"No."

"He'll check."

"Then he'll realize I made a polite excuse because I didn't want to go."

"You should go to his parties."

Tanya did not want to have this argument. There were more important things on her mind. She needed to write her articles, get out of there, and save the life of Ustin Bodian. But Daniil was a good boss and liberal minded, so she suppressed her impatience. "Pyotr doesn't care whether I attend his party or not," she said. "He wants my brother, who works for Khrushchev." Tanya was used to people trying to befriend her because of her influential family. Her late father had been a colonel in the KGB, the secret police; and her uncle Volodya was a general in Red Army Intelligence.

Daniil had a journalist's persistence. "Pyotr gave in to us over the Siberia articles. You should show that you're grateful."

"I hate his parties. His friends get drunk and paw each other's wives."

"I don't want him to bear a grudge against you."

"Why would he do that?"

"You're very attractive." Daniil was not coming on to Tanya. He lived with a male friend and she was sure he was one of those men not drawn to women. He spoke in a matter-of-fact tone. "Beautiful, and talented, and—worst of all—young. Pyotr won't find it difficult to hate you. Try a little harder with him." Daniil drifted away.

Tanya realized he was probably right, but she decided to think about it later, and returned her attention to her typewriter.

At midday she got a plate of potato salad with pickled herrings from the canteen and ate at her desk.

She finished her third article soon afterward. She handed the sheets of paper to Daniil. "I'm going home to bed," she said. "Please don't call."

"Good work," he said. "Sleep well."

She put her notebook in her shoulder bag and left the building.

Now she had to make sure she was not being followed. She was tired, and that meant she was likely to make foolish mistakes. She felt worried.

She went past the bus stop, walked several blocks to the previous stop on the route, and caught the bus there. It made no sense, which meant that anyone who did the same had to be following her.

No one was.

She got off near a grand pre-revolutionary palace now converted to apartments. She walked around the block, but no one appeared to be watching the building. Anxiously she went around again to make sure. Then she entered the gloomy hall and climbed the cracked marble staircase to the apartment of Vasili Yenkov.

Just as she was about to put her key in the lock the door opened, and a slim blond girl of about eighteen stood there. Vasili was behind her. Tanya cursed inwardly. It was too late for her to run away or pretend she was going to a different apartment.

The blonde gave Tanya a hard, appraising stare, taking in her hairstyle, her figure, and her clothes. Then she kissed Vasili on the mouth, threw a triumphant look at Tanya, and went down the staircase.

Vasili was thirty but he liked girls young. They yielded to him because he was tall and dashing, with carved good looks and thick dark hair always a little too long and soft brown bedroom eyes. Tanya admired him for a completely different set of reasons: because he was bright, brave, and a world-class writer.

She walked into his study and dropped her bag on a chair. Vasili worked as a radio script editor and was a naturally untidy man. Papers covered his desk, and books were stacked on the floor. He seemed to be working on a radio adaptation of Maxim Gorky's first play, *The Philistines.* His gray cat, Mademoiselle, was sleeping on the couch. Tanya pushed her off and sat down. "Who was that little tart?" she said.

"That was my mother."

Tanya laughed despite her annoyance.

"I'm sorry she was here," Vasili said, though he did not look very sad about it.

"You knew I was coming today."

"I thought you'd be later."

"She saw my face. No one is supposed to know there is a connection between you and me."

"She works at the GUM department store. Her name is Varvara. She won't suspect anything."

"Please, Vasili, don't let it happen again. What we're doing is dangerous enough. We shouldn't take additional risks. You can screw a teenager any day."

"You're right, and it won't happen again. Let me make you some tea. You look tired." Vasili busied himself at the samovar.

"I am tired. But Ustin Bodian is dying."

"Hell. What of?"

"Pneumonia."

Tanya did not know Bodian personally, but she had interviewed him, before he got into trouble. As well as being extraordinarily talented, he was a warm and kindhearted man. A Soviet artist admired all over the world, he had lived a life of great privilege, but he was still able to get publicly angry about injustice done to people less fortunate than himself—which was why they had sent him to Siberia.

Vasili said: "Are they still making him work?"

Tanya shook her head. "He can't. But they won't send him to the hospital. He just lies on his bunk all day, getting worse."

"Did you see him?"

"Hell, no. Asking about him was dangerous enough. If I'd gone to the prison camp they would have kept me there."

Vasili handed her tea and sugar. "Is he getting any medical treatment at all?"

"No."

"Did you get any idea of how long he might have to live?"

Tanya shook her head. "You now know everything I know."

"We have to spread this news."

Tanya agreed. "The only way to save his life is to publicize his illness and hope that the government will have the grace to be embarrassed."

"Shall we put out a special edition?"

"Yes," said Tanya. "Today."

Vasili and Tanya together produced an illegal news sheet called *Dissidence*. They reported on censorship, demonstrations, trials, and political prisoners. In his office at Radio

Moscow, Vasili had his own stencil duplicator, normally used for making multiple copies of scripts. Secretly he printed fifty copies of each issue of *Dissidence*. Most of the people who received one made more copies on their own typewriters, or even by hand, and circulation mushroomed. This self-publishing system was called *samizdat* in Russian and was widespread: whole novels had been distributed the same way.

"I'll write it." Tanya went to the cupboard and pulled out a large cardboard box full of dry cat food. Pushing her hands into the pellets, she drew out a typewriter in a cover. This was the one they used for *Dissidence*.

Typing was as unique as handwriting. Every machine had its own characteristics. The letters were never perfectly aligned: some were a little raised, some off center. Individual letters became worn or damaged in distinctive ways. In consequence, police experts could match a typewriter to its product. If *Dissidence* had been typed on the same machine as Vasili's scripts, someone might have noticed. So Vasili had stolen an old machine from the scheduling department, brought it home, and buried it in the cat's food to hide it from casual observation. A determined search would find it, but if there should be a determined search Vasili would be finished anyway.

Also in the box were sheets of the special waxed paper used in the duplicating machine. The typewriter had no ribbon: instead, its letters pierced the paper, and the duplicator worked by forcing ink through the letter-shaped holes.

Tanya wrote a report on Bodian, saying that General Secretary Nikita Khrushchev would be personally responsible if one of the USSR's greatest tenors died in a prison camp. She recapitulated the main points of Bodian's trial for anti-Soviet activity, including his impassioned defense of artistic freedom. To divert suspicion away from herself, she misleadingly credited the information about Bodian's illness to an imaginary opera lover in the KGB.

When she had done, she handed two sheets of stencil paper to Vasili. "I've made it concise," she said.

"Concision is the sister of talent. Chekov said that." He read the report slowly, then nodded approval. "I'll go in to Radio Moscow now and make copies," he said. "Then we should take them to Mayakovsky Square."

Tanya was not surprised, but she was uneasy. "Is it safe?"

"Of course not. It's a cultural event that isn't organized by the government. Which is why it suits our purpose."

Earlier in the year, young Muscovites had started to gather informally around the statue of Bolshevik poet Vladimir Mayakovsky. Some would read poems aloud, attracting more people. A permanent rolling poetry festival had come into being, and some of the works declaimed from the monument were obliquely critical of the government.

Such a phenomenon would have lasted ten minutes under Stalin, but Khrushchev was a reformer. His program included a limited degree of cultural tolerance, and so far no action had been taken against the poetry readings. But liberalization proceeded by two steps forward and one back. Tanya's brother said it depended on whether Khrushchev was doing well, and felt strong politically, or was suffering setbacks, and feared a coup by his conservative enemies within the Kremlin. Whatever the reason, there was no predicting what the authorities would do.

Tanya was too tired to think about this, and she guessed that any alternative location would be as dangerous. "While you're at the radio station, I'm going to sleep."

She went into the bedroom. The sheets were rumpled: she guessed Vasili and Varvara had spent the morning in bed. She pulled the coverlet over the top, removed her boots, and stretched out.

Her body was tired but her mind was busy. She was afraid, but she still wanted to go to Mayakovsky Square. *Dissidence* was an important publication, despite its amateurish production and small circulation. It proved the Communist government was not all-powerful. It showed dissidents they were not alone. Religious leaders struggling against persecution read about folksingers arrested for protest songs, and vice versa. Instead of feeling like a single voice in a monolithic society, the dissident realized that he or she was part of a great network, thousands of people who wanted a government that was different and better.

And it could save the life of Ustin Bodian.

At last Tanya fell asleep.

She was awakened by someone stroking her cheek. She opened her eyes to see Vasili stretched out beside her. "Get lost," she said.

"It's my bed."

She sat upright. "I'm twenty-two—far too old to interest you."

"For you, I'll make an exception."

"When I want to join a harem, I'll let you know."

"I'd give up all the others for you."

"No, you wouldn't."

"I would, really."

"For five minutes, maybe."

"Forever."

"Do it for six months, and I'll reconsider."

"Six months?"

"See? If you can't be chaste for half a year, how can you promise forever? What the hell time is it?"

"You slept all afternoon. Don't get up. I'll just take off my clothes and slip into bed with you."

Tanya stood up. "We have to leave now."

Vasili gave up. He probably had not been serious. He felt compelled to proposition young women. Having gone through the motions he would now forget about it, for a while at least. He handed her a small bundle of about twenty-five sheets of paper, printed on both sides with slightly blurred letters: copies of the new issue of *Dissidence*. He wound a red cotton scarf around his neck, despite the fine weather. It made him look artistic. "Let's go, then," he said.

Tanya made him wait while she went to the bathroom. The face in the mirror looked at her with an intense blue-eyed stare framed by pale-blond hair in a short gamine crop. She put on sunglasses to hide her eyes and tied a non-descript brown scarf around her hair. Now she could have been any youngish woman.

She went into the kitchen, ignoring Vasili's impatient foot-tapping, and drew a glass of water from the tap. She drank it all, then said: "I'm ready."

They walked to the Metro station. The train was crowded with workers heading home. They went to Mayakovsky Station on the Garden Ring orbital road. They would not linger here: as soon as they had given out all fifty copies of their news sheet they would leave. "If there should be any trouble," Vasili said, "just remember, we don't know each other." They separated and emerged aboveground a minute apart. The sun was low and the summer day was cooling.

Vladimir Mayakovsky had been a poet of international stature as well as a Bolshevik, and the Soviet Union was proud of him. His heroic statue stood twenty feet high in the middle of the square named after him. Several hundred people milled about on the grass, mostly young, some dressed in vaguely Western fashions, blue jeans and roll-neck sweaters. A boy in a cap was selling his own novel, carbon-copy pages hole-punched and tied with string. It was called *Growing Up Backward*. A long-haired girl carried a guitar but made no attempt to play it: perhaps it was an accessory, like a handbag. There was only one uniformed cop, but the secret policemen were comically obvious, wearing leather jackets in the mild air to conceal their guns. Tanya avoided their eyes, though: they were not that funny.

People were taking turns to stand up and speak one or two poems each. Most were men but there was a sprinkling of women. A boy with an impish grin read a piece about a clumsy farmer trying to herd a flock of geese, which the crowd quickly realized was a metaphor for the Communist Party organizing the nation. Soon everyone was roaring with laughter except the KGB men, who just looked puzzled.

Tanya drifted inconspicuously through the crowd, half-listening to a poem of adolescent angst in Mayakovsky's futurist style, drawing the sheets of paper one at a time from her pocket and discreetly slipping them to anyone who looked friendly. She kept an eye on Vasili as he did the same. Right away she heard exclamations of shock and concern as people started to talk about Bodian: in a crowd such as this, most people would know who he was and why he had been imprisoned. She gave the sheets away as fast as she could, eager to get rid of them all before the police got wind of what was going on.

A man with short hair who looked ex-army stood at the front and, instead of reciting a poem, began to read aloud Tanya's article about Bodian. Tanya was pleased: the news was getting around even faster than she had hoped. There were shouts of indignation as he got to the part about Bodian not getting medical attention. But the men in the leather jackets noticed the change in atmosphere and looked more alert. She spotted one speaking urgently into a walkie-talkie.

She had five sheets left and they were burning a hole in her pocket.

The secret police had been on the edges of the crowd, but now they moved in, converging on the speaker. He waved his copy of *Dissidence* defiantly, shouting about Bodian as the cops came closer. Some in the audience crowded the plinth, making it difficult for the police to get near. In response the KGB men got rough, shoving people out of the way. This was how riots started. Tanya nervously backed away toward the fringe of the crowd. She had one more copy of *Dissidence*. She dropped it on the ground.

Suddenly half a dozen uniformed police arrived. Wondering fearfully where they had come from, Tanya looked across the road to the nearest building and saw more running out through its door: they must have been concealed within, waiting in case they were needed. They drew their nightsticks and pushed through the crowd, hitting people indiscriminately. Tanya saw Vasili turn and walk away, moving through the throng as fast as he could, and she did the same. Then a panicking teenager cannoned into her, and she fell to the ground.

She was dazed for a moment. When her vision cleared she saw more people running. She got to her knees, but she felt dizzy. Someone tripped over her, knocking her flat again. Then suddenly Vasili was there, grabbing her with both hands, lifting her to her feet. She had a moment of surprise: she would not have expected him to risk his own safety to help her.

Then a cop hit Vasili over the head with a truncheon and he fell. The cop knelt down, pulled Vasili's arms behind his back and handcuffed him with swift, practiced movements. Vasili looked up, caught Tanya's eye, and mouthed: "Run!"

She turned and ran but, an instant later, she collided with a uniformed policeman. He grabbed her by the arm. She tried to pull away, screaming: "Let me go!"

He tightened his grip and said: "You're under arrest, bitch."

CHAPTER SIX

The Nina Onilova Room in the Kremlin was named after a female machine-gunner killed at the Battle of Sevastopol. On the wall was a framed black-and-white photo of a Red Army general placing the Order of the Red Banner medal on her tombstone. The picture hung over a white marble fireplace that was stained like a smoker's fingers. All around the room, elaborate plaster moldings framed squares of light paintwork where other pictures had once hung, suggesting that the walls had not been painted since the revolution. Perhaps the room had once been an elegant salon. Now it was furnished with canteen tables pushed together to form a long rectangle and twenty or so cheap chairs. On the tables were ceramic ashtrays that looked as if they were emptied daily but never wiped.

Dimka Dvorkin walked in with his mind in a whirl and his stomach in knots.

The room was the regular meeting place of aides to the ministers and secretaries who formed the Presidium of the Supreme Soviet, the governing body of the USSR.

Dimka was an aide to Nikita Khrushchev, first secretary and chairman of the Presidium, but all the same he felt he should not be here.

The Vienna Summit was a few weeks away. It would be the dramatic first encounter between Khrushchev and the new American president, John Kennedy. Tomorrow, at the most important Presidium of the year, the leaders of the USSR would decide strategy for the summit. Today, the aides were gathering to prepare for the Presidium. It was a planning meeting for a planning meeting.

Khrushchev's representative had to present the leader's thinking so that the other aides could prepare their bosses for tomorrow. His unspoken task was to uncover any latent opposition to Khrushchev's ideas and, if possible, quash it. It was his solemn duty to ensure that tomorrow's discussion went smoothly for the leader.

Dimka was familiar with Khrushchev's thinking about the summit, but all the same he felt he could not possibly cope with this meeting. He was the youngest and most inexperienced of Khrushchev's aides. He was only a year out of university. He had never been to the pre-Presidium meeting before: he was too junior. But ten minutes ago his secretary had informed him that one of the senior aides had called in sick and the other two had just been in a car crash, so he, Dimka, had to stand in.

Dimka had got a job working for Khrushchev for two reasons. One was that he had come top of every class he had ever attended, from nursery school through university. The other was that his uncle was a general. He did not know which factor was the more important.

The Kremlin presented a monolithic appearance to the outside world but, in truth, it was a battlefield. Khrushchev's hold on power was not strong. He was a Communist heart and soul, but he was also a reformer who saw failings in the Soviet system and wanted to implement new ideas. But the old Stalinists in the Kremlin were not yet defeated. They were alert for any opportunity to weaken Khrushchev and roll back his reforms.

The meeting was informal, the aides drinking tea and smoking with their jackets off and their ties undone—most were men, though not all. Dimka spotted a friendly face: Natalya Smotrov, aide to Foreign Minister Andrei Gromyko. She was in her midtwenties, and attractive despite a drab black dress. Dimka did not know her well but he had spoken to her a few times. Now he sat down next to her. She looked surprised to see him. "Konstantinov and Pajari have been in a car crash," he explained.

"Are they hurt?"

"Not badly."

"What about Alkaev?"

"Off sick with shingles."

"Nasty. So you're the leader's representative."

"I'm terrified."

"You'll be fine."

He looked around. They all seemed to be waiting for something. In a low voice he said to Natalya: "Who chairs this meeting?"

One of the others heard him. It was Yevgeny Filipov, who worked for conservative defense minister Rodion Malinovsky. Filipov was in his thirties but dressed older, in a baggy postwar suit and a gray flannel shirt. He repeated Dimka's question loudly, in a scornful tone. "Who chairs this meeting? You do, of course. You're aide to the chairman of the Presidium, aren't you? Get on with it, college boy."

Dimka felt himself redden. For a moment he was lost for words. Then inspiration struck, and he said: "Thanks to Major Yuri Gagarin's remarkable space flight, Comrade Khrushchev will go to Vienna with the congratulations of the world ringing in his ears." Last month Gagarin had been the first human being to travel into outer space in a rocket, beating the Americans by just a few weeks, in a stunning scientific and propaganda coup for the Soviet Union and for Nikita Khrushchev.

The aides around the table clapped, and Dimka began to feel better.

Then Filipov spoke again. "The first secretary might do better to have ringing in his ears the inaugural speech of President Kennedy," he said. He seemed incapable of speaking without a sneer. "In case comrades around the table have forgotten, Kennedy accused us of planning world domination, and he vowed to pay any price to stop us. After all the friendly moves we have made—unwisely, in the opinion of some experienced comrades—Kennedy could hardly have made clearer his aggressive intentions." He raised his arm with a finger in the air, like a schoolteacher. "Only one response is possible from us: increased military strength."

Dimka was still thinking up a rejoinder when Natalya beat him to it. "That's a race we can't win," she said with a brisk commonsense air. "The United States is richer than the Soviet Union, and they can easily match any increase in our military forces."

She was more sensible than her conservative boss, Dimka inferred. He shot her a grateful look and followed up. "Hence Khrushchev's policy of peaceful coexistence, which enables us to spend less on the army, and instead invest in agriculture and industry." Kremlin conservatives hated peaceful coexistence. For them, the conflict with capitalist imperialism was a war to the death.

Out of the corner of his eye, Dimka saw his secretary, Vera, a bright, nervy woman of forty, enter the room. He waved her away.

Filipov was not so easily disposed of. "Let's not permit a naïve view of world politics to encourage us to reduce our army too fast," he said scornfully. "We can hardly claim to be winning on the international stage. Look at how the Chinese defy us. That weakens us at Vienna."

Why was Filipov trying so hard to prove that Dimka was a fool? Dimka suddenly recalled that Filipov had wanted a job in Khrushchev's office—the job that Dimka had got.

"As the Bay of Pigs weakened Kennedy," Dimka replied. The American president had authorized a crackpot CIA plan for an invasion of Cuba at a place called the Bay of Pigs: the scheme had gone wrong and Kennedy had been humiliated. "I think our leader's position is stronger."

"All the same, Khrushchev has failed—" Filipov stopped, realizing he was going too far. These premeeting discussions were frank, but there were limits.

Dimka seized on the moment of weakness. "What has Khrushchev failed to do, comrade?" he said. "Please enlighten us all."

Filipov amended quickly. "We have failed to achieve our main foreign policy objective: a permanent resolution of the Berlin situation. East Germany is our frontier post in Europe. Its borders secure the borders of Poland and Czechoslovakia. Its unresolved status is intolerable."

"All right," Dimka said, and he was surprised to hear a note of confidence in his own voice. "I think that's enough discussion of general principles. Before I close the meeting I will explain the trend of the first secretary's current thinking on the problem."

Filipov opened his mouth to protest against this abrupt termination, but Dimka cut him off. "Comrades will speak when invited by the chair," he said, deliberately making his voice a harsh grind; and they all went quiet.

"In Vienna, Khrushchev will tell Kennedy we can wait no longer. We have made reasonable proposals for regulating the situation in Berlin, and all we hear from the Americans is that they want no changes." Around the table, several men nodded. "If they will not agree to a plan, Khrushchev will say, then we will take unilateral action; and if the Americans try to stop us, we will meet force with force."

There was a long moment of silence. Dimka took advantage of it by standing up. "Thank you for your attendance," he said.

Natalya said what everyone was thinking. "Does that mean we are willing to go to war with the Americans over Berlin?"

"The first secretary does not believe there will be a war," said Dimka, giving them the evasive answer that Khrushchev had given him. "Kennedy is not mad."

He caught a look of mingled surprise and admiration from Natalya as he walked away from the table. He could not believe he had been so tough. He had never been a pussycat, but this was a powerful and smart group of men, and he had bullied them. His position helped: new though he was, his desk in the first secretary's suite of offices gave him power. And, paradoxically, Filipov's hostility had helped. They could all sympathize with the need to come down hard on someone who was trying to undermine the leader.

Vera was hovering in the anteroom. She was an experienced political assistant who would not panic unnecessarily. Dimka had a flash of intuition. "It's my sister, isn't it?" he said.

Vera was spooked. Her eyes widened. "How do you do that?" she said in awe.

It was not supernatural. He had feared for some time that Tanya was heading for trouble. He said: "What has she done?"

"She's been arrested."

"Oh, hell."

Vera pointed to a phone off the hook on a side table and

Dimka picked it up. His mother, Anya, was on the line. "Tanya's in the Lubyanka!" she said, using the shorthand name for KGB headquarters in Lubyanka Square. She was close to hysteria.

Dimka was not taken totally by surprise. His twin sister and he agreed that there was a lot wrong with the Soviet Union, but whereas he believed reform was needed, she thought Communism should be abolished. It was an intellectual disagreement that made no difference to their affection for one another. Each was the other's best friend. It had always been that way.

You could be arrested for thinking as Tanya did—which was one of the things that was wrong. "Be calm, Mother, I can get her out of there," Dimka said. He hoped he would be able to justify that assurance. "Do you know what happened?"

"There was a riot at some poetry meeting!"

"I bet she went to Mayakovsky Square. If that's all . . ." He did not know everything his sister got up to, but he suspected her of worse than poetry.

"You have to do something, Dimka! Before they . . ."

"I know." Before they start to interrogate her, Mother meant. A chill of fear passed over him like a shadow. The prospect of interrogation in the notorious basement cells of KGB headquarters terrified every Soviet citizen.

His first instinct had been to say he would get on the phone, but now he decided that would not be enough. He had to show up in person. He hesitated momentarily: it could harm his career, if people knew he had gone to the Lubyanka to spring his sister. But that thought barely gave him pause. She came before himself and Khrushchev and the entire Soviet Union. "I'm on my way, Mother," he said. "Call Uncle Volodya and tell him what's happened."

"Oh, yes, good idea! My brother will know what to do."

Dimka hung up. "Phone the Lubyanka," he said to Vera. "Tell them very clearly that you're calling from the office of the first secretary, who is concerned about the arrest of leading journalist Tanya Dvorkin. Tell them that Comrade Khrushchev's aide is on his way to question them about it, and they should do nothing until he arrives."

She was making notes. "Shall I order up a car?"

Lubyanka Square was less than a mile from the Kremlin

compound. "I have my motorcycle downstairs. That will be quicker." Dimka was privileged to own a Voskhod 175 bike with a five-speed gearbox and twin tailpipes.

He had known Tanya was heading for trouble because, paradoxically, she had ceased to tell him everything, he reflected as he rode. Normally they had no secrets from one another. Dimka had an intimacy with his twin that they shared with no one else. When Mother was away, and they were alone, Tanya would walk through the flat naked, to fetch clean underwear from the airing cupboard, and Dimka would pee without bothering to close the bathroom door. Occasionally Dimka's male friends would sniggeringly suggest that their closeness was erotic, but in fact it was the opposite. They could be so intimate only because there was no sexual spark.

But for the past year he had known she was hiding something from him. He did not know what it was, but he could guess. Not a boyfriend, he felt sure: they told each other everything about their romantic lives, comparing notes, sympathizing. Almost certainly it was political, he thought. The only reason she might keep something from him would be to protect him.

He drew up outside the dreaded building, a yellow brick palace erected before the revolution as the headquarters of an insurance company. The thought of his sister imprisoned in this place made him feel ill. For a moment he was afraid he was going to puke.

He parked right in front of the main entrance, took a moment to recover his self-possession, and walked inside.

Tanya's editor, Daniil Antonov, was already there, arguing with a KGB man in the lobby. Daniil was a small man, slightly built, and Dimka thought of him as harmless, but he was being assertive. "I want to see Tanya Dvorkin, and I want to see her *right now*," he said.

The KGB man wore an expression of mulish obstinacy. "That may not be possible."

Dimka butted in. "I'm from the office of the first secretary," he said.

The KGB man refused to be impressed. "And what do you do there, son—make the tea?" he said rudely. "What's your name?" It was an intimidating question: people were terrified to give their names to the KGB.

"Dmitri Dvorkin, and I'm here to tell you that Comrade Khrushchev is personally interested in this case."

"Fuck off, Dvorkin," said the man. "Comrade Khrushchev knows nothing about this case. You're here to get your sister out of trouble."

Dimka was taken aback by the man's confident rudeness. He guessed that many people trying to spring family or friends from KGB arrest would claim personal connections with powerful people. But he renewed his attack. "What's your name?"

"Captain Mets."

"And what are you accusing Tanya Dvorkin of?"

"Assaulting an officer."

"Did a girl beat up one of your goons in leather jackets?" Dimka said jeeringly. "She must have taken his gun from him first. Come off it, Mets, don't be a prick."

"She was attending a seditious meeting. Anti-Soviet literature was circulated." Mets handed Dimka a crumpled sheet of paper. "The meeting became a riot."

Dimka looked at the paper. It was headed *Dissidence*. He had heard of this subversive news sheet. Tanya might easily have something to do with it. This edition was about Ustin Bodian, the opera singer. Dimka was momentarily distracted by the shocking allegation that Bodian was dying of pneumonia in a Siberian labor camp. Then he recalled that Tanya had returned from Siberia today, and realized she must have written this. She could be in real trouble. "Are you alleging that Tanya had this paper in her possession?" he demanded. He saw Mets hesitate and said: "I thought not."

"She should not have been there at all."

Daniil put in: "She's a reporter, you fool. She was observing the event, just as your officers were."

"She's not an officer."

"All TASS reporters cooperate with the KGB, you know that."

"You can't prove she was there officially."

"Yes, I can. I'm her editor. I sent her."

Dimka wondered whether that was true. He doubted it. He felt grateful to Daniil for sticking his neck out in defense of Tanya.

Mets was losing confidence. "She was with a man called

Vasili Yenkov, who had five copies of that sheet in his pocket."

"She doesn't know anyone called Vasili Yenkov," said Dimka. It might have been true: certainly he had never heard the name. "If it was a riot, how could you tell who was with whom?"

"I'll have to talk to my superiors," said Mets, and he turned away.

Dimka made his voice harsh. "Don't be long," he barked. "The next person you see from the Kremlin may not be the boy who makes the tea."

Mets went down a staircase. Dimka shuddered: everyone knew the basement contained the interrogation rooms.

A moment later Dimka and Daniil were joined in the lobby by an older man with a cigarette dangling from his mouth. He had an ugly, fleshy face with an aggressively jutting chin. Daniil did not seem pleased to see him. He introduced him as Pyotr Opotkin, features editor in chief.

Opotkin looked at Dimka with eyes screwed up to keep out the smoke. "So, your sister got herself arrested at a protest meeting," he said. His tone was angry, but Dimka sensed that underneath it Opotkin was for some reason pleased.

"A poetry reading," Dimka corrected him.

"Not much difference."

Daniil put in: "I sent her there."

"On the day she got back from Siberia?" said Opotkin skeptically.

"It wasn't really an assignment. I suggested she drop by sometime to see what was going on, that's all."

"Don't lie to me," said Opotkin. "You're just trying to protect her."

Daniil raised his chin and gave a challenging look. "Isn't that what you're here to do?"

Before Opotkin could reply, Captain Mets returned. "The case is still under consideration," he said.

Opotkin introduced himself and showed Mets his identity card. "The question is not whether Tanya Dvorkin should be punished, but how," he said.

"Exactly, sir," said Mets deferentially. "Would you like to come with me?"

Opotkin nodded and Mets led him down the stairs.

Dimka said in a quiet voice: "He won't let them torture her, will he?"

"Opotkin was mad at Tanya already," Daniil said worriedly.

"What for? I thought she was a good journalist."

"She's brilliant. But she turned down an invitation to a party at his house on Saturday. He wanted you to go, too. Pyotr loves important people. A snub really hurts him."

"Oh, shit."

"I told her she should have accepted."

"Did you really send her to Mayakovsky Square?"

"No. We could never do a story about such an unofficial gathering."

"Thanks for trying to protect her."

"My privilege—but I don't think it's working."

"What do you think will happen?"

"She might be fired. More likely, she'll be posted somewhere disagreeable, such as Kazakhstan." Daniil frowned. "I must think of some compromise that will satisfy Opotkin but not be too hard on Tanya."

Dimka glanced at the entrance door and saw a man in his forties with a brutally short military haircut and wearing the uniform of a Red Army general. "At last, Uncle Volodya," he said.

Volodya Peshkov had the same intense blue-eyed stare as Tanya. "What is this shit?" he said angrily.

Dimka filled him in. As he was finishing, Opotkin reappeared. He spoke obsequiously to Volodya. "General, I have discussed this problem of your niece with our friends in the KGB and they are content for me to deal with it as an internal TASS matter."

Dimka slumped with relief. Then he wondered whether Opotkin's entire approach had been to maneuver himself into a position where he could appear to do a favor for Volodya.

"Allow me to make a suggestion," said Volodya. "You might mark the incident as serious, without attaching blame to anyone, simply by transferring Tanya to another post."

That was the punishment Daniil had mentioned a moment ago.

Opotkin nodded thoughtfully, as if considering this idea;

though Dimka was sure he would eagerly comply with any "suggestion" from General Peshkov.

Daniil said: "Perhaps a foreign posting. She speaks German and English."

This was an exaggeration, Dimka knew. Tanya had studied both languages in school, but that was not the same as speaking them. Daniil was trying to save her from banishment to some remote Soviet region.

Daniil added: "And she could still write features for my department. I'd rather not lose her to news—she's too good."

Opotkin looked dubious. "We can't send her to London or Bonn. That would seem like a reward."

It was true. Assignments in the capitalist countries were prized. The living allowances were colossal and, even though they did not buy as much as in the USSR, Soviet citizens still lived much better in the West than at home.

Volodya said: "East Berlin, perhaps, or Warsaw."

Opotkin nodded. A move to another Communist country was more like a punishment.

Volodya said: "I'm glad we've been able to resolve this."

Opotkin said to Dimka: "I'm having a party on Saturday evening. Perhaps you would like to come?"

Dimka guessed this would seal the deal. He nodded. "Tanya told me about it," he said with false enthusiasm. "We'll both be there. Thank you."

Opotkin beamed.

Daniil said: "I happen to know of a post in a Communist country that's vacant right now. We need someone there urgently. She could go tomorrow."

"Where's that?" said Dimka.

"Cuba."

Opotkin, now in a sunny frame of mind, said: "That might be acceptable."

It was certainly better than Kazakhstan, Dimka thought.

Mets reappeared in the lobby with Tanya beside him. Dimka's heart lurched: she looked pale and scared, but unharmed. Mets spoke with a mixture of deference and defiance, like a dog that barks because it is frightened. "Allow me to suggest that young Tanya stay away from poetry readings in future," he said.

Uncle Volodya looked as if he could strangle the fool, but he put on a smile. "Very sound advice, I'm sure."

They all went out. Darkness had fallen. Dimka said to Tanya: "I've got my bike—I'll take you home."

"Yes, please," she said. She obviously wanted to talk to Dimka.

Uncle Volodya could not read her mind as Dimka could, and he said: "Let me take you in my car—you look too shaken for a motorcycle ride."

To Volodya's surprise, Tanya said: "Thank you, Uncle, but I'll go with Dimka."

Volodya shrugged and got into a waiting ZIL limousine. Daniil and Opotkin said good-bye.

As soon as they were all out of earshot, Tanya turned to Dimka with a frantic look. "Did they say anything about Vasili Yenkov?"

"Yes. They said you were with him. Is that true?"

"Yes."

"Oh, shit. But he's not your boyfriend, is he?"

"No. Do you know what happened to him?"

"He had five copies of *Dissidence* in his pocket, so he's not getting out of the Lubyanka soon, even if he has friends in high places."

"Hell! Do you think they will investigate him?"

"I'm sure of it. They'll want to know whether he merely hands out *Dissidence,* or actually produces it, which would be much more serious."

"Will they search his flat?"

"They would be remiss if they didn't. Why—what will they find there?"

She looked around, but no one was near. All the same she lowered her voice. "The typewriter on which *Dissidence* is written."

"Then I'm glad that Vasili isn't your boyfriend, because he's going to spend the next twenty-five years in Siberia."

"Don't say that!"

Dimka frowned. "You're not in love with him, I can tell . . . but you're not wholly indifferent to him, either."

"Look, he's a brave man, and a wonderful poet, but our relationship is not a romance. I've never even kissed him. He's one of those men who has to have lots of different women."

"Like my friend Valentin." Dimka's roommate at university, Valentin Lebedev, had been a real Lothario.

"Exactly like Valentin, yes."

"So . . . how much do you care if they search Vasili's apartment and find this typewriter?"

"A lot. We produced *Dissidence* together. I wrote today's edition."

"Shit. I was afraid of that." Now Dimka knew the secret she had been keeping from him for the past year.

Tanya said: "We have to go to the apartment, now, and take that typewriter and get rid of it."

Dimka took a step back from her. "Absolutely not. Forget it."

"We must!"

"No. I'd risk anything for you, and I might risk a lot for someone you loved, but I'm not going to stick my neck out for this guy. We could all end up in fucking Siberia."

"I'll do it on my own, then."

Dimka frowned, trying to evaluate the risks of different actions. "Who else knows about you and Vasili?"

"No one. We were careful. I made sure I wasn't followed when I went to his place. We never met in public."

"So the KGB investigation will not link you to him."

She hesitated, and at that point he knew they were in deep trouble.

"What?" he said.

"It depends how thorough the KGB are."

"Why?"

"This morning, when I went to Vasili's flat, there was a girl there—Varvara."

"Oh, fuck."

"She was just going out. She doesn't know my name."

"But, if the KGB shows her photographs of people arrested at Mayakovsky Square today, will she pick you out?"

Tanya looked distraught. "She gave me a real up-and-down look, assuming I might be a rival. Yes, she would know my face again."

"Oh, God, then we have to get the typewriter. Without that, they'll think Vasili is no more than a distributor of *Dissidence,* so they probably won't track down his every casual girlfriend, especially as there seem to be a lot. You may get away with it. But if they find the typewriter, you're finished."

"I'll do it alone. You're right, I can't put you in this much danger."

"But I can't leave you in this much danger," he said. "What's the address?"

She told him.

"Not too far," he said. "Get on the bike." He climbed on and kicked the engine into life.

Tanya hesitated, then got on behind him.

Dimka switched on the headlight and they pulled away.

As he drove, he wondered if the KGB might already be at Vasili's place, searching the apartment. It was a possibility, he decided, but unlikely. Assuming they had arrested forty or fifty people, it would take them most of the night to do initial interviews, get names and addresses, and decide whom to prioritize. All the same, it would be wise to be cautious.

When he reached the address Tanya had given him he drove past it without slowing down. The streetlights showed a grand nineteenth-century house. All such buildings were now either converted to government offices or divided into apartments. There were no cars parked outside and no leather-coated KGB men lurking at the entrance. He drove all around the block without seeing anything suspicious. Then he parked a couple of hundred yards from the door.

They got off the bike. A woman walking a dog said: "Good evening," and passed on. They went into the building.

Its lobby had once been an imposing hall. Now a lone electric bulb revealed a marble floor that was chipped and scratched, and a grand staircase with several balusters missing from the banister.

They went up the stairs. Tanya took out a key and opened the apartment door. They stepped inside and closed the door.

Tanya led the way into the living room. A gray cat observed them warily. Tanya took a large box from a cupboard. It was half full of cat food pellets. She rummaged inside and pulled out a typewriter in a cover. Then she withdrew some sheets of stencil paper.

She ripped up the sheets of paper, threw them in the fireplace, and put a match to them. Watching them burn, Dimka said angrily: "Why the hell do you risk everything for the sake of an empty protest?"

"We live in a brutal tyranny," she said. "We have to do something to keep hope alive."

"We live in a society that is developing Communism," Dimka rejoined. "It's difficult and we have problems. But you should help solve those problems instead of inflaming discontent."

"How can you have solutions if no one is allowed to talk about the problems?"

"In the Kremlin we talk about the problems all the time."

"And the same few narrow-minded men always decide not to make any major changes."

"They're not all narrow-minded. Some are working hard to change things. Give us time."

"The revolution was forty years ago. How much time do you need before you finally admit that Communism is a failure?"

The sheets in the fireplace had quickly burned to black ashes. Dimka turned away in frustration. "We've had this argument so many times. We need to get out of here." He picked up the typewriter.

Tanya scooped up the cat and they went out.

As they were leaving, a man with a briefcase came into the lobby. He nodded as he passed them on the stairs. Dimka hoped the light was too dim for him to have seen their faces properly.

Outside the door, Tanya put the cat down on the pavement. "You're on your own, now, Mademoiselle," she said.

The cat walked off disdainfully.

They hurried along the street to the corner, Dimka trying ineffectually to conceal the typewriter under his jacket. The moon had risen, to his dismay, and they were clearly visible. They reached the motorcycle.

Dimka handed her the typewriter. "How are we going to get rid of it?" he whispered.

"The river?"

He racked his brains, then recalled a spot on the riverbank where he and some fellow students had gone, a couple of times, to stay up all night drinking vodka. "I know somewhere."

They got on the bike and Dimka drove out of the city

center toward the south. The place he had in mind was on the outskirts of the city, but that was all to the good: they were less likely to be noticed.

He drove fast for twenty minutes and pulled up outside the Nikolo-Perervinsky Monastery.

The ancient institution, with its magnificent cathedral, was now a ruin, disused for decades and stripped of its treasures. It was located on a neck of land between the main southbound railway line and the Moskva River. The fields around it were being turned into building sites for new high-rise apartment buildings, but at night the neighborhood was deserted. There was no one in sight.

Dimka wheeled the bike off the road into a clump of trees and parked it on its stand. Then he led Tanya through the copse to the ruined monastery. The derelict buildings were eerily white in the moonlight. The onion domes of the cathedral were falling in, but the green tiled roofs of the monastery buildings were mostly intact. Dimka could not shake the feeling that the ghosts of generations of monks were watching him through the smashed windows.

He headed west across a swampy field to the river.

Tanya said: "How do you know about this place?"

"We came here when we were students. We used to get drunk and watch the sun rise over the water."

They reached the edge of the river. This was a sluggish channel in a wide bend, and the water was placid in the moonlight. But Dimka knew it was deep enough for the purpose.

Tanya hesitated. "What a waste," she said.

Dimka shrugged. "Typewriters are expensive."

"It's not just money. It's a dissident voice, an alternative view of the world, a different way of thinking. A typewriter is freedom of speech."

"Then you're better off without it."

She handed it to him.

He moved the roller rightward to its maximum extension, giving himself a handle by which to hold the machine. "Here goes," he said. He swung his arm back, then with all his might he flung the typewriter out over the river. It did not go far, but it landed with a satisfying splash and immediately disappeared from sight.

They both stood and watched the ripples in the moonlight.

"Thank you," said Tanya. "Especially as you don't believe in what I'm doing."

He put his arm around her shoulders, and together they walked away.

CHAPTER SEVEN

Geography Jakes was in a sour mood. His arm still hurt like hell although it was encased in plaster and supported by a sling around his neck. He had lost his coveted job before starting it: just as Greg had predicted, the law firm of Fawcett Renshaw had withdrawn its offer after he appeared in the newspapers as an injured Freedom Rider. Now he did not know what he was going to do with the rest of his life.

The graduation ceremony, called commencement, was held in Harvard University's Old Yard, a grassy plaza surrounded by gracious redbrick university buildings. Members of the Board of Overseers wore top hats and cutaway tailcoats. Honorary degrees were presented to the British foreign secretary, a chinless aristocrat called Lord Home, and to the oddly named McGeorge Bundy, one of President Kennedy's White House team. Despite his mood, George felt a mild sadness at leaving Harvard. He had been here seven years, first as an undergraduate, then as a law student. He had met some extraordinary people, and made a few good friends. He had passed every exam he took. He had dated many women and slept with three. He had got drunk once, and hated the feeling of being out of control.

But today he was too angry to indulge in nostalgia. After the mob violence in Anniston, he had expected a strong response from the Kennedy administration. Jack Kennedy had presented himself to the American people as a liberal, and had won the black vote. Bobby Kennedy was attorney

general, the highest law enforcement officer in the land.
George had expected Bobby to say, loud and clear, that the
Constitution of the United States was in force in Alabama
the same as everywhere else.

He had not.

No one had been arrested for attacking the Freedom
Riders. Neither the local police nor the FBI had investigated any of the many violent crimes that had been committed. In America in 1961, while the police looked on,
white racists could attack civil rights protesters, break their
bones, try to burn them to death—and get away with it.

George had last seen Maria Summers in a doctor's office.
The wounded Freedom Riders had been turned away from
the nearest hospital, but eventually they had found people
willing to treat them. George had been with a nurse, having
his broken arm treated, when Maria had come to say that
she had got a flight to Chicago. He would have got up and
thrown his arms around her if he could. As it was she had
kissed his cheek and vanished.

He wondered if he would ever see her again. I could
have fallen hard for her, he thought. Maybe I already did.
In ten days of nonstop conversation he had never once felt
bored: she was at least as smart as he was, maybe smarter.
And although she seemed innocent, she had velvet brown
eyes that made him picture her in candlelight.

The commencement ceremony came to an end at eleven
thirty. Students, parents, and alumni began to drift away
through the shadows of the tall elms, heading for the formal
lunches at which graduating students would be given their
degrees. George looked out for his family but did not at first
see them.

However, he did see Joseph Hugo.

Hugo was alone, standing by the bronze statue of John
Harvard, lighting one of his long cigarettes. In the black
ceremonial robe his white skin looked even more pasty.
George clenched his fists. He wanted to beat the crap out of
that rat. But his left arm was useless and, anyway, if he and
Hugo had a fistfight in the Old Yard, today of all days, there
would be hell to pay. They might even lose their degrees.
George was already in enough trouble. He would be wise to
ignore Hugo and walk on.

Instead he said: "Hugo, you piece of shit."

Hugo looked scared, despite George's injured arm. He was the same size as George, and probably as strong, but George had rage on his side, and Joseph knew it. He looked away and tried to walk around George, muttering: "I don't wish to speak to you."

"I'm not surprised." George moved to stand in his way. "You watched while a crazed mob attacked me. Those thugs broke my goddamned arm."

Hugo took a step back. "You had no business going to Alabama."

"And you had no business pretending to be a civil rights activist when all the time you were spying for the other side. Who was paying you, the Ku Klux Klan?"

Hugo lifted his chin defensively, and George wanted to punch it. "I volunteered to give information to the FBI," Hugo said.

"So you did it without pay! I don't know whether that makes it better or worse."

"But I won't be a volunteer much longer. I start work for the Bureau next week." He said it in the half-embarrassed, half-defiant tone of someone admitting that he belongs to a religious sect.

"You were such a good snitch that they gave you a job."

"I always wanted to work in law enforcement."

"That's not what you were doing in Anniston. You were on the side of the criminals there."

"You people are Communists. I've heard you talking about Karl Marx."

"And Hegel, and Voltaire, and Gandhi, and Jesus Christ. Come on, Hugo, even you aren't that stupid."

"I hate disorder."

And that was the problem, George reflected bitterly. People hated disorder. Press coverage had blamed the Riders for stirring up trouble, not the segregationists with their baseball bats and their bombs. It drove him mad with frustration: did no one in America think about what was *right*?

Across the grass he spotted Verena Marquand, waving at him. He abruptly lost interest in Joseph Hugo.

Verena was graduating from the English Department. However, there were so few people of color at Harvard that they all knew one another. And she was so gorgeous that he would have noticed her if she had been one of a thousand colored girls at Harvard. She had green eyes and skin the color of toffee ice cream. Under her robe she was wearing a green dress with a short skirt that showed off long, smooth legs. The mortarboard was perched on her head at a cute angle. She was dynamite.

People said she and George were a good match, but they had never dated. Whenever he had been unattached, she had been in a relationship, and vice versa. Now it was too late.

Verena was an ardent civil rights campaigner, and was going to work for Martin Luther King in Atlanta after graduation. Now she said enthusiastically: "You really started something with that Freedom Ride!"

It was true. After the firebombing at Anniston, George had left Alabama by plane with his arm in plaster; but others had taken up the challenge. Ten students from Nashville had caught a bus to Birmingham, where they had been arrested. New Riders had replaced the first group. There had been more mob violence by white racists. Freedom Riding had become a mass movement.

"But I lost my job," George said.

"Come to Atlanta and work for King," Verena said immediately.

George was startled. "Did he tell you to ask me?"

"No, but he needs a lawyer, and no one half as bright as you has applied."

George was intrigued. He had almost fallen in love with Maria Summers, but he would do well to forget her: he would probably never see her again. He wondered whether Verena would go out with him if they were both working for King. "That's an idea," he said. But he wanted to think about it.

He changed the subject. "Are your folks here today?"

"Of course, come and meet them."

Verena's parents were celebrity supporters of Kennedy. George was hoping they would now come out and criticize the president for his feeble reaction to segregationist violence. Perhaps George and Verena together could persuade them to make a public statement. That would do a lot to ease the pain of his arm.

He walked across the lawn beside Verena.

"Mom, Dad, this is my friend George Jakes," said Verena.

Her parents were a tall, well-dressed black man and a white woman with an elaborate blond coiffure. George had seen their photographs many times: they were a famous interracial couple. Percy Marquand was "the Negro Bing Crosby," a movie star as well as a smooth crooner. Babe Lee was a theater actress specializing in gutsy female roles.

Percy spoke in a warm baritone familiar from a dozen hit records. "Mr. Jakes, down there in Alabama you took that broken arm for all of us. I'm honored to shake your hand."

"Thank you, sir, but please call me George."

Babe Lee held his hand and looked into his eyes as if she wanted to marry him. "We're so grateful to you, George, and proud, too." Her manner was so seductive that George glanced uneasily at her husband, thinking he might be angered, but neither Percy nor Verena showed any reaction, and George wondered whether Babe did this to every man she met.

As soon as he could free his hand from Babe's grasp, George turned to Percy. "I know you campaigned for Kennedy in the presidential election last year," he said. "Aren't you angry now about his record on civil rights?"

"We're all disappointed," Percy said.

Verena broke in. "I should think so! Bobby Kennedy asked the Riders for a cooling-off period. Can you imagine? Of course CORE refused. America is ruled by laws, not mobs!"

"A point that should have been made by the attorney general," George said.

Percy nodded, unperturbed by this two-person attack. "I hear the administration has made a deal with the Southern states," he said. George pricked up his ears: this had not been in the newspapers. "The state governors have agreed to restrain the mobs, which is what the Kennedy brothers want."

George knew that in politics no one ever gave something for nothing. "What was the quid pro quo?"

"The attorney general will turn a blind eye to the illegal arrest of Freedom Riders."

Verena was outraged, and irritated with her father. "I

wish you had told me about this before, Daddy," she said sharply.

"I knew it would make you mad, honey."

Verena's face darkened at this condescension, and she looked away.

George concentrated on the key question: "Will you protest publicly, Mr. Marquand?"

"I've thought about it," said Percy. "But I don't think it would have much impact."

"It might influence black voters against Kennedy in 1964."

"Are we sure we want to do that? We'd all be worse off with someone like Dick Nixon in the White House."

Verena said indignantly: "Then what *can* we do?"

"What's happened in the South in the past month has proved, beyond doubt, that the law as it stands is too weak. We need a new civil rights bill."

George said: "Amen to that."

Percy went on: "I might be able to help make that happen. Right now I have a little influence in the White House. If I criticize the Kennedys I'll have none."

George felt Percy should speak out. Verena voiced the same thought. "You ought to say what's right," she said. "America is full of people being judicious. That's how we got into this mess."

Her mother was offended. "Your daddy is famous for saying what's right," she said indignantly. "He has stuck his neck out again and again."

George saw that Percy was not to be persuaded. But perhaps he was right. A new civil rights bill, making it impossible for the Southern states to oppress Negroes, might be the only real solution.

"I'd better find my folks," George said. "An honor to meet you both."

"Think about working for Martin," Verena called after him as he walked away.

He went to the park where law degrees would be presented. A temporary stage had been built, and trestle tables had been set up in tents for the lunch afterward. He found his parents right away.

His mother had a new yellow dress. She must have saved up for it: she was proud, and would not allow the rich Peshkovs to buy things for her, only for George. She looked him up and down, in his academic robe and mortarboard. "This is the happiest day of my life," she said. Then, to his astonishment, she burst into tears.

George was surprised. This was unusual. She had spent the last twenty-five years refusing to show weakness. He put his arms around her and hugged her. "I'm so lucky to have you, Mom," he said.

He detached himself gently from her embrace and blotted her tears with a clean white handkerchief. Then he turned to his father. Like most of the alumni, Greg was wearing a straw boater that had a hatband printed with the year of his graduation from Harvard—in his case, 1942. "Congratulations, my boy," he said, shaking George's hand. Well, George thought, he's here, which is something.

George's grandparents appeared a moment later. Both were Russian immigrants. His grandfather, Lev Peshkov, had started out running bars and nightclubs in Buffalo, and now owned a Hollywood studio. Grandfather had always been a dandy, and today he wore a white suit. George never knew what to think of him. People said he was a ruthless businessman with little respect for the law. On the other hand, he had been kind to his black grandson, giving him a generous allowance as well as paying his tuition.

Now he took George's arm and said confidentially: "I have one piece of advice for you in your law career. Don't represent criminals."

"Why not?"

"Because they're losers," Grandfather chuckled.

Lev Peshkov was widely believed to have been a criminal himself, a bootlegger in the days of Prohibition. George said: "Are *all* criminals losers?"

"The ones who get caught are," said Lev. "The rest don't need lawyers." He laughed heartily.

George's grandmother, Marga, kissed him warmly. "Don't you listen to your grandfather," she said.

"I have to listen," George said. "He paid for my education."

Lev pointed a finger at George. "I'm glad you don't forget that."

Marga ignored him. "Just look at you," she said to George in a voice full of affection. "So handsome, and a lawyer now!"

George was Marga's only grandchild, and she doted on

him. She would probably slip him fifty bucks before the end of the afternoon.

Marga had been a nightclub singer, and at sixty-five she still moved as if she were going onstage in a slinky dress. Her black hair was probably dyed that color nowadays. She was wearing more jewelry than was appropriate for an outdoor occasion, George knew; but he guessed that as the mistress, rather than the wife, she felt the need for status symbols.

Marga had been Lev's lover for almost fifty years. Greg was the only child they had had together.

Lev also had a wife, Olga, in Buffalo, and a daughter, Daisy, who was married to an Englishman and lived in London. So George had English cousins he had never met — white, he assumed.

Marga kissed Jacky, and George noticed people nearby giving them looks of surprise and disapproval. Even at liberal Harvard it was unusual to see a white person embrace a Negro. But George's family always drew stares on the rare occasions when they all appeared in public together. Even in places where all races were accepted, a mixed family could still bring out white people's latent prejudices. He knew that before the end of the day he would hear someone mutter the word *mongrel.* He would ignore the insult. His black grandparents were long dead, and this was his entire family. To have these four people bursting with pride at his graduation was worth any price.

Greg said: "I had lunch with old Renshaw yesterday. I talked him into renewing Fawcett Renshaw's job offer."

Marga said: "Oh, that's wonderful! George, you'll be a Washington lawyer after all!"

Jacky gave Greg a rare smile. "Thank you, Greg," she said.

Greg lifted a warning finger. "There are conditions," he said.

Marga said: "Oh, George will agree to anything reasonable. This is such a great opportunity for him."

She meant *for a black kid,* George knew, but he did not protest. Anyway, she was right. "What conditions?" he said guardedly.

"Nothing that doesn't apply to every lawyer in the world,"

Greg replied. "You have to stay out of trouble, is all. A lawyer can't get on the wrong side of the authorities."

George was suspicious. "Stay out of trouble?"

"Just take no further part in any kind of protest movement, marches, demonstrations, like that. As a first-year associate, you'll have no time for that stuff anyway."

The proposal angered George. "So I would begin my working life by vowing never to do anything in the cause of freedom."

"Don't look at it that way," said his father.

George bit back an irate retort. His family only wanted what was best for him, he knew. Trying to keep his voice neutral, he said: "Which way should I look at it?"

"Your role in the civil rights movement won't be as a frontline soldier, that's all. Be a supporter. Send a check once a year to the NAACP." The National Association for the Advancement of Colored People was the oldest and most conservative civil rights group: they had opposed Freedom Rides as being too provocative. "Just keep your head down. Let someone else go on the bus."

"There might be another way," said George.

"What's that?"

"I could work for Martin Luther King."

"Has he offered you a job?"

"I've received an approach."

"What would he pay you?"

"Not much, I'm guessing."

Lev said: "Don't think you can turn down a perfectly good job, then come to me for an allowance."

"Okay, Grandfather," said George, although that was exactly what he had been thinking. "But I believe I'll take the job anyway."

His mother joined the argument. "Oh, George, don't," she said. She was going to say more, but the graduating students were called to line up for their degrees. "Go," she said. "We'll talk more later."

George left the family group and found his place in line. The ceremony began, and he shuffled forward. He recalled working at Fawcett Renshaw last summer. Mr. Renshaw had thought himself heroically liberal for hiring a black law clerk. But George had been given work that was demeaningly easy even for an intern. He had been patient and looked for an opportunity, and one had come. He had done a piece of legal research that won a case for the firm, and they had offered him a job on graduation.

This kind of thing happened to him a lot. The world assumed that a student at Harvard must be intelligent and capable—unless he was black, in which case all bets were off. All his life George had had to prove that he was not an idiot. It made him resentful. If he ever had children, his hope was that they would grow up in a different world.

His turn came to go onstage. As he mounted the short flight of steps, he was astonished to hear hissing.

Hissing was a Harvard tradition, normally used against professors who lectured badly or were rude to students. George was so horrified that he paused on the steps and looked back. He caught the eye of Joseph Hugo. Hugo was not the only one—the hissing was too loud for that—but George felt sure Hugo had orchestrated this.

George felt hated. He was too humiliated to mount the stage. He stood there, frozen, and the blood rushed to his face.

Then someone began clapping. Looking across the rows of seats, George saw a professor standing up. It was Merv West, one of the younger faculty. Others joined him in applauding, and they quickly drowned out the hissing. Several more people stood up. George imagined that even people who did not know him had guessed who he was by the plaster cast on his arm.

He found his courage again and walked onto the stage. A cheer went up as he was handed his certificate. He turned slowly to face the audience and acknowledged the applause with a modest bow of his head. Then he went off.

His heart was hammering as he joined the other students. Several men shook his hand silently. He was horrified by the hissing, and at the same time elated by the applause. He realized he was perspiring, and he wiped his face with a handkerchief. What an ordeal.

He watched the rest of the ceremony in a daze, glad to have time to recover. As the shock of the hissing wore off, he could see that it had been done by Hugo and a handful of right-wing lunatics, and the rest of liberal Harvard had honored him. He should feel proud, he told himself.

The students rejoined their families for lunch. George's mother hugged him. "They cheered you," she said.

"Yes," Greg said. "Though for a moment there it looked as if it was going to be something else."

George spread his hands in a gesture of appeal. "How can I not be part of this struggle?" he said. "I really want the job at Fawcett Renshaw, and I want to please the family that has supported me through all these years of education—but that's not all. What if I have children?"

Marga put in: "That would be nice!"

"But, Grandmother, my children will be colored. What kind of world will they grow up in? Will they be second-class Americans?"

The conversation was interrupted by Merv West, who shook George's hand and congratulated him on getting his degree. Professor West was a little underdressed in a tweed suit and a button-down collar.

George said: "Thank you for starting the applause, Professor."

"Don't thank me, you deserved it."

George introduced his family. "We were just talking about my future."

"I hope you haven't made any final decisions."

George's curiosity was piqued. What did that mean? "Not yet," he said. "Why?"

"I've been talking to the attorney general, Bobby Kennedy—a Harvard graduate, as you know."

"I hope you told him that his handling of what happened in Alabama was a national disgrace."

West smiled regretfully. "Not in those words, not quite. But he and I agreed that the administration's response was inadequate."

"Very. I can't imagine he . . ." George trailed off as he was struck by a thought. "What does this have to do with decisions about my future?"

"Bobby has decided to hire a young black lawyer to give the attorney general's team a Negro perspective on civil rights. And he asked me if there was anyone I could recommend."

George was momentarily stunned. "Are you saying . . ."

West raised a warning hand. "I'm not offering you the

job—only Bobby can do that. But I can get you an interview . . . if you want it."

Jacky said: "George! A job with Bobby Kennedy! That would be fantastic."

"Mother, the Kennedys have let us down so badly."

"Then go to work for Bobby and change things!"

George hesitated. He looked at the eager faces around him: his mother, his father, his grandmother, his grandfather, and back to his mother again.

"Maybe I will," he said at last.

CHAPTER EIGHT

Dimka Dvorkin was abashed to be a virgin at the age of twenty-two.

He had dated several girls while at university, but none of them had let him go all the way. Anyway, he was not sure he should. No one had actually told him that sex should be part of a long-term loving relationship, but he sort of felt it anyway. He had never been in a frantic hurry to do it, the way some boys were. However, his lack of experience was now becoming an embarrassment.

His friend Valentin Lebedev was the opposite. Tall and confident, he had black hair and blue eyes and buckets of charm. By the end of their first year at Moscow State University he had bedded most of the girl students in the Politics Department and one of the teachers.

Early on in their friendship, Dimka had said to him: "What do you do about, you know, avoiding pregnancy?"

"That's the girl's problem, isn't it?" Valentin had said carelessly. "Worse comes to the worst, it's not that difficult to get an abortion."

Talking to others, Dimka found out that many Soviet boys took the same attitude. Men did not get pregnant, so it was not their problem. And abortion was available on demand during the first twelve weeks. But Dimka could not get comfortable with Valentin's approach, perhaps because his sister was so scornful about it.

Sex was Valentin's main interest, and studying took sec-

ond place. With Dimka it had been the other way around—
which was why Dimka was now an aide in the Kremlin and
Valentin worked for the Moscow City Parks Department.

It was through his connections in Parks that Valentin had
been able to arrange for the two of them to spend a week
at the V. I. Lenin Holiday Camp for Young Communists in
July 1961.

The camp was a bit military, with tents pitched in ruler-
straight rows and a curfew at ten thirty, but it had a swimming pool and a boating lake and loads of girls, and a week
there was a privilege much sought after.

Dimka felt he deserved a holiday. The Vienna Summit
had been a victory for the Soviet Union, and he shared the
credit.

Vienna had actually begun badly for Khrushchev. Kennedy and his dazzling wife had entered Vienna in a fleet of
limousines flying dozens of stars-and-stripes flags. When the
two leaders met, television viewers all over the world saw
that Kennedy was several inches taller, towering over Khrushchev, looking down his patrician nose at the bald top of
Khrushchev's head. Kennedy's tailored jackets and skinny
ties made Khrushchev look like a farmer in his Sunday suit.
America had won a glamour contest that the Soviet Union
had not even known it was entering.

But once the talks began, Khrushchev had dominated.
When Kennedy tried to have an amiable discussion, as between two reasonable men, Khrushchev became loudly aggressive. Kennedy suggested it was not logical for the Soviet
Union to encourage Communism in Third World countries,
then protest indignantly about American efforts to roll
back Communism in the Soviet sphere. Khrushchev replied
scornfully that the spread of Communism was a historic inevitability, and nothing that either leader did could stand in
its way. Kennedy's grasp of Marxist philosophy was weak,
and he had not known what to say.

The strategy developed by Dimka and other advisers
had triumphed. When Khrushchev returned to Moscow he
ordered dozens of copies of the summit minutes to be distributed, not only to the Soviet bloc, but to the leaders of
countries as far away as Cambodia and Mexico. Since then
Kennedy had been silent, not even responding to Khru-

shchev's threat to take over West Berlin. And Dimka went on holiday.

On the first day Dimka put on his new clothes, a checked short-sleeved shirt and a pair of shorts his mother had sewn from the trousers of a worn-out blue serge suit. "Are shorts like that fashionable in the West?" Valentin said.

Dimka laughed. "Not as far as I know."

While Valentin was shaving, Dimka went for supplies.

When he emerged he was pleased to see, right next door, a young woman lighting the small portable stove that was provided with each tent. She was a little older than Dimka; he guessed twenty-seven. She had thick red-brown hair cut in a bob, and an attractive scatter of freckles. She looked alarmingly fashionable in an orange blouse and a pair of tight black pants that ended just below the knee.

"Hello!" Dimka said with a smile. She looked up at him. He said: "Do you need a hand with that?"

She lit the gas with a match, then went inside her tent without speaking.

Well, I'm not going to lose my virginity with her, Dimka thought, and he walked on.

He bought eggs and bread in the store next to the communal bathroom block. When he got back there were two girls outside the next tent: the one he had spoken to, and a pretty blonde with a trim figure. The blonde wore the same style of black pants, but with a pink blouse. Valentin was talking to them, and they were laughing.

He introduced them to Dimka. The redhead was called Nina, and she made no reference to their earlier encounter, though she still seemed reserved. The blonde was Anna, and she was obviously the outgoing one, smiling and pushing her hair back with a graceful gesture.

Dimka and Valentin had brought with them one iron saucepan in which they planned to do all the cooking, and Dimka had filled it with water to boil the eggs; but the girls were better equipped, and Nina took the eggs from him to make blinis.

Things were looking up, Dimka thought.

Dimka studied Nina while they ate. Her narrow nose, small mouth, and daintily protruding chin gave her a guarded look, as if she were perpetually weighing things up.

But she was voluptuous, and when Dimka realized he might see her in a swimsuit, his throat went dry.

Valentin said: "Dimka and I are going to take a boat and row across to the other side of the lake." This was the first Dimka had heard of such a plan, but he said nothing. "Why don't the four of us go together?" Valentin went on. "We could take a picnic lunch."

It could not possibly be that easy, Dimka thought. They had only just met!

The girls looked at one another for a telepathic moment, then Nina said briskly: "We'll see. Let's clear away." She began to pick up plates and cutlery.

That was disappointing, but perhaps not the end of the matter.

Dimka volunteered to carry the dirty dishes to the bath-room block.

"Where did you get those shorts?" Nina asked while they were walking.

"My mother sewed them."

She laughed. "Sweet."

Dimka asked himself what his sister would have implied by calling a man sweet, and he decided it meant he was kind but not attractive.

A concrete blockhouse contained toilets, showers, and large communal sinks. Dimka watched while Nina washed the dishes. He tried to think of things to say, but nothing came. If she had asked him about the crisis in Berlin he could have talked all day. But he had no gift for the mildly amusing nonsense that Valentin produced in an effortless stream. Eventually he managed: "Have you and Anna been friends long?"

"We work together," she said. "We're both administra-tors at the steel union headquarters in Moscow. I got di-vorced a year ago, and Anna was looking for someone to share her apartment, so now we live together."

Divorced, Dimka thought; that meant she was sexually experienced. He felt intimidated. "What was your husband like?"

"He's a shit," said Nina. "I don't like talking about him."

"Okay." Dimka searched desperately for something bland to say. "Anna seems like a really nice person," he tried.

"She's well connected."

That seemed an odd remark to make about your friend. "How so?"

"Her father got us this holiday. He's Moscow district secretary of the union." Nina seemed proud of this.

Dimka carried the clean dishes back to the tents. When they arrived, Valentin said cheerily: "We've made sandwiches—ham and cheese." Anna looked at Nina and made a gesture of helplessness, as if to say that she had been unable to halt the Valentin steamroller; but it was clear to Dimka that she had not really wanted to. Nina shrugged, and so it was settled that they would picnic.

They had to stand in line an hour for a boat, but Muscovites were accustomed to queuing, and by late morning they were out on the clear, cold water. Valentin and Dimka took turns rowing, and the girls soaked up the sun. No one seemed to feel the need for small talk.

On the far side of the lake they tied up the boat at a small beach. Valentin pulled off his shirt, and Dimka followed suit. Anna took off her blouse and pants. Underneath she was wearing a sky blue two-piece swimsuit. Dimka knew it was called a bikini, and was fashionable in the West, but he had never actually seen one, and he was embarrassed by how aroused he felt. He could hardly take his eyes off her smooth, flat stomach and her navel.

To his disappointment, Nina kept her clothes on.

They ate their sandwiches, and Valentin produced a bottle of vodka. No alcohol was sold in the camp store, Dimka knew. Valentin explained: "I bought it from the boat supervisor. He has a small capitalist enterprise going." Dimka was not surprised: most things people really wanted were sold on the black market, from television sets to blue jeans.

They passed the bottle around, and both girls took a long swallow.

Nina wiped her mouth on the back of her hand. "So, you two work together in the Parks Department?"

"No," Valentin laughed. "Dimka's too clever for that."

Dimka said: "I work at the Kremlin."

Nina was impressed. "What do you do?"

Dimka did not really like to say, because it sounded like boasting. "I'm an assistant to the first secretary."

"You mean to Comrade Khrushchev!" Nina said in astonishment.

"Yes."

"How the hell did you get a job like that?"

Valentin put in: "I told you, he's smart. He was top of every class."

"You don't land a job like that just by getting top marks," Nina said crisply. "Who do you know?"

"My grandfather, Grigori Peshkov, stormed the Winter Palace in the October Revolution."

"That doesn't get you a good job."

"Well, my father was in the KGB—he died last year. My uncle is a general. *And* I'm smart."

"Modest, too," she said, but her sarcasm was genial. "What's your uncle's name?"

"Vladimir Peshkov. We call him Volodya."

"I've heard of General Peshkov. So he's your uncle. With a family like that, how come you wear homemade shorts?"

Dimka was confused now. She was interested in him for the first time, but he could not make out whether she was admiring or scornful. Perhaps it was just her manner.

Valentin stood up. "Come and explore with me," he said to Anna. "We'll leave these two here to discuss Dimka's shorts." He held out his hand. Anna took it and let him pull her to her feet. Then they walked off into the woods, holding hands.

"Your friend doesn't like me," said Nina.

"He likes Anna, though."

"She's pretty."

Dimka said quietly: "You're beautiful." He had not planned to say it: it just came out. But he meant it.

Nina looked at him thoughtfully, as if reappraising him. Then she said: "Do you want to swim?"

Dimka did not care much for water, but he was keen to see her in her swimsuit. He pulled off his clothes: he was wearing swimming trunks under his shorts.

Nina had on a brown nylon one-piece, rather than a bikini, but she filled it out so well that Dimka was not disappointed. She was the opposite of slim Anna. Nina had deep breasts and wide hips, and there were freckles on her throat. She saw his gaze on her body, and she turned away and ran into the water.

Dimka followed.

It was bitingly cold despite the sun, yet Dimka enjoyed the sensual feel of the water all over his body. They both swam energetically to keep warm. They went out into the lake, then returned more slowly to the shore. They stopped short of the beach, and Dimka let his feet drift to the bottom. The water came to their waists. Dimka looked at Nina's breasts. The cold water made her nipples stick out, showing through her swimsuit.

"Stop staring," she said, and playfully splashed his face.

He splashed her back.

"Right!" she said, and grabbed his head, trying to duck him.

Dimka struggled and caught her around the waist. They wrestled in the water. Nina's body was heavy but firm, and he relished its solidity. He got both arms around her and lifted her feet off the bottom. When she thrashed, laughing and trying to free herself, he pulled her more firmly to him, and felt her soft breasts pressing against his face.

"I give in!" she yelled.

Reluctantly he put her down. For a moment they looked at one another. In her eyes he saw a gleam of desire. Something had changed her attitude to him: the vodka, the realization that he was a high-powered apparatchik, the exhilaration of horseplay in the water, or perhaps all three. He hardly cared. He saw the invitation in her smile, and kissed her mouth.

She kissed him back with enthusiasm.

He forgot the cold water, lost in the sensations of her lips and tongue, but after a few minutes she shivered and said: "Let's get out."

He held her hand as they waded through the shallows onto dry ground. They lay on the grass side by side and started kissing again. Dimka touched her breasts, and began to wonder whether this was the day he would lose his virginity.

Then they were interrupted by a harsh voice speaking through a megaphone: "Return your boat to the dock! Your time is up!"

Nina murmured: "It's the sex police."

Dimka chuckled, despite his disappointment.

He looked up to see a small rubber dinghy with an outboard motor passing a hundred yards offshore.

He waved acknowledgment. They were supposed to keep the boat for two hours. He guessed that a bribe to the supervisor would have secured an extension but he had not thought of it. Indeed, he had hardly dreamed that his relationship with Nina would progress so fast.

"We can't go back without the others," Nina said; but a moment later Valentin and Anna emerged from the woods. They had been only just out of sight, Dimka guessed, and had heard the megaphone summons.

The boys moved a little apart from the girls and they all put on their outer clothes over their swimsuits. Dimka heard Nina and Anna talking in low voices, Anna speaking urgently and Nina giggling and nodding agreement.

Then Anna gave Valentin a meaningful look. It seemed to be a prearranged signal. Valentin nodded and turned to Dimka. Quietly he said: "The four of us are going to the folk-dancing evening tonight. When we come back, Anna will come into our tent with me. You're to go with Nina in their tent. Okay?"

It was more than okay, it was thrilling. Dimka said: "You've arranged it all with Anna?"

"Yes, and Nina has just agreed."

Dimka could hardly believe it. He would be able to spend all night embracing Nina's firm body. "She likes me!"

"Must be the shorts."

They got into the boat and rowed back. The girls announced that they wanted to shower as soon as they returned. Dimka wondered how he could make the time pass quickly until evening.

When they reached the dock, they saw a man in a black suit waiting.

Dimka knew instinctively that this was a messenger for him. I might have known, he thought regretfully; things were going too well.

They all got out of the boat. Nina looked at the man sweating in his suit and said: "Are we going to be arrested for keeping the boat too long?" She was only half joking.

Dimka said: "Are you here for me? I'm Dmitri Dvorkin."

"Yes, Dmitri Ilich," the man said, respectfully using his patronymic. "I'm your driver. I'm here to take you to the airport."

"What's the emergency?"

The driver shrugged. "The first secretary wants you."

"I'll get my bag," said Dimka regretfully.

By way of a small consolation, Nina looked awestruck.

.   .   .

The car took Dimka to Vnukovo airport, southwest of Moscow, where Vera Pletner was waiting with a large envelope and a ticket to Tbilisi, capital of the Georgian Soviet Socialist Republic.

Khrushchev was not in Moscow but at his dacha, or second home, in Pitsunda, a resort for top government officials on the Black Sea, and that was where Dimka was headed.

He had never flown before.

He was not the only aide whose holiday had been cut short. In the departure lounge, about to open the envelope, he was approached by Yevgeny Filipov, wearing a gray flannel shirt as usual despite the summer weather. Filipov looked pleased, which had to be a bad sign.

"Your strategy has failed," he said to Dimka with evident satisfaction.

"What's happened?"

"President Kennedy has made a television speech."

Kennedy had said nothing for seven weeks, since the Vienna Summit. The United States had not responded to Khrushchev's threat to sign a treaty with East Germany and take West Berlin back. Dimka had assumed that the American president was too cowed to stand up to Khrushchev. "What was the speech about?"

"He told the American people to prepare for war."

So that was the emergency.

They were called to board. Dimka said to Filipov: "What did Kennedy say, exactly?"

"Speaking of Berlin, he said: 'An attack upon that city will be regarded as an attack upon us all.' The full transcript is in your envelope."

They went on board, Dimka still wearing his holiday shorts. The plane was a Tupolev Tu-104 jetliner. Dimka looked out of the window as they took off. He knew how aircraft worked, the curved upper surface of the wing creating an air-pressure difference, but all the same it seemed like magic when the plane lifted into the air.

At last he tore his gaze away and opened the envelope.

Filipov had not exaggerated.

Kennedy was not merely making threatening noises. He proposed to triple the draft, call up reservists, and increase the American army to a million men. He was preparing a new Berlin airlift, moving six divisions to Europe, and planning economic sanctions on Warsaw Pact countries.

And he had increased the military budget by more than three *billion* dollars.

Dimka realized that the strategy Khrushchev and his advisers had mapped out had failed catastrophically. They had all underestimated the handsome young president. He could not be bullied, after all.

What could Khrushchev do?

He might have to resign. No Soviet leader had ever done that—both Lenin and Stalin had died in office—but there was a first time for everything in revolutionary politics.

Dimka read the speech twice and mulled it for the rest of the two-hour journey. There was only one alternative to Khrushchev's resignation, he thought: the leader could sack all his aides, take on new advisers, and reshuffle the Presidium, giving his enemies more power, as an acknowledgment that he had been wrong and a promise to seek wiser counsel in the future.

Either way, Dimka's short career in the Kremlin was over. Perhaps it had been too ambitious, he thought dismally. No doubt a more modest future awaited him.

He wondered whether the voluptuous Nina would still want to spend a night with him.

The flight landed at Tbilisi and a small military aircraft shuttled Dimka and Filipov to an airstrip on the coast.

Natalya Smotrov from the Foreign Ministry was waiting for them there. The humid seaside air had curled her hair, giving her a wanton air. "There's bad news from Pervukhin," she said as she drove them away from the plane. Mikhail Pervukhin was the Soviet ambassador to East Germany. "The flow of emigrants to the West has turned into a flood."

Filipov looked annoyed, probably because he had not received this news before Natalya. "What numbers are we talking about?"

"It's approaching a thousand people a day."

Dimka was flabbergasted. "A thousand a *day*?"

Natalya nodded. "Pervukhin says the East German government is no longer stable. The country is approaching collapse. There could be a popular uprising."

"You see?" Filipov said to Dimka. "This is what your policy has led to."

Dimka had no answer.

Natalya drove along the coast road to a forested peninsula and turned in at a massive iron gate in a long stucco wall. Set amid immaculate lawns was a white villa with a long balcony on the upper floor. Beside the house was a full-size swimming pool. Dimka had never seen a home with its own pool.

"He's down by the sea," a guard told Dimka, jerking his head toward the far side of the house.

Dimka found his way through the trees to a shingle beach. A soldier with a submachine gun looked hard at him, then waved him on.

He found Khrushchev under a palm tree. The second-most powerful man in the world was short, fat, bald, and ugly. He wore the trousers of a suit, held up by suspenders, and a white shirt with the sleeves rolled. He was sitting on a wicker beach chair, and on a small table in front of him were a jug of water and a glass tumbler. He seemed to be doing nothing.

He looked at Dimka and said: "Where did you get those shorts?"

"My mother made them."

"I should have a pair of shorts."

Dimka said the words he had rehearsed. "Comrade First Secretary, I offer you my immediate resignation."

Khrushchev ignored that. "We will overtake the United States, in military might and economic prosperity, within the next twenty years," he said, as if he were continuing an ongoing discussion. "But, meanwhile, how do we prevent the stronger power from dominating global politics and holding back the spread of world Communism?"

"I don't know," said Dimka.

"Watch this," said Khrushchev. "I am the Soviet Union." He picked up the jug and poured water slowly into the glass until it was full to the brim. Then he handed the jug to Dimka. "You are the United States," he said. "Now you pour water into the glass."

Dimka did as he was told. The glass overflowed, and water soaked into the white tablecloth.

"You see?" said Khrushchev as if he had proved a point. "When the glass is full, no more can be added without making a mess."

Dimka was mystified. He asked the expected question. "What's the significance of this, Nikita Sergeyevich?"

"International politics is like a glass. Aggressive moves by either side pour water in. The overflow is war."

Dimka saw the point. "When tension is at its maximum, no one can make a move without causing a war."

"Well done. And the Americans do not want war, any more than we do. So, if we maintain international tension at the maximum—full to the brim—the American president is helpless. He cannot do anything without causing war, so he must do nothing!"

Dimka realized this was brilliant. It showed how the weaker power could dominate. "So Kennedy is now powerless?" he said.

"Because his next move is war!"

Had this been Khrushchev's long-term plan? Dimka wondered. Or had he just made it up as a hindsight justification? He was nothing if not an improviser. But it hardly mattered. "So, what are we going to do about the crisis in Berlin?" he said.

"We're going to build a wall," said Khrushchev.

CHAPTER NINE

George Jakes took Verena Marquand to the Jockey Club for lunch. It was not a club, but a swanky new restaurant in the Fairfax Hotel that had found favor with the Kennedy crowd. George and Verena were the best-dressed couple in the room, she ravishing in a gingham check frock with a wide red belt, he in a tailored dark blue linen blazer with a striped tie. Nevertheless, they were given a table by the kitchen door. Washington was integrated, but not unprejudiced. George did not let it get to him.

Verena was in town with her parents. They had been invited to the White House later today for a cocktail party being given to thank high-profile supporters such as the Marquands—and, George knew, to keep their goodwill for the next campaign.

Verena looked around appreciatively. "It's a long time since I was in a decent restaurant," she said. "Atlanta is a desert." With parents who were Hollywood stars, she had been raised to think lavish was normal.

"You should move here," George told her, looking into her startling green eyes. The sleeveless dress showed off the perfection of her café-au-lait skin, and she surely knew it. If she were to move to Washington, he would ask her for a date.

George was trying to forget Maria Summers. He was dating Norine Latimer, a history graduate who worked as a secretary at the National Museum of American History. She was attractive and intelligent, but it was not working: he still thought about Maria all the time. Perhaps Verena might be a more effective cure.

He kept all that to himself, naturally. "You're out of the swim, all the way down there in Georgia," he said.

"Don't be so sure," she said. "I'm working for Martin Luther King. He's going to change America more than John F. Kennedy."

"That's because Dr. King has only one issue, civil rights. The president has a hundred. He's the defender of the free world. Right now his major worry is Berlin."

"Curious, isn't it?" she said. "He believes in freedom and democracy for German people in East Berlin, but not for American Negroes in the South."

George smiled. She was always combative. "It's not just about what he believes," he said. "It's what he can achieve."

She shrugged. "So how much difference can *you* make?"

"The Justice Department employs nine hundred and fifty lawyers. Before I arrived, only ten were black. Already I'm a ten percent improvement."

"So what have you achieved?"

"Justice is taking a tough line with the Interstate Commerce Commission. Bobby has asked them to ban segregation in the bus service."

"And what makes you think this ruling will be enforced any better than all the previous ones?"

"Not much, so far." George was frustrated, but he wanted to hide the full extent of that from Verena. "There's a guy called Dennis Wilson, a young white lawyer on Bobby's personal team, who sees me as a threat, and keeps me out of the really important meetings."

"How can he do that? You were hired by Robert Kennedy—doesn't he want your input?"

"I need to win Bobby's confidence."

"You're cosmetic," she said scornfully. "With you there, Bobby can tell the world he's got a Negro advising him on civil rights. He doesn't have to listen to you."

George feared she might be right, but he did not admit it. "That depends on me. I have to make him listen."

"Come to Atlanta," she said. "The job with Dr. King is still open."

George shook his head. "My career is here." He remembered what Maria had said, and repeated it. "Protesters can have a big impact but, in the end, it's governments that reshape the world."

"Some do, some don't," said Verena.

When they left, they found George's mother waiting in the hotel lobby. George had arranged to meet her here, but had not expected her to wait outside the restaurant. "Why didn't you join us?" he asked.

She ignored his question and spoke to Verena. "We met briefly at the Harvard commencement," she said. "How are you, Verena?" She was going out of her way to be polite, which was a sign, George knew, that she did not really like Verena.

George saw Verena to a taxi and kissed her cheek. "It was great to see you again," he said.

He and his mother went on foot, heading for the Justice Department. Jacky Jakes wanted to see where her son worked. George had arranged for her to visit on a quiet day, when Bobby Kennedy was at CIA headquarters at Langley, Virginia, seven or eight miles out of town.

Jacky had taken a day off work. She was dressed for the occasion in a hat and gloves, as if she were going to church. As they walked he said: "What do you think of Verena?"

"She's a beautiful girl," Jacky replied promptly.

"You'd like her politics," George said. "You and Khrushchev." He was exaggerating, but both Verena and Jacky were ultraliberal. "She thinks the Cubans have the right to be Communists if they want."

"And so they do," Jacky said, proving his point.

"So what don't you like?"

"Nothing."

"Mom, we men aren't very intuitive, but I've been studying you all my life, and I know when you have reservations."

She smiled and touched his arm affectionately. "You're attracted to her, and I can see why. She's irresistible. I don't want to badmouth a girl you like, but . . ."

"But what?"

"It might be difficult to be married to Verena. I get the feeling she considers her own inclinations first, last, and in between."

"You think she's selfish."

"We're all selfish. I think she's spoiled."

George nodded and tried not to be offended. His mother was probably right. "You don't need to worry," he said. "She's determined to stay down there in Atlanta."

"Well, perhaps that's for the best. I only want you to be happy."

The Department of Justice was housed in a grand classical building across the street from the White House. Jacky seemed to swell a little with pride as they walked in. It pleased her that her son worked in such a prestigious place. George enjoyed her reaction. She was entitled: she had devoted her life to him, and this was her reward.

They entered the Great Hall. Jacky liked the famous murals showing scenes of American life, but she looked askance at the aluminum statue *Spirit of Justice,* which depicted a woman showing one breast. "I'm not a prude, but I don't see why Justice has to have her bosom uncovered," she said. "What's the reason for that?"

George considered. "To show that Justice has nothing to hide?"

She laughed. "Nice try."

They went up in the elevator. "How is your arm?" Jacky asked.

The plaster was off, and George no longer needed a sling. "It still hurts," he said. "I find it helps to keep my left hand in my pocket. Gives the arm a little support."

They got off at the fifth floor. George took Jacky to the room he shared with Dennis Wilson and several others. The attorney general's office was next door.

Dennis was at his desk near the door. He was a pale man whose blond hair was receding prematurely. George said to him: "When's he coming back?"

Dennis knew he meant Bobby. "Not for an hour, at least."

George said to his mother: "Come and see Bobby Kennedy's office."

"Are you sure it's okay?"

"He's not there. He wouldn't mind."

George led Jacky through an anteroom, nodding to two secretaries, and into the attorney general's office. It looked more like the drawing room of a large country house, with walnut paneling, a massive stone fireplace, patterned carpet and curtains, and lamps on occasional tables. It was a huge room, but Bobby had managed to make it look cluttered. The furnishings included an aquarium and a stuffed tiger. His enormous desk was a litter of papers, ashtrays, and family photographs. On a shelf behind the desk chair were four telephones.

Jacky said: "Remember that place by Union Station where we lived when you were a little boy?"

"Of course I do."

"You could fit the whole house in here."

George looked around. "You could, I guess."

"And that desk is bigger than the bed where you and I used to sleep until you were four."

"Both of us and the dog, too."

On the desk was a green beret, headgear of the U.S. Army Special Forces that Bobby admired so much. But Jacky was more interested in the photographs. George picked up a framed picture of Bobby and Ethel sitting on a lawn in front of a big house, surrounded by their seven children. "This is taken outside Hickory Hill, their home in McLean, Virginia." He handed it to her.

"I like that," she said, studying the photo. "He cares for his family."

A confident voice with a Boston accent said: "Who cares for his family?"

George spun round to see Bobby Kennedy walking into the room. He wore a crumpled light gray summer suit. His tie was loose and his shirt collar unbuttoned. He was not as handsome as his older brother, mainly because of his large rabbity front teeth.

George was flustered. "I'm sorry, sir," he said. "I thought you were out for the afternoon."

"That's all right," said Bobby, though George was not sure he meant it. "This place is owned by the American people—they can look at it if they like."

"This is my mother, Jacky Jakes," George said.

Bobby shook her hand vigorously. "Mrs. Jakes, you have a fine son," he said, turning on the charm, as he did whenever talking to a voter.

Jacky's face had darkened with embarrassment, but she spoke without hesitation. "Thank you," she said. "You have several—I was looking at them in this picture."

"Four sons and three daughters. They're all wonderful, and I speak with complete objectivity."

They all laughed.

Bobby said: "It was a pleasure to meet you, Mrs. Jakes. Come and see us anytime."

Though he was gracious, that was clearly a dismissal, and George and his mother left the room.

They walked along the corridor to the elevator. Jacky said: "That was embarrassing, but Bobby was kind."

"It was also planned," George said angrily. "Bobby's never early for anything. Dennis deliberately misled us. He wanted to make me look uppity."

His mother patted his arm. "If that's the worst thing that happens today, we'll be in good shape."

"I don't know." George recalled Verena's accusation, that his job was cosmetic. "Do you think my role here could be just to make Bobby look like he's listening to Negroes when he's not?"

Jacky considered. "Maybe."

"I might do more good working for Martin Luther King in Atlanta."

"I understand how you feel, but I think you should stay here."

"I knew you'd say that."

He saw her out of the building. "How is your apartment?" she said. "I have to see that next."

"It's great." George had rented the top floor of a high, narrow Victorian row house in the Capitol Hill neighborhood. "Come over on Sunday."

"So I can cook you dinner in your kitchen?"

"What a kind offer."

"Will I meet your girlfriend?"

"I'll invite Norine."

They kissed good-bye. Jacky would get a commuter train to her home in Prince George's County. Before she walked away she said: "Remember this. There are a thousand smart young men willing to work for Martin Luther King. But there's only one Negro sitting in the office next to Bobby Kennedy's."

She was right, he thought. She usually was.

When he returned to the office he said nothing to Dennis, but sat at his desk and wrote a summary for Bobby of a report on school integration.

At five o'clock Bobby and his aides jumped into limousines for the short ride to the White House, where Bobby was scheduled to meet with the president. This was the first time George had been taken along to a White House meeting, and he wondered whether that was a sign that he was becoming more trusted—or just that the meeting was less important.

They entered the West Wing and went to the Cabinet Room. It was a long room with four tall windows on one side. Twenty or so dark blue leather chairs stood around a coffin-shaped table. World-shaking decisions were made in this room, George thought solemnly.

After fifteen minutes there was no sign of President Kennedy. Dennis said to George: "Go and make certain Dave Powers knows where we are, will you?" Powers was the president's personal assistant.

"Sure," said George. Seven years at Harvard and I'm a messenger boy, he thought.

Before the meeting with Bobby, the president had been due to drop in on a cocktail party for celebrity supporters. George made his way to the main house and followed the noise. Under the massive chandeliers in the East Room, a hundred people were into their second hour of drinking. George waved to Verena's parents, Percy Marquand and Babe Lee, who were talking to someone from the Democratic National Committee.

The president was not in the room.

George looked around and spotted a kitchen entrance. He had learned that the president often used staff doors and back corridors, to avoid constantly being buttonholed and delayed.

He went through the staff door and found the presidential party right outside. The handsome, tanned president, only forty-four years old, wore a navy blue suit with a white shirt and a skinny tie. He looked tired and edgy. "I can't be photographed with an interracial couple!" he said in a frustrated tone, as if forced to repeat himself. "I'd lose ten million votes!"

George had seen only one interracial couple in the ballroom: Percy Marquand and Babe Lee. He felt outraged. So the liberal president was scared to be photographed with them!

Dave Powers was an amiable middle-aged man with a big nose and a bald head, about as different from his boss as could be imagined. He said to the president: "What am I supposed to do?"

"Get them out of there!"

Dave was a personal friend, and not scared to let Kennedy know when he was irritated. "What am I going to tell them, for Christ's sake?"

Suddenly George stopped being angry and started to think. Was this an opportunity for him? Without forming any definite plan, he said: "Mr. President, I'm George Jakes. I work for the attorney general. May I take care of this problem for you?"

He watched their faces and knew what they were thinking. If Percy Marquand was going to be insulted in the White House, how much better it would be if the offender were black.

"Hell, yes," said Kennedy. "I'd appreciate that, George."

"Yes, sir," said George, and he went back into the ballroom.

But what was he going to do? He racked his brains as he crossed the polished floor toward where Percy and Babe stood. He had to get them out of the room for fifteen or twenty minutes, that was all. What could he tell them?

Anything but the truth, he guessed.

When he reached the conversational group, and touched Percy Marquand gently on the arm, he still didn't know what he was going to say.

Percy turned, recognized him, smiled, and shook his hand. "Everybody!" he said to the people around him. "Meet a Freedom Rider!"

Babe Lee grabbed his arm with both hands, as if afraid someone was going to steal him. "You're a hero, George," she said.

At that moment George realized what he had to say. "Mr. Marquand, Miss Lee, I work for Bobby Kennedy now, and he would like to talk to you for a few minutes about civil rights. May I take you to him?"

"Of course," said Percy, and a few seconds later they were out of the room.

George regretted his words immediately. His heart thumped as he walked them to the West Wing. How was Bobby going to take this? He might say *Hell, no, I don't have time.* If an embarrassing incident resulted, George would be to blame. Why had he not kept his mouth shut?

"I had lunch with Verena," he said, making small talk.

Babe Lee said: "She loves her job in Atlanta. The Southern Christian Leadership Conference has a small headquarters organization, but they're doing great things."

Percy said: "Dr. King is a great man. Of all the civil rights leaders I've met, he's the most impressive."

They reached the Cabinet Room and went in. The half-dozen men there were sitting at one end of the long table, chatting, some smoking. They looked in surprise at the newcomers. George located Bobby and watched his face. He looked puzzled and irritated. George said: "Bobby, you know Percy Marquand and Babe Lee. They would be happy to talk to us about civil rights for a few minutes."

For a moment Bobby's face darkened with rage. George realized this was the second time today he had surprised his boss with an uninvited guest. Then Bobby smiled. "What a privilege!" he said. "Sit down, folks, and thank you for supporting my brother's election campaign."

George was relieved, for the moment. There would be no embarrassment. Bobby had switched to automatic charm. He asked Percy and Babe their views, and talked candidly about the difficulties the Kennedys were having with Southern Democrats in Congress. The guests were flattered.

A few minutes later the president came in. He shook hands with Percy and Babe, then asked Dave Powers to take them back to the party.

As soon as the door closed behind them, Bobby rounded on George. "Never do that to me again!" he said. His face showed the strength of his pent-up fury.

George saw Dennis Wilson smother a grin.

"Who the fuck do you think you are?" Bobby stormed.

George thought Bobby was going to hit him. He balanced on the balls of his feet, ready to dodge a blow. He said desperately: "The president wanted them out of the room! He didn't want to be photographed with Percy and Babe."

Bobby looked at his brother, who nodded.

George said: "I had thirty seconds to think of a pretext that wouldn't insult them. I told them you wanted to meet them. And it worked, didn't it? They're not offended—in fact they think they got VIP treatment!"

The president said: "It's true, Bob. George here got us out of a tight situation."

George said: "I wanted to make sure we didn't lose their support for the reelection campaign."

Bobby looked blank for a moment, taking it in. "So," he said, "you told them I wanted to talk to them, just as a way of keeping them out of the presidential photographs."

"Yes," said George.

The president said: "That was quick thinking."

Bobby's face changed. After a moment he started to laugh. His brother joined in, then the other men in the room followed suit.

Bobby put his arm around George's shoulders.

George still felt shaky. He had feared he would be fired.

Bobby said: "Georgie boy, you're one of us!"

George realized he had been accepted into the inner circle. He slumped with relief.

He was not as proud as he might have been. He had carried out a shabby little deception, and helped the president to pander to racial prejudice. He wanted to wash his hands.

Then he saw the look of rage on Dennis Wilson's face, and he felt better.

That August, Rebecca was summoned to secret police headquarters for a second time.

She wondered fearfully what the Stasi wanted now. They had already ruined her life. She had been tricked into a sham marriage, and now she could not get a job, no doubt because they were ordering schools not to hire her. What else could they do to her? Surely they could not put her in jail just because she had been their victim?

But they could do anything they liked.

She took the bus across town on a hot Berlin day. The new headquarters building was as ugly as the organization it represented, a rectilinear concrete box for people whose minds were all straight edges. Once again she was escorted up in the lift and along the sickly yellow corridors, but this time she was taken to a different office. Waiting for her there she found her husband, Hans. When she saw him, her fear was displaced by even stronger rage. Even though he had the power to hurt her, she was too angry to kowtow to him.

He was wearing a new blue-gray suit that she had not seen before. He had a large room with two windows and new modern furniture: he was more senior than she had thought.

Needing time to gather her wits, she said: "I was expecting to see Sergeant Scholz."

Hans looked away. "He was not suitable for security work."

Rebecca could see that Hans was hiding something. Presumably Scholz had been fired, or perhaps demoted to the traffic police. "I suppose he made a mistake in interviewing me here, rather than at the local police station."

"He should not have interviewed you at all. Sit there." He pointed to a chair in front of his big, ugly desk.

The chair was made of metal tubing and hard orange plastic—designed to make his victims even more uncomfortable, Rebecca guessed. Her suppressed fury gave her the strength to defy him. Instead of sitting, she went to the window and looked out over the car park. "You wasted your time, didn't you?" she said. "You went to all that trouble to watch my family, and you didn't find a single spy or saboteur." She turned to look at him. "Your bosses must be angry with you."

"On the contrary," he said. "This is considered one of the most successful operations the Stasi has ever conducted."

Rebecca could not imagine how that could be possible. "You can't have learned anything very interesting."

"My team has produced a chart showing every Social Democrat in East Germany, and the links between them," he said proudly. "And the key information was obtained in your house. Your parents know all the most important reactionaries, and many came to visit."

Rebecca frowned. It was true that most of the people who came to the house were former Social Democrats: that was only natural. "But they're just friends," she said.

Hans let out a mocking hoot of laughter. "Just friends!" he jeered. "Please, I know you think we're not very bright— you said so, many times, when I was living with you—but we're not completely brainless."

It occurred to Rebecca that Hans and all secret policemen were obliged to believe—or at least, to pretend to believe— in fantastic conspiracies against the government. Otherwise their work was a waste of time. So Hans had constructed an imaginary network of Social Democrats based on the Franck family house, all plotting to bring down the Communist government.

If only it were true.

Hans said: "Of course, it was never intended that I

should marry you. A flirtation, just enough to get me into the house, was all that we planned."

"My proposal of marriage must have presented you with a problem."

"Our project was going so well. The information I was getting was crucial. Each person I saw at your house led us to more Social Democrats. If I declined your proposal the tap would have been turned off."

"How brave you were," Rebecca said. "You must be proud."

He stared at her. For a moment she could not read him. Something was going on in his mind, and she did not know what it was. It crossed her mind that he might want to touch her or kiss her. The thought made her flesh creep. Then he shook his head as if to clear it. "We're not here to talk about the marriage," he said with irritation.

"Why are we here?"

"You caused an incident at the employment exchange."

"An incident? I asked the man standing in front of me in the line how long he had been unemployed. The woman behind the counter stood up and yelled at me. 'There is no unemployment in Communist countries!' she screeched. I looked at the queue in front of me and behind, and I laughed. That's an incident?"

"You laughed hysterically and refused to stop, and you were ejected from the building."

"It's true that I couldn't stop laughing. What she said was so absurd."

"It was not absurd!" Hans fumbled a cigarette from a packet of f6. Like all bullies, he became nervous when someone stood up to him. "She was right," he said. "No one is out of work in East Germany. Communism has solved the problem of unemployment."

"Don't, please," said Rebecca. "You'll make me laugh again, and then I'll have to be ejected from this building as well."

"Sarcasm will do you no good."

She looked at a framed photograph on the wall showing Hans shaking hands with Walter Ulbricht, the East German leader. Ulbricht had a bald dome, and he cultivated a Van-dyke beard and mustache: the resemblance to Lenin was faintly comic. Rebecca asked: "What did Ulbricht say to you?"

"He congratulated me on my promotion to captain."

"Also part of your reward for cruelly misleading your wife. So, tell me, if I'm not unemployed, what am I?"

"You are under investigation as a social parasite."

"That's outrageous! I have worked continuously since graduating. Eight years without a day of sick leave. I've been promoted and given extra responsibilities, including the supervision of new teachers. And then one day I discovered my husband was a Stasi spy, and soon afterward I was fired. Since then I have been to six job interviews. Each time, the school was desperate for me to start as soon as possible. And yet—for no reason they could give me—each time they wrote afterward telling me they were not able to offer me the post. Do you know why?"

"No one wants you."

"Everyone wants me. I am a good teacher."

"You are ideologically unreliable. You would be a bad influence on impressionable youngsters."

"I have a glowing reference from my last employer."

"From Bernd Held, you mean. He, too, is under investigation for ideological unreliability."

Rebecca felt a chill of dread deep in her chest. She tried to keep her face expressionless. How terrible it would be if kind, capable Bernd were to get into trouble on her account. I must warn him, she thought.

She failed to hide her feelings from Hans. "That's rocked you, hasn't it?" he said. "I always had my suspicions about him. You were fond of him."

"He wanted to have an affair with me," Rebecca said. "But I was unwilling to deceive you. Just fancy that."

"I would have found you out."

"Instead of which, I found you out."

"I was doing my duty."

"So, you're making sure I can't get a job, and accusing me of social parasitism. What do you expect me to do—go west?"

"Emigration without permission is a crime."

"And yet so many people do it! I hear the number has risen to almost a thousand a day. Teachers, doctors, engineers—even police officers. Oh!" She was struck by an insight. "Is that what happened to Sergeant Scholz?"

Hans looked shifty. "None of your business."

"I can tell by your face. So Scholz went west. Why do all these respectable people turn criminal, do you suppose? Is it because they want to live in a country that has free elections, and so on?"

Hans raised his voice angrily. "Free elections gave us Hitler—is that what they want?"

"Perhaps they don't like living in a place where the secret police can do anything they like. You can imagine how uneasy that makes people."

"Only those who have guilty secrets!"

"And what's my secret, Hans? Come on, you must know."

"You are a social parasite."

"So you prevent my getting a job, then you threaten to jail me for not having a job. I suppose I'd be sent to a work camp, would I? Then I would have a job, except that I wouldn't be paid. I love Communism—it's so logical! Why are people so desperate to escape from it? I wonder."

"Your mother told me many times that she would never emigrate to the West. She would consider it running away."

Rebecca wondered what he was getting at. "So . . . ?"

"If you commit the crime of illegal emigration, you will never be able to come back."

Rebecca saw what was coming, and she was filled with despair.

Hans said triumphantly: "You would never see your family again."

. . .

Rebecca was crushed. She left the building and stood at the bus stop. Whichever way she looked at it, she was forced to either lose her family or lose her freedom.

Despondent, she took the bus to the school where she used to work. She was unprepared for the nostalgia that struck her like a blow when she walked in: the sound of young people's chatter, the smell of chalk dust and cleaning fluid, the notice boards and football boots and signs saying: NO RUNNING. She realized how happy she had been as a teacher. It was vitally important work, and she was good at it. She could not bear the thought of giving it up.

Bernd was in the head teacher's office, wearing a black

corduroy suit. The cloth was worn but the color flattered him. He beamed happily when she opened the door. "Have they made you head?" she asked, although she could guess the answer.

"That will never happen," he replied. "But I'm doing the job anyway, and loving it. Meanwhile our old boss, Anselm, is head of a big school in Hamburg—and making double the salary. How about you? Take a seat."

She sat down and told him about her job interviews. "It's Hans's revenge," she said. "I never should have thrown his damn matchstick model out of the window."

"It may not be that," Bernd said. "I've seen this before. A man hates the person he has wronged, paradoxically. I think it's because the victim is a perpetual reminder that he behaved shamefully."

Bernd was very smart. She missed him. "I'm afraid Hans may hate you, too," she said. "He told me you're being investigated for ideological unreliability, because you wrote me a reference."

"Oh, hell." He rubbed the scar on his forehead, always a sign that he was worried. Involvement with the Stasi never had a happy ending.

"I'm sorry."

"Don't be. I'm glad I wrote that reference. I'd do it again. Someone has to tell the truth in this damn country."

"Hans also figured out, somehow, that you were ... attracted to me."

"And he's jealous?"

"Hard to imagine, isn't it?"

"Not in the least. Even a spy couldn't fail to fall for you."

"Don't be absurd."

"Is that why you came?" Bernd said. "To warn me?"

"And to say ..." She had to be discreet, even with Bernd. "To say that I probably won't see you for some time."

"Ah." He nodded understanding.

People rarely said they were going to the West. You could be arrested just for planning it. And someone who found out that you were intending to go was committing a crime if he failed to inform the police. So no one but your immediate family wanted the guilty knowledge.

Rebecca stood up. "So, thank you for your friendship."

He came around the desk and took both her hands. "No, thank *you*. And good luck."

"To you, too."

She realized that in her unconscious mind she had already made the decision to go west; and she was thinking of that, with surprise and anxiety, when unexpectedly Bernd bent his head and kissed her.

She was not expecting this. It was a gentle kiss. He let his lips linger on hers, but did not open his mouth. She closed her eyes. After a year of fake marriage it was good to know that someone genuinely found her desirable, even lovable. She felt an urge to throw her arms around him, but suppressed it. It would be madness now to start a doomed relationship. After a few moments she broke away.

She felt herself near to tears. She did not want Bernd to see her cry. She managed to say: "Good-bye." Then she turned away and quickly left the room.

. . .

She decided she would leave two days later, early on Sunday morning.

Everyone got up to see her off.

She could not eat any breakfast. She was too upset. "I'll probably go to Hamburg," she said, faking good spirits. "Anselm Weber is head of a school there now, and I'm sure he'll hire me."

Her grandmother Maud, in a purple silk robe, said: "You could get a job anywhere in West Germany."

"But it will be nice to know at least one person in the city," Rebecca said forlornly.

Walli chipped in: "There's supposed to be a great music scene in Hamburg. I'm going to join you as soon as I can leave school."

"If you leave school, you'll have to work," their father said to Walli in a sarcastic tone. "That will be a new experience for you."

"No quarreling this morning," said Rebecca.

Father gave her an envelope of money. "As soon as you're on the other side, get a taxi," he said. "Go straight to Marienfelde." There was a refugee center at Marienfelde, in the south of the city near Tempelhof airport. "Start the process of emigration. I'm sure you'll have to wait in line for hours, maybe days. As soon as you have everything in order, come to the factory. I'll set you up with a West German bank account, and so on."

Her mother was in tears. "We *will* see you," she said. "You can fly to West Berlin any time you want, and we can just walk across the border and meet you. We'll have picnics on the beach at the Wannsee."

Rebecca was trying not to cry. She put the money in a small shoulder bag that was all she was taking. Anything more in the way of luggage might get her arrested by the Vopos at the border. She wanted to linger, but she was afraid she might lose her nerve altogether. She kissed and hugged each of them: Grandmother Maud; her adoptive father, Werner; her adoptive brother and sister, Lili and Walli; and last of all Carla, the woman who had saved her life, the mother who was not her mother, and was for that reason even the more precious.

Then, her eyes full of tears, she left the house.

It was a bright summer morning, the sky blue and cloudless. She tried to feel optimistic: she was beginning a new life, away from the grim repression of a Communist regime. And she would see her family again, one way or another.

She walked briskly, threading through the streets of the old city center. She passed the sprawling campus of the Charité hospital and turned on to Invaliden Strasse. To her left was the Sandkrug Bridge, which carried traffic over the Berlin-Spandau Ship Canal to West Berlin.

Except that today it did not.

At first Rebecca was not sure what she was looking at. There was a line of cars that stopped short of the bridge. Beyond the cars, a crowd of people stood looking at something. Perhaps there had been a crash on the bridge. But to her right, in the Platz vor dem Neuen Tor, twenty or thirty East German soldiers stood around doing nothing. Behind them were two Soviet tanks.

It was puzzling and frightening.

She pushed through the crowd. Now she could see the problem. A crude barbed-wire fence had been erected across the near end of the bridge. A small gap in the fence was manned by police who seemed to be refusing to let anyone through.

Rebecca was tempted to ask what was going on, but she did not want to draw attention to herself. She was not far from Friedrich Strasse Station: from there she could go by subway directly to Marienfelde.

She turned south, walking faster now, and took a zigzag course around a series of university buildings to the station.

There was something wrong here, too.

Several dozen people were crowded around the entrance. Rebecca fought her way to the front and read a notice pasted to the wall that said only what was obvious: the station was closed. At the top of the steps, a line of police with guns formed a barrier. No one was being admitted to the platforms.

Rebecca began to be fearful. Perhaps it was a coincidence that the first two crossing places she had chosen were blocked. And perhaps not.

There were eighty-one places where people could cross from East to West Berlin. The next nearest was the Brandenburg Gate, where the broad Unter den Linden passed through the monumental arch into the Tiergarten. She walked south on Friedrich Strasse.

As soon as she turned west on Unter den Linden she knew she was in trouble. Here again there were tanks and soldiers. Hundreds of people were gathered in front of the famous gateway. When she got to the front of the crowd, Rebecca saw another barbed-wire fence. It was strung across wooden sawhorses and guarded by East German police.

Young men who looked like Walli—leather jackets, narrow trousers, Elvis hairstyles—were shouting insults from a safe distance. On the West Berlin side, similar types were yelling angrily, and occasionally throwing stones at the police.

Looking more closely, Rebecca saw that the various policemen—Vopos, border police, and factory militia—were making holes in the road, planting tall concrete posts, and stringing barbed wire from post to post in a more permanent arrangement.

Permanent, she thought, and her spirits sank into an abyss.

She spoke to a man next to her. "Is it everywhere?" she said. "This fence?"

"Everywhere," he said. "The bastards."

The East German regime had done what everyone said could not be done: they had built a wall across the middle of Berlin.

And Rebecca was on the wrong side.

PART TWO

BUG

1961-1962

George felt wary when he went to lunch with Larry Mawhinney at the Electric Diner. George was not sure why Larry had suggested this, but he agreed out of curiosity. He and Larry were the same age and had similar jobs: Larry was an aide in the office of air force chief of staff General Curtis LeMay. But their bosses were at loggerheads: the Kennedy brothers mistrusted the military.

Larry wore the uniform of an air force lieutenant. He was all soldier: clean shaven, with buzz-cut fair hair, his tie knotted tightly, his shoes shiny. "The Pentagon hates segregation," he said.

George raised his eyebrows. "Really? I thought the army was traditionally reluctant to trust Negroes with guns."

Mawhinney lifted a placatory hand. "I know what you mean. But, one, that attitude was always overtaken by necessity: Negroes have fought in every conflict since the War of Independence. And two, it's history. The Pentagon today needs men of color in the military. And we don't want the expense and inefficiency of segregation: two sets of bathrooms, two sets of barracks, prejudice and hatred between men who are supposed to be fighting side by side."

"Okay, I buy that," said George.

Larry cut into his grilled-cheese sandwich and George took a forkful of chili con carne. Larry said: "So, Khrushchev got what he wanted in Berlin."

George sensed that this was the real subject of the lunch.

"Thank God we don't have to go to war with the Soviets," he said.

"Kennedy chickened out," Larry said. "The East German regime was close to collapse. There might have been a counterrevolution, if the president had taken a tougher line. But the Wall has stopped the flood of refugees to the West, and now the Soviets can do anything they like in East Berlin. Our West German allies are mad as hell about it."

George bristled. "The president avoided World War Three!"

"At the cost of letting the Soviets tighten their grip. It's not exactly a triumph."

"Is that the Pentagon's view?"

"Pretty much."

Of course it was, George thought irritably. He now understood: Mawhinney was here to argue the Pentagon's line, in the hope of winning George as a supporter. I should be flattered, he told himself: it shows that people now see me as part of Bobby's inner circle.

But he was not going to listen to an attack on President Kennedy without hitting back. "I suppose I should expect nothing less of General LeMay. Don't they call him 'Bombs Away' LeMay?"

Mawhinney frowned. If he found his boss's nickname funny, he was not going to show it.

George thought the overbearing, cigar-chewing LeMay deserved mockery. "I believe he once said that if there's a nuclear war, and at the end of it there are two Americans and one Russian left, then we've won."

"I never heard him say anything like that."

"Apparently President Kennedy told him: 'You better hope the Americans are a man and a woman.'"

"We have to be strong!" Mawhinney said, beginning to get riled. "We've lost Cuba and Laos and East Berlin, and we're in danger of losing Vietnam."

"What do you imagine we can do about Vietnam?"

"Send in the army," Larry said promptly.

"Don't we already have thousands of military advisers there?"

"It's not enough. The Pentagon has asked the president again and again to send in ground combat troops. It seems he doesn't have the guts."

That annoyed George because it was so unfair. "President Kennedy does not lack courage," he snapped.

"Then why won't he attack the Communists in Vietnam?"

"He doesn't believe we can win."

"He should listen to experienced and knowledgeable generals."

"Should he? They told him to back the stupid Bay of Pigs invasion. If the Joint Chiefs are experienced and knowledgeable, how come they didn't tell the president that an invasion by Cuban exiles was bound to fail?"

"We *told* him to send air cover—"

"Excuse me, Larry, but the whole idea was to avoid involving Americans. Yet as soon as it went wrong, the Pentagon wanted to send in the marines. The Kennedy brothers suspect you people of a sucker punch. You led him into a doomed invasion by exiles because you wanted to force him to send in U.S. troops."

"That's not true."

"Maybe, but he thinks that now you're trying to lure him into Vietnam by the same method. And he's determined not to be fooled a second time."

"Okay, so he's got a grudge against us because of the Bay of Pigs. Seriously, George, is that a good enough reason to let Vietnam go Communist?"

"We'll have to agree to disagree."

Mawhinney put down his knife and fork. "Do you want dessert?" He had realized he was wasting his time: George was never going to be a Pentagon ally.

"No dessert, thanks," George said. He was in Bobby's office to fight for justice, so that his children could grow up as American citizens with equal rights. Someone else would have to fight Communism in Asia.

Mawhinney's face changed and he waved across the restaurant. George glanced back over his own shoulder and got a shock.

The person Mawhinney was waving at was Maria Summers.

She did not see him. She was already turning back to her companion, a white girl of about the same age.

"Is that Maria Summers?" he said incredulously.

"Yeah."

"You know her."

"Sure. We were at Chicago Law together."

"What's she doing in Washington?"

"Funny story. She was originally turned down for a job in the White House press office. Then the person they appointed didn't work out, and she was the second choice."

George was thrilled. Maria was in Washington—permanently! He made up his mind to speak to her before leaving the restaurant.

It occurred to him that he might find out more about her from Mawhinney. "Did you date her at law school?"

"No. She only went out with colored guys, and not many of them. She was known as an iceberg."

George did not take that remark at face value. Any girl who said no was an iceberg, to some men. "Did she have anyone special?"

"There was one guy she was seeing for about a year, but he dumped her because she wouldn't put out."

"I'm not surprised," George said. "She comes from a strict family."

"How do you know that?"

"We were on the first Freedom Ride together. I talked to her a bit."

"She's pretty."

"That's the truth."

They got the check and split it. On the way out George stopped at Maria's table. "Welcome to Washington," he said.

She smiled warmly. "Hello, George. I've been wondering how soon I'd run into you."

Larry said: "Hi, Maria. I was just telling George how you were known as an iceberg at Chicago Law." Larry laughed.

It was a typical male jibe, nothing unusual, but Maria flushed.

Larry walked out of the restaurant, but George stayed behind. "I'm sorry he said that, Maria. And I'm embarrassed that I heard it. It was really crass."

"Thank you." She gestured toward the other woman. "This is Antonia Capel. She's a lawyer, too."

Antonia was a thin, intense woman with hair severely drawn back. "Good to know you," George said.

Maria said to Antonia: "George got a broken arm protecting me from an Alabama segregationist with a crow-bar."

Antonia was impressed. "George, you're a real gentleman," she said.

George saw that the girls were ready to leave: their check was on the table in a saucer, covered with a few bills. He said to Maria: "Can I walk you back to the White House?"

"Sure," she said.

Antonia said: "I have to run to the drugstore."

They stepped out into the mild air of a Washington autumn. Antonia waved good-bye. George and Maria headed for the White House.

George studied her out of the corner of his eye as they crossed Pennsylvania Avenue. She wore a smart black raincoat over a white turtleneck, clothing for a serious political operator, but she could not cover up her warm smile. She was pretty, with a small nose and chin, and her big brown eyes and soft lips were sexy.

"I was arguing with Mawhinney about Vietnam," George said. "I think he hoped to persuade me as a way of indirectly getting to Bobby."

"I'm sure of it," said Maria. "But the president isn't going to give in to the Pentagon on this."

"How do you know?"

"He's making a speech tonight saying that there are limits to what we can achieve in foreign policy. We cannot right every wrong or reverse every adversity. I've just written the press release for the speech."

"I'm glad he's going to stand firm."

"George, you didn't hear what I said. I wrote a press release! Don't you understand how unusual that is? Normally the men write them. The women just type them out."

George grinned. "Congratulations." He was happy to be with her, and they had quickly slipped back into their friendly relationship.

"Mind you, I'll find out what they think of it when I get back to the office. What's happening at Justice?"

"It looks like our Freedom Ride really achieved something," George said eagerly. "Soon all interstate buses will have a sign saying: 'Seating aboard this vehicle is without regard to race, color, creed, or national origin.' The same words have to be printed on bus tickets." He was proud of this achievement. "How about that?"

"Well done." But Maria asked the key question. "Will the ruling be enforced?"

"That's up to us in Justice, and we're trying harder than ever before. We've already acted several times to oppose the authorities in Mississippi and Alabama. And a surprising number of towns in other states are just giving in."

"It's hard to believe we're really winning. The segregationists always seem to have another dirty trick in reserve."

"Voter registration is our next campaign. Martin Luther King wants to double the number of black voters in the South by the end of the year."

Maria said thoughtfully: "What we really need is a new civil rights bill that makes it difficult for Southern states to defy the law."

"We're working on that."

"So you're telling me Bobby Kennedy is a civil rights supporter?"

"Hell, no. A year ago the issue wasn't even on his agenda. But Bobby and the president hated those photographs of white mob violence in the South. They made the Kennedys look bad on the front pages of newspapers all over the world."

"And global politics is what they really care about."

"Exactly."

George wanted to ask her for a date, but he held back. He was going to break up with Norine Latimer as soon as possible: that was inevitable, now that Maria was here. But he felt he had to tell Norine their romance was over before he asked Maria out. Anything else would seem dishonest. And the delay would not be long: he would see Norine within a few days.

They entered the West Wing. Black faces in the White House were unusual enough for people to stare at them. They went to the press office. George was surprised to find it a small room jammed with desks. Half a dozen people worked intently with gray Remington typewriters and phones with rows of flashing lights. From an adjoining room came the chatter of teletype machines, punctuated by the bells they rang to herald particularly important messages. There was an inner office that George presumed must belong to press secretary Pierre Salinger.

Everyone seemed to be concentrating hard, no one chatting or looking out of the window.

Maria showed him her desk and introduced the woman at the next typewriter, an attractive redhead in her midthirties. "George, this is my friend Miss Fordham. Nelly, why is everyone so quiet?"

Before Nelly could answer, Salinger came out of his office, a small, chubby man in a tailored European-style suit. With him was President Kennedy.

The president smiled at everyone, nodded to George, and spoke to Maria. "You must be Maria Summers," he said. "You've written a good press release—clear and emphatic. Well done."

Maria flushed with pleasure. "Thank you, Mr. President."

He seemed in no hurry. "What were you doing before you came here?" He asked the question as if there was nothing in the world more interesting.

"I was at Chicago Law."

"Do you like it in the press office?"

"Oh, yes, it's exciting."

"Well, I appreciate your good work. Keep it up."

"I'll do my very best."

The president went out, and Salinger followed.

George looked at Maria with amusement. She seemed dazed.

After a moment, Nelly Fordham spoke. "Yeah, it takes you like that," she said. "For a minute there, you were the most beautiful woman in the world."

Maria looked at her. "Yes," she said. "That's exactly how I felt."

. . .

Maria was a little lonely, but otherwise happy.

She loved working at the White House, surrounded by bright, sincere people who wanted only to make the world a better place. She felt she could achieve a lot in government. She knew she would have to struggle with prejudice—against women and against Negroes—but she believed she could overcome that with intelligence and determination.

Her family had a history of prevailing against the odds. Her grandfather Saul Summers had walked to Chicago from his hometown of Golgotha, Alabama. On the way he had been arrested for "vagrancy" and sentenced to thirty days' labor in a coal mine. While there, he saw a man clubbed to death by guards for trying to escape. After thirty days he was not released, and when he complained he was flogged. He risked his life, escaped, and made it to Chicago. There he eventually became pastor of the Bethlehem Full Gospel Church. Now eighty years old, he was semiretired, still preaching occasionally.

Maria's father, Daniel, had gone to a Negro college and law school. In 1930, in the Depression, he had opened a storefront law firm in the South Side neighborhood, where no one could afford a postage stamp, let alone a lawyer. Maria had often heard him reminisce about how his clients had paid him in kind: homemade cakes, eggs from their backyard hens, a free haircut, some carpentry around his office. By the time Roosevelt's New Deal kicked in and the economy improved, he was the most popular black lawyer in Chicago.

So Maria was not afraid of adversity. But she was lonely. Everyone around her was white. Grandfather Summers often said: "There's nothing wrong with white people. They just ain't black." She knew what he meant. White people did not know about "vagrancy." Somehow it slipped their minds that Alabama had continued to send Negroes to forced labor camps until 1927. If she spoke about such things, they looked sad for a moment, then turned away, and she knew they thought she was exaggerating. Black people who talked about prejudice were boring to whites, like sick people who recited their symptoms.

She had been delighted to see George Jakes again. She would have sought him out as soon as she got to Washington, except that a modest girl did not chase after a man, no matter how charming he was; and anyway she would not have known what to say. She liked George more than any man she had met since she broke up with Frank Baker two years ago. She would have married Frank if he had asked her, but he wanted sex without marriage, a proposal she had rejected. When George had walked her back to the press office, she had felt sure he was about to ask her for a date, and she had been disappointed when he had not.

She shared an apartment with two black girls, but did not have much in common with them. Both were secretaries, and mainly interested in fashions and movies.

Maria was used to being exceptional. There had not been many black women at her college, and at law school she had been the only one. Now she was the only black woman in the White House, not counting cleaners and cooks. She had no complaints: everyone was friendly. But she was lonely.

On the morning after she met George she was studying a speech by Fidel Castro, looking for nuggets the press office could use, when her phone rang and a man said: "Would you like to go swimming?"

The flat Boston accent was familiar, but she could not identify it for a moment. "Who is this?"

"Dave."

It was Dave Powers, the president's personal aide, sometimes called the First Friend. Maria had spoken to him two or three times. Like most people in the White House, he was amiable and charming.

But now Maria was taken by surprise. "Where?" she said.

He laughed. "Here in the White House, of course."

She recalled that there was a pool in the west gallery, between the White House and the West Wing. She had never seen it, but she knew it had been built for President Roosevelt. She had heard that President Kennedy liked to swim at least once a day because the water relieved the pressure on his bad back.

Dave added: "There will be some other girls."

Maria's first thought was of her hair. Just about every black woman in an office job wore a hairpiece or a wig to work. Blacks and whites alike felt that the natural look of black hair just was not businesslike. Today Maria had a beehive, with a hairpiece carefully braided into her own hair, which itself had been relaxed with chemicals to mimic the smooth, straight texture of white women's hair. It was not a secret: it would be obvious to every black woman who glanced at her. But a white man such as Dave would never even notice.

How could she go swimming? If she got her hair wet it would turn into a mess that she would not be able to rescue.

She was too embarrassed to say what the problem was, but she quickly thought of an excuse. "I don't have a swimsuit."

"We have swimsuits," Dave replied. "I'll pick you up at noon." He hung up.

Maria looked at her watch. It was ten to twelve.

What was she going to do? Would she be allowed to ease herself carefully into the water at the shallow end, and keep her hair dry?

She had asked all the wrong questions, she realized. She really needed to know why she had been invited and what might be expected of her—and whether the president would be there.

She looked at the woman at the next desk. Nelly Fordham was a single woman who had worked at the White House for a decade. She hinted that years ago she had been disappointed in love. She had been helpful to Maria from the start. Now she was looking curious. "'I don't have a swimsuit'?" she quoted.

"I'm invited to the president's pool," Maria said. "Should I go?"

"Of course! Just as long as you tell me all about it when you come back."

Maria lowered her voice. "He said there will be some other girls. Do you think the president will be there?"

Nelly looked around, but no one was listening. "Does Jack Kennedy like to swim surrounded by pretty girls?" she said. "No prizes for answering that one."

Maria still was not sure whether to go. Then she remembered Larry Mawhinney calling her an iceberg. That had stung. She was not an iceberg. She was a virgin at twenty-five because she had never met a man to whom she wanted to give herself body and soul, but she was not frigid.

Dave Powers appeared at the door and said: "Coming?"

"Heck, yes," said Maria.

Dave walked her along the arcade at the edge of the Rose Garden to the pool entrance. Two other girls arrived at the same time. Maria had seen them before, always together: both were White House secretaries. Dave introduced them. "Meet Jennifer and Geraldine, known as Jenny and Jerry," he said.

The girls led Maria into a changing room where a dozen or more swimsuits hung on hooks. Jenny and Jerry stripped off quickly. Maria noticed that both had superb figures. She did not often see white girls naked. Although blondes, both had dark pubic hair in a neat triangle. Maria wondered whether they trimmed it with scissors. She had never thought of doing that.

The swimsuits were all one-pieces and made of cotton. Maria rejected the more flamboyant colors and picked a modest dark navy. Then she followed Jenny and Jerry to the pool.

The walls on three sides were painted with Caribbean scenes, palm trees and sailing ships. The fourth wall was mirrored, and Maria checked her reflection. She was not too fat, she thought, except for her ass, which was too big. The navy blue looked good against her dark brown skin.

She noticed a table of drinks and sandwiches to one side. She was too nervous to eat.

Dave was sitting on the edge, barefoot with his pants rolled up, paddling his feet in the water. Jenny and Jerry were bobbing around, talking and laughing. Maria sat opposite Dave and put her feet in. The pool was as warm as a bath.

A minute later, President Kennedy appeared, and Maria's heart beat faster.

He was wearing the usual dark suit, white shirt, and narrow tie. He stood at the edge, smiling at the girls. Maria caught a lemon whiff of his 4711 cologne. He said: "Mind if I join you?" just as if it was their pool, not his.

Jenny said: "Please do!" She and Jerry were not surprised to see him, and Maria deduced that this was not the first time they had swum with the president.

He went into the dressing room and came out again wearing blue swimming trunks. He was lean and tanned, in great shape for a man of forty-four, probably on account of all the sailing he did at Hyannis Port on Cape Cod, where he had a holiday home. He sat on the edge, then eased himself into the water with a sigh.

He swam for a few minutes. Maria wondered what her mother would say. Ma would disapprove of her daughter going swimming with a married man if he were anyone other than the president. But surely nothing bad could happen here, in the White House, in front of Dave Powers and Jenny and Jerry?

The president swam over to where she sat. "How are you getting on in the press office, Maria?" He asked this as if it were the most important question in the world.

"Fine, thank you, sir."

"Is Pierre a good boss?"

"Very good. Everyone likes him."

"I like him, too."

This close, Maria could see the faint wrinkles at the corners of his eyes and mouth, and the touch of gray in his thick red-brown hair. His eyes were not quite blue, she saw, more like hazel.

He knew she was scrutinizing him, she thought, and he did not mind. Perhaps he was used to it. Perhaps he liked it. He smiled and said: "What kind of work are you doing?"

"A mixture." She was overwhelmingly flattered. Maybe he was just being nice, but he seemed genuinely interested in her. "Mostly I do research for Pierre. This morning I've been combing through a speech by Castro."

"Rather you than me. His speeches are long!"

Maria laughed. In the back of her mind a voice said, *The president is joking with me about Fidel Castro! In a swimming pool!* She said: "Sometimes Pierre asks me to write a press release, which is the part I like best."

"Tell him to give you more releases to write. You're good at it."

"Thank you, Mr. President. I can't tell you how much that means to me."

"You're from Chicago—is that right?"

"Yes, sir."

"Where are you living now?"

"In Georgetown. I share an apartment with two girls who work in the State Department."

"Sounds good. Well, I'm glad you're settled. I value your work, and I know Pierre does too."

He turned and talked to Jenny, but Maria did not hear what he said. She was too excited. The president remembered her name; he knew she was from Chicago; he thought highly of her work. And he was *so* attractive. She felt light enough to float up to the moon.

Dave looked at his watch and said: "Twelve thirty, Mr. President."

Maria could not believe she had been here for half an

hour. It seemed like two minutes. But the president got out of the pool and went into the changing room.

The three girls got out. "Have a sandwich," Dave said. They all went to the table. Maria tried to eat something—this was her lunch break—but her stomach seemed to have shrunk to nothing. She drank a bottle of sugary soda pop.

Dave left, and the three girls changed back into their work clothes. Maria looked in the mirror. Her hair was a little damp, from the humidity, but it was still perfectly in place.

She said good-bye to Jenny and Jerry, then went back to the press office. On her desk was a thick report on health care and a note from Salinger asking for a two-page summary in an hour.

She caught the eye of Nelly, who said: "Well? What was that all about?"

Maria thought for a moment, then said: "I have no idea."

. . .

George Jakes got a message asking him to drop in on Joseph Hugo at FBI headquarters. Hugo was now working as personal assistant to FBI director J. Edgar Hoover. The message said that the Bureau had important information about Martin Luther King that Hugo wished to share with the attorney general's staff.

Hoover hated Martin Luther King. Not a single FBI agent was black. Hoover hated Bobby Kennedy, too. He hated a lot of people.

George considered refusing to go. The last thing he wanted was to speak to that creep Hugo, who had betrayed the civil rights movement and George personally. George's arm still hurt occasionally from the injury he had received in Anniston while Hugo looked on, chatting to the police and smoking.

On the other hand, if it was bad news George wanted to hear it first. Perhaps the FBI had caught King out in an extramarital affair, or something of that kind. George would welcome the chance to manage the dissemination of any negative information about the civil rights movement. He did not want someone such as Dennis Wilson spreading the word. For that reason he would have to see Hugo, and probably suffer his gloating.

FBI headquarters was on another floor of the Justice Department building. George found Hugo in a small office near the director's suite of rooms. Hugo had a short FBI haircut and wore a plain midgray suit with a white nylon shirt and a navy blue tie. On his desk was a pack of menthol cigarettes and a file folder.

"What do you want?" said George.

Hugo grinned. He could not conceal his pleasure. He said: "One of Martin Luther King's advisers is a Communist."

George was shocked. This accusation could blight the entire civil rights movement. He felt cold with worry. You could never prove that someone was *not* a Communist—and anyway, the truth hardly mattered: just the suggestion was deadly. Like the accusation of witchcraft in the Middle Ages, it was an easy way to stir up hatred among stupid and ignorant people.

"Who is this adviser?" George asked Hugo.

Hugo looked at a file, as if he had to refresh his memory. "Stanley Levison," he said.

"That doesn't sound like a Negro name."

"He's a Jew." Hugo took a photograph from the file and handed it over.

George saw an undistinguished white face with receding hair and large spectacles. The man was wearing a bow tie. George had met King and his people in Atlanta, and none of them looked like this. "Are you sure he works for the Southern Christian Leadership Conference?"

"I didn't say he *worked* for King. He's a New York attorney. Also a successful businessman."

"So in what sense is he an 'adviser' to Dr. King?"

"He helped King get his book published, and defended him from a tax-evasion lawsuit in Alabama. They don't meet often, but they talk on the phone."

George sat upright. "How would you know a thing like that?"

"Sources," Hugo said smugly.

"So, you claim that Dr. King sometimes telephones a New York attorney and gets advice on tax and publishing matters."

"From a Communist."

"How do you know he's a Communist?"

"Sources."

"What sources?"

"We can't reveal the identities of informants."

"You can to the attorney general."

"You're not the attorney general."

"Do you know Levison's card number?"

"What?" Hugo was momentarily flustered.

"Communist Party members have a card, as you know. Each card has a number. What's Levison's card number?"

Hugo pretended to search for it. "I don't think that's in this file."

"So you can't prove Levison is a Communist."

"We don't need *proof*," Hugo said, showing irritation. "We're not going to prosecute him. We're simply informing the attorney general of our suspicions, as is our duty."

George's voice rose. "You're blackening Dr. King's name by claiming that a lawyer he consulted is a Communist— and you offer no evidence whatsoever?"

"You're right," said Hugo, surprising George. "We need more evidence. That's why we'll be asking for a wiretap on Levison's phone." The attorney general had to authorize wiretaps. "The file is for you." He proffered it.

George did not take it. "If you wiretap Levison you'll be listening to some of Dr. King's calls."

Hugo shrugged. "People who talk to Communists take the risk of being wiretapped. Anything wrong with that?"

George thought there *was* something wrong with that, in a free country, but he did not say so. "We don't know that Levison is a Communist."

"So we need to find out."

George took the file, stood up, and opened the door.

Hugo said: "Hoover will undoubtedly mention this next time he meets with Bobby. So don't try to keep it to yourself."

That thought had crossed George's mind, but now he said: "Of course not." It had been a bad idea anyway.

"So what will you do?"

"I'll tell Bobby," George said. "He'll decide." He left the room.

He went up in the elevator to the fifth floor. Several Justice Department officials were just coming out of Bobby's office. George looked in. As usual, Bobby had his jacket off, his shirtsleeves rolled, and his glasses on. He had evidently just finished a meeting. George checked his watch: he had a few minutes before his next meeting. He walked in.

Bobby greeted him warmly. "Hi, George, how are things with you?"

It had been like this ever since the day George had imagined Bobby was about to hit him. Bobby treated him like a bosom pal. George wondered if that was a pattern. Maybe Bobby had to quarrel with someone before becoming close.

"Bad news," George said.

"Sit down and tell me."

George closed the door. "Hoover says he's found a Communist in Martin Luther King's circle."

"Hoover is a troublemaking cocksucker," said Bobby.

George was startled. Did Bobby mean that Hoover was queer? It seemed impossible. Maybe Bobby was just being insulting. "Name of Stanley Levison," George said.

"Who is he?"

"A lawyer Dr. King has consulted about tax and other matters."

"In Atlanta?"

"No, Levison is based in New York."

"It doesn't sound like he's really close to King."

"I don't believe he is."

"But that hardly matters," Bobby said wearily. "Hoover can always make it sound worse than it is."

"The FBI says Levison is a Communist, but they won't tell me what evidence they have, though they might tell you."

"I don't want to know anything about their sources of information." Bobby held up his hands, palms outward, in a defensive gesture. "I'd be blamed for every goddamn leak forever after."

"They don't even have Levison's party card number."

"They don't fucking know," Bobby said. "They're just guessing. But it makes no difference. People will believe it."

"What are we going to do?"

"King has to break with Levison," Bobby said decisively. "Otherwise Hoover will leak this, King will be damaged, and the whole civil rights mess will just get worse."

George did not think of the civil rights campaign as a "mess," but the Kennedy brothers did. However, that was not the point. Hoover's accusation was a threat that had to be dealt with, and Bobby was right: the simplest solution was for King to break with Levison. "But how are we going to get Dr. King to do that?" George asked.

Bobby said: "You're going to fly down to Atlanta and tell him to."

George was daunted. Martin Luther King was famous for defying authority, and George knew from Verena that in private as well as in public King could not easily be talked into anything. But George hid his apprehension behind a calm veneer. "I'll call now and make an appointment." He went to the door.

"Thank you, George," Bobby said with evident relief. "It's so great to be able to rely on you."

. . .

The day after she went swimming with the president, Maria picked up the phone and heard the voice of Dave Powers again. "There's a staff get-together at five thirty," he said. "Would you like to come?"

Maria and her flatmates had plans to see Audrey Hepburn and the dishy George Peppard in *Breakfast at Tiffany's*. But junior White House staffers did not say no to Dave Powers. The girls would have to drool over Peppard without her. "Where do I go?" she said.

"Upstairs."

"Upstairs?" That usually meant the president's private residence.

"I'll pick you up." Dave hung up.

Maria immediately wished she had put on a more fancy outfit today. She was wearing a plaid pleated skirt and a plain white blouse with little gold-colored buttons. Her hairpiece was a simple bob, short in the back with long scimitars of hair either side of her chin, in the current fashion. She feared she looked like every other office girl in Washington.

She spoke to Nelly. "Have you been invited to a staff get-together this evening?"

"Not me," said Nelly. "Where is it?"

"Upstairs."

"Lucky you."

At five fifteen, Maria went to the ladies' room to adjust

her hair and makeup. She noticed that none of the other women was making any special effort, and she deduced that they had not been invited. Perhaps the get-together was for the newest recruits.

At five thirty, Nelly picked up her handbag to leave. "You take care of yourself, now," she said to Maria.

"You, too."

"No, I mean it," said Nelly, and she walked out before Maria could ask what she meant by that.

Dave Powers appeared a minute later. He led her out of doors, along the West Colonnade, past the entrance to the pool, then back inside and up in an elevator.

The doors opened on a grand hallway with two chandeliers. The walls were painted a color between blue and green that Maria thought might be called *eau de nil*. She hardly had time to take it in. "We're in the West Sitting Hall," Dave said, and led her through an open doorway into an informal room with a scatter of comfortable couches and a large arched window facing the sunset.

The same two secretaries were here, Jenny and Jerry, but no one else. Maria sat down, wondering whether others were going to join them. On the coffee table was a tray with cocktail glasses and a jug. "Have a daiquiri," Dave said, and poured it without waiting for her answer. Maria did not drink alcohol often, but she sipped it and liked it. She took a cheese puff from the tray of snacks. What was this all about?

"Will the First Lady be joining us?" she asked. "I'm longing to meet her."

There was a moment of silence, making her feel as if she had said something tactless; then Dave said: "Jackie's gone to Glen Ora."

Glen Ora was a farm in Middleburg, Virginia, where Jackie Kennedy kept horses and rode with the Orange County Hunt. It was about an hour from Washington.

Jenny said: "She's taken Caroline and John John."

Caroline Kennedy was four and John John was one.

If I were married to him, Maria thought, I wouldn't leave him to ride my horse.

Suddenly he walked in, and they all stood up.

He looked tired and strained, but his smile was as warm as ever. He took off his jacket, threw it over the back of a chair, sat on the couch, leaned back, and put his feet on the coffee table.

Maria felt she had been admitted to the most exclusive social group in the world. She was in the president's home, having drinks and snacks while he put his feet up. Whatever else happened, she would always have the memory of this.

She drained her glass, and Dave topped it up.

Why was she thinking, Whatever else happened? There was something off here. She was just a researcher, hoping for an early promotion to assistant press officer. The atmosphere was relaxed, but she was not really among friends. None of these people knew anything about her. What was she doing here?

The president stood up and said: "Maria, would you like a tour of the residence?"

A tour of the residence? From the president himself? Who would say no?

"Of course." She stood up. The daiquiri went to her head, and for a moment she felt dizzy, but it passed.

The president went through a side door, and she followed.

"This used to be a guest bedroom, but Mrs. Kennedy has converted it into a dining room," he said. The room was papered with battle scenes from the American Revolution. The square table in the middle looked too small for the room, Maria thought, and the chandelier too big for the table. But mostly she thought: I'm alone with the president in the White House residence—me! Maria Summers!

He smiled and looked into her eyes. "What do you think?" he said, as if he could not make up his own mind until he had heard her opinion.

"I love it," she said, wishing she could think of a more intelligent compliment.

"This way." He led her back across the West Sitting Hall and through the opposite door. "This is Mrs. Kennedy's bedroom," he said, and he closed the door behind them.

"It's beautiful," Maria breathed.

Opposite the door were two long windows with light blue drapes. To Maria's left was a fireplace with a couch placed on a rug patterned with the same blue. Over the mantel was a collection of framed drawings that looked tasteful and highbrow, just like Jackie. At the other end, the bedcovers and the canopy also matched, as did the cloth that covered the round occasional table in the corner. Maria had never seen a room like it, even in magazines.

But she was thinking: Why did he call it "Mrs. Kennedy's bedroom"? Did he not sleep here? The big double bed was made up in two separate halves, and Maria recalled that the president had to have a hard mattress because of his back.

He led her to the window and they looked out. The evening light was soft over the South Lawn and the fountain where the Kennedy children sometimes paddled. "So beautiful," Maria said.

He put a hand on her shoulder. It was the first time he had touched her, and she trembled a little with the thrill. She smelled his cologne, close enough now to pick up the rosemary and musk under the citrus. He looked at her with the faint smile that was so alluring. "This is a very private room," he murmured.

She looked into his eyes. "Yes," she whispered. She felt a deep sense of intimacy with him, as if she had known him all her life, as if she knew beyond doubt that she could trust and love him without limit. She had a momentary guilty thought about George Jakes. But George had not even asked her for a date. She put him out of her mind.

The president put his other hand on the opposite shoulder and gently pushed her back. When her legs touched the bed she sat down.

He pushed her farther back, until she had to lean on her elbows. Still gazing into her eyes, he began to undo her blouse. For a moment she felt ashamed of those cheap gold-colored buttons, here in this unspeakably elegant room. Then he put his hands on her breasts.

Suddenly she hated the nylon brassiere that came between his skin and hers. Swiftly she undid the rest of the buttons, slipped her blouse off, reached behind her back to undo her bra, and threw that aside too. He gazed adoringly at her breasts, then took them in his soft hands, stroking them gently at first, then grasping them firmly.

He reached under her plaid skirt and pulled down her panties. She wished she had remembered to trim her pubic hair, as Jenny and Jerry did.

He was breathing hard, and so was she. He unfastened his suit pants and dropped them, then he lay on top of her.

Was it always this quick? She did not know.

He entered her smoothly. Then, feeling resistance, he stopped. "Haven't you done this before?" he said with surprise.

"No."

"Are you okay?"

"Yes." She was more than okay. She was happy, eager, yearning.

He pushed more gently. Something gave way, and she felt a sharp pain. She could not suppress a soft cry.

"Are you okay?" he repeated.

"Yes." She did not want him to stop.

He continued with closed eyes. She studied his face, the look of concentration, the smile of pleasure. Then he gave a sigh of satisfaction, and it was over.

He stood upright and pulled up his pants.

Smiling, he said: "The bathroom is through there." He pointed to a door in the corner, then did up his fly.

Suddenly Maria felt embarrassed, lying on the bed with her nakedness exposed to view. She stood up quickly. She grabbed her blouse and bra, stooped to pick up her panties, and ran into the bathroom.

She looked in the mirror and said: "What just happened?"

I lost my virginity, she thought. I had intercourse with a wonderful man. He happens to be the president of the United States. I enjoyed it.

She put her clothes on, then adjusted her makeup. Fortunately he had not mussed her hair.

This is Jackie's bathroom, she thought guiltily; and suddenly she wanted to leave.

The bedroom was empty. She went to the door, then turned and looked back at the bed.

She realized he had not once kissed her.

She went into the West Sitting Hall. The president sat there alone, his feet up on the coffee table. Dave and the girls had gone, leaving behind a tray of used glasses and the remains of the snacks. Kennedy seemed relaxed, as if nothing momentous had happened. Was this an everyday occurrence for him?

"Would you like something to eat?" he said. "The kitchen's right here."

"No, thank you, Mr. President."

She thought: He just fucked me, and I'm still calling him Mr. President.

He stood up. "There's a car at the South Portico waiting to take you home," he said. He walked her out into the main hall. "Are you okay?" he said for the third time.

"Yes."

The elevator came. She wondered if he would kiss her good night.

He did not. She got into the elevator.

"Good night, Maria," he said.

"Good night," she said, and the doors closed.

.　.　.

It took a while for George to tell Norine Latimer that their affair was over.

He was dreading it.

He had broken up with girls before, of course. After one or two dates it was easy: you just didn't call. After a longer relationship, in his experience, the feeling was usually mutual: both of you knew that the thrill had gone. But Norine fell between the two extremes. He had been seeing her only for a few months, and they were getting on fine. He had been hoping that they would spend a night together soon. She would not be expecting the brush-off.

He met her for lunch. She asked to be taken to the restaurant in the basement of the White House, known as the mess, but women were not allowed in. George did not want to take her somewhere swanky such as the Jockey Club, for fear she would imagine he was about to propose. In the end they went to Old Ebbitt's, a traditional politicians' restaurant that had seen better days.

Norine looked more Arabic than African. She was dramatically handsome, with wavy black hair and olive skin and a curved nose. She wore a fluffy sweater that really did not suit her: George guessed she was trying not to intimidate her boss. Men were uncomfortable with authoritative-looking women in their offices.

"I'm really sorry about canceling last night," he said when they had ordered. "I was summoned to a meeting with the president."

"Well, I can't compete with the president," she said.

That struck him as kind of a dumb thing to say. Of course she couldn't compete with the president; no one could. But he did not want to get into that discussion. He went right to the point. "Something's happened," he said. "Before I met you, there was another girl."

"I know," said Norine.

"What do you mean?"

"I like you, George," Norine said: "You're smart and funny and kind. And you're handsome, apart from that ear."

"But . . ."

"But I can tell when a man is carrying a torch for someone else."

"You can?"

"I guess it's Maria," said Norine.

George was astonished. "How the heck did you know that?"

"You've mentioned the name four or five times. And you've never talked about any other girl from your past. So it doesn't take a genius to figure out that she's still important to you. But she's in Chicago, so I thought maybe I could win you away from her." Norine suddenly looked sad.

George said: "She's come to Washington."

"Smart girl."

"Not for me. For a job."

"Whichever, you're dumping me for her."

He could hardly say yes to that. But it was true, so he said nothing.

Their food came, but Norine did not pick up her fork. "I wish you well, George," she said. "Take care of yourself."

It seemed very sudden. "Uh . . . you too."

She stood up. "Good-bye."

There was only one thing to say. "Good-bye, Norine."

"You can have my salad," she said, and she walked out.

George toyed with his food for a few minutes, feeling bad. Norine had been gracious, in her own way. She had made it easy for him. He hoped she was okay. She did not deserve to be hurt.

He went from the restaurant to the White House. He had to attend the President's Committee on Equal Employment Opportunity, chaired by Vice President Lyndon Johnson. George had formed an alliance with one of Johnson's advisers, Skip Dickerson. But he had half an hour to spare before the meeting started, so he went to the press office in search of Maria.

Today she was wearing a polka-dot dress with a matching hair band. The band was probably holding in place a wig: Maria's cute bob was definitely not natural.

When she asked him how he was, he did not know how to answer. He felt guilty about Norine; but now he could ask Maria out with a good conscience. "Pretty good, on balance," he said. "You?"

She lowered her voice. "Some days I just hate white people."

"What brought this on?"

"You haven't met my grandfather."

"Never met any of your family."

"Grandpa still preaches in Chicago now and again, but he spends most of his time in his hometown, Golgotha, Alabama. Says he never really got used to the cold wind in the Midwest. But he's still feisty. He put on his best suit and went down to the Golgotha courthouse to register to vote."

"What happened?"

"They humiliated him." She shook her head. "You know their tricks. They give people a literacy test: you have to read part of the state constitution aloud, explain it, then write it down. The registrar picks which clause you have to read. He gives whites a simple sentence, like: 'No person shall be imprisoned for debt.' But Negroes get a long, complicated paragraph that only a lawyer could understand. Then it's up to the registrar to say whether you're literate or not, and of course he always decides the whites are literate and the Negroes aren't."

"Sons of bitches."

"That's not all. Negroes who try to register get fired from their jobs, as a punishment, but they couldn't do that to Grandpa because he's retired. So, as he was leaving the courthouse, they arrested him for loitering. He spent the night in jail—no picnic when you're eighty." There were tears in her eyes.

The story hardened George's resolve. What did he have to complain about? So, some of the things he had to do made him want to wash his hands. Working for Bobby was still the most effective thing he could do for people like

Grandpa Summers. One day those Southern racists would be smashed.

He looked at his watch. "I have a meeting with Lyndon."

"Tell him about my grandpa."

"Maybe I will." The time George spent with Maria always seemed too short. "I'm sorry to hurry away, but do you want to meet up after work?" he said. "We could have drinks, maybe go for dinner somewhere?"

She smiled. "Thank you, George, but I have a date tonight."

"Oh." George was taken aback. Somehow it had not occurred to him that she might already be dating. "Uh, I have to go to Atlanta tomorrow, but I'll be back in two or three days. Maybe over the weekend?"

"No, thanks." She hesitated, then explained: "I'm kind of going steady."

George was devastated—which was stupid: why would a girl as attractive as Maria *not* have a steady date? He had been a fool. He felt disoriented, as if he had lost his footing. He managed to say: "Lucky guy."

She smiled. "It's nice of you to say so."

George wanted to know about the competition. "Who is he?"

"You don't know him."

No, but I will as soon as I can learn his name. "Try me."

She shook her head. "I prefer not to say."

George was frustrated beyond measure. He had a rival and did not even know the man's name. He wanted to press her, but he was wary of acting like a bully: girls hated that. "Okay," he said reluctantly. With massive insincerity he added: "Have a great evening."

"I sure will."

They separated, Maria heading for the press office and George toward the vice president's rooms.

George was heartsick. He liked Maria more than any girl he had ever met, and he had lost her to someone else.

He thought: I wonder who he is?

.   .   .

Maria took off her clothes and got into the bath with President Kennedy.

Jack Kennedy took pills all day but nothing relieved his

back pain like being in water. He even shaved in the tub in the mornings. He would have slept in a pool if he could.

This was his bathtub, in his bathroom, with his turquoise-and-gold bottle of 4711 cologne on the shelf over the wash-basin. Since the first time, Maria had never been back inside Jackie's quarters. The president had a separate bedroom and bathroom, connected to Jackie's suite by a short corridor where—for some reason—the record player was housed.

Jackie was out of town, again. Maria had learned not to torture herself with thoughts of her lover's wife. Maria knew she was cruelly betraying a decent woman, and it grieved her, so she did not think about it.

Maria loved the bathroom, which was luxurious beyond dreams, with soft towels and white bathrobes and expensive soap—and a family of yellow rubber ducks.

They had slipped into a routine. Whenever Dave Powers invited her, which was about once a week, she would take the elevator up to the residence after work. There was always a pitcher of daiquiris and a tray of snacks waiting in the West Sitting Hall. Sometimes Dave was there, sometimes Jenny and Jerry, sometimes no one. Maria would pour a drink and wait, eager but patient, until the president arrived.

Soon afterward they would move to the bedroom. It was Maria's favorite place in the world. It had a four-poster bed with a blue canopy, two chairs in front of a real fire, and piles of books, magazines, and newspapers everywhere. She felt she could cheerfully live in this room for the rest of her life.

He had gently taught her to give oral sex. She had been an eager pupil. That was usually what he wanted when he arrived. He was often in a hurry for it, almost desperate; and there was something arousing about his urgency. But she liked him best afterward, when he would relax and become warmer, more affectionate.

Sometimes he put a record on. He liked Sinatra and Tony Bennett and Percy Marquand. He had never heard of the Miracles or the Shirelles.

There was always a cold supper in the kitchen: chicken, shrimp, sandwiches, salad. After they ate they would un-dress and get into the bath.

She sat at the opposite end of the tub. He put two ducks in the water and said: "Bet you a quarter my duck can go faster than yours." In his Boston accent he said *quarter* like an Englishman, not pronouncing the letter *r*.

She picked up a duck. She loved him most when he was like this: playful, silly, childish. "Okay, Mr. President," she said. "But make it a dollar, if you got the moxie."

She still called him Mr. President most of the time. His wife called him Jack; his brothers sometimes called him Johnny. Maria called him Johnny only at moments of great passion.

"I can't afford to lose a dollar," he said, laughing. But he was sensitive, and he could tell she was not in the right mood. "What's the matter?"

"I don't know." She shrugged. "I don't usually talk to you about politics."

"Why not? Politics is my life, and yours, too."

"You get pestered all day. Our time together is about relaxing and having fun."

"Make an exception." He picked up her foot, lying alongside his thigh in the water, and stroked her toes. She had beautiful feet, she knew; and she always put varnish on her toenails. "Something has upset you," he said quietly. "Tell me what it is."

When he looked at her so intensely, with his hazel eyes and his wry smile, she was helpless. She said: "The day before yesterday, my grandfather was jailed for trying to register to vote."

"Jailed? They can't do that. What was the charge?"

"Loitering."

"Oh. This happened somewhere in the South."

"Golgotha, Alabama, his hometown." She hesitated, but decided to tell him the whole truth, although he would not like it. "Do you want to know what he said when he came out of jail?"

"What?"

"He said: 'With President Kennedy in the White House, I thought I could vote, but I guess I was wrong.' That's what Grandma told me."

"Hell," said the president. "He believed in me, and I failed him."

"That's what he thinks, I guess."

"What do you think, Maria?" He was still stroking her toes.

She hesitated again, looking at her dark foot in his white hands. She feared that this discussion could become acrimonious. He was touchy about the least suggestion that he was insincere or untrustworthy, or that he failed to keep his promises as a politician. If she pushed him too hard, he might end their relationship. And then she would die.

But she had to be honest. She took a deep breath and tried to remain calm. "Far as I can see, the issue is not complicated," she began. "Southerners do this because they can. The law, as it stands, lets them get away with it, despite the Constitution."

"Not entirely," he interrupted. "My brother Bob has stepped up the number of lawsuits brought by the Justice Department for voting rights violations. He has a bright young Negro lawyer working with him."

She nodded. "George Jakes. I know him. But what they're doing isn't enough."

He shrugged. "I can't deny that."

She pressed on. "Everyone agrees that we have to change the law by bringing in a new civil rights act. A lot of people thought you promised that in your election campaign. And ... nobody understands why you haven't done it yet." She bit her lip, then risked the ultimate. "Including me."

His face hardened.

She immediately regretted being so candid. "Don't be mad," she pleaded. "I wouldn't upset you for the world—but you asked me the question, and I wanted to be honest." Tears came to her eyes. "And my poor grandpa spent all night in jail, in his best suit."

He forced a smile. "I'm not mad, Maria. Not at you, anyway."

"You can tell me anything," she said. "I adore you. I would never sit in judgment on you—you must know that. Just say how you feel."

"I'm angry because I'm weak, I guess," he said. "We have a majority in Congress only if we include conservative Southern Democrats. If I bring in a civil rights bill, they'll sabotage it—and that's not all. In revenge, they'll vote against all the rest of my domestic legislation program, including Medicare. Now, Medicare could improve the lives of colored Americans even more than civil rights legislation."

"Does that mean you've given up on civil rights?"

"No. We have midterm elections next November. I'll be asking the American people to send more Democrats to Congress so that I can fulfill my campaign promises."

"Will they?"

"Probably not. The Republicans are attacking me on foreign policy. We've lost Cuba, we've lost Laos, and we're losing Vietnam. I had to let Khrushchev put up a barbed-wire fence right across the middle of Berlin. Right now my back is up against the goddamn wall."

"How strange," Maria reflected. "You can't let Southern Negroes vote because you're vulnerable on foreign policy."

"Every leader has to look strong on the world stage, otherwise he can't get anything done."

"Couldn't you just try? Bring in a civil rights bill, even though you'll probably lose it. At least then people would know how sincere you are."

He shook his head. "If I bring in a bill and get defeated I'll look weak, and that will jeopardize everything else. And I'd never get a second chance on civil rights."

"So what should I tell Grandpa?"

"That doing the right thing is not as easy as it looks, even when you're president."

He stood up, and she did the same. They toweled each other dry, then went into his bedroom. Maria put on one of his soft blue cotton nightshirts.

They made love again. If he was tired, it was brief, like the very first time; but tonight he was at ease. He reverted to a playful mood, and they lay back on the bed, toying with one another, as if nothing else in the world mattered.

Afterward he went to sleep quickly. She lay beside him, blissfully happy. She did not want the morning to come, when she would have to get dressed and go to the press office and begin her day's work. She lived in the real world as if it were a dream, waiting only for the call from Dave Powers that meant she could wake up and come back to the only reality that mattered.

She knew that some of her colleagues must have guessed what she was doing. She knew he was never going to leave his wife for her. She knew she should be worried about getting pregnant. She knew that everything she was doing was foolish and wrong and could not possibly have a happy ending.

And she was too much in love to care.

. . .

George understood why Bobby was so pleased to be able to send him to talk to King. When Bobby needed to put pressure on the civil rights movement, he had more chance of success using a black messenger. George thought Bobby was right about Levison but, nevertheless, he was not entirely comfortable with his role—a feeling that was beginning to be familiar.

Atlanta was cold and rainy. Verena met George at the airport, wearing a tan coat with a black fur collar. She looked beautiful, but George was still hurting too much from Maria's rejection to be attracted. "I know Stanley Levison," Verena said, driving George through the urban sprawl of the city. "A very sincere guy."

"He's a lawyer, right?"

"More than that. He helped Martin with the writing of *Stride Toward Freedom*. They're close."

"The FBI says Levison is a Communist."

"Anyone who disagrees with J. Edgar Hoover is a Communist, according to the FBI."

"Bobby referred to Hoover as a cocksucker."

Verena laughed. "Do you think he meant it?"

"I don't know."

"Hoover, a powder puff?" She shook her head in disbelief. "It's too good to be true. Real life is never that funny."

She drove through the rain to the Old Fourth Ward neighborhood, where there were hundreds of black-owned businesses. There seemed to be a church on every block. Auburn Avenue had once been called the most prosperous Negro street in America. The Southern Christian Leadership Conference had its headquarters at number 320. Verena pulled up at a long two-story building of red brick.

George said: "Bobby thinks Dr. King is arrogant."

Verena shrugged. "Martin thinks Bobby is arrogant."

"What do you think?"

"They're both right."

George laughed. He liked Verena's sharp wit.

They hurried across the wet sidewalk and went inside. They waited outside King's office for fifteen minutes, then they were called.

Martin Luther King was a handsome man of thirty-three, with a mustache and prematurely receding black hair. He was short, George guessed about five foot six, and a little plump. He wore a well-pressed dark-gray suit with a white shirt and a narrow black satin tie. There was a white silk handkerchief in his breast pocket, and he had large cuff links. George caught a whiff of cologne. He got the impression of a man whose dignity was important to him. George sympathized: he felt the same.

King shook George's hand and said: "Last time we met, you were on the Freedom Ride, heading for Anniston. How's the arm?"

"It's completely healed, thank you," George said. "I've given up competitive wrestling, but I was ready to do that anyway. Now I coach a high school team in Ivy City." Ivy City was a black neighborhood in Washington.

"That's a good thing," King said. "To teach Negro boys to use their strength in a disciplined sport, with rules. Please have a seat." He waved at a chair and retreated behind his desk. "Tell me why the attorney general has sent you to speak to me." There was a hint of injured pride in his voice. Perhaps King thought Bobby should have come himself. George recalled that King's nickname within the civil rights movement was De Lawd.

George outlined the Stanley Levison problem briskly, leaving out nothing but the wiretap request. "Bobby sent me here to urge you, as strongly as I can, to break all ties with Mr. Levison," he said in conclusion. "It's the only way to protect yourself from the charge of being a fellow traveler with the Communists—an accusation that can do untold harm to the movement that you and I both believe in."

When he had finished, King said: "Stanley Levison is not a Communist."

George opened his mouth to ask a question.

King held up a hand to silence him: he was not a man to tolerate interruption. "Stanley has never been a member of the Communist Party. Communism is atheistical, and I as a follower of the Lord Jesus Christ would find it impossible to be the close friend of an atheist. But—" He leaned forward across the desk. "That is not the whole truth."

He was silent for a few moments, but George knew that he was not supposed to speak.

"Let me tell you the whole truth about Stanley Levison," King went on at last, and George felt he was about to hear a sermon. "Stanley is good at making money. This embarrasses him. He feels he should spend his life helping others. So, when he was young, he became ... entranced. Yes, that's the word. He was entranced by the ideals of Communism. Although he never joined, he used his remarkable talents to help the Communist Party of the USA in various ways. Soon he saw how wrong he was, broke the association, and gave his support to the cause of freedom and equality for the Negro. And so he became my friend."

George waited until he was sure King had finished, then he said: "I'm deeply sorry to hear this, Reverend. If Levison has been a financial adviser to the Communist Party, he is forever tainted."

"But he has changed."

"I believe you, but others will not. By continuing a relationship with Levison you will be giving ammunition to our enemies."

"So be it," said King.

George was flabbergasted. "What do you mean?"

"Moral rules must be obeyed when it doesn't suit us. Otherwise, why would we need rules?"

"But if you balance—"

"We don't balance," King said. "Stanley did wrong to help the Communists. He has repented and is making amends. I'm a preacher in the service of the Lord. I must forgive as Jesus does and welcome Stanley with open arms. Joy shall be in heaven over one sinner that repenteth, more than over ninety and nine just persons. I myself am too often in need of God's grace to refuse mercy to another."

"But the cost—"

"I'm a Christian pastor, George. The doctrine of forgiveness goes deep into my soul, deeper even than freedom and justice. I could not go back on it for any prize."

George realized his mission was doomed. King was completely sincere. There was no prospect of changing his mind.

George stood up. "Thank you for taking the time to explain your point of view. I appreciate it, and so does the attorney general."

"God bless you," said King.

George and Verena left the office and walked outside. Without speaking, they got into Verena's car. "I'll drop you at your hotel," she said.

George nodded. He was thinking about King's words. He did not want to talk.

They drove in silence until she pulled up at the hotel entrance. Then she said: "Well?"

He said: "King made me ashamed of myself."

.   .   .

"That's what preachers do," said his mother. "It's their job. It's good for you." She poured a glass of milk for George and gave him a slice of cake. He did not want either.

He had told her the whole thing, sitting in her kitchen. "He was so strong," George said. "Once he knew what was right, he was going to do it, no matter what."

"Don't set him up too high," Jacky said. "No one's an angel—especially if he's a man." It was late afternoon, and she was still wearing her work clothes, a plain black dress and flat shoes.

"I know that. But there I was, trying to persuade him to break with a loyal friend for cynical political reasons, and he just talked about right and wrong."

"How was Verena?"

"I wish you could have seen her, in that coat with a black fur collar."

"Did you take her out?"

"We had dinner." He had not kissed her good night.

Out of the blue, Jacky said: "I like that Maria Summers."

George was startled. "How do you know her?"

"She belongs to the club." Jacky was supervisor of the colored staff at the University Women's Club. "It doesn't have many black members, so of course we talk. She mentioned she worked at the White House. I told her about you, and we realized you two already know each other. She has a nice family."

George was amused. "How do you know *that*?"

"She brought her parents in for lunch. Her father's a big

lawyer in Chicago. He knows Mayor Daley there." Daley was a big Kennedy supporter.

"You know more about her than I do!"

"Women listen. Men talk."

"I like Maria, too."

"Good." Jacky frowned, remembering the original topic of conversation. "What did Bobby Kennedy say when you got back from Atlanta?"

"He's going to okay the wiretap on Levison. That means the FBI will be listening to some of Dr. King's phone calls."

"How much does that matter? Everything King does is intended to be publicized."

"They may find out, in advance, what King is going to do next. If they do, they'll tip off the segregationists, who will be able to plan ahead, and may find ways to undermine what King does."

"It's bad, but it's not the end of the world."

"I could tip King off about the wiretap. Tell Verena to warn King to be careful what he says on the phone to Levison."

"You'd be betraying the trust of your work colleagues."

"That's what bothers me."

"In fact, you'd probably have to resign."

"Exactly. Because I'd feel a traitor."

"Besides, they might find out about the tip-off, and when they looked around for the culprit they'd see one black face in the room—yours."

"Maybe I should do it anyway, if it's the right thing."

"If you leave, George, there's *no* black face in Bobby Kennedy's inner circle."

"I knew you'd say I should shut up and stay."

"It's hard, but yes, I think you should."

"So do I," said George.

CHAPTER TWELVE

"You live in an amazing house," Beep Dewar said to Dave Williams.

Dave was thirteen years old; he had lived here as long as he could remember; and he had never really noticed the house. He looked up at the brick façade of the garden front, with its regular rows of Georgian windows. "Amazing?" he said.

"It's so old."

"It's eighteenth century, I think. So it's only about two hundred years old."

"Only!" She laughed. "In San Francisco, nothing is two hundred years old!"

The house was in Great Peter Street, London, a couple of minutes' walk from Parliament. Most of the houses in the neighborhood were eighteenth century, and Dave knew vaguely that they had been built for members of Parliament and peers who had to attend the House of Commons and the House of Lords. Dave's father, Lloyd Williams, was an M.P.

"Do you smoke cigarettes?" said Beep, taking out a packet.

"Only when I get the chance."

She gave him one and they both lit up.

Ursula Dewar, known as Beep, was also thirteen, but she seemed older than Dave. She wore nifty American clothes, tight sweaters and narrow jeans and boots. She claimed she could drive. She said British radio was square: only three stations, none playing rock and roll—and they went off the air at midnight! When she caught Dave staring at the small bumps her breasts made in the front of her black turtleneck, she was not even embarrassed; she just smiled. But she never quite gave him an opportunity to kiss her.

She would not be the first girl he had kissed. He would have liked to let her know that, just in case she thought he was inexperienced. She would be the third, counting Linda Robertson, whom he did count even though she had not actually kissed him back. The point was, he knew what to do.

But he had not managed it with Beep, not yet.

He had come close. He had discreetly put his arm around her shoulders in the back of his father's Humber Hawk, but she had turned her face away and looked out at the lamplit streets. She did not giggle when tickled. They had jived to the Dansette record player in the bedroom of his fifteen-year-old sister, Evie; but Beep had declined to slow-dance when Dave put on Elvis singing "Are You Lonesome To-night?"

Still he lived in hope. Sadly, this was not the moment, standing in the small garden on a winter afternoon, Beep hugging herself to keep warm, both of them stiffly dressed in their best clothes. They were off to a formal family occasion. But there would be a party later. Beep had a quarter bottle of vodka in her handbag to spike the soft drinks they would be given while their parents hypocritically glugged whisky and gin. And then anything might happen. He stared at her pink lips closing around the filter tip of her Chesterfield, and imagined yearningly what it would be like.

His mother's American accent called from the house: "Get in here, you kids—we're leaving!" They dropped their cigarettes into the flower bed and went inside.

The two families were assembling in the hall. Dave's grandmother Eth Leckwith was to be "introduced" to the House of Lords. This meant she would become a baroness, be addressed as Lady Leckwith, and sit as a Labour peer in the upper chamber of Parliament. Dave's parents, Lloyd and Daisy, were waiting, with his sister, Evie, and a young family friend, Jasper Murray. The Dewars, wartime friends, were here too. Woody Dewar was a photographer on a one-year assignment in London, and had brought his wife, Bella, and their children, Cameron and Beep. All Americans seemed fascinated by the pantomime of British public life, so the Dewars were joining in the celebration. They formed a large group as they left the house and headed for Parliament Square.

Walking through the misty London streets, Beep transferred her attention from Dave to Jasper Murray. He was eighteen and a Viking, tall and broad with blond hair. He wore a heavy tweed jacket. Dave longed to be so grown-up and masculine, and to have Beep look up at him with that expression of admiration and desire.

Dave treated Jasper like an older brother, and asked his advice. He had confessed to Jasper that he adored Beep and could not figure out how to win her heart. "Keep trying," Jasper had said. "Sometimes sheer persistence works."

Dave could hear their conversation. "So you're Dave's cousin?" Beep said to Jasper as they crossed Parliament Square.

"Not really," Jasper replied. "We're no relation."

"So how come you live here rent-free and everything?"

"My mother was at school with Dave's mother in Buffalo. That's where they met your father. Since then they've all been friends."

There was more to it than that, Dave knew. Jasper's mother, Eva, had been a refugee from Nazi Germany and Dave's mother, Daisy, had taken her in, with characteristic generosity. But Jasper preferred to underplay the extent to which his family was indebted to the Williamses.

Beep said: "What are you studying?"

"French and German. I'm at St. Julian's, which is one of the larger colleges of London University. But mostly I write for the student newspaper. I'm going to be a journalist."

Dave was envious. He would never learn French or go to university. He was bottom of the class at everything. His father despaired.

Beep said to Jasper: "Where are your parents?"

"Germany. They move around the world with the army. My father's a colonel."

"A colonel!" said Beep admiringly.

Dave's sister, Evie, muttered in his ear: "Little tart, what does she think she's doing? First she flutters her eyelashes at you, then she flirts with a man five years older!"

Dave made no comment. He knew that his sister had a

massive crush on Jasper. He could have taunted her, but he refrained. He liked Evie and, besides, it was better to save up stuff like this and use it next time she was mean to him.

"Don't you have to be born an aristocrat?" Beep was saying.

"Even in the oldest families there has to be a first one," Jasper said. "But nowadays we have life peers, who don't pass the title to their heirs. Mrs. Leckwith will be a life peer."

"Will we have to curtsey to her?"

Jasper laughed. "No, idiot."

"Will the queen be there for the ceremony?"

"No."

"How disappointing!"

Evie whispered: "Stupid bitch."

They went into the Palace of Westminster by the Lords Entrance. They were greeted by a man in court dress, including knee breeches and silk stockings. Dave heard his grandmother say in her lilting Welsh accent: "Obsolete uniforms are a sure sign of an institution in need of reform."

Dave and Evie had been coming to the Parliament building all their lives, but it was a new experience for the Dewars, and they marveled. Beep forgot to be charmingly dizzy and said: "Every surface is decorated! Floor tiles, patterned carpets, wallpaper, wood paneling, stained glass, and carved stone!"

Jasper looked at her with more interest. "It's typical Victorian Gothic."

"Oh, really?"

Dave was beginning to get irritated with the way Jasper was impressing Beep.

The party split, most of them following an usher up several flights to a gallery overlooking the debating chamber. Ethel's friends were already there. Beep sat next to Jasper, but Dave managed to sit the other side of her, and Evie slid in beside him. Dave had often visited the House of Commons, at the other end of the same palace, but this was more ornate, and had red leather benches instead of green.

After a long wait there was a stir of activity below and his grandmother came in, walking in line with four other people, all dressed in funny hats and extremely silly robes with fur trimmings. Beep said: "This is amazing!" but Dave and Evie giggled.

The procession stopped in front of a throne, and Grandmam knelt down, not without difficulty—she was sixty-
eight. There was a lot of passing round of scrolls that had to
be read aloud. Dave's mother, Daisy, was explaining the
ceremony in a low voice to Beep's parents, tall Woody and
plump Bella, but Dave tuned her out. It was all bollocks
really.

After a while Ethel and two of her escorts went and sat
on one of the benches. Then followed the funniest part of
all.

They sat down, then immediately stood up again. They
took off their hats and bowed. They sat down and put their
hats back on again. Then they went through the whole thing
again, looking for all the world like three marionettes on
strings: stand up, hats off, bow, sit down, hats on. By this
time Dave and Evie were helpless with suppressed laughter.
Then they did it a third time. Dave heard his sister splutter:
"Stop, please stop!" which made him giggle even more.
Daisy directed a stern blue-eyed glare at them, but she was
too full of fun herself not to see the funny side, and in the
end she grinned too.

At last it was over and Ethel left the chamber. Her family and friends stood up. Dave's mother led them through a
maze of corridors and staircases to a basement room for the
party. Dave checked that his guitar was safe in a corner. He
and Evie were going to perform, though she was the star: he
was merely her accompanist.

Within a few minutes there were about a hundred people in the room.

Evie buttonholed Jasper and started asking him about
the student newspaper. The subject was close to his heart,
and he answered with enthusiasm, but Dave was sure Evie
was onto a loser. Jasper was a boy who knew how to look
after his own interests. Right now he had luxurious lodg-
ings, rent-free, a short bus ride from his college. He was not
likely to destabilize that comfortable situation by beginning
a romance with the daughter of the house, in Dave's cynical
opinion.

However, Evie took Jasper's attention away from Beep,
leaving the field clear for Dave. He got her a ginger beer
and asked her what she thought of the ceremony. Surreptitiously, she poured vodka into their soft drinks. A minute

later everyone applauded as Ethel came in, dressed now in normal clothes, a red dress and matching coat with a small hat perched on her silver curls. Beep whispered: "She must have been drop-dead gorgeous, once upon a time."

Dave found it creepy to think about his grandmother as an attractive woman.

Ethel began to speak. "It's such a pleasure to share this occasion with all of you," she said. "I'm only sorry my beloved Bernie didn't live to see this day. He was the wisest man I ever knew."

Granddad Bernie had died a year ago.

"It is strange to be addressed as 'my lady,' especially for a lifelong socialist," she went on, and everyone laughed. "Bernie would ask me whether I had beaten my enemies or just joined them. So let me assure you that I have joined the peerage in order to abolish it."

They applauded.

"Seriously, comrades, I gave up being the member of Parliament for Aldgate because I felt it was time to let someone younger take over, but I haven't retired. There is too much injustice in our society, too much bad housing and poverty, too much hunger in the world—and I may have only twenty or thirty campaigning years left!"

That got another laugh.

"I've been advised that here in the House of Lords it's wise to take up one issue and make it your own, and I've decided what my issue will be."

They went quiet. People were always keen to know what Eth Leckwith would do next.

"Last week my dear old friend Robert von Ulrich died. He fought in the First World War, got in trouble with the Nazis in the thirties, and ended up running the best restaurant in Cambridge. Once, when I was a young seamstress working in a sweatshop in the East End, he bought me a new dress and took me to dinner at the Ritz. And . . ." She lifted her chin defiantly. "And he was a homosexual."

There was an audible susurration of surprise in the room.

Dave muttered: "Blimey!"

Beep said: "I like your grandmother."

People were not used to hearing this subject discussed so openly, especially by a woman. Dave grinned. Good old Grandmam, still making trouble after all these years.

"Don't mutter—you're not really shocked," she said crisply. "You all know there are men who love men. Such people do no harm to anyone—in fact, in my experience they tend to be gentler than other men—yet what they do is a crime according to the laws of our country. Even worse, plainclothes police detectives pretending to be men of the same sort entrap them, arrest them, and put them in jail. In my opinion this is as bad as persecuting people for being Jewish or pacifist or Catholic. So my main campaign here in the House of Lords will be homosexual law reform. I hope you will all wish me luck. Thank you."

She got an enthusiastic round of applause. Dave figured that almost everyone in the room genuinely did wish her luck. He was impressed. He thought jailing queers was stupid. The House of Lords went up in his estimation: if you could campaign for that sort of change here, maybe the place was not completely ludicrous.

Finally Ethel said: "And now, in honor of our American relatives and friends, a song."

Evie went to the front and Dave followed her. "Trust Grandmam to give them something to think about," Evie murmured to Dave. "I bet she'll succeed, too."

"She generally gets what she wants." He picked up his guitar and strummed the chord of G.

Evie began immediately:

O say can you see, by the dawn's early light,

Most of the people in the room were British, not American, but Evie's voice made them all listen.

What so proudly we hail'd at the twilight's last gleaming,

Dave thought nationalist pride was bollocks, really, but despite himself he felt a little choked up. It was the song.

Whose broad stripes and bright stars through the perilous fight
O'er the ramparts we'd watch'd were so gallantly streaming?

The room was so quiet that Dave could hear his own

breathing. Evie could do this. When she was onstage, everyone watched.

> *And the rocket's red glare, the bombs bursting in air,*
> *Gave proof through the night that our flag was still there,*

Dave looked at his mother and saw her wipe away a tear.

> *O say does that star-spangled banner yet wave*
> *O'er the land of the free and the home of the brave?*

They clapped and cheered. Dave had to give his sister
credit: she was a pain in the neck at times, but she could
hold an audience spellbound.

He got another ginger beer, then looked around for Beep,
but she was not in the room. He saw her older brother, Cameron, who was a creep. "Hey, Cam, where did Beep go?"

"Out for a smoke, I guess," he said.

Dave wondered if he could find her. He decided to go
and look. He put down his drink.

He approached the exit at the same time as his grandmother, so he held the door for her. She was probably heading
for the ladies' room: he had a vague notion that old women
had to go a lot. She smiled at him and turned up a red-carpeted
staircase. He had no idea where he was so he followed her.

On the half landing she was stopped by an elderly man
leaning on a cane. Dave noticed that he was wearing an elegant suit in a pale gray material with a chalk stripe. A patterned silk handkerchief spilled out of the breast pocket.
His face was mottled and his hair was white, but obviously
he had once been a good-looking man. He said: "Congratulations, Ethel," and shook her hand.

"Thank you, Fitz." They seemed to know each other well.

He held on to her hand. "So you're a baroness now."

She smiled. "Isn't life strange?"

"Baffles me."

They were blocking the way, and Dave hovered, waiting.
Although their words were trivial, their conversation had
an undertone of passion. Dave could not put his finger on
what it was.

Ethel said: "You don't mind that your housekeeper has
been elevated to the peerage?"

Housekeeper? Dave knew that Ethel had started out as a maid in a big house in Wales. This man must have been her employer.

"I stopped minding that sort of thing a long time ago," the man said. He patted her hand and released it. "During the Attlee government, to be precise."

She laughed. Clearly she liked talking to him. There was a powerful undertone to their conversation, neither love nor hate, but something else. If they had not been so old, Dave would have thought it was sex.

Getting impatient, Dave coughed.

Ethel said: "This is my grandson, David Williams. If you really have stopped minding, you might shake his hand. Dave, this is Earl Fitzherbert."

The earl hesitated, and for a moment Dave thought he was going to refuse to shake; then he seemed to make up his mind, and stuck out his hand. Dave shook it and said: "How do you do?"

Ethel said: "Thank you, Fitz." Or, rather, she almost said it, but seemed to choke before finishing the sentence. Without saying anything more, she walked on. Dave nodded politely at the old earl and followed.

A moment later Ethel disappeared through a door marked LADIES.

Dave guessed there was some history between Ethel and Fitz. He decided to ask his mother about it. Then he spotted an exit that might lead outside, and forgot all about the old folk.

He stepped through the door and found himself in an irregular-shaped internal courtyard with rubbish bins. This would be the perfect place for a surreptitious smooch, he thought. It was not a thoroughfare, no windows overlooked it, and there were odd little corners. His hopes rose.

There was no sign of Beep, but he smelled tobacco smoke.

He stepped past the bins and looked around the corner.

She was there, as he had hoped, and there was a cigarette in her left hand. But she was with Jasper, and they were locked in an embrace. Dave stared at them. Their bodies seemed glued together, and they were kissing passionately, her right hand in his hair, his right hand on her breast.

"You're a treacherous bastard, Jasper Murray," said Dave, then he turned and went back into the building.

• • •

In the school production of *Hamlet,* Evie Williams proposed to play Ophelia's mad scene in the nude.

Just the idea made Cameron Dewar feel uncomfortably warm.

Cameron adored Evie. He just hated her views. She joined every bleeding-heart cause in the news, from animal cruelty to nuclear disarmament, and she talked as if people who did not do the same must be brutal and stupid. But Cameron was used to this: he disagreed with most people his age, and all of his family. His parents were hopelessly liberal, and his grandmother had once been editor of a newspaper with the unlikely title *The Buffalo Anarchist.*

The Williamses were just as bad, leftists every one. The only halfway sensible resident of the house in Great Peter Street was the sponger Jasper Murray, who was more or less cynical about everything. London was a nest of subversives, even worse than Cameron's hometown of San Francisco. He would be glad when his father's assignment was over and they could go back to America.

Except that he would miss Evie. Cameron was fifteen years old and in love for the first time. He did not *want* a romance: he had too much to do. But as he sat at his school desk trying to memorize French and Latin vocabulary, he found himself remembering Evie singing "The Star-Spangled Banner."

She liked him, he felt sure. She realized he was clever, and asked him earnest questions: How did nuclear power stations work? Was Hollywood an actual place? How were Negroes treated in California? Better still, she listened attentively to his answers. She was not making small talk: like him, she had no interest in chitchat. They would be a well-known intellectual couple, in Cameron's fantasy.

For this year Cameron and Beep were going to the school Evie and Dave attended, a progressive London establishment where—as far as Cameron could see—most of the teachers were Communists. The controversy about Evie's mad scene went all around the school in a flash. The drama teacher, Jeremy Faulkner, a beardie in a striped college scarf, actually approved of the idea. However, the head teacher was not so foolish, and he stamped on it decisively.

This was one instance in which Cameron would have been glad to see liberal decadence prevail.

The Williams and Dewar families went together to see the play. Cameron hated Shakespeare but he was looking forward eagerly to seeing what Evie would do onstage. She had an air of intensity that seemed to be brought out by an audience. She was like her great-grandfather Dai Williams, the pioneering trade unionist and evangelical preacher, according to Ethel, Dai's daughter. Ethel had said: "My father had the same bound-for-glory light in his eyes."

Cameron had studied *Hamlet* conscientiously—the way he studied everything, in order to get good marks—and he knew that Ophelia was a notoriously difficult part. Supposedly pathetic, she could easily become comic, with her obscene songs. How was a fifteen-year-old going to play this role and carry an audience with her? Cameron did not want to see her fall on her face (although there was, in the back of his mind, a little fantasy in which he put his arms around her delicate shoulders and comforted her as she wept for her humiliating failure).

With his parents and his kid sister, Beep, he filed into the school hall, which doubled as the gym, so that it smelled equally of dusty hymn books and sweaty sneakers. They took their seats next to the Williams family: Lloyd Williams, the Labour M.P.; his American wife, Daisy; Eth Leckwith, the grandmother; and Jasper Murray, the lodger. Young Dave, Evie's kid brother, was somewhere else, organizing an intermission bar.

Several times in the past few months Cameron had heard the story of how his mother and father had first met here in London, during the war, at a party given by Daisy. Papa had walked Mama home: when he told the story, a strange light came into his eye, and Mama gave him a look that said *Shut the hell up right now,* and he said no more. Cameron and Beep wondered pruriently what their parents had done on the walk home.

A few days later Papa had parachuted into Normandy, and Mama had thought she would never see him again; but all the same she had broken off her engagement to another man. "My mother was furious," Mama said. "She never forgave me."

Cameron found the school hall seats uncomfortable even

for the half hour of morning assembly. Tonight was going to be purgatory. He knew all too well that the full play was five hours long. Evie had assured him that this was a shortened version. Cameron wondered how short.

He spoke to Jasper, sitting next to him. "What's Evie going to wear for the mad scene?"

"I don't know," said Jasper. "She won't tell anyone."

The lights went down and the curtain rose on the battlements of Elsinore.

The painted backdrops that formed the scenery were Cameron's work. He had a strong visual sense, presumably inherited from his father, the photographer. He was particularly pleased with the way the painted moon concealed a spotlight that picked out the sentry.

There was not much else to like. Every school play Cameron had ever seen had been dreadful, and this was no exception. The seventeen-year-old boy playing Hamlet tried to seem enigmatic but succeeded only in being wooden. However, Evie was something else.

In her first scene Ophelia had little to do other than listen to her condescending brother and her pompous father, until at the end she cautioned her brother against hypocrisy in a short speech that Evie delivered with waspish delight. But in her second scene, telling her father about Hamlet's crazy invasion of her private room, she blossomed. At the start she was frantic, then she became calmer, quieter, and more concentrated, until it seemed the audience hardly dared to breathe while she said: "He raised a sigh so piteous and profound." And then, in her next scene, when the enraged Hamlet raved at her about joining a nunnery, she seemed so bewildered and hurt that Cameron wanted to leap onstage and punch him out. Jeremy Faulkner had wisely decided to end the first half at that point, and the applause was tremendous.

Dave was presiding over an intermission bar selling soft drinks and candy. He had a dozen friends serving as fast as they could. Cameron was impressed: he had never seen school pupils work so hard. "Did you give them pep pills?" he asked Dave as he got a glass of cherry pop.

"Nope," said Dave. "Just twenty percent commission on everything they sell."

Cameron was hoping Evie might come and talk to her

family during the intermission, but she still had not appeared when the bell rang for the second half, and he returned to his seat, disappointed but eager to see what she would do next.

Hamlet improved when he had to badger Ophelia with dirty jokes in front of everyone. Perhaps it came naturally to the actor, Cameron thought unkindly. Ophelia's embarrassment and distress increased until it bordered on hysteria.

But it was her mad scene that brought the house down.

She entered looking like an inmate of an asylum, in a stained and torn nightdress of thin cotton that reached only to midthigh. So far from being pitiable, she was jeering and aggressive, like a drunk whore on the street. When she said: "The owl was a baker's daughter," a sentence that in Cameron's opinion meant nothing at all, she made it sound like a vile taunt.

Cameron heard his mother murmur to his father: "I can't believe that girl is only fifteen."

On the line "Young men may do it if they come to it, by cock they are to blame," Ophelia made a grab for the king's genitals that provoked a nervous titter from the audience.

Then came a sudden change. Tears rolled down her cheeks, and her voice sank almost to a whisper as she spoke of her dead father. The audience fell silent. She was a child again as she said: "I cannot choose but weep, to think they should lay him in the cold ground."

Cameron wanted to cry too.

Then she rolled her eyes, staggered, and cackled like an old witch. "Come, my coach!" she cried insanely. She put both hands to the neckline of her dress and ripped it down the front. The audience gasped. "Good night, ladies!" she cried, letting the garment fall to the floor. Stark naked, she cried: "Good night, good night, good night!" Then she ran off.

After that the play was dead. The gravedigger was not funny and the sword fight at the end so artificial as to be boring. Cameron could think of nothing but the naked Ophelia raving at the front of the stage, her small breasts proud, the hair at her groin a flaming auburn; a beautiful girl driven insane. He guessed every man in the audience felt the same. No one cared about Hamlet.

At the curtain call the biggest applause was for Evie. But the head teacher did not come onstage to offer the lavish praise and extensive thanks normally given to the most hopeless of amateur dramatic productions.

As they left the hall, everyone looked at Evie's family. Daisy chatted brightly to other parents, putting a brave face on it. Lloyd, in a severe dark gray suit with a waistcoat, said nothing but looked grim. Evie's grandmother Eth Leckwith smiled faintly: perhaps she had reservations, but she was not going to complain.

Cameron's family also had mixed reactions. His mother's lips were pursed in disapproval. His father wore a smile of tolerant amusement. Beep was bursting with admiration.

Cameron said to Dave: "Your sister's brilliant."

"I like yours, too," said Dave with a grin.

"Ophelia stole the show from Hamlet!"

"Evie's a genius," Dave replied. "Drives our parents up the wall."

"Why?"

"They don't believe show business is serious work. They want us both to go into politics." He rolled his eyes.

Cameron's father, Woody Dewar, overheard. "I had the same problem," he said. "My father was a United States senator, and so was my grandfather. They couldn't understand why I wanted to be a photographer. It just didn't seem like a real job to them." Woody worked for *Life* magazine, probably the best photo journal in the world after *Paris Match*.

Both families went backstage. Evie emerged from the girls' dressing room looking demure in a twinset and a below-the-knee skirt, an outfit obviously chosen to say *I am not a sexual exhibitionist, that was Ophelia*. But she also wore an expression of quiet triumph. Whatever people said about her nudity, no one could deny that her acting had captivated the audience.

Her father was the first to speak. Lloyd said: "I just hope you don't get arrested for indecent exposure."

"I didn't really plan it," Evie said as if he had paid her a compliment. "It was kind of a last-minute thing. I wasn't even sure the nightdress would rip."

Crap, thought Cameron.

Jeremy Faulkner appeared in his trademark college scarf.

He was the only teacher who allowed pupils to call him by his first name. "That was fabulous!" he raved. "A peak moment!" His eyes were bright with excitement. The thought occurred to Cameron that Jeremy, too, was in love with Evie.

Evie said: "Jerry, these are my parents, Lloyd and Daisy Williams."

For a moment the teacher looked scared, but he recovered quickly. "Mr. and Mrs. Williams, you must be even more surprised than I was," he said, deftly disclaiming responsibility. "You should know that Evie is the most brilliant pupil I have ever taught." He shook hands with Daisy, then with a visibly reluctant Lloyd.

Evie spoke to Jasper. "You're invited to the cast party," she said. "My special guest."

Lloyd frowned. "Party?" he said. "After that?" Clearly he felt a celebration was not appropriate.

Daisy touched his arm. "It's okay," she said.

Lloyd shrugged.

Jeremy said brightly: "Just for an hour. School in the morning!"

Jasper said: "I'm too old. I'd feel out of place."

Evie protested: "You're only a year older than the sixth-formers."

Cameron wondered why the hell she wanted him there. He *was* too old. He was a university student: he did not belong at a high school party.

Fortunately, Jasper agreed. "I'll see you back at the house," he said firmly.

Daisy put in: "No later than eleven o'clock, please."

The parents left. Cameron said: "My God, you got away with it!"

Evie grinned. "I know."

They celebrated with coffee and cake. Cameron wished Beep was there to put some vodka into the coffee, but she had not taken part in the production so she had gone home, as had Dave.

Evie was the center of attention. Even the boy playing Hamlet admitted she was the star of the evening. Jeremy Faulkner could not stop talking about how her nakedness had expressed Ophelia's vulnerability. His praise for Evie became embarrassing and eventually kind of creepy.

Cameron waited patiently, letting them monopolize her,

knowing that he had the ultimate advantage: he would be taking her home.

At ten thirty they left. "I'm glad my father got this assignment in London," Cameron said as they zigzagged through the back streets. "I hated leaving San Francisco, but it's pretty cool here."

"That's good," she said without enthusiasm.

"The best part is getting to know you."

"How sweet. Thank you."

"It's really changed my life."

"Surely not."

This was not going the way Cameron had imagined. They were alone in the deserted streets, speaking in low voices as they walked close together through circles of lamplight and pools of darkness, but there was no feeling of intimacy. They were more like people making small talk. All the same he was not giving up. "I want us to be close friends," he said.

"We already are," she replied with a touch of impatience.

They reached Great Peter Street and still he had not said what he wanted to say. As they approached the house he stopped. She took another step forward, so he grabbed her arm and held her back. "Evie," he said, "I'm in love with you."

"Oh, Cam, don't be ridiculous."

Cameron felt as if he had been punched.

Evie tried to walk on. Cameron gripped her arm more tightly, not caring now if he hurt her. "Ridiculous?" he said. There was an embarrassing quaver in his voice, and he spoke again more firmly. "Why should it be ridiculous?"

"You don't know anything," she said in a tone of exasperation.

This was a particularly hurtful reproach. Cameron prided himself on knowing a great deal, and he had imagined she liked him for that. "What don't I know?" he said.

She pulled her arm out of his grasp with a vigorous jerk. "I'm in love with Jasper, you idiot," she said, and she went into the house.

CHAPTER THIRTEEN

In the morning, while it was still dark, Rebecca and Bernd made love again.

They had been living together three months, in the old town house in Berlin-Mitte. It was a big house, which was fortunate, for they shared it with her parents, Werner and Carla, plus her brother, Walli, and her sister, Lili, and Grandmother Maud.

For a while, love had consoled them for all they had lost. Both were out of work, prevented from getting jobs by the secret police—despite East Germany's desperate shortage of schoolteachers.

But both were under investigation for social parasitism, the crime of being unemployed in a Communist country. Sooner or later they would be convicted and jailed. Bernd would go to a prison labor camp, where he would probably die.

So they were going to escape.

Today was their last full day in East Berlin.

When Bernd slid his hand gently up Rebecca's nightdress, she said: "I'm too nervous."

"We may not have many more chances," he said.

She grabbed him and clung to him. She knew he was right. They might both die attempting to flee.

Worse, one might die and one might live.

Bernd reached for a condom. They had agreed that they would marry when they reached the free world, and avoid pregnancy until then. If their plans should go wrong, Rebecca did not want to raise a child in East Germany.

Despite all the fears that troubled her, Rebecca was overcome by desire, and responded energetically to Bernd's touch. Passion was a recent discovery for her. She had mildly enjoyed sex with Hans, most of the time, and with two previous lovers, but she had never before been flooded with desire, possessed by it so completely that for a while she forgot everything else. Now the thought that this could be the last time made her desire even more intense.

After it was over he said: "You're a tiger."

She laughed. "I never was before. It's you."

"It's us," he said. "We're right."

When she had caught her breath, she said: "People escape every day."

"No one knows how many."

Escapers swam across canals and rivers, they climbed barbed wire, or they hid in cars and trucks. West Germans, who were allowed into East Berlin for their relatives. Allied troops could go anywhere, so one East German man bought a U.S. army uniform at a theatrical costume shop and walked through a checkpoint unchallenged.

Rebecca said: "And many die."

The border guards showed no mercy and no shame. They shot to kill. They sometimes left the wounded to bleed to death in no-man's-land, as a lesson to others. Death was the penalty for trying to leave the Communist paradise.

Rebecca and Bernd were planning to escape via Bernauer Strasse.

One of the grim ironies of the Wall was that in some streets the buildings were in East Berlin but the sidewalk was in the West. Residents of the east side of Bernauer Strasse had opened their front doors on Sunday, August 13, 1961, to find a barbed-wire fence preventing them from stepping outside. At first, many leaped from upstairs windows to freedom—some injuring themselves, others jumping onto a blanket held by West Berlin firemen. Now all those buildings had been evacuated, their doors and windows boarded up.

Rebecca and Bernd had a different plan.

They got dressed and went down to breakfast with the

family—probably their last for a long time. It was a tense repeat of the same meal on August 13 last year. On that occasion the family had been sad and anxious: Rebecca had been planning to leave, but not at the risk of her life. This time they were scared.

Rebecca tried to be cheerful. "Maybe you'll all follow us across the border one day," she said.

Carla said: "You know we aren't going to do that. You *must* go—you have no life left here. But we're staying."

"What about Father's work?"

"For now, I carry on," Werner said. He was no longer able to go to the factory he owned because it was in West Berlin. He was trying to manage it remotely, but that was nearly impossible. There was no telephone service between the two Berlins, so he had to do everything by mail, which was always liable to be delayed by the censors.

This was agony for Rebecca. Her family was the most important thing in the world to her, but she was being forced to leave them. "Well, no wall lasts forever," she said. "One day Berlin will be reunited, and then we can be together again."

There was a ring at the doorbell, and Lili jumped up from the table. Werner said: "I hope that's the postman with the factory accounts."

Walli said: "I'm going to cross the Wall as soon as I can. I'm not going to spend my life in the East, with some old Communist telling me what music to play."

Carla said: "You can make your own decision—as soon as you're an adult."

Lili came back into the kitchen looking scared. "It's not the postman," she said. "It's Hans."

Rebecca let out a small scream. Surely her estranged husband could not know about her escape plan?

Werner said: "Is he alone?"

"I think so."

Grandma Maud said to Carla: "Remember how we dealt with Joachim Koch?"

Carla looked at the children. Obviously they were not supposed to know how Joachim Koch had been dealt with.

Werner went to the kitchen cupboard and opened the bottom drawer. It contained heavy pans. He pulled the drawer all the way out and set it on the floor. Then he reached deep into the cavity and brought out a black pistol with a brown grip and a small box of ammunition.

Bernd said: "Jesus."

Rebecca did not know much about guns, but she thought it was a Walther P38. Werner must have kept it after the war.

What had happened to Joachim Koch? Rebecca wondered. Had he been killed?

By Mother? And *Grandma*?

Werner said to Rebecca: "If Hans Hoffmann takes you out of this house we will never see you again." Then he began to load the gun.

Carla said: "He may not be here to arrest Rebecca."

"True," said Werner. He said to Rebecca: "Talk to him. Find out what he wants. Scream if you need to."

Rebecca stood up. Bernd did the same. "Not you," Werner said to Bernd. "The sight of you might anger him."

"But—"

Rebecca said: "Father's right. Just be ready to come if I call."

"All right."

Rebecca took a deep breath, made herself calm, and went into the hall.

Hans stood there in his new blue-gray suit, wearing a striped tie that Rebecca had given him for his last birthday. He said: "I got the divorce papers."

Rebecca nodded. "You were expecting them, of course."

"Can we talk about it?"

"Is there anything to say?"

"Perhaps."

She opened the door of the dining room, used occasionally for formal dinners and otherwise for doing homework. They went in and sat down. Rebecca did not close the door.

"Are you sure you want to do this?" Hans said.

Rebecca was scared. Did he mean escape? Did he know? She managed to say: "Do what?"

"Get divorced," he said.

She was confused. "Why not?" she said. "It's what you want, too."

"Is it?"

"Hans, what are you trying to say?"

"That we don't have to be divorced. We could start again. This time there would be no deceptions. Now that you know I am an officer of the Stasi, there would be no need for lies."

This felt like a stupid dream in which impossible things happen. "But why?" she said.

Hans leaned forward across the table. "Don't you know? Can't you at least guess?"

"No, I can't!" she said, although she had the glimmering of a creepy suspicion.

"I love you," said Hans.

"For God's sake!" Rebecca shouted. "How can you say such a thing? After all you've done!"

"I mean it," he said. "I was faking it at first. But I realized after a while what a wonderful woman you are. I *wanted* to marry you—that wasn't just work. You're beautiful, and smart, and dedicated to teaching—I admire dedication. I've never met a woman like you. Come back to me, Rebecca—please."

"No!" she shouted.

"Think about it. Take a day. Take a week."

"No!"

She was yelling her refusal at the top of her voice, but he acted as if she were coyly pretending reluctance. "We'll talk again," he said with a smile.

"No!" she yelled. "Never! Never! Never!" And she ran from the room.

They were all at the open door of the kitchen, looking scared. Bernd said: "What? What happened?"

"He doesn't want a divorce," Rebecca wailed. "He says he loves me. He wants to start again—give it another chance!"

Bernd said: "I'm going to fucking strangle him."

But there was no need to restrain Bernd. At that moment they heard the front door slam.

"He's gone," Rebecca said. "Thank God."

Bernd put his arms around her and she buried her face in his shoulder.

"Well," said Carla in a shaky voice, "I wasn't expecting *that.*"

Werner unloaded the pistol.

Grandma Maud said: "That's not the end of it. Hans will

come back. Stasi officers do not believe that ordinary people can say no to them."

"And they're right," said Werner. "Rebecca, you have to leave today."

She detached herself from Bernd's embrace. "Oh, no—today?"

"Now," her father said. "You're in terrible danger."

Bernd said: "He's right. Hans may come back with reinforcements. We have to do now what we planned to do tomorrow morning."

"All right," said Rebecca.

Rebecca and Bernd ran upstairs to their room. Bernd put on his black corduroy suit with a white shirt and a black tie, as if going to a funeral. Rebecca, too, dressed all in black. They both put on black gym shoes. From under the bed Bernd took a coiled washing line he had bought last week. He slung it across his body like a bandolier, then put on a brown leather jacket to hide it. Rebecca donned a dark short coat over her black roll-neck sweater and black pants.

They were ready in a few short minutes.

The family was waiting in the hall. Rebecca hugged and kissed them all. Lili was crying. "Don't get killed," she sobbed.

Bernd and Rebecca put on leather gloves and went to the door.

They waved to the family one more time, then they went out.

· · ·

Walli followed them at a distance.

He wanted to see how they did it. They had not told anyone their plan, not even the family. Mother said the only way to keep a secret was to tell nobody. She and Father were ardent about this, leading Walli to suspect that it came from those mysterious wartime experiences that they never explained.

Walli had told the family he was going to play the guitar in his room. He had an electric instrument now. Hearing no noise, his parents would assume he was practicing without plugging in.

He slipped out through the back door.

the roof. Rebecca felt dizzyingly conspicuous, but when she looked around she saw no one but a single distant figure back in the cemetery.

The next part was forbidding. Bernd got one knee up on the window ledge, but it was narrow. Fortunately the curtains were drawn, so that if there were people in the room they would not see anything—unless they heard a noise and came to investigate. With some difficulty he got his other knee on the sill. Leaning on Rebecca's shoulder for support, he contrived to stand upright. With his feet now firmly planted, albeit on a narrow footing, he helped Rebecca up.

She knelt on the ledge and tried not to look down.

Bernd reached out to the sloping edge of the pitched roof, their next step up. He could not climb onto the roof from where he was: there was nothing to grab but the edge of a slate. They had already discussed this problem. Still kneeling, Rebecca braced herself. Bernd put one foot on her right shoulder. Holding the roof edge for balance, he put all his weight on her. It hurt, but she took the strain. A moment later his left foot was on her left shoulder. Evenly balanced, she could hold him—for a few moments.

A second later he cocked his leg over the edge of the slates and rolled up onto the roof.

He splayed his body out, for maximum traction, then reached down. With one gloved hand he grabbed the collar of Rebecca's coat, and she grasped his upper arm.

The curtains were suddenly pulled apart, and a woman's face stared at Rebecca from a distance of a few inches.

The woman screamed.

With an effort, Bernd lifted Rebecca until she was able to get her leg over the sloping edge of the roof; then he pulled her toward him until she was safe.

But they both lost control and started to slide down.

Rebecca spread her arms and pressed the palms of her gloved hands to the slates, trying to brake her slide. Bernd did the same. But they continued to slip, slowly but relentlessly—then Rebecca's sneakers touched an iron gutter. It did not feel sturdy, but it held, and they both came to a stop.

"What was that scream?" Bernd asked urgently.

"A woman in the bedroom saw me. I don't think she could have been heard on the street, though."

"But she might raise the alarm."

"Nothing we can do. Let's keep going."

They edged crabwise across the pitched roof. The houses were old and some of the roof slates were broken. Rebecca tried not to put weight on the gutter that her feet were touching. Their progress was painfully slow.

She imagined the woman at the window talking to her husband. "If we do nothing we'll be accused of collaborating. We could say we were fast asleep and didn't hear anything, but they'll probably arrest us anyway. And even if we call the police they might arrest us on suspicion. When things go wrong they arrest everyone in sight. Best just to keep our heads down. I'll draw the curtains again."

Ordinary people avoided any contact with the police—but the woman at the window might not be ordinary. If she or her husband was a party member, with a soft job and privileges, they would have a degree of immunity from police harassment, and in those circumstances they would undoubtedly raise a hue and cry.

But the seconds ticked by, and Rebecca heard no sound of a commotion. Perhaps she and Bernd had got away with it.

They came to an angle in the roof. Bracing his feet on the opposing sides, Bernd was able to crawl upward until he got his hands over the roof ridge. Now he had a safer grip, though he ran the risk that his dark-gloved fingertips might be noticed by the police on the street.

He turned the angle and crawled on, every second getting nearer to Bernauer Strasse and freedom.

Rebecca followed. She glanced over her shoulder, wondering if anyone could see her and Bernd. Their dark clothing was inconspicuous against the gray slates, but they were not invisible. Was anyone watching? She could see the backyards and the cemetery. The dark figure she had noticed a minute ago was now running from the chapel toward the cemetery gate. A leaden fear made her stomach cold. Had he seen them, and was he hurrying to warn the police?

She suffered a moment of panic, then she realized the figure was familiar.

"Walli?" she said.

What the hell was he up to? Obviously he had followed her and Bernd. But to what end? And where was he heading in such a hurry?

There was nothing she could do but worry.

They came to the back wall of the apartment building on Bernauer Strasse.

The windows were boarded up. Bernd and Rebecca had talked about breaking through the boards to get in, then breaking through another set at the front to get out, but they had decided it would be too noisy, time-consuming, and difficult. Easier, they guessed, to go over the top.

The ridge of the roof they were on was at the level of the gutters of the high adjacent building, so they could easily step from one roof to the next.

From then on they would be clearly visible to the guards with the machine guns on the side street below.

This was their most vulnerable moment.

Bernd crawled up the house roof to the ridge, straddled it, then scrambled up onto the higher roof of the apartment building, heading for the top.

Rebecca followed. She was breathing hard now. Her knees were bruised and her shoulders ached where Bernd had stood on them.

When she was straddling the lower roof she took a look down. She was alarmingly close to the policemen on the street. They were lighting cigarettes: if one should glance upward, all would be lost. Both she and Bernd would be easy targets for their submachine guns.

But they were only a few steps from freedom.

She braced herself to wriggle onto the roof in front of her. Beneath her left foot something moved. Her sneaker slipped, and she fell. She was still astride the ridge, and the impact hurt her groin. She gave a muffled cry, leaned vertiginously sideways for a horrifying moment, then regained her balance.

Unfortunately the cause of her stumble, a loose slate, slipped down the roof, tumbled over the gutter, and fell to the street, where it shattered noisily.

The cops heard the sound and looked at the fragments on the pavement.

Rebecca froze.

The police looked around. Any second now it would occur to them that the slate must have fallen from the roof, and they would look up. But, before they did, one was hit by a flung stone. A second later, Rebecca heard her brother's voice yelling: "All cops are cunts!"

. . .

Walli picked up another stone and threw it at the police. This one missed.

Baiting East German policemen was suicidally stupid—he knew that. He was likely to be arrested, beaten up, and jailed. But he had to do it.

He could see that Bernd and Rebecca were hopelessly exposed. The police would spot them any second now. They never hesitated to shoot escapers. The range was short, about fifty feet. Both fugitives would be riddled with machine-gun bullets in a few seconds.

Unless the cops could be distracted.

They were not much older than Walli. He was sixteen; they seemed about twenty. They were looking around in confusion, their newly lit cigarettes between their lips, unable to figure out why a slate had shattered and two stones had been thrown.

"Pig-faces!" Walli yelled. "Shitheads! Your mothers are whores!"

They saw him then. He was a hundred yards away, visible despite the mist. As soon as they set eyes on him they started to move toward him.

He backed away.

They started to run.

Walli turned and fled.

At the cemetery gate he looked back. One of the men had stopped, no doubt realizing they should not both leave their post at the Wall to chase someone who had merely thrown stones. They had not yet got around to wondering why anyone would do something so rash.

The second cop knelt down and aimed his gun.

Walli slipped into the cemetery.

. . .

Bernd looped the clothesline around a brick chimney, pulled it tight, and tied a secure knot.

Rebecca lay flat on the roof ridge, looking down, panting. She could see one cop pounding along the street after Walli, and Walli running across the cemetery. The second cop was returning to his post, but—luckily—he kept looking back, watching his colleague. Rebecca did not know whether to be relieved or horrified that her brother was risking his life to divert the attention of the police for the next few crucial seconds.

She looked the other way, into the free world. In Bernauer Strasse, on the far side of the street, a man and a woman stood watching her and talking excitedly.

Holding the rope, Bernd sat down, then slid on his bottom down the west slope of the roof to the edge. Next he wound the rope twice around his chest under his arms, leaving a long tail of fifty or so feet. He could now lean out over the edge, supported by the rope tied to the chimney.

He returned to Rebecca and straddled the ridge. "Sit upright," he said. He tied the free end of the clothesline around her and tied a knot. He held the rope firmly in his leather-gloved hands.

Rebecca took a last look into East Berlin. She saw Walli nimbly scaling the fence at the far end of the cemetery. His figure crossed a road and vanished into a side street. The cop gave up and turned back.

Then the man happened to look up, toward the roof of the apartment building, and his jaw dropped in astonishment.

Rebecca was in no doubt about what he had seen. She and Bernd were perched on top of the roof, clear against the skyline.

The cop shouted and pointed, then broke into a run.

Rebecca rolled off the ridge and slowly slid down the slope of the roof until her sneakers touched the gutter at the front.

She heard a burst of machine-gun fire.

Bernd stood upright beside her, bracing himself with the rope tied to the chimney.

Rebecca felt him take her weight.

Here goes, she thought.

She rolled over the gutter and slid into thin air.

The rope pulled painfully around her chest, above her breasts. She dangled in the air for a moment, then Bernd played out the rope and she began to descend in short jerks.

They had practiced this at her parents' house. Bernd had let her down from the highest window all the way to the backyard. It hurt his hands, he said, but he could do it, if he had good gloves. All the same, she was instructed to pause

briefly anytime she could rest her weight on a window surround to give him a moment's respite.

She heard shouts of encouragement, and guessed that a
crowd had now gathered down on Bernauer Strasse, on the
west side of the Wall.

Below her she could see the pavement and the barbed
wire that ran along the façade of the building. Was she in
West Berlin yet? The frontier police would shoot anyone on
the east side, but they had strict instructions not to fire into
the West, for the Soviets did not want any diplomatic inci-
dents. But she was dangling immediately above the barbed
wire, neither in one country nor the other.

She heard another burst of machine-gun fire. Where
were the cops, and who were they shooting at? She guessed
they would try to get up on the roof and shoot her and
Bernd before it was too late. If they followed the same la-
borious route as their quarry they would not catch up in
time. But they could probably save time by entering the
building and simply running up the stairs.

She was almost there. Her feet touched the barbed wire.
She pushed away from the building, but her legs did not
quite clear the wire. She felt the barbs rip her trousers and
tear her skin painfully. Then a crowd gathered around and
helped her, taking her weight, disentangling her from the
barbed wire, unwinding the rope around her chest, and setting her on the ground.

As soon as she was steady on her feet, she looked up.
Bernd was on the edge of the roof, loosening the rope
around his chest. She stepped backward across the road so
that she could see better. The policemen had not yet
reached the roof.

Bernd got the rope firmly in both hands, then stepped
backward off the roof. He rappelled slowly down the wall,
slipping the rope through his hands as he went. This was
extremely difficult, because all his weight was supported by
his grip on the rope. He had practiced at home, walking
down the back wall of the town house at night when he
would not be seen. But this building was taller.

The crowd in the street cheered him.

Then a cop appeared on the roof.

Bernd came down faster, risking his grip on the rope for
more speed.

Someone shouted: "Get a blanket!"

Rebecca knew there was not enough time for that.

The cop aimed his submachine gun at Bernd, but hesitated. He could not fire into West Germany. He might well hit people other than the escapers. It was the kind of incident that could start a war.

The man turned and looked at the rope around the chimney. He might have untied it, but Bernd would reach the ground first.

Did the cop have a knife?

Apparently not.

Then he was inspired. He put the barrel of his gun against the taut rope and fired a single round.

Rebecca screamed.

The rope split, its end flying into the air over Bernauer Strasse.

Bernd fell like a stone.

The crowd scattered.

Bernd hit the sidewalk with a sickening thump.

Then he lay still.

.   .   .

Three days later Bernd opened his eyes, looked at Rebecca, and said: "Hello."

Rebecca said: "Oh, thank God."

She had been out of her mind with worry. The doctors had told her that he would recover consciousness, but she had not been able to believe it until she saw it. He had undergone several operations, and in between he had been heavily drugged. This was the first time she had seen the light of intelligence in his face.

Trying not to cry, she leaned over the hospital bed and kissed his lips. "You're back," she said. "I'm so glad."

He said: "What happened?"

"You fell."

He nodded. "The roof. I remember. But . . ."

"The policeman broke your rope."

He looked along the length of his body. "Am I in plaster?"

She had been longing for him to come round, but she had also been dreading this moment. "From the waist down," she said.

"I . . . I can't move my legs. I can't feel them." He looked panicky. "Have my legs been amputated?"

"No." Rebecca took a deep breath. "You've broken most of the bones in your legs, but you can't feel them because your spinal cord is partially severed."

He was thoughtful for a long moment. Then he said: "Will it heal?"

"The doctors say that nerves may heal, albeit slowly."

"So . . ."

"So you may get some below-the-waist functions back, eventually. But you will be in a wheelchair when you leave this hospital."

"Do they say how long?"

"They say . . ." She had to make an effort not to cry. "You must prepare for the possibility that it may be permanent."

He looked away. "I'm a cripple."

"But we're free. You're in West Berlin. We've escaped."

"Escaped to a wheelchair."

"Don't think of it that way."

"What the hell am I going to do?"

"I've thought about this." She made her voice firm and confident, more so than she felt. "You're going to marry me and return to teaching."

"That's not likely."

"I've already phoned Anselm Weber. You'll remember that he's now head of a school in Hamburg. He has jobs for both of us, starting in September."

"A teacher in a wheelchair?"

"What difference will that make? You'll still be able to explain physics so that the dullest child in the class understands. You don't need legs for that."

"You don't want to marry a cripple."

"No," she said. "But I want to marry you. And I will."

His tone became bitter. "You can't marry a man with no below-the-waist functions."

"Listen to me," she said fiercely. "Three months ago I didn't know what love was. I've only just found you, and I'm not going to lose you. We've escaped, we've survived, and we're going to live. We'll get married, we'll teach school, and we'll love each other."

"I don't know."

"I want only one thing from you," she said. "You must

not lose hope. We'll confront all difficulties together, and we'll solve all problems together. I can put up with any hardship as long as I've got you. Promise me, now, Bernd Held, that you'll never give up. Never."

There was a long pause.

"Promise," she said.

He smiled. "You're a tiger," he said.

PART THREE

ISLAND

1962

CHAPTER FOURTEEN

Dimka and Valentin rode the Ferris wheel in Gorky Park with Nina and Anna.

After Dimka had been called away from the holiday camp, Nina had taken up with an engineer and had dated him for several months, but then they broke up, so now she was free again. Meanwhile, Valentin and Anna had become a couple: he slept over at the girls' apartment most weekends. Also, significantly, Valentin had told Dimka a couple of times that having sex with one woman after another was just a phase men went through when they were young.

I should be so lucky, Dimka thought.

On the first warm weekend of the short Moscow summer, Valentin proposed a double date. Dimka agreed eagerly. Nina was smart and strong-minded, and she challenged him: he liked that. But mainly she was sexy. He often thought about how enthusiastically she had kissed him. He wanted very much to do that again. He recalled how her nipples had stuck out in the cold water. He wondered whether she ever thought about that day on the lake.

His problem was that he could not share Valentin's cheerfully exploitative attitude to girls. Valentin, at least until he met Anna, would say anything to get a girl into bed. Dimka felt it was wrong to manipulate or bully people. He also believed that if someone said no, you should accept it, whereas Valentin always took no to mean "Maybe not yet."

Gorky Park was an oasis in the desert of earnest Communism, a place Muscovites could go simply to have fun. People put on their best clothes, bought ice cream and candy, flirted with strangers, and kissed in the bushes.

Anna pretended to be scared on the Ferris wheel, and Valentin went along with the charade, putting his arm around her and telling her it was perfectly safe. Nina looked comfortable and unworried, which Dimka preferred to phony terror, but it gave him no chance to get intimate.

Nina looked good in a cotton shirtwaist dress with orange and green stripes. The back view was particularly alluring, Dimka thought as they climbed off the wheel. For this date he had managed to get a pair of American jeans and a blue checked shirt. In exchange he had given two ballet tickets that Khrushchev did not want: *Romeo and Juliet* at the Bolshoi.

"What have you been doing since I saw you last?" Nina asked him as they strolled around the park, drinking lukewarm orange cordial bought from a stall.

"Working," he said.

"Is that all?"

"I usually get to the office an hour before Khrushchev, to make sure everything is ready for him: the documents he needs, the foreign newspapers, any files he might want. He often works until late into the evening, and I rarely go home before he does." He wished he could make his job sound as exciting as it really was. "I don't have much time for anything else."

Valentin said: "Dimka was the same at university—work, work, work."

Happily, Nina did not seem to think that Dimka's life was dull. "You're really with Comrade Khrushchev every day?"

"Most days."

"Where do you live?"

"Government House." It was an elite apartment building not far from the Kremlin.

"Very nice."

"With my mother," he added.

"I'd live with my mother for the sake of a place in that building."

"My twin sister normally lives with us, also, but she's gone to Cuba—she's a reporter with TASS."

"I'd like to go to Cuba," Nina said wistfully.

"It's a poor country."

"I could live with that, in a climate where there's no winter. Imagine dancing on the beach in January."

Dimka nodded. He was thrilled by Cuba in a different way. Castro's revolution showed that rigid Soviet orthodoxy was not the only possible form of Communism. Castro had new, different ideas. "I hope Castro survives," he said.

"Why shouldn't he?"

"The Americans have invaded once already. The Bay of Pigs was a disaster, but they will try again, with a bigger army—probably in 1964, while President Kennedy is running for reelection."

"That's terrible! Can't something be done?"

"Castro is trying to make peace with Kennedy."

"Will he succeed?"

"The Pentagon is against it, and conservative congressmen are making a fuss, so the whole idea is getting nowhere."

"We have to support the Cuban revolution!"

"I agree—but our conservatives don't like Castro either. They're not sure he's a real Communist."

"What will happen?"

"It depends on the Americans. They may leave Cuba alone. But I don't think they're that smart. My guess is they'll keep harassing Castro until he feels the only place he can look for help is the Soviet Union. So he'll end up asking us for protection, sooner or later."

"What can we do?"

"Good question."

Valentin interrupted them. "I'm hungry. Have you girls got any food at home?"

"Of course," said Nina. "I bought a knuckle of bacon for a stew."

"Then what are we waiting for? Dimka and I will buy some beer on the way."

They took the Metro. The girls had an apartment in a building controlled by the steel union, their employer. Their place was small: a bedroom with two single beds, a living room with a couch in front of a television set, a kitchen with a tiny dining table, and a bathroom. Dimka guessed that Anna was responsible for the lacy cushions on the couch and the plastic flowers in the vase on top of the TV, and Nina had bought the striped curtains and the posters on the wall showing mountain scenery.

Dimka worried about the shared bedroom. If Nina wanted to sleep with him, would the two couples make love in the same room? Such arrangements had not been unknown when Dimka was a university student in crowded accommodations. All the same he did not like the idea. Apart from anything else, he did not want Valentin to know just how inexpert he was.

He wondered where Nina slept when Valentin stayed over. Then he noticed a small stack of blankets on the living room floor, and he deduced that she slept on the couch.

Nina put the joint in a big saucepan; Anna chopped up a large turnip; Valentin put out cutlery and plates; and Dimka poured the beer. Everyone but Dimka seemed to know what was going to happen next. He was a little unnerved, but he went along.

Nina made a tray of snacks: pickled mushrooms, blinis, sausage, and cheese. While the stew was cooking they went into the living room. Nina sat on the couch and patted the place beside her to indicate that Dimka should sit there. Valentin took the easy chair and Anna sat on the floor at his feet. They listened to music on the radio while they drank their beer. Nina had put some herbs in the pot, and the aroma from the kitchen made Dimka hungry.

They talked about their parents. Nina's were divorced, Valentin's were separated, and Anna's hated one another. "My mother didn't like my father," said Dimka. "Nor did I. Nobody likes a KGB man."

"I've been married once—never again," Nina said. "Do you know anyone who is happily married?"

"Yes," said Dimka. "My uncle Volodya. Mind you, my aunt Zoya is gorgeous. She's a physicist, but she looks like a film star. When I was little I called her Magazine Auntie, because she resembled the impossibly beautiful women in magazine photos."

Valentin stroked Anna's hair, and she laid her head on his thigh in a way Dimka found sexy. He wanted to touch Nina, and surely she would not mind—why else had she invited him to her apartment?—but he felt awkward and embarrassed. He wished she would do something: she was the experienced one. But she seemed content to listen to the music and sip beer, a faint smile on her face.

At last supper was ready. The stew was delicious: Nina was a good cook. They ate it with black bread.

When they had finished and cleared away, Valentin and Anna went into the bedroom and closed the door.

Dimka went to the bathroom. The face in the mirror over the washbasin was not handsome. His best feature was a pair of large blue eyes. His dark brown hair was cut short in the military style approved for young apparatchiks. He looked like a serious young man whose thoughts were far above sex.

He checked the condom in his pocket. Such things were in short supply and he had gone to a lot of trouble to get some. However, he did not agree with Valentin's contention that pregnancy was the woman's problem. He felt sure he would not enjoy sex if he felt he might be forcing the girl to go through either childbirth or abortion.

He returned to the living room. To his surprise, Nina had her coat on.

"I thought I'd walk you to the Metro station," she said.

Dimka was baffled. "Why?"

"I don't think you know this neighborhood—I wouldn't like you to get lost."

"I mean, why do you want me to leave?"

"What else would you do?"

"I'd like to stay here and kiss you," he said.

Nina laughed. "What you lack in sophistication, you make up for in enthusiasm." She took off her coat and sat down.

Dimka sat beside her and kissed her hesitantly.

She kissed him back with reassuring enthusiasm. He realized with mounting excitement that she did not care if he was inexpert. Soon he was eagerly fumbling with the buttons of her shirtwaist. She had wonderfully large breasts. They were encased in a formidable utilitarian brassiere, but she took that off, then offered them to be kissed.

Things moved quickly after that.

When the big moment arrived, she lay on the couch with her head on the armrest and one foot on the floor, a position she assumed so readily that Dimka thought she must have done it before.

He hastily took out his condom and fumbled it out of the packet, but she said: "No need for that."

He was startled. "What do you mean?"

"I can't bear children. I've been told by doctors. It's why my husband divorced me."

He dropped the condom on the floor and lay on top of her.

"Easy does it," she said, guiding him inside.

I've done it, Dimka thought; I've lost my virginity at last.

.   .   .

The speedboat was the kind once known as a rumrunner: long and narrow, extremely fast, and painfully uncomfortable to ride in. It crossed the Straits of Florida at eighty knots, hitting every wave with the impact of a car knocking down a wooden fence. The six men aboard were strapped in, the only way to be halfway safe in an open boat at such a speed. In the small cargo hold they had M3 submachine guns, pistols, and incendiary bombs. They were going to Cuba.

George Jakes really should not have been with them.

He stared across the moonlit water, feeling seasick. Four of the men were Cubans living in exile in Miami: George knew only their first names. They hated Communism, hated Castro, and hated everyone who did not agree with them. The sixth man was Tim Tedder.

It had started when Tedder walked into the office at the Justice Department. He was vaguely familiar, and George had placed him as a CIA man, although he was officially "retired" and working as a freelance security consultant.

George had been on his own in the room. "Help you?" he had said politely.

"I'm here for the Mongoose meeting."

George had heard of Operation Mongoose, a project that the untrustworthy Dennis Wilson was involved in, but he did not know the full details. "Come in," he had said, waving at a chair. Tedder had walked in with a cardboard folder under his arm. He was about ten years older than George, but looked as if he had got dressed in the 1940s: he wore a double-breasted suit and his wavy hair was brilliantined with a high side parting. George said: "Dennis will be back any second."

"Thanks."

"How's it going? Mongoose, I mean."

Tedder looked guarded and said: "I'll report at the meeting."

"I won't be there." George looked at his wristwatch. He was deceitfully implying that he had been invited, which he had not; but he was curious. "I have a meeting at the White House."

"Too bad."

George recalled a fragment of information. "According to the original plan, you should now be in phase two, the buildup."

Tedder's face cleared as he inferred that George was in the loop. "Here's the report," he said, opening the cardboard folder.

George was pretending to know more than he did. Mongoose was a project to help anti-Communist Cubans foment a counterrevolution. The plan had a timetable whose climax was the overthrow of Castro in October of this year, just before the midterm congressional elections. CIA-trained infiltration teams were supposed to undertake political organization and anti-Castro propaganda.

Tedder handed George two sheets of paper. Pretending to be less interested than he was, George said: "Are we keeping to our timetable?"

Tedder avoided the question. "It's time to pile on the pressure," he said. "Furtively circulating leaflets that poke fun at Castro is not achieving what we want."

"How can we increase the pressure?"

"It's all in there," Tedder said, pointing at the paper.

George looked down. What he read was worse than he expected. The CIA was proposing to sabotage bridges, oil refineries, power plants, sugar mills, and shipping.

At that moment Dennis Wilson walked in. He had his shirt collar undone, his tie loose, and his sleeves rolled, just like Bobby, George noticed, although his receding hairline would never rival Bobby's vigorous thatch. When Wilson saw Tedder talking to George he looked surprised, then anxious.

George said to Tedder: "If you blow up an oil refinery, and people are killed, then anyone here in Washington who approved the project is guilty of murder."

Dennis Wilson spoke angrily to Tedder. "What have you told him?"

"I thought he was cleared!" said Tedder.

"I am cleared," said George. "My security clearance is the same as Dennis's." He turned to Wilson. "So why have you been so careful to keep this from me?"

"Because I knew you'd make a fuss."

"And you were right. We're not at war with Cuba. Killing Cubans is murder."

"We are at war," said Tedder.

"Oh?" said George. "So, if Castro sent agents here to Washington, and they bombed a factory and killed your wife, that wouldn't be a crime?"

"Don't be ridiculous."

"Apart from the fact that it's murder, can't you imagine the stink if this gets out? There would be an international scandal! Picture Khrushchev at the United Nations, calling on our president to stop financing international terrorism. Think of the articles in *The New York Times.* Bobby might have to resign. And what about the president's reelection campaign? Has no one even thought about the politics of all this?"

"Of course we have. That's why it's top secret."

"And how's that working out?" George turned a page. "Am I really reading this?" he said. "We're trying to assassinate Fidel Castro with poisoned cigars?"

"You're not on the team for this project," said Wilson. "So just forget about it, okay?"

"Hell, no. I'm going straight to Bobby with this."

Wilson laughed. "You asshole. Don't you realize? Bobby's in charge of it!"

George was flattened.

All the same, he had gone to Bobby, who had said calmly: "Go down to Miami and take a look at the operation, George. Have Tedder show you around. Come back and tell me what you think."

So George had visited the large new CIA camp in Florida where Cuban exiles were trained for their infiltration missions. Then Tedder had said: "Maybe you should come on a mission. See for yourself."

It was a dare, and Tedder had not expected George to accept it. But George felt that if he refused he would be putting himself in a weak position. Right now he had the high ground: he was against Mongoose on moral and political grounds. If he refused to go on a raid, he would be seen as timid. And perhaps there was a part of him that could not resist the challenge of proving his courage. So, foolishly, he had said: "Yes. Will you be coming along?"

That had surprised Tedder, and George had seen clearly that Tedder wished he could withdraw the offer. But now he, too, had been challenged. It was what Greg Peshkov would call a pissing contest. And Tedder, too, had felt unable to back down; although he had said, as an afterthought: "Of course, we can't tell Bobby you came."

So here they were. It was a pity, George reflected, that President Kennedy was so fond of the spy novels of the British writer Ian Fleming. The president seemed to think the world could be saved by James Bond in reality as well as in thrillers. Bond was "licensed to kill." That was crap. No one was licensed to kill.

Their target was a small town called La Isabela. It lay along a narrow peninsula that stuck like a finger out of Cuba's north coast. It was a port, and had no business other than trade. Their aim was to damage the harbor facilities.

Their arrival was timed for first light. The sky to the east was turning gray when the skipper, Sanchez, throttled back the powerful engine, and its roar faded to a low burble. Sanchez knew this stretch of coast well: his father had owned a sugar plantation in the neighborhood, before the revolution. The silhouette of a town began to emerge on the dim horizon, and he killed the engine and unshipped a pair of oars.

The tide took them toward the town; the oars were mainly for steering. Sanchez had judged his approach perfectly. A line of concrete piers came into view. Behind the piers, George could dimly see large warehouses with pitched roofs. There were no big ships in port: farther along the coast, a few small fishing boats were moored. A low surf whispered on the beach; otherwise the world was hushed. The silent speedboat bumped against a pier.

The hatch was opened and the men armed themselves. Tedder offered George a pistol. George shook his head. "Take it," Tedder said. "This is dangerous."

George knew what Tedder was up to. Tedder wanted him

to get blood on his hands. That way he would lose the ability to criticize Mongoose. But George was not so easy to manipulate. "No, thanks," he said. "I'm strictly an observer."

"I'm in charge of this mission, and I'm ordering you."

"And I'm telling you to fuck off."

Tedder gave in.

Sanchez tied up the boat and they all disembarked. No one spoke. Sanchez pointed to the nearest warehouse, which also seemed to be the largest. They all ran toward it. George brought up the rear.

No one else was in sight. George could see a row of houses that looked little more than timber shacks. A tethered ass was cropping the sparse grass at the side of the dirt road. The only vehicle in sight was a rusty pickup truck of 1940s vintage. This was a very poor place, he realized. Clearly it had once been a busy port. George guessed it had been ruined by President Eisenhower, who had imposed an embargo on trade between the USA and Cuba in 1960.

Somewhere, a dog started barking.

The warehouse had timber sides and a corrugated-iron roof, but no windows. Sanchez found a small door and kicked it in. They all ran inside. The place was empty but for packaging litter: broken packing cases, cardboard boxes, short lengths of rope and string, discarded sacks and torn netting.

"Perfect," said Sanchez.

The four Cubans threw incendiary bombs around the floor. A moment later they flamed up. The litter caught fire immediately. The timber walls would light in moments. They all ran outside again.

A voice said in Spanish: "Hey! What's this?"

George turned to see a white-haired Cuban man in some kind of uniform. He was too old to be a cop or a soldier, so George guessed he was the night watchman. He wore sandals. However, he had a handgun on his belt, and he was fumbling to open the holster.

Before he could get his gun out, Sanchez shot him. Blood bloomed from the breast of his white uniform shirt and he fell backward.

"Let's go!" Sanchez said, and the five men ran toward the speedboat.

George knelt over the old man. The eyes stared up at the brightening sky, seeing nothing.

Behind him, Tedder yelled: "George! Let's go!"

Blood pumped from the chest wound for a few moments, then slowed to a trickle. George felt for a pulse, but there was none. At least the man had died fast.

The blaze in the warehouse was spreading rapidly, and George could feel its heat.

Tedder said: "George! We'll leave you behind!"

The speedboat's engine started with a roar.

George closed the dead man's eyes. He stood up. For a few seconds he remained standing, head bowed. Then he ran for the speedboat.

As soon as he was aboard, the boat veered away from the dock and headed across the bay. George strapped himself in.

Tedder yelled in his ear: "What the fuck did you think you were doing?"

"We killed an innocent man," George said. "I thought he deserved a moment of respect."

"He was working for the Communists!"

"He was the night watchman—he probably didn't know Communism from cheesecake."

"You're a goddamn pussy."

George looked back. The warehouse was now a giant bonfire. People were swarming around it, presumably trying to put out the blaze. He returned his gaze to the sea in front, and did not look back again.

When at last they reached Miami and stood on solid ground again, George said to Tedder: "While we were at sea, you called me a pussy." He knew this was stupid, almost as stupid as going on the raid, but he was too proud to let it pass. "We're on dry land, now, with no safety issues. Why don't you say it again, here?"

Tedder stared at him. Tedder was taller than George, but not so broad. He must have had some kind of training in unarmed combat, and George could see him weighing the odds, while the Cubans looked on with neutral interest.

Tedder's gaze flicked to George's cauliflower ear and back again and he said: "I think we'll just forget it."

"I thought so," said George.

On the plane back to Washington he drafted a short report for Bobby, saying that in his opinion Operation Mongoose was ineffective, as there was no sign that people in

Cuba (as opposed to exiles) wanted to overthrow Castro. It was also a threat to the global prestige of the United States, as it would cause anti-American hostility if it ever became public. When he handed Bobby the report, he said succinctly: "Mongoose is useless, and it's dangerous."

"I know," Bobby said. "But we have to do something."

*   *   *

Dimka was seeing all women differently.

He and Valentin spent most weekends with Nina and Anna at the girls' apartment, the couples taking turns to sleep in the bed or on the floor of the living room. In the course of a night he and Nina would have sex twice and even three times. He knew, in more detail than he had ever dreamed of, how a woman's body looked and smelled and tasted.

Consequently he looked at other women in a new, more knowing way. He could imagine them naked, speculate how their breasts curved, visualize their body hair, imagine their faces when they made love. In a way he knew all women, knowing one.

He felt a little disloyal to Nina when he admired Natalya Smotrov on the beach at Pitsunda, wearing a canary yellow swimsuit, with wet hair and sandy feet. Her trim figure was not as curvy as Nina's, but it was no less delightful. Perhaps his interest was pardonable: he had been here on the Black Sea coast for two weeks with Khrushchev, living the life of a monk. Anyway, he was not seriously courting temptation, for Natalya wore a wedding ring.

She was reading a typed report while he took a midday swim, and then she slipped a dress on over her swimsuit at the same time as he changed into his homemade shorts, so they walked together from the beach up to what they called the Barracks.

It was an ugly new building with bedrooms for relatively low-status visitors such as themselves. They met with the other aides in the empty dining room, which smelled of boiled pork and cabbage.

This was a jockeying-for-position meeting ahead of next week's Politburo. The purpose, as always, was to identify controversial issues and assess the support for one side or another. Then an aide could save his boss from the embarrassment of arguing in favor of a proposal that would be subsequently rejected.

Dimka went on the attack right away. "Why is the Defense Ministry so slow in sending arms to our comrades in Cuba?" he said. "Cuba is the only revolutionary state in the American continent. It is proof that Marxism applies all over the world, not just in the East."

Dimka's fondness for the Cuban revolution was more than ideological. He was thrilled by the bearded heroes with their combat fatigues and their cigars—such a contrast to the grim-faced Soviet leaders in their gray suits. Communism was supposed to be a joyous crusade to make a better world. Sometimes the Soviet Union was more like a medieval monastery where everyone had taken vows of poverty and obedience.

Yevgeny Filipov was aide to the defense minister, and he bristled. "Castro is not a true Marxist," he said. "He ignores the correct line laid down by the Popular Socialist Party of Cuba." The PSP was the pro-Moscow party. "He goes his own revisionist way."

Communism was badly in need of revision, in Dimka's opinion, but he did not say that. "The Cuban revolution is a massive blow to capitalist imperialism. We should support it if only because the Kennedy brothers so hate Castro!"

"Do they?" said Filipov. "I don't know so much. The Bay of Pigs invasion happened a year ago. What have the Americans done since?"

"They have spurned Castro's peace feelers."

"True: the conservatives in Congress would not let Kennedy make a pact with Castro even if he wanted to. But that doesn't mean he's going to war."

Dimka looked around the room at the assembled aides in their short-sleeved shirts and sandals. They were watching him and Filipov, discreetly remaining silent until they could tell who was going to win this gladiatorial contest. Dimka said: "We have to make sure the Cuban revolution is not overthrown. Comrade Khrushchev believes there will be another American invasion, this one better organized and more lavishly financed."

"But where is your evidence?"

Dimka was defeated. He had been aggressive and done his best, but his position was weak. "We don't have evidence either way," he admitted. "We have to argue from probabilities."

"Or we could delay arming Castro until the position becomes clearer."

Around the table several people nodded agreement. Filipov had scored heavily against Dimka.

At that moment Natalya spoke. "As a matter of fact, there is some evidence," she said. She passed Dimka the typed pages she had been reading on the beach.

Dimka scanned the document. It was a report from the KGB station chief in the USA, and it was headed: "Operation Mongoose."

While he was rapidly reading the pages, Natalya said: "Contrary to what Comrade Filipov from the Defense Ministry argues, the KGB is sure the Americans have *not* given up on Cuba."

Filipov was furious. "Why has this document not been circulated to us all?"

"It's only just in from Washington," Natalya said coolly. "You'll get a copy this afternoon, I'm sure."

Natalya always seemed to get hold of key information a little ahead of everyone else, Dimka reflected. It was a great skill for an aide. Clearly she must be very valuable to her boss, Foreign Minister Gromyko. No doubt that was why she had such a high-powered job.

Dimka was astonished by what he was reading. It meant he would win today's argument, thanks to Natalya, but it was bad news for Cuba's revolution. "This is even worse than Comrade Khrushchev feared!" he said. "The CIA has sabotage teams in Cuba ready to destroy sugar mills and power stations. It's guerrilla warfare! And they're plotting to assassinate Castro!"

Filipov said desperately: "Can we rely on this information?"

Dimka looked at him. "What's your opinion of the KGB, comrade?"

Filipov shut up.

Dimka got to his feet. "I'm sorry to draw this meeting to a premature close," he said. "But I think the first secretary needs to see this right away." He left the building.

He followed a path through the pine forest to Khrushchev's white stucco villa. Inside, it was strikingly furnished with white curtains and furniture made of timber bleached like drift-wood. He wondered who had picked such a radically con-temporary style: certainly not the peasant Khrushchev, who, if he noticed decor at all, would probably have preferred velvet upholstery and flower-patterned carpets.

Dimka found the leader on the upstairs balcony that looked over the bay. Khrushchev was holding a pair of pow-erful Komz binoculars.

Dimka was not nervous. Khrushchev had taken a liking to him, he knew. The boss was pleased with the way he stood up to the other aides. "I thought you would want to see this report right away," Dimka said. "Operation Mon-goose—"

"I just read it," Khrushchev interrupted. He handed the binoculars to Dimka. "Look over there," he said, pointing across the water toward Turkey.

Dimka put the binoculars to his eyes.

"American nuclear missiles," said Khrushchev. "Aimed at my dacha!"

Dimka could not see any missiles. He could not see Tur-key, which was one hundred fifty miles away in that direction. But he knew that this characteristically theatrical gesture by Khrushchev was essentially right. In Turkey the USA had deployed Jupiter missiles, obsolete but certainly not harm-less: Dimka had this information from his uncle Volodya in Red Army Intelligence.

Dimka was not sure what to do. Should he pretend he could see the missiles through the binoculars? But Khru-shchev must know he could not.

Khrushchev solved the problem by snatching the binoc-ulars back. "And do you know what I'm going to do?" he said.

"Please tell me."

"I'm going to let Kennedy know how it feels. I will de-ploy nuclear missiles in Cuba—aimed at *his* dacha!"

Dimka was speechless. He had not been expecting this. And he could not see it as a good idea. He agreed with his boss in wanting more military aid for Cuba, and he had been battling the Defense Ministry over that issue—but now Khrushchev was going too far. "Nuclear missiles?" he repeated, trying to gain time to think.

"Exactly!" Khrushchev pointed to the KGB report on

Operation Mongoose that Dimka was still clutching. "And that will convince the Politburo to support me. Poisoned cigars. Ha!"

"Our official line has been that we will not deploy nuclear weapons in Cuba," Dimka said, in the manner of one who presents incidental information, rather than in an argumentative tone. "We have given the Americans that reassurance several times, and publicly."

Khrushchev grinned with impish delight. "Then Kennedy will be all the more surprised!"

Khrushchev scared Dimka in this mood. The first secretary was not a fool, but he was a gambler. If this scheme went wrong it could lead to a diplomatic humiliation that might bring about Khrushchev's downfall as leader—and, by way of collateral damage, end Dimka's career. Worse, it might provoke the American invasion of Cuba that it was intended to prevent—and his beloved sister was in Cuba. There was even a chance that it would spark the nuclear war that would end capitalism, Communism, and quite possibly the human race.

On the other hand, Dimka could not help feeling excited. What a tremendous blow would be struck against the rich, smug Kennedy boys, against the global bully that was the United States, and against the whole capitalist-imperialist power bloc. If the gamble paid off, what a triumph it would be for the USSR and Khrushchev.

What should he do? He switched to practical mode and strained to think of ways to reduce the apocalyptic risks of the scheme. "We could start by signing a peace treaty with Cuba," he said. "The Americans could hardly object to that without admitting that they were planning to attack a poor Third World country." Khrushchev looked unenthusiastic but said nothing, so Dimka went on. "Then we could step up the supply of conventional weapons. Again it would be awkward for Kennedy to protest: why shouldn't a country buy guns for its army? Finally we could send the missiles—"

"No," said Khrushchev abruptly. He never liked gradualism, Dimka reflected. "This is what we'll do," Khrushchev went on. "We'll ship the missiles secretly. We'll put them in boxes labeled 'drainage pipes,' anything. Even the ships' captains won't know what's inside. We'll send our artillerymen over to Cuba to assemble the launchers. The Americans won't have any idea what we're up to."

Dimka felt a little sick, with both fear and exhilaration. It would be extraordinarily difficult to keep such a big project secret, even in the Soviet Union. Thousands of men would be involved in crating the weapons, sending them by train to the ports, opening them in Cuba, and deploying them. Was it even possible to keep them all quiet?

However, he said nothing.

Khrushchev went on: "And then, when the weapons are launch-ready, we'll make an announcement. It will be a fait accompli—the Americans will be helpless to do anything about it."

It was just the kind of grand dramatic gesture Khrushchev loved, and Dimka realized he would never talk him out of it. He said cautiously: "I wonder how President Kennedy will react to such an announcement."

Khrushchev made a scornful noise. "He's a boy—inexperienced, timid, weak."

"Of course," said Dimka, though he feared Khrushchev might be underestimating the young president. "But they have midterm elections on November sixth. If we revealed the missiles during the campaign, Kennedy would come under heavy pressure to do something drastic, to avoid humiliation at the polls."

"Then you have to keep the secret until November sixth."

Dimka said: "Who does?"

"You do. I'm putting you in charge of this project. You'll be my liaison with the Defense Ministry, who will have to carry it out. It will be your job to make sure they don't let the secret leak before we're ready."

Dimka was shocked enough to blurt out: "Why me?"

"You hate that prick Filipov. Therefore I can trust you to ride him hard."

Dimka was too aghast to wonder how Khrushchev knew he hated Filipov. The army was being given a near-impossible task—and Dimka would get the blame if it went wrong. This was a catastrophe.

But he knew better than to say so. "Thank you, Nikita Sergeyevich," he said formally. "You can rely on me."

CHAPTER FIFTEEN

The GAZ-13 limousine was called a Seagull because of its streamlined American-style rear wings. It could reach one hundred miles per hour, just, although it was uncomfortable at such speeds on Soviet roads. It was available in two-tone burgundy and cream with whitewall tires, but Dimka's was black.

He sat in the back as it drove onto the quayside at Sevastopol, Ukraine. The town stood on the tip of the Crimean Peninsula, where it poked out into the Black Sea. Twenty years ago it had been flattened by German bombing and artillery fire. After the war it had been rebuilt as a cheerful seaside resort with Mediterranean balconies and Venetian arches.

Dimka got out and looked at the ship moored at the dock, a timber freighter with oversize hatches designed to take tree trunks. Under the hot summer sun, stevedores were loading skis and clearly labeled cartons of cold-weather clothing, to give the impression that the ship was headed to the frozen north. Dimka had devised the deliberately misleading code name Operation Anadyr, after a town in Siberia.

A second Seagull pulled onto the dock and parked behind Dimka's. Four men in Red Army Intelligence uniforms got out and stood waiting for his instructions.

A railway line ran alongside the dock, and a massive gantry straddled the line, positioned to shift cargo directly from railcar to ship. Dimka looked at his wristwatch. "The fucking train should be here by now."

Dimka was wound up tight. He had never been so tense in all his life. He had not even known what stress was until he started this project.

The senior Red Army man was a colonel called Pankov. Despite his rank, he addressed Dimka with formal respect. "You want me to make a call, Dmitri Ilich?"

A second officer, Lieutenant Meyer, said: "I think it's coming."

Dimka looked along the track. In the distance he could see, approaching slowly, a line of low-slung open railcars loaded with long wooden crates.

Dimka said: "Why does everyone think it's all right to be fifteen fucking minutes late?"

Dimka was worried about spies. He had visited the chief of the local KGB station and reviewed his list of suspected people in the area. They were all dissidents: poets, priests, painters of abstract art, and Jews who wanted to go to Israel—typical Soviet malcontents, about as threatening as a cycling club. Dimka had them all arrested anyway, but not one looked dangerous. Almost certainly there were real CIA agents in Sevastopol, but the KGB did not know who they were.

A man in captain's uniform came from the ship across the gangway and addressed Pankov. "Are you in charge here, Colonel?"

Pankov inclined his head toward Dimka.

The captain became less deferential. "My ship can't go to Siberia," he said.

"Your destination is classified information," Dimka said. "Do not speak of it." In Dimka's pocket was a sealed envelope that the captain was to open after he had sailed from the Black Sea into the Mediterranean. At that point he would learn he was going to Cuba.

"I need cold-weather lubricating oil, antifreeze, deicing equipment—"

Dimka said: "Shut the fuck up."

"But I have to protest. Siberian conditions—"

Dimka said to Lieutenant Meyer: "Punch him in the mouth."

Meyer was a big man and he hit hard. The captain fell back, his lips bleeding.

Dimka said: "Go back aboard your ship, wait for orders, and keep your stupid mouth shut."

The captain left, and the men on the quay turned their attention back to the approaching train.

Operation Anadyr was huge. The approaching train was the first of nineteen similar, all required to bring just this first missile regiment to Sevastopol. Altogether, Dimka was sending fifty thousand men and two hundred thirty thousand tons of equipment to Cuba. He had a fleet of eighty-five ships.

He still did not see how he was to keep the whole thing secret.

Many of the men in authority in the Soviet Union were careless, lazy, drunk, and just plain stupid. They misunderstood their instructions, they forgot, they approached challenging tasks halfheartedly and then gave up, and sometimes they just decided they knew better. Reasoning with them was useless; charm was worse. Being nice to them made them think you were a fool who could be ignored.

The train inched alongside the ship, its steel-on-steel brakes squealing. Each purpose-built railcar carried just one wooden crate eighty feet long and nine feet square. A crane operator mounted the gantry and entered its control cabin. Stevedores leaped onto the railcars and began readying the crates for loading. A company of soldiers had traveled with the train, and now they began to help the stevedores. Dimka was relieved to see that the missile regiment flashes had been removed from their uniforms, in accordance with his instructions.

A man in a civilian suit jumped down off a car, and Dimka was irritated to see that it was Yevgeny Filipov, his opposite number at the Defense Ministry. Filipov approached Pankov, as the captain had, but Pankov said: "Comrade Dvorkin is in command here."

Filipov shrugged. "Just a few minutes late," he said with a satisfied air. "We were delayed—"

Dimka noticed something. "Oh, no," he said. "Fuck it."

Filipov said: "Something wrong?"

Dimka stamped his foot on the concrete quay. "Fuck, fuck, fuck!"

"What is it?"

Dimka looked at him in fury. "Who's in charge on the train?"

"Colonel Kats is with us."

"Bring the dumb bastard here to me right away."

Filipov did not like to do Dimka's bidding, but he could hardly refuse such a request, and he went away.

Pankov looked an inquiry at Dimka.

Dimka said with weary rage: "Do you see what is stenciled on the side of each crate?"

Pankov nodded. "It's an army code number."

"Exactly," Dimka said bitterly. "It means: 'R-12 ballistic missile.'"

"Oh, shit," said Pankov.

Dimka shook his head in impotent fury. "Torture is too good for some people."

He had feared that sooner or later he would have a showdown with the army, and on balance it suited him to have it now, over the very first shipment. And he was prepared for it.

Filipov returned with a colonel and a major. The senior man said: "Good morning, comrades. I'm Colonel Kats. Slight delay, but otherwise everything is going smoothly—"

"No, it's not, you dimwitted prick," said Dimka.

Kats was incredulous. "What did you say?"

Filipov said: "Look here, Dvorkin, you can't talk to an army officer like that."

Dimka ignored Filipov and spoke to Kats. "You have endangered the security of this entire operation by your disobedience. Your orders were to paint over the army numbers on the crates. You were provided with new stencils reading 'Construction-Grade Plastic Pipe.' You were to paint new markings on all the crates."

Kats said indignantly: "There wasn't time."

Filipov said: "Be reasonable, Dvorkin."

Dimka suspected Filipov might be happy for the secret to leak, for then Khrushchev would be discredited and might even fall from power.

Dimka pointed south, out to sea. "There is a NATO country just one hundred and fifty miles in that direction, Kats, you fucking idiot. Don't you know that the Americans have spies? And that they send them to places such as Sevastopol, which is a naval base and a major Soviet port?"

"The markings are in code—"

"In code? What is your brain made of, dog shit? What

training do you imagine is given to capitalist-imperialist spies? They are taught to recognize uniform badges—such as the missile regiment flash you are wearing on your collar, also against orders—as well as other military insignia and equipment markings. You stupid turd, every traitor and CIA informant in Europe can read the army code on these crates."

Kats tried standing on his dignity. "Who do you think you are?" he said. "Don't you dare speak to me like that. I've got children older than you."

"You are relieved of your command," said Dimka.

"Don't be ridiculous."

"Show him, please."

Colonel Pankov took a sheet of paper from his pocket and handed it to Kats.

Dimka said: "As you see from the document, I have the necessary authority."

Filipov's jaw was hanging open, Dimka saw.

Dimka said to Kats: "You are under arrest as a traitor. Go with these men."

Lieutenant Meyer and another of Pankov's group smoothly positioned themselves either side of Kats, took his arms, and marched him to the limousine.

Filipov recovered his wits. "Dvorkin, for God's sake—"

"If you can't say anything helpful, shut your fucking mouth," Dimka said to him. He turned to the missile regiment major, who had not said a word so far. "Are you Kats's second-in-command?"

The man looked terrified. "Yes, comrade. Major Spektor at your service."

"You are now in command."

"Thank you."

"Take this train away. North of here is a large complex of train sheds. Arrange with the railway management to stop there for twelve hours while you repaint the crates. Bring the train back here tomorrow."

"Yes, comrade."

"Colonel Kats is going to a labor camp in Siberia for the rest of his life, which will not be very long. So, Major Spektor, don't make a mistake."

"I won't."

Dimka got into his limousine. As he drove away, he passed Filipov standing on the quay, looking as if he was not sure what had just happened.

.   .   .

Tanya Dvorkin stood on the dock at Mariel, on Cuba's north coast, twenty-five miles from Havana, where a narrow inlet opened into a huge natural harbor hidden among hills. She looked anxiously at a Soviet ship moored at a concrete pier. Parked on the pier was a Soviet ZIL-130 truck pulling an eighty-foot trailer. A crane was lifting a long wooden crate from the ship's hold and moving it through the air, with painful slowness, toward the truck. The crate was marked in Russian: CONSTRUCTION-GRADE PLASTIC PIPE.

She saw all this by floodlights. The ships had to be unloaded at night, by order of her brother. All other shipping had been cleared out of the harbor. Patrol boats had closed the inlet. Frogmen searched the waters around the ship to guard against an underwater threat. Dimka's name was mentioned in tones of fear: his word was law and his wrath terrible to behold, they said.

Tanya was writing articles for TASS that told how the Soviet Union was helping Cuba, and how grateful the Cuban people were for the friendship of their ally on the far side of the globe. But she reserved the real truth for the coded cables she sent, via the KGB's telegraph system, to Dimka in the Kremlin. And now Dimka had given her the unofficial task of making sure his instructions were carried out without fail. That was why she was anxious.

With Tanya was General Paz Oliva, the most beautiful man she had ever met.

Paz was breathtakingly attractive: tall and strong and a little scary, until he smiled and spoke in a soft bass voice that made her think of the strings of a cello being caressed by a bow. He was in his thirties: most of Castro's military men were young. With his dark skin and soft curls he looked more Negro than Hispanic. He was a poster boy for Castro's policy of racial equality, such a contrast with Kennedy's.

Tanya loved Cuba, but it had taken a while. She missed Vasili more than she had expected. She realized how fond she was of him, even though they had never been lovers. She worried about him in his Siberian labor camp, hungry and cold. The campaign for which he had been punished — publicizing the illness of Ustin Bodian, the opera singer — had been successful, sort of: Bodian had been released from prison, though he had died soon afterward in a Moscow hospital. Vasili would find the irony telling.

Some things she could not get used to. She still put on a coat to go out, although the weather was never cold. She got bored with beans and rice and, to her surprise, found herself longing for a bowl of kasha with sour cream. After endless days of hot summer sun, she sometimes hoped for a downpour to freshen the streets.

Cuban peasants were as poor as Soviet peasants, but they seemed happier, perhaps because of the weather. And eventually the Cuban people's irrepressible joie de vivre bewitched Tanya. She smoked cigars and drank rum with tuKola, the local substitute for Coke. She loved to dance with Paz to the irresistibly sexy rhythms of the traditional music they called *trova*. Castro had closed most of the nightclubs, but no one could prevent Cubans playing guitars, and the musicians had moved to small bars called *casas de la trova*.

But she worried for the Cuban people. They had defied their giant neighbor, the United States, only ninety miles away across the Straits of Florida, and she knew that one day they might be punished. When she thought about it, Tanya felt like the crocodile bird, bravely perched between the open jaws of the great beast, pecking food from a row of teeth like broken knives.

Was the Cubans' defiance worth the price? Only time would tell. Tanya was pessimistic about the prospects for reforming Communism, but some of the things Castro had done were admirable. In 1961, the Year of Education, ten thousand students had flocked to the countryside to teach farmers to read, a heroic crusade to wipe out illiteracy in one campaign. The first sentence in the primer was "The peasants work in the cooperative," but so what? People who could read were better equipped to recognize government propaganda for what it was.

Castro was no Bolshevik. He scorned orthodoxy and restlessly sought out new ideas. That was why he annoyed the Kremlin. But he was no democrat either. Tanya had been saddened when he had announced that the revolution had made elections unnecessary. And there was one area in which he had imitated the Soviet Union slavishly: with advice from the KGB he had created a ruthlessly efficient secret police force to stamp out dissent.

On balance, Tanya wished the revolution well. Cuba had to escape from underdevelopment and colonialism. No one wanted the Americans back, with their casinos and their prostitutes. But Tanya wondered whether Cubans would ever be allowed to make their own decisions. American hostility drove them into the arms of the Soviets; but as Castro moved closer to the USSR, it became increasingly likely that the Americans would invade. What Cuba really needed was to be left alone.

But perhaps now it had a chance. She and Paz were among a mere handful of people who knew what was in these long wooden crates. She was reporting directly to Dimka on the effectiveness of the security blanket. If the plan worked it might protect Cuba permanently from the danger of an American invasion, and give the country breathing space in which to find its own way into the future.

That was her hope, anyway.

She had known Paz a year. "You never talk about your family," she said as they watched the crate being positioned in the trailer. She addressed him in Spanish: she was now fairly fluent. She had also picked up a smattering of the American-accented English that many Cubans used occasionally.

"The revolution is my family," he said.

Bullshit, she thought.

All the same, she was probably going to sleep with him.

Paz might turn out to be a dark-skinned version of Vasili, handsome and charming and faithless. There was probably a string of lissome Cuban girls with flashing eyes taking turns to fall into his bed.

She told herself not to be cynical. Just because a man was gorgeous he did not have to be a mindless Lothario. Perhaps Paz was simply waiting for the right woman to become his life partner and toil alongside him in the mission to build a new Cuba.

The missile in its crate was lashed to the bed of the

trailer. Paz was approached by a small, obsequious lieutenant called Lorenzo, who said: "Ready to move out, General."

"Carry on," said Paz.

The truck moved slowly away from the dock. A herd of
motorcycles roared into life and went ahead of the truck to
clear the road. Tanya and Paz got into his army car, a green
Buick LeSabre station wagon, and followed the convoy.

Cuba's roads had not been designed for eighty-foot trucks.
In the last three months, Red Army engineers had built new
bridges and reconfigured hairpin bends, but still the convoy
moved at walking pace much of the time. Tanya noted with
relief that all other vehicles had been cleared from the
roads. In the villages through which they passed, the low-
built two-room wooden houses were dark, and the bars were
shut. Dimka would be satisfied.

Tanya knew that back at the dockside another missile was
already being eased onto another truck. The process would
go on until first light. Unloading the entire cargo would take
two nights.

So far, Dimka's strategy was working. It seemed no one
suspected what the Soviet Union was up to in Cuba. There
was no whisper of it on the diplomatic circuit or in the un-
controlled pages of Western newspapers. The feared explosion of outrage in the White House had not yet happened.

But there were still two months to go before the American midterm elections; two more months during which
these huge missiles had to be made launch-ready in total
secrecy. Tanya did not know whether it could be done.

After two hours they drove into a broad valley that had
been taken over by the Red Army. Here engineers were
building a launch site. This was one of more than a dozen
tucked away out of sight in the folds of the mountains all
across the 777-mile-long island of Cuba.

Tanya and Paz got out of the car to watch the crate being
off-loaded from the truck, again under floodlights. "We did
it," said Paz in a tone of satisfaction. "We now have nuclear
weapons." He took out a cigar and lit it.

Sounding a note of caution, Tanya said: "How long will
it take to deploy them?"

"Not long," he said dismissively. "A couple of weeks."

He was not in the mood to think about problems, but to

Tanya the task looked as if it might take more than two
weeks. The valley was a dusty construction site where little
had so far been achieved. All the same, Paz was right: they
had done the hard part, which was bringing nuclear weapons into Cuba without the Americans finding out.

"Look at that baby," Paz said. "One day it could land in
the middle of Miami. Bang."

Tanya shuddered at the thought. "I hope not."

"Why?"

Did he really need to be told? "These weapons are
meant to be a threat. They're supposed to make the Americans afraid to invade Cuba. If ever they are used, they will
have failed."

"Perhaps," he said. "But if they do attack us, we will be
able to wipe out entire American cities."

Tanya was unnerved by the evident relish with which he
contemplated this dreadful prospect. "What good would
that do?"

He seemed surprised by the question. "It will maintain
the pride of the Cuban nation." He uttered the Spanish
word *dignidad* as if it were sacred.

She could hardly believe what she was hearing. "So you
would start a nuclear war for the sake of your pride?"

"Of course. What could be more important?"

Indignantly she said: "The survival of the human race,
for one thing!"

He waved his lighted cigar in a dismissive gesture. "You
worry about the human race," he said. "My concern is my
honor."

"Shit," said Tanya. "Are you mad?"

Paz looked at her. "President Kennedy is prepared to use
nuclear weapons if the United States is attacked," he said.
"Secretary Khrushchev will use them if the Soviet Union is
attacked. The same for De Gaulle of France and whoever is
the leader of Great Britain. If one of them said anything
different he would be deposed within hours." He drew on
his cigar, making the end glow red, then blew out smoke. "If
I'm mad," he said, "they all are."

.   .   .

George Jakes did not know what the emergency was. Bobby
Kennedy summoned him and Dennis Wilson to a crisis

meeting in the White House on the morning of Tuesday, October 16. His best guess was that the subject would be on the front page of today's *New York Times*, with the headline:

Eisenhower Calls President
Weak on Foreign Policy

The unwritten rule was that ex-presidents did not attack their successors. However, George was not surprised that Eisenhower had flouted the convention. Jack Kennedy had won by calling Eisenhower weak and inventing a nonexistent "missile gap" in the Soviets' favor. Clearly Ike was still hurting from this punch below the belt. Now that Kennedy was vulnerable to a similar charge, Eisenhower was getting his revenge—exactly three weeks before the midterm elections.

The other possibility was worse. George's great fear was that Operation Mongoose might have leaked. The revelation that the president and his brother were organizing international terrorism would be ammunition for every Republican candidate. They would say the Kennedys were criminals for doing it and fools for letting the secret out. And what reprisals might Khrushchev dream up?

George could see that his boss was furious. Bobby was not good at hiding his feelings. Rage showed in the set of his jaw and the hunch of his shoulders and the arctic blast of his blue-eyed gaze.

George liked Bobby for the openness of his emotions. People who worked with Bobby saw into his heart, frequently. It made him more vulnerable but also more lovable.

When they walked into the Cabinet Room, President Kennedy was already there. He sat on the other side of the long table, on which were several large ashtrays. He was in the center, with the presidential seal on the wall above and behind him. Either side of the seal, tall arched windows looked out onto the Rose Garden.

With him was a little girl in a white dress who was obviously his daughter, Caroline, not quite five years old. She had short light brown hair parted at the side—like her father's—and held back with a simple clip. She was speaking to him, solemnly explaining something, and he was listening raptly, as if her words were as vital as anything else said in this room of power. George was profoundly struck by the intensity of the connection between parent and child. If ever I have a daughter, he thought, I will listen like that, so that she will know she is the most important person in the world.

The aides took their seats against the wall. George sat next to Skip Dickerson, who worked for Vice President Lyndon Johnson. Skip had very fair straight hair and pale skin, almost like an albino. He pushed his blond forelock out of his eyes and spoke in a Southern accent. "Any idea where the fire is?"

"Bobby isn't saying," George replied.

A woman George did not know came into the room and took Caroline away. "The CIA has some news for us," the president said. "Let's begin."

At one end of the room, in front of the fireplace, stood an easel displaying a large monochrome photograph. The man standing next to it introduced himself as an expert photointerpreter. George had not known that such a profession existed. "The pictures you are about to see were taken on Sunday by a high-altitude U-2 aircraft of the CIA flying over Cuba."

Everyone knew about the CIA's spy planes. The Soviets had shot one down over Siberia two years ago, and had put the pilot on trial for espionage.

Everyone peered at the photo on the easel. It seemed blurred and grainy, and showed nothing that George could recognize except maybe trees. They needed an interpreter to tell them what they were looking at.

"This is a valley in Cuba about twenty miles inland from the port of Mariel," the CIA man said. He pointed with a little baton. "A good-quality new road leads to a large open field. These small shapes scattered around are construction vehicles: bulldozers, backhoes, and dump trucks. And here"—he tapped the photo for emphasis—"here, in the middle, you see a group of shapes like planks of wood in a row. They are in fact crates eighty feet long by nine feet across. That is exactly the right size and shape to contain a Soviet R-12 intermediate-range ballistic missile, designed to carry a nuclear warhead."

George just managed to stop himself from saying *Holy*

shit, but others were not so restrained, and for a moment the room was full of astonished curses.

Someone said: "Are you sure?"

The photointerpreter replied: "Sir, I have been studying air reconnaissance photographs for many years, and I can assure you of two things: one, this is exactly what nuclear missiles look like, and two, nothing else looks like this."

God save us, George thought fearfully; the goddamn Cubans have nukes.

Someone said: "How the hell did they get there?"

The photointerpreter said: "Clearly the Soviets transported them to Cuba in conditions of utter secrecy."

"Snuck them in under our fucking noses," said the questioner.

Someone else asked: "What is the range of those missiles?"

"More than a thousand miles."

"So they could hit . . ."

"This building, sir."

George had to repress an impulse to get up and leave right away.

"And how long would it take?"

"To get here from Cuba? Thirteen minutes, we calculate."

Involuntarily, George glanced at the windows, as if he might see a missile coming across the Rose Garden.

The president said: "That son of a bitch Khrushchev lied to me. He told me he would not deploy nuclear missiles in Cuba."

Bobby added: "And the CIA told us to believe him."

Someone else said: "This is bound to dominate the rest of the election campaign—three more weeks."

With relief, George turned his mind to the domestic political consequences: the possibility of nuclear war was somehow too terrible to contemplate. He thought of this morning's *New York Times.* How much more Eisenhower could say now! At least when he was president he had not allowed the USSR to turn Cuba into a Communist nuclear base.

This was a disaster, and not just for foreign policy. A Republican landslide in November would mean that Kennedy was hamstrung for the last two years of his presidency, and that would be the end of the civil rights agenda. With more

Republicans joining Southern Democrats in opposing equality for Negroes, Kennedy would have no chance of bringing in a civil rights bill. How long would it be then before Maria's grandfather would be allowed to register to vote without getting arrested?

In politics, everything was connected.

We have to do something about the missiles, George thought.

He had no idea what.

Fortunately Jack Kennedy did.

"First, we need to step up U-2 surveillance of Cuba," the president said. "We have to know how many missiles they have and where they are. And then, by God, we're going to take them out."

George perked up. Suddenly the problem did not seem so great. The USA had hundreds of aircraft and thousands of bombs. And President Kennedy taking decisive, violent action to protect America would do no harm to the Democrats in the midterms.

Everyone looked at General Maxwell Taylor, chairman of the Joint Chiefs of Staff and America's most senior military commander after the president. His wavy hair, slick with brilliantine and parted high on his head, made George think he might be vain. He was trusted by both Jack and Bobby, though George was not sure why. "An air strike would need to be followed by a full-scale invasion of Cuba," Taylor said.

"And we have a contingency plan for that."

"We can land one hundred fifty thousand men there within a week of the bombing."

Kennedy was still thinking about taking out the Soviet missiles. "Could we guarantee to destroy every launch site in Cuba?" he asked.

Taylor replied: "It will never be one hundred percent, Mr. President."

George had not thought of that snag. Cuba was 777 miles long. The air force might not be able to find every site, let alone destroy them all.

President Kennedy said: "And I guess any missiles remaining after our air strike would be fired at the USA immediately."

"We would have to assume that, sir," said Taylor.

The president looked bleak, and George had a sudden vivid sense of the dreadful weight of responsibility he bore. "Tell me this," said Kennedy. "If one missile landed on a medium-size American city, how bad would that be?"

Election politics were driven from George's mind, and once again his heart was chilled by the dreaded thought of nuclear war.

General Taylor conferred with his aides for a few moments, then turned back to the table. "Mr. President," he said, "our calculation is that six hundred thousand people would die."

CHAPTER SIXTEEN

Dimka's mother, Anya, wanted to meet Nina. This surprised him. His relationship with Nina was exciting, and he slept with her every chance he got, but what did that have to do with his mother?

He put that to her, and she answered in tones of exasperation. "You were the cleverest boy in school, but you're such a fool sometimes," she said. "Listen. Every weekend that you're not away somewhere with Khrushchev, you're with this woman. Obviously she's important. You've been seeing her for three months. Of course your mother wants to know what she's like! How can you even ask?"

He supposed she was right. Nina was not just a date nor even merely a girlfriend. She was his lover. She had become part of his life.

He loved his mother, but he did not obey her in everything: she disapproved of the motorcycle, the blue jeans, and Valentin. However, he would do anything reasonable to please her, so he invited Nina to the apartment.

At first Nina refused. "I'm not going to be inspected by your family, like a used car you're thinking of buying," she said resentfully. "Tell your mother I don't want to get married. She'll soon lose interest in me."

"It's not my family, it's just her," Dimka told her. "My father's dead and my sister's in Cuba. Anyway, what have you got against marriage?"

"Why, are you proposing to me?"

Dimka was embarrassed. Nina was thrilling and sexy, and he had never been anywhere near so deeply involved with a woman, but he had not thought about marriage. Did he want to spend the rest of his life with her?

He dodged the question. "I'm just trying to understand you."

"I've tried marriage, and I didn't like it," she said. "Satisfied?"

Challenge was her default setting. He did not mind. It was part of what made her so exciting. "You prefer being single," he said.

"Obviously."

"What's so great about it?"

"I don't have to please a man, so I can please myself. And when I want something else I can see you."

"I fit neatly into the slot."

She grinned at the double meaning. "Exactly."

However, she was thoughtful for a while; then she said: "Oh, hell, I don't want to make an enemy of your mother. I'll go."

On the day, Dimka felt nervous. Nina was unpredictable. When something happened to displease her—a plate carelessly broken, a real or imagined slight, a note of reproof in Dimka's voice—her disapproval was a blast like Moscow's north wind in January. He hoped she would get on with his mother.

Nina had not previously been inside Government House. She was impressed by the lobby, which was the size of a small ballroom. The apartment was not large but it was luxuriously finished, by comparison with most Moscow homes, having thick rugs and expensive wallpaper and a radiogram—a walnut cabinet containing a record player and a radio. These were the privileges of senior KGB officers such as Dimka's father.

Anya had prepared a lavish spread of snacks, which Muscovites preferred to a formal dinner: smoked mackerel and hard-boiled eggs with red pepper on white bread; little rye bread sandwiches with cucumber and tomatoes; and her pièce de résistance, a plate of "sailboats," ovals of toast with triangles of cheese held upright by a toothpick like a mast.

Anya wore a new dress and put on a touch of makeup. She had gained a little weight since the death of Dimka's father, and it suited her. Dimka felt his mother was happier since her husband had died. Maybe Nina was right about marriage.

The first thing Anya said to Nina was: "Twenty-three years old, and this is the first time my Dimka has ever brought a girl home."

He wished his mother had not told her that. It made him seem a beginner. He *was* a beginner, and Nina had figured that out long ago, but all the same he did not need her to be reminded. Anyway, he was learning fast. Nina said he was a good lover, better than her husband, though she would not go into details.

To his surprise, Nina went out of her way to be pleasant to his mother, politely calling her Anya Grigorivitch, helping in the kitchen, asking her where she got her dress.

When they had had some vodka, Anya felt relaxed enough to say: "So, Nina, my Dimka tells me you don't want to get married."

Dimka groaned. "Mother, that's too personal!"

But Nina did not seem to mind. "I'm like you. I've already been married," she said.

"But I'm an old woman."

Anya was forty-five, which was generally considered too old for remarriage. Women of that age were thought to have left desire behind—and, if they had not, they were regarded with distaste. A respectable widow who remarried in middle age would be careful to tell everyone it was "just for companionship."

"You don't look old, Anya Grigorivitch," Nina said. "You might be Dimka's big sister."

This was rubbish, but Anya liked it all the same. Perhaps women always enjoyed such flattery, regardless of whether it was credible. Anyway, she did not deny it. "I'm too old to have more children, anyway."

"I can't have children, either."

"Oh!" Anya was shaken by that revelation. It upturned all her fantasies. For a moment she forgot to be tactful. "Why not?" she asked bluntly.

"Medical reasons."

"Oh."

Clearly Anya would have liked to know more. Dimka had noticed that medical details were of great interest to many women. But Nina clammed up, as she always did on this subject.

There was a knock at the door. Dimka sighed: he could guess who it was. He opened up.

On the doorstep were his grandparents, who lived in the same building. "Oh! Dimka—you're here!" said his grandfather Grigori Peshkov, feigning surprise. He was in uniform. He was nearly seventy-four, but he would not retire. Old men who did not know when to quit were a major problem in the Soviet Union, in Dimka's opinion.

Dimka's grandmother Katerina had had her hair done. "We brought you some caviar," she said. Clearly this was not the casual drop-in they were pretending. They had found out that Nina was coming and they were here to check her out. Nina was being inspected by the family, just as she had feared.

Dimka introduced them. Grandmother kissed Nina and Grandfather held her hand longer than necessary. To Dimka's relief, Nina continued to be charming. She called Grandfather "comrade General." Realizing immediately that he was susceptible to attractive girls, she flirted with him, to his delight, at the same time giving Grandmother a woman-to-woman look that said *You and I know what men are like.*

Grandfather asked her about her job. She had recently been promoted, she told him, and now she was publishing manager, organizing the printing of the steel union's various newsletters. Grandmother asked about her family, and she said she did not see much of them as they all lived in her hometown of Perm, a twenty-four-hour train journey eastward.

She soon got Grandfather onto his favorite subject, historical inaccuracies in Eisenstein's film *October,* especially the scenes depicting the storming of the Winter Palace, in which Grandfather had participated.

Dimka was pleased they were all getting on so well, yet at the same time he had the uneasy sensation that he was not in control of whatever was happening here. He felt as if he were on a ship sailing through calm waters to an unknown destination: all was well for the moment, but what lay ahead?

The phone rang, and Dimka answered. He always did in

the evenings: it was usually the Kremlin calling for him. The voice of Natalya Smotrov said: "I've just heard from the KGB station in Washington."

Talking to her while Nina was in the room made Dimka feel awkward. He told himself not to be stupid: he had never touched Natalya. He had thought about it, though. But surely a man need not feel guilty for his thoughts? "What's happened?" he asked.

"President Kennedy has booked television time this evening to talk to the American people."

As usual, she had the hot news first. "Why?"

"They don't know."

Dimka thought immediately of Cuba. Most of his missiles were there now, and the nuclear warheads to go with them. Tons of ancillary equipment and thousands of troops had arrived. In a few days the weapons would be launch-ready. The mission was almost complete.

But two weeks remained before the American midterm elections. Dimka had been considering flying to Cuba—there was a scheduled air service from Prague to Havana—to make sure the lid was screwed on tight for a few more days. It was vital that the secret be kept just a little longer.

He prayed that Kennedy's surprise TV appearance would be about something else: Berlin, perhaps, or Vietnam.

"What time is the broadcast?" Dimka asked Natalya.

"Seven in the evening, Eastern time."

That would be two o'clock tomorrow morning in Moscow. "I'll phone him right away," he said. "Thank you." He broke the connection, then dialed Khrushchev's residence.

The phone was answered by Ivan Tepper, head of the household staff, the equivalent of a butler. "Hello, Ivan," said Dimka. "Is he there?"

"On his way to bed," said Ivan.

"Tell him to put his trousers back on. Kennedy is going to speak on television at two A.M. our time."

"Just a minute, he's right here."

Dimka heard a muttered conversation, then Khrushchev's voice. "They have found your missiles!"

Dimka's heart sank. Khrushchev's spontaneous intuition was usually right. The secret was out—and Dimka was going to take the blame. "Good evening, comrade First Secretary," he said, and the four people in the room with him went silent. "We don't yet know what Kennedy will be speaking about."

"It's the missiles, bound to be. Call an emergency meeting of the Presidium."

"What time?"

"In an hour."

"Very good."

Khrushchev hung up.

Dimka dialed the home of his secretary. "Hello, Vera," he said. "Emergency Presidium at ten tonight. He's on his way to the Kremlin."

"I'll start calling people," she said.

"You have the numbers at your home?"

"Yes."

"Of course you do. Thank you. I'll be at the office in a few minutes." He hung up.

They were all staring at him. They had heard him say "Good evening, comrade First Secretary." Grandfather looked proud, Grandmother and Mother were concerned, and Nina had a gleam of excitement in her eye. "I've got to go to work," Dimka said unnecessarily.

Grandfather said: "What's the emergency?"

"We don't know yet."

Grandfather patted him on the shoulder and looked sentimental. "With men such as you and my son, Volodya, in charge, I know the revolution is safe."

Dimka was tempted to say he wished he felt so confident. Instead he said: "Grandfather, will you get an army car to take Nina home?"

"Of course."

"Sorry to break up the party . . ."

"Don't worry," said Grandfather. "Your work is more important. Go, go."

Dimka put on his coat, kissed Nina, and left.

Going down in the elevator, he wondered despairingly whether he had somehow let out the secret of the Cuban missiles, despite all his efforts. He had run the entire operation with formidable security. He had been brutally efficient. He had been a tyrant, punishing mistakes severely, humiliating fools, ruining the careers of men who failed to follow orders meticulously. What more could he have done?

Outside, a nighttime rehearsal was in progress for the military parade scheduled for Revolution Day, in two weeks' time. An endless line of tanks, artillery, and soldiers rumbled along the embankment of the Moskva River. None of this will do us any good if there's a nuclear war, he thought. The Americans did not know it, but the Soviet Union had few nuclear weapons, nowhere near the numbers the USA had. The Soviets could hurt the Americans, yes, but the Americans could wipe the Soviet Union off the face of the earth.

As the road was blocked by the procession, and the Kremlin was less than a mile away, Dimka left his motorcycle at home and walked.

The Kremlin was a triangular fortress on the north side of the river. Within were several palaces now converted to government buildings. Dimka went to the senate building, yellow with white pillars, and took the elevator to the third floor. He followed a red carpet along a high-ceilinged corridor to Khrushchev's office. The first secretary had not yet arrived. Dimka went two doors farther along to the Presidium Room. Fortunately, it was clean and tidy.

The Presidium of the Supreme Soviet was in practice the ruling body of the Soviet Union. Khrushchev was its chairman. This was where the power lay. What would Khrushchev do?

Dimka was first, but soon Presidium members and their aides began to trickle in. No one knew what Kennedy was going to say. Yevgeny Filipov arrived with his boss, Defense Minister Rodion Malinovsky. "This is a fuckup," Filipov said, hardly able to hide his glee. Dimka ignored him.

Natalya came in with the black-haired, dapper foreign minister Andrei Gromyko. She had decided that the late hour licensed casual clothing, and she looked cute in tight American-style blue jeans and a loose-fitting wool sweater with a big rolled collar.

"Thank you for the early warning," Dimka murmured to her. "I really appreciate it."

She touched his arm. "I'm on your side," she said. "You know that."

Khrushchev arrived and opened the meeting by saying: "I believe Kennedy's television address will be about Cuba."

Dimka sat up against the wall behind Khrushchev, ready

to run errands. The leader might need a file, a newspaper, or a report; he might ask for tea or beer or a sandwich. Two other Khrushchev aides sat with Dimka. None of them knew the answers to the big questions. Had the Americans found the missiles? And, if they had, who had let the secret out? The future of the world hung in the balance but Dimka, somewhat to his shame, was equally worried about the future of Dimka.

Impatience was driving him mad. Kennedy would speak four hours from now. Surely the Presidium could learn the content of his speech before then? What was the KGB for?

Defense Minister Malinovsky looked like a veteran movie star, with his regular features and thick silver hair. He argued that the USA was not about to invade Cuba. Red Army Intelligence had people in Florida. There was a buildup of troops there, but nowhere near enough for an invasion, he thought. "This is some kind of election campaign trick," he said. Dimka thought he sounded overconfident.

Khrushchev, too, was skeptical. Perhaps it was true that Kennedy did not want war with Cuba, but was he free to act as he wished? Khrushchev believed that the American president was at least partly under the control of the Pentagon and capitalist-imperialists such as the Rockefeller family. "We must have a contingency plan in case the Americans do invade," he said. "Our troops must be prepared for every eventuality." He ordered a ten-minute break for committee members to consider the options.

Dimka was horrified by the rapidity with which the Presidium had begun to discuss war. This was never the plan! When Khrushchev decided to send missiles to Cuba, he had not intended to provoke combat. How did we get here from there? Dimka thought despairingly.

He saw Filipov in an ominous huddle with Malinovsky and several others. Filipov was writing something down. When they reconvened, Malinovsky read a draft order for the Soviet commander in Cuba, General Issa Pliyev, authorizing him to use "all available means" to defend Cuba.

Dimka wanted to say: *Are you mad?*

Khrushchev felt the same. "We would be giving Pliyev the authority to start a nuclear war!" he said angrily.

To Dimka's relief Anastas Mikoyan backed Khrushchev. Always a peacemaker, Mikoyan looked like a lawyer in a country town, with a neat mustache and receding hair. But he was the man who could talk Khrushchev out of his most reckless schemes. Now he opposed Malinovsky. Mikoyan had extra authority because he had visited Cuba shortly after its revolution.

"What about handing over control of the missiles to Castro?" said Khrushchev.

Dimka had heard his boss say some crazy things, especially during hypothetical discussions, but this was irresponsible even by his standards. What was he thinking?

"May I counsel against?" said Mikoyan mildly. "The Americans know that we don't want nuclear war, and as long as we control the weapons they will try to solve this problem by diplomacy. But they will not trust Castro. If they know he has his finger on the trigger they may try to destroy all the missiles in Cuba with one massive first strike."

Khrushchev accepted that, but he was not prepared to rule out nuclear weapons altogether. "That would mean the Americans can have Cuba back!" he said indignantly.

At that point, Alexei Kosygin spoke up. He was Khrushchev's closest ally, though ten years younger. His receding hair had left a gray quiff on top of his head like the prow of a ship. He had the red face of a drinker, but Dimka thought he was the smartest man in the Kremlin. "We should not be thinking about when to use nuclear weapons," Kosygin said. "If we get to that point, we will have failed catastrophically. The question to discuss is this: What moves can we make today to ensure that the situation does not deteriorate into nuclear war?"

Thank God, Dimka thought, someone talking sense at last.

Kosygin went on: "I propose that General Pliyev be authorized to defend Cuba by all means *short of* nuclear weapons."

Malinovsky had doubts, fearing that U.S. intelligence might somehow learn of this order; but despite his reservations the proposal was agreed on, to Dimka's great relief, and the message was sent. The danger of a nuclear holocaust still loomed, but at least the Presidium was focused on avoiding a war rather than fighting it.

Soon afterward, Vera Pletner looked into the room and beckoned Dimka. He slipped out. In the broad corridor she handed him six sheets of paper. "This is Kennedy's speech," she said quietly.

"Thank heaven!" He looked at his watch. It was one fifteen A.M., forty-five minutes before the American president was due to go on television. "How did we get this?"

"The American government kindly provided our Washington embassy with advance copies, and the Foreign Ministry has quickly translated it."

Standing in the corridor, alone but for Vera, Dimka read fast. "This government, as promised, has maintained the closest surveillance of the Soviet military buildup on the island of Cuba."

Kennedy called Cuba an island, Dimka noticed, as if it did not count as a real country.

"Within the past week, unmistakable evidence has established the fact that a series of offensive missile sites is now in preparation on that imprisoned island."

Evidence, Dimka thought; what evidence?

"The purpose of these bases can be none other than to provide a nuclear strike capability against the Western Hemisphere."

Dimka read on but, infuriatingly, Kennedy did not say how he had come by the information, whether from traitors or spies, in the Soviet Union or Cuba, or by some other means. Dimka still did not know whether this crisis was his fault.

Kennedy made much of Soviet secrecy, calling it deception. That was fair, Dimka thought; Khrushchev would have made the same accusation in the reverse situation. But what was the American president going to do? Dimka skipped pages until he came to the important part.

"First, to halt this offensive buildup, a strict quarantine on all offensive military equipment under shipment to Cuba is being initiated."

Ah, Dimka thought; a blockade. That was against international law, which was why Kennedy was calling it a quarantine, as if he were combating some plague.

"All ships of any kind bound for Cuba from whatever nation or port will, if found to contain cargoes of offensive weapons, be turned back."

Dimka saw immediately that this was just a preliminary. The quarantine would make no difference: most of the mis-

siles were already in place and nearly ready to be fired—
and Kennedy must know that, if his intelligence was as
good as it seemed. The blockade was symbolic.

There was also a threat. "It shall be the policy of this
nation to regard any nuclear missile, launched from Cuba,
against any nation in the Western Hemisphere, as an attack
by the Soviet Union on the United States, requiring a full
retaliatory response upon the Soviet Union."

Dimka felt as if something cold and heavy had settled in
his stomach. This was a terrible threat. Kennedy would not
trouble to find out whether the missile had been launched
by the Cubans or the Red Army; it was all the same to him.
Nor would he care what the target was. If they bombed
Chile it would be the same as bombing New York.

Any time one of Dimka's nukes was fired, the USA
would turn the Soviet Union into a radioactive desert.

Dimka saw in his mind the picture everyone knew, the
mushroom cloud of a nuclear bomb; and in his imagination
it rose over the center of Moscow, where the Kremlin and
his home and every familiar building lay in ruins, and
scorched corpses floated like a hideous scum on the poisoned water of the Moskva River.

Another sentence caught his eye. "It is difficult to settle
or even discuss these problems in an atmosphere of intimidation." The hypocrisy of the Americans took Dimka's breath
away. What was Operation Mongoose if not intimidation?

It was Mongoose that had persuaded a reluctant Presidium
to send the missiles in the first place. Dimka was beginning to
suspect that aggression was self-defeating in international
politics.

He had read enough. He went back into the Presidium
Room, walked quickly up to Khrushchev, and handed him
the sheaf of papers. "Kennedy's television speech," he said,
clearly enough for everyone to hear. "An advance copy, provided by the USA."

Khrushchev snatched the papers and began to read. The
room fell silent. There was no point in saying anything until
they knew what was in the document.

Khrushchev took his time reading the formal, abstract
language. Now and again he snorted with derision or grunted
with surprise. As he progressed through the pages, Dimka
sensed that his mood was changing from anxiety to relief.

After several minutes he put down the last page. Still he said nothing, thinking. At last he looked up. A smile broke over his lumpy peasant face as he looked around the table at his colleagues. "Comrades," he said, "we have saved Cuba!"

. . .

As usual, Jacky interrogated George about his love life. "Are you dating anyone?"

"I only just broke up with Norine."

"Only just? That was almost a year ago."

"Oh . . . I guess it was."

She had made fried chicken with okra and the deep-fried cornmeal dumplings she called hush puppies. This had been his favorite meal when he was a boy. Now at twenty-six he preferred rare beef and salad, or pasta with clam sauce. Also, he normally had dinner at eight in the evening, not six. But he tucked in and did not tell her any of this. He preferred not to spoil the pleasure she took in feeding him.

She sat opposite him at the kitchen table, as she always had. "How is that nice Maria Summers?"

George tried not to wince. He had lost Maria to another man. "Maria has a steady," he said.

"Oh? Who is he?"

"I don't know."

Jacky made a frustrated noise. "Didn't you ask?"

"I sure did. She wouldn't tell me."

"Why not?"

George shrugged.

"It's a married man," his mother said confidently.

"Mom, you can't possibly know that," George said, but he had a horrible suspicion she might be right.

"Normally a girl boasts about the man she's seeing. If she clams up, she's ashamed."

"There could be another reason."

"Such as?"

For the moment George could not think of one.

Jacky went on: "He's probably someone she works with. I sure hope her preacher grandfather doesn't find out."

George thought of another possibility. "Maybe he's white."

"Married and white too, I'll bet. What is that press officer like, Pierre Salinger?"

"An affable guy in his thirties, good French clothes, a little heavy. He's married, and I hear he's up to no good with his secretary, so I'm not sure he has time for another girlfriend."

"He might, if he's French."

George grinned. "Have you ever met a French person?"

"No, but they have a reputation."

"And Negroes have a reputation for being lazy."

"You're right. I shouldn't talk that way, people are individuals."

"That's what you always taught me."

George had only half his mind on the conversation. The news about the missiles in Cuba had been kept secret from the American people for a week, but it was about to be revealed. It had been a week of intense debate within the small circle who knew, but little had been resolved. Looking back, George realized that when he had first heard he had underreacted. He had thought mainly of the imminent midterm elections and their effect on the civil rights campaign. For a moment he had even relished the prospect of American retaliation. Only later had the truth sunk in: that civil rights would no longer matter, and no more elections would ever be held, if there was a nuclear war.

Jacky changed the subject. "The chef where I work has a lovely daughter."

"Is that so?"

"Cindy Bell."

"What is Cindy short for, Cinderella?"

"Lucinda. She graduated this year from Georgetown University."

Georgetown was a neighborhood of Washington, but few of the city's black majority attended its prestigious university. "She white?"

"No."

"Must be bright, then."

"Very."

"Catholic?" Georgetown University was a Jesuit foundation.

"Nothing wrong with Catholics," Jacky said with a touch of defiance. Jacky attended Bethel Evangelical Church, but she was broad-minded. "Catholics believe in the Lord, too."

"Catholics don't believe in birth control, though."

"I'm not sure I do."

"What? You're not serious."

"If I'd used birth control, I wouldn't have you."

"But you don't want to deny other women the right to a choice."

"Oh, don't be so argumentative. I don't want to ban birth control." She smiled fondly. "I'm just glad I was ignorant and reckless when I was sixteen." She stood up. "I'll put some coffee on." The doorbell rang. "Would you see who that is?"

George opened the front door to an attractive black girl in her early twenties, wearing tight Capri pants and a loose sweater. She was surprised to see him. "Oh!" she said. "I'm sorry, I thought this was Mrs. Jakes's house."

"It is," said George. "I'm visiting."

"My father asked me to drop this off as I was passing." She handed him a book called *Ship of Fools*. He had heard the title before: it was a bestseller. "I guess Dad borrowed it from Mrs. Jakes."

"Thank you," George said, taking the book. Politely he added: "Won't you come in?"

She hesitated.

Jacky came to the kitchen door. From there she could see who was outside: it was not a large house. "Hello, Cindy," she said. "I was just talking about you. Come in, I've made fresh coffee."

"It sure smells good," said Cindy, and she crossed the threshold.

George said: "Can we have coffee in the living room, Mom? It's almost time for the president."

"You don't want to watch TV, do you? Sit and talk to Cindy."

George opened the living room door. He said to Cindy: "Would you mind if we watched the president? He's going to say something important."

"How do you know?"

"I helped write his speech."

"Then I have to watch," she said.

They went in. George's grandfather Lev Peshkov had bought and furnished this house for Jacky and George in 1949. After that Jacky proudly refused to take anything more from Lev except George's school and college costs. On her modest salary she could not afford to redecorate, so the living room had changed little in thirteen years. George liked it this way: fringed upholstery, an Oriental rug, a china cabinet. It was old-fashioned, but homey.

The main innovation was the RCA Victor television set. George turned it on, and they waited for the green screen to warm up.

Cindy said: "Your mom works at the University Women's Club with my dad, doesn't she?"

"That's right."

"So he didn't really need me to drop off the book. He could have given it back to her tomorrow at work."

"Yes."

"We've been set up."

"I know."

She giggled. "Oh, well, what the heck."

He liked her for that.

Jacky brought in a tray. By the time she had poured coffee, President Kennedy was on the monochrome screen, saying: "Good evening, my fellow citizens." He was sitting at a desk. In front of him was a small lectern with two microphones. He wore a dark suit, white shirt, and narrow tie. George knew that the shadows of terrible strain on his face had been concealed by television makeup.

When he said Cuba had "a nuclear strike capability against the Western Hemisphere," Jacky gasped and Cindy said: "Oh, my Lord!"

He read from sheets of paper on the lectern in his flat Boston accent, *hard* pronounced "haad," and *report* pronounced "repoat." His delivery was deadpan, almost boring, but his words were electrifying. "Each of these missiles, in short, is capable of striking Washington, DC—"

Jacky gave a little scream.

"—the Panama Canal, Cape Canaveral, Mexico City—"

Cindy said: "What are we going to do?"

"Wait," said George. "You'll see."

Jacky said: "How could this happen?"

"The Soviets are sneaky," George said.

Kennedy said: "We have no desire to dominate or conquer any other nation or impose our system on its people."

At that point, normally Jacky would have made a derisive remark about the Bay of Pigs invasion; but she was beyond political point-scoring now.

The camera zoomed in for a close-up as Kennedy said: "To halt this offensive buildup, a strict quarantine on all offensive military equipment under shipment to Cuba is being initiated."

"What use is that?" said Jacky. "The missiles are there already—he just said so!"

Slowly and deliberately, the president said: "It shall be the policy of this nation to regard any nuclear missile, launched from Cuba, against any nation in the Western Hemisphere, as an attack by the Soviet Union on the United States, requiring a full retaliatory response upon the Soviet Union."

"Oh, my Lord," said Cindy again. "So if Cuba launches just one missile, it's all-out nuclear war."

"That's right," said George, who had attended the meetings where this had been thrashed out.

As soon as the president said, "Thank you and good night," Jacky turned off the set and rounded on George. "What is going to happen to us?"

He longed to reassure her, to make her feel safe, but he could not. "I don't know, Mom."

Cindy said: "This quarantine makes no difference to anything, even I can see that."

"It's just a preliminary."

"So what comes next?"

"We don't know."

Jacky said: "George, tell me the truth, now. Is there going to be war?"

George hesitated. Nuclear weapons were being loaded on jets and flown around the country, to ensure that some at least would survive a Soviet first strike. The invasion plan for Cuba was being refined, and the State Department was sifting candidates to lead the pro-American government that would take charge of Cuba afterward.

Strategic Air Command had moved its alert status to DEFCON 3—Defense Condition Three, ready to start a nuclear attack in fifteen minutes.

On balance, what was the likeliest outcome of all this?

With a heavy heart, George said: "Yes, Mom. I think there will be war."

. . .

In the end the Presidium ordered all Soviet missile ships still on their way to Cuba to turn around and come home.

Khrushchev reckoned he lost little by this, and Dimka agreed. Cuba had nukes now; it hardly mattered how many. The Soviet Union would avoid a confrontation on the high seas, claim to be a peacemaker in this crisis—and still have a nuclear base ninety miles from the USA.

Everyone knew that would not be the end of the matter. The two superpowers had not yet addressed the real question, what to do about the nuclear weapons already in Cuba. All Kennedy's options were still open, and as far as Dimka could see, most of them led to war.

Khrushchev decided not to go home tonight. It was too dangerous to be even a few minutes' car journey away: if war broke out he had to be here, ready to make instant decisions.

Next to his grand office was a small room with a comfortable couch. The first secretary lay down there in his clothes. Most of the Presidium made the same decision, and the leaders of the world's second-most powerful country settled down to an uneasy sleep in their offices.

Dimka had a small cubbyhole down the corridor. There was no couch in his office: just a hard chair, a utilitarian desk, and a file cabinet. He was trying to figure out where would be the least uncomfortable place to lay his head when there was a tap at the door and Natalya came in. She brought with her a light fragrance unlike any Soviet perfume.

She had been wise to dress casually, Dimka realized: they were all going to sleep in their clothes. "I like your sweater," he said.

"It's called a Sloppy Joe." She used the English words.

"What does that mean?"

"I don't know, but I like how it sounds."

He laughed. "I was just trying to figure out where to sleep."

"Me, too."

"On the other hand, I'm not sure I'll be able to sleep."

"You mean, knowing you might never wake up?"

"Exactly."

"I feel the same."

Dimka thought for a moment. Even if he spent the night awake, worrying, he might as well find somewhere to be comfortable. "This is a palace, and it's empty," he said. He hesitated, then added: "Shall we explore?" He was not sure why he said that. It was the kind of thing his lady-killer friend Valentin might come out with.

"Okay," said Natalya.

Dimka picked up his overcoat, to use as a blanket.

The spacious bedrooms and boudoirs of the palace had been inelegantly subdivided into offices for bureaucrats and typists, and filled with cheap furniture made of pine and plastic. There were upholstered chairs in a few of the larger rooms for the most important men, but nothing you could sleep on. Dimka began to think of ways to make a bed on the floor. Then, at the far end of the wing, they passed along a corridor cluttered with buckets and mops and came to a grand room full of stored furniture.

The room was unheated, and their breath turned to white vapor. The large windows were frosted over. The gilded wall lights and chandeliers had sockets for candles, all empty. A dim light came from two naked bulbs hanging from the painted ceiling.

The stacked furniture looked as if it had been here since the revolution. There were chipped tables with spindly legs, chairs with rotting brocade upholstery, and carved bookcases with empty shelves. Here were the treasures of the tsars, turned to junk.

The furniture was rotting away here because it was too ancien régime to be used in the offices of commissars, although Dimka guessed it was the kind of stuff that might sell for fortunes in the antique auctions of the West.

And there was a four-poster bed.

Its hangings were full of dust but the faded blue coverlet appeared intact and it even had a mattress and pillows.

"Well," said Dimka, "here's one bed."

"We may have to share," said Natalya.

That thought had crossed Dimka's mind, but he had dismissed it. Pretty girls sometimes casually offered to share a bed with him in his fantasies, but never in real life.

Until now.

But did he want to? He was not married to Nina, but she undoubtedly wanted him to be faithful to her, and he certainly expected the same of her. On the other hand, Nina was not here, and Natalya was.

Foolishly, he said, "Are you suggesting we sleep together?"

"Just for warmth," she said. "I can trust you, can't I?"

"Of course," he said. That made it all right, he supposed.

Natalya drew back the ancient coverlet. Dust rose, making her sneeze. The sheets beneath had yellowed with age, but seemed intact. "Moths don't like cotton," she remarked.

"I didn't know that."

She stepped out of her shoes. In her jeans and sweater she slipped between the sheets. She shivered. "Come on," she said. "Don't be shy."

Dimka put his coat over her. Then he unlaced his shoes and pulled them off. This was strange but exciting. Natalya wanted to sleep with him, but without sex.

Nina would never believe it.

But he had to sleep somewhere.

He took off his tie and got into bed. The sheets were icy. He put his arms around Natalya. She laid her head against his shoulder and pressed her body to his. Her bulky sweater and his suit coat made it impossible for him to feel the contours of her body, but all the same he got an erection. If she felt it, she did not react.

In a few minutes they stopped shivering and felt warmer. Dimka's face was pressed into her hair, which was wavy and abundant and smelled of lemon soap. His hands were on her back, but he got no sense of her skin through the chunky sweater. He could feel her breath on his neck. The rhythm of her breathing changed, becoming regular and shallow. He kissed the top of her head, but she made no response.

He could not figure Natalya out. She was just an aide, like Dimka, and not more than three or four years his senior, but she drove a Mercedes, twelve years old and beautifully preserved. She usually dressed in conventionally dowdy Kremlin clothes yet she wore costly imported perfume. She was charming to the point of flirtatiousness, but she went home and cooked dinner for her husband.

She had inveigled Dimka into bed with her, then she had fallen asleep.

He was sure he would not sleep, lying in bed with a warm girl in his arms.

But he did.

It was still dark outside when he woke up.

Natalya mumbled: "What's the time?"

She was still in his arms. He craned his neck to look at his wrist, which was behind her left shoulder. "Six thirty."

"And we're still alive."

"The Americans didn't bomb us."

"Not yet."

"We'd better get up," Dimka said; and he immediately regretted it. Khrushchev would not be awake yet. And even if he was, Dimka did not have to bring this delicious moment to a premature end. He was bewildered, but happy. Why the hell had he suggested getting up?

But she was not ready. "In a minute," she said.

He was pleased by the thought that she liked lying in his arms.

Then she kissed his neck.

It was the lightest possible touch of her lips on his skin, as if a moth had flown out of the ancient hangings and brushed him with its wings; but he had not imagined it.

She had kissed him.

He stroked her hair.

She tilted her head back and looked at him. Her mouth was slightly open, the full lips a little parted, and she was smiling faintly, as if at a pleasant surprise. Dimka was no expert on women but even he could not mistake the invitation. Still he hesitated to kiss her.

Then she said: "Today we're probably going to be bombed to oblivion."

So Dimka kissed her.

The kiss heated up in a flash. She bit his lip and pushed her tongue into his mouth. He rolled her onto her back and put his hands up inside her baggy sweater. She unfastened her brassiere with a swift movement. Her breasts were delightfully small and firm, with big pointed nipples that were already hard to his fingertips. When he sucked them she gasped with pleasure.

He tried to take off her jeans, but she had another idea.

She pushed him onto his back and feverishly undid his trousers. He was afraid he would come right away—something that happened to a lot of men, according to Nina—but he did not. Natalya pulled his cock out of his underwear. She stroked it with both hands, pressed it to her cheek, and kissed it, then put it in her mouth.

When he felt himself about to explode he tried to withdraw, pushing her head away: this was how Nina preferred it. But Natalya made a protesting noise, then rubbed and sucked harder, so that he lost control and came in her mouth.

After a minute she kissed him. He tasted his semen on her lips. Was that peculiar? It felt simply affectionate.

She pulled off her jeans and underwear, and he realized it was his turn to please her. Fortunately Nina had tutored him in this.

Natalya's hair was as curly and plentiful here as on her head. He buried his face, longing to return the delight she had given him. She guided him with her hands on his head, indicating by slight pressure when his kisses should be lighter or heavier, moving her hips up or down to tell him where to concentrate his attention. She was only the second woman he had done this to, and he luxuriated in the taste and the smell of her.

With Nina this was only a preliminary, but in a surprisingly short time Natalya cried out, first pressing his head hard against her, then, as if the pleasure were too much, pushing him away.

They lay side by side, catching their breath. This had been a totally new experience for Dimka, and he said reflectively: "This whole question of sex is more complicated than I thought."

To his surprise, this made her laugh heartily.

"What did I say?" he said.

She laughed all the more, and all she would say was: "Oh, Dimka, I adore you."

· · ·

La Isabela was a ghost town, Tanya saw. Once a thriving Cuban port, it had been hit hard by Eisenhower's trade embargo. It was miles from anywhere, and surrounded by salt marshes and mangrove swamps. Scraggy goats roamed the streets. Its harbor hosted a few shabby fishing boats—and the *Aleksandrovsk,* a fifty-four-hundred-ton Soviet freighter packed to the gunwales with nuclear warheads.

The ship had been headed for Mariel. After President Kennedy announced the blockade, most of the Soviet ships had turned back, but a few that were only hours from landfall had been ordered to make a dash for the nearest Cuban port.

Tanya and Paz watched the ship inch up to the concrete dock in a shower of rain. The antiaircraft guns on deck were concealed beneath coils of rope.

Tanya was terrified. She had no idea what was going to happen. All her brother's efforts had failed to stop the secret getting out before the American midterm elections—and the trouble Dimka might be in as a result was only the least of her worries. Clearly the blockade was no more than an opening shot. Now Kennedy had to appear strong. And with Kennedy being strong and the Cubans defending their precious *dignidad* anything could happen, from an American invasion to a worldwide nuclear holocaust.

Tanya and Paz had become more intimate. They had told one another about their childhoods and their families and their past lovers. They touched each other frequently. They often laughed. But they held back from romance. Tanya was tempted, but she resisted. The idea of having sex with a man just because he was so beautiful seemed wrong. She liked Paz—despite his *dignidad*—but she did not love him. In the past she had kissed men she did not love, especially while she was at university, but she had not had sex with them. She had gone to bed with only one man, and she had loved him, or at least she had thought she did at the time. But she might sleep with Paz, if only to have someone's arms around her when the bombs fell.

The largest of the dockside warehouses was burned out. "I wonder how that happened," Tanya said, pointing.

"The CIA set fire to it," said Paz. "We get a lot of terrorist attacks here."

Tanya looked around. The quayside buildings were empty and derelict. Most of the homes were one-story wooden shacks. Rain pooled on the dirt roads. The Americans could blow the whole place up without doing noticeable damage to the Castro regime. "Why?" she said.

Paz shrugged. "It's an easy target, here on the end of the

peninsula. They come over from Florida in a speedboat, sneak ashore, blow something up, shoot one or two innocent people, and go back to America." In English he added: "Fuckin' cowards."

Tanya wondered if all governments were the same. The Kennedy brothers spoke of freedom and democracy yet they sent armed gangs across the water to terrorize the Cuban people. The Soviet Communists talked of liberating the proletariat while they imprisoned or murdered everyone who disagreed with them, and they sent Vasili to Siberia for protesting. Was there an honest regime anywhere in the world?

"Let's go," said Tanya. "It's a long way back to Havana, and I need to tell Dimka that this ship has arrived safely." Moscow had decided the *Aleksandrovsk* was close enough to reach port, but Dimka was anxious for confirmation.

They got into Paz's Buick and drove out of town. On either side of the road were tall thickets of sugarcane. Turkey vultures floated above, hunting the fat rats in the fields. In the distance, the high chimney of a sugar mill pointed like a missile at the sky. The flat landscape of central Cuba was crosshatched with single-track railway lines built to transport cane from the fields to the mills. Where the land was uncultivated it was mostly tropical jungle, flame trees and jacarandas and towering royal palms; or rough scrub grazed by cattle. The slim white egrets that followed the cows were grace notes on the dun landscape.

Transport in rural Cuba was still mostly horse-drawn, but as they approached Havana the roads became crowded with military trucks and buses taking reservists to their bases. Castro had declared a full combat alert. The nation was on a war footing. As Paz's Buick sped by, the men waved and called out: "*Patria o muerte!* Motherland or death! *Cuba sí, yanqui no!*"

On the outskirts of the capital she saw that a new poster had appeared overnight and now blanketed every wall. In simple black and white, it showed a hand clutching a machine gun and the words A LAS ARMAS—"To Arms." Castro really understood propaganda, she reflected, unlike the old men in the Kremlin, whose idea of a slogan was: "Implement the resolutions of the twentieth party congress!"

Tanya had written and encoded her message earlier, and

had only to fill in the exact time that the *Aleksandrovsk* had docked. She took the message into the Soviet embassy and gave it to the KGB communications officer, whom she knew well.

Dimka would be relieved, but Tanya was still fearful. Was it really good news that Cuba had another shipload of nuclear weapons? Might not the Cuban people—and Tanya herself—be safer with none?

"Do you have other duties today?" Tanya asked Paz when she came out.

"My job is liaison with you."

"But in this crisis . . ."

"In this crisis, nothing is more important than clear communication with our Soviet allies."

"Then let's walk along the Malecón together."

They drove to the sea front. Paz parked at the Hotel Nacional. Soldiers were stationing an antiaircraft gun outside the famous hotel.

Tanya and Paz left the car and walked along the promenade. A wind from the north whipped the sea into angry surges that crashed against the stone wall, throwing up explosions of spray that fell on the promenade like rain. This was a popular place to stroll, but today there were more people than usual, and their mood was not leisurely. They clustered in small crowds, sometimes talking but often silent. They were not flirting or telling jokes or showing off their best clothes. Everyone was looking in the same direction, north, toward the United States. They were watching for the *yanquis*.

Tanya and Paz watched with them for a while. She felt in her heart that the invasion had to happen. Destroyers would come slicing through the waves; submarines would surface a few yards away; and the gray planes with the blue-and-white stars would appear out of the clouds, loaded with bombs to drop on the Cuban people and their Soviet friends.

At last Tanya took Paz's hand in her own. He squeezed gently. She looked up into his deep brown eyes. "I think we're going to die," she said calmly.

"Yes," he said.

"Do you want to go to bed with me first?"

"Yes," he said again.

"Shall we go to my apartment?"

"Yes."

They returned to the car and drove to a narrow street in the old town, near the cathedral, where Tanya had upstairs rooms in a colonial building.

Tanya's first and only lover had been Petr Iloyan, a lecturer at her university. He had worshipped her young body, gazing at her breasts and touching her skin and kissing her hair as if he had never come across anything so marvelous. Paz was the same age as Petr but, Tanya quickly realized, making love with him was going to be different. It was *his* body that was the center of attention. He took his clothes off slowly, as if teasing her, then stood naked in front of her, giving her time to take in his perfect skin and the curves of his muscles. Tanya was happy to sit on the edge of the bed and admire him. The display seemed to excite him, for his penis was already fat with arousal and half erect, and Tanya could hardly wait to get her hands on it.

Petr had been a slow, gentle lover. He had been able to work Tanya up into a fever of anticipation, then hold back tantalizingly. He would change positions several times, rolling her on top, then kneeling behind her, then getting her to straddle him. Paz was not rough but he was vigorous, and Tanya gave herself up to excitement and pleasure.

Afterward Tanya made eggs and coffee. Paz turned on the TV and they watched Castro's speech while they ate.

Castro sat in front of a Cuban national flag, its bold blue and white stripes appearing black and white in the monochrome television picture. As always, he wore battle-dress drab, the only sign of rank a single star on the epaulet: Tanya had never seen him in a civilian suit, nor in the kind of pompous medal-encrusted uniform beloved of Communist leaders elsewhere.

Tanya felt a rush of optimism. Castro was no fool. He knew he could not defeat the United States in a war, even with the Soviet Union on his side. Surely he would come up with some dramatic gesture of reconciliation, some initiative that would transform the situation and defuse the time bomb.

His voice was high and reedy, but he spoke with overwhelming passion. The bushy beard gave him the air of a messiah crying in the wilderness, even though he was obviously in a studio. His black eyebrows moved expressively in a high forehead. He gestured with his big hands, sometimes raising a schoolmasterly forefinger to forbid dissent, often clenching a fist. At times he grasped the arms of his chair as if to prevent himself taking off like a rocket. He appeared to have no script, not even any notes. His expression showed indignation, pride, scorn, rage—but never doubt. Castro lived in a universe of certainty.

Point by point, Castro attacked Kennedy's television speech, which had been broadcast on live radio beamed at Cuba. He scorned Kennedy's appeal to the "captive people of Cuba." "We are not sovereign by the grace of the *yanquis,*" he said contemptuously.

But he said nothing about the Soviet Union and nothing about nuclear weapons.

The speech lasted ninety minutes. It was a performance of Churchillian magnetism: brave little Cuba would defy big bullying America and would never give in. It must have boosted the morale of the Cuban people. But otherwise it changed nothing. Tanya was bitterly disappointed and even more scared. Castro had not even tried to prevent war.

At the end he cried: "Motherland or death, we will win!" Then he jumped out of the chair and rushed out as if he had not a minute to lose on his way to save Cuba.

Tanya looked at Paz. His eyes were glistening with tears.

She kissed him, then they made love again, on the couch in front of the flickering screen. This time it was slower and more satisfying. She treated him the way Petr had treated her. It was not difficult to adore his body, and he undoubtedly liked adoration. She squeezed his arms and kissed his nipples and pushed her fingers into his curls. "You're so beautiful," she murmured as she sucked his earlobe.

Afterward, as they lay sharing a cigar, they heard noises from outside. Tanya opened the door leading to the balcony. The city had been quiet while Castro was on television, but now people were coming out onto the narrow streets. Night had fallen, and some were carrying candles and torches. Tanya's journalistic instincts returned. "I have to go out there," she said to Paz. "This is a big story."

"I'll come with you."

They pulled on their clothes and left the building. The streets were wet but the rain had stopped. More and more people appeared. There was a carnival atmosphere. Every-

one was cheering and shouting slogans. Many were singing
the national anthem, "La Bayamesa." There was nothing
Latin about the tune—it sounded more like a German
drinking song—but the singers meant every word.

> *To live in chains is to live*
> *In dishonor and ignominy*
> *Hear the call of the bugle:*
> *Hasten, brave ones, to arms!*

As Tanya and Paz marched through the alleys of the old
city with the crowd, Tanya noticed that many of the men
had armed themselves. Lacking guns, they carried garden
tools and machetes, and had kitchen knives and meat cleav-
ers in their belts, as if they were going to fight the Americans hand-to-hand on the Malecón.

Tanya recalled that one Boeing B-52 Stratofortress of
the United States Air Force carried seventy thousand
pounds of bombs.

You poor fools, she thought bitterly, how much use do
you think your knives will be against that?

CHAPTER SEVENTEEN

George had never felt nearer death than he did in the Cabinet Room of the White House on Wednesday, October 24.

The morning meeting began at ten, and George thought war would break out before eleven.

Technically this was the Executive Committee of the National Security Council, called ExComm for short. In practice President Kennedy summoned anyone he felt could help in the crisis. His brother Bobby was always among them.

The advisers sat on leather chairs around the long table. Their aides sat on similar chairs up against the walls. The tension in the room was suffocating.

The alert status of the Strategic Air Command had moved to DEFCON 2, the level just below imminent war. Every bomber of the air force was ready. Many were continuously in the air, loaded with nukes, patrolling over Canada, Greenland, and Turkey, as close as they could get to the borders of the USSR. Every bomber had a preassigned Soviet target.

If war broke out, the Americans would unleash a nuclear firestorm that would flatten every major town in the Soviet Union. Millions would die. Russia would not recover in a hundred years.

And the Soviets had to have something similar planned for the United States.

Ten o'clock was the moment the blockade went into ef-

fect. Any Soviet vessel within five hundred miles of Cuba
was now fair game. The first interception of a Soviet missile
ship, by the USS *Essex,* was expected between ten thirty
and eleven. By eleven they might all be dead.

CIA chief John McCone began by reviewing all Soviet
shipping en route to Cuba. He spoke in a drone that heightened the tension by making everyone impatient. Which Soviet ships should the navy intercept first? What would
happen then? Would the Soviets allow their ships to be inspected? Would they fire on American ships? What should
the navy do then?

While the group tried to second-guess their opposite
numbers in Moscow, an aide brought McCone a note. Mc-
Cone was a dapper, white-haired man of sixty. He was a
businessman, and George suspected that the CIA career
professionals did not tell him everything they were doing.

Now McCone peered through his rimless glasses at the
note, which seemed to puzzle him. Eventually he said: "Mr.
President, we've just received information from the Office
of Naval Intelligence that all six Soviet ships currently in
Cuban waters have either stopped or reversed course."

George thought: What the hell does that mean?

Dean Rusk, the bald, pug-nosed secretary of state, asked:
"What do you mean, Cuban waters?"

McCone did not know.

Bob McNamara, the Ford president whom Kennedy had
made secretary of defense, said: "Most of these ships are
outbound, from Cuba to the Soviet Union—"

"Why don't we find out?" the president interrupted tetchily.
"Are we talking about ships leaving Cuba or ships coming
in?"

McCone said: "I'll find out," and he left the room.

The tension rose another notch.

George had always imagined that crisis meetings in the
White House would be supernaturally high-powered, with
everyone supplying the president with accurate information so that he could make a wise judgment. But this was
the greatest crisis ever, and all was confusion and misunderstanding. That made George even more afraid.

When McCone came back in he said: "These ships are all
westbound, all inbound for Cuba." He listed the six vessels
by name.

McNamara spoke next. He was forty-six, and the phrase *whiz kid* had been invented for him when he turned the Ford Motor Company from loss to profit. President Kennedy trusted him more than anyone else in the room except Bobby. Now from memory McNamara reeled off the positions of all six ships. Most were still hundreds of miles from Cuba.

The president was impatient. "Now, what do they say they're doing with those, John?"

McCone replied: "They either stopped or reversed direction."

"Is this *all* the Soviet ships, or just selected ones?"

"This is a selected bunch. There are twenty-four altogether."

Once again McNamara interrupted with the key information. "It looks as though these are the ships closest to the quarantine barrier."

George whispered to Skip Dickerson, sitting next to him: "The Soviets seem to be pulling back from the brink."

"I sure hope you're right," Skip murmured.

The president said: "We're not planning to grab any of those, are we?"

McNamara said: "We're not planning to grab any ship that is not proceeding to Cuba."

General Maxwell Taylor, the chairman of the Joint Chiefs, picked up a phone and said: "Get me George Anderson." Admiral Anderson was the chief of naval operations and was in charge of the blockade. After a few seconds Taylor began speaking quietly.

There was a pause. Everyone was trying to absorb the news and figure out what it meant. Were the Soviets giving in?

The president said: "We ought to check first. How do we find out if six ships are simultaneously turning? General, what does the navy say about this report?"

General Taylor looked up and said: "Three ships are definitely turning back."

"Be in touch with the *Essex* and tell them to wait an hour. We have to move quickly because they're going to intercept between ten thirty and eleven."

Every man in the room looked at his watch.

It was ten thirty-two.

George got a glimpse of Bobby's face. He looked like a man reprieved from a death sentence.

The immediate crisis was over, but George realized over the next few minutes that nothing had been resolved. While the Soviets were clearly moving to avoid confrontation at sea, their nuclear missiles were still in Cuba. The clock had been turned back an hour, but it was still ticking.

ExComm discussed Germany. The president feared Khrushchev might announce a blockade of West Berlin to parallel the American blockade of Cuba. There was nothing they could do about that, either.

The meeting broke up. George was not needed at Bobby's next appointment. He left with Skip Dickerson, who said: "How's your friend Maria?"

"Fine, I think."

"I was in the press office yesterday. She called in sick."

George's heart missed a beat. He had given up all hope of a romance with Maria, but all the same the news that she was ill made him feel panicky. He frowned. "I didn't know that."

"None of my business, George, but she's a nice gal, and I thought maybe someone should check up on her."

George squeezed Skip's arm. "Thanks for letting me know," he said. "You're a pal."

White House staffers did not call in sick in the middle of the greatest crisis of the Cold War, George reflected, not unless they were seriously ill. His anxiety deepened.

He hurried to the press office. Maria's chair was empty. Nelly Fordham, the friendly woman at the next desk, said: "Maria's not well."

"I heard. Did she say what the trouble was?"

"No."

George frowned. "I wonder if I could get away for an hour and go see her."

"I wish you would," Nelly said. "I'm worried too."

George looked at his watch. He was pretty sure Bobby would not need him until after lunch. "I guess I could manage it. She lives in Georgetown, doesn't she?"

"Yes, but she moved from her old place."

"Why?"

"Said her flatmates were too nosy."

That made sense to George. Other girls would be desperate to learn the identity of a clandestine lover. Maria was so determined to keep the secret that she had moved out. That indicated how serious she was about the guy.

Nelly was flicking through her Rolodex. "I'll write down the address for you."

"Thanks."

She handed him a piece of paper and said: "You're Georgy Jakes, aren't you?"

"Yes." He smiled. "It's a long time since anyone called me Georgy, though."

"I used to know Senator Peshkov."

The fact that she mentioned Greg meant, almost certainly, that she knew he was George's father. "Really?" George said. "How did you know him?"

"We dated, if you want to know the truth. But nothing came of it. How is he?"

"Pretty well. I have lunch with him about once a month."

"I guess he never married."

"Not yet."

"And he must be past forty."

"I believe there is a lady in his life."

"Oh, don't worry. I'm not after him. I made that decision a long time ago. All the same, I wish him well."

"I'll tell him that. Now I'm going to jump in a cab and go check on Maria."

"Thank you, Georgy—or George, I should say."

George hurried out. Nelly was an attractive woman with a kind heart. Why had Greg not married her? Perhaps it suited him to be a bachelor.

George's taxi driver said: "You work in the White House?"

"I work for Bobby Kennedy. I'm a lawyer."

"No kidding!" The driver did not trouble to hide his surprise that a Negro should be a lawyer with a high-powered job. "You tell Bobby we ought to bomb Cuba to dust. That's what we ought to do. Bomb them to goddamn dust."

"Do you know how big Cuba is, end to end?" George said.

"What is this, a quiz show?" the driver said resentfully.

George shrugged and said no more. Nowadays he avoided political discussions with outsiders. They usually had easy answers: send all the Mexicans home, put Hells Angels in the army, castrate the queers. The greater their ignorance, the stronger their opinions.

Georgetown was only a few minutes away, but the journey seemed long. George imagined Maria collapsed on the floor, or lying in bed on the edge of death, or in a coma.

The address Nelly had given George turned out to be a gracious old house divided into studio apartments. Maria did not answer her downstairs doorbell, but a black girl who looked like a student let George in and pointed out Maria's room.

Maria came to the door in a bathrobe. She certainly looked sick. Her face was bloodless and her expression dejected. She did not say *Come in,* but she walked away, leaving the door open, and he entered. At least she was ambulatory, he thought with relief: he had feared worse.

It was a tiny place, one room with a kitchenette. He guessed she shared the bathroom down the hall.

He looked hard at her. It pained him to see her this way, not just sick, but miserable. He longed to take her in his arms, but he knew that would be unwelcome. "Maria, what's the matter?" he said. "You look terrible!"

"Just feminine problems, that's all."

That phrase was normally code for a menstrual period, but he was pretty sure this was something else.

"Let me make you a cup of coffee—or maybe tea?" He took off his coat.

"No, thanks," she said.

He decided to make it anyway, just to show her that he cared. But then he glanced at the chair she was about to sit on, and saw that the seat was stained with blood.

She noticed it at the same time, blushed, and said: "Oh, hell."

George knew a little about women's bodies. Several possibilities passed through his mind. He said: "Maria, have you suffered a miscarriage?"

"No," she said tonelessly. She hesitated.

George waited patiently.

At last Maria said: "An abortion."

"You poor thing." He grabbed a towel from the kitchenette, folded it, and placed it on the bloodstain. "Sit on this, for now," he said. "Rest." He looked at the shelf over the refrigerator and saw a packet of jasmine tea. Figuring that must be what she liked, he put water on to heat. He said no more until he had made the tea.

Abortion law varied from state to state. George knew that in DC it was legal for the purpose of protecting the health of the mother. Many doctors interpreted this liberally, to include the woman's health and general well-being. In practice, anyone who had the money could find a doctor willing to perform an abortion.

Although she had said she did not want tea, she took a cup.

He sat opposite her with a cup for himself. "Your secret lover," he said. "I guess he's the father."

She nodded. "Thank you for the tea. I presume World War Three hasn't started yet, otherwise you wouldn't be here."

"The Soviets turned their ships back, so the danger of a showdown at sea has receded. But the Cubans still have nukes, aimed at us."

Maria seemed too depressed to care.

George said: "He wouldn't marry you."

"No."

"Because he's already married?"

She did not answer.

"So he found you a doctor and paid the bill."

She nodded.

George thought that was a despicable way to behave, but if he said so she would probably throw him out for insulting the man she loved. Trying to control his anger, George said: "Where is he now?"

"He'll call." She glanced at the clock. "Soon, probably."

George decided not to ask any more questions. It would be unkind to interrogate her. And she did not need to be told how foolish she had been. What *did* she need? He decided to ask. "Is there anything you need? Anything I can do for you?"

She started to cry. Between sobs she said: "I hardly know you! How come you're my only real friend in the whole city?"

He knew the answer to that question. She had a secret that she would not share. That made it difficult for others to be close to her.

She said: "Lucky for me you're so kind."

Her gratitude embarrassed him. "Does it hurt?" he said.

"Yes, it hurts like hell."

"Should I call a doctor?"

"It's not that bad. They told me to expect this."

"Do you have any aspirin?"

"No."

"Why don't I step out and get you some?"

"Would you? I hate to ask a man to run errands."

"It's okay, this is an emergency."

"There's a drugstore right on the corner of the block."

George put down his cup and shrugged on his coat.

Maria said: "Could I ask you an even bigger favor?"

"Sure."

"I need sanitary napkins. Do you think you could buy a box?"

He hesitated. A man, buying sanitary napkins?

She said: "No, it's too much to ask, forget it."

"Hell, what are they going to do, arrest me?"

"The brand name is Kotex."

George nodded. "I'll be right back."

His bravado did not last long. When he reached the drugstore he felt stricken with embarrassment. He told himself to shape up. So, it was uncomfortable. Men his age were risking their lives in the jungles of Vietnam. How bad could this be?

The store had three self-service aisles and a counter. Aspirins were not displayed on the open shelves, but sold from the counter.

To George's dismay, feminine sanitary products were the same.

He picked up a cardboard container with six bottles of Coke. She was bleeding, so she needed fluids. But he could not postpone the moment of mortification for long.

He went up to the counter.

The pharmacist was a middle-aged white woman. Just my luck, he thought.

He put the Cokes on the counter and said: "I need some aspirin, please."

"What size? We have small, medium, and large bottles."

George was thrown. What if she asked him what size sanitary towels he wanted? "Uh, large, I guess," he said.

The pharmacist put a large bottle of aspirin on the counter. "Anything else?"

A young woman shopper came and stood behind him, holding a wire basket containing cosmetics. She was obviously going to hear everything.

"Anything else?" the pharmacist repeated.

Come on, George, be a man, he thought. "I need a box of sanitary napkins," he said. "Kotex."

The young woman behind him stifled a giggle.

The pharmacist looked at him over her spectacles. "Young man, are you doing this for a bet?"

"No, ma'am!" he said indignantly. "They are for a lady who is too sick to come to the store."

She looked him up and down, taking in the dark gray suit, the white shirt, the plain tie, and the folded white handkerchief in the breast pocket of the jacket. He was glad he did not look like a student involved in a jape. "All right, I believe you," she said. She reached below the counter and picked up a box.

George stared at it in horror. The word *Kotex* was printed on the side in large letters. Was he going to have to carry that out in the street?

The pharmacist read his mind. "I guess you'd like me to wrap this for you."

"Yes, please."

With quick, practiced movements she wrapped the box in brown paper, then she put it in a bag with the aspirin.

George paid.

The pharmacist gave him a hard look, then seemed to relent. "I'm sorry I doubted you," she said. "You must be a good friend to some girl."

"Thank you," he said, and he hurried out.

Despite the October cold, he was perspiring.

He returned to Maria's place. She took three aspirins, then went along the corridor to the bathroom, clutching the wrapped box.

George put the Cokes in the refrigerator, then looked around. He saw a shelf of law books over a small desk with framed photographs. A family group showed her parents, he presumed, and an elderly clergyman who must have been her distinguished grandfather. Another showed Maria in graduation robes. There was also a picture of President

Kennedy. She had a television set, a radio, and a record player. He looked through her discs. She liked the latest pop music, he saw: the Crystals; Little Eva; Booker T and the MGs. On the table beside her bed was the novel *Ship of Fools*.

While she was out, the phone rang.

George picked it up. "This is Maria's phone."

A man's voice said: "May I speak with Maria, please?"

The voice was vaguely familiar, but George could not place it. "She stepped out," he said. "Who is—wait a minute, she just walked in."

Maria snatched the phone from him. "Hello? Oh, hi . . . He's a friend, he brought me some aspirins . . . Oh, not too bad, I'll get by . . ."

George said: "I'll step outside, give you some privacy."

He strongly disapproved of Maria's lover. Even if the jerk was married he should have been here. He had made her pregnant, so he should have taken care of her after the abortion.

That voice . . . George had heard it before. Had he actually met Maria's lover? It would not be surprising, if the man was a work colleague, as George's mother surmised. But the voice on the phone was not Pierre Salinger's.

The girl who had let him in now walked by, on her way out again. She grinned at him standing outside the door like a naughty boy. "Have you been misbehaving in class?" she said.

"No such luck," said George.

She laughed and walked on.

Maria opened the door and he went back inside. "I really have to get back to work," he said.

"I know. You came to visit me in the middle of the Cuba crisis. I'll never forget that." She was visibly happier now that she had talked to her man.

Suddenly George had a flash of realization. "That voice!" he said. "On the phone."

"You recognized it?"

He was astonished. "Are you having an affair with Dave Powers?"

To George's consternation, Maria laughed out loud. "Please!" she said.

He saw right away how unlikely it was. Dave, the president's personal assistant, was a homely-looking man of about fifty who still wore a hat. He was not likely to win the heart of a beautiful and lively young woman.

A moment later, George realized who Maria *was* having an affair with.

"Oh, my God," he said, staring. He was astonished at what he had just figured out.

Maria said nothing.

"You're sleeping with President Kennedy," George said in amazement.

"Please don't tell!" she begged. "If you do, he'll leave me. Promise, please!"

"I promise," said George.

. . .

For the first time in his adult life, Dimka had done something truly, indisputably, shamefully wrong.

He was not married to Nina, but she expected him to be faithful, and he assumed she was faithful to him; so there was no question that he had betrayed her trust by spending the night with Natalya.

He had thought it might be the last night of his life but, since it had not been, the excuse seemed feeble.

He had not had sexual intercourse with Natalya, but that, too, was a lousy excuse. What they had done was, if anything, even more intimate and loving than regular sex. He felt wretchedly guilty. Never before had he seen himself as untrustworthy, dishonest, and unreliable.

His friend Valentin would probably handle this situation by cheerfully carrying on affairs with both women until he was found out. Dimka did not even consider that option. He felt bad enough after one night of deception: he could not possibly do it on a regular basis. He would end up throwing himself in the Moskva River.

He had to either tell Nina, or break up with her, or both. He could not live with such a mammoth deception. But he found that he was scared. This was ludicrous. He was Dmitri Ilich Dvorkin, hatchet man to Khrushchev, hated by some, feared by many. How could he be afraid of a girl? But he was.

And what about Natalya?

He had a hundred questions for Natalya. He wanted to

know how she felt about her husband. Dimka knew nothing about him except his name, Nik. Was she getting divorced? If so, did the breakdown of the marriage have anything to do with Dimka? Most importantly, did Natalya see Dimka playing any role in her future?

He kept seeing her around the Kremlin, but there was no chance for them to be alone. The Presidium met three times on Tuesday—morning, afternoon, and evening—and the aides were even busier during the meal breaks. Each time Dimka looked at Natalya she seemed more wonderful. He was still wearing the suit he had slept in, as were all the men, but Natalya had changed into a dark blue dress with a matching jacket that made her look both authoritative and alluring at the same time. Dimka had trouble concentrating on the meetings, even though their task was to prevent World War III. He would gaze at her, remember what they had done to one another, and look away in embarrassment; then, a minute later, he would stare at her again.

But the pace of work was so intense that he was not able to talk privately to her even for a few seconds.

Khrushchev went home to his own bed late on Tuesday night, so everyone else did the same. First thing on Wednesday, Dimka gave Khrushchev the glad news—hot from his sister in Cuba—that the *Aleksandrovsk* had docked safely at La Isabela. The rest of the day was equally busy. He saw Natalya constantly, but neither of them had a minute to spare.

By this time Dimka was asking himself questions. What did *he* think Monday night meant? What did he want in the future? If any of them were alive in a week's time, did he want to spend the rest of his life with Natalya, or Nina—or neither?

By Thursday he was desperate for some answers. He felt, irrationally, that he did not want to be killed in a nuclear war before he had resolved this.

He had a date with Nina that evening: they were to go to a movie with Valentin and Anna. If he could get away from the Kremlin, and keep the date, what would he say to Nina?

The morning Presidium normally began at ten, so the aides got together informally at eight in the Onilova Room. On Thursday morning Dimka had a new proposal from Khrushchev to put to the others. He was also hoping for a private talk with Natalya. He was about to approach her when Yevgeny Filipov appeared with the early editions of the European newspapers. "The front pages are all equally bad," he said. He was pretending to be distraught with grief, but Dimka knew he was feeling the opposite. "The turning back of our ships is portrayed as a humiliating climb-down by the Soviet Union!"

He was hardly exaggerating, Dimka saw, looking at the papers spread on the cheap modern tables.

Natalya sprang to Khrushchev's defense. "Of course they say that," she countered. "All those newspapers are owned by capitalists. Did you expect them to praise our leader's wisdom and restraint? How naïve are you?"

"How naïve are *you*? The London *Times,* the Italian *Corriere della Sera,* and *Le Monde* of Paris—these are the papers read and believed by the leaders of the Third World countries whom we hope to win to our side."

That was true. Unfair though it was, people around the world trusted the capitalist press more than Communist publications.

Natalya replied: "We cannot decide our foreign policy based on the probable reactions of Western newspapers."

"This operation was supposed to be top secret," Filipov said. "Yet the Americans found out about it. We all know who was responsible for security." He meant Dimka. "Why is that person sitting at this table? Should he not be under interrogation?"

Dimka said: "Army security may be to blame." Filipov worked for the defense minister. "When we know how the secret got out, then we will be able to decide who should be interrogated." It was feeble, he knew, but he still had no idea what had gone wrong.

Filipov changed his tack. "At this morning's Presidium, the KGB will report that the Americans have massively stepped up their mobilization in Florida. The railroad tracks are jammed with railcars carrying tanks and artillery. The racetrack in Hallandale has been taken over by the 1st Armored Division, thousands of men sleeping in the grandstands. Ammunition factories are working twenty-four hours a day producing bullets for their planes to strafe Soviet and Cuban troops. Napalm bombs— "

Natalya interrupted him. "This, too, was expected."

"But what will we do when they invade Cuba?" Filipov
said. "If we respond using only conventional weapons, we
cannot win: the Americans are too strong. Will we respond
with nuclear weapons? President Kennedy has stated that
if one nuclear weapon is launched from Cuba he will bomb
the Soviet Union."

"He cannot mean it," said Natalya.

"Read the reports from Red Army Intelligence. The
American bombers are circling us now!" He pointed at the
ceiling, as if they might look up and see the planes. "There
are only two possible outcomes for us: international humiliation, if we're lucky, and nuclear death if we're not."

Natalya fell silent. No one around the table had an answer to that.

Except Dimka.

"Comrade Khrushchev has a solution," he said.

They all looked at him in surprise.

He went on: "At this morning's meeting, the first secre-
tary will propose making an offer to the United States."
There was dead silence. "We will dismantle our missiles in
Cuba—"

He was interrupted by a chorus of reaction around the
table, from gasps of surprise to cries of protest. He held up
a hand for quiet.

"We will dismantle our missiles *in exchange* for a guarantee of what we have wanted all along. The Americans
must promise not to invade Cuba."

They took a few moments to digest this.

Natalya was the quickest to get it. "This is brilliant," she
said. "How can Kennedy refuse? He would be admitting his
intention to invade a poor Third World country. He would
be universally condemned for colonialism. And he would
be proving our point that Cuba needs nuclear missiles to
defend itself." She was the smartest person at the table, as
well as the prettiest.

Filipov said: "But if Kennedy accepts, we have to bring
the missiles home."

"They will no longer be necessary!" Natalya said. "The
Cuban revolution will be safe."

Dimka could see that Filipov wanted to argue against
this but could not. Khrushchev had got the Soviet Union
into a fix, but he had devised an honorable way out.

When the meeting broke up, Dimka at last managed to grab Natalya. "We need a minute to discuss the wording of Khrushchev's offer to Kennedy," he said.

They retreated to a corner of the room and sat down. He gazed at the front of her dress, remembering her little breasts with their pointed nipples.

She said: "You have to stop staring at me."

He felt foolish. "I wasn't staring at you," he said, though it was obviously not true.

She ignored that. "If you keep it up even the men will notice."

"I'm sorry, I can't help it." Dimka was downcast. This was not the intimate, happy conversation he had foreseen.

"No one must know what we did." She looked scared.

Dimka felt as if he were talking to a different person from the cheerfully sexy girl who had seduced him only the day before yesterday. He said: "Well, I'm not planning to go around telling people, but I didn't know it was a state secret."

"I'm married!"

"Are you planning to stay with Nik?"

"What kind of question is that?"

"Do you have any children?"

"No."

"People get divorced."

"My husband would never agree to a divorce."

Dimka stared at her. Obviously that was not the end of the matter: a woman might get a divorce against her husband's will. But this discussion was not really about the legal situation. Natalya was in some kind of panic. Dimka said: "Why did you do it, anyway?"

"I thought we were all going to die!"

"And now you regret it?"

"I'm married!" she said again.

That did not answer his question, but he guessed he was not going to get any more from her.

Boris Kozlov, another of Khrushchev's aides, called across the canteen: "Dimka! Come on!"

Dimka stood up. "Can we talk again soon?" he murmured.

Natalya looked down and said nothing.

Boris said: "Dimka, let's go!"

He left.

The Presidium discussed Khrushchev's proposal for most of the day. There were complications. Would the Americans insist on inspecting the launch sites to verify that they had been deactivated? Would Castro accept inspection? Would Castro promise not to accept nuclear weapons from any other source, for example China? Still Dimka thought it represented the best yet hope of peace.

Meanwhile, Dimka thought about Nina and Natalya. Before this morning's conversation, he had thought it was up to him which of the two women he wanted. He now realized he had deluded himself into thinking the choice was his to make.

Natalya was not going to leave her husband.

He realized he was crazy for Natalya in a way he had never been for Nina. Every time there was a tap on his office door he hoped it was Natalya. In his memory he replayed their time together over and over, obsessively hearing again everything she said, up to the unforgettable words: "Oh, Dimka, I adore you."

It was not *I love you* but it was close.

But she would not get a divorce.

All the same, Natalya was the one he wanted.

That meant he had to tell Nina their affair was over. He could not carry on an affair with a girl he liked second best: it would be dishonest. In his imagination he could hear Valentin mocking his scruples, but he could not help them.

But Natalya intended to stay with her husband. So Dimka would have no one.

He would tell Nina tonight. The four were due to meet at the girls' apartment. He would take Nina aside and tell her . . . what? It seemed more difficult when he tried to think of the actual words. Come on, he told himself; you've written speeches for Khrushchev, you can write one for yourself.

Our affair is over . . . I don't want to see you anymore . . . I thought I was in love with you, but I've realized I'm not . . . It was fun while it lasted . . .

Everything he thought of sounded cruel. Was there no kind way to say this? Perhaps not. What about the naked truth? I've met someone else, and I really love her . . .

That sounded worst of all.

At the end of the afternoon, Khrushchev decided the Presidium should put on a public display of international goodwill by going en masse to the Bolshoi Theater, where the American Jerome Hines was singing *Boris Godunov,* the most popular of Russian operas. Aides were invited too. Dimka thought it was a stupid idea. Who was going to be fooled? On the other hand, he found himself relieved to have to call off his date with Nina, which he was now dreading.

He phoned her place of work and caught her just before she left. "I can't make it tonight," he said. "I've got to go to the Bolshoi with the boss."

"Can't you get out of it?" she said.

"Are you joking?" A man who worked for the first secretary would miss his mother's funeral rather than disobey.

"I want to see you."

"It's out of the question."

"Come after the opera."

"It will be late."

"No matter how late it is, come to my place. I'll be up, if I have to wait all night."

He was puzzled. She was not normally so insistent. She almost sounded needy, and that was not like her. "Is anything wrong?"

"There's something we have to discuss."

"What?"

"I'll tell you tonight."

"Tell me now."

Nina hung up.

Dimka put on his overcoat and walked to the theater, which was only a few steps from the Kremlin.

Jerome Hines was six foot six, and wore a crown with a cross on top: his presence was immense. His astonishingly powerful bass filled the theater and made its echoing spaces seem small. Yet Dimka sat through Mussorgsky's opera without hearing much. He ignored the spectacle onstage. He spent the evening worrying alternately about how the Americans would respond to Khrushchev's peace proposal and how Nina would respond to his ending their affair.

When at last Khrushchev said good night, Dimka walked to the girls' apartment, which was a mile or so from the theater. On the way he tried to guess what Nina wanted to talk about. Perhaps she was going to end their relationship: that would be a relief. She might have been offered a promotion that required her to move to Leningrad. She might even have met someone else, as he had, and decided the new man was Mr. Right. Or she could be ill: a fatal disease, perhaps connected with the mysterious reasons why she could not get pregnant. All these possibilities offered Dimka an easy way out, and he realized he would be gladdened by any one, perhaps even—to his shame—the fatal illness.

No, he thought, I don't really wish her dead.

As promised, Nina was waiting for him.

She was wearing a green silk robe, as if about to go to bed, but her hair was perfect and she wore a little light makeup. She kissed him on the lips, and he kissed her back with shame in his heart. He was betraying Natalya by relishing the kiss, and betraying Nina by thinking of Natalya. The double guilt gave him a pain in his stomach.

Nina poured a glass of beer and he drank half of it quickly, eager for some Dutch courage.

She sat beside him on the couch. He was pretty sure she had nothing on under the robe. Desire stirred in him, and the picture of Natalya in his mind began to fade a little.

"We're not at war yet," he said. "That's my news. What's yours?"

Nina took the beer from him and set it on the coffee table, then she held his hand. "I'm pregnant," she said.

Dimka felt as if he had been punched. He stared at her in uncomprehending shock. "Pregnant," he said stupidly.

"Two months and a bit."

"Are you sure?"

"I've missed two consecutive periods."

"Even so . . ."

"Look." She opened her robe to show him her breasts. "They're bigger."

They were, he saw, feeling a mixture of desire and dismay.

"And they hurt." She closed the robe, but not very tight. "And smoking makes me sick to my stomach. Damn it, I *feel* pregnant."

This could not be true. "But you said . . ."

"That I couldn't have children." She looked away. "That's what my doctor told me."

"Have you seen him?"

"Yes. It's confirmed."

Incredulously, Dimka said: "What does he say now?"

"That it's a miracle."

"Doctors don't believe in miracles."

"That's what I thought."

Dimka tried to stop the room spinning around him. He swallowed hard and struggled to get over the shock. He had to be practical. "You don't want to get married, and I sure as hell don't," he said. "What are you going to do about it?"

"You have to give me the money for an abortion."

Dimka swallowed. "All right." Abortions were readily available in Moscow, but they were not free. Dimka considered how he would get the money. He had been planning to trade in his motorcycle and buy a used car. If he postponed that he could probably manage it. He might borrow from his grandparents. "I can do that," he said.

She immediately relented. "We should pay half each. We made this baby together."

Suddenly Dimka felt different. It was her use of the word *baby*. He found himself conflicted. He pictured himself holding a baby, watching a child take its first steps, teaching it to read, taking it to school. He said: "Are you sure an abortion is what you want?"

"How do *you* feel?"

"Uncomfortable." He asked himself why he felt this way. "I don't think it's a sin, or anything like that. I just started imagining, you know, a little baby." He was not sure where these feelings had come from. "Could we have the child adopted?"

"Give birth, and then hand the baby over to strangers?"

"I know, I don't like it either. But it's hard, to raise a child on your own. I'd help you, though."

"Why?"

"It will be my child, too."

She took his hand. "Thank you for saying that." She looked very vulnerable suddenly, and his heart lurched. She said: "We love each other, don't we?"

"Yes." At that moment he did. He thought of Natalya, but somehow his picture of her was vague and distant, whereas Nina was here—in the flesh, he thought, and that phrase seemed more vivid than usual.

"We'll both love the child, won't we?"

"Yes."

"Well, then . . ."

"But you don't want to get married."

"I didn't."

"Past tense."

"I felt that way when I wasn't pregnant."

"Have you changed your mind?"

"Everything feels different now."

Dimka was bewildered. Were they talking about getting married? Desperate for something to say, he tried a joke. "If you're proposing to me, where's the bread and salt?" The traditional betrothal ceremony required the exchange of gifts of bread and salt.

To his astonishment, she burst into tears.

His heart melted. He put his arms around her. At first she resisted, but after a moment she allowed herself to be hugged. Her tears wet his shirt. He stroked her hair.

She lifted her head to be kissed. After a minute she broke away. "Will you make love to me, before I get too fat and hideous?" Her robe gaped, and he could see one soft breast, charmingly freckled.

"Yes," he said recklessly, pushing the picture of Natalya even farther back in his mind.

Nina kissed him again. He grasped her breast: it felt even heavier than before.

She pulled away again. "You didn't mean what you said at the start, did you?"

"What did I say?"

"That you sure as hell didn't want to get married."

He smiled, still holding her breast. "No," he said. "I didn't mean it."

· · ·

On Thursday afternoon George Jakes felt a faint optimism.

The pot was boiling, but the lid was still on. The quarantine was in force, the Soviet missile ships had turned back, and there had been no showdown on the high seas. The United States had not invaded Cuba and no one had fired any nuclear weapons. Perhaps World War III could be averted after all.

The feeling lasted just a little longer.

Bobby Kennedy's aides had a television set in their office at the Justice Department, and at five o'clock they watched a broadcast from United Nations headquarters in New York. The Security Council was in session, twenty chairs around a horseshoe table. Inside the horseshoe sat interpreters wearing headphones. The rest of the room was crowded with aides and other observers, watching the head-to-head confrontation between the two superpowers.

The American ambassador to the UN was Adlai Stevenson, a bald intellectual who had sought the Democratic presidential nomination in 1960 and been defeated by the more telegenic Jack Kennedy.

The Soviet representative, the colorless Valerian Zorin, was speaking in his usual drone, denying that there were any nuclear weapons in Cuba.

Watching on television in Washington, George said in exasperation: "He's a goddamn liar! Stevenson should just produce the photographs."

"That's what the president told him to do."

"Then why doesn't he?"

Wilson shrugged. "Men like Stevenson always think they know best."

On-screen, Stevenson stood up. "Let me ask one simple question," he said. "Do you, Ambassador Zorin, deny that the USSR has placed and is placing medium- and intermediate-range missiles and sites in Cuba? Yes or no?"

George said: "Attaboy, Adlai," and there was a murmur of agreement from the men watching TV with him.

In New York, Stevenson looked at Zorin, who was sitting just a few seats away from him around the horseshoe. Zorin continued to write notes on his pad.

Impatiently, Stevenson said: "Don't wait for the translation—yes or no?"

The aides in Washington laughed.

Eventually Zorin replied in Russian, and the interpreter translated: "Mr. Stevenson, continue your statement, please, you will receive the answer in due course, do not worry."

"I am prepared to wait for my answer until hell freezes over," said Stevenson.

Bobby Kennedy's aides cheered. At last, America was giving them what for!

Then Stevenson said: "And I'm also prepared to present the evidence in this room."

George said: "Yes!" and punched the air.

"If you will indulge me for a moment," Stevenson went on, "we will set up an easel here at the back of the room where I hope it will be visible to everyone."

The camera moved in to focus on half a dozen men in suits who were swiftly mounting a display of large blow-up photographs.

"Now we've got the bastards!" said George.

Stevenson's voice continued, measured and dry, but somehow infused with aggression. "The first of these exhibits shows an area north of the village of Candelaria, near San Cristobal, southwest of Havana. The first photograph shows the area in late August 1962; it was then only peaceful countryside."

Delegates and others were crowding around the easels, trying to see what Stevenson was referring to.

"The second photograph shows the same area one day last week. A few tents and vehicles had come into the area, new spur roads had appeared, and the main road had been improved."

Stevenson paused, and the room was quiet. "The third photograph, taken only twenty-four hours later, shows facilities for a medium-range missile battalion," he said.

Exclamations from the delegates combined into a hum of surprise.

Stevenson went on. More photographs were put up. Until this moment some national leaders had believed the Soviet ambassador's denial. Now everyone knew the truth.

Zorin sat stone-faced, saying nothing.

George glanced up from the TV to see Larry Mawhinney enter the room. George looked askance at him: the one time they had talked, Larry had got angry with him. But now he seemed friendly. "Hi, George," he said, as if they had never exchanged harsh words.

George said neutrally: "What's the news from the Pentagon?"

"I came to warn you that we're going to board a Soviet ship," Larry said. "The president made the decision a few minutes ago."

George's heartbeat quickened. "Shit," he said. "Just when I thought things might be calming down."

Mawhinney went on: "Apparently he thinks the quarantine means nothing if we don't intercept and inspect at least one suspicious vessel. He's already getting flak because we let an oil tanker through."

"What kind of ship are we going to arrest?"

"The *Marucla*, a Lebanese freighter with a Greek crew, under charter to the Soviet government. She left from Riga, ostensibly carrying paper, sulfur, and spare parts for Soviet trucks."

"I can't imagine the Soviets entrusting their missiles to a Greek crew."

"If you're right, there'll be no trouble."

George looked at his watch. "When will it happen?"

"It's dark in the Atlantic now. They'll have to wait until morning."

Larry left, and George wondered how dangerous this was. It was hard to know. If the *Marucla* were as innocent as she pretended to be, perhaps the interception would go off without violence. But if she were carrying nuclear weapons, what would happen? President Kennedy had made another knife-edge decision.

And he had seduced Maria Summers.

George was not very surprised that Kennedy was having an affair with a black girl. If half the gossip were true, the president was not in any way picky about his women. Quite the contrary: he liked mature women and teenagers, blondes and brunettes, socialites who were his equal and empty-headed typists.

George wondered for a moment whether Maria had any idea that she was one among so many.

President Kennedy had no strong feelings about race, always considering it as a purely political issue. Although he had not wanted to be photographed with Percy Marquand and Babe Lee, fearing it would lose him votes, George had seen him cheerfully shaking hands with black men and women, chatting and laughing, relaxed and comfortable. George had also been told that Kennedy attended parties where there were prostitutes of all colors, though he did not know whether those rumors were true.

But the president's callousness had shocked George. It

was not the procedure she had undergone—though that was unpleasant enough—but the fact that she had been alone. The man who made her pregnant should have picked her up after the operation and driven her home and stayed with her until he was sure she was okay. A phone call was not enough. His being president was not a sufficient excuse. Jack Kennedy had fallen a long way in George's estimation.

Just as he was thinking about men who irresponsibly get girls pregnant, his own father walked in.

George was startled. Greg had never before visited this office.

"Hello, George," he said, and they shook hands just as if they were not father and son. Greg was wearing a rumpled suit made of a soft blue pinstripe fabric that looked as if it had some cashmere in the mix. If I could afford a suit like that, George thought, I'd keep it pressed. He often thought that when he looked at Greg.

George said: "This is unexpected. How are you?"

"I was just passing your door. Do you want to get a cup of coffee?"

They went to the cafeteria. Greg ordered tea and George got a bottle of Coke and a straw. As they sat down, George said: "Someone was asking after you the other day. A lady in the press office."

"What's her name?"

"Nell something. I'm trying to remember. Nelly Ford?"

"Nelly Fordham." Greg looked into the distance, his expression showing nostalgia for half-forgotten delights.

George was amused. "A girlfriend, evidently."

"More than that. We were engaged."

"But you didn't get married."

"She broke it off."

George hesitated. "This may be none of my business . . . but why?"

"Well . . . if you want to know the truth, she found out about you, and she said she didn't want to marry a man who already had a family."

George was fascinated. His father rarely opened up about those days.

Greg looked thoughtful. "Nelly was probably right," he said. "You and your mother were my family. But I couldn't marry your mom—couldn't have a career in politics and a black wife. So I chose the career. I can't say it's made me happy."

"You've never talked to me about this."

"I know. It's taken the threat of World War Three to make me tell you the truth. How do you think things are going, anyway?"

"Wait a minute. Was it ever really in the cards that you might marry Mom?"

"When I was fifteen I wanted to, more than anything else in the world. But my father made damn sure it didn't happen. I had another chance, a decade later, but at that point I was old enough to see what a crazy idea it was. Listen, mixed-race couples have a hard enough time of it now, in the sixties. Imagine what it would have been like in the forties. All three of us would probably have been miserable." He looked sad. "Besides, I didn't have the guts—and *that's* the truth. Now tell me about the crisis."

With an effort, George turned his mind to the Cuban missiles. "An hour ago I was beginning to believe we might get through this—but now the president has ordered the navy to intercept a Soviet ship tomorrow morning." He told Greg about the *Marucla.*

Greg said: "If she's genuine, there should be no problem."

"Correct. Our people will go aboard and look at the cargo, then give out some candy bars and leave."

"Candy?"

"Each interception vessel has been allocated two hundred dollars for 'people-to-people materials'—that means candy, magazines, and cheap cigarette lighters."

"God bless America. But . . ."

"But if the crew is Soviet military and the cargo is nuclear warheads, the ship probably won't stop when requested. Then the shooting starts."

"I better let you get back to saving the world."

They got up and left the cafeteria. In the hall they shook hands again. Greg said: "The reason I came by . . ."

George waited.

"We may all die this weekend, and before we do there's something I want you to know."

"Okay." George wondered what the hell was coming.

"You are the best thing that ever happened to me."

"Wow," George said quietly.

"I haven't been much of a father, and I wasn't kind to your mother, and . . . you know all that. But I'm proud of you, George. I don't deserve any credit, I know, but, my God, I'm proud." He had tears in his eyes.

George had had no idea Greg felt so strongly. He was stunned. He did not know what to say in response to such unexpected emotions. In the end he just said: "Thank you."

"Good-bye, George."

"Good-bye."

"God bless and keep you," said Greg, and he walked away.

. . .

Early Friday morning George went to the White House Situation Room.

President Kennedy had created this suite in the West Wing basement where previously there had been a bowling alley. Its ostensible purpose was to speed communications in a crisis. The truth was that Kennedy believed the military had kept information from him during the Bay of Pigs crisis, and he wanted to make sure they never got another chance to do that.

This morning the walls were covered with large-scale maps of Cuba and its sea approaches. The teletype machines chattered like cicadas on a warm night. Pentagon telegrams were copied here. The president could listen in to military communications. The quarantine operation was being run from a room in the Pentagon known as Navy Flag Plot, but radio conversations between that room and the ships could be overheard here.

The military hated the Situation Room.

George sat on an uncomfortable modern chair at a cheap dining table and listened. He was still mulling over last night's conversation with Greg. Had Greg expected George to throw his arms around him and cry: "Daddy!" Probably not. Greg seemed comfortable with his avuncular role. George had no wish to change that. At the age of twenty-six he could not suddenly start treating Greg like a regular father. All the same, George *was* kind of happy about what Greg had said. My father loves me, he thought; that can't be bad.

The USS *Joseph P. Kennedy* hailed the *Marucla* at dawn.

The *Kennedy* was a twenty-four-hundred-ton destroyer armed with eight missiles, an antisubmarine rocket launcher, six torpedo tubes, and twin five-inch gun mounts. It also had nuclear depth charge capability.

The *Marucla* immediately cut its engines, and George breathed easier.

The *Kennedy* lowered a boat and six men crossed to the *Marucla.* The sea was rough, but the crew of the *Marucla* obligingly threw a rope ladder over the side. All the same, the chop made it difficult to board. The officer in charge did not want to look ridiculous by falling in the water, but eventually he took a chance, leaped for the ladder, and boarded the ship. His men followed.

The Greek crew offered them coffee.

They were delighted to open the hatches for the Americans to inspect their cargo, which was pretty much what they had said. There was a tense moment when the Americans insisted on opening a crate labeled SCIENTIFIC INSTRUMENTS, but it turned out to contain laboratory equipment no more sophisticated than what might be found in a high school.

The Americans left and the *Marucla* resumed course for Havana.

George reported the good news to Bobby Kennedy by phone, then hopped a cab.

He told the driver to take him to the corner of Fifth and K Streets, in one of the city's worst slum neighborhoods. Here, above a car showroom, was the CIA's National Photographic Interpretation Center. George wanted to understand this art and had asked for a special briefing, and since he worked for Bobby, he got it. He picked his way across a sidewalk littered with beer bottles, entered the building, and passed through a security turnstile; then he was escorted to the fourth floor.

He was shown around by a gray-haired photointerpreter called Claud Henry, who had learned his trade in the Second World War, analyzing aerial photographs of bomb damage from Germany.

Claud told George: "Yesterday the navy sent Crusader jets over Cuba, so we now have low-level photographs, much easier to read."

George did not find it so easy. To him the photos pinned up around Claud's room still looked like abstract art, meaningless shapes arranged in a random pattern. "This is a Soviet military base," Claud said, pointing at a photo.

"How do you know?"

"Here's a soccer pitch. Cuban soldiers don't play soccer. If it was a Cuban camp it would have a baseball diamond."

George nodded. Clever, he thought.

"Here's a row of T-54 tanks."

They just looked like dark squares to George.

"These tents are missile shelters," Claud said. "According to our tentologists."

"Tentologists?"

"Yes. I'm actually a cratologist. I wrote the CIA handbook on crates."

George smiled. "You're not kidding, are you?"

"When the Soviets are shipping very large items such as fighter aircraft, they have to be carried on deck. They disguise them by putting them in crates. But we can usually work out the dimensions of the crate. And a MiG-15 comes in a different-size crate than a MiG-21."

"Tell me something," said George. "Do the Soviets have this kind of expertise?"

"We don't think so. Consider this. They shot down a U-2 plane, so they know we have high-altitude planes with cameras. Yet they thought they could send missiles to Cuba without us finding out. They were still denying the existence of the missiles until yesterday, when we showed them the photos. So, they know about the spy planes and they know about the cameras, but until now they didn't know we could see their missiles from the stratosphere. That leads me to think they're behind us in photointerpretation."

"That sounds right."

"But here's last night's big revelation." Claud pointed to an object with fins in one of the photos. "My boss will be briefing the president about this within the hour. It's thirty-five feet long. We call it a Frog, for Free Rocket over Ground. It's a short-range missile, intended for battlefield situations."

"So this will be used against American troops if we invade Cuba."

"Yes. And it's designed to carry a nuclear warhead."

"Oh, shit," said George.

"That's probably what President Kennedy is going to say," said Claud.

CHAPTER EIGHTEEN

The radio was on in the kitchen of the house in Great Peter Street on Friday evening. All over the world, people were keeping their radios on, listening fearfully for news flashes.

It was a big kitchen, with a long scrubbed-pine table in the center. Jasper Murray was making toast and reading the newspapers. Lloyd and Daisy Williams got all the London papers and several Continental ones as well. Lloyd's main interest as a member of Parliament was foreign affairs, and had been ever since he fought in the Spanish Civil War. Jasper was scanning the pages for some reason to hope.

Tomorrow, Saturday, there would be a protest march in London, if London was still standing in the morning. Jasper would be there as a reporter for *St. Julian's News*, the student paper. Jasper did not really like doing news reports: he preferred features, longer, more reflective pieces, in which the writing could be a little more fancy. He hoped one day to work in magazines, or maybe even television.

But first he wanted to be editor of *St. Julian's News*. The post came with a small salary and a sabbatical year off studies. It was much coveted, as it practically guaranteed the student a good job in journalism after graduation. Jasper had applied but had been defeated by Sam Cakebread. The Cakebread name was famous in British journalism: Sam's father was assistant editor of *The Times* and his uncle was a much-loved radio commentator. He had a younger sister at

St. Julian's College who had interned with *Vogue* magazine. Jasper suspected that it was Sam's name, not his ability, that had won him the job.

But ability was never enough in Britain. Jasper's grandfather had been a general, and his father had been on course for a similar career, until he made the mistake of marrying a Jewish girl, and in consequence had never been promoted above the rank of colonel. The British establishment never forgave people who broke their rules. Jasper had heard it was different in the United States.

Evie Williams was in the kitchen with Jasper, sitting at the table, making a placard that read HANDS OFF CUBA.

Evie no longer had a schoolgirl crush on Jasper. He was relieved. She was sixteen now, and beautiful in a pale, ethereal way; but she was too solemn and intense for his taste. Anyone who dated her would have to share her passionate commitment to a wide range of campaigns against cruelty and injustice, from apartheid in South Africa to experiments on animals. Jasper had no commitment to anything, and anyway he preferred girls like the impish Beep Dewar, who even at the age of thirteen had put her tongue in his mouth and rubbed herself against his erection.

As Jasper watched, Evie inscribed, inside the *O* of OFF, the four-branched symbol of the Campaign for Nuclear Disarmament. Jasper said: "So your slogan supports two idealistic causes for the price of one!"

"There's nothing idealistic about it," she said sharply. "If war breaks out tonight, do you know what the first target of Soviet nuclear bombs will be? Britain. That's because we have nuclear weapons, which they need to eliminate before they attack the United States. They won't be bombing Norway, or Portugal, or any country that has the sense to stay out of the nuclear competition. Anyone who thinks logically about the defense of our country knows that nuclear weapons don't protect us—they put us in danger."

Jasper had not intended his remark to be taken seriously, but Evie took everything seriously.

Evie's fourteen-year-old brother, Dave, was also at the table, making miniature Cuban flags. He had used a stencil to paint the stripes onto sheets of heavy paper, and now he was attaching the sheets to small sticks of plywood with a borrowed staple gun. Jasper resented Dave's privileged life, with wealthy, easygoing parents, but he worked hard to be friendly. "How many are you making?" he asked.

Dave said: "Three hundred and sixty."

"Not a random number, presumably."

"If we don't all get killed by bombs tonight, I'm going to sell them at the demonstration tomorrow for sixpence each. Three hundred and sixty sixpences are one hundred and eighty shillings, or nine pounds, which is the price of the guitar amplifier I want to buy."

Dave had a nose for business. Jasper remembered his soft drinks stall at the school play, staffed by teenage boys who worked at top speed because Dave was paying them a commission. But Dave did badly at his lessons, coming at or near the bottom of the class in all academic subjects. It drove his father wild, for in other respects Dave seemed bright. Lloyd accused Dave of laziness, but Jasper thought it was more complicated. Dave had trouble making sense of anything written down. His own writing was dire, full of spelling mistakes and even reversed letters. It reminded Jasper of his best friend at school, who had been incapable of singing the school song, and found it hard to hear the difference between his one-note drone and the melody the other boys were singing. Likewise, Dave had to make an effort of concentration to see the difference between the letters *d* and *b*. He longed to fulfill the expectations of his high-achieving parents, but always fell short.

As he stapled his sixpenny flags together, his mind evidently wandered, for apropos of nothing he said: "Your mother and mine can't have had much in common when they first met."

"No," said Jasper. "Daisy Peshkov was the child of a Russian-American gangster. Eva Rothmann was a doctor's daughter from a middle-class Jewish family in Berlin, sent to America to escape the Nazis. Your mother took my mother in."

Evie, who had been named after Eva, said: "My mother just has a big heart."

Jasper said half to himself: "I wish someone would send me to America."

"Why don't you just go?" said Evie. "You could tell them to leave the Cuban people alone."

Jasper did not care a damn about the Cubans. "I can't afford it." Even living rent-free he was too broke to buy a ticket to the United States.

At that moment the woman with the big heart walked into the room. Daisy Williams at forty-six was still attractive, with big blue eyes and fair curls: when she was young she must have been irresistible, Jasper thought. Tonight she was dressed modestly, in a midblue skirt with matching jacket and no jewelry; hiding her wealth, Jasper thought sardonically, the better to play the part of a politician's wife. Her figure was still trim, though not as slim as it used to be. Picturing her naked, he thought she would be better in bed than her daughter, Evie. Daisy would be like Beep, ready for anything. He was surprised to catch himself in such a fantasy about someone his mother's age. It was a good thing women could not read men's minds.

"What a nice picture," she said fondly. "Three kids working quietly." She still had a distinctive American accent, though its edges had been worn smooth by her living in London for a quarter of a century. She looked with surprise at Dave's flags. "You don't often take an interest in world affairs."

"I'm going to sell them for sixpence each."

"I might have guessed your efforts had nothing to do with world peace."

"I leave world peace to Evie."

Evie said with spirit: "Someone has to worry about it. We could all be dead before this march begins, you know—just because Americans are such hypocrites."

Jasper looked at Daisy, but she was not offended. She was used to her daughter's abrasive ethical pronouncements. Mildly, she said: "I guess Americans have been badly scared by the missiles in Cuba."

"Then they should imagine how other people feel, and take their missiles out of Turkey."

"I think you're right, and it was a mistake for President Kennedy to put them there. All the same, there's a difference. Here in Europe we're used to having missiles pointed at us—on both sides of the Iron Curtain. But when Khrushchev secretly sent missiles to Cuba he made a shocking change in the status quo."

"Justice is justice."

"And practical politics is something else. But look how history repeats itself. My son is like my father, always alert for an opportunity to make a few bucks, even on the brink of World War Three. My daughter is like my Bolshevik uncle Grigori, determined to change the world."

Evie looked up. "If he was a Bolshevik, he did change the world."

"But was it for the better?"

Lloyd came in. Like his coal-mining ancestors, he was short in stature with broad shoulders. Something about the way he walked reminded Jasper that he had once been a champion boxer. He was dressed with old-fashioned flair, in a black suit with a faint herringbone stripe, a crisp white linen handkerchief in his breast pocket. The two parents were obviously going to a political event. "I'm ready if you are, my darling," he said to Daisy.

Evie said: "What's your meeting about?"

"Cuba," said her father. "What else?" He noticed her placard. "I see you've already made up your mind about the issue."

"It's not complicated, is it?" she said. "The Cuban people should be allowed to choose their own destiny—isn't that a basic democratic principle?"

Jasper saw a row looming. In this family, half the rows were about politics. Bored by Evie's idealism, he interrupted. "Hank Remington is going to sing 'Poison Rain' in Trafalgar Square tomorrow." Remington, an Irish boy whose real name was Harry Riley, was leader of a pop group called the Kords. The song was about nuclear fallout.

"He's wonderful," said Evie. "So clear thinking." Hank was one of her heroes.

"He came to see me," said Lloyd.

Evie immediately changed her tone. "You didn't tell me!"

"It happened only today."

"What did you think of him?"

"He's a genuine working-class genius."

"What did he want?"

"He wanted me to stand up in the House of Commons and denounce President Kennedy as a warmonger."

"So you should!"

"And what happens if Labour wins the next general election? Suppose I become foreign secretary. I might have to go to the White House and ask the president's support for something the Labour government wants to do, perhaps a resolution in the United Nations against racial discrimination in South Africa. Kennedy might remember how I insulted him, and tell me to drop dead."

Evie said: "You should do it anyway."

"Calling someone a warmonger usually doesn't help. If I thought it would resolve the current crisis, I would do it. But it's a card you can play only once, and I prefer to save it for a winning hand."

Jasper reflected that Lloyd was a pragmatic politician. He approved.

Evie did not. "I believe that people should stand up and tell the truth," she said.

Lloyd smiled. "I'm proud to have such a daughter," he said. "I hope you will hold on to that belief all your life. But now I must go and explain the crisis to my supporters in the East End."

Daisy said: "Bye, kids. See you later."

They went out.

Evie said: "Who won that argument?"

Your father did, Jasper thought, hands down; but he did not say so.

. . .

George returned to downtown Washington in a state of high anxiety. Everyone had been working on the assumption that an invasion of Cuba was bound to succeed. The Frogs changed everything. U.S. troops would now face battlefield nuclear weapons. Perhaps the Americans would still prevail, but the war would be harder and would cost more lives, and the result was no longer a foregone conclusion.

He got out of his taxi at the White House and stopped by the press office. Maria was at her desk. He was happy to see that she looked much better than she had three days earlier. "I'm fine, thank you," she said in answer to George's query. A small weight of worry lifted from his heart, leaving the larger still heavy on him. She was recovering physically, but he did not know what spiritual damage was being caused by her secret love affair.

He was not able to ask her more intimate questions because she had company. With her was a young black man in a tweed jacket. "Meet Leopold Montgomery," she said. "He's with Reuters. He came by to pick up a press release."

"Call me Lee," the man said.

George said: "I guess there aren't many colored reporters covering Washington."

"I'm the only one," Lee said.

Maria said: "George Jakes works with Bobby Kennedy."

Lee suddenly became more interested. "What's he like?"

"It's a great job," George said, avoiding the question. "Mainly I advise on civil rights. We take legal action against Southern states that prevent Negroes from voting."

"But we need a new civil rights act."

"Say that, brother." George turned to Maria. "I can't stay. I'm glad you're feeling better."

Lee said: "I'll walk with you, if you're going over to Justice."

George avoided the company of newsmen, but he felt a camaraderie with Lee, who was trying to make it in white Washington just as George was, so he said: "Okay."

Maria said: "Thanks for dropping by, Lee. Please call me if you need any clarification on that release."

"Sure will," he said.

George and Lee left the building and went along Pennsylvania Avenue. George said: "What's in your press release?"

"Although the ships have turned around, the Soviets are still constructing missile launch sites in Cuba, and they're doing it at top speed."

George thought of the aerial reconnaissance photographs he had just seen. He was tempted to tell Lee about them. He would have liked to give a scoop to a young black reporter. However, it would have been a breach of security, and he resisted the impulse. "I guess that's so," he said noncommittally.

Lee said: "The administration seems to be doing nothing."

"What do you mean?"

"The quarantine is clearly ineffective, and the president isn't doing anything else."

George was stung. He was part of the administration, albeit a small part, and he felt unjustly accused. "In his television speech on Monday the president said the quarantine was just the beginning."

"So he will be taking further action?"

"That's obviously what he meant."

"But what will he do?"

George smiled, realizing he was being pumped. "Watch this space," he said.

When he got back to Justice, Bobby was in a rage. It was not Bobby's way to yell and curse and throw objects across the room. His fury was cold and mean. People talked about his terrifying blue-eyed stare.

"Who's he mad at?" George asked Dennis Wilson.

"Tim Tedder. He's sent three infiltration teams into Cuba, six men to a team. More are waiting to go."

"What? Why? Who told the CIA to do that?"

"It's part of Operation Mongoose, and apparently no one told them to *stop*."

"But they might start World War Three all on their own!"

"That's why Bobby's spitting nails. Also, they sent in a two-man team to blow up a copper mine—and, unfortunately, they've lost contact."

"So those two guys are probably in jail now, drawing floor plans of the CIA station in Miami for their Soviet interrogators."

"Yeah."

"This is a stupid time to do that stuff for so many reasons," George said. "Cuba's preparing for war. Castro's security is always good, but right now it must be on high alert."

"Exactly. Bobby's going to a Mongoose meeting at the Pentagon in a few minutes, and I expect he will nail Tedder to a cross."

George did not go with Bobby to the Pentagon. He still was not invited to Mongoose meetings—somewhat to his relief: his trip to La Isabela had convinced him that the whole operation was criminal, and he wanted nothing more to do with it.

He sat at his desk, but found it difficult to concentrate. Civil rights had taken a backseat anyway: no one was thinking about equality for Negroes this week.

George felt the crisis was slipping out of President Kennedy's control. Against his better judgment the president had ordered the *Marucla* to be boarded. The event had gone off without trouble, but what would happen next time? Now there were battlefield nuclear weapons in Cuba:

America might still invade, but the price would be high. And just to add an extra element of risk, the CIA was playing its own games.

Everyone was desperate to cool the temperature, but the opposite kept happening, a nightmarish escalation of the crisis that no one wanted.

Later in the afternoon, Bobby came back from the Pentagon with a wire service report in his hand. "What the hell is this?" he said to the aides. He began to read: "In response to the speeded-up campaign to build missile launch sites in Cuba, fresh action by President Kennedy is expected imminently"—he held his hand in the air, finger pointing up—"according to sources close to the attorney general." Bobby looked around the room. "Who blabbed?"

George said: "Oh, fuck."

Everyone looked at him.

Bobby said: "Do you have something to tell me, George?"

George wanted to sink through the floor. "I'm sorry," he said. "All I did was quote the president's speech, saying the quarantine was only the beginning."

"You can't say that sort of thing to reporters! You've given him a new story."

"Oh, boy, I know that now."

"And you've escalated the crisis just when we were all trying to calm things down. The next story will speculate what action the president has in mind. Then if he does nothing they'll say he's dithering."

"Yes, sir."

"Why were you talking to him at all?"

"He was introduced to me at the White House and he walked along Pennsylvania Avenue with me."

Dennis Wilson said to Bobby: "Is that a Reuters report?"

"Yes, why?"

"It was probably written by Lee Montgomery."

George groaned inwardly. He knew what was coming next. Wilson was deliberately making the incident look worse.

Bobby said: "What makes you say that, Dennis?"

Wilson hesitated, so George answered the question. "Montgomery is a Negro."

Bobby said: "Is that why you talked to him, George?"

"I guess I didn't want to tell him to drop dead."

"Next time, that's exactly what you say to him, and to

any other reporter who tries to get a story out of you, no matter what his color."

George was relieved to hear the words *next time*. It meant that he was not going to be fired. "Thank you," he said. "I'll remember that."

"You'd better." Bobby went into his office.

"You got away with it," Wilson said to George. "Lucky bastard."

"Yeah," said George. He added sarcastically: "Thanks for your help, Dennis."

Everyone returned to their work. George could hardly believe what he had done. He, too, had inadvertently poured fuel on the flames.

He was still feeling depressed when the switchboard put through a long-distance call from Atlanta. "Hi, George, this is Verena Marquand."

Her voice cheered him up. "How are you?"

"Worried."

"You and the whole world."

"Dr. King asked me to call you and find out what's happening."

"You probably know as much as we do," George said. He was still smarting from Bobby's reprimand, and he was not about to risk another indiscretion. "Pretty much everything is in the newspapers."

"Are we really going to invade Cuba?"

"Only the president knows that."

"Will there be a nuclear war?"

"Even the president doesn't know that."

"I miss you, George. I wish I could sit down with you and just, you know, talk."

That surprised him. He had not known her well at Harvard, and he had not seen her for a half a year. He was not aware that she was fond enough of him to miss him. He did not know what to say.

She said: "What am I going to tell Dr. King?"

"Tell him . . ." George paused. He thought of all the people around President Kennedy: the hotheaded generals who wanted war now, the CIA men trying to be James Bond, the reporters who complained of inaction when the president was being cautious. "Tell him the smartest man in the

United States is in charge, and we can't ask for better than that."

"Okay," said Verena, and she hung up.

George asked himself if he believed what he had said. He wanted to hate Jack Kennedy for the way he had treated Maria. But could anyone else handle this crisis better than Kennedy? No. George could not think of another man with the right combination of courage, wisdom, restraint, and calm.

Late in the afternoon, Wilson took a phone call, then said to everyone in the room: "We're getting a letter from Khrushchev. It's coming through to the State Department."

Someone asked: "What does it say?"

"Not much, so far," Wilson said. He looked at his note-book. "We don't have it all yet. 'You are threatening us with war, but you well know that the least you would receive in reply would be to experience the same consequences . . .' It was delivered to our embassy in Moscow just before ten this morning, our time."

George said: "Ten o'clock! It's six in the evening now. What's taking so long?"

Wilson answered with weary condescension, as if tired of explaining elementary procedures to beginners. "Our people in Moscow have to translate the letter into English, then encrypt it, then key it. After it's received here in Washington, State Department officials must decrypt it and then type it. And every word must be triple-checked before the president acts. It's a long process."

"Thank you," said George. Wilson was a smug prick. However, he knew a lot.

It was Friday night, but no one was going home.

Khrushchev's message arrived in bits. Predictably, the important part was at the end. If the United States would promise not to invade Cuba, Khrushchev said, "the necessity for the presence of our military specialists would disappear."

It was a compromise proposal, and that had to be good news. But what, exactly, did it mean?

Presumably the Soviets would withdraw their nuclear weapons from Cuba. Nothing less would count for anything.

But could the United States promise never to invade Cuba? Would President Kennedy even consider tying his own hands like that? George thought he would be loath to give up all hope of getting rid of Castro.

And how would the world react to such a deal? Would they see it as a foreign policy coup for Khrushchev? Or would they say Kennedy had forced the Soviets to back down?

Was this good news? George could not decide.

Larry Mawhinney put his buzz-cut head around the door. "Cuba has short-range nuclear weapons now," he said.

"We know," said George. "The CIA found them yesterday."

"That means we have to have the same," said Larry.

"What do you mean?"

"The Cuba invasion force must be equipped with battle-field nukes."

"Must it?"

"Of course! The Joint Chiefs are about to demand them. Would you send our men into battle less well armed than the enemy?"

He had a point, George saw; but there was a terrible consequence. "So now any war with Cuba must be a nuclear war, from the start."

"Damn right," said Larry, and he left.

. . .

Last thing, George dropped by his mother's house. Jacky made coffee and put a plate of cookies in front of him. He did not take one. "I saw Greg yesterday," he said.

"How is he?"

"Same as ever. Except . . . Except that he told me I was the best thing that ever happened to him."

"Hm!" she said in a disparaging tone. "What brought that on?"

"He wanted me to know how proud he is of me."

"Well, well. There is still some good in that man."

"How long is it since you last saw Lev and Marga?"

Jacky narrowed her eyes in suspicion. "What kind of question is that?"

"You get along well with Grandmother Marga."

"That's because she loves you. When a person loves your child, it's endearing. You'll find that out when you have kids."

"You haven't seen her since Harvard commencement, more than a year ago."

"That's true."

"You don't work on the weekend."

"The club is closed Saturdays and Sundays. When you were small I had to have weekends off, to take care of you when you weren't in school."

"The First Lady has taken Caroline and John Junior to Glen Ora."

"Oh, and I suppose you think I ought to go to my country house in Virginia and spend a couple of days riding my horses?"

"You could go and see Marga and Lev in Buffalo."

"Go to Buffalo for the weekend?" she said incredulously. "For pity's sake, child! I'd spend all Saturday on the train there and all Sunday on the train back."

"You could fly."

"I can't afford to."

"I'll buy you a ticket."

"Oh, my good Lord," she said. "You think the Russians are going to bomb us this weekend, don't you?"

"It's never been closer than this. Go to Buffalo."

She drained her cup, then got up and went to the sink to wash it. After a moment she said: "And what about you?"

"I have to stay here and do what I can to prevent it happening."

Jacky shook her head decisively. "I'm not going to Buffalo."

"It would ease my heart mightily, Mom."

"If you want to ease your heart, pray to the Lord."

"You know what the Arabs say? 'Trust in Allah, but tether your camel.' I'll pray if you'll go to Buffalo."

"How do you know the Russians won't bomb Buffalo?"

"I don't know for sure. But I'd guess it's a secondary target. And it may be out of range of those missiles in Cuba."

"You make a weak case, for a lawyer."

"I'm serious, Mom."

"So am I," she said. "And you're a good son, to worry about your mother. But listen to me, now. From the age of sixteen I've given my life to nothing but raising you. If everything I've done is going to be wiped out in a nuclear flash, I don't want to be alive afterward to know about it. I'm staying where you are."

"Either we'll both survive, or we'll both die."

" 'The Lord giveth, and the Lord taketh away,' " she quoted. " 'Blessed be the name of the Lord.' "

.   .   .

The United States had more than two hundred nuclear missiles that could reach the Soviet Union, according to Dimka's uncle Volodya in Red Army Intelligence. The Americans believed the Soviet Union had about half that many intercontinental missiles, Volodya said. In truth, the USSR had precisely forty-two.

And some of them were obsolete.

When the United States did not immediately reply to the Soviet Union's compromise offer, Khrushchev ordered even the oldest and most unreliable missiles to be made launch-ready.

In the early hours of Saturday morning, Dimka telephoned the missile testing range at Baikonur in Kazakhstan. The army base there had two five-engined Semyorkas, obsolete R-7 rockets of the type that had taken the *Sputnik* into orbit five years ago. They were being readied for a Mars probe.

Dimka called off the Mars expedition. The Semyorkas were included in the Soviet Union's forty-two intercontinental missiles. They were needed for World War III.

He ordered the scientists to fit both rockets with nuclear warheads and fuel them.

Preparation for launch would take twenty hours. The Semyorkas used an unstable liquid propellant, and they could not be kept on alert for more than a day. They would be used this weekend or not at all.

Semyorka rockets often exploded on takeoff. However, if they did not, they could reach Chicago.

Each was to be fitted with a 2.8-megaton bomb.

If one managed to hit its target, it would destroy everything within seven miles of the center of Chicago, from the lake shore to Oak Park, according to Dimka's atlas.

When he was sure the commanding officer had understood the orders, Dimka went to bed.

CHAPTER NINETEEN

The phone woke Dimka. His heart pounded: was it war? How many minutes did he have to live? He snatched up the receiver. It was Natalya. First with the news, as usual, she said: "There's a flash from Pliyev."

General Pliyev was in command of Soviet forces in Cuba.

"What?" said Dimka. "What does it say?"

"They think the Americans are going to attack today, at dawn their time."

It was still dark in Moscow. Dimka turned on the bedside light and looked at his watch. It was eight in the morning: he should be at the Kremlin. But dawn in Cuba was still five and a half hours away. His heart slowed a little. "How do they know?"

"That's not the point," she said impatiently.

"What is the point?"

"I'll read you the last sentence. 'We have decided that in the event of a U.S. attack on our installations, we will employ all available means of air defense.' They will use nuclear weapons."

"They can't do that without our permission!"

"But that's exactly what they're proposing."

"Malinovsky won't let them."

"Don't bet on that."

Dimka cursed under his breath. Sometimes the military seemed actually to want nuclear annihilation. "I'll meet you in the canteen."

"Give me half an hour."

Dimka showered fast. His mother offered him breakfast, but he refused, so she gave him a piece of black rye bread to take with him. "Don't forget there's a party for your grandfather today," Anya said.

It was Grigori's birthday: he was seventy-four. There would be a big lunch at his apartment. Dimka had promised to bring Nina. They were planning to surprise everyone by announcing their engagement.

But there would be no party if the Americans attacked Cuba.

As Dimka was leaving, Anya stopped him. "Tell me the truth," she said. "What's going to happen?"

He put his arms around her. "I'm sorry, Mother, I don't know."

"Your sister's over there in Cuba."

"I know."

"She's right in the line of fire."

"The Americans have intercontinental missiles, Mother. We're all in the line of fire."

She hugged him, then turned away.

Dimka drove to the Kremlin on his motorcycle. When he got to the Presidium building, Natalya was waiting in the canteen. Like Dimka, she had dressed in a hurry, and she looked a little disheveled. Her untidy hair fell over her face in a way he found charming. I must stop thinking like this, he told himself: I'm going to do the right thing, and marry Nina and raise our child.

He wondered what Natalya would say when he told her that.

But this was not the moment. He took his piece of rye bread from his pocket. "I wish I could get some tea," he said. The canteen doors were open but no one was serving yet.

"I've heard that restaurants in the United States open when people want food and drinks, not when the staff wants to work," said Natalya. "Do you think it's true?"

"Probably just propaganda," said Dimka. He sat down.

"Let's draft a reply to Pliyev," she said, and opened a notebook.

Chewing, Dimka concentrated on the issue. "The Presidium should forbid Pliyev to launch nuclear weapons without specific orders from Moscow."

"I'd rather forbid him even to mount the warheads on the rockets. Then they can't be fired by accident."

"Good thinking."

Yevgeny Filipov came into the room. He was wearing a brown pullover under a gray suit jacket. Dimka said: "Good morning, Filipov, have you come to apologize to me?"

"For what?"

"You accused me of allowing the secret of our Cuban missiles to leak out. You even said I should be arrested. Now we know the missiles were photographed by a spy plane of the CIA. Obviously you owe me a groveling apology."

"Don't be ridiculous," Filipov blustered. "We didn't think their high-altitude photographs would show something as small as a missile. What are you two plotting?"

Natalya answered with the truth. "We're discussing this morning's flash message from Pliyev."

"I've already spoken to Malinovsky about it." Filipov worked for Defense Minister Malinovsky. "He is in agreement with Pliyev."

Dimka was horrified. "Pliyev can't be allowed to start World War Three on his own initiative!"

"He won't be starting it. He'll be defending our troops from American aggression."

"The level of response can't be a local decision."

"There may be no time for anything else."

"Pliyev must make time, rather than trigger a nuclear exchange."

"Malinovsky believes we must protect the weapons we have in Cuba. If they were destroyed by the Americans, it would weaken our ability to defend the USSR."

Dimka had not thought of that. A significant part of the Soviet nuclear stockpile was now in Cuba. The Americans could wipe out all those costly weapons, leaving the Soviets seriously weakened.

"No," said Natalya. "Our whole strategy must be based on *not* using nuclear weapons. Why? Because we have so few, by comparison with the American arsenal." She leaned forward across the canteen table. "Listen to me, Yevgeny. If it comes to all-out nuclear war, *they win*." She sat back. "So we may brag, we may bluster, we may threaten, but we may not fire our weapons. For us, nuclear war is suicide."

"That's not how the Defense Ministry sees it."

Natalya hesitated. "You speak as if a decision has already been made."

"It has. Malinovsky has endorsed Pliyev's proposal."

Dimka said: "Khrushchev won't like that."

"On the contrary," said Filipov. "He agreed with it."

Dimka realized he had missed out on early-morning discussions because he had been up so late last night. That put him at a disadvantage. He stood up. "Let's go," he said to Natalya.

They left the cafeteria. Waiting for the elevator, Dimka said: "Damn. We've got to reverse that decision."

"I'm sure Kosygin will want to raise it at the Presidium today."

"Why don't you type the order we drafted and suggest Kosygin bring it to the meeting? I'll try to soften Khrushchev up."

"All right."

They parted and Dimka went to Khrushchev's office. The first secretary was reading translations of Western newspaper articles, each one stapled to the original clipping. "Have you read Walter Lippmann's article?"

Lippmann was a syndicated American columnist of liberal views. He was said to be close to President Kennedy.

"No." Dimka had not yet looked at the papers.

"Lippmann proposes a swap: we withdraw our missiles from Cuba, and they remove theirs from Turkey. It's a message to me from Kennedy!"

"Lippmann is only a journalist—"

"No, no. He's a mouthpiece for the president."

Dimka doubted that American democracy worked that way, but he said nothing.

Khrushchev went on: "It means that if we propose this swap, Kennedy will accept."

"But we have already demanded something different— their promise not to invade Cuba."

"So, we will keep Kennedy guessing!"

We'll certainly keep him confused, Dimka thought. But that was Khrushchev's way. Why be consistent? It only made life easier for the enemy.

Dimka changed the subject. "There will be questions at

the Presidium about Pliyev's message. Giving him the power to fire nuclear weapons—"

"Don't worry," said Khrushchev with a deprecating wave. "The Americans are not going to attack now. They're even talking to the United Nations general secretary. They want peace."

"Of course," said Dimka deferentially. "So long as you know it's going to come up."

"Yes, yes."

The leaders of the Soviet Union gathered in the paneled Presidium Room a few minutes later. Khrushchev opened the meeting with a long speech arguing that the time for an American attack had passed. Then he raised what he called the Lippmann Proposal. There was little enthusiasm for it around the long table, but no one opposed him. Most people realized the leader had to conduct diplomacy in his own style.

Khrushchev was so excited about the new idea that he dictated his letter to Kennedy there and then, while the others listened. Then he ordered that it should be read out on Radio Moscow. That way the American embassy here could forward it to Washington without the time-consuming chore of encoding it.

Finally Kosygin raised the issue of Pliyev's flash. He argued that control of nuclear weapons must remain in Moscow, and read out the order to Pliyev that Dimka and Natalya had drafted.

"Yes, yes, send it," said Khrushchev impatiently; and Dimka breathed easier.

An hour later Dimka was with Nina, going up in the elevator at Government House. "Let's try to forget our woes for a while," he said to her. "We won't talk about Cuba. We're going to a party. Let's enjoy ourselves."

"That suits me," Nina said.

They went to the apartment of Dimka's grandparents. Katerina opened the door in a red dress. Dimka was startled to see that it was knee length, in the latest Western fashion, and that his grandmother still had slim legs. She had lived in the West, while her husband was on the diplomatic circuit, and she had learned to dress more stylishly than most Soviet women.

She looked Nina up and down with the unapologetic curiosity of old people. "You look well," she said, and Dimka wondered why her tone of voice sounded a little odd.

Nina took it as a compliment. "Thank you, so do you. Where did you get that dress?"

Katerina led them into the living room. Dimka remembered coming here as a boy. His grandmother had always given him *belev* candy, a traditional Russian kind of apple confection. His mouth watered: he would have liked a piece right then.

Katerina seemed a little unsteady in her high-heeled shoes. Grigori was sitting in the easy chair opposite the television, as always, though the set was off. He had already opened a bottle of vodka. Perhaps that was why Grandmother was wobbling a little.

"Birthday greetings, Grandfather," said Dimka.

"Have a drink," said Grigori.

Dimka had to be careful. He would be no use to Khrushchev drunk. He knocked back the vodka Grigori gave him, then put the glass down out of Grandfather's reach, to avoid a refill.

Dimka's mother was already there, helping Katerina. She came out of the kitchen carrying a plate of crackers with red caviar. Anya had not inherited Katerina's stylishness. She always looked comfortably dumpy, whatever she wore.

She kissed Nina.

The doorbell rang and Uncle Volodya came in with his family. He was forty-eight, and his close-cropped hair was now gray. He was in uniform: he might be called to duty at any moment. Aunt Zoya followed him, approaching fifty but still a pale Russian goddess. Behind her trailed their two teenagers, Dimka's cousins, Kotya and Galina.

Dimka introduced Nina. Both Volodya and Zoya greeted her warmly.

"Now we're all here!" said Katerina.

Dimka looked around: at the old couple who had started it all; at his plain mother and her handsome blue-eyed brother; at his beautiful aunt and his teenage cousins; and at the voluptuous redhead he was going to marry. This was his family. And it was the most precious part of everything that would be lost today if his fears came true. They all lived within a mile of the Kremlin. If the Americans fired their nuclear weapons at Moscow tonight, the people in this room would all be lying dead in the morning, their brains boiled, their bodies crushed, their skin burned black. And the only consolation was that he would not have to mourn them because he, too, would be dead.

They all drank to Grigori's birthday.

"I wish my little brother, Lev, could be with us," said Grigori.

"And Tanya," said Anya.

Volodya said: "Lev Peshkov is not so little anymore, Father. He's sixty-seven years old and a millionaire in America."

"I wonder if he has grandchildren in America."

"Not in America, no," said Volodya. Red Army Intelligence could find out this sort of thing easily, Dimka knew. "Lev's illegitimate son, Greg, the senator, is a bachelor. But his legitimate daughter, Daisy, who lives in London, has two adolescents, a boy and a girl, about the same age as Kotya and Galina."

"So, I'm a great-uncle to two British kids," Grigori said, musing in a pleased tone. "What are they called? Jane and Bill, perhaps." The others laughed at the odd sounds of the English names.

"David and Evie," said Volodya.

"You know, I was supposed to be the one to go to America," Grigori said. "But at the last minute I had to give my ticket to Lev." He went into a reminiscence. His family had heard the story before, but they listened again, happy to indulge him on his birthday.

After a moment, Volodya took Dimka aside and said: "How was this morning's Presidium?"

"They ordered Pliyev not to fire nuclear weapons without specific orders from the Kremlin."

Volodya grunted disparagingly. "Waste of time."

Dimka was surprised. "Why?"

"It will make no difference."

"Are you saying Pliyev will disobey orders?"

"I think any commander would. You haven't been in battle, have you?" Volodya gave Dimka a searching look with those intense blue eyes. "When you're under attack, fighting for your life, you defend yourself with any means that come to hand. It's visceral, you can't help it. If the Americans invade Cuba, our forces there will throw everything at them, regardless of orders from Moscow."

"Shit," said Dimka. All this morning's efforts had been wasted, if Volodya was right.

Grandfather's story wound down, and Nina touched Dimka's arm. "Now might be a good moment."

Dimka addressed the assembled family. "Now that we have honored my grandfather's birthday, I have an announcement. Quiet, please." He waited for the teenagers to stop talking. "I have asked Nina to marry me, and she has accepted."

They all cheered.

Another round of vodka was poured, but Dimka managed not to drink this one.

Anya kissed Dimka. "Well done, my son," she said. "She didn't want to get married—until she met you!"

"Maybe I'll have great-grandchildren soon!" said Grigori, and he winked broadly at Nina.

Volodya said: "Father, don't embarrass the poor girl."

"Embarrass? Rubbish. Nina and I are friends."

"Don't worry about that," said Katerina, who was now drunk. "She's already pregnant."

Volodya protested: "Mother!"

Katerina shrugged. "A woman can tell."

So that was why Grandmother looked Nina up and down so hard when we arrived, Dimka thought. He saw a glance pass between Volodya and Zoya: Volodya raised an eyebrow, Zoya gave a slight nod, and Volodya made a momentary "Oh!" with his mouth.

Anya looked shocked. She said to Nina: "But you told me . . ."

Dimka said: "I know. We thought Nina couldn't have children. But the doctors were wrong!"

Grigori raised yet another glass. "Hooray for wrong doctors! I want a boy, Nina—a great-grandson to carry on the Peshkov-Dvorkin line!"

Nina smiled. "I'll do my best, Grigori Sergeivitch."

Anya still looked troubled. "The doctors made a mistake?"

"You know doctors, they never admit to mistakes," said Nina. "They say it's a miracle."

"I just hope I live to see my great-grandchild," said Grigori. "Damn the Americans to hell." He drank.

Kotya, the sixteen-year-old boy, spoke up. "Why do the Americans have more missiles than we do?"

Zoya answered: "When we scientists began to work on nuclear energy, back in 1940, and we told the government that it could be used to create a super-powerful bomb, Stalin did not believe us. So the West got ahead of the USSR, and they're still ahead. That's what happens when governments don't listen to scientists."

Volodya added: "But don't repeat what your mother says when you go to school, okay?"

Anya said: "Who cares? Stalin killed half of us, now Khrushchev will kill the other half."

"Anya!" protested Volodya. "Not in front of the children!"

"I feel for Tanya," said Anya, ignoring her brother's remonstrances. "Over there in Cuba, waiting for the Americans to attack." She began to weep. "I wish I could have seen my pretty little girl again," she said, sudden tears streaming down her cheeks. "Just once more, before we die."

. . .

By Saturday morning the U.S. was ready to attack Cuba.

Larry Mawhinney gave George the details in the basement Situation Room at the White House. President Kennedy called this area a pigpen, because he found it cramped; but he had been raised in grand spacious homes: the suite was larger than George's apartment.

According to Mawhinney, the air force had five hundred seventy-six planes at five different bases ready for the air strike that would turn Cuba into a smoking wasteland. The army had mobilized one hundred fifty thousand troops for the invasion that would follow. The navy had twenty-six destroyers and three aircraft carriers circling the island nation. Mawhinney said all this proudly, as if it were his own personal achievement.

George thought Mawhinney was too glib. "None of that will be any use against nuclear missiles," George said.

"Fortunately, we have nukes of our own," Mawhinney replied.

Like that made everything all right.

"How do we fire them, exactly?" said George. "I mean, what does the president do, physically?"

"He has to call the Joint War Room at the Pentagon. His phone in the Oval Office has a red button that connects him instantly."

"And what would he say?"

"He has a black leather briefcase containing a set of codes that he has to use. The briefcase goes everywhere with him."

"And then ... ?"

"It's automatic. There's a program called the Single Integrated Operational Plan. Our bombers and missiles take off with about three thousand nuclear weapons, and head for a thousand targets in the Communist bloc." Mawhinney made a flattening motion with his hand. "Wipe them out," he said with relish.

George was not buying this attitude. "And they do the same to us."

Mawhinney looked annoyed. "Listen, if we get the first punch in, we can destroy most of their weapons before they get off the ground."

"But we're not likely to get the first punch in, because we're not barbarians, and we don't want to start a nuclear war that would kill millions."

"That's where you politicians go wrong. A first strike is the way to win."

"Even if we do what you want, we'll only destroy *most* of their weapons, you said."

"Obviously, we won't get a hundred percent."

"So, whatever happens, the USA gets nuked."

"War is not a picnic," Mawhinney said angrily.

"If we avoid war, we can carry on having picnics."

Larry looked at his watch. "ExComm at ten," he said.

They left the Situation Room and went upstairs to the Cabinet Room. The president's senior advisers were gathering, with their aides. President Kennedy entered a few minutes after ten. This was the first time George had seen him since Maria's abortion. He stared at the president with new eyes. This middle-aged man in the dark suit with the faint stripe had fucked a young woman, then let her go to the abortion doctor on her own. George felt a momentary flash of pure vitriolic rage. At that moment he could have killed Jack Kennedy.

All the same, the president did not look evil. He was bearing the strain of the cares of the world, literally, and George, against his will, felt a pang of sympathy, too.

As usual, CIA chief McCone opened the meeting with an intelligence summary. In his customary soporific drone he announced news frightening enough to keep everyone wide awake. Five medium-range missile sites in Cuba were now fully operational. Each had four missiles, so there were now twenty nuclear weapons pointed at the United States and ready to be fired.

At least one had to be targeted on this building, George thought grimly, and his stomach cramped in fear.

McCone proposed round-the-clock surveillance of the sites. Eight U.S. Navy jets were ready to take off from Key West to overfly the launchpads at low level. Another eight would travel the same circuit this afternoon. When it got dark they would go again, illuminating the sites with flares. In addition, high-altitude reconnaissance flights by U-2 spy planes would continue.

George wondered what good that would do. The overflights might detect prelaunch activity, but what could the U.S. do about that? Even if the American bombers took off immediately, they would not reach Cuba before the missiles were fired.

And there was another problem. As well as nuclear missiles aimed at the USA, the Red Army in Cuba had SAMs, surface-to-air missiles designed to bring down aircraft. All twenty-four SAM batteries were operational, McCone reported, and their radar equipment had been switched on. So American planes overflying Cuba would now be tracked and targeted.

An aide came into the room with a long sheet of paper torn off a teletype machine. He gave it to President Kennedy. "This is from the Associated Press in Moscow," said the president, and he read it aloud. "'Premier Khrushchev told President Kennedy yesterday he would withdraw offensive weapons from Cuba if the United States withdrew its rockets from Turkey.'"

Mac Bundy, the national security adviser, said: "He did not."

George was as puzzled as everyone else. Khrushchev's letter yesterday had demanded that the USA promise not to invade Cuba. It had said nothing about Turkey. Had the Associated Press made a mistake? Or was Khrushchev up to his usual tricks?

The president said: "He may be putting out another letter."

That turned out to be the truth. In the next few minutes, further reports made the situation clearer. Khrushchev was making a completely separate new proposal, and had broadcast it on Radio Moscow.

"He's got us in a pretty good spot here," said President Kennedy. "Most people would regard this as not an unreasonable proposal."

Mac Bundy did not like that idea. "What 'most people,' Mr. President?"

The president said: "I think you're going to find it difficult to explain why we want to take hostile military action in Cuba when he's saying: 'Get yours out of Turkey and we'll get ours out of Cuba.' I think you've got a very touchy point there."

Bundy argued for going back to Khrushchev's first offer. "Why pick that track when he's offered us the other track in the last twenty-four hours?"

Impatiently, the president said: "This is their new and latest position—and it's a public one." The press did not yet know about Khrushchev's letter, but this new proposal had been made through the media.

Bundy persisted. America's NATO allies would feel betrayed if the U.S. traded missiles, he said.

Defense Secretary Bob McNamara expressed the bewilderment and fear that they all felt. "We had one deal in the letter, now we've got a different one," he said. "How can we negotiate with somebody who changes his deal before we even get a chance to reply?"

No one knew the answer.

    . . .

That Saturday, the royal poinsettia trees in the streets of Havana blossomed with brilliant red flowers like bloodstains on the sky.

Early in the morning Tanya went to the store and grimly laid in provisions for the end of the world: smoked meat, canned milk, processed cheese, a carton of cigarettes, a bottle of rum, and fresh batteries for her flashlight. Although it was daybreak there was a line, but she waited only fifteen minutes, which was nothing to someone accustomed to Moscow queues.

There was a doomsday air in the narrow streets of the old town. Habaneros were no longer waving machetes and singing the national anthem. They were collecting sand in buckets for putting out fires, sticking gummed paper over their windows to minimize flying shards, toting sacks of flour. They had been so foolish as to defy their superpower neighbor, and now they were going to be punished. They should have known better.

Were they right? Was war unavoidable now? Tanya felt sure no world leader really wanted it, not even Castro, who was beginning to sound borderline crazy. But it could happen anyway. She thought gloomily of the events of 1914. No one had wanted war then. But the Austrian emperor had seen Serbian independence as a threat, in the same way that Kennedy saw Cuban independence as a threat. And once Austria declared war on Serbia the dominoes fell with deadly inevitability until half the planet was involved in a conflict more cruel and bloody than any the world had previously known. But surely that could be avoided this time?

She thought of Vasili Yenkov, in a prison camp in Siberia. Ironically, he might have a chance of surviving a nuclear war. His punishment might save his life. She hoped so.

When she got back to her apartment she turned on the radio. It was tuned to one of the American stations broadcasting from Florida. The news was that Khrushchev had offered Kennedy a deal. He would withdraw the missiles from Cuba if Kennedy would do the same in Turkey.

She looked at her canned milk with a feeling of overwhelming relief. Maybe she would not need emergency rations after all.

She told herself it was too soon to feel safe. Would Kennedy accept? Would he prove wiser than the ultraconservative Emperor Franz Joseph of Austria?

A car honked outside. She had a long-standing date to fly to the eastern end of Cuba with Paz today to write about a Soviet antiaircraft battery. She had not really expected him to show up, but when she looked out of the window she saw his Buick station wagon at the curb, its wipers struggling to cope with a tropical rainstorm. She picked up her raincoat and bag and went out.

"Have you seen what your leader has done?" he asked angrily as soon as she got into the car.

She was surprised by his rage. "You mean the Turkey offer?"

"He didn't even consult us!" Paz pulled away, driving too fast along the narrow streets.

Tanya had not even thought about whether the Cuban leaders should be part of the negotiation. Obviously Khrushchev, too, had overlooked the need for this courtesy. The world saw the crisis as a conflict of superpowers, but naturally the Cubans still imagined it was about them. And this faint prospect of a peace deal seemed to them a betrayal.

She needed to calm Paz down, if only to prevent a road accident. "What would you have said, if Khrushchev had asked you?"

"That we will not trade our security for Turkey's!" he said, and banged the steering wheel with the heel of his hand.

Nuclear weapons had not brought security to Cuba, Tanya reflected. They had done the opposite. Cuba's sovereignty was more threatened today than ever. But she decided not to enrage Paz further by pointing this out.

He drove to a military airstrip outside Havana where their plane was waiting, a Yakovlev Yak-16 propeller-driven Soviet light transport aircraft. Tanya looked at it with interest. She had never intended to be a war correspondent but, to avoid appearing ignorant, she had taken pains to learn the stuff men knew, especially how to identify aircraft, tanks, and ships. This was the military modification of the Yak, she saw, with a machine gun mounted in a ball turret on top of the fuselage.

They shared the ten-seat cabin with two majors of the 32nd Guards air fighter regiment, dressed in the loud check shirts and peg-top pants that had been issued in a clumsy attempt to disguise Soviet troops as Cubans.

Takeoff was a little too exciting: it was the rainy season in the Caribbean, and there were gusty winds, too. When they could see the land below, through gaps in the clouds, they glimpsed a collage of brown and green patches crazed with crooked yellow lines of dirt road. The little plane was tossed around in a storm for two hours. Then the sky cleared, with the rapidity characteristic of tropical weather changes, and they landed smoothly near the town of Banes.

They were met by a Red Army colonel called Ivanov who already knew all about Tanya and the article she was writing. He drove them to an antiaircraft base. They arrived at ten A.M., Cuban time.

The site was laid out as a six-pointed star, with the command post in the center and the launchers at the points. Beside each launcher stood a transporter trailer bearing a single surface-to-air missile. The troops looked miserable in their waterlogged trenches. Inside the command post, officers stared intently at green radar screens that beeped monotonously.

Ivanov introduced them to the major in command of the battery. He was obviously tense. No doubt he would have preferred not to have visiting VIPs on a day such as this.

A few minutes after they arrived, a foreign aircraft was sighted at high altitude entering Cuban airspace two hundred miles west. It was given the tag Target No. 33.

Everyone was speaking Russian, so Tanya had to translate for Paz. "It must be a U-2 spy plane," he said. "Nothing else flies that high."

Tanya was suspicious. "Is this a drill?" she asked Ivanov.

"We were planning to fake something, for your benefit," he said. "But actually this is the real thing."

He looked so worried that Tanya believed him. "We're not going to shoot it down, are we?" she said.

"I don't know."

"The arrogance of these Americans!" Paz raved. "Flying right above us! What would they say if a Cuban plane overflew Fort Bragg? Imagine their indignation!"

The major ordered a combat alert, and Soviet troops began to move missiles from transporters to launchers, and to attach the cables. They did it with calm efficiency, and Tanya guessed they had practiced many times.

A captain was plotting the course of the U-2 on a map. Cuba was long and thin, 777 miles from east to west but only fifty to a hundred miles from north to south. Tanya saw that the spy plane was already fifty miles inside Cuba. "How fast do they fly?" she asked.

Ivanov answered: "Five hundred miles an hour."

"How high?"

"Seventy thousand feet, roughly double the altitude of a regular jet airline flight."

"Can we really hit a target that far away and moving so fast?"

"We don't need a direct hit. The missile has a proximity fuse. It explodes when it gets close."

"I know we're targeting this plane," she said. "But please tell me we're not actually going to fire at it."

"The major is calling for instructions."

"But the Americans might retaliate."

"Not my decision."

The radar was tracking the intruder plane, and a lieutenant reading from a screen called out its height, speed, and distance. Outside the command post, the Soviet artillerymen adjusted the aim of the launchers to follow Target No. 33. The U-2 crossed Cuba from north to south, then turned east, following the coast, coming closer to Banes. Outside, the missile launchers turned slowly on their pivoting bases, tracking the target like wolves sniffing the air. Tanya said to Paz: "What if they fire by accident?"

That was not what he was thinking about. "It's taking pictures of our positions!" he said. "Those photographs will be used to guide their army when they invade—which could be in a few hours' time."

"The invasion is much more likely to happen if you kill an American pilot!"

The major had the phone to his ear while he watched the fire-control radar. He looked up at Ivanov and said: "They're checking with Pliyev." Tanya knew that Pliyev was the Soviet commander in chief in Cuba. But surely Pliyev would not shoot down an American plane without authorization from Moscow?

The U-2 reached the southernmost tip of Cuba and turned, following the north coast. Banes was near the coast. The U-2's course would bring it directly overhead. But at any instant it could turn north—and then, traveling at about a mile a second, it could quickly be out of range.

"Shoot it down!" said Paz. "Now!"

Everyone ignored him.

The plane turned north. It was almost directly above the battery, though thirteen miles high.

Just a few more seconds, please, Tanya thought, praying to she knew not what god.

Tanya, Paz, and Ivanov stared at the major, who stared at the screen. The room was silent but for the beeping of the radar.

Then the major said: "Yes, sir."

What was it—reprieve or doom?

Without putting down the phone, he spoke to the men in the room. "Destroy Target No. 33. Fire two missiles."

"No!" said Tanya.

There was a roar of sound. Tanya looked through the window. A missile rose from its launcher and was gone in a blink. Another followed seconds later. Tanya put her hand to her mouth, feeling she might vomit in fear.

They would take about a minute to reach an altitude of thirteen miles.

Something might go wrong, Tanya thought. The missiles could malfunction, veer off course, and land harmlessly in the sea.

On the radar screen, two small dots approached a larger one.

Tanya prayed they would miss.

They went fast, then all three dots merged.

Paz let out a yell of triumph.

Then a scatter of smaller dots sprayed across the screen.

Speaking into the phone, the major said: "Target No. 33 is destroyed."

Tanya looked out of the window, as if she might see the U-2 crashing to earth.

The major raised his voice. "It's a kill. Well done, everyone."

Tanya said: "And what will President Kennedy do to us now?"

.   .   .

George was full of hope on Saturday afternoon. Khrushchev's messages were inconsistent and confusing, but the Soviet leader seemed to be seeking a way out of the crisis. And President Kennedy certainly did not want war. Given goodwill on both sides, it seemed inconceivable that they would fail.

On his way to the Cabinet Room, George stopped by the press office and found Maria at her desk. She was wearing a smart gray dress, but she had on a bright pink headband, as if to announce to the world that she was well and happy. George decided not to ask how she was: clearly she did not want to be treated as an invalid. "Are you busy?" he said.

"We're waiting for the president's reply to Khrushchev," she said. "The Soviet offer was made publicly, so we're assuming the American response will be released to the press."

"That's the meeting I'm going to with Bobby," George said. "To draft the response."

"Swapping missiles in Cuba for missiles in Turkey seems like a reasonable proposal," she said. "Especially as it may save all our lives."

"Praise be."

"Your mom says that."

He laughed and moved on. In the Cabinet Room, advisers and their aides were gathering for the four o'clock meeting of ExComm. Among a knot of military aides by the door, Larry Mawhinney was saying: "We have to stop them giving Turkey to the Communists!"

George groaned. The military saw everything as a fight to the death. In truth, nobody was going to give Turkey away. The proposal was to scrap some missiles that were obsolete anyway. Was the Pentagon really going to oppose a peace deal? He could hardly believe it.

President Kennedy came in and took his usual place, in the middle of the long table with the windows behind him. They all had copies of a draft response put together earlier. It said that the USA could not discuss missiles in Turkey until the Cuba crisis had been resolved. The president did not like the wording of this reply to Khrushchev. "We're rejecting his message," he complained. "He" was always Khrushchev: Kennedy saw this as a personal conflict. "This is not going to be successful. He's going to announce that we've rejected his proposal. Our position ought to be that we're *glad* to discuss this matter—once we get a positive indication that they have ceased their work in Cuba."

Someone said: "That really injects Turkey as a quid pro quo."

National Security Adviser Mac Bundy chimed in: "That's my worry." Bundy, whose hair was receding although he was only forty-three, came from a Republican family and tended to be hard-line. "If we sound, to NATO and other allies, as if we want to make this trade, then we're in real trouble."

George was disheartened: Bundy was lining up with the Pentagon, against a deal.

Bundy went on: "If we appear to be trading the defense of Turkey for a threat to Cuba, we'll just have to face a radical decline in the effectiveness of the alliance."

That was the problem, George realized. The Jupiter missiles might have been obsolete, but they symbolized American determination to resist the spread of Communism.

The president was not convinced by Bundy. "The situation is moving there, Mac."

Bundy persisted. "The justification for this message is that we expect it to be turned down."

Really? thought George. He was pretty sure President Kennedy and his brother did not see it that way.

"We expect to be acting against Cuba tomorrow or the next day," Bundy went on. "What's our military plan?"

This was not how George had thought the meeting would go. They should be talking about peace, not war.

Defense Secretary Bob McNamara, the whiz kid from Ford, answered the question. "A large air strike leading to invasion." Then he turned the argument back to Turkey. "To minimize the Soviet response against NATO following a U.S. attack on Cuba, we get those Jupiters out of Turkey before the Cuban attack—and let the Soviets know. On that basis, I don't believe the Soviets would strike Turkey."

That was ironic, George thought: to protect Turkey, it was necessary to take away its nuclear weapons.

Secretary of State Dean Rusk, who George thought was one of the smarter men in the room, warned: "They might take some other action—in Berlin."

George marveled that the American president could not attack a Caribbean island without calculating the repercussions five thousand miles away in Eastern Europe. It showed how the entire planet was a chess board for the two super-powers.

McNamara said: "I'm not prepared at this moment to recommend air attacks on Cuba. I'm just saying we must now begin to look at it more realistically."

General Maxwell Taylor spoke. He had been in touch

with the Joint Chiefs of Staff. "The recommendation they give is that the big strike, Operations Plan 312, be executed no later than Monday morning, unless there is irrefutable evidence in the meantime that offensive weapons are being dismantled."

Sitting behind Taylor, Mawhinney and his friends looked pleased. Just like the military, George thought: they could hardly wait to go into battle, even though it might mean the end of the world. He prayed that the politicians in the room would not be guided by the soldiers.

Taylor continued: "And that the execution of this strike plan be followed by the execution of 316, the invasion plan, seven days later."

Bobby Kennedy said sarcastically: "Well, I'm surprised."

There was loud laughter around the table. Everyone thought the military's recommendations were absurdly predictable, it seemed. George felt relieved.

But the mood became grim again when McNamara, reading a note passed to him by an aide, suddenly said: "The U-2 was shot down."

George gasped. He knew that a CIA spy plane had gone silent during a mission over Cuba, but everyone was hoping it had suffered a radio problem and was on its way home.

President Kennedy evidently had not been briefed about the missing plane. "A U-2 was shot down?" he said, and there was fear in his voice.

George knew why the president was appalled. Until this moment, the superpowers had been nose to nose, but all they had done was threaten one another. Now the first shot had been fired. From this point on, it would be much more difficult to avoid war.

"Wright just said it was found shot down," McNamara said. Colonel John Wright was with the Defense Intelligence Agency.

Bobby said: "Was the pilot killed?"

As so often, he had asked the key question.

General Taylor said: "The pilot's body is in the plane."

President Kennedy said: "Did anyone see the pilot?"

"Yes, sir," Taylor replied. "The wreckage is on the ground and the pilot's dead."

The room went quiet. This changed everything. An American was dead, shot down in Cuba by Soviet guns.

Taylor said: "That raises the question of retaliation."

It certainly did. The American people would demand revenge. George felt the same. Suddenly he yearned for the president to launch the massive air attack that the Pentagon had demanded. In his mind he saw hundreds of bombers in close formation sweeping across the Florida Straits and dropping their deadly payload on Cuba like a hailstorm. He wanted every missile launcher blown up, all the Soviet troops slaughtered, Castro killed. If the entire Cuban nation suffered, so be it: that would teach them not to kill Americans.

The meeting had been going on for two hours, and the room was foggy with tobacco smoke. The president announced a break. It was a good idea, George thought. George himself certainly needed to calm down. If the others were feeling as bloodthirsty as he was, they were in no state to make rational decisions.

The more important reason for the break, George knew, was that President Kennedy had to take his medicine. Most people knew he had a bad back, but few understood that he fought a constant battle against a whole range of ailments, including Addison's disease and colitis. Twice a day the doctors shot him up with a cocktail of steroids and antibiotics to keep him functioning.

Bobby undertook to redraft the letter to Khrushchev, with the help of the president's cheerful young speechwriter Ted Sorensen. The two of them went with their aides to the president's study, a cramped room next to the Oval Office. George took a pen and yellow pad and wrote down everything Bobby told him to. With only two people discussing it, the draft was done quickly.

The key paragraphs were:

1. You would agree to remove these weapons systems from Cuba under appropriate United Nations observation and supervision; and undertake, with suitable safeguards, to halt the further introduction of such weapons systems into Cuba.
2. We, on our part, would agree—upon the establishment of adequate arrangements through the United Nations to ensure the carrying out and continuation of these commitments—(a) to remove promptly the

quarantine arrangements now in effect and (b) to give assurances against an invasion of Cuba and I am confident that other nations of the Western Hemisphere would be prepared to do likewise.

The USA was accepting Khrushchev's first offer. But what about his second? Bobby and Sorensen agreed to say:

The effect of such a settlement on easing world tensions would enable us to work toward a more general arrangement regarding "other armaments" as proposed in your second letter.

It was not much, just a hint of a promise to discuss something, but it was probably the most that ExComm would allow.

George privately wondered how this could possibly be enough.

He gave his handwritten draft to one of the president's secretaries and asked her to get it typed. A few minutes later, Bobby was summoned to the Oval Office, where a smaller group was gathering: the president, Dean Rusk, Mac Bundy, and two or three others, with their closest aides. Vice President Lyndon Johnson was excluded: he was a smart political operator, in George's opinion, but his rough Texas manners grated on the refined Boston Kennedy brothers.

The president wanted Bobby to carry the letter personally to the Soviet ambassador in Washington, Anatoly Dobrynin. Bobby and Dobrynin had had several informal meetings in the last few days. They did not much like one another, but they were able to speak frankly, and had formed a useful back channel that bypassed the Washington bureaucracy. In a face-to-face meeting, perhaps Bobby could expand on the hint of a promise to discuss the missiles in Turkey—without getting prior approval from ExComm.

Dean Rusk suggested that Bobby could go a little further with Dobrynin. In today's meetings it had become clear that no one really wanted the Jupiter missiles to remain in Turkey. From a strictly military point of view they were useless. The problem was cosmetic: the Turkish government and the other NATO allies would be angered if the USA traded those missiles in a Cuba settlement. Rusk suggested a solution that George thought was very smart. "Offer to pull the Jupiters out later—say, in five or six months' time," said Rusk. "Then we can do it quietly, with the agreement of our allies, and step up the Mediterranean activity of our nuclear-armed submarines to compensate. But the Soviets have to promise to keep that deal deadly secret."

It was a startling suggestion, but brilliant, George thought.

Everyone agreed with remarkable speed. ExComm discussions had rambled all over the globe for most of the day, but this smaller group here in the Oval Office had suddenly become decisive. Bobby said to George: "Call Dobrynin." He looked at his watch, and George did the same: it was seven fifteen P.M. "Ask him to meet me at the Justice Department in half an hour," Bobby said.

The president added: "And release the letter to the press fifteen minutes later."

George stepped into the secretaries' office next to the Oval Office and picked up a phone. "Get me the Soviet embassy," he said to the switchboard operator.

The ambassador agreed instantly to the meeting.

George took the typed letter to Maria and told her the president wanted it released to the press at eight P.M.

She looked anxiously at her watch, then said: "Okay, girls, we'd better go to work."

Bobby and George left the White House and a car drove them the few blocks to the Justice Department. In the gloomy weekend lighting, the statues in the Great Hall seemed to watch the two men suspiciously. George explained to the security staff that an important visitor would shortly arrive to see Bobby.

They went up in the elevator. George thought Bobby looked exhausted, and undoubtedly he was. The corridors of the huge building echoed emptily. Bobby's cavernous office was dimly lit, but he did not bother to switch on more lamps. He slumped behind his wide desk and rubbed his eyes.

George looked out of the window at the streetlights. The center of Washington was a pretty park full of monuments and palaces, but the rest of it was a densely populated metropolis with five million residents, more than half of them black. Would the city be here this time tomorrow? George had seen pictures of Hiroshima: miles of buildings flattened to rubble, and burned and maimed survivors on the out-skirts, staring with uncomprehending eyes at the unrecognizable world around them. Would Washington look like that in the morning?

Ambassador Dobrynin was shown in at exactly a quarter to eight. He was a bald man in his early forties, and he clearly relished his informal meetings with the president's brother.

"I want to lay out the current alarming situation the way the president sees it," Bobby said. "One of our planes has been shot down over Cuba and the pilot is dead."

"Your planes have no right to fly over Cuba," Dobrynin said quickly.

Bobby's discussions with Dobrynin could be combative, but today the attorney general was in a different mood. "I want you to understand the political realities," he said. "There is now strong pressure on the president to respond with fire. We can't stop these overflights: it's the only way we can check the state of construction of your missile bases. But if the Cubans shoot at our planes, we're going to shoot back."

Bobby told Dobrynin what was in the letter from President Kennedy to Secretary Khrushchev.

"And what about Turkey?" Dobrynin said sharply.

Bobby replied carefully. "If that is the only obstacle to achieving the regulation I mentioned earlier, the president doesn't see any insurmountable difficulties. The greatest difficulty for the president is the public discussion of the issue. If such a decision were announced now it would tear NATO apart. We need four to five months to remove the missiles from Turkey. But this is extremely confidential: only a hand-ful of people know that I am saying this to you."

George watched Dobrynin's face carefully. Was it his imagination, or was the diplomat concealing a rush of excitement?

Bobby said: "George, give the ambassador the phone numbers we use to get to the president directly."

George grabbed a pad, wrote down three numbers, tore off the sheet, and handed it to Dobrynin.

Bobby stood up, and the ambassador did the same. "I need an answer tomorrow," Bobby said. "That's not an ulti-matum, it's the reality. Our generals are itching for a fight.

And don't send us one of those long Khrushchev letters that take all day to translate. We need a clear, businesslike answer from you, Mr. Ambassador. And we need it fast."

"Very well," said the Russian, and he went out.

    . . .

On Sunday morning, the KGB station chief in Havana reported to the Kremlin that the Cubans now thought an American attack was inevitable.

Dimka was at a government dacha at Novo-Ogaryevo, a picturesque village on the outskirts of Moscow. The dacha was a small place with white columns that made it look a bit like the White House in Washington. Dimka was preparing for the Presidium meeting to be held here in a few minutes, at twelve noon. He went around the long oak table with eighteen briefing folders, putting one in each place. They contained President Kennedy's latest message to Khrushchev, translated into Russian.

Dimka felt hopeful. The American president had agreed to everything Khrushchev had originally demanded. If this letter had arrived, miraculously, minutes after Khrushchev's first message had been sent, the crisis would have been over instantly. But the delay had permitted Khrushchev to add to his demands. And, unfortunately, Kennedy's letter did not directly mention Turkey. Dimka did not know whether that would be a sticking point for his boss.

The Presidium members were assembling when Natalya Smotrov came into the room. Dimka noticed first that her curly hair was getting longer and sexier, and second that she looked scared. He had been trying to get a few minutes with her to tell her about his engagement. He felt he could not give the news to anyone in the Kremlin until he had told Natalya. But once again this was not a good moment. He needed her alone.

She came straight to him and said: "Those imbeciles have shot down an American plane."

"Oh, no!"

She nodded. "A U-2 spy plane. The pilot is dead."

"Shit! Who did it, us or the Cubans?"

"No one will say, which means it was probably us."

"But no such order was given!"

"Exactly."

This was what they had both feared: that someone would start the shooting without authorization.

The members were taking their seats, aides behind them as usual. "I'll go and tell him," Dimka said but, as he spoke, Khrushchev came in. Dimka hurried to his side and murmured the news in the leader's ear as he sat down. Khrushchev did not reply, but looked grim.

He opened the meeting with what was clearly a prepared speech. "There was a time when we advanced, as in October 1917; but in March 1918 we had to retreat, having signed the Brest-Litovsk agreement with the Germans," he began. "Now we find ourselves face-to-face with the danger of war and nuclear catastrophe, with the possible result of destroying the human race. In order to save the world, we must retreat."

That sounded like the beginning of an argument for compromise, Dimka thought.

But Khrushchev quickly turned to military considerations. What should the Soviet Union do if the Americans were to attack Cuba today, as the Cubans themselves fully expected? General Pliyev must be instructed to defend Soviet forces in Cuba. But he should ask permission before using nuclear weapons.

While the Presidium was discussing that possibility, Dimka was called out of the room by Vera Pletner, his secretary. There was a phone call for him.

Natalya followed him out.

The Foreign Ministry had news that must be passed to Khrushchev immediately—yes, in the middle of the meeting. A cable had just been received from the Soviet ambassador in Washington. Bobby Kennedy had told him the missiles in Turkey would be removed in four or five months—but this must be kept deadly secret.

"This is good news!" Dimka said delightedly. "I'll tell him right away."

"One more thing," said the Foreign Ministry official. "Bobby kept stressing the need for speed. Apparently the American president is under severe pressure from the Pentagon to attack Cuba."

"Just as we thought."

"Bobby kept saying there is very little time. They must have their answer today."

"I'll tell him."

He hung up. Natalya was standing beside him, looking expectant. She had a nose for news. He told her: "Bobby Kennedy offered to remove the missiles from Turkey."

She smiled broadly. "It's over!" she said. "We've won!" Then she kissed him on the lips.

Dimka went back into the room in high excitement. Malinovsky, the defense minister, was speaking. Dimka went up to Khrushchev and said in a low voice: "A cable from Dobrynin—he's received a new offer from Bobby Kennedy."

"Tell everyone," Khrushchev said, interrupting the speaker.

Dimka repeated what he had been told.

Presidium members rarely smiled, but Dimka now saw broad grins around the table. Kennedy had given them everything they had asked for! It was a triumph for the Soviet Union and for Khrushchev personally.

"We must accept as quickly as possible," Khrushchev said. "Bring in a stenographer. I will dictate our letter of acceptance immediately, and it must be broadcast on Radio Moscow."

Malinovsky said: "When should I instruct Pliyev to start dismantling the missile launchers?"

Khrushchev looked at him as if he were stupid. "Now," he said.

. . .

After the Presidium, Dimka at last got Natalya alone. She was sitting in an anteroom, going through her notes of the meeting. "I have something to tell you," he said. For some reason he had a feeling of discomfort in his stomach, though he had nothing to be nervous about.

"Go ahead." She turned a page in her notebook.

He hesitated, feeling he did not have her attention.

Natalya put down the book and smiled.

Now or never.

Dimka said: "Nina and I are engaged to be married."

Natalya went pale and her mouth dropped open in shock.

Dimka felt the need to say something else. "We told my family yesterday," he said. "At my grandfather's birthday party." Stop gabbling, shut up, he told himself. "He's seventy-four."

When Natalya spoke, her words shocked him. "What about me?" she said.

He hardly understood what she meant. "You?" he said.

Her voice dropped to a whisper. "We spent a night together."

"I'll never forget it." Dimka was baffled. "But afterward, all you would say to me was that you were married."

"I was scared."

"Of what?"

Her face showed genuine distress. Her wide mouth was twisted in a grimace, almost as if she were in pain. "Don't get married, please!"

"Why not?"

"Because I don't want you to."

Dimka was flabbergasted. "Why didn't you tell me?"

"I didn't know what to do."

"But now it's too late."

"Is it?" She looked at him with pleading eyes. "You can break off an engagement . . . if you want to."

"Nina is going to have a baby."

Natalya gasped.

Dimka said: "You should have said something . . . before . . ."

"And if I had?"

He shook his head. "There is no point in discussing it."

"No," she said. "I see that."

"Well," said Dimka, "at least we avoided a nuclear war."

"Yes," she said. "We're alive. That's something."

CHAPTER TWENTY

The smell of coffee woke Maria. She opened her eyes. President Kennedy was in bed beside her, sitting upright with several pillows propping him, drinking coffee and reading the Sunday edition of *The New York Times*. He was wearing a light blue nightshirt, as was she. "Oh!" she said.

He smiled. "You sound surprised."

"I am," she said. "To be alive. I thought we might die in the night."

"Not this time."

She had gone to sleep half-hoping it would happen. She dreaded the end of their love affair. She knew it had no future. For him to leave his wife would destroy him politically; to do so for a black woman was unthinkable. Anyway, he did not even want to leave Jackie: he loved her, and he loved their children. He was happily married. Maria was his mistress, and when he tired of her he would discard her. Sometimes she felt she would prefer to die before that came to pass—especially if death could come while she was at his side, in bed, in a flash of nuclear destruction that would be over before they knew what was happening.

She said none of this: her role was to make him happy, not sad. She sat upright, kissed his ear, looked over his shoulder at the newspaper, took his cup from his hand, and drank some of his coffee. Despite everything, she was glad she was still alive.

He had not mentioned her abortion. It was almost as if

he had forgotten about it. She had never raised it with him. She had called Dave Powers and said she was pregnant; and Dave had given her a phone number and said he would take care of the doctor's fee. The only time the president had spoken about it had been when he phoned her after the procedure. He had bigger worries on his mind.

Maria thought about raising the subject herself, but quickly decided against it. Like Dave, she wanted to shield the president from care, not give him additional burdens. She felt sure this was the right decision, though she could not help feeling sorry, and even hurt, that she was not able to talk to him about something so important.

She had feared that sex might be painful after the procedure. However, when Dave had asked her to go to the residence last night, she had been so reluctant to decline the invitation that she had decided to take the risk; and it had been fine—wonderful, in fact.

"I'd better move," the president said. "I'm going to church this morning."

He was about to get up when the bedside phone rang. He picked it up. "Good morning, Mac," he said.

Maria guessed he was talking to McGeorge Bundy, the national security adviser. She jumped out of bed and went to the bathroom.

Kennedy often took calls in bed in the morning. Maria assumed that the people who phoned either did not know or did not care whether he had company. She saved the president embarrassment by making herself scarce during such conversations, just in case they were top secret.

She peeped out of the door in time to see him hang up the phone. "Great news!" he said. "Moscow Radio announced that Khrushchev is dismantling the Cuban missiles and sending them back to the USSR."

Maria had to restrain herself from shouting for joy. It was over!

"I feel like a new man," said the president.

She threw her arms around him and kissed him. "You saved the world, Johnny," she said.

He looked reflective. After a minute he said: "Yeah, I guess I did."

. . .

Tanya was standing on her balcony, leaning on the wrought-iron parapet, breathing deeply of the damp Havana morning air, when Paz's Buick pulled up below, completely blocking the narrow street. He jumped out of the car, looked up, saw her, and yelled: "You betrayed me!"

"What?" She was astonished. "How?"

"You know."

He was a passionate and mercurial character, but she had never seen him this angry, and she was glad he had not come up the stairs to the apartment. However, she was baffled as to the reason for his rage. "I've told no secrets, and I haven't slept with another man," she said. "So I'm sure I haven't betrayed you."

"Then why are they dismantling the missile launchers?"

"Are they?" If that was so, the crisis was over. "Are you sure?"

"Don't pretend you don't know."

"I'm not pretending anything. But if it's true, we're saved." Out of the corner of her eye she noticed neighbors opening windows and doors, to watch the row with unabashed curiosity. She ignored them. "Why are you angry?"

"Because Khrushchev made a deal with the *yanquis*—and never even discussed it with Castro!"

The neighbors made disapproving noises.

"Of course I didn't know," she said with annoyance. "Do you imagine Khrushchev talks to me about such things?"

"He sent you here."

"Not personally."

"He talks to your brother."

"You really believe I'm some kind of special emissary of Khrushchev?"

"Why do you suppose I have gone everywhere with you for months?"

In a quieter voice, she replied: "I imagined it was because you liked me."

The listening women made sympathetic cooing sounds.

"You're not welcome here any longer," he yelled. "Pack your suitcase. You are to leave Cuba immediately. Today!"

With that he jumped back into his car and roared away.

"It was nice knowing you," said Tanya.

.   .   .

Dimka and Nina celebrated by going to a bar near her apartment that evening.

Dimka was determined not to think about his unsettling conversation with Natalya. It changed nothing. He put her to the back of his mind. They had had a brief fling and it was over. He loved Nina, and she was going to be his wife.

He bought a couple of bottles of weak Russian beer and sat beside her on a bench. "We're going to be married," he said tenderly. "I want you to have a wonderful dress."

"I don't want a lot of fuss," Nina said.

"Nor do I, for myself, but that could be a problem," Dimka said with a frown. "I'm the first of my generation to get married. My mother and grandparents will want to throw a big party. What about your family?" He knew that Nina's father had died in the war, but her mother was still alive, and she had a brother a couple of years younger than she.

"I hope Mother will be well enough to come." Nina's mother lived in Perm, nine hundred miles east of Moscow. But something told Dimka that Nina did not really want her mother to come.

"What about your brother?"

"He'll ask for leave, but I don't know if he'll get it." Nina's brother was in the Red Army. "I have no idea where he's stationed. He could be in Cuba, for all I know."

"I'll find out," Dimka said. "Uncle Volodya can pull a few strings."

"Don't go to too much trouble."

"I want to. This will probably be my only wedding!"

She snapped: "What do you mean by that?"

"Nothing." He had meant it lightheartedly, and he was sorry to have irritated her. "Forget I said it."

"Do you think I'm going to divorce you as I did my first husband?"

"I said exactly the opposite, didn't I? What's the matter with you?" He forced a smile. "We should be happy today. We're getting married, we're having a baby, and Khrushchev has saved the world."

"You don't understand. I'm not a virgin."

"I guessed that."

"Will you be serious?"

"All right."

"A wedding is normally two young people promising to love one another forever. You can't say that twice. Don't you see that I'm embarrassed to be doing this again because I've already failed at it once?"

"Oh!" he said. "Yes, I do see, now that you've explained it." Nina's attitude was a little old-fashioned—lots of people got divorced nowadays—but perhaps that was because she came from a provincial town. "So you want a celebration appropriate to a second marriage: no extravagant promises, no newlywed jokes, an adult awareness that life doesn't always go according to plan."

"Exactly."

"Well, my beloved, if that's what you want, I will make sure you have it."

"Will you, really?"

"Whatever made you think I wouldn't?"

"I don't know," she said. "Sometimes I forget what a good man you are."

. . .

That morning, at the last ExComm of the crisis, George heard Mac Bundy invent a new way of describing the opposite sides among the president's advisers. "Everyone knows who were the hawks and who were the doves," he said. Bundy himself was a hawk. "Today was the day of the doves."

But there were few hawks this morning: everyone was full of praise for President Kennedy's handling of the crisis, even some who had recently argued that he was being dangerously weak, and had pressed him to commit the United States to a war.

George summoned up the nerve to banter with the president. "Maybe you should solve the India-China border war next, Mr. President."

"I don't think either of them, or anyone else, wants me to."

"But today you're ten feet tall."

President Kennedy laughed. "That'll last about a week."

Bobby Kennedy was pleased at the prospect of seeing more of his family. "I've almost forgotten my way home," he said.

The only unhappy people were the generals. The Joint Chiefs of Staff, meeting at the Pentagon to finalize plans for the air attack on Cuba, were furious. They sent the president an urgent message saying that Khrushchev's acceptance was a trick to gain time. Curtis LeMay said this was the greatest defeat in American history. No one took any notice.

George had learned something, and he felt it was going to take him a while to digest it. Political issues were interlinked more closely than he had previously imagined. He had always thought that problems such as Berlin and Cuba were separate from each other and had little connection with such issues as civil rights and health care. But President Kennedy had been unable to deal with the Cuban missile crisis without thinking of the repercussions in Germany. And if he had failed to deal with Cuba, the imminent midterm elections would have crippled his domestic program, and made it impossible for him to pass a civil rights bill. Everything was connected. This realization had implications for George's career that he needed to mull over.

When ExComm broke up George kept his suit on and went to his mother's house. It was a sunny autumn day, and the leaves had turned red and gold. She cooked him supper, as she loved to do. She made steak and mashed potatoes. The steak was overdone: he could not persuade her to serve it in the French style, medium rare. He enjoyed the food anyway, because of the love with which it was made.

Afterward she washed the dishes and he dried, then they got ready to go to the evening service at Bethel Evangelical Church. "We must thank the Lord for saving us all," she said as she stood in front of the mirror by the door, putting on her hat.

"You thank the Lord, Mom," George said amiably. "I'll thank President Kennedy."

"Why don't we just agree to be grateful to both?"

"I'll buy that," said George, and they went out.

PART FOUR

GUN

1963

CHAPTER TWENTY-ONE

J oe Henry's Dance Band had a regular Saturday night gig in the restaurant of the Europe Hotel in East Berlin, playing jazz standards and show tunes for the East German elite and their wives. Joe, whose real name was Josef Heinried, was not much of a drummer, in Walli's opinion; but he could keep the beat, even when drunk, and besides, he was an official of the musicians' union, so he could not be fired.

Joe arrived at the staff entrance of the hotel at six P.M. in an old black Framo V901 van with his precious drums in the back packed tight with cushions. While Joe sat at the bar drinking beer, it was Walli's job to carry the drums from the van to the stage, unpack them from their leather cases, and set up the kit the way Joe liked it. There was a bass drum with a kick pedal, two tom-toms, a snare drum, a high hat, a crash cymbal, and a cowbell. Walli handled them as gently as if they were eggs: they were American Slingerland drums that Joe had won from a GI in a card game back in the 1940s, and he would never get another set like it.

The pay was lousy, but as part of the deal Walli and Karolin performed for twenty minutes in the interval, as the Bobbsey Twins, and, most importantly, they got musicians' union cards, even though Walli at seventeen was too young.

Walli's English grandmother, Maud, had chortled when he told her the name of the duo. "Are you Flossie and Freddie, or Bert and Nan?" she had said. "Oh, Walli, you do make me laugh." It turned out that the Bobbsey Twins were not a bit like the Everly Brothers. There was a series of old-fashioned books for children about the impossibly perfect Bobbsey family with two sets of beautiful rosy-cheeked twins.

Walli and Karolin had decided to stick with the name anyway.

Joe was an idiot but Walli was learning from him just the same. Joe made sure the band was too loud to be ignored, though not so loud that people complained they could not converse. He gave each band member the spotlight in one number, keeping the musicians happy. He always opened with a well-known number, and he liked to finish while the dance floor was packed, leaving people wanting more.

Walli did not know what the future held, but he knew what he wanted. He was going to be a musician, the leader of a band, popular and famous; and he was going to play rock music. Perhaps the Communists would soften their attitude to American culture, and permit pop groups. Maybe Communism would fall. Best of all, Walli might find a way to go to America.

All that was a long way off. Right now his ambition was that the Bobbsey Twins would become popular enough for him and Karolin to become full-time professionals.

Joe's musicians drifted in while Walli was setting up, and they began to play at seven sharp.

Communists were ambivalent about jazz. They were suspicious of everything American, but the Nazis had banned jazz, which made jazz anti-Fascist. In the end they permitted it because so many people liked it. Joe's band had no vocalist, so there was no problem about songs that celebrated bourgeois values, such as "Top Hat, White Tie and Tails" or "Puttin' on the Ritz."

Karolin arrived a minute later, and her presence lit up the shabby backstage area with a glow like candlelight, bathing the gray walls in a rosy wash and making the grimy corners vanish into shadow.

For the first time, there was something in Walli's life that mattered as much as music. He had had girlfriends before; in fact they came without much effort by him. And they had usually been willing to have sex with him, so intercourse for Walli was not the unattainable dream it was for most of his schoolmates. But he had experienced nothing like the overwhelming love and passion he felt for Karolin. "We think the same way—we even say the same thing sometimes," he had told Grandmother Maud, and she had said: "Ah—soul mates." Walli and Karolin could talk about sex as easily as they talked about music, confiding what they liked and did not like—though there was not much that Karolin did not like.

The band would play for another hour. Walli and Karolin got into the back of Joe's van and lay down. It became a boudoir, dimly lit by the yellow glow from the car park lights; Joe's cushions were a velvet divan, and Karolin a languorous odalisque, opening her robes to offer her body to Walli's kisses.

They had tried sex using a condom, but neither of them liked it. Sometimes they had intercourse without a condom, and Walli withdrew at the last moment, but Karolin said that was not really safe. Tonight they used their hands. After Walli had come into Karolin's handkerchief, she showed him how to please her, guiding his fingers, and she came with a little "Oh!" that sounded more like surprise than anything else.

"Sex with the one you love is the second-best thing in the world," Maud had said to Walli. Somehow a grandmother could say things that a mother could not.

"If that's second best, what's first?" he had asked.

"Seeing your children happy."

"I thought you were going to say: 'Playing ragtime,'" Walli had said, and she had laughed.

As always, Walli and Karolin went from sex to music with no break, as if it were all one. Walli taught Karolin a new song. He had a radio in his bedroom and he listened to American stations broadcasting from West Berlin, so he knew all the popular numbers. This one was called "If I Had a Hammer," and it was a hit for an American trio called Peter, Paul and Mary. It had a compelling beat, and he felt sure the audience would love it.

Karolin was doubtful about the lyrics, which mentioned justice and freedom.

Walli said: "In America, Pete Seeger is called a Communist for writing it! I think it annoys bullies everywhere."

"How does that help us?" Karolin said with remorseless practicality.

"No one here will understand the English words."

"All right," she said, giving in reluctantly. Then she said: "I have to stop doing this, anyway."

Walli was shocked. "What do you mean?"

She looked somber. She had saved some piece of bad news so that it would not spoil the sex, Walli realized. Karolin had impressive self-control. She said: "My father has been questioned by the Stasi."

Karolin's father was a supervisor at a bus station. He seemed uninterested in politics, and was an unlikely suspect for the secret police. "Why?" said Walli. "What did they question him about?"

"You," she said.

"Oh, shit."

"They told him you were ideologically unreliable."

"What was the name of the man who interrogated him? Was it Hans Hoffmann?"

"I don't know."

"I bet it was." If Hans was not the actual interviewer, he was surely responsible, Walli thought.

"They said Dad would lose his job if I continued to be seen in public singing with you."

"Do you have to do what your parents say? You're nineteen."

"I'm still living with them, though." Karolin had left school but was at a technical college studying to be a bookkeeper. "Anyway, I can't be responsible for my father getting the sack."

Walli was devastated. This blighted his dream. "But . . . we're so good! People love us!"

"I know. I'm so sorry."

"How do the Stasi even know about your singing?"

"Do you remember the man in the cap who followed us the night we met? I see him occasionally."

"Do you think he follows me all the time?"

"Not all the time," she said in a lowered voice. People always spoke quietly when mentioning the Stasi, even if there was no one to overhear. "Maybe just now and again. But I suppose that sooner or later he noticed me with you, and started tailing me, and found out my name and address, and that's how they got to my father."

Walli refused to accept what was happening. "We'll go to the West," he said.

Karolin looked agonized. "Oh, God, I wish we could."

"People escape all the time."

Walli and Karolin had talked of this often. Escapers swam

canals, obtained false papers, hid themselves in truckloads
of produce, or just sprinted across. Sometimes their stories
were told on West German radio stations; more often there
were all kinds of rumors.

Karolin said: "People die all the time, too."

At the same time as Walli was eager to leave, he was
tortured by the possibility that Karolin would be hurt, or
worse, in the escape. The border guards shot to kill. And the
Wall changed constantly, becoming more and more formidable. Originally it had been a barbed-wire fence. Now in
many places it was a double barrier of concrete slabs with a
broad floodlit middle patrolled by dogs and guarded by
watchtowers. It even had tank traps. No one had ever tried
to cross in a tank, though border guards fled frequently.

Walli said: "My sister escaped."

"But her husband was crippled."

Rebecca and Bernd were married now and living in Hamburg. Both were schoolteachers, even though Bernd was in
a wheelchair: he had not yet recovered completely from his
fall. Their letters to Carla and Werner were always delayed
by the censors, but they got through in the end.

"I don't want to live here, anyway," said Walli derisively.
"I'll spend my life singing songs that are approved by the
Communist Party, and you'll be a bookkeeper so that your
father can keep his job in the bus garage. I'd rather be
dead."

"Communism can't last forever."

"Why not? It's lasted since 1917. And what if we have
children?"

"What makes you say that?" she asked sharply.

"If we stay here, we're not just condemning ourselves to
a life in prison. Our children will suffer, too."

"Do you want to have children?"

Walli had not intended to raise this subject. He did not
know whether he wanted children. First he needed to save
his own life. "Well, I don't want to have children in East
Germany," he said. He had not thought of this before, but
now that he had said it he felt sure of it.

Karolin looked serious. "Then maybe we should escape,"
she said. "But how?"

Walli had toyed with many ideas, but he had a favorite.
"Have you seen the checkpoint near my school?"

"I've never really looked."

"It's used by vehicles carrying goods to West Berlin—meat, vegetables, cheese, and so on." The East German government did not like feeding West Berlin, but they needed the money, according to Walli's father.

"And . . . ?"

Walli had worked out some details in his fantasy. "The barrier is a single length of timber about six inches thick. You show your papers, then the guard swings up the barrier to let your truck in. They inspect your load in the compound, then there's another similar barrier to the exit."

"Yes, I recall the setup."

Walli made his voice more confident than he felt. "It strikes me that a driver who had trouble with the guards could probably crash through both barriers."

"Oh, Walli, it's so dangerous!"

"There's no safe way to get out."

"You don't have a truck."

"We'll steal this van." After the show, Joe always sat in the bar while Walli packed up the drum kit and loaded the van. By the time Walli was finished, Joe was more or less drunk, and Walli would drive him home. Walli did not have a license, but Joe did not know that, and he had never been sober enough to notice Walli's erratic driving. After helping Joe into his apartment, Walli had to stash the kit in the hallway, then garage the van. "I could take it tonight, after the show," he said to Karolin. "We could go across first thing in the morning, as soon as the checkpoint opens."

"If I'm late home my father will come looking for me."

"Go home, go to bed, and get up early. I'll wait for you outside the school. Joe won't surface before midday. By the time he realizes his van is missing, we'll be strolling in the Tiergarten."

Karolin kissed him. "I'm scared, but I love you," she said.

Walli heard the band playing "Avalon," the closing number of the first set, and he realized they had been talking a long time. "We're on in five minutes," he said. "Let's go."

The band left the stage and the dance floor emptied. It took Walli less than a minute to set up the microphones and the small guitar amplifier. The audience returned to their drinks and their conversations. Then the Bobbsey Twins came on. Some customers took no notice; others looked on with interest: Walli and Karolin made an attractive couple, and that was always a good start.

As usual they began with "Noch Einen Tanz," which got people's attention and made them laugh. They sang some folk songs, two Everly Brothers numbers, and "Hey Paula," a hit for an American duo very like themselves called Paul and Paula. Walli had a high voice, and sang harmonies over Karolin's tune. He had developed a fingerpicking guitar style that was rhythmic as well as melodic.

They finished with "If I Had a Hammer." Most of the audience loved it, clapping along with the beat, though there were a few stern faces at the words *justice* and *freedom* in the refrain.

They came off to loud applause. Walli's head swam with the euphoria of knowing he had enchanted an audience. It was better than being drunk. He was flying.

Passing them in the wings, Joe said: "If you ever sing that song again, you're fired."

Walli's elation was punctured. He felt as if he had been slapped. Furious, he said to Karolin: "That settles it. I'm leaving tonight."

They returned to the van. Often they made love a second time, but tonight both were too tense. Walli was boiling with rage. "What's the earliest you could meet me in the morning?" he said to Karolin.

She thought for a minute. "I'll go home now and tell them I need an early night, because I have to get up early in the morning . . . for a rehearsal of my college's May Day parade."

"Good," he said.

"I could be with you by seven without arousing suspicion."

"That's perfect. There won't be much traffic through the checkpoint at that hour on a Sunday morning."

"Kiss me again, then."

They kissed long and hard. Walli touched her breasts, then pulled away. "Next time we make love, we'll be free," he said.

They got out of the van. "Seven o'clock," Walli repeated.

Karolin waved and disappeared into the night.

Walli got through the rest of the evening on a wave of hope mingled with rage. He was constantly tempted to show his scorn for Joe, but also fearful that for some reason he would not be able to steal the van. However, if he showed his feelings Joe did not notice, and by one o'clock Walli was parked in the street outside his school. He was out of sight of the checkpoint, around two corners, which was good: he did not want the guards to see him and get suspicious.

He lay on the cushions in the back of the van with his eyes shut, but it was too cold to sleep. He spent much of the night thinking about his family. His father had been bad-tempered for more than a year. Father no longer owned the television factory in West Berlin: he had made it over to Rebecca, so that the East German government could not find a way to take it from the family. He was still trying to run the place, even though he could not go there. He had hired a Danish accountant to be his liaison. As a foreigner, Enok Andersen was able to cross between West and East Berlin once a week for a meeting with Father. It was no way to run a business, and it drove Father crazy.

Walli did not think his mother was happy either. She was mostly absorbed in her work, as head of nursing at a large hospital. She hated the Communists as much as the Nazis, but there was nothing she could do about it.

Grandmother Maud was as stoical as ever. Germany had been fighting Russia for as long as she could remember, she said, and she only hoped to live long enough to see who won. She thought that playing the guitar was an achievement, unlike Walli's parents, who saw it as a waste of time.

The one Walli would miss most was Lili. She was four-teen now, and he liked her a lot better than he had when they were kids and she was a pest.

He tried not to think too much about the dangers ahead of him. He did not want to lose his nerve. In the small hours, when he felt his determination weakening, he thought of Joe's words: "If you ever sing that song again, you're fired." The recollection stoked Walli's rage. If he stayed in East Germany he would spend his life being told what to play by numbskulls such as Joe. It would be no life at all; it would be hell; it would be impossible. He had to leave, whatever else happened. The alternative was unthinkable.

That thought gave him courage.

At six o'clock he left the van and went in search of a hot

drink and something to eat. However, there was nothing open, even at the railway stations, and he returned to the van hungrier than ever. The walking had warmed him, though.

Daylight took the chill off. He sat in the driving seat, so that he could look out for Karolin. She would find him without difficulty: she knew the vehicle, and anyway there were no other vans parked near the school.

Over and over again he visualized what he was about to do. He would take the guards by surprise. It would be several seconds before they realized what was happening. Then, presumably, they would shoot.

With any luck, by that time the guards would be behind Walli and Karolin, shooting at the back of the van. How dangerous was that? Walli really had no idea. He had never been shot at. He had never seen anyone fire a gun, for any reason. He did not know whether bullets could pass through cars or not. He recalled his father saying that hitting someone with a firearm was not as easy as it seemed in the movies. That was the extent of Walli's knowledge.

He suffered an anxious moment when a police car drove past. The cop in the passenger seat gave Walli a hard stare. If they asked to see his driving license he was done for. He cursed his foolishness in not staying in the back of the van. But they drove on without stopping.

In Walli's imagination, both he and Karolin would be killed by the guards if something went wrong. But now for the first time it occurred to him that one might be hit while the other survived. That was a terrible prospect. They often said "I love you" to one another, but Walli was feeling it in a different way. To love someone, he now realized, was to have something so precious that you could not bear to lose it.

An even worse possibility struck him: one of them might be crippled, like Bernd. How would Walli feel if Karolin were paralyzed and it was his fault? He would want to commit suicide.

At last his watch said seven o'clock. He wondered if any of these thoughts had occurred to her. Almost certainly they had. What else would she have been thinking of in the night? Would she come walking along the street, sit next to him in the van, and quietly tell him she was not willing to take the risk? What would he do then? He could not give up, and live out his life behind the Iron Curtain. But could he leave her and go alone?

He was disappointed when seven fifteen came around and she had not appeared.

By seven thirty he was worried, and by eight he was in despair.

What had gone wrong?

Had Karolin's father discovered there was no rehearsal tomorrow for the college's May Day parade? Why would he trouble to check a thing like that?

Was Karolin ill? She had been perfectly well last night.

Had she changed her mind?

She might have.

She had never been as sure as he of the need to escape. She voiced doubts and foresaw difficulties. When they had talked about it last night, he had suspected she was against the whole idea until he mentioned raising their children in East Germany. That was when she had come round to Walli's way of thinking. But now it looked as if she had had second thoughts.

He decided to give her until nine o'clock.

Then what? Go alone?

He no longer felt hungry. The tension in his guts was such that he knew he could not eat. He was thirsty, though. He would almost have given his guitar for hot coffee with cream in it.

At eight forty-five, a slim girl with long fair hair came walking along the street toward the van, and Walli's heart beat faster; but as she came closer he saw that she had dark eyebrows and a small mouth and an overbite. It was not Karolin.

At nine Karolin still had not appeared.

Go or stay?

If you ever sing that song again, you're fired.

Walli started the engine.

He moved forward slowly and turned the first corner.

He would need to be traveling fast to bust through the timber barrier. On the other hand, if he approached at top speed the guards would be forewarned. He needed to begin at normal speed, slow down a little to lull them, then stamp on the gas.

Unfortunately, not much happened when you stamped on the gas in this vehicle. The Framo had a 900 cc three-cylinder two-stroke engine. Walli thought maybe he should have kept the drums on board, so that their weight would give the van more impetus when it hit.

He turned a second corner, and the checkpoint stood ahead of him. About three hundred yards away, the road was blocked by a barrier that lifted to give access to a compound with a guardhouse. The compound was about fifty yards long. Another wooden barrier blocked the exit. Beyond that, the road was bare for thirty yards, then turned into a regular West Berlin street.

West Berlin, he thought; then West Germany; then America.

There was a truck waiting at the near barrier. Walli hurriedly stopped the van. If he got into a queue he was in trouble, for he would have little opportunity to build up speed.

As the truck passed through the barrier, a second vehicle pulled up. Walli waited. But he saw a guard staring his way, and realized his presence had been noted. In an attempt to cover up, he got out of the van, went around to the back, and opened the rear door. From there he could see through the windscreen. As soon as the second vehicle passed into the compound, he returned to the driving seat.

He put the van in gear and hesitated. It was not too late to turn around. He could take the van back to Joe's garage, leave it there, and walk home, his only problem to explain to his parents why he had been out all night.

Life or death.

If he waited now, another truck might come along and block his way; and then a guard might stroll along the street and ask him what the hell he thought he was doing, loitering within sight of a checkpoint; and his opportunity would be lost.

If you ever sing that song again . . .

He let out the clutch and moved forward.

He reached thirty miles an hour, then slowed down a little. The guard standing by the barrier was watching him. He touched the brake. The guard looked away.

Walli floored the accelerator pedal.

The guard heard the change in the engine note and turned around, wearing a slight frown of puzzlement. As the van picked up speed, he waved at Walli with a *Slow down* gesture. Pointlessly, Walli pressed harder on the pedal. The Framo gained pace lumberingly, like an elephant. Walli saw the guard's expression change in slow motion, from curiosity to disapproval to alarm. Then the man panicked. Even though he was not in the way of the van, he took three steps backward and flattened himself against a wall.

Walli let out a yell that was half war cry, half sheer terror.

The van hit the barrier with a crash of deforming metal. The impact threw Walli forward onto the steering wheel, which struck his ribs painfully. He had not anticipated that. Suddenly it was hard to catch his breath. But the timber bar fractured with a crack like a gunshot, and the van moved on, its pace only a little reduced by the impact.

Walli changed into first gear and accelerated. The two vehicles ahead of him had both pulled over for inspection, leaving a clear path to the exit. The other people in the compound, three guards and two drivers, turned to see what the noise was. The Framo picked up speed.

Walli experienced a rush of confidence. He was going to make it! Then a guard with more than average presence of mind knelt down and aimed his submachine gun.

He was just to one side of Walli's route to the exit. In a flash Walli realized he would pass the guard at point-blank range. He was sure to be shot and killed.

Without thinking, he swung the wheel and drove straight at the guard.

The guard fired a burst. The windscreen shattered, but to Walli's astonishment he was not hit. Then he was almost on top of the man. He was suddenly struck by the horror of driving a vehicle over a living human body, and he swung the wheel again to avoid the guard. But he was too late, and the front of the van hit the man with a sickening thump, knocking him down. Walli cried: "No!" The vehicle lurched as its front offside wheel rolled over the guard. "Oh, Christ!" Walli wailed. He had never wanted to hurt anyone.

The van slowed as Walli yielded to despair. He wanted to jump out and see if the guard was alive, and if so help him. Then gunfire broke out again, and he realized they were going to kill him now if they could. Behind him, he heard bullets hit the metal of the van.

He pressed the pedal down and swung the wheel again, trying to get back on track. He had lost momentum. He managed to steer toward the exit barrier. He did not know whether he was going fast enough to break it. Resisting the impulse to change gear, he let the engine shriek in first.

He felt a sudden pain as if someone had stuck a knife in his leg. He shouted out in shock and agony. His foot came up off the pedal, and the van immediately slowed. He had to force himself to press down again, despite how it hurt. He screamed in pain. He felt hot blood run down his calf into his shoe.

The van hit the second timber barrier. Again Walli was thrown forward; again the wheel bruised his ribs; again the wooden bar splintered and fell away; and again the van kept going.

The van crossed a patch of concrete. The gunfire ceased. Walli saw a street with shops, advertisements for Lucky Strike and Coca-Cola, shiny new cars, and, best of all, a small group of startled soldiers in American uniforms. He took his foot off the accelerator and tried to brake. Suddenly the pain was too much. His leg felt paralyzed, and he was unable to press down on the brake pedal. In desperation he steered the van into a lamppost.

The soldiers rushed to the van and one threw open the door. "Well done, kid, you made it!" he said.

I made it, Walli thought. I'm alive, and I'm free. But without Karolin.

"Hell of a ride," the soldier said admiringly. He was not much older than Walli.

As Walli relaxed, the pain became overwhelming. "My leg hurts," he managed to say.

The soldier looked down. "Jeez, look at all that blood." He turned and spoke to someone behind him. "Hey, call an ambulance."

Walli passed out.

⋅   ⋅   ⋅

Walli got his bullet wound stitched up and was discharged from hospital the next day with bruised ribs and a bandage around the calf of his right leg.

According to the newspapers, the border guard he had run over had died.

Limping, Walli went to the Franck television factory and told his story to the Danish accountant, Enok Andersen, who undertook to tell Werner and Carla that he was all right. Enok gave Walli some West German deutschmarks, and Walli got a room at the YMCA.

His ribs hurt every time he turned over in bed, and he slept badly.

Next day he retrieved his guitar from the van. The instrument had survived the crossing without damage, unlike Walli. However, the vehicle was a write-off.

Walli applied for a West German passport, granted automatically to escapers.

He was free. He had escaped from the suffocating puritanism of Walter Ulbricht's Communist regime. He could play and sing anything he chose.

And he was miserable.

He missed Karolin. He felt as if he had lost a hand. He kept thinking of things he would tell her or ask her tonight or tomorrow, then suddenly remember that he could not speak to her; and the dreadful recollection hit him every time like a kick in the stomach. He would see a pretty girl on the street, and think about what he and Karolin might do next Saturday in the back of Joe's van; then he would realize that there would be no more evenings in the back of the van, and he would feel stricken by grief. He walked past clubs where he might get a gig, then wondered if he could bear to perform without Karolin at his side.

He spoke on the phone to his sister Rebecca, who urged him to come and live in Hamburg with her and her husband; but he thanked her and declined. He could not bring himself to leave Berlin while Karolin was still in the East.

Missing her grievously, he took his guitar a week later to the Minnesänger folk club, where he had met her two years ago. A sign outside said it was not open on Mondays, but the door stood ajar, so he went in anyway.

Sitting at the bar, adding up figures in a ledger, was the club's young compere and owner, Danni Hausmann. "I remember you," said Danni. "The Bobbsey Twins. You were great. Why did you never come back?"

"The Vopos smashed up my guitar," Walli explained.

"But now you have another, I see."

Walli nodded. "But I've lost Karolin."

"That was careless. She was a pretty girl."

"We both lived in the East. She's still there, but I escaped."

"How?"

"I drove a van through the barrier."

"That was you? I read about it in the newspapers. Hey, man, cool! But why didn't you bring the chick?"

"She didn't show up at the rendezvous."

"Too bad. Want a drink?" Danni went behind the bar.

"Thanks. I'd like to go back for her, but I'm wanted for murder there now."

Danni pumped two glasses of draft beer. "The Communists made a huge fuss about that. They're calling you a violent criminal."

They had also demanded Walli's extradition. The government of West Germany had refused, saying that the guard had shot at a German citizen who merely wanted to go from one Berlin street to the next, and responsibility for his death lay with the unelected East German regime that illegally imprisoned its population.

In his head Walli did not believe that he had done wrong, but in his heart he could not get used to the idea that he had killed a man.

He said to Danni: "If I crossed the border they would arrest me."

"Man, you're fucked."

"And I still don't know why Karolin didn't come."

"And you can't go back to ask her. Unless . . ."

Walli pricked up his ears. "Unless what?"

Danni hesitated. "Nothing."

Walli put down his glass. He was not going to let a thing like that pass him by. "Come on, man—what?"

Danni said thoughtfully: "Of all the people in Berlin, I guess the one I could trust is a guy who killed an East German border guard."

This was maddening. "What are you talking about?"

Danni made up his mind. "Oh, just something I heard."

If it were just something he had heard, he would not be so secretive about it, Walli thought. "What did you hear?"

"There might be a way to go back without passing through a checkpoint."

"How?"

"I can't tell you."

Walli was angered. Danni seemed to be toying with him. "Then why the fuck did you say it?"

"Take it easy, okay? I can't tell you, but I could take you to see someone."

"When?"

Danni thought for a minute, then answered the question with a question. "Are you willing to go back today? Like, now?"

Walli was scared, but he did not hesitate. "Yes. But why the rush?"

"So that you have no chance to tell anyone. They're not exactly professional about security, but they're not completely stupid either."

He was talking about an organized group. It sounded promising. Walli got off his stool. "Can I leave my guitar here?"

"I'll put it in the store." Danni picked up the instrument in its case and locked it in a cupboard with several other instruments and some amplification gear. "Let's go," he said.

The club was just off the Ku'damm. Danni closed up and they walked to the nearest subway station. Danni noticed his limp. "You were shot in the leg, according to the newspapers."

"Yeah. Hurts like fuck."

"I guess I can trust you. A Stasi undercover agent wouldn't go so far as to wound himself."

Walli did not know whether to be thrilled or terrified. Might he really be able to return to East Berlin—today? It seemed too much to hope for. Yet it also filled him with dread. East Germany still had the death penalty. If he were caught, he would probably be executed by guillotine.

Walli and Danni took the subway across the city. It occurred to Walli that this could be a trap. The Stasi probably had agents in West Berlin, and the owner of the Minnesänger could be one. Would they go to so much trouble to catch Walli? It was a stretch; but, knowing how vengeful Hans Hoffmann was, Walli thought it was possible.

He studied Danni covertly as they rode the underground train. Could *he* be a Stasi agent? It was hard to imagine. Danni was about twenty-five, and had longish hair combed forward in the latest style. He wore elastic-sided boots with

pointed toes. He had a successful club. He was too cool to
be a cop.

On the other hand, he was perfectly placed to spy on
West Berlin's young anti-Communists. Most of them probably came to his club. He must know just about every student leader in West Berlin. Did the Stasi care about what
such young people were doing?

Of course they did. They were obsessed, like medieval
priests hunting witches.

Yet Walli could not pass up this opportunity, if it meant
he might speak to Karolin just one more time.

He vowed to be alert.

The sun was going down when they came out of the subway in the district called Wedding. They walked south, and
Walli quickly realized they were heading for Bernauer Strasse,
where Rebecca had escaped.

The street had changed, he saw in the fading daylight.
On the south side, in place of the barbed-wire fence, there
was now a concrete wall; and the buildings on the Communist side were in the process of being demolished. On the
free side, where Walli and Danni were, the street seemed
blighted. The ground-floor shops in the apartment buildings
looked run-down. Walli guessed that nobody wanted to live
so close to the Wall, repellent to the eye and to the heart.

Danni led him to the back of a building and they went in
by the rear entrance of a disused shop. It seemed to have
been a grocery store, for on the walls were enamel advertisements for canned salmon and cocoa. However, the shop
and the rooms around it were full of loose earth, piled high,
leaving only a narrow passage through; and Walli began to
guess what was going on here.

Danni opened a door and went down a concrete stair lit
by an electric bulb. Walli followed. Danni called out a phrase
that might have been code: "Submariners coming in!" At
the foot of the stairs was a large cellar, undoubtedly used by
the grocer for storage. Now there was a hole a yard square
in the floor, and a surprisingly professional-looking hoist
over it.

They had dug a tunnel.

"How long has this been here?" Walli asked. If his sister
had known about it last year she might have escaped this
way, and avoided Bernd's crippling injury.

"Too long," said Danni. "We finished it a week ago."

"Oh." That was too late to have been any use to Rebecca.

Danni added: "We only use it in twilight. In daytime we would be too visible, and at night we would have to use flashlights, which might call attention to us. All the same, the risk of discovery increases every time we bring people across."

A young man in jeans came up a ladder out of the hole: presumably one of the student tunnelers. He looked hard at Walli, then said: "Who's this, Danni?"

"I vouch for him, Becker," said Danni. "I've known him since before the Wall went up."

"Why is he here?" Becker was hostile and suspicious.

"To go across."

"He wants to go to the East?"

Walli explained: "I escaped last week, but I need to go back for my girlfriend. I can't cross by a regular checkpoint because I killed a border guard, so I'm wanted for murder."

"You're that guy?" Becker looked at him again. "Yeah, I recognize you from the photograph in the paper." His attitude changed. "You can go, but you haven't got much time." He looked at his watch. "They'll start coming through from the East in ten minutes exactly. There's hardly room to pass someone in the tunnel, and I don't want you to cause a traffic jam and slow down the escapers."

Walli was scared, but he did not want to lose this chance. "I'll go right away," he said, concealing his fear.

"Okay, go."

He shook Danni's hand. "Thanks," he said. "I'll be back for my guitar."

"Good luck with your girl."

Walli scrambled down the ladder.

The shaft was three yards deep. At the bottom was the entrance to a tunnel about a yard square. It was neatly built, Walli saw immediately. There was a plank floor, and the roof was propped at intervals. He dropped to his hands and knees and began to crawl.

After a few seconds he realized there were no lights. He kept crawling as it became completely dark. He felt viscerally scared. He knew that the real danger would come when he emerged into East Germany at the other end of the tunnel, but his animal instincts told him to be frightened now, as he crawled forward unable to see an inch in front of his face.

To distract himself, he tried to picture the streetscape above. He was passing beneath the road, then the Wall, then the half-demolished houses on the Communist side; but he did not know how much farther the tunnel went, nor where it terminated.

He was breathing hard with the effort, his hands and knees were sore from crawling on planks, and the bullet wound in his calf was burning with pain; but all he could do was grit his teeth and go on.

The tunnel could not be infinite. It must end eventually. He just had to keep crawling. The sense that he was lost in endless darkness was just childish panic. He had to stay calm. He could do that. Karolin was at the end of this tunnel—not literally, but all the same the thought of her sexy, wide-mouthed smile gave him strength to combat his fear.

Was there a glimmer ahead, or did he imagine it? For a long time it remained too faint to be sure of; but at last it strengthened, and a couple of seconds later he emerged into electric light.

There was another shaft above his head. He went up a ladder and found himself in another basement. Three people stood staring at him. Two had luggage: he guessed they were escapers. The third, presumably one of the student organizers, looked at him and said: "I don't know you!"

"Danni brought me," he said. "I'm Walli Franck."

"Too many people know about this tunnel!" the man said. His voice was shrill with anxiety.

Well, of course, Walli thought; everyone who escapes through it obviously knows the secret. He understood why Danni had said that the danger increased every time it was used. He wondered whether it would still be open when he wanted to return. The thought of being trapped in East Germany again almost made him want to turn around and crawl all the way back.

The man turned to the two with bags. "Go," he said. They went down the shaft. Returning his attention to Walli, he pointed to a flight of stone steps. "Go to the top and wait," he said. "When the coast is clear, Cristina will open the hatch from the outside. You get out. Then you're on your own."

"Thanks." Walli went up the steps until his head came up against an iron trapdoor in the ceiling. This had originally been used for deliveries of some kind, he guessed. He crouched on the steps and forced himself to be patient. Lucky for him there was someone keeping watch on the outside, otherwise he might be seen leaving.

After a couple of minutes, the hatch opened. In the evening light, Walli saw a young woman in a gray head scarf. He scrambled out, and two more people with bags hurried down the steps. The young woman called Cristina closed the hatch. She had a pistol stuffed into her belt, he saw with surprise.

Walli looked around. He was in a small walled yard at the back of a derelict apartment building. Cristina pointed to a wooden door in the wall. "Go that way," she said.

"Thank you."

"Get lost," she said. "Fast."

They were all too stressed to be polite.

Walli opened the door and passed through to the street. To his left, a few yards away, was the Wall. He turned right and started walking.

At first he looked around constantly, expecting to see a police car screech up. Then he tried to act normally and saunter along the pavement as he used to. No matter how he tried, he could not lose the limp: his leg hurt too much.

His first impulse was to go straight to Karolin's house. But he could not knock on her door. Her father would call the police.

He had not thought this out.

Perhaps it would be better if he met her leaving class tomorrow afternoon. There was nothing suspicious about a boy waiting outside the college for his girlfriend, and Walli had done it often. Somehow he would have to make sure none of her classmates saw his face. He was agonizingly impatient to see her, but he would be mad not to take precautions.

What would he do in the meantime?

The tunnel had come out in Strelitzer Strasse, which ran southward into the old city center, Berlin-Mitte, where his family lived. He was only a few blocks from his parents' house. He could go home.

They might even be pleased to see him.

As he approached their street, he wondered whether the house might be under surveillance. If that was so, he could not go there. He thought again about changing his appearance, but he had nothing with which to disguise himself: when he left his room at the YMCA this morning he had not dreamed he might be back in East Berlin by nightfall. At his family home there would be hats and scarves and other useful items of attire—but first he had to get there safely.

Happily it was now dark. He walked along his parents' street on the opposite side, scanning for people who might be Stasi snoops. He saw no loiterers, no one sitting in a parked car, no one stationed at a window. All the same he went to the end of the street and walked around the block. Coming back, he ducked down the alley that led to the backyards. He opened a gate, crossed his parents' yard, and came to the kitchen entrance. It was nine thirty: his father had not yet locked up the house. Walli opened the door and stepped inside.

The light was on but the kitchen was empty. Dinner was long over and his family would be upstairs in the drawing room. Walli crossed the hall and went up. The drawing room door was open, and he stepped inside. His mother, father, sister, and grandmother were watching television. Walli said: "Hello, everyone."

Lili screamed.

Grandmother Maud said in English: "Oh, my goodness!"

Carla went pale and her hands flew to her mouth.

Werner stood up. "My boy," he said. In two strides he crossed the room and folded Walli into his arms. "My boy, thank God."

In Walli's heart a dam of pent-up feeling burst, and he wept.

His mother hugged him next, tears flowing freely. Then Lili, then Grandmother Maud. Walli wiped his eyes with the sleeve of his denim shirt, but more kept coming. His overwhelming emotion had taken him by surprise. He had thought himself hardened, at the age of seventeen, to being alone and separated from his family. Now he saw that he had only been postponing the tears.

At last they all calmed down and dried their eyes. Mother rebandaged Walli's bullet wound, which had bled while he was in the tunnel. Then she made coffee and brought some cake, and Walli realized he was starving. When he had eaten and drunk his fill, he told them the story. Then, when they had asked all their questions, he went to bed.

. . .

Next day at half past three he was leaning against a wall across the street from Karolin's college, wearing a cap and sunglasses. He was early: the girls came out at four.

The sun was shining optimistically on Berlin. The city was a mixture of grand old buildings, hard-edged modern concrete, and slowly disappearing vacant lots where bombs had fallen during the war.

Walli's heart was full of longing. In a few minutes he would see Karolin's face, framed by long curtains of fair hair, the wide mouth smiling. He would kiss her hello, and feel the soft roundness of her lips on his. Perhaps they would lie down together, before the night was over, and make love.

He was also consumed by curiosity. Why had she not turned up at their rendezvous, nine days ago, to escape with him? He was almost certain something had happened to spoil their plan: her father had somehow divined what was afoot and locked her in her room, or a similar stroke of bad luck. But he also suffered a fear, faint but not negligible, that she had changed her mind about coming with him. He could hardly contemplate the possible reason why. Did she still love him? People could change. In the East German media he had been portrayed as a heartless killer. Had that affected her?

Soon he would know.

His parents were devastated by what had happened, but they had not tried to make him change his plans. They had not wanted him to leave home, feeling that he was much too young, but they knew that now he could not stay in the East without being jailed. They had asked what he was going to do in the West—study, or work—and he had said he could not make any decisions until he had talked to Karolin. They had accepted that, and for the first time his father had not tried to tell him what to do. They were treating him like a grown-up. He had been demanding this for years, but now that it had happened he felt lost and scared.

People began to come out of the college.

The building was an old bank converted into classrooms. The students were all girls in their late teens, learning to be typists and secretaries and bookkeepers and travel agents. They carried bags and books and folders. They wore spring sweater-and-skirt combinations, a bit old-fashioned: trainee secretaries were expected to dress modestly.

At last Karolin emerged, wearing a green twinset, carrying her books in an old leather briefcase.

She looked different, Walli thought; a bit more round-faced. She could not have put on much weight in a week, could she? She was with two other girls, chatting, though she did not laugh when they did. Walli feared that if he spoke to her now the other girls would notice him. That would be dangerous: even though he was disguised, they might know that the notorious murderer and escaper Walli Franck had been Karolin's boyfriend, and suspect that this boy in dark glasses was he.

He felt panic rise: surely his purpose could not be so easily frustrated, now at the last moment, after all he had been through? Then the two friends turned left and waved good-bye, and Karolin crossed the street on her own.

As she came near, Walli took off his sunglasses and said: "Hello, baby."

She looked, recognized him, and gave a squeal of shock, stopping in her tracks. He saw astonishment and fear on her face, and something else—could it be guilt? Then she ran to him, dropped her briefcase, and threw herself into his arms. They hugged and kissed, and Walli was swamped by relief and happiness. His first question was answered: she still loved him.

After a minute he realized passersby were staring—some smiling, others looking with disapproval. He put his sunglasses back on. "Let's go," he said. "I don't want people to recognize me." He picked up her dropped briefcase.

They walked away from the college, holding hands. "How did you get back?" she said. "Is it safe? What are you going to do? Does anyone know you're here?"

"We've got so much to talk about," he said. "We need a place to sit down and be private." Across the street he spotted a church. Perhaps it would be open for people seeking spiritual calm.

He led Karolin to the door. "You're limping," she said.

"That border guard shot me in the leg."

"Does it hurt?"

"You bet it does."

The church door was unlocked, and they went in.

It was a plain Protestant hall, dimly lit, with rows of hard benches. At the far end a woman in a head scarf was dusting the lectern. Walli and Karolin sat in the back row and spoke in low voices.

"I love you," Walli said.

"I love you, too."

"What happened on Sunday morning? You were supposed to meet me."

"I got scared," she said.

This was not the answer he had been expecting, and he found it hard to understand. "I was scared, too," he said. "But we made each other a promise."

"I know."

He could see that she was in an agony of remorse; but there was something else. He did not want to torture her, but he had to know the truth. "I took a terrible risk," he said. "You shouldn't have backed out without a word."

"I'm sorry."

"I wouldn't have done it to you," he said. Then he added accusingly: "I love you too much."

She flinched as if he had struck her. But her answer was spirited. "I'm not a coward," she said.

"If you love me, how could you have let me down?"

"I'd give my life for you."

"If that was true, you would have come with me. How can you say it, now?"

"Because it's not just my life at risk."

"It's mine, too."

"And someone else's."

Walli was baffled. "Whose, for God's sake?"

"I'm talking about the life of our child."

"What?"

"We're going to have a baby. I'm pregnant, Walli."

Walli's mouth fell open. He could not speak. His world turned upside down in an instant. Karolin was pregnant. A baby was coming into their lives.

His child.

"Oh, my God," he said at last.

"I was so torn, Walli," she said in anguish. "You have to try to understand that. I wanted to go with you, but I couldn't put the baby in danger. I couldn't get in the van, knowing you were going to crash through the barrier. I wouldn't care if I got injured, but not the child." She was pleading with him. "Say you understand."

"I understand," he said. "I think."

"Thank you."

He took her hand. "All right, let's talk about what we're going to do."

"I know what I'm going to do," she said firmly. "I already love this baby. I'm not going to get rid of it."

She had been living with the knowledge for some weeks, he guessed, and she had thought long and hard. All the same he was taken aback by her strength of purpose. "You speak as if it's nothing to do with me," he said.

"This is my body!" she said fiercely. The cleaner looked round, and Karolin lowered her voice, though she continued to speak forcefully. "I will not be told what to do with my body by any man, you or my father!"

Walli guessed that her father had tried to persuade her to have an abortion. "I'm not your father," Walli said. "I'm not going to tell you what to do, and I don't want to talk you into an abortion."

"I'm sorry."

"But is this our baby, or just yours?"

She began to cry. "Ours," she said.

"Then shall we talk about what we're going to do—together?"

She squeezed his hand. "You're so grown-up," she said. "It's a good thing—you're going to be a father before you're eighteen."

That was a shocking thought. He pictured his own father, with his short haircut and his waistcoats. Now Walli would be required to play that role: commanding, authoritative, reliable, always able to provide for the family. He was not ready, no matter what Karolin said.

But he had to do it, anyway.

"When?" he said.

"November."

"Do you want to get married?"

She smiled through her tears. "Do you want to marry me?"

"More than anything in the world."

"Thank you." She hugged him.

The cleaner coughed reprovingly. Conversation was permitted, but physical contact was not.

Walli said: "You know I can't stay here in the East."

"Couldn't your father get a lawyer?" she said. "Or exert some political pressure? The government might issue a pardon, if all the circumstances were explained."

Karolin's family was not political. Walli's was, and he knew with total certainty that he was never going to receive a pardon for killing a border guard. "It's impossible," he said. "If I stay here they'll execute me for murder."

"So what can you do?"

"I have to go back to the West, and I have to stay there, unless Communism collapses, and I don't see that happening in my lifetime."

"No."

"You'll have to come with me to West Berlin."

"How?"

"We'll go out the way I came in. Some students have dug a tunnel under Bernauer Strasse." He looked at his watch. Time was passing quickly. "We need to be there around sundown."

She looked horrified. "Today?"

"Yes, right away."

"Oh, God."

"Wouldn't you prefer our child to grow up in a free country?"

She grimaced as if in pain at the conflict within her. "I'd prefer not to take terrible risks."

"So would I. But we have no choice."

She looked away from him, at the rows of pews and the assiduous cleaner, and at a plaque on the wall saying I AM THE WAY, THE TRUTH, AND THE LIFE. It was not helpful, Walli thought, but Karolin made up her mind. "Then let's go," she said, and she stood up.

They left the church. Walli headed north. Karolin was subdued, and he tried to cheer her up. "The Bobbsey Twins are having an adventure," he said. She smiled briefly.

Walli considered whether they might be under surveillance. He was pretty sure no one had seen him leave his parents' house this morning: he had gone out the back way and no one had followed him. But did Karolin have a tail? Perhaps there had been another man waiting outside her college for her to emerge, someone expert at making himself inconspicuous.

Walli started to look behind him every minute or so to check whether there might be one person always in view. He did not see anyone suspicious, but he succeeded in spooking Karolin. "What are you doing?" she said fearfully.

"Checking for a tail."

"You mean the man in the cap?"

"Maybe. Let's catch a bus." They were passing a stop, and Walli pulled Karolin to the end of the queue.

"Why?"

"To see if anyone gets on and off with us."

Unfortunately it was rush hour, and millions of Berliners were catching buses and trains home. By the time a bus came, there were several people in line behind Walli and Karolin. As they boarded he looked hard at each of them. There was a woman in a raincoat, a pretty girl, a man in blue overalls, a man in a suit with a trilby hat, and two teenagers.

They rode the bus three stops east, then got off. The woman in the raincoat and the man in overalls got off behind them. Walli headed west, going back the way they had come, figuring that anyone who followed them on such an illogical route must be suspicious.

But no one did.

"I'm pretty sure we're not being tailed," he said to Karolin.

"I'm so scared," she said.

The sun was going down. They needed to hurry. They turned north, heading for Wedding. Walli checked behind him again. He saw a middle-aged man in the brown canvas coat of a warehouseman, but no one he had noticed earlier. "I think we're all right," he said.

"I'm not going to see my family again, am I?" Karolin said.

"Not for a while," Walli replied. "Unless they escape, too."

"My father would never leave. He loves his buses."

"They have buses in the West."

"You don't know him."

Walli did know him, and Karolin was right. Her father was as different as could be from the clever, strong-willed

Werner. Karolin's father had no political or religious ideas and cared nothing for freedom of speech. If he lived in a democracy he probably would not bother to vote. He liked his work and his family and his pub. His favorite food was bread. Communism gave him everything he needed. He would never escape to the West.

It was twilight when Walli and Karolin reached Strelitzer Strasse.

Karolin became increasingly jumpy as they walked along the street toward where it dead-ended at the Wall.

Ahead Walli noticed a young couple with a child. He wondered if they, too, were escaping. Yes, they were: they opened the door to the yard and disappeared.

Walli and Karolin reached the place, and Walli said: "We go in here."

Karolin said: "I want my mother with me when I have the baby."

"We're almost there!" Walli said. "Through this door there's a yard with a hatch. We go down the shaft and along the tunnel to freedom!"

"I'm not scared of escaping," she said. "I'm scared of giving birth."

"You'll be fine," Walli said desperately. "They have great hospitals in the West. You'll be surrounded by doctors and nurses."

"I want my mother," she said.

Over her shoulder Walli saw, four hundred yards away at the corner of the street, the man in the brown canvas coat talking to a policeman. "Shit!" he said. "We *were* followed." He looked at the door, then at Karolin. "It's now or never," he said. "I have no choice, I have to go. Are you coming with me, or not?"

She was crying. "I want to, but I can't," she said.

A car came around the corner, traveling fast. It stopped beside the policeman and the tail. A familiar figure jumped out of the car, a tall man with a stoop: Hans Hoffmann. He spoke to the man in the brown coat.

Walli said to Karolin: "Either follow me, or walk quickly away from here. There's going to be trouble." He stared at her. "I love you," he said. Then he dashed through the door.

Standing over the hatch was Cristina, still wearing the head scarf and the gun in her belt. When she saw Walli she threw the iron doors open. "You may need that gun," Walli said to her. "The police are coming."

He took one look back. The wooden door in the wall remained shut. Karolin had not followed him. Pain twisted in his stomach: it was the end.

He scrambled down the steps.

In the cellar the young couple with the child were standing with one of the students. "Hurry!" Walli yelled. "The police are coming!"

They went down the shaft: mother first, then child, then father. The child was slow on the ladder.

Cristina came down the steps and shut the iron trapdoor behind her with a clang. "How did the police get onto us?" she said.

"The Stasi were following my girlfriend."

"You stupid fool, you've betrayed us all."

"Then I'll go last," Walli said.

The male student went down the shaft, and Cristina made to follow.

"Give me your gun," Walli said.

She hesitated.

Walli said: "If I'm behind you, you won't be able to use it."

She handed it to him.

He took it gingerly. It looked exactly like the pistol his father had pulled from its hiding place in the kitchen, the day Rebecca and Bernd had escaped.

Cristina noticed his unease. "Have you ever fired a gun?" she said.

"Never."

She took it back from him and moved a lever near the hammer. "Now the safety catch is off," she said. "All you do is point it and pull the trigger." She put the safety catch on again and handed the gun back to him. Then she went down the ladder.

Walli could hear shouts and car engines outside. He could not guess what the police were doing, but it was clear he was running out of time.

He saw how things had gone wrong. Hans Hoffmann had had Karolin under surveillance, no doubt hoping that Walli might come back for her. The tail had seen her meet a boy and go off with him. Someone had decided not to arrest them immediately, but to see whether they would lead their watchers to a group of coconspirators. There had been a slick change of personnel after they got off the bus, and a new follower had taken over, the man in the brown coat. At some point he had realized they were heading for the Wall, and had pressed the panic button.

Now the police and the Stasi were outside, searching the rear of the derelict buildings, trying to figure out where Walli and Karolin had gone. They would find the trapdoor any second now.

With the pistol in his hand Walli went down the shaft, following the others.

As he reached the foot of the ladder he heard the clang of the iron hatch. The police had located the entrance. A moment later there were gruff shouts of surprise and triumph as they saw the hole in the floor.

Walli had to wait a long, agonizing moment at the mouth of the tunnel, until Cristina disappeared inside. He followed her, then stopped. He was slim, and he was just about able to turn in the narrow passage. He peeked out, looking up the shaft, and saw the bulk of a policeman stepping onto the ladder.

This was hopeless. The police were too close. All they had to do was point their guns into the tunnel and fire. Walli himself would be shot, and when he fell the bullets would pass over him and hit the next in line—and so on: the slaughter would be bloody. And he knew they would not hesitate to shoot, for no mercy was shown to escapers, ever. It would be carnage.

He had to keep them out of the shaft.

But he did not want to kill another man.

Kneeling just inside the mouth of the tunnel, he moved the safety catch of the Walther. Then he put his hand holding the gun outside the tunnel, pointed it upward, and pulled the trigger.

The gun kicked in his hand. The bang was very loud in the confined space. Immediately afterward he heard shouts of dismay and fear, but not of pain, and he guessed he had scared them without actually hitting anyone. He peeped out and saw the cop scrambling back up the ladder and out of the shaft.

He waited. He knew the escapers ahead of him would be

slow, because of the child. He could hear the cops discussing in angry tones what they were going to do. None of them was willing to go down the shaft: it was suicide, one said. But they could not just let people escape!

To reinforce the danger to them, Walli fired the gun again. He heard sudden panic movements as if they had all pulled back from the shaft. He thought he had succeeded in scaring them off. He turned to crawl away.

Then he heard a voice he knew well. Hans Hoffmann said: "We need grenades."

"Oh, fuck," said Walli.

He stuck the gun in his belt and began to crawl along the tunnel. There was nothing for it now but to get as far along as possible. In no time he felt Cristina's shoes in front of him. "Hurry up!" he yelled. "The cops are getting grenades!"

"I can't go faster than the guy in front of me!" she yelled back.

All Walli could do was follow. It was dark now. He heard no sound from the cellar to his rear. Regular cops were not normally equipped with grenades, he guessed, but Hans could get some from nearby border guards in a couple of minutes.

Walli could see nothing, but he could hear the panting of his fellow fugitives, and the scrape of their knees on the boards. The child began to cry. Yesterday Walli would have cursed it for a dangerous nuisance, but today he was a father-to-be, and he felt only pity for the frightened kid.

What would the police do with their grenades? Would they play safe, and drop one into the shaft, where it might do little damage? Or would one have the nerve to climb down the ladder and throw one lethally into the tunnel? That might kill all the escapers.

Walli decided he had to do more to discourage the cops. He lay down, rolled over, pulled the gun, and raised himself on his left elbow. He could see nothing, but he pointed the gun back along the tunnel and pulled the trigger.

Several people screamed.

Cristina said: "What was that?"

Walli put the gun away and resumed crawling. "I was just discouraging the cops."

"Warn us next time, for Christ's sake."

He saw light ahead. The tunnel seemed shorter going back. He heard cries of relief as people realized they were at the end. He found himself going faster, pushing up against Cristina's shoes.

Behind him, there was an explosion.

He felt the shock wave, but it was weak, and he knew immediately that they had dropped the first grenade into the down shaft. He had never paid enough attention to physics in school, but he guessed that in those circumstances nearly all the explosive force would go upward.

However, he could foresee what Hans would do next. Having made sure there was no longer someone lying in wait inside the tunnel entrance, he would now send a cop down the ladder to throw a grenade into the tunnel.

Ahead the group was emerging into the cellar of the disused grocery. "Quickly!" Walli yelled. "Climb the ladder fast!"

Cristina exited the tunnel and stood in the shaft, smiling. "Relax," she said. "This is the West. We're out—we're free!"

"Grenades!" Walli yelled. "Go up, fast as you can!"

The couple with the child was climbing the ladder with painful slowness. The male student and Cristina followed. Walli stood at the foot of the ladder, trembling with impatience and fear. He went up right behind Cristina, his face at her knees. He reached the top and saw them all standing around, laughing and hugging. "Lie flat!" he yelled. "Grenades!" He threw himself to the floor.

There was a terrific boom. The shock wave seemed to rock the cellar. Then there was a gushing sound like a fountain, and he guessed that earth was spurting from the mouth of the tunnel. Confirming his guess, a rain of mud and small stones fell on him. The hoist over the shaft collapsed and fell into the hole.

The noise died away. The cellar was quiet except for the sobbing of the child. Walli looked around. The kid had a nosebleed, but seemed otherwise unhurt, and no one else appeared injured. He looked over the lip of the shaft and saw that the tunnel had fallen in.

He stood upright, shakily. He had made it. He was alive and free.

And alone.

. . .

Rebecca had spent a lot of her father's money on the apartment in Hamburg. The place was the ground floor of a grand old merchant's house. All the rooms were big enough to allow Bernd to turn the wheelchair—even the bathroom. She had installed every known aid for a man paralyzed from the waist down. Walls and ceilings were festooned with ropes and grab handles that enabled him to wash and dress himself and get in and out of bed. He could even cook in the kitchen, if he wanted to, though like most men he could not prepare anything more complicated than eggs.

She was determined—furiously determined—that she and Bernd were going to live as normal an existence as possible, despite his injury. They would enjoy their marriage and their work and their freedom. Life for them would be busy and varied and satisfying. Anything less would give the victory to the tyrants on the other side of the Wall.

Bernd's condition had not changed since he left the hospital. The doctors said he might improve, and he should keep hoping. One day, they insisted, he might be able to father children. Rebecca should never stop trying.

She felt she had a lot to be happy about. She was teaching again, doing what she was good at, opening the minds of young people to the intellectual riches of the world they lived in. She was in love with Bernd, whose kindness and humor made every day a pleasure. They were free to read what they liked, think what they liked, and say what they liked, without having to worry about police spies.

Rebecca had a long-term aim, too. She yearned to be reunited with her family one day. Not her original family: the memory of her biological parents was poignant, but distant and vague. However, Carla had rescued her from the hell of war, and had made her feel safe and loved, even when they were all hungry and cold and scared. Over the years the house in Mitte had filled with people to love and be loved by Rebecca: baby Walli; then her new father, Werner; then a baby girl, Lili. Even Grandmother Maud, that impossibly dignified old English lady, had loved and cared for Rebecca.

She would be reunited with them when all West Germans were reunited with all East Germans. Many people thought that day might never come. Perhaps they were right. But Carla and Werner had taught Rebecca that if you wanted change you had to take political action to get it. "In my family, apathy isn't an option," Rebecca had said to Bernd. So they had joined the Free Democratic Party, which was liberal, though not as socialist as Willy Brandt's Social Democratic Party. Rebecca was branch secretary and Bernd was treasurer.

In West Germany you could join any party you liked except the Communist Party, which was banned. Rebecca disapproved of that prohibition. She hated Communism, but banning it was the kind of thing Communists did, not democrats.

Rebecca and Bernd drove to work together every day. They came home after school, and Bernd laid the table while Rebecca prepared dinner. Some days, after they had eaten, Bernd's masseur came. Because Bernd could not move his legs, they had to be massaged regularly to improve the circulation and prevent, or at least slow, the wasting of nerves and muscles. Rebecca cleared away while Bernd went into the bedroom with the masseur, Heinz.

This evening she sat down with a pile of exercise books and began marking. She had asked her pupils to write an imaginary advertisement about the attractions of Moscow as a holiday destination. They liked tongue-in-cheek assignments.

After an hour Heinz departed, and Rebecca went into the bedroom.

Bernd lay naked on the bed. His upper body was strongly muscular, because he constantly had to use his arms to move himself. His legs looked like those of an old man, thin and pale.

He usually felt good, physically and mentally, after massage. Rebecca leaned over him and kissed his lips, long and slow. "I love you," she said. "I'm so happy to be with you." She said it often, because it was true, and because he needed reassurance: she knew that sometimes he wondered how she could love a cripple.

She stood facing him and took off her clothes. He liked her to do this, he said, even though it never gave him a hard-on. She had learned that paralyzed men rarely got psychogenic erections, the kind caused by sexy sights or thoughts.

All the same his eyes followed her with evident enjoyment as she unfastened her bra, slid her stockings off, and stepped out of her panties.

"You look great," he said.

"And I'm all yours."

"Lucky me."

She lay beside him and they caressed each other languorously. Sex with Bernd, before and after his accident, had always been about soft kisses and murmured endearments, not just fucking. In that way he was different from her first husband. Hans had had a program: kiss, undress, get hard, come. Bernd's philosophy was anything you like, in any order.

After a while she straddled him, then maneuvered so that he could kiss her breasts and suck her nipples. He had adored her breasts right from the start, and now he enjoyed them with the same intensity and relish as before the accident; and that aroused her more than anything.

When she was ready, she said: "Do you want to try?"

"Sure," he said. "We should always try."

She moved back, so that she was astride his withered legs, and bent over his penis. She manipulated it with her hand. It grew a little, and he got what was called a reflex erection. For a few moments it was hard enough to go inside her, then it quickly subsided. "Never mind," she said.

"I don't mind," he said, but she knew it was not true. He would have liked to have an orgasm. He wanted children, too.

She lay beside him, took his hand, and placed it on her vagina. He positioned his fingers in the way she had taught him, then she pressed his hand with her own and moved rhythmically. It was like masturbation, but using his hand. He stroked her hair fondly with his other hand. It worked, as it always did, and she had a delightful orgasm.

Lying beside him afterward, she said: "Thank you."

"You're welcome."

"Not just for that."

"What, then?"

"For coming with me. For escaping. I can never tell you enough how grateful I am."

"Good."

The doorbell rang. They looked at one another in puzzlement: they expected no one. Bernd said: "Maybe Heinz left something behind."

Rebecca was mildly annoyed. Her euphoria had been shattered. She put on a robe and went to the door, feeling grumpy.

There stood Walli. He looked thin and smelled ripe. He wore jeans, American baseball shoes, and a grubby shirt—no coat. He was carrying a guitar and nothing else.

"Hello, Rebecca," he said.

Her grumpiness evaporated in a flash. She smiled broadly. "Walli!" she said. "What a wonderful surprise! I'm so happy to see you!"

She stood back and he stepped into the hallway.

"What are you doing here?" she said.

"I've come to live with you," he said.

CHAPTER TWENTY-TWO

The most racist city in America was probably Birmingham, Alabama. George Jakes flew there in April 1963.

Last time he came to Alabama, he recalled vividly, they had tried to kill him.

Birmingham was a dirty industrial city, and from the plane it had a delicate rose-pink aura of pollution, like the chiffon scarf around the neck of an old prostitute.

George felt the hostility as he walked through the terminal. He was the only colored man in a suit. He remembered the attack on him and Maria and the Freedom Riders in Anniston, just sixty miles away: the bombs, the baseball bats, the whirling lengths of iron chain, and most of all the faces, twisted and deformed into masks of hatred and madness.

He walked out of the airport, located the taxi stand, and got into the first car in line.

"Get out of the car, boy," said the driver.

"I beg your pardon?"

"I don't drive for no goddamn nigras."

George sighed. He was reluctant to get out. He felt like sitting there in protest. He did not like to make things easy for racists. But he had a job to do in Birmingham, and he could not do it in jail. So he got out.

Standing by the open door, he looked down the line. The car behind had a white driver: he assumed he would get the same treatment again. Then, three cars back, a dark brown arm came out of the window and waved at him.

He stepped away from the first cab.

"Close the door!" the driver yelled.

George hesitated, then said: "I don't close doors for no goddamn segregationists." It was not a very good line, but it gave him some small satisfaction, and he walked away leaving the door wide open.

He jumped into the cab with the black driver. "I know where you're going," the man said. "Sixteenth Street Baptist Church."

The church was the base of fiery preacher Fred Shuttlesworth. He had founded the Alabama Christian Movement for Human Rights, after the state courts outlawed the moderate National Association for the Advancement of Colored People. Clearly, George thought, any Negro arriving at the airport was assumed to be a civil rights campaigner.

But George was not going to the church. "Take me to the Gaston Motel, please," he said.

"I know the Gaston," said the driver. "I saw Little Stevie Wonder in the lounge there. It's just a block from the church."

It was a hot day and the cab had no air-conditioning. George wound down the window and let the slipstream cool his perspiring skin.

He had been sent by Bobby Kennedy with a message for Martin Luther King. The message was stop pushing, calm things down, end your protests, things are changing. George had a feeling that Dr. King was not going to like it.

The Gaston was a low-built modern hotel. Its owner, A. G. Gaston, was a coal miner who had become Birmingham's leading black businessman. George knew that Gaston was nervous about the disruption being brought to Birmingham by King's campaign, but gave his qualified support nonetheless. George's taxi drove through the entrance into a motor court.

Martin Luther King was in Room 30, the motel's only suite; but before seeing him George had lunch with Verena Marquand in the nearby Jockey Boy Restaurant. When he asked for his hamburger medium rare, the waitress looked at him as if he were speaking a foreign language.

Verena ordered a salad. She looked more alluring than ever in white pants and a black blouse. George wondered if she had a boyfriend. "You're on a downhill slope," he said to her while they were waiting for their food. "First Atlanta, now Birmingham. Come to Washington, before you find yourself stuck in Mudslide, Mississippi." He was teasing, but he did think that if she came to Washington he might ask her out on a date.

"I go where the movement takes me," she replied seriously.

Their lunch arrived. "Why did King decide to target this town?" George asked while they were eating.

"The commissioner of public safety—effectively the chief of police—is a vicious white racist called Eugene 'Bull' Connor."

"I've seen his name in the papers."

"The nickname tells you all you need to know about him. As if that were not enough, Birmingham also has the most violent chapter of the Ku Klux Klan."

"Any idea why?"

"This is a steel town, and the industry is in decline. Skilled, high-wage jobs have always been reserved for white men, while blacks do low-paid work such as cleaning. Now the whites are desperately trying to maintain their prosperity and privileges—just at the moment when blacks are asking for their fair share."

It was a crisp analysis, and George's respect for Verena went up a notch. "How does that show itself?"

"Klan members throw homemade bombs at the homes of prosperous Negroes in mixed neighborhoods. Some people call this town Bombingham. Needless to say, the police never arrest anyone for the bombings, and the FBI somehow just can't seem to figure out who might be doing it."

"No surprise there. J. Edgar Hoover can't find the Mafia, either. But he knows the name of every Communist in America."

"However, white rule is weakening here. Some people are beginning to realize it does the town no good. Bull Connor just lost an election for mayor."

"I know. The White House view is that Birmingham's Negroes will get what they want in due course, if they're patient."

"Dr. King's view is that now is the time to pile on the pressure."

"And how is that working out?"

"To be frank, we're disappointed. When we sit in at a lunch counter, the waitresses turn out the lights and say sorry, they're closing."

"A clever move. Some towns did something similar to the Freedom Riders. Instead of making a fuss, they just ignored what was happening. But that level of restraint is too much for most segregationists, and they soon reverted to beating people up."

"Bull Connor won't give us a permit to demonstrate, so our marches are illegal, and the protesters are usually jailed; but they're too few to make the national news."

"So maybe it's time for another change of tactics."

A young black woman came into the café and approached their table. "The Reverend Dr. King is free to see you now, Mr. Jakes."

George and Verena left their lunches half-eaten. As with the president, you did not ask Dr. King to wait while you finished what you were doing.

They returned to the Gaston and went upstairs to King's suite. As always, he was dressed in a dark business suit: the heat seemed to make little difference to him. George was struck again by how small he was, and how handsome. This time King was less wary, more welcoming. "Sit down, please," he said, waving to a couch. His voice was mild even when his words were barbed: "What has the attorney general got to tell me that he can't say over the phone?"

"He wants you to consider delaying your campaign here in Alabama."

"Somehow I'm not surprised."

"He supports what you're trying to achieve, but he feels the protest may be ill timed."

"Tell me why."

"Bull Connor has just lost the election for mayor to Albert Boutwell. There's a new city government. Boutwell is a reformer."

"Some people feel Boutwell is just a more dignified version of Bull Connor."

"Reverend, that may be so; but Bobby would like you to give Boutwell the chance to prove himself—one way or the other."

"I see. So that message is: Wait."

"Yes, sir."

King looked at Verena, as if inviting her to comment, but she said nothing.

After a moment King said: "Last September, Birmingham businessmen promised to remove humiliating WHITES ONLY signs from their stores and, in return, Fred Shuttlesworth agreed to a moratorium on demonstrations. We kept our promise, but the businessmen broke theirs. As has happened so many times, our hopes were blasted."

"I'm sorry to hear that," said George. "But—"

King ignored the interruption. "Nonviolent direct action seeks to create so much tension, and sense of crisis, that a community is forced to confront the issue and open the door to sincere negotiation. You ask me to give Boutwell time to show his true colors. Boutwell may be less of a brute than Connor, but he is a segregationist, dedicated to keeping the status quo. He needs to be prodded to act."

This was so reasonable that George could not even pretend to disagree, though the likelihood of his changing King's mind seemed to be fading rapidly.

"We have never made a gain, in civil rights, without pressure," King went on. "Frankly, George, I have yet to engage in a campaign that was 'well timed' in the eyes of men such as Bobby Kennedy. For years now I have heard the word 'Wait.' It rings in my ears with piercing familiarity. This 'Wait' always means 'Never.' We have waited three hundred and forty years for our rights. African nations are moving with jetlike speed toward independence, but we still creep at horse-and-buggy pace toward gaining a cup of coffee at a lunch counter."

George realized now that he was hearing a sermon being rehearsed, but he was no less mesmerized. He had abandoned all hope of fulfilling his mission for Bobby.

"Our great stumbling block, in our stride toward freedom, is not the White Citizens' Councilor or the Ku Klux Klanner. It's the white moderate who is more devoted to order than to justice; who constantly says, like Bobby Kennedy: 'I agree with the goal you seek, but I cannot condone your methods.' He paternalistically believes he can set the timetable for another man's freedom."

Now George felt ashamed, for he was Bobby's messenger.

"We will have to repent, in this generation, not merely for the hateful words and actions of bad people, but for the appalling silence of the good," King said, and George had to struggle against tears. "The time is always ripe to do right. 'Let justice roll down like waters, and righteousness like an ever-flowing stream,' said the prophet Amos. You tell Bobby Kennedy that, George."

"Yes, sir, I will," said George.

.   .   .

When George got back to Washington he called Cindy Bell, the girl his mother had tried to fix him up with, and asked her for a date. She said: "Why not?"

It would be his first date since he had dumped Norine Latimer in the doomed hope of romancing Maria Summers.

He took a taxi to Cindy's place the following Saturday evening. She was still living at her parents' home, a small working-class house. Her father opened the door. He had a bushy beard: George guessed a chef did not need to look neat. "I'm glad to meet you, George," he said. "Your mother is one of the finest people I've ever known. I hope you don't mind me saying something so personal."

"Thank you, Mr. Bell," said George. "I agree with you."

"Come in, Cindy's almost ready."

George noticed a small crucifix on the wall in the hallway, and remembered that the Bells were Catholic. He recalled being told, as a teenager, that convent schoolgirls were the hottest.

Cindy appeared in a tight sweater and a short skirt that made her father frown a little, though he said nothing. George had to smother a smile. She was curvy and did not want to hide it. A small silver cross on a chain hung between her generous breasts—for protection, perhaps?

George handed her a small box of chocolates tied up with a blue ribbon.

Outside, she raised her eyebrows at the taxi.

"I'm going to buy a car," George said. "I just haven't had time."

As they drove downtown, Cindy said: "My father admires your mother for raising you on her own, and making such a good job of it."

"And they lend each other books," said George. "Is your mom okay with all that?"

Cindy giggled. The idea of sexual jealousy in the parental generation was naturally comical. "You're sharp. Mom knows nothing else is going on—but all the same she's on her guard."

George felt glad he had asked her out. She was intelligent and warm, and he was beginning to think how pleasant it would be to kiss her. The thought of Maria became dim in his mind.

They went to an Italian restaurant. Cindy confessed that she loved all kinds of pasta. They had tagliatelle with mushrooms, then veal escalopes in a sherry sauce.

She had a degree from Georgetown University, but she told him she was working as a secretary to a black insurance broker. "Girls get hired as secretaries, even after college," she said. "I'd like to do government work. I know people think it's dull, but Washington runs this whole country. Unfortunately, the government hires mostly white people for the important jobs."

"That's true."

"How did you break in?"

"Bobby Kennedy wanted a black face on his team, to make him look sincere about civil rights."

"So you're a symbol."

"I was, at the start. It's better now."

After dinner they went to see Tippi Hedren and Rod Taylor in Alfred Hitchcock's latest film, *The Birds*. During the scary scenes, Cindy clung to George in a way he found delightful.

On the way out, they disagreed amiably about the ending of the movie. Cindy hated it. "I was so disappointed!" she said. "I was looking forward to the explanation."

George shrugged. "Not everything in life has an explanation."

"Yes, it does, but sometimes we just don't know it."

They went to the bar of the Fairfax Hotel for a nightcap. He ordered Scotch and she had a daiquiri. Her silver cross caught his eye. "Is that just jewelry, or something more?" he said.

"Something more," she replied. "It makes me feel safe."

"Safe from . . . anything in particular?"

"No. It just guards me, generally."

George was skeptical. "You don't believe that."

"Why not?"

"Uh . . . I don't want to offend you, if you're sincere, but it seems superstitious to me."

"I thought you were religious. You go to church, don't you?"

"I go with my mother because it's important to her, and I love her. To make her happy, I'll sing hymns and listen to prayers and hear a sermon, all of which seem to me to be just . . . mumbo jumbo."

"Don't you believe in God?"

"I think there's probably a controlling intelligence in the universe, a being that decided the rules, such as E equals MC squared, and the value of pi. But that being isn't likely to care whether we sing its praise or not, I doubt whether its decisions can be manipulated by praying to a statue of the Virgin Mary, and I don't believe it will organize special treatment for you on account of what you have around your neck."

"Oh."

He saw that he had shocked her. He realized he had been arguing as if at a White House meeting, where the issues were too important for anyone to care about other people's feelings. "I probably shouldn't be so direct," he said. "Are you offended?"

"No," she said. "I'm glad you told me." She finished her drink.

George put some money down on the bar and slid off his stool. "I've enjoyed talking to you," he said.

"Nice movie, disappointing ending," she said.

That summed up the evening. She was likable and attractive, but he could not see himself falling for a woman whose beliefs about the universe were so much at odds with his own.

They went outside and got a cab.

On the ride back, George realized that in his heart of hearts he was not sorry the date had not worked out. He still had not fully got over Maria. He wondered how much longer it was going to take.

When they reached Cindy's house she said: "Thank you for a lovely evening." She kissed his cheek and got out of the car.

Next day Bobby sent George back to Alabama.

George and Verena stood in Kelly Ingram Park, in the heart of black Birmingham, at twelve noon on Friday, May 3, 1963. Across the road was the famous Sixteenth Street Baptist Church, a magnificent redbrick Byzantine building designed by a black architect. The park was crowded with civil rights campaigners, bystanders, and anxious parents.

They could hear singing from inside the church: "Ain't Gonna Let Nobody Turn Me Round." A thousand black high school students were getting ready to march.

To the east of the park, the avenues leading downtown were blocked by hundreds of police. Bull Connor had commandeered school buses to take the marchers to jail, and he had attack dogs in case anyone refused to go. The police were backed up by firemen with hoses.

There were no colored men in the police force or the fire brigade.

The civil rights campaigners always applied, in the correct way, for permission to march. Every time, they were refused. When they marched nevertheless, they were arrested and sent to jail.

In consequence, most of Birmingham's Negroes were reluctant to join the demonstrations—permitting the all-white city government to claim that Martin Luther King's movement had little support.

King himself had gone to jail here exactly three weeks ago, on Good Friday. George had marveled at how crass the segregationists were: did they not know who else had been arrested on Good Friday? King had been put in solitary confinement, for no reason other than sheer malice.

But King's jailing had hardly made the papers. A Negro being mistreated for demanding his rights as an American was not news. King had been criticized by white clergymen in a letter that got big publicity. From the jail he had written a reply that smoldered with righteousness. No newspapers had printed it, though perhaps they yet would. Overall, the campaign had got little publicity.

Birmingham's black teenagers clamored to join the demonstrations, and at last King agreed to permit schoolchildren to march, but nothing changed: Bull Connor just jailed the children, and no one cared.

The sound of the hymns from inside the church was thrilling, but that was not enough. Martin Luther King's campaign in Birmingham was going nowhere, just like George's love life.

George was studying the firemen on the streets to the east of the park. They had a new type of weapon. The device appeared to take water from two inlet hoses and force it out through a single nozzle. Presumably that gave the jet supercharged force. It was mounted on a tripod, suggesting that it was too powerful for a man to hold. George was glad he was strictly an observer, and would not be taking part in the march. He suspected that the jet would do more than soak you.

The doors of the church flew open and a group of students emerged through the triple arches, dressed in their Sunday best, singing. They marched down the long, broad flight of steps to the street. There were about sixty of them, but George knew that this was only the first contingent: there were hundreds more inside. Most were high school seniors, with a sprinkling of younger kids.

George and Verena followed them at a distance. The watching crowd in the park cheered and clapped as the marchers paraded down Sixteenth, passing mostly black-owned stores and businesses. They turned east along Fifth Avenue and came to the corner of Seventeenth, where their way was blocked by police barricades.

A police captain spoke through a bullhorn. "Disperse, get off the street," he said. He pointed to the firemen behind him. "Otherwise you're going to get wet."

On previous occasions the police had simply herded demonstrators into paddy wagons and buses and taken them to jail. But, George knew, the jails were now full and overcrowded, and Bull Connor was hoping to minimize arrests today: he would prefer them all to go home.

Which was the last thing they were going to do. The sixty kids stood in the road, facing the massed ranks of white authority, and sang at the tops of their voices.

The police captain made a signal to the firemen, who turned on the water. George noted that they deployed regular hoses, not the tripod-mounted water cannon. Nevertheless the spray drove most of the marchers back, and sent the bystanders scurrying across the park and into doorways.

Through his bullhorn the captain kept repeating: "Evacuate the area! Evacuate the area!"

Most of the marchers retreated—but not all. Ten simply sat down. Already soaked to the skin, they ignored the water and continued singing.

That was when the firemen turned on the water cannon.

The effect was instant. Instead of a spurt of water, unpleasant but harmless, the seated pupils were blasted with a high-powered jet. They were knocked backward and cried out in pain. Their hymn turned to screams of fright.

The smallest of them was a little girl. The water lifted her physically from the ground and blasted her backward. She rolled along the street like a blown leaf. Her arms and legs flailed helplessly. Bystanders began yelling and cursing.

George swore and ran into the street.

The firemen relentlessly directed their tripod-mounted hose to follow the child, so that she could not escape from its force. They were trying to wash her away like a scrap of litter. George was the first of several men to reach her. He got between the hose and her, and turned his back.

It was like being punched.

The jet knocked him to his knees. But the little girl was now protected, and she got to her feet and ran toward the park. However, the fire hose followed her and tumbled her down again.

George was enraged. The firemen were like hunting dogs bringing down a young deer. Shouts of protest from bystanders told him that they, too, were infuriated.

George ran after the girl and shielded her again. This time he was prepared for the impact of the jet, and he managed to keep his balance. He knelt and picked up the child. Her pink churchgoing dress was sodden. Carrying her, he staggered toward the sidewalk. The firemen chased him with the jet, trying to knock him down again, but he stayed on his feet long enough to get to the other side of a parked car.

He set the girl on her feet. She was screaming in terror. "It's okay, you're safe now," George told her, but she could not be consoled. Then a distraught woman rushed to her and picked her up. The girl clung to the woman, and George guessed that this was her mother. Weeping, the mother carried her away.

George was bruised and sodden. He turned around to see what was happening. The marchers had all been trained in nonviolent protest, but the furious onlookers had not, and now they were retaliating, he saw, throwing rocks at the firemen. This was turning into a riot.

He could not see Verena.

Police and firemen advanced along Fifth Avenue, trying to disperse the crowd, but their progress was slowed by the hail of missiles. Several men went into the buildings along the south side of the street and bombarded the police from upstairs windows, throwing stones, bottles, and garbage. George hurried away from the fracas. He stopped on the next corner, outside the Jockey Boy Restaurant, and stood with a small group of reporters and spectators, black and white.

Looking north, he saw that more contingents of young marchers were coming out of the church and taking different southbound streets to avoid the violence. That would create a problem for Bull Connor by splitting his forces.

Connor responded by deploying the dogs.

They came out of the vans snarling, baring their teeth, and straining against their leather leashes. Their handlers looked just as vicious: thickset white men in police caps and sunglasses. Dogs and handlers alike were animals eager to attack.

Cops and dogs rushed forward in a pack. Marchers and bystanders tried to flee, but the crowd on the street was now tightly packed, and many people could not get away. The dogs were hysterical with excitement, snapping and biting and drawing blood from people's legs and arms.

Some people fled west, into the depths of the black neighborhood, chased by cops. Others took sanctuary in the church. No more marchers were emerging from the triple arches, George saw: the demonstration was coming to an end.

But the police had not yet had enough.

From nowhere, two cops with dogs appeared beside George. One grabbed hold of a tall young Negro: George had noticed him because he was wearing an expensive-looking cardigan sweater. The boy was about fifteen, and had taken no part in the demonstration other than to watch. Nevertheless the cop spun him round, and the dog leaped up and sunk its teeth into the boy's middle. He cried out in fear and pain. One of the reporters snapped a picture.

George was about to intervene when the cop pulled the dog off. Then he arrested the boy for parading without a permit.

George noticed a big-bellied white man, dressed in a shirt and no jacket, watching the arrest. From photographs in the newspapers he recognized Bull Connor. "Why didn't you bring a meaner dog?" Connor said to the arresting officer.

George felt like remonstrating with the man. He was supposed to be the commissioner of public safety, but he was acting like a street hoodlum.

But George realized he was in danger of getting arrested himself, especially now that his smart suit was a drenched rag. Bobby Kennedy would not be pleased if George ended up in jail.

With an effort, George suppressed his anger, clamped his mouth shut, turned, and walked briskly back to the Gaston.

Fortunately he had a spare pair of pants in his luggage. He took a shower, dressed again in dry clothes, and sent his suit for pressing. He called the Justice Department and dictated to a secretary his report on the day's events for Bobby Kennedy. He made his report dry and unemotional, and left out the fact that he had been fire-hosed.

He found Verena again in the lounge of the hotel. She had escaped without injury, but she looked shaken. "They can do anything they like to us!" she said, and there was a note of hysteria in her voice. He felt the same, but it was worse for her. Unlike George, she had not been a Freedom Rider, and he guessed this might be the first time she had seen violent racial hatred in its naked horror.

"Let me buy you a drink," he said, and they went to the bar.

Over the next hour he talked her down. Mostly he just listened; every now and again he said something sympathetic or reassuring; he helped her become calm by being calm himself. The effort brought his own boiling passions under control.

They had dinner together quietly in the hotel restaurant. It was just dark when they went upstairs. In the corridor Verena said: "Will you come to my room?"

He was surprised. It had not been a romantic or sexy evening, and he had not regarded it as a date. They were just two fellow-campaigners commiserating.

She saw his hesitation. "I just want someone to hold me," she said. "Is that all right?"

He was not sure he understood, but he nodded.

The image of Maria flashed into his mind. He suppressed it. It was time he forgot her.

When they were in the room she closed the door and put her arms around him. He pressed her body to his and kissed her forehead. She turned her face away and laid her cheek against his shoulder. Okay, he thought, you want to hug but you don't want to kiss. He made up his mind to simply follow her cues. Whatever she wanted would be all right with him.

After a minute she said: "I don't want to sleep alone."

"Okay," he said neutrally.

"Can we just cuddle?"

"Yes," he said, though he could not believe it would happen that way.

She drew away from his embrace. Then, quickly, she stepped out of her shoes and pulled her dress over her head. She was wearing a white brassiere and panties. He stared at her perfect creamy skin. She took off her underwear in a couple of seconds. Her breasts were flat and firm with tiny nipples. Her pubic hair had an auburn tinge. She was the most beautiful woman he had ever seen naked—by far.

He took it all in at a glance, for she immediately got into bed.

George turned away and took off his shirt.

Verena said: "Your back! Oh, God—it's awful!"

George felt sore from the fire hose, but it had not occurred to him that the damage would show. He stood with his back to the mirror by the door and looked over his shoulder. He saw what Verena meant: his skin was a mass of purple bruises.

He took off his shoes and socks slowly. He had an erection, and he was hoping it would go down, but it did not. He could not help it. He stood up and took off his pants and undershorts, then he got into bed as quickly as she had.

They hugged. His erection pressed into her belly, but she showed no reaction. Her hair tickled his neck and her breasts were squashed against his chest. He was madly aroused, but instinct told him to be still, and he obeyed it.

Verena began to cry. At first she made small moaning noises, and George was not sure whether they indicated sexual feelings. Then he felt her warm tears on his chest, and she began to shake with sobbing. He patted her back in the primal gesture of comfort.

A part of his mind marveled at what he was doing. He was naked in bed with a beautiful woman and all he could do was pat her back. But on a deeper level it made sense. He had a vague but sure feeling that they were giving one another a kind of comfort stronger than sex. They were both in the grip of an intense emotion, albeit one for which George did not have a name.

Verena's sobs gradually eased. After a while her body relaxed, her breathing became regular and shallow, and she drifted into the helplessness of sleep.

George's erection subsided. He closed his eyes and concentrated on the warmth of her body against his, and the light feminine aroma that rose from her skin and her hair. With such a girl in his arms he felt sure he would not sleep.

But he did.

When he woke up in the morning, she was gone.

.   .   .

On that Saturday morning Maria Summers went to work in a pessimistic mood.

While Martin Luther King had been in jail in Alabama, the Commission on Civil Rights had produced a horrifying report on abuse of Negroes in Mississippi. But the Kennedy administration had cleverly undermined the report. A Justice Department lawyer called Burke Marshall had written a memo quibbling with its findings; Maria's boss, Pierre Salinger, had portrayed its proposals as extremist; and the American press had been fooled.

And the man Maria loved was in charge. President Kennedy had a good heart, she believed, but his eye was always on the next election. He had done well in last year's midterms: his coolheaded handling of the Cuban missile crisis had won him popularity, and the expected Republican landslide had been averted. But now he was worrying about his reelection contest next year. He did not like Southern segregationists, but he was not willing to sacrifice himself in the battle against them.

So the civil rights campaign was fizzling out.

Maria's brother had four children of whom she was very fond. They, and any children Maria herself might have in the future, were going to grow up to be second-class Americans. If they traveled in the South they would have trouble finding a hotel willing to take them in. If they went to a white church they would be turned away, unless the pastor considered himself a liberal and directed them to a special roped-off seating area for Negroes. They would see a sign saying WHITES ONLY outside public toilets, and a sign directing COLOREDS to a bucket in the backyard. They would ask why there were no black people on television, and their parents would not know how to answer them.

Then she reached the office and saw the newspapers.

On the front page of *The New York Times* was a photograph from Birmingham that made Maria gasp with horror. It showed a white policeman with a savage German shepherd dog. The dog was biting a harmless-looking Negro teenager while the cop held the boy by his cardigan sweater. The cop's teeth were bared in a grin of eager malice, as if he wanted to bite someone too.

Nelly Fordham heard Maria's gasp and looked up from *The Washington Post*. "Ugly, ain't it?" she commented.

The same picture was on the front of many other American newspapers, and the airmail editions of foreign papers too.

Maria sat at her desk and began to read. The tone had altered, she noticed with a gleam of hope. It was no longer possible for the press to point the finger of blame at Martin Luther King and say that his campaign was ill timed and Negroes should be patient. The story had changed, with the unstoppable chemistry of media coverage, a mysterious process that Maria had learned to respect and fear.

Her excitement grew as she began to suspect that the white Southerners had gone too far. The press was now talking about violence against children on the streets of America. They still quoted men who said it was all the fault of King and his agitators, but the segregationists' customary tone of confident deprecation had gone, and now there was a note of desperate denial. Was it possible that one photograph could change everything?

Salinger came into the room. "Everybody," he said. "The president looked at the papers this morning, saw the photographs from Birmingham, and felt sickened—and he would like the press to know it. This is not an official statement, but it is an off-the-record briefing. The key word is *sickened*. Put it out right away, please."

Maria looked at Nelly and they both raised their eyebrows. This was a change.

Maria picked up the phone.

. . .

By Monday morning, George was moving like an old man, cautiously, trying to minimize the twinges of pain. The Birmingham Fire Department's water cannon produced a pressure of one hundred pounds per square inch, according to the newspapers, and George could feel every pound on every inch of his back.

He was not the only one hurting on Monday morning. Hundreds of demonstrators were bruised. Some had been dog-bitten badly enough to need stitches. Thousands of schoolchildren were still in jail.

George prayed their sufferings would prove worthwhile.

There was hope now. The wealthy white businessmen of Birmingham wanted to end the conflict. No one was shopping: a black boycott of downtown stores had been made more effective by the fear of whites that they might get caught up in a riot. Even the hard-nosed owners of steel mills and factories felt that their businesses were being damaged by the city's reputation as the world capital of violent racism.

And the White House hated the continuing global headlines. Foreign newspapers, taking for granted the Negroes' right to justice and democracy, could not understand why the American president seemed unable to enforce his own laws.

Bobby Kennedy sent Burke Marshall to try to make a deal with Birmingham's leading citizens. Dennis Wilson was his aide. George did not trust either. Marshall had undermined the Commission on Civil Rights report with legal quibbles, and Dennis had always been jealous of George.

Birmingham's white elite would not negotiate directly with Martin Luther King, so Dennis and George had to act as go-betweens, with Verena representing King.

Burke Marshall wanted King to call off Monday's demonstration. "And take the pressure off, just when we're gaining the advantage?" said Verena incredulously to Dennis Wilson in the swanky lounge of the Gaston Motel. George nodded agreement.

"The city government can't do anything right now anyway," Dennis responded.

The city government was going through a separate but related crisis: Bull Connor had mounted a legal challenge to the election he had lost, so there were two men claiming to be mayor. Verena said: "So they're divided and weakened—good! If we wait for them to resolve their differences, they'll come back stronger and more determined. Don't you White House people know anything about politics?"

Dennis pretended that the civil rights campaigners were muddled about what they wanted. That, too, infuriated Verena. "We have four simple demands," she said. "One: immediate desegregation of lunch counters, restrooms, water fountains, all facilities in stores. Two: nondiscriminatory hiring and promotion of black employees in the stores. Three: all demonstrators to be released from jail, and charges dropped. Four: for the future, a biracial committee to negotiate desegregation of the police, schools, parks, movie theaters, and hotels." She glared at Dennis. "Anything muddled there?"

King was asking for things that should have been taken for granted, but all the same it was too much for the whites. That evening, Dennis came back to the Gaston and told George and Verena the counterproposals. The store owners were willing to desegregate fitting rooms immediately, other facilities after a delay. Five or six black employees could be promoted to "tie jobs" as soon as the demonstrations ended. The businessmen could do nothing about the prisoners, because that was a matter for the courts. Segregation of schools and other city facilities had to be referred to the mayor and the city council.

Dennis was pleased. For the first time ever, the whites were negotiating!

But Verena was scornful. "This is nothing," she said. "They never ask two women to share a fitting room, so they're hardly segregated in the first place. And there are more than five Negro men in Birmingham capable of putting on a tie. As for the rest—"

"They say they have no power to reverse the decisions of the courts or change the laws."

"How naïve are you?" said Verena. "In this town, the courts and the city government do what the businessmen ask them to do."

Bobby Kennedy asked George to put together a list of the most influential white businessmen in town, with their phone numbers. The president was going to call them personally and tell them they needed to compromise.

George noted other exciting signs. Mass meetings in Birmingham churches on Monday evening collected an amazing $40,000 in donations to the campaign: it took King's people most of the night to count it all, which they did in a motel room rented for the purpose. Even more money was pouring in by mail. The movement normally lived from hand to mouth, but Bull Connor and his dogs had brought a massive windfall.

Verena and King's people settled in for a late-night session in the sitting room of King's suite, discussing how to keep the pressure on. George was not invited—he did not want to learn things he might feel obliged to report to Bobby—so he went to bed.

In the morning he put on his suit and went downstairs to King's ten o'clock press conference. He found the motel courtyard crammed with more than a hundred journalists from all over the world, sweating under the Alabama sun. King's Birmingham campaign was hot news—again thanks to Bull Connor. "The activities which have taken place in Birmingham over the last few days mark the nonviolent movement's coming of age," King said. "This is the fulfillment of a dream."

George could not see Verena anywhere, and the suspicion grew in him that the real action might be elsewhere. He left the motel and went around the corner to the church. He did not find Verena, but he did notice schoolchildren coming out of the church basement and getting into cars parked in a line along Fifth Avenue. He sensed an air of forced nonchalance about the adults supervising them.

He ran into Dennis Wilson, who had news. "The Senior

Citizens Committee is having an emergency meeting at the chamber of commerce."

George had heard of this unofficial group, nicknamed the Big Mules. They were the men who held the real power in the town. If they were panicking, something would have to change.

Dennis said: "What are King's people planning?"

George was glad he did not know. "I wasn't invited to the meeting," he said. "But they've cooked up something."

He parted from Dennis and walked downtown. Even strolling alone he knew he might be arrested for parading without a permit, but he had to take the risk: he would be of no use to Bobby if he hid in the Gaston.

In ten minutes he reached Birmingham's typical Southern-town business district: department stores, cinemas, civic buildings, and a railway line running through the middle.

George figured out what King's plan was only when he saw it going into operation.

Suddenly Negroes walking alone, or in twos and threes, began to congregate, brandishing placards that they had until now kept hidden. Some sat down, blocking the sidewalk; others knelt to pray on the steps of the massive art deco city hall. Conga lines of hymn-singing teenagers wove in and out of segregated stores. Traffic slowed to a halt.

The police were caught unawares: they were concentrated around Kelly Ingram Park, half a mile away, and the demonstrators had blindsided them. But George felt sure that this air of good-natured protest could last only as long as Bull Connor remained off balance.

As morning turned into afternoon he returned to the Gaston. He found Verena looking worried. "This is great, but it's out of control," she said. "Our people are trained in nonviolent protest, but thousands of others are just joining in, and they have no discipline."

"It's increasing the pressure on the Big Mules," George said.

"But we don't want the governor to declare martial law." The governor of Alabama was George Wallace, an unyielding segregationist.

"Martial law means federal control," George pointed out. "Then the president would have to order at least partial integration."

"If it's forced on the Big Mules from the outside they'll find ways to undermine it. Better that it's their decision."

Verena was a subtle political thinker, George could tell. No doubt she had learned a lot from King. But he was not sure whether she was right on this point.

He ate a ham sandwich and went out again. The atmosphere around Kelly Ingram Park was now more tense. There were hundreds of police in the park, swinging their nightsticks and restraining their eager dogs. The fire brigade hosed anyone headed downtown. The Negroes, resenting the hoses, began to throw stones and Coke bottles at the police. Verena and others of King's team moved through the crowd, begging people to stay calm and refrain from violence, but they had little effect. A strange white vehicle that people called the Tank drove up and down Sixteenth Street, with Bull Connor bellowing through a loudspeaker: "Disperse! Get off the streets!" It was not a tank, George had been told, but an army surplus armored car Connor had bought.

George saw Fred Shuttlesworth, King's rival as leader of the campaign. At forty-one he was a wiry, tough-looking man, smartly dressed with a trim mustache. He had survived two bombings, and his wife had been stabbed by a Ku Klux Klansman, but he seemed to have no fear, and refused to leave town. "I wasn't saved to run," he liked to say. Although a fighter by nature, he was now trying to marshal some of the youngsters. "You mustn't taunt the police," he was saying. "Don't act like you intend to strike them." It was good advice, George figured.

Kids gathered around Shuttlesworth and he led them, like the Pied Piper, back toward his church, waving a white handkerchief in the air in an attempt to show the police his peaceful intent.

It almost worked.

Shuttlesworth led the kids past the fire trucks outside the church to the basement entrance, which was at street level, and ushered them inside and down the stairs. When they were all in, he turned to follow. At that moment George heard a voice say: "Let's put some water on the reverend."

Shuttlesworth turned, frowning, to look back. A jet from a water cannon hit him squarely in the chest. He staggered and fell backward down the stairs with a clatter and a roar.

Someone yelled: "Oh, my God, Shuttlesworth is struck!"

George rushed in. Shuttlesworth lay at the foot of the stairs, gasping. "Are you okay?" George yelled, but Shuttlesworth could not answer. "Get an ambulance, somebody, fast!" George shouted.

George was astonished that the authorities had been so stupid. Shuttlesworth was a hugely popular figure. Did they actually *want* to provoke a riot?

Ambulances were near at hand, and it was only a minute or two later that two men came in with a stretcher and carried Shuttlesworth out.

George followed them up to the sidewalk. Black bystanders and white police were milling around dangerously. Reporters had gathered and press photographers clicked as the stretcher was eased into the ambulance. They all watched it drive away.

A moment later, Bull Connor appeared. "I waited a week to see Shuttlesworth hit by a hose," he said jovially. "I'm sorry I missed it."

George was furious. He hoped one of the bystanders would punch Connor's fat face.

A white newspaper reporter said: "He left in an ambulance."

"I wish it was a hearse," said Connor.

George had to turn away to control his fury. He was saved by Dennis Wilson, who appeared from nowhere and grabbed his arm. "Good news!" he said. "The Big Mules caved!"

George spun around. "What do you mean, they caved?"

"They formed a committee to negotiate with the campaigners."

That *was* good news. Something had changed them: the demonstrations, or the phone calls from the president, or the threat of martial law. Whatever the reason, they were now desperate enough to sit down with black people and discuss a truce. Perhaps it could be agreed before the rioting turned seriously nasty.

"But they need someplace to meet," Dennis added.

"Verena will know. Let's go find her." George turned to leave, then paused and looked back at Bull Connor. He was becoming irrelevant, George now saw. Connor was on the streets, jeering at civil rights campaigners, but at the chamber of commerce the city's most powerful men had changed course—and they had done so without consulting Connor. Maybe the time was coming when fat white bullies would no longer rule the South.

And then again, maybe not.

. . .

The compromise was announced at a press conference on Friday. Fred Shuttlesworth attended, with cracked ribs from the water cannon, and announced: "Birmingham reached an accord with its conscience today!" Shortly afterward he fainted and had to be carried out. Martin Luther King declared a victory and flew home to Atlanta.

Birmingham's white elite had at last agreed to some measure of desegregation. Verena complained that it was not much, and in a way she was right: they were making a few minor concessions. But George believed that a huge change of principle had occurred: the whites had accepted that they needed to negotiate with the Negroes about segregation. They could no longer simply lay down the law. Those negotiations would continue, and they could go in only one direction.

Whether this was a small advance or a major turning point, every colored person in Birmingham was celebrating on Saturday night, and Verena invited George to her room.

He soon learned that she was not one of those girls who liked the man to take charge in bed. She knew what she wanted and she was comfortable asking for it. That was fine with George.

Almost anything would have been fine with him. He was enchanted by her lovely pale body and her witchy green eyes. She talked a lot while they made love, telling him how she felt, asking him if this pleased him or that embarrassed him; and the talk heightened their intimacy. He realized, more strongly than ever, how sex could be a way of getting to know the other person's character as well as her body.

Near the end she wanted to get on top. This, too, was new: no woman had done that with him before. She knelt astride him, and he held her hips and moved with her. She closed her eyes, but he did not. He watched her face, fascinated and enthralled, and when at last she reached her climax, he did too.

A few minutes before midnight he stood at the window in a robe, looking down on the streetlights of Fifth Avenue, while Verena was in the bathroom. His mind returned to the agreement King had struck with Birmingham's whites. If it was a triumph for the civil rights movement, die-hard segregationists would not accept defeat, he guessed; but what *would* they do? Bull Connor undoubtedly had a plan for sabotaging the agreement. So presumably did George Wallace, the racist governor.

That day the Ku Klux Klan had held a rally at Bessemer, a small town eighteen miles from Birmingham. According to Bobby Kennedy's intelligence, supporters had come from Georgia, Tennessee, South Carolina, and Mississippi. No doubt their speakers had spent the evening working them up into a frenzy of indignation about Birmingham giving in to the blacks. By now the women and children must have gone home, but the men would have started drinking and bragging to one another about what they were going to do.

Tomorrow would be Mother's Day, Sunday, May 12. George recalled Mother's Day two years ago, when white people had tried to kill him and other Freedom Riders by firebombing their bus at Anniston, sixty miles from here.

Verena emerged from the bathroom. "Come back to bed," she said, getting under the sheet.

George was eager. He hoped to make love to her at least once more before dawn. But just as he was about to turn away from the window, something caught his eye. The headlights of two cars were approaching along Fifth Avenue. The first vehicle was a white Birmingham Police Department patrol car, clearly marked with the number 25. It was followed by an old round-nosed Chevrolet from the early fifties. Both cars slowed as they drew level with the Gaston.

George suddenly noticed that the cops and state troopers who had been patrolling the streets around the motel had vanished. There was no one on the sidewalk.

What the hell . . . ?

A second later something was thrown from the open rear window of the Chevrolet, across the sidewalk, to the wall of the motel. The object landed right underneath the windows of the corner suite, Room 30, which Martin Luther King had occupied until he left earlier today.

Then both cars accelerated.

George turned from the window, crossed the room in two strides, and threw himself on top of Verena.

Her yell of protest was just beginning when it was drowned by a tremendous boom. The entire building shook as if in an earthquake. The air filled with the sounds of smashing glass and the rumble of falling masonry. The window of their room shattered with a tinkling noise like death chimes. There was a creepy moment of quiet. As the sound of the two cars faded, George heard shouts and screams from within the building.

He said to Verena: "Are you okay?"

She said: "What the fuck happened?"

"Someone threw a bomb from a car." He frowned. "The car had a police escort. Can you believe that?"

"In this goddamn town? You bet I can."

George rolled off her and looked around the room. He saw broken glass all over the floor. A piece of green cloth was draped over the end of the bed, and after a moment he realized it was the curtain. A picture of President Roosevelt had been blown off the wall by the force of the blast, and lay faceup on the carpet, crazed glass over the president's smile.

Verena said: "We have to go downstairs. People may be hurt."

"Wait a minute," George said. "I'll get your shoes." He put his feet down on a clear patch of the rug. To cross the room he had to pick up shards of glass and throw them aside. His shoes and hers were side by side in the closet: he liked that. He put his feet into his black leather oxfords, then picked up Verena's white kitten-heels and took them to her.

The lights went out.

They both dressed quickly in the dark. They discovered there was no water in the bathroom. They went downstairs.

The darkened lobby was full of panicking hotel staff and guests. Several people were bleeding but it seemed no one was dead. George pushed his way outside. By the street-lights he saw a hole five feet across in the wall of the building, and a spill of heavyweight rubble across the sidewalk. Trailers parked in the adjacent lot had been wrecked by the force of the blast. But, by a miracle, no one had been badly injured.

A cop arrived with a dog, then an ambulance drew up, then more police. Ominously, groups of Negroes began to gather outside the motel and in Kelly Ingram Park on the next block. These people were not the nonviolent Christians who had marched joyfully out of the Sixteenth Street Baptist Church singing hymns, George noted anxiously. This crowd had spent Saturday evening drinking in bars and pool halls and juke joints, and they did not subscribe to the Gandhian philosophy of passive resistance favored by Martin Luther King.

Someone said there had been another bomb, a few blocks away, at the parsonage occupied by Martin Luther King's brother, Alfred, always known as A. D. King. An eyewitness had seen a uniformed cop place a package on the porch a few seconds before the blast. Clearly the Birmingham police had tried to murder both King brothers at the same time.

The crowd got angrier.

Soon they were throwing bottles and rocks. Dogs and water cannon were the favorite targets. George went back inside the motel. Verena was helping to rescue an elderly black woman from a wrecked ground-floor room by flashlight.

"It's getting nasty out there," George said to Verena. "They're throwing rocks at the police."

"So they damn well should. The police are the bombers."

"Think about this," George said urgently. "Why do the whites want a riot tonight? To sabotage the agreement."

She wiped plaster dust off her forehead. George watched her face and saw rage replaced by calculation. "Damn, you're right," she said.

"We can't let them do it."

"But how can we stop it?"

"We have to get all the movement leaders out there calming people down."

She nodded. "Hell, yes. I'll start rounding people up."

George went back outside. The riot had escalated fast. A taxicab had been overturned and torched, and was blazing in the middle of the road. A block away, a grocery store was alight. Squad cars approaching from downtown were halted at Seventeenth Street by a hail of missiles.

George grabbed a megaphone and addressed the crowd. "Everybody stay calm!" he said. "Don't jeopardize our deal! The segregationists are trying to provoke a riot—don't give them what they want! Go home to bed!"

A black man standing nearby said to him: "How come *we* have to go home every time *they* start violence!"

George jumped on the hood of a parked car and stood on the roof. "This is not helping us!" he said. "Our movement is nonviolent! Everybody go home!"

Someone yelled: "We're nonviolent, but they ain't!"

Then an empty whisky bottle flew through the air and hit George's forehead. He climbed down from the roof of the car. He touched his head. It hurt, but it was not bleeding.

Others took up his cry. Verena appeared with several movement leaders and preachers, and they all mingled with the crowd, trying to talk people down. A. D. King got up on a car. "Our home was just bombed," he cried. "We say, Father, forgive them, for they know not what they do. But you are not helping—you are hurting us! Please, clear this park!"

Slowly, it began to work. Bull Connor was nowhere to be seen, George noted: the man in charge was Chief of Police Jamie Moore—a law enforcement professional rather than a political appointee—and that helped. The police attitude seemed to have changed. Dog handlers and firemen no longer seemed eager for a fight. George heard a cop saying to a group of Negroes: "We're your friends!" It was bullshit, but a new kind of bullshit.

There were hawks and doves among the segregationists, George realized. Martin Luther King had allied himself with the doves, and thereby outflanked the hawks. Now the hawks were trying to reignite the fires of hatred. They could not be allowed to succeed.

Lacking the stimulus of police aggression, the crowd lost the will to riot. George began to hear a different kind of comment. When the burning grocery store collapsed, people sounded penitent. "That's a doggone shame," said one man, and another said: "We gone too far."

At last the preachers got them singing, and George relaxed. It was all over, he felt.

He found Chief Moore on the corner of Fifth Avenue and Seventeenth Street. "We need to get repair crews to the motel, Chief," he said politely. "Power and water are out, and it's going to get unsanitary in there pretty quickly."

"I'll see what I can do," said Moore, and put his walkie-talkie to his ear.

But before he could speak into it, the state troopers arrived.

They wore blue helmets and they carried carbines and double-barreled shotguns. They arrived in a rush, most in cars, some on horseback. Within seconds there were two hundred or more. George stared in horror. This was a catastrophe—they would restart the riot. But that was what Governor George Wallace wanted, he realized. Wallace, like Bull Connor and the bombers, saw that the only hope now for the segregationists was a complete breakdown of law and order.

A car drew up and Wallace's director of public safety, Colonel Al Lingo, jumped out, toting a shotgun. Two men with him, apparently bodyguards, had Thompson submachine guns.

Chief Moore holstered his walkie-talkie. He spoke softly, but carefully did not address Lingo by his military rank. "If you'd leave, Mr. Lingo, I'd appreciate it."

Lingo did not trouble to be courteous. "Get your cowardly ass back to your office," he said. "I'm in charge now, and my orders are to put those black bastards to bed."

George expected them to tell him to get lost, but they were too intent on their argument to care about him.

"Those guns are not needed," said Moore. "Will you please put them up? Somebody's going to get killed."

"You're damn right!" said Lingo.

George walked away quickly, heading back to the motel.

Just before he went inside he turned to look, just in time to see the state troopers charge the crowd.

Then the riot started all over again.

George found Verena in the motel courtyard. "I have to go to Washington," he said.

He did not want to go. He wanted to spend time with Verena, talking to her, deepening their newfound intimacy. He wanted to make her fall in love with him. But that would have to wait.

She said: "What are you going to do in Washington?"

"Make sure the Kennedy brothers understand what's hap-

pening. They have to be told that Governor Wallace is pro-
voking violence in order to undermine the deal."

"It's three o'clock in the morning."

"I'd like to get to the airport as early as possible and
catch the first flight out. I might have to go via Atlanta."

"How will you get to the airport?"

"I'm going to look for a taxi."

"No cab will pick up a black man tonight—especially
one with a lump on his forehead."

George touched his face exploratively and found a bump
just where she said. "How did that happen?" he said.

"I seem to remember seeing a bottle hit you."

"Oh, yes. Well, it may be dumb, but I have to try to get to
the airport."

"What about your luggage?"

"I can't pack in the dark. Besides, I don't have much. I'm
just going to go."

"Be careful," she said.

He kissed her. She put her arms around his neck and
pressed her slim body to his. "It was great," she whispered.
Then she let him go.

He left the motel. The avenues heading directly downtown were blocked to the east: he would have to take a
circuitous route. He walked west, then north, then turned
east when he felt he was well clear of the rioting. He did not
see any taxis. He might have to wait for the first bus of Sunday morning.

A faint light was showing in the eastern sky when a car
screeched to a halt alongside him. He got ready to run, fearing white vigilantes, then changed his mind when three state
troopers got out, rifles at the ready.

They won't need much of an excuse to kill me, he thought
fearfully.

The leader was a short man with a swagger. George noticed he had a sergeant's chevrons on his sleeve. "Where are
you going, boy?" the sergeant said.

"I'm trying to get to the airport, Sarge," George said. "Maybe
you can tell me where I can find a taxicab."

The leader turned to the others with a grin. "He's trying
to get to the airport," he repeated, as if the idea were risible.
"He thinks we can help him find a taxi!"

His subordinates laughed appreciatively.

"What are you going to do at the airport?" the sergeant asked George. "Clean the toilets?"

"I'm going to catch a plane to Washington. I work at the Department of Justice. I'm a lawyer."

"Is that so? Well, I work for George Wallace, the governor of Alabama, and we don't pay too much mind to Washington, down here. So get in the goddamn car before I break your woolly head."

"What are you arresting me for?"

"Don't get smart with me, boy."

"If you seize me without good cause, you're a criminal, not a trooper."

With a sudden quick motion the sergeant swung his rifle, butt first. George ducked and instinctively raised his hand to protect his face. The wooden butt of the rifle struck his left wrist painfully. The other two troopers seized his arms. He offered no resistance, but they dragged him along as if he were struggling. The sergeant opened the rear door of the car and they threw him on the backseat. They slammed the door before he was fully inside, and it jammed his leg, causing him to shout in pain. They opened the door again, shoved his injured leg inside, and closed the door.

He lay slumped on the backseat. His leg hurt but his wrist was worse. They can do anything they like to us, he thought, because we're black. At that moment he wished he had thrown rocks and bottles at the police instead of running around telling people to calm down and go home.

The troopers drove to the Gaston. There they opened the back door of the car and pushed George out. Holding his left wrist in his right hand, he limped back into the courtyard.

. . .

Later that Sunday morning George at last found a working taxi with a black driver and went to the airport, where he caught a flight to Washington. His left wrist hurt so badly that he could not use his arm, and he kept his hand in his pocket for support. The wrist was swollen, and to ease the pain he took off his watch and unbuttoned his shirt cuff.

From a pay phone at National Airport he called the Department of Justice and learned that there would be an emergency meeting at the White House at six P.M. The president was flying in from Camp David, and Burke Marshall had been helicoptered in from West Virginia. Bobby was on his way to Justice and urgently required a briefing, and no, there was no time for George to go home and change his clothes.

Vowing to keep a clean shirt in his desk drawer from now on, George got a taxi to the Justice Department and went straight to Bobby's office.

George insisted that his injuries were too trivial to require medical treatment, though he winced every time he tried to move his left arm. He summarized the night's events for the attorney general and a group of advisers including Marshall. For some reason Bobby's huge black Newfoundland dog, Brumus, was there too.

"The truce that was agreed on with such difficulty this week is now in jeopardy," George told them in conclusion. "The bombings, and the brutality of the state troopers, have weakened the Negroes' commitment to nonviolence. On the other side, the riots threaten to undermine the position of the whites who negotiated with Martin Luther King. The enemies of integration, George Wallace and Bull Connor, hope that one side or both will renounce the agreement. Somehow we have to prevent that happening."

"Well, that's pretty clear," said Bobby.

They all got into Bobby's car, a Ford Galaxie 500. It was spring, and he had the top down. They drove the short distance to the White House. Brumus enjoyed the ride.

Several thousand demonstrators were outside the White House, noticeably a mixture of black and white, carrying placards that said SAVE THE SCHOOLCHILDREN OF BIRMINGHAM.

President Kennedy was in the Oval Office, sitting in his favorite chair, a rocker, waiting for the group from Justice. With him was a powerful trio of military men: Bob McNamara, the whiz kid secretary of defense, plus the army secretary and the army chief of staff.

This group had gathered here today, George realized, because the Negroes of Birmingham had started fires and thrown bottles last night. Such an emergency meeting had never been called during all the years of nonviolent civil rights protest, even when the Ku Klux Klan bombed the homes of Negroes. Rioting brought results.

The military men were present to discuss sending the army into Birmingham. Bobby focused as always on the political reality. "People are going to be calling for the president to take action," he said. "But here's the problem. We can't admit that we're sending federal troops to control the state troopers—that would be the White House declaring war on the state of Alabama. So we'd have to say it was to control the rioters—and that would be the White House declaring war on Negroes."

President Kennedy got it right away. "Once the white people have the protection of federal troops, they might just tear up the agreement they just made," he said.

In other words, George thought, the threat of Negro riots is keeping the agreement alive. He did not like this conclusion, but it was hard to escape.

Burke Marshall spoke up. He saw the agreement as his baby. "If that agreement blows up," he said wearily, "the Negroes will be, uh . . ."

The president finished his sentence. "Uncontrollable," he said.

Marshall added: "And not only in Birmingham."

The room went quiet as they all contemplated the prospect of similar riots in other American cities.

President Kennedy said: "What is King doing today?"

George said: "Flying back to Birmingham." He had learned this just before leaving the Gaston. "By now, I have no doubt, he's making the rounds of the big churches, urging people to go home peacefully after the service and stay indoors tonight."

"Will they do what he says?"

"Yes, provided there are no further bombings, and the state troopers are brought under control."

"How can we guarantee that?"

"Could you deploy U.S. troops *near* Birmingham, but not actually *in* the city? That would demonstrate support for the agreement. Connor and Wallace would know that if they misbehave, they will forfeit their power. But it would not give the whites the chance to renege on the deal."

They talked it up and down for a while, and in the end that was what they decided to do.

George and a small subgroup moved to the Cabinet Room to draft a statement for the press. The president's secretary typed it. Press conferences were usually held in Pierre Salinger's office, but today there were too many reporters and television cameras for that room, and it was a warm spring evening, so the announcement was made in the Rose Garden. George watched President Kennedy step outside, stand in front of the world's press, and say: "The Birmingham agreement was and is a just accord. The federal government will not permit it to be sabotaged by a few extremists on either side."

Two steps forward, one step back, and two more forward, George thought; but we make progress.

CHAPTER TWENTY-THREE

Dave Williams had a plan for Saturday night. Three girls from his class at school were going to the Jump Club in Soho, and Dave and two other boys had said, casually, that they might meet the girls there. Linda Robertson was one of the girls. Dave thought she liked him. Most people assumed he was thick, because he always came bottom of the class in exams, but Linda talked to him intelligently about politics, which he knew about because of his family.

Dave was going to wear a new shirt with startlingly long collar points. He was a good dancer—even his male friends conceded that he had a stylish way of doing the Twist. He thought he had a good chance of starting a romance with Linda.

Dave was fifteen but, to his intense annoyance, most girls of his age preferred older boys. He still winced when he remembered how, more than a year ago, he had followed the enchanting Beep Dewar, hoping to steal a kiss, and had found her locked in a passionate embrace with eighteen-year-old Jasper Murray.

On Saturday mornings the Williams children went to their father's study to receive their weekly allowances. Evie, who was seventeen, was given a pound; Dave got ten shillings. Like Victorian paupers, they often had to listen to a sermon first. Today Evie was given her money and dismissed, but Dave was told to wait. When the door closed, his father, Lloyd, said: "Your exam results are very bad."

Dave knew that. In ten years of schooling he had failed every written test he had ever taken. "I'm sorry," he said. He did not want to get into an argument: he just wanted to take his money and go.

Dad was wearing a check shirt and a cardigan, his Saturday morning outfit. "But you're not stupid," he said.

"The teachers think I'm thick," Dave said.

"I don't believe that. You're intelligent, but lazy."

"I'm not lazy."

"What are you, then?"

Dave did not have an answer. He was a slow reader, but worse than that he always forgot what he had read as soon as he turned the page. He was a poor writer, too: when he wanted to put "bread" his pen would write "beard" and he would not notice the difference. His spelling was atrocious. "I got top marks in oral French and German," he said.

"Which only proves you can do it when you try."

It did not prove any such thing, but Dave did not know how to explain that.

Lloyd said: "I've thought long and hard about what to do, and your mother and I have talked about it endlessly."

This sounded ominous to Dave. What the hell was coming now?

"You're too old to be spanked, and anyway we never had much faith in physical punishment."

That was true. Most kids were smacked when they misbehaved, but Dave's mother had not struck him for years; his father, never. What bothered Dave now, however, was the word *punishment*. Clearly he was in for it.

"The only thing I can think of, to force you to concentrate on your studies, is to withdraw your allowance."

Dave could not believe what he was hearing. "What do you mean, withdraw?"

"I'm not giving you any more money until I see an improvement in your schoolwork."

Dave had not seen this coming. "But how am I supposed to get around London?" And buy cigarettes, and get into the Jump Club, he thought in a panic.

"You walk to school anyway. If you want to go anywhere else, you'll have to do better in your lessons."

"I can't live like that!"

"You get fed for nothing, and you have a wardrobe full of

clothes, so you won't lack for much. Just remember that if you don't study, you'll never have the money to get around."

Dave was outraged. His plan for this evening was ruined. He felt helpless and infantile. "So that's it?"

"Yes."

"I'm wasting my time here, then."

"You're listening to your father trying to guide you as best he can."

"Same bloody thing," Dave said, and he stamped out.

He took his leather jacket off the hook in the hall and left the house. It was a mild spring morning. What was he going to do? His plan for the day had been to meet some friends in Piccadilly Circus, stroll along Denmark Street looking at guitars, have a pint of beer in a pub, then come home and put on the shirt with the long collar points.

He had some change in his pocket—enough for half a pint of beer. How could he get the money for admission to the Jump Club? Perhaps he could work. Who would employ him at short notice? Some of his friends had jobs on Saturday or Sunday, working in shops and restaurants that needed extra people at the weekend. He considered walking into a café and offering to wash up in the kitchen. It was worth a try. He turned his steps toward the West End.

Then he had another idea.

He had relatives who might employ him. His father's sister, Millie, was in the fashion business, with three shops in affluent north London suburbs: Harrow, Golders Green, and Hampstead. She might give him a Saturday job, though he did not know how good he would be at selling frocks to ladies. Millie was married to a leather wholesaler, Abie Avery, and his warehouse in east London might be a better bet. But both Auntie Millie and Uncle Abie would probably check with Lloyd, who would tell them that Dave was supposed to be studying, not working. However, Millie and Abie had a son, Lenny, aged twenty-three, who was a small-time businessman and hustler. On Saturdays Lenny operated a market stall in Aldgate, in the East End. He sold Chanel No. 5 and other expensive perfumes at ludicrously low prices. He whispered to his customers that they were stolen, but in fact they were simple fakes, cheap scent in expensive-looking bottles.

Lenny might give Dave a day's work.

Dave had just enough money for the Tube fare. He turned into the nearest station and bought his ticket. If Lenny turned him down he did not know how he was going to get back. He guessed he could walk a few miles if necessary.

The train took him underneath London from the affluent west to the working-class east. The market was already crowded with shoppers eager to buy at prices lower than those in the regular stores. Some of the goods *were* stolen, Dave guessed: electric kettles, shavers, irons, and radio sets slipped out of the back door of the factory. Others were surplus production sold off cheaply by the makers: records no one wanted, books that had failed to become bestsellers, ugly photo frames, ashtrays in the shape of seashells. But most were defective. There were boxes of stale chocolates, striped scarves with a flaw in the weave, piebald leather boots that had been unevenly dyed, china plates decorated with half a flower.

Lenny resembled his and Dave's grandfather, the late Bernie Leckwith, with thick dark hair and brown eyes. Lenny's hair was oiled and combed into an Elvis Presley pompadour. His greeting was warm. "Hello, young Dave! Want some scent for the girlfriend? Try Fleur Sauvage." He pronounced it "flewer savidge." "Guaranteed to make her knickers fall down, yours for two shillings and sixpence."

"I need a job, Lenny," said Dave. "Can I work for you?"

"Need a job? Your mother's a millionaire, ain't she?" said Lenny evasively.

"Dad cut off my allowance."

"Why did he do that?"

"Because my schoolwork is poor. So I'm broke. I just want to earn enough money to go out tonight."

For the third time, Lenny replied with a question. "What am I, the Labour Exchange?"

"Give me a chance. I bet I could sell perfume."

Lenny turned to a customer. "You, madam, have got very good taste. Yardley perfumes are the classiest on the market—yet that bottle in your hand is only three shillings, and I had to pay two-and-six to the bloke that stole it, I mean to say supplied it to me."

The woman giggled and bought the perfume.

"I can't pay you a wage," Lenny said to Dave. "But I tell

you what I'll do: I'll give you ten percent of everything you take."

"It's a deal," said Dave, and he joined Lenny behind the display.

"Keep the money in your pockets and we'll settle up later." Lenny gave him a "float" of a pound in coins to make change.

Dave picked up a bottle of Yardley, hesitated, smiled at a passing woman, and said: "The classiest perfume on the market."

She smiled back and walked on.

He kept trying, imitating Lenny's patter, and after a few minutes he sold a bottle of Joy by Patou for two-and-six. He soon knew all Lenny's lines: "Not every woman has the flair to wear this one, but you . . . Only buy this if there's a man you *really* want to please . . . Discontinued line, the government banned this scent because it's too sexy . . ."

The crowds were cheerful and always ready to laugh. They dressed up to come to the market: it was a social event. Dave learned a whole range of new slang for money: a sixpenny piece was a Tilbury, five shillings was a dollar, and a ten-shilling note was half a knicker.

The time passed quickly. A waitress from a nearby café brought two sandwiches of thick white bread with fried bacon and ketchup, and Lenny paid her and gave one of the sandwiches to Dave, who was surprised to learn that it was lunchtime. The pockets of his drainpipe jeans grew heavy with coins, and he recalled with pleasure that 10 percent of the money was his. At midafternoon he noticed that there were hardly any men on the streets, and Lenny explained that they had all gone to a football match.

Toward the end of the afternoon, business slowed to almost nothing. Dave thought the money in his pockets might amount to as much as five pounds, in which case he had made ten shillings, the amount of his normal allowance—and he could go to the Jump Club.

At five o'clock Lenny began to dismantle the stall, and Dave helped to put the unsold goods in cardboard boxes, then they loaded everything into Lenny's yellow Bedford van.

When they counted Dave's money, he had taken just

over nine pounds. Lenny gave him a pound, a little more than the agreed ten percent, "because you helped me pack up." Dave was delighted: he had made twice the amount his father should have given him this morning. He would gladly do this every Saturday, he thought, especially if it meant he did not have to listen to his father's preaching.

They went to the nearest pub and got pint glasses of beer. "You play the guitar a bit, don't you?" Lenny said as they sat at a grimy table with a full ashtray.

"Yes."

"What sort of instrument have you got?"

"An Eko. It's a cheap copy of a Gibson."

"Electric?"

"It's semihollow."

Lenny looked impatient: perhaps he did not know much about guitars. "Can you plug it in, is what I'm asking."

"Yes—why?"

"Because I need a rhythm guitarist for my group."

That was exciting. Dave had not thought of joining a group, but the idea appealed to him instantly. "I didn't know you had a group," he said.

"The Guardsmen. I play piano and do most of the singing."

"What kind of music?"

"Rock and roll—the only kind."

"By which you mean . . ."

"Elvis, Chuck Berry, Johnny Cash . . . All the greats."

Dave could play three-chord songs without difficulty. "What about the Beatles?" Their chords were more difficult.

Lenny said: "Who?"

"A new group. They're fab."

"Never heard of them."

"Well, anyway, I can play rhythm guitar on old rock songs."

Lenny looked mildly offended at the phrase, but he said: "So, do you want to audition for the Guardsmen?"

"I'd love to!"

Lenny looked at his watch. "How long will it take you to go home and get your guitar?"

"Half an hour, and half an hour to get back."

"Meet me at the Aldgate Workingmen's Club at seven.

We'll be setting up. We can audition you before we play. Have you got an amplifier?"

"Small one."

"It'll have to do."

Dave got the Tube. His success as a salesman, and the beer he had drunk, gave him an inner glow. He smoked a cigarette on the train, rejoicing at his victory over his father. He imagined saying casually to Linda Robertson: "I play guitar in a beat group." That could hardly fail to impress her.

He arrived home and entered the house by the back door. He managed to slip up to his room without seeing either of his parents. It took him only a few moments to put his guitar in its carrying case and pick up his amplifier.

He was about to leave when his sister, Evie, came into his room, dressed up for Saturday night. She wore a short skirt and knee boots, and her hair was back-combed in a beehive. She had heavy eye makeup in the panda style made fashionable by Dusty Springfield. She looked older than seventeen. "Where are you going?" Dave asked her.

"To a party. Hank Remington is supposed to be there."

Remington, lead singer of the Kords, sympathized with some of Evie's causes, and had said so in interviews.

"You've caused a stir today," Evie said. She was not accusing him: she always took his side in arguments with the parents, and he did the same for her.

"What makes you say that?"

"Dad's really upset."

"Upset?" Dave was not sure what to make of that. His father could be angry, disappointed, stern, authoritarian, or tyrannical, and he knew how to react; but upset? "Why?"

"I gather you and he had a row."

"He wouldn't give me my allowance because I failed all my exams."

"What did you do?"

"Nothing. I walked out. I probably slammed the door."

"Where have you been all day?"

"I worked on Lenny Avery's market stall and earned a pound."

"Good for you! Where are you off to now, with your guitar?"

"Lenny has a beat group. He wants me to play rhythm

guitar." That was an exaggeration: Dave did not have the job yet.

"Good luck!"

"I suppose you'll tell Mum and Dad where I've gone."

"Only if you want me to."

"I don't care." Dave went to the door, then hesitated. "He's upset?"

"Yes."

Dave shrugged and left.

He got out of the house without being seen.

He was looking forward to the audition. He played and sang a lot with his sister, but he had never sat in with a real group that had a drummer. He hoped he was good enough—though rhythm guitar was not difficult.

On the Tube his thoughts kept wandering back to his father. He was a bit shocked to learn that he could upset Dad. Fathers were supposed to be invulnerable—but that attitude was childish, he now saw. Irritatingly, he might have to change his outlook. He could no longer be merely indignant and resentful. He was not the only sufferer. Dad had hurt him, but he had hurt Dad as well, and they were both responsible. Feeling responsible was not as comfortable as feeling outraged.

He found the Aldgate Workingmen's Club and carried his guitar and amplifier inside. It was a drab place, with bright neon strips throwing a harsh light on Formica tables and tubular chairs lined up in rows that made him think of a factory canteen: hardly the place for rock and roll.

The Guardsmen were onstage, tuning up. As well as Lenny on piano there was Lew on drums, Buzz on bass, and Geoffrey on lead guitar. Geoffrey had a microphone in front of him, so presumably he also did some singing. All three were older than Dave, in their early twenties, and he feared they might be much better musicians than he was. Suddenly, playing rhythm did not seem so easy.

He tuned his guitar to the piano and plugged into his amplifier. Lenny said: "Do you know 'Mess of Blues'?"

Dave did, and he felt relieved. It was a rock-steady number in the key of C, led by a rolling piano part, easy to accompany on the guitar. He strummed along with it effortlessly, and found a special kick in playing with others that he had never experienced on his own.

Lenny sang well, Dave thought. Buzz and Lew made a solid rhythm section, very steady. Geoff had some fancy licks on lead guitar. The group was competent, if a bit unimaginative.

At the end of the song, Lenny said: "The chords round out the sound of the group nicely, but can you play more rhythmically?"

Dave was surprised to be criticized. He thought he had done well. "Okay," he said.

The next number was "Shake, Rattle and Roll," a Jerry Lee Lewis hit that was also piano-led. Geoffrey sang in unison with Lenny on the chorus. Dave played choppy chords on the offbeat, and Lenny seemed to like that better.

Lenny announced "Johnny B. Goode," and without being asked Dave enthusiastically played the Chuck Berry introduction. When he got to the fifth bar he expected the group to join in, as on the record, but the Guardsmen remained silent. Dave stopped, and Lenny said: "I usually play the intro on the piano."

"Sorry," Dave said, and Lenny restarted the number.

Dave felt dispirited. He was not doing well.

The next number was "Wake Up, Little Susie." To Dave's surprise, Geoffrey did not sing the Everly Brothers harmony. After the first verse, Dave moved to Geoffrey's microphone and began to sing with Lenny. A minute later, two young waitresses who were putting ashtrays out on the tables stopped their work to listen. At the end of the song they clapped. Dave grinned with pleasure. It was the first time he had been applauded by anyone outside his family.

One of the girls said to Dave: "What's your group called?"

Dave pointed at Lenny. "It's his group, and they're called the Guardsmen."

"Oh." She seemed mildly disappointed.

Lenny's last choice was "Take Good Care of My Baby," and again Dave sang the harmony. The waitresses danced along the aisles between the rows of tables.

Afterward, Lenny got up from the piano. "Well, you're not much of a guitarist," he said to Dave. "But you sing nicely, and those girls really went for it."

"So am I in, or out?"

"Can you play tonight?"

"Tonight!" Dave was pleased, but he had not expected to start immediately. He was looking forward to seeing Linda Robertson later.

"You got something better to do?" Lenny looked a bit offended that Dave had not accepted instantly.

"Well, I was going to see a girl, but she'll just have to wait. What time will we be through?"

"This is a workingmen's club. They don't stay up late. We come offstage at half past ten."

Dave calculated that he could be at the Jump Club by eleven. "That's okay," he said.

"Good," said Lenny. "Welcome to the group."

.   .   .

Jasper Murray still could not afford to go to America. At St. Julian's College, London, there was a group called the North America Club that chartered flights and sold cheap tickets. Late one afternoon he went to their little office in the student union and inquired about prices. He learned that he could go to New York for ninety pounds. It was too much, and he left disconsolate.

He spotted Sam Cakebread in the coffee bar. For several days he had been looking for a chance to speak to Sam outside the office of the student newspaper, *St. Julian's News*. Sam was the paper's editor, Jasper its news editor.

With Sam was his younger sister, Valerie, also a student at St. Julian's, wearing a tweed cap and a minidress. She wrote articles about fashion for the paper. She was attractive: in other circumstances Jasper would have flirted with her, but today he had other matters on his mind. He would have preferred to talk to Sam on his own, but he decided that Valerie's presence was no real problem.

He carried his coffee to Sam's table. "I want your advice," he said. He wanted information, not advice, but people were sometimes reluctant to share information, whereas they were always flattered to be asked for advice.

Sam was wearing a herringbone jacket with a tie and smoking a pipe: perhaps he wanted to look older. "Take a seat," he said, folding the paper he had been reading.

Jasper sat down. His relationship with Sam was awkward. They had been rivals for the post of editor, and Sam had won. Jasper had concealed his resentment, and Sam had made him news editor. They had become colleagues, but not friends. "I want to be next year's editor," Jasper said. He hoped that Sam would help him, either because he was the right man for the job—which he was—or out of guilt.

"That's up to Lord Jane," said Sam evasively. Jane was provost of the college.

"Lord Jane will ask your opinion."

"There's a whole appointment committee."

"But you and the provost are the members who count."

Sam did not argue with that. "So you want my advice."

"Who else is in the running?"

"Toby, obviously."

"Really?" Toby Jenkins was the features editor, a plodder who had commissioned a dull series of worthy articles about the work of university officials such as the registrar and the treasurer.

"He will apply."

Sam himself had got the job partly because of the distinguished journalists among his relations. Lord Jane was impressed by such connections. This irritated Jasper, but he did not mention it.

Jasper said: "Toby's stuff is pedestrian."

"He's an accurate reporter, if unimaginative."

Jasper recognized this remark as a dig at himself. He was the opposite of Toby. He prized sensation over accuracy. In his reports a scuffle always became a fight, a plan was a conspiracy, and a slip of the tongue was never less than a blatant lie. He knew that people read newspapers for excitement, not information.

Cakebread added: "And he did write that piece about rats in the refectory."

"So he did." Jasper had forgotten. The article had caused an uproar. It had been luck, really: Toby's father worked for the local council and knew about the efforts of the pest control department to eradicate vermin in the eighteenth-century cellars of St. Julian's College. Nevertheless the article had secured the job of features editor for Toby, who had written nothing half as good since. "So I need a scoop," Jasper said thoughtfully.

"Perhaps."

"You mean, like, revealing that the provost is skimming off university funds to pay his gambling debts."

"I doubt that Lord Jane gambles." Sam did not have a great sense of humor.

Jasper thought about Lloyd Williams. Might he provide some kind of tip-off? Lloyd was frightfully discreet, unfortunately.

Then he thought of Evie. She had applied to attend the Irving School of Drama, which was part of St. Julian's College, so she was of interest to the student newspaper. She had just got her first acting job, in a film called *All Around Miranda*. And she was going out with Hank Remington, of the Kords. Perhaps . . .

Jasper stood up. "Thanks for your help, Sam. I really appreciate it."

"Anytime," said Sam.

Jasper caught the Tube home. The more he thought about interviewing Evie, the more excited he became.

Jasper knew the truth about Evie and Hank. They were not just dating, they were having a passionate affair. Her parents knew she went out with Hank two or three evenings a week, and came home at midnight on Saturdays. But Jasper and Dave also knew that most days after school Evie went to Hank's flat in Chelsea and had sex with him. Hank had already written a song about her, "Too Young to Smoke."

But would she give Jasper an interview?

When he got home to the house in Great Peter Street, Evie was in the red-tiled kitchen, learning lines. Her hair was pinned up untidily, and she wore a faded old shirt, but she still looked fabulous. Jasper's relationship with her was warm. Throughout her girlish crush on him, he had always been kind, though never encouraging. His motive for being so careful was that he did not want a crisis that would cause a rift between him and her generously hospitable parents. Now he was even more glad he had kept her goodwill. "How's it going?" he said with a nod at her script.

She shrugged. "The part isn't difficult, but film will be a new challenge."

"Maybe I should interview you."

She looked troubled. "I'm supposed to do only the publicity arranged by the studio."

Jasper felt a mild panic. What kind of journalist would he

make if he failed to secure an interview with Evie even though he lived in her house? "It's only for the student paper," he said.

"I suppose that doesn't really count."

His hopes rose. "I'm sure not. And it might help you get accepted by the Irving drama school."

She put down the script. "All right. What do you want to know?"

Jasper suppressed his feeling of triumph. Coolly he said: "How did you get the part in *All Around Miranda*?"

"I went to an audition."

"Tell me about that." Jasper took out a notebook and started writing.

He was careful not to mention her nude scene in *Hamlet*. He feared she would tell him not to mention it. Fortunately he did not need to question her about it, for he had seen it himself. Instead he asked her about the stars of the movie, and other famous people she had met, and gradually worked around to Hank Remington.

When Jasper mentioned Hank, Evie's eyes lit up with a characteristic intensity of feeling. "Hank is the most courageous and dedicated person I know," she said. "I admire him so much."

"But you don't just admire him."

"I adore him."

"And you are dating."

"Yes, but I don't want to say too much about that."

"Of course, no problem." She had said "Yes," and that was enough.

Dave came in from school and made instant coffee with boiling milk. "I thought you weren't supposed to do publicity," he said to Evie.

Jasper thought: Shut your mouth, you overprivileged little shit.

Evie replied to Dave. "This is only for *St. Julian's News*," she said.

Jasper wrote the article that evening.

As soon as he saw it typed out, he realized it could be more than just a piece for the student paper. Hank was a star, Evie was a minor actress, and Lloyd was a member of Parliament: this could be a big story, he thought with mounting excitement. If he could get something published in a national newspaper it would give his career prospects a major boost.

It could also get him in trouble with the Williams family.

He gave his article to Sam Cakebread the next day.

Then, with trepidation, he phoned the tabloid *Daily Echo*.

He asked for the news editor. He did not get the news editor, but he was put through to a reporter called Barry Pugh. "I'm a student journalist, and I've got a story for you," he said.

"Okay, go ahead," said Pugh.

Jasper hesitated only a moment. He was betraying Evie and the entire Williams family, he knew; but he plunged on anyway. "It's about the daughter of a member of Parliament who is sleeping with a pop star."

"Good," said Pugh. "Who are they?"

"Could we meet?"

"I suppose you want some money?"

"Yes, but that's not all."

"What else?"

"I want my name on the article when it appears."

"Let's get the story down first, then we'll see."

Pugh was trying to employ the kind of blandishments Jasper had used on Evie. "No, thanks," Jasper said firmly. "If you don't like the story, you don't have to print it, but if you do use it you must put my name on it."

"All right," said Pugh. "When can we meet?"

. . .

Two days later, at breakfast in Great Peter Street, Jasper read in the *Guardian* that Martin Luther King was planning a massive demonstration of civil disobedience in Washington in support of a civil rights bill. King was forecasting that there would be one hundred thousand people. "Boy, I'd love to see that," said Jasper.

Evie said: "Me, too."

It was to take place in August, during the university vacation, so Jasper would be free. But he could not afford ninety pounds for the fare to the USA.

Daisy Williams opened an envelope and said: "My goodness! Lloyd, here's a letter from your German cousin Rebecca!"

Dave, the youngest, swallowed a mouthful of Sugar Puffs and said: "Who the heck is Rebecca?"

His father had been leafing through newspapers with the speed of a professional politician. Now he looked up and said: "Not really a cousin. She was adopted by some distant relations of mine after her parents died in the war."

"I'd forgotten we had German relatives," Dave said. "*Gott im Himmel!*"

Jasper had noticed that Lloyd was suspiciously vague about his relatives. The late Bernie Leckwith had been his stepfather, but no one ever mentioned his real father. Jasper felt sure Lloyd had been illegitimate. It was not quite a tabloid story: bastardy was not as much of a disgrace as formerly. All the same, Lloyd never gave details.

Lloyd went on: "Last time I saw Rebecca was in 1948. She was about seventeen. By then she had been adopted by my relation Carla Franck. They lived in Berlin-Mitte, so now their house must be on the wrong side of the Wall. What's become of her?"

Daisy answered: "She's obviously got out of East Germany, somehow, and moved to Hamburg. Oh ... her husband was injured escaping, and he's in a wheelchair."

"What prompted her to write to us?"

"She's trying to trace Hannelore Rothmann." Daisy looked at Jasper. "She was your grandmother. Apparently she was kind to Rebecca in the war, the day Rebecca's real parents were killed."

Jasper had never met his mother's family. "We don't know exactly what happened to my German grandparents, but Mother is sure they're dead," he said.

Daisy said: "I'll show this letter to your mother. She should write to Rebecca."

Lloyd opened the *Daily Echo* and said: "Bloody hell, what's this?"

Jasper had been waiting for this moment. He clasped his hands together in his lap to stop them shaking.

Lloyd spread the newspaper on the table. On page three was a photograph of Evie coming out of a nightclub with Hank Remington, and the headline:

Kords Star Hank
& Labour MP's
Nudie Daughter, 17

by Barry Pugh and Jasper Murray

"I didn't write that!" Jasper lied. His indignation sounded forced, to him; what he really felt was elation at the sight of his own name over a report in a national newspaper. The others did not seem to notice his mixed emotions.

Lloyd read aloud: "'Pop star Hank Remington's latest flame is the just-seventeen daughter of Lloyd Williams, member of Parliament for Hoxton. Movie starlet Evie Williams is famous for appearing nude onstage at Lambeth Grammar, the posh school for top people's children.'"

Daisy said: "Oh, dear, how embarrassing."

Lloyd read on: "'Evie said: "Hank is the most courageous and dedicated person I have ever known." Both Evie and Hank support the Campaign for Nuclear Disarmament, despite the disapproval of her father, who is Labour spokesman on military affairs.'" Lloyd looked at Evie severely. "You know a lot of courageous and dedicated people, including your mother, who drove an ambulance during the Blitz, and your great-uncle Billy Williams, who fought at the Somme. Hank must be remarkable, to overshadow them."

"Never mind that," said Daisy. "I thought you weren't supposed to do interviews without asking the studio, Evie."

"Oh, God, this is my fault," Jasper said. They all looked at him. He had known there would be a scene like this, and he was ready for it. He had no difficulty looking distraught: he felt horribly guilty. "I interviewed Evie for the student paper. The *Echo* must have lifted my story—and rewritten it to make it sensational." He had prepared this fiction in advance.

"First lesson of public life," Lloyd said. "Journalists are treacherous."

That's me, Jasper thought—treacherous. But the Williams family seemed to accept that he had not intended the *Echo* to run the story.

Evie was close to tears. "I might lose the part."

Daisy said: "I can't imagine this will do the movie any damage—quite the reverse."

"I hope you're right," said Evie.

"I'm so sorry, Evie," said Jasper, with all the sincerity he could muster. "I feel I've really let you down."

"You didn't mean to," Evie said.

Jasper had got away with it. Around the table, no one was looking accusingly at him. They saw the *Echo* report as nobody's fault. The only one he was not sure of was Daisy, who wore a slight frown and avoided his eye. But she loved Jasper for his mother's sake, and she would not accuse him of duplicity.

Jasper stood up. "I'm going to the *Daily Echo* office," he said. "I want to meet this Pugh bastard and see what explanation he can offer."

He was glad to get out of the house. He had successfully lied his way through a difficult scene, and the release of tension was enormous.

An hour later he was in the newsroom of the *Echo*. He was thrilled to be there. This was what he wanted: the news desk, the typewriters, the ringing phones, the pneumatic tubes carrying copy across the room, the air of excitement.

Barry Pugh was about twenty-five, a small man with a squint, wearing a rumpled suit and scuffed suede shoes. "You did well," he said.

"Evie still doesn't know I gave the story to you."

Pugh had little time for Jasper's scruples. "Bloody few stories would ever be published if we asked permission every time."

"She was supposed to refuse all interviews except those arranged by the studio publicist."

"Publicists are your enemies. Be proud you outwitted one."

"I am."

Pugh handed him an envelope. Jasper tore it open. It contained a check. "Your payment," Pugh said. "That's what you get for a page three lead."

Jasper looked at the amount. It was ninety pounds.

He remembered the march on Washington. Ninety pounds was the fare to the USA. Now he could go to America.

His heart lifted.

He put the check in his pocket. "Thank you very much," he said.

Barry nodded. "Let us know if you have any more stories like that."

. . .

Dave Williams was nervous about playing the Jump Club. It
was a deeply cool central London venue, just off Oxford
Street. It had a reputation for breaking new stars, and had
launched several groups now in the hit parade. Famous musicians went there to listen to new talent.

Not that it looked special. There was a small stage at
one end and a bar at the other. In between was room for
a couple of hundred people to dance buttock-to-buttock.
The floor was an ashtray. The only decoration consisted of
a few tattered posters of famous acts that had played
there in the past—except in the dressing room, where the
walls bore the most obscene graffiti Dave had ever come
across.

Dave's performance with the Guardsmen had improved,
thanks in part to helpful advice from his cousin. Lenny had
a soft spot for Dave, and talked like an uncle to him, although he was only eight years older. "Listen to the drummer," Lenny had told him. "Then you'll always be on the
beat." And: "Learn to play without looking at your guitar,
so that you can meet the eyes of people in the audience."
Dave was grateful for any tips he could get, but he knew he
was still far short of seeming professional. All the same he
felt wonderful onstage. There was nothing to read or write,
so he was no longer a dunce; in fact, he was competent, and
getting better. He had even fantasized about becoming a
musician, and never having to study, ever again; but he
knew the chances were small.

The group was improving, however. When Dave sang in
harmony with Lenny they sounded modern, more like the
Beatles. And Dave had persuaded Lenny to try some different material, authentic Chicago blues and danceable Detroit soul, the kind of thing the younger groups were playing.
As a result they were getting more dates. Instead of once a
fortnight, they were now booked every Friday and Saturday
night.

But Dave had another reason for anxiety. He had got
this gig by asking Evie's boyfriend, Hank Remington, to

recommend the group. But Hank had turned his nose up at their name. "The Guardsmen sounds old-fashioned, like the Four Aces, and the Jordanaires," he had said.

"We might change it," Dave had said, willing to do anything for a booking at the Jump Club.

"The latest vogue is a name from an old blues, like the Rolling Stones."

Dave recalled a track by Booker T. and the MGs that he had heard a few days earlier. He had been struck by its oddball name. "How about Plum Nellie?" he had said.

Hank had liked that, and told the club they should try out a new group called Plum Nellie. A suggestion from someone as famous as Hank was like a command, and the group got the gig.

But when Dave had proposed the name change, Lenny had turned it down flat. "The Guardsmen we are, and the Guardsmen we stay," he had said mulishly, and started talking about something else. Dave had not dared to tell him the Jump Club already thought they were called Plum Nellie.

Now the crisis was approaching.

At the sound check they played "Lucille." After the first verse, Dave stopped and turned to the lead guitarist, Geoffrey. "What the fuck was that?" Dave said.

"What?"

"You played something weird halfway through."

Geoffrey gave a knowing smile. "Nothing. It's just a passing chord."

"It's not on the record."

"What's the matter, can't you play C sharp diminished?"

Dave knew exactly what was going on. Geoffrey was trying to show him up as a beginner. But unfortunately Dave had never heard of a diminished chord.

Lenny said: "Known to pub pianists as a double minor, Dave."

Swallowing his pride, Dave said to Geoffrey: "Show me."

Geoffrey rolled up his eyes and sighed, but he demonstrated the chord shape. "Like that, all right?" he said wearily, as if tired of dealing with amateurs.

Dave copied the chord. It was not difficult. "Next time, tell me before we play the fucking song," he said.

After that it went well. Phil Burleigh, the owner of the

club, entered in the middle and listened. Being prematurely bald, he was naturally known as Curly Burleigh. At the end he nodded approval. "Thank you, Plum Nellie," he said.

Lenny shot a filthy look at Dave. "The group is called the Guardsmen," he said firmly.

Dave said: "We discussed changing it."

"You discussed it. I said no."

Curly said: "The Guardsmen is a terrible name, mate."

"It's what we're called."

"Listen, Byron Chesterfield is coming in tonight," Curly said with a note of desperation. "He's the most important promoter in London—in Europe, probably. You might get work from him—but not with that name."

"Byron Chesterfield?" said Lenny, laughing. "I've known him all my life. His real name is Brian Chesnowitz. His brother's got a stall in Aldgate Market."

Curly said: "It's your name I'm worried about, not his."

"Our name is fine."

"I can't put on a group called the Guardsmen. I've got a reputation." Curly stood up. "I'm sorry, lads," he said. "Pack up your gear."

Dave said: "Come on, Curly, you don't want to piss off Hank Remington."

"Hank's an old mate," said Curly. "We played skiffle together at the 2i's Coffee Bar in the fifties. But he recommended me a group called Plum Nellie, not the Guardsmen."

Dave was distraught. "All my friends are coming!" he said. He was thinking of Linda Robertson in particular.

Curly said: "I'm sorry about that."

Dave turned to Lenny. "Be reasonable," he said. "What's in a name?"

"It's my group, not yours," said Lenny stubbornly.

So that was the issue. "Of course it's your group," said Dave. "But you taught me that the customer is always right." He was struck by inspiration. "And you can change the name back to the Guardsmen tomorrow morning, if you want."

Lenny said: "Naah," but he was weakening.

"Better than not playing," said Dave, pressing his advantage. "It would be a real comedown to go home now."

"Oh, fuck it, all right," said Lenny.

And the crisis was over, to Dave's intense relief and pleasure.

They stood at the bar drinking beer while the first customers trickled in. Dave limited himself to one pint: enough
to relax him, not enough to make him fumble the chords.
Lenny had two pints, Geoffrey three.

Linda Robertson showed up, to Dave's delight, in a short
purple dress and white knee boots. She and all Dave's
friends were legally too young to drink alcohol in bars, but
they went to great lengths to look older, and anyway the
law was not enforced strictly.

Linda's attitude to Dave had changed. In the past she
had treated him like a bright kid brother, even though they
were the same age. The fact that he was playing at the Jump
Club turned him into a different person in her eyes. Now
she saw him as a sophisticated grown-up, and asked him
excited questions about the group. If this was what he got
for being in Lenny's crummy outfit, Dave thought, what
must it be like to be a real pop star?

With the others he returned to the dressing room to change.
Professional groups usually appeared wearing identical suits,
but that was expensive. Lenny compromised with red shirts
for everyone. Dave thought that group uniforms were going
out of fashion: the anarchic Rolling Stones dressed individ-
ually.

Plum Nellie was bottom of the bill, and played first. Lenny,
as leader of the group, introduced the songs. He was seated
at the side of the stage, with the upright piano angled so
that he could look at the audience. Dave stood in the middle, playing and singing, and most eyes were on him. Now
that the worry about the group's name was out of the way—
at least for the moment—he could relax. He moved as he
played, swinging the guitar as if it were his dance partner;
and when he sang he imagined he was speaking to the audience, emphasizing the words with his facial expressions
and the movements of his head. As always, the girls responded to that, watching him and smiling as they danced
to the beat.

After the set, Byron Chesterfield came to the dressing
room.

He was about forty, and wore a beautiful light blue suit
with a waistcoat. His tie had a pattern of daisies. His hair
was receding either side of an old-fashioned brilliantined
quiff. He brought a cloud of cologne into the room.

He spoke to Dave. "Your group is not bad," he said.

Dave pointed to Lenny. "Thank you, Mr. Chesterfield, but it's Lenny's group."

Lenny said: "Hello, Brian, don't you remember me?"

Byron hesitated a moment, then said: "My life! It's Lenny Avery." His London accent became broader. "I never recognized you. How's the stall?"

"Doing great, never better."

"The group is good, Lenny: bass and drums solid, nice guitars and piano. I like the vocal harmonies." He jerked a thumb at Dave. "And the girls love the kid. You getting much work?"

Dave was excited. Byron Chesterfield liked the group!

Lenny said: "We're busy every weekend."

"I might be able to get you an out-of-town gig for six weeks in the summer, if you're interested," Byron said. "Five nights a week, Tuesday to Saturday."

"I don't know," said Lenny with indifference. "I'd have to get my sister to run the stall for me while I was away."

"Ninety pound a week in your hand, no deductions."

That was more than they had ever been paid, Dave calculated. And with luck it would fall in the school holiday.

Dave was annoyed to see Lenny still looking dubious. "What about board and lodging?" he said. Dave realized he was not uninterested, he was negotiating.

"You get lodging but not board," Byron said.

Dave wondered if this was at a seaside resort, where there was seasonal work for entertainers.

Lenny said: "I couldn't leave the stall for that kind of money, Brian. Pity it's not a hundred and twenty pound a week. Then I could consider it."

"The venue might go to ninety-five, as a personal favor to me."

"Say a hundred and ten."

"If I forgo my own fee I can make it a hundred."

Lenny looked at the rest of the group. "What do you say, lads?"

They all wanted to take the job.

"What's the venue?" Lenny said.

"A club called the Dive."

Lenny shook his head. "Never heard of it. Where is it?"

"Didn't I mention that?" said Byron Chesterfield. "It's in Hamburg."

. . .

Dave could hardly contain his excitement. A six-week gig—in Germany! Legally, he was old enough to quit school. Was there a chance he might become a professional musician?

In exuberant mood, he took his guitar and amplifier and Linda Robertson to the house in Great Peter Street, intending to drop off his gear before walking her home to her parents' place in Chelsea. Unfortunately his parents were still up, and his mother waylaid him in the hall. "How did it go?" she asked brightly.

"Great," he said. "I'm just dropping off my gear, and I'm going to walk Linda home."

"Hello, Linda," said Daisy. "How nice to see you again."

"How do you do?" Linda said politely, morphing into a demure schoolgirl; but Dave could see his mother taking in the short dress and the sexy boots.

"Will the club hire you again?" Daisy asked.

"Well, a promoter called Byron Chesterfield offered us a summer job at another club. It's great because it's all during the school holiday."

His father came out of the drawing room, still wearing his suit from whatever Saturday night political meeting he had attended. "What's happening in the school holiday?"

"Our group has a six-week engagement."

Lloyd frowned. "You need to do some revision in the vacation. Next year you have the all-important O-level exams. To date, your grades are nowhere near good enough to permit you to take the whole summer off."

"I can study in the day. We'll be playing in the evenings."

"Hmm. You obviously don't care about missing the annual holiday with your family in Tenby."

"I do," Dave lied. "I love Tenby. But this is a great opportunity."

"Well, I don't see how we can leave you alone in this house for two weeks while we're in Wales. You're still only fifteen."

"Er, the club isn't in London," Dave said.

"Where is it?"

"Hamburg."

Daisy said: "What?"

Lloyd said: "Don't be ridiculous. Do you imagine we're going to allow you to do that at your age? It must be illegal under German employment law, for one thing."

"Not all laws are strictly enforced," Dave argued. "I bet you illegally bought drinks in pubs before you were eighteen."

"I went to Germany with my mother when I was eighteen. I certainly never spent six weeks unsupervised in a foreign country at the age of fifteen."

"I won't be unsupervised. Cousin Lenny will be with me."

"I don't see him as a reliable chaperone."

"Chaperone?" said Dave indignantly. "What am I, a Victorian maiden?"

"You're a child, according to the law, and an adolescent, in reality. You're certainly not an adult."

"You've got a cousin in Hamburg," Dave said desperately. "Rebecca. She wrote to Mam. You could ask her to look after me."

"She's a distant cousin by adoption, and I haven't seen her for sixteen years. That's not a sufficiently close connection for me to dump an unruly teenager on her for the summer. I'd hesitate to do it to my sister."

Daisy adopted a conciliatory tone. "From her letter I got the impression of a kind person, Lloyd, dear. And I don't think she has children of her own. She might not mind being asked."

Lloyd looked annoyed. "Do you actually want Dave to do this?"

"No, of course not. If I had my wish, he would come to Tenby with us. But he is growing up, and we may have to loosen the apron strings." She looked at Dave. "He's going to find it harder work and less fun than he imagines, but he may learn some life lessons from it."

"No," said Lloyd with an air of finality. "If he were eighteen, perhaps I'd agree. But he's too young, much too young."

Dave wanted to scream with rage and burst into tears at the same time. Surely they would not spoil this opportunity?

"It's late," said Daisy. "Let's talk about it in the morning. Dave needs to get Linda home before her parents start to worry."

Dave hesitated, reluctant to leave the argument unresolved.

Lloyd went to the foot of the stairs. "Don't get your hopes up," he said to Dave. "It isn't going to happen."

Dave opened the front door. If he walked out now, without saying anything else, he would leave them with the wrong impression. He needed them to know they could not stop him going to Hamburg easily. "Listen to me," he said, and his father looked startled. Dave made up his mind. "For the first time in my life, I'm a success at something, Dad," he said. "Just understand me. If you try to take this from me, I'll leave home. And, I swear, if I leave I will never, ever, come back."

He led Linda out and slammed the door.

CHAPTER TWENTY-FOUR

T anya Dvorkin was back in Moscow, but Vasili Yenkov
was not.

After the two of them had been arrested at the
poetry reading in Mayakovsky Square, Vasili had
been convicted of "anti-Soviet activities and propaganda" and sentenced to two years in a Siberian labor
camp. Tanya felt guilty: she had been Vasili's partner in
crime, but she had got away with it.

Tanya assumed Vasili had been beaten and interrogated.
But she was still free and working as a journalist, therefore
he had not given her away. Perhaps he had refused to talk.
More likely, he might have named plausible fictitious col-
laborators who the KGB believed were simply difficult to
track down.

By the spring of 1963 Vasili had served his sentence. If he
was alive—if he had survived the cold, hunger, and disease
that killed many prisoners in labor camps—he should be
free now. Ominously, he had not reappeared.

Prisoners were normally allowed to send and receive
one letter per month, heavily censored; but Vasili could not
write to Tanya, for that would betray her to the KGB; so she
had no information; and no doubt the same applied to most
of his friends. Perhaps he wrote to his mother in Leningrad.
Tanya had never met her: Vasili's association with Tanya
was secret even from his mother.

Vasili had been Tanya's closest friend. She lay awake
nights worrying about him. Was he ill, or even dead? Per-

haps he had been convicted of another crime, and had his sentence extended. Tanya was tortured by the uncertainty. It gave her a headache.

One afternoon she took the risk of mentioning Vasili to her boss, Daniil Antonov. The features department of TASS was a large, noisy room, with journalists typing, talking on the phone, reading newspapers, and walking in and out of the reference library. If she spoke quietly she would not be overheard. She began by saying: "What happened about Ustin Bodian, in the end?" The ill treatment of Bodian, a dissident opera singer, was the subject of the edition of *Dissidence* Vasili had been giving out when arrested—an issue written by Tanya.

"Bodian died of pneumonia," Daniil said.

Tanya knew that. She was pretending ignorance only to bring the conversation around to Vasili. "There was a writer arrested with me that day—Vasili Yenkov," she said in a musing tone. "Any idea what happened to him?"

"The script editor. He got two years."

"Then he must be free by now."

"Perhaps. I haven't heard. He won't get his old job back, so I'm not sure where he'd go."

He would come to Moscow, Tanya felt sure. But she shrugged, pretending indifference, and went back to typing an article about a woman bricklayer.

She had made several discreet inquiries among people who would have known if Vasili had returned. The answer had been the same in all cases: no one had heard anything.

Then, that afternoon, Tanya got word.

Leaving the TASS building at the end of the working day, she was accosted by a stranger. A voice said: "Tanya Dvorkin?" and she turned to see a pale, thin man in dirty clothes.

"Yes?" she said, a little anxiously: she could not imagine what such a man would want with her.

"Vasili Yenkov saved my life," he said.

It was so unexpected that for a moment she did not know how to respond. Too many questions raced through her mind: How do you know Vasili? Where and when did he save your life? Why have you come to me?

He thrust into her hand a grubby envelope the size of a regular sheet of paper, then he turned away.

It took Tanya a moment to gather her wits. At last she realized there was one question more important than all the rest. While the man was still within earshot she said: "Is Vasili alive?"

The stranger stopped and looked back. The pause struck fear into Tanya's heart. Then he said: "Yes," and she felt the sudden lightness of relief.

The man walked away.

"Wait!" Tanya called, but he quickened his pace, turned a corner, and disappeared from view.

The envelope was not sealed. Tanya looked inside. She saw several sheets of paper covered with handwriting that she recognized as Vasili's. She pulled them halfway out. The first sheet was headed:

Frostbite

by Ivan Kuznetsov

She pushed the sheets back into the envelope and walked on to the bus stop. She felt scared and excited at the same time. "Ivan Kuznetsov" was an obvious pseudonym, the commonest name imaginable, like Hans Schmidt in German or Jean Lefevre in French. Vasili had written something, an article or a story. She could hardly wait to read it, yet at the same time she had to resist the impulse to hurl it away from her like something contaminated, for it was sure to be subversive.

She shoved it into her shoulder bag. When the bus came it was crowded—this was the evening rush hour—so she could not look at the manuscript on her way home without the risk that someone would read it over her shoulder. She had to suppress her impatience.

She thought about the man who had handed it to her. He had been badly dressed, half starved, and in poor health, with a look of permanent wary fearfulness: just like a man recently released from jail, she thought. He had seemed glad to get rid of the envelope, and reluctant to say more to her than he had to. But he had at least explained why he had undertaken his dangerous errand. He was repaying a debt. "Vasili Yenkov saved my life," he had said. Again she wondered how.

She got off the bus and walked to Government House. On her return from Cuba she had moved back into her mother's flat. She had no reason to get her own apartment and, if she had, it would have been a lot less luxurious.

She spoke briefly to Anya, then went to her bedroom and sat down on the bed to read what Vasili had written.

His handwriting had altered. The letters were smaller, the risers shorter, the loops less flamboyant. Did that reflect a change of personality, she wondered, or just a shortage of writing paper?

She began to read.

Josef Ivanovich Maslov, called Soso, was overjoyed when the food arrived spoiled.

Normally, the guards stole most of the consignment and sold it. The prisoners were left with plain gruel in the morning and turnip soup at night. Food rarely went bad in Siberia, where the ambient temperature was usually below freezing—but Communism could work miracles. So when, occasionally, the meat was crawling with maggots and the fat rancid, the cook threw it all into the pot, and the prisoners rejoiced. Soso gobbled down kasha that was oily with stinking lard, and longed for more.

Tanya was nauseated, but at the same time she had to read on.

With each page she was more impressed. The story was about an unusual relationship between two prisoners, one an intellectual dissident, the other an uneducated gangster. Vasili had a simple, direct style that was remarkably effective. Life in the camp was described in brutally vivid language. But there was more than just description. Perhaps because of his experience in radio drama, Vasili knew how to keep a story moving, and Tanya found that her interest never flagged.

The fictional camp was located in a forest of Siberian larch, and its work was chopping down the trees. There were no safety rules and no protective clothing or equipment, so accidents were frequent. Tanya particularly noted an episode in which the gangster severed an artery in his arm with a saw and was saved by the intellectual, who tied a tourniquet around his arm. Was that how Vasili had saved the life of the messenger who had brought his manuscript to Moscow from Siberia?

Tanya read the story twice. It was almost like talking to Vasili: the phrasing was familiar from a hundred discussions and arguments, and she recognized the kinds of things he found funny or dramatic or ironic. It made her heart ache with missing him.

Now that she knew Vasili was alive, she had to find out why he had not returned to Moscow. The story contained no clue to that. But Tanya knew someone who could find out almost anything: her brother.

She put the manuscript in the drawer of her bedside table. She left the bedroom and said to her mother: "I have to go and see Dimka—I won't be long." She went down in the elevator to the floor on which her brother lived.

The door was opened by his wife, Nina, nine months pregnant. "You look well!" Tanya said.

It was not true. Nina was long past the stage when people said a pregnant woman looked "blooming." She was huge, her breasts pendulous, her belly stretched taut. Her fair skin was pale under the freckles, and her red-brown hair was greasy. She looked older than twenty-nine. "Come in," she said in a tired voice.

Dimka was watching the news. He turned off the television, kissed Tanya, and offered her a beer.

Nina's mother, Masha, was there, having come from Perm by train to help her daughter with the baby. Masha was a small, prematurely wrinkled peasant woman dressed in black, visibly proud of her citified daughter in her swanky apartment. Tanya had been surprised when she first met Masha, having previously got the impression that Nina's mother was a schoolteacher; but it turned out that she merely worked in the village school, cleaning it in fact. Nina had pretended that her parents were somewhat higher in status—a practice so common as to be almost universal, Tanya supposed.

They talked about Nina's pregnancy. Tanya wondered how to get Dimka alone. There was no way she was going to talk about Vasili in front of Nina or her mother. Instinctively she mistrusted her brother's wife.

Why did she feel that so strongly? she wondered guiltily.

It was because of the pregnancy, she decided. Nina was not intellectual, but she was clever: not the type to suffer an accidental pregnancy. Tanya had a suspicion, never voiced, that Nina had manipulated Dimka into the marriage. Tanya knew that her brother was sophisticated and savvy about almost everything: he was naïve and romantic only about women. Why would Nina have wanted to entrap him? Because the Dvorkins were an elite family, and Nina was ambitious?

Don't be such a bitch, Tanya told herself.

She made small talk for half an hour, then got up to go.

There was nothing supernatural about the twins' relationship, but they knew each other so well that each could usually guess what the other was thinking, and Dimka intuited that Tanya had not come to talk about Nina's pregnancy. Now he stood up too. "I've got to take out the garbage," he said. "Give me a hand, would you, Tanya?"

They went down in the elevator, each carrying a bucket of rubbish. When they were outside, at the back of the building, with no one else around, Dimka said: "What is it?"

"Vasili Yenkov's sentence is up, but he hasn't come back to Moscow."

Dimka's face hardened. He loved Tanya, she knew, but he disagreed with her politics. "Yenkov did his best to undermine the government I work for. Why would I care what happens to him?"

"He believes in freedom and justice, as you do."

"That kind of subversive activity just gives the hardliners an excuse to resist reform."

Tanya knew she was defending herself, as well as Vasili. "If it were not for people like Vasili, the hard-liners would say everything was all right, and there would be no pressure for change. How would anyone know that they killed Ustin Bodian, for example?"

"Bodian died of pneumonia."

"Dimka, that's not worthy of you. He died of neglect, and you know it."

"True." Dimka looked chastened. In a softer voice he said: "Are you in love with Vasili Yenkov?"

"No. I *like* him. He's funny and smart and brave. But he's the kind of man that needs a succession of young girls."

"Or he *was*. There are no nymphets in a prison camp."

"Anyway, he is a friend, and he's served his sentence."

"The world is full of injustice."

"I want to know what has happened to him, and you can find out for me. If you will."

Dimka sighed. "What about my career? In the Kremlin, compassion for dissidents unjustly treated is not considered admirable."

Tanya's hopes rose. He was weakening. "Please. It means a lot to me."

"I can't make any promises."

"Just do your best."

"All right."

Tanya felt overcome by gratitude, and kissed his cheek. "You're a good brother," she said. "Thank you."

. . .

Just as the Eskimos were said to have numerous different words for snow, so the citizens of Moscow had many phrases for the black market. Everything other than life's most basic necessities had to be bought "on the left." Many such purchases were straightforwardly criminal: you found a man who smuggled blue jeans from the West and you paid him an enormous price. Others were neither legal nor illegal. To buy a radio or a rug, you might have to put your name down on a waiting list; but you could leap to the top of the list "through pull," by being a person of influence and having the power to return the favor; or "through friends," by having a relative or pal in a position to manipulate the list. So widespread was queue-jumping that most Muscovites believed no one *ever* got to the top of a list just by waiting.

One day Natalya Smotrov asked Dimka to go with her to buy something on the black market. "Normally I'd ask Nik," she said. Nikolai was her husband. "But it's a present for his birthday, and I want it to be a surprise."

Dimka knew little about Natalya's life outside the Kremlin. She was married with no children, but that was about the extent of his knowledge. Kremlin apparatchiks were part of the Soviet elite, but Natalya's Mercedes and her imported perfume indicated some other source of privilege and money. However, if there was a Nikolai Smotrov in the upper reaches of the Communist hierarchy, Dimka had never heard of him.

Dimka asked: "What are you going to give him?"

"A tape recorder. He wants a Grundig—that's a German brand."

Only on the black market could a Soviet citizen buy a German tape recorder. Dimka wondered how Natalya could afford such an expensive gift. "Where are you going to find one?" he asked.

"There's a guy called Max at the Central Market." This bazaar, in Sadovaya-Samotyochnaya, was a lawful alternative to state stores. Produce from private gardens was sold at higher prices. Instead of long queues and unattractive displays, there were mountains of colorful vegetables—for those who could afford them. And the sale of legitimate produce masked even more profitable illegal business at many of the stalls.

Dimka understood why Natalya wanted company. Some of the men who did this kind of work were thugs, and a woman had reason to be wary.

Dimka hoped that was her only motive. He did not want to be led into temptation. He felt close to Nina just now, her time being near. They had not had sex for a couple of months, which made him more vulnerable to Natalya's charms. But that paled beside the drama of pregnancy. The last thing Dimka wanted was a dalliance with Natalya. But he could hardly refuse her this simple favor.

They went in the lunch hour. Natalya drove Dimka to the market in her ancient Mercedes. Despite its age it was fast and comfortable. How did she get parts for it? he wondered.

On the way she asked him about Nina. "The baby is due any day," he said.

"Let me know if you need baby supplies," Natalya said. "Nik's sister has a three-year-old who no longer needs feeding bottles and suchlike."

Dimka was surprised. Baby feeding bottles were a luxury more rare than tape recorders. "Thank you, I will."

They parked and walked through the market to a shop selling secondhand furniture. This was a semilegal business. People were allowed to sell their own possessions, but it was against the law to be a middleman, which made the trade cumbersome and inefficient. To Dimka, the difficulties of imposing such Communist rules illustrated the practical necessity of many capitalist practices—hence the need for liberalization.

Max was a heavy man in his thirties dressed American style in blue jeans and a white T-shirt. He sat at a pine kitchen table, drinking tea and smoking. He was surrounded by cheap used couches and cabinets and beds, mostly elderly and damaged. "What do you want?" he said brusquely.

"I spoke to you last Wednesday about a Grundig tape recorder," said Natalya. "You said to come back in a week."

"Tape recorders are difficult to get hold of," he said.

Dimka intervened. "Don't piss about, Max," he said, making his voice as harsh and contemptuous as Max's. "Have you got one or not?"

Men such as Max considered it a sign of weakness to give a direct answer to a simple question. He said: "You'll have to pay in American dollars."

Natalya said: "I agreed to your price. I've brought exactly that much. No more."

"Show me the money."

Natalya took a wad of American bills from the pocket of her dress.

Max held out his hand.

Dimka took Natalya's wrist to prevent her handing over the money prematurely. He said: "Where is the tape recorder?"

Max spoke over his shoulder. "Josef!"

There was a movement in the back room. "Yes?"

"Tape recorder."

"Yes."

Josef came out, carrying a plain cardboard box. He was a younger man, maybe nineteen, with a cigarette dangling from his lip. Although small, he was muscular. He put the box down on a table. "It's heavy," he said. "Have you got a car?"

"Around the corner."

Natalya counted out the cash.

Max said: "It cost me more than I expected."

"I don't have any more money," Natalya said.

Max picked up the bills and counted them. "All right," he

said resentfully. "It's yours." He stood up and stuffed the wad into the pocket of his jeans. "Josef will carry it to your car." He went into the back room.

Josef grasped the box to pick it up.

Dimka said: "Just a minute."

Josef said: "What? I haven't got time to waste."

"Open the box," said Dimka.

Josef took the weight of the box, ignoring him, but Dimka put his hand on it and leaned on it, making it impossible for Josef to lift it. Josef gave him a look of blazing fury, and for a moment Dimka wondered if there would be violence. Then Josef stood back and said: "Open the damn thing yourself."

The lid was stapled and taped. Dimka and Natalya got it open with some difficulty. Inside was a reel-to-reel tape recorder. The brand name was Magic Tone.

"This is not a Grundig," Natalya said.

"These are better than Grundigs," Josef said. "Nicer sound."

"I paid for a Grundig," she said. "This is a cheap Japanese imitation."

"You can't get Grundigs these days."

"Then I'll have the money back."

"You can't, not once you've opened the box."

"Until we opened the box, we didn't know you were trying to defraud us."

"Nobody defrauded you. You wanted a tape recorder."

Dimka said: "Bugger this." He went to the door of the back room.

Josef said: "You can't go in there!"

Dimka ignored him and went in. The room was full of cardboard boxes. A few were open, showing television sets, record players, and radios, all foreign brands. But Max was not there. Dimka saw a back door.

He returned to the front room. "Max has run off with your money," he told Natalya.

Josef said: "He's a busy man. He has a lot of customers."

"Don't be so fucking stupid," Dimka said to him. "Max is a thief, and so are you."

Josef pointed a finger close to Dimka's face. "Don't you call me stupid," he said in a threatening tone.

"Give her the money back," Dimka said. "Before you get into real trouble."

Josef grinned. "What are you going to do—call the police?"

They could not do that. They were engaged in an illegal transaction. And the police would probably arrest Dimka and Natalya but not Josef and Max, who were undoubtedly paying bribes to protect their business.

"There's nothing we can do," Natalya said. "Let's go."

Josef said: "Take your tape recorder."

"No, thanks," Natalya said. "It's not what I want." She went to the door.

Dimka said. "We're coming back—for the money."

Josef laughed. "What are you going to do?"

"You'll see," Dimka said weakly, and he followed Natalya out.

He was seething with frustration as Natalya drove back to the Kremlin. "I'm going to get your money back," he said to her.

"Please don't," she said. "Those men are dangerous. I don't want you to get hurt. Just leave it."

He was not going to leave it, but he said no more.

When he got to his office, the KGB file on Vasili Yenkov was on his desk.

It was not thick. Yenkov was a script editor who had never been in trouble nor even under suspicion until the day in May 1961 when he had been arrested carrying five copies of a subversive news sheet called *Dissidence*. Under interrogation he claimed he had been handed a dozen copies a few minutes earlier and had begun to pass them out under a sudden impulse of compassion for the opera singer who had pneumonia. A thorough search of his apartment had revealed nothing to contradict his story. His typewriter did not match the one used to produce the newsletter. With electrical terminals attached to his lips and his fingertips, he had given the names of other subversives, but innocent and guilty people alike did that under torture. As was usual, some of the people named had been impeccable Communist Party members, while others the KGB had failed to trace. On balance, the secret police were inclined to believe Yenkov was not the illegal publisher of *Dissidence*.

Dimka had to admire the grit of a man who could maintain a lie under KGB interrogation. Yenkov had protected Tanya even while suffering agonizing torture. Perhaps he deserved his freedom.

Dimka knew the truth that Yenkov had kept hidden. On the night of Yenkov's arrest, Dimka had driven Tanya on his motorcycle to Yenkov's apartment, where she had picked up a typewriter, undoubtedly the machine used to produce *Dissidence*. Dimka had hurled it into the Moskva River half an hour later. Typewriters did not float. He and Tanya had saved Yenkov from a longer sentence.

Yenkov was no longer at the logging camp in the larch forest, according to the file. Someone had discovered that he had a little technical expertise. His first job at Radio Moscow had been studio production assistant, so he knew about microphones and electrical connections. The shortage of technicians in Siberia was so chronic that this had been enough to get him a job as an electrician in a power station.

He had probably been pleased, at first, to move to inside work at which he did not have to risk losing a limb to a careless axe. But there was a downside. The authorities were reluctant to permit a competent technician to leave Siberia. When his sentence was up, he had applied in the usual way for a travel visa to return to Moscow. And his application had been refused. That left him no choice but to continue in his job. He was stuck.

It was unjust; but injustice was everywhere, as Dimka had pointed out to Tanya.

Dimka studied the photograph in the file. Yenkov looked like a movie star, with a sensual face, fleshy lips, black eyebrows, and thick dark hair. But there seemed more to him than that. A faint expression of wry amusement around the corners of his eyes suggested that he did not take himself too seriously. It would not be surprising if Tanya were in love with this man, despite her denials.

Anyway, Dimka would try to get him released for her sake.

He would speak to Khrushchev about the case. However, he needed to wait until the boss was in a good mood. He put the file in his desk drawer.

He did not get an opportunity that afternoon. Khrushchev left early, and Dimka was getting ready to go home when Natalya put her head around his door. "Come for a drink," she said. "We need one after our horrible experience in the Central Market."

Dimka hesitated. "I need to get home to Nina. Her time is near."

"Just a quick one."

"Okay." He screwed the cap onto his fountain pen and spoke to his secretary. "We can go, Vera."

"I've got a few more things to do," she said. She was conscientious.

The Riverside Bar was patronized by the young Kremlin elite, so it was not as dismal as the average Moscow drinking hole. The chairs were comfortable, the snacks were edible, and for the better-paid apparatchik with exotic tastes there were bottles of Scotch and bourbon behind the bar. Tonight it was crowded with people whom Dimka and Natalya knew, mostly aides like themselves. Someone thrust a glass of beer into Dimka's hand and he drank gratefully. The mood was boisterous. Boris Kozlov, a Khrushchev aide like Dimka, told a risky joke. "Everybody! What will happen when Communism comes to Saudi Arabia?"

They all cheered and begged him to tell them.

"After a while there will be a shortage of sand!"

Everyone laughed. The people in this group were keen workers for Soviet Communism, as Dimka was, but they were not blind to its faults. The gap between party aspirations and Soviet reality bothered them all, and jokes released the tension.

Dimka finished his beer and got another.

Natalya raised her glass as if about to give a toast. "The best hope for world revolution is an American company called United Fruit," she said. The people around her laughed. "No, seriously," she said, though she was smiling. "They persuade the United States government to support brutal right-wing dictatorships all over Central and South America. If United Fruit had any sense they would foster gradual progress toward bourgeois freedoms—the rule of law, freedom of speech, trade unions—but, happily for world Communism, they're too dumb to see that. They stamp ruthlessly on reform movements, so the people have nowhere to turn but to Communism—just as Karl Marx predicted." She clinked glasses with the nearest person. "Long live United Fruit!"

Dimka laughed. Natalya was one of the smartest people in the Kremlin, as well as the prettiest. Flushed with gaiety, her wide mouth open in a laugh, she was enchanting. Dimka could not help comparing her with the weary, bulging, sex-averse woman at home, though he knew the thought was cruelly unjust.

Natalya went to the bar to order snacks. Dimka realized he had been here more than an hour: he had to leave. He went up to Natalya with the intention of saying good-bye. But the beer was just enough to make him incautious and, when Natalya smiled warmly at him, he kissed her.

She kissed him back, enthusiastically.

Dimka did not understand her. She had spent a night with him; then she yelled at him that she was married; then she asked him to go for a drink with her; then she kissed him. What next? But he hardly cared about her inconsistency when her warm mouth was on his and the tip of her tongue was teasing his lips.

She broke the embrace, and Dimka saw his secretary standing beside them.

Vera's expression was severely judgmental. "I've been looking for you," she said with a note of accusation. "There was a phone call just after you left."

"I'm sorry," said Dimka, not sure whether he was apologizing for being hard to find or for kissing Natalya.

Natalya took a plate of pickled cucumbers from the bartender and returned to the group.

"Your mother-in-law called," Vera went on.

Dimka's euphoria had now evaporated.

"Your wife has gone into labor," Vera said. "All is well, but you should join her at the hospital."

"Thank you," said Dimka, feeling that he was the worst kind of faithless husband.

"Good night," said Vera, and she left the bar.

Dimka followed her out. He stood breathing the cool night air for a moment. Then he got on his motorcycle and headed for the hospital. What a moment to be caught kissing a colleague. He deserved to feel humiliated: he had done something stupid.

He parked his bike in the hospital car park and went in. He found Nina in the maternity ward, sitting up in bed. Masha was on a chair beside the bed, holding a baby wrapped in a white shawl. "Congratulations," Masha said to Dimka. "It's a boy."

"A boy," Dimka said. He looked at Nina. She smiled, weary but triumphant.

He looked at the baby. He had a lot of damp dark hair. His eyes were a shade of blue that made Dimka think of his grandfather Grigori. All babies had blue eyes, he recalled. Was it his imagination that this baby seemed already to look at the world with Grandfather Grigori's intense stare?

Masha held the baby out to Dimka. He took the little bundle as if handling a large eggshell. In the presence of this miracle, the day's dramas faded to nothing.

I have a son, he thought, and tears came to his eyes.

"He's beautiful," Dimka said. "Let's call him Grigor."

. . .

Two things kept Dimka awake that night. One was guilt: just when his wife was giving birth in bloodshed and agony, he had been kissing Natalya. The other was rage at the way he had been outwitted and humiliated by Max and Josef. It was not he but Natalya who had been robbed, but he felt no less indignant and resentful.

Next morning on the way to work he drove his motorcycle to the Central Market. For half the night he had rehearsed what he would say to Max. "My name is Dmitri Ilich Dvorkin. Check who I am. Check who I work for. Check who my uncle is and who my father was. Then meet me here tomorrow with Natalya's money, and beg me not to take the revenge you deserve." He wondered whether he had the nerve to say all that; whether Max would be impressed or scornful; whether the speech would be threatening enough to retrieve Natalya's money and Dimka's pride.

Max was not sitting at the pine table. He was not in the room. Dimka did not know whether to be disappointed or relieved.

Josef was standing by the door to the back room. Dimka wondered whether to unleash his speech on the youngster. He probably did not have the power to get the money back, but it might relieve Dimka's feelings. While Dimka hesitated he noticed that Josef had lost the threatening arrogance he had displayed yesterday. To Dimka's astonishment, before he had a chance to open his mouth Josef backed away from him, looking scared. "I'm sorry!" Josef said. "I'm sorry!"

Dimka could not account for this transformation. If Josef had found out, overnight, that Dimka worked in the Kremlin and came from a politically powerful family, he might be apologetic and conciliatory, and he might even give the money back, but he would not look as if he were afraid for his life. "I just want Natalya's money," Dimka said.

"We gave it back! We already did!"

Dimka was puzzled. Had Natalya been here before him? "Who did you give it to?"

"Those two men."

Dimka could not make sense of this. "Where is Max?" he said.

"In the hospital," said Josef. "They broke both his arms. Isn't that enough for you?"

Dimka reflected for a moment. Unless this was all some charade, it seemed that two unknown men had beaten Max severely and forced him to give them the money he had taken from Natalya. Who were they? And why had they done this?

Clearly Josef knew no more. Bemused, Dimka turned and left the store.

It was not the police who had done this, he reasoned as he walked back to his bike, nor the army nor the KGB. Anyone official would have arrested Max and taken him to prison and broken his arms in private. Someone unofficial, then.

Unofficial meant gangland. So there were nasty criminals among Natalya's friends or family.

No wonder she never said much about her private life.

Dimka drove fast to the Kremlin but still he was dismayed to find that Khrushchev had got there before him. However, the boss was in a good mood: Dimka could hear him laughing. Perhaps this was the moment to mention Vasili Yenkov. He opened his desk drawer and took out Yenkov's KGB file. He picked up a folder of documents for Khrushchev to sign, then he hesitated. He was a fool to do this, even for his beloved sister. But he suppressed his anxiety and went into the main office.

The first secretary sat behind a big desk speaking on the telephone. He did not much like the phone, preferring face-to-face contact: that way, he said, he could tell when people were lying. However, this conversation was jovial. Dimka put the letters in front of him, and he began to sign while continuing to talk and laugh into the mouthpiece.

When he hung up, Khrushchev said: "What's that in your hand? Looks like a KGB file."

"Vasili Yenkov. Sentenced to two years in a labor camp for possessing a leaflet about Ustin Bodian, the dissident singer. He's served his time, but they're keeping him there."

Khrushchev stopped signing and looked up. "Do you have some personal interest?"

Dimka felt a chill of fear. "None whatsoever," he lied, managing to keep the anxiety out of his voice. If he revealed his sister's link to a convicted subversive it could end his career and hers.

Khrushchev narrowed his eyes. "So why should we let him come home?"

Dimka wished he had refused Tanya. He should have known Khrushchev would see through him: a man did not become leader of the Soviet Union without being suspicious to the point of paranoia. Dimka backpedaled desperately. "I don't say we should bring him home," he said as calmly as he could. "I just thought you might like to know about him. His crime was trivial, he has suffered his punishment, and for you to grant justice to a minor dissident would accord with your general policy of cautious liberalization."

Khrushchev was not fooled. "Someone has asked you for a favor." Dimka opened his mouth to protest his innocence, but Khrushchev held up a hand to silence him. "Don't deny it, I don't mind. Influence is your reward for hard work."

Dimka felt as if a death sentence had been lifted. "Thank you," he said, sounding more pathetically grateful than he wished.

"What job is Yenkov doing in Siberia?" Khrushchev asked.

Dimka realized that the hand holding the file was trembling. He pressed his arm against his side to stop it. "He's an electrician in a power station. He's not qualified, but he used to work in radio."

"What was his job in Moscow?"

"He was a script editor."

"Oh, for fuck's sake!" Khrushchev threw down his pen.

"A script editor? What the hell use is a script editor? They're desperate for electricians in Siberia. Leave him there. He's doing something useful."

Dimka stared at him in dismay. He did not know what to say.

Khrushchev picked up his pen and resumed signing. "A script editor," he muttered. "My arse."

. . .

Tanya typed out Vasili's short story, "Frostbite," with two carbon copies.

But it was too good merely for samizdat publication. Vasili evoked the world of the prison camps with brutal vividness—but he did more. Copying it, she had realized, with an ache in her heart, that the camp stood for the Soviet Union, and the story was a savage critique of Soviet society. Vasili was telling the truth in a way that Tanya could not, and she burned with remorse. Every day she wrote articles that were published in newspapers and magazines all over the USSR; every day she carefully avoided reality. She did not tell outright lies, but she always skirted around the poverty, injustice, repression, and waste that were the actual characteristics of her country. Vasili's writing showed her that her life was a fraud.

She took the typescript to her editor, Daniil Antonov. "This came to me in the mail, anonymously," she said. He might well guess that she was lying, but he would not betray her. "It's a short story set in a prison camp."

"We can't publish it," he said quickly.

"I know. But it's very good—the work of a great writer, I think."

"Why are you showing it to me?"

"You know the editor of *New World* magazine."

Daniil looked thoughtful. "He occasionally publishes something unorthodox."

Tanya lowered her voice. "I don't know how far Khrushchev's liberalization is intended to go."

"The policy has vacillated, but the overall instruction is that the excesses of the past should be discussed and condemned."

"Would you read it and, if you like it, show it to the editor?"

"Sure." Daniil read a few lines. "Why do you think it was sent to *you*?"

"It's probably written by someone I met when I went to Siberia two years ago."

"Ah." He nodded. "That would explain it." He meant *Not a bad cover.*

"The author will probably reveal his identity if the story is accepted for publication."

"Okay," said Daniil. "I'll do my best."

CHAPTER TWENTY-FIVE

The University of Alabama was the last all-white state university in the USA. On Tuesday, June 11, two young Negroes arrived at the campus in Tuscaloosa to register as students. George Wallace, the diminutive governor of Alabama, stood at the doors of the university with his arms folded and his legs astride, and vowed to keep them out.

At the Department of Justice in Washington, George Jakes sat with Bobby Kennedy and others listening to telephone reports from people at the university. The television was on, but for the moment none of the networks was showing the scene live.

Less than a year ago, two people had been shot dead during riots at the University of Mississippi after its first colored student enrolled. The Kennedy brothers were determined to prevent a repeat.

George had been to Tuscaloosa, and had seen the university's leafy campus. He had been frowned at as he walked across the green lawns, the only dark face among the pretty girls in bobby socks and the smart young men in blazers. He had drawn for Bobby a sketch of the grand portico of the Foster Auditorium, with its three doors, in front of which Governor Wallace now stood, at a portable lectern, surrounded by highway patrolmen. The June temperature in Tuscaloosa was rising toward a hundred degrees. George could visualize the reporters and photographers crowded in front of Wallace, sweating in the sun, waiting for violence to break out.

The confrontation had long been anticipated and planned by both sides.

George Wallace was a Southern Democrat. Abraham Lincoln, who freed the slaves, had been a Republican, while proslavery Southerners had been Democrats. Those Southerners were still in the party, helping Democratic presidents get elected, then undermining them once in office.

Wallace was a small, ugly man, going bald except for a patch at the front of his head that he greased and combed into a ludicrous quiff. But he was cunning, and George Jakes could not figure out what he was up to today. What result did Wallace hope for? Mayhem—or something more subtle?

The civil rights movement, which had seemed moribund two months ago, had taken wing after the Birmingham riots. Money was pouring in: at a Hollywood fund-raiser, movie stars such as Paul Newman and Tony Franciosa had written checks for a thousand dollars each. The White House was terrified of more disorder, and desperate to appease the protesters.

Bobby Kennedy had at last come round to the belief that there must be a new civil rights bill. He now admitted that the time had come for Congress to outlaw segregation in all public places—hotels, restaurants, buses, restrooms—and to protect the right of Negroes to vote. But he had not yet convinced his brother the president.

Bobby was pretending to be calm and in charge this morning. A television crew was filming him, and three of his seven children were running around the office. But George knew how fast Bobby's relaxed openness could turn to cold fury when things went wrong.

Bobby was resolved that there would be no rioting—but he was equally determined to get the two students enrolled. A judge had issued a court order to admit the students, and Bobby, as attorney general, could not let himself be defeated by a state governor intent on flouting the law. He was ready to send in troops to remove Wallace by force—but that, too, would be an unhappy ending, Washington bullying the South.

Bobby was in his shirtsleeves, bent over the speaker-phone on his wide desk, with wet marks of perspiration under his arms. The army had set up mobile communications, and someone in the crowd was telling Bobby what was happening. "Nick has arrived," the voice on the speaker said. Nicholas Katzenbach was deputy attorney general, and Bobby's representative on the scene. "He's going up to Wallace . . . he's handing him the cease-and-desist." Katzenbach was armed with a presidential proclamation ordering Wallace to cease illegally defying a court order. "Now Wallace is making a speech."

George Jakes's left arm was in a discreet black silk sling. State troopers had cracked a bone in his wrist in Birmingham, Alabama. Two years earlier a racist rioter had broken the same arm in Anniston, which was also in Alabama. George hoped never to go to Alabama again.

"Wallace isn't talking about segregation," said the voice on the speaker. "He's talking about states' rights. He says Washington doesn't have the right to interfere in Alabama schools. I'm going to try to get close enough so you can hear him."

George frowned. In his inaugural speech as governor, Wallace had said: "Segregation now, segregation tomorrow, segregation forever." But then he had been speaking to white Alabamans. Who was he trying to impress today? Something was going on here that the Kennedy brothers and their advisers had not yet understood.

Wallace's speech was long. When at last it was over, Katzenbach once again demanded that Wallace obey the court, and Wallace refused. Stalemate.

Katzenbach then left the scene—but the drama was not over. The two students, Vivian Malone and James Hood, were waiting in a car. By prior arrangement, Katzenbach escorted Vivian to her dormitory, and another Justice Department lawyer did the same for James. This was only temporary. To register formally, they had to enter the Foster Auditorium.

The lunchtime news came on television, and in Bobby Kennedy's office someone turned up the sound. Wallace stood at the lectern, looking taller than he was in real life. He said nothing about colored people or segregation or civil rights. He talked of the might of central government oppressing the sovereignty of the state of Alabama. He spoke indignantly about freedom and democracy, as if there were no Negroes being denied the vote. He quoted the American Constitution as if he did not spurn it every day of his life. It was a bravura performance, and it worried George.

Burke Marshall, the white lawyer who headed the civil rights division, was in Bobby's office. George still did not trust him, but Marshall had become more radical since Birmingham, and now he proposed resolving the stalemate in Tuscaloosa by sending troops in. "Why don't we just go ahead and do it?" he said to Bobby.

Bobby agreed.

It took time. Bobby's aides ordered sandwiches and coffee. On the campus, everyone held their positions.

News came in from Vietnam. At a road junction in Saigon a Buddhist monk called Thich Quang Duc, doused in five gallons of gasoline, had calmly struck a match and set himself alight. His suicide was a protest at the persecution of the Buddhist majority by the American-sponsored president Ngo Dinh Diem, who was a Catholic.

There was no end to the travails of President Kennedy.

At last the voice on Bobby's speakerphone said: "General Graham has arrived . . . with four soldiers."

"Four?" said George. "That's our show of force?"

They heard a new voice, presumably that of the general addressing Wallace. He said: "Sir, it is my sad duty to ask you to step aside under orders from the president of the United States."

Graham was the commander of the Alabama National Guard, and he was clearly doing his duty against his inclination.

But the voice on the phone now said: "Wallace is walking away . . . Wallace is leaving! Wallace is leaving! It's over!"

There was cheering and handshaking in the office.

After a minute the others noticed that George was not joining in. Dennis Wilson said: "What's the matter with you?"

In George's opinion, the people around him were not thinking hard enough. "Wallace planned this," he said. "All along, he intended to give in as soon as we called in the troops."

"But why?" said Dennis.

"That's the question that's been bothering me. All morning, I've had this suspicion that we're being used."

"So what did Wallace gain by this charade?"

"A showcase. He's just been on television, posing as the ordinary man standing up to a bullying government."

"Governor Wallace, complaining about being bullied?" said Wilson. "That's a joke!"

Bobby had been following the argument, and now he intervened. "Listen to George," he said. "He's asking the right questions."

"It's a joke to you and me," said George. "But many working-class Americans feel that integration is being shoved down their throats by Washington do-gooders such as all of us in this room."

"I know," said Wilson. "Though it's unusual to hear that from . . ." He was going to say from a Negro, but changed his mind. "From someone who campaigns for civil rights. What's your point?"

"What Wallace was doing, today, was talking to those white working-class voters. They'll remember him standing there, defying Nick Katzenbach—a typical East Coast liberal, they'll say—and they'll remember the soldiers making Governor Wallace withdraw."

"Wallace is the governor of Alabama. Why would he need to address the nation?"

"I suspect he will oppose Jack Kennedy in next year's Democratic primaries. He's running for president, folks. And he opened his campaign today on national television—with our help."

There was a moment of quiet in the office as that sank in. George could tell that they were convinced by his argument, and worried by its implications.

"Right now, Wallace leads the news, and he looks like a hero," George finished. "Maybe President Kennedy needs to seize back the initiative."

Bobby touched the intercom on his desk and said: "Get me the president." He lit a cigar.

Dennis Wilson took a call on another phone and said: "The two students have entered the auditorium and registered."

A few moments later Bobby picked up the phone to talk to his brother. He reported a nonviolent victory. Then he began to listen. "Yes!" he said at one stage. "George Jakes said the same thing . . ." There was another long pause. "Tonight? But there's no speech . . . Of course it can be written. No, I think you've made the right decision. Let's do it." He hung up and looked around the room. "The president is going to introduce a new civil rights bill," he said.

George's heart leaped. That was what he and Martin Luther King and everyone in the civil rights movement had been asking for.

Bobby went on: "And he's going to announce it on live television—tonight."

"Tonight?" said George in surprise.

"In a few hours' time."

That made sense, George thought, though it would be a rush. The president would be back at the top of the news, where he belonged—ahead of both George Wallace and Thich Quang Duc.

Bobby added: "And he wants you to go over there and work on the speech with Ted."

"Yes, sir," said George.

He left the Justice Department in a state of high excitement. He walked so fast that he was panting when he reached the White House. He took a minute to catch his breath on the ground floor of the West Wing. Then he went upstairs. He found Ted Sorensen in his office with a group of colleagues. George took off his jacket and sat down.

Among the papers scattered on the table was a telegram from Martin Luther King to President Kennedy. In Danville, Virginia, when sixty-five Negroes had protested segregation, forty-eight of them had been so badly beaten by the police that they had ended up in the hospital. "The Negro's endurance may be at breaking point," King's cable said. George underlined that sentence.

The group worked intensely on the speech. It would begin with a reference to the day's events in Alabama, emphasizing that the troops had been enforcing a court order. However, the president would not linger on the details of this particular squabble, but move quickly to a strong appeal to the moral values of all decent Americans. At intervals, Sorensen took handwritten pages to the secretaries to be typed.

George felt frustrated that something so important had

to be done in a last-minute rush, but he understood why. Drafting legislation was a rational process; politics, by contrast, was an intuitive game. Jack Kennedy had good instincts, and his gut feelings told him that he needed to take the initiative today.

Time passed too quickly. The speech was still being written when the TV crews moved into the Oval Office and began to set up their lights. President Kennedy walked along the corridor to Sorensen's room and asked how it was coming. Sorensen showed him some pages, and the president did not like them. They moved into the secretaries' office, and Kennedy started dictating changes to be typed. Then it was eight o'clock, and the speech was unfinished, but the president was on the air.

George watched the TV in Sorensen's room, biting his nails.

And President Kennedy gave the performance of his life.

He started off a little too formally, but he warmed up when he spoke of the life prospects of a Negro baby: half as much chance of completing high school, one-third of the chance of graduating college, twice as much chance of being unemployed, and a life expectancy seven years shorter than that of a white baby.

"We are confronted primarily with a moral issue," he said. "It is as old as the scriptures and as clear as the American Constitution."

George marveled. Much of this was unscripted, and it showed a new Jack Kennedy. The slick modern president had discovered the power of sounding biblical. Perhaps he had learned from the preacher Martin Luther King. "Who among us would be content to have the color of his skin changed?" he said, reverting to short, plain words. "Who among us would then be content with the counsels of patience and delay?"

It was Jack Kennedy and his brother Bobby who had counseled patience and delay, George reflected. He rejoiced that now at last they had seen the painful inadequacy of such advice.

"We preach freedom around the world," the president said. He was about to go to Europe, George knew. "But are we to say to the world, and much more importantly to each other, that this is the land of the free—except for the Negroes? That we have no second-class citizens—except Negroes? That we have no class or caste system, no ghettoes, no master race—except with respect to Negroes?"

George exulted. This was strong stuff—especially the reference to the master race, which called the Nazis to mind. It was the kind of speech he had always wanted the president to make.

"The fires of frustration are burning in every city, north and south, where legal remedies are not at hand," Kennedy said. "Next week I shall ask the Congress of the United States to act, to make a commitment it has not fully made this century, to the proposition that"—he had gone formal, but now he reverted to plain language—"race has no place in American life or law."

That was a quote for the newspapers, George thought immediately: race has no place in American life or law. He was excited beyond measure. America was changing, right now, minute by minute, and he was part of that change.

"Those who do nothing are inviting shame as well as violence," the president said, and George thought he meant it, even though doing nothing had been his policy until a few hours ago.

"I ask the support of all our citizens," Kennedy finished.

The broadcast ended. Along the corridor, the TV lights were switched off and the crews began to pack their gear. Sorensen congratulated the president.

George was euphoric but exhausted. He went home to his apartment, ate scrambled eggs, and watched the news. As he had hoped, the president's broadcast was the main item. He went to bed and fell asleep.

The phone woke him. It was Verena Marquand. She was weeping and barely coherent. "What happened?" George asked her.

"Medgar," she said, and then something he could not understand.

"Are you talking about Medgar Evers?" George knew the man, a black activist in Jackson, Mississippi. He was a full-time employee of the National Association for the Advancement of Colored People, the most moderate of the civil rights groups. He had investigated the murder of Emmett Till and organized a boycott of white stores. His work had made him a national figure.

"They shot him," Verena sobbed. "Right outside his house."

"Is he dead?"

"Yes. He has three children, George—three! His kids heard the shot and went out and found their father bleeding to death on their driveway."

"Oh, Christ."

"What is *wrong* with these white people? Why do they do this to us, George? Why?"

"I don't know, baby," said George. "I just don't know."

. . .

Once again, Bobby Kennedy sent George to Atlanta with a message for Martin Luther King.

When George called Verena to make the appointment, he said: "I'd love to see your apartment."

He could not figure Verena out. That night in Birmingham they had made love and survived a racist bomb, and he had felt very close to her. But days had gone by, then weeks, without another opportunity to make love, and their intimacy had evaporated. Yet, when she had been distraught with the news of the murder of Medgar Evers, she had not phoned Martin Luther King, nor her father, but George. Now he did not know what their relationship was.

"Sure," she said. "Why not?"

"I'll bring a bottle of vodka." He had learned that vodka was her favorite booze.

"I share the place with another girl."

"Shall I bring two bottles?"

She laughed. "Easy, tiger. Laura will be happy to go out for the evening. I've done it often enough for her."

"Does that mean you'll make dinner?"

"I'm not much of a cook."

"How about if you fry a couple of steaks and I make a salad?"

"You have sophisticated taste."

"That's why I like *you*."

"Smooth talker."

He flew there the next day. He was hoping to spend the night with her, but he did not want her to feel taken for granted, so he checked into a hotel, then got a taxi to her place.

He had more than seduction on his mind. Last time he had brought a message from Bobby to King, he had felt ambivalent about it. This time Bobby was right and King was wrong, and George was determined to change King's mind. So first he would try to change Verena's.

Atlanta in June was hot, and she greeted him wearing a sleeveless tennis dress that showed her long light tan arms. Her feet were bare, and that made him wonder whether she had anything on under the dress. She kissed him on the lips, but briefly, so that he was not sure what it meant.

She had a classy modern apartment with contemporary furniture. She could not afford it on the salary Martin Luther King was giving her, George guessed. Percy Marquand's record royalties must have been paying the rent.

He put the vodka down on the kitchen counter and she handed him a bottle of vermouth and a cocktail shaker. Before making the drinks he said: "I want to be sure you understand something. President Kennedy is in the greatest trouble of his political career. This is much worse than the Bay of Pigs."

She was shocked, as he had intended. "Tell me why," she said.

"Because of his civil rights bill. The morning after his television broadcast—the morning after you called to tell me that Medgar had been murdered—the House majority leader telephoned the president. He said it was going to be impossible to pass the farm bill, mass-transit funding, foreign aid, and the space budget. Kennedy's program of legislation has been completely derailed. Just as we feared, those Southern Democrats are taking their revenge. And the president's rating in the opinion polls dropped ten points overnight."

"It's done him good internationally, though," she pointed out. "You may just have to tough it out at home."

"Believe me, we are," George said. "Lyndon Johnson has come into his own."

"Johnson? Are you kidding me?"

"No, I'm not." George was friendly with one of the vice president's aides, Skip Dickerson. "Did you know that the city of Houston shut off dockside electricity to protest the navy's new policy on shore leave integration?"

"Yes, the bastards."

"Lyndon solved that problem."

"How?"

"NASA is planning to build a tracking station worth millions of dollars in Houston. Lyndon just threatened to cancel it. The city turned the power back on seconds later. Never underestimate Lyndon Johnson."

"We could do with more of that attitude in the administration."

"True." But the Kennedy brothers were fastidious. They did not want to dirty their hands. They preferred to win the argument by sweet reason. Consequently, they did not make much use of Johnson; in fact they looked down on him for his arm-twisting skills.

George filled the cocktail shaker with ice, then poured in some vodka and shook it up. Verena opened the refrigerator and took out two cocktail glasses. George poured a teaspoonful of vermouth into each frosted glass, swirled it around to coat the sides, then added the cold vodka. Verena dropped an olive into each glass.

George liked the feeling of doing something together. "We make a good team, don't we?" he said.

Verena raised her glass and drank. "You make a good martini," she said.

George smiled ruefully. He had been hoping for a different answer, one that affirmed their relationship. He sipped and said: "Yeah, I do."

Verena got out lettuce and tomatoes and two sirloin steaks. George began to wash the lettuce. As he did so he turned the conversation to the real purpose of his visit. "I know that we've talked about this before, but it doesn't help the White House that Dr. King has Communist associates."

"Who says he does?"

"The FBI."

Verena snorted contemptuously. "That famously reliable source of information on the civil rights movement. Knock it off, George. You know that J. Edgar Hoover believes that anyone who disagrees with him is a Communist, including Bobby Kennedy. Where's the evidence?"

"Apparently the FBI has evidence."

"Apparently? So you haven't seen any. Has Bobby?"

George felt embarrassed. "Hoover says the source is sensitive."

"Hoover has refused to show the evidence to the attorney general? Who does Hoover think he's working for?" She sipped her drink thoughtfully. "Has the *president* seen the evidence?"

George said nothing.

Verena's incredulity mounted. "Hoover can't say no to the president."

"I believe the president decided not to push the matter to a confrontation."

"How naïve are you people? George, listen to me. *There is no evidence.*"

George decided to concede the point. "You're probably right. I don't believe that Jack O'Dell and Stanley Levison are Communists, though probably they used to be; but don't you see that the truth doesn't matter? There are grounds for suspicion, and that's enough to discredit the civil rights movement. And, now that the president has proposed a civil rights bill, he gets discredited too." George wrapped the washed lettuce in a towel and windmilled his arm to dry the leaves. Irritation made him do it more energetically than necessary. "Jack Kennedy has put his political life on the line for civil rights, and we can't let him be brought down by charges of Communist association." He tipped the lettuce into a bowl. "Just get rid of those two guys, and solve the problem!"

Verena spoke patiently. "O'Dell is an employee of Martin Luther King's organization, just as I am, but Levison isn't even on the payroll. He's just a friend and adviser to Martin. Do you really want to give J. Edgar Hoover the power to choose Martin's friends?"

"Verena, they're standing in the way of the civil rights bill. Just tell Dr. King to get rid of them—please."

Verena sighed. "I think he will. It's taking a while for his Christian conscience to get around to the idea of spurning loyal longtime supporters, but in the end he'll do it."

"Thank the Lord for that." George's spirits lifted: for once he could go back to Bobby with good news.

Verena salted the steaks and put them in a frying pan. "And now I'll tell you something," she said. "It won't make any goddamn difference. Hoover will continue to leak stories to the press about how the civil rights movement is a Communist front. He would do it if we were all lifelong Republicans. J. Edgar Hoover is a pathological liar who hates Negroes, and it's a damn shame your boss doesn't have the balls to fire him."

George wanted to protest but unfortunately the accusation was true. He sliced a tomato into the salad.

Verena said: "Do you like your steak well cooked?"

"Not too much."

"The French way? So do I."

George made a couple more drinks and they sat at the small table to eat. George embarked on the second half of his message. "It would help the president if Dr. King would call off this damn Washington sit-in."

"That isn't going to happen."

King had called for a "massive, militant, and monumental sit-in demonstration" in Washington, coinciding with nationwide acts of civil disobedience. The Kennedy brothers were appalled. "Consider this," George said. "In Congress, there are some people who will always vote for civil rights and some who never will. The ones who matter are those who could go either way."

"Swing voters," said Verena, using a phrase that had come into vogue.

"Exactly. They know that the bill is morally right but politically unpopular, and they're looking for excuses to vote against it. Your demonstration will give them the chance to say: 'I'm for civil rights, but not at the point of a gun.' The timing is wrong."

"As Martin says, the timing is always wrong for white people."

George grinned. "You're whiter than I am."

She tossed her head. "And prettier."

"That's the truth. You're just about the prettiest sight I've ever seen."

"Thank you. Eat up."

George picked up his knife and fork. They ate mostly in silence. George complimented Verena on the steaks, and she said he made a good salad, for a man.

When they had finished they carried their drinks into the living room and sat on the couch, and George resumed the argument. "It's different, now, don't you see? The administration is on our side. The president is trying his best to pass the bill we've been demanding for years."

She shook her head. "If we've learned one thing, it's that

change comes faster when we keep up the pressure. Did you know that Negroes are getting served by white waitresses in Birmingham restaurants now?"

"Yes, I did know that. What an incredible turnaround."

"And it wasn't achieved by waiting patiently. It happened because they threw rocks and started fires."

"The situation has changed."

"Martin won't cancel the demonstration."

"Would he modify it?"

"What do you mean?"

This was George's Plan B. "Could it become a simple law-abiding march, rather than a sit-in? Congressmen might feel less threatened."

"I don't know. Martin might consider that."

"Hold it on a Wednesday, to discourage people from staying in the city all weekend, and end it early so that the marchers leave well before nightfall."

"You're trying to draw the sting."

"If we must have a demonstration, we should do everything possible to make sure the occasion is nonviolent and makes a good impression, especially on television."

"In that case, how about stationing portable toilets all along the route? I guess Bobby can get that done, even if he can't fire Hoover."

"Great idea."

"And how about rounding up some white supporters? The whole thing will look better on TV if there are white marchers as well as black."

George considered. "I bet Bobby could get the unions to send contingents."

"If you can promise both of those things as sweeteners, I think we have a chance of changing Martin's mind."

George saw that Verena had come around to his point of view and was now discussing how to persuade King. That was half a victory. He said: "And if you can persuade Dr. King to change the sit-in to a march, I think we might get the president to endorse it." He was sticking his neck out, but it was possible.

"I'll do my best," she said.

George put his arm around her. "See, we *are* a good team," he said. She smiled and said nothing. He persisted. "Don't you agree?"

She kissed him. It was the same as the last kiss: more than just friendly, less than sexy. She said thoughtfully: "After that bomb smashed the window of my hotel room, you crossed the room barefoot to fetch my shoes."

"I remember," he said. "There was broken glass all over the floor."

"That was it," she said. "That was your mistake."

George frowned. "I don't get it. I thought I was being nice."

"Exactly. You're too good for me, George."

"What? That's insane!"

She was serious. "I sleep around, George. I get drunk. I'm unfaithful. I had sex with Martin, once."

George raised his eyebrows but said nothing.

"You deserve better," Verena went on. "You're going to have a wonderful career. You might be our first Negro president. You need a wife who will be true to you and work alongside you and support you and be a credit to you. That's not me."

George was bemused. "I wasn't looking that far ahead," he said. "I was just hoping to kiss you some more."

She smiled. "That, I can do," she said.

He kissed her long and slow. After a while he stroked the outside of her thigh, up inside the skirt of her tennis dress. His hand went as far as her hip. He had been right: no underwear.

She knew what he was thinking. "See?" she said. "Bad girl."

"I know," he said. "I'm crazy about you anyway."

CHAPTER TWENTY-SIX

It had been hard for Walli to leave Berlin. Karolin was there, and he wanted to be near her. But that made no sense when they were separated by the Wall. Although they had been only a mile apart he could never see her. He could not risk crossing the border again: it was only by luck that he had not been killed last time. All the same it had been hard for him to move to Hamburg.

Walli told himself he understood why Karolin had chosen to stay with her family to have the baby. Who was best qualified to help her when she gave birth—her mother, or a seventeen-year-old guitar player? But the logic of her decision was small consolation to him.

He thought about her when he went to bed at night and as soon as he woke up in the morning. When he saw a pretty girl in the street it just made him sad about Karolin. He wondered how she was. Did the pregnancy make her uncomfortable and nauseous, or was she glowing? Were her parents angry with her, or thrilled at the prospect of a grandchild?

They exchanged letters, and both always wrote "I love you." But they hesitated to say more about their emotions, knowing that every word would be scrutinized by a secret policeman in the censorship office, perhaps someone they knew, such as Hans Hoffmann. It was like declaring your feelings in front of a scornful audience.

They were on opposite sides of the Wall, and they might as well have been a thousand miles apart.

So Walli came to Hamburg and moved into his sister's spacious apartment.

Rebecca never nagged him. His parents, in their letters, badgered him to go back to school, or perhaps college. Their stupid suggestions had included that he should study to become an electrician, a lawyer, and a schoolteacher like Rebecca and Bernd. But Rebecca herself said nothing. If he spent all day in his room practicing the guitar, she made no objection, just asked him to wash up his coffee cup instead of leaving it dirty in the sink. If ever he talked to her about his future, she said: "What's the rush? You're seventeen. Do what you want, and see what happens." Bernd was equally tolerant. Walli adored Rebecca and liked Bernd more every day.

He had not yet got used to West Germany. People had bigger cars and newer clothes and nicer homes. The government was openly criticized in the newspapers and even on television. Reading some attack on the aging Chancellor Adenauer, Walli would find himself looking guiltily over his shoulder, fearful that someone might observe him reading subversive material; and he would have to remind himself that this was the West, where he had freedom of speech.

He was sad to move away from Berlin but, he now discovered to his delight, Hamburg was the pounding heart of the German music scene. It was a port city, entertaining sailors from all over the world. A street called the Reeperbahn was the center of the red-light district, with bars, strip joints, semisecret homosexual clubs, and many music venues.

Walli longed for only two things in life: to live with Karolin, and to be a professional musician.

One day soon after moving to Hamburg he walked along the Reeperbahn with his guitar slung over his shoulder and went into every bar to ask if they would like a singer-guitarist to entertain their customers. He believed he was good. He could sing, he could play, and he could please an audience. All he needed was a chance.

After a dozen or so rejections he struck lucky at a beer cellar called El Paso. The decor was evidently intended to be American, with the skull of a longhorn steer over the door and posters of cowboy films on the walls. The proprietor wore a Stetson, but his name was Dieter and he spoke with a Low German accent. "Can you play American music?" he said.

"You betcha," said Walli in English.

"Come back at seven thirty. I'll give you a trial."

"How much would you pay me?" said Walli. Although he still got an allowance from Enok Andersen, the accountant at his father's factory, he was desperate to prove he could be financially independent, and justify his refusal to follow his parents' career advice.

But Dieter looked mildly offended, as if Walli had said something impolite. "Play for half an hour or so," he said airily. "If I like you, then we can talk about money."

Walli was inexperienced, but not stupid, and he felt sure that such evasiveness was a sign that the money would be low. However, this was the only offer he had got in two hours, and he accepted it.

He went home and spent the afternoon putting together half an hour of American songs. He would start with "If I Had a Hammer," he decided; the audience at the Europe Hotel had liked it. He would do "This Land Is Your Land" and "A Mess of Blues." He practiced all his choices several times, though he hardly needed to.

When Rebecca and Bernd came home from work and heard his news, Rebecca announced that she would go with him. "I've never seen you play to an audience," she said. "I've just heard you messing about at home and never finishing the song you started."

It was kind of her, particularly as tonight she and Bernd were excited about something else: the visit to Germany of President Kennedy.

Walli and Rebecca's parents believed that only American firmness had prevented the Soviet Union from taking over West Berlin and incorporating it into East Germany. Kennedy was a hero to them. Walli himself liked anyone who gave the tyrannical East German government a hard time.

Walli laid the table while Rebecca prepared supper. "Mother always taught us that if you want something you join a political party and campaign for it," she said. "Bernd and I want East and West Germany to be reunited, so that we and thousands more Germans can be with their families again. That's why we've joined the Free Democratic Party."

Walli wanted the same thing, with all his heart, but he could not imagine how it might happen. "What do you think Kennedy will do?" he asked.

"He may say that we have to learn to live with East Germany, at least for now. That's true, but it's not what we want to hear. I'm hoping he'll give the Communists a poke in the eye, if you want to know the truth."

They watched the news after they ate. The picture was in clear shades of gray on the screen of their up-to-the-minute Franck television—not blurred green like the old sets.

Today Kennedy had been in West Berlin.

He had made a speech from the steps of Schöneberg town hall. In front of the building was a vast plaza that was jam-packed with spectators. According to the newsreader, there were four hundred fifty thousand people in the crowd.

The handsome young president spoke in the open air, a huge stars-and-stripes flag behind him, the breeze tousling his thick hair. He came out fighting. "There are some who say that Communism is the wave of the future," he said. "Let them come to Berlin!" The audience roared their agreement. The cheers were even louder when he repeated the sentence in German. "*Lass' sie nach Berlin kommen!*"

Walli saw that Rebecca and Bernd were delighted by this. "He's not talking about normalization, or realistically accepting the status quo," Rebecca said approvingly.

Kennedy was defiant. "Freedom has many difficulties, and democracy is not perfect," he said.

Bernd commented: "He's referring to the Negroes."

Then Kennedy said scornfully: "But we have never had to put up a wall to keep our people in!"

"Right!" Walli shouted.

The June sun shone down on the president's head. "All free men, wherever they live, are citizens of Berlin," he said. "And therefore, as a free man, I take pride in the words: *Ich bin ein Berliner!*"

The crowd went wild. Kennedy stepped back from the microphone and slid his notes into his jacket pocket.

Bernd was smiling broadly. "I think the Soviets will get that message," he said.

Rebecca said: "Khrushchev is going to be mad as hell."

Walli said: "The madder the better."

He and Rebecca were in an upbeat mood as they drove

to the Reeperbahn in the van she had adapted for Bernd
and his wheelchair. El Paso had been empty during the afternoon, and now it had only a handful of customers. Dieter
in the Stetson had been less than friendly earlier, and this
evening he was grumpy. He pretended to have forgotten to
ask Walli to come back, and Walli feared he was going to
withdraw the offer of a tryout; but then he jerked his thumb
toward a tiny stage in the corner.

As well as Dieter there was a middle-aged barmaid with
a big bust wearing a check shirt and a bandanna: Dieter's
wife, Walli guessed. Clearly they wanted to give their bar a
distinctive character, but neither had much charm, and they
were not attracting many customers, American or otherwise.

Walli hoped that he might be the magic ingredient that
pulled in the crowds.

Rebecca bought two beers. Walli plugged in his amplifier
and switched the microphone on. He felt excited. This was
what he loved, and what he was good at. He looked at Dieter and his wife, wondering when they wanted him to begin,
but neither showed any interest in him, so he strummed a
chord and started singing "If I Had a Hammer."

The few customers glanced at him with curiosity for a moment, then went back to their conversations. Rebecca
clapped along with the beat enthusiastically, but no one else
did. Nevertheless Walli gave it everything, strumming rhythmically and singing loudly. It might take two or three numbers, but he could win this crowd over, he told himself.

Halfway through the song, the microphone went dead.
So did Walli's amplifier. The power to the stage had obviously failed. Walli finished the song without amplification,
figuring that was slightly less embarrassing than stopping in
the middle.

He put down his guitar and went to the bar. "The power's gone dead onstage," he said to Dieter.

"I know," said Dieter. "I switched it off."

Walli was baffled. "Why?"

"I don't want to listen to that rubbish."

Walli felt as if he had been slapped. Every time he had
ever performed in public, people had liked what he did. He
had never been told that his music was rubbish. His stomach went cold with shock. He hardly knew what to do or say.

Dieter added: "I asked for American music."

That made no sense. Walli said indignantly: "That song was a number one hit in America!"

"This place is named after 'El Paso' by Marty Robbins—the greatest song ever written. I thought you would play that sort of thing. 'Tennessee Waltz,' or 'On Top of Old Smoky,' songs by Johnny Cash, Hank Williams, Jim Reeves."

Jim Reeves was the most boring musician the world had ever known. "You're talking about country-and-western music," Walli said.

Dieter did not feel he needed to be enlightened. "I'm talking about American music," he said with the confidence of ignorance.

There was no point in arguing with such a fool. Even if Walli had realized what was wanted, he would not have played it. He was not going into the music business to play "On Top of Old Smoky."

He returned to the stage and put his guitar in its case.

Rebecca looked bewildered. "What happened?" she said.

"The landlord didn't like my repertoire."

"But he didn't even listen to one song all through!"

"He feels he knows a lot about music."

"Poor Walli!"

Walli could deal with Dieter's boneheaded scorn, but Rebecca's sympathy made him want to cry. "It doesn't matter," he said. "I wouldn't want to work for such an asshole."

"I'm going to give him a piece of my mind," said Rebecca.

"No, please don't," Walli said. "It won't help to have my big sister tell him off."

"I suppose not," she said.

"Come on." Walli picked up his guitar and amplifier. "Let's go home."

• • •

Dave Williams and Plum Nellie arrived in Hamburg with high hopes. They were on a roll. They were becoming popular in London, and now they were going to wow Germany.

The manager of the Dive was called Herr Fluck, which Plum Nellie found hilarious. Not so funny was the fact that he did not like Plum Nellie much. Even worse, after two evenings Dave thought he was right. The group was not giving the punters what they wanted.

"Make dance!" Herr Fluck said in English. "Make dance!" The people in the club, all in their teens and twenties, were mainly interested in dancing. The most successful numbers were the ones that got the girls out on the floor, bopping with one another, so that the men could then cut in and get paired off.

But mostly the group fell short of generating the kind of excitement that got everyone moving. Dave was appalled. This was their big chance and they were fluffing it. If they did not improve, they would be sent home. "For the first time in my life, I'm a success at something," he had said to his skeptical father; and in the end his father had let him come to Hamburg. Would he have to go home and admit that he had failed at this, too?

He could not figure out what the problem was, but Lenny could. "It's Geoff," he said. Geoffrey was the lead guitarist. "He's homesick."

"Does that make him play badly?"

"No, it makes him drink, and the drink makes him play badly."

Dave took to standing right next to the drum kit and hitting his guitar strings harder and more rhythmically, but it did not make much difference. He realized that when one musician underperformed, it brought down the whole group.

On his fourth day he went to visit Rebecca.

He was delighted to discover that he had not one but two relations in Hamburg, and the second was a guitar-playing seventeen-year-old boy. Dave had schoolboy German, and Walli had picked up some English from his grandmother Maud; but they both spoke the language of music, and they spent an afternoon trading chords and guitar licks. That evening Dave took Walli to the Dive, and suggested that the club hire Walli to play in the intervals between Plum Nellie's sets. Walli played a new American hit called "Blowin' in the Wind," which the manager liked, and he got the job.

A week later, Rebecca and Bernd invited the group for a meal. Walli explained to her that the boys worked late into the night and got up at midday, so they liked to eat at around six in the evening, before going onstage. That was fine with Rebecca.

Four of the five accepted the invitation: Geoff would not come.

Rebecca had cooked a pile of pork chops in a rich sauce, with great bowls of fried potatoes, mushrooms, and cabbage. Dave guessed she wanted, in a motherly way, to make sure they got one good meal in the course of a week. She was right to worry: they were living mainly on beer and cigarettes.

Her husband, Bernd, helped with the cooking and serving, moving himself around with surprising agility. Dave was struck by how happy Rebecca was, and how much in love with Bernd.

The group tucked into the food eagerly. They all talked in mixed English and German, and the atmosphere was amiable even if they did not understand everything that was said.

After eating they all thanked Rebecca profusely, then got the bus to the Reeperbahn.

Hamburg's red-light district was like London's Soho but more open, less discreet. Until he came here, Dave had not known that there were male prostitutes as well as female.

The Dive was a grubby basement. By comparison, the Jump Club was plush. At the Dive the furniture was broken, there was no heating or ventilation, and the toilets were in the backyard.

When they arrived, still full of Rebecca's food, they found Geoff in the bar, drinking beer.

The group went onstage at eight. With breaks, they would play until three in the morning. Every night they played every song they knew at least once, and their favorites three times. Herr Fluck made them work hard.

Tonight they played worse than ever.

Throughout the first set Geoff was all over the place, playing wrong notes and fumbling his solos; and that put everyone else off. Instead of concentrating on entertaining people, they were struggling to cover Geoff's mistakes. By the end of the set Lenny was angry.

In the interval, Walli sat on a stool, front of stage, and played the guitar and sang Bob Dylan songs. Dave sat and watched. Walli had a cheap harmonica on a rack that fitted around his neck, so that he could blow and strum at the same time, just as Dylan did. Walli was a good musician,

Dave thought, and smart enough to recognize that Dylan was the latest craze. The clientele of the Dive mostly preferred rock and roll, but some listened, and when Walli went offstage he got a round of enthusiastic applause from a table of girls in the corner.

Dave accompanied Walli to the dressing room, and there they discovered a full-scale crisis.

Geoff was on the floor, drunk and incapable of standing upright without assistance. Lenny, kneeling over him, slapped his face hard every now and again. That probably relieved Lenny's feelings, but it did not bring Geoff round. Dave got a mug of black coffee from the bar, and they forced Geoff to drink some, but that made no difference either.

"We'll have to go on without no fucking lead guitarist," said Lenny. "Unless you can play Geoff's solos, Dave."

"I can do the Chuck Berry stuff, but that's all," said Dave.

"We'll just have to leave the rest out. This fucking audience probably won't notice."

Dave was not sure Lenny was right. Guitar solos were part of the dynamic of good dance music, creating light and shade and preventing the repetitive pop tunes from becoming boring.

Walli said: "I can play Geoff's part."

Lenny looked scornful. "You've never played with us."

"I hear your whole act three nights," Walli said. "I can play all those songs."

Dave looked at Walli and saw in his eyes an eagerness that was touching. He was evidently yearning for this opportunity.

Lenny was skeptical. "Really?"

"I can play. Is not difficult."

"Oh, isn't it?" Lenny was a bit miffed.

Dave was keen to give Walli a chance. "He's a better guitarist than I am, Lenny."

"That's not saying fucking much."

"He's better than Geoff, too."

"Has he ever been in a group?"

Walli understood the question. "In a duo. With a girl singer."

"He hasn't worked with a drummer, then."

That was a key point, Dave knew. He recalled how star-

tled he had been, the first time he played with the Guardsmen, to discover the tight discipline imposed on his playing
by the drumbeat. But he had managed, and Walli could
surely do the same. "Let him try, Lenny," Dave pleaded. "If
you don't like what he does, you can send him off after the
first number."

Herr Fluck put his head around the door and said: "*Raus!
Raus!* It's showtime!"

"All right, all right, *wir kommen*," Lenny replied. He
stood up. "Pick up your axe and get onstage, Walli."

Walli went on.

The opening number of the second set was "Dizzy, Miss
Lizzy," which was guitar-led. Dave said to Walli: "Do you
want to warm up with an easier one?"

"No, thanks," said Walli.

Dave hoped his confidence was justified.

Lew, the drummer, counted: "Three, four, *one.*"

Walli came in right on cue and played the riff.

The group came in a bar later. They played the intro. Just
before Lenny started to sing, Dave caught his eye, and
Lenny nodded approvingly.

Walli played the guitar part perfectly without apparent
effort.

At the end of the song, Dave gave Walli a wink.

They did the set. Walli played every number well, and even
joined in some of the backing vocals. His performance lifted
the group's energy and they got the girls out on the floor.

It was the best set they had played since they got to Germany.

As they went off, Lenny put his arm around Walli and
said: "Welcome to the group."

. . .

Walli hardly slept that night. Playing with Plum Nellie, he
had felt he belonged, musically, and that he enhanced the
group. It had made him so happy that he began to fear it
might not last. Had Lenny really meant it when he said:
"Welcome to the group"?

Next day Walli went to the cheap boardinghouse in the
St. Pauli district where the group lodged. He arrived at midday, just as they were getting up.

He hung out for a couple of hours with Dave and Buzz,

the bass player, going through the group's repertoire, polishing up beginnings and endings of songs. They seemed to assume he would be playing with them again. He wanted confirmation.

Lenny and Lew, the drummer, surfaced around three in the afternoon. Lenny was direct. "Do you definitely want to join this group?"

"Yes," Walli said.

"That's it, then," said Lenny. "You're in."

Walli was not convinced. "What about Geoff?"

"I'll talk to him when he gets up."

They went to a café called Harald's on Grosse Freiheit and had coffee and cigarettes for an hour, then they came back and woke Geoff. He looked ill, which was not surprising after drinking so much that he had passed out. He sat on the edge of his bed while Lenny talked to him and the others listened from the doorway. "You're out of the group," Lenny said. "I'm sorry about it, but you let us down badly last night. You were too drunk to stand up, let alone play. Walli took your place and I'm making him permanent."

"He's just a punk kid," Geoff managed.

Lenny said: "Not only is he sober, he's a better guitarist than you."

"I need coffee," said Geoff.

"Go to Harald's."

They did not see Geoff again before they left for the club.

They were setting up onstage just before eight when Geoff walked in, sober, guitar in hand.

Walli stared at him in consternation. Earlier he had got the impression Geoff had accepted that he was fired. Maybe he had just been too hungover to argue.

Whatever the reason, he had not packed his bag and left, and Walli became anxious. He had suffered so many setbacks: the police smashing up his guitar so that he could not appear at the Minnesänger; Karolin withdrawing from the gig at the Europe Hotel; and the proprietor of El Paso pulling the plug halfway through his first song. Surely this would not turn into another disappointment?

They all stopped what they were doing and watched as Geoff climbed onstage and opened his guitar case.

At that point Lenny said: "What are you doing, Geoff?"

"I'm going to show you that I'm the best guitarist you've ever heard."

"For Pete's sake! You're fired and that's that. Just fuck off to the station and catch a train to Hook."

Geoff changed his tone and became wheedling. "We've been playing together for six years, Lenny. That has to count for something. You have to give me one chance."

This seemed so reasonable that Walli, to his alarm, felt sure Lenny would agree. But Lenny shook his head. "You're an all-right guitar player, but you're no genius, and you're an awkward bastard too. Since we got here you've been playing so badly that we were on the point of being fired last night when Walli joined us."

Geoff looked around. "What do the others think?" he said.

"Who told you this group was a democracy?" Lenny said.

"Who told you it's not?" Geoff turned to Lew, the drummer, who was adjusting a foot pedal. "What do you think?"

Lew was Geoff's cousin. "Give him another chance," Lew said.

Geoff addressed the bassist. "What about you, Buzz?"

Buzz was an easygoing character who would go along with whoever shouted loudest. "I'd give him a chance."

Geoff looked triumphant. "That makes three of us against one of you, Lenny."

Dave put in: "No, it doesn't. In a democracy, you have to be able to count. It's you three against Lenny, me, and Walli—which makes it even."

Lenny said: "Don't bother about the votes. This is my group and I make the decisions. Geoff is fired. Put your instrument away, Geoff, or I'll sling it right out the fucking door."

At this point Geoff seemed to accept that Lenny was serious. He put his guitar back in its case and slammed the lid. Picking it up, he said: "I'll promise you something, you bastards. If I go, you'll all go."

Walli wondered what that meant. Perhaps it was just an empty threat. Anyway, there was no time to think about it. A couple of minutes later they started to play.

All Walli's fears departed. He could tell he was good and the group was good with him in it. Time passed quickly. In the interval, he went back onstage alone and sang Bob

Dylan songs. He included a number he had written himself, called "Karolin." The audience seemed to like it. Afterward he went straight back onstage to open the second set with "Dizzy, Miss Lizzy."

While he was playing "You Can't Catch Me" he saw a couple of uniformed policemen at the back talking to the proprietor, Herr Fluck, but he thought nothing of it.

When they came off at midnight, Herr Fluck was waiting in their dressing room. Without preamble he said to Dave: "How old are you?"

"Twenty-one," said Dave.

"Don't give me that shit."

"What do you care?"

"In Germany we have laws about employing minors in bars."

"I'm eighteen."

"The police say you're fifteen."

"What do the police know about it?"

"They've been talking to the guitar player you just fired—Geoff."

Lenny said: "The bastard, he's shopped us."

Herr Fluck said: "I run a nightclub. Prostitutes come in here, drug dealers, criminals of all kinds. I must constantly prove to the police that I do my best to obey the law. They say I have to send you home—all of you. So, good-bye."

Lenny said: "When do we have to go?"

"You leave the club now. You leave Germany tomorrow."

Lenny said: "That's outrageous!"

"When you're a club owner, you do as the police tell you." He pointed at Walli. "He does not have to leave the country, being German."

"Fuck it," said Lenny. "I've lost two guitarists in one day."

"No, you haven't," said Walli. "I'm coming with you."

CHAPTER TWENTY-SEVEN

Jasper Murray fell in love with the USA. They had all-night radio and three channels of television and a different morning newspaper in every city. The people were generous and their houses were spacious and their manners were relaxed and informal. Back home, English people acted as if they were perpetually taking tea in a Victorian drawing room, even when they were doing business deals or giving television interviews or playing sports. Jasper's father, an army officer, could not see this, but his German-Jewish mother did. Here in the States, people were direct. In restaurants, waiters were efficient and helpful without bowing and scraping. No one was obsequious.

Jasper was planning a series of articles about his travels for *St. Julian's News*, but he also had a higher ambition. Before leaving London, he had spoken to Barry Pugh and asked if the *Daily Echo* might be interested to see what he wrote. "Yeah, sure, if you come across something, you know, special," Pugh had said without enthusiasm. Last week in Detroit, Jasper had got an interview with Smokey Robinson, lead singer of the Miracles, and had sent the article to the *Echo* by express post. He reckoned it should have got there by now. He had given the Dewars' number, but Pugh had not phoned. Jasper was still hopeful, though, and he would call Pugh today.

He was staying at the Dewar family apartment in Washington. It was a big place in a swanky building a few blocks from the White House. "My grandfather Cameron Dewar bought this before the First World War," Woody Dewar explained to Jasper at the breakfast table. "Both he and my father were senators."

A colored maid called Miss Betsy poured orange juice for Jasper and asked if he would like some eggs. "No, thanks, just coffee," he said. "I'm meeting a family friend for breakfast in an hour."

Jasper had met the Dewars at the house in Great Peter Street during the year the family had spent in London. He had not been close to them except, briefly, to Beep, but all the same they had welcomed him to their home, more than a year later, with open-handed hospitality. Like the Williamses, they were casually generous, especially toward young people. Lloyd and Daisy were always happy to accommodate stray teenagers for a night or a week—or, in Jasper's case, several years. The Dewars seemed the same. "It's so kind of you to let me stay here," Jasper said to Bella.

"Oh, you're welcome, it's nothing," she said, and she meant it.

Jasper turned to Woody. "I assume you'll be photographing today's civil rights march for *Life* magazine?"

"That's right," said Woody. "I'll mingle with the crowd, taking discreet candid shots with a small thirty-five-millimeter camera. Someone else will do the essential formal pictures of the celebrities on the platform."

He was dressed casually, in chinos and a short-sleeved shirt, but all the same it would be difficult for such a tall man to be inconspicuous. However, Woody's revealing news photographs were world famous. "I'm familiar with your work, as is everyone who's interested in journalism," said Jasper.

"Does any particular subject attract you?" Woody asked. "Crime, politics, war?"

"No. I'd be happy to cover everything—as you seem to."

"I'm interested in faces. Whatever the story—a funeral, a football game, a murder investigation—I photograph faces."

"What do you expect today?"

"No one knows. Martin Luther King is predicting a hundred thousand people. If he gets that many, it will be the biggest civil rights march ever. We all hope it will be happy and peaceful, but we're not counting on it. Look what happened in Birmingham."

"Washington is different," Bella put in. "We have colored police officers here."

"Not many," Woody said. "Although you can bet they will all be at the forefront today."

Beep Dewar came into the dining room. She was fifteen and petite. "Who's going to be at the forefront?" she said.

"Not you, I hope," said her mother. "You stay clear of trouble, please."

"Of course, Mama."

Jasper noted that Beep had learned a measure of discretion in the two years since he had last seen her. Today she looked cute, but not especially sexy, in tan jeans and a loose-fitting cowboy shirt—a sensible outfit for a day that might turn disorderly.

She acted toward Jasper as if she had completely forgotten about their flirtation in London. She was signaling that he should not expect to take up where he had left off. No doubt she had had boyfriends since then. For his part, he was relieved that she did not feel he belonged to her.

The last member of the Dewar family to appear at breakfast was Cameron, Beep's older brother by two years. He was dressed like a middle-aged man, in a linen jacket with a white shirt and a tie. "You stay out of trouble too, Cam," said his mother.

"I have no intention of going anywhere near the march," he said prissily. "I'm planning to visit the Smithsonian."

Beep said: "Don't you believe colored people should be able to vote?"

"I don't believe they should cause trouble."

"If they were allowed to vote, they wouldn't need to make their point in other ways."

Bella said: "That's enough, you two."

Jasper finished his coffee. "I need to make a transatlantic phone call," he said. He felt obliged to add: "I'll pay for it, of course," though he was not sure he had enough money.

"Go right ahead," Bella said. "Use the phone in the study. And please don't trouble about paying."

Jasper was relieved. "You're so kind," he said.

Bella waved that aside. "I think *Life* magazine probably takes care of our phone bill, anyway," she said vaguely.

Jasper went into the study. He called the *Daily Echo* in London and reached Barry Pugh, who said: "Hi, Jasper, how are you enjoying the USA?"

"It's great." Jasper swallowed nervously. "Did you get my Smokey Robinson piece?"

"Yes, thanks. Well written, Jasper, but it doesn't make it for the *Echo*. Try the *New Musical Express*."

Jasper was disheartened. He had no interest in writing for the pop press. "Okay," he said. Not ready to give up, he added: "I thought the fact that Smokey is the Beatles' favorite singer might give the interview extra interest."

"Not enough. Nice try, though."

Jasper tried hard to keep the disappointment out of his voice. "Thanks."

Pugh said: "Isn't there some kind of demonstration in Washington today?"

"Yes, civil rights." Jasper's hopes rose again. "I'll be there—if you'd like a report?"

"Hmm . . . Give us a ring if it gets violent."

And not otherwise, Jasper inferred. Disappointed, he said: "Okay, will do."

Jasper cradled the phone and stared at it pensively. He had worked hard on the Smokey Robinson piece and he felt the Beatles connection made it special. But he had been wrong, and all he could do was try again.

He returned to the dining room. "I must go," he said. "I'm meeting Senator Peshkov at the Willard Hotel."

Woody said: "The Willard is where Martin Luther King stays."

Jasper brightened. "Maybe I could get an interview." The *Echo* would surely be interested in that.

Woody smiled. "There will be several hundred reporters hoping for an interview with King today."

Jasper turned to Beep. "Will I see you later?"

"We're meeting at the Washington Monument at ten," she said. "There's a rumor that Joan Baez is going to sing."

"I'll look for you there."

Woody said: "Did you say you're meeting Greg Peshkov?"

"Yes. He's the half brother of Daisy Williams."

"I know. The domestic arrangements of Greg's father, Lev Peshkov, were hot gossip when your mother and I were teenagers in Buffalo. Please give Greg my regards."

"Of course," said Jasper, and he went out.

. . .

George Jakes entered the coffee shop at the Willard and looked around for Verena, but she had not yet arrived. However, he saw his father, Greg Peshkov, having breakfast with a good-looking man of about twenty who had a blond Beatle haircut. George sat at their table and said: "Good morning."

Greg said: "This is Jasper Murray, a student from London, England. He's the son of an old friend. Jasper, meet George Jakes."

They shook hands. Jasper looked faintly startled, as people often did when they saw Greg and George together; but, like most people, he was too polite to ask for an explanation.

Greg said to George: "Jasper's mother was a refugee from Nazi Germany."

Jasper said: "My mother has never forgotten how the American people welcomed her that summer."

George said to Jasper: "So the subject of racial discrimination is familiar to you, I guess."

"Not really. My mother doesn't like to talk about the old days too much." He smiled engagingly. "At school in England I was called Jasper Jewboy for a while, but it didn't stick. Are you involved in today's march, George?"

"Kind of. I work for Bobby Kennedy. Our concern is to make sure the day goes smoothly."

Jasper was interested. "How are you able to do that?"

"The Mall is full of temporary drinking fountains, first aid stations, portable toilets, and even a check-cashing facility. A church in New York has made eighty thousand sandwich lunches for the organizers to distribute free. All speeches are limited to seven minutes, so that the event will end on time and visitors can leave town well before dark. And Washington has banned the sale of liquor for the day."

"Will it work?"

George did not know. "Frankly, everything depends on the white people. It only takes a few cops to start throwing their weight around, using billy clubs or fire hoses or attack dogs, to turn a prayer meeting into a riot."

Greg said: "Washington isn't the Deep South."

"It isn't the North, either," said George. "So there's no telling what will happen."

Jasper persisted with his questions. "And if there is a riot?"

Greg answered him. "There are four thousand troops stationed in the suburbs, and fifteen thousand paratroopers close by in North Carolina. Washington hospitals have canceled all nonurgent surgery to make room for the wounded."

"Blimey," said Jasper. "You're serious."

George frowned. These precautions were not public knowledge. Greg had been briefed, as a senator; but he should not have told Jasper.

Verena appeared and came to their table. All three men stood up. She spoke to Greg. "Good morning, Senator. Good to see you again."

Greg introduced her to Jasper, whose eyes were popping out. Verena had that effect on white and black men. "Verena works for Martin Luther King," Greg said.

Jasper turned a hundred-watt smile on Verena. "Could you get me an interview with him?"

George snapped: "Why?"

"I'm a student journalist. Didn't I mention that?"

"No, you did not," George said with irritation.

"I'm sorry."

Verena was not immune to Jasper's charm. "I'm so sorry," she said with a rueful smile. "An interview with the Reverend Dr. King is out of the question today."

George was annoyed. Greg should have warned him that Jasper was a journalist. Last time George talked to a reporter he had embarrassed Bobby Kennedy. He hoped he had not said anything indiscreet today.

Verena turned to George, and her tone changed to annoyance. "I just talked to Charlton Heston. FBI agents are phoning our celebrity supporters this morning, telling them to stay in their hotel rooms for the day because there's going to be violence."

George made a disgusted noise. "The FBI is worried, not that the march will be violent, but that it will be a success."

Verena was not satisfied with that. "Can't you stop them trying to sabotage the whole event?"

"I'll speak to Bobby, but I don't think he'll want to cross swords with J. Edgar Hoover on something so minor." George touched Greg's arm. "Verena and I have to talk. Excuse us, please."

Verena said: "My table is over there."

They crossed the room. George forgot about the sneaky Jasper Murray. As they sat down, he said to Verena: "What's the situation?"

She leaned across the table and spoke in a low voice, but she was bursting with excitement. "It's going to be bigger than we thought," she said, her eyes shining. "A hundred thousand people is an underestimate."

"How do you know?"

"Every scheduled bus, train, and plane to Washington today is full," she said. "At least twenty chartered trains arrived this morning. At Union Station you can't hear yourself think for the people singing 'We Shall Not Be Moved.' Special buses are coming through the Baltimore tunnel at the rate of one hundred per hour. My father chartered a plane from Los Angeles for all the movie stars. Marlon Brando is here, and James Garner. CBS is broadcasting the whole thing live."

"How many people do you think will show up altogether?"

"Right now we're guessing double the original estimate."

George was flabbergasted. "Two hundred thousand people?"

"That's what we think now. It could go higher."

"I don't know whether that's good or bad."

She frowned in irritation. "How could it be bad?"

"We just haven't planned for that many. I don't want trouble."

"George, this is a protest movement—it's *about* trouble."

"I wanted us to show that a hundred thousand Negroes could meet in a park without starting a goddamn fight."

"We're in a fight already, and the whites started it. Hell, George, they broke your wrist for trying to go to the airport."

George touched his left arm reflexively. The doctor said it had healed, but it still gave him a twinge sometimes. "Did you see *Meet the Press*?" he asked her. Dr. King had been questioned by a panel of journalists on the NBC news show.

"Of course I did."

"Every question was about either Negro violence or Communists in the civil rights movement. We must not let these become the issues!"

"We can't let our strategy be dictated by *Meet the Press*. What do you think those white journalists are going to talk about? Don't expect them to ask Martin about violent white cops, dishonest Southern juries, corrupt white judges, and the Ku Klux Klan!"

"Let me put it to you another way," George said calmly. "Suppose today goes off peacefully, but Congress rejects the civil rights bill, and *then* there are riots. Dr. King will be able to say: 'A hundred thousand Negroes came here in peace, singing hymns, giving you the chance to do the right thing—but you spurned the opportunity we offered, and now you see the consequences of your obstinacy. If there are riots now, you have no one to blame but yourselves.' How about that?"

Verena smiled reluctantly and nodded assent. "You're pretty smart, George," she said. "Did you know that?"

. . .

The National Mall was a three-hundred-acre park, long and narrow, stretching for two miles from the Capitol at one end to the Lincoln Memorial at the other. The marchers assembled in the middle, at the Washington Monument, an obelisk more than five hundred feet tall. A stage had been set up and, when George arrived, the pure, thrilling voice of Joan Baez was ringing out "Oh, Freedom."

Jasper looked for Beep Dewar, but the crowd was already at least fifty thousand strong, and not surprisingly he could not see her.

He was having the most interesting day of his life, and it was not yet eleven in the morning. Greg Peshkov and George Jakes were Washington insiders who had casually given him exclusive information: how he wished the *Daily Echo* was interested. And green-eyed Verena Marquand was possibly the most beautiful woman Jasper had ever seen. Was George sleeping with her? Lucky man, if so.

Joan Baez was followed by Odetta and Josh White, but the crowd went wild when Peter, Paul and Mary appeared. Jasper could hardly believe he was seeing these huge stars live onstage without even buying a ticket. Peter, Paul and Mary sang their latest hit, "Blowin' in the Wind," a song written by Bob Dylan. It seemed to be about the civil rights movement, and included the line: "How many years can some people exist before they're allowed to be free?"

The audience became even more madly enthusiastic when Dylan himself walked on. He sang a new song about the murder of Medgar Evers, called "Only a Pawn in Their Game." The song sounded enigmatic to Jasper, but the listeners were oblivious to ambiguity, and rejoiced that the hottest new music star in America seemed to be on their side.

The throng was swelling minute by minute. Jasper was tall, and could look over most heads, but he could no longer see the edge of the multitude. To the west, the famous long reflecting pool led to the Greek temple commemorating Abraham Lincoln. The demonstrators were supposed to march to the Lincoln Memorial later, but Jasper could see that many were already migrating to the western end of the park, probably intent on securing the best seats for the speeches.

So far there had been no hint of violence, despite media pessimism—or had it been media wishful thinking?

There seemed to be news photographers and television cameras everywhere. They often focused on Jasper, perhaps because of his pop-star haircut.

He started to write an article in his head. The event was a picnic in a forest, he decided, with revelers lunching in a sunlit glade while bloodthirsty predators skulked in the deep shade of the surrounding woods.

He strolled west with the crowd. The Negroes were dressed in their Sunday best, he noticed, the men in ties and straw hats, the women in bright print dresses and head scarves, whereas the whites were casual. The issue had widened from segregation, and the placards called for votes, jobs, and housing. There were delegations from trade unions, churches, and synagogues.

Near the Lincoln Memorial he ran into Beep. She was with a group of girls heading in the same direction. They found a spot where they had a clear view of the stage that had been set up on the steps.

The girls passed around a large bottle of warm Coca-Cola. Some of them were Beep's friends, Jasper discovered; others had simply tagged along. They were interested in him as an exotic foreigner. He lay in the August sun chatting idly to them until the speeches began. By that time the crowd stretched farther than Jasper could see. He felt sure there were more than the one hundred thousand expected.

The lectern stood in front of the giant statue of the brooding President Lincoln, seated on a huge marble throne, his massive hands on the arms of the chair, his beetle brows drawn, his expression stern.

Most of the speakers were black, but there were a few whites, including a rabbi. Marlon Brando was on the platform, brandishing an electric cattle prod of the kind used on Negroes by the police in Gadsden, Alabama. Jasper liked the sharp-tongued union leader Walter Reuther, who said scathingly: "We cannot defend freedom in Berlin as long as we deny freedom in Birmingham."

But the crowd grew restless and began to shout for Martin Luther King.

He was almost the last speaker.

King was a preacher, and a good one, Jasper knew immediately. His diction was crisp, his voice a vibrant baritone. He had the power to move the crowd's emotions, a valuable skill that Jasper admired.

However, King had probably never before preached to so many people. Few men had.

He cautioned that the demonstration, triumphant though it was, meant nothing if it did not lead to real change. "Those who hope that the Negro needed to blow off steam, and will now be content, will have a rude awakening if the nation returns to business as usual." The audience cheered and whooped at every resonant phrase. "There will be neither rest nor tranquillity in America until the Negro is granted his citizenship rights," King warned. "The whirlwinds of revolt will continue to shake the foundations of our nation until the bright day of justice emerges."

As he drew near to the end of his seven minutes, King became more biblical. "We can never be satisfied as long as our children are stripped of their selfhood, and robbed of their dignity, by signs stating 'For Whites Only,'" he said. "We will not be satisfied until justice runs down like waters, and righteousness like a mighty stream."

On the platform behind him, the gospel singer Mahalia Jackson cried: "My Lord! My Lord!"

"Even though we face the difficulties of today and to-morrow, I still have a dream," he said.

Jasper sensed that King had thrown away his prepared speech, for he was no longer manipulating his audience emotionally. Instead, he seemed to be drawing his words from a deep, cold well of suffering and pain, a well created by centuries of cruelty. Jasper realized that Negroes described their suffering in the words of the Old Testament prophets, and bore their pain with the consolation of Jesus's gospel of hope.

King's voice shook with emotion as he said: "I have a dream that one day this nation will rise up and live out the true meaning of its creed: 'We hold these truths to be self-evident, that all men are created equal.'

"I have a dream that one day, on the red hills of Georgia, the sons of former slaves and the sons of former slave owners will be able to sit down together at the table of brother-hood—I have a dream.

"That one day even the state of Mississippi—a state sweltering with the heat of injustice, sweltering with the heat of oppression—will be transformed into an oasis of freedom and justice. I have a dream."

He had hit a rhythm, and two hundred thousand people felt it sway their souls. It was more than a speech: it was a poem and a canticle and a prayer as deep as the grave. The heartbreaking phrase "I have a dream" came like an amen at the end of each ringing sentence.

"That my four little children will one day live in a nation where they will not be judged by the color of their skin but by the content of their character—I have a dream today.

"I have a dream that one day down in Alabama—with its vicious racists, with its governor having his lips dripping with the words of interposition and nullification—one day right there in Alabama, little black boys and black girls will be able to join hands with little white boys and white girls as sisters and brothers—I have a dream today.

"With this faith we will be able to hew, out of the mountain of despair, a stone of hope.

"With this faith we will be able to transform the jangling discords of our nation into a beautiful symphony of broth-erhood.

"With this faith we will be able to work together, to pray together, to struggle together, to go to jail together, to stand up for freedom together, knowing that we will be free one day."

Looking around, Jasper saw that black and white faces alike were running with tears. Even he felt moved, and he had thought himself immune to this kind of thing.

"And when this happens; when we allow freedom to ring; when we let it ring from every village and every hamlet, from every state and every city; we will be able to speed up that day when *all* of God's children, black men and white men, Jews and Gentiles, Protestants and Catholics, will be able to join hands . . ."

Here he slowed down, and the crowd was almost silent.

King's voice trembled with the earthquake force of his passion. ". . . and sing, in the words of the old Negro spiritual:

"Free at last!

"Free at last!

"Thank God Almighty, we are free at last!"

He stepped back from the microphone.

The crowd gave a roar such as Jasper had never heard. They rose to their feet in a surge of rapturous hope. The applause rolled on, seeming as endless as the ocean waves.

It went on until King's distinguished white-haired mentor, Benjamin Mays, stepped up to the microphone and pronounced a blessing. Then people knew it was over, and at last they turned away reluctantly from the stage to go home.

Jasper felt as if he had come through a storm, or a battle, or a love affair: he was spent but jubilant.

He and Beep headed for the Dewar apartment, hardly speaking. Surely, Jasper thought, the *Echo* would be interested in this? Hundreds of thousands of people had heard a heart-stopping plea for justice. Surely British politics, with its dismal sex scandals, could not compete with this for space on the front page of a newspaper?

He was right.

Beep's mother, Bella, was sitting at the kitchen table, shelling peas, while Miss Betsy peeled potatoes. As soon as Jasper walked in, Bella said to him: "The *Daily Echo* in London has called twice for you. A Mr. Pugh."

"Thank you," said Jasper, his heart beating faster. "Do you mind if I return the call?"

"Of course not, go right ahead."

Jasper went to the study and phoned Pugh. "Did you take part in the march?" said Pugh. "Did you hear the speech?"

"Yes, and yes," said Jasper. "It was incredible—"

"I know. We're going all out with it. Can you give us an I-was-there piece? As personal and impressionistic as you like. Don't worry too much about facts and figures, we'll have all those in the main report."

"I'd be happy to," said Jasper. It was an understatement: he was ecstatic.

"Let it run. About a thousand words. We can always cut if necessary."

"All right."

"Call me in half an hour and I'll put you through to a copy taker."

"Couldn't I have longer?" said Jasper; but Pugh had already hung up.

"Blimey," said Jasper to the wall.

There was an American-style yellow legal pad on Woody Dewar's desk. Jasper pulled it toward him and picked up a pencil. He thought for a minute, then wrote:

"Today I stood in a crowd of two hundred thousand people and heard Martin Luther King redefine what it means to be American."

. . .

Maria Summers felt high.

The television set had been on in the press office, and she had stopped work to watch Martin Luther King, as had just about everyone else in the White House, including President Kennedy.

When it ended she was walking on air. She could hardly wait to hear what the president thought of the speech. A few minutes later she was summoned to the Oval Office. The temptation to hug Kennedy was even harder for her to resist than usual. "He's damn good," was Kennedy's slightly detached reaction. Then he said: "He's on his way here now," and Maria was overjoyed.

Jack Kennedy had changed. When Maria had first fallen in love with him, he had been in favor of civil rights intellectually, but not emotionally. The change was not due to their affair. Rather, it was the relentless brutality and lawlessness of the segregationists that had shocked him into a heartfelt personal commitment. And he had risked everything by bringing forward the new civil rights bill. She knew better than anyone how worried he was about it.

George Jakes came in, immaculately dressed as always, today in a dark blue suit with a pale gray shirt and a striped tie. He smiled warmly at her. She was fond of him: he had been a friend in need. He was, she thought, the second-most attractive man she had ever met.

Maria knew that she and George were here for show, because they were among the small number of colored people in the administration. They were both reconciled to being used as symbols. It was not dishonest: though their number was small, Kennedy had appointed more Negroes to high-level posts than any previous president.

When Martin Luther King walked in, President Kennedy shook his hand and said: "I have a dream!"

It was meant well, Maria knew, but she felt it was ill judged. King's dream came from the depths of vicious repression. Jack Kennedy had been born into America's privileged elite, powerful and rich: how could he claim to have a dream of freedom and equality? Dr. King obviously felt this too, for he looked embarrassed and changed the subject. Later, in bed, the president would ask Maria where he had taken a wrong step, she knew; and she would have to find a loving and reassuring way to explain it to him.

King and the other civil rights leaders had not eaten since breakfast. When the president realized this, he ordered coffee and sandwiches for them from the White House kitchen.

Maria got them all to line up for a formal photograph, then the discussion began.

King and the others were riding a wave of elation. After today's demonstration, they told the president, the civil rights bill could be toughened up. There should be a new section banning racial discrimination in employment. Young black men were dropping out of school at an alarming rate, seeing no future.

President Kennedy suggested that Negroes should copy the Jews, who valued education and made their kids study.

Maria came from a Negro family who did exactly that, and she agreed with him. If black kids dropped out of school, was that the government's problem? But she also saw how cleverly Kennedy had shifted the discussion away from the real issue, which was millions of jobs that were reserved for whites only.

They asked Kennedy to lead the crusade for civil rights. Maria knew that he was thinking something he could not say: that if he became too strongly identified with the Negro cause, then all the white people would vote Republican.

The shrewd Walter Reuther offered different advice. Identify the businessmen behind the Republican party and pick them off in small groups, he said. Tell them that if they don't cooperate, their profits will suffer. Maria knew this as the Lyndon Johnson approach, a combination of cajolery and threats. The advice went over the president's head: it just was not his style.

Kennedy went through the voting intentions of congressmen and senators, ticking off on his fingers those likely to oppose the civil rights bill. It was a dismal register of prejudice, apathy, and timidity. He was going to have trouble passing even a watered-down version of the bill, he made clear; anything tougher was doomed.

Gloom seemed to fall on Maria like a funeral shawl. She felt tired, depressed, and pessimistic. Her head ached and she wanted to go home.

The meeting lasted more than an hour. By the time it finished, all the euphoria had evaporated. The civil rights leaders filed out, their faces showing disenchantment and frustration. It was all very well for King to have a dream, but it seemed the American people did not share it.

Maria could hardly believe it but, despite all that had happened today, it seemed the great cause of equality and freedom was no farther forward.

CHAPTER TWENTY-EIGHT

Jasper Murray felt confident he would get the post of editor of *St. Julian's News*. With his application he had sent in a clipping of his article in the *Daily Echo* about Martin Luther King's "I have a dream" speech. Everyone said it was a great piece. He had been paid twenty-five pounds, less than he had got for the interview with Evie: politics was not as lucrative as celebrity scandal.

"Toby Jenkins has never had a paragraph published anywhere outside the student press," Jasper told Daisy Williams, sitting in the kitchen in Great Peter Street.

"Is he your only rival?" she asked.

"As far as I know, yes."

"When will you hear the decision?"

Jasper looked at his watch, although he knew the time. "The committee is meeting now. They'll put up a notice outside Lord Jane's office when they break for lunch at twelve thirty. My friend Pete Donegan is there. He'll be my deputy editor. He's going to phone me immediately."

"Why do you want the post so badly?"

Because I know how bloody good I am, Jasper thought; twice as good as Cakebread and ten times better than Toby Jenkins. I deserve this job. But he did not open his heart to Daisy Williams. He was a little wary of her. She loved his mother, not him. When the interview with Evie had appeared in the *Echo,* and Jasper had pretended to be dismayed, it had seemed to him that Daisy had not been completely deceived. He worried that she saw through him.

However, she always treated him kindly, for his mother's sake.

Now he gave her a softened version of the truth. "I can turn *St. Julian's News* into a better paper. Right now it's like a parish magazine. It tells you what's going on, but it's frightened of conflict and controversy." He thought of something that would appeal to Daisy's ideals. "For example, St. Julian's College has a board of governors, some of whom have investments in apartheid South Africa. I'd publish that information and ask what such men are doing governing a famous liberal college."

"Good idea," Daisy said with relish. "That'll stir them up."

Walli Franck came into the kitchen. It was midday, but he had evidently just got up: he kept rock-and-roll hours.

Daisy said to him: "Now that Dave's back in school, what are you going to do?"

Walli put instant coffee into a cup. "Practice the guitar," he said.

Daisy smiled. "If your mother were here, I guess she would ask if you shouldn't try to earn some money."

"I don't want to earn money. But I must. That's why I have a job."

Walli's grammar was sometimes so correct that it was hard to understand. Daisy said: "You don't want money, but you do have a job?"

"Washing beer glasses at the Jump Club."

"Well done!"

The doorbell rang, and a minute later a maid showed Hank Remington into the kitchen. He had classic Irish charm. He was a chirpy redhead with a big smile for everyone. "Hello, Mrs. Williams," he said. "I've come to take your daughter out to lunch—unless you're available!"

Women enjoyed Hank's flattery. "Hello, Hank," Daisy said warmly. She turned to the maid and said: "Make sure Evie knows Mr. Remington is here."

"Is it *Mr.* Remington, now?" said Hank. "Don't give people the idea that I'm respectable—it could ruin my reputation." He shook hands with Jasper. "Evie showed me your article about Martin Luther King—that was great, well done." Then he turned to Walli. "Hi, I'm Hank Remington."

Walli was awestruck, but managed to introduce himself. "I'm Dave's cousin, and I play guitar in Plum Nellie."

"How was Hamburg?"

"Great, until we got thrown out because Dave was too young."

"The Kords used to play in Hamburg," Hank said. "It was great. I was born in Dublin but I grew up on the Reeperbahn, if you know what I mean."

Jasper found Hank fascinating. He was rich and famous, one of the biggest pop stars in the world, yet he was working hard to be nice to everyone in the room. Did he have an insatiable desire to be liked—and was that the secret of his success?

Evie came in looking great. Her hair had been cut in a short bob that mimicked the Beatles, and she wore a simple Mary Quant A-line dress that showed off her legs. Hank pretended to be bowled over: "Jesus, I'll have to take you somewhere posh, looking like that," he said. "I was thinking of a Wimpy bar."

"Wherever we go, it will have to be quick," Evie said. "I've got an audition at three thirty."

"What for?"

"A new play called *A Woman's Trial*. It's a courtroom drama."

Hank was pleased. "You'll be making your stage debut!"

"If I get the part."

"Oh, you'll get it. Come on, we'd better go, my Mini's parked on a yellow line."

They went out and Walli returned to his room. Jasper looked at his watch: it was twelve thirty. The editor would be announced any minute now.

Making conversation, he said: "I loved the States."

"Would you like to live there?" Daisy asked.

"More than anything. And I want to work in television. *St. Julian's News* will be a great first step, but basically newspapers are obsolete. TV news is the thing now."

"America is my home," Daisy said musingly, "but I found love in London."

The phone rang. The editor had been chosen. Was it Jasper, or Toby Jenkins?

Daisy answered. "He's right here," she said, and handed the receiver to Jasper, whose heart was thudding.

The caller was Pete Donegan. He said: "Valerie Cakebread got it."

At first Jasper did not understand. "What?" he said. "Who?"

"Valerie Cakebread is the new editor of *St. Julian's News*. Sam Cakebread fixed it for his sister."

"Valerie?" When Jasper understood he was flabbergasted. "She's never written anything but fashion puffs!"

"And she made the tea at *Vogue* magazine."

"How could they do this?"

"Beats me."

"I knew Lord Jane was a prick, but this . . ."

"Shall I come to your place?"

"What for?"

"We should go out and drown our sorrows."

"Okay." Jasper hung up the phone.

Daisy said: "Bad news, obviously. I'm sorry."

Jasper was rocked. "They gave the job to the current editor's sister! I never saw that coming." He recalled his conversation with Sam and Valerie in the coffee bar of the student union. The treacherous pair, neither had even hinted that Valerie was in the running.

He had been outmaneuvered by someone more guileful than himself, he realized bitterly.

Daisy said: "What a shame."

It was the British way, Jasper thought resentfully; family connections were more important than talent. His father had fallen victim to the same syndrome, and in consequence was still only a colonel.

"What will you do?" Daisy said.

"Emigrate," Jasper said. His resolve was now stronger than ever.

"Finish college first," Daisy said. "Americans value education."

"I suppose you're right," Jasper said. But his studies had always come second to his journalism. "I can't work for *St. Julian's News* under Valerie. I gave in gracefully last year, after Sam beat me to the job, but I can't do it again."

"I agree," Daisy said. "It makes you look like a second-rater."

Jasper was struck by a thought. A plan began to form in his mind. He said: "The worst of it is that now there won't be a newspaper to expose such things as the scandal of college governors having investments in South Africa."

Daisy took the bait. "Maybe someone will start a rival newspaper."

Jasper pretended to be skeptical. "I doubt it."

"It's what Dave's grandmother and Walli's grandmother did in 1916. It was called *The Soldier's Wife.* If they could do it . . ."

Jasper put on an innocent face and asked the key question. "Where did they get the money?"

"Maud's family was rich. But it can't cost much to print a couple of thousand copies. Then you pay for the second issue with the income from the first."

"I got twenty-five pounds from the *Echo* for my piece on Martin Luther King. But I don't think that would be enough . . ."

"I might help."

Jasper pretended reluctance. "You might never get your money back."

"Draw up a budget."

"Jack's on his way over here now. We can make some calls."

"If you put in your own money, I'll match it."

"Thank you!" Jasper had no intention of spending his own money. But a budget was like a newspaper gossip column: most of it could be fiction, because no one ever knew the truth. "We could get the first issue together for the beginning of term, if we're quick."

"You should run that story about South African investments on the front page."

Jasper's spirits had lifted again. This might even be better. "Yeah . . . *St. Julian's News* will have a bland front page saying 'Welcome to London,' or something. Ours will be the real newspaper." He began to feel excited.

"Show me your budget as soon as you can," Daisy said. "I'm sure we can work something out."

"Thank you," said Jasper.

CHAPTER TWENTY-NINE

In September of 1963 George Jakes bought a car. He could afford it and he liked the idea, even though in Washington it was easy enough to get around on public transport. He preferred foreign cars: he thought they were more stylish. He found a dark blue five-year-old two-door Mercedes-Benz 220S convertible that had a classy look. On the third Sunday in September he drove to Prince George's County, Maryland, to visit his mother. She would cook him dinner, then they would drive together to Bethel Evangelical Church for the evening service. These days it was not often he had time to visit her, even on a Sunday.

Driving along Suitland Parkway with the top down in the mild September sunshine, he thought about all the questions she would ask him and what answers he would give. First, she would want to know about Verena. "She says she's not good enough for me, Mom," he would say. "What do you think of that?"

"She's right," his mother would probably say. Not many girls were good enough for her son, in her opinion.

She would ask how he was getting on with Bobby Kennedy. The truth was that Bobby was a man of extremes. There were people he hated implacably: J. Edgar Hoover was one. That was fine by George: Hoover was contemptible. But Lyndon Johnson was another. George thought it was a pity that Bobby hated Johnson, who could have been a powerful ally. Sadly, they were oil and water. George tried to imagine the big, boisterous vice president hanging out with the ultrachic Kennedy clan on a boat at Hyannis Port. The image made him smile: Lyndon would be like a rhinoceros in a ballet class.

Bobby liked as hard as he hated, and fortunately George

was someone he liked. George was one of a small inner group who were trusted so much that even when they made mistakes it was assumed they were well intentioned and so they were forgiven. What would George say to his mother about Bobby? "He's a smart man who sincerely wants to make America a better country."

She would want to know why the Kennedy brothers were moving so slowly on civil rights. George would say: "If they push harder there will be a white backlash, and that will have two results. One, we'll lose the civil rights bill in Congress. Two, Jack Kennedy will lose the 1964 presidential election. And if Kennedy loses, who will win? Dick Nixon? Barry Goldwater? It could even be George Wallace, heaven forbid."

These were his musings as he parked in the driveway of Jacky Jakes's small, pleasant ranch-style house and let himself in at the front door.

All those thoughts fled his mind instantly when he heard the sound of his mother weeping.

He suffered a moment of childish fear. He had not often known his mother to cry: she had always been a tower of strength in the landscape of his youth. But, on the few occasions when she had given in, and howled her grief and fear uncontrollably, little Georgy had been bewildered and terrified. And now, just for a second, he had to suppress the revival of that boyhood terror, and remind himself that he was a grown man, not to be scared by a mother's tears.

He slammed the door and strode across the little hallway into the living room. Jacky was sitting on the tan velvet couch in front of the television set. Her hands were pressed to her cheeks as if to hold her head on. Tears streamed down her face. Her mouth was open, and she was wailing. She was staring wide-eyed at the TV.

George said: "Mama, what is it, for God's sake, what happened?"

"Four little girls!" she sobbed.

George looked at the monochrome picture on the screen. He saw two cars that looked as if they had been in a smash. Then the camera moved to a building and panned along damaged walls and broken windows. It pulled back, and he recognized the building. His heart lurched. "My God, that's the Sixteenth Street Baptist Church in Birmingham!" he said. "What did they do?"

His mother said: "The whites bombed the Sunday school!"

"No! No!" George's mind refused to accept it. Even in Alabama, men would not bomb a Sunday school.

"They killed four girls," Jacky said. "Why did God let this happen?"

On television, a newsreader's voice-over said: "The dead have been identified as Denise McNair, aged eleven—"

"Eleven!" said George. "This can't be true!"

"—Addie Mae Collins, fourteen; Carole Robertson, fourteen; and Cynthia Wesley, fourteen."

"But they're children!" said George.

"More than twenty other people were injured by the blast," the newsreader intoned in a voice devoid of emotion, and the camera showed an ambulance pulling away from the scene.

George sat down next to his mother and put his arms around her. "What are we going to do?" he said.

"Pray," she replied.

The newsreader continued remorselessly. "This was the twenty-first bomb attack on Negroes in Birmingham in the last eight years," he said. "The city police have never brought any perpetrators to justice for any of the bombings."

"Pray?" said George, his voice trembling with grief.

Right then he wanted to kill someone.

. . .

The Sunday school bomb horrified the world. As far away as Wales, a group of coal miners started a collection to pay for a new stained-glass window to replace one smashed in the Sixteenth Street Baptist Church.

At the funeral, Martin Luther King said: "In spite of the darkness of this hour, we must not lose faith in our white brothers." George tried to follow that counsel, but he found it hard.

For a while George felt public opinion swinging toward civil rights. A congressional committee toughened Kennedy's bill, adding the ban on employment discrimination that the campaigners wanted so badly.

But a few weeks later the segregationists came out of their corner fighting.

In mid-October an envelope was delivered to the Justice

Department and passed to George. It contained a slim bound report from the FBI entitled:

COMMUNISM AND THE NEGRO MOVEMENT
A CURRENT ANALYSIS

"What the fuck?" George murmured to himself.

He read it quickly. The report was eleven pages long and devastating. It called Martin Luther King "an unprincipled man." It claimed that he took advice from Communists "knowingly, willingly and regularly." With an assured air of inside knowledge it said: "Communist Party officials visualize the possibility of creating a situation whereby it could be said that, as the Communist Party goes, so goes Martin Luther King."

These confident assertions were not backed up by a single scrap of evidence.

George picked up the phone and called Joe Hugo at FBI headquarters, which was on another floor in the same Justice Department building. "What is this shit?" he said.

Joe knew immediately what he was talking about and did not bother to pretend otherwise. "It's not my fault your friends are Commies," he said. "Don't shoot the messenger."

"This is not a report. It's a smear of unsupported allegations."

"We have evidence."

"Evidence that can't be produced is not evidence, Joe, it's hearsay—weren't you listening in law school?"

"Sources of intelligence have to be protected."

"Who have you sent this crap to?"

"Let me check. Ah ... the White House, the secretary of state, the defense secretary, the CIA, the army, the navy, and the air force."

"So it's all over Washington, you asshole."

"Obviously we don't try to *conceal* information about our nation's enemies."

"This is a deliberate attempt to sabotage the president's civil rights bill."

"We would never do a thing like that, George. We're just a law enforcement agency." Joe hung up.

George took a few minutes to recover his temper. Then he went through the report underlining the most outrageous allegations. He typed a note listing the government departments to which the report had been sent, according to Joe. Then he took the document in to Bobby.

As always, Bobby sat at his desk with his jacket off, his tie loosened, and his glasses on. He was smoking a cigar. "You're not going to like this," George said. He handed over the report, then summarized it.

"That cocksucker Hoover," said Bobby.

It was the second time George had heard Bobby call Hoover a cocksucker. "You don't mean that literally," George said.

"Don't I?"

George was startled. "Is Hoover a homo?" It was hard to imagine. Hoover was a short, overweight man with thinning hair, a squashed nose, lopsided features, and a thick neck. He was the opposite of a fairy.

Bobby said: "I hear the Mob has photos of him in a woman's dress."

"Is that why he goes around saying there is no such thing as the Mafia?"

"It's one theory."

"Jesus."

"Make an appointment for me to see him tomorrow."

"Okay. In the meantime, let me go through the Levison wiretaps. If Levison is influencing King toward Communism, there must be evidence in those phone calls. Levison would have to talk about the bourgeoisie, the masses, class struggle, revolution, the dictatorship of the proletariat, Lenin, Marx, the Soviet Union, like that. I'll make a note of every such reference and see what they add up to."

"That's not a bad idea. Let me have a memo before I meet with Hoover."

George returned to his office and sent for the transcripts of the wiretap on Stanley Levison's phone—faithfully copied to the Justice Department by Hoover's FBI. Half an hour later a file clerk wheeled a cart into the room.

George started work. Next time he looked up was when a cleaner opened his door and asked if she could sweep his office. He stayed at his desk while she worked around him.

He remembered "pulling all-nighters" at Harvard Law, especially during the absurdly demanding first year.

Long before he finished, it was clear to him that Levison's conversations with King had nothing to do with Communism. They did not use a single one of George's key words, from *alienation* to *Zapata.* They talked about a book King was writing; they discussed fund-raising; they planned the march on Washington. King admitted fears and doubts to his friend: even though he advocated nonviolence, was he to blame for riots and bombings provoked by peaceful demonstrations? They rarely touched on wider political issues, never on the Cold War conflicts that obsessed every Communist: Berlin, Cuba, Vietnam.

At four A.M. George put his head down on the desk and napped. At eight he took a clean shirt from his desk drawer, still in its laundry wrapper, and went to the men's room to wash. Then he typed the note Bobby had requested, saying that in two years of phone calls Stanley Levison and Martin Luther King had never spoken about Communism or any subject remotely associated therewith. "If Levison is a Moscow propagandist, he must be the worst one in history," George finished.

Later that day, Bobby went to see Hoover at the FBI. When he came back he said to George: "He agreed to withdraw the report. Tomorrow his liaison men will go to every recipient and retrieve all copies, saying it needs to be revised."

"Good," George said. "But it's too late, isn't it?"

"Yes," said Bobby. "The damage is done."

. . .

As if President Kennedy did not have enough to worry about in the autumn of 1963, the crisis in Vietnam boiled over on the first Saturday in November.

Encouraged by Kennedy, the South Vietnamese military deposed their unpopular president, Ngo Dinh Diem. In Washington, National Security Adviser McGeorge Bundy woke Kennedy at three A.M. to tell him the coup he had authorized had now taken place. Diem and his brother, Nhu, had been arrested. Kennedy ordered that Diem and his family be given safe passage to exile.

Bobby summoned George to go with him to a meeting in the Cabinet Room at ten A.M.

During the meeting an aide came in with a cable announcing that both Ngo Dinh brothers had committed suicide.

President Kennedy was more shocked than George had ever seen him. He looked stricken. He paled beneath his tan, jumped to his feet, and rushed from the room.

"They didn't commit suicide," Bobby said to George after the meeting. "They're devout Catholics."

George knew that Tim Tedder was in Saigon, liaising between the CIA and the Army of the Republic of Vietnam, the ARVN, pronounced "Arvin." No one would be surprised if it turned out that Tedder had fouled up.

Around midday a CIA cable revealed that the Ngo Dinh brothers had been executed in the back of an army personnel carrier.

"We can't control anything over there," George said to Bobby in frustration. "We're trying to help those people find their way to freedom and democracy, but nothing we do works."

"Just hang on another year," said Bobby. "We can't lose Vietnam to the Communists now—my brother would be defeated in the presidential election next November. But as soon as he's reelected, he'll pull out faster than you can blink. You'll see."

. . .

A gloomy group of aides sat in the office next to Bobby's one evening that November. Hoover's intervention had worked, and the civil rights bill was in trouble. Congressmen who were ashamed to be racists were looking for a pretext to vote against the bill, and Hoover had given them one.

The bill had been routinely passed to the Committee on Rules, whose chair, Howard W. Smith, from Virginia, was one of the more rabid conservative Southern Democrats. Emboldened by the FBI's accusations of Communism in the civil rights movement, Smith had announced that his committee would keep the bill bottled up indefinitely.

It made George furious. Could these men not see that their attitudes had led to the murder of the Sunday school girls? As long as respectable people said it was all right to treat Negroes as if they were not quite human, ignorant thugs would think they had permission to kill children.

And there was worse. With a year to go before the presidential election, Jack Kennedy was losing popularity. He and Bobby were especially worried about Texas. Kennedy had won Texas in 1960 because he had a popular Texan running mate, Lyndon Johnson. Unfortunately, three years of association with the liberal Kennedy administration had just about destroyed Johnson's credibility with the conservative business elite.

"It's not just civil rights," George argued. "We're proposing to abolish the oil depletion allowance. Texas oilmen haven't paid the taxes they ought to for decades, and they hate us for wanting to scrap their privileges."

"Whatever it is," said Dennis Wilson, "thousands of Texas conservatives have left the Democrats and joined the Republicans. And they love Senator Goldwater." Barry Goldwater was a right-wing Republican who wanted to scrap Social Security and drop nuclear bombs on Vietnam. "If Barry runs for president, he's going to take Texas."

Another aide said: "We need the president to go down there and romance those shitkickers."

"He will," said Dennis. "And Jackie's going with him."

"When?"

"They're going to Houston on November twenty-first," Dennis replied. "And then, the next day, they'll go to Dallas."

CHAPTER THIRTY

Maria Summers was watching on TV, in the White House press office, as Air Force One touched down in brilliant sunshine at the Dallas airport called Love Field.

A ramp was maneuvered into place at the rear door. Vice President Lyndon Johnson and his wife, Lady Bird Johnson, took up their positions at the foot of the ramp, waiting to greet the president. A chain-link fence kept back a crowd of two thousand.

The aircraft door opened. There was a suspenseful pause, then Jackie Kennedy emerged, wearing a Chanel suit and a matching pillbox hat. Right behind her was her husband, Maria's lover, President John F. Kennedy. Secretly, Maria thought of him as Johnny, the name his brothers occasionally used.

The television commentator, a local man, said: "I can see his suntan all the way from here!" He was a novice, Maria guessed: although the television picture was monochrome he failed to tell his audience the colors of things. Every woman watching would have been interested to know that Jackie's outfit was pink.

Maria asked herself whether she would change places with Jackie, given the chance. In her heart Maria yearned to own him, to tell people she loved him, to point to him and say: "That's my husband." But there would be sadness as well as pleasure in the marriage. President Kennedy betrayed his wife constantly, and not just with Maria. Although he never admitted it, Maria had gradually realized that she was only one of a number of girlfriends, maybe dozens. It was hard enough to be his mistress and share him: how much more painful it must be to be his wife, knowing that he was intimate with other women, that he kissed them and touched their private parts and put his cock in their mouths every chance he got. Maria had to be content: she got what a mistress was entitled to. But Jackie did *not* have what a wife was entitled to. Maria did not know which was worse.

The presidential couple descended the ramp and began to shake hands with the Texas bigwigs waiting for them. Maria wondered how many of the people who were so pleased to be seen with Kennedy today would support him in next year's election—and how many were already planning, behind their smiles, to betray him.

The Texas press was hostile. *The Dallas Morning News,* owned by a rabid conservative, had in the past two years called Kennedy a crook, a Communist sympathizer, a thief, and "fifty times a fool." This morning it was struggling to find something negative to say about the triumphant tour by Jack and Jackie. It had settled for the feeble STORM OF POLITICAL CONTROVERSY SWIRLS AROUND KENNEDY ON VISIT. Inside, however, there was a pugnacious full-page advertisement paid for by "the American Fact-Finding Committee" with a list of sinister questions addressed to the president, such as: "Why has Gus Hall, head of the U.S. Communist Party, praised almost every one of your policies?" The political ideas were about as stupid as could be, Maria thought. Anyone who believed that President Kennedy was a secret Communist had to be certifiably insane, in her opinion. But the tone was deeply nasty, and she shivered.

A press officer interrupted her thoughts. "Maria, if you're not busy . . ."

She was not, evidently, since she was watching television. "What can I do for you?" she said.

"I want you to run down to the archives." The National Archives building was less than a mile from the White House. "Here's what I need." He handed her a sheet of paper.

Maria often wrote press releases, or at least drafted them, but she had not been promoted to press officer: no woman ever had. She was still a researcher after more than two years. She would have moved on long ago, were it not for her love affair. She looked at the list and said: "I'll get on it right away."

"Thanks."

She took a last glance at the television. The president moved away from the official party and went to the crowd, reaching over the fence to shake hands, Jackie behind him in her pillbox hat. The people roared with excitement at the prospect of actually touching the golden couple. Maria could see the Secret Service men she knew well trying to stay close to the president, hard eyes scanning the throng, alert for trouble.

In her mind she said: *Please take good care of my Johnny.* Then she left.

. . .

That morning George Jakes drove his Mercedes convertible out to McLean, Virginia, eight miles from the White House. Bobby Kennedy lived there with his large family in a thirteen-bedroom white-painted brick house called Hickory Hill. The attorney general had scheduled a lunch meeting there to discuss organized crime. This subject was outside George's area of expertise, but he was getting invited to a wider range of meetings as he became closer to Bobby.

George stood in the living room with his rival Dennis Wilson, watching the TV coverage from Dallas. The president and Jackie were doing what George and everyone else in the administration wanted them to do, charming the socks off the Texans, chatting with them and touching them, Jackie giving her famous irresistible smile and extending a gloved hand to shake.

George glimpsed his friend Skip Dickerson in the background, close to Vice President Johnson.

At last the Kennedys retreated to their limousine. It was a stretched Lincoln Continental four-door convertible, and the top was down. The people were going to see their president in the flesh, without even a window intervening. Texas governor John Connally stood at the open door wearing a white ten-gallon hat. The president and Jackie got into the rear seat. Kennedy rested his right elbow on the edge, looking relaxed and happy. The car pulled away slowly, and the motorcade followed. Three buses of reporters brought up the rear.

The convoy drove out of the airport and onto the road, and the television coverage came to an end. George switched off the set.

It was a fine day in Washington, too, and Bobby had decided to have the meeting outside, so they all trooped through the back door and across the lawn to the pool patio, where chairs and tables had been set out ready. Looking back toward the house, George saw that a new wing had been built. It was not finished, for some workmen were painting it, and they had a transistor radio playing, its sound a mere susurration at this distance.

George admired what Bobby had done about organized crime. He had different government departments working together to target individual heads of crime families. The Federal Bureau of Narcotics had been gingered up. The Bureau of Alcohol, Tobacco and Firearms had been enlisted. Bobby had ordered the Internal Revenue Service to investigate mobsters' tax returns. He had got the Immigration and Naturalization Service to deport those who were not citizens. It all amounted to the most effective attack ever on American crime.

Only the FBI let him down. The man who should have been the attorney general's staunchest ally in the fight, J. Edgar Hoover, stood aloof, claiming there was no such thing as the Mafia, perhaps—George now knew—because the Mob was blackmailing him over his homosexuality.

Bobby's crusade, like so much that the Kennedy administration did, was disdained in Texas. Illegal gambling, prostitution, and drug use were popular among many leading citizens. *The Dallas Morning News* had attacked Bobby for making the federal government too powerful, and argued that crime should remain the responsibility of local law enforcement authorities—who were mostly incompetent or corrupt, as everyone knew.

The meeting was interrupted when Bobby's wife, Ethel, brought out lunch: tuna sandwiches and chowder. George looked at her with admiration. She was a slim, attractive woman of thirty-five, and it was hard to believe that four months ago she had given birth to their eighth child. She was dressed with the understated chic that George now recognized as the trademark of the Kennedy women.

A phone beside the pool rang and Ethel picked it up. "Yes," she said, and she carried the phone on its long lead to Bobby. "It's J. Edgar Hoover," she said.

George was startled. Was it possible that Hoover *knew* they were discussing organized crime without him, and was calling to reprimand them? Could he have bugged Bobby's patio?

Bobby took the phone from Ethel. "Hello?"

Across the grass, George noticed one of the house painters behaving oddly. He picked up his portable radio, spun around, and started running toward Bobby and the group on the patio.

George looked again at the attorney general. A look of horror came over Bobby's face, and suddenly George felt scared. Bobby turned away from the group and clasped his hand over his mouth. George thought, What is that bastard Hoover saying to him?

Then Bobby turned back to the group eating lunch and cried: "Jack's been shot! It might be fatal!"

George's thoughts moved with underwater slowness. Jack. That means the president. He's been shot. Shot in Dallas, it must be. It might be fatal. He might be dead.

The president might be dead.

Ethel ran to Bobby. All the men jumped to their feet. The painter arrived at the poolside, holding up his radio, unable to speak.

Then everyone began talking at the same time.

George still felt submerged. He thought of the important people in his life. Verena was in Atlanta, and she would hear the news on the radio. His mother was at work, in the University Women's Club; she would hear in minutes. Congress was in session, and Greg would be there. Maria—

Maria Summers. Her secret lover had been shot. She would be grief-stricken—and she would have no one to comfort her.

George had to go to her.

He ran across the lawn and through the house to the parking lot in front, jumped into his open Mercedes, and drove off at top speed.

It was just before two in the afternoon in Washington, one in Dallas, and eleven in the morning in San Francisco, where Cam Dewar was in a math class, studying differential equations and finding them hard to understand—a new experience for him, for until now all schoolwork had been easy.

His year in a London school had done him no harm. In fact the English kids were a little ahead, because they started school younger. Only his ego had been damaged, by Evie Williams's scornful rejection.

Cameron had little respect for the hip young math teacher, Mark "Fabian" Fanshore, with his crew cut and his knitted ties. He wanted to be the pupils' friend. Cameron thought a teacher should be authoritative.

The principal, Dr. Douglas, stepped into the room. Cameron liked him better. The school's leader was a dry, aloof academic, who did not care whether people liked him or not as long as they did what he told them.

"Fabian" looked up in surprise: Dr. Douglas was not often seen in classrooms. Douglas said something to him in a low voice. It must have been shocking, for Fabian's handsome face paled beneath his tan. They talked for a minute, then Fabian nodded and Douglas walked out.

The bell rang for the midmorning break, but Fabian said firmly: "Stay in your seats, please, and listen to me in silence, all right?" He had the odd speech habit of muttering "All right?" and "Okay?" with unnecessary frequency. "I've got some bad news for you," he went on. "Terribly bad news, in fact, okay? There has been a dreadful event in Dallas, Texas."

Cameron said: "The president is in Dallas today."

"Correct, but don't interrupt me, okay? The very shocking news is that our president has been shot. We don't yet know if he's dead, all right?"

Someone said: "Fuck!" out loud but, astonishingly, Fabian ignored it.

"Now I want you to keep calm. Some of the girls in the school may be very upset." There were no girls in the math class. "The younger children will need reassurance. I expect you to behave like the young men you are and help others who may be more vulnerable, okay? Take your break now as usual, and look out for alterations in the school timetable later. Off you go."

Cameron picked up his books and walked out into the corridor, where all hope of quiet and order evaporated in seconds. The voices of children and adolescents pouring out of classrooms rose to a roar. Some kids were running, some standing dumbstruck, some crying, most shouting.

Everyone was asking whether the president was dead.

Cam did not like Jack Kennedy's liberal politics, but suddenly that did not matter. If Cam had been old enough, he would have voted for Nixon, but all the same he felt personally outraged. Kennedy was the American president, elected by the American people, and an attack on him was an attack on them.

Who shot my president? he thought. Was it the Russians? Fidel Castro? The Mafia? The Ku Klux Klan?

He spotted his younger sister, Beep. She yelled: "Is the president dead?"

"Nobody knows," Cam said. "Who's got a radio?"

She thought for a moment. "Dr. Duggie has one."

That was true, there was an old-fashioned mahogany wireless set in the head's study. "I'm going to see him," Cam said.

He made his way through the corridors to the head's room and knocked on the door. Dr. Douglas's voice called: "Come!" Cameron went in. The head was there with three other teachers, listening to the radio. "What do you want, Dewar?" said Douglas in his customary irritated tone.

"Sir, everyone in the school would like to listen to the radio."

"Well, we can't get them all in here, boy."

"I thought you might put the radio in the school hall and turn up the volume."

"Oh, did you, now?" Douglas looked about to issue a scornful dismissal.

But his deputy, Mrs. Elcot, murmured: "Not a bad idea."

Douglas hesitated a moment, then nodded. "All right, Dewar. Good thinking. Go to the hall and I'll bring the radio."

"Thank you, sir," said Cameron.

· · ·

Jasper Murray was invited to the opening night of *A Woman's Trial* at the King's Theatre in London's West End. Student journalists did not normally get such invitations, but Evie Williams was in the cast, and she had made sure he was on the list.

Jasper's newspaper, *The Real Thing*, was going well, so well that he had dropped out of classes to run it for a year. The first issue had sold out after Lord Jane attacked it, in an uncharacteristically incontinent outburst during Freshers' Week, for smearing members of the governing body. Jasper was delighted to have enraged Lord Jane, who was a pillar of the British establishment that disfavored people such as Jasper and his father. The second issue, containing further revelations about college bigwigs and their dubious investments, had broken even financially, and the third had made a profit. Jasper had been obliged to conceal the extent of his success from Daisy Williams, who might have wanted her loan repaid.

The fourth issue would go to the printer tomorrow. He was not so happy with this one: there was no big controversy.

He put that out of his mind for the moment and settled in his seat. Evie's career had overtaken her education: there was no point in going to drama school when you were already getting film parts and West End roles. The girl who had once had an adolescent crush on Jasper was now a confident adult, still discovering her powers but in no doubt about where she was going.

Her distinguished boyfriend sat next to Jasper. Hank Remington was the same age as Jasper. Although Hank was a millionaire and world famous, he did not look down on a mere student. In fact, having left school at the age of fifteen, he was inclined to defer to people he thought were educated. This pleased Jasper, who did not say what he knew to be true, that Hank's raw genius counted for a lot more than school exams.

Evie's parents were in the same row, as was her grandmother Eth Leckwith. The major absence was her brother, Dave, whose group had a gig.

The curtain went up. The play was a legal drama. Jasper had heard Evie learning her lines, and he knew that the third act took place in a courtroom; but the action started in the prosecuting barrister's chambers. Evie, playing his daughter, came in halfway through the first act and had an argument with her father.

Jasper was awestruck by Evie's confidence and the authority of her performance. He had to keep reminding himself that this was the kid who lived in the same house as he. He found himself resenting the father's smug condescension and sharing the daughter's indignation and frustration. Evie's anger grew and, as the end of the act drew near, she began an impassioned plea for mercy that had the audience silently mesmerized.

Then something happened.

People began to mutter.

At first the actors onstage did not notice. Jasper looked around, wondering whether someone had fainted or thrown up, but he could see nothing to explain the talking. On the other side of the auditorium two people left their seats and walked out with a third man who appeared to have come to summon them. Hank, sitting beside Jasper, hissed: "Why don't these bastards keep quiet?"

After a minute Evie's magisterial performance faltered, and Jasper knew that she had become aware of something going on. She tried to win back the attention of the audience by becoming more histrionic: she spoke louder, her voice cracked with emotion, and she strode about the stage, making large gestures. It was a brave effort, and Jasper's admiration rose even higher; but it did not work. The murmur of conversation rose to a buzz, then to a roar.

Hank stood up, turned around, and said to the people behind him: "Will you lot just bloody well shut up?"

Onstage, Evie stumbled. "Think of what that woman ..." She hesitated. "Think of how that woman has lived—has suffered—has been through ..." She fell silent.

The veteran actor playing her barrister father got up from behind his desk, saying, "There, there, dear," a line that might or might not have been in the script. He came downstage to where Evie was standing and put his arm around her shoulder. Then he turned, squinting into the spotlights, and spoke directly to the audience.

"If you please, ladies and gentlemen," he said in the fruity baritone for which he was famous, "will someone kindly tell us what on earth has happened?"

. . .

Rebecca Held was in a hurry. She came home from work with Bernd, made supper for them both, and got ready to go to a meeting while Bernd cleared away. She had recently been elected to the parliament that governed the Hamburg city-state—one of a growing number of female members. "Are you sure you don't mind me rushing out?" she said to Bernd.

He spun his wheelchair around to face her. "Never give anything up for me," he said. "Never sacrifice anything. Never say you can't go somewhere or do something because you have to take care of your crippled husband. I want you to have a full life that gives you everything you ever hoped for. That way you'll be happy, you'll stay with me, and you'll go on loving me."

Rebecca's question had been little more than a courtesy, but clearly Bernd had been thinking about this. His speech moved her. "You're so good," she said. "You're like Werner, my father. You're strong. And you must be right, because I do love you, now more than ever."

"Speaking of Werner," he said, "what do you make of Carla's letter?"

All post in East Germany was liable to be read by the secret police. The sender could be jailed for saying the wrong thing, especially in letters to the West. Any mention of hardship, shortages, unemployment, or the secret police themselves would get you in trouble. So Carla wrote in hints. "She says that Karolin is now living with her and Werner," Rebecca said. "So I think we have to infer that the poor girl was thrown out by her parents—probably under pressure from the Stasi, maybe from Hans himself."

"Is there no end to that man's vengefulness?" said Bernd.

"Anyway, Karolin has been befriended by Lili, who is almost fifteen, just the right age to be fascinated by a pregnancy. And the mother-to-be will get plenty of good advice from Grandma Maud. That house will be a safe haven for Karolin, the way it was for me when my parents were killed."

Bernd nodded. "Are you not tempted to get back in touch with your roots?" he asked. "You never talk about being Jewish."

She shook her head. "My parents were secular. I know that Walter and Maud used to go to church, but Carla got out of the habit, and religion has never meant anything to me. And race is best forgotten. I want to honor my parents' memory by working for democracy and freedom through-out Germany, East and West." She smiled wryly. "Sorry to make a speech. I should save it for the parliament." She picked up her briefcase with the papers for the meeting.

Bernd looked at his watch. "Check the news before you go, in case there's something you need to know about."

Rebecca turned on the TV. The bulletin was just begin-ning. The newsreader said: "The American president, John F. Kennedy, was shot and killed today in Dallas, Texas."

"No!" Rebecca's exclamation was almost a scream.

"The young president and his wife, Jackie, were driving through the city in an open car when a gunman fired several shots, hitting the president, who was pronounced dead min-utes later at a local hospital."

"His poor wife!" said Rebecca. "His children!"

"Vice President Lyndon B. Johnson, who was in the mo-torcade, is believed to be on his way back to Washington to take over as the new president."

"Kennedy was the defender of West Berlin," said Rebecca, distraught. "He said: 'I am a Berliner.' He was our champion."

"He was," said Bernd.

"What will happen to us now?"

. . .

"I made a terrible mistake," said Karolin to Lili, sitting in the kitchen of the town house in Berlin-Mitte. "I should have gone with Walli. Would you fill a hottie for me? I've got a backache again."

Lili took a rubber bottle from the cupboard and filled it at the hot tap. She felt Karolin was too hard on herself. She said: "You did what you thought was best for your baby."

"I was timid," Karolin said.

Lili arranged the bottle behind Karolin. "Would you like some warm milk?"

"Yes, please."

Lili poured milk into a pan and put it on to heat.

"I acted from fear," Karolin went on. "I thought Walli

was too young to be trustworthy. I thought my parents could be relied upon. It was the reverse of the truth."

Karolin's father had thrown her out after the Stasi threatened to get him fired from his job as a bus station supervisor. Lili had been shocked. She had not known there were parents who would do such things. "I can't imagine my parents turning on me," Lili said.

"They never would," Karolin said. "And when I turned up on their doorstep, homeless and penniless and six months pregnant, they took me in without a moment's hesitation." She winced at another pang.

Lili poured warm milk into a cup and gave it to Karolin.

Karolin took a sip and said: "I'm so grateful to you and your family. But the truth is I'll never trust anyone again. The only person you can rely upon in this life is yourself. That's what I've learned." She frowned, then she said: "Oh, God!"

"What?"

"I've wet myself." A damp patch spread across the front of her skirt.

"Your waters have broken," Lili said. "That means the baby is coming."

"I've got to clean myself up." Karolin stood up, then groaned. "I don't think I can make it to the bathroom," she said.

Lili heard the front door open, then shut. "Mother's home," she said. "Thank God!" A moment later Carla came into the kitchen. She took in the scene at a glance and said: "How often are the pains coming?"

"Every minute or two," Karolin replied.

"Goodness, we don't have much time," said Carla. "I'm not even going to try to get you upstairs." Briskly, she started putting towels on the floor. "Lie down right here," she said. "I gave birth to Walli on this floor," she added brightly, "so I expect it will do for you." Karolin lay down, and Carla pulled off the soaked underwear.

Lili was frightened, even though her competent mother was now here. Lili could not imagine how a whole baby could emerge through such a tiny opening. Her fear grew worse, not better, a few minutes later when she saw the opening begin to enlarge.

"This is nice and quick," said Carla calmly. "Lucky you."

Karolin's groans of agony seemed restrained: Lili felt she would have been screaming her head off.

Carla said to Lili: "Put your hand here, and hold the head when it comes out." Lili hesitated, and Carla said: "Go on, it will be all right."

The kitchen door opened, and Lili's father appeared. "Have you heard the news?" he said.

"This is no place for men," Carla said without looking at him. "Go to the bedroom, open the bottom drawer of the chest, and bring me the light blue cashmere shawl."

"All right," Werner said. "But someone shot President Kennedy. He's dead."

"Tell me later," said Carla. "Bring me that shawl."

Werner disappeared.

"What did he say about Kennedy?" Carla asked a minute later.

"I think the baby's coming out," Lili said fearfully.

Karolin gave a huge wail of pain and effort, and the baby's head squeezed out. Lili supported it with one hand. It was wet and slimy and warm. "It's alive!" she said. She found herself overflowing with an emotion of love and protectiveness for the tiny scrap of new life.

And she was no longer frightened.

.   .   .

Jasper's newspaper was produced in a tiny office in the student union building. The room contained one desk, two phones, and three chairs. Jasper met Pete Donegan there half an hour after leaving the theater.

"There are five thousand students in this college and another twenty thousand or more at other London colleges, and a lot are American," Jasper said as soon as Pete walked in. "We need to call all our writers and get them working straightaway. They must talk to every American student they can think of, preferably tonight, tomorrow morning at the latest. If we do this right we can make a huge profit."

"What's the splash?"

"Probably HEARTBREAK OF U.S. STUDENTS. Get a mug shot of anyone who gives a good quote. I'll do the American teachers: Heslop in English, Rawlings in engineering ... Cooper in philosophy will say something outrageous, he always does."

"We ought to have a biography of Kennedy as a side-bar," said Donegan. "And maybe a page of pictures of his life—Harvard, the navy, his wedding to Jackie—"

"Wait a minute," said Jasper. "Didn't he study in London at one point? His father was American ambassador here—a right-wing Hitler-supporting bastard, apparently—but I seem to recall that the son went to the London School of Economics."

"That's right, it comes back to me now," said Donegan. "But his studies were cut short, after only a few weeks."

"It doesn't matter," said Jasper excitedly. "Someone there must have met him. It makes no difference if they spoke to him for less than five minutes. We just need one quote, I don't care if it's only: 'He was quite tall.' Our splash is THE STUDENT JFK I KNEW, BY LSE PROF."

"I'll get on it right away," said Donegan.

. . .

When George Jakes was a mile from the White House, traffic slowed to a stop for no apparent reason. He banged on his steering wheel in frustration. He pictured Maria weeping alone somewhere.

People started to blare their horns. Several cars ahead, a driver got out and spoke to someone on the sidewalk. At the corner, half a dozen people were gathered around a parked car with its windows open, listening, presumably to the car radio. George saw a well-dressed woman clap her hand to her mouth in horror.

In front of George's Mercedes was a new white Chevrolet Impala. The door opened and the driver got out. He was wearing a suit and hat, and might have been a salesman making calls. He looked around, saw George in his open-top car, and said: "Is it true?"

"Yes," George said. "The president has been shot."

"Is he dead?"

"I don't know." There was no radio in George's car.

The salesman approached the open window of a Buick. "Is the president dead?"

George did not hear the reply.

The traffic was not moving.

George turned off his engine, jumped out of the car, and started to run.

He was dismayed to realize that he had got out of shape.
He always seemed too busy to work out. He tried to think
when was the last time he had done some vigorous exercise,
and he could not remember. He found himself perspiring
and breathing hard. Despite his impatience, he had to alternate jogging with fast walking.

His shirt was soaked with sweat when he reached the
White House. Maria was not in the press office. "She went
to the National Archives Building to do some research,"
said Nelly Fordham, whose face was wet with tears. "She
probably hasn't even heard the news yet."

"Do we know whether the president is dead?"

"Yes, he is," said Nelly, and she sobbed afresh.

"I don't want Maria to hear it from a stranger," George
said, and he left the building and ran along Pennsylvania
Avenue toward the National Archives.

. . .

Dimka had been married to Nina for a year, and their child,
Grigor, was six months old, when he finally admitted to
himself that he was in love with Natalya.

She and her friends frequently went for a drink at the
Riverside Bar after work, and Dimka got into the habit of
joining the group when Khrushchev did not keep him late.
Sometimes it was more than one drink, and often Dimka
and Natalya were the last two left.

He found he was able to make her laugh. He was not
generally considered a comedian, but he relished the many
ironies of Soviet life, and so did she. "A worker showed how
a bicycle factory could make mudguards more quickly by
molding one long strip of tin, then cutting it, instead of cutting it first, then bending the pieces one by one. He was
reprimanded and disciplined for endangering the five-year
plan."

Natalya laughed, opening her wide mouth and showing
her teeth. The way she laughed suggested a potential for
reckless abandon that made Dimka's heart beat faster. He
imagined her throwing her head back like that while they
were making love. Then he imagined seeing her laugh like
that every day for the next fifty years, and he realized that
was the life he wanted.

He did not tell her, though. She had a husband, and

seemed to be happy with him; at least, she said nothing bad about him, although she was never in a hurry to go home to him. More importantly, Dimka had a wife and a child, and he owed them his loyalty.

He wanted to say: *I love you. I'm going to leave my family. Will you leave your husband, live with me, and be my friend and lover for the rest of our lives?*

Instead he said: "It's late, I'd better go."

"Let me drive you," she said. "It's too cold for your motorcycle."

She pulled up at the corner near Government House. He leaned across to kiss her good night. She let him kiss her lips, briefly, then pulled back. He got out of the car and went into the building.

On the way up in the elevator he thought about the excuse he would make to Nina for being late. There was a genuine crisis at the Kremlin: this year's grain harvest had been a catastrophe, and the Soviet government was desperately trying to buy foreign wheat to feed its people.

When he entered the apartment, Grigor was asleep and Nina was watching TV. He kissed her forehead and said: "I was kept late at the office, sorry. We had to finish a report on the bad harvest."

"You shit-faced liar," said Nina. "Your office has been calling here every ten minutes, trying to find you, to tell you that President Kennedy has been killed."

· · ·

Maria's tummy rumbled. She looked at her watch and realized she had forgotten to have lunch. The work she was doing had absorbed her, and for two or three hours no one had come into this area to disturb her. But she was almost done, so she decided to finish off, then get a sandwich.

She bent her head over the old-fashioned ledger she was reading, then looked up again when she heard a noise. She was astonished to see George Jakes come in, panting, his suit jacket wet with perspiration, his eyes a little wild. "George!" she said. "What the heck . . . ?" She stood up.

"Maria," he said, "I'm so sorry." He came around the table and put his hands on her shoulders, a gesture that was a little too intimate for their strictly platonic friendship.

"Why are you sorry?" she said. "What have you done?"

"Nothing." She tried to pull back, but he tightened his grip. "They shot him," he said.

Maria saw that George was close to tears. She stopped resisting him and stepped closer. "Who was shot?" she said.

"In Dallas," he said.

Then she began to understand, and a terrible dread rose inside her. "No," she said.

George nodded. In a quiet voice he said: "The president is dead. I'm so sorry."

"Dead," Maria said. "He can't be dead." Her legs felt weak, and she sank to her knees. George knelt with her and folded her in his arms. "Not my Johnny," she said, and a huge sob erupted from inside her. "Johnny, my Johnny," she moaned. "Don't leave me, please. Please, Johnny. Please don't leave." She saw the world turn gray, she slumped helplessly, then her eyes closed and she lost consciousness.

·   ·   ·

Onstage at the Jump Club in London, Plum Nellie performed a storming version of "Dizzy, Miss Lizzy" and came off to shouts of: "More!"

Backstage, Lenny said: "That was great, lads, best we've ever played!"

Dave looked at Walli and they both grinned. The group was getting better fast, and every gig was the best ever.

Dave was surprised to find his sister waiting in the dressing room. "How did the play go?" he said. "I'm sorry I couldn't be there."

"It stopped in the first act," she said. "President Kennedy has been shot dead."

"The president!" said Dave. "When did this happen?"

"A couple of hours ago."

Dave thought of their American mother. "Is Mam upset?"

"Terribly."

"Who shot him?"

"No one knows. He was in Texas, in a place called Dallas."

"Never heard of it."

Buzz, the bass player, said: "What shall we do for an encore?"

Lenny said: "We can't do an encore, it would be disrespectful. President Kennedy has been assassinated. We have to do a minute's silence, or something."

Walli said: "Or a sad song."

Evie said: "Dave, you know what we should do."

"Do I?" He thought for a second, then said: "Oh, yeah."

"Come on, then."

Dave went onstage with Evie and plugged in his guitar. They stood at the microphone together. The rest of the group watched from the wings.

Dave spoke into the microphone. "My sister and I are half British, half American, but we feel very American to-night." He paused. "Most of you probably know by now that President Kennedy has been shot dead."

He heard several gasps from the audience, indicating that some had not heard, and the room went quiet. "We would like to play a special song now, a song for all of us, but especially for Americans."

He played a G chord.

Evie sang:

O say can you see, by the dawn's early light,
What so proudly we hail'd at the twilight's last gleaming,

The room was dead silent.

Whose broad stripes and bright stars through the perilous
    fight
O'er the ramparts we watch'd were so gallantly streaming?

Evie's voice rose thrillingly.

And the rocket's red glare, the bombs bursting in air,
Gave proof through the night that our flag was still there,

Several people in the audience were crying openly now, Dave saw.

O say does that star-spangled banner yet wave
O'er the land of the free and the home of the brave?

"Thank you for listening," said Dave. "And God bless America."

PART FIVE

SONG

1963-1967

aria was not allowed to go to the funeral.

The day after the assassination was a Saturday, but like most White House staff she went into work, performing her duties in the press office with tears streaming down her face. It was not noticed: half the people there were crying.

She was better off here than at home alone. Work distracted her a little from her grief, and there was no end of work: the world's press wanted to know every detail of the funeral arrangements.

Everything was on TV. Millions of American families sat in front of their sets all weekend. The three networks canceled all their regular programs. The news consisted entirely of stories linked to the assassination, and between bulletins there were documentaries about John F. Kennedy, his life, his family, his career, and his presidency. With merciless pathos they reran the happy footage of Jack and Jackie greeting the crowds at Love Field on Friday morning, an hour before his death. Maria recalled how she had idly asked herself if she would change places with Jackie. Now both of them had lost him.

At midday on Sunday, in the basement of the Dallas police station, the prime suspect, Lee Harvey Oswald, was himself murdered, live on television, by a minor mobster called Jack Ruby; a sinister mystery piled on top of an insupportable tragedy.

On Sunday afternoon Maria asked Nelly Fordham if

they needed tickets for the funeral. "Oh, honey, I'm sorry, no one from this office is invited," Nelly said gently. "Only Pierre Salinger."

Maria felt panicky. Her heart fluttered. How could she not be there when they lowered the man she loved into his grave? "I have to go!" she said. "I'll speak to Pierre."

"Maria, you can't go," Nelly said. "You absolutely can't."

Something in Nelly's tone rang an alarm bell. She was not just giving advice. She almost sounded scared.

Maria said: "Why not?"

Nelly lowered her voice. "Jackie knows about you."

This was the first time anyone in the office had acknowledged that Maria had had a relationship with the president; but in her distress Maria hardly noticed that milestone. "She can't possibly know! I was always careful."

"Don't ask me how, I have no idea."

"I don't believe you."

Nelly might have been offended, but she just shook her head sadly. "From what little I understand of such things, I believe the wife always knows."

Maria wanted to deny it indignantly, but then she thought of the secretaries Jenny and Jerry, and the socialites Mary Meyer and Judith Campbell, and others. Maria was sure they all had sexual relations with President Kennedy. She had no proof, but when she saw them with him she just sort of knew. And Jackie had feminine intuition too.

Which meant Maria could not go to the funeral. She saw that now. The widow could not be forced to face her husband's mistress at such a time. Maria understood that with total, miserable certainty.

So she stayed at home on Monday to watch it on TV.

The body had been lying in state in the rotunda at the Capitol. At half past ten the flag-draped coffin was carried out of the building and placed on a caisson, a type of gun carriage, drawn by six white horses. The procession then headed toward the White House.

Two men stood out in the funeral cortege, being inches taller than the rest: French president Charles de Gaulle, and the new American president, Lyndon Johnson.

Maria was all cried out. She had been sobbing for almost three days. Now when she looked at the television she just saw a pageant, a show organized for the benefit of the world. For her this was not about drums and flags and uniforms. She had lost a man; a warm, smiling, sexy man; a man with a bad back and faint wrinkles in the corners of his hazel eyes and a set of rubber ducks on the edge of his bathtub. She would never look at him again. Life without him stretched long and empty ahead of her.

When the cameras zoomed in on Jackie, her beautiful face visible despite the veil, Maria thought that she, too, looked numb. "I wronged you," Maria said to the face on the screen. "God forgive me."

She was startled by a ring at the door. It was George Jakes. He said: "You shouldn't be alone for this."

She felt a surge of helpless gratitude. When she really needed a friend, George was there. "Come in," she said. "I'm sorry I look like a slattern." She was wearing a night-dress and an old bathrobe.

"You look fine to me." George had seen her worse than shabby.

He had brought a bag of Danish pastries. Maria put them on a plate. She had not had breakfast but, all the same, she did not eat a pastry. She did not feel hungry.

A million people lined the route, according to the television commentary. The coffin was taken from the White House to St. Matthew's Cathedral, where there was a mass.

At twelve noon there was a five-minute silence, and traffic stopped all over America. The cameras showed crowds standing silent on city streets. It was strange to be in Washington and hear no cars outside. Maria and George stood in front of the TV set in her little apartment. They bowed their heads. George took her hand and held it. She felt a wave of affection for him.

When the five-minute silence ended, Maria made coffee. Her appetite returned, and they ate the pastries. No cameras were allowed in the church, so for a while there was nothing to watch. George talked to distract her, and she appreciated it. He said: "Will you stay in the press office?"

She had hardly thought about it, but she knew the answer. "No. I'm going to leave the White House."

"Good idea."

"Apart from everything else, I don't see a future for myself in the press office. They never promote women, and I'm not going to spend my life as a researcher. I'm in government because I want to get things done."

"There's an opening in the Justice Department that might suit you." George spoke as if the thought had just occurred to him, but Maria suspected he had planned to say this. "Dealing with corporations that disobey government regulations. They call it compliance. Could be interesting."

"Do you think I'd have a chance?"

"With a degree from Chicago Law and two years' experience in the White House? Absolutely."

"They don't hire many Negroes, though."

"You know something? I think Lyndon may change that."

"Really? He's a Southerner!"

"Don't prejudge him. To be honest, our people have treated him badly. Bobby hates him, don't ask me why. Maybe because he calls his dick Jumbo."

Maria giggled for the first time in three days. "You're kidding."

"Apparently it's large. If he wants to intimidate someone, he pulls it out and says: 'Meet Jumbo.' That's what people say."

Men told such stories, Maria knew. It might be true and it might not. She grew serious again. "Everyone in the White House thinks Johnson's behavior has been callous, especially toward the Kennedys."

"I don't buy that. Look, when the president had just died and no one knew what to do next, America was terribly vulnerable. What if the Soviets had chosen that moment to take over West Berlin? We are the government of the most powerful country in the world, and we have to do our job, without a second's pause, no matter how deep our sadness. Lyndon picked up the reins immediately, and a darn good thing he did, because no one else was thinking about it."

"Not even Bobby?"

"Least of all Bobby. I love the man, you know that, but he surrendered to his grief. He's comforting Jackie and he's organizing his brother's funeral, and he's not governing America. Frankly, most of our people are just as bad. They may think Lyndon is being callous. I think he's being presidential."

At the end of the mass, the coffin was brought out of the church and again placed on the caisson for the journey to Arlington National Cemetery. This time the mourners traveled in a long line of black limousines. The procession passed the Lincoln Memorial and crossed the Potomac River.

Maria said: "What will Johnson do about the civil rights bill?"

"That's the big question. Right now the bill is doomed. It's with the rules committee, whose chairman, Howard Smith, won't even say when they will begin discussing it."

Maria thought of the Sunday school bombing. How could anyone side with those Southern racists? "Can't his committee overrule him?"

"Theoretically, yes, but when the Republicans ally with the Southern Democrats they have a majority, and they always defeat civil rights, no matter what the public thinks. I don't know how these people can pretend they believe in democracy."

On television, Jackie Kennedy lit an eternal flame to burn perpetually over the grave. George took Maria's hand again, and she saw tears in his eyes. They watched in silence as the casket was slowly lowered into the ground.

Jack Kennedy was gone.

Maria said: "Oh, God, what will happen to us all now?"

"I don't know," said George.

.   .   .

George left Maria reluctantly. She was sexier than she knew in her cotton nightdress and her old velvet bathrobe, with her hair naturally curly and untidy instead of laboriously straightened. But she no longer needed him: she was planning to meet Nelly Fordham and some other girls from the White House at a Chinese restaurant that evening for a private wake, so she would not be alone.

George had dinner with Greg. They ate at the dark-paneled Occidental Grill, a stone's throw from the White House. George smiled at his father's appearance: as always, he wore expensive clothes as if they were rags. His slim black satin tie was awry, his shirt cuffs were unbuttoned, and there was a whitish mark on the lapel of his black suit. Fortunately, George had not inherited his slovenliness.

"I thought we might need cheering up," said Greg. He loved high-class restaurants and refined cuisine, and this was a trait George *had* inherited. They ordered lobster and Chablis.

George had felt closer to his father since the Cuban missile crisis, when the threat of imminent annihilation had caused Greg to open his heart. George had always felt, as an illegitimate child, that he was an embarrassment, and that when Greg played the role of father he did so dutifully but without enthusiasm. However, since that surprising conversation he had understood that Greg really loved him. Their relationship continued to be unusual and rather distant, but George now believed it was founded on something genuine and lasting.

While they were waiting for their food, George's friend Skip Dickerson approached their table. He was dressed for the funeral in a dark suit and a black tie, which looked dramatic against his white-blond hair and pale skin. In his Southern accent, he drawled: "Hi, George. Good evening, Senator. May I join you for just a minute?"

George said: "This is Skip Dickerson, who works for Lyndon. For the president, I should say."

"Pull up a chair," said Greg.

Skip drew up a red leather chair, leaned forward, and spoke intensely to Greg. "The president knows you're a scientist."

Now, thought George, what the heck is this about? Skip never wasted time in small talk.

Greg smiled. "My major in college was physics, yes."

"You graduated summa cum laude from Harvard."

"Lyndon is more impressed by that sort of thing than he should be."

"But you were one of the scientists who developed the atom bomb."

"I worked on the Manhattan Project, that's true."

"President Johnson wants to make sure you approve of the plans for the Lake Erie study."

George knew what Skip was talking about. The federal government was financing a waterfront study for the city of Buffalo that would probably lead to a major harbor construction project. It was worth millions of dollars to several companies in upstate New York.

Greg said: "Well, Skip, we'd like to be sure the study isn't going to be pruned in the budget."

"You can count on that, sir. The president feels this project is top priority."

"I'm glad to hear that, thank you."

The conversation had nothing to do with science, George felt sure. It was about what congressmen called "pork"— the allocation of federal spending projects to favored states.

Skip said: "You're welcome, and enjoy your dinner. Oh, before I go—can we count on you to support the president on this darn wheat bill?"

The Soviets had had a bad harvest, and they were desperate for grain. As part of the process of trying to get along a little better with the Soviet Union, President Kennedy had sold them surplus American wheat on credit.

Greg sat back and spoke thoughtfully. "Members of Congress feel that if the Communists can't feed their people it's not up to us to help them out. Senator Mundt's wheat bill would cancel Kennedy's deal, and I kind of think Mundt is right."

"And President Johnson agrees with you!" said Skip. "He sure doesn't want to help Communists. But this will be the first vote after the funeral. Do we really want it to be a slap in the face for the dead president?"

George put in: "Is that really President Johnson's concern? Or does he want to send a message saying that he's in charge of foreign policy now, and he's not going to have Congress second-guess every nickel-and-dime decision he makes?"

Greg chuckled. "Sometimes I forget how smart you are, George. That's exactly what Lyndon wants."

Skip said: "The president wants to work hand in glove with Congress on foreign policy. But he would really appreciate being able to count on your support tomorrow. He feels it would be a terrible dishonor to the memory of President Kennedy if the wheat bill passes."

Neither man was willing to say what was really going on here, George noted. The simple truth was that Johnson was threatening to cancel the Buffalo dock project if Greg voted for the wheat bill.

And Greg caved. "Please tell the president that I understand his concern and he can count on my vote," he said.

Skip stood up. "Thank you, Senator," he said. "He'll be very pleased."

George said: "Before you go, Skip . . . I know the new president has a lot on his mind, but sometime in the next few days he's going to turn his thoughts to the civil rights bill. Please call me if you think I can help in any way at all."

"Thanks, George. I appreciate that." Skip left.

Greg said: "Nicely done."

"Just making sure he knows the door is open."

"That kind of thing is so important in politics."

Their food came. When the waiters had retreated, George picked up his knife and fork. "I'm a Bobby Kennedy man, through and through," he said as he began to carve his lobster. "But Johnson shouldn't be underestimated."

"You're right, but don't overestimate him either."

"What does that mean?"

"Lyndon has two failings. He's intellectually weak. Oh, listen, he's as cunning as a Texas polecat, but that's not the same thing. He went to schoolteacher college, and never learned abstract thinking. He feels inferior to us Harvard-educated types, and he's right. His grasp of international politics is feeble. The Chinese, the Buddhists, Cubans, Bolsheviks—such people have different ways of thinking that he will never understand."

"What's his other failing?"

"He's morally weak, too. He has no principles. His support of civil rights is genuine, but it's not ethical. He sympathizes with colored people as underdogs, and he thinks he's an underdog, too, because he comes from a poor Texas family. It's a gut reaction."

George smiled: "He just got you to do exactly what he wanted."

"Correct. Lyndon knows how to manipulate people one at a time. He's the most skillful parliamentary politician I've ever met. But he's not a statesman. Jack Kennedy was the opposite: hopelessly incompetent at managing Congress, superb on the international stage. Lyndon will deal with Congress masterfully, but as leader of the free world? I don't know."

"Do you think he has any chance of getting the civil rights bill past Congressman Howard Smith's committee?"

Greg grinned. "I can't wait to see what Lyndon will do. Eat your lobster."

Next day Senator Mundt's wheat bill was defeated by fifty-seven votes to thirty-six.

The headline on the day after read:

Wheat Bill—First Johnson Victory

. . .

The funeral was over. Kennedy was gone, and Johnson was president. The world had changed, but George did not know what that meant, and nor did anyone else. What kind of president would Johnson be? How would he be different? A man most people did not know had suddenly become leader of the free world and ruler of its most powerful country. What was he going to do?

He was about to say.

The chamber of the House of Representatives was packed full. Television lights glared on the assembled congressmen and senators. The justices of the Supreme Court wore their black robes, and the Joint Chiefs of Staff glittered with medals.

George was seated next to Skip Dickerson in the gallery, which was equally full, with people sitting on the steps in the aisles. George studied Bobby Kennedy, down below at one end of the cabinet row, head bent, staring at the floor. Bobby had got thinner in the five days since the assassination. Also, he had taken to wearing his dead brother's clothes, which did not fit him, and added to the impression of a man who had shrunk.

In the presidential box sat Lady Bird Johnson with her two daughters, one plain, one pretty, all three women having old-fashioned hairstyles. With them in the box were several Democratic Party luminaries: Mayor Daley of Chicago, Governor Lawrence of Pennsylvania, and Arthur Schlesinger, the Kennedys' in-house intellectual, who—George happened to know—was already conspiring to unseat Johnson in next year's presidential race. Surprisingly, there were also two black faces in the box. George knew who they were: Zephyr and Sammy Wright, cook and chauffeur to the Johnson family. Was that a good sign?

The big double doors swung open. A doorkeeper with

the comic name of Fishbait Miller shouted: "Mr. Speaker! The president of the United States!" Then Lyndon Johnson walked in, and everyone stood up and applauded.

George had two worrying questions about Lyndon Johnson, and both would be answered today. The first was: Would he abandon the troublesome civil rights bill? Pragmatists in the Democratic Party were urging him to do just that. Johnson would have a good excuse, if he wanted one: President Kennedy had failed to get congressional support for the bill and it was doomed to failure. The new president was entitled to give it up as a bad job. Johnson could say that legislation on the crippling, divisive issue of segregation must wait until after the election.

If he did say that, the civil rights movement would be set back years. The racists would celebrate victory, the Ku Klux Klan would feel that everything they had done was justified, and the corrupt white police, judges, church leaders, and politicians of the South would know they could carry on persecuting and beating and torturing and murdering Negroes with no fear of justice.

But if Johnson did not say that, if he affirmed his support for civil rights, there was another question: Would he have the authority to fill Kennedy's shoes? That question, too, would be answered in the next hour, and the prospects were poor. Lyndon was a smooth operator one-on-one; he was at his least impressive when speaking to large groups on formal occasions—which was precisely what he had to do in a few moments' time. For the American people, this was his first major appearance as their leader, and it would define him, for better or worse.

Skip Dickerson was biting his nails. George said to him: "Did you write the speech?"

"A few lines of it. It was a team effort."

"What's he going to say?"

Skip shook his head anxiously. "Wait and see."

Washington insiders expected Johnson to screw up. He was a bad public speaker, tedious and stiff. Sometimes he rushed his words, sometimes he sounded ponderous. When he wanted to emphasize something he just shouted. His gestures were embarrassingly awkward: he would lift one hand and jab a finger in the air, or raise both arms and wave his fists. Speeches generally revealed Lyndon at his worst.

George could not read anything in Johnson's demeanor as he walked through the applauding crowd, went up to the dais, stood at the lectern, and opened a black loose-leaf notebook. He showed neither confidence nor nervousness as he put on a pair of rimless spectacles, then waited patiently until the applause died down and the audience settled in their seats.

At last he spoke. In an even, measured tone of voice he said: "All I have I would have given, gladly, not to be standing here today."

The chamber became hushed. He had struck exactly the right note of sorrowful humility. It was a good start, George thought.

Johnson continued in the same vein, speaking with slow dignity. If he felt the impulse to rush, he was controlling it firmly. He wore a dark blue suit and tie, and a shirt with a tab-fastened collar, a style considered formal in the South. He looked occasionally from one side to the other, speaking to the whole of the chamber and at the same time seeming to command it.

Echoing Martin Luther King, he talked of dreams: Kennedy's dreams of conquering space, of education for all children, of the Peace Corps. "This is our challenge," he said. "Not to hesitate, not to pause, not to turn about and linger over this evil moment, but to continue on our course so that we may fulfill the destiny that history has set for us."

He had to stop, then, because of the applause.

Then he said: "Our most immediate tasks are here on this hill."

This was the crunch. Capitol Hill, where Congress sat, had been at war with the president for most of 1963. Congress had the power to delay legislation, and used it often, even when the president had campaigned and won public support for his plans. But since John Kennedy announced his civil rights bill they had gone on strike, like a factory full of militant workers, delaying everything, mulishly refusing to pass even routine bills, scorning public opinion and the democratic process.

"First," said Johnson, and George held his breath while he waited to hear what the new president would put first.

"No memorial oration or eulogy could more eloquently honor President Kennedy's memory than the earliest possible passage of the civil rights bill for which he fought so long."

George leaped to his feet, clapping for joy. He was not the only one: the applause burst out again, and this time went on longer than previously.

Johnson waited for it to die down, then said: "We have talked long enough in this country about civil rights. We have talked for one hundred years or more. It is time, *now,* to write the next chapter—and to write it in the books of law."

They applauded again.

Euphoric, George looked at the few black faces in the chamber: five Negro congressmen, including Gus Hawkins of California, who actually looked white; Mr. and Mrs. Wright in the presidential box, clapping; a scatter of dark faces among the spectators in the gallery. Their expressions showed relief, hope, and gladness.

Then his eye fell on the rows of seats behind the cabinet, where the senior senators sat, most of them Southerners, sullen and resentful.

Not a single one was joining in the applause.

. . .

Skip Dickerson laid it out to George six days later in the small study next to the Oval Office. "Our only chance is a discharge petition."

"What's that?"

Dickerson pushed his blond forelock out of his eyes. "It's a resolution passed by Congress discharging the rules committee from control of the bill and forcing it to be sent to the floor for debate."

George felt frustrated that these arcane procedures had to be gone through so that Maria's grandfather would not be thrown in jail for registering to vote. "I've never heard of that," he said.

"We need a majority vote. Southern Democrats will be against us, so I calculate we're fifty-eight votes short."

"Shit. We need fifty-eight Republicans to support us before we can do the right thing?"

"Yes. And that's where you come in."

"Me?"

"A lot of Republicans claim to support civil rights. After all, theirs is the party of Abraham Lincoln, who freed the slaves. We want Martin Luther King and all the Negro leaders to call their Republican supporters, explain this situation to them, and tell them to vote for the petition. The message is that you can't be in favor of civil rights unless you're in favor of the petition."

George nodded. "That's good."

"Some will say they're in favor of civil rights but they don't like this procedural hurry-up. They need to understand that Senator Howard Smith is a hard-core segregationist who will make sure his committee debates the rules until it's too late to pass the bill. What he's doing is not *delay*, it's *sabotage*."

"Okay."

A secretary put her head around the door and said: "He's ready for you."

The two young men stood up and walked into the Oval Office.

As always, George was struck by the sheer size of Lyndon Johnson. He was six foot three, but height was only part of it. His head was big, his nose was long, his earlobes were like pancakes. He shook George's hand, then held on to it, grasping George's shoulder with his other hand, standing close enough to make George feel uncomfortable at the intimacy.

Johnson said: "George, I've asked all the Kennedy people to stay on at the White House and help me. You're all Harvard educated and I went to Southwest Texas State Teachers' College. See, I need y'all more than he did."

George did not know what to say. This level of humility was embarrassing. After a hesitation he said: "I'm here to help you any way I can, Mr. President."

By now a thousand people must have said that or something similar, but Johnson reacted as if he had never heard it before. "I sure appreciate you saying that, George," he said fervently. "Thank you." Then he got down to business. "A lot of people have asked me to soften up the civil rights bill to make it easier for Southerners to swallow. They've suggested taking out the prohibition against segregation in public accommodations. I'm not willing to do that, George, for two reasons. The first is that they're going to hate the bill regardless of how hard or soft it is, and I don't believe they'll support it no matter how much I draw its teeth."

That sounded right to George. "If you're going to have a fight, you might as well fight for what you really want."

"Exactly. And I'll tell you the second reason. I have a friend and employee called Mrs. Zephyr Wright."

George recalled Mr. and Mrs. Wright, who had been in the presidential box at the House of Representatives.

Johnson went on: "One time when she was about to drive to Texas I asked her to take my dog with her. She said: 'Please don't ask me to do that.' I had to ask why. 'Driving through the South is tough enough just being black,' she said. 'You can't find a place to eat or sleep or even go to the bathroom. With a dog it's going to be just impossible.' That hurt me, George; it almost brought me to tears. Mrs. Wright is a college graduate, you know. That was when I realized how important public accommodations are when we're talking about segregation. I know what it is to be looked down on, George, and I sure don't wish it on anyone else."

"It's good to hear that," said George.

He knew he was being romanced. Johnson still had hold of his hand and shoulder, was still leaning in a little too close, his dark eyes looking at George with remarkable intensity. George knew what Johnson was doing—but it was working just the same. George felt moved by the story about Zephyr, and believed Johnson when he said he knew what it was to be looked down upon. He felt a surge of admiration and affection for this big, awkward, emotional man who seemed to be on the side of the Negroes.

"It's going to be tough, but I think we can win it," said Johnson. "Do your best, George."

"Yes, sir," said George. "I will."

. . .

George explained President Johnson's strategy to Verena Marquand shortly before Martin Luther King went to the Oval Office. She looked stunning in a bright red PVC raincoat but, for once, George was not distracted by her beauty. "We have to put everything we've got into this effort," he said urgently. "If the petition fails, the bill fails, and Southern Negroes will be back where they started."

He gave Verena a list of Republican congressmen who had not yet signed the petition.

She was impressed. "President Kennedy talked to us about votes, but he never had a list like this," she said.

"That's Lyndon," said George. "If the whips tell him how many votes they think they've got, he says: 'Thinking isn't good enough—I need to know!' He has to have the names. And he's right. This is too important for guesswork."

He told her that civil rights leaders had to put pressure on liberal Republicans. "Every one of these men must get a call from someone whose approval he cares about."

"Is that what the president is going to tell Dr. King this morning?"

"Precisely." Johnson had seen all the most important civil rights leaders one by one. Jack Kennedy would have had them all in a room together, but Lyndon could not work his magic so well in large groups.

"Does Johnson think the civil rights leaders can turn all these Republicans around?" Verena said skeptically.

"Not on their own, but he's enlisting others. He's seeing all the union leaders. He had breakfast with George Meany this morning."

Verena shook her beautiful head in wonder. "You have to give him credit for energy." She looked thoughtful. "Why couldn't President Kennedy do this?"

"Same reason Lyndon can't sail a yacht—he doesn't know how."

Johnson's meeting with King went well. But next morning George's optimism was punctured by a segregationist backlash.

Leading Republicans denounced the petition. McCulloch of Ohio said it had irritated people who might otherwise have supported the civil rights bill. Gerald Ford told reporters that the rules committee should be allowed time to hold hearings, which was rubbish: everyone knew that Smith wanted to kill the bill, not debate it. All the same, reporters were briefed that the petition had failed.

But Johnson was not discouraged. Wednesday morning he spoke to the Business Advisory Council, eighty-nine of the most important American businessmen, and he said: "I am the only president you have; if you would have me fail, then you fail, for the country fails."

Then he addressed the executive council of the AFL-

CIO, the largest federation of unions, and said: "I need you, I want you, and I believe you should be at my side." He got a standing ovation, and the Steelworkers' thirty-three lobbyists stormed Capitol Hill.

George was sitting down to dinner with Verena in one of the restaurants there when Skip Dickerson passed their table and hissed: "Clarence Brown has gone to see Howard Smith."

George explained to Verena: "Brown is the senior Republican on Smith's committee. Either he's telling Smith to tough it out, and ignore the lobbying . . . or he's saying that Republicans can't take this pressure much longer. If two people on the committee turn against Smith, his decisions can be overturned by a majority vote."

"Could it all be over so quickly?" Verena marveled.

"Smith may jump before he's pushed. It looks more dignified." George moved his plate away. Tension had ruined his appetite.

Half an hour later Dickerson came by again. "Smith caved," he crowed. "There will be a formal statement tomorrow." He walked on, spreading the news.

George and Verena grinned at one another. Verena said: "Well, God bless Lyndon Johnson."

"Amen," said George. "We have to celebrate."

"What shall we do?"

"Come to my apartment," said George. "I'll think of something."

CHAPTER THIRTY-TWO

There was no uniform at Dave's school, but boys were mocked for being overdressed. Dave took some ribbing on the day he showed up in a four-button jacket, a white shirt with long collar points, a paisley tie, and blue hipster trousers with a white plastic belt. He did not care about the teasing. He had a mission.

Lenny's group had been on the fringes of show business for years. As things stood, they could spend another decade playing rock and roll in clubs and pubs. Dave wanted more than that in 1964. And the way forward was to make a record.

After school he took the Tube to Tottenham Court Road and walked from there to an address in Denmark Street. On the ground floor of the building was a guitar shop, but beside it was a door leading to an office above, and a nameplate that said CLASSIC RECORDS.

Dave had spoken to Lenny about getting a recording contract, but Lenny had been discouraging. "I've tried that," he had said. "You can't get through the door. It's a closed circle."

That made no sense. There had to be a way in, otherwise no one would ever make records. But Dave knew better than to chop logic with Lenny. So he decided to do it on his own.

He had begun by studying the names of the record companies in the hit parade. It was a complicated exercise, because there were many labels, all owned by a few companies.

The phone book had helped him sort them out, and he had picked Classic as his target.

He had called their number and said: "This is British Railways Lost Property. We have a tape in a box marked: 'Head of Artists and Recording, Classic Records.' Who should we send it to?" The girl who answered the phone had given him a name and this address in Denmark Street.

At the top of the stairs he found a receptionist, probably the one he had spoken to on the phone. Assuming a confident air, he used the name she had given him. "I'm here to see Eric Chapman," he said.

"What name shall I say?"

"Dave Williams. Tell him Byron Chesterfield sent me."

This was a lie, but Dave had nothing to lose.

The receptionist disappeared through a door. Dave looked around. The lobby was decorated with framed gold and silver discs. A photograph of Percy Marquand, the Negro Bing Crosby, was inscribed: "To Eric, with thanks for everything." Dave noticed that all the discs were at least five years old. Eric needed fresh talent.

Dave felt nervous. He was not accustomed to deception. He told himself not to be timid. He was not breaking the law. If he were found out, the worst that could happen was that he would be told to get out and stop wasting people's time. It was worth risking that.

The secretary came out, and a middle-aged man stood in the doorway. He wore a green cardigan over a white shirt and a nondescript tie. He had thinning gray hair. He leaned on the doorpost, looking Dave up and down. After a moment he said: "So Byron sent you to me, did he?"

His tone was skeptical: obviously he did not believe the story. Dave avoided repeating the lie by telling another. "Byron said: 'EMI has the Beatles, Decca has the Rolling Stones, Classic needs Plum Nellie.'" Byron had said nothing of the kind. Dave had figured it out for himself, reading the music press.

"Plum what?"

Dave handed Chapman a photo of the group. "We've done a stint at the Dive in Hamburg, as the Beatles did, and we've played the Jump Club in London, like the Stones." He was surprised he had not yet been thrown out, and he wondered how much longer his luck would hold.

"How do you know Byron?"

"He's our manager." Another lie.

"What sort of music?"

"Rock and roll, but with a lot of vocal harmonies."

"Just like every other pop group at the moment."

"But we're better."

There was a long pause. Dave was pleased that Chapman was even talking to him. Lenny had said: "You can't get through the door." Dave had proved him wrong there.

Then Chapman said: "You're a bloody liar."

Dave opened his mouth to protest, but Chapman held up a hand to silence him. "Don't tell me any more whoppers. Byron isn't your manager and he didn't send you here. You might have met him, but he didn't say Classic Records needs Plum Nellie."

Dave said nothing. He had been caught out. This was humiliating. He had tried to bluff his way into a record company and he had failed.

Chapman said: "What's your name, again?"

"Dave Williams."

"What do you want from me, Dave?"

"A recording contract."

"There's a surprise."

"Give us an audition. I promise you won't regret it."

"I'll tell you a secret, Dave. When I was eighteen, I got my first job in a recording studio by saying I was a qualified electrician. I lied. The only qualification I had was grade seven piano."

Dave's heart leaped in hope.

"I like your cheek," Chapman said. A little sadly, he added: "If I could turn back the clock, I wouldn't mind being a young chancer all over again."

Dave held his breath.

"I'll audition you."

"Thanks!"

"Come into the recording studio after Christmas." He jerked a thumb at the receptionist. "Cherry will give you an appointment." He went back into his room and closed the door.

Dave could hardly believe his luck. He had been caught out in his silly lies—but he had got an audition just the same!

He made a provisional appointment with Cherry, and said he would phone to confirm when he had checked with the rest of the group. Then he went home, walking on air.

As soon as he got back to the house in Great Peter Street he picked up the phone in the hall and called Lenny. "I got us an audition with Classic Records!" he said triumphantly.

Lenny was not as enthusiastic as Dave expected. "Who told you to do that?" He was miffed because Dave had taken the initiative.

Dave refused to be deflated. "What have we got to lose?"

"How did you manage it?"

"Bluffed my way in. I saw Eric Chapman, and he said okay."

"Blind luck," said Lenny. "It happens sometimes."

"Yeah," said Dave, though he was thinking: I wouldn't have got lucky if I'd stayed home sitting on my arse.

"Classic isn't really a pop label," Lenny said.

"That's why they need us." Dave was running out of patience. "Lenny, how can this be bad?"

"No, it's fine, we'll see if it comes to anything."

"Now we have to decide what to play at the audition. The secretary told me we'll get to record two songs."

"Well, we should do 'Shake, Rattle and Roll,' obviously." Dave's heart sank. "Why?"

"It's our best number. Always goes down well."

"You don't think it's a bit old-fashioned?"

"It's a classic."

Dave knew he could not fight Lenny about this, not right now. Lenny had already swallowed his pride once. He could be pushed, but not too far. However, they could do two songs: perhaps the second could be more distinctive. "How about a blues?" Dave said desperately. "For a contrast. Show our range."

"Yeah. 'Hoochie Coochie Man.'"

That was a bit better, more like the material the Rolling Stones were doing. "Okay," said Dave.

He went into the drawing room. Walli was there with a guitar on his knee. He had been living with the Williams family ever since coming from Hamburg with the group. He and Dave often sat in this room, playing and singing, between school and dinner.

Dave told him the news. Walli was pleased, but worried

about Lenny's choice of material. "Two songs that were hits in the fifties," he said. His English was improving fast.

"It's Lenny's group," said Dave helplessly. "If you think you can change his mind, please try."

Walli shrugged. He was a great musician but a bit passive, Dave found. Evie said everyone was passive by comparison with the Williams family.

They were pondering Lenny's taste when Evie came in with Hank Remington. *A Woman's Trial* was a hit, despite the catastrophic opening on the day President Kennedy was killed. Hank was recording a new album with the Kords. They spent their afternoons together, then went off to their separate jobs.

Hank was wearing crushed-velvet hipster trousers and a polka-dot shirt. He sat with Dave and Walli while Evie went upstairs to change. As always he was charming and amusing, telling stories about the Kords on tour.

He picked up Walli's guitar and strummed some chords absentmindedly, then said: "Do you want to hear a new song?"

They did, of course.

It was a sentimental ballad called "Love Is It." The appeal was instant. It was a lovely melody with a little shuffle in the beat. They asked him to play it again, and he did.

Walli said: "What was that chord at the start of the bridge?"

"C sharp minor." Hank showed him, then passed him the guitar.

Walli played the chords, and Hank sang it a third time. Dave improvised a harmony.

"That sounded nice," Hank said. "Such a pity we're not going to record it."

"What?" Dave was incredulous. "It's beautiful!"

"The Kords think it's soppy. We're a rock outfit, they say; we don't want to sound like Peter, Paul and Mary."

"I think it's a number one hit," said Dave.

His mother put her head around the door. "Walli," she said. "Phone call for you—from Germany."

It would be Walli's sister Rebecca in Hamburg, Dave guessed. Walli's family in East Berlin could not phone him: the regime there did not allow phone calls to the West.

While Walli was out of the room, Evie reappeared. She had put her hair up and wore jeans and a T-shirt, ready for makeup and wardrobe artists to go to work on her. Hank was going to drop her at the theater on his way to the recording studio.

Dave was distracted, thinking about "Love Is It," a great song that the Kords did not want.

Walli came back in, followed by Daisy. He said: "That was Rebecca."

"I like Rebecca," said Dave, remembering pork chops and fried potatoes.

"She just received a letter, very delayed, from Karolin in East Berlin." Walli paused. He seemed to be in the grip of some emotion. At last he managed to say: "Karolin had the baby. It's a girl."

Everyone jumped up and congratulated him. Daisy and Evie kissed him. Daisy said: "When did this happen?"

"The twenty-second of November. Easy to remember: it was the day Kennedy was shot."

"How much did she weigh?" Daisy asked.

"Weigh?" said Walli as if that was an incomprehensible question.

Daisy laughed. "It's something people always tell you about new babies."

"I didn't ask what she weighed."

"Never mind. What about her name?"

"Karolin suggests Alice."

"That's lovely," said Daisy.

"Karolin will send me a photograph," said Walli. "Of my daughter," he added dazedly. "But she sends it via Rebecca, because letters to England are even more held up in the censor's office."

Daisy said: "I can't wait to see the picture!"

Hank rattled his car keys impatiently. Maybe he found baby talk boring. Or, Dave thought, perhaps he did not like the baby taking the spotlight away from him.

Evie said: "Oh, my God, look at the time. Bye, everyone. Congratulations again, Walli."

As they were leaving, Dave said: "Hank, are the Kords really not going to record 'Love Is It'?"

"Really. When they take against something, they're a stubborn lot."

"In that case . . . could Walli and I have the song for

Plum Nellie? We've got an audition in January with Classic Records."

"Sure," said Hank with a shrug. "Why not?"

. . .

Lloyd Williams asked Dave to step into his study on Saturday morning.

Dave was about to go out. He was wearing a horizontally striped blue-and-white sweater, jeans, and a leather jacket. "Why?" he said pugnaciously. "You're no longer giving me an allowance." The money he earned playing with Plum Nellie was not much, but it was enough for Tube fares, drinks, and occasionally a shirt or a new pair of boots.

"Is money the only reason for speaking to your father?"

Dave shrugged and followed him into the room. It had an antique desk and some leather chairs. A fire smoldered in the grate. On the wall was a picture of Lloyd at Cambridge in the thirties. The room was a shrine to everything that was out-of-date. It seemed to smell of obsolescence.

Lloyd said: "I ran into Will Furbelow at the Reform Club yesterday."

Will Furbelow was the head of Dave's school. Being bald, he was inevitably known as None Above.

"He says you're in danger of failing all your exams."

"He's never been my biggest fan."

"If you fail, you will not be allowed to continue at the school. That will be the end of your formal education."

"Thank God for that."

Lloyd was not going to be riled. "Every profession will be closed to you, from accountant to zoologist. They all require you to pass exams. The next possibility, for you, is an apprenticeship. You could learn to do something useful, and you should think about what you might like: bricklaying, cooking, motor mechanics . . ."

Dave wondered whether Dad was out of his mind. "Bricklaying?" he said. "Do you even *know* me? I'm Dave."

"Don't sound incredulous. These are the jobs people do if they can't pass exams. Below that level, you could be a shop assistant or a factory hand."

"I can't believe I'm hearing this."

"I was afraid you would do this, close your eyes to reality."

Dad was the one closing his eyes, Dave thought.

"I realize you're getting beyond the age where I can expect you to obey me."

Dave was startled. This was a new approach. He said nothing.

"But I want you to be clear about where we stand. When you leave school, I expect you to work."

"I am working, quite hard. I play three or four nights a week, and Walli and I have started trying to write songs."

"I mean that I expect you to support yourself. Although your mother has inherited wealth, we agreed long ago that we would never support our children in idleness."

"I'm not idle."

"You think that what you do is work, but the world may not see it that way. In any event, if you want to continue living here you'll have to pay your share."

"You mean rent?"

"If you want to call it that, yes."

"Jasper's never paid rent, and he's lived here for years!"

"He's still a student. And he passes his exams."

"What about Walli?"

"A special case, because of his background; but sooner or later he must pay his share, too."

Dave was working out the implications. "So, if I don't become a bricklayer or a shop assistant, and I don't make enough money with the group to pay your rent, then . . ."

"Then you will have to look for alternative accommodation."

"You'll throw me out."

Lloyd looked pained. "All your life, you've had the best of everything handed to you on a plate: a lovely home, a great school, the best food, toys and books, piano lessons, skiing holidays. But that was when you were a child. Now you're almost an adult, and you have to face reality."

"My reality, not yours."

"You scorn the kind of work that ordinary people do. You're different, you're a rebel. Fine. Rebels pay a price. Sooner or later, you have to learn that. That's all."

Dave sat thoughtful for a minute. Then he stood up. "Okay," he said. "I get the message." He went to the door.

As he left, he glanced back, and saw his father watching him with an odd expression.

He thought about that as he went out of the house and slammed the front door. What was that look? What did it mean?

He was still thinking about it as he bought his Tube ticket. Going down on the escalator, he saw an advertisement for a play called *Heartbreak House*. That was it, he thought. That was his father's facial expression.

He had looked heartbroken.

•   •   •

A small color photograph of Alice arrived in the post, and Walli studied it eagerly. It showed a baby like any other: a tiny pink face with alert blue eyes, a cap of thin dark brown hair, a blotchy throat. The rest of her was tightly wrapped in a sky blue blanket. All the same Walli felt an upsurge of love and a sudden need to protect and care for the helpless creature he had made.

He wondered if he would ever see her.

With the picture was a note from Karolin. She said that she loved Walli and missed him, and she was going to apply to the East German government for permission to emigrate to the West.

In the picture, Karolin was holding Alice and looking at the camera. Karolin had put on weight, and her face was more round. Her hair was pulled back, instead of framing her face like curtains. She no longer resembled all the other pretty girls in the Minnesänger folk club. She was a mother now. It made her even more desirable in Walli's eyes.

He showed the photograph to Dave's mother, Daisy. "Well, now, what a beautiful baby!" she said.

Walli smiled, though in his opinion no babies were beautiful, not even his own.

"I think she has your eyes, Walli," Daisy went on.

Walli's eyes had a slight Oriental look. He figured some long-ago ancestor must have been Chinese. He could not tell whether or not Alice's eyes were similar.

Daisy continued to gush. "And this is Karolin." Daisy had not seen her before: Walli had no photos. "What a pretty young woman."

"Wait till you see her dressed up," Walli said proudly. "People stop and stare."

"I hope we will see her, sometime."

A shadow fell over Walli's happiness, as if a cloud had hidden the sun. "So do I," he said.

He followed the news from East Berlin, reading the German newspapers in the public library, and he often questioned Lloyd Williams, whose specialty as a politician was foreign affairs. Walli knew that getting out of East Germany was ever more difficult: the Wall was being made larger and more formidable, with more guards and more towers. Karolin would never try to escape, especially now that she had a child. However, there might be another way. Officially, the East German government would not say whether legal emigration was possible; indeed, they would not even say which department dealt with applications. But Lloyd had learned, from the British embassy in Bonn, that about ten thousand people a year were given permission. Perhaps Karolin would be one of them.

"One day, I feel certain," said Daisy; but she was just being nice.

Walli showed the picture to Evie and Hank Remington, who were sitting in the drawing room, reading a script. The Kords were hoping to make a movie, and Hank wanted Evie to be in it. They put down their papers to coo over the baby.

"We have our audition with Classic Records today," Walli told Hank. "I'm meeting Dave after school."

"Hey, good luck with that," Hank said. "Are you going to do 'Love Is It'?"

"I hope so. Lenny wants to do 'Shake, Rattle and Roll.' "

Hank shook his head, making his long red hair swirl in a way that had caused a million adolescent girls to scream for joy. "Too old-fashioned."

"I know."

People were constantly coming and going at the house in Great Peter Street, and now Jasper came in with a woman Walli had not seen before. "This is my sister, Anna," he said.

Anna was a dark-eyed beauty in her middle twenties. Jasper was good-looking, too: they must be a handsome family, Walli thought. Anna had a generously rounded figure, unfashionable now that all models were flat-chested like Jean "the Shrimp" Shrimpton.

Jasper introduced everyone. Hank stood up to shake hands with Anna and said: "I've been hoping to meet you. Jasper tells me you're a book editor."

"That's right."

"I'm thinking of writing my life story."

Walli thought Hank was a bit young, at twenty, to be writing his autobiography; but Anna had a different view. "What a wonderful idea," she said. "Millions of people would want to read it."

"Oh, do you think so?"

"I know it, even though biography isn't my field—I specialize in translations of German and East European literature."

"I had a Polish uncle, would that help?"

Anna laughed, a rich chuckle, and Walli warmed to her. So did Hank, and they sat down to discuss the book.

Carrying two guitars, Walli left the house.

He had found Hamburg a startling contrast to East Germany, but London was unnervingly different, an anarchic riot. People wore all styles of clothing, from bowler hats to miniskirts. Boys with long hair were too commonplace even to be stared at. Political commentary was not just free, it was outrageous: Walli had been shocked to see a man on television impersonating Prime Minister Harold Macmillan, talking in his voice and wearing a little silver mustache and making idiotic pronouncements, though the Williams family had laughed heartily.

Walli was also struck by the number of dark faces. Germany had a few coffee-colored Turkish immigrants, but London had thousands of people from the Caribbean islands and the Indian subcontinent. They came to work in hospitals and factories and on the buses and trains. Walli noticed that the Caribbean girls were very stylishly dressed and sexy.

He met Dave at the school gates and they took the Tube to north London.

Dave was nervous, Walli could tell. Walli was not nervous. He knew he was a good musician. Working at the Jump Club every night he heard dozens of guitarists, and it was rare to come across one who was more accomplished than he. Most got by with a few chords and a lot of enthusiasm. When he did hear someone good he would stop washing glasses and watch the group, studying the guitarist's technique, until the boss told him to get back to work; then, when he got home, he would sit in his room and imitate what he had heard until he could play it perfectly.

Unfortunately, virtuosity did not make you a pop star.

There was more to it than that: charm, good looks, the right clothes, publicity, clever management, and, most of all, good songs.

And Plum Nellie had a good song. Walli and Dave had played "Love Is It" to the rest of the group, and they had performed it at several gigs over the busy Christmas season. It went down well, although—as Lenny pointed out—you could not dance to it.

But Lenny did not want to audition it. "Not our type of material," he had said. He felt the same as the Kords: it was too pretty and sentimental for a rock group.

From the Tube station, Walli and Dave walked to a big old house that had been soundproofed and converted into recording studios. They waited in the hall. The others turned up a few minutes later. A receptionist asked them all to sign a piece of paper that she said was "for insurance." To Walli it looked more like a contract. Dave frowned as he read it, but they all signed.

After a few minutes, an inner door opened and an unprepossessing young man slouched out. He wore a V-neck sweater with a shirt and tie, and he was smoking a hand-rolled cigarette. "Right," he said by way of introduction, and pushed his hair out of his eyes. "We're almost ready for you. Is this your first time in a recording studio?"

They admitted that it was.

"Well, our job is to make you sound your best, so just follow our guidance, okay?" He seemed to feel he was granting them a great favor. "Come into the studio and plug in, and we'll take it from there."

Dave said: "What's your name?"

"Laurence Grant." He did not say exactly what his role was, and Walli guessed he was a lowly assistant trying to make himself seem important.

Dave introduced himself and the group, which made Laurence fidget impatiently; then they went in.

The studio was a large room with low lighting. At one side was a full-size Steinway piano, very like the one in Walli's home in East Berlin. It had a padded cover and was partly hidden by a screen draped in blankets. Lenny sat at it and played a series of chords all the way up the keyboard. It had the warm tone characteristic of Steinways. Lenny looked impressed.

A drum kit was set up ready. Lew had brought his own snare drum, and he set about making the change.

Laurence said: "Something wrong with our drums?"

"No, it's just that I'm used to the feel of my own snare."

"Ours is more suitable for recording."

"Oh, okay." Lew removed his own drum and put the studio snare back on its stand.

Three amplifiers stood on the floor, their lights showing that they were on and ready. Walli and Dave plugged into the two Vox AC30 models and Buzz took the larger Ampeg bass amp. They tuned to the piano.

Lenny said: "I can't see the rest of the group. Do we have to have this screen?"

"Yeah, we do," said Laurence.

"What's it for?"

"It's a baffle."

Walli could tell, from Lenny's expression, that he was none the wiser; but he let it drop.

A middle-aged man in a cardigan entered through a different door. He was smoking. He shook hands with Dave, who obviously had met him before, then introduced himself to the rest of the group. "I'm Eric Chapman, and I'll be producing your audition," he said.

This is the man who holds our future in his hands, Walli thought. If he thinks we're good, we'll make records. If not, there's no court of appeal. I wonder what he likes. He doesn't look like a rock-and-roller. More the Frank Sinatra type.

"I gather you haven't done this before," Eric said. "But there's really not much to it. At first it's best to ignore the equipment, and try to relax and play as if this was a regular gig. If you make a minor mistake, just play through." He pointed at Laurence. "Larry here is our general dogsbody, so ask him for anything you need: tea, coffee, extra leads, whatever."

Walli had not heard the English word *dogsbody* before, but he could guess what it meant.

Dave said: "There is one thing, Eric. Our drummer, Lew, brought his own snare, because he's more comfortable with it."

"What type is it?"

Lew answered. "Ludwig Oyster Black Pearl."

"Should be fine," Eric said. "Go ahead and switch."

Lenny said: "Do we have to have this baffle here?"

"I'm afraid we do," Eric said. "It keeps the piano mike from picking up too much drum sound."

So, Walli thought, Eric knows what he's talking about, and Larry is full of shit.

Eric said: "If I like you, we'll talk about what to do next. If not, I won't beat about the bush: I'll tell you straight that you're not what I'm looking for. Is that okay with everybody?"

They all said it was.

"All right, let's give it a whirl."

Eric and Larry retreated through a soundproofed door and reappeared behind an internal window. Eric put on headphones and spoke into a microphone, and the group heard his voice coming from a small speaker on the wall. "Are you ready?"

They were ready.

"Tape is rolling. Plum Nellie audition, take one. In your own time, lads."

Lenny started to play boogie-woogie piano. It sounded wonderful on the Steinway. After four bars the group came in like clockwork. They played this number at every gig: they could do it in their sleep. Lenny went all out, doing the Jerry Lee Lewis vocal flourishes. When they had finished, Eric played back the recording without comment.

Walli thought it sounded good. But what did Eric think?

"You play that well," he said over the intercom when they had finished. "Now, have you got something more modern?"

They played "Hoochie Coochie Man." Once again the piano sounded marvelous to Walli, the minor chords thundering out.

Eric asked them to play both songs again, and they did so. Then he came out of the control booth. He sat on an amplifier and lit a cigarette. "I said I would tell you straight, and I will," he said, and Walli knew then that he was going to reject them. "You play well, but you're old-fashioned. The world doesn't need another Jerry Lee Lewis or Muddy Waters. I'm looking for the next greatest thing, and you're not it. I'm sorry." He took a long drag on his cigarette and blew out smoke. "You can have the tape, and do what you like with it. Thanks for coming in." He stood up.

They all looked at one another. Disappointment was written on every face.

Eric went back into the control room, and Walli saw him, through the glass, taking the reel-to-reel tape off the machine.

Walli stood up, about to pack his guitar away.

Dave blew on his microphone, and the sound was amplified: everything was still on. He strummed a chord. Walli hesitated. What was Dave up to?

Dave began to sing "Love Is It."

Walli joined in immediately, and they sang in harmony. Lew came in with a quiet drum pattern, and Buzz played a simple walking bass. Finally Lenny joined in on the piano.

They played for two minutes, then Larry switched everything off, and the group was silenced.

It was all over, and they had failed. Walli was more disappointed than he would have expected. He was so sure the group was good. Why could Eric not see it? He undid the strap of his guitar.

Then Eric came back. "What the fuck was that?" he said.

Dave said: "A new song we've just learned. Did you like it?"

"It's completely different," Eric said. "Why did you stop?"

"Larry turned us off."

"Turn them on again, Larry, you prick," said Eric. He turned back to Dave. "Where did you get the song?"

"Hank Remington wrote it for us," said Dave.

"Of the Kords?" Eric was frankly skeptical. "Why would he write a song for you?"

Dave was equally candid. "Because he's going out with my sister."

"Oh. That explains it."

Before going back into the booth, Eric spoke quietly to Larry. "Go and phone Paulo Conti," he said. "He only lives around the corner. If he's at home, ask him to pop in right away."

Larry left the studio.

Eric went back into the booth. "Tape rolling," he said over the intercom. "Whenever you're ready."

They did the song again.

All Eric said was: "Again, please."

After the second time he came out again. Walli feared he

would say it was not good enough after all. "Let's do it again," he said. "This time we'll record the backing first time around, and the vocals after."

Dave said: "Why?"

"Because you play better when you don't have to sing, and you sing better when you don't have to play."

They recorded the instruments, then they sang the song while the recording was played to them through headphones. Afterward Eric came out of the booth to listen with them. They were joined by a well-dressed young man with a Beatle haircut: Paulo Conti, Walli presumed. Why was he here?

They listened to the combined track, Eric sitting on an amp and smoking.

When it ended, Paulo said in a London accent: "I like it. Nice song."

He seemed confident and authoritative, though he was only about twenty. Walli wondered what right he had to an opinion.

Eric dragged on his cigarette. "Now, we might have something here," he said. "But there's a problem. The piano part is wrong. No offense, Lenny, but the Jerry Lee Lewis style is a bit heavy-handed. Paulo is here to show you what I mean. Let's record it again with Paulo on the piano."

Walli looked at Lenny. He was angry, Walli could tell; but he was keeping it under control. He remained sitting on the piano stool and said: "Let's get something straight, Eric. This is my group. You can't shove me out and bring Paulo in."

"I wouldn't worry too much about that if I were you, Lenny," said Eric. "Paulo plays with the Royal National Symphony Orchestra and he's released three albums of Beethoven sonatas. He doesn't want to join a pop group. I wish he did—I know half a dozen outfits that would take him on quicker than you can say *hit parade*."

Lenny looked foolish and said aggressively: "All right, so long as we understand each other."

They played the song again, and Walli could see immediately what Eric meant. Paulo played light trills with his right hand and simple chords with his left, and it suited the song much better.

They recorded it again with Lenny. He tried to play like Paulo, and made a decent job of it, but he did not really have the touch.

They recorded the backing twice more, once with Paulo and once with Lenny; then they recorded the vocal part three times. Finally Eric was satisfied. "Now," he said, "we need a B side. What have you got that's similar?"

"Wait a minute," Dave said. "Does that mean that we've passed the audition?"

"Of course you have," said Eric. "Do you think I go to this much trouble with groups I'm about to turn down?"

"So . . . 'Love Is It' by Plum Nellie will be released as a record?"

"I bloody well hope so. If my boss turns it down I'll quit."

Walli was surprised to learn that Eric had a boss. Until now he had given the impression that he *was* the boss. It was a trivial deception, but Walli marked it.

Dave said: "Do you think it will be a hit?"

"I don't make predictions—I've been in this business too long. But if I thought it was going to be a miss, I wouldn't be here talking to you, I'd be down the pub."

Dave looked around at the group, grinning. "We passed the audition," he said.

"You did," Eric said impatiently. "Now, what have you got for the B side?"

.   .   .

"Are you ready for some good news?" said Eric Chapman over the phone to Dave Williams a month later. "You're going to Birmingham."

At first Dave did not know what he meant. "Why?" he said. Birmingham was an industrial city one hundred twenty miles north of London. "What's in Birmingham?"

"The television studio where they make *It's Fab!*, you idiot."

"Oh!" Dave suddenly felt breathless with excitement. Eric was talking about a popular show that featured pop groups miming to their records. "Are we on it?"

"Of course you are! 'Love Is It' will be their Hot Tip for the week."

The record had been out five days. It had been played on the BBC Light Programme once, and several times on Radio Luxembourg. To Dave's surprise, Eric did not know how many copies had actually been bought: the record business was not that good at tracking sales.

Eric had released the version with Paulo on the piano. Lenny had pretended not to notice.

Eric treated Dave as the leader of the group, despite what Lenny had told him. Now he said: "Have you got decent outfits to wear?"

"We normally wear red shirts and black jeans."

"It's black-and-white television, so that'll probably look fine. Make sure you all wash your hair."

"When are we going?"

"Day after tomorrow."

"I'll have to get off school," Dave said worriedly. There might be trouble about that.

"You may have to *leave* school, Dave."

Dave gulped. He wondered if that was true.

Eric finished: "Meet me at Euston station at ten in the morning. I'll have your tickets."

Dave hung up the phone and stared at it. He was going to be on *It's Fab!*

It was beginning to look as if he might actually make a living by singing and playing the guitar. As that prospect came to seem more real, his dread of the alternatives grew. What a comedown it would be now, if he had to get a regular job after all.

He called the rest of the group immediately, but he decided not to tell his family until afterward. There was too much risk that his father would try to stop him going.

He kept the exciting secret to himself all evening. Next day at lunchtime he asked to see the head teacher, old None Above.

Dave felt intimidated in the headmaster's study. In his early days at school he had been caned in this office several times for such offenses as running in the corridor.

He explained the situation and pretended there had not been time to get a note from his father.

"It seems to me you have to choose between getting a decent education and becoming a pop singer," said Mr. Furbelow, pronouncing the words *pop singer* with a grimace of distaste. He looked as if he had been asked to eat a can of cold dog food.

Dave thought of saying: *Actually, my ambition is to become a prostitute's minder,* but Furbelow's sense of humor was as scant as his hair. "You told my father I'm going to fail all my exams and be thrown out of the school."

"If your work does not improve rapidly, and if you consequently fail to gain any O-level qualifications, you will not be admitted to the sixth form," the head said with prissy exactness. "All the more reason why you may not take days off school to appear on trashy television programs."

Dave thought of arguing about "trashy" and decided it was a lost cause. "I thought you might regard a trip to a television studio as an educational experience," he said reasonably.

"No. There is far too much talk nowadays about educational 'experiences.' Education takes place in the classroom."

Despite Furbelow's mulish obstinacy, Dave continued to try to reason with him. "I'd like to have a career in music."

"But you don't even belong to the school orchestra."

"They don't use any instruments invented in the last hundred years."

"And all the better for it."

Dave was finding it harder and harder to keep his temper. "I play the electric guitar quite well."

"I don't call that a musical instrument."

Against his better judgment, Dave allowed his voice to rise in a challenge. "What is it, then?"

Furbelow's chin lifted and he looked superior. "More a sort of nigger noisemaker."

For a moment, Dave was silenced. Then he lost his cool. "This is just willful ignorance!" he said.

"Don't you dare speak to me like that."

"Not only are you ignorant, you're a racist!"

Furbelow stood up. "Get out this instant."

"You think it's all right for you to come out with your crude prejudices, just because you're the burned-out head of a school for rich kids!"

"Be silent!"

"Never," said Dave, and he left the room.

In the corridor outside the head's study, it occurred to him that he could not now go to class.

A moment later he realized he could not stay in the school.

He had not planned this, but in a moment of madness he had, in fact, left school.

So be it, he thought; and he left the building.

He went to a café nearby and ordered eggs and chips. He had burned his boats. After he had called the head ignorant and burned-out and a racist they would not have him back, no matter what. He felt scared as well as liberated.

But he did not regret what he had done. He had a chance of becoming a pop star—and the school had wanted him to let it slip by!

Ironically, he was at a loss to know what to do with his newfound freedom. He wandered around the streets for a couple of hours, then returned to the school gates to wait for Linda Robertson.

He walked her home after school. Naturally the whole class had noticed his absence, but the teachers had said nothing. When Dave told her what had happened, she was awestruck. "So you're going to Birmingham anyway?"

"You bet."

"You'll have to leave school."

"I've left."

"What will you do?"

"If the record is a hit, I'll be able to afford to get a flat with Walli."

"Wow. And if it's not?"

"Then I'm in trouble."

She invited him in. Her parents were out, so they went to her bedroom, as they had done before. They kissed, and she let him feel her breasts; but he could tell she was troubled. "What's the matter?" he said.

"You're going to be a star," she said. "I know it."

"Aren't you glad?"

"You'll be mobbed by dolly birds who will let you go all the way."

"I hope so!"

She burst into tears.

"I was kidding," he said. "I'm sorry!"

She said: "You used to be this cute little kid I liked to talk to. None of the girls even wanted to kiss you. Then you joined a group and turned into the coolest boy in school, and they all envied me. Now you'll be famous and I'll lose you."

He thought she wanted him to say that he would be faithful to her, no matter what, and he was tempted to swear undying love; but he held back. He really liked her, but he was not yet sixteen, and he knew he was too young to be tied down. However, he did not want to hurt her feelings, so he said: "Let's just see what happens, okay?"

He saw the disappointment on her face, though she covered it up quickly. "Good idea," she said. She dried her tears, then they went down to the kitchen and had tea and chocolate biscuits until her mother came home.

When he got back to Great Peter Street there was no sign of anything unusual, so he deduced that the school had not telephoned his parents. No doubt None Above would prefer to write a letter. That gave Dave a day of grace.

He said nothing to his parents until the following morning. His father left at eight. Then Dave spoke to his mother. "I'm not going to school," he said.

She did not fly off the handle. "Try to understand the journey that your father has made," she said. "He was illegitimate, as you know. His mother worked in a sweatshop in the East End, before she went into politics. His grandfather was a coal miner. Yet your father went to one of the world's great universities, and by the time he was thirty-one he was a minister in the British government."

"But I'm different!"

"Of course you are, but to him it looks as if you just want to throw away everything he and his parents and grandparents have achieved."

"I have to live my own life."

"I know."

"I've left school. I had a row with old None Above. You'll probably get a letter from him today."

"Oh, dear. Your father will find that hard to forgive."

"I know. I'm leaving home, too."

She began to cry. "Where will you go?"

Dave felt tearful, too, but he kept control. "I'll stay at the YMCA for a few days, then get a flat with Walli."

She put a hand on his arm. "Just don't be angry with your father. He loves you so much."

"I'm not angry," said Dave, though he was, really. "I'm just not going to be held back by him, that's all."

"Oh, God," she said. "You're as wild as I was, and just as pigheaded."

Dave was surprised. He knew she had made an unhappy first marriage, but all the same he could not imagine his mother being wild.

She added: "I hope your mistakes won't be as bad as mine."

As he was leaving, she gave him all the money in her purse.

Walli was waiting in the hall. They left the house carrying their guitars. As soon as they were outside in the street all feelings of regret vanished, and Dave began to feel both excited and apprehensive. He was going to be on television! But he had gambled everything. He felt a little dizzy every time he remembered that he had left home and school.

They got the Tube to Euston. Dave had to ensure the television appearance was a success. This was paramount. If the record did not sell, he thought fearfully, and Plum Nellie was a failure, what then? He might have to wash glasses at the Jump Club, like Walli.

What could he do that would make people buy the record?

He had no idea.

Eric Chapman was waiting at the railway station in a pin-striped suit. Buzz, Lew, and Lenny were already there. They loaded their guitars onto the train. The drums and amplifiers were going separately, being driven in a van to Birmingham by Larry Grant; but no one would trust him with the precious guitars.

On the train, Dave said to Eric: "Thanks for buying our tickets."

"Don't thank me. The cost will be deducted from your fee."

"So . . . the television company will pay our fee to you?"

"Yes, and I'll deduct twenty-five percent, plus expenses, and pay you the rest."

"Why?" said Dave.

"Because I'm your manager, that's why."

"Are you? I didn't know."

"Well, you signed the contract."

"Did I?"

"Yes. I wouldn't have recorded you otherwise. Do I look like a charity worker?"

"Oh—that piece of paper we signed before the audition?"

"Yes."

"She said it was for insurance."

"Among other things."

Dave had a feeling he had been tricked.

Lenny said: "The show's on Saturday, Eric. How come we're going on a Thursday?"

"Most of it's prerecorded. Just one or two of the acts perform live on the day."

Dave was surprised. The show gave the impression of a fun party full of kids dancing and having a great time. He said: "Will there be an audience?"

"Not today. You've got to pretend you're singing to a thousand screaming girls all wetting their knickers for you."

Buzz, the bass player, said: "That's easy. I've been performing for imaginary girls since I was thirteen."

It was a joke, but Eric said: "No, he's right. Look at the camera and picture the prettiest girl you know standing right there taking her bra off. I promise you, it will put just the right sort of smile on your face."

Dave realized he was smiling already. Maybe Eric's trick worked.

They reached the studio at one. It was not very smart. Much of it was dingy, like a factory. The parts that appeared on camera had a tawdry glamour, but everything out of shot was scuffed and grubby. Busy people walked around ignoring Plum Nellie. Dave felt as though everyone knew he was a beginner.

A group called Billy and the Kids was onstage when they arrived. A record was playing loudly, and they were singing and playing along, but they had no microphones and their guitars were not plugged in. Dave knew, from his friends, that most viewers did not realize the acts were miming, and he wondered how people could be so dumb.

Lenny was scornful of the jolly Billy and the Kids record, but Dave was impressed. They smiled and gestured to the nonexistent audience, and when the song came to an end they bowed and waved as if acknowledging gales of applause. Then they did the whole thing all over again, with no less energy and charm. That was the professional way, Dave realized.

Plum Nellie's dressing room was large and clean, with big mirrors surrounded by Hollywood lights, and a fridge full of soft drinks. "This is better than what we're used to," said Lenny. "There's even a toilet roll in the bog!"

Dave put on his red shirt, then went back to watch the filming. Mickie McFee was performing now. She had had a string of hits in the fifties and was making a comeback. She was at least thirty, Dave guessed, but she looked sexy in a pink sweater stretched tight across her breasts. She had a great voice. She did a soul ballad called "It Hurts Too Much," and she sounded like a black girl. What must it be like, Dave wondered, to have so much confidence? He was so anxious he felt as if his stomach was full of worms.

The cameramen and technicians liked Mickie—they were mostly the older generation—and they clapped when she finished.

She came down off the stage and saw Dave. "Hello, kid," she said.

"You were great," Dave said, and introduced himself.

She asked him about the group. He was telling her about Hamburg when they were interrupted by a man in an Argyle sweater. "Plum Nellie onstage, please," the man said in a soft voice. "Sorry to butt in, Mickie, darling." He turned to Dave. "I'm Kelly Jones, producer." He looked Dave up and down. "You look fab. Get your guitar." He turned back to Mickie. "You can eat him up later."

She protested: "Give a girl a chance to play hard to get."

"That'll be the day, duckie."

Mickie waved a good-bye and disappeared.

Dave wondered whether they had meant a single word they had said.

He had little time to think about it. The group got onstage and were shown their places. As usual, Lenny turned up his shirt collar, the way Elvis did. Dave told himself not to be nervous: he would be miming, so he didn't even have to play the song right! Then they were into it and Walli was fingering the introduction as the record began.

Dave looked at the rows of empty seats and imagined Mickie McFee pulling the pink sweater off over her head to reveal a black brassiere. He grinned happily into the camera and sang the harmony.

The record was two minutes long, but it seemed to be over in five seconds.

He expected to be asked to do it again. They all waited

onstage. Kelly Jones was talking earnestly to Eric. After a minute they both came over to the group. Eric said: "Technical problem, lads."

Dave feared there was something wrong with their performance, and the television appearance might be canceled.

Lenny said: "What technical problem?"

Eric said: "It's you, Lenny, I'm sorry."

"What are you talking about?"

Eric looked at Kelly, who said: "This show is about kids with groovy clothes and Beatle haircuts raving to the latest hits. I'm sorry, Lenny, but you're not a kid, and your haircut is five years out-of-date."

Lenny said angrily: "Well, I'm very sorry."

Eric said: "They want the group to appear without you, Lenny."

"Forget it," said Lenny. "It's my group."

Dave was terrified. He had sacrificed everything for this! He said: "Listen, what if Lenny combs his hair forward and turns down the collar of his shirt?"

Lenny said: "I'm not doing it."

Kelly said: "And he would still look too old."

"I don't care," said Lenny. "It's all of us or none of us." He looked around the group. "Right, lads?"

No one said anything.

"Right?" Lenny repeated.

Dave felt scared, but forced himself to speak. "I'm sorry, Lenny, but we can't miss this chance."

"You bastards," Lenny said furiously. "I should never have let you change the name. The Guardsmen were a great little rock-and-roll combo. Now it's a schoolboy group called Plum fucking Nellie."

"So," Kelly said impatiently. "You'll go back onstage without Lenny and do the number again."

Lenny said: "Am I being fired from my own group?"

Dave felt like a traitor. He said: "It's only for today."

"No, it's not," said Lenny. "How can I tell my friends that my group is on telly but I'm not in it? Fuck that. It's all or nothing. If I leave now, I leave forever."

No one said anything.

"Right, then," said Lenny, and he walked out of the studio.

They all looked shamefaced.

Buzz said: "That was brutal."

Eric said: "That's show business."

Kelly said: "Let's go for another take, please."

Dave feared he would not be able to jig about merrily, after such a traumatic row, but to his surprise he managed fine.

They went through the song twice, and Kelly said he loved their performance. He thanked them for their understanding, and hoped they would come back on the show soon.

When the group returned to the dressing room, Dave hung back in the studio and sat in the empty audience section for a few minutes. He was emotionally exhausted. He had made his television debut, and he had betrayed his cousin. He could not help remembering all the helpful advice Lenny had given him. I'm an ungrateful rotter, he thought.

Heading back to join the others, he looked in at an open door and saw Mickie McFee in her dressing room, holding a glass in her hand. "Do you like vodka?" she said.

"I don't know what it tastes like," said Dave.

"I'll show you." She kicked the door shut, put her arms around his neck, and kissed him with her mouth open. Her tongue had a booze taste a bit like gin. Dave kissed her back enthusiastically.

She broke the embrace and poured more vodka into her glass, then offered it to him.

"No, you drink it," he said. "I prefer it that way."

She emptied the glass, then kissed him again. After a minute she said: "Oh, boy, you are a living doll."

She stepped back, then, to Dave's astonishment and delight, she pulled her tight pink sweater over her head and threw it aside.

She was wearing a black bra.

CHAPTER THIRTY-THREE

Dimka's grandmother, Katerina, died of a heart attack at the age of seventy. She was buried in Novodevichy Cemetery, a small park full of monuments and little chapels. The tombstones were prettily topped with snow, like slices of iced cake.

This prestigious resting place was reserved for leading citizens: Katerina was here because one day Grandfather Grigori, a hero of the October Revolution, would be buried in the same grave. They had been married almost fifty years. Dimka's grandfather seemed dazed and uncomprehending as his lifelong companion was lowered into the frozen ground.

Dimka wondered what it must be like, to love a woman for half a century and then lose her, suddenly, between one beat of the heart and the next. Grigori kept saying: "I was so lucky to have her. I was so lucky."

A marriage such as that was probably the best thing in the world, Dimka thought. They had loved one another and had been happy together. Their love had survived two world wars and a revolution. They had had children and grandchildren.

What would people say about Dimka's marriage, he wondered, when he was lowered into the Moscow earth, perhaps fifty years from now? "Call no man happy until he is dead," said the playwright Aeschylus: Dimka had heard that quote at university and always remembered it. Youthful promise could be blighted by later tragedy; suffering was often rewarded by wisdom. According to family legend, the young Katerina had preferred Grigori's gangster brother, Lev, who had fled to America, leaving her pregnant. Grigori had married her and raised Volodya as his son. Their happiness had had an inauspicious beginning, proving Aeschylus's point.

Another surprise pregnancy had triggered Dimka's own marriage. Perhaps he and Nina could end up as happy as Grigori and Katerina. It was what he longed for, despite his feelings for Natalya. He wished he could forget her.

He looked across the grave at his uncle Volodya and aunt Zoya and their two teenagers. Zoya at fifty was serenely beautiful. There was another marriage that seemed to have brought lasting happiness.

He was not sure about his own parents. His late father had been a cold man. Perhaps that was a consequence of being in the secret police: how could people who did such cruel work be loving and sympathetic? Dimka looked at his mother, Anya, weeping for the loss of her own mother. She had seemed happier since his father died.

Out of the corner of his eye he looked at Nina. She was solemn but dry-eyed. Was she happy being married to him? She had been divorced once, and when Dimka met her she had said she never wanted to marry again and was unable to have children. Now she stood beside him as his wife and carried Grigor, their nine-month-old son, wrapped in a bearskin blanket. Dimka sometimes felt he had no idea what was going on in her mind.

Because Grandfather Grigori had stormed the Winter Palace in 1917, a lot of people had showed up to say a last farewell to his wife. Some were important Soviet dignitaries. Here was the bushy-eyebrowed Leonid Brezhnev, secretary of the Central Committee, glad-handing the mourners. There was Marshal Mikhail Pushnoy, who had been a young protégé of Grigori's in the Second World War. Pushnoy, an overweight Lothario, was stroking his luxuriant gray mustache and turning his charm on Aunt Zoya.

Anticipating this crowd, Uncle Volodya had paid for a reception in a restaurant just off Red Square. Restaurants were dismal places, with surly waiters and poor food. Dimka had heard, from both Grigori and Volodya, that they were different in the West. However, this one was typically Soviet. The ashtrays were full when they arrived. The snacks were stale: dry blinis and curling old pieces of toast with perfunctory slices of boiled egg and smoked fish. Fortunately, even Russians could not spoil vodka, and there was plenty of that.

The Soviet food crisis was over. Khrushchev had succeeded in buying grain from the United States and elsewhere, and there would be no famine this winter. But the emergency had highlighted a long-term disappointment. Khrushchev had pinned his hopes on making Soviet agriculture modern and productive—and he had failed. He ranted about inefficiency, ignorance, and clumsiness, but he had made no headway against such problems. And agriculture symbolized the general miscarriage of his reforms. For all his maverick ideas and sudden radical changes, the USSR was still decades behind the West in everything except military might.

Worst of all, the opposition to Khrushchev within the Kremlin came from men who wanted not more reform but less, hidebound conservatives such as preening Marshal Pushnoy and back-slapping Brezhnev, both now roaring with laughter at one of Grigori's war stories. Dimka had never been so worried about the future of his country, his leader, and his own career.

Nina handed the baby to Dimka and got a drink. A minute later she was with Brezhnev and Marshal Pushnoy, joining in their laughter. People always laughed a lot at funeral wakes, Dimka had noticed: it was the reaction after the solemnity of the burial.

Nina was entitled to party, he felt: she had carried Grigor and given birth to him and breast-fed him, so she had not had much fun for a year.

She had got over her anger with Dimka for lying to her on the night Kennedy died. Dimka had calmed her with another lie. "I did work late, but then I went for a drink with some colleagues." She had remained angry for a while, but less so, and now she seemed to have forgotten the incident. He was pretty sure she had no suspicion of his illicit feelings for Natalya.

Dimka took Grigor around the family, proudly showing people his first tooth. The restaurant was in an old house, with tables spread through several ground-floor rooms of different sizes. Dimka ended up in the farthest room with his uncle Volodya and aunt Zoya.

That was where his sister cornered him. "Have you seen how Nina is behaving?" Tanya said.

Dimka laughed. "Is she getting drunk?"

"And flirting."

Dimka was not perturbed. Anyway, he was in no position to condemn Nina: he did the same when he went to the Riverside Bar with Natalya. He said: "It is a party."

Tanya had no inhibitions about what she said to her twin. "I noticed that she went straight for the most high-ranking men in the room. Brezhnev just left, but she's still making eyes at Marshal Pushnoy—who must be twenty years older than her."

"Some women find power attractive."

"Did you know that her first husband brought her to Moscow from Perm and got her the job with the steel union?"

"No, I didn't."

"Then she left him."

"How do you know?"

"Her mother told me."

"All Nina got from me was a baby."

"And an apartment in Government House."

"You think she's some kind of gold digger?"

"I worry about you. You're so smart about everything—except women."

"Nina is a little materialistic. It's not the worst of sins."

"So you don't mind."

"No, I don't."

"Okay. But if she hurts my brother I'll scratch her eyes out."

. . .

Daniil came and sat opposite Tanya in the canteen at the TASS building. He put down his tray and tucked a handkerchief into his shirt collar to protect his tie. Then he said: "The people at *New World* like 'Frostbite.'"

Tanya was thrilled. "Good!" she said. "It took them long enough—it must be at least six months. But that's great news!"

Daniil poured water into a plastic tumbler. "It will be one of the most daring things they've ever printed."

"So they're going to publish?"

"Yes."

She wished she could tell Vasili. But he would have to find out on his own. She wondered if he was able to get the magazine. It must be available at libraries in Siberia. "When?"

"They haven't decided. But they don't do anything in a hurry."

"I'll be patient."

Dimka was awakened by the phone. A woman's voice said: "You don't know me, but I have information for you."

Dimka was confused. The voice belonged to Natalya. He threw a guilty look at his wife, Nina, lying beside him. Her eyes were still closed. He looked at the clock: it was five thirty in the morning.

Natalya said: "Don't ask questions."

Dimka's brain started to work. Why was Natalya pretending to be a stranger? She wanted him to do the same, obviously. Was it for fear that his tone of voice would betray his fondness for her to the wife beside him in bed?

He played along. "Who are you?"

"They're plotting against your boss," she said.

Dimka realized that his first interpretation had been wrong. What Natalya feared was that the phone might be tapped. She wanted to be sure Dimka did not say anything to reveal her identity to the listening KGB.

He felt the chill of fear. True or false, this meant trouble for him. He said: "Who is plotting?"

Beside him, Nina opened her eyes.

Dimka shrugged helplessly, miming: *I have no idea what is going on.*

"Leonid Brezhnev is approaching other Presidium members about a coup."

"Shit." Brezhnev was one of the half-dozen most powerful men under Khrushchev. He was also conservative and unimaginative.

"He has Podgorny and Shelepin on his side already."

"When?" said Dimka, disobeying the instruction not to ask questions. "When will they strike?"

"They will arrest Comrade Khrushchev when he returns from Sweden." Khrushchev was planning a trip to Scandinavia in June.

"But why?"

"They think he's losing his mind," said Natalya, and then the connection was broken.

Dimka hung up and said *Shit* again.

"What is it?" Nina said sleepily.

"Just work problems," Dimka said. "Go back to sleep."

Khrushchev was not losing his mind, though he was depressed, seesawing between manic cheerfulness and deep gloom. At the root of his disquiet was the agricultural crisis. Unfortunately, he was easily seduced by quick-fix solutions: miracle fertilizers, special pollination, new strains. The one proposal he would not consider was relaxing central control. All the same, he was the Soviet Union's best hope. Brezhnev was no reformer. If he became leader the country would go backward.

It was not just Khrushchev's future that worried Dimka now: it was his own. He had to reveal this phone call to Khrushchev: on balance that was less dangerous than concealing it. But Khrushchev was still enough of a peasant to punish the bringer of bad news.

Dimka asked himself whether this was the moment to jump ship, and leave Khrushchev's service. It would not be easy: apparatchiks generally went where they were told. But there were ways. Another senior figure could be persuaded to request that a young aide be transferred to his office, perhaps because the aide's special skills were needed. It could be arranged. Dimka could try for a job with one of the conspirators, Brezhnev perhaps. But what was the point of that? It might save his career, but to no purpose. Dimka was not going to spend his life helping Brezhnev hold back progress.

However, if he was to survive, he and Khrushchev needed to be ahead of this conspiracy. The worst thing they could do would be to wait and see what happened.

Today was April 17, 1964, Khrushchev's seventieth birthday. Dimka would be the first to congratulate him.

In the next room, Grigor began to cry.

Dimka said: "The phone woke him."

Nina sighed and got up.

Dimka washed and dressed quickly, then wheeled his motorcycle out of the garage and rode fast to Khrushchev's residence in the suburb called Lenin Hills.

He arrived at the same time as a van bringing a birthday present. He watched as security men carried into the living room a huge new radio-television console with a metal plaque inscribed:

> FROM YOUR COMRADES AT WORK
> IN THE CENTRAL COMMITTEE
> AND THE COUNCIL OF MINISTERS

Khrushchev often grumpily told people not to waste public money buying him presents, but everyone knew he was secretly happy to receive them.

Ivan Tepper, the butler, showed Dimka upstairs to Khrushchev's dressing room. A new dark suit hung ready to be put on for the day of congratulatory ceremonies. Khrushchev's three Hero of Socialist Labor stars were already pinned to the breast of the jacket. Khrushchev sat in a robe drinking tea and looking at the newspapers.

Dimka told him about the phone call while Ivan helped Khrushchev on with his shirt and tie. The KGB wiretap on Dimka's phone, if there was one, would confirm his story that the call was anonymous, supposing that Khrushchev checked. Natalya had been clever, as always.

"I don't know whether it's important or not, and I didn't think it was for me to decide," Dimka said cautiously.

Khrushchev was dismissive. "Aleksandr Shelepin isn't ready to be leader," he said. Shelepin was a deputy prime minister and former head of the KGB. "Nikolai Podgorny is narrow. And Brezhnev isn't suited either. Do you know they used to call him the Ballerina?"

"No," said Dimka. It was hard to imagine anyone less like a dancer than the stocky, graceless Brezhnev.

"Before the war, when he was secretary of Dnepropetrovsk Province."

Dimka saw that he was supposed to ask the obvious question. "Why?"

"Because anyone could turn him round!" said Khrushchev. He laughed heartily and put his jacket on.

So the threatened coup was dismissed with a joke. Dimka was relieved that he was not being condemned for crediting stupid reports. But one worry was replaced by another. Was Khrushchev's intuition right? His instincts had proved reliable in the past. But Natalya always got news first, and Dimka had never known her to be wrong.

Then Khrushchev picked up another thread. His sly peasant eyes narrowed and he said: "Do these petty plotters have a reason for their discontent? The anonymous caller must have told you."

This was an embarrassing question. Dimka did not dare tell Khrushchev that people thought he was mad. Desperately improvising, he said: "The harvest. They blame you for last year's drought." He hoped this was so implausible it would be inoffensive.

Khrushchev was not offended, but irritated. "We need new methods!" he said angrily. "They must listen to Lysenko!" He fumbled his jacket buttons, then let Tepper do them up.

Dimka kept his face expressionless. Trofim Lysenko was a scientific charlatan, a clever self-promoter who had won Khrushchev's favor even though his research was worthless. He promised improved yields that never materialized, but he managed to persuade political leaders that his opponents were "antiprogress," an accusation that was as fatal in the USSR as "Communist" was in the USA.

"Lysenko performs experiments on cows," Khrushchev went on. "His rivals use fruit flies! Who gives a shit about fruit flies?"

Dimka recalled his aunt Zoya talking about scientific research. "I believe the genes evolve faster in fruit flies—"

"Genes?" said Khrushchev. "Rubbish! No one has ever seen a gene."

"No one has ever seen an atom, but that bomb destroyed Hiroshima." Dimka regretted the words as soon as they were out of his mouth.

"What do you know about it?" Khrushchev roared. "You're just repeating what you've heard, parrot-fashion! Unscrupulous people use innocents like you to spread their lies." He shook his fist. "We will get improved yields. You'll see! Get out of my way."

Khrushchev pushed past Dimka and left the room.

Ivan Tepper gave Dimka an apologetic shrug.

"Don't worry," said Dimka. "He's got mad at me before. He won't remember this tomorrow." He hoped it was true.

Khrushchev's rage was not as worrying as his misapprehensions. He was wrong about agriculture. Alexei Kosygin, who was the best economist in the Presidium, had plans for reform that involved loosening the grip that ministries held on agriculture and other industries. That was the way to go, in Dimka's opinion; not miracle cures.

Was Khrushchev just as wrong about the plotters? Dimka did not know. He had done his best to warn his boss. He could not start a countercoup on his own.

Going down the stairs, he heard applause from the open door of the dining room. Khrushchev was receiving congratulations from the Presidium. Dimka paused in the hall. When the applause died down, he heard the slow bass voice of Brezhnev. "Dear Nikita Sergeyevitch! We, your close comrades in arms, members and candidate members of the Presidium and secretaries of the Central Committee, extend special greetings and fervently congratulate you, our closest personal friend and comrade, on your seventieth birthday."

It was fulsome even by Soviet standards.

Which was a bad sign.

. . .

A few days later, Dimka was given a dacha.

He had to pay, but the rent was nominal. As with most luxuries in the Soviet Union, the difficulty was not the price but getting to the head of the queue.

A dacha—a weekend home or holiday villa—was the first ambition of upwardly mobile Soviet couples. (The second was a car.) Dachas were normally granted only to Communist Party members, naturally.

"I wonder how we got it," Dimka mused after opening the letter.

Nina thought there was no mystery. "You work for Khrushchev," she said. "You should have been given one long ago."

"Not necessarily. It generally takes a few more years of service. I can't think of anything I've done recently that has been especially pleasing to him." He recalled the argument about genes. "In fact just the opposite."

"He likes you. Someone handed him a list of vacant dachas and he put your name next to one. He didn't think about it for longer than five seconds."

"You're probably right."

A dacha could be anything from a palace by the sea to a hut in a field. The following Sunday, Dimka and Nina went to find out what theirs was like. They packed a picnic lunch, then, with baby Grigor, took the train to a village thirty miles outside Moscow. They were full of eager curiosity. A station attendant gave them directions to their place, which was called the Lodge. It took them fifteen minutes to walk there.

The house was a one-story timber cabin. It had a large kitchen-cum-living-room and two bedrooms. It was set in a small garden that ran down to a stream. Dimka thought it was paradise. He wondered again what he had done to get so lucky.

Nina liked it, too. She was excited, moving through the rooms and opening cupboards. Dimka had not seen her so happy for months.

Grigor, who was not so much walking as staggering, seemed delighted to have a new place in which to stumble and fall.

Dimka was imbued with optimism. He envisioned a future in which he and Nina came here on summer weekends year after year. Every season they would marvel over how different Grigor was from last year. Their son's growth would be measured in summers: he would talk next season, count the summer after, then catch a ball, then read, then swim. He would be a toddler here at the dacha, then a boy climbing a tree in the garden, then an adolescent with spots, then a young man charming the girls in the village.

The place had not been used for a year or more, and they threw open all the windows, then set about dusting surfaces and sweeping floors. It was partly furnished, and they started a list of things they would bring next time: a radio, a samovar, a bucket.

"I could come here with Grigor on Friday mornings in the summer," Nina said. She was washing pottery bowls in the sink. "You could join me on Friday night, or Saturday morning if you have to work late."

"You wouldn't mind being here on your own at night?"

said Dimka as he scrubbed ancient grease off the kitchen range. "It's a bit lonely."

"I'm not nervous, you know that."

Grigor cried for his lunch, and Nina sat down to feed him. Dimka took a look around outside. He would have to erect a fence at the bottom of the garden, he saw, to prevent Grigor falling into the stream. It was not deep, but Dimka had read somewhere that a child could drown in three inches of water.

A gate in a wall led to a larger garden beyond. Dimka wondered who his neighbors were. The gate was not locked, so he opened it and went through. He found himself in a small wood. Exploring, he came within sight of a larger house. He speculated that his dacha might once have been the home of the gardener at the big house.

Not wanting to intrude on someone's privacy, he turned back—and came face-to-face with a soldier in uniform.

"Who are you?" said the man.

"Dmitri Dvorkin. I'm moving into the little house next door."

"Lucky you—it's a jewel."

"I was just exploring. I hope I haven't trespassed."

"You'd better stay on your own side of that wall. This place belongs to Marshal Pushnoy."

"Oh!" said Dimka. "Pushnoy? He's a friend of my grandfather."

"Then that's how you got the dacha," said the soldier.

"Yes," said Dimka, and he felt vaguely troubled. "I suppose it is."

CHAPTER THIRTY-FOUR

George's apartment was the top floor of a high, narrow Victorian row house in the Capitol Hill neighborhood. He preferred this to a modern building: he liked the proportions of the nineteenth-century rooms. He had leather chairs, a high-fidelity record player, plenty of bookshelves, and plain canvas blinds at the windows instead of fussy drapes.

It looked even better with Verena in it.

He loved to see her doing everyday things in his home: sitting on the couch and kicking off her shoes, making coffee in her bra and panties, standing naked in the bathroom brushing her perfect teeth. Best of all he liked to see her asleep in his bed, as she was now, with her soft lips slightly parted, her lovely face in repose, one long, slender arm thrown back to reveal the strangely sexy armpit. He leaned over her and kissed her armpit. She made a noise in her throat but did not wake up.

Verena stayed here every time she came to Washington, which was about once a month. It was driving George crazy. He wanted her all the time. But she was not willing to give up her job with Martin Luther King in Atlanta, and George could not leave Bobby Kennedy. So they were stuck.

George got up and walked naked into the kitchen. He started a pot of coffee and thought about Bobby, who was wearing his brother's clothes, spending too much time at the graveside holding hands with Jackie, and letting his political career go to hell.

Bobby was the public's favorite choice for vice president. President Johnson had not asked Bobby to be his running mate in November, nor had he ruled him out. The two men disliked one another, but that did not necessarily prevent their teaming up for a Democratic victory.

Anyway, Bobby needed to make only a small effort to become Johnson's friend. A little sucking up went a long way with Lyndon. George had planned it with his friend Skip Dickerson, who was close to Johnson. A dinner party for Johnson at Bobby and Ethel's Virginia mansion, Hickory Hill; a few warm handshakes in full view in the corridors of the Capitol; a speech in which Bobby said Lyndon was a worthy successor to his brother; it could be easily done.

George hoped it would happen. A campaign might bring Bobby out of his grief-stricken torpor. And George himself relished the prospect of working in a presidential election campaign.

Bobby could make something special of the normally insignificant post of vice president, just as he had revolutionized the role of attorney general. He would become a high-profile advocate for the things he believed in, such as civil rights.

But first Bobby needed somehow to be reanimated.

George poured two mugs of coffee and returned to the bedroom. Before getting back under the covers he turned on the television. He had a TV set in every room, like Elvis: he felt uneasy if he was away from the news too long. "Let's see who won the California Republican primary," he said.

Verena said sleepily: "You so romantic, baby, I like to die."

George laughed. Verena often made him laugh. It was one of the best things about her. "Who are you trying to kid?" he said. "You want to watch the news, too."

"Okay, you're right." She sat up and sipped coffee. The sheet fell off her, and George had to tear his gaze away to look at the screen.

The leading candidates for the Republican nomination were Barry Goldwater, the right-wing senator from Arizona, and Nelson Rockefeller, the liberal governor of New York. Goldwater was an extremist who hated labor unions, welfare, the Soviet Union, and—most of all—civil rights.

Rockefeller was an integrationist and an admirer of Martin Luther King.

They had fought a close contest so far, but the result of yesterday's California primary would be decisive. The winner would take all the state's delegates, about 15 percent of the total attending the Republican convention. Whoever had won last night would almost certainly be the Republican candidate for president.

The commercial break ended, the news came on, and the primary was the top story. Goldwater had won. It was a narrow victory—52 percent to 48 percent—but Goldwater had all the California delegates.

"Hell," said George.

"Amen to that," said Verena.

"This is really bad news. A serious racist is going to be one of the two presidential candidates."

"Maybe it's good news," Verena argued. "Could be all the sensible Republicans will vote Democrat to keep Goldwater out."

"That's worth hoping for."

The phone rang and George picked up the bedside extension. He immediately recognized the Southern drawl of Skip Dickerson, saying: "Did you see the result?"

"Fucking Goldwater won," said George.

"We think it's good news," said Skip. "Rockefeller might have beaten our man, but Goldwater is too conservative. Johnson will wipe the floor with him in November."

"That's what Martin Luther King's people think."

"How do you know that?"

George knew because Verena had told him. "I talked to . . . some of them."

"Already? The result has only just been announced. You're not actually in bed with Dr. King, are you, George?"

George laughed. "Never mind who I'm in bed with. What did Johnson say when you told him the result?"

Skip hesitated. "You won't like it."

"Now I *have* to know."

"Well, he said: 'Now I can win without the help of that little runt.' I apologize, but you did ask."

"Damn."

The little runt was Bobby. George saw immediately the political calculation Johnson had made. If Rockefeller had been his opponent, Johnson would have had to work hard for liberal votes, and having Bobby on the ticket would have helped him win them. But running against Goldwater he could automatically count on all the liberal Democrats and many liberal Republicans too. His problem now would be securing the votes of the white working class, many of whom were racist. So he no longer needed Bobby—in fact, Bobby would now be a liability.

Skip said: "I'm sorry, George, but it's, you know, realpolitik."

"Yeah. I'll tell Bobby. Though he's probably guessed. Thanks for letting me know."

"You bet."

George hung up and said to Verena: "Johnson doesn't want Bobby for his running mate now."

"It makes sense. He doesn't like Bobby, and now he doesn't need him. Who will he pick instead?"

"Gene McCarthy, Hubert Humphrey, or Thomas Dodd."

"Where does this leave Bobby?"

"That's the problem." George got up and turned the volume of the television down to a murmur, then returned to bed. "Bobby's been useless as attorney general since the assassination. I still push on with lawsuits against Southern states that prevent Negroes from voting, but he's not really interested. He's also forgotten all about organized crime—and he was doing so well! We got Jimmy Hoffa convicted, and Bobby hardly noticed."

Shrewdly, Verena asked: "Where does that leave *you*?" She was one of only a few people who thought ahead as fast as George himself.

"I may quit," George said.

"Wow."

"I've been treading water for six months, and I'm not going to do it much longer. If Bobby really is a spent force I'll move on. I admire him more than any man, but I'm not going to sacrifice my life to him."

"What will you do?"

"I could probably get a great job with a Washington law firm. I've had three years' experience in the Department of Justice, and that's worth a lot."

"They don't hire many Negroes."

"That's true, and a lot of firms wouldn't even give me an

interview. But others might hire me just to prove they're liberal."

"Really?"

"Things are changing. Lyndon is really hot on equal opportunities. He sent Bobby a note complaining about how few female lawyers the Justice Department hires."

"Good for Johnson!"

"Bobby was mad as hell."

"So you'll work for a law firm."

"If I stay in Washington."

"Where else would you go?"

"Atlanta. If Dr. King still wants me."

"You'd move to Atlanta," Verena said thoughtfully.

"I could."

There was a silence. They both looked at the screen. Ringo Starr had tonsillitis, the newsreader told them. George said: "If I moved to Atlanta, we could be together all the time."

She looked pensive.

"Would you like that?" he asked her.

Still she said nothing.

He knew why. He had not said *how* they would be together. He had not planned this, but they had got to the point where they had to decide whether to get married.

Verena was waiting for him to propose.

An image of Maria Summers came into his mind, unbidden, unwanted. He hesitated.

The phone rang.

George picked it up. It was Bobby. "Hey, George, wake up," he said jocularly.

George concentrated, trying to put the thought of marriage out of his mind for a minute. Bobby sounded happier than he had for a long time. George said: "Did you see the California result?"

"Yes. It means Lyndon doesn't need me. So I'm going to run for senator. What do you think of that?"

George was startled. "Senator! For what state?"

"New York."

So Bobby would be in the Senate. Maybe he could shake up those crusty old conservatives, with their filibusters and their delaying tactics. "That's great!" said George.

"I want you to join my campaign team. What do you say?"

George looked at Verena. He had been on the brink of proposing marriage. But now he was not moving to Atlanta. He was going on the campaign trail, and if Bobby won he would be back in Washington, working for Senator Kennedy. Everything had changed, again.

"I say yes," George said. "When do we start?"

CHAPTER THIRTY-FIVE

Dimka was with Khrushchev at the Black Sea holiday resort of Pitsunda, on Monday, October 12, 1964, when Brezhnev called.

Khrushchev was not at his best. He lacked energy and talked about the need for old men to retire and make way for the next generation. Dimka missed the old Khrushchev, the podgy gnome full of mischievous ideas, and wondered when he would come back.

The study was a paneled room with an Oriental rug and a bank of telephones on a mahogany desk. The phone that rang was a special high-frequency instrument connecting party and government offices. Dimka picked it up, heard the subterranean rumble of Brezhnev's voice, and handed the phone to Khrushchev.

Dimka heard only Khrushchev's half of the conversation. Whatever Brezhnev was saying, it caused the leader to say: "Why? ... On what issue? ... I'm on vacation, what could be so urgent? What do you mean, you all got together? ... Tomorrow? ... All right!"

After he hung up, he explained. The Presidium wanted him to return to Moscow to discuss urgent agricultural problems. Brezhnev had been insistent.

Khrushchev sat thoughtfully for a long time. He did not dismiss Dimka. Eventually he said: "They haven't got any urgent agricultural problems. This is what you warned me of six months ago, on my birthday. They're going to throw me out."

Dimka was shocked. So Natalya had been right.

Dimka had believed Khrushchev's reassurances, and his faith had seemed justified in June, when Khrushchev came back from Scandinavia and the threatened arrest did not take place. At that point, Natalya had admitted that she no longer knew what was happening. Dimka assumed the plot had come to nothing.

Now it seemed that it had merely been postponed.

Khrushchev had always been a fighter. "What will you do?" Dimka asked him.

"Nothing," said Khrushchev.

That was even more shocking.

Khrushchev went on: "If Brezhnev thinks he can do better, let him try, the big turd."

"But what will happen with him in charge? He doesn't have the imagination and energy to drive reforms through the bureaucracy."

"He doesn't even see much need for change," the old man said. "Maybe he's right."

Dimka was aghast.

Back in April he had considered whether to leave Khrushchev and try for a job with another senior Kremlin figure, but he had decided against it. Now that was beginning to look like a mistake.

Khrushchev became practical. "We'll leave tomorrow. Cancel my lunch with the French minister of state."

Beneath a thundercloud of gloom Dimka set about making the arrangements: getting the French delegation to come earlier, ensuring the plane and Khrushchev's personal pilot would be ready, and altering tomorrow's diary. But he did it all as if in a trance. How could the end come so easily?

No previous Soviet leader had retired. Both Lenin and Stalin had died in office. Would Khrushchev be killed now? What about his aides?

Dimka asked himself how much longer he had to live.

He wondered if they would even let him see little Grigor again.

He pushed the thought to the back of his mind. He could not operate if he were paralyzed by fear.

They took off at one the following afternoon.

The flight to Moscow took two and a half hours, with no change of time zone. Dimka had no idea what awaited them at the end of the trip.

They flew to Vnukovo-2, south of Moscow, the airport for official flights. When Dimka got off the plane behind Khrushchev, a small group of minor officials greeted them, instead of the usual crowd of top government ministers. At that point, Dimka knew for sure that it was all over.

Two cars were parked on the runway: a ZIL-111 limousine and a five-seater Moskvitch 403. Khrushchev walked to the limousine, and Dimka was ushered to the modest saloon.

Khrushchev realized they were being separated. Before getting into his car, he turned and said: "Dimka."

Dimka felt close to tears. "Yes, comrade First Secretary?"

"I may not see you again."

"Surely that cannot be!"

"Something I should tell you."

"Yes, comrade?"

"Your wife is fucking Pushnoy."

Dimka stared at him, speechless.

"Better you should know," Khrushchev said. "Goodbye." He got into his car and it pulled away.

Dimka sat in the back of the Moskvitch, dazed. He might never see the impish Nikita Khrushchev again. And Nina was sleeping with a stout middle-aged general with a gray mustache. It was all too much to take in.

After a minute, the driver said: "Home or office?"

Dimka was surprised he had a choice. That meant he was not being taken to the basement prison of the Lubyanka, at least not today. He was reprieved.

He considered his options. He could hardly work. There was no point in making appointments and preparing briefings for a leader who was about to fall. "Home," he said.

When he got there, he found himself surprisingly reluctant to accuse Nina. He was embarrassed, as if he were the wrongdoer.

And he *was* guilty. One night of oral sex with Natalya was not the same as the ongoing affair that Khrushchev's words implied, but it was bad enough.

Dimka said nothing while Nina fed Grigor. Then Dimka bathed him and put him to bed, and Nina made supper. While they ate, he told her that Khrushchev would resign tonight or tomorrow. It would be in the newspapers in a couple of days, he guessed.

Nina was alarmed. "What about your job?"

"I don't know what will happen," he said anxiously. "Right now no one is worrying about aides. They're probably deciding whether or not to kill Khrushchev. They'll deal with the small fry later."

"You'll be all right," she said after a moment's reflection. "Your family is influential."

Dimka was not so sure.

They cleared away. She noticed he had not eaten much. "Don't you like the stew?"

"I'm on edge," he said. Then he blurted it out. "Are you Marshal Pushnoy's mistress?"

"Don't be stupid," she said.

"No, I'm serious," Dimka said. "Are you?"

She put the plates in the sink with a bang. "What gave you that stupid idea?"

"Comrade Khrushchev told me. I assume he got the information from the KGB."

"How would they know?"

Dimka noticed that she was answering questions with questions, usually a sign of deceit. "They watch the movements of all senior government figures, looking for nonconformist behavior."

"Don't be ridiculous," she said again. She sat down and took out her cigarettes.

"You flirted with Pushnoy at my grandmother's funeral."

"Flirting is one thing—"

"And then we got a dacha right next to his."

She put a cigarette in her mouth and struck a match, but it went out. "That did seem a coincidence—"

"You're a cool one, Nina, but your hands are shaking."

She threw the dead match on the floor. "Well, how do you think I feel?" she said angrily. "I'm in this apartment all day with nobody to talk to but a baby and your mother. I wanted a dacha and you weren't going to get us one!"

Dimka was taken aback. "So you admit that you prostituted yourself?"

"Oh, be realistic, how else does anyone get anything in Moscow?" She got the cigarette alight and drew on it hard. "You work for a general secretary who is mad. I open my legs for a marshal who is horny. There's not much difference."

"So why did you open your legs for me?"

She said nothing, but involuntarily looked around the room.

He understood instantly. "For an apartment in Government House?"

She did not deny it.

"I thought you loved me," he said.

"Oh, I was fond of you, but since when was that enough? Don't be such a baby. This is the real world. If you want something, you pay the price."

He felt a hypocrite, accusing her, so he confessed. "Well, I might as well tell you that I've been unfaithful too."

"Ha!" she said. "I didn't think you had the nerve. Who with?"

"I'd rather not say."

"Some little typist in the Kremlin, of course."

"It was just one night, and we didn't have intercourse, but I don't feel that makes it much better."

"Oh, for God's sake, do you think I care? Go ahead—enjoy it!"

Was Nina raving in her anger, or revealing her true feelings? Dimka felt bewildered. He said: "I never foresaw that kind of marriage for us."

"Take it from me, there's no other kind."

"Yes, there is," he said.

"You dream your dreams, I'll dream mine." She switched on the television.

Dimka sat staring at the screen for a while, not seeing or hearing the program. After a while he went to bed, but he did not sleep. Later, Nina got into bed next to him, but they did not touch.

Next day Nikita Khrushchev left the Kremlin forever.

Dimka continued to go into work every morning. Yevgeny Filipov, walking around in a new blue suit, had been promoted. Obviously he had been part of the plot against Khrushchev, and had earned his reward.

Two days later, on Friday, the newspaper *Pravda* announced Khrushchev's resignation.

Sitting in his office with little to do, Dimka noticed that Western newspapers for the same day announced that the British prime minister had also been deposed. Upper-class Conservative Sir Alec Douglas-Home had been replaced by Harold Wilson, leader of the Labour Party, in a national election.

To Dimka in a cynical mood there was something askew when a rampantly capitalist country could fire its aristocratic premier and install a social democrat at the will of the people, whereas in the world's leading Communist state such things were plotted in secrecy by a tiny ruling elite and then announced, days later, to an impotent and docile population.

The British did not even ban Communism. Thirty-six Communist candidates had stood for Parliament. None had been elected.

A week ago, Dimka would have balanced these thoughts against the overwhelming superiority of the Communist system, especially as it would be when reformed. But now the hope of reform had withered, and the Soviet Union had been preserved with all its flaws for the foreseeable future. He knew what his sister would say: barriers to change were an integral part of the system, just another of its faults. But he could not bring himself to accept that.

The following day *Pravda* condemned subjectivism and drift, harebrained scheming, bragging and bluster, and several other sins of Khrushchev's. All that was crap, in Dimka's opinion. What was happening was a lurch backward. The Soviet elite was rejecting progress and opting for what they knew best: rigid control of the economy, repression of dissenting voices, avoidance of experiment. It would make them feel comfortable—and keep the Soviet Union trailing behind the West in wealth, power, and global influence.

Dimka was given minor tasks to perform for Brezhnev. Within a few days he was sharing his small office with one of Brezhnev's aides. It was only a matter of time before he was ousted. However, Khrushchev was still in the Lenin Hills residence, so Dimka began to feel that his boss and he might live.

After a week Dimka was reassigned.

Vera Pletner brought him his orders in a sealed envelope, but she looked so sad that Dimka knew the envelope contained bad news before he opened it. He read it immediately. The letter congratulated him on being appointed assistant secretary of the Kharkov Communist Party.

"Kharkov," he said. "Fuck it."

His association with the disgraced leader had clearly outweighed the influence of his distinguished family. This was a serious demotion. There would be a salary increase, but money was not worth much in the Soviet Union. He would be assigned an apartment and a car, but he would be in Ukraine, a long way from the center of power and privilege.

Worst of all, he would be living four hundred fifty miles from Natalya.

Sitting at his desk, he sank into a depression. Khrushchev was finished, Dimka's career had gone backward, the Soviet Union was heading downhill, his marriage to Nina was a train wreck, and he was to be sent away from Natalya, the bright spot in his life. Where had he gone wrong?

There was not much drinking in the Riverside Bar these days, but that evening he met Natalya there for the first time since coming back from Pitsunda. Her boss, Andrei Gromyko, was unaffected by the coup, and remained foreign minister, so she had kept her job.

"Khrushchev gave me a parting gift," Dimka said to her.

"What?"

"He told me Nina is having an affair with Marshal Pushnoy."

"Do you believe it?"

"I presume the KGB told Khrushchev."

"Still, it might be a mistake."

Dimka shook his head. "She admitted it. That wonderful dacha we got is right next door to Pushnoy's place."

"Oh, Dimka, I'm sorry."

"I wonder who watches Grigor while they're in bed."

"What are you going to do?"

"I can't feel very indignant. I'd be having an affair with you if I had the nerve."

Natalya looked troubled. "Don't talk like that," she said. Her face showed different emotions in quick succession: sympathy, sadness, longing, fear, and uncertainty. She pushed back her unruly hair in a nervous gesture.

"Too late now, anyhow," said Dimka. "I've been posted to Kharkov."

"What?"

"I heard today. Assistant secretary of the Kharkov Communist Party."

"But when will I see you?"

"Never, I imagine."

Her eyes filled with tears. "I can't live without you," she said.

Dimka was astonished. She liked him, he knew that, but she had never spoken this way, even during the single night they had spent together. "What do you mean?" he said idiotically.

"I love you, didn't you know that?"

"No, I didn't," he said, stupefied.

"I've loved you for a long time."

"Why did you never tell me?"

"I'm frightened."

"Of . . . ?"

"My husband."

Dimka had suspected something like this. He assumed, though he had no proof, that Nik was responsible for the savage beating of the black-marketeer who had tried to cheat Natalya. It was no surprise if Nik's wife was terrified of declaring her love for another man. This was the reason for Natalya's changeability, from sexy warmth one day to cold distance the next. "I guess I'm frightened of Nik, too," he said.

"When do you leave?"

"The furniture van will come on Friday."

"So soon!"

"In the office, I'm a loose cannon. They don't know what I might do. They want me out of the way."

She took out a white handkerchief and touched her eyes with it. Then she leaned closer to him across the little table. "Do you remember that room with all the old Tsarist furniture?"

He smiled. "I'll never forget it."

"And the four-poster bed?"

"Of course."

"It was so dusty."

"And cold."

Her mood had changed again, and now she was playful, teasing. "What do you remember most?"

An answer sprang to mind instantly: her little breasts with their big pointed nipples. But he suppressed it.

She said: "Go on, you can tell me."

What did he have to lose? "Your nipples," he said. He was half embarrassed, half inflamed.

She giggled. "Do you want to see them again?"

Dimka swallowed hard. Trying to match her light mood, he said: "Guess."

She stood up, suddenly looking decisive. "Meet me there at seven," she said. Then she walked out.

. . .

Nina was furious. "Kharkov?" she yelled. "What am I supposed to do in fucking Kharkov?"

Nina did not normally use bad language: she felt it was coarse. She had risen above such low habits. Her lapse was a sign of how strongly she felt.

Dimka was unsympathetic. "I'm sure the steel union there will give you a job." In any case it was time she sent Grigor to a day nursery and returned to work, something that was expected of Soviet mothers.

"I don't want to be exiled to a provincial city."

"Nor do I. Do you imagine I volunteered?"

"Didn't you see this coming?"

"I did, and I even considered switching jobs, but I thought the putsch had been canceled, when it had only been postponed. Naturally the plotters did all they could to keep me in the dark."

She gave him a calculating look. "I suppose you spent last night saying good-bye to your typist."

"You told me you didn't care."

"All right, smart mouth. When do we have to go?"

"Friday."

"Hell." Looking furious, Nina started packing.

On Wednesday, Dimka spoke to his uncle Volodya about the move. "It's not just about my career," he said. "I'm not in government for myself. I want to prove that Communism can work. But that means it has to change and improve. Now I'm afraid we could go backward."

"We'll get you back to Moscow as soon as we can," Volodya said.

"Thank you," Dimka said with fervent gratitude. His uncle had always been supportive.

"You deserve it," Volodya said warmly. "You're smart

and you get things done, and we don't have a surplus of such people. I wish I had you in my office."

"I was never the military type."

"But, listen. After something like this has happened, you have to prove your loyalty by working hard and not complaining—and, most of all, not constantly begging to be sent back to Moscow. If you do all that for five years, I can start working on your return."

"Five years?"

"Until I can *start*. Don't count on less than ten. In fact, don't count on anything. We don't know how Brezhnev is going to work out."

In ten years the Soviet Union could slide back all the way to poverty and underdevelopment, Dimka thought. But there was no point in saying so. Volodya was not just his best chance—he was his only chance.

Dimka saw Natalya again on Thursday. She had a split lip. "Did Nik do that?" said Dimka angrily.

"I slipped on icy steps and fell on my face," she said.

"I don't believe you."

"It's true," she said, but she would not meet him in the furniture storeroom again.

On Friday morning a ZIL-130 panel truck arrived and parked outside Government House, and two men in overalls began to carry Dimka's and Nina's possessions down in the elevator.

When the truck was almost full, they stopped for a break. Nina made them sandwiches and tea. The phone rang, and the doorman said: "There's a messenger here from the Kremlin, has to deliver personally."

"Send him up," said Dimka.

Two minutes later, Natalya appeared at the door in a coat of champagne-colored mink. With her damaged lip, she looked like a ravaged goddess.

Dimka stared at her uncomprehendingly. Then he glanced at Nina.

She caught his guilty look, and glared at Natalya. Dimka wondered if the two women would fly at one another. He got ready to intervene.

Nina folded her arms across her chest. "So, Dimka," she said, "I suppose this is your little typist."

What was Dimka supposed to say? *Yes*? *No*? *She's my lover*?

Natalya looked defiant. "I'm not a typist," she said.

"Don't worry," said Nina. "I know exactly what you are."

That jibe was rich, Dimka thought, coming from the woman who had slept with a fat old general in order to get a dacha. But he did not say so.

Natalya looked haughty and handed him an official-looking envelope.

He tore it open. It was from Alexei Kosygin, the reforming economist. He had a strong power base so, despite his radical ideas, he had been made chairman of the Council of Ministers in the Brezhnev government.

Dimka's heart leaped. The letter offered him a job as aide to Kosygin—here in Moscow.

"How did you manage this?" he said to Natalya.

"Long story."

"Well, thank you." He wanted to throw his arms around her and kiss her, but refrained. He turned to Nina. "I'm saved," he said. "I can stay in Moscow. Natalya has got me a job with Kosygin."

The two women stared at one another, each hating the other. No one knew what to say.

After a long pause, one of the removal men said: "Does that mean we have to unload the truck?"

.   .   .

Tanya flew Aeroflot to Siberia, touching down at Omsk on the way to Irkutsk. The plane was a comfortable Tupolev Tu-104 jet. The overnight flight took eight hours, and she dozed most of the way.

Officially, she was on assignment for TASS. Secretly, she was going to look for Vasili.

Two weeks ago Daniil Antonov had come to her desk and discreetly handed her the typescript of "Frostbite." "*New World* can't publish this after all," he had said. "Brezhnev is clamping down. Orthodoxy is the watchword now."

Tanya had shoved the sheets of paper into a drawer. She was disappointed, but she had been half prepared for this. She said: "Do you remember the articles I wrote three years ago about life in Siberia?"

"Of course," he said. "It was one of the most popular

series we ever did—and the government got a surge of applications from families wanting to go there."

"Maybe I should do a follow-up. Talk to some of the same people and ask how they're getting on. Also interview some newcomers."

"Great idea." Daniil lowered his voice. "Do you know where he is?"

So he had guessed. It was not surprising. "No," she said. "But I can find out."

Tanya was still living at Government House. She and her mother had moved up a floor into the grandparents' large apartment, after the death of Katerina, so that they could look after Grandfather Grigori. He claimed he did not need looking after: he had cooked and cleaned for himself and his kid brother, Lev, when they were factory workers before the First World War and living in one room in a St. Petersburg slum, he said proudly. But the truth was that he was seventy-six, and he had not cooked a meal nor swept a floor since the revolution.

That evening Tanya went down in the elevator and knocked on the door of her brother's apartment.

Nina opened up. "Oh," she said rudely. She retreated into the apartment, leaving the door open. She and Tanya had never liked one another.

Tanya stepped into the little hallway. Dimka appeared from the bedroom. He smiled, pleased to see her. She said: "A quiet word?"

He picked up his keys from a small table and led her outside, closing the apartment door. They went down in the elevator and sat on a bench in the spacious lobby. Tanya said: "I want you to find out where Vasili is."

He shook his head. "No."

Tanya almost cried. "Why not?"

"I've just avoided being exiled to Kharkov, by the skin of my teeth. I'm in a new job. What impression will I give if I start making inquiries about a criminal dissident?"

"I have to talk to Vasili!"

"I don't see why."

"Imagine how he must feel. He finished his sentence more than a year ago, yet he's still there. He may fear being forced to remain there the rest of his life! I have to tell him that we haven't forgotten about him."

Dimka took her hand. "I'm sorry, Tanya. I know you're fond of him. But what good will it do to put myself at risk?"

"On the strength of 'Frostbite,' he could be a great author. And he writes about our country in a way that encapsulates everything that's wrong. I have to tell him to write more."

"So what?"

"You work in the Kremlin: you can't change anything. Brezhnev is never going to reform Communism."

"I know. I'm in despair."

"Politics in this country is finished. Literature could be our only hope, now."

"Is a short story going to make any difference?"

"Who knows? But what else can we do? Come on, Dimka. We've always disagreed about whether Communism should be reformed or abolished, but neither of us has ever just given up."

"I don't know."

"Check where Vasili Yenkov lives and works. Say it's a confidential political inquiry for a report you're working on."

Dimka sighed. "You're right, we can't just give up."

"Thank you."

He got the information two days later. Vasili had been released from the prison camp but for some reason there was no new address on file. However, he was working at a power station a few miles outside Irkutsk. The recommendation of the authorities was that he should be refused a travel visa for the foreseeable future.

Tanya was met at the airport by a representative of the Siberian recruitment agency, a woman in her thirties called Irina. Tanya would have preferred a man. Women were intuitive: Irina might suspect Tanya's true mission.

"I thought we could start at the Central Department Store," Irina said brightly. "We have a lot of things you can't easily buy in Moscow, you know!"

Tanya forced enthusiasm. "Great!"

Irina drove her into the town in a four-wheel-drive Moskvitch 410. Tanya dropped her bag at the Central Hotel, then let herself be shown around the store. Curbing her impatience, she interviewed the manager and a counter assistant.

Then she said: "I want to see the Chenkov power station."

"Oh!" said Irina. "But why?"

"I went there last time I was here." This was a lie, but Irina would not know that. "One of my themes will be how things have changed. Also, I'm hoping to reinterview people I saw last time."

"But the power station has not been forewarned of your visit."

"That's all right. I'd prefer not to disrupt their work. We'll look around, then I'll talk to people during the lunch break."

"As you wish." Irina did not like it, but she was obliged to do everything possible to please an important journalist. "I'll just call ahead."

The Chenkov was an old coal-fired electricity-generating station, built in the thirties when cleanliness was not a consideration. The smell of coal was in the air, and its dust coated all surfaces, turning white to gray and gray to black. They were greeted by the manager, in a suit and a dirty shirt, clearly taken by surprise.

As Tanya was shown around she looked for Vasili. He should be easy to spot, a tall man with thick dark hair and movie-star looks. But she must not reveal, to Irina or anyone else nearby, that she knew him well and had come to Siberia to look for him. "You seem familiar," she would say. "I believe I must have interviewed you last time I was here." Vasili was quick-witted, and he would readily understand what was going on, but she would keep talking as long as possible, to give him time to get over his shock at seeing her.

An electrician would probably work in the control room, or on the furnace floor, she speculated; then she realized he could be fixing a power outlet or a lighting circuit anywhere in the complex.

She wondered how he might have changed in the intervening years. Presumably he still felt she was a friend: he had sent his story to her. No doubt he had a girlfriend here—perhaps several, knowing him. Would he be philosophical about his extended imprisonment, or enraged by the injustice done to him? Would he be pathetic, or rail at her for not getting him out?

She did her job thoroughly, asking workers how they and their families felt about life in Siberia. They all mentioned the high salaries and rapid promotion consequent on the shortage of skilled people. Many spoke cheerfully of the hardships: there was a spirit of pioneering camaraderie.

By midday she still had not seen Vasili. It was frustrating: he could not be far away.

Irina took her to the management dining room, but Tanya insisted on having lunch in the canteen with the workers. People relaxed while they were eating, and they spoke more honestly and colorfully. Tanya made notes of what they said, and kept looking around the room, choosing the next interviewee and at the same time keeping an eye out for Vasili.

However, the lunch hour went by and he did not appear. The canteen began to empty out. Irina proposed moving on to their next appointment, a visit to a school where Tanya would be able to speak to young mothers. Tanya could not think of a reason for refusing.

She would have to ask for him by name. She imagined saying: *I seem to remember an interesting man I met last time, an electrician, I think, called Vasili . . . Vasili, um, Yenkov? Could you find out whether he still works here?* It was barely plausible. Irina would make the inquiry, but she was not stupid, and she was sure to wonder what was Tanya's special interest in this man. It would not take her long to find out that Vasili had come to Siberia as a political prisoner. Then the question would be whether Irina decided to shut up and mind her own business—often the preferred way in the Soviet Union—or to curry favor by mentioning Tanya's query to someone above her in the Communist Party hierarchy.

For years no one had known of the friendship between Tanya and Vasili. That was their protection. It was why they had not been sentenced to life imprisonment for publishing a subversive magazine. After Vasili's arrest, Tanya had let one person into the secret, her twin brother. And Daniil had guessed. But now she was in danger of arousing the suspicions of a stranger.

She steeled her nerve to speak, and then Vasili appeared.

Tanya clamped her hand over her mouth to stop herself screaming.

Vasili looked like an old man. He was thin and bent. His hair was long and straggly and streaked with gray. His formerly fleshy, sensual face was drawn and lined. He wore grubby overalls with screwdrivers in the pockets. He dragged his feet as he walked.

Irina said: "Is something wrong, Comrade Tanya?"

"Toothache," said Tanya, improvising.

"I'm so sorry."

Tanya could not tell whether Irina believed her.

Her heart was thudding. She was overjoyed to have found Vasili, but horrified by his ravaged appearance. And she had to conceal this storm of emotions from Irina.

She stood up, letting Vasili see her. Few people were left in the canteen, so he could not miss her. She turned her face aside, not looking at him, to divert Irina's suspicion. She picked up her bag as if to go. "I must see a dentist as soon as I get home," she said.

Out of the corner of her eye she saw Vasili stop suddenly, staring at her. So that Irina would not notice, she said: "Tell me about the school we're going to. What age are the pupils?"

They began walking toward the door as Irina answered her question. Tanya tried to observe Vasili without looking directly at him. He remained frozen, staring, for several moments. As the two women approached him, Irina gave him a quizzical look.

Tanya then looked directly at Vasili again.

His sunken face was now looking stunned. His mouth hung open and he stared unblinkingly at her. But there was something in his eyes other than shock. Tanya realized it was hope—astonished, incredulous, yearning hope. He was not completely defeated: something had given this wreck of a man the strength to write that wonderful story.

She remembered the words she had prepared. "You look familiar—did I talk to you last time I was here, three years ago? My name is Tanya Dvorkin and I work for TASS."

Vasili closed his mouth and started to collect himself, but still he seemed dumbstruck.

Tanya kept on talking. "I'm writing a follow-up to my series on emigrants to Siberia. I'm afraid I don't remember your name, though—I've interviewed hundreds of people in the last three years!"

"Yenkov," he said at last. "Vasili Yenkov."

"We had a most interesting talk," Tanya said. "It's coming back to me. I must interview you again."

Irina looked at her watch. "We're short of time. The schools close early here."

Tanya nodded at her and said to Vasili: "Could we meet this evening? Would you mind coming to the Central Hotel? Perhaps we could have a drink together."

"At the Central Hotel," Vasili repeated.

"At six?"

"Six o'clock at the Central Hotel."

"I'll see you then," Tanya said, and she went out.

. . .

Tanya wanted to reassure Vasili that he had not been forgotten. She had done that already, but was it enough? Could she offer him any hope? She also wanted to tell him that his story was wonderful and he should write more, but again she had no encouragement to offer him: "Frostbite" could not be published and the same would probably be true of anything else he produced. She feared she might end up making him feel worse, not better.

She waited for him in the bar. The hotel was not bad. All visitors to Siberia were VIPs—no one came here for a holiday—so the place had the level of luxury expected by the Communist elite.

Vasili came in, looking a bit better than he had earlier. He had combed his hair and put on a clean shirt. He still looked like a man recovering from an illness, but the light of intelligence shone in his eyes.

He took both her hands in his. "Thank you for coming here," he said, his voice trembling with emotion. "I can't begin to tell you how much it means to me. You're a friend, a solid-gold friend."

She kissed his cheek.

They ordered beer. Vasili ate the free peanuts like a starving man.

"Your story is wonderful," Tanya said. "Not just good, but extraordinary."

He smiled. "Thank you. Perhaps something worthwhile can come out of this terrible place."

"I'm not the only person who admires it. The editors of *New World* accepted it for publication." He lit up with gladness, and she had to bring him down again. "But they changed their minds when Khrushchev was deposed."

Vasili looked crestfallen, then he took another handful of nuts. "I'm not surprised," he said, recovering his equanimity. "At least they liked it—that's the important thing. It was worth writing."

"I've made a few copies and mailed them—anonymously, of course—to some of the people who used to receive *Dissidence*," she added. She hesitated. What she planned to say next was bold. Once said, it could not be retracted. She took the plunge. "The only other thing I could do is try to get a copy out to the West."

She saw the light of optimism in his eyes, but he pretended to be dubious. "That would be dangerous for you."

"And for you."

Vasili shrugged. "What are they going to do to me—send me to Siberia? But you could lose everything."

"Could you write some more stories?"

From underneath his jacket he took a large used envelope. "I have already," he said, and he gave the envelope to her. He drank some beer, emptying his glass.

She glanced into the envelope. The pages were covered with Vasili's small, neat handwriting. "Why," she said with elation, "it's enough for a book!" Then she realized that if she were caught with this material she, too, could end up stuck in Siberia. She slipped the envelope into her shoulder bag quickly.

"What will you do with them?" he asked.

Tanya had given this some thought. "There's an annual book fair in Leipzig, in East Germany. I could arrange to cover it for TASS—I speak German, after a fashion. Western publishers attend the fair—editors from Paris and London and New York. I might be able to get your work published in translation."

His face lit up. "Do you think so?"

"I believe 'Frostbite' is good enough."

"That would be so wonderful. But you would be taking a terrible risk."

She nodded. "So would you. If somehow the Soviet authorities found out who the author was, you'd be in trouble."

He laughed. "Look at me—starving, dressed in rags, living alone in a hostel for men that is always cold—I'm not worried."

It had not occurred to her that he might not be getting enough to eat. "There's a restaurant here," she said. "Shall we have dinner?"

"Yes, please."

Vasili ordered beef Stroganoff with boiled potatoes. The waitress put a small bowl of bread rolls on the table, as was done at banquets. Vasili ate all the rolls. After the Stroganoff he ordered pirozhki, a fried bun filled with stewed plums. He also ate everything Tanya left on her plate.

She said: "I thought skilled people were highly paid here."

"Volunteers are, yes. Not ex-prisoners. The authorities submit to the price mechanism only when forced."

"Can I send you food?"

He shook his head. "Everything is stolen by the KGB. Parcels arrive ripped open, marked 'Suspicious package, officially inspected,' and everything decent is gone. The guy in the room next to mine received six jars of jam, all empty."

Tanya signed the bill for dinner.

Vasili said: "Does your hotel room have its own bathroom?"

"Yes."

"Does it have hot water?"

"Of course."

"Can I take a shower? At the hostel we get hot water only once a week, and then we have to rush before it runs out."

They went upstairs.

Vasili was a long time in the bathroom. Tanya sat on the bed, looking out at the grimy snow. She felt stunned. She knew, in a vague way, what labor camps were like, but seeing Vasili had brought it home to her in a devastatingly vivid way. Her imagination had not previously stretched to the extent of the prisoners' suffering. And yet, despite everything, Vasili had not succumbed to despair. In fact, he had summoned, from somewhere, the strength and courage to write about his experiences with passion and humor. She admired him more than ever.

When at last he emerged from the bathroom, they said good-bye. In the old days he would have made a pass at her, but today the thought did not seem to cross his mind.

She gave him all the money in her purse, a bar of chocolate, and two pairs of long underwear that would be too short but otherwise would fit him. "They might be better than what you've got," she said.

"They certainly are," he said. "I don't have any underwear."

After he left, she cried.

CHAPTER THIRTY-SIX

Every time they played "Love Is It" on Radio Luxembourg, Karolin cried.

Lili, now sixteen, thought she knew how Karolin felt. It was like having Walli back home, singing and playing in the next room, except that they could not walk in and see him and tell him how good it sounded.

If Alice was awake they would sit her close to the radio and say: "That's your daddy!" She did not understand, but she knew it was something exciting. Sometimes Karolin sang the song to her, and Lili accompanied her on the guitar and sang the harmony.

Lili's mission in life was to help Karolin and Alice emigrate to the West and be reunited with Walli.

Karolin was still living at the Franck family house in Berlin-Mitte. Her parents would have nothing to do with her. They said she had disgraced them by giving birth to an illegitimate child. But the truth was that the Stasi had told her father he would lose his job as a bus station supervisor because of Karolin's involvement with Walli. So they had thrown her out, and she had moved in with Walli's family.

Lili was glad to have her there. Karolin was like an older sister to replace Rebecca. And Lili adored the baby. Every day when she came home from school she watched Alice for a couple of hours, to give Karolin a break.

Today was Alice's first birthday, and Lili made a cake. Alice sat in her high chair and happily banged a bowl with a wooden spoon while Lili mixed a light sponge cake that the baby could eat.

Karolin was upstairs in her room, listening to Radio Luxembourg.

Alice's birthday was also the anniversary of the assassination. West German radio and television had programs about President Kennedy and the impact of his death. East German stations were playing it down.

Lyndon Johnson had been president by default for almost a year, but three weeks ago he had won an election by a landslide, defeating the Republican ultraconservative Barry Goldwater. Lili was glad. Although Hitler had died before she was born, she knew her country's history, and she was frightened by politicians who made excuses for racial hatred.

Johnson was not as inspiring as Kennedy, but he seemed equally determined to defend West Berlin, which was what mattered most to Germans on both sides of the Wall.

As Lili was taking the cake out of the oven, her mother arrived home from work. Carla had managed to keep her job as nursing manager in a large hospital, even though she was known to have been a Social Democrat. One time when a rumor had gone around that she was to be fired, the nurses had threatened to go on strike, and the hospital director had been obliged to avert trouble by reassuring them that Carla would continue to be their boss.

Lili's father had been forced to take a job, even though he was still trying to run his business in West Berlin by remote control. He had to work as an engineer in a state-owned factory in East Berlin, making televisions that were far inferior to the West German sets. At the outset he had made some suggestions for improving the product, but this was seen as a way of criticizing his superiors, so he stopped. This evening as soon as he arrived home from work he came into the kitchen and they all sang "Hoch Soll Sie Leben," the traditional German birthday song meaning: "Long may she live."

Then they sat around the kitchen table and talked about whether Alice would ever see her father.

Karolin had applied to emigrate. Escape was becoming more difficult every year: Karolin might have tried to cross, all the same, had she been alone; but she was not willing to risk Alice's life. Every year a few people were allowed out legally. No one could find out the grounds on which applications were judged, but it seemed that most of those allowed to leave were unproductive dependents, children and old people.

Karolin and Alice were unproductive dependents, but their application had been refused.

As always, no reason was given.

Naturally, the government would not say whether any appeal was possible. Once again, rumor filled the information gap. People said you could petition the country's leader, Walter Ulbricht.

He seemed an unlikely savior, a short man with a beard that imitated Lenin's, slavishly orthodox in everything. He was rumored to be happy about the coup in Moscow because he had thought Khrushchev insufficiently doctrinaire. All the same, Karolin had written him a personal letter, explaining that she needed to emigrate in order to marry the father of her child.

"They say he's a believer in old-fashioned family morality," Karolin said. "If that's true, he ought to help a woman who only wants her child to have a father."

People in East Germany spent half their lives trying to guess what the government planned or wanted or thought. The regime was unpredictable. They would allow a few rock-and-roll records to be played in youth clubs, then suddenly ban them altogether. For a while they would be tolerant about clothing, then they would start arresting boys in blue jeans. The country's constitution guaranteed the right to travel, but very few people got permission to visit their relatives in West Germany.

Grandmother Maud joined in the conversation. "You can't tell what a tyrant is going to do," she said. "Uncertainty is one of their weapons. I've lived under the Nazis as well as the Communists. They're depressingly similar."

There was a knock at the front door. Lili opened it and was horrified to see, standing on the doorstep, her former brother-in-law, Hans Hoffmann.

Lili held the door a few inches ajar and said: "What do you want, Hans?"

He was a big man, and could easily have shoved her out

of the way, but he did not. "Open up, Lili," he said in a voice of weary impatience. "I'm with the police, you can't keep me out."

Lili's heart was pounding, but she stayed where she was and shouted over her shoulder: "Mother! Hans Hoffmann is at the door!"

Carla came running. "Did you say Hans?"

"Yes."

Carla took Lili's place at the door. "You're not welcome here, Hans," she said. She spoke with calm defiance, but Lili could hear her breathing, fast and anxious.

"Is that so?" Hans said coolly. "All the same, I need to speak to Karolin Koontz."

Lili gave a small cry of fear. Why Karolin?

Carla asked the question. "Why?"

"She has written a letter to the comrade general secretary, Walter Ulbricht."

"Is that a crime?"

"On the contrary. He is the leader of the people. Anyone may write to him. He is glad to hear from them."

"So why have you come here to bully and frighten Karolin?"

"I'll explain my purpose to Fräulein Koontz. Don't you think you'd better ask me in?"

Carla murmured to Lili: "He might have something to tell us about her application to emigrate. We'd better find out." She opened the door wide.

Hans stepped into the hall. He was in his late thirties, a big man who stooped slightly. He wore a heavy double-breasted dark blue coat of a quality not generally available in East German shops. It made him look larger and more menacing. Lili instinctively moved away from him.

He knew the house, and now he acted as if he still lived here. He took off his coat and hung it on a hook in the hall, then without invitation he walked into the kitchen.

Lili and Carla followed him.

Werner was standing up. Lili wondered fearfully if he had taken his pistol from its hiding place behind the saucepan drawer. Perhaps Carla had been arguing on the doorstep in order to give him time to do just that. Lili tried to stop her hands shaking.

Werner did not hide his hostility. "I'm surprised to see you in this house," he said to Hans. "After what you did, you should be ashamed to show your face."

Karolin was looking puzzled and anxious, and Lili realized she did not know who Hans was. In an aside Lili explained: "He's with the Stasi. He married my sister and lived here for a year, spying on us."

Karolin's hand went to her mouth and she gasped. "That's him?" she whispered. "Walli told me. How could he do such a thing?"

Hans heard them whispering. "You must be Karolin," he said. "You wrote to the comrade general secretary."

Karolin looked scared but defiant. "I want to marry the father of my child. Are you going to let me?"

Hans looked at Alice in her high chair. "Such a lovely baby," he said. "Boy or girl?"

It made Lili shake with fear just that Hans was looking at Alice.

Reluctantly, Karolin said: "Girl."

"And what's her name?"

"Alice."

"Alice. Yes, I think you said that in your letter."

Somehow this pretense of being nice about the baby was even more frightening than a threat.

Hans pulled out a chair and sat at the kitchen table. "So, Karolin, you seem to want to leave your country."

"I should think you'd be glad—the government disapproves of my music."

"But why do you want to play decadent American pop songs?"

"Rock and roll was invented by American Negroes. It's the music of oppressed people. It's revolutionary. That's why it's so strange to me that Comrade Ulbricht hates rock and roll."

When Hans was defeated by an argument he always just ignored it. "But Germany has such a wealth of beautiful traditional music," he said.

"I love traditional German songs. I'm sure I know more than you do. But music is international."

Grandmother Maud leaned forward and said waspishly: "Like socialism, comrade."

Hans ignored her.

Karolin said: "And my parents threw me out of the house."

"Because of your immoral way of life."

Lili was outraged. "They threw her out because you, Hans, threatened her father!"

"Not at all," he said blandly. "What are respectable parents to do when their daughter becomes antisocial and promiscuous?"

Angry tears came to Karolin's eyes. "I have never been promiscuous."

"But you have an illegitimate child."

Maud spoke again. "You seem a little confused about biology, Hans. Only one man is required to make a baby, legitimate or otherwise. Promiscuity has nothing to do with it."

Hans looked stung, but once again he refused to rise to the bait. Still addressing Karolin, he said: "The man you wish to marry is wanted for murder. He killed a border guard and fled to the West."

"I love him."

"So, Karolin, you beg the general secretary to grant you the privilege of emigration."

Carla said: "It's not a privilege, it's a right. Free people may go where they like."

That got to Hans. "You people think you can do anything! You don't realize that you belong to a society that has to act as one. Even fish in the sea know enough to swim in schools!"

"We're not fish."

Hans ignored that and turned back to Karolin. "You are an immoral woman who has been rejected by her family because of outrageous behavior. You have taken refuge in a family with known antisocial tendencies. And you wish to marry a murderer."

"He's not a murderer," Karolin whispered.

"When people write to Ulbricht, their letters are passed to the Stasi for evaluation," Hans said. "Yours, Karolin, was given to a junior officer. Being young and inexperienced, he took pity on an unmarried mother, and recommended that permission be granted." This sounded like good news, Lili thought, but she felt sure there would be a twist in the tail. She was right. Hans went on: "Fortunately, his superior passed his report to me, recalling that I have had previous dealings with this"—he looked around with an expression of disgust—"with this undisciplined, nonconformist, trou-blemaking group."

Lili knew what he was going to say now. It was heart-breaking. Hans had come here to tell them that he had been responsible for the rejection of Karolin's application—and to rub it in personally.

"You will receive a formal reply—everyone does," he said. "But I can tell you now that you will not be permitted to emigrate."

"Can I visit Walli?" Karolin begged. "Just for a few days? Alice has never even seen her father!"

"No," said Hans with a tight smile. "People who have applied for emigration are never subsequently allowed to take holidays abroad." His hatred showed through momen-tarily as he added: "What do you think we are, stupid?"

"I will apply again in a year's time," said Karolin.

Hans stood up, a smile of triumphant superiority playing around his lips. "The answer will be the same next year, and the year after, and always." He looked around at all of them. "None of you will be given permission to leave. Ever. I promise you."

With that he left.

. . .

Dave Williams phoned Classic Records. "Hello, Cherry, this is Dave," he said. "Can I speak to Eric?"

"He's out at the moment," she said.

Dave was disappointed and indignant. "This is the third time I've phoned!"

"Unlucky."

"He could phone me back."

"I'll ask him."

Dave hung up.

He was not unlucky. Something was wrong.

Plum Nellie had had a great 1964. "Love Is It" had gone to number one on the hit parade, and the group—without Lenny—had done a tour of Britain with a package of pop stars including the legendary Chuck Berry. Dave and Walli had moved into a two-bedroom apartment in the theater district.

But things had now cooled right down. It was frustrating. Plum Nellie had a second record out. Classic had released "Shake, Rattle and Roll," with "Hoochie Coochie Man" on the B side, rushing it out for Christmas. Eric had not consulted the group, and Dave would have preferred to record a new song.

Dave had proved right. "Shake, Rattle and Roll" had flopped. Now it was January 1965, and as Dave thought about the year ahead he had a sense of panic. At night he had dreams about falling—from a roof, out of a plane, off a ladder—and woke up feeling that his life was about to end. The same sensation came over him when he contemplated his future.

He had allowed himself to believe that he was going to be a musician. He had left his parents' home and his school. He was sixteen, old enough to get married and pay taxes. He had thought he had a career. And suddenly it was all falling apart. He did not know what to do. He was no good at anything other than music. He could not face the humiliation of going back to live in his parents' house. In old-fashioned stories the boy hero would "run away to sea." Dave loved the idea of disappearing, then returning five years later, bronzed and bearded and telling tales of faraway places. But in his heart he knew he would hate the discipline of the navy. It would be worse than school.

He did not even have a girlfriend. When he left school he had ended his romance with Linda Robertson. She said she had been expecting it, though she cried all the same. When he received the money from Plum Nellie's appearance on *It's Fab!* he had got Mickie McFee's phone number from Eric and asked her if she wanted to go out with him, maybe to dinner and a movie. She had thought for a long moment, then said: "No. You're really sweet, but I can't be seen out with a sixteen-year-old. I already have a bad reputation, but I don't want to look quite such a fool." Dave had been hurt.

Walli was sitting next to Dave now, guitar in hand as usual. He was playing with a metal tube fitted over the middle finger of his left hand, and singing: "Woke up this morning, believe I'll dust my broom."

Dave frowned. "That's the Elmore James sound!" he said after a minute.

"It's called bottleneck guitar," Walli said. "They used to do it with the neck of a broken bottle, but now someone makes these metal things."

"It sounds great."

"Why do you keep phoning Eric?"

"I want to know how many copies we sold of 'Shake, Rattle and Roll,' what's happening about the American release of 'Love Is It,' and whether we've got any tour dates coming up—and our manager won't speak to me!"

"Fire him," said Walli. "He is a breast."

Walli's English was almost perfect now. "A tit, you mean," Dave said. "We say he's a tit, not a breast."

"Thank you."

"How can I fire him if I can't get him on the phone?" Dave said gloomily.

"Go round to his office."

Dave looked at Walli. "You know, you're not as dumb as you sound." Dave began to feel better. "That's exactly what I'm going to do."

The downhearted feeling left him as he stepped outside. Something about the streets of London always cheered him. This was one of the world's great cities: anything could happen.

Denmark Street was less than a mile away. Dave was there in fifteen minutes. He went up the stairs to the office of Classic Records. "Eric is out," Cherry said.

"Are you sure?" said Dave. Feeling bold, he opened Eric's door.

Eric was there, behind the desk. He looked a bit foolish, having been caught out in deceit. Then his expression changed to anger and he said: "What do you want?"

Dave did not say anything immediately. His father sometimes said: "Just because someone asks you a question, don't think you have to answer. I've learned that in politics." Dave just stepped into the room and closed the door behind him.

If he remained standing, he thought, it would look as if he expected to be told to leave at any moment. So he sat on the chair in front of Eric's desk and crossed his legs.

Then he said: "Why are you avoiding me?"

"I've been busy, you arrogant little sod. What is it?"

"Oh, all kinds of things," Dave said expansively. "What's happening to 'Shake, Rattle and Roll'? What are we doing in the New Year? What news from America?"

"Nothing, nothing, and nothing," said Eric. "Satisfied?"

"Why would I be satisfied with that?"

"Look." Eric put his hand in his pocket and took out a roll of bills. "Here's twenty quid. That's what you've got coming for 'Shake, Rattle and Roll.'" He threw four five-pound notes on the desk. "Now are you satisfied?"

"I'd like to see the figures."

Eric laughed. "The figures? Who do you think you are?"

"I'm your client, and you're my manager."

"Manager? There's nothing to manage, you twerp. You were a one-hit wonder. We have them all the time in our business. You had a stroke of luck. Hank Remington gave you a song, but you never had real talent. It's over, forget it, go back to school."

"I can't go back to school."

"Why ever not? What are you, sixteen, seventeen?"

"I failed every exam I ever took."

"Then get a job."

"Plum Nellie is going to be one of the most successful acts in the world, and I'm going to be a musician for the rest of my life."

"Keep dreaming, son."

"I will." Dave stood up. He was about to leave when he thought of a snag. He had signed a contract with Eric. If the group really did do well, Eric might claim a percentage. He said: "So, Eric, you're not Plum Nellie's manager anymore, is that what you're telling me?"

"Hallelujah! He's got the message at last."

"I'll take back that contract, then."

Eric suddenly looked suspicious. "What? Why?"

"The contract we signed, the day we recorded 'Love Is It.' You don't want to keep it, do you?"

Eric hesitated. "Why do you want it back?"

"You've just told me I have no talent. Of course, if you see a great future for the group—"

"Don't make me laugh." Eric picked up the phone. "Cherry, my love, get the Plum Nellie contract out of the file and give it to young Dave on his way out." He cradled the handset.

Dave picked up the money from the desk. "One of us is a fool, Eric," he said. "I wonder which?"

Walli loved London. There was music everywhere: folk clubs, beat clubs, theaters, concert halls, and opera houses. Every night Plum Nellie was not playing he went out to hear music, sometimes with Dave, sometimes alone. Every now and again he went to a classical recital, where he would hear new chords.

The English were strange. When he said he was German, they always started talking about the Second World War. They thought they had won the war, and they got offended if he pointed out that it was actually the Soviets who had defeated the Germans. Sometimes he said he was Polish, just to avoid having the same boring conversation again.

But half the people in London were not English anyway: they were Irish, Scottish, Welsh, Caribbean, Indian, and Chinese. All the drug dealers came from islands: Maltese men sold pep pills, heroin pushers were from Hong Kong, and you could buy marijuana from Jamaicans. Walli liked to go to Caribbean clubs, where they played music with a different beat. He was approached by lots of girls at all these places, but he always told them he was engaged.

One day the phone rang, while Dave was out, and the caller said: "May I speak to Walter Franck?"

Walli almost replied that his grandfather had been dead for more than twenty years. "I am Walli," he said after a hesitation.

The caller switched to German. "This is Enok Andersen calling from West Berlin."

Andersen was the Danish accountant who managed Walli's father's factory. Walli recalled a bald man with glasses and a ballpoint pen in the breast pocket of his jacket. "Is something wrong?"

"All your family is well, but I am the bringer of disappointing news. Karolin and Alice have been refused permission to emigrate."

Walli felt as if he had been punched. He sat down heavily. "Why?" he said. "What reason?"

"The government of East Germany does not give reasons for their decisions. However, a Stasi man visited the house—Hans Hoffmann, whom you know."

"A jackal."

"He told the family that none of them would ever get permission to emigrate or travel to the West."

Walli covered his eyes with his hand. "Never?"

"That's what he said. Your father asked me to convey this to you. I'm very sorry."

"Thank you."

"Is there any message I can give your family? I cross to East Berlin once a week still."

"Say I love them all, please." Walli choked up.

"Very well."

Walli swallowed. "And say that I *will* see them all again one day. I feel sure of it."

"I'll tell them that. Good-bye."

"Good-bye." Walli hung up, feeling desolate.

After a minute he picked up his guitar and played a minor chord. Music was consoling. It was abstract, just notes and their relationships. There were no spies, no traitors, no policemen, no walls. He sang: "I miss you, Alice . . ."

. . .

Dave was glad to see his sister again. He met her outside the office of her agency, International Stars. Evie was wearing a purple derby hat. She said: "Home is pretty dull without you."

"Nobody has rows with Dad?" said Dave with a grin.

"He's so busy, since Labour won the election. He's in the cabinet now."

"And you?"

"I'm doing a new film."

"Congratulations!"

"But you fired your manager."

"Eric felt Plum Nellie was a one-hit wonder. But we haven't given up. However, we must get some more gigs. All we've got in the diary is a few nights at the Jump Club, and that won't even pay the rent."

"I can't promise that International Stars will take you on," Evie said. "They agreed to talk to you, that's all."

"I know." But agents did not meet people just to blow them off, Dave figured. And clearly the agency wanted to be nice to Evie Williams, the hottest young actress in London. So he had high hopes.

They went inside. The place was different from Eric Chapman's office. The receptionist was not chewing gum. There were no trophies on the lobby walls, just some tasteful watercolors. It was classy, though not very rock-and-roll.

They did not have to wait. The receptionist took them into the office of Mark Batchelor, a tall man in his twenties wearing a shirt with a fashionable tab collar and a knitted tie. His secretary brought coffee on a tray. "We love Evie, and we'd like to help her brother," Batchelor said when the initial pleasantries were out of the way. "But I'm not sure we can. 'Shake, Rattle and Roll' has damaged Plum Nellie."

Dave said: "I don't disagree, but tell me exactly what you mean."

"If I may be frank . . ."

"Of course," said Dave, thinking how different this was from a conversation with Eric Chapman. .

"You look like an average pop group who had the good luck to get your hands on a Hank Remington song. People think the song was great, not you. We live in a small world — a few record companies, a handful of tour promoters, two television shows — and everyone thinks the same. I can't sell you to any of them."

Dave swallowed. He had not expected Batchelor to be this candid. He tried not to show his disappointment. "We *were* lucky to get a Hank Remington song," he admitted. "But we're not an average pop group. We have a first-class rhythm section and a virtuoso lead guitarist, and we look good, too."

"Then you have to prove to people that you're not one-hit wonders."

"I know. But with no recording contract and no big gigs I'm not sure how we do that."

"You need another great song. Can you get another from Hank Remington?"

Dave shook his head. "Hank doesn't write songs for other people. 'Love Is It' was a one-off, a ballad that the Kords didn't want to record."

"Perhaps he could write another ballad." Batchelor spread his hands in a who-knows gesture. "I'm not creative, that's why I'm an agent, but I know enough to realize that Hank is a prodigy."

"Well . . ." Dave looked at Evie. "I suppose I could ask him."

Batchelor said breezily: "What harm could it do?"

Evie shrugged. "I don't mind," she said.

"All right, then," said Dave.

Batchelor stood up and put out his hand to shake. "Good luck," he said.

As they left the building, Dave said to Evie: "Can we go and see Hank now?"

"I've got some shopping to do," Evie said. "I told him I'd see him tonight."

"This is really important, Evie. My whole life is in ruins."

"All right," she said. "My car's around the corner."

They drove to Chelsea in Evie's Sunbeam Alpine. Dave chewed his lip. Batchelor had done him the favor of being brutally honest. But Batchelor did not believe in Plum Nellie's talent—just Hank Remington's. All the same, if Dave could get just one more good song from Hank, the group would be back on course.

What was he going to say?

Hi, Hank, got any more ballads? That was too casual.

Hank, I'm in a fix. Too needy.

Our record company made a real mistake releasing 'Shake, Rattle and Roll.' But we could rescue the situation—with a little help from you. Dave did not like any of these approaches, mainly because he hated to beg.

But he would do it.

Hank had an apartment by the river. Evie led the way into a big old house and up in a creaking elevator. She spent most nights here now. She opened the apartment door with her own key. "Hank!" she called out. "It's only me."

Dave walked in behind her. There was a hallway with a splashy modern painting. They passed a gleaming kitchen and looked into a living room with a grand piano. No one was there.

"He's out," Dave said despondently.

Evie said: "He might be taking an afternoon nap."

Another door opened, and Hank emerged from what was obviously the bedroom, pulling his jeans on. He closed the door behind him. "Hello, love," he said. "I was in bed. Hello, Dave, what are you doing here?"

"Evie brought me to ask you a really big favor," said Dave.

"Yeah," said Hank, looking at Evie. "I was expecting you later."

"Dave couldn't wait."

Dave said: "We need a new song."

"It's not a good time, Dave," said Hank. Dave expected him to explain, but he did not.

Evie said: "Hank, is something wrong?"

"Yeah, actually," said Hank.

Dave was startled. No one ever answered yes to that question.

Evie's feminine intuition was far ahead of Dave. "Is there someone in the bedroom?"

"I'm sorry, love," said Hank. "I wasn't expecting you back."

At that point the bedroom door opened and Anna Murray came out.

Dave's mouth fell open in shock. Jasper's sister had been in bed with Evie's boyfriend!

Anna was fully dressed in business clothes, including stockings and high heels, but her hair was mussed and her jacket buttons were misaligned. She did not speak and avoided meeting anyone's eye. She went into the living room and came back out carrying a briefcase. She went to the apartment door, lifted a coat off the hook, and went out without speaking a word.

Hank said: "She came round to talk about my autobiography, and one thing led to another . . ."

Evie was crying. "Hank, how could you?"

"I didn't plan it," he said. "It just happened."

"I thought you loved me."

"I did. I do. This was just . . ."

"Just what?"

Hank looked to Dave for support. "There are some temptations a man can't resist."

Dave thought of Mickie McFee, and nodded.

Evie said angrily: "Dave's a boy. I thought you were a man, Hank."

"Now," he said, suddenly looking aggressive, "watch your mouth."

Evie was incredulous. "Watch my mouth? I've just caught you in bed with another girl, and you're telling me to watch my mouth?"

"I mean it," he said threateningly. "Don't go too far."

Dave was suddenly scared. Hank looked as if he might

punch Evie. Was that what working-class Irish people did? And what was Dave supposed to do—protect his sister from her lover? Would Dave be expected to fight the greatest musical genius since Elvis Presley?

"Too far?" Evie said angrily. "I'm going too far now—right out of the fucking door. How's that?" She turned and marched away.

Dave looked at Hank. "Erm . . . about that song . . ."

Hank shook his head silently.

"Okay," said Dave. "Right." He could not think of a way to continue the conversation.

Hank held the door for him and he went out.

Evie cried in the car for five minutes, then dried her eyes. "I'll drive you home," she said.

When they got back to the West End, Dave said: "Come up to the flat. I'll make you a cup of coffee."

"Thanks," she said.

Walli was on the couch, playing the guitar. "Evie's a bit upset," Dave told him. "She broke up with Hank." He went into the kitchen and put the kettle on.

Walli said: "In English, the phrase 'a bit upset' means very unhappy. If you were only a little unhappy, say because I forgot your birthday, you would say you were 'terribly upset,' wouldn't you?"

Evie smiled. "Bless you, Walli, you're so logical."

"Creative, too," said Walli. "I'll cheer you up. Listen to this." He started to play, then he sang: "I miss ya, Alicia."

Dave came in from the kitchen to listen. Walli sang a sad ballad in D minor, with a couple of chords Dave did not recognize.

When it ended, Dave said: "It's a beautiful song. Did you hear it on the radio? Who's it by?"

"It's by me," Walli said. "I made it up."

"Wow," said Dave. "Play it again."

This time, Dave improvised a harmony.

Evie said: "You two are great. You didn't need that bastard Hank."

Dave said: "I want to sing this song to Mark Batchelor." He looked at his watch. It was half past five. He picked up the phone and called International Stars. Batchelor was still at his desk. "We have a song," Dave said. "Can we come to your office and play it to you?"

"I'd love to hear it, but I was just leaving for the day."

"Can you drop in at Henrietta Street on your way home?"

There was a hesitation, then Batchelor said: "Yes, I could, it's near my train station."

"What's your drink?"

"Gin and tonic, please."

Twenty minutes later Batchelor was on the sofa with a glass in his hand, and Dave and Walli were playing the song on two guitars and singing in harmony, with Evie joining in on the chorus.

When the song ended he said: "Play it again."

After the second time they looked at him expectantly. There was a pause. Then he said: "I wouldn't be in this business if I didn't know a hit when I heard it. This is a hit."

Dave and Walli grinned. Dave said: "That's what I thought."

"I love it," Batchelor said. "With this, I can get you a recording contract."

Dave put down his guitar, stood up, and shook hands with Batchelor to seal the deal. "We're in business," he said.

Mark took a long sip of his drink. "Did Hank just write the song on the spot, or did he have it in a drawer somewhere?"

Dave grinned. Now that they had shaken hands, he could level with Batchelor. "It's not a Hank Remington song," he said.

Batchelor raised his eyebrows.

Dave said: "You assumed it was, and I apologize for not correcting you, but I wanted you to have an open mind."

"It's a good song, and that's all that matters. But where did you get it?"

"Walli wrote it," said Dave. "This afternoon, while I was in your office."

"Great," said Batchelor. He turned to Walli. "What have you got for the B side?"

· · · ·

"You ought to go out," Lili Franck said to Karolin.

This was not Lili's own idea. In fact it was her mother's. Carla was worried about Karolin's health. Since Hans Hoffmann's visit, Karolin had lost weight. She looked pale and listless. Carla had said: "Karolin is only twenty years old.

She can't shut herself up like a nun for the rest of her life. Can't you take her out somewhere?"

They were in Karolin's room, now, playing their guitars and singing to Alice, who was sitting on the floor surrounded by toys. Occasionally she clapped her hands enthusiastically, but mostly she ignored them. The song she liked best was "Love Is It."

Karolin said: "I can't go out, I've got Alice to look after."

Lili was prepared to deal with objections. "My mother can watch her," she said. "Or even Grandmother Maud. Alice's not much trouble in the evenings." Alice was now fourteen months and sleeping all night.

"I don't know. It wouldn't feel right."

"You haven't had a night out for years—literally."

"But what would Walli think?"

"He doesn't expect you to hide away and never enjoy yourself, does he?"

"I don't know."

"I'm going to the St. Gertrud Youth Club tonight. Why don't you come with me? There's music and dancing and usually a discussion—I don't think Walli would mind."

The East German leader, Walter Ulbricht, knew that young people needed entertainment, but he had a problem. Everything they liked—pop music, fashion, comics, Hollywood movies—was either unavailable or banned. Sports were approved of, but usually involved separating the boys from the girls.

Lili knew that most people of her age hated the government. Teenagers did not care much about Communism or capitalism, but they were passionate about haircuts, fashion, and pop music. Ulbricht's puritan dislike of everything they held dear had alienated Lili's generation. Worse, they had developed a fantasy, probably wholly unrealistic, about the lives of their contemporaries in the West, whom they imagined to have record players in their bedrooms and cupboards full of hip new clothes and ice cream every day.

Church youth clubs were permitted as a feeble attempt to fill the gap in the lives of adolescents. Such clubs were safely uncontroversial, but not as suffocatingly righteous as the Communist Party youth organization, the Young Pioneers.

Karolin looked thoughtful. "Perhaps you're right," she said. "I can't spend my life being a victim. I've had bad luck, but I mustn't let that define me. The Stasi think I'm just the girl whose boyfriend killed a border guard, but I don't have to accept what they say."

"Exactly!" Lili was pleased.

"I'm going to write to Walli and tell him all about it. But I'll go with you."

"Then let's get changed."

Lili went to her own room and put on a short skirt—not quite a miniskirt, as worn by girls on the Western television shows watched by everyone in East Germany, but above the knee. Now that Karolin had agreed, Lili asked herself whether this was the right course. Karolin certainly needed a life of her own: she had been dead right in what she said about not letting the Stasi define her. But what would Walli think, when he found out? Would he worry that Karolin was forgetting him? Lili had not seen her brother for almost two years. He was nineteen now, and a pop star. She did not know what he might think.

Karolin borrowed Lili's blue jeans, then they made up their faces together. Lili's older sister, Rebecca, had sent them black eyeliner and blue eye shadow from Hamburg, and by a miracle the Stasi had not stolen it.

They went to the kitchen to take their leave. Carla was feeding Alice, who waved good-bye to her mother so cheerfully that Karolin was a little put out.

They walked to a Protestant church a few streets away. Only Grandmother Maud was a regular churchgoer, but Lili had been twice previously to the youth club held in the crypt. It was run by a new young pastor called Odo Vossler, who wore his hair like the Beatles. He was dishy, though he was too old for Lili, at least twenty-five.

For music Odo had a piano, two guitars, and a record player. They started with a folk dance, something the government could not possibly disapprove of. Lili was paired with Berthold, a boy of about her own age, sixteen. He was nice but not sexy. Lili had her eye on Thorsten, who was a bit older and looked like Paul McCartney.

The dance steps were energetic, with much clapping and twirling. Lili was pleased to see Karolin entering into the spirit of the dance, smiling and laughing. She already looked better.

But the folk dancing was only a token, something to talk about in response to hostile inquiries. Someone put on "I Feel Fine" by the Beatles, and they all started to do the Twist.

After an hour they paused for a rest and a glass of Vita Cola, the East German Coke. To Lili's great satisfaction, Karolin looked flushed and happy. Odo went around talking to each person. His message was that if anyone had any problems, including issues about personal relationships and sex, he was there to listen and give advice. Karolin said to him: "My problem is that the father of my child is in the West," and they got into a deep discussion until the dancing started again.

At ten, when the record player was switched off, Karolin surprised Lili by picking up one of the guitars. She gestured to Lili to take the other. The two had been playing and singing together at home, but Lili had never imagined doing it in public. Now Karolin started an Everly Brothers number, "Wake Up, Little Susie." The two guitars sounded good together, and Karolin and Lili sang in harmony. Before they got to the end, everyone in the crypt was jiving. At the end of the song, the dancers called for more.

They played "I Want to Hold Your Hand" and "If I Had a Hammer," then for a slow dance they did "Love Is It." The kids did not want them to stop, but Odo asked them to play one more number, then go home before the police came and arrested him. He said it with a smile, but he meant it.

For a finale they played "Back in the USA."

CHAPTER THIRTY-SEVEN

Early in 1965, as Jasper Murray prepared for his final university exams, he wrote to every broadcasting organization in the USA whose address he could find.

They all got the same letter. He sent them his article about Evie dating Hank, his piece on Martin Luther King, and the assassination special edition of *The Real Thing*. And he asked for a job. Any job, as long as it was in American television.

He had never wanted anything this much. Television news was better than print—faster, more engaging, more vivid—and American television was better than British. And he knew he would be good at it. All he needed was a start. He wanted it so much it hurt.

When he had mailed the letters—at considerable expense—he let his sister, Anna, buy him lunch. They went to the Gay Hussar, a Hungarian restaurant favored by left-wing writers and politicians. "What will you do if you don't get a job in the States?" Anna asked him after they had ordered.

The prospect depressed him. "I really don't know. In this country, you're expected to work for provincial newspapers first, covering cat shows and the funerals of long-serving aldermen, but I don't think I can face that."

Anna got the restaurant's signature cold cherry soup. Jasper had fried mushrooms with tartar sauce. Anna said: "Listen, I owe you an apology."

"Yes," said Jasper. "You damn well do."

"Look, Hank and Evie weren't even engaged, let alone married."

"But you knew perfectly well that they were a couple."

"Yes, and I was wrong to go to bed with him."

"You were."

"There's no need for you to be so bloody sanctimonious. It's uncharacteristic for me, but it's just the kind of thing you'd do."

He did not argue with that because it was true. He had on occasion gone to bed with women who were married or engaged. Instead he said: "Does Mother know?"

"Yes, and she's furious. Daisy Williams has been her best friend for thirty years, and has also been extraordinarily kind to you, letting you live there rent-free—and now I've done this to her daughter. What did Daisy say to you?"

"She's angry, because you caused her daughter such pain. But she also said that when she fell in love with Lloyd she was already married to someone else, so she does not feel entitled to too much moral indignation."

"Well, anyway, I'm sorry."

"Thank you."

"Except that I'm not really sorry."

"What do you mean?"

"I went to bed with Hank because I fell in love with him. Since that first time, I've spent almost every night with him. He's the most wonderful man I've ever met, and I'm going to marry him, if ever I can nail his foot to the floor."

"As your brother, I'm entitled to ask what on earth he sees in you."

"Other than big tits, you mean?" She laughed.

"Not that you aren't good-looking, but you are a few years older than Hank, and there are about a million nubile maidens in England who would jump into his bed at a snap of his fingers."

She nodded. "Two things. First, he's clever but undereducated. I'm his tour guide to the world of the mind: art, theater, politics, literature. He's enchanted by someone who talks to him about that stuff without condescending."

Jasper was not surprised. "He used to love to talk to Daisy and Lloyd about all that. But what's the other thing?"

"You know he's my second lover."

Jasper nodded. Girls were not supposed to admit this

sort of thing, but he and Anna had always known about each other's exploits.

She went on: "Well, I was with Sebastian almost four years. In that length of time, a girl learns a lot. Hank knows very little about sex, because he's never kept a girlfriend long enough to develop real intimacy. Evie was his longest relationship, and she was too young to teach a man much."

"I see." Jasper had never thought this way about relationships, but it made sense. He was a bit like Hank. He wondered whether women thought him unsophisticated in bed.

"Hank learned a lot from a singer called Mickie McFee, but he only slept with her twice."

"Really? Dave Williams shagged her in a dressing room."

"And Dave told you?"

"I think he told everyone. It may have been his first shag."

"Mickie McFee gets around."

"So, you're Hank's love tutor."

"He learns fast. And he's growing up quickly. What he did to Evie, he will never do again."

Jasper was not sure he believed that, but he did not voice his misgivings.

. . .

Dimka Dvorkin flew to Vietnam in February 1965 along with a large group of Foreign Ministry officials and aides, including Natalya Smotrov.

It was Dimka's first trip outside the Soviet Union. But he was even more excited about being with Natalya. He was not sure what was going to happen, but he had an exhilarating sense of liberation, and he could tell she felt the same. They were far away from Moscow, out of range of his wife and Natalya's husband. Anything could happen.

Dimka was feeling more optimistic in general. Kosygin, his boss since the fall of Khrushchev, understood that the Soviet Union was losing the Cold War because of its economy. Soviet industry was inefficient, and Soviet citizens were poor. Kosygin's aim was to make the USSR more productive. The Soviets had to learn how to manufacture things that people of other countries might want to buy. They had to compete with the Americans in prosperity, not just in tanks and missiles. Only then would they have a hope of converting the world to their way of life. This attitude heartened Dimka. Brezhnev, the leader, was woefully conservative, but perhaps Kosygin could reform Communism.

Part of the economic problem was that so much of the national income was spent on the military. In the hope of reducing this crippling expense, Khrushchev had come up with the policy of peaceful coexistence, living side by side with the capitalists without fighting wars. Khrushchev had not done much to implement the idea: his quarrels in Berlin and Cuba had required more military expenditure, not less. But progressive thinkers in the Kremlin still believed in the strategy.

Vietnam would be a severe test.

On stepping out of the plane, Dimka was assailed by a warm, wet atmosphere unlike anything he had experienced. Hanoi was the ancient capital of an ancient country, long oppressed by foreigners, first the Chinese, then the French, then the Americans. Vietnam was more crowded and more colorful than any place Dimka had ever seen.

It was also split in two.

Vietnamese leader Ho Chi Minh had defeated France in the anticolonial war of the fifties. But Ho was an undemocratic Communist, and the Americans refused to accept his authority. President Eisenhower had sponsored a puppet government in the south, based in the provincial capital of Saigon. The unelected Saigon regime was tyrannical and unpopular, and was under attack by resistance fighters called the Vietcong. The South Vietnamese army was so weak that now, in 1965, it had to be propped up by twenty-three thousand American troops.

The Americans were pretending that South Vietnam was a separate country, just as the Soviet Union pretended that East Germany was a country. Vietnam was a mirror image of Germany, though Dimka would never dare say that aloud.

While the ministers attended a banquet with North Vietnamese leaders, the Soviet aides ate a less formal dinner with their Vietnamese opposite numbers—all of whom spoke Russian, some having visited Moscow. The food was mostly vegetables and rice, with small amounts of fish and meat, but it was tasty. There were no female Vietnamese staffers, and the men seemed surprised to see Natalya and the two other Soviet women.

Dimka sat next to a dour middle-aged apparatchik called Pham An. Natalya, sitting opposite, asked the man what he hoped to get from the talks.

An replied with a shopping list. "We need aircraft, artillery, radar, air defense systems, small arms, ammunition, and medical supplies," he said.

This was exactly what the Soviets were hoping to avoid. Natalya said: "But you won't need those things if the war comes to an end."

"When we have defeated the American imperialists our needs will be different."

"We would all like to see a smashing victory for the Vietcong," said Natalya. "But there might be other possible outcomes." She was trying to broach the idea of peaceful coexistence.

"Victory is the only possibility," said Pham An dismissively.

Dimka was dismayed. An was stubbornly refusing to engage in the discussion for which the Soviets had come here. Perhaps he felt it was beneath his dignity to argue with a woman. Dimka hoped that was the only reason for his obstinacy. If the Vietnamese would not talk about alternatives to war, the Soviet mission would fail.

Natalya was not easily deflected from her purpose. She now said: "Military victory most certainly is *not* the only possible outcome." Dimka found himself feeling proud of her gutsy persistence.

"You speak of defeat?" said An, bristling—or at least pretending to bristle.

"No," she said calmly. "But war is not the only road to victory. Negotiations are an alternative."

"We negotiated with the French many times," An said angrily. "Every agreement was designed only to gain time while they prepared further aggression. This was a lesson to our people, a lesson on dealing with imperialists, a lesson we will never forget."

Dimka had read the history of Vietnam and knew that An's anger was justified. The French had been as dishonest and perfidious as any other colonialists. But that was not the end of the story.

Natalya persisted—quite rightly, since this was the message Kosygin was undoubtedly giving Ho Chi Minh. "Imperialists are treacherous, we all know that. But negotiations can also be used by revolutionaries. Lenin negotiated at Brest-Litovsk. He made concessions, stayed in power, and reversed all those concessions when he was stronger."

An parroted Ho Chi Minh's line. "We will not consider negotiations until there is a neutral coalition government in Saigon that includes Vietcong representatives."

"Be reasonable," Natalya said mildly. "To make major demands as preconditions is just a way of avoiding negotiations. You must consider compromise."

An said angrily: "When the Germans invaded Russia and marched all the way to the gates of Moscow, did you compromise?" He banged the table with his fist, a gesture that surprised Dimka coming from a supposedly subtle Oriental. "No! No negotiations, no compromise—and no Americans!"

Soon after that the banquet ended.

Dimka and Natalya returned to their hotel. He walked with her to her room. At the door, she said simply: "Come in."

It would be only their third night together. The first two they had spent on a four-poster bed in a dusty storeroom full of old furniture at the Kremlin. But somehow being together in a bedroom seemed as natural as if they had been lovers for years.

They kissed and took off their shoes, and kissed again and brushed their teeth, and kissed again. They were not crazed with uncontrollable lust: rather, they were relaxed and playful. "We've got all night to do anything we like," Natalya said, and Dimka thought those were the sexiest words he had ever heard.

They made love, then had some caviar and vodka she had brought with her, then made love again.

Afterward, lying on the twisted sheets, looking up at the slow-moving ceiling fan, Natalya said: "I assume someone is eavesdropping on us."

"I hope so," Dimka said. "We sent a KGB team over here at great expense to teach them how to bug hotel rooms."

"Perhaps it's Pham An listening," Natalya said, and giggled.

"If so, I hope he enjoyed it more than the dinner."

"Hmm. That was kind of a disaster."

"They'll have to change their attitude to get weapons from us. Even Brezhnev doesn't want us involved in a massive war in Southeast Asia."

"But if we refuse to arm them, they could go to the Chinese."

"They hate the Chinese."

"I know. Still . . ."

"Yes."

They drifted off to sleep and were awakened by the phone. Natalya picked it up and gave her name. She listened for a while, then said: "Hell." Another minute went by and she hung up. "News from South Vietnam," she said. "The Vietcong attacked an American base last night."

"Last night? Only hours after Kosygin arrived in Hanoi? That's no coincidence. Where?"

"A place called Pleiku. Eight Americans were killed and a hundred or so wounded. And they destroyed ten U.S. aircraft on the ground."

"How many Vietcong casualties?"

"Only one body was left behind in the compound."

Dimka shook his head in amazement. "You've got to give it to the Vietnamese, they're terrific fighters."

"The Vietcong are. The South Vietnamese army is hopeless. That's why they need the Americans to fight for them."

Dimka frowned. "Isn't there some American big shot in South Vietnam right now?"

"McGeorge Bundy, national security adviser, one of the worst of the capitalist-imperialist warmongers."

"He'll be on the phone to President Johnson right now."

"Yes," said Natalya. "I wonder what he's saying."

She had her answer later the same day.

American planes from the aircraft carrier USS *Ranger* bombed an army camp called Dong Hoi on the coast of North Vietnam. It was the first time the Americans had bombed the north, and it began a new phase in the conflict.

Dimka watched in despair as Kosygin's position crumbled, bit by bit, during the course of the day.

After the bombing, American aggression was condemned by Communist and nonaligned countries around the world.

Third World leaders now expected Moscow to come to the aid of Vietnam, a Communist country being directly attacked by American imperialism.

Kosygin did not want to escalate the Vietnam War, and the Kremlin could not afford to give massive military aid to Ho Chi Minh, but that was exactly what they now did.

They had no choice. If they drew back the Chinese would step in, eager to supplant the USSR as the mighty friend of small Communist countries. The position of the Soviet Union as defender of world Communism was now at stake, and everyone knew it.

All talk of peaceful coexistence was forgotten.

Dimka and Natalya were thrown into gloom, as was the entire Soviet delegation. Their negotiating position with the Vietnamese was fatally undermined. Kosygin had no cards to play: he had to grant everything Ho Chi Minh asked for.

They remained in Hanoi three more days. Dimka and Natalya made love all night, but during the daytime all they did was make detailed notes of Pham An's shopping list. Even before they left, a consignment of Soviet surface-to-air missiles was on its way.

Dimka and Natalya sat together on the plane home. Dimka dozed, delightfully recalling four humid nights of love under a lazy ceiling fan.

"What are you smiling about?" Natalya said.

He opened his eyes. "You know."

She giggled. "Apart from that . . ."

"What?"

"When you review this trip in your mind, don't you get a feeling . . . ?"

"That we were totally managed and exploited? Yes, from the first day."

"In fact, that Ho Chi Minh deftly manipulated the two most powerful countries in the world, and ended up getting everything he wanted."

"Yes," said Dimka. "That's exactly the feeling I get."

.   .   .

Tanya went to the airport with Vasili's subversive typescript in her suitcase. She was scared.

She had done dangerous things before. She had published a seditious newspaper; she had been arrested in Mayakovsky Square and dragged off to the notorious basement of the KGB's Lubyanka building; and she had made contact with a dissident in Siberia. But this was the most frightening.

Communicating with the West was a crime of a higher order. She was taking Vasili's typescript to Leipzig, where she hoped to place it with a Western publisher.

The news sheet that she and Vasili had published had been distributed only in the USSR. The authorities would be much angrier about dissident material that found its way to the West. Those responsible would be considered not just rebels but traitors.

Thinking about the danger, sitting in the back of the taxi, she felt nauseated by fear, and clamped her hand over her mouth in a panic until the sensation faded.

On arrival she almost told the driver to turn around and take her home. Then she remembered Vasili in Siberia, hungry and cold, and she steeled her nerve and carried her case into the terminal.

The Siberia trip had changed her. Before, she had thought of Communism as a well-intentioned experiment that had failed and ought to be scrapped. Now, she saw it as a brutal tyranny whose leaders were evil. Every time she thought of Vasili, her heart was filled with hatred for the people who had done this to him. She even had trouble talking to her twin brother, who still hoped that Communism could be improved rather than abolished. She loved Dimka, but he was closing his eyes to reality. And she had realized that wherever there was cruel oppression—in the Deep South of the USA, in British Northern Ireland, and in East Germany—there had to be many nice ordinary people like her family who looked away from the grisly truth. But Tanya would not be one of them. She was going to fight it to the end.

Whatever the risk.

At the desk she handed over her papers and placed her case on the scale. If she had believed in God, she would have prayed.

Check-in staff were all KGB. This one was a man in his thirties with the blue shadow of a heavy beard. Tanya sometimes assessed people by imagining what they would be like to interview. This one would be assertive to the point of aggression, she thought, answering neutral questions as if they were hostile, constantly on the lookout for hidden implications and veiled accusations.

He looked hard at her face, comparing it with her photograph. She tried not to seem scared. However, she told herself, even innocent Soviet citizens were scared when KGB men looked at them.

He put her passport down on his desk and said: "Open the bag."

There was no knowing why. They might do it because you appeared suspicious or because they had nothing better to do or because they liked pawing through women's underwear. They did not have to give a reason.

Heart pounding, Tanya opened her case.

The clerk knelt down and began to rifle through her things. It took him less than a minute to discover Vasili's typescript. He took it out and read the title page: *Stalag: A Novel of the Nazi Concentration Camps* by Klaus Holstein.

This was fake, as was the contents list, the preface, and the prologue.

The clerk said: "What is this?"

"A partial translation of an East German work. I'm going to the Leipzig Book Fair."

"Has this been approved?"

"In East Germany, of course, otherwise it would not have been published."

"And in the Soviet Union?"

"Not yet. Works may not be submitted for approval before they are finished, obviously."

She tried to breathe normally as the clerk flicked through the pages.

"These people have Russian names," he said.

"There were many Russians in the Nazi camps, as you know," Tanya said.

If her story were to be checked it would fall flat in no time, she knew. If the clerk took the time to read more than the first few pages he would see that the stories were not about the Nazis but about the Gulag; and then it would take the KGB only a few hours to learn that there was no East German book nor a publisher, at which point Tanya would be taken back to that cellar in the Lubyanka.

He riffled the pages idly, as if wondering whether to make a fuss about this or not. Then there was a commotion at the next desk: a passenger was objecting to the confiscation of an icon. Tanya's clerk returned her papers with her boarding card and waved her away, then went to assist his colleague.

Her legs felt so weak she feared she might not be able to walk away.

She recovered her strength and made it through the rest of the formalities. The plane was the familiar Tupolev Tu-104, this one configured for civilian passengers, a bit cramped with six seats abreast. The flight to Leipzig was a thousand miles, and took a little over three hours.

When Tanya picked up her suitcase at the other end she looked carefully at it but saw no signs that it had been opened. But she was not yet in the clear. She carried it into the customs and immigration zone, feeling as if she were holding something radioactive. She recalled that the East German government was said to be harsher than the Soviet regime. The Stasi was even more omnipresent than the KGB.

She showed her papers. An official studied them carefully, then dismissed her with a discourteous gesture.

She headed for the exit, not looking at the faces of the uniformed officials, all men, who stood scrutinizing passengers.

Then one of them stepped in front of her. "Tanya Dvorkin?"

She almost burst into guilty tears. "Y-yes."

He addressed her in German. "Please come with me."

This is it, she thought; my life is over.

She followed him through a side door. To her surprise, it led to a parking area. "The director of the book fair has sent a car for you," the official said.

A driver was waiting. He introduced himself and put the incriminating suitcase into the trunk of a two-tone green-and-white Wartburg 311 limousine.

Tanya fell into the backseat and slumped, as helpless as if she were drunk.

She began to recover as the car took her into the city center. Leipzig was an ancient crossroads that had hosted trade fairs since the Middle Ages. Its railway station was the biggest in Europe. In her article Tanya would mention the city's strong Communist tradition, and its resistance to Nazism, which continued into the 1940s. She would not include the thought that occurred to her now, that Leipzig's grand nineteenth-century buildings looked even more gracious beside the brutalist Soviet-era architecture.

The taxi took her to the fair. In a large hall like a warehouse, publishers from Germany and abroad had erected stalls where they displayed their books. Tanya was shown around by the director. He explained to her that the main business of the fair was the buying and selling, not of physical books, but of licenses to translate them and publish them in other countries.

Toward the end of the afternoon she managed to get away from him and look around on her own.

She was astonished by the enormous number and bewildering variety of books: car manuals, scientific journals, almanacs, children's stories, Bibles, art books, atlases, dictionaries, school textbooks, and the complete works of Marx and Lenin in every major European language.

She was looking for someone who might want to translate Russian literature and publish it in the West.

She began to scan the stalls for Russian novels in other languages.

The Western alphabet was different from the Russian, but Tanya had learned German and English at school, and had studied German at university, so she could read the names of the authors and generally guess at the titles.

She spoke to several publishers, telling them she was a journalist for TASS and asking them how they were benefiting from the fair. She got some quotes useful for her article. She did not even hint that she had a Russian book to offer them.

At the stall of a London publisher called Rowley she picked up an English translation of *The Young Guard,* a popular Soviet novel by Alexander Fadeyev. She knew it well, and amused herself by deciphering the English of the first page until she was interrupted. An attractive woman of about her own age addressed her in German. "Please let me know if I can answer any questions."

Tanya introduced herself and interviewed the woman about the fair. They quickly discovered that the editor spoke Russian better than Tanya spoke German, so they switched.

Tanya asked about English translations of Russian novels. "I'd like to publish more of them," said the editor. "But many contemporary Soviet novels—including the one you're holding in your hand—are too slavishly pro-Communist."

Tanya pretended to be prickly. "You wish to publish anti-Soviet propaganda?"

"Not at all," the editor said with a tolerant smile. "Writers are permitted to like their governments. My company publishes many books that celebrate the British Empire and its triumphs. But an author who sees nothing at all wrong in the society around him may not be taken seriously. It's wiser to throw in a soupçon of criticism, if only for the sake of credibility."

Tanya liked this woman. "Can we meet again?"

The editor hesitated. "Do you have something for me?"

Tanya did not answer the question. "Where are you staying?"

"The Europa."

Tanya had a room reserved at the same hotel. That was convenient. "What's your name?"

"Anna Murray. What's yours?"

"We'll talk again," said Tanya, and she walked away.

She felt drawn to Anna Murray on instinct, an instinct refined by a quarter of a century of life in the Soviet Union; but her feeling was supported by evidence. First, Anna was clearly British, not a Russian or East German posing as British. Second, she was neither Communist nor strenuously pretending to be the opposite. Her relaxed neutrality was impossible for a KGB spy to fake. Third, she used no jargon. People brought up in Soviet orthodoxy could not help talking about party, class, cadres, and ideology. Anna used none of the key words.

The green-and-white Wartburg was waiting outside. The driver took her to the Europa, where she checked in. Almost immediately she left her room and returned to the lobby.

She did not want to draw attention to herself even by merely asking at reception for Anna Murray's room number. At least one of the desk clerks would be an informant for the Stasi, and might make a note of a Soviet journalist seeking out an English publisher.

However, behind the reception desk was a bank of numbered pigeonholes where the staff deposited room keys and messages. Tanya simply sealed an empty envelope, wrote on it "Frau Anna Murray," and handed it in without speaking. The clerk immediately put it in the pigeonhole for Room 305.

There was a key in the space, which meant that Anna Murray was not in her room right now.

Tanya went into the bar. Anna was not there. Tanya sat for an hour, sipping a beer, roughing out her article on a notepad. Then she went into the restaurant. Anna was not there either. She had probably gone out to dinner with colleagues at a restaurant in the city. Tanya sat alone and ordered the local speciality, *allerlei,* a vegetable dish. She sat over her coffee for an hour, then left.

Passing through the lobby, she looked again at the pigeonholes. The key for 305 had gone.

Tanya returned to her own room, picked up the typescript, and walked to the door of Room 305.

There she hesitated. Once she had done this, she was committed. No cover story would explain or excuse her action. She was distributing anti-Soviet propaganda to the West. If she were caught, her life would be over.

She knocked on the door.

Anna opened it. She was barefoot and there was a toothbrush in her hand: clearly she had been getting ready for bed.

Tanya put her finger on her lips, indicating silence. Then she handed Anna the typescript. She whispered: "I'll come back in two hours." Then she walked away.

She returned to her own room and sat on the bed, shaking.

If Anna simply rejected the work, that would be bad enough. But if Tanya had misjudged her, Anna might feel obliged to tell someone in authority that she had been offered a dissident book. She might fear that, if she kept quiet about it, she could be accused of taking part in a conspiracy. She might think that the only sensible thing to do was to report the illicit approach that had been made to her.

But Tanya believed most Westerners did not think that way. Despite Tanya's dramatic precautions, Anna would have no real sense that she was guilty of a crime just by reading a typescript.

So the main question was whether Anna would like Vasili's work. Daniil had, and so had the editors of *New World*. But they were the only people who had read the stories, and they were all Russian. How would a foreigner react? Tanya felt confident that Anna would see that the material was well written, but would it move her? Would it break her heart?

At a few minutes past eleven, Tanya returned to Room 305.

Anna opened the door with the typescript in her hand.

Her face was wet with tears.

She spoke in a whisper. "It's unbearable," she said. "We have to tell the world."

.   .   .

One Friday night Dave found out that Lew, the drummer in Plum Nellie, was homosexual.

Until then he had thought that Lew was just shy. A lot of girls wanted to have sex with boys who played in pop groups, and the dressing room was sometimes like a brothel, but Lew never took advantage. This was not astonishing: some did, some did not. Walli never went with "groupies." Dave occasionally did, and Buzz, the bass player, never said no.

Plum Nellie was getting gigs again. "I Miss Ya, Alicia" was in the top twenty at number nineteen, and rising. Dave and Walli were writing songs together, and hoping to make a long-playing record. Late one afternoon they went to the BBC studios in Portland Place and prerecorded a radio performance. The money was peanuts but it was an opportunity to promote "I Miss Ya, Alicia." Maybe the song would go to number one. And, as Dave sometimes said, you could live on peanuts.

They came out blinking into the evening sunshine and decided to go for a drink at a nearby pub called the Golden Horn.

"I don't fancy a drink," said Lew.

"Don't be daft," Buzz said. "When have you ever said no to a pint of beer?"

"Let's go to a different pub, then," said Lew.

"Why?"

"I don't like the look of that one."

"If you're afraid of being pestered, put your sunglasses on."

They had been on television several times, and they were sometimes recognized by fans in restaurants and bars, but there was rarely any trouble. They had learned to stay away from places where young teenagers might gather, such as coffee bars near schools, for that could lead to a mob scene; but they were all right in grown-up pubs.

They went into the Golden Horn and approached the bar. The bartender smiled at Lew and said: "Hello, Lucy, dear, what'll it be, vod and ton?"

The group looked at Lew in surprise.

Buzz said: "So you're a regular here?"

Walli said: "What's a vod and ton?"

Dave said: "Lucy?"

The barman looked nervous. "Who are your friends, Lucy?"

Lew looked at the other three and said: "You bastards, you've found me out."

Buzz said: "Are you queer?"

Having been found out, Lew threw caution to the winds. "I'm as queer as a clockwork orange, a three-pound note, a purple unicorn, or a football bat. If you weren't all blind as well as stupid you would have figured it out years ago. Yes, I kiss men and go to bed with them whenever I can without getting caught. But please don't worry that I might make advances to you: you're all much too fucking ugly. Now let's have a drink."

Dave cheered and clapped, and after a moment of shocked hesitation Buzz and Walli followed his lead.

Dave was intrigued. He knew about queers, but only in a theoretical way. He had never had a homosexual friend, as far as he knew—though most of them kept it secret, as Lew had, because what they did was a crime. Dave's grandmother Lady Leckwith was campaigning for the law to be changed, but so far she had not succeeded.

Dave was in favor of his grandmother's campaign, mainly because he hated the kind of people who opposed her: pompous clergymen, indignant Tories, and retired colonels. He had never really thought about the law as something that might affect his friends.

They had a second round of drinks, and a third. Dave's money was running low, but he had high hopes. "I Miss Ya,

Alicia" was going to be released in the USA. If it was a hit there the group would be made. And he would never again have to worry about spelling.

The pub filled up quickly. Most of the men had something in common: a way of walking and talking that was a bit theatrical. They called one another "lovey" and "precious." After a while it became easy to tell who was queer and who was not. Perhaps that was why they did it. There were also a few girls in couples, most with short haircuts and trousers. Dave felt he was seeing a new world.

However, they were not exclusive, and seemed happy to share their favorite pub with heterosexual men and women. About half the people there knew Lew, and the group found themselves at the center of a conversational cluster. The queers bantered in a distinctive way that made Dave laugh. A man in a shirt similar to Lew's said: "Ooh, Lucy, you're wearing the same shirt as me! How nice." Then he added in a stage whisper: "Unimaginative bitch," and the others laughed, including Lew.

Dave was approached by a tall man who said in a low voice: "Listen, mate, do you know who could sell me some pills?"

Dave knew what he was talking about. A lot of musicians took pep pills. Various kinds could be bought at places such as the Jump Club. Dave had tried some but did not really like the effect.

He looked hard at the stranger. Although he was dressed in jeans and a striped sweater, the jeans were cheap and did not go with the sweater, and the man had a short military-style haircut. Dave had an uneasy feeling. "No," he said curtly, and turned away.

In one corner stood a tiny stage with a microphone. At nine o'clock a comedian came on, to enthusiastic applause. It was a man dressed as a woman, although the hair and makeup were so good that in a different setting Dave might not have twigged.

"Could I have everybody's attention, please?" the comic said. "I'd just like to make an important public announcement. Jerry Robertson's got VD."

They all laughed. Walli said to Dave: "What's VD?"

"Venereal disease," Dave said. "Spots on your cock."

The comedian paused, then added: "I know, because I gave it to him."

This got another laugh, then there was a commotion at the door. Dave looked that way and saw several uniformed policemen coming in, pushing people out of the way.

The comic said: "Ooh, it's the law! I do like a uniform. The police come here a lot, have you noticed? I wonder what attracts them?"

He was making a joke of it, but the police were unpleasantly serious. They shoved their way through the crowd, seeming to enjoy being unnecessarily rough. Four went into the men's toilets. "Perhaps they've just come for a pee," said the comic. An officer got up on the stage. "You're an inspector, aren't you?" the comic said flirtatiously. "Have you come to inspect me?"

Two more cops dragged the comic away. "Don't worry!" he cried. "I'll come quietly!"

The inspector grabbed the microphone. "Right, you filthy pansies," he said. "I have information that illegal drugs are being sold on these premises. If you don't want to get hurt, stand face to the wall and get ready to be searched."

The police were still pouring in. Dave looked around for a way out, but all the doors were blocked by blue uniforms. Some of the customers moved to the edges of the room and stood facing the walls, looking resigned, as if all this had happened to them before. The police never raided the Jump Club, Dave reflected, even though drugs were sold there almost openly.

The cops who had gone into the toilet came out frog-marching two men, one of whom was bleeding from the nose. One of the cops said to the inspector: "They were in the same cubicle, governor."

"Charge them with public indecency."

"Right you are, guv."

Dave was struck painfully in the back, and cried out. A policeman wielding a nightstick said: "Get over by the wall."

Dave said: "What did you do that for?"

The cop stuck the club close to Dave's nose. "Shut your mouth, queer boy, or I'll shut it with my truncheon."

"I'm not a—" Dave stopped himself. Let them believe

what they like, he thought. I'd rather be with the queers than with the police. He stepped to the wall and stood as ordered, rubbing the painful spot in his back.

He found himself next to Lew, who said: "Are you all right?"

"Just a bit bruised. You?"

"Nothing much."

Dave was learning about why his grandmother wanted to change the law. He felt ashamed for having lived so long in ignorance.

Lew said in a low voice: "At least the cops haven't recognized the group."

Dave nodded. "They're not the type to be familiar with the faces of pop stars."

Out of the corner of his eye he saw the inspector talking to the badly dressed man who had asked about buying pills. Now he understood the cheap jeans and the military haircut: the man was an undercover detective, poorly disguised. He was shrugging his shoulders and spreading his arms in a helpless gesture, and Dave guessed he had failed to find anyone selling drugs.

The police searched everyone, making them turn out their pockets. The one who examined Dave felt his crotch a good deal longer than was necessary. Are these cops queer too? Dave wondered. Is that why they do this?

Several men objected to the intimate searching. They were beaten with truncheons, then arrested for assaulting the police. Another man had a packet of pills he said were prescribed by his doctor, but he was arrested all the same.

Eventually the police left. The barman announced drinks on the house, but few people took up the offer. The members of Plum Nellie left the pub. Dave decided to go home for an early night.

"Does that sort of thing happen a lot to you queers?" he asked Lew as they were saying good-bye.

"All the time, mate," said Lew. "All the fucking time."

.   .   .

Jasper went to visit his sister at Hank Remington's Chelsea flat one evening at seven o'clock, when he was sure Anna would be home from work but the couple would not yet have gone out. He felt nervous. He wanted something from Anna and Hank, something vital to his future.

He sat in the kitchen and watched Anna make Hank his favorite food, a fried-potato sandwich. "How's your work?" he asked her, making small talk.

"Wonderful," she said, and her eyes gleamed with enthusiasm. "I've discovered a new writer, a Russian dissident. I don't even know his real name, but he's a genius. I'm publishing his stories set in a Siberian prison camp. The title is *Frostbite.*"

"Doesn't sound like much of a laugh."

"It is funny in parts, but it will break your heart. I'm having it translated right now."

Jasper was skeptical. "Who wants to read about people in a prison camp?"

"The whole world," said Anna. "You wait and see. How about you—do you know what you'll do after graduation?"

"I've been offered a job as junior reporter on the *Western Mail,* but I don't want to take it. I've been editor and publisher of my own paper, for Christ's sake."

"Did you get any replies from America?"

"One," said Jasper.

"Only one? What did they say?"

Jasper took the letter out of his pocket and showed it to her. It was from a television news show called *This Day.*

Anna read it. "It just says they don't hire people without an interview. How disappointing."

"I plan to take them at their word."

"What do you mean?"

Jasper pointed to the address on the letterhead. "I'm going to show up at their office with this letter in my hand and say: 'I've come for my interview.'"

Anna laughed. "They'll have to admire your cheek."

"There's only one snag." Jasper swallowed. "I need ninety pounds for the airfare. And I've only got twenty."

She lifted a basket of potatoes out of the fryer and set them to drain. Then she looked at Jasper. "Is that why you've come here?"

He nodded. "Can you lend me seventy pounds?"

"Certainly not," she said. "I don't have seventy pounds. I'm a book editor. That's almost a month's salary."

Jasper had known that would be the answer. But it was not the end of the conversation. He gritted his teeth and said: "Can you get it from Hank?"

Anna layered the fried potatoes on a slice of buttered white bread. She sprinkled malt vinegar over them, then salted them heavily. She put a second slice of bread on top, then cut the sandwich in halves.

Hank walked in, tucking his shirt into a pair of orange corduroy hipster trousers. His long red hair was wet from the shower. "Hi, Jasper," he said with his usual cordiality. Then he kissed Anna and said: "Wow, baby, something smells good."

Anna said: "Hank, this could be the most expensive sandwich you will ever eat."

CHAPTER THIRTY-EIGHT

Dave Williams was looking forward to meeting his notorious grandfather, Lev Peshkov.

Plum Nellie was on the road in the States in the autumn of 1965. The All-Star Touring Beat Revue gave performers a hotel room every second night. Alternate nights were spent on the bus.

They would do a show, get on the bus at midnight, and drive to the next city. Dave never slept properly on the bus. The seats were uncomfortable and there was a smelly toilet at the back. The only refreshment was a cooler full of sugary soda pop supplied free by Dr Pepper, the sponsor of the tour. A soul group from Philadelphia called the Topspins ran a poker game on the bus: Dave lost ten dollars one night and never played again.

In the morning they would arrive at a hotel. If they were lucky, they could check in right away. If not, they had to hang around the lobby, bad-tempered and unwashed, waiting for last night's guests to vacate their rooms. They would do the next evening's show, spend the night at the hotel, and get back on the bus in the morning.

Plum Nellie loved it.

The money was not much, but they were touring America: they would have done it for nothing.

And there were the girls.

Buzz, the bass player, often had several fans in his hotel bedroom during the course of a single day and night. Lew was enthusiastically exploring the queer scene—though

Americans preferred the word gay to queer. Walli remained faithful to Karolin, but even he was happy, living his dream of being a pop star.

Dave did not much like sex with groupies, but there were several terrific girls on the tour. He made a play for blond Joleen Johnson from the Tamettes, who turned him down, explaining that she had been happily married since she was thirteen. Then he tried Little Lulu Small, who was flirty but would not go to his room. Finally one evening he got talking to Mandy Love from the Love Factory, a black girl group from Chicago. She had big brown eyes and a wide mouth and smooth midbrown skin that felt like silk under Dave's fingertips. She introduced him to marijuana, which he liked better than beer. They spent every hotel night together after Indianapolis, though they had to be discreet: interracial sex was a crime in some states.

The bus rolled into Washington, DC, on a Wednesday morning. Dave had an appointment for lunch with Grandfather Peshkov. This had been arranged by his mother, Daisy.

He dressed for the engagement like the pop star he was: a red shirt, blue hipster trousers, a gray tweed jacket with a red overcheck, and narrow-toed boots with a Cuban heel. He got a cab from the cheap hotel where the groups were staying to the swankier place where his grandfather had a suite.

Dave was intrigued. He had heard so many bad things about this old man. If the family legends were true, Lev had killed a policeman in St. Petersburg, then fled Russia, leaving a pregnant girlfriend behind. In Buffalo he made his boss's daughter pregnant, married her, and inherited a fortune. He had been suspected of murdering his father-in-law, but never charged. During Prohibition he had been a bootlegger. While married to Daisy's mother he had had numerous mistresses, including the movie star Gladys Angelus. It went on and on.

Waiting in the hotel lobby, Dave wondered what Lev looked like. They had never met. Apparently Lev had visited London once, for Daisy's wedding to her first husband, Boy Fitzherbert; but he had never returned.

Daisy and Lloyd came to the USA about every five years, mainly to see her mother, Olga, now in a retirement home in Buffalo. Dave knew that Daisy did not have much love for her father. Lev had been absent most of Daisy's childhood. He had had a second family in the same city—a mistress, Marga, and an illegitimate son, Greg—and apparently he had always preferred them to Daisy and her mother.

Across the lobby Dave saw a man in his early seventies dressed in a silver-gray suit with a red-and-white-striped tie. He recalled his mother saying that her father had always been a dandy. Dave smiled and said: "Are you Grandfather Peshkov?"

They shook hands, and Lev said: "Don't you have a tie?"

Dave got this sort of thing all the time. For some reason the older generation felt they had the right to be rude about young people's clothes. Dave had a number of stock replies, ranging from charming to hostile. Now he said: "When you were a teenager in St. Petersburg, Grandfather, what did cool kids like you wear?"

Lev's stern expression broke into a grin. "I had a jacket with mother-of-pearl buttons, a waistcoat and a brass watch chain, and a velvet cap. And my hair was long and parted in the middle, just like yours."

"So we're alike," Dave said. "Except that I've never killed anyone."

Lev was startled for a moment, then he laughed. "You're a smart kid," he said. "You've inherited my brains."

A woman in a chic blue coat and hat came to Lev's side, walking like a fashion model although she had to be near Lev's age. Lev said: "This is Marga. She ain't your grandma."

The mistress, Dave thought. "You're obviously too young to be anyone's grandmother," he said with a smile. "What should I call you?"

"You are a charmer!" she replied. "You can call me Marga. I used to be a singer, too, you know, though I never had your kind of success." She looked nostalgic. "In those days I ate handsome boys like you for breakfast."

Girl singers haven't changed, Dave thought, remembering Mickie McFee.

They went into the restaurant. Marga asked a lot of questions about Daisy, Lloyd, and Evie. They were excited to hear about Evie's acting career, especially as Lev owned a Hollywood studio. But Lev was most interested in Dave and his business. "They say you're a millionaire, Dave," he said.

"They lie," said Dave. "We're selling a lot of records, but there's not as much money in it as people imagine. We get about a penny a record. So if we sell a million copies, we earn enough maybe for each of us to buy a small car."

"Someone's robbing you," said Lev.

"I wouldn't be surprised," Dave said. "But I don't know what to do about it. I fired our first manager, and this one is much better, but I still can't afford to buy a house."

"I'm in the movie business, and sometimes we sell records of our soundtrack music, so I've seen how music people work. You want some advice?"

"Yes, please."

"Set up your own record company."

Dave was intrigued. He had been thinking along the same lines, but it seemed like a fantasy. "Do you think that's possible?"

"You can rent a recording studio, I guess, for a day or two, or however long it takes."

"We can record the music, and I suppose we can get a factory to make the discs, but I'm not so sure about selling them. I wouldn't want to spend time managing a team of sales representatives, even if I knew how."

"You don't need to do that. Get the big record company to do sales and distribution for you on a percentage basis. They'll get the peanuts and you'll get the profits."

"I wonder if they would agree to that."

"They won't like it, but they'll do it, because they can't afford to lose you."

"I guess."

Dave found himself drawn to this shrewd old man, despite his criminal reputation.

Lev had not finished. "What about publishing? You write the songs, don't you?"

"Walli and I do it together, usually." Walli was the one who actually put the songs down on paper, for Dave's handwriting and spelling were so bad that no one could ever read what he wrote; but the creative act was a collaboration. "We make a little extra from songwriting royalties."

"A little? You should make a lot. I bet your publisher employs a foreign agent who takes a cut."

"True."

"If you look into it, you'll find the foreign agent also employs a subagent who takes another cut, and so on. And all the people taking cuts are part of the same corporation. By the time they've taken twenty-five percent three or four times you got zip." Lev shook his head in disgust. "Set up your own publishing company. You'll never make money until you're in control."

Marga said: "How old are you, Dave?"

"Seventeen."

"So young. But at least you're smart enough to pay attention to business."

"I wish I was smarter."

After lunch they went into the lounge. "Your uncle Greg is going to join us for coffee," Lev said. "He's your mother's half brother."

Dave recalled that Daisy spoke fondly of Greg. He had done some foolish things in his youth, she said, but so had she. Greg was a Republican senator, but she even forgave him that.

Marga said: "My son, Greg, never married, but he has a son of his own, called George."

Lev said: "It's kind of an open secret. Nobody mentions it, but everyone in Washington knows. Greg ain't the only congressman with a bastard kid."

Dave knew about George. His mother had told him, and Jasper Murray had actually met George. Dave felt it was cool to have a colored cousin.

Dave said: "So George and I are your two grandsons."

"Yeah."

Marga said: "Here come Greg and George now."

Dave looked up. Walking across the lounge was a middle-aged man wearing a stylish gray flannel suit that needed a good brush and press. Beside him was a handsome Negro of about thirty, immaculately dressed in a dark gray mohair suit and a narrow tie.

They came up to the table. Both men kissed Marga. Lev said: "Greg, this is your nephew, Dave Williams. George, meet your English cousin."

They sat down. Dave noticed that George was poised and confident, despite being the only dark-skinned person in the room. Negro pop stars were growing their hair longer, like everyone else in show business, but George still had a short crop, probably because he was in politics.

Greg said: "Well, Daddy, did you ever imagine a family like this?"

Lev said: "Listen to me, I'll tell you something. If you could go back in time, to when I was the age Dave is now, and you could meet the young Lev Peshkov, and tell him how his life was going to turn out, do you know what he'd do? He'd say you were out of your goddamn mind."

. . .

That evening George took Maria Summers out to dinner for her twenty-ninth birthday.

He was worried about her. Maria had changed her job and moved to a different apartment, but she did not yet have a boyfriend. She socialized with girls from the State Department about once a week, and she went out with George now and again, but she had no romantic life. George feared she was still mourning. The assassination was almost two years ago, but a person could easily take longer than that to recover from the murder of her lover.

His affection for Maria was definitely not that of a brother. He found her sexy and alluring, and had ever since that bus ride to Alabama. He felt about her the way he felt about Skip Dickerson's wife, who was gorgeous and charming. Like his best friend's wife, Maria was simply not available. If life had turned out differently, he felt sure he might be happily married to her. But he had Verena; and Maria wanted no one.

They went to the Jockey Club. Maria wore a gray wool dress, smart but plain. She had no jewelry on, and wore her glasses all the time. Her hairpiece was a little old-fashioned. She had a pretty face and a sexy mouth, and—more importantly—she had a warm heart: she could have found a man easily, if only she had tried. However, people were beginning to say that she was a career girl, a woman whose job was the most important thing in her life. George did not really think that could make her happy, and he fretted about her.

"I just got a promotion," she said as they sat down at the restaurant table.

"Congratulations!" said George. "Let's have champagne."

"Oh, no, thank you, I have to work tomorrow."

"It's your birthday!"

"All the same, I won't. I might have a small brandy later, to help me sleep."

George shrugged. "Well, I guess your seriousness explains your promotion. I know you're intelligent, capable, and extremely well educated, but none of that counts, normally, if your skin is dark."

"Absolutely. It's always been next to impossible for people of color to get high posts in government."

"Well done for overcoming that prejudice. It's quite an achievement."

"Things have changed since you left the Justice Department—and you know why? The government is trying to persuade Southern police forces to hire Negroes, but the Southerners say: 'Look at your own staff—they're all white!' So senior officials are under pressure. To prove they're not prejudiced, they need to promote people of color."

"They probably think one example is enough."

Maria laughed. "Plenty."

They ordered. George reflected that both he and Maria had succeeded in breaking the color bar, but that did not show that it was not there. On the contrary, they were the exceptions that proved the rule.

Maria was thinking along the same lines. "Bobby Kennedy seems all right," she said.

"When I first met him he regarded civil rights as a distraction from more important issues. But the great thing about Bobby is that he'll see reason, and change his mind if necessary."

"How's he doing?"

"Early days yet," George said evasively. Bobby had been elected as the senator from New York, and George was one of his close aides. George felt that Bobby was not adjusting well to his new role. He had been through so many changes—leading adviser to his brother the president, then sidelined by President Johnson, and now a junior senator—that he was in danger of losing track of who he was.

"He ought to speak out against the Vietnam War!" Maria clearly felt passionately about this, and George sensed that she had been planning to lobby him. "President Kennedy was *reducing* our effort in Vietnam, and he refused again and again to send ground combat troops," she said.

"But as soon as Johnson was elected he sent thirty-five hundred marines, and the Pentagon immediately asked for more. In June, they demanded another one hundred seventy-five thousand troops—and General Westmoreland said it probably wouldn't be enough! But Johnson just lies about it all the time."

"I know. And the bombing of the north was supposed to bring Ho Chi Minh to the negotiating table, but it just seems to have made the Communists more resolute."

"Which is exactly what was predicted when the Pentagon war-gamed it."

"Did they? I don't think Bobby knows that." George would tell him tomorrow.

"It's not generally known, but they ran two war games on the effect of bombing North Vietnam. Both showed the same result: an *increase* in Vietcong attacks in the south."

"This is exactly the spiral of failure and escalation that Jack Kennedy feared."

"And my brother's eldest boy is coming up to draft age." Maria's face showed her fear for her nephew. "I don't want Stevie to be killed! Why doesn't Senator Kennedy speak out?"

"He knows it will make him unpopular."

Maria was not willing to accept that. "Will it? People don't like this war."

"People don't like politicians who undermine our troops by criticizing the war."

"He can't let public opinion dictate to him."

"Men who ignore public opinion don't remain in politics long, not in a democracy."

Maria raised her voice in frustration. "So no one can ever oppose a war?"

"Maybe that's why we have so many of them."

Their food came, and Maria changed the subject. "How is Verena?"

George felt he knew Maria well enough to be frank. "I adore her," he said. "She stays at my apartment every time she comes to town, which is about once a month. But she doesn't seem to want to settle down."

"If she settled down with you, she'd have to live in Washington."

"Is that so bad?"

"Her job is in Atlanta."

George did not see the problem. "Most women live where their husband's job is."

"Things are changing. If Negroes can be equal, why not women?"

"Oh, come on!" George said indignantly. "It's not the same."

"It certainly is not. Sexism is worse. Half the human race are enslaved."

"Enslaved?"

"Think how many housewives work hard all day for no pay! And in most parts of the world, a woman who leaves her husband is liable to be arrested and brought home by the police. Someone who works for nothing and can't leave the job is called a slave, George."

George was annoyed by this argument, the more so as Maria seemed to be winning it. But he saw an opportunity to bring up the subject that was really worrying him. He said: "Is this why you're single?"

Maria looked uncomfortable. "Partly," she said, not meeting his eye.

"When do you think you might start dating again?"

"Soon, I guess."

"Don't you want to?"

"Yes, but I work hard, and don't have much spare time."

George did not buy this. "You think no one can ever live up to the man you lost."

She did not deny it. "Am I wrong?" she said.

"I believe you could find someone who would be kinder to you than he was. Someone smart and sexy and also faithful."

"Maybe."

"Would you go out on a blind date?"

"I might."

"Do you care if he's black or white?"

"Black. It's too much trouble, dating white guys."

"Okay." George was thinking of Leopold Montgomery, the reporter. But he did not say so yet. "How was your steak?"

"It melted in the mouth. Thank you for bringing me here. And for remembering my birthday."

They ate dessert, then had brandy with coffee. "I have a

white cousin," said George. "How about that? Dave Williams. I met him today."

"How come you haven't seen him before?"

"He's a British pop singer, here on tour with his group, Plum Nellie."

Maria had never heard of them. "Ten years ago I knew every act in the hit parade. Am I growing old?"

George smiled. "You're twenty-nine today."

"Only a year off thirty! Where did the time go?"

"Their big hit was called 'I Miss Ya, Alicia.'"

"Oh, sure, I've heard that song on the radio. So your cousin is in that group?"

"Yeah."

"Do you like him?"

"I do. He's young, not yet eighteen, but he's mature, and he charmed our cantankerous Russian grandfather."

"Have you seen him perform?"

"No. He offered me a free ticket, but they're in town tonight only, and I already had a date."

"Oh, George, you could have canceled me."

"On your birthday? Heck, no." He called for the check.

He drove her home in his old-fashioned Mercedes. She had moved to a larger apartment in the same neighborhood, Georgetown.

They were surprised to see a police car outside the building with its lights flashing.

George walked Maria to the door. A white cop was standing outside. George said: "Is there something wrong, Officer?"

"Three apartments in this building were burglarized this evening," the cop said. "Do you live here?"

"I do!" said Maria. "Was number four robbed?"

"Let's go look."

They entered the building. Maria's door had been forced open. Her face looked bloodless as she walked into the apartment. George and the cop followed.

Maria looked around, bewildered. "It looks the way I left it." After a second she added: "Except that all the drawers are open."

"You need to check what's missing."

"I don't own anything worth stealing."

"They generally take money, jewelry, liquor, and fire-arms."

"I'm wearing my watch and ring, I don't drink, and I sure don't own a gun." She went into the kitchen, and George watched through the open door. She opened a coffee tin. "I had eighty dollars in here," she told the cop. "It's gone."

He wrote in his notebook. "Exactly eighty?"

"Three twenties and two tens."

There was one more room. George crossed the living room and opened the door to the bedroom.

Maria cried: "George! Don't go in there!"

She was too late.

George stood in the doorway, looking around the bedroom in amazement. "Oh, my God," he said. Now he saw why she was not dating.

Maria turned away, mortified with embarrassment.

The cop went past George into the bedroom. "Wow," he said. "You must have a hundred pictures of President Kennedy in here! I guess you were a fan of his, right?"

Maria struggled to speak. "Yes," she said, sounding choked up. "A fan."

"I mean, with the candles, and flowers, and like that, it's amazing."

George turned away from the sight. "Maria, I'm sorry I looked," he said quietly.

She shook her head, meaning he had no need to apologize: it had been an accident. But George knew he had violated a secret, sacred place. He wanted to kick himself.

The cop was still talking. "It's almost like a, what do you call it, in a Catholic church? A shrine, is the word."

"That's right," said Maria. "It's a shrine."

. . .

The program *This Day* was part of a network of television and radio stations and studios, some of which were housed in a downtown skyscraper. In the personnel department was an attractive middle-aged woman called Mrs. Salzman who fell victim to Jasper Murray's charm. She crossed her shapely legs and looked at him archly over the top of her blue-framed spectacles and called him Mr. Murray. He lit her cigarettes and called her Blue Eyes.

She felt sorry for him. He had come all the way from Britain in the hope of being interviewed for a job that did not exist. *This Day* never hired beginners: all its staff was experienced television reporters, producers, cameramen, and researchers. Several of them were distinguished in their profession. Even the secretaries were news veterans. In vain Jasper protested that he was not a beginner: he had been editor of his own paper. The student press did not count, Mrs. Salzman told him, oozing compassion.

He could not go back to London: it would be too humiliating. He would do anything to stay in the USA. His job on the *Western Mail* would have been filled by someone else by now.

He begged Mrs. Salzman to find him a job, any job, no matter how menial, somewhere in the network of which *This Day* was a part. He showed her his green card, obtained from the American embassy in London, which meant he had permission to seek employment in the States. She told him to come back in a week.

He was staying at an international student hostel on the Lower East Side, paying a dollar a night. He spent a week exploring New York, walking everywhere to save cash. Then he went back to see Mrs. Salzman, taking with him a single rose. And she gave him a job.

It was *very* menial. He was a clerk-typist on a local radio station, his task to listen to the radio all day and log everything that happened: which advertisements were aired, which records were played, who was interviewed, the length of the news bulletins and the weather forecasts and the traffic reports. Jasper did not care. He had got a foot in the door. He was working in America.

The personnel office, the radio station, and the *This Day* studio were all in the same skyscraper, and Jasper hoped he might get to know the people on *This Day* socially, but it never happened. They were an elite group who kept themselves separate.

One morning Jasper found himself in the elevator with Herb Gould, editor of *This Day,* a man of about forty with the permanent shadow of a blue-black beard. Jasper introduced himself and said: "I'm a great admirer of your show."

"Thank you," Gould said politely.

"It's my ambition to work for you," Jasper went on.

"We don't need anyone right now," Gould said.

"One day if you have time I'd like to show you my articles for British national newspapers." The elevator came to a halt. Desperately, Jasper kept going. "I've written—"

Gould held up a hand to silence him and stepped out of the lift. "Thanks all the same," he said, and he walked away.

A few days later, Jasper was at his typewriter with his headphones on and heard the mellifluous voice of Chris Gardner, the host of the midmorning show, say: "The British group Plum Nellie is in the city today for a show tonight with the All-Star Touring Beat Revue." Jasper pricked up his ears. "We were hoping to bring you an interview with these guys, who are being called the new Beatles, but the promoter said they wouldn't have time. Here instead is their latest hit, written by Dave and Walli: 'Good-bye London Town.'"

As the record began, Jasper tore off his headphones, jumped up from his desk—in a little booth in the corridor—and went into the studio. "I can get an interview with Plum Nellie," he said.

On air, Gardner sounded like the kind of movie star who always played the romantic lead, but in fact he was a homely-looking man with dandruff on the shoulders of his cardigan. "How would you manage that, Jasper?" he said with mild skepticism.

"I know the group. I grew up with Dave Williams. My mother and his are best friends."

"Can you get the group to come into the studio?"

Jasper probably could, but that was not what he wanted. "No," he said. "But if you give me a microphone and a tape recorder I'll guarantee to interview them in their dressing room."

There was a certain amount of bureaucratic fuss—the station manager was reluctant to let an expensive tape recorder leave the building—but at six that evening Jasper was backstage at the theater with the group.

Chris Gardner wanted no more than a few minutes of bland remarks from the group: how they liked the United States, what they thought about girls screaming at their concerts, whether they felt homesick. But Jasper hoped to give the radio station more than that. He intended this interview to be his passport to a real job in television. It had to be a sensation that rocked America.

First he interviewed them all together, doing the vanilla questions, talking about the early days back in London, getting them relaxed. He told them the station wanted to show them as fully rounded human beings: this was journalists' code for intrusive personal questions, but they were too young and inexperienced to know that. They were open with him, except for Dave, who was guarded, perhaps remembering the fuss caused by Jasper's article about Evie and Hank Remington. The others trusted him. Something else they had yet to learn was that no journalist could be trusted.

Then he asked them for individual interviews. He did Dave first, knowing that he was the leader. He gave Dave an easy ride, avoiding probing questions, not challenging any of the answers. Dave returned to the dressing room looking tranquil, and that gave the others confidence.

Jasper interviewed Walli last.

Walli was the one with a real story to tell. But would he open up? All Jasper's preparations were aimed at that result.

Jasper placed their chairs close together, and spoke to Walli in a low voice, to create the illusion of privacy, even though their words would be heard by millions. He put an ashtray next to Walli's chair to encourage him to smoke, guessing that a cigarette would make him feel more at ease. Walli lit up.

"What kind of child were you?" Jasper said, smiling as if this was just a lighthearted conversation. "Well-behaved, or naughty?"

Walli grinned. "Naughty," he said, and laughed.

They were off to a good start.

Walli talked about his childhood in Berlin after the war and his early interest in music, then about going to the Minnesänger club, where he came second in the contest. This brought Karolin into the conversation in a natural way, as she and Walli had paired up that night. Walli became passionate as he spoke about the two of them as a musical duo, their choice of material and the way they performed together, and it was clear how much he loved her, even though he did not say it.

This was great stuff, a lot better than the average pop star interview, but still not enough for Jasper.

"You were enjoying yourselves, you were making good music, and you were pleasing audiences," Jasper said. "What went wrong?"

"We sang 'If I Had a Hammer.'"

"Explain to me why that was a mistake."

"The police didn't like it. Karolin's father was afraid he would lose his job because of us, so he made her quit."

"So, in the end, the only place you could play your music was the West."

"Yes," Walli said briefly.

Jasper sensed that Walli was trying to dam the flow of passion.

Sure enough, after a moment's hesitation Walli added: "I don't want to say too much about Karolin—it could get her into trouble."

"I don't think the East German secret police listen to our radio station," Jasper said with a smile.

"No, but still . . ."

"I won't broadcast anything risky, I guarantee."

It was a worthless promise, but Walli accepted it. "Thanks," he said.

Jasper moved on quickly. "I believe the only thing you took with you, when you left, was your guitar."

"That's right. It was a sudden decision."

"You stole a vehicle."

"I was roadying for the bandleader. I used his van."

Jasper knew that this story, although big in the German press, had not been widely reported in the United States. "You drove to the checkpoint . . ."

"And smashed through the wooden barrier."

"And the guards shot at you."

Walli just nodded.

Jasper lowered his voice. "And the van hit a guard."

Walli nodded again. Jasper wanted to yell at him: *This is radio—stop nodding!* Instead he said: "And . . ."

"I killed him," Walli said at last. "I killed the guy."

"But he was trying to kill you."

Walli shook his head, as if Jasper were missing the point. "He was my age," Walli said. "I read about him in the news-papers later. He had a girlfriend."

"And that's important to you . . ."

Walli nodded again.

Jasper said: "What does that signify?"

"He was similar to me," Walli said. "Except that I liked guitars and he liked guns."

"But he was working for the regime that imprisoned you in East Germany."

"We were just two boys. I escaped because I had to. He shot me because he had to. It's the Wall that is evil."

That was such a great quote that Jasper had to suppress his elation. In his head he was already writing the article he would offer to the tabloid *New York Post*. He could see the headline:

Secret Anguish of
Pop Star Walli

But he wanted yet more. "Karolin didn't leave with you."

"She didn't show up. I had no idea why. I was so disappointed, and I couldn't understand it. So I escaped anyway." In the pain of remembering, Walli had lost sight of the need to be cautious.

Jasper prompted him again. "But you went back for her."

"I met some people who were digging a tunnel for escapers. I had to know why she had not shown up. So I went through the tunnel the wrong way, into the East."

"That was dangerous."

"If I had been caught, yes."

"And you met up with Karolin, then . . ."

"She told me she was pregnant."

"And she didn't want to escape with you."

"She was afraid for the baby."

"Alicia."

"Her name is Alice. I changed it in the song. For the rhyme, you know?"

"I understand. And what is your situation now, Walli?"

Walli choked up. "Karolin can't get permission to leave East Germany, not even for a short visit; and I can't go back."

"So you are a family split in two by the Berlin Wall."

"Yes." Walli let out a sob. "I may never see Alice."

Jasper thought: *Gotcha.*

· · · ·

Dave Williams had not seen Beep Dewar since her visit to London four years ago. He was eager to meet her again.

The last date of the Beat Revue tour was in San Francisco, where Beep lived. Dave had got the Dewars' address from his mother, and had sent them four tickets and a note inviting them to come backstage afterward. They had not been able to reply, for he was in a different city every day, so he did not know whether they were going to turn up.

He was no longer sleeping with Mandy Love—much to his regret. She had taught him a lot, including oral sex. But she had never really felt comfortable walking around with a white British boyfriend, and she had now gone back to her long-term lover, a piano player. They would probably get married when the tour was over, Dave thought.

Since then Dave had had no one.

By now Dave knew what kinds of sex he did and did not like. In bed girls could be intense, or slutty, or soulful, or sweetly submissive, or briskly practical. Dave was happiest when they were playful.

He had a feeling Beep would be playful.

He wondered what would happen if Beep showed up tonight.

He recalled her at thirteen, smoking Chesterfield cigarettes in the garden in Great Peter Street. She had been pretty and petite, and sexier than anyone had a right to be at that age. To Dave at thirteen, hypersensitized by adolescent hormones, she had been impossibly alluring. He had been flat crazy for her. However, although they had got on well, she had not been interested in him romantically. To his immense frustration, she had preferred the older Jasper Murray.

His thoughts drifted to Jasper. Walli had been upset when the interview was broadcast on the radio. Even worse had been the story in the *New York Post,* headlined:

**"I May Never
See My Kid"
—Pop Star Dad**

by Jasper Murray

Walli was afraid the publicity might cause trouble for

Karolin in East Germany. Dave recalled Jasper's interview with Evie, and made a mental note never to trust a word Jasper said.

He wondered how much Beep might have changed in four years. She might be taller, or she might have grown fat. Would he still find her overwhelmingly desirable? Would she be more interested in him now that he was older?

She might have a boyfriend, of course. She might go out with that guy tonight instead of coming to the gig.

Before the show, Plum Nellie had a couple of hours to look around. They quickly realized that San Francisco was the coolest city of them all. It was full of young people in radically stylish clothes. Miniskirts were out. The girls wore dresses that trailed the floor, flowers in their hair, and tiny bells that tinkled as they moved. The men's hair was longer here than anywhere else, even London. Some of the young black men and women had grown it into a huge fuzzy cloud that looked amazing.

Walli in particular loved the town. He said he felt as if he could do anything here. It was at the opposite end of the universe from East Berlin.

There were twelve acts in the Beat Revue. Most of them played two or three songs, then went off. The top-of-the-bill act had twenty minutes at the end. Plum Nellie was big enough stars to close the first half with fifteen minutes, during which they played five short songs. No amplifiers were carried on tour: they played through whatever was available at the venue, often primitive speakers designed for sports announcements. The audience, almost all teenage girls, screamed loudly all the way through, so that the group could not hear themselves. It hardly mattered: no one was listening.

The thrill of working in the USA was wearing off. The group was getting bored, and looking forward to going back to London, where they were due to record a new album.

After the performance they returned backstage. The venue was a theater, so their dressing room was large enough, and the toilet was clean—quite different from the beat clubs in London and Hamburg. The only refreshment available was the free Dr Pepper from the sponsor, but the doorman was usually willing to send out for beer.

Dave told the group that friends of his parents might come backstage, so they had to behave. They all groaned: that meant no drugs and no fumbling with groupies until the old people had gone.

During the second half, Dave saw the doorman at the artists' entrance and made sure he had the names of the guests: Mr. Woody Dewar, Mrs. Bella Dewar, Mr. Cameron Dewar, and Miss Ursula "Beep" Dewar.

Fifteen minutes after the end of the show, they appeared in the doorway of his dressing room.

Beep had hardly changed at all, Dave saw with delight. She was still petite, no taller than she had been at thirteen, although she was curvier. Her jeans were tight around her hips but flared below the knee, the latest fashion, and she wore a closely fitting sweater with broad blue and white stripes.

Had she dressed up for Dave? Not necessarily. What teenage girl would *not* dress up to go backstage at a pop concert?

He shook hands with all four visitors and introduced them to the rest of the group. He was afraid the other guys might disgrace him, but in fact they were on their best behavior. They all invited family guests occasionally, and each appreciated the others being restrained in the presence of older relatives and friends of their parents.

Dave had to force himself to stop staring at Beep. She still had that look in her eye. Mandy Love had it, too. People called it sex appeal or je ne sais quoi or just "It." Beep had an impish grin, a sway in her walk, and an air of lively curiosity. Dave was as consumed with desperate desire as he had been when he was a thirteen-year-old virgin.

He tried to talk to Cameron, who was two years older than Beep and already studying at the University of California at Berkeley, just outside San Francisco. But Cam was difficult. He was in favor of the Vietnam War, he thought civil rights should progress more gradually, and he felt it was right that homosexual acts should be crimes. He also preferred jazz.

Dave gave the Dewars fifteen minutes, then said: "This is the last night of our tour. There's a farewell get-together at the hotel starting in a few minutes. Beep and Cam, would you like to come?"

"Not me," said Cameron immediately. "Thanks all the same."

"Shame," said Dave with polite insincerity. "What about you, Beep?"

"I'd love to come," said Beep, and looked at her mother.

"In by midnight," said Bella.

Woody said: "Use our taxi service to get home, please."

"I'll make sure of it," Dave reassured them.

The parents and Cameron left, and the musicians got on the bus with their guests for the short ride to the hotel.

The party was in the hotel bar, but in the lobby Dave murmured in Beep's ear: "Have you ever tried smoking marijuana?"

"You mean pot?" she said. "You bet!"

"Not so loud—it's against the law!"

"Have you got some?"

"Yes. We should probably smoke it in my room. Then we can join the party."

"Okay."

They went to his room. Dave rolled a joint while Beep found a rock station on the radio. They sat on the bed, passing the roach back and forth. Mellowing out, Dave smiled and said: "When you came to London . . ."

"What?"

"You weren't interested in me."

"I liked you, but you were too young."

"*You* were too young, for the things I wanted to do to you."

She grinned mischievously. "What did you want to do to me?"

"There was a long list."

"What came first?"

"First?" Dave was not going to tell her. Then he thought: Why not? So he said: "I wanted to see your tits."

She handed him the joint, then pulled the striped sweater over her head with a swift movement. She had nothing on underneath it.

Dave was astounded and overjoyed. He got a hard-on just looking. "They're so beautiful," he said.

"Yes, they are," she said dreamily. "So pretty I sometimes have to touch them myself."

"Oh, my God," Dave groaned.

"On your list," Beep said, "what was second?"

. . .

Dave changed his flight to a week later and stayed on at the hotel. He saw Beep after school every weekday and all day Saturday and Sunday. They went to movies, they shopped for cool clothes, and they walked around the zoo. They made love two or three times a day, always using condoms.

One evening while he was undressing she said: "Take off your jeans."

He looked at her, lying on the hotel bed wearing just her panties and a denim cap. "What are you talking about?"

"Tonight you're my slave. Do as you're told. Take off your jeans."

He was already taking them off, and he was about to say so when he realized that this was a fantasy. The thought amused him, and he decided to play along. He pretended to be reluctant, and said: "Aw, do I have to?"

"You have to do everything I say, because you belong to me," she said. "Take off your goddamn jeans."

"Yes, ma'am," Dave said.

She sat upright, watching him. He saw the mischievous lust in her faint smile. "Very good," she said.

Dave said: "What should I do next?"

Dave knew why he had fallen so hard for Beep, both when he was thirteen and again a few days ago. She was full of fun, ready to try anything, hungry for new experiences. With some girls, Dave had been bored after two fucks. He felt he could never get bored with Beep.

They made love, Dave pretending reluctance while Beep ordered him to do things he was already longing for. It was weirdly exciting.

Afterward he said idly: "Where did you get your nickname, anyway?"

"Have I never told you?"

"No. There's so much I don't know about you. Yet I feel as if we've been close for years."

"When I was little I had a toy car, the kind you sit in and pedal. I don't even remember it, but apparently I loved it. I spent hours driving it, and I used to say: 'Beep! Beep!'"

They got dressed and went for hamburgers. Dave saw her bite into hers, watched the juice run down her chin, and realized that he was in love.

"I don't want to go back to London," he said.

She swallowed and said: "Then stay."

"I can't. Plum Nellie has to make a new album. Then we go on tour in Australia and New Zealand."

"I adore you," she said. "When you go, I'll cry. But I'm not going to spoil today by being miserable about tomorrow. Eat your hamburger. You need the protein."

"I feel we're soul mates. I know I'm young, but I've had a lot of different girls."

"No need to brag. I've done pretty well, too."

"I didn't mean to brag. I'm not even proud of it—it's too easy when you're a pop singer. I'm trying to explain, to myself as well as to you, why I feel so sure."

She dipped a French fry into ketchup. "Sure of what?"

"That I want this to be permanent."

She froze with the French fry halfway to her mouth, then put it back on the plate. "What do you mean?"

"I want us to be together always. I want us to live together."

"Live together . . . how?"

"Beep," he said.

"Still here."

He reached across the table and took her hand. "Would you think about maybe getting married?"

"Oh, my God," she said.

"I know it's crazy, I know."

"It's not crazy," she said. "But it's sudden."

"Does that mean you want to? Get married?"

"You're right. We're soul mates. I've never had half this much fun with a boyfriend."

She was still not answering the question. He said slowly and distinctly: "I love you. Will you marry me?"

She hesitated for a long moment, then she said: "Hell, yes."

. . .

"Don't even ask me," said Woody Dewar angrily. "You two are not getting married."

He was a tall man, dressed in a tweed jacket with a button-down shirt and a tie. Dave had to work hard not to be intimidated.

Beep said: "How did you know?"

"It doesn't matter."

"My creep of a brother told you," Beep said. "What a dick I was to confide in him."

"There's no need for bad language."

They were in the drawing room of the Dewars' Victorian mansion on Gough Street in the Nob Hill district. The handsome old furniture and expensive but faded curtains reminded Dave of the house in Great Peter Street. Dave and Beep sat together on the red velvet couch, Bella was in an antique leather chair, and Woody stood in front of the carved stone fireplace.

Dave said: "I know it's sudden, but I have obligations: recording in London, a tour of Australia, and more."

"Sudden?" said Woody. "It's totally irresponsible! The mere fact that you can make the suggestion at all, after a week of dating, proves that you're nowhere near mature enough for marriage."

Dave said: "I hate to boast, but you force me to say that I've been living independently from my parents for two years; in that time I've built up a multimillion-dollar international business; and although I'm not as rich as people imagine, I am able to keep your daughter in comfort."

"Beep is seventeen! And so are you. She can't marry without my permission, and I'm not giving it. And I'm betting Lloyd and Daisy will take the same attitude to you, young Dave."

Beep said: "In some states you can get married at eighteen."

"You're not going anywhere like that."

"What are you going to do, Daddy, put me in a nunnery?"

"Are you threatening to elope?"

"Just pointing out that, in the end, you don't really have the power to stop us."

She was right. Dave had checked, at the San Francisco public library on Larkin Street. The age of majority was twenty-one, but several states allowed women to marry at eighteen without parental consent. And in Scotland the age was sixteen. In practice it was difficult for parents to prevent the marriage of two people who were determined.

But Woody said: "Don't you bet on that. This is not going to happen."

Dave said mildly: "We don't want to quarrel with you about this, but I think Beep's just saying that yours is not the only opinion that counts here."

He thought his words were inoffensive, and he had spoken in a courteous tone of voice, but that seemed to infuriate Woody more. "Get out of this house before I throw you out."

Bella intervened for the first time. "Stay where you are, Dave."

Dave had not moved. Woody had a bad leg from a war wound: he was not throwing anyone anywhere.

Bella turned to her husband. "Darling, twenty-one years ago you sat in this room and confronted my mother."

"I wasn't seventeen, I was twenty-five."

"Mother accused you of causing the breaking-off of my engagement to Victor Rolandson. She was right: you were the cause of it, though at that point you and I had spent only one evening together. We had met at Dave's mother's party, after which you went off to invade Normandy and I didn't see you for a year."

Beep said: "One evening? What did you do to him, Mom?"

Bella looked at her daughter, hesitated, then said: "I blew him in a park, honey."

Dave was astonished. Bella and Woody? It was unimaginable!

Woody protested: "Bella!"

"This is no time to mince words, Woody, dear."

Beep said: "On the first date? Wow, Mom! Way to go!"

Woody said: "For God's sake . . ."

Bella said: "My darling, I'm just trying to remind you of what it was like to be young."

"I didn't propose marriage right away!"

"That's true, you were painfully slow."

Beep giggled and Dave smiled.

Woody said to Bella: "Why are you undermining me?"

"Because you're being just a little pompous." She took his hand, smiled, and said: "We were in love. So are they. Lucky us, lucky them."

Woody became a little less angry. "So we should let them do anything they like?"

"Certainly not. But perhaps we can compromise."

"I don't see how."

"Suppose we tell them to ask us again in a year. In the meantime, Dave will be welcome to come and live here, in our house, whenever he can get a break from working with the group. While he's here he can share Beep's bed, if that's what they want."

"Certainly not!"

"They're going to do it, either here or elsewhere. Don't fight battles you can't win. And don't be a hypocrite. You slept with me before we were married, and you slept with Joanne Rouzrokh before you met me."

Woody got up. "I'll think about it," he said, and he walked out of the room.

Bella turned to Dave. "I'm not giving orders, Dave, either to you or to Beep. I'm asking you—begging you—to be patient. You're a good man from a fine family, and I will be happy when you marry my daughter. But please wait a year."

Dave looked at Beep. She nodded.

"All right," said Dave. "A year."

. . .

On the way out of the hostel in the morning, Jasper checked his pigeonhole. There were two letters. One was a blue airmail envelope addressed in his mother's graceful handwriting. The other had a typed address. Before he could open them he was called. "Telephone for Jasper Murray!" He stuffed both envelopes into the inside pocket of his jacket.

The caller was Mrs. Salzman. "Good morning, Mr. Murray."

"Hello, Blue Eyes."

"Are you wearing a tie, Mr. Murray?" she said.

Ties had become unfashionable, and anyway a clerk-typist was not required to be smart. "No," he said.

"Put one on. Herb Gould wants to see you at ten."

"He does? Why?"

"There's a vacancy for a researcher on *This Day*. I showed him your clippings."

"Thank you—you're an angel!"

"Put on a tie." Mrs. Salzman hung up.

Jasper returned to his room and put on a clean white shirt and a sober dark tie. Then he put his jacket and topcoat back on and went to work.

At the newsstand in the lobby of the skyscraper, he bought a small box of chocolates for Mrs. Salzman.

He went to the offices of *This Day* at ten minutes to ten. Fifteen minutes later, a secretary took him to Gould's office.

"Good to meet you," Gould said. "Thanks for coming in."

"I'm glad to be here." Jasper guessed that Gould had no memory of their conversation in the elevator.

Gould was reading the assassination edition of *The Real Thing*. "In your résumé it says you started this newspaper."

"Yes."

"How did that come about?"

"I was working on the official university student newspaper, *St. Julian's News.*" Jasper's nervousness receded as he began to talk. "I applied for the post of editor, but it went to the sister of the previous editor."

"So you did it in a fit of pique."

Jasper grinned. "Partly, yes, though I felt sure I could do a better job than Valerie. So I borrowed twenty-five pounds and started a rival paper."

"And how did it work out?"

"After three issues we were selling more than *St. Julian's News.* And we made a profit, whereas *St. Julian's News* was subsidized." This was only slightly exaggerated. *The Real Thing* had just about broken even over a year.

"That's a real achievement."

"Thank you."

Gould held up the *New York Post* clipping of the interview with Walli. "How did you get this story?"

"What had happened to Walli wasn't a secret. It had already appeared in the German press. But in those days he was not a pop star. If I may say so . . ."

"Go on."

"I believe the art of journalism is not always finding out facts. Sometimes it's *realizing* that certain already-known facts, written up the right way, add up to a big story."

Gould nodded agreement. "All right. Why do you want to switch from print to television?"

"We know that a good photograph on the front page sells more copies than the best headline. Moving pictures are even better. No doubt there will always be a market for long in-depth newspaper articles, but for the foreseeable future most people are going to get their news from television."

Gould smiled. "No argument here."

The speaker on his desk beeped and his secretary said: "Mr. Thomas is calling from the Washington bureau."

"Thanks, sweetie. Jasper, good talking to you. We'll be in touch." He picked up the phone. "Hey, Larry, what's up?"

Jasper left the office. The interview had gone well, but it had ended with frustrating suddenness. He wished he had had the chance to ask how soon he would hear. But he was a supplicant: no one was worried about how he felt.

He returned to the radio station. While he was at the interview, his job had been done by the secretary who regularly relieved him at lunchtime. Now he thanked her and took over. He took off his jacket, and remembered the mail in his pocket. He put on his headphones and sat at the little desk. On the radio, a sports reporter was previewing a ball game. Jasper took out his letters and opened the one with the typewritten address.

It was from the president of the United States.

It was a form letter, with his name handwritten in a box. It read:

Greeting:
You are hereby ordered for induction into the Armed
Forces of the United States

Jasper said aloud: "What?"

and to report at the address below on January 20,
1966, at 7 A.M. for forwarding to an Armed Forces
Induction Station.

Jasper fought down panic. This was obviously a bureaucratic foul-up. He was British: the U.S. Army surely would not conscript foreign citizens.

But he needed to get this sorted out as soon as possible. American bureaucrats were as maddeningly incompetent as any, and equally capable of causing endless unnecessary trouble. You had to pretend to take them seriously, like a red light at a deserted crossroads.

The reporting station was just a few blocks from the radio station. When the secretary came back to relieve him for lunch, he put on his jacket and topcoat and walked out of the building.

He turned up his collar against the cold New York wind and hurried through the streets to the federal building. There he entered an army office on the third floor and found a man in a captain's uniform sitting at a desk. The short-back-and-sides haircut looked more ridiculous than ever, now that even middle-aged men were growing their hair longer. "Help you?" said the captain.

"I'm pretty sure this letter has been sent to me in error," Jasper said, and he handed over the envelope.

The captain scanned it. "You know there's a lottery system?" he said. "The number of men liable for service is greater than the number of soldiers required, so the recruits are selected randomly." He handed the letter back.

Jasper smiled. "I don't think I'm eligible for service, do you?"

"And why would that be?"

Perhaps the captain had not noticed his accent. "I'm not an American citizen," Jasper said. "I'm British."

"What are you doing in the United States?"

"I'm a journalist. I work for a radio station."

"And you have a work permit, I presume."

"Yes."

"You're a resident alien."

"Exactly."

"Then you are liable to be drafted."

"But I'm not American!"

"Makes no difference."

This was becoming exasperating. The army had screwed up, Jasper was almost certain. The captain, like many petty officials, was simply unwilling to admit a mistake. "Are you telling me that the United States army conscripts foreigners?"

The captain was unperturbed. "Conscription is based on residence, not citizenship."

"That can't be right."

The captain began to look irritated. "If you don't believe me, check it out."

"That's exactly what I'm going to do."

Jasper left the building and returned to the office. The

personnel department would know about this kind of thing. He would go and see Mrs. Salzman.

He gave her the box of chocolates.

"You're sweet," she said. "Mr. Gould likes you, too."

"What did he say?"

"Just thanked me for sending you to him. He hasn't made up his mind yet. But I don't know of anyone else under consideration."

"That's great news! But I have a little problem you might be able to help me with." He showed her the letter from the army. "This must be a mistake, surely?"

Mrs. Salzman put her glasses on and read the letter. "Oh, dear," she said. "How unlucky. And just when you were getting along so well!"

Jasper could hardly believe his ears. "You're not saying I'm really liable for military service?"

"You are," she said sadly. "We've had this trouble before with foreign employees. The government says that if you want to live and work in the United States, you ought to help defend the country from Communist aggression."

"Are you telling me I'm going in the army?"

"Not necessarily."

Jasper's heart leaped with hope. "What's the alternative?"

"You can go home. They won't try to stop you from leaving the country."

"This is outrageous! Can't you get me out of it?"

"Do you have a hidden medical condition of any kind? Flat feet, tuberculosis, a hole in the heart?"

"Never been ill."

She lowered her voice. "And I presume you're not homosexual."

"No!"

"Your family doesn't belong to a religion that forbids military service?"

"My father's a colonel in the British army."

"I'm so sorry."

Jasper began to believe it. "I'm really leaving. Even if I get the job on *This Day,* I won't be able to take it up." He was struck by a thought. "Don't they have to give you your job back when you've finished your military service?"

"Only if you've held the job for a year."

"So I might not even be able to return to my job as clerk-typist on the radio station!"

"There's no guarantee."

"Whereas if I leave the United States now . . ."

"You can just go home. But you'll never work in the USA again."

"Jesus."

"What will you do? Leave, or join the army?"

"I really don't know," he said. "Thank you for your help."

"Thank you for the chocolates, Mr. Murray."

Jasper left her office in a daze. He could not return to his desk: he had to think. He went outside again. Normally he loved the streets of New York: the high buildings, the mighty Mack trucks, the extravagantly styled cars, the glittering window displays of the fabulous stores. Today it had all turned sour.

He walked toward the East River and sat in a park from which he could see the Brooklyn Bridge. He thought about leaving all this and going home to London with his tail between his legs. He thought about spending two long years working for a provincial British newspaper. He thought about never again being able to work in the USA.

Then he thought about the army: short hair, marching, bullying sergeants, violence. He thought about the hot jungles of Southeast Asia. He might have to shoot small, thin peasant men in pajamas. He might be killed, or crippled.

He thought of all the people he knew in London who had envied his going to the States. Anna and Hank had taken him to dinner at the Savoy to celebrate. Daisy had given a farewell party for him at the house in Great Peter Street. His mother had cried.

He would be like a bride who comes home from the honeymoon and announces a divorce. The humiliation seemed worse than the risk of death in Vietnam.

What was he going to do?

CHAPTER THIRTY-NINE

The St. Gertrud Youth Club had changed.

It had started out more or less harmless, Lili recalled. The East German government approved of traditional dancing, even if it took place in the basement of a church. And the government was happy for a Protestant pastor such as Odo Vossler to chat to youngsters about relationships and sex, since his views were likely to be as puritanical as their own.

Two years later the club was not so innocent. They no longer began the evening with a folk dance. They played rock music and danced in the energetic individualist style that youngsters all over the world called freaking out. Later, Lili and Karolin would play guitars and sing songs about freedom. The evening always ended with a discussion, led by Pastor Odo; and these discussions regularly strayed into forbidden territory: democracy, religion, the shortcomings of the East German government, and the overwhelming attraction of life in the West.

Such talk was commonplace at Lili's home, but for some of the kids it was a new and liberating experience to hear the government criticized and the ideas of Communism challenged.

This was not the only place where such things went on. Three or four evenings a week, Lili and Karolin took their guitars to a different church hall or a private house in or near Berlin. They knew that what they were doing was dangerous, but both felt they had little to lose. Karolin knew that she would never be reunited with Walli while the Berlin Wall remained standing. After the American newspapers ran stories about Walli and Karolin, the Stasi had punished the family by having Lili expelled from college: now she worked as a waitress in the canteen of the Ministry of Transport. Both young women had been determined not to let the government stifle them. Now they were famous among young people who secretly opposed the Communists. They made tape recordings of their songs that were passed around from one fan to another. Lili felt they were keeping the flame alight.

For Lili there was another attraction at St. Gertrud's: Thorsten Greiner. He was twenty-two, but he had a baby face like Paul McCartney's that made him look younger. He shared Lili's passion for music. He had recently broken up with a girl called Helga who was just not intelligent enough for him—in Lili's opinion.

One evening in 1967 Thorsten brought to the club the latest record by the Beatles. On one side was a bouncingly happy number called "Penny Lane," which they all danced to energetically; on the other a weirdly fascinating song, "Strawberry Fields Forever," to which Lili and others did a kind of slow dream-dance, swaying to the music and waving their arms and hands like underwater plants. They played both sides of the disc again and again.

When people asked Thorsten how he got the record, he tapped the side of his nose in a mysterious gesture and said nothing. But Lili knew the truth. Once a week Thorsten's uncle Horst drove across the border into West Berlin in a van full of bolts of cloth and cheap clothing, the East's largest export. Horst always gave the border guards a share of the comic books, pop records, makeup, and fashionable clothes he brought back.

Lili's parents thought the music was frivolous. For them only politics was serious. But they failed to understand that for Lili and her generation the music was political, even when the songs were about love. New ways of playing guitars and singing were all tied up with long hair and different clothes, racial tolerance and sexual freedom. Every song by the Beatles or Bob Dylan said to the older generation: "We don't do things your way." For teenagers in East Germany that was a stridently political message, and the government knew it and banned the records.

They were all freaking out to "Strawberry Fields Forever" when the police arrived.

Lili was dancing opposite Thorsten. She understood English, and she was intrigued by John Lennon singing: "Living is easy with eyes closed, misunderstanding all you see." It so vividly described most people in East Germany, she thought.

Lili was among the first to spot the uniforms coming through the street door. She knew right away that the Stasi had at last caught up with the St. Gertrud Youth Club. It was inevitable: young people were bound to talk about exciting things they did. No one knew how many East German citizens were informers for the secret police, but Lili's mother said it was more than the Gestapo had. "We couldn't do now what we did in the war," Carla had said; though when Lili had asked what she did in the war her mother had clammed up, as always. Anyway, it had been likely all along that sooner or later the Stasi would get wind of what was going on in the basement of St. Gertrud's Church.

Lili immediately stopped dancing and looked around for Karolin, but could not see her. Odo was not in sight either. They must have left the basement. In the corner opposite the street door was a staircase that led directly to the pastor's house alongside the church. They had probably gone out that way for some reason.

Lili said to Thorsten: "I'm going to fetch Odo."

She was able to push through the crowd of dancers and slip away before most people realized they were being raided. Thorsten followed her. They got to the top of the staircase before Lennon sang: "Let me take you down—" and stopped abruptly.

The harsh voice of a police officer began to give orders below as they crossed the hall of the pastor's residence. It was a large house for a single man: Odo was lucky. Lili had not been here often, but she knew he had a study on the ground floor at the front, and she guessed this was the likeliest place to find him. The door was ajar, and she pushed it wide and stepped inside.

There, in an oak-paneled room with bookshelves full of works of biblical scholarship, Odo and Karolin were locked in a passionate embrace. They were kissing with their mouths open. Karolin's hands were on Odo's head, her fingers buried in his long, thick hair. Odo was stroking and squeezing Karolin's breasts. She pressed against him, her body curved tautly like an archer's bow.

Lili was shocked silent. She thought of Karolin as her brother's wife, the fact that they were not actually married a mere technicality. It had never occurred to her that Karolin could become fond of another man—let alone the pastor! For a moment her mind searched wildly for some alternative explanation: they were rehearsing a play, or doing calisthenics.

Then Thorsten said: "My God!"

Odo and Karolin jumped apart with a suddenness that was almost comic. Shock and guilt showed on their faces. After a moment they spoke together. Odo said: "We were going to tell you." At the same time Karolin said: "Oh, Lili, I'm so sorry . . ."

For a frozen moment, Lili was vividly conscious of details: the check pattern of Odo's jacket, Karolin's nipples poking through her dress, Odo's theological degree in a brass frame on the wall, the old-fashioned flowered carpet with a threadbare patch in front of the fireplace.

Then she remembered the emergency that had brought her upstairs. "The police have come," she said. "They're in the basement."

Odo said: "Hell!" He strode out and Lili heard him hurrying down the stairs.

Karolin stared at Lili. Neither woman knew what to say. Then Karolin broke the spell. "I must go with him," she said, and followed Odo.

Lili and Thorsten were left in the study. It was a nice place for kissing, Lili thought sadly: the oak paneling, the fireplace, the books, the carpet. She wondered how often Odo and Karolin had done this, and when it had started. She thought about Walli. Poor Walli.

She heard shouting from downstairs, and that energized her. She had no reason to return to the basement, she realized. Her coat was down there but the evening was not bitterly cold: she could manage without it. She might escape.

The front door of the house was on the opposite side of the building from the basement entrance. She wondered whether the police had the whole place surrounded, and decided probably not.

She crossed the hall and opened the front door. There were no police in sight.

She said to Thorsten: "Shall we leave?"

"Yes, quickly."

They went out, closing the door quietly.

"I'll see you home," Thorsten said.

They hurried around the corner, then slowed their pace when they were out of sight of the church. Thorsten said: "That must have been a shock for you."

"I thought she loved Walli!" Lili wailed. "How could she do this to him?" She began to cry.

Thorsten put his arm around her shoulders as they walked along. "When was it that Walli left?"

"Almost four years ago."

"Have Karolin's prospects of emigrating got any better?"

Lili shook her head. "Worse."

"She needs someone to help her raise Alice."

"She has me, and my family!"

"Perhaps she feels that Alice needs a father."

"But . . . the pastor!"

"Most men wouldn't even think about taking on an unmarried mother. Odo is different just because he is a pastor."

At the house, Lili had to ring the doorbell because her key was in her coat. Her mother came to the door, saw her face, and said: "What on earth has happened?"

Lili and Thorsten stepped inside. Lili said: "The police raided the church, and I went to warn Karolin and found her kissing Odo!" She burst into fresh tears.

Carla closed the front door. "You mean *really* kissing him?"

"Yes, like mad!" said Lili.

"Come into the kitchen and have a cup of coffee, both of you."

As soon as they had told their story, Lili's father left, intending to do what he could to ensure that Karolin did not spend the night in jail. Carla then pointed out that Thorsten probably ought to go home in case his parents had heard of the raid and were worrying about him. Lili saw him to the door and he kissed her on the lips, briefly but delightfully, before walking away.

Then the three women were alone in the kitchen: Lili, Carla, and Grandmother Maud. Alice, now three years old, was asleep upstairs.

Carla said to Lili: "Don't be too hard on Karolin."

"Why not?" said Lili. "She's betrayed Walli!"

"It's been four years—"

"Grandmother waited four years for Grandfather Walter," Lili said. "And she didn't even have a baby!"

"That's true," said Maud. "Although I thought about Gus Dewar."

"Woody's father?" said Carla, surprised. "I didn't know that."

"Walter was tempted, too," Maud went on, with the cheerful indiscretion characteristic of people too old to be embarrassed. "By Monika von der Helbard. But nothing happened."

The way she made light of this annoyed Lili. "It's easy for you, Grandmother," she said. "Everything is so far in the past."

Carla said: "I'm sad about this, Lili, but I don't see how we can be angry. Walli may never come home, and Karolin may never leave East Germany. Can we really expect her to spend her life waiting for someone she may never see again?"

"I thought that was what she was going to do. I thought she was committed." Though Lili realized she could not remember Karolin actually saying it.

"I think she's already waited a long time."

"Is four years a long time?"

"It's long enough for a young woman to start asking herself whether she wants to sacrifice her life to a memory."

Both Carla and Maud sympathized with Karolin, Lili realized with dismay.

They discussed the matter until midnight, when Werner came home, accompanied by Karolin—and Odo.

Werner said: "Two of the boys managed to get into fights with police officers, but other than them nobody went to jail, I'm happy to say. However, the youth club is closed."

Everyone sat at the kitchen table. Odo sat beside Karolin. To Lili's horror, he held Karolin's hand in front of everybody. He said: "Lili, I'm sorry you found out by accident just when we were getting ready to tell you."

"Tell me what?" she said aggressively, though she thought grimly that she could guess.

"We love each other," Odo said. "I expect this is hard for you to accept, and we're sorry about that. But we have thought and prayed about it."

"Prayed?" Lili said incredulously. "I've never known Karolin to pray for anything!"

"People change."

Weak women change to please men, Lili thought. But before she could say it her mother spoke up. "This is hard for us all, Odo. Walli loves Karolin and the baby he's never seen. We know that from his letters. And we could guess it from Plum Nellie's songs: so many of them are about separation and loss."

Karolin said: "If you wish, I will leave this house to-night."

Carla shook her head. "It's hard for us, but it's harder for you, Karolin. I can't ask a normal young woman to dedicate her life to someone she may never see again—even though that person is our beloved son. Werner and I have talked about this. We knew it was coming sooner or later."

Lili was shocked. Her parents had foreseen this! They had said nothing to her. How could they be so heartless?

Or were they just more sensible? She did not want to believe that.

Odo said: "We want to get married."

Lili stood up. "No!" she cried.

Odo said: "And we hope you will all give us your blessing: Maud, Werner, Carla, and most of all Lili, who has been such a great friend to Karolin through her years of trouble."

"Go to hell," said Lili, and she left the room.

. . .

Dave Williams pushed his grandmother around Parliament Square in her wheelchair, followed by a flock of photographers. Plum Nellie's publicist had tipped off the newspapers, so Dave and Ethel had expected the cameras, and they posed cooperatively for ten minutes. Then Dave said: "Thank you, gentlemen," and turned into the car park of the Palace of Westminster. He paused at the Peers' Entrance, waved for one more shot, then pushed the chair into the House of Lords.

The usher said: "Good afternoon, m'lady."

Grandmam Ethel, Baroness Leckwith, had lung cancer. She was taking powerful drugs to control the pain, but her mind was clear. She could still walk a little way, though she quickly became breathless. She had every reason to retire from active politics. But today the Lords were discussing the Sexual Offences Bill 1967.

Ethel felt strongly about this partly because of her gay friend Robert. To Dave's surprise his father, whom Dave considered an old stick-in-the-mud, was also passionately in favor of reforming the law. Apparently Lloyd had witnessed the Nazi persecution of homosexuals and had never forgotten it, although he refused to discuss the details.

Ethel would not speak in the debate—she was too ill for that—but she was determined to vote. And when Eth Leckwith was determined, there was no stopping her.

Dave pushed her along the entrance hall, which was a cloakroom, each coat hook having a pink ribbon loop on which members were supposed to hang their swords. The House of Lords did not even pretend to move with the times.

It was a crime in Britain for a man to have sex with another man, and every year hundreds of men who did so were prosecuted, jailed, and—worst of all—humiliated in the newspapers. The bill under discussion today would legalize homosexual acts by consenting adults in private.

The issue was controversial, and the bill was unpopular with much of the general public; but the tide was running in favor of reform. The Church of England had decided not to oppose a change in the law. They still said homosexuality was a sin, but they agreed it should not be a crime. The bill had a good chance, but its supporters feared a last-minute backlash—hence Ethel's determination to vote.

Ethel asked Dave: "Why are you so keen to be the one who takes me to this debate? You've never shown much interest in politics."

"Our drummer, Lew, is gay," Dave said, using the American word. "I was with him once in a pub called the Golden Horn when the police raided it. I was so disgusted with the way the cops behaved that I've been looking, ever since, for a way to show that I'm on the side of the homosexuals."

"Good for you," Ethel said; then she added, with the waspishness characteristic of her later years: "I'm glad to see that the crusading spirit of your forebears hasn't been entirely obliterated by rock and roll."

Plum Nellie was more successful than ever. They had released a "concept album" called *For Your Pleasure Tonight* that pretended to be a recording of a show featuring groups of different kinds: old-time music hall, folk, blues, swing, gospel, Motown—all in fact Plum Nellie. It was selling millions all over the world.

A policeman helped Dave carry the wheelchair up a flight of steps. Dave thanked him, wondering whether he had ever raided a gay pub. They reached the Peers' Lobby and Dave wheeled Ethel as far as the threshold of the debating chamber.

Ethel had planned this and got the agreement of the leader of the Lords to her appearing in her wheelchair. But Dave himself was not allowed to push her into the chamber, so they waited for one of her friends to notice her and take over.

The debate was already under way, with the peers sitting on red leather benches either side of a room whose decorations seemed ludicrously rich, like a palace in a Disney movie.

A peer was speaking, and Dave listened. "The bill is a queers' charter and will encourage that most loathsome creature, the male prostitute," the man said pompously. "It will increase the temptations that lie in the path of adolescents." That was strange, Dave thought. Did this guy believe that all men were queer, but most simply resisted temptation? "It is not that I lack compassion for the unfortunate homosexual—I am also not lacking in compassion for those who are dragged into his net."

Dragged into his net? What a lot of rubbish, Dave thought.

A man got up from the Labour side and took the handles of Ethel's wheelchair. Dave left the chamber and went up a staircase to the spectators' gallery.

When he got there another peer was speaking. "In one of the more popular Sunday newspapers last week there appeared an account, which some of Your Lordships may have seen, of a homosexual wedding in a Continental country." Dave had read this story in the *News of the World.* "I think the newspaper concerned is to be congratulated on highlighting this very nasty happening." How could a wedding be a nasty happening? "I only hope that, if this bill becomes law, the most vigilant eye will be kept on practices of this kind. I do not think these things could happen in this country, but it is possible."

Dave thought: Where do they dig up these dinosaurs?

Fortunately not all the peers were this bad. A formidable-looking woman with silver hair got up. Dave had met her at his mother's house: her name was Dora Gaitskell. She said: "As a society, we gloss over many perversions between men and women in private. The law, and society, are very tolerant towards these and turn a blind eye." Dave was astonished. What did she know about perversions between men and women? "Those men who are born, conditioned, or tempted irrevocably into homosexuality should have extended to them the same degree of tolerance as is extended to any other so-called perversion between men and women." Good for you, Dora, thought Dave.

But Dave's favorite was another white-haired old woman, this one with a twinkle in her eye. She, too, had been a guest at the house in Great Peter Street: her name was Barbara Wootton. After one of the men had gone on at great length about sodomy, she struck a note of irony. "I ask myself: What are the opponents of this bill afraid of?" she said. "They cannot be afraid that disgusting practices will be thrown upon their attention, because these acts are legalized only if they are performed in private. They cannot be afraid that there will be a corruption of youth, because these acts will be legalized only if they are performed by consenting adults. I can only suppose that the opponents of the bill will be afraid that their imagination will be tormented by visions of what will be going on elsewhere." The clear implication was that men who tried to keep homosexuality criminal did so as a way of policing their own fantasy life, and Dave laughed out loud—and was quickly told to keep quiet by an usher.

The vote was taken at half past six. It seemed to Dave that more people had spoken against than for the bill. The process of voting took an inordinately long time. Instead of putting slips of paper in a box, or pressing buttons, the peers had to get up and leave the chamber, passing through one of two lobbies, for either the "Contents" or the "Not Contents." Ethel's wheelchair was pushed into the "Content" lobby by another peer.

The bill was passed by one hundred eleven votes to forty-eight. Dave wanted to cheer, but it would have seemed wrong, like applauding in church.

Dave met Ethel at the entrance to the chamber and took

over the wheelchair from one of her friends. She looked triumphant but exhausted, and he could not help wondering how long she had to live.

What a life she had had, he thought as he pushed her through the ornate corridors toward the exit. His own transformation from class dunce to pop star was nothing by comparison with her journey, from a two-bedroom cottage beside the slag heap in Aberowen all the way to the gilded debating chamber of the House of Lords. And she had transformed her country as well as herself. She had fought and won political battles—for votes for women, for welfare, for free health care, for girls' education, and now freedom for the persecuted minority of homosexual men. Dave had written songs that were loved around the world, but that seemed nothing compared with what his grandmother had achieved.

An elderly man walking with two canes stopped them in a paneled hallway. His air of decrepit elegance rang a bell, and Dave recalled seeing him once before, here in the House of Lords, on the day Ethel had become a baroness, about five years ago. The man said amiably: "Well, Ethel, I see you got your buggery bill passed. Congratulations."

"Thank you, Fitz," she said.

Dave remembered, now. This was Earl Fitzherbert, who had once owned a big house in Aberowen called Tŷ Gwyn, now the College of Further Education.

"I'm sorry to hear you've been ill, my dear," said Fitz. He seemed fond of her.

"I won't mince words with you," Ethel said. "I haven't got long to go. You'll probably never see me again."

"That makes me terribly sad." To Dave's surprise, tears rolled down the old earl's wrinkled face, and he pulled a large white handkerchief from his breast pocket to wipe his eyes. And now Dave recalled that the previous time he had witnessed a meeting between them he had been struck by an undercurrent of intense emotion, barely controlled.

"I'm glad I knew you, Fitz," Ethel said, in a tone that suggested he might have assumed the opposite.

"Are you?" Fitz said. Then to Dave's astonishment he added: "I never loved anyone the way I loved you."

"I feel the same," she said, doubling Dave's amazement. "I can say it now that my dear Bernie's gone. He was my soul mate, but you were something else."

"I'm so glad."

"I have only one regret," Ethel said.

"I know what it is," said Fitz. "The boy."

"Yes. If I have a dying wish, it is that you will shake his hand."

Dave wondered who "the boy" might be. Not himself, presumably.

The earl said: "I knew you would ask me that."

"Please, Fitz."

He nodded. "At my age, I ought to be able to admit when I've been wrong."

"Thank you," she said. "Knowing that, I can die happy."

"I hope there's an afterlife," he said.

"I have no idea," said Ethel. "Good-bye, Fitz."

The old man bent over the wheelchair, with difficulty, and kissed her lips. He pulled himself upright again and said: "Farewell, Ethel."

Dave pushed the wheelchair away.

After a minute he said: "That was Earl Fitzherbert, wasn't it?"

"Yes," said Ethel. "He's your grandfather."

.   .   .

The girls were Walli's only problem.

Young, pretty, and sexy in a wholesome way that seemed to him uniquely American, they trooped through his front door in dozens, all eager to have sex with him. The fact that he was remaining faithful to his girlfriend in East Berlin seemed only to make him more desirable.

"Buy a house," Dave had said to the members of the group. "Then, when the bubble bursts and nobody wants Plum Nellie anymore, at least you'll have somewhere to live."

Walli was beginning to realize that Dave was very smart. Since he had set up the two companies, Nellie Records and Plum Publishing, the group was making a lot more money. Walli was still not the millionaire people thought he was, though he would be when the royalties started to come in from *For Your Pleasure Tonight*. Meanwhile, he could at last afford to buy a home of his own.

Early in 1967 he bought a bow-fronted Victorian house in San Francisco, on Haight Street near the corner of Ashbury.

In this neighborhood, property values had been blighted by a years-long battle over a proposed freeway that was never built. Low rents drew students and other young people, who created a laid-back ambience that then attracted musicians and actors. Members of the Grateful Dead and Jefferson Airplane lived there. It was common to see rock stars, and Walli could walk around almost like a normal person.

The Dewars, the only people Walli knew in San Francisco, expected him to gut the house and modernize it; but he thought the old-fashioned coffered ceilings and wood paneling were cool, and he kept everything, though he had it all painted white.

He installed two luxurious bathrooms and a custom kitchen with a dishwashing machine. He shopped for a television set and a state-of-the-art record player. Otherwise he bought little normal furniture. He put rugs and cushions on the polished wood floors, mattresses and coat rails in the bedrooms. He had no chairs other than six stools of the kind used by guitarists in recording studios.

Both Cameron and Beep Dewar were students at Berkeley, the San Francisco branch of the University of California. Cam was a weirdo who dressed like a middle-aged man and was more conservative than Barry Goldwater. But Beep was cool, and she introduced Walli to her friends, some of whom lived in his neighborhood.

Walli lived here when he was not touring with the group or recording in London. While here, he spent most of his time playing the guitar. To play as apparently effortlessly as he did onstage required a high order of skill, and he never let a day go by without practicing for at least a couple of hours. After that he would work on songs: trying out chords, putting together fragments of melody, struggling to decide which were wonderful and which merely tuneful.

He wrote to Karolin once a week. It was difficult to think of things to say. It seemed unkind to tell her about movies and concerts and restaurants of the kind that she could never enjoy.

With Werner's help he had arranged to send monthly payments so that Karolin could support herself and Alice. A modest allowance in a foreign currency bought a lot in East Germany.

Karolin wrote back once a month. She had learned guitar and formed a duo with Lili. They did protest songs and circulated tapes of their music. Otherwise her life seemed empty in comparison with his own, and most of her news was about Alice.

Like most people in the neighborhood, Walli did not lock his doors. Friends and strangers wandered in and out. He kept his favorite guitars in a locked room at the top of the house: otherwise he owned little worth stealing. Once a week, a local store filled his refrigerator and food cupboard with groceries. Guests helped themselves, and when the food ran out Walli went to restaurants.

In the evenings he saw movies and plays, went to hear bands, or hung out with other musicians, drinking beer and smoking marijuana, in their homes or his own. There was a lot to see on the street: impromptu gigs, street theater, and performance art events that people called "happenings." In the summer of 1967 the neighborhood suddenly became famous as the world center of the hippie movement. When schools and colleges closed for the vacation, youngsters from all over America hitchhiked to San Francisco and headed for the corner of Haight and Ashbury. The police decided to turn a blind eye to the widespread use of marijuana and LSD, and to people having sex more or less publicly in Buena Vista Park. And all the girls were taking the contraceptive pill.

The girls were Walli's only problem.

Tammy and Lisa were typical. They came from Dallas, Texas, on a Greyhound bus. Tammy was blond; Lisa was Hispanic; both were eighteen. They had planned just to ask for Walli's autograph and had been amazed to find his door open and him sitting on a giant cushion on the floor playing an acoustic guitar.

After their bus ride they needed a shower, they said, and he told them to go right ahead. They had showered together without closing the bathroom door, as Walli discovered in an absentminded moment, thinking about harmonies, when he went in there to pee. Was it coincidence that at that very moment Tammy was soaping Lisa's olive-skinned little breasts with her white hands?

Walli left and used the other bathroom, but it took all his strength.

The postman brought his mail, including letters forwarded from London by Mark Batchelor, Plum Nellie's manager. One was addressed in Karolin's handwriting and had an East German stamp. Walli set it aside to read later.

It was a normal day in Haight-Ashbury. A musician friend strolled in and they started writing a song together, but it came to nothing. Dave Williams and Beep Dewar stopped by: Dave was living at her parents' house and looking for a property to buy. A dealer called Jesus dropped off a pound of marijuana and Walli hid most of it in the cabinet of a guitar amplifier. He did not mind sharing; but, if he did not ration it, all of it would be gone by nightfall.

In the evening Walli went to a diner with a few friends, taking Tammy and Lisa. Four years after leaving the Soviet bloc he still marveled at the abundance of food in America: big steaks, juicy hamburgers, piles of French fries, mountainous crisp salads, thick milk shakes, all for next to nothing, and coffee with free refills! Not that such food was expensive in East Germany—it just did not exist there at all. Butchers were always short of the best cuts of meat, and restaurants grumpily served mean portions of unappealing food. Walli had never seen a milk shake there.

Over dinner Walli learned that Lisa's father was a doctor serving the Mexican community in Dallas, and that she hoped to study medicine and follow in his footsteps. Tammy's family ran a profitable gas station, but her brothers would take it over, and she was going to art school to study fashion design with the aim of opening a clothing store. They were ordinary girls, but this was 1967 and they were taking the pill and they wanted to get laid.

It was a warm night. After eating they all went to the park. They sat down with a group of people singing gospel songs. Walli joined in, and no one recognized him in the dark. Tammy was tired after the bus journey, and she lay down with her head in his lap. He stroked her long blond hair and she went to sleep.

A little after midnight, people began to leave. Walli strolled home, not noticing until he got there that Tammy and Lisa were still with him. "Do you to have a place to spend the night?" he said.

Tammy said in her Texas accent: "We could sleep in the park."

Walli said: "You can crash on my floor if you want."

Lisa said: "Would you like to sleep with one of us?"

Tammy said: "Or both?"

Walli smiled. "No, I have a girlfriend, Karolin, back in Berlin."

"Is that true?" said Lisa. "I read it in the paper, but . . ."

"It's true."

"And you have a baby daughter?"

"She's three years old, now. Her name is Alice."

"But no one still believes in fidelity, and all that crap, do they? Especially not in San Francisco. All you need is love, right?"

"Good night, girls."

He went upstairs to the bedroom he normally used and got undressed. He could hear the girls moving around downstairs. It was just after one thirty when he got into bed—an early night for a musician.

This was the time of day when he liked to read and re-read Karolin's letters. It soothed him to think about her, and he often fell asleep imagining that she was in his arms. He settled on his mattress, sitting upright with his back to a pillow propped against the wall, and pulled the sheet up under his chin. Then he opened the envelope.

He read:

Dear Walli—

That was strange. She normally wrote "My beloved Walli" or "My love."

I know this letter will bring you pain and distress, and for that I am so sorry that my heart is almost breaking.

What on earth could have happened? He read on fast.

You left four years ago and there is no hope of us being together in the foreseeable future. I'm weak, and I cannot face a lifetime alone.

She was ending their affair—she was breaking up with him. It was the last thing he expected.

I have met someone, a good man who loves me.

She had a boyfriend! This was even worse. She had betrayed Walli. He began to feel angry. Lisa had been right: no one still believed in fidelity and all that crap.

Odo is the pastor of St. Gertrud's Church in Berlin-Mitte.

Walli said aloud: "A fucking clergyman!"

He will love and care for my baby.

"She calls her 'my baby'—but Alice is my baby too!"

We are going to get married. Your parents are upset but they have not ceased to be kind to me, as they always are to everyone. Even your sister Lili tries to understand, though she finds it difficult.

I bet she does, thought Walli. Lili would hold out longest.

You made me happy for a short while, and you gave me my precious Alice, and for that I will always love you.

Walli felt hot tears on his cheeks.

I hope that in years to come you will find it in your heart to forgive me and Odo, and that one day we may meet as friends, perhaps when we are old and gray.

"In hell, maybe," said Walli.

> *With love,*
> *Karolin*

The door opened and Tammy and Lisa came in.
Walli's vision was blurred with tears, but it seemed to him that they were both naked.

Lisa said: "What's the matter?"

Tammy said: "Why are you crying?"

Walli said: "Karolin broke up with me. She's going to marry the pastor."

Tammy said: "I'm so sorry," and Lisa said: "Poor you."

Walli was ashamed of his tears but he could not stop them. He threw the letter down, rolled sideways, and pulled the sheet over his head.

They got into bed either side of him. He opened his eyes. Tammy, facing him, touched the tears on his face with a gentle finger. Behind him, Lisa pressed her warm body against his back.

He managed to say: "I don't want this."

Tammy said: "You shouldn't be alone, feeling so sad. We'll just cuddle you. Close your eyes."

He yielded, and shut his eyes. Slowly his anguish turned to numbness. His mind emptied and he drifted into a doze.

When he woke up, Tammy was kissing his mouth and Lisa was sucking his penis.

He made love to each of them in turn. Tammy was gentle and sweet; Lisa was energetic and passionate. He was grateful to them for consoling him in his grief.

But, for all that, no matter how he tried, he could not come.

CHAPTER FORTY

The mine dog was getting tired.

He was a thin Vietnamese boy wearing nothing but cotton shorts. He had to be about thirteen years old, Jasper Murray guessed. The boy had been so foolish as to go into the jungle to gather nuts this morning just when a platoon of D Company—"Desperadoes"—was setting out on its mission.

His hands were tied behind his back and attached by a string, thirty yards long, to a corporal's web belt. The boy walked along the path ahead of the company. But it had been a long morning, and he was still a kid, and now his steps were faltering, causing the men to catch up with him inadvertently. When that happened, Sergeant Smithy threw a bullet at him, hitting him on the head or back, and the kid would cry out and go faster.

The jungle trails were mined and booby-trapped by the resistance, the Vietcong insurgents, usually called Charlie. The mines were all improvised: reloaded American artillery shells; old U.S. Army Bouncing Betties; dud bombs turned into real ones; even French army pressure mines left over from the fifties.

Using a Vietnamese peasant as a mine dog was not very unusual, although no one would admit it back in the States. Sometimes the slants knew which stretches of the trail had been mined. Other times they were somehow able to see warning signs invisible to the grunts. And if the mine dog failed to spot the trap he would get killed instead of them. No downside.

Jasper was disgusted, but he had seen worse things in the six months he had so far spent in Vietnam. In Jasper's opinion, men of all nations were capable of savage cruelty, especially when they were scared. He knew that the British army had committed gruesome atrocities in Kenya: his father had been there, and now, whenever Kenya was mentioned, Dad looked pale and muttered something feeble about brutality on both sides.

However, D Company was special.

It was part of Tiger Force, the Special Forces unit of the 101st Airborne Division. Supreme commander General William Westmoreland proudly called them "my fire brigade." Instead of regular uniforms they wore tiger-striped battle dress without insignia. They were allowed to grow beards and carry handguns openly. Their specialty was pacification.

Jasper had joined D Company a week ago. The assignment was probably a bureaucratic error: he did not particularly belong here, but Tiger Force mixed men from many different units and divisions. This was his first mission with them. In this platoon there were twenty-five men, about half black and half white.

They did not know Jasper was British. Most GIs had never met a Brit, and he had got bored with being an object of curiosity. He had changed his accent, and to them he sounded Canadian, or something. Never again did he want to explain that he did not actually know the Beatles.

Their mission today was to "cleanse" a village.

They were in Quang Ngai Province, in the northern part of South Vietnam known to the army as I Corps Tactical Zone, or just "the northern region." Like about half of South Vietnam, it was ruled not by the regime in Saigon but by the Vietcong guerrillas, who organized village government and even collected taxes.

"The Vietnamese people just don't understand the American way," said the man walking alongside Jasper. He was Neville, a tall Texan with an ironic sense of humor. "When the Vietcong took over this region there was a lot of uncultivated land, owned by rich people in Saigon who couldn't be bothered to farm it, so Charlie gave it to the peasants. Then, when we started to win territory back, the Saigon government returned the land to the original owners. Now the peasants are mad at us, can you believe that? They don't get the concept of private property. That tells you how dumb they are."

Corporal John Donellan, a black soldier known as Donny, overheard and said: "You're just a fucking Communist, Neville."

"I am not—I voted for Goldwater," Neville said mildly. "He promised to keep uppity Negroes in their place."

The others within earshot laughed: this kind of banter was enjoyed by soldiers. It helped them deal with their fear.

Jasper, too, liked Neville's subversive sarcasm. But during their first rest stop this morning he had noticed Neville rolling a joint, and sprinkling into the marijuana some of the unrefined heroin they called brown sugar. If Neville was not a junkie, he soon would be.

Guerrilla fighters moved among the people as fish swam in the sea, according to the Chinese Communist leader Chairman Mao. General Westmoreland's strategy for defeating the Vietcong fish was to take away their sea. Three hundred thousand peasants in Quang Ngai were being rounded up and moved to sixty-eight fortified concentration camps, to leave the landscape deserted but for the Vietcong.

Except that it was not working. As Neville said: "These people! They act as if we have no right to come to their country and order them to leave their homes and their fields and go live in a prison camp. What is wrong with them?" Many peasants evaded the roundup and stayed close to their land. Others went, then escaped from the crowded, unsanitary camps and came home. Either way, they were now legitimate targets in the eyes of the army. "If there are people who are out there—and not in the camps—they're pink as far as we're concerned," General Westmoreland said. "They're Communist sympathizers." The lieutenant briefing the platoon had put it even more clearly. "There are no friendlies," he had said. "Do you hear me? There are no friendlies. No one is supposed to be here. Shoot anything that moves."

The target this morning was a village that had been evacuated and then reoccupied. Their job was to clean it out and level it.

First they had to find it. Navigation was difficult in the jungle. Landmarks were few and visibility was restricted.

And Charlie could be anywhere, maybe a yard away. The knowledge kept them all on edge. Jasper had learned to look *through* the foliage, from one layer to the next, scanning for a color, a shape, or a texture that did not fit. It was difficult to stay vigilant when you were tired, dripping with sweat, and pestered by bugs, but men who let their guard down at the wrong moment got killed.

There were different kinds of jungle, too. Bamboo thickets and elephant grass were impassable in practice, though the army high command refused to admit it. Canopy forests were easier, for the dim light restricted the undergrowth. Rubber plantations were best: the trees in neat rows, the undergrowth kept down, usable roads. Today Jasper was in a mixed forest, with banyan, mangrove, and jackfruit trees, the green backdrop splashed with the bright colors of tropical forest flowers, orchids and arums and chrysanthemums. Hell has never looked so pretty, Jasper was thinking when the bomb went off.

He was deafened by a bang and thrown to the ground. His shock did not last long. He rolled away from the trail, stopped in the flimsy shelter of a bush, deployed his M16 rifle, and looked around.

At the head of the line of men, five bodies lay on the ground. None was moving. Jasper had seen death in combat several times since arriving in Vietnam, but he would never get used to it. A moment ago there had been five walking, talking human beings, men who had told him a joke or bought him a drink or given him a hand scrambling over a deadfall; and now there was just a mess of mangled bloody chunks of meat on the ground.

He could guess what had happened. Someone had stepped on a hidden pressure mine. Why had the mine dog not set it off? The boy must have spotted it and had the presence of mind to keep quiet and walk around it. Now he was nowhere to be seen. He had got the better of his captors in the end.

Another of the men came to the same conclusion. He was Mad Jack Baxter, a tall Midwesterner with a black beard. Screaming, "That fucking slant led us into it!" he ran forward, firing his rifle, sending rounds uselessly into the greenery, wasting ammunition. "I'll kill the motherfucker!"

he screamed. Then his twenty-round magazine was empty and he stopped.

They were all angry, but others were more sensible. Sergeant Smithy was already on the radio, calling in medevac. Corporal Donny was kneeling down, optimistically looking for a pulse in one of the prone bodies. Jasper saw that a chopper could not possibly land on this narrow trail. He jumped up and yelled to Smithy: "I'll look for a clearing!"

Smithy nodded. "McCain and Frazer, go with Murray," he shouted.

Jasper checked that he had a couple of Willie Petes, white phosphorus grenades, then struck out from the path, followed by the other two.

He looked for signs that the terrain might be turning rocky or sandy so that the vegetation might thin out and form a clearing. He was careful to note what landmarks he could, so as not to get lost. After a couple of minutes they emerged from the jungle onto the banked edge of a rice paddy.

At the far side of the field Jasper saw three or four figures wearing the thin cotton pajamas that were the everyday clothing of peasants. Before he could count them they had spotted him and melted into the jungle.

He wondered whether they were from the target village. If so, he had inadvertently warned them of the company's approach. Well, that was too bad: saving the injured took priority.

McCain and Frazer ran around the edge of the paddy, securing the perimeter. Jasper exploded a Willie Pete. It set fire to the rice, but the shoots were green and the flames soon went out. However, a column of thick white phosphorus smoke rose into the air, signaling his location.

Jasper looked around. Charlie knew that when the Americans were preoccupied with their dead and wounded it was a good time to attack them. Jasper held his M16 in two hands and scanned the jungle, ready to drop to the ground and shoot back if they were fired on. McCain and Frazer were doing the same, he saw. In all probability none of them would get the chance to duck. A sniper in the trees would have all the time in the world to draw a bead and fire an accurate deadly shot. It was always like that in this fucking war, Jasper thought. Charlie sees us but we don't see him. He hits and runs. Next day the sniper is pulling up weeds in a rice paddy and pretending to be a simple farmer who wouldn't know one end of a Kalashnikov from the other.

While he waited he thought of home. I could be working for the *Western Mail* now, he mused, sitting in a comfortable council chamber, dozing while an alderman drones on about the dangers of inadequate street lighting, instead of sweating in a rice paddy wondering if I'll take a bullet in the next few seconds.

He thought of his family and friends. His sister, Anna, had become a big shot in the book world after discovering a brilliant Russian dissident writer who went under the pseudonym of Ivan Kuznetsov. Evie Williams, who had once had an adolescent crush on Jasper, was now a movie star living in Los Angeles. Dave and Walli were millionaire rock stars. But Jasper was a foot soldier on the losing side in a cruel, stupid war a thousand miles from nowhere.

He wondered about the antiwar movement in the States. Were they making headway? Or were people still fooled by the propaganda that protesters were all Communists and drug addicts who wanted to undermine America? There would be a presidential election next year, 1968. Would Johnson be defeated? Would the winner stop the war?

The chopper landed and Jasper led the stretcher team through the jungle to the site of the explosion. He remembered his landmarks and found the platoon without difficulty. As soon as he arrived he could see, from the attitudes of the men standing around, that all the casualties were dead. The medevac team would be taking back five body bags.

The survivors were fuming. "That slant led us right into a goddamn trap," said Corporal Donny. "Ain't that some kind of fuckin' us around?"

"Fuckin'-A," said Mad Jack.

As always, Neville pretended to agree while implying the contrary. "Fool kid probably thought we might kill him when we had no more use for him," he said. "Too dumb to realize that Sergeant Smithy was planning to take him home to Philadelphia and put him through college." No one laughed.

Jasper told Smithy about the peasants he had seen in the

rice paddy. "Our village must be in that direction," Smithy said.

The company went with the bodies back to the chopper. After it took off, Donny deployed an M2 flamethrower to napalm the rice field, burning the entire crop in a few minutes. "Good work," said Smithy. "Now they know that if they come back they won't have anything to eat."

Jasper said to him: "I guess the chopper will have warned the villagers. We'll probably find the place empty." Or, Jasper thought, there could be an ambush; but he did not say that.

"Empty is okay," said Smithy. "We'll flatten the place anyway. And intelligence says there are tunnels. We have to find those and destroy them."

The Vietnamese had been digging tunnels since the start of their war against the French colonists in 1946. Beneath the jungle were literally hundreds of miles of passageways, ammunition dumps, dormitories, kitchens, workshops, and even hospitals. They were difficult to destroy. Water traps at regular intervals protected the inhabitants from being smoked out. Aerial bombing usually missed the target. The only way to damage them was from the inside.

But first the tunnel had to be found.

Sergeant Smithy led the platoon along a trail from the rice field into a small plantation of coconut palms. When they emerged from the palms they could see the village, about a hundred houses overlooking cultivated fields. There was no sign of life, but all the same they entered cautiously.

The place appeared deserted.

The men went from house to house, yelling: *"Didi mau!"* which was Vietnamese for "Get out!" Jasper looked into a house and saw the shrine that was the center of most Vietnamese homes: a display of candles, scrolls, incense pots, and tapestries dedicated to the family's ancestors. Then Corporal Donny deployed the flamethrower. The building had walls of woven bamboo daubed with mud, and a roof of palm leaves, and the napalm quickly set the whole place blazing.

Walking toward the center of the village, rifle at the ready, Jasper was surprised to hear a rhythmic thumping noise. He realized he was listening to the beat of a drum, probably a *mo,* a hollow wooden instrument struck with a stick. He guessed that someone had used the *mo* to warn the villagers to flee. But why was he still drumming?

With the others he followed the noise to the middle of the village. There they found a ceremonial pond with lotus flowers in front of a small *dinh,* the building that was the center of village life: temple, meeting hall, and schoolroom.

Inside, sitting cross-legged on a floor of beaten earth, they found a shaven-headed Buddhist monk drumming on a wooden fish about eighteen inches long. He saw them enter but did not stop.

The company had one soldier who spoke a little Vietnamese. He was a white American from Iowa, but they called him Slope. Now Smith said: "Slope, ask the slant where the tunnels are."

Slope shouted at the monk in Vietnamese. The man ignored him and continued drumming.

Smithy nodded to Mad Jack, who stepped forward and kicked the monk in the face with a heavyweight U.S. Army M-1966 jungle combat boot. The man fell backward, blood coming from his mouth and nose, and his drum and stick flew in opposite directions. Creepily, he made no sound.

Jasper swallowed. He had seen Vietcong guerrillas tortured for information: it was commonplace. Though he did not like it, he thought it was reasonable; they were men who wanted to kill him. Any man in his early twenties captured in this zone was probably one of the guerrillas or someone who actively supported them, and Jasper was reconciled to such men being tortured even when there was no proof they had ever fought against the Americans. This monk might have looked like a noncombatant, but Jasper had seen a ten-year-old girl throw a grenade into a parked helicopter.

Smithy picked up the monk and held him upright, facing the soldiers. His eyes were closed but he was breathing. Slope asked him the question again.

The monk made no response.

Mad Jack picked up the wooden fish, held it by its tail, and started to beat the monk with it. He hit the man on the head, shoulders, chest, groin, and knees, pausing every now and again for Slope to ask the question.

Jasper was really uncomfortable now. Just by watching this he was committing a war crime, but it was not so much the illegality that bothered him: he knew that when U.S. Army investigators looked into allegations of atrocities they always found insufficient evidence. He just did not see that this monk deserved it. Jasper was sickened, and turned away.

He did not blame the men. In every place, in every time, in every country there were men who would do this kind of thing, given the right circumstances. Jasper blamed the officers who knew what was happening and did nothing, the generals who lied to the press and the people back in Washington, and most of all the politicians who did not have the courage to stand up and say: "This is wrong."

A moment later Slope said: "Give it up, Jack, the fucker's dead."

Smithy said: "Shit." He let go of the monk, who fell lifeless to the ground. "We have to find the fucking tunnels."

Corporal Donny and four others came into the temple dragging three Vietnamese: a man and a woman of middle age, and a girl of about fifteen. "This family thought they could hide from us in the coconut shed," said Donny.

The three Vietnamese stared in horror at the body of the monk, his robes soaked in blood, his face a pulpy mass that hardly looked human.

Smithy said: "Tell them they're going to look like that unless they show us the tunnels."

Slope translated. The peasant man answered him. Slope said: "He says there are no tunnels in this village."

"Lying motherfucker," said Smithy.

Jack said: "Shall I . . . ?"

Smithy looked thoughtful. "Do the girl, Jack," he said. "Make the parents watch."

Jack looked eager. He ripped the girl's pajamas off, causing her to scream. He threw her to the ground. Her body was pale and slender. Donny held her down. Jack pulled out his penis, already half erect, and rubbed it to stiffen it.

Once again Jasper was horrified but not surprised. Rape was not commonplace, but it happened too frequently. Men occasionally reported it, usually when they were new to Vietnam. The army would investigate and find the allegations unsupported by evidence, meaning that all the other soldiers said they did not want any trouble and anyway they had seen nothing, and the matter would end there.

The older woman started talking, a stream of hysterical, pleading words. Slope said: "She says the girl is a virgin and really only a child."

"She's no child," said Smithy. "Look at the black fur on that little snatch."

"The mother swears by all the gods that there are no tunnels here. She says she doesn't support the Vietcong because she used to be the village moneylender but Charlie stopped her."

Smithy said: "Do it, Jack."

Jack lay on the girl, his big frame hiding most of her slight body. He seemed to be having difficulty penetrating. The other men shouted encouragement and made jokes. Jack gave a powerful thrust, and the girl screamed.

He pumped vigorously for a minute. The mother continued to plead, though Slope did not bother to translate. The father was silent, but Jasper saw tears streaming down his face. Jack grunted a couple of times, then stopped and withdrew. There was blood on the girl's thighs, bright red on her ivory skin.

Smithy said: "Who's next?"

"I'll do her," said Donny, unzipping.

Jasper left the temple.

This was not normal. Any pretext of getting the father to talk was now redundant: if he had known anything he would have revealed it before the rape began. Jasper had run out of excuses for the men of this platoon. They were out of control. General Westmoreland had created a monster and deliberately let it loose. They were beyond sanity. They were not even animals; they were worse than that; they were mad, evil fiends.

Neville followed him out. "Remember, Jasper," he said, "this is necessary to win the hearts and minds of the Vietnamese people."

Jasper knew that this was Neville's way of bearing the unbearable, but all the same he could not stomach Neville's humor at this moment. "Why don't you shut the fuck up?" he said, and walked away.

He was not the only one sickened by the scene in the temple. About half the platoon was out here, watching the village burn. A pall of black smoke lay over the village like a shroud. Jasper could hear the girl screaming in the temple, but after a while she stopped. Minutes later, he heard a shot, then another.

But what was he going to do about it? If he made a complaint, nothing would be done except that the army would find ways to punish him for stirring up trouble. But maybe, he thought, he should do it anyway. In any case, he vowed to go back to the States and spend the rest of his life exposing the liars and fools who made this kind of atrocity happen.

Then Donny came out of the temple and approached him. "Smithy wants you," he said.

Jasper followed the corporal back into the temple.

The girl lay splayed on the floor, a bullet hole in her forehead. Jasper also noticed a bleeding bite mark on her small breast.

The father was dead, too.

The mother was on her knees, begging, presumably, for mercy.

Smithy said: "You haven't lost your cherry yet, Murray."

He meant that Jasper had not yet committed a war crime.

Jasper knew what was coming.

Smithy said: "Shoot the old woman."

"Fuck you, Smithy," said Jasper. "Shoot her yourself."

Mad Jack raised his rifle and pressed the end of the barrel into the side of Jasper's neck.

Suddenly everyone was silent and still.

Smithy said: "Shoot the old woman, or Jack will shoot you."

Jasper had no doubt that Smithy was willing to give the order, and that Jack would obey. And he understood why. They needed him to be complicit. Once he had killed the woman he would be as guilty as any of them, and that would prevent him making trouble.

He looked around. All eyes were on him. No one protested or even looked uneasy. This was a rite they had performed before, he could tell. No doubt they did it with every newcomer to the company. Jasper wondered how many men had refused the order, and died. They would have been recorded as killed by enemy fire. No downside.

Smithy said: "Don't take too long making up your mind, we have work to do."

They were going to kill the woman anyway, Jasper knew.

He would not save her by refusing to do it himself. He would be sacrificing his own life for nothing.

Jack prodded him with the rifle.

Jasper raised his M16 and pointed it at the woman's forehead. She had dark brown eyes, he saw, and a little gray in her black hair. She did not move away from his gun, or even flinch, but continued pleading in words he could not comprehend.

Jasper touched the selector lever on the left side of the gun, moving it from "Safe" to "Semi," allowing it to fire a single round.

His hands were quite steady.

He pulled the trigger.

PART SIX

FLOWER

1968

J asper Murray spent two years in the army, one year of training in the USA and one of combat in Vietnam. He was discharged in January 1968 without ever having been wounded. He felt lucky.

Daisy Williams paid for him to fly to London to see his family. His sister, Anna, was now editorial director of Rowley Publishing. She had at last married Hank Remington, who was proving to be more enduring than most pop stars. The house in Great Peter Street was strangely quiet: the youngsters had all moved out, leaving only Lloyd and Daisy in residence. Lloyd was now a minister in the Labour government and therefore rarely home. Ethel died that January, and her funeral was held a few hours before Jasper was due to fly to New York.

The service was at the Calvary Gospel Hall in Aldgate, a small wooden shack where she had married Bernie Leckwith fifty years earlier, when her brother, Billy, and countless boys like him were fighting in the frozen mud trenches of the First World War.

The little chapel could seat a hundred or so worshippers, with another twenty or thirty standing at the back; but more than a thousand people turned up to say good-bye to Eth Leckwith.

The pastor moved the service outside and the police closed the street to cars. The speakers got up on chairs to address the crowd. Ethel's two children, Lloyd Williams and Millie

Avery, both in their fifties, stood at the front with most of her grandchildren and a handful of great-grandchildren.

Evie Williams read the parable of the Good Samaritan from the Gospel of Luke. Dave and Walli brought guitars and sang "I Miss Ya, Alicia." Half the cabinet were there. So was Earl Fitzherbert. Two buses from Aberowen brought a hundred Welsh voices to swell the hymn singing.

But most of the mourners were ordinary Londoners whose lives had been touched by Ethel. They stood in the January cold, the men holding their caps in their hands, the women shushing their children, the old people shivering in their cheap coats; and when the pastor prayed for Ethel to rest in peace, they all said amen.

George Jakes had a simple plan for 1968: Bobby Kennedy would become president and stop the war.

Not all of Bobby's aides were in favor. Dennis Wilson was happy for Bobby to remain simply the senator from New York. "People will say that we already have a Democratic president and Bobby should support Lyndon Johnson, not run against him," he said. "It's unheard-of."

They were at the National Press Club in Washington on January 30, 1968, waiting for Bobby, who was about to have breakfast with fifteen reporters.

"That's not true," George said. "Truman was opposed by Strom Thurmond and Henry Wallace."

"That was twenty years ago. Anyway, Bobby can't win the Democratic nomination."

"I think he'll be more popular than Johnson."

"Popularity has nothing to do with it," Wilson said. "Most of the convention delegates are controlled by the party's power brokers: labor leaders, state governors, and city mayors. Men like Daley." The mayor of Chicago, Richard Daley, was the worst kind of old-fashioned politician, ruthless and corrupt. "And the one thing Johnson is good at is infighting."

George shook his head in disgust. He was in politics to defy those old power structures, not give in to them. So was Bobby, in his heart. "Bobby will get such a bandwagon rolling in the country that the power brokers won't be able to ignore him."

"Haven't you talked to him about this?" Wilson was pretending to be incredulous. "Haven't you heard him say that people will see him as selfish and ambitious if he runs against a Democratic incumbent?"

"More people think he's the natural heir to his brother."

"When he spoke at Brooklyn College, the students had a placard that said: HAWK, DOVE — OR CHICKEN?"

This jibe had stung Bobby and dismayed George. But now George tried to put it in an optimistic light. "That means they want him to run!" he said. "They know that he's the only contender who can unite old and young, black and white, and rich and poor, and can get everyone working together to end the war and give blacks the justice they deserve."

Wilson's mouth twisted in a sneer but, before he could pour scorn on George's idealism, Bobby walked in, and everyone sat down to breakfast.

George's feelings about Lyndon Johnson had undergone a reverse. Johnson had started so well, passing the Civil Rights Act of 1964 and the Voting Rights Act of 1965, and planning the War on Poverty. But Johnson failed to understand foreign policy, as George's father, Greg, had forecast. All Johnson knew was that he did not want to be the president who lost Vietnam to the Communists. Consequently he was now hopelessly mired in a dirty war and dishonestly telling the American people he was winning it.

The words had also changed. When George was young, *black* was a vulgar term, *colored* was more dainty, and *Negro* was the polite word, used by the liberal *New York Times*, always with a capital letter, like *Jew*. Now *Negro* was considered condescending and *colored* evasive, and everyone talked about black people, the black community, black pride, and even black power. Black is beautiful, they said. George was not sure how much difference the words made.

He did not eat much breakfast: he was too busy making notes of the questions and Bobby's answers in preparation for a press release.

One of the journalists asked: "How do you feel about the pressure on you to run for president?"

George looked up from his notes and saw Bobby give a brief, humorless grin, then say: "Badly. Badly."

George tensed. Bobby was too damn honest sometimes.

The journalist said: "What do you think about Senator McCarthy's campaign?"

He was talking not about the notorious Senator Joe Mc-Carthy, who had hunted down Communists in the fifties, but a completely opposite character, Senator Eugene McCarthy, a liberal who was a poet as well as a politician. Two months ago Gene McCarthy had declared his intention of seeking the Democratic nomination, running as the antiwar candidate against Johnson. He had already been dismissed as a no-hoper by the press.

Now Bobby replied: "I think McCarthy's campaign is going to help Johnson." Bobby still would not call Lyndon the president. George's friend Skip Dickerson, who worked for Johnson, was scornful about this.

"Well, will you run?"

Bobby had lots of ways of not answering this question, a whole repertoire of evasive responses; but today he did not use any of them. "No," he said.

George dropped his pencil. Where the hell had that come from?

Bobby added: "In no conceivable circumstances would I run."

George wanted to say: *In that case, what the fuck are we all doing here?*

He noticed Dennis Wilson smirking.

He was tempted to walk out there and then. But he was too polite. He stayed in his seat and carried on making notes until the breakfast ended.

Back in Bobby's office on Capitol Hill, he wrote the press release, working like an automaton. He changed Bobby's quote to: "In no foreseeable circumstances would I run," but it made little difference.

Three staffers resigned from Bobby's team that afternoon. They had not come to Washington to work for a loser.

George was angry enough to quit, but he kept his mouth shut. He wanted to think. And he wanted to talk to Verena.

She was in town, and staying at his apartment as always. She now had her own closet in his bedroom, where she kept cold-weather clothes she never needed in Atlanta.

She was so upset she was near tears that evening. "He's all we have!" she said. "Do you know how many casualties we suffered in Vietnam last year?"

"Of course I do," said George. "Eighty thousand. I put it in one of Bobby's speeches, but he didn't use that part."

"Eighty thousand men killed or wounded or missing," Verena said. "It's awful—and now it will go on."

"Casualties will certainly be higher this year."

"Bobby has missed his shot at greatness. But why? Why did he do it?"

"I'm too angry to talk to him about it, but I believe he genuinely suspects his own motives. He's asking himself whether he wants this for the sake of his country, or his ego. He's tormented by such questions."

"Martin is too," Verena said. "He asks himself whether inner-city riots are his fault."

"But Dr. King keeps those doubts to himself. You have to, as a leader."

"Do you think Bobby planned this announcement?"

"No, he did it on impulse, I'm sure. That's one of the things that make him difficult to work for."

"What will you do?"

"Quit, probably. I'm still thinking about it."

They were getting changed to go out for a quiet dinner, and at the same time waiting for the news to come on TV. Tying a wide tie with bold stripes, George watched Verena in the mirror as she put on her underwear. Her body had changed in the five years since he had first seen her naked. She would be twenty-nine this year, and she no longer had the leggy charm of a foal. Instead she had gained poise and grace. George thought her mature look was even more beautiful. She had grown her hair in the bushy style called a "natural," which somehow emphasized the allure of her green eyes.

Now she sat in front of his shaving mirror to do her eye makeup. "If you quit, you could come to Atlanta and work for Martin," she said.

"No," said George. "Dr. King is a single-issue campaigner. Protesters protest, but politicians change the world."

"So what would you do?"

"Run for Congress, probably."

Verena put down her mascara brush and turned to look directly at him. "Wow," she said. "That came out of left field."

"I came to Washington to fight for civil rights, but the

injustice suffered by blacks isn't just a matter of rights," George said. He had been thinking about this a long time. "It's about housing and unemployment and the Vietnam War, where young black men are being killed every day. Black people's lives are affected even by events in Moscow and Peking, in the long term. A man like Dr. King inspires people, but you have to be an all-around politician in order to do any real good."

"I guess we need both," Verena said, and went back to doing her eyes.

George put on his best suit, which always made him feel better. He would have a martini later, maybe two. For seven years his life had been bound up inextricably with Robert Kennedy's. Maybe it was time to move on.

He said: "Does it ever occur to you that our relationship is peculiar?"

She laughed. "Of course! We live apart and meet every month or two for mad passionate sex. And we've being doing this for years!"

"A man might do what you do, and meet his mistress on business trips," George said. "Especially if he were married. That would be normal."

"I kind of like that idea," she said. "Meat and potatoes at home, and a little caviar when away."

"I'm glad to be the caviar, anyway."

She licked her lips. "Mm, salty."

George smiled. He would not think about Bobby anymore this evening, he decided.

The news came on TV, and George turned up the volume. He expected Bobby's announcement to be the first report, but there was a bigger story. During the New Year holiday that the Vietnamese called Tet, the Vietcong had launched a massive offensive. They had attacked five of the six largest cities, thirty-six provincial capitals, and sixty small towns. The assault had astounded the U.S. military by its size: no one had imagined the guerrillas capable of such a large-scale operation.

The Pentagon said the Vietcong forces had been repelled, but George did not believe it.

The newscaster said further major attacks were expected tomorrow.

George said to Verena: "I wonder what this will do for Gene McCarthy's campaign."

. . .

Beep Dewar persuaded Walli Franck to make a political speech.

At first he refused. He was a guitar player, and he feared he would make a fool of himself, like a senator singing pop songs in public. But he came from a political family, and his upbringing would not allow him to be apathetic. He remembered his parents' scorn for those West Germans who failed to protest about the Berlin Wall and the repressive East German government. They were as guilty as the Communists, his mother said. Now Walli realized that if he turned down a chance to speak a few words in favor of peace, he was as bad as Lyndon Johnson.

Plus he found Beep pretty much irresistible.

So he said yes.

She picked him up in Dave's red Dodge Charger and drove him to Gene McCarthy's San Francisco campaign headquarters, where he talked to a small army of young enthusiasts who had spent the day knocking on doors.

He felt nervous when he stood up in front of the audience. He had prepared his opening line. He spoke slowly, but informally. "Some people told me I should stay out of politics because I'm not American," he said in a conversational tone. Then he gave a little shrug and said: "But those people think it's okay if Americans go to Vietnam and kill people, so I guess it's not so bad for a German to come to San Francisco and just talk . . ."

To his surprise there was a howl of laughter and a round of applause. Maybe this would be all right.

Young people had been flocking to support McCarthy's campaign since the Tet Offensive. They were all neatly dressed. The boys were clean shaven and had midlength hair. The girls wore twinsets and saddle shoes. They had changed their appearance to persuade voters that McCarthy was the right president not just for hippies but for middle Americans too. Their slogan was: "Neat and clean for Gene."

Walli paused, making them wait, then he touched his shoulder-length blond locks and said: "Sorry about my hair."

They laughed and clapped again. This was just like show business, Walli realized. If you were a star, they would love you just for being more or less normal. At a Plum Nellie concert, the audience would cheer wildly at literally anything Walli or Dave said into the microphone. And a joke became ten times as funny when told by a celebrity.

"I'm not a politician. I can't make a political speech . . . but I guess you guys hear as many of those as you want."

"Right on!" shouted one of the boys, and they laughed again.

"But I have some experience, you know? I used to live in a Communist country. One day the police caught me singing a Chuck Berry song called 'Back in the USA.' So they smashed up my guitar."

The audience went quiet.

"It was my first guitar. In those days I had only one. Broke my guitar, broke my heart. So, you see, I know about Communism. I probably know more about it than Lyndon Johnson. I hate Communism." He raised his voice a little. "And I'm *still* against the war."

They broke out into cheers again.

"You know some people believe Jesus is coming back to earth one day. I don't know if that's true." They were uneasy with this, not sure how to take it. Then Walli said: "If he comes to America he'll probably be called a Communist."

He glanced sideways at Beep, who was laughing along with the rest. She was wearing a sweater and a short but respectable skirt. Her hair was cut in a neat bob. She was still sexy, though: she could not hide that.

"Jesus will probably be arrested by the FBI for un-American activities," Walli went on. "But he won't be surprised: it's pretty similar to what happened to him the first time he came to earth."

Walli had hardly planned beyond his first sentence, and now he was making it up as he went along, but they were delighted. However, he decided to quit while he was ahead.

He had prepared his ending. "I just came here to say one thing to you, and that's: Thank you. Thank you on behalf of millions of people all over the world who want to end this evil war. We appreciate the hard work you're doing here. Keep it up, and I hope to God you win. Good night."

He stepped back from the microphone. Beep came up to

him and took his arm, and together they left by the back door, with cheers and applause still ringing out. As soon as they were in Dave's car, Beep said: "My God—you were brilliant! You should run for president!"

He smiled and shrugged. "People are always pleased to find that a pop star is a human being. That's really all it is."

"But you spoke sincerely—and you were so witty!"

"Thanks."

"Maybe you get it from your mother. Didn't you tell me she was in politics?"

"Not really. There's no normal politics in East Germany. She was a city councilor, before the Communists cracked down. By the way, did you notice my accent?"

"Just a little bit."

"I was afraid of that." He was sensitive about his accent. People associated it with Nazis in war movies. He tried to speak like an American, but it was difficult.

"Actually it's charming," Beep said. "I wish Dave could have heard you."

"Where is he, anyway?"

"London, I think. I imagined you would know."

Walli shrugged. "I know he's taking care of business somewhere. He'll show up as soon as we need to write some songs, or make a film, or go on the road again. I thought you two were going to get married."

"We are. We just haven't gotten around to it yet, he's been so busy. And, you know, my parents are cool about us sharing a bedroom when he's here, so it's not like we're desperate to get away from them."

"Nice." They reached Haight-Ashbury and Beep stopped the car outside Walli's house. "You want a cup of coffee or something?" Walli did not know why he said that: it just came out.

"Sure." Beep turned off the throaty engine.

The house was empty. Tammy and Lisa had helped Walli deal with his grief about Karolin's engagement, and he would always be grateful to them, but they had been living a fantasy life that had lasted only as long as the vacation. When summer turned to fall they had left San Francisco and gone home to attend college, like most of the hippies of 1967.

While it lasted, it had been an idyllic time.

Walli put on the new Beatles album, *Magical Mystery*

Tour, then made coffee and rolled a joint. They sat on a giant cushion, Walli cross-legged, Beep with her feet tucked under her, and passed the roach. Soon Walli drifted into the mellow mood he liked so much. "I hate the Beatles," he said after a while. "They are so fucking good."

Beep giggled.

Walli said: "Weird lyrics."

"I know!"

"What does that line mean? 'Four of fish and finger pies.' It sounds like, you know, cannibalism."

"Dave explained that to me," Beep said. "In England they have seafood restaurants that sell fish in batter with French fries to go. They call it 'fish and chips.' And 'four of fish' means four pennies' worth."

"What about 'finger pie'?"

"Okay, that's when a boy puts his finger up a girl's, you know, vagina."

"And the connection?"

"It means that if you bought fish and chips for a girl she would let you finger her."

"Remember the days when that was daring?" Walli said nostalgically.

"Everything's different now, thank God," said Beep. "The old rules don't apply anymore. Love is free."

"Now it's oral sex on the first date."

"What do you like best?" Beep mused. "Giving oral sex, or receiving?"

"What a difficult question!" Walli was not sure he ought to be talking about this with his best friend's fiancée. "But I think I like receiving." He could not resist the temptation to add: "What about you?"

"I prefer giving," she said.

"Why?"

She hesitated. For a moment she looked guilty: perhaps she, too, was not sure they should be discussing this, despite her hippie talk about free love. She took a long draw on the joint and blew out smoke. Her face cleared, and she said: "Most boys are so bad at oral sex that receiving is never as exciting as it should be."

Walli took the joint from her. "If you could tell the boys of America what they need to know about giving oral sex, what would you say?"

She laughed. "Well, first of all, don't start licking right away."

"No?" Walli was surprised. "I thought it was all about licking."

"Not at all. You should be gentle at first. Just kiss it!"

Walli knew, then, that he was lost.

He looked down at Beep's legs. Her knees were pressed close together. Was that defensive? Or a sign of excitement?

Or both?

"No girl ever told me that," he said. He gave her back the joint.

He was feeling an irresistible rush of sexual excitement. Was she feeling it, too, or just playing a game with him?

She sucked the last of the smoke from the roach and dropped it in the ashtray. "Most girls are too shy to talk about what they like," she said. "The truth is that even a kiss can be too much, right at the start. In fact . . ." She gave him a direct look, and at that moment he knew that she, too, was lost. She said in a lower voice: "In fact, you can give her a thrill just by breathing on it."

"Oh, my God."

"Even better," she said, "is to breathe on it through the cotton of her underwear."

She moved slightly, parting her knees at last, and he saw that under her short skirt she was wearing white panties.

"That's amazing," he said hoarsely.

"Do you want to try it?" she said.

"Yes," said Walli. "Please."

. . .

When Jasper Murray returned to New York he went to see Mrs. Salzman. She got him an interview with Herb Gould, for a job as a researcher on the television news show *This Day*.

He was now a different proposition. Two years ago he had been a supplicant, a student journalist desperate for a job, someone to whom nobody owed anything. Now he was a veteran who had risked his life for the USA. He was older and wiser, and he was owed a debt, especially by men who had not fought. He got the job.

It was strange. He had forgotten what cold weather felt

like. His clothes bothered him: a suit and a white shirt with a button-down collar and a tie. His regular business oxford shoes were so light in weight he kept thinking he was barefoot. Walking from his apartment to the office he found himself scanning the sidewalk for concealed mines.

On the other hand, he was busy. The civilian world had few of the long, infuriating periods of inactivity that characterized army life: waiting for orders, waiting for transport, waiting for the enemy. From his first day back Jasper was making phone calls, checking files, looking up information in libraries, and conducting preinterviews.

In the office of *This Day* a mild shock awaited Jasper. Sam Cakebread, his old rival on the student newspaper, was now working for the program. He was a fully fledged reporter, not having had to take time out to fight a war. Irksomely, Jasper often had to do preparatory research for stories that Sam would then report on camera.

Jasper worked on fashion, crime, music, literature, and business. He researched a story about his sister's bestseller, *Frostbite,* and its pseudonymous author, speculating about which of the known Soviet dissidents might have written it, based on writing style and prison camp experiences; concluding it was probably someone nobody had heard of.

Then they decided to do a show about the astonishing Vietcong operation that had been dubbed the Tet Offensive.

Jasper was still angry about Vietnam. His rage burned low in his guts like a damped furnace, but he had forgotten nothing, least of all his vow to expose men who lied to the American people.

When the fighting began to die down, during the second week of February, Herb Gould told Sam Cakebread to plan a summing-up report, assessing how the offensive had changed the course of the war. Sam presented his preliminary conclusions to an editorial meeting attended by the whole team, including researchers.

Sam said the Tet Offensive had been a failure for the North Vietnamese in three ways. "First, Communist forces were given the general order: 'Move forward to achieve final victory.' We know this from documents found on captured enemy troops. Second: although fighting is still going on in Hue and Khe Sanh, the Vietcong have proved unable to hold a single city. And third, they have lost more than twenty thousand men, all for nothing."

Herb Gould looked around for comment.

Jasper was very junior in this group, but he was unable to keep quiet. "I have one question for Sam," he said.

"Go ahead, Jasper," said Herb.

"What fucking planet are you living on?"

There was a moment of shocked silence at his rudeness. Then Herb said mildly: "A lot of people are skeptical about this, Jasper, but explain why—maybe without the profanity?"

"Sam has just given us President Johnson's line on Tet. Since when did this program become a propaganda agency for the White House? Shouldn't we be challenging the government's view?"

Herb did not disagree. "How would you challenge it?"

"First, documents found on captured troops cannot be taken at face value. The written orders given to soldiers are not a reliable guide to the enemy's strategic objectives. I have a translation here: 'Display to the utmost your revolutionary heroism by surmounting all hardships and difficulties.' This is not strategy, it's a pep talk."

Herb said: "So what *was* their objective?"

"To demonstrate their power and reach, and thereby to demoralize the South Vietnam regime, our troops, and the American people. And they have succeeded."

Sam said: "They still didn't take any cities."

"They don't need to hold cities—they're already there. How do you think they got to the American embassy in Saigon? They didn't parachute in, they walked around the corner! They were probably living on the next block. They don't *take* cities because they already *have* them."

Herb said: "What about Sam's third point—their casualties?"

"No Pentagon figures on enemy casualties are trustworthy," Jasper said.

"It would be a big step, for our show to tell the American people that the government lies to us about this."

"Everyone from Lyndon Johnson to the grunt on patrol in the jungle is lying about this, because they all need high kill figures to justify what they're doing. But I know the truth because I was there. In Vietnam, any dead person counts as an enemy casualty. Throw a grenade into a bomb shelter, kill everyone inside—two young men, four women, an old man, and a baby—that's eight Vietcong dead, in the official report."

Herb was dubious. "How can we be sure this is true?"

"Ask any veteran," said Jasper.

"It's hard to credit."

Jasper was right and Herb knew it, but Herb was anxious about taking such a strong line. However, Jasper judged he was ready to be talked round. "Look," said Jasper. "It's now four years since we sent the first ground combat troops to South Vietnam. Throughout that period, the Pentagon has been reporting one victory after another, and *This Day* has been repeating their statements to the American people. If we've had four years of victory, how come the enemy can penetrate to the heart of the capital city and surround the U.S. embassy? Open your eyes, will you?"

Herb was thoughtful. "So, Jasper, if you're right, and Sam's wrong, what's our story?"

"That's easy," said Jasper. "The story is the administration's credibility after the Tet Offensive. Last November Vice President Humphrey told us we're winning. In December General Palmer said the Vietcong had been defeated. In January Secretary of Defense McNamara told us the North Vietnamese were losing their will to fight. General Westmoreland himself told reporters the Communists were unable to mount a major offensive. Then one morning the Vietcong attacked almost every major city and town in South Vietnam."

Sam said: "We've never questioned the president's honesty. No television show ever has."

Jasper said: "Now's the time. Is the president lying? Half of America is asking that."

Everyone looked at Herb. It was his decision. He was silent for a long moment. Then he said: "All right. That's the title of our report. 'Is the President Lying?' Let's do it."

. . .

Dave Williams got an early flight from New York to San Francisco and ate an American breakfast of pancakes with bacon in first class.

Life was good. Plum Nellie was successful and he would

never have to take another exam for the rest of his life. He loved Beep and he was going to marry her as soon as he could find the time.

He was the only member of the group who had not yet bought a house, but he hoped to do so today. It would be more than a house, though. His idea was to buy a place in the country, with some land, and build a recording studio. The whole group could live there while they were making an album, which took several months nowadays. Dave often recalled with a smile how they had recorded their first album in one day.

Dave was excited: he had never bought a house before. He was looking forward eagerly to seeing Beep, but he had decided to take care of business first, so that his time with her would be uninterrupted. He was met at the airport by his business manager, Mortimer Schulman. Dave had hired Morty to take care of his personal finances separately from those of the group. Morty was a middle-aged man in relaxed California clothes, a navy blazer with a blue shirt open at the neck. Because Dave was only twenty he often found that lawyers and accountants condescended to him and tried to give him instructions rather than information. Morty treated him as the boss, which he was, and laid out options, knowing that it was up to Dave himself to make the decisions.

They got into Morty's Cadillac, drove across the Bay Bridge, and headed north, passing the university town of Berkeley, where Beep was a student. As he drove, Mort said: "I received a proposition for you. It's not really my role, but I guess they thought I was the nearest thing to your personal agent."

"What proposition?"

"A television producer called Charlie Lacklow wants to talk to you about doing your own TV show."

Dave was surprised: he had not seen that one coming. "What kind of show?"

"You know, like *The Danny Kaye Show* or *The Dean Martin Show.*"

"No kidding?" This was big news. Sometimes it seemed to Dave that success was falling on him like rain: hit songs, platinum albums, sellout tours, successful movies—and now this.

There were a dozen or more variety shows on American

television every week, most of them headlined by a movie
star or a comic. The host would introduce a guest and chat
for a minute, then the guest would sing his or her latest hit,
or do a comedy routine. The group had appeared as guests
on many such programs, but Dave did not see how they
could fit into that format as hosts. "So it would be *The Plum
Nellie Show*?"

"No. *Dave Williams and Friends*. They don't want the
group, just you."

Dave was dubious. "That's flattering, but . . ."

"It's a major opportunity, if you ask me. Pop groups generally have a short life, but this is your chance to become an
all-around family entertainer—which is a role you can play
until you're seventy."

That struck a chord. Dave had thought about what he
might do when Plum Nellie were no longer popular. It happened to most pop acts, though there were exceptions—
Elvis was still big. Dave was planning to marry Beep and
have children, a prospect he found daunting. The time
might come when he needed another way to earn a living.
He had thought about becoming a record producer and artist manager: he had done well in both roles for Plum Nellie.

But this was too soon. The group was hugely popular and
now, at last, making real money. "I can't do it," he said to
Morty. "It might break up the group, and I can't risk that
while we're doing so well."

"Should I tell Charlie Lacklow you're not interested?"

"Yeah. With regrets."

They crossed another long bridge and entered hilly country with orchards on the lower slopes, the plum and almond
trees frothing pink and white blossoms. "We're in the valley
of the Napa River," said Morty. He turned onto a dusty side
road that wound upward. After a mile he drove through an
open gate and pulled up outside a big ranch house.

"This is the first one on my list, and the nearest to San
Francisco," Morty said. "I don't know if it's the kind of thing
you had in mind."

They got out of the car. The place was a rambling timber-
framed building that went on forever. It looked as if two or
three outbuildings had been joined to the main residence at
different times. Walking around to the far side, they came

upon a spectacular view across the valley. "Wow," said Dave. "Beep is going to love this."

Cultivated fields fell away from the grounds of the house. "What do they grow here?" said Dave.

"Grapes."

"I don't want to be a farmer."

"You'd be a landlord. Thirty acres are rented out."

They went inside. The place was barely furnished with ill-assorted tables and chairs. There were no beds. "Does anyone live here?" Dave asked.

"No. For a few weeks every fall the grape pickers use it as a dormitory."

"And if I move in . . ."

"The farmer will find other accommodation for his seasonal workers."

Dave looked around. The place was ramshackle and derelict, but beautiful. The woodwork seemed solid. The main house had high ceilings and an elegant staircase. "I can't wait for Beep to see it," he said.

The main bedroom had the same spectacular view over the valley. He pictured himself and Beep getting up in the morning and looking out together, making coffee, and having breakfast with two or three barefoot children. It was perfect.

There was space for half a dozen guest rooms. The large detached barn, currently full of agricultural machinery, was the right size for a recording studio.

Dave wanted to buy it immediately. He told himself not to get enthusiastic too soon. He said: "What's the asking price?"

"Sixty thousand dollars."

"That's a lot."

"Two thousand dollars an acre is about the market price for a producing vineyard," Morty said. "They'll throw in the house for free."

"Plus it wants a lot of work."

"You said it. Central heating, electrical rewiring, insulation, new bathrooms . . . You could spend almost as much again fixing it up."

"Say a hundred thousand dollars, not including recording equipment."

"It's a lot of money."

Dave grinned. "Fortunately, I can afford it."

"You certainly can."

When they went outside, a pickup truck was parking. The man who got out had broad shoulders and a weathered face. He looked Mexican but he spoke without an accent. "I'm Danny Medina, the farmer here," he said. He wiped his hands on his dungarees before shaking.

"I'm thinking of buying the place," Dave said.

"Good. It will be nice to have a neighbor."

"Where do you live, Mr. Medina?"

"I have a cottage at the other end of the vineyard, just out of sight over the lip of the ridge. Are you European?"

"Yes, British."

"Europeans usually like wine."

"Do you make wine here?"

"A little. We sell most of the grapes. Americans don't like wine, except for Italian Americans, and they import it. Most people prefer cocktails or beer. But our wine is good."

"White or red?"

"Red. Would you like a couple of bottles to try?"

"Sure."

Danny reached into the cab of the pickup, pulled out two bottles, and handed them to Dave.

Dave looked at the label. "Daisy Farm Red?" he said.

Morty said: "That's the name of the place, didn't I tell you? Daisy Farm."

"Daisy is my mother's name."

Danny said: "Maybe it's an omen." He climbed back into the vehicle. "Good luck!"

As Danny drove away, Dave said: "I like this place. Let's buy it."

Morty protested: "I have five more to show you!"

"I'm in a hurry to see my fiancée."

"You might like one of the other places even more than this."

Dave gestured over the vine fields. "Do any of them have this view?"

"No."

"Let's go back to San Francisco."

"You're the boss."

On the way back, Dave began to feel daunted by the

project he had embarked on. "I guess I need to find a builder," he said.

"Or an architect," said Morty.

"Really? Just to fix a place up?"

"An architect would talk to you about what you want, draw up plans, then get bids from a number of builders. He would also supervise the work, in theory—though in my experience they tend to lose interest."

"Okay," said Dave. "Do you know anyone?"

"Do you want an old established firm, or someone young and hip?"

Dave considered. "How about someone young and hip who works for an old established firm?"

Morty laughed. "I'll ask around."

They drove back to San Francisco and, shortly after midday, Morty dropped Dave off at the Dewar family house on Nob Hill.

Beep's mother let Dave in. "Welcome!" she said. "You're early—which is great, except that Beep's not here."

Dave was disappointed, but not surprised. He had anticipated spending the whole day looking at properties with Morty, and had told Beep to expect him at the end of the afternoon. "I guess she's gone to school," Dave said. She was a sophomore at Berkeley. Dave knew—though her parents did not—that she studied very little, and was in danger of failing her exams and getting expelled.

He went to the bedroom they shared and put down his suitcase. Beep's contraceptive pills were on the bedside table. She was careless, and sometimes forgot to take the tablet, but Dave did not mind. If she got pregnant, they would just get married in a hurry.

He returned downstairs and sat in the kitchen with Bella, telling her all about Daisy Farm. She was infected by his enthusiasm and eager to view the place.

"Would you like some lunch?" she offered. "I was about to make soup and a sandwich."

"No, thanks, I had a huge breakfast on the plane." Dave was hyped up. "I'll go and tell Walli about Daisy Farm."

"Your car's in the garage."

Dave got in his red Dodge Charger and zigzagged across San Francisco from its wealthiest neighborhood to its poorest.

Walli was going to love the idea of a farmhouse where they could all live and make music, Dave thought. They would have all the time they wanted to perfect their recordings. Walli was itching to work with one of the new eight-track tape recorders—and people were already talking about even bigger sixteen-track machines—but today's more complex music took longer to make. Studio time was costly, and musicians sometimes felt rushed. Dave believed he had found the solution.

As Dave drove, a fragment of a tune came into his head, and he sang: "We're all going to Daisy Farm." He smiled. Perhaps it would be a song. "Daisy Farm Red" would be a good title. It could be a girl or a color or a type of marijuana. He sang: "We're all going to see Daisy Farm Red, where the fruit hangs on the vine."

He parked outside Walli's house in Haight-Ashbury. The front door was unlocked, as always. The living room on the ground floor was empty, but littered with the debris of the previous night: pizza boxes, dirty coffee cups, full ashtrays, and empty beer bottles.

Dave was disappointed not to find Walli up. He was itching to discuss Daisy Farm. He decided to wake Walli.

He went upstairs. The house was quiet. It was possible Walli had got up earlier and gone out without cleaning up.

The bedroom door was closed. Dave knocked and opened it. Walking in, he sang: "We're all going to Daisy Farm," then he stopped dead.

Walli was in bed, half sitting up, clearly startled.

Next to him on the mattress was Beep.

For a moment Dave was too shocked to speak.

Walli said: "Hey, man . . ."

Dave's stomach lurched, as if he were in an elevator that had dropped too fast. He suffered a feeling of panicky weightlessness. Beep was in bed with Walli, and there was no ground beneath Dave's feet. Stupidly, he said: "What the fuck is this?"

"It's nothing, man . . ."

Shock turned to anger. "What are you talking about? You're in bed with my fiancée! How can it be *nothing*?"

Beep sat upright. Her hair was tousled. The sheet fell away from her breasts. "Dave, let us explain," she said.

"Okay, explain," said Dave, folding his arms.

She got up. She was naked, and the perfect beauty of her body brought home to Dave, with the force and shock of a punch in the face, that he had lost her. He wanted to weep.

Beep said: "Let's all have coffee and—"

"No coffee," Dave said, speaking harshly to save himself from the humiliation of tears. "Just explain."

"I don't have any clothes on!"

"That's because you've been fucking your fiancé's best friend." Dave found that angry words masked his pain. "You said you were going to explain that to me. I'm still waiting."

Beep pushed her hair out of her eyes. "Look, jealousy is out-of-date, okay?"

"And what does that mean?"

"I love you and I want to marry you, but I like Walli too, and I like going to bed with him, and love is free, isn't it? So why lie about it?"

"That's it?" said Dave incredulously. "That's your explanation?"

Walli said: "Take it easy, man, I think I'm still tripping a little."

"You two took acid last night—is that how this happened?" Dave felt a glimmer of hope. If they had only done it once . . .

"She loves you, man. She just passes the time with me, while you're away, you know?"

Dave's hope was dashed. This was not the only time. It was a regular thing.

Walli stood up and pulled on a pair of jeans. "My feet grew bigger in the night," he said. "Weird."

Dave ignored the druggy talk. "You haven't even said you're sorry—either of you!"

"We're not sorry," said Walli. "We felt like screwing, so we did. It doesn't change anything. No one is faithful anymore. All you need is love—didn't you understand that song?" He stared at Dave intently. "Did you know you have an aura? Kind of like a halo. I never noticed that before. It's blue, I think."

Dave had taken LSD himself, and he knew there was little prospect of getting any sense out of Walli in this state. He turned to Beep, who seemed to be coming down from the high. "Are you sorry?"

"I don't believe that what we did was wrong. I've grown past that mentality."

"So you'd do it again?"

"Dave, don't break up with me."

"What's to break up?" Dave said wildly. "We don't have a relationship. You screw anyone you fancy. Live that way if you want, but it's not marriage."

"You have to leave those old ideas behind."

"I have to get out of this house." Dave's rage was turning to grief. He realized he had lost Beep: lost her to drugs and free love, lost her to the hippie culture his music had helped to create. "I have to get away from you." He turned away.

"Don't go," she said. "Please."

Dave went out.

He ran down the stairs and out of the house. He jumped into his car and roared away. He almost ran over a long-haired boy staggering across Ashbury Street, smiling vacantly, stoned out of his mind in the afternoon. To hell with all hippies, Dave thought, especially Walli and Beep. He did not want to see either of them again.

Plum Nellie was finished, he realized. He and Walli were the essence of the group, and now that they had quarreled there was no group. Well, so be it, Dave thought. He would start his solo career today.

He saw a phone booth and pulled up. He opened the glove box and took out the roll of quarters he kept there. He dialed Morty's office.

Morty said: "Hey, Dave, I talked to the Realtor already. I offered fifty grand and we settled on fifty-five, how's that?"

"Great news, Morty," said Dave. He would need the recording studio for his solo work. "Listen, what was the name of that TV producer?"

"Charlie Lacklow. But I thought you were worried about breaking up the group."

"Suddenly I'm not so worried about it," Dave said. "Set up a meeting."

.   .   .

By March the future was looking bleak for George and for America.

George was in New York with Bobby Kennedy on Tuesday, March 12, the day of the New Hampshire primary, the first major clash between rival Democratic hopefuls. Bobby had a late supper with old friends at the fashionable "21"

restaurant on Fifty-second Street. While Bobby was upstairs, George and the other aides ate downstairs.

George had not resigned. Bobby seemed liberated by
announcing that he would not run for president. After the
Tet Offensive, George wrote a speech that openly attacked
President Johnson, and for the first time Bobby did not censor himself, but used every coruscating phrase. "Half a million American soldiers with seven hundred thousand
Vietnamese allies, backed by huge resources and the most
modern weapons, are unable to secure even a single city
from the attacks of an enemy whose strength is about two
hundred and fifty thousand!"

Just as Bobby seemed to be getting his fire back, George's
disillusionment with President Johnson had been completed by the president's reaction to the Kerner Commission, appointed to examine the causes of racial unrest
during the long, hot summer of 1967. Their report pulled no
punches: the cause of the rioting was white racism, it said. It
was sharply critical of government, the media, and the police, and it called for radical action on housing, jobs, and
segregation. It was published as a paperback and sold two
million copies. But Johnson simply rejected the report. The
man who had heroically championed the Civil Rights Act
of 1964 and the Voting Rights Act of 1965—the keystones
of Negro advancement—had given up the fight.

Bobby, having made the decision not to run, continued
to torment himself with worry about whether he had done
the right thing—as was his characteristic way. He talked
about it to his oldest friends and his most casual acquaintances, his closest advisers—including George—and newspaper reporters. Rumors began to circulate that he had
changed his mind. George would not believe it unless he
heard it from Bobby's own lips.

Primaries were local races between people from the
same party who wanted to be that party's presidential candidate. The first Democratic primary was held in New
Hampshire. Gene McCarthy was the hope of the young, but
he was doing badly in opinion polls, trailing a long way behind President Johnson, who wanted to run for reelection.
McCarthy had little money. Ten thousand enthusiastic young
volunteers had arrived in New Hampshire to campaign for
him, but George and the other aides around the table at

"21" confidently expected tonight's result to be a victory for Johnson by a huge margin.

George looked forward to the presidential election in November with trepidation. On the Republican side the leading moderate, George Romney, had dropped out of the race, leaving the field clear for the flaky conservative Richard Nixon. So the presidential election would almost certainly be fought between Johnson and Nixon, both pro-war.

Toward the end of the gloomy meal George was summoned to the phone by a staffer who had the New Hampshire result.

Everyone had been wrong. The result was completely unexpected. McCarthy had gained 42 percent of the vote, astonishingly close to Johnson's 49.

George realized that Johnson could be beaten after all.

He rushed upstairs and gave Bobby the news.

Bobby's reaction was downbeat. "It's too much!" he said. "Now how am I going to get McCarthy to drop out?"

That was when George understood that, after all, Bobby was going to run.

• • •

Walli and Beep went to Bobby Kennedy's rally to disrupt it.

Both were angry at Bobby. For months he had refused to declare himself a presidential candidate. He did not think he could win, and—they believed—he had not had the guts to try. So Gene McCarthy had stuck his neck out, and had done so well that he now had a real chance of beating President Johnson.

Until now. For Bobby Kennedy had declared his candidacy and stepped in to exploit all the work McCarthy's supporters had done and snatch the victory for himself. They thought he was a cynical opportunist.

Walli was contemptuous, Beep was incandescent. Walli's response was more moderate because he saw the political reality behind the personal morality. McCarthy's base consisted mostly of students and intellectuals. His masterstroke had been to conscript his young followers into a volunteer army of election campaigners, and that had given him a burst of success no one had expected. But would those volunteers be enough to take him all the way to the White

House? All through his youth Walli had heard his parents making judgments like this, talking about elections—not those in East Germany, which were a sham, but in West Germany and France and the United States.

Bobby's support was broader. He pulled in the Negroes, who believed he was on their side, and the vast Catholic working class—Irish, Polish, Italian, and Hispanic. Walli hated Bobby's moral shallowness, but he had to admit—though it made Beep angry—that Bobby had a better chance than Gene of beating President Johnson.

All the same, they agreed that the right thing to do was to boo Bobby Kennedy tonight.

The audience included a lot of people like themselves: young men with long hair and beards, hippie girls with bare feet. Walli wondered how many of them had come to jeer. There were also blacks of all ages, the young ones with their hair in the style now called an Afro, their parents in the colorful dresses and smart suits they wore to church. The breadth of Bobby's appeal was shown by a substantial minority of middle-class, middle-aged white people, dressed in chinos and sweaters in the chill of a San Francisco spring.

Walli himself had his hair tucked up inside a denim cap, and wore sunglasses to hide his identity.

The stage was surprisingly bare. Walli had been expecting flags, streamers, posters, and giant photographs of the candidate, such as he had seen on television for other campaign rallies. Bobby just had a bare stage with a lectern and a microphone. In another candidate that would have been a sign that he had run out of money, but everyone knew Bobby had unlimited access to the Kennedy fortune. So what did it mean? To Walli it said: "No bullshit, this is the real me." Interesting, he thought.

Right now the lectern was occupied by a local Democrat who was warming up the crowd for the big star. It was a lot like show business, Walli reflected. The audience was getting used to laughing and clapping, and at the same time becoming more eager for the appearance of the act they had come to see. For the same reason, Plum Nellie concerts featured a lesser group as support.

But Plum Nellie no longer existed. The group should by now have been working on a new album for Christmas, and Walli had a few songs that had reached the stage where he wanted to play them for Dave, so that Dave could write a bridge or change a chord or say: "Great, let's call it 'Soul Kiss.'" But Dave had dropped out of sight.

He had sent a coldly polite note to Beep's mother, thanking her for letting him stay at the house and asking her to pack his clothes and have them ready to be picked up by an assistant. Walli knew, from a phone call to Daisy in London, that Dave was renovating a farmhouse in Napa Valley and planning a recording studio there. And Jasper Murray had phoned Walli, trying to check a rumor that Dave was making a television special without the group.

Dave was suffering from old-fashioned jealousy, quite out-of-date now according to hippie thinking. He needed to realize that people could not be tied down, they should make love to anyone they wanted. Strongly as Walli believed this he could not help feeling guilty. He and Dave had been close, they liked and trusted one another, they had stuck together all the way from the Reeperbahn. Walli was unhappy about having wounded his friend.

It was not as if Beep was the love of Walli's life. He liked her a lot—she was beautiful and fun and great in the sack, and they were a much-admired couple—but she was not the only girl in the world. Walli probably would not have screwed her if he had known it would destroy the group. But he had not been thinking about consequences; he had instead been living for the moment, the way people should. It was especially easy to give in to such careless impulses when you were stoned.

She was still shaken from having been dumped by Dave. Perhaps that was why she and Walli were comfortable together: she had lost Dave and he had lost Karolin.

Walli's mind was wandering, but he was jerked back to the present moment when Bobby Kennedy was announced.

Bobby was smaller than Walli had imagined, and less confident. He walked up to the lectern with a half smile and a wave that was almost shy. He put his hand in the pocket of his suit jacket, and Walli recalled President Kennedy doing exactly the same.

Several people in the audience immediately held up signs. Walli saw KISS ME, BOBBY! and BOBBY IS GROOVY. Beep now drew a rolled-up sheet of paper from her pants leg, and she and Walli held it up. It read simply: TRAITOR.

Bobby began to speak, referring to a small pack of file cards he took from his inside pocket. "Let me begin with an apology," he said. "I was involved in many of the early decisions on Vietnam, decisions which set us on our present path."

Beep yelled out: "Too damn right!" and the people around her laughed.

Bobby went on in his flat Boston accent. "I am willing to bear my share of the responsibility. But past error is no excuse for its own perpetuation. Tragedy is a tool for the living to gain wisdom. 'All men make mistakes,' said the ancient Greek Sophocles. 'But a good man yields when he knows his course is wrong, and repairs the evil. The only sin is pride.'"

The audience liked that, and applauded. As they did so, Bobby looked down at his notes, and Walli saw that he was making a theatrical mistake. This should be a two-way exchange. The crowd wanted their star to look at them and acknowledge their praise. Bobby seemed embarrassed by them. This kind of political rally did not come easily to him, Walli realized.

Bobby continued on the subject of Vietnam but, despite the initial success of his opening confession, he did not do well. He was tentative, he stammered, and he repeated himself. He stood still, looking wooden, seeming reluctant to move his body or gesture with his hands.

A few opponents in the hall heckled him, but Walli and Beep did not join in. There was no need. Bobby was killing himself without assistance.

During a quiet moment, a baby cried. Out of the corner of his eye, Walli saw a woman get up and move toward the exit. Bobby stopped in midsentence and said: "Please don't leave, ma'am!"

The audience tittered. The woman turned in the aisle and looked at Bobby up on the stage.

He said: "I'm used to the sound of babies crying."

They laughed at that: everyone knew he had ten children.

"Besides," he added, "if you go the newspapers will say that I ruthlessly threw a mother and baby out of the hall."

They cheered at that: many young people hated the press for its biased coverage of demonstrations.

The woman smiled and returned to her seat.

Bobby looked down at his notes. For a moment he had come across as a warm human being. At that point he might have turned the crowd. But he would lose them again by returning to his prepared speech. Walli thought he had missed his opportunity.

Then Bobby seemed to realize the same thing. He looked up again and said: "I'm cold in here. Are you cold?"

They roared their agreement.

"Clap," he said. "Come on, that'll warm us up." He began to clap his hands, and the audience did the same, laughing.

After a minute he stopped and said: "I feel better now. Do you?" And they shouted their assent again.

"I want to talk about decency," he said. He was back to his speech, but now he was not referring to his notes. "Some people think that long hair is indecent, and bare feet, and smooching in the park. I'll tell you what I think." He raised his voice. "Poverty is indecent!" The crowd shouted approval. "Illiteracy is indecent!" They applauded again. "And I say, right here in California, that it is indecent for a man to work in the fields with his back and his hands without ever having hope of sending his son to college."

No one in the room could doubt that Bobby believed what he was saying. He had put away his file cards. He became passionate, waving his arms, pointing, banging the lectern with a fist; and the listeners responded to the strength of his emotion, acclaiming every fervent phrase. Walli looked at their faces and recognized the expressions he saw when he himself was up onstage: young men and women staring in rapture, eyes wide, mouths open, faces shining with adoration.

No one ever looked at Gene McCarthy that way.

At some point, Walli realized, he and Beep had quietly dropped their TRAITOR banner to the floor.

Bobby was speaking about poverty. "In the Mississippi Delta I have seen children with distended stomachs and facial sores from starvation." He raised his voice. "I don't think that's acceptable!

"Indians living on their bare and meager reservations have so little hope for the future that the greatest cause of death among teenagers is suicide. I believe we can do better!

"The people of the black ghettoes listen to ever greater promises of equality and justice as they sit in the same decaying schools and huddle in the same filthy rooms warding off the rats. I am convinced that America can do better than that!"

He was building up to the climax, Walli saw. "I come here today to ask for your help over the next few months," Bobby said. "If you, too, believe that poverty is indecent, give me your support."

They yelled that they would.

"If you, too, think it is unacceptable that children starve in our country, work for my campaign."

They hurrahed again.

"Do you believe, as I do, that America can do better?"

They roared their agreement.

"Then join me—and America *will* do better!"

He stepped back from the lectern, and the crowd went wild.

Walli looked at Beep. He could tell that she felt the way he did. "He's going to win, isn't he?" said Walli.

"Yes," said Beep. "He's going all the way to the White House."

.   .   .   .

Bobby's ten-day tour took him to thirteen states. At the end of the last day, he and his entourage boarded a plane in Phoenix to fly to New York. By then George Jakes was sure Bobby was going to be president.

The public response had been overwhelming. Thousands mobbed Bobby at airports. They crowded the streets to watch his motorcade go by, Bobby always standing on the backseat of a convertible, with George and others sitting on the floor holding his legs so that the people could not pull him out of the car. Gangs of children ran alongside shouting: "Bobby!" Whenever the car stopped, people flung themselves at him. They ripped off his cuff links and his tie pins and the buttons on his suits.

On the plane, Bobby sat down and emptied his pockets. Out came a snowstorm of paper like confetti. George picked up some of the scraps from the carpet. They were notes, dozens of them, neatly written and carefully folded small and thrust into Bobby's pockets. They begged him to attend college graduations or visit sick children in city hospitals, and they told him that prayers were being said for him in suburban homes, and candles lit in country churches.

Bobby took off his suit coat and rolled up his sleeves, as was his habit. That was when George noticed his arms. Bobby had hairy forearms, but that was not what struck George. His hands were swollen and his skin was webbed with angry red scratches. It happened when the crowds were touching him, George realized. They did not want to injure him, but they adored him so much that they drew blood.

The people had found the hero they needed—but Bobby, too, had found himself. That was why George and the other aides called it the Free at Last tour. Bobby had struck a style that was all his own. He had a new version of the Kennedy charisma. His brother had been charming but contained, self-possessed, private—the right manner for 1963. Bobby was more open. At his best, he gave the audience the feeling that he was laying bare his own soul, confessing himself to be a flawed human being who wanted to do the right thing but was not always certain what it was. The catchphrase of 1968 was: "Let it all hang out." Bobby felt comfortable doing that, and they loved him for it.

Half the people on the plane flying back to New York were newsmen. For ten days they had been photographing and filming the ecstatic crowds, and filing reports on how the new, reborn Bobby Kennedy was winning voters' hearts. The power brokers of the Democratic Party might not like Bobby's youthful liberalism, but they would not be able to ignore the phenomenon of his popularity. How could they blandly select Lyndon Johnson to run a second time when the American people were clamoring for Bobby? And if they ran an alternative pro-war candidate—Vice President Hubert Humphrey, say, or Senator Muskie—he would take votes from Johnson without denting Bobby's support. George did not see how Bobby could fail to get the nomination.

And Bobby would beat the Republican. It would almost certainly be "Tricky" Dick Nixon, a has-been who had been beaten by a Kennedy once already.

The road to the White House seemed clear of obstacles. As the plane approached John F. Kennedy airport in

New York, George wondered what Bobby's opponents would do to try to stop him. President Johnson had been scheduled to make a national television broadcast this evening while the plane was in the air. George looked forward to finding out what Johnson had said. He could not think of anything that would make a difference.

"It must be quite something," one of the journalists said to Bobby, "to land at an airport named for your brother."

It was an unkind, intrusive question from a reporter hoping to spark an intemperate response that would make a story. But Bobby was used to this. All he said was: "I wish it was still called Idlewild."

The plane taxied to the gate. Before the seat belt sign was switched off, a familiar figure came on board and ran down the aisle to Bobby. It was the New York State chairman of the Democratic Party. Before he reached Bobby he shouted: "The president is not going to run! The president is not going to run!"

Bobby said: "Say that again."

"The president is not going to run!"

"You must be kidding."

George was stunned. Lyndon Johnson, who hated the Kennedys, had realized that he could not win the Democratic nomination, doubtless for all the reasons that had occurred to George. But he hoped that another pro-war Democrat could beat Bobby. Johnson had figured, then, that the only way he could sabotage Bobby's run for the presidency was to withdraw from the race himself.

And now all bets were off.

CHAPTER FORTY-TWO

Dave Williams knew that his sister was up to something.

He was making the pilot of *Dave Williams and Friends,* his own television show. When first it was proposed he had taken the idea lightly: it seemed a superfluous augmentation of the tidal wave of Plum Nellie's success. Now the group had split and Dave needed the show. It was the beginning of his solo career. It had to be good.

The producer had suggested inviting Dave's movie-star sister to appear as a guest. Evie was hotter than ever. Her latest film, a comedy about a snobby girl who hired a black lawyer, was a huge hit.

Evie proposed to sing a duet with her costar in the movie, Percy Marquand. The producer, Charlie Lacklow, loved the idea but worried about the choice of song. Charlie was a small, belligerent man with a grating voice. "It has to be a comedy song," he said. "They can't sing 'True Love' or 'Baby, It's Cold Outside.'"

"Easier said than done," said Dave. "Most duets are romantic."

Charlie had shaken his head. "Forget it. This is television. We can't even hint at sex between a white woman and a black man."

"They could sing 'Anything You Can Do, I Can Do Better.' That's comic."

"No. People will think it's a comment on civil rights."

Charlie Lacklow was smart, but Dave did not like him. Nobody did. He was a bad-tempered bully, and his occasional attempts to be ingratiatingly nice only made it worse.

Dave tried: "How about 'Mockingbird'?"

Charlie thought for a minute. "'If that mockingbird don't sing, he's gonna buy me a diamond ring,'" he sang. He reverted to speech. "I guess we can get away with that."

"Sure we can," Dave said. "The original recording was by a brother-and-sister duo, Inez and Charlie Foxx. No one thought it suggested incest."

"Okay."

Dave discussed the sensitivities of the American television audience with Evie, and explained the choice of song, and she agreed—except that she had a gleam in her eye that Dave knew too well. It meant trouble. It was how she had looked just before the school production of *Hamlet,* when she had played Ophelia in the nude.

They also discussed his breakup with Beep. "Everybody reacts as if it was just a typical teenage romance that didn't last," Dave complained. "But I stopped having teenage romances long before I stopped being a teenager, and I never much liked screwing around. I was serious about Beep. I wanted kids."

"You grew up faster than Beep," Evie said. "And I grew up faster than Hank Remington. Hank has settled down with Anna Murray—I hear he doesn't screw around anymore. Maybe Beep will do the same."

"And it will be too late for me, just as it was for you," Dave said bitterly.

Now the orchestra was tuning up, Evie was in makeup, and Percy was putting on his costume. Meanwhile the director, Tony Peterson, asked Dave to record his introduction.

The show was in color, and Dave was dressed in a burgundy velvet suit. He looked into the camera, imagined Beep walking back into his life with her arms reaching out to embrace him, and smiled warmly. "Now, fans, a special kick. We have both stars of the hit movie *My Client and I*: Percy Marquand, and my very own sister, Evie Williams!" He clapped his hands. The studio was quiet, but the sound of an audience applauding would be dubbed onto the soundtrack before the show was broadcast.

"I love the smile, Dave," said Tony. "Do it again."

Dave did it three times, and Tony pronounced himself satisfied.

At that point Charlie came in with a gray-suited man in his forties. Dave saw immediately that Charlie was in obsequious mode. "Dave, I want you to meet our sponsor," he said. "This is Albert Wharton, the top man at National Soap and one of the leading businessmen in America. He's flown here all the way from Cleveland, Ohio, to meet you, isn't that great of him?"

"It sure is," said Dave. People flew halfway around the world to see him every time he did a concert, but he always acted pleased.

Wharton said: "I have two teenage children, a boy and a girl. They're going to be envious that I met you."

Dave was trying to concentrate on making a great show, and the last thing he needed was to talk to a laundry detergent magnate; but he realized he had to be polite to this man. "I should sign a couple of autographs for your kids," he said.

"That would give them a thrill."

Charlie snapped his fingers at Miss Pritchard, his secretary, who was following behind him. "Jenny, sweetie," he said, even though she was a prim forty-year-old. "Get a couple of Dave's photos from the office."

Wharton looked like a typical conservative businessman with short hair and boring clothes. That prompted Dave to say: "What made you decide to sponsor my show, Mr. Wharton?"

"Our leading product is a detergent called Foam," Wharton began.

"I've seen the ads," Dave said with a smile. " 'Foam washes cleaner than white!' "

Wharton nodded. Probably everyone he met quoted his advertising to him. "Foam is well known and trusted, and has been for many years," he said. "For that reason, it's also a bit fuddy-duddy. Young housewives tend to say: 'Foam, yes, my mother always used it.' Which is nice, but it has its dangers."

Dave was amused to hear him talk about the character of a box of detergent as if it were a person. But Wharton spoke with no hint of humor or irony, and Dave suppressed the impulse to take it lightly. He said: "So I'm here to let them know that Foam is young and groovy."

"Exactly," said Wharton. Then he smiled at last. "And, at the same time, to bring some popular music and wholesome humor into American homes."

Dave grinned. "It's a good thing I'm not in the Rolling Stones!"

"It certainly is," said Wharton in deadly earnest.

Jenny came back with two eight-by-ten color photographs of Dave, and a felt-tipped pen.

Dave said to Wharton: "What are your children called?"

"Caroline and Edward."

Dave dedicated one photo to each child and signed.

Tony Peterson said: "Ready for the 'Mockingbird' segment."

A little set had been built for this number. It looked like a corner of a swanky store, with glass cupboards full of glittery luxuries. Percy came on in a dark suit and a silver tie, like a floorwalker. Evie was a wealthy shopper with hat, gloves, and handbag. They took their positions either side of a counter. Dave smiled at the pains Charlie had taken to make sure their relationship was not seen as amorous.

They rehearsed with the orchestra. The song was upbeat and lighthearted. Percy's baritone and Evie's contralto harmonized nicely. At the appropriate moments, Percy produced from under the counter a caged bird and a tray of rings. "We'll add canned laughter at that point, to let the audience know it's intended to be funny," said Charlie.

They did it for the cameras. The first take was perfect, but they did it again for safety, as always.

As they were coming to the end, Dave felt good. This was ideal family entertainment for the American audience. He began to believe that his show would succeed.

In the last bar of the song, Evie leaned across the counter, stood on tiptoe, and kissed Percy's cheek.

"Wonderful!" said Tony, walking onto the set. "Thank you, everybody. Set up for Dave's next introduction, please." He had a distinct air of embarrassed haste, and Dave wondered why.

Evie and Percy stepped off the set.

Beside Dave, Mr. Wharton said: "We can't broadcast that kiss."

Before Dave could say anything, Charlie Lacklow said fawningly: "Of course not, don't worry, Mr. Wharton, we can lose it, we'll cut to Dave applauding, probably."

Dave said mildly: "I thought the kiss was charming and kind of innocent."

"Did you?" said Wharton severely.

Dave wondered apprehensively if this was going to become an issue.

Charlie said: "Drop it, Dave. We can't show an interracial kiss on American television."

Dave was surprised. But, thinking about it, he realized that those few black people who appeared on TV were rarely if ever touched by white people. "Is that, like, a policy, or something?" he asked.

"More of an unwritten rule," Charlie said. "Unwritten, and unbreakable," he added firmly.

Evie heard the exchange and said challengingly: "Why is that?"

Dave saw the look on her face and groaned inwardly. Evie was not going to let this pass. She wanted a fight.

But for a few moments there was silence. No one was sure what to say, especially with Percy right there.

Eventually Wharton answered Evie's question in his dry accountant's tone. "The audience would disapprove," he said. "Most Americans believe the races should not intermarry."

Charlie Lacklow added: "Exactly. What happens on television is happening in your home, in your living room, with your kids watching, and your mother-in-law."

Wharton looked at Percy and remembered that he was married to Babe Lee, a white woman. "I'm sorry if this offends you, Mr. Marquand," he said.

"I'm used to it," Percy said mildly; not denying that he was offended, but declining to make a big deal of it. Dave thought that was remarkably gracious.

Evie said indignantly: "Maybe television should work to alter people's prejudices."

"Don't be naïve," Charlie said rudely. "If we show them something they don't like, they'll just change the goddamn channel."

"Then *all* the networks should do the same, and portray America as a place where all men are equal."

"It won't work," said Charlie.

"Perhaps it won't," said Evie. "But we have to try, don't we? We have a responsibility." She looked around the group: Charlie, Tony, Dave, Percy, and Wharton. Dave felt guilty when he met her eye, for he knew she was right. "All of us," she went on. "We make television programs, which influence how people think."

Charlie said: "Not necessarily—"

Dave interrupted him. "Knock it off, Charlie. We influence people. If we didn't, Mr. Wharton would be wasting his money."

Charlie looked angry, but he had no answer.

"Now we have a chance, today, to make the world a better place," Evie went on. "Nobody would mind if I kissed Bing Crosby on prime-time television. Let's help people to see that it's no different if the cheek I kiss is a little darker in color."

They all looked at Mr. Wharton.

Dave felt perspiration break out under his skintight frilled shirt. He did not want Wharton to be offended.

"You argue well, young lady," said Wharton. "But my duty is to my shareholders and my employees. I'm not here to make the world a better place, I'm here to sell Foam to housewives. And I won't achieve that if I associate my product with interracial sex, with all due respect to Mr. Marquand. I'm a big fan, by the way, Percy—I have all your records."

Dave found himself thinking of Mandy Love. He had been crazy about her. She was black—not golden tan like Percy, but a beautiful deep coaly brown. Dave had kissed her skin until his lips were sore. He might have proposed to her, if she had not gone back to her old boyfriend. And Dave would now be in Percy's position, straining to tolerate a conversation that insulted his marriage.

Charlie said: "I think the duet works as a beautiful symbol of interracial harmony without hinting at the prickly topic of sex between the races. I believe we've done a wonderful job here—provided we leave out the kiss."

Evie said: "Nice try, Charlie, but that's bullshit, and you know it."

"It's the reality."

Trying to lighten the mood, Dave said: "Did you call sex a 'prickly topic,' Charlie? That's funny."

No one laughed.

Evie looked at Dave. "Aside from making jokes, what are you going to do, Dave?" she said, almost taunting him. "You and I were raised to stand up for what's right. Our father fought in the Spanish Civil War. Our grandmother won women the right to vote. Are you going to give in?"

Percy Marquand said: "You're the talent, Dave. They need you. Without you they don't have a show. You have power. Use it to do good."

Charlie said: "Get real. There's no show without National Soap. We'll have trouble finding a new sponsor—especially after people find out why Mr. Wharton pulled out."

Wharton had not actually said he would withdraw his sponsorship over the kiss, Dave noted. Nor had Charlie said that finding a new sponsor would be impossible—just difficult. If Dave insisted on keeping the kiss, the show might go on, and Dave's television career might survive.

Perhaps.

"Is this really my decision?" he said.

Evie said: "Looks like it."

Was he prepared to take the risk?

No, he was not.

"The kiss comes out," he said.

. . . .

Jasper Murray flew to Memphis in April to check out a strike by sanitation workers that was becoming violent.

Jasper knew about violence. All men, including himself, had it in them to be either peaceable or vicious, according to circumstances, he believed. Their natural inclination was to lead a quiet, law-abiding life; but given the right sort of encouragement most of them were capable of committing torture, rape, and murder. He knew.

So when he came to Memphis he listened to both sides. The city hall spokesman said that outside agitators were inciting the strikers to violent behavior. The campaigners blamed police brutality.

Jasper asked: "Who is in charge?"

The answer was Henry Loeb.

Loeb, the Democrat mayor of Memphis, was openly racist, Jasper learned. He believed in segregation, supported "separate but equal" facilities for whites and blacks, and publicly railed against court-ordered integration.

And almost all the sanitation workers were black.

Their wages were so low that many qualified for welfare. They had to do compulsory unpaid overtime. And the city would not recognize their union.

But it was the issue of safety that started the strike. Two men had been crushed to death by a malfunctioning truck. Loeb refused to retire obsolete trucks or tighten safety rules.

The city council voted to end the strike by recognizing the union, but Loeb overrode the council.

The protest spread.

It got national attention when Martin Luther King weighed in on the side of the sanitation men.

King flew in for his second visit on the same day as Jasper, April 3, 1968, a Wednesday. That evening a storm darkened the city. In pounding rain, Jasper went to hear King speak to a rally at the Mason Temple.

Ralph Abernathy was the warm-up man. Taller and darker than King, less handsome and more aggressive, he was—according to gossip—King's drinking and womanizing buddy as well as his closest ally and friend.

The audience consisted of sanitation workers and their families and supporters. Looking at their worn shoes and their old coats and hats, Jasper realized that these were some of the poorest people in America. They were ill-educated and they did dirty jobs and they lived in a city that called them second-class citizens, nigras, boys. But they had spirit. They were not going to take it any longer. They believed in a better life. They had a dream.

And they had Martin Luther King.

King was thirty-nine, but he looked older. He had been a little chubby when Jasper saw him speak in Washington, but he had put on weight in the five years since then, and now he looked plump. If his suit had not been so smart he might have been a shopkeeper. But that was before he opened his mouth. When he spoke, he became a giant.

Tonight he was in an apocalyptic mood. As lightning flashed outside the windows, and the crash of thunder interrupted his speech, he told the audience that his plane that morning had been delayed by a bomb threat. "But it doesn't matter with me, now, because I've been to the mountain-top," he said, and they cheered. "I just want to do God's will." And then he was seized by the emotion of his own words, and his voice trembled with urgency the way it had on the steps of the Lincoln Memorial. "And he's allowed me to go up to the mountain," he cried. "And I've looked over." His voice rose again. "And I've *seen* the Promised Land!"

King was genuinely moved, Jasper could see. He was perspiring heavily and shedding tears. The crowd shared his passion and responded, shouting out: "Yes!" and "Amen!"

"I may not get there with you," King said, his voice shaking with feeling, and Jasper recalled that in the Bible, Moses had never reached Canaan. "But I want you to know, to-night, that we as a people will get to the Promised Land." Two thousand listeners erupted in applause and amens. "And so I'm happy tonight. I'm not worried about anything. I'm not fearing any man." He paused, then said slowly: "Mine eyes have seen the glory of the coming of the Lord."

With that he seemed to stagger back from the pulpit. Ralph Abernathy, behind him, leaped up to support him, and led him to his seat amid a hurricane of approbation that rivaled the storm outside.

Jasper spent the next day covering a legal dispute. The city was trying to get the courts to ban a demonstration King had planned for the following Monday, and King was working on a compromise that would guarantee a small, peaceful march.

At the end of the afternoon, Jasper talked to Herb Gould in New York. They agreed that Jasper would try to arrange for Sam Cakebread to interview both Loeb and King on Saturday or Sunday, and Herb would send a crew to get footage of Monday's demonstration, for a report to be broadcast on Monday evening.

After talking to Gould, Jasper went to the Lorraine Mo-tel, where King was staying. It was a low two-story building with balconies overlooking the parking lot. Jasper spotted a white Cadillac that, he knew, was loaned to King, along with a chauffeur, by a black-owned Memphis funeral home. Near the car was a group of King's aides, and among them Jasper spotted Verena Marquand.

She was as breathtakingly gorgeous as she had been five years ago, but she looked different. Her hairdo was an Afro, and she wore beads and a caftan. Jasper saw tiny lines of strain around her eyes, and wondered what it was like working for a man who was so passionately adored and at the same time so bitterly hated as Martin Luther King.

Jasper gave her his most winning smile, introduced himself, and said: "We've met before."

She looked suspicious. "I don't think so."

"Sure we have. But you could be forgiven for not remembering. The date was the twenty-eighth of August, 1963. A lot else happened on that day."

"Especially Martin's 'I have a dream' speech."

"I was a student reporter and I asked you to get me an interview with Dr. King. You gave me the brush-off." Jasper also remembered how mesmerized he had been by Verena's beauty. He was feeling the same enchantment now.

She softened. With a smile she said: "And I guess you still want that interview."

"Sam Cakebread will be here at the weekend. He's going to talk to Herb Loeb. He really should interview Dr. King as well."

"I'll do my best, Mr. Murray."

"Please call me Jasper."

She hesitated. "Satisfy my curiosity. How did we come to meet, that day in Washington?"

"I was having breakfast with Congressman Greg Peshkov, a family friend. You were with George Jakes."

"And where have you been since then?"

"Vietnam, some of the time."

"You fought?"

"Saw some action, yes." He hated talking about that. "May I ask you a personal question?"

"Try me. I don't promise to answer."

"Are you and George still an item?"

"I'm not going to answer."

At that moment they both heard King's voice, and looked up. He was standing on the balcony outside his room, looking down, saying something to one of the aides near Jasper and Verena in the parking lot. King was tucking his shirt in, as if dressing after a shower. He was probably getting ready to go out for dinner, Jasper thought.

King put both hands on the rail and leaned over, joshing with someone below. "Ben, I want you to sing 'My Precious Lord' for me tonight like you've never sung it before—want you to sing it real pretty."

The driver of the white Cadillac called up to him: "The air's turning cool, Reverend. You might want a topcoat tonight."

King said: "Okay, Jonesy." He straightened up from the rail.

A shot rang out.

King staggered back, threw up his arms like a man on a cross, hit the wall behind him, and fell.

Verena screamed.

King's aides took cover around the white Cadillac.

Jasper dropped to one knee. Verena crouched down in front of him. He put both arms around her, pulling her head to his chest protectively, and looked for the source of the shot. There was a building across the street that might be a rooming house.

There was no second shot.

Jasper was torn for a moment. He released Verena from his protective embrace. "Are you okay?" he asked her.

"Oh, Martin!" she said, looking up at the balcony.

They both stood up warily, but the shooting seemed to have stopped.

Without speaking, they both dashed up the exterior staircase to the balcony.

King lay on his back, his feet up against the railing. Ralph Abernathy was bent over him, as was another campaigner, the amiable, bespectacled Billy Kyles. Screams and moans were coming from the people in the parking lot who had seen the shooting.

The bullet had smashed King's neck and jaw and ripped off his necktie. The wound was terrible, and Jasper knew immediately that King had been struck by an expanding slug known as a dumdum. Blood was pooling around King's shoulders.

Abernathy was yelling: "Martin! Martin! Martin!" He patted King's cheek. Jasper thought he saw a faint sign of awareness on King's face. Abernathy said: "Martin, this is Ralph, don't worry, it's going to be all right." King's lips moved but there was no sound.

Kyles was first to the phone in the room. He picked it up, but apparently there was no one at the switchboard. Kyles started banging on the wall with his fist, shouting: "Answer the phone! Answer the phone! Answer the phone!"

Then he gave up and ran back out to the balcony. He shouted to the people in the parking lot: "Call an ambulance, Dr. King has been shot!"

Someone wrapped King's shattered head in a towel from the bathroom.

Kyles took an orange-colored spread from the bed and put it over King, covering his body up to his destroyed neck.

Jasper knew wounds. He knew how much blood a man could lose, and what a man could and could not recover from.

He had no hope for Martin Luther King.

Kyles lifted King's hand, prized open his fingers, and took away a pack of cigarettes. Jasper had never seen King smoking: obviously he did it only in private. Even now Kyles was protecting his friend. The gesture touched Jasper's heart.

Abernathy was still talking to King. "Can you hear me?" he said. "Can you hear me?"

Jasper saw the color of King's face alter dramatically. The brown skin paled and turned a grayish tan. The handsome features became unnaturally still.

Jasper knew death, too, and this was it.

Verena saw the same thing. She turned away and stepped inside the room, sobbing.

Jasper put his arms around her.

She slumped against him, weeping, and her hot tears soaked into his white shirt.

"I'm so sorry," Jasper whispered. "So sorry." Sorry for Verena, he thought. Sorry for Martin Luther King.

Sorry for America.

· · ·

That night, the inner cities of the United States exploded.

Dave Williams, in the bungalow at the Beverly Hills Hotel where he was living, watched the television coverage with horror. There were riots in one hundred ten cities. In Washington, twenty thousand people overwhelmed the police and set fire to buildings. In Baltimore, six people died and seven hundred were injured. In Chicago, two miles of West Madison Street were reduced to rubble.

All the next day Dave stayed in his room, sitting on the couch in front of the TV, smoking cigarettes. Who was to blame? It was not just the gunman. It was all the white racists who stirred up hatred. And it was all the people who did nothing about cruel injustice.

People such as Dave.

In his life he had been given one chance to stand up against racism. It had happened a few days ago in a television studio in Burbank. He had been told that a white woman could not kiss a black man on American television. His sister had demanded that he challenge that racist rule. But he had caved in to prejudice.

He had killed Martin Luther King, as surely as Henry Loeb and Barry Goldwater and George Wallace had killed him.

The show would be broadcast tomorrow, Saturday, at eight in the evening, without the kiss.

Dave ordered a bottle of bourbon from room service and fell asleep on the couch.

In the morning he woke up early, knowing what he had to do.

He showered, took a couple of aspirins for his hangover, and dressed in his most conservative outfit, a green check suit with broad lapels and flared pants. He ordered a limousine and went to the studio in Burbank, arriving at ten.

He knew Charlie Lacklow would be in his office, even though it was the weekend, because Saturday was broadcast day, and there were sure to be last-minute panics—just like the one Dave was about to create.

Charlie's middle-aged secretary, Jenny, was at her desk in the outer office. "Good morning, Miss Pritchard," Dave said. He treated her with extra respect because Charlie was so rude to her. In consequence she adored Dave and would do anything for him. "Would you please check flights to Cleveland?"

"In Ohio?"

He grinned. "Is there another Cleveland?"

"You want to go there today?"

"As soon as possible."

"Do you know how far it is?"

"About two thousand miles."

She picked up her phone.

Dave added: "Order a limousine to meet me at the airport there."

She made a note, then spoke into the phone. "When is the next flight to Cleveland? . . . Thank you, I'll hold." She looked at Dave again. "Where in Cleveland do you want to go?"

"Give the driver Albert Wharton's home address."

"Is Mr. Wharton expecting you?"

"It's going to be a surprise." He winked at her and went into the inner office.

Charlie was behind the desk. In honor of Saturday he was wearing a tweed jacket and no tie. "Could you make two edits of the show?" Dave said. "One with the kiss and one without?"

"Easily," said Charlie. "We already have an edit without the kiss, ready to broadcast. We could make the alternative this morning. But we're not going to do it."

"Later today you're going to get a phone call from Albert Wharton, asking you to leave the kiss in. I just want you to be ready. You wouldn't want to disappoint our sponsor."

"Of course not. But what makes you so sure he's going to change his mind?"

Dave was not at all sure, but he did not tell Charlie that. "Having both versions ready, what would be the latest time you could make the change?"

"About ten minutes to eight, Eastern time."

Jenny Pritchard put her head around the door. "You're booked on the eleven o'clock plane, Dave. The airport is seven miles from here, so you need to leave now."

"I'm on my way."

"The flight takes four and a half hours, and there's a three-hour time difference, so you land at six thirty." She handed him a slip of paper with Mr. Wharton's address. "You should be there by seven."

"That gives me just enough time," said Dave. He waved a good-bye at Charlie and said: "Stay by the phone."

Charlie looked bemused. He was not used to being pushed around. "I'm not going anywhere," he said.

In the outer office, Miss Pritchard said: "His wife is Susan and his children are Caroline and Edward."

"Thank you." Dave closed Charlie's door. "Miss Pritchard, if you ever get fed up with working for Charlie, I need a secretary."

"I'm fed up now," she said. "When do I start?"

"Monday."

"Should I come to the Beverly Hills Hotel at nine?"

"Make it ten."

The hotel limousine took Dave to LAX. Miss Pritchard had called the airline, and there was a stewardess waiting to take him through the VIP channel, to avoid mob scenes in the departure lounge.

He had had nothing but aspirins for breakfast, so he was glad of the in-flight lunch. As the plane came down toward the flat city by Lake Erie, he ruminated over what he was going to say to Mr. Wharton. This was going to be difficult. But if he handled it well perhaps he could turn Wharton around. That would make up for his earlier cowardice. He longed to tell his sister that he had redeemed himself.

Miss Pritchard's arrangements worked well, and a car was waiting for him at Hopkins International Airport. It took him to a leafy suburb not far away. A few minutes after seven the limousine pulled into the driveway of a large but unostentatious ranch-style house. Dave walked up to the entrance and rang the bell.

He felt nervous.

Wharton himself came to the door in a gray V-neck sweater and slacks. "Dave Williams?" he said. "What the hey . . . ?"

"Good evening, Mr. Wharton," Dave said. "I'm sorry to intrude, but I'd really like to speak to you."

When he got over his surprise, Wharton seemed pleased. "Come on in," he said. "Meet the family."

Wharton ushered Dave into the dining room. The family appeared to be finishing dinner. Wharton had a pretty wife in her thirties, a daughter of about sixteen, and a spotty son a couple of years younger. "We have a surprise visitor," Wharton said. "This is Mr. Dave Williams, of Plum Nellie."

Mrs. Wharton put a small white hand to her mouth and said: "Oh my golly gosh."

Dave shook hands with her, then turned to the youngsters. "You must be Caroline and Edward."

Wharton looked pleased that Dave had remembered his children's names.

The kids were awestruck to get a surprise visit from a real pop star they had seen on TV. Edward could hardly speak. Caroline pulled back her shoulders, making her breasts stick out, and gave Dave a look that he had seen before in a thousand teenage girls. It said: *You can do anything you like to me.*

Dave pretended not to notice.

Mr. Wharton said: "Sit down, Dave, please. Join us."

Mrs. Wharton said: "Would you like some dessert? We're having strawberry shortcake."

"Yes, please," Dave said. "I'm living in a hotel—some home cooking would be a real treat."

"Oh, you poor thing," she said, and she went off to the kitchen.

"Have you come from Los Angeles today?" Wharton asked.

"Yes."

"Not just to call on me, I'm sure."

"Actually, yes. I want to talk to you one more time about tonight's show."

"Okay," Wharton said dubiously.

Mrs. Wharton returned with the dessert on a platter and began to serve.

Dave wanted the children on his side. He said to them: "In the show that your dad and I made, there's a part where Percy Marquand does a duet with my sister, Evie Williams."

Edward said: "I saw their movie—it was a blast!"

"At the end of the song, Evie kisses Percy on the cheek." Dave paused.

Caroline said: "So? Big deal!"

Mrs. Wharton raised a flirtatious eyebrow as she passed Dave a large wedge of strawberry shortcake.

Dave went on: "Mr. Wharton and I talked about whether this would offend our audience—something neither of us wants to do. We decided to leave out the kiss."

Wharton said: "I think it was a wise choice."

Dave said: "I've come here to see you today, Mr. Wharton, because I believe that, since we made that decision, the situation has changed."

"You're talking about the assassination of Martin Luther King."

"Dr. King was killed, but America is still bleeding." That sentence came into Dave's head from nowhere, the way song lyrics sometimes did.

Wharton shook his head, and his mouth set in a stubborn line. Dave's optimism lost its fizz. Wharton said ponderously: "I have more than a thousand employees—many of them Negroes, by the way. If sales of Foam plummet because we offended viewers, some of those people will lose their jobs. I can't risk that."

"We would both be taking a risk," Dave said. "My own popularity is also at stake. But I want to do something to help this country heal."

Wharton smiled indulgently, as he might have if one of his children said something hopelessly idealistic. "And you think a kiss can do that?"

Dave made his voice lower and harsher. "It's Saturday night, Albert. Picture this: all over America, young black men are wondering whether to go out tonight and start fires and smash windows, or kick back and stay out of trouble. Before making up their minds, a lot of them will watch *Dave Williams and Friends,* just because it's hosted by a rock star. How do you want them feeling at the end of the show?"

"Well, obviously—"

"Think of how we built that set for Percy and Evie. Everything about the scene says that white and black have to be kept apart: their costumes, the roles they're playing, and the counter between them."

"That was the intention," said Wharton.

"We emphasized their separateness, and I don't want to throw that in black people's faces, especially not tonight, when their great hero has been murdered. But Evie's kiss, right at the end, undermines the whole setup. The kiss says we don't have to exploit one another and beat one another and murder one another. It says we *can* touch one another. That shouldn't be a big thing, but it is."

Dave held his breath. In truth he was not sure the kiss was going to stop many riots. He wanted the kiss left in just because it stood for right against wrong. But he thought maybe this argument might convince Wharton.

Caroline said: "Dave's so right, Dad. You really ought to do it."

"Yeah," said Edward.

Wharton was not much moved by his children's opinions, but he turned to his wife, somewhat to Dave's surprise, and asked: "What do you think, dear?"

"I wouldn't tell you to do anything that would harm the company," she said. "You know that. But I think this could even benefit National Soap. If you're criticized, tell them you did it because of Martin Luther King. You could end up a hero."

Dave said: "It's seven forty-five, Mr. Wharton. Charlie Lacklow is waiting by the phone. If you call him in the next five minutes, he'll have time to switch the tapes. The decision is yours."

The room went quiet. Wharton thought for a minute. Then he got up. "Heck, I think you might be right," he said.

He went out into the hall.

They all heard him dialing. Dave bit his lip. "Mr. Lacklow, please . . . Hello, Charlie . . . Yes, he's here, having dessert with us . . . We've had a long discussion about it, and I'm calling to ask you to put the kiss back in the show . . . Yes, that's what I said. Thank you, Charlie. Good night."

Dave heard the sound of the phone being cradled, and allowed a warm sense of triumph to suffuse him.

Mr. Wharton came back into the room. "Well, it's done," he said.

Dave said: "Thank you, Mr. Wharton."

· · ·

"The kiss got huge publicity, nearly all of it good," Dave said to Evie over lunch in the Polo Lounge on Tuesday.

"So National Soap benefited?"

"That's what my new friend Mr. Wharton tells me. Sales of Foam have gone up, not down."

"And the show?"

"Also a success. They have already commissioned a season."

"And all because you did the right thing."

"My solo career is off to a great start. Not bad for a kid who failed all his exams."

Charlie Lacklow joined them at their table. "Sorry I'm

late," he said insincerely. "I've been working on a joint press release with National Soap. A bit late, three days after the show, but they want to capitalize on the good publicity." He handed two sheets of paper to Dave.

Evie said: "May I see?" She knew Dave had trouble reading. He handed the papers to her. After a minute she said: "Dave! They have you saying: 'I wish to pay tribute to the managing director of National Soap, Mr. Albert Wharton, for his courage and vision in insisting that the show be broadcast including the controversial kiss.' The nerve!"

Dave took back the paper.

Charlie handed him a ballpoint pen.

Dave wrote: "OK" at the top of the sheet, then signed it and handed it to Charlie.

Evie was apoplectic. "It's outrageous!" she said.

"Of course it is," said Dave. "That's show business."

CHAPTER FORTY-THREE

On the day Dimka's divorce became final, there was a meeting of top Kremlin aides to discuss the crisis in Czechoslovakia.

Dimka was bucked. He longed to marry Natalya, and now one major obstacle was out of the way. He could hardly wait to tell her the news, but when he arrived at the Nina Onilova Room several other aides were already there, and he had to wait.

When she came in, with her curly hair falling around her face in the way he found so enchanting, he gave her a big smile. She did not know what it was for, but she smiled back happily.

Dimka was almost as happy about Czechoslovakia. The new leader in Prague, Alexander Dubček, had turned out to be a reformer after Dimka's own heart. For the first time since Dimka had been working in the Kremlin, a Soviet satellite had announced that its version of Communism might not be exactly the same as the Soviet model. On April 5 Dubček had announced an action program that included freedom of speech, the right to travel to the West, an end to arbitrary arrests, and greater independence for industrial enterprises.

And if it worked in Czechoslovakia it might work in the USSR too.

Dimka had always thought that Communism could be reformed—unlike his sister and the dissidents, who believed it should be scrapped.

The meeting began, and Yevgeny Filipov presented a

KGB report that said bourgeois elements were attempting to undermine the Czech revolution.

Dimka sighed heavily. This was typical of the Kremlin under Brezhnev. When people resisted their authority, they never asked whether there were legitimate reasons, but always looked for—or invented—malign motives.

Dimka's response was scornful. "I doubt if there are many bourgeois elements left in Czechoslovakia, after twenty years of Communism," he said.

As evidence Filipov produced two pieces of paper. One was a letter from Simon Wiesenthal, director of the Jewish Documentation Center in Vienna, praising the work of Zionist colleagues in Prague. The other was a leaflet printed in Czechoslovakia calling for Ukraine to secede from the USSR.

Across the table, Natalya Smotrov was derisive. "These documents are such obvious forgeries as to be laughable! It's not remotely plausible that Simon Wiesenthal is organizing a counterrevolution in Prague. Surely the KGB can do better than this?"

Filipov said angrily: "Dubček has turned out to be a snake in the grass!"

There was a grain of truth in that. When the previous Czech leader became unpopular, Dubček had been approved by Brezhnev as a replacement because he seemed dull and reliable. His radicalism had come as a nasty shock to Kremlin conservatives.

Filipov went on. "Dubček has allowed newspapers to attack Communist leaders!" he said indignantly.

Filipov was on weak ground here. Dubček's predecessor, Antonín Novotný, had been a crook. Now Dimka said: "The newly liberated newspapers revealed that Novotný was using government import licenses to buy Jaguar cars that he then sold to his party colleagues at a huge profit." He pretended incredulity. "Do you really want to protect such men, Comrade Filipov?"

"I want Communist countries to be governed in a disciplined and rigorous way," Filipov replied. "Subversive newspapers will soon start demanding Western-style so-called democracy, in which political parties representing rival bourgeois factions create the illusion of choice but unite to repress the working class."

"Nobody wants that," said Natalya. "But we do want Czechoslovakia to be a culturally advanced country attractive to Western tourists. If we crack down and tourism declines, the Soviet Union will be forced to pay out even more money to support the Czech economy."

Filipov sneered: "Is that the Foreign Ministry view?"

"The Foreign Ministry wants a negotiation with Dubček to ensure that the country remains Communist, not a crude intervention that will alienate capitalist and Communist countries alike."

In the end the economic arguments prevailed with the majority around the table. The aides recommended to the Politburo that Dubček be questioned by other Warsaw Pact members at their next meeting in Dresden, East Germany. Dimka was exultant: the threat of a hard-line purge had been warded off, at least for the moment. The thrilling Czech experiment in reformed Communism could continue.

Outside the room, Dimka said to Natalya: "My divorce has come through. I am no longer married to Nina, and that's official."

Her response was muted. "Good," she said, but she looked anxious.

Dimka had been living apart from Nina and little Grigor for a year. He had his own small place, where he and Natalya snatched a few hours of togetherness once or twice a week. It was unsatisfactory to both of them. "I want to marry you," he said.

"I want the same."

"Will you talk to Nik?"

"Yes."

"Tonight?"

"Soon."

"What are you scared of?"

"I'm not frightened for myself," she said. "I don't care what he does to me." Dimka winced, remembering her split lip. "It's you I'm worried about," she went on. "Remember the tape recorder man."

Dimka remembered. The black market trader who had cheated Natalya had been so badly beaten that he ended up in hospital. Natalya's implication was that the same might happen to Dimka if she asked Nik for a divorce.

Dimka did not believe this. "I'm not some lowlife crimi-

nal, I'm right-hand man to the premier. Nik can't touch me."
He was 99 percent sure of this.

"I don't know," Natalya said unhappily. "Nik has high-up
contacts too."

Dimka spoke more quietly. "Do you still have sex with
him?"

"Not often. He has other girls."

"Do you enjoy it?"

"No!"

"Does he?"

"Not much."

"Then what's the problem?"

"His pride. He'll be angry to think I could prefer another
man."

"I'm not afraid of his anger."

"I am. But I will talk to him. I promise."

"Thank you." Dimka lowered his voice to a whisper. "I
love you."

"I love you, too."

Dimka returned to his office and summarized the aides'
meeting for his boss, Alexei Kosygin.

"I don't believe the KGB, either," Kosygin said. "Andropov wants to suppress Dubček's reforms, and he's fabricating evidence to support that move." Yuri Andropov was
the new head of the KGB, and a fanatical hard-liner. Kosygin went on: "But I need reliable intelligence from Czechoslovakia. If the KGB is untrustworthy, who can I turn to?"

"Send my sister there," said Dimka. "She's a reporter for
TASS. In the Cuban missile crisis she sent Khrushchev su-
perb intelligence from Havana via the Red Army telegraph.
She can do the same for you from Prague.

"Good idea," said Kosygin. "Organize it, will you?"

.   .   .

Dimka did not see Natalya the next day, but the day after
that she phoned just as he was leaving the office at seven.

"Did you talk to Nik?" he asked her.

"Not yet." Before Dimka could express his disappointment she went on: "But something else happened. Filipov
came to see him."

"Filipov?" Dimka was astonished. "What does a Defense Ministry official want with your husband?"

"Mischief. I think he told Nik about you and me."

"Why would he do that? I know we're always clashing in meetings, but still . . ."

"There's something I haven't told you. Filipov made a pass at me."

"The stupid prick. When?"

"Two months ago, at the Riverside Bar. You were away with Kosygin."

"Incredible. He thought you might go to bed with him just because I was out of town?"

"Something like that. It was embarrassing. I told him I wouldn't sleep with him if he were the last man in Moscow. I probably should have been gentler."

"You think he talked to Nik for revenge?"

"I'm sure of it."

"What did Nik say to you?"

"Nothing. That's what worries me. I wish he'd bust my lip again."

"Don't say that."

"I'm afraid for you."

"I'll be fine, don't worry."

"Be careful."

"I will."

"Don't walk home, drive."

"I always do."

They said good-bye and hung up. Dimka put on his heavy coat and fur hat and left the building. His Moskvitch 408 was in the Kremlin car park, so he was safe there. He drove home, wondering whether Nik would have the nerve to ram his car, but nothing happened.

He reached his building and parked on the street a block away. This was the moment of greatest vulnerability. He had to walk from the car door to the building door under the streetlights. If they were going to beat him up they might do it here.

There was no one in sight, but they might be hiding.

Nik himself would not be the one to carry out the attack, Dimka presumed. He would send some of his thugs. Dimka wondered how many. Should he fight back? Against two he might have a chance: he was no pussy. If there were three or more he might as well lie down and take it.

He got out of the car and locked it.

He walked along the pavement. Would they burst out of the back of that parked van? Come around the corner of the next building? Be lurking in this doorway?

He reached his building and went inside. Perhaps they would be in the lobby.

He had to wait a long time for the elevator.

When it arrived and the doors closed he wondered if they would be in his apartment.

He unlocked his front door. The place was silent and still. He looked into the bedroom, the living room, the kitchen, and the bathroom.

The place was empty.

He bolted the door.

.   .   .

For two weeks Dimka walked around fearing he could be attacked at any minute. Eventually he decided it was not going to happen. Perhaps Nik did not care that his wife was having an affair; or perhaps he was too wise to make an enemy of someone who worked in the Kremlin. Either way, Dimka began to feel safer.

He still wondered at the spite of Yevgeny Filipov. How could the man even have been surprised that Natalya rejected him? He was dull and conservative and homely-looking and badly dressed: what did he imagine he had to tempt an attractive woman who already had a lover as well as a husband? But clearly Filipov's feelings had been deeply wounded. However, his revenge seemed not to have worked.

But the main thing on Dimka's mind was the Czech reform movement that was being called the Prague Spring. It had caused the most bitter Kremlin split since the Cuban missile crisis. Dimka's boss, Soviet premier Alexei Kosygin, was the leader of the optimists, who hoped the Czechs could find a way out of the bog of inefficiency and waste that was the typical Communist economy. Muting their enthusiasm for tactical reasons, they proposed that Dubček be watched carefully, but that confrontation should be avoided if possible. However, conservatives such as Filipov's boss, Defense Minister Andrei Grechko, and KGB chief Andropov were unnerved by Prague. They feared that radical ideas would undermine their authority, infect other countries, and subvert the Warsaw Pact military alliance. They wanted to send in the tanks, depose Dubček, and install a rigid Communist regime slavishly loyal to Moscow.

The real boss, Leonid Brezhnev, was sitting on the fence, as he so often did, waiting for a consensus to emerge.

Despite being some of the most powerful people in the world, the top men in the Kremlin were scared of stepping out of line. Marxism-Leninism answered all questions, so the eventual decision would be infallibly correct. Anyone who had argued for a different outcome was therefore revealed to be culpably out of touch with orthodox thinking. Dimka sometimes wondered if it was this bad in the Vatican.

Because no one wanted to be the first to express an opinion on the record, as always they had to get their aides to thrash things out informally ahead of any Politburo meeting.

"It's not just Dubček's revisionist ideas about freedom of the press," said Yevgeny Filipov to Dimka one afternoon in the broad corridor outside the Presidium Room. "He's a Slovak who wants to give more rights to the oppressed minority he comes from. Imagine if *that* idea starts to get around places such as Ukraine and Belarus."

As always, Filipov looked ten years out-of-date. Nowadays almost everyone was wearing their hair longer, but he still had an army crop. Dimka tried to forget for a moment that he was a malicious troublemaking bastard. "These dangers are remote," Dimka argued. "There's no immediate threat to the Soviet Union—certainly nothing to justify ham-fisted military intervention."

"Dubček has undermined the KGB. He's expelled several agents from Prague and authorized an investigation into the death of the old foreign minister Jan Masaryk."

"Is the KGB entitled to murder ministers in friendly governments?" Dimka asked. "Is that the message you want to send to Hungary and East Germany? That would make the KGB worse than the CIA. At least the Americans only murder people in enemy countries such as Cuba."

Filipov became petulant. "What is to be gained by allowing this foolishness in Prague?"

"If we invade Czechoslovakia, there will be a diplomatic freeze—you know that."

"So what?"

"It will damage our relations with the West. We're trying to reduce tension with the United States, so that we can spend less on our military. That whole effort could be sabotaged. An invasion might even help Richard Nixon get elected president—and he could *increase* American defense spending. Think what that could cost us!"

Filipov tried to interrupt, but Dimka overrode him. "The invasion will also shock the Third World. We're trying to strengthen our ties with nonaligned countries in the face of rivalry from China, which wants to replace us as leader of global Communism. That's why we're organizing the World Communist Conference in November. That conference could become a humiliating failure if we invade Czechoslovakia."

Filipov sneered: "So you would simply let Dubček do what he likes?"

"On the contrary." Dimka now revealed the proposal favored by his boss. "Kosygin will go to Prague and negotiate a compromise—a nonmilitary solution."

Filipov in his turn put his cards on the table. "The Defense Ministry will support that plan in the Politburo—on condition that we immediately begin preparations for an invasion in case the negotiation should fail."

"Agreed," said Dimka, who felt sure the military would make such preparations anyway.

The decision made, they went in opposite directions. Dimka returned to his office just as his secretary, Vera Pletner, was picking up the phone. He saw her face turn the color of the paper in her typewriter. "Has something happened?" he said.

She gave him the receiver. "Your ex-wife," she said.

Suppressing a groan, Dimka took the instrument and spoke into it. "What is it, Nina?"

"Come at once!" she screamed. "Grisha's gone!"

Dimka's heart seemed to stop. Grigor, whom they called Grisha, was not quite five years old, and had not yet started school. "What do you mean, gone?"

"I can't find him, he's disappeared, I've looked everywhere!"

There was a pain in Dimka's chest. He struggled to remain calm. "When and where did you last see him?"

"He went upstairs to see your mother. I let him go on his own—I always do, it's only three floors in the lift."

"When was that?"

"Less than an hour ago—you have to come!"

"I'm coming. Phone the police."

"Come quickly!"

"Phone the police, okay?"

"Okay."

Dimka dropped the phone and left the room. He raced out of the building. He had not paused to put on his coat, but he hardly noticed the cold Moscow air. He jumped into his Moskvitch, shoved the steering-column gearshift into first, and tore out of the compound. Even with his foot flat to the floor, the little car did not go fast.

Nina still had the apartment they had lived in together at Government House, less than a mile from the Kremlin. Dimka double-parked and ran in.

There was a KGB doorman in the lobby. "Good afternoon, Dmitri Ilich," the man said politely.

"Have you seen Grisha, my little boy?" said Dimka.

"Not today."

"He's disappeared—could he have gone out?"

"Not since I came back from my lunch break at one."

"Have any strangers entered the building today?"

"Several, as always. I have a list—"

"I'll look at it later. If you see Grisha, call the apartment immediately."

"Yes, of course."

"The police will be here any minute."

"I'll send them right up."

Dimka waited for the elevator. He was slick with perspiration. He was so jumpy he pressed the wrong button and had to wait while the lift stopped at an intermediate floor. When he reached Nina's floor she was in the corridor with Dimka's mother, Anya.

Anya was wiping her hands compulsively in her flower-print apron. She said: "He never reached my apartment. I don't understand what happened!"

"Could he have got lost?" said Dimka.

Nina said: "He's gone there twenty times before—he knows the way—but yes, he could have got distracted by something and gone to the wrong place, he's five years old."

"The doorman is sure he hasn't left the building. So we just have to search. We'll knock at every apartment door.

No, wait, most of the residents have telephones. I'll go down and use the doorman's phone to call them."

Anya said: "He might not be in an apartment."

"You two search every corridor and staircase and cleaning closet."

"All right," said Anya. "We'll take the elevator to the top floor and work down."

They got in the lift and Dimka ran down the stairs. In the lobby he told the doorman what was happening and began to phone apartments. He was not sure how many there were in the building: maybe a hundred? "A little boy is lost, have you seen him?" he said each time his call was answered. As soon as he heard "No" he hung up and dialed the next apartment. He made a note of the apartments where there was no answer or no phone.

He had done four floors without a glimmer of hope when the police arrived, a fat sergeant and a young constable. They were maddeningly calm. "We'll take a look around," the sergeant said. "We know this building."

"It'll need more than two of you to search properly!" Dimka said.

"We'll send for reinforcements if necessary, sir," the sergeant said.

Dimka did not want to spend time arguing with them. He went back to phoning, but he was beginning to think that Nina and Anya had the best chance of finding Grisha. If the boy had wandered into the wrong apartment, surely the occupier would have phoned the doorman by now. Grisha might be going up and down staircases, lost. Dimka wanted to weep when he thought of how scared the little boy would be.

After he had been phoning for another ten minutes, the two policemen came up the stairs from the basement with Grisha walking between them, holding the sergeant's hand.

Dimka dropped the phone and ran to him.

Grisha said: "I couldn't open the door, and I cried!"

Dimka picked him up and hugged him, striving not to weep with relief.

After a minute he said: "What happened, Grisha?"

"The policemen found me," he said.

Anya and Nina appeared from the stairwell and came running, ecstatic with relief. Nina snatched Grisha from Dimka and crushed the boy to her bosom.

Dimka turned to the sergeant. "Where did you find him?"

The man looked pleased with himself. "Down in the cellar, in a storeroom. The door wasn't locked, but he couldn't reach the handle. He's had a scare, but otherwise he seems to have come to no harm."

Dimka addressed the boy. "Tell me, Grisha, why did you go down to the basement?"

"The man said there was a puppy—but I couldn't find the puppy!"

"The man?"

"Yes."

"Someone you know?"

Grisha shook his head.

The sergeant put his cap on to leave. "All's well that ends well, then."

"Just a minute," Dimka said. "You heard the boy. A man lured him down there with talk of a puppy."

"Yes, sir, he told me that. But no crime seems to have been committed, as far as I can see."

"The child was abducted!"

"Difficult to know exactly what happened, especially when the information comes from one so young."

"It's not difficult at all. A man inveigled the child down to the cellar, then abandoned him there."

"But what would be the point of that?"

"Look, I'm grateful to you for finding him, but don't you think you're taking the whole thing rather lightly?"

"Children do go astray every day."

Dimka began to be suspicious. "How did you know where to look?"

"A lucky guess. As I say, we're familiar with this building."

Dimka decided not to voice his suspicions while he was still in a state of high emotion. He turned away from the officer and spoke to Grisha again. "Did the man tell you his name?"

"Yes," said Grisha. "His name is Nik."

.   .   .   .   .

Next morning, Dimka sent for the KGB file on Nik Smotrov.

He was in a rage. He wanted to get a gun and kill Nik. He had to keep telling himself to remain calm.

It would not have been difficult for Nik to get past the doorman yesterday. He could have faked a delivery, entered close behind some legitimate residents so that he looked part of the group, or just flashed a Communist Party card. Dimka found it a little more difficult to figure out how Nik could have known that Grisha would be moving from one part of the building to another on his own, but on reflection he decided Nik had probably reconnoitered the building a few days earlier. He could have chatted to some neighbors, figured out the child's daily schedule, and picked the best opportunity. He had probably paid off those local policemen, too. His aim was to scare Dimka half to death.

He had succeeded.

But he was going to regret it.

In theory, Alexei Kosygin as premier could look at any file he liked. In practice, KGB chief Yuri Andropov would decide what Kosygin could and could not see. However, Dimka felt sure that Nik's activities, though criminal, had no political dimension, so there was no reason for the file to be withheld. Sure enough, it arrived on his desk that afternoon.

It was thick.

As Dimka suspected, Nik was a black market trader. Like most such men, he was an opportunist. He would buy and sell whatever came his way: flowered shirts, costly perfume, electric guitars, lingerie, Scotch whisky—any illegally imported luxury difficult to obtain in the Soviet Union. Dimka went carefully through the reports, looking for something he could use to destroy Nik.

The KGB dealt in rumors, and Dimka needed something definite. He could go to the police, report what the KGB file said, and demand an investigation. But Nik was sure to be bribing the police—otherwise he could not have got away with his crimes for so long. And his protectors would naturally want the bribes to continue. So they would make sure the investigation got nowhere.

The file contained plenty of material on Nik's personal life. He had a mistress and several girlfriends, including one with whom he smoked marijuana. Dimka wondered how much Natalya knew about the girlfriends. Nik met business associates most afternoons at the Bar Madrid near the Central Market. He had a pretty wife, who—

Dimka was shocked to read that Nik's wife was having a

long-term affair with Dmitri Ilich "Dimka" Dvorkin, aide
to Premier Kosygin.

Seeing his own name felt horrible. Nothing was private,
it seemed.

At least there were no pictures or tape recordings.

There was, however, a photo of Nik, whom Dimka had
never seen. He was a good-looking man with a charming
smile. In the picture he wore a jacket with epaulets, a high-
fashion item. According to the notes he was just under six
feet tall with an athletic build.

Dimka wanted to pound him into jelly.

He put revenge fantasies out of his mind and read on.

Soon he struck gold.

Nik was buying television sets from the Red Army.

The Soviet military had a colossal budget that no one
dared question for fear of being thought unpatriotic. Some
of the money was spent on high-technology equipment
bought from the West. In particular, every year the Red
Army bought hundreds of expensive televisions. Their preferred brand was Franck, of West Berlin, whose sets had a
superior picture and great sound. According to the file, most
of these TVs were not needed by the army. They were ordered by a small group of midranking officers, who were
named in the file. The officers then declared the televisions
obsolete and sold them cheaply to Nik, who resold them at
a huge price on the black market and shared out the profits.

Most of Nik's dealings were penny-ante, but this scam
had been making him serious money for years.

There was no proof that the story was true, but it made
total sense to Dimka. The KGB had reported the story to
the army, but an army investigation had turned up no proof.
Most likely, Dimka thought, the investigator had been cut
in on the deal.

He phoned Natalya's office. "Quick question," he said.
"What brand of TV do you have at home?"

"Franck," she said immediately. "It's great. I can get you
one, if you like."

"No, thanks."

"Why do you ask?"

"I'll explain later." Dimka hung up.

He looked at his watch. It was five. He left the Kremlin
and drove to the street called Sadovaya-Samotyochnaya.

He had to scare Nik. It would not be easy, but he had to do it. Nik had to be made to understand that he must never, ever, threaten Dimka's family.

He parked his Moskvitch but did not get out immediately. He recalled the frame of mind he had been in throughout the Cuban missile project, when he had to keep the mission secret at all costs. He had destroyed men's careers and ruined their lives without hesitation, because the job had to be done. Now he was going to ruin Nik.

He locked his car and walked to the Bar Madrid.

He pushed open the door and stepped inside. He stood still and looked around. It was a bleak modern place, cold and plastic, insufficiently warmed by an electric fire and some photographs of flamenco dancers on the walls. The handful of customers gazed at him with interest. They looked like petty crooks. None resembled the photo of Nik in the file.

At the far end of the room was a corner bar with a door next to it marked PRIVATE.

Dimka strode through the room as if he owned it. Without stopping he spoke to the man behind the bar. "Nik in the back?"

The man looked as if he might be about to tell Dimka to stop and wait, but then he looked again at Dimka's face and changed his mind. "Yes," he said.

Dimka pushed open the door.

In a small back room four men were playing cards. There was a lot of money on the table. To one side, on a couch, two young women in cocktail dresses and heavy makeup were smoking long American cigarettes and looking bored.

Dimka recognized Nik immediately. The face was as handsome as the photograph had suggested, but the camera had failed to capture the cold expression. Nik looked up and said: "This is a private room. Piss off."

Dimka said: "I've got a message for you."

Nik put his cards facedown on the table and sat back. "Who the fuck are you?"

"Something bad is going to happen."

Two of the card players stood up and turned to face Dimka. One reached inside his jacket. Dimka thought he might be about to draw a weapon. But Nik held up a cautionary hand, and the man hesitated.

Nik kept his eyes on Dimka. "What are you talking about?"

"When the bad thing happens, you'll ask who's causing it."

"And you'll tell me?"

"I'm telling you now. It's Dmitri Ilich Dvorkin. He's the cause of your problems."

"I don't have any problems, asshole."

"You didn't, until yesterday. Then you made a mistake— asshole."

The men around Nik tensed, but he remained calm. "Yesterday?" His eyes narrowed. "Are you the creep she's fucking?"

"When you find yourself in so much trouble that you don't know what to do, remember my name."

"You're Dimka!"

"You'll see me again," said Dimka, and he turned slowly and walked out of the room.

As he walked through the bar, all eyes were on him. He looked straight ahead, expecting a bullet in the back at any moment.

He reached the door and went out.

He grinned to himself. I got away with it, he thought.

Now he had to make good on his threat.

He drove six miles from the city center to the Khodynka airfield and parked at the headquarters of Red Army Intelligence. The old building was a bizarre piece of Stalin-era architecture, a nine-story tower surrounded by a two-story outer ring. The directorate had expanded into a newer fifteen-story building nearby: intelligence organizations never got smaller.

Carrying the KGB file on Nik, Dimka went into the old building and asked for General Volodya Peshkov.

A guard said: "Do you have an appointment?"

Dimka raised his voice. "Don't fuck around, son. Just call the general's secretary and say I'm here."

After a flurry of anxious activity—few people dropped by this place without a summons—he was directed through a metal detector and led up in the lift to an office on the top floor.

This was the highest building around and it had a fine view over the roofs of Moscow. Volodya welcomed Dimka and offered him tea. Dimka had always liked his uncle. Now in his midfifties, Volodya had silver-gray hair. Despite the hard blue-eyed stare, he was a reformer—unusual among the generally conservative military. But he had been to America.

"What's on your mind?" said Volodya. "You look ready to kill someone."

"I've got a problem," Dimka told him. "I've made an enemy."

"Not unusual, in the circles within which you work."

"This is nothing to do with politics. Nik Smotrov is a gangster."

"How did you come to fall foul of such a man?"

"I'm sleeping with his wife."

Volodya looked disapproving. "And he's threatening you."

Volodya had probably never been unfaithful to Zoya, his scientist wife, who was as beautiful as she was brilliant. But that meant he had scant sympathy for Dimka. Volodya might have felt differently if he had been so foolish as to marry someone like Nina.

Dimka said: "Nik kidnapped Grisha."

Volodya sat upright. "What? When?"

"Yesterday. We got him back. He was only shut in the cellar of Government House. But it was a warning."

"You have to give up this woman!"

Dimka ignored that. "There's a particular reason why I've come to you, Uncle. There's a way you could help me and do the army some good at the same time."

"Go on."

"Nik is behind a fraud that costs the army millions every year." Dimka explained about the TV sets. When he had finished he put the file on Volodya's desk. "It's all in there—including the names of the officers who are organizing the whole thing."

Volodya did not pick up the file. "I'm not a policeman. I can't arrest this Nik. And if he's bribing police officers, there's not much I can do about it."

"But you can arrest the army officers involved."

"Oh, yes. They will all be in army jails within twenty-four hours."

"And you can shut down the whole business."

"Very quickly."

And then Nik will be ruined, Dimka thought. "Thank you, Uncle," he said. "That's very helpful."

. . .

Dimka was in his apartment, packing for Czechoslovakia, when Nik came to see him.

The Politburo had approved Kosygin's plan. Dimka was flying with him to Prague to negotiate a nonmilitary solution to the crisis. They would find a way to allow the liberalization experiment to continue while at the same time reassuring the diehards that there was no fundamental threat to the Soviet system. But what Dimka hoped was that in the long term the Soviet system *would* change.

Prague in May would be mild and wet. Dimka was folding his raincoat when the doorbell rang.

There was no doorman in his building, and no intercom system. The street door was permanently unlocked and visitors walked upstairs to the apartments unannounced. It was not as luxurious as Government House, where his ex-wife was living in their old apartment. Dimka occasionally felt resentful, but he was glad Grisha was near his grandmother.

Dimka opened the door and was shocked to see his lover's husband standing there.

Nik was an inch taller than Dimka, and heavier, but Dimka was ready to take him on. He stepped back a pace and picked up the nearest heavy object, a glass ashtray, to use as a weapon.

"No need for that," said Nik, but he stepped into the hall and shut the door behind him.

"Piss off," said Dimka. "Go now, before you get into any more trouble." He managed to sound more confident than he felt.

Nik glared at him with hot hatred in his eyes. "You've made your point," he said. "You're not afraid of me. You're powerful enough to turn my life to shit. I should be scared of you. All right, I get it. I'm scared."

He did not sound it.

Dimka said: "What have you come here for?"

"I don't give a toss for the bitch. I only married her to please my mother, who's dead now. But a man's pride is hurt when another man pokes his fire. You know what I mean."

"Get to the point."

"My business is ruined. No one in the army will speak to me, let alone sell me TV sets. Men who have built four-bedroom dachas from the money I've made for them now walk past me in the street without speaking—those who aren't in jail."

"You shouldn't have threatened my son."

"I know it now. I thought my wife was opening her legs for some little apparatchik. I didn't know he was a fucking warlord. I underestimated you."

"So bugger off home and lick your wounds."

"I have to make a living."

"Try working."

"No jokes, please. I've found another source of Western TV sets—nothing to do with the army."

"Why should I care?"

"I can rebuild the business you destroyed."

"So what?"

"Can I come in and sit down?"

"Don't be so fucking stupid."

Rage flared again in Nik's eyes, and Dimka feared he had gone too far, but the flame died down, and Nik said meekly: "Okay, here's the deal. I'll give you ten percent of the profits."

"You want me to go into business with you? In a criminal enterprise? You must be mad."

"All right, twenty percent. And you don't have to do anything except leave me alone."

"I don't want your money, you fool. This is the Soviet Union. You can't just buy anything you want, like in America. My connections are worth far more than you could ever pay me."

"There must be something you want."

Until this moment Dimka had been arguing with Nik just to keep him off balance, but now he saw an opportunity. "Oh, yes," he said. "There is something I want."

"Name it."

"Divorce your wife."

"What?"

"I want you to get a divorce."

"Divorce Natalya?"

"Divorce your wife," Dimka said again. "Which of those three words are you having trouble understanding?"

"Fuck me, is that all?"

"Yes."

"You can marry her. I wouldn't touch her now anyway."

"If you divorce her, I'll leave you alone. I'm not a cop, and I'm not running a crusade against corruption in the USSR. I have more important work to do."

"It's a deal." Nik opened the door. "I'll send her up."

That took Dimka by surprise. "She's here?"

"Waiting in the car. I'll have her things packed up and sent around tomorrow. I don't want her in my place ever again."

Dimka raised his voice. "Don't you dare hurt her. If she's even bruised, the whole deal is off."

Nik turned in the doorway and pointed a threatening finger. "And don't you renege. If you try to screw me I'll cut off her nipples with the kitchen scissors."

Dimka believed he would. He suppressed a shudder. "Get out of my flat."

Nik left without closing the door.

Dimka was breathing hard, as if he had been running. He stood still in the small hall of the apartment. He heard Nik clattering down the stairs. He put the ashtray down on the hall table. His fingers were slippery with perspiration, and he almost dropped it.

What just happened seemed like a dream. Had Nik really stood in this hallway and agreed to a divorce? Had Dimka really scared him off?

A minute later he heard footsteps of a different kind on the stairs: lighter, faster, coming up. He did not go out of the apartment: he felt stuck where he was.

Natalya appeared in the doorway, her broad smile lighting up the whole place. She threw herself into his arms. He buried his face in her mass of curls. "You're here," he said.

"Yes," she said. "And I'm never going to leave."

CHAPTER FORTY-FOUR

Rebecca was tempted to be unfaithful to Bernd. But she could not lie to him. So she told him everything in a convulsion of repentance. "I've met someone I really like," she said. "And I've kissed him. Twice. I'm so sorry. I'll never do it again."

She was scared of what he would say next. He might immediately ask for a divorce. Most men would. Bernd was better than most men, though. But it would break her heart if he were not angry but simply humiliated. She would have hurt the person she loved most in the world.

However, Bernd's response to her confession was shockingly different from anything she had expected. "You should go ahead," he said. "Have an affair with the guy."

They were in bed, last thing at night, and she turned over and stared at him. "How can you say that?"

"This is 1968, the age of free love. Everyone is having sex with everyone else. Why should you miss out?"

"You don't mean that."

"I didn't mean it to sound so trivial."

"What did you mean?"

"I know you love me," he said, "and I know you like having sex with me, but you mustn't go through the rest of your life without experiencing the real thing."

"I don't believe in the real thing," she said. "It's different for everyone. It's much better with you than it was with Hans."

"It will always be good, because we love each other. But I think you need a really good fuck."

And he was right, she thought. She loved Bernd and she liked the peculiar sex they had, but when she thought about Claus lying on top of her, kissing her and moving inside her, and how she would lift her hips to meet his thrusts, she immediately got wet. She was ashamed of this feeling. Was she an animal? Perhaps she was, but Bernd was right about what she needed.

"I think I'm weird," she said. "Maybe it's because of what happened to me in the war." She had told Bernd—but no one else, ever—how Red Army soldiers had been about to rape her when Carla had offered herself instead. German women rarely spoke of that time, even to one another. But Rebecca would never forget the sight of Carla going up that staircase, head held high, with the Soviet soldiers following her like eager dogs. Rebecca, thirteen years old, had known what they were going to do, and she had wept with relief that it was not happening to her.

Bernd asked perceptively: "Do you also feel guilty that you escaped while Carla suffered?"

"Yes, isn't that strange?" she said. "I was a child, and a victim, but I feel as if I did something shameful."

"It's not unusual," Bernd said. "Men who survive battles feel remorse because others died and not them." Bernd had got the scar on his forehead during the battle of Seelow Heights.

"I felt better after Carla and Werner adopted me," Rebecca said. "Somehow that made it all right. Parents make sacrifices for their children, don't they? Women suffer to bring children into the world. Perhaps it doesn't make much sense, but once I became Carla's daughter I felt entitled."

"It makes sense."

"Do you really want me to go to bed with another man?"

"Yes."

"But why?"

"Because the alternative is worse. If you don't do it, you'll always feel, in your heart, that you missed out on something because of me, that you made a sacrifice for my sake. I'd rather you went ahead and tried it. You don't have to reveal the details: just come home and tell me you love me."

"I don't know," Rebecca said, and she slept uneasily that night.

On the evening of the next day she was sitting next to the man who wanted to become her lover, Claus Krohn, in a meeting room in Hamburg's enormous green-roofed neo-Renaissance town hall. Rebecca was a member of the parliament that ran the Hamburg city-state. The committee was discussing a proposal to demolish a slum and build a new shopping center. But all she could think about was Claus.

She was sure that after tonight's meeting Claus would invite her to a bar for a drink. This would be the third time. After the first he had kissed her good night. The second had ended with a passionate clinch in a car park, when they had kissed with mouths open and he had touched her breasts. Tonight, she felt sure, he would ask her to go to his apartment.

She did not know what to do. She could not concentrate on the debate. She doodled on her agenda. She was both bored and anxious: the meeting was tedious but she did not want it to end because she was scared of what would happen next.

Claus was an attractive man: intelligent, kind, charming, and exactly her age, thirty-seven. His wife had died in a car crash two years ago, and he had no children. He was not good-looking in the movie-star sense, but he had a warm smile. Tonight he was wearing a politician's blue suit, but he was the only man in the room with a shirt open at the neck. Rebecca wanted to make love to him, wanted it badly. And at the same time she dreaded it.

The meeting came to an end and, as she expected, Claus asked her if she would like to meet him at the Yacht Bar, a quiet place well away from city hall. They drove there in their separate cars.

The bar was small and dark, busiest in the daytime, when it was used by people who had sailboats, quiet and almost deserted now. Claus ordered a beer, Rebecca asked for a glass of Sekt. As soon as they were settled she said: "I told my husband about us."

Claus was startled. "Why?" he said. Then he added: "Not that there's much to tell." All the same he looked guilty.

"I can't lie to Bernd," she said. "I love him."

"And you obviously can't lie to me, either," Claus said.

"I'm sorry."

"It isn't something to apologize for—just the opposite. Thank you for being honest. I appreciate it." Claus looked crestfallen, and amid all her other emotions Rebecca felt pleased that he liked her enough to be so disappointed. He said ruefully: "If you've confessed to your husband, why are you here with me now?"

"Bernd told me to go ahead," she said.

"Your husband wants you to kiss me?"

"He wants me to become your lover."

"That's creepy. Is it to do with his paralysis?"

"No," she lied. "Bernd's condition makes no difference to our sex life." This was the story she had told her mother and a few other women whom she was really close to. She deceived them for Bernd's sake: she felt it would be humiliating for him if people knew the truth.

"Well," said Claus, "if this is my lucky day, shall we go straight to my apartment?"

"Let's not rush, if you don't mind."

He put his hand over hers. "It's okay to be nervous."

"I haven't done this often."

He smiled. "That's not a bad thing, you know, even if we are living in the age of free love."

"I slept with two boys at university. Then I married Hans, who turned out to be a police spy. Then I fell in love with Bernd and we escaped together. There, that's my entire love life."

"Let's talk about something else for a while," he said. "Are your parents still in the East?"

"Yes, they'll never get permission to leave. Once you make an enemy of someone like Hans Hoffmann—my first husband—he never forgets."

"You must miss them."

She could not express how much she missed her family. The Communists had blocked calls to the West the day they built the Wall, so she could not even speak to her parents on the phone. All she had was letters—opened and read by the Stasi, usually delayed, often censored, any enclosure of value stolen by the police. A few photos had got through, and Rebecca had them next to her bed: her father turning gray, her mother getting heavier, Lili growing into a beautiful woman.

Instead of trying to explain her grief she said: "Tell me about yourself. What happened to you in the war?"

"Nothing much, except that I starved, like most kids," he said. "The house next door was destroyed and everyone in it killed, but we were all right. My father is a surveyor: he spent much of the war assessing bomb damage and making buildings safe."

"Do you have brothers and sisters?"

"One of each. You?"

"My sister, Lili, is still in East Berlin. My brother, Walli, escaped soon after I did. He's a guitar player in a group called Plum Nellie."

"That Walli? He's your brother?"

"Yes. I was there when he was born, on the floor of our kitchen, which was the only warm room in the house. Quite an experience for a fourteen-year-old girl."

"So he escaped."

"And came to live with me, here in Hamburg. He joined the group when they were playing some grimy club on the Reeperbahn."

"And now he's a pop star. Do you see him?"

"Of course. Every time Plum Nellie plays in West Germany."

"What a thrill!" Claus looked at her glass and saw that it was empty. "Would you like another Sekt?"

Rebecca felt a tightness in her chest. "No, thanks, I don't think so."

"Listen," he said. "Something I want you to understand. I'm desperate to make love to you, but I know you're torn. Just remember that you can change your mind at any moment. There's no such thing as the point of no return. If you feel uncomfortable, just say so. I won't be angry or insistent, I promise. I would hate to feel I'd pushed you into something you weren't ready for."

It was exactly the right thing for him to say. The tightness eased. Rebecca had been afraid of getting in too deep, realizing she had made the wrong decision, and feeling unable to back out. Claus's promise set her mind at rest. "Let's go," she said.

They got into their cars and Rebecca followed Claus. Driving along she felt a wild exhilaration. She was about to give herself to Claus. She pictured his face as she took off her blouse: she was wearing a new bra, black with lace trimming. She thought of how they would kiss—frantically before, lovingly after. She imagined his sigh as she took his penis in her mouth. She felt she had never wanted anything so badly, and she had to clamp her teeth together to prevent herself crying out.

Claus had a small apartment in a modern building. Going up in the elevator, Rebecca was assailed by doubts again. What if he didn't like what he saw when she took off her clothes? She was thirty-seven: she no longer had the firm breasts and perfect skin of her teenage years. What if he had a hidden dark side? He might produce handcuffs and a whip, then lock the door—

She told herself not to be silly. She had the normal woman's ability to know when she was with a weirdo, and Claus was delightfully normal. All the same, she felt apprehensive as he opened the apartment door and ushered her in.

It was a typical man's home, a bit bare of ornament, with utilitarian furniture except for a large television and an expensive record player. Rebecca said: "How long have you lived here?"

"A year."

As she had guessed, it was not the home he had shared with his late wife.

He had undoubtedly planned what to do next. Moving quickly, he ignited the gas fire, put a Mozart string quartet on the record deck, and assembled a tray with a bottle of schnapps, two glasses, and a bowl of salted nuts.

They sat side by side on the couch.

She wanted to ask him how many other girls he had seduced on this couch. It would have struck a wrong note, but all the same she wondered. Was he enjoying being single, or did he long to marry again? Another question she was not going to ask.

He poured drinks and she took a sip just for something to do.

He said: "If we kiss now, we'll taste the liquor on each other's tongues."

She grinned. "All right."

He leaned toward her. "I don't like to waste money," he murmured.

She said: "I'm so glad you're frugal."

For a moment they could not kiss because they were giggling too much.

Then they did.

.   .   .

People thought Cameron Dewar was mad when he invited Richard Nixon to speak at Berkeley. It was the most famously radical campus in the country. Nixon would be crucified, they said. There would be a riot. Cam did not care.

Cam thought Nixon was the only hope for America. Nixon was strong and determined. People said he was unscrupulous and sly: so what? America needed such a leader. God forbid that the president should be a man such as Bobby Kennedy who could not stop asking himself what was right and what was wrong. The next president had to destroy the rioters in the ghettos and the Vietcong in the jungle, not search his own conscience.

In his letter to Nixon, Cam said that the liberals and the crypto-Communists on campus got all the attention in the left-leaning media, but in truth most students were conservative and law-abiding, and there would be a huge turnout for Nixon.

Cam's family was furious. His grandfather and his great-grandfather had both been Democratic senators. His parents had always voted Democrat. His sister was so outraged she could barely speak. "How can you campaign for injustice and dishonesty and war?" Beep said.

"There's no justice without order on the streets, and there's no peace while we're threatened by international Communism."

"Where have you *been* the last few years? When the blacks were nonviolent they just got attacked with nightsticks and dogs! Governor Reagan praises the police for beating up student demonstrators!"

"You're so against the police."

"No, I'm not. I'm against criminals. Cops who beat up demonstrators are criminals, and they should go to jail."

"There, that's why I support such men as Nixon and

Reagan: because their opponents want to put cops in jail instead of troublemakers."

Cam was pleased when Vice President Hubert Humphrey declared that he would seek the Democratic nomination. Humphrey had been Johnson's yes-man for four years, and no one would trust him either to win the war or to negotiate peace, so he was unlikely to be elected, but he might spoil things for the more dangerous Bobby Kennedy.

Cam's letter to Nixon got a reply from one of the campaign team, John Ehrlichman, suggesting a meeting. Cam was thrilled. He wanted to work in politics: maybe this was the beginning!

Ehrlichman was Nixon's advance man. He was intimidatingly tall, six foot two, with black eyebrows and receding hair. "Dick loved your letter," he said.

They met at a fragrant coffee shop on Telegraph Avenue and sat outside under a tree in new leaf, watching students go by on bicycles in the sunshine. "A nice place to study," Ehrlichman said. "I went to UCLA."

He asked Cam a lot of questions. He was intrigued by Cam's Democratic forebears. "My grandmother was editor of a newspaper called the *Buffalo Anarchist*," Cam admitted.

"It's a sign of how America is becoming more conservative," Ehrlichman said.

Cam was relieved to learn that his family would not be an obstruction to a career in the Republican Party.

"Dick won't speak on the Berkeley campus," Ehrlichman said. "It's too risky."

Cam was disappointed. He thought Ehrlichman was wrong: the event could be a big success.

He was about to argue when Ehrlichman said: "But he wants you to start a group called Berkeley Students for Nixon. It will show that not all young people are fooled by Gene McCarthy or in love with Bobby Kennedy."

Cam was flattered to be taken so seriously by a presidential campaigner, and he quickly agreed to do what Ehrlichman asked.

His closest friend on campus was Jamie Mulgrove, who like Cam was majoring in Russian and a member of the Young Republicans. They announced the formation of the group, and got some publicity in *The Daily Californian*, the student news-paper, but only ten people joined.

Cam and Jamie organized a lunchtime meeting to attract members. With Ehrlichman's help, Cam got three promi-nent California Republicans to speak. He booked a hall that would hold two hundred fifty.

He sent out a press release and this time got a wider re-sponse from local newspapers and radio stations intrigued by the counterintuitive idea of Berkeley students support-ing Nixon. Several ran stories about the meeting and prom-ised to send reporters.

Sharon McIsaac from the *San Francisco Examiner* called Cam. "How many members do you have so far?" she asked.

Cam took an instinctive dislike to her pushy tone. "I can't tell you that," he said. "It's like a military secret. Be-fore a battle, you don't let the enemy know how many guns you've got."

"Not many, then," she said sarcastically.

The meeting was shaping up to be a minor media event. Unfortunately, they could not sell the tickets.

They could have given them away, but that was risky: it could attract left-wing students who would heckle.

Cam still believed that thousands of students were con-servative, but he realized they were unwilling to admit it in today's atmosphere. That was cowardly, but politics did not matter much to most people, he knew.

But what was he going to do?

The day before the meeting he had more than two hun-dred tickets left—and Ehrlichman called. "Just checking, Cam," he said. "How's it shaping up?"

"It's going to be terrific, John," Cam lied.

"Any press interest?"

"Some. I'm expecting a few reporters."

"Sold many tickets?" It was almost as if Ehrlichman could read Cam's mind over the phone.

Cam was caught in his deception and could not back-track. "A few more to go and we'll be sold out." With luck, Ehrlichman would never know.

Then Ehrlichman dropped his bombshell. "I'll be in San Francisco tomorrow, so I'll come along."

"Great!" said Cam, his heart sinking.

"See you then."

That afternoon, after a class on Dostoevsky, Cam and Jamie stayed in the lecture theater and scratched their heads. Where could they find two hundred Republican students?

"They don't have to be real students," Cam said.

"We don't want the press saying the meeting was packed with stooges," Jamie said anxiously.

"Not stooges. Just Republicans who don't happen to be students."

"I still think it's risky."

"I know. But better than a flop."

"Where are we going to get the bodies?"

"Do you have a number for the Oakland Young Republicans?"

"I do."

They went to a pay phone and Cam called. "I need two hundred people just to make the event look like a success," he confessed.

"I'll see what I can do," the man said.

"Tell them not to speak to reporters, though. We don't want the press finding out that Berkeley Students for Nixon consists mainly of people who aren't students."

After Cam hung up, Jamie said: "Isn't this kind of dishonest?"

"What do you mean?" Cam knew exactly what he meant, but he was not going to admit it. He was not willing to jeopardize his big chance with Ehrlichman just for the sake of a petty lie.

Jamie said: "Well, we're telling people that Berkeley students support Nixon, but we're faking it."

"But we can't back out now!" Cameron was scared that Jamie would want to cancel the whole thing.

"I guess not," Jamie said dubiously.

Cam was in suspense all the next morning. At half past twelve there were only seven people in the hall. When the speakers arrived Cam took them to a side room and offered them coffee and cookies baked by Jamie's mother. At a quarter to one the place was still almost deserted. But then at ten to one, people started to trickle in. By one the room was almost full, and Cam breathed a little easier.

He invited Ehrlichman to chair the meeting. "No," said Ehrlichman. "It looks better if a student does it."

Cam introduced the speakers but hardly heard what they said. His meeting was a success, and Ehrlichman was impressed—but it could still go wrong.

At the end he summed up and said that the popularity of the meeting was a sign of a student backlash against demonstrations, liberalism, and drugs. He got an enthusiastic round of applause.

When it was over he could hardly wait to get them all out the door.

The reporter Sharon McIsaac was there. She had a crusading look, reminding him of Evie Williams, who had spurned his adolescent love. Sharon was approaching students. A couple declined to speak to her; then, to Cam's relief, she buttonholed one of the few genuine Berkeley Republicans. By the time the interview was over, everyone else had left.

At two thirty Cam and Ehrlichman stood in an empty room. "Well done," said Ehrlichman. "Are you sure all those people were students?"

Cam hesitated. "Are we on the record?"

Ehrlichman laughed. "Listen," he said. "When the semester ends, do you want to come and work on Dick's presidential election campaign? We could use a guy like you."

Cam's heart leaped. "I'd love to," he said.

. . .

Dave was in London, staying with his parents in Great Peter Street, when Fitz knocked on the door.

The family was in the kitchen: Lloyd, Daisy, and Dave—Evie was in Los Angeles. It was six, the hour at which the children had used to eat their evening meal, which they called "tea," when they were small. In those days the parents would sit with them for a while and talk about the day, before going out for the evening, usually to some political meeting. Daisy would smoke and Lloyd would sometimes make cocktails. The habit of meeting in the kitchen to chat at that hour had persisted long after the children grew too old to have "tea."

Dave was talking to his parents about his breakup with Beep when the maid came in and said: "It's Earl Fitzherbert."

Dave saw his father tense up.

Daisy put her hand on Lloyd's arm and said: "It will be all right."

Dave was consumed with curiosity. He knew, now, that the earl had seduced Ethel when she was his housekeeper, and that Lloyd was the illegitimate child of their affair. He knew, too, that Fitz had angrily refused to acknowledge Lloyd as his son for more than half a century. So what was the earl doing here tonight?

Fitz walked into the room using two canes and said: "My sister, Maud, has died."

Daisy sprang up. "I'm so sorry to hear that, Fitz," she said. "Come and sit down." She took his arm.

But Fitz hesitated and looked at Lloyd. "I have no right to sit down in this house," he said.

Dave could tell that humility did not come naturally to Fitz.

Lloyd was controlling intense emotion. This was the father who had rejected him all his life. "Please sit down," Lloyd said stiffly.

Dave pulled out a kitchen chair and Fitz sat at the table. "I'm going to her funeral," he said. "It's in two days' time."

Lloyd said: "She was living in East Germany, wasn't she? How did you hear that she had died?"

"Maud has a daughter, Carla. She telephoned the British embassy in East Berlin. They were so kind as to phone me and give me the news. I was a minister in the Foreign Office until 1945, and that still counts for something, I'm glad to say."

Without being asked, Daisy took a bottle of Scotch from a cupboard, poured an inch into a glass, and put it in front of Fitz with a small jug of tap water. Fitz poured a little water into the whisky and took a sip. "How kind of you to remember, Daisy," he said. Dave recalled that Daisy had lived with Fitz for a while, when she was married to his son, Boy Fitzherbert. That was why she knew how he liked his whisky.

Lloyd said: "Lady Maud was my late mother's best friend." He sounded a little less uptight. "I last saw her when Mam took me to Berlin in 1933. At that time Maud was a journalist, writing articles that annoyed Hitler."

Fitz said: "I haven't seen my sister or spoken to her since 1919. I was angry with her for marrying without my permission, and marrying a German, too; and I stayed angry for almost fifty years." His discolored old face showed profound sadness. "Now it's too late for me to forgive her. What a fool I was." He looked directly at Lloyd. "A fool about that, and other things."

Lloyd gave a brief, silent nod of acknowledgment.

Dave caught his mother's eye. He felt that something important had just happened, and her expression confirmed it. Fitz's regret was so deep it could hardly be spoken, but he had come as near as he could to apologizing.

It was hard to imagine that this feeble old man had once been swept by tidal waves of passion. But Fitz had loved Ethel, and Dave knew that Ethel had felt the same, for he had heard her say it. Fitz had rejected their child and now, after a lifetime of denial, he was looking back and comprehending how much he had lost. It was unbearably sad.

"I'll go with you," Dave said impulsively.

"What?"

"To the funeral. I'll go to Berlin with you." Dave was not sure why he wanted to do this, except he sensed it might have a healing effect.

"You're very kind, young Dave," said Fitz.

Daisy said: "That would be a wonderful thing to do, Dave."

Dave glanced at his father, nervous that Lloyd would disapprove; but there were surprising tears in Lloyd's eyes.

Next day Dave and Fitz flew to Berlin. They stayed overnight at a hotel on the west side.

"Do you mind if I call you Fitz?" Dave said over dinner. "We always called Bernie Leckwith 'Grandpa,' even though we knew he was my father's stepfather. And as a child I never met you. So it feels, like, too late to change."

"I'm in no position to dictate to you," said Fitz. "And anyway, I really don't mind."

They talked about politics. "We Conservatives were right about Communism," said Fitz. "We said it wouldn't work, and it doesn't. But we were wrong about social democracy. When Ethel said we should give everyone free education and free health care and unemployment insurance, I told her she was living in a dream world. But now look: everything she campaigned for has come to pass, and yet England is still England."

Fitz had a charming ability to admit his mistakes, Dave

thought. Clearly the earl had not always been this way: his quarrels with his family had lasted decades. Perhaps it was a quality that came with old age.

The following morning a black Mercedes with a driver, ordered by Dave's secretary, Jenny Pritchard, was waiting to take them across the border and into the East.

They drove to Checkpoint Charlie.

They went through a barrier and into a long shed where they had to hand over their passports. Then they were asked to wait.

The border guard who had taken their passports went away. After a while a tall, stooped man in a civilian suit ordered them to get out of their Mercedes and follow him.

The man strode ahead, then looked around, irritated at Fitz's slowness. "Please hurry," he said in English.

Dave remembered the German he had learned in school and improved in Hamburg. "My grandfather is old," he said indignantly.

Fitz spoke in a low voice. "Don't argue," he said to Dave. "This arrogant bastard is with the Stasi." Dave raised an eyebrow: he had not previously heard Fitz use bad language. "They're like the KGB, only not so softhearted," Fitz added.

They were taken to a bare office with a metal table and hard wooden chairs. They were not asked to sit, but Dave held a chair for Fitz, who sank into it gratefully.

The tall man spoke German to an interpreter, who smoked cigarettes as he translated the questions. "Why do you wish to enter East Germany?"

"To attend the funeral of a close relative at eleven this morning," Fitz answered. He looked at his wristwatch, a gold Omega. "It's ten now. I hope this won't take long."

"It will take as long as necessary. What is your sister's name?"

"Why do you ask that?"

"You say you wish to attend the funeral of your sister. What is her name?"

"I said I wanted to attend the funeral of a close relative. I did not say it was my sister. You obviously know all about it already."

This secret policeman had been waiting for them, Dave realized. It was hard to imagine why.

"Answer the question. What is your sister's name?"

"She was Frau Maud von Ulrich, as your spies have obviously informed you."

Dave noticed that Fitz was getting annoyed, and breaking his own injunction to say as little as possible.

The man said: "How is it that Lord Fitzherbert has a German sister?"

"She married a friend of mine called Walter von Ulrich, who was a German diplomat in London. He was killed by the Gestapo during the Second World War. What did you do in the war?"

Dave saw, from the look of fury on the tall man's face, that he had understood; but he did not answer the question. Instead he turned to Dave. "Where is Walli Franck?"

Dave was astonished. "I don't know."

"Of course you know. He is in your music group."

"The group has split. I haven't seen Walli for months. I don't know where he is."

"This is not believable. You are partners."

"Partners fall out."

"What is the reason for your quarrel?"

"Personal and musical differences." In truth the differences were purely personal. Dave and Walli had never had any musical differences.

"Yet now you wish to attend the funeral of his grandmother."

"She was my great-aunt."

"Where did you last see Walli Franck?"

"In San Francisco."

"The address, please."

Dave hesitated. This was getting nasty.

"Answer, please. Walli Franck is wanted for murder."

"I last saw him in Buena Vista Park. That's on Haight Street. I don't know where he lives."

"Do you realize that it is a crime to obstruct the police in the course of their duty?"

"Of course."

"And that if you commit such a crime in East Germany, you may be arrested and tried and put in jail here?"

Dave was suddenly frightened, but he tried to remain calm. "And then millions of fans all over the world would demand my release."

"They will not be allowed to interfere with justice."

Fitz put in: "Are you sure your comrades in Moscow would be pleased with you for creating a major international diplomatic incident over this?"

The tall man laughed scornfully, but he was not convincing.

Dave had a flash of insight. "You're Hans Hoffmann, aren't you?"

The interpreter did not translate this, but instead said quickly: "His name is of no concern to you."

But Dave could tell by the tall man's face that his guess had been right. He said: "Walli told me about you. His sister threw you out, and you've been taking revenge on her family ever since."

"Just answer the question."

"Is this part of your revenge? Harassing two innocent men on their way to a funeral? Is that the kind of people you Communists are?"

"Wait here, please." Hans and his interpreter left the room, and Dave heard from the other side of the door the sound of a bolt being shot.

"I'm sorry," Dave said. "This seems to be about Walli. You would have been better off on your own."

"Not your fault. I just hope we don't miss the funeral." Fitz took out his cigar case. "You don't smoke, Dave, do you?"

Dave shook his head. "Not tobacco, anyhow."

"Marijuana is bad for you."

"And I suppose cigars are healthy?"

Fitz smiled. "Touché."

"I've had this argument with my father. He drinks Scotch. You parliamentarians have a clear policy: all dangerous drugs are illegal, except the ones you like. And then you complain that young people won't listen."

"You're right, of course."

It was a big cigar, and Fitz smoked it all and dropped the stub in a stamped-tin ashtray. Eleven o'clock came and went. They had missed the funeral for which they had flown from London.

At half past eleven the door opened again. Hans Hoffmann stood there. With a little smile he said: "You may enter East Germany." Then he walked away.

Dave and Fitz found their car. "We'd better go straight to the house, now," said Fitz. He gave the driver the address.

They drove along Friedrich Strasse to Unter den Linden. The old government buildings were fine but the sidewalks were deserted. "My God," said Fitz. "This used to be one of the busiest shopping streets in Europe. Look at it now. Merthyr Tydfil on a Monday."

The car pulled up outside a town house in better condition than the other homes. "Maud's daughter seems to be more affluent than her neighbors," Fitz remarked.

Dave explained. "Walli's father owns a television factory in West Berlin. Somehow he manages to run it from here. I guess it still makes money."

They went into the house. The family introduced themselves. Walli's parents were Werner and Carla, a handsome man and a plain woman with strong features. Walli's sister, Lili, was nineteen and attractive, and did not look like Walli at all. Dave was intrigued to meet Karolin, who had long fair hair parted in the center and forming curtains either side of her face. With her was Alice, the inspiration for the song, a shy four-year-old with a black ribbon in her hair for mourning. Karolin's husband, Odo, was a little older, about thirty. He had fashionably long hair but wore a clerical collar.

Dave explained why they had missed the funeral. They mixed languages, though the Germans spoke English better than the English spoke German. Dave sensed that the family's attitude to Fitz was equivocal. It was understandable: he had after all been harsh to Maud, and her daughter might think it was too late to make amends. However, it was also too late to remonstrate, and no one spoke of the fifty-year estrangement.

A dozen friends and neighbors who had attended the funeral were having coffee and snacks served by Carla and Lili. Dave talked to Karolin about guitars. It turned out she and Lili were underground stars. They were not allowed to make records, because their songs were about freedom, but people made tape recordings of their performances and loaned them to one another. It was a bit like samizdat publishing in the Soviet Union. They discussed cassette tapes, a new format, more convenient though with poor sound quality. Dave offered to send Karolin some cassettes and a deck, but she said they would only be stolen by the secret police.

Dave had assumed Karolin must be a hard-hearted woman, to break off her relationship with Walli and marry Odo, but to his surprise he liked her. She seemed kind and smart. She spoke of Walli with great affection and wanted to know all about his life.

Dave told her how he and Walli had quarreled. She was distressed by the story. "It's not like him," she said. "Walli was never the type to fool around. Girls used to fall for him all the time, and he could have had a different one every weekend, but he never did."

Dave shrugged. "He's changed."

"What about your former fiancée? What's her name?"

"Ursula, but everyone calls her Beep. To be honest, it's not surprising that she should be unfaithful. She's kind of wild. It's part of what makes her so attractive."

"I think you still have feelings for her."

"I was crazy about her." Dave gave an evasive answer because he did not know how he felt now. He was angry with Beep, enraged by her betrayal, but if she wanted to come back to him he was not sure what he would do.

Fitz came over to where the two of them were sitting. "Dave," he said, "I'd like to see the grave before we return to West Berlin. Would you mind?"

"Of course not." Dave stood up. "We should probably go soon."

Karolin said to Dave: "If you do speak to Walli, please give him my love. Tell him I long for the day when he can meet Alice. I will tell her all about him when she's old enough."

They all had messages for Walli: Werner, Carla, and Lili. Dave guessed he would have to speak to Walli just to pass them on.

As they were leaving, Carla said to Fitz: "You should have something of Maud's."

"I'd like that."

"I know just the thing." She disappeared for a minute and came back with an old leather-bound photograph album. Fitz opened it. The pictures were all monochrome, some sepia, many faded. They had captions in large, loopy handwriting, presumably Maud's. The oldest had been taken in a grand country house. Dave read: "Tŷ Gwyn, 1905." That was the Fitzherbert country residence, now Aberowen College of Further Education.

Seeing photos of himself and Maud as young people made Fitz cry. Tears rolled down the papery old skin of his wrinkled face and soaked into the collar of his immaculate white shirt. He spoke with difficulty. "Good times never come back," he said.

They took their leave. The chauffeur drove them to a large and charmless municipal cemetery, and they found Maud's grave. The earth had already been returned to the pit, forming a small mound that was, pathetically, the size and approximate shape of a human being. They stood side by side for a few minutes, saying nothing. The only sound was birdsong.

Fitz wiped his face with a large white handkerchief. "Let's go," he said.

At the checkpoint they were again detained. Hans Hoffmann watched, smiling, while they and their cars were thoroughly searched.

"What are you looking for?" Dave asked. "Why would we smuggle something out of East Germany? You don't have anything here that anyone wants!" No one answered him.

A uniformed officer seized on the photograph album and handed it to Hoffmann.

Hoffmann looked through it casually and said: "This will have to be examined by our forensic department."

"Of course," Fitz said sadly.

They had to leave without it.

As they drove away, Dave looked back and saw Hans drop the album into a rubbish bin.

. . .

George Jakes flew from Portland to Los Angeles to meet Verena with a diamond ring in his pocket.

He had been on the road with Bobby Kennedy, and had not seen Verena since the funeral of Martin Luther King in Atlanta seven weeks earlier.

George was devastated by the assassination. Dr. King had been the bright burning hope of black Americans, and now he was gone, murdered by a white racist with a hunting rifle. President Kennedy had given hope to blacks and he, too, had been killed by a white man with a gun. What was the point of politics if great men could be so easily wiped out? But, George thought, at least we still have Bobby.

Verena was even harder hit. At the funeral she had been

bewildered, angry, and lost. The man she had admired, cherished, and served for seven years was gone.

To George's consternation she had not wanted him to console her. He was hurt deeply by this. They lived six hundred miles apart, but he was the man in her life. He figured that her rejection was part of her grief, and would pass.

There was nothing for her in Atlanta—she did not want to work for King's successor, Ralph Abernathy—so she had resigned. George had thought she might move into his apartment in Washington. However, without explanation she had gone back to her parents' home in Los Angeles. Perhaps she needed time alone to grieve.

Or perhaps she wanted something more than just an invitation to move into his place.

Hence the ring.

The next primary was California, which gave George a chance to visit Verena.

At LAX he rented a white Plymouth Valiant, a cheap compact—the campaign was paying—and drove to North Roxbury Drive in Beverly Hills.

He passed through tall gates and parked in front of a Tudor-style brick house that he guessed was the size of five genuine Tudor houses. Verena's parents, Percy Marquand and Babe Lee, lived like the stars they were.

A maid let him in and showed him into a living room that had nothing Tudor about it: a white carpet, air-conditioning, and a floor-to-ceiling window that looked out onto a swimming pool. The maid asked if he would like a drink. "A soda, please," he said. "Any kind."

When Verena came in he suffered a shock.

She had cut off her wonderful Afro, and her hair was now cropped close to her head, as short as his. She wore black pants, a blue shirt, a leather blazer, and a black beret. It was the uniform of the Black Panther Party for Self-Defense.

George suppressed his outrage in order to kiss her. She gave him her lips, but only briefly, and he knew right away that she had not moved on from her mood at the funeral. He hoped his proposal would bring her out of it.

They sat on a couch covered in a swirly pattern of burnt orange, primrose yellow, and chocolate brown. The maid brought George a Coke with ice in a tall glass on a silver tray. When she had gone he took Verena's hand. Holding in his anger, he said as gently as he could: "Why are you wearing that uniform?"

"Isn't it obvious?"

"Not to me."

"Martin Luther King led a nonviolent campaign, and they shot him."

George was disappointed in her. He had expected a better argument than that. He said: "Abraham Lincoln fought a civil war, and they shot him, too."

"Blacks have a right to defend themselves. No one else will—especially not the police."

George could barely conceal his contempt for these ideas. "You just want to scare whitey. Nothing has ever been achieved by this kind of grandstanding."

"What has nonviolence achieved? Hundreds of black people lynched and murdered, thousands beaten and jailed."

George did not want to fight with her—on the contrary, he wanted to bring her back to normal—but he could not help raising his voice. "Plus the Civil Rights Act of 1964, the Voting Rights Act of 1965, and six black congressmen and a senator!"

"And now white people are saying it's gone far enough. No one has been able to pass a law against housing discrimination."

"Maybe the whites are afraid they'll have Panthers in Gestapo outfits walking around their nice suburbs carrying guns."

"The police have guns. We need them too."

George realized that this argument, which seemed to be about politics, was really about their relationship. And he was losing her. If he could not talk her out of the Black Panthers, he could not bring her back into his life. "Look, I know that police forces all over America are full of violent racists. But the solution to that problem is to improve the police, not shoot them. We have to get rid of politicians such as Ronald Reagan who encourage police brutality."

"I refuse to accept a situation where the whites have guns and we don't."

"Then campaign for gun control and more black cops in senior positions."

"Martin believed in that and he's dead." Verena's words were defiant, but she could not keep it up, and she began to cry.

George tried to embrace her, but she pushed him away. Nevertheless he strove to make her see reason. "If you want to protect black people, come and work on our campaign," he said. "Bobby is going to be president."

"Even if he wins, Congress won't let him do anything."

"They'll try to stop him, and we'll have a political battle, and one side will win and the other will lose. It's how we change things in America. It's a lousy system, but all the others are worse. And shooting each other is the worst of all."

"We're not going to agree."

"Okay." He lowered his voice. "We've disagreed before, but always kept on loving each other, haven't we?"

"This is different."

"Don't say that."

"My whole life has changed."

George looked hard at her face, and saw there a mixture of defiance and guilt that gave him a clue to what was going on. "You're sleeping with one of the Panthers, aren't you?"

"Yes."

George had a heavy feeling in his guts, as if he had drunk a tankard of cold ale. "You should have told me."

"I'm telling you now."

"My God." George was sad. He fingered the ring in his pocket. Was it going to stay there? "Do you realize it's seven years since we graduated from Harvard?" He fought back tears.

"I know."

"Police dogs in Birmingham, 'I have a dream' in Washington, President Johnson backing civil rights, two assassinations . . ."

"And blacks are still the poorest Americans, living in the lousiest houses, getting the most perfunctory health care—and doing more than their share of the fighting in Vietnam."

"Bobby's going to change all that."

"No, he's not."

"Yes, he is. And I'm going to invite you to the White House to admit that you were wrong."

Verena went to the door. "Good-bye, George."

"I can't believe it ends like this."

"The maid will see you out."

George found it difficult to think straight. He had loved Verena for years, and had assumed they would marry sooner or later. Now she had ditched him for a Black Panther. He felt lost. Although they had lived apart, he had always been able to think about what he would say to her and how he would caress her next time they were together. Now he was alone.

The maid came in and said: "This way, Mr. Jakes, if you please."

Automatically he followed her to the hall. She opened the front door.

"Thank you," he said.

"Good-bye, Mr. Jakes."

George got into his rented car and drove away.

. . .

On voting day in the California primary, George was with Bobby Kennedy at the Malibu beach home of John Frankenheimer, the movie director. The weather was overcast that morning, but nevertheless Bobby swam in the ocean with his twelve-year-old son, David. They both got caught in the undertow and emerged with scratches and scrapes from being dragged over the pebbles. After lunch Bobby fell asleep beside the pool, stretched out across two chairs, his mouth open. Looking through the glass patio doors, George noticed an angry mark on Bobby's forehead from the swimming incident.

He had not told Bobby that he had broken up with Verena. He had told only his mother. He barely had time to think on the campaign trail, and California had been nonstop: airport mob scenes, motorcades, hysterical crowds, and packed meetings. George was glad to be so busy. He had the luxury of feeling sad only for a few minutes every night before falling asleep. Even then he found himself imagining conversations with Verena in which he persuaded her to return to legitimate politics and campaign for Bobby. Perhaps their different approaches had always been a manifestation of fundamental incompatibility. He had never wanted to believe that.

At three o'clock the results of the first exit poll were broadcast on TV. Bobby led Gene McCarthy 49 percentage points to 41. George was elated. I can't win my girl, but I can win elections, he thought.

Bobby showered and shaved and put on a blue pin-striped suit and a white shirt. Either the suit, or perhaps his increased confidence, made him seem more presidential than ever before, George thought.

The bruise on Bobby's forehead was unsightly, but John Frankenheimer found some professional movie makeup in the house and covered up the mark.

At half past six the Kennedy entourage got into cars and drove into Los Angeles. They went to the Ambassador Hotel, where the victory celebration was already getting under way in the ballroom. George went with Bobby to the Royal Suite on the fifth floor. There in a large living room a hundred or more friends, advisers, and privileged journalists were downing cocktails and congratulating one another. Every TV set in the suite was on.

George and the closest advisers followed Bobby through the living room and into one of the bedrooms. As always, Bobby mixed partying with hard political talk. Today, as well as California, he had won a low-profile primary in South Dakota, birthplace of Hubert Humphrey. After California he felt confident of winning New York, where he had the advantage of being one of the state's senators. "We're beating McCarthy, damn it," he said exultantly, sitting on the floor in a corner of the room, keeping an eye on the TV.

George was beginning to worry about the convention. How could he make sure that Bobby's popularity was reflected in the votes of delegates from states where there were no primaries? "Humphrey is working hard on states such as Illinois, where Mayor Daley controls the delegate votes."

"Yeah," said Bobby. "But in the end men like Daley can't ignore popular feeling. They want to win. Hubert can't beat Dick Nixon, and I can."

"It's true, but do the Democratic power brokers know that?"

"They will by August."

George shared Bobby's sense that they were riding a wave, but he saw the dangers ahead all too clearly. "We need McCarthy to withdraw so that we can concentrate on beating Humphrey. We have to make a deal with McCarthy."

Bobby shook his head. "I can't offer him the vice presidency. He's a Catholic. Protestants might vote for one Catholic, but not two."

"You could offer him the top job in cabinet."

"Secretary of State?"

"If he pulls out now."

Bobby frowned. "It's hard to imagine working with him in the White House."

"If you don't win, you won't be in the White House. Should I put out feelers?"

"Let me think about it some more."

"Of course."

"You know something else, George?" Bobby said. "For the first time I don't feel I'm here as Jack's brother."

George smiled. That was a big step.

George went into the main room to talk to reporters, but he did not get a drink. When he was with Bobby he preferred to stay sharp. Bobby himself liked bourbon. But incompetence on his team infuriated him, and he could lacerate someone who let him down. George felt comfortable drinking alcohol only when Bobby was far away.

He was still stone-cold sober a few minutes before midnight when he accompanied Bobby down to the ballroom to give his victory speech. Bobby's wife, Ethel, looked groovy in an orange-and-white minidress with white tights, despite being pregnant with their eleventh child.

The crowd went wild, as always. The boys all wore Kennedy straw hats. The girls had a uniform: blue skirt, white blouse, and red Kennedy sash. A band blared a campaign song. Powerful television lights added to the heat in the room. Led by bodyguard Bill Barry, Bobby and Ethel pushed through the crowd, their young supporters reaching out to touch them and pull their clothes, until they reached a small platform. Jostling photographers added to the chaos.

The crowd hysteria was a problem for George and others, but it was Bobby's strength. His ability to get this emotional reaction from people was going to take him to the White House.

Bobby stood behind a bouquet of microphones. He had not asked for a written speech, just some notes. His performance was lackluster, but no one cared. "We are a great country, an unselfish country, and a compassionate country," he said. "I intend to make that my basis for running." These were not inspiring words, but the crowd adored him too much to care.

George decided he would not go with Bobby to the Factory discotheque afterward. Seeing couples dance would only remind him that he was alone. He would get a good night's sleep before flying to New York in the morning to launch the campaign there. Work was the cure for his heartache.

"I thank all of you who made this possible this evening," Bobby said. He flashed the Churchillian V-for-victory sign, and around the room hundreds of young people repeated the gesture. He reached down from the platform to shake some of the outstretched hands.

Then there was a glitch. His next appointment was with the press in a nearby room. The plan was for him to pass through the crowd as he left, but George could see that Bill Barry was unable to clear a path between the hysterical teenage girls shouting: "We want Bobby! We want Bobby!"

A hotel employee in the uniform of a maître d'hôtel solved the problem, pointing Bobby to a pair of swinging doors that evidently led through staff quarters to the press room. Bobby and Ethel followed the man into a dim corridor, and George and Bill Barry and the rest of the entourage hurried after them.

George was wondering how soon he could again raise with Bobby the need to make a deal with Gene McCarthy. It was the strategic priority, in George's opinion. But personal relationships were so important to the Kennedys. If Bobby could have made a friend of Lyndon Johnson everything would have been different.

The corridor led to a brightly lit pantry zone with gleaming stainless-steel steam tables and a huge ice maker. A radio reporter was interviewing Bobby as they walked, saying: "Senator, how are you going to counter Mr. Humphrey?" Bobby shook hands with smiling staff on his way through. A young kitchen worker turned from a tray stacker as if to greet Bobby.

Then, in a lightning flash of terror, George saw a gun in the young man's hand.

It was a small black revolver with a short barrel.

The man pointed the gun at Bobby's head.

George opened his mouth to yell but the shot came first.

The little weapon made a noise that was more of a pop than a bang.

Bobby threw his hands up to his face, staggered back, then fell to the concrete floor.

George roared: "No! No!" It could not be happening—it could not be happening again!

A moment later came a volley of shots like a Chinese firecracker. Something stung George's arm, but he ignored it.

Bobby lay on his back beside the ice machine, hands above his head, feet apart. His eyes were open.

People were yelling and screaming. The radio reporter was babbling into his microphone: "Senator Kennedy has been shot! Senator Kennedy has been shot! Is that possible? Is that possible?"

Several men jumped on the gunman. Someone was shouting: "Get the gun! Get the gun!" George saw Bill Barry punch the shooter in the face.

George knelt by Bobby. He was alive, but bleeding from a wound just behind his ear. He looked bad. George loosened his tie to help him breathe. Someone else put a folded coat under Bobby's head.

A man's voice was moaning: "God, no ... Christ, no ..."

Ethel pushed through the crowd, knelt beside George, and spoke to her husband. There was a flicker of recognition in Bobby's face, and he tried to speak. George thought he said: "Is everyone else all right?" Ethel stroked his face.

George looked around. He could not tell whether anyone else had been hit by the volley of bullets. Then he noticed his own forearm. The sleeve of his suit was ripped and blood was seeping from a wound. He had been hit. Now that he noticed, it hurt like hell.

The far door opened, and reporters and photographers from the press room burst through. The cameramen mobbed the group around Bobby, shoving each other and climbing on the stoves and sinks to get better shots of the bleeding victim and his stricken wife. Ethel pleaded: "Give him some air, please! Let him breathe!"

An ambulance crew arrived with a stretcher. They took Bobby by the shoulders and feet. Bobby cried weakly: "Oh, no, don't . . ."

"Gently!" Ethel begged the crew. "Gently."

They lifted him onto the stretcher and strapped him in. Bobby's eyes closed.

He never opened them again.

CHAPTER FORTY-FIVE

That summer Dimka and Natalya painted the apartment, with the sun shining through the open windows. It took longer than necessary because they kept stopping for sex. Her glorious hair was tied up and hidden in a rag, and she wore an old shirt of his with a frayed collar; but her shorts were tight, and every time he saw her up a ladder he had to kiss her. He pulled down her shorts so often that after a while she just wore the shirt; and then they had even more sex.

They could not marry until her divorce was finalized, and for the sake of appearances Natalya had her own tiny apartment nearby, but unofficially they were already embarking on their new life together in Dimka's place. They rearranged the furniture to Natalya's liking and bought a couch. They developed routines: he made breakfast, she cooked dinner; he polished her shoes, she ironed his shirts; he shopped for meat, she for fish.

They never saw Nik, but Natalya began to establish a relationship with Nina. Dimka's ex-wife was now the accepted lover of Marshal Pushnoy, and spent many weekends with him at his dacha, hosting dinners with his intimate friends, some of whom brought *their* mistresses. Dimka did not know how Pushnoy arranged matters with his wife, a pleasant-looking elderly woman who always appeared at his side on formal state occasions. During Nina's country weekends, Dimka and Natalya looked after Grisha. At first Natalya was nervous, never having had children of her own—

Nik hated kids. But she quickly became fond of Grisha, who looked a lot like Dimka; and, not surprisingly, she turned out to have the usual maternal instincts.

Their private life was happy but their public life was not. The diehards in the Kremlin only pretended to accept the Czechoslovakia compromise. As soon as Kosygin and Dimka got back from Prague the conservatives went to work to undermine the agreement, pressing for an invasion that would crush Dubček and his reforms. The argument raged through June and July in the heat of Moscow and in the Black Sea breezes at the dachas to which the Communist Party elite migrated for their summer holidays.

For Dimka this was not really about Czechoslovakia. It was about his son and the world in which he would grow up. In fifteen years Grisha would be at university; in twenty he would be working; in twenty-five he might have children of his own. Would Russia have a better system, something like Dubček's idea of Communism with a human face? Or would the Soviet Union still be a tyranny in which the unchallengeable authority of the party was brutally enforced by the KGB?

Infuriatingly Leonid Brezhnev, general secretary, sat on the fence. Dimka had come to despise him. Terrified of being caught on the losing side, Brezhnev would never make up his mind until he knew which way the collective decision was likely to go. He had no vision, no courage, no plan for making the Soviet Union a better country. He was no leader.

The conflict came to a head at a two-day meeting of the Politburo starting on Thursday, August 15. As always, the formal meeting consisted mostly of polite interchanges of platitudes, while the real battles were fought outside.

It was in the plaza that Dimka had his face-off with Yevgeny Filipov, standing in the sunshine outside the yellow-and-white palace of the senate building among the parked cars and waiting limousines. "Look at the KGB reports from Prague," Filipov said. "Counterrevolutionary student rallies! Clubs where the overthrow of Communism is openly discussed! Secret weapons caches!"

"I don't believe all the stories," Dimka said. "True, there is discussion of reform, but the dangers are being exaggerated by the failed leaders of the past who are now being pushed aside." The truth was that Andropov, the hard-line head of the KGB, was fabricating sensational intelligence reports to bolster the conservatives; but Dimka was not foolhardy enough to say so out loud.

Dimka had a source of reliable intelligence: his twin sister. Tanya was in Prague, sending carefully noncommittal articles to TASS and, at the same time, supplying Dimka and Kosygin with reports saying that Dubček was a hero to all Czechs except the old party apparatchiks.

It was almost impossible for people to get at the truth in a closed society. Russians told so many lies. In the Soviet Union almost every document was deceitful: production figures, foreign policy assessments, police interviews with suspects, economic forecasts. Behind their hands people murmured that the only true page in the newspaper was the one with the radio and television programs.

"I can't tell which way it's going to go," Natalya said to Dimka on Thursday night. She still worked for Foreign Minister Andrei Gromyko. "All the signals from Washington say President Johnson will do nothing if we invade Czechoslovakia. He has too many problems of his own — riots, assassinations, Vietnam, and a presidential election."

They had finished painting for the evening and were sitting on the floor sharing a bottle of beer. Natalya had a single smudge of yellow paint on her forehead. For some reason that made Dimka want to fuck her. He was wondering whether to do it now or get washed and go to bed first when she said: "Before we get married . . ."

That was ominous. "Yes?"

"We should talk about children."

"We probably should have done that before we spent all summer screwing our brains out." They had never used birth control.

"Yes. But you already have a child."

"We have a child. He's ours. You'll be his stepmother."

"And I'm very fond of him. It's easy to love a boy who looks so much like you. But how do you feel about having more?"

Dimka could see that for some reason she was worried about this, and he needed to reassure her. He put down the beer and embraced her. "I adore you," he said. "And I would love to have children with you."

"Oh, thank God," she said. "Because I'm pregnant."

. . .

It was difficult to get newspapers in Prague, Tanya found. This was an ironic consequence of Dubček's abolition of censorship. Previously, few people had bothered to read the anodyne and dishonest reports in the state-controlled press. Now that the papers could tell the truth, they could never print enough copies to keep up with the demand. She had to get up early in the morning to buy them before they sold out.

Television had been freed, too. On current affairs programs, workers and students questioned and criticized government ministers. Released political prisoners were allowed to confront the secret policemen who had thrown them in jail. Around the television set in the lobby of any large hotel there was often a small crowd of eager viewers watching the discussion on the screen.

Similar exchanges were taking place in every café, works canteen, and town hall. People who had suppressed their true feelings for twenty years were suddenly allowed to say what was in their hearts.

The air of liberation was infectious. Tanya was tempted to believe that the old days were over and there was no danger. She had to keep reminding herself that Czechoslovakia was still a Communist country with secret police and torture basements.

She had with her the typescript of Vasili's first novel.

It had arrived, shortly before she left Moscow, in the same way as his first short story, handed to her in the street outside her office by a stranger who was unwilling to answer questions. As before, it was written in small handwriting—no doubt to save paper. Its sardonic title was *A Free Man*.

Tanya had typed it out on airmail paper. She had to assume that her luggage would be opened. Although she was a trusted reporter for TASS, it was still possible that any hotel room she stayed in would be turned over, and the apartment allocated to her in the old town of Prague would be thoroughly searched. But she had devised a clever hiding place, she thought. All the same she lived in fear. It was like possessing a nuclear bomb. She was desperate to pass it on as soon as possible.

She had befriended the Prague correspondent of a British newspaper, and at the first opportunity she had said to him: "There's a book editor in London who specializes in translations of East European novels—Anna Murray, of Rowley Publishing. I'd love to interview her about Czech literature. Do you think you could get a message to her?"

This was dangerous, for it established a traceable connection between Tanya and Anna; but Tanya had to take some risks, and it seemed to her that this one was minimal.

Two weeks later the British journalist had said: "Anna Murray's coming to Prague next Tuesday. I couldn't give her your phone number because I don't have it, but she'll be at the Palace Hotel."

On Tuesday Tanya called the hotel and left a message for Anna saying: "Meet Jakub at the Jan Hus monument at four." Jan Hus was a medieval philosopher burned at the stake by the Pope for arguing that mass should be said in the local language. He remained a symbol of Czech resistance to foreign control. His memorial was in Old Town Square.

The secret police agents in all hotels took special interest in guests from the West, and Tanya had to assume that they were shown all messages, therefore they might stake out the monument to see whom Anna was meeting. So Tanya did not go to the rendezvous. Instead she intercepted Anna on the street and slipped her a card with the address of a restaurant in the Old Town and the message: "Eight P.M. tonight. Table booked in the name of Jakub."

There was still the possibility that Anna would be followed from her hotel to the restaurant. It was unlikely: the secret police did not have enough men to tail every foreigner all the time. Nevertheless Tanya continued to take precautions. That evening she put on a loose-fitting leather jacket, despite the warm weather, and went to the restaurant early. She sat at a different table from the one she had reserved. She kept her head down when Anna arrived, and watched as Anna was seated.

Anna was unmistakably foreign. No one in Eastern Europe was that well dressed. She had a dark red pantsuit tailored to her voluptuous figure. She wore it with a glorious multicolored scarf that had to come from Paris. Anna had dark hair and eyes that probably came from her German-

Jewish mother. She must be close to thirty, Tanya calculated, but she was one of those women who became more beautiful as they left their youth behind.

No one followed Anna into the restaurant. Tanya stayed put for fifteen minutes, watching the arrivals, while Anna ordered a bottle of Hungarian Riesling and sipped a glass. Four people came in, an elderly married couple and two youngsters on a date: none looked remotely like police. Finally Tanya got up and joined Anna at the reserved table, draping her jacket over the back of her chair.

"Thank you for coming," Tanya said.

"Please don't mention it. I'm glad to."

"It's a long way."

"I'd travel ten times as far to meet the woman who gave me *Frostbite*."

"He's written a novel."

Anna sat back with a satisfied sigh. "That's what I was hoping you'd say." She poured wine into Tanya's glass. "Where is it?"

"Hidden. I'll give it to you before we leave."

"Okay." Anna was puzzled, for she could see no sign of a typescript, but she accepted what Tanya said. "You've made me very happy."

"I always knew that *Frostbite* was brilliant," Tanya said reflectively. "But even I didn't anticipate the international success you've had. In the Kremlin they're furious about it, especially as they still can't figure out who the author is."

"You should know that there's a fortune in royalties due to him."

Tanya shook her head. "If he received money from overseas that would give the game away."

"Well, maybe one day. I've asked the largest London firm of literary agents to represent him."

"What is a literary agent?"

"Someone who looks after the author's interests, negotiates contracts, and makes sure the publisher pays on time."

"I never heard of that."

"They've opened a bank account in the name of Ivan Kuznetsov. But you should think about whether the money should be invested somehow."

"How much is it?"

"More than a million pounds."

Tanya was shocked. Vasili would be the richest man in Russia if he could get his hands on the money.

They ordered dinner. Prague restaurants had improved in recent months, but the food was still traditional. Their beef and sliced dumplings came in a rich gravy garnished with whipped cream and a spoonful of cranberry jam.

Anna asked: "What's going to happen here in Prague?"

"Dubček is a sincere Communist who wants the country to remain part of the Warsaw Pact, so he presents no fundamental threat to Moscow; but the dinosaurs in the Kremlin don't see it that way. No one knows what's going to happen."

"Do you have children?"

Tanya smiled. "Key question. Perhaps we may choose to suffer the Soviet system, for the sake of a quiet life; but do we have the right to bequeath such misery and oppression to the next generation? No, I don't have children. I have a nephew, Grisha, whom I love, the son of my twin brother. And this morning in a letter my brother told me that the woman who will soon be his second wife is already pregnant, so I'll have another nephew or a niece. For their sakes, I have to hope that Dubček will succeed, and other Communist countries will follow the Czech example. But the Soviet system is inherently conservative, much more resistant to change than capitalism. That may be its most fundamental flaw, in the long run."

When they had finished, Anna said: "If we can't pay our author, can we perhaps give you a present to pass to him? Is there anything from the West he would like?"

A typewriter was what he needed, but that would blow his cover. "A sweater," she said. "A really thick, warm sweater. He's always cold. And some underwear, the kind with long sleeves and long legs."

Anna looked aghast at this peep into the life of Ivan Kuznetsov. "I'll go to Vienna tomorrow and get him the best quality."

Anna nodded, pleased. "Shall we meet again here on Friday?"

"Yes."

Tanya stood up. "We should leave separately."

A look of panic crossed Anna's face. "What about the typescript?"

"Wear my jacket," said Tanya. It might be a bit small for Anna, who was heavier than Tanya; but she could get it on. "When you reach Vienna, unpick the lining." She shook Anna's hand. "Don't lose it," she said. "I don't have a copy."

. . .

In the middle of the night Tanya was awakened by her bed shaking. She sat up, terrified, thinking the secret police had come to arrest her. When she turned on the light she saw that she was alone, but the shaking had not been a dream. The framed photograph of Grisha on her bedside table seemed to be dancing, and she could hear the tinkling sound of small jars of makeup vibrating on the glass top of her dressing table.

She jumped out of bed and went to the open window. It was first light. There was a loud rumbling noise coming from the nearby main street, but she could not see what was causing it. She was filled with a vague dread.

She looked for her leather jacket, and remembered that she had given it to Anna. She quickly pulled on blue jeans and a sweater, stepped into her shoes, and hurried out. Despite the early hour there were people on the street. She walked swiftly in the direction of the noise.

As soon as she reached the main street she knew what had happened.

The noise was caused by tanks. They were rolling along the street, slowly but unstoppably, their caterpillar tracks making a hideous din. Riding on the tanks were soldiers in Soviet uniforms, most young, just boys. Looking along the street in the gentle light of dawn, Tanya saw that there were dozens of tanks, perhaps hundreds, the incoming line stretching all the way to the Charles Bridge and beyond. Along the sidewalks small groups of Czech men and women stood, many in their nightwear, watching with dismay and stupefaction as their city was overrun.

The conservatives in the Kremlin had won, Tanya realized. Czechoslovakia had been invaded by the Soviet Union. The brief season of reform and hope was over.

Tanya caught the eye of a middle-aged woman standing next to her. The woman wore an old-fashioned hairnet like the one Tanya's mother put on every night. Her face was streaming with tears.

That was when Tanya felt the wetness on her own cheeks and realized that she, too, was weeping.

.   .   .

A week after the tanks rolled into Prague, George Jakes was sitting on his couch in Washington, in his underwear, watching television coverage of the Democratic convention in Chicago.

For lunch he had heated a can of tomato soup and eaten it straight from the pan, which now stood on the coffee table, with the red remains of the glutinous liquid congealing inside.

He knew what he ought to do. He should put on a suit and go out and get himself a new job and a new girlfriend and a new life.

Somehow he just could not see the point.

He had heard of depression and he knew this was it.

He was only mildly diverted by the spectacle of the Chicago police running amok. A few hundred demonstrators were peacefully sitting down in the road outside the convention center. The police were wading into them with nightsticks, savagely beating everyone, as if they did not realize they were committing criminal assault live on television — or, more likely, they knew but did not care.

Someone, presumably Mayor Richard Daley, had let the dogs off the leash.

George idly speculated on the political consequences. It was the end of nonviolence as a political strategy, he guessed. Martin Luther King and Bobby Kennedy had both been wrong, and now they were dead. The Black Panthers were right. Mayor Daley, Governor Ronald Reagan, presidential candidate George Wallace, and all their racist police chiefs would use violence against anyone whose ideas they found distasteful. Black people needed guns to protect themselves. So did anyone else who wanted to challenge the bull elephants of American society. Right now in Chicago the police were treating middle-class white kids the way they had always treated blacks. That had to change attitudes.

There was a ring at his doorbell. He frowned, puzzled. He was not expecting a visitor and did not want to talk to anyone. He ignored the sound, hoping the caller would go away. The bell rang again. I might be out, he thought; how do they know I'm here? It rang a third time, long and insistently, and he realized the person was not going to give up.

He went to the door. It was his mother. She was carrying a covered casserole dish.

Jacky looked him up and down. "I thought so," she said, and she walked in uninvited.

She put her casserole in his oven and turned on the heat. "Take a shower," she ordered him. "Shave your sorry face and put on some decent clothing."

He thought of arguing but did not have the energy. It seemed easier just to do as she said.

She began clearing up the room, putting his soup pan in the kitchen sink, folding newspapers, opening windows.

George retired to his room. He took off his underwear, showered, and shaved. It would make no difference. He would slob out again tomorrow.

He put on chinos and a blue button-down shirt, then returned to the living room. The casserole smelled good, he could not deny that. Jacky had laid the dining table. "Sit down," she said. "Supper's ready."

She had made King Ranch chicken in a tomato-cream sauce with green chilies and a cheese crust. George could not resist it, and he had two platefuls. Afterward his mother washed up and he dried the dishes.

She sat with him to watch the convention coverage. Senator Abraham Ribicoff was speaking, nominating George McGovern, a last-minute alternative peace candidate. He caused a stir by saying: "With George McGovern as president of the United States, we would not have to have Gestapo tactics in the streets of Chicago."

Jacky said: "My, that's telling them."

The convention hall went quiet. The television director cut to a shot of Mayor Daley. He looked like a giant frog, with bulging eyes, a jowly face, and a neck that was all rolls of fat. For a moment he forgot he was on television—just like his cops—and yelled vituperatively at Ribicoff.

The microphones did not pick up his words. "I wonder what he said," George mused.

"I can tell you," said Jacky. "I can lip-read."

"I never knew that."

"When I was nine years old I went deaf. Took them a long time to figure out what was wrong. Eventually I had an operation that restored my hearing. But I never forgot how to lip-read."

"Okay, Mom, prove it. What did Mayor Daley say to Abe Ribicoff?"

"He said: 'Fuck you, you Jew son of a bitch,' that's what he said."

.   .   .

Walli and Beep were staying in the Chicago Hilton, on the fifteenth floor, where the McCarthy campaign had its headquarters. They were tired and dispirited when they went to their room at midnight on the last day of the convention, Thursday. They had lost: Hubert Humphrey, Johnson's vice president, had been chosen as the Democratic candidate. The presidential election would be fought between two men who supported the Vietnam War.

They did not even have any dope to smoke. They had given that up, temporarily, for fear of giving the press a chance to smear McCarthy. They watched TV for a while, then went to bed, too miserable to make love.

Beep said: "Shit, I'll be back in class in a couple of weeks. I don't know if I can face it."

"I guess I'll make a record," Walli said. "I've got some new songs."

Beep was dubious. "You think you can patch things up with Dave?"

"No. I'd like to, but he won't. When he called me to tell me he had seen my folks in East Berlin, he was real cold, even though he was doing a nice thing."

"Oh, God, we really hurt him," Beep said sadly.

"Besides, he's doing fine on his own, with his TV show and everything."

"So how will you make an album?"

"I'll go to London. I know Lew will drum for me, and Buzz will play bass: they're both pissed at Dave for breaking up the group. I'll lay down the basic tracks with them, then record the vocals on my own, and spend some time adding overdubs, guitar licks, and vocal harmonies and maybe even strings and horns."

"Wow, you've really thought about this."

"I've had time. I haven't been inside a studio for half a year."

There was a bang and a crash and the room was flooded with light from the hall. Walli realized with incredulity and terror that someone had beaten the door in. He threw back the sheets and jumped out of bed, yelling: "What the fuck?"

The room lights came on and he saw two uniformed Chicago policemen entering through the wreckage of the door. He said: "What the hell is going on?"

By way of reply one of them hit him with a nightstick.

Walli managed to dodge, and instead of hitting his head the truncheon landed painfully on his shoulder. He yelled in agony and Beep screamed.

Grasping his injured shoulder, Walli backed toward the bed. The cop swung his stick again. Walli jumped back, falling on the bed, and the club hit his leg. He roared in pain.

Both cops lifted their clubs. Walli rolled over, covering Beep. One nightstick smashed into his back and the other his hip. Beep screamed: "Stop it, please, stop, we haven't done anything wrong, stop hitting him!"

Walli felt two more excruciating blows and thought he would pass out. Then suddenly it stopped, and two pairs of heavily booted footsteps sounded across the room and out.

Walli rolled off Beep. "Ah, fuck, it hurts," he said.

Beep knelt up, trying to see his injuries. "Why did they do it?" she said.

Walli heard, from outside the room, sounds of more doors being broken down and more screaming people being dragged from their beds and beaten. "The Chicago police can do anything they like," he said. "It's worse than East Berlin."

. . .

In October, on a plane to Nashville, Dave Williams sat next to a Nixon supporter.

Dave was going to Nashville to make a record. His own studio in Napa, Daisy Farm, was still under construction. Besides, some of the best musicians in the business were in Nashville. Dave felt that rock music was becoming too cerebral, with psychedelic sounds and twenty-minute guitar solos, so he planned an album of classic two-minute pop songs, "The Girl of My Best Friend" and "I Heard It Through the Grapevine" and "Woolly Bully." Besides, he knew that Walli was making a solo album in London and he did not want to be left behind.

And he had another reason. Little Lulu Small, who had flirted with him on the All-Star Touring Beat Revue, now lived in Nashville and worked as a backing singer. He needed someone to help him forget Beep.

On the front page of his newspaper was a photograph from the Olympic Games in Mexico City. It was of the medal ceremony for the two hundred meters race. The gold medal winner was Tommie Smith, a black American, who had broken the world record. A white Australian took silver, and another black American bronze. All three men wore human rights badges on their Olympic jackets. While "The Star-Spangled Banner" was being played, the two American athletes had bowed their heads and raised their fists in the Black Power salute, and that was the photo in all the papers.

"Disgraceful," said the man sitting next to Dave in first class.

He looked about forty, and was dressed in a business suit with a white shirt and a tie. He had taken from his briefcase a thick typed document and was annotating it with a ballpoint pen.

Dave normally avoided talking to people on planes. The conversation usually turned into an interview about what it was really like to be a pop star, and that was boring. But this guy did not appear to know who Dave was. And Dave was curious to know what went on in the head of such a man.

His neighbor went on: "I see that the president of the International Olympic Committee has thrown them out of the games. Damn right."

"The president's name is Avery Brundage," Dave said. "It says in my paper that back in 1936, when the games were held in Berlin, he defended the right of the Germans to give the Nazi salute."

"I don't agree with that either," said the businessman. "The games are nonpolitical. Our athletes compete as Americans."

"They're Americans when they win races, and when they get conscripted into the army," Dave said. "But they're Negroes when they want to buy the house next door to yours."

"Well, I'm for equality, but slow change is usually better than fast."

"Maybe we should have an all-white army in Vietnam,

just until we're sure American society is ready for complete equality."

"I'm against the war, too," the man said. "If the Vietnamese are dumb enough to want to be Communists, let them. It's Communists in America we should be worried about."

He was from a distant planet, Dave felt. "What line of business are you in?"

"I sell advertising for radio stations." He offered his hand to shake. "Ron Jones."

"Dave Williams. I'm in the music business. If you don't mind my asking, who will you vote for in November?"

"Nixon," said Jones without hesitation.

"But you're against the war, and you favor civil rights for Negroes, albeit not too soon; so you agree with Humphrey on the issues."

"To hell with the issues. I have a wife and three kids, a mortgage and a car loan; they're my issues. I've fought my way up to regional sales manager and I have a shot at national sales director in a few years' time. I've worked my socks off for this and no one's going to take it away from me: not rioting Negroes, not drug-taking hippies, not Communists working for Moscow, and certainly not a soft-hearted liberal like Hubert Humphrey. I don't care what you say about Nixon, he stands for people like me."

At that moment Dave felt, with an overwhelming sense of impending doom, that Nixon was going to win.

. . .

George Jakes put on a suit and a white shirt and a tie, for the first time in months, and went for lunch with Maria Summers at the Jockey Club. It was her invitation.

He could guess what was going to happen. Maria had been talking to his mother. Jacky had told Maria that George spent all day moping in his apartment, doing nothing. Maria was going to tell him to pull himself together.

He could not see the point. His life was wrecked. Bobby was dead and the next president would be either Humphrey or Nixon. Nothing could be done, now, to end the war or to bring equality for blacks or even to stop the police beating up anyone they took a dislike to.

All the same he agreed to have lunch with Maria. They went back a long way.

Maria was looking attractive in a mature way. She wore a black dress with a matching jacket and a row of pearls. She projected confidence and authority. She looked like what she was, a successful midlevel bureaucrat at the Department of Justice. She refused a cocktail and they ordered lunch.

When the waiter had gone, she said to George: "You never get over it."

He understood that she was comparing his grief for Bobby to her own bereavement over Jack.

"There's a hole in your heart, and it doesn't go away," she said.

George nodded. She was so right that it was difficult not to cry.

"Work is the best cure," she said. "That and time."

She had survived, George realized. Her loss was the greater, for Jack Kennedy had been her lover, not just her friend.

"You helped me," she said. "You got me the job at Justice. That was my salvation: a new environment, a new challenge."

"But not a new boyfriend."

"No."

"You still live alone?"

"I have two cats," she said. "Julius and Loopy."

George nodded. Her being single would have helped her at the Justice Department. They hesitated to promote a married woman who might get pregnant and leave, but a confirmed spinster had a better chance.

Their food came and they ate in silence for a few minutes. Then Maria put down her fork. "I want you to go back to work, George."

George was moved by her loving concern, and he admired the steady determination with which she had rebuilt her life. But he could not work up any enthusiasm. He gave a helpless shrug. "Bobby's gone, McCarthy lost the nomination. Who would I work for?"

Maria surprised him by saying: "Fawcett Renshaw."

"Those bastards?" Fawcett Renshaw was the Washington law firm that had offered George a job when he graduated, only to withdraw the offer because he went on the Freedom Ride.

"You'd be their civil rights expert," she added.

George relished the irony. Seven years ago, involvement with civil rights had debarred him from working at Fawcett Renshaw; now it qualified him. We have won some victories, he thought, despite everything. He began to feel better.

"You've worked at Justice and on Capitol Hill, so you have priceless inside knowledge," she went on. "And, you know what? Suddenly it's become fashionable for a Washington law firm to have one black lawyer on the team."

"How do you know what Fawcett Renshaw wants?" he asked.

"At the Justice Department we have a lot to do with them. Usually trying to get their clients to comply with government legislation."

"I'd end up defending corporations who violate civil rights legislation."

"Think of it as a learning experience. You'll gain first-hand knowledge of how equalities legislation works on the ground. That would be valuable if ever you returned to politics. Meanwhile you'll be making good money."

George wondered if he ever would return to politics.

He looked up to see his father approaching across the restaurant. Greg said: "I've just finished lunch—may I join you for coffee?"

George wondered whether this apparently accidental meeting had in fact been planned by Maria. He also recalled that old Renshaw, the senior partner at the law firm, was a boyhood friend of Greg's.

Maria said to Greg: "We were just talking about George going back to work. Fawcett Renshaw wants him."

"Renshaw mentioned it to me. You'll be invaluable to them. Your contacts are matchless."

"Nixon looks like he's winning," George said dubiously. "Most of my contacts are with the Democrats."

"They're still useful. Anyway, I don't expect Nixon to last long. He'll crash and burn."

George raised his eyebrows. Greg was a liberal Republican who would have preferred someone such as Nelson Rockefeller as presidential candidate. Even so, he was being surprisingly disloyal to his party. "You think the peace movement will destroy Nixon?" George asked.

"In your dreams. The other way around, more likely. Nixon isn't Lyndon Johnson. Nixon understands foreign policy—

better than most people in Washington, probably. Don't be
fooled by his dumb-ass talk about Commies, that's just for
the benefit of his supporters in the trailer parks." Greg was
a snob. "Nixon will get us out of Vietnam, and he'll say we
lost the war because the peace movement undermined the
military."

"So what will bring him down?"

"Dick Nixon lies," Greg said. "He lies just about every
time he opens his damn mouth. When a Republican administration came into office in 1952, Nixon claimed we had
discovered thousands of subversives in the government."

"How many had you found?"

"None. Not a single one. I know, I was a young congressman. Then he told the press we had come across a blueprint
for socializing America in the files of the outgoing Democratic administration. Reporters asked to see it."

"He didn't have a copy."

"Correct. He also said he had a secret Communist mem-
orandum about how they planned to work through the
Democratic Party. No one ever saw that, either. I suspect
that Dick's mother never told him it's a sin to tell a lie."

"There's a lot of dishonesty in politics," George said.

"And in many other walks of life. But few people lie as
much and as shamelessly as Nixon. He's a cheat and a
crook. He's gotten away with it until now. People do. But it's
different when you're president. Reporters know they've
been lied to about Vietnam, and more and more they scru-
tinize everything the government says. Dick will get caught
out, and then he'll fall. And you know something else? He'll
never understand why. He'll say the press was out to get
him all along."

"I sure hope you're right."

"Take the job, George," Greg pleaded. "There's so much
to be done."

George nodded. "Maybe I will."

.   .   .

Claus Krohn was a redhead. On his head, his hair was a
dark reddish-brown, but on the rest of his body it was ginger. Rebecca was particularly fond of the triangle that grew
from his groin up to a point near his navel. It was what she

looked at when she was giving him oral sex, which she enjoyed at least as much as he did.

Now she lay with her head on his belly and tangled her fingernails idly in the curls. They were in his apartment on a Monday night. Rebecca had no meetings on Monday nights, but she pretended she did, and her husband pretended to believe her.

The physical arrangements were easy. Her feelings were harder to manage. It was so difficult to keep these two men in separate compartments in her head that she often wanted to give up. She felt miserably guilty about being unfaithful to Bernd. But her reward was passionate and satisfying sex with a charming man who adored her. And Bernd had given her permission. She reminded herself of that again and again.

This year everyone was doing it. Love was all you needed. Rebecca was no hippie—she was a schoolteacher and a respected city politician—but all the same she was affected by the atmosphere of promiscuity, almost as if she were inadvertently inhaling some of the marijuana in the air. Why not? she asked herself. What's the harm?

When she looked back on the thirty-seven years of her life so far, all her regrets were for things she had *not* done: she had not been unfaithful to her rotten first husband; she had not got pregnant with Bernd's child while it was still possible; she had not escaped from the East German tyranny years earlier.

At least she would never look back and regret not having fucked Claus.

Claus said: "Are you happy?"

Yes, she thought, when I forget about Bernd for a few minutes. "Of course," she said. "I wouldn't be toying with your pubic hair otherwise."

"I love our time together, except that it's always too short."

"I know. I'd like to have a second life, so that I could spend it all with you."

"I'd settle for a weekend."

Too late, Rebecca saw where the conversation was going. For a moment, she stopped breathing.

She had been afraid of this. Monday evenings were not

enough. Perhaps there had never really been a chance that Claus would be satisfied with once a week. "I wish you hadn't said that," she said.

"You could get a nurse to take care of Bernd."

"I know I could."

"We could drive to Denmark, where nobody knows us. Stay in a small seaside hotel. Walk along one of those endless beaches and breathe the salt air."

"I knew this would happen." Rebecca stood up. Distractedly, she looked for her underwear. "It was only a question of when."

"Hey, slow down! I'm not forcing you."

"I know you're not, you sweet, kind man."

"If you're not comfortable taking a weekend away, we won't do it."

"We won't do it." She found her panties and pulled them on, then reached for her bra.

"Then why are you getting dressed? We have another half hour at least."

"When we began doing this I swore I'd stop before it got serious."

"Listen! I'm sorry I wanted a weekend away with you. I'll never mention it again, I promise."

"That's not the problem."

"Then what is?"

"I *want* to go away with you. That's what bothers me. I want it more than you do."

He looked baffled. "Then . . . ?"

"So I have to choose. I can't love you both any longer." She zipped her dress and stepped into her shoes.

"Choose me," he pleaded. "You've given six long years to Bernd. Isn't that enough? How could he be dissatisfied?"

"I made a promise to him."

"Break it."

"A person who breaks a promise diminishes herself. It's like losing a finger. It's worse than being paralyzed, which is merely physical. Someone whose promises are worthless has a disabled soul."

He looked ashamed. "You're right."

"Thank you for loving me, Claus. I'll never forget a single second of our Monday evenings."

"I can't believe I'm losing you." He turned away.

She wanted to kiss him one more time, but she decided not to.

"Good-bye," she said, and she went out.

. . .

In the end, the election was nail-bitingly close.

In September Cam had been ecstatically confident that Richard Nixon would win. He was far ahead in the polls. The police riot in Democratic Chicago, fresh in the minds of television viewers, tainted his opponent, Hubert Humphrey. Then, through September and October, Cam learned that voters' memories were maddeningly short. To Cam's horror, Humphrey began to close the gap. On the Friday before the election, the Harris poll had Nixon ahead 40–37; on Monday, Gallup said Nixon 42–40; on election day, Harris put Humphrey ahead "by a nose."

On election night, Nixon checked into a suite in the Waldorf Towers in New York. Cam and other key volunteers gathered in a more modest room with a TV and a refrigerator full of beer. Cam looked around the room and wondered excitedly how many of them would get jobs in the White House if Nixon won tonight.

Cam had got to know a plain, serious girl called Stephanie Maple, and he was hoping she might go to bed with him, either to celebrate Nixon's victory or for consolation in defeat.

At half past eleven they saw longtime Nixon press aide Herb Klein speaking from the cavernous press room several floors below them. "We still think we can win by three to five million, but it looks closer to three million at this point." Cam caught Stephanie's eye and raised his eyebrows. They knew Herb was bullshitting. By midnight Humphrey was ahead, in the votes already counted, by six hundred thousand. Then, at ten minutes past midnight, came news that deflated Cam's hopes: CBS reported that Humphrey had won New York—not by a whisker, but by half a million votes.

All eyes turned to California, where voting went on for three more hours after the polls closed in the East. But California went to Nixon, and it all came down to Illinois.

No one could predict the Illinois result. Mayor Daley's Democratic Party machine always cheated brazenly. But had Daley's power been diminished by the sight of his police bludgeoning kids on live television? Was his support of Humphrey even reliable? Humphrey had uttered the mildest of veiled criticism of Daley, saying: "Chicago last August was filled with pain," but bullies were thin-skinned, and there were rumors that Daley was so disgruntled that his backing for Humphrey was halfhearted.

Whatever the reason, in the end Daley did not deliver Illinois for Humphrey.

When the TV announced that Nixon had taken the state by one hundred forty thousand votes, the Nixon volunteers erupted with joy. It was over, and they had won.

They congratulated one another for a while, then the party broke up and they headed for their rooms, to get a few hours' sleep before Nixon's victory speech in the morning. Cam said quietly to Stephanie: "How about one more drink? I have a bottle in my room."

"Oh, gosh, no, thanks," she said. "I'm beat."

He hid his disappointment. "Maybe another time."

"Sure."

On his way to his room Cam ran into John Ehrlichman. "Congratulations, sir!"

"And to you, too, Cam."

"Thank you."

"When do you graduate?"

"June."

"Come and see me then. I might be able to offer you a job."

It was what Cam dreamed of. "Thank you!"

He entered his room in high spirits, despite Stephanie's refusal. He set his alarm and fell on the bed, exhausted but triumphant. Nixon had won. The decadent, liberal sixties were coming to an end. From now on people would have to work for what they wanted, not demand it by going on demonstrations. America was once again going to become strong, disciplined, conservative, and rich. There would be a new regime in Washington.

And Cam would be part of it.

PART SEVEN

TAPE

1972-1974

J acky Jakes cooked fried chicken, sweet potatoes, collard greens, and corn bread. "To heck with my diet," said Maria Summers, and tucked in. She loved this kind of food. She noticed that George ate sparingly, a little chicken and some greens, no bread. He had always had refined tastes.

It was Sunday. Maria visited the Jakes house almost as if she were family. It had started four years ago, after Maria helped George get his job at Fawcett Renshaw. That Thanksgiving, he had invited Maria to his mother's house for the traditional turkey dinner, in an attempt to cheer them all up after their hopes had crashed in Nixon's election victory. Maria had been missing her own family, so far away in Chicago, and had been grateful. She loved Jacky's combination of warmth and feistiness, and Jacky had seemed to take to her, too. Since then Maria had visited every couple of months.

After dinner they sat in the living room. When George was out of the room, Jacky said: "Something's eating you, child. What's on your mind?"

Maria sighed. Jacky was perceptive. "I've got a hard decision to make," Maria said.

"Romance, or work?"

"Work. You know, at first it seemed President Nixon wouldn't be as bad as we all feared. He's done more for black people than anyone ever expected." She ticked off items on her fingers. "One: He forced the construction unions to accept more blacks in their industry. The unions fought him hard on that but he held out. Two: He helped minority businesses. In three years, minorities' share of government contracts has gone from eight million dollars to two hundred forty-two million dollars. Three: He desegregated our schools. We had the laws in place already, but Nixon enforced them. By the time Nixon's first term ends, the proportion of children in all-black schools in the South will be below ten percent, down from sixty-eight percent."

"Okay, I'm convinced. What's the problem?"

"The administration *also* does things that are just plain wrong—I mean criminal. The president acts as if the law doesn't apply to him!"

"Believe me, honey, all criminals think that."

"But we public servants are supposed to be discreet. Silence is part of our code. We don't rat on the politicians, even when we disagree with what they're doing."

"Hmm. Two moral principles in conflict. Your duty to your boss contradicts your duty to your country."

"I could just resign. I'd probably earn more outside the government anyway. But Nixon and his people would just carry on, like Mafia hoodlums. And I don't *want* to work in the private sector. I want to make America a better society, especially for blacks. I've dedicated my life to that. Why should I give it up just because Nixon's a crook?"

"Plenty of government people talk to the press. I read stories all the time about what 'sources' are telling reporters."

"We're so shocked because Nixon and Agnew got elected by promising law and order. The blatant hypocrisy of it all makes us kind of furious."

"So, you have to decide whether to 'leak' to the media."

"I guess that's what I'm thinking."

"If you do," said Jacky anxiously, "please be careful."

Maria and George went with Jacky to the evening service at Bethel Evangelical Church, then George drove Maria home. He still had the old dark blue Mercedes convertible he had bought when he first came to Washington. "Just about every part of this car has been replaced," he said. "Cost me a fortune."

"Then it's a good thing you're earning a fortune at Fawcett Renshaw."

"I do okay."

Maria realized she was holding her shoulders so rigidly that her back hurt. She tried to relax her muscles. "George, I have something serious to talk about."

"All right."

She hesitated. Now or never. "In the past month, in the Justice Department, antitrust investigations into three separate corporations have been canceled on the direct orders of the White House."

"Any reason?"

"None given. But all three were major donors to Nixon's campaign in 1968, and are expected to finance his reelection campaign this year."

"But that's straightforward perverting the course of justice! It's a crime."

"Exactly."

"I knew Nixon was a liar, but I didn't think he was an actual crook."

"It's hard to believe, I know."

"Why are you telling me?"

"I want to give the story to the press."

"Wow, Maria, that's kind of dangerous."

"I'm prepared to take the risk. But I'm going to be very, very careful."

"Good."

"Do you know any reporters?"

"Of course. There's Lee Montgomery, for a start."

Maria smiled. "I dated him a few times."

"I know—I fixed you up."

"But that means he knows of the connection between you and me. Think of someone who's never met me."

"You're right, bad idea. How about Jasper Murray?"

"Head of the Washington bureau of *This Day*? He'd be ideal. How do you know him?"

"I met him years ago, when he was a student journalist, pestering Verena for an interview with Martin Luther King. Then, six months ago, he approached me at a press conference given by one of my clients. Turns out he was at that motel in Memphis, talking to Verena, when they both saw Dr. King shot. He asked me what had become of her. I had to tell him I had no idea. I think he was kind of taken with her."

"Most men are."

"Including me."

"Will you go see Murray?" Maria was tense, fearing that George would refuse, saying he did not want to get involved. "Will you tell him what I've told you?"

"So I would be, like, your cutout. There would be no direct connection between you and Jasper."

"Yes."

"It's like a James Bond movie."

"But will you do it?" She held her breath.

He grinned. "Absolutely," he said.

. . .

President Nixon was mad as hell.

He stood behind his large two-pedestal desk in the Oval Office, framed by the gold window drapes. His back was hunched, his head down, his bushy eyebrows drawn together in a frown. His jowly face was dark, as always, with the shadow of a beard he could never quite shave off. His lower lip was thrust out in his most characteristic expression, defiance that always seemed on the point of turning into self-pity.

His voice was deep, grating, gravelly. "I don't give a damn how it's done," he said. "Do whatever has to be done to stop these leaks and prevent further unauthorized disclosures."

Cam Dewar and his boss, John Ehrlichman, stood listening. Cam was tall, like his father and grandfather, but Ehrlichman was taller. Ehrlichman was domestic affairs assistant to the president. His modest job title was misleading: he was one of Nixon's closest advisers.

Cam knew why the president was angry. They had all watched *This Day* the evening before. Jasper Murray had turned the lens of his prying camera on Nixon's financial backers. He claimed that Nixon had canceled antitrust investigations into three large corporations, all of which had made substantial donations to his campaign.

It was true.

Worse, Murray had implied that any company that needed to divert an investigation in this presidential election year only had to make a large enough contribution to the Committee to Reelect the President, known as CREEP.

Cam guessed that was probably true, too.

Nixon used the power of the presidency to help his friends. He also attacked his enemies, directing tax audits and other investigations at corporations that donated to the Democrats.

Cam had found Murray's report sickening in its hypocrisy. Everybody knew this was how politics worked. Where did they think the money for election campaigns would come from otherwise? The Kennedy brothers would have done the same, if they had not already had more money than God.

Leaks to the press had plagued Nixon's presidency. *The New York Times* had exposed Nixon's top secret bombing raids on Vietnam's neighbor Cambodia, citing anonymous White House sources. Syndicated reporter Seymour Hersh had revealed that U.S. troops had murdered hundreds of innocent people at a Vietnamese village called My Lai—an atrocity the Pentagon had tried desperately to cover up. Now, in January 1972, Nixon's popularity was at an all-time low.

Dick Nixon took it personally. He took everything personally. This morning he looked hurt, betrayed, outraged. He believed the world was full of people who had it in for him, and the leaks confirmed his paranoia.

Cam, too, was enraged. When he got the White House job he had hoped to be part of a group that would change America. But everything the Nixon administration tried to do was undermined by liberals in the media and their traitorous "sources" within the government. It was agonizingly frustrating.

"This Jasper Murray," said Nixon.

Cam remembered Jasper. The man had been living at the Williams house in London a decade ago when the Dewar family visited. Now *there* was a nest of crypto-Communists.

Nixon said: "Is he a Jew?"

Cam felt impatient, and kept his face rigidly expressionless. Nixon had some crackpot ideas, and one was that Jews were natural spies.

Ehrlichman said: "I don't think so."

Cam said: "I met Murray years ago in London. His mother is half Jewish. His father is a British army officer."

"Murray is British?"

"Yes, but we can't use that against him because he served with the U.S. Army in Vietnam. Saw action, has the medals to prove it."

"Well, find a way to stop these leaks. I don't want to be told why it can't be done. I don't want excuses. I want results. I want it done, whatever the cost."

This was the kind of fighting talk Cam liked to hear. He felt bucked.

Ehrlichman said: "Thank you, Mr. President," and they went out.

"Well, that's clear enough!" Cam said eagerly as soon as they were outside the Oval Office.

"We need surveillance on Murray," Ehrlichman said decisively.

"I'll get on it," said Cam.

Ehrlichman headed for his office. Cam left the White House and walked along Pennsylvania Avenue toward the Department of Justice.

"Surveillance" meant a lot of things. It was not against the law to "bug" a room by placing a hidden recording device. However, getting into the room secretly to place the bug almost always involved the crime of breaking and entering, or burglary. And wiretapping, recording telephone conversations, *was* illegal—with exceptions. The Nixon administration believed wiretapping was legal if approved by the attorney general. In the last two years the White House had placed a total of seventeen wiretaps, all approved by the attorney general on grounds of national security and installed by the FBI. Cam was on his way to get authorization for number eighteen.

His memory of Jasper Murray as a youngster was vague, but he vividly recollected the beautiful Evie Williams, who had brutally spurned the advances of fifteen-year-old Cam. When he had told her that he was in love with her she had said: "Don't be ridiculous." And then, when he pressed her for a reason, she had said: "I'm in love with Jasper, you idiot."

He told himself these were silly adolescent dramas. Evie was a movie star now, and a supporter of every Communist cause from civil rights to sex education. In a famous incident on her brother's television show she had kissed Percy Marquand, scandalizing an audience who was not used to seeing whites even touch blacks. And she was certainly no longer in love with Jasper. She had dated pop star Hank Remington for a long time, though they were not together now.

But the memory of her scornful rebuff stung Cam like a burn. And women were still rejecting him. Even Stephanie Maple, who was not beautiful at all, had turned him down on the night of Nixon's victory. Later, when they both came to Washington to work, Stephanie had at last agreed to go to bed with Cam; but she had ended the romance after one night, which in a way was worse.

Cam knew he was tall and awkward, but so was his father, who apparently had never had trouble attracting women. Cam had talked to his mother about this indirectly. "How come you fell for Dad?" he had said. "He's not handsome or anything."

"Oh, but he was so *nice,*" she had said.

Cam had no idea what she was talking about.

He arrived at the Department of Justice and entered the high Great Hall with its art deco aluminum light fixtures. He anticipated no problem with the authorization: the attorney general, John Mitchell, was a Nixon crony, and had been Nixon's campaign manager in 1968.

The elevator's aluminum door opened. Cam got in and pressed the button for the fifth floor.

.   .   .

In ten years in the Washington bureaucracy, Maria had learned to be watchful. Her office was in the corridor leading to the attorney general's suite of rooms, and she kept her door open, so that she could see who came and went. She was especially alert on the day after the broadcast of the edition of *This Day* based on her leak. She knew there would be an explosive reaction from the White House, and she was waiting to see what form it would take.

As soon as she saw one of John Ehrlichman's aides go by, she jumped out of her chair.

"The attorney general is in a meeting and can't be disturbed," she said, catching him up. She had seen him before. He was an awkward, gangling white boy, tall and thin, his shoulders like a wire coat hanger for his suit. She knew the type: he would be clever and naïve at the same time. She put on her most friendly smile. "Perhaps I can do something for you?"

"It's not the kind of thing that can be discussed with a secretary," he said irritably.

Maria's antennae quivered. She sensed danger. But she pretended to be eager to help. "Then it's a good thing I'm not a secretary," she said. "I'm an attorney. My name is Maria Summers."

He clearly had difficulty with the concept of a black woman lawyer. "Where did you study?" he asked skeptically.

He probably expected her to name an obscure Negro college, so she took pleasure in saying casually: "Chicago Law." But she could not resist asking: "How about you?"

"I'm not a lawyer," he admitted. "I majored in Russian at Berkeley. Cam Dewar."

"I've heard of you. You work for John Ehrlichman. Why don't we talk in my office?"

"I'll wait for the attorney general."

"Is this about that TV show last night?"

Cam glanced around furtively. No one was listening.

"We have to do something about that," Maria said emphatically. "The business of government can't go on with these leaks all the time," she went on, feigning indignation. "It's impossible!"

The young man's attitude warmed. "That's what the president thinks."

"But what are we going to do about it?"

"We need a wiretap on Jasper Murray."

Maria swallowed. Thank God I found out about this, she thought. But she said: "Great—some tough action at last."

"A journalist who admits to receiving confidential information from within the government is clearly a danger to national security."

"Absolutely. Now don't you worry about the paperwork. I'll put an authorization form in front of Mitchell today. He'll be glad to sign it, I know."

"Thank you."

She caught him looking at her chest. Having seen her first as a secretary and then as a Negro, he was now regarding her as a pair of breasts. Young men were so predictable. "This will be what they call a black bag job," she said. The phrase meant illegal breaking and entering. "Joe Hugo is in charge of that for the FBI."

"I'll go and see him now." The headquarters of the Bureau was in the same building. "Thank you for your help, Maria."

"You're welcome, Mr. Dewar."

She watched him retreat down the corridor, then she closed her office door. She picked up the phone and dialed Fawcett Renshaw. "I'd like to leave a message for George Jakes," she said.

.   .   .

Joe Hugo was a pale man with prominent blue eyes. He was somewhere in his thirties. Like all FBI agents he wore excruciatingly conservative clothes: a plain gray suit, a white shirt, a nondescript tie, black toe-capped shoes. Cam himself was conventional in his tastes, but his unremarkable brown chalk-stripe suit with wide lapels and flared trousers suddenly seemed radical.

Cam told Hugo he worked for Ehrlichman and said right out: "I need a wiretap on Jasper Murray, the television journalist."

Joe frowned. "Tap the office of *This Day*? If *that* story got out . . ."

"Not his office, his home. The leakers we're talking about most likely sneak out late in the evening and go to a pay phone and call him at home."

"Either way it's a problem. The FBI doesn't do black bag jobs anymore."

"What? Why?"

"Mr. Hoover feels the Bureau is in danger of taking the rap for other people in government."

Cam could not contradict that. If the FBI was caught burglarizing the home of a journalist, naturally the president would deny all knowledge. That was how things worked. J. Edgar Hoover had been breaking the law for years, but now for some reason he had got a bug up his ass about it. There was no telling with Hoover, seventy-seven years old and no saner than he had ever been.

Cam raised his voice. "The president has asked for this wiretap, and the attorney general is happy to authorize it. Are you going to refuse?"

"Relax," said Hugo. "There's always a way to give the president what he needs."

"You mean you'll do it?"

"I mean there's a way." Hugo wrote something on a pad and tore off the sheet. "Call this guy. He used to do these jobs officially. He's retired now, which just means he does them unofficially."

Cam was uncomfortable with the idea of doing things unofficially. What did that mean? he wondered. But he sensed this was not the moment to quibble.

He took the piece of paper. It bore the name "Tim Tedder" and a phone number. "I'll call him today," Cam said.

"From a pay phone," said Hugo.

·   ·   ·

The mayor of Roath, Mississippi, sat in George Jakes's office at Fawcett Renshaw. His name was Robert Denny, but he said: "Call me Denny. Everyone knows Denny. Even my little lady wife calls me Denny." He was the kind of man George had been fighting for a decade: an ugly, fat, foul-mouthed, stupid white racist.

His city was building an airport, with help from the government. But recipients of federal funding had to be equal-opportunity employers. And Maria in the Justice Department had learned that the new airport would have no black staff other than skycaps.

This was typical of the kind of work George got.

Denny was as condescending as a man could be. "We do things a little differently in the South, George," he said.

Don't I fucking know it, George thought; you thugs broke my arm eleven years ago, and it still aches like a bastard on a cold day.

"People in Roath wouldn't have confidence in an airport run by coloreds," Denny went on. "They would fear things might not be done right, you know, from a safety point of view. I'm sure you understand me."

You bet I do, you racist fool.

"Old Renshaw is a good friend of mine."

Renshaw was not a friend of Denny's, George knew. The senior partner had met this client just twice. But Denny was hoping to make George nervous. *If you mess up, your boss is going to be real mad at you.*

Denny went on: "He tells me that you're the best person in Washington to get the Justice Department off my back."

George said: "Mr. Renshaw is right. I am."

With Denny were two city councilors and three aides, all white. Now they sat back, showing relief. George had reassured them that their problem could be solved.

"Now," George said, "there are two ways we could achieve this. We could go to court and challenge the Justice Department's ruling. They're not that smart over there, and we can find flaws in their methodology, mistakes in their reports, and bias. Litigation is good for my firm, because our fees would be high."

"We can pay," said Denny. The airport was clearly a lucrative project.

"Two snags with litigation," George said. "One, there are always delays—and you want to get your airport built and operating as soon as you can. Two, no lawyer can put his hand on his heart and tell you what the court's decision will be. You never know."

"Not here in Washington, anyhow," said Denny.

Clearly the courts in Roath were more amenable to Denny's wishes.

"Alternatively," George said, "we could negotiate."

"What would that involve?"

"A phased introduction of more black employees at all levels."

"Promise them anything!" said Denny.

"They're not completely stupid, and payments would be tied to compliance."

"What do you think they'll want?"

"The Justice Department doesn't really care, so long as they can say they've made a difference. But they will consult with black organizations in your town." George glanced down at the file on his desk. "This case was brought to the Justice Department by Roath Christians for Equal Rights."

"Fucking Communists," said Denny.

"The Justice Department will probably agree to any compromise that has the approval of that group. It gets them and you out of the department's hair."

Denny reddened. "You better not be telling me I have to negotiate with the goddamn Roath Christians."

"It's the smart way to go if you want a quick solution to your problem."

Denny bristled.

George added: "But you don't have to see them personally. In fact I recommend you don't speak to them at all."

"Then who will negotiate with them?"

"I will," said George. "I'll fly down there tomorrow."

The mayor grinned. "And you being, you know, the color you are, you'll be able to talk them into backing down."

George wanted to strangle the dumb prick. "I don't want you to misunderstand me, Mr. Mayor—Denny, I should say. You will have to make some real changes. My job is to make sure they're as painless as possible. But you're an experienced political leader, and you know the importance of public relations."

"That's the truth."

"If there's any talk of the Roath Christians backing down, it could sabotage the whole deal. Better for you to take the line that you've graciously made some small concessions, much against your will, in order to get your airport built for the good of the town."

"Gotcha," Denny said with a wink.

Without realizing it, Denny had agreed to reverse a decades-old practice and employ more blacks at his airport. This was a small victory, but George relished it. However, Denny would not be happy unless he could tell himself and others that he had pulled a fast one. Best, perhaps, to go along with the delusion.

George winked back.

As the delegation from Mississippi was leaving the office, George's secretary gave him a strange look and a slip of paper.

It was a typed phone message: "There will be a prayer meeting at the Barney Circle Full Gospel Church tomorrow at six."

The secretary's look said this was a strange way for a high-powered Washington lawyer to spend the cocktail hour.

George knew the message was from Maria.

. . .

Cam did not like Tim Tedder. He wore a safari suit and had a soldier's short haircut. He had no sideburns, at a time when almost everyone wore sideburns. Cam felt Tedder was too gung ho. He clearly relished everything clandestine. Cam wondered what Tedder would have said if asked to kill Jasper Murray rather than just wiretap him.

Tedder had no scruples about breaking the law, but he was used to working with the government, and within twenty-four hours he appeared in Cam's office with a written plan and a budget.

The plan provided for three men to watch Jasper Murray's apartment over two days to determine his routine. Then they would enter at a time they knew to be safe and plant a transmitter in his phone. They would also place a tape recorder nearby, probably on the roof of the building, in a casing marked 50,000 VOLTS—DO NOT TOUCH to discourage investigation. Then they would change the tapes once every twenty-four hours for a month, and Tedder would provide transcripts of all conversations.

The price for all this was five thousand dollars. Cam would get the money from the slush fund operated by the Committee to Reelect the President.

Cam took the proposal to Ehrlichman, sharply conscious that he was crossing a line. He had never done anything criminal in his life. Now he was about to become a conspirator in a burglary. It was necessary: the leaks had to be stopped, and the president had said: "I don't give a damn how it's done." All the same, Cameron did not feel good about it. He was jumping off a diving board in the dark, and could not see the water below.

John Ehrlichman wrote "E" in the approve box.

Then he added an anxious little note: "If done under your assurance that it is not traceable."

Cam knew what that meant.

If it all went wrong, he was to take the blame.

. . .

George left his office at five thirty and drove to Barney Circle, a low-rent residential neighborhood east of Capitol Hill. The church was a shack on a lot surrounded by a high chicken-wire fence. Inside, the rows of hard chairs were half full. The worshippers were all black, mostly women. It was a good place for a clandestine meeting: an FBI agent in here would be as conspicuous as a turd on a tablecloth.

One of the women turned around, and George recognized Maria Summers. He sat next to her.

"What is it?" he whispered. "What's the emergency?"

She put her finger to her lips. "Afterward," she said.

He smiled wryly. He would have to sit through an hour of prayers. Well, it would probably do his soul good.

George was delighted to be part of this cloak-and-dagger plot with Maria. His work at Fawcett Renshaw did not satisfy his passion for justice. He was helping to advance the cause of equality for blacks, but piecemeal, and slowly. He was now thirty-six, old enough to know that youthful dreams of a better world are rarely fulfilled, but all the same he thought he ought to be able to do more than get a few extra blacks hired at Roath airport.

A robed pastor entered and began with an extempore prayer that lasted ten or fifteen minutes. Then he invited the congregation to sit in silence and hold their own conversations with God. "We will be glad to hear the voice of any man who feels moved by the Holy Spirit to share his prayers with the rest of us. In accordance with the teaching of the Apostle Paul, women remain silent in the church."

George nudged Maria, knowing she would be bristling at that piece of sanctified sexism.

George's mother adored Maria. George suspected that Jacky thought she might have been like Maria, if she had been born a generation later. She might have had a good education and a high-powered job and a black dress with a row of pearls.

During the prayers George's thoughts wandered to Verena. She had disappeared into the Black Panthers. He would have liked to believe that she was responsible for the more humane side of their mission, such as cooking free breakfasts for inner-city schoolchildren whose mothers spent the early mornings cleaning white people's offices. But, knowing Verena, she might just as easily be robbing banks.

The pastor closed the meeting with another long prayer. As soon as he said amen, the members of the congregation turned to one another and began to chat. The hum of their conversations was loud, and George felt he could talk to Maria without fear of being overheard.

Maria said immediately: "They're going to tap Jasper

Murray's home phone. One of Ehrlichman's boys came over from the White House."

"Obviously Jasper's last TV show triggered this."

"You bet your socks."

"And it's not really Jasper they're after."

"I know. It's the person who's giving him information. It's me."

"I'll see Jasper tonight and warn him to be careful what he says on his home phone."

"Thanks." She looked around. "We're not as unobtrusive as I'd hoped."

"Why not?"

"We're too well dressed. We obviously don't belong here."

"And my secretary now thinks I'm born again. Let's get out of here."

"We can't leave together. You go first."

George left the little church and drove back toward the White House.

Maria was not the only insider leaking to the press, he reflected: there were many. George figured that the president's casual disregard of the law had shocked some government workers into breaking a lifelong discretion. Nixon's criminality was particularly horrifying in a president who had campaigned on a law-and-order ticket. George felt as if the American people were victims of a gigantic hoax.

George tried to think where would be the best place to meet Jasper. Last time he had simply gone to the office of *This Day*. Doing that once might not have been dangerous, but he should avoid a repeat visit. He did not want to be seen with Jasper too often by Washington insiders. On the other hand, their meeting had to seem casual, not furtive, just in case they were spotted.

He drove to the parking garage nearest to Jasper's office. A block of spaces on the third floor was reserved for the staff of *This Day*. George parked nearby and went to a pay phone.

Jasper was at his desk.

George did not give his name. "It's Friday night," he said without preamble. "When were you thinking of leaving the office?"

"Soon."

"Now would be good."

"Okay."

George hung up.

A few minutes later Jasper came out of the elevator, a big man with a mane of fair hair, carrying a raincoat. He walked to his vehicle, a bronze Lincoln Continental with a black fabric roof.

George got into the Lincoln beside him and told him about the wiretap.

Jasper said: "I'll have to take the phone to pieces, and remove the bug."

George shook his head. "If you do that they'll know, because they won't get any transmissions."

"So what?"

"So they'll find another way to bug you, and next time we might not be so lucky as to find out about it."

"Shit. I take all my most important calls at home. What am I going to do?"

"When an important source calls, say you're busy and you'll call back; then go out to a pay phone."

"I guess I'll figure something out. Thanks for the tip. Does it come from the usual source?"

"Yes."

"He's well informed."

"Yes," said George, "he is."

eep Dewar came to see Dave Williams at Daisy Farm, his recording studio in Napa Valley.

The rooms were plain yet comfortable, but there was nothing plain about the studio, which had state-of-the-art equipment. Several hit albums had been made here, and renting the place to bands had turned into a small but profitable business. Sometimes they asked Dave to be their producer, and he found that he seemed to have a talent for helping them achieve the sounds they wanted.

Which was just as well, for Dave was not making as much money as he once had. Since the breakup of Plum Nellie there had been a greatest hits album, a live album, and an album of outtakes and alternate versions. Each had sold less than the previous one. Solo albums by former members had done modestly well. Dave was not in trouble, but he was no longer buying a new Ferrari every year. And the trend was down.

When Beep called and asked if she could drive up and see him the next day he had been so surprised that he had not asked whether she had some special reason.

That morning he shampooed his beard in the shower, put on clean jeans, and picked out a bright blue shirt. Then he asked himself why he was making a fuss. He was no longer in love with Beep. Why did he care what she thought of his appearance? He realized that he wanted her to look at him and regret jilting him. "Bloody fool," he said aloud to himself, and put on an old T-shirt.

All the same, he wondered what she wanted.

He was in the studio, working with a young singer-song-writer making his first album, when the gate phone flashed silently. He left the artist working on the middle eight and stepped outside. Beep drove up to the house in a red Mercury Cougar with the top down.

He expected her to have changed, and was intrigued to see what she would look like, but in fact she was the same: small and pretty with an impish look in her eye. She hardly seemed different from when he had first met her, a decade ago, when she had been a disturbingly sexy thirteen-year-old. Today she wore blue matador pants and a striped tank top, and her hair was cut in a short bob.

First he took her to the back of the house and showed her the view across the valley. It was winter, and the vines were bare, but the sun was shining, and the rows of brown plants threw blue shadows, making curvilinear patterns like brushstrokes.

She said: "What kind of grapes do you grow?"

"Cabernet sauvignon, the classic red grape. It's hardy, and this stony soil suits it."

"Do you make wine?"

"Yes. It's not great, but it's improving. Come inside and try a glass."

She liked the all-wood kitchen, which looked traditional despite having all the latest gadgets. The cabinets were natural hand-scraped pine, washed with a light stain to give the wood a golden glow. Dave had removed the flat ceiling, opening up the height of the room to the underside of the pitched roof.

He had spent a lot of time designing this room because he wanted it to be like the kitchen of the house in Great Peter Street, a room where everyone came to hang out, eat and drink and talk.

They sat at the antique pine table and Dave opened a bottle of Daisy Farm Red 1969, the first one he and Danny Medina had produced as partners. It was still too tannic, and Beep made a face. Dave laughed. "I guess you have to appreciate its potential."

"I'll take your word for that."

She took out a pack of Chesterfields. Dave said: "You were smoking Chesterfields when you were thirteen."

"I ought to give it up."

"I had never seen such long cigarettes."

"You were sweet at that age."

"And the sight of your lips sucking on a Chesterfield was strangely arousing to me, though I could not have said why."

She laughed. "I could have told you."

He took another sip of the wine. It might be better in a couple more years. He said: "How is Walli?"

"Fine. He does more dope than he should, but what can I tell you? He's a rock star."

Dave smiled. "I smoke a joint most evenings myself."

"Are you dating anyone?"

"Sally Dasilva."

"The actress. I saw a picture of the two of you, arriving at some premiere, but I didn't know if it was serious."

It was not very serious. "She's in LA, and we both work a lot. But we get a weekend together once in a while."

"By the way, I have to tell you how much I admire your sister."

"Evie's a good actress."

"She made me weep with laughter in that movie where she played a rookie cop. But it's her activism that makes her a hero. A lot of people oppose the war, but not many have the guts to go to North Vietnam."

"She was scared shitless."

"I bet."

Dave put down his glass and gave Beep a direct look. He could not contain his curiosity any longer. "What's really on your mind, Beep?"

"First, thanks for seeing me. You didn't have to, and I appreciate it."

"You're welcome." He had almost said no, but inquisitiveness had overcome resentment.

"Second, I apologize for what I did back in 1968. I'm sorry I hurt you. It was cruel, and I'll never cease to be ashamed."

Dave nodded. He was not going to disagree. To let her fiancé find her in bed with his best friend was about as cruel as a girl could be, and the fact that she had been only twenty at the time was not enough of an excuse.

"Third, Walli is sorry too. He and I still love each other, don't get me wrong, but we know what we did. Walli will tell you so himself, if you ever give him the chance."

"Okay." She was beginning to churn up Dave's emotions. He felt echoes of long-forgotten passions: anger, resentment, loss. He was impatient to find out where this was leading.

Beep said: "Could you ever forgive us?"

He was unprepared for the question. "I don't know, I haven't thought about it," he said weakly. Before today he might have said that he no longer cared, but somehow Beep's questions were reawakening dormant grief. "What would forgiving you involve?"

Beep took a breath. "Walli wants to re-form the group."

"Oh!" Dave had not been expecting that.

"He misses working with you."

Dave found that gratifying, in a mean-minded sort of way.

Beep added: "The solo albums haven't done so well."

"His sold better than mine."

"But it's not even the sales that bother him. He doesn't care about the money, doesn't spend half of what he earns. What matters to him is that the music was better when the two of you made it together."

"I can't disagree with that," said Dave.

"He's got some songs he'd like to share with you. You could get Lew and Buzz over from London. We could all live here at Daisy Farm. Then, when the album comes out, maybe you could do a reunion concert, even a tour."

Against his will Dave felt excited. Nothing had ever been as thrilling as the Plum Nellie years, all the way from Hamburg to Haight-Ashbury. The group had been exploited and cheated and ripped off, and they had loved every minute of it. Now he was respected and fairly paid, a television personality, a family entertainer, a show business entrepreneur. But it was not half so much fun.

"Go back on the road?" he mused. "I don't know."

"Think about it," Beep pleaded. "Don't say yes or no."

"Okay," Dave said. "I'll think about it."

But he already knew the answer.

He walked her out to her car. There was a newspaper

lying on the passenger seat. Beep picked it up and handed it to him. "Have you seen this?" she said. "It's a photo of your sister."

• • •

The picture showed Evie Williams in camouflage fatigues.

The first thing that struck Cam Dewar was how alluring she looked. The baggy clothing only reminded him that underneath was the perfect body the world had seen in the movie *The Artist's Model*. The heavy boots and the utilitarian cap just made her more cute.

She was sitting on a tank. Cam did not know much about armaments, but the caption told him this was a Soviet T-54 with a 100 mm gun.

All around her were uniformed soldiers of the North Vietnamese army. She seemed to be telling them something amusing, and her face was alight with animation and humor. They were smiling and laughing the way people anywhere in the world did around a Hollywood celebrity.

She was on a peace mission, according to the accompanying article. She had learned that Vietnamese people did not wish to be at war with the United States. "There's a fucking surprise," Cam said sarcastically. All they wanted was to be left alone, Evie said.

The picture was a public relations triumph for the antiwar movement. Half the girls in America wanted to be Evie Williams, half the boys wanted to marry her, and they all admired her courage in going to North Vietnam. Worse yet, the Communists were doing her no harm. They were talking to her and telling her that they wanted to be friends with the American people.

How could the wicked president drop bombs on these nice folks?

It made Cam want to puke.

But the White House was not taking this lying down.

Cam was working the phones, calling sympathetic journalists. There were not too many of those: the liberal media hated Nixon, and a part of the conservative media found him too moderate. But there were enough supporters, Cam thought, to start a backlash, if only they would play along.

Cam had in front of him a list of points to make, and he

chose from the list depending on whom he was talking to. "How many American boys do you think have been killed by that tank?" he asked a writer for a talk show.

"I don't know, you tell me," the man replied.

The correct answer was probably none, since North Vietnamese tanks generally did not meet American forces, but engaged the South Vietnamese army. However, that was not the point. "It's a question liberals ought to be asked on your show," Cam said.

"You're right, it's a good question."

Speaking to a columnist for a right-wing tabloid he asked: "Did you know that Evie Williams is British?"

"Her mother is American," the journalist pointed out.

"Her mother hates America so much that she left in 1936 and has never lived here since."

"Good point!"

Speaking to a liberal journalist who often attacked Nixon, Cam said: "Even you have to admit she's naïve, to let herself be used like this by the North Vietnamese for anti-American propaganda. Or do you take her peace mission seriously?"

The results were spectacular. Next day began a backlash against Evie Williams that was larger in scale than her original triumph. She became public enemy number one, replacing Eldridge Cleaver, the serial rapist and Black Panther leader. Letters vilifying her poured into the White House—and not all of them were whipped up by local Republican Parties around the country. She became a hate figure to the people who had voted for Nixon, people who clung to the simple belief that you were either for America or against it.

Cam found the whole thing deeply gratifying. Every time he read another tabloid diatribe against her, he remembered how she had called his love ridiculous.

But he was not through with her yet.

When the backlash was at its height, he called Melton Faulkner, a pro-Nixon businessman who was on the board of one of the television networks. He got the switchboard to dial the call, so that Faulkner's secretary would say to him: "The White House is on the line!"

When he reached Faulkner he gave his name and said:

"The president has asked me to call you, sir, about a special the network is planning on Jane Addams."

Jane Addams, who died in 1935, had been a progressive campaigner, suffragette, and winner of the Nobel Peace Prize.

"That's right," said Faulkner. "Is the president a fan of hers?"

The hell he is, Cam thought; Jane Addams was just the kind of woolly-minded liberal he hated. "Yes, he is," Cam said. "But *The Hollywood Reporter* says you're thinking of casting Evie Williams as Jane."

"That's right."

"You probably saw the recent news about Evie Williams and the way she let herself be exploited for propaganda by America's enemies."

"Sure, I read that story."

"Are you sure this anti-American British actress with socialist views is the right person to play an American hero?"

"As a board member, I don't have any say in casting . . ."

"The president has no power to take any action about this, heaven forbid, but he thought you might be interested to hear his opinion."

"I most certainly am."

"Good to talk to you, Mr. Faulkner." Cam hung up.

He had heard people say that revenge is sweet. But no one had told him how sweet.

. . .

Dave and Walli sat in the recording studio on high stools, holding guitars. They had a song called "Back Together Again." It was in two parts, the different parts in different keys, and they needed a hinge chord for the transition. They sang the song over and over, trying different things.

Dave was happy. They still had it. Walli was an original, coming up with melodies and harmonic progressions that no one else used. They bounced ideas off one another and the result was better than anything either did alone. They were going to make a triumphant comeback.

Beep had not changed, but Walli had. He was gaunt. His high cheekbones and almond eyes were accentuated by his thinness, and he looked vampirishly handsome.

Buzz and Lew sat nearby, smoking, listening, waiting. They were patient. As soon as Dave and Walli had the song figured out, Buzz and Lew would move to their instruments and work out the drum and bass parts.

It was ten in the evening, and they had been working for three hours. They would keep going until three or four in the morning, then sleep until midday. Those were rock-and-roll hours.

This was their third day in the studio. They had spent the first jamming, playing old favorites, enjoying getting used to one another again. Walli had played wonderful melodic guitar lines. Unfortunately, on the second day Walli had suffered a stomach upset and retired early. So this was their first day of serious work.

On an amplifier beside Walli stood a bottle of Jack Daniel's and a tall glass with ice cubes. In the old days they had often drunk booze or smoked joints while they worked on songs. It had been part of the fun. These days Dave preferred to work straight, but Walli had not changed his habits.

Beep came in with four beers on a tray. Dave guessed she wanted Walli to drink beer instead of whisky. She often brought food into the studio: blueberries with ice cream, chocolate cake, bowls of peanuts, bananas. She wanted Walli to live on something other than booze. He would take a spoonful of ice cream or a handful of peanuts, then return to his Jack Daniel's.

Fortunately he was still brilliant, as the new song showed. However, he was getting irritated with their inability to come up with the right transition chord. "Fuck," he said. "I have it in my head, you know? But it won't come out."

Buzz said: "Musical constipation, mate. You need a rock laxative. What would be the equivalent of a bowl of prunes?"

Dave said: "A Schoenberg opera."

Lew said: "A drum solo by Dave Clark."

Walli said: "A Demis Roussos album."

The phone flashed and Beep picked it up. "Come on in," she said, and hung up. Then she said to Walli: "It's Hilton."

"Okay." Walli got off his stool, put his guitar in a stand, and went out.

Dave looked inquiringly at Beep, who said: "A dealer."

Dave kept playing the song. There was nothing unusual

about a dope dealer calling at a recording studio. He did not
know why musicians used drugs so much more than the
general population, but it had always been so: Charlie
Parker had been a heroin addict, and he was the generation
before last.

While Dave strummed, Buzz picked up his bass and
played along, and Lew sat behind the kit and began to drum
quietly, looking for the groove. They had been improvising
for fifteen or twenty minutes when Dave stopped and said:
"What the fuck has happened to Walli?"

He left the studio, followed by the others, and returned
to the main house.

They found Walli in the kitchen. He was stretched out on
the floor, stoned, with a hypodermic syringe still stuck in his
arm. He had shot up as soon as his supply arrived.

Beep bent over him and gently pulled out the needle.
"He'll be out now until morning," she said. "I'm sorry."

Dave cursed. That was the end of the day's work.

Buzz said to Lew: "Shall we go to the cantina?"

There was a bar at the bottom of the hill, mostly used by
Mexican farm workers. It had the ridiculous name of the
Mayfair Lounge, so they referred to it as the cantina.

"Might as well," said Lew.

The rhythm section left.

Beep said: "Help me get him to bed."

Dave picked up Walli by the shoulders, Beep took his
legs, and they carried him to the bedroom. Then they returned to the kitchen. Beep leaned against the counter
while Dave put on coffee.

"He's an addict, isn't he?" Dave said, fiddling with a paper filter.

Beep nodded.

"Do you think we can even make this album?"

"Yes!" she said. "Please don't give up on him. I'm afraid ..."

"Okay, stay calm." He switched the machine on.

"I can manage him," she said desperately. "He maintains
in the evenings, just keeping going on small amounts while
he works, then in the early hours he shoots up and nods out.
This was unusual, today. He doesn't often just crash like
that. Normally I score the stuff and ration it."

Dave was appalled. He looked at her. "You've become
nursemaid to a junkie."

"We make these decisions when we're too young to know better, then we have to live with them," she said, and she started to cry.

Dave put his arms around her, and she wept on his chest. He gave her time, while the front of his shirt got wet and the kitchen filled with the aroma of coffee. Then he gently disengaged himself and poured two cups.

"Don't worry," he said. "Now that we know about the problem, we can work around it. While Walli's at his best we'll do the difficult stuff: writing the songs, the guitar solos, the vocal harmonies. When he's not around we'll lay down backing tracks and do a rough mix. We can get it together."

"Oh, thank you. You've saved his life. I can't tell you how relieved I am. You're such a good man." She stood on tiptoe and kissed his lips.

Dave felt weird. She was thanking him for saving her boyfriend's life and, at the same time, kissing him.

Then she said: "I was such a fool to give you up."

That was disloyal to the man in the bedroom. But loyalty had never been her strength.

She put her arms around his waist and pressed her body to his.

For a moment he held his hands in the air, away from her; then he gave in, and put his arms around her again. Perhaps loyalty was not his strength either.

"Junkies don't have much sex," she said. "It's been a while."

Dave felt shaky. At some level, he realized, he had known this was going to happen, from the moment she drove up in that red convertible.

He was shaking because he wanted her so badly.

Still he said nothing.

"Take me to bed, Dave," she said. "Let's fuck like we used to, just once, for old times' sake."

"No," he said.

But he did.

⋅ ⋅ ⋅

They finished the album the day FBI director J. Edgar Hoover died.

Over breakfast at noon the following day, in the kitchen

of Daisy Farm, Beep said: "My grandfather is a senator, and he says J. Edgar liked to suck cock."

They were all amazed.

Dave grinned. He was pretty sure old Gus Dewar had never said "suck cock" to his granddaughter. But Beep liked to talk that way in front of guys. She knew it turned them on. She was mischievous. It was one of the things that made her exciting.

She went on: "Grandpapa told me Hoover lived with his associate director, a guy called Tolson. They went everywhere together, like husband and wife."

Lew said: "It's people like Hoover give us queers a bad name."

Walli, up unusually early, said: "Hey, listen, we're going to do a reunion concert when the album comes out, right?"

Dave said: "Yeah. What's on your mind?"

"Let's make it a fund-raiser for George McGovern."

The idea of rock bands raising money for liberal politicians was catching on, and McGovern was the leading contender for the Democratic nomination in this year's presidential election, running as a peace candidate.

Dave said: "Great idea. Doubles our publicity, and helps to end the war as well."

Lew said: "I'm for it."

Buzz said: "Okay, I'm outvoted, I concede."

Lew and Buzz left soon after to catch a plane to London. Walli went into the studio to pack his guitars into their cases, a job he did not like to leave to roadies.

Dave said to Beep: "You can't just go."

"Why not?"

"Because for the last six weeks we've been fucking our brains out every time Walli nodded out."

She grinned. "Been great, hasn't it?"

"And because we love each other." Dave waited to see whether she would confirm or deny this.

She did neither.

He repeated: "You can't just go."

"What else am I going to do?"

"Talk to Walli. Tell him to get a new nursemaid. Come and live here with me."

Beep shook her head.

"I met you a decade ago," Dave said. "We've been lovers. We were engaged to get married. I think I know you."

"So?"

"You're fond of Walli, you care for him, you want him to be okay. But you rarely have sex with him and, what's even more telling, you don't mind that. Which tells me you don't love him."

Once again she did not confirm or deny what he said.

Dave said: "I think you love me."

She looked into her empty coffee cup, as if she might see answers there in the dregs.

"Shall we get married?" Dave said. "Is that why you're hesitating—you want me to propose? Then I will. Marry me, Beep. I love you. I loved you when we were thirteen years old and I don't think I ever stopped."

"What, not even when you were in bed with Mandy Love?"

He smiled ruefully. "I might have forgotten about you just for a few moments now and again."

She grinned. "Now I believe you."

"What about children? Would you like to have kids? I would."

She said nothing.

Dave said: "I'm pouring my heart out here, and I'm getting nothing back. What's going on in your head?"

She looked up, and he saw that she was crying. She said: "If I leave Walli, he'll die."

"I don't believe he will," Dave said.

Beep held up a hand to silence him. "You asked me what's going on in my head. If you really want to know, don't contradict what I say."

Dave shut up.

"I've done a lot of selfish bad things in my life. Some you know about, but there are more."

Dave could believe that. But he wanted to tell her that she had also brought joy and laughter into many people's lives, including his own. However, she had asked him just to listen, so he did.

"I hold Walli's life in my hands."

Dave bit back a retort, but Beep said what had been on the tip of his tongue. "Okay, it's not my fault he's a junkie, I'm not his mother, I don't have to save him."

Dave thought Walli might be tougher than Beep reckoned. On the other hand Jimi Hendrix had died, Janis Joplin had died, Jim Morrison had died . . .

"I want to change," Beep said. "More, I want to make up for my mistakes. It's time for me to do something that isn't just what grabs me at the moment. It's time for me to do something good. So I'm going to stay with Walli."

"Is that your last word?"

"Yes."

"Good-bye, then," said Dave, and he hurried out of the room so that she would not see him cry.

he Kremlin is in a panic about Nixon's visit to China," said Dimka to Tanya.

They were in Dimka's apartment. His three-year-old daughter, Katya, was on Tanya's knee, and they were looking through a book with pictures of farm animals.

Dimka and Natalya had moved back into Government House. The Peshkov-Dvorkin clan now occupied three apartments in the same building. Grandfather Grigori was still in his original place, living now with his daughter, Anya, and granddaughter, Tanya. Dimka's ex-wife, Nina, lived there with Grisha, eight years old and a little schoolboy. And now Dimka and Natalya and little Katya had moved in. Tanya adored her nephew and niece and was always happy to babysit. Government House was almost like a peasant village, Tanya sometimes thought, with the extended family minding the children.

People often asked Tanya whether she did not want children of her own. "There's plenty of time," she always answered. She was still only thirty-two. But she did not feel she was free to marry. Vasili was not her lover, but she had dedicated her life to the undercover work they did together, first in publishing *Dissidence,* then in smuggling Vasili's books to the West. Occasionally she was courted by one of the diminishing number of eligible bachelors her age, and sometimes she would go on a few dates and even go to bed with one of them. But she could not let them into her clandestine life.

And Vasili's life was now more important than her own. With the publication of *A Free Man* he had become one of the world's leading writers. He interpreted the Soviet Union to the rest of the planet. After his third book, *The Age of Stagnation,* there was talk of a Nobel Prize, except that apparently they could not award it to a pseudonym. Tanya was the conduit by which his work reached the West, and it would be impossible to keep such a big, terrible secret from a husband.

The Communists hated "Ivan Kuznetsov." The whole world knew that he could not reveal his real name for fear that his work would be suppressed, and this made the Kremlin leaders look like the Philistines they were. Every time his work was mentioned in the Western media, people pointed out that it had never been published in Russian, the language in which it had been written, because of Soviet censorship. It drove the Kremlin mad.

"Nixon's trip was a big success," Tanya said to Dimka. "In our office we get news feeds from the West. People can't stop congratulating Nixon on his vision. This is a giant leap forward for the stability of the world, they say. Also, his poll ratings have jumped—and this is election year in the United States."

The idea that the capitalist-imperialists might link with the maverick Chinese Communists to gang up on the USSR was a terrifying prospect to the Soviet leadership. They immediately invited Nixon to Moscow in an attempt to redress the balance.

"Now they're desperate to make sure Nixon's visit here is also a success," Dimka said. "They'll do anything to keep the USA from siding with China."

Tanya was struck by a thought. "Anything?"

"I exaggerate. But what did you have in mind?"

Tanya felt her heart beat faster. "Would they release dissidents?"

"Ah." Dimka knew, but would not say, that Tanya was thinking of Vasili. Dimka was one of a very few people who knew of Tanya's connection to a dissident. He was too cautious to mention it casually. "The KGB is proposing the opposite—a clampdown. They want to jail everyone who might possibly wave a protest placard at the American president's passing limousine."

"That's stupid," said Tanya. "If we suddenly put hundreds of people in jail, the Americans will find out—they have spies, too—and they won't like it."

Dimka nodded. "Nixon doesn't want his critics saying that he came here and ignored the whole issue of human rights—not in an election year."

"Exactly."

Dimka looked thoughtful. "We must make the most of this opportunity. I have a meeting tomorrow with some people from the U.S. embassy. I wonder if I can use that . . ."

. . .

Dimka had changed. The invasion of Czechoslovakia had done it. Until that moment he had clung stubbornly to the belief that Communism could be reformed. But he had seen, in 1968, that as soon as a few people began to make progress in changing the nature of Communist government, their efforts would be crushed by those who had a stake in keeping things just the same. Men such as Brezhnev and Andropov enjoyed power, status, and privilege: why would they risk all that? Dimka now agreed with his sister: Communism's biggest problem was that the all-embracing authority of the party always stifled change. The Soviet system was helplessly frozen in a terrified conservatism, just as the regime of the tsars had been sixty years earlier, when his grandfather had been a foreman at the Putilov Machine Works in St. Petersburg.

How ironic that was, Dimka reflected, when the first philosopher to explain the phenomenon of social change had been Karl Marx.

Next day Dimka chaired another in a long series of discussions about Nixon's visit to Moscow. Natalya was there, but unfortunately so was Yevgeny Filipov. The American team was led by Ed Markham, a middle-aged career diplomat. Everyone spoke through interpreters.

Nixon and Brezhnev would sign two arms limitation treaties and an environmental protection agreement. "The environment" was not an issue in Soviet politics, but apparently

Nixon felt strongly about it, and had promoted pioneering legislation in the States. Those three documents would be sufficient to guarantee that the visit would be hailed as a historic triumph, and go a long way toward guarding against the dangers of a Chinese-American alliance. Mrs. Nixon would visit schools and hospitals. Nixon was insisting on having a meeting with a dissident poet, Yevgeny Yev- tushenko, whom he had met previously in Washington.

At today's meeting the Soviets and the Americans dis- cussed security and protocol, as always. In the middle of the meeting Natalya said the words she had previously agreed on with Dimka. Speaking in a casual tone to the Americans, she said: "We have been carefully considering your demand that we release a large number of so-called political prisoners, as a token gesture toward what you call human rights."

Ed Markham threw a startled look at Dimka, who was chair of the meeting. Markham knew nothing of this. That was because the Americans had made no such demand. Dimka made a quick, surreptitious brushing-away gesture, indicating that Markham should keep quiet. A skilled and experienced negotiator, the American said nothing.

Filipov was equally surprised. "I have no knowledge of any such—"

Dimka raised his voice. "Please, Yevgeny Davidovitch, do not interrupt Comrade Smotrov! I insist that one person speaks at a time."

Filipov looked furious, but his Communist Party training forced him to follow the rules.

Natalya went on: "We have no political prisoners in the Soviet Union, and we cannot see the logic of releasing crim- inals onto the streets to coincide with the visit of a foreign head of state."

"Quite," said Dimka.

Markham was clearly mystified. Why raise a fictitious demand only to refuse it? But he waited in silence to see where Natalya was going. Meanwhile Filipov drummed his fingers on his writing pad in frustration.

Natalya said: "However, a small number of persons are denied internal travel visas because of connections with an- tisocial groups and troublemakers."

That was precisely the situation of Tanya's friend Vasili. Dimka had tried once before to get him released, but had failed. Perhaps he would have more luck this time.

Dimka watched Markham intently. Would he realize what was going on and play his part? Dimka needed the Americans to pretend they had made demands about releasing dissidents. He could then go back to the Kremlin and say the USA was insisting on this as a precondition of Nixon's visit. At that point any objections from the KGB or any other group would fall away, for everyone in the Kremlin was desperate to get Nixon here to woo him away from the hated Chinese.

Natalya went on: "As these people have not actually been sentenced by the courts, there is no legal bar to action by the government, so we offer to ease the restraints, permitting them to travel, as a gesture of goodwill."

Dimka said to the Americans: "Would that action on our part satisfy your president?"

Markham's face had cleared, and he had now understood the game Natalya and Dimka were playing. He was happy to be used that way, and he said: "Yes, I think that might be sufficient."

"That's agreed, then," said Dimka, and sat back in his chair with a profound sense of accomplishment.

. . .

President Nixon came to Moscow in May, when the snow had thawed and the sun shone.

Tanya had been hoping to see a large-scale release of political prisoners to coincide with the visit, but she had been disappointed. This was the best chance in years to get Vasili out of his hovel in Siberia and back to Moscow. Tanya knew that her brother had tried, but it seemed he had failed. It made her want to weep.

Her boss, Daniil Antonov, said: "Follow the president's wife around today, please, Tanya."

"Fuck off," she said. "Just because I'm a woman doesn't mean I have to do stories about women all the time."

Throughout her career Tanya had fought against being given "feminine" assignments. Sometimes she won, sometimes she lost.

Today she lost.

Daniil was a good guy, but he was not a pushover. "I'm not asking you to cover women all the time, and I never have, so don't talk shit. I'm asking you to cover Pat Nixon today. Now just do as you're told."

Daniil was actually a great boss. Tanya gave in.

Today Pat Nixon was taken to Moscow State University, a thirty-two-story yellow stone building with thousands of rooms. It seemed mostly empty.

Mrs. Nixon said: "Where are all the students?"

The rector of the university, speaking through interpreters, said: "It's exam time, they're all studying."

"I'm not getting to meet the Russian people," Mrs. Nixon complained.

Tanya wanted to say: *You bet you're not meeting the people—they might tell you the truth.*

Mrs. Nixon looked conservative even by Moscow standards. Her hair was piled high and sprayed rigid, like a Viking helmet and almost as hard. She wore clothes that were too young-looking for her and at the same time out of fashion. She had a fixed smile that rarely faltered, even when the press corps following her became unruly.

She was taken into a study room where three students sat at tables. They seemed surprised to see her and clearly did not know who she was. It was evident they did not want to meet her.

Poor Mrs. Nixon probably had no idea that any contact with Westerners was dangerous for ordinary Soviet citizens. They were liable to be arrested afterward and interrogated about what was said and whether the meeting was prearranged. Only the most foolhardy Muscovites wanted to exchange words with foreign visitors.

Tanya composed her article in her head while she followed the visitor around. *Mrs. Nixon was clearly impressed by the new modern Moscow State University. The USA does not have a university building of comparable size.*

The real story was in the Kremlin, which was why Tanya had been bad-tempered with Daniil. Nixon and Brezhnev were signing treaties that would make the world a safer place. That was the story Tanya wanted to cover.

She knew from reading the foreign press that Nixon's

China visit and this Moscow trip had transformed his prospects in the November presidential election. From a January low, his approval rating had soared. He now had a strong chance of getting reelected.

Mrs. Nixon was dressed in a two-piece check suit with a short jacket and discreetly below-the-knee skirt. Her white shoes had a low heel. A chiffon neck scarf completed her outfit. Tanya hated doing fashion. She had covered the Cuban missile crisis, for God's sake—from Cuba!

At last the First Lady was whisked away in a Chrysler LeBaron limousine, and the press pack dispersed.

In the car park Tanya saw a tall man wearing a long, threadbare coat in the spring sunshine. He had unkempt iron gray hair, and his lined face looked as if it might once have been handsome.

It was Vasili.

She stuffed her fist into her mouth and bit her hand to suppress the scream that bubbled up in her throat.

He saw that she had recognized him, and he smiled, showing gaps where he had lost teeth.

She walked slowly over to where he stood, hands in the pockets of his coat. He had no hat, and he squinted because of the sun.

"They let you out," Tanya said.

"To please the American president," he said. "Thank you, Dick Nixon."

He should have thanked Dimka Dvorkin. But it was probably better not to tell anyone that, not even Vasili.

She looked around warily, but there was no one else in sight.

"Don't worry," said Vasili. "For two weeks this place has been crawling with security police, but they all left five minutes ago."

She could restrain herself no longer, and threw herself into his arms. He patted her back as if to comfort her. She hugged him hard.

"My," he said, "you smell good."

She broke the embrace. She was bursting with a hundred questions and had to restrain her enthusiasm and pick one. "Where are you living?"

"They gave me a Stalin apartment—old, but nice."

Apartments from the Stalin era had bigger rooms and

higher ceilings than the more compact flats built in the late fifties and sixties.

She was overflowing with exhilaration. "Shall I visit you there?"

"Not yet. Let's find out how closely they're watching me."

"Do you have work?" It was a favorite trick of the Communists to make sure a man could not get a job, then accuse him of being a social parasite.

"I'm at the Agriculture Ministry. I write pamphlets for peasants explaining new farming techniques. Don't pity me: it's important work, and I'm good at it."

"And your health?"

"I'm fat!" He opened his coat to show her.

She laughed happily. He was not fat, but perhaps he was not as thin as he had been. "You're wearing the sweater I sent you. I'm amazed it reached you." It was the one Anna Murray had bought in Vienna. Tanya would now have to explain all that to him. She did not know where to start.

"I've hardly taken this off for four years. I don't need it, in Moscow in May, but it's hard to get used to the idea that the weather is not always freezing."

"I can get you another sweater."

"You must be making big money!"

"No, I'm not," she said with a wide smile. "But you are."

He frowned, puzzled. "How come?"

"Let's go to a bar," she said, taking his arm. "I've got such a lot to tell you."

. . .

The front page of *The Washington Post* carried an odd story on the morning of Sunday, June 18. To most readers it was a bit baffling. To a handful it was utterly unnerving.

5 Held in Plot to Bug Democrats' Office Here

by Alfred E. Lewis
Washington Post Staff Writer

Five men, one of whom said he is a former employee of the Central Intelligence Agency, were arrested at 2:30 A.M. yesterday in what authorities described as an elab-

orate plot to bug the offices of the Democratic National Committee here.

Three of the men were native-born Cubans and another was said to have trained Cuban exiles for guerrilla activity after the 1961 Bay of Pigs invasion.

They were surprised at gunpoint by three plain-clothes officers of the metropolitan police department in a sixth floor office at the plush Watergate, 2600 Virginia Ave., NW, where the Democratic National Committee occupies the entire floor.

There was no immediate explanation as to why the five suspects would want to bug the Democratic National Committee offices or whether or not they were working for any other individuals or organizations.

Cameron Dewar read the story and said: "Oh, shit."

He pushed away his cornflakes, too tense now to eat. He knew exactly what this was about, and it presented a terrible threat to President Nixon. If people knew or believed that the law-and-order president had ordered a burglary, it could even derail his reelection.

Cam scanned the paragraphs until he came to the names of the accused men. He feared that Tim Tedder would be among them. To Cam's relief, Tedder was not mentioned.

But most of the men named were Tedder's friends and associates.

Tedder and a group of former FBI and CIA agents formed the White House Special Investigations Unit. They had a high-security office on the ground floor of the Executive Office Building, across the street from the White House. Taped to their door was a piece of paper marked: PLUMBERS. It was a joke: their job was to stop leaks.

Cam had not known they planned to bug the Democrats' offices. However, he was not surprised: it was quite a good idea, and might lead to information about sources of leaks.

But the stupid idiots were not supposed to get themselves arrested by the Washington fucking police.

The president was in the Bahamas, due back tomorrow.

Cam called the Plumbers' office. Tim Tedder answered. "What are you doing?" Cam said.

"Weeding files."

In the background, Cam heard the whine of a shredder. "Good," he said.

Then he got dressed and went to the White House.

At first it seemed that none of the burglars had any direct connection with the president, and throughout Sunday Cam thought the scandal might be managed. Then it turned out that one of them had given a false name. "Edward Martin" was in fact James McCord, a retired CIA agent employed full-time by CREEP, the Committee to Reelect the President.

"That does it," Cam said. He felt crushed and devastated. This was terrible.

Monday's *Washington Post* carried the information about McCord in a story bylined Bob Woodward and Carl Bernstein.

Still Cam hoped the president's involvement might be covered up.

Then the FBI stepped in. The Bureau began to investigate the five burglars. In the old days, Cam thought regretfully, J. Edgar Hoover would have done no such thing; but Hoover was dead. Nixon had installed a crony, Patrick Gray, as acting director, but Gray did not know the Bureau and was struggling to control it. The upshot was that the FBI was beginning to act like a law enforcement agency.

The burglars had been found in possession of large amounts of cash, new bills with sequential numbers. This meant that sooner or later the FBI would be able to trace the money and find out who had given it to them.

Cam already knew. This money, like the payments for all the administration's undercover projects, came from the CREEP slush fund.

The FBI inquiry had to be shut down.

. . .

When Cam Dewar walked into Maria Summers's office at the Department of Justice, she suffered a moment of fear. Had she been found out? Had the White House somehow discovered that she was Jasper Murray's source of inside information? She was standing at her file cabinet, and for a moment her legs felt so weak she feared she might fall.

But Cam was friendly, and she calmed down. He smiled,

took a seat, and gave her the adolescent up-and-down look that indicated he found her attractive.

Keep on dreaming, white boy, she thought.

What was he up to now? She sat at her desk, took off her glasses, and gave him a warm smile. "Hi, Mr. Dewar," she said. "How did that wiretap work out?"

"In the end it didn't give us much information," Cam said. "We think Murray may have a secure phone somewhere else that he uses for confidential calls."

Thank God, she thought. "That's too bad," she said.

"We appreciate your help, all the same."

"You're very kind. Is there something else I can do for you?"

"Yes. The president wants the attorney general to order the FBI to stop investigating the Watergate burglary."

Maria tried to conceal her shock as her mind reeled with the implications. So it *was* a White House caper. She was amazed. No president other than Nixon would have been so arrogant and stupid.

Once again, she would find out the most if she pretended to be supportive. "Okay," she said, "let's think about this. Kleindienst isn't Mitchell, you know." John Mitchell had resigned as attorney general in order to run CREEP. His replacement, Richard Kleindienst, was another Nixon crony, but not as biddable. "Kleindienst will want a reason," Maria said.

"We can give him one. The FBI investigation may lead to confidential matters of foreign policy. In particular, it may reveal damaging information about CIA involvement in President Kennedy's Bay of Pigs invasion."

That was typical of Tricky Dick, Maria thought with disgust. Everyone would pretend they were protecting American interests when in reality they were saving the president's sorry ass. "So it's a matter of national security."

"Yes."

"Good. That will justify the attorney general in ordering the FBI to back off." But Maria did not want it to be so easy for the White House. "However, Kleindienst may want concrete assurance."

"We can provide that. The CIA is prepared to make a formal request. Walters will do it." General Vernon Walters was deputy director of the CIA.

"If the request is formal, I think we can go ahead and do exactly what the president wants."

"Thank you, Maria." The boy stood up. "You've been very helpful, again."

"You're welcome, Mr. Dewar."

Cam left the room.

Maria stared thoughtfully at the chair he had vacated. The president must have authorized this burglary, or at least turned a blind eye to it. That was the only possible reason for Cam Dewar to be working so hard on a cover-up. If someone in the administration had okayed the burglary in defiance of Nixon's wishes, that person would by now have been named and shamed and fired. Nixon was not squeamish about getting rid of embarrassing colleagues. The only person he cared to protect was himself.

Was she going to let him get away with it?

Like hell she was.

She picked up the phone and said: "Call Fawcett Renshaw, please."

CHAPTER FORTY-NINE

Dave Williams was nervous. It was almost five years since Plum Nellie had played to a live audience. Now they were about to face sixty thousand fans at Candlestick Park in San Francisco.

Performing in a studio was not the same at all. The tape recorder was forgiving: if you played a bum note or your voice cracked or you forgot the lyrics, you could just erase the error and try again.

Anything that went wrong here tonight would be heard by everyone in the stadium and never corrected.

Dave told himself not to be silly. He had done this a hundred times. He recalled playing with the Guardsmen in pubs in the East End of London, when he had known only a handful of chords. Looking back, he marveled at his youthful audacity. He remembered the night Geoffrey had passed out, dead drunk, at the Dive in Hamburg, and Walli had come onstage and played lead guitar throughout the set with no rehearsal. Happy-go-lucky days.

Dave now had nine years' experience. That was longer than the entire career of many pop stars. All the same, as the fans streamed in, buying beer and T-shirts and hot dogs, all trusting Dave to ensure they would have a great evening, he felt shaky.

A young woman from the music company that distributed Nellie Records came into his dressing room to ask if there was anything he needed. She wore loon pants and a crop top, showing off a perfect figure. "No, thanks, darling," he said. All the dressing rooms had a small bar with beer and liquor, soft drinks and ice, and a carton of cigarettes.

"If you want a little something to relax you, I have supplies," she said.

He shook his head. He did not want drugs right now. He might smoke a joint afterward.

She persisted. "Or if I can, you know, do anything . . ."

She was offering him sex. She was as gorgeous as a slim California blonde could be, which was very beautiful indeed, but he was not in the mood.

He had not been in the mood since the last time he saw Beep.

"Maybe after the show," he said. If I get drunk enough, he thought. "I appreciate the offer, but right now I want you to get lost," he said firmly.

She was not offended. "Let me know if you change your mind!" she said cheerfully, and she went out.

Tonight's gig was a benefit for George McGovern. His election campaign had succeeded in bringing young people back into politics. In Europe he would have been middle-of-the-road, Dave knew, but here he was considered left-wing. His tough criticism of the Vietnam War delighted liberals, and he spoke with authority because of his combat experience in World War II.

Dave's sister, Evie, came to his dressing room to wish him luck. She was dressed to avoid recognition, with her hair pinned up under a tweed cap, sunglasses, and a biker jacket. "I'm going back to England," she said.

That surprised him. "I know you've had some bad press since that Hanoi photo, but . . ."

She shook her head. "It's worse than bad press. I'm hated today as passionately as I was loved a year ago. It's the phenomenon Oscar Wilde noticed: one turns to the other with bewildering suddenness."

"I thought you might ride it out."

"So did I, for a while. But I haven't been offered a decent part in six months. I could play the plucky girl in a spaghetti Western, a stripper in an off-Broadway improvisation, or any part I like in the Australian tour of *Jesus Christ Superstar*."

"I'm sorry—I had no idea."

"It wasn't exactly spontaneous."

"What do you mean?"

"A couple of journalists told me they got calls from the White House."

"This was organized?"

"I think so. Look, I was a popular celebrity who attacked Nixon at every opportunity. It's not surprising that he stuck the knife in me when I was foolish enough to give him a chance. It isn't even unfair: I'm doing my best to put *him* out of a job."

"That's pretty big of you."

"And it might not even be Nixon. Who do we know who works at the White House?"

"Beep's brother?" Dave was incredulous. "Cam did this to you?"

"He fell for me, all those years ago in London, and I turned him down kind of roughly."

"And he's held a grudge all these years?"

"I could never prove it."

"The bastard!"

"So, I've put my swanky Hollywood home on the market, sold my convertible, and packed up my collection of modern art."

"What will you do?"

"Lady Macbeth, for a start."

"You'll be terrifying. Where?"

"Stratford-upon-Avon. I'm joining the Royal Shakespeare Company."

"One door closes and another opens."

"I'm so happy to be doing Shakespeare again. It's ten years since I played Ophelia at school."

"In the nude."

Evie smiled ruefully. "What a little show-off I was."

"You were also a good actor, even then."

She stood up. "I'll leave you to get ready. Enjoy yourself tonight, little brother. I'll be in the audience, bopping."

"When are you leaving for England?"

"I'm on a plane tomorrow."

"Let me know when *Macbeth* opens. I'll come and see you."

"That would be nice."

Dave walked out with Evie. The stage had been built on

a temporary scaffold at one end of the field. Behind the stage, a crowd of roadies, sound men, record company people, and privileged journalists milled on the grass. The dressing rooms were tents pitched in a roped-off area.

Buzz and Lew had arrived, but there was no sign of Walli. Dave was relying on Beep to get Walli here on time. He wondered anxiously where they were.

Soon after Evie left, Beep's parents came backstage. Dave was again on good terms with Bella and Woody. He decided not to tell them what Evie had said about Cam stirring up the press against her. Lifelong Democrats, they were already annoyed that their son was working for Nixon.

Dave wanted to know what Woody thought of McGovern's chances. "George McGovern has a problem," Woody said. "In order to defeat Hubert Humphrey and get the nomination, he had to break the power of the old Democratic Party barons, the city mayors and the state governors and the union bosses."

Dave had not followed this closely. "How did he manage that?"

"After the mess of Chicago 1968 the party rewrote the rules, and McGovern chaired the commission that did that."

"Why's that a problem?"

"Because the old power brokers won't work for him. Some detest him so much that they started a movement called Democrats for Nixon."

"Young people like him."

"We have to hope that will be enough."

At last Beep arrived with Walli. The Dewar parents went off to Walli's dressing room. Dave put on his stage outfit, a red one-piece jumpsuit and engineer boots. He did some exercises to warm up his voice. While he was singing scales, Beep came in.

She gave him a sunny smile and kissed his cheek. As always, she lit up the room just by walking in. I should never have let her go, Dave thought. What kind of an idiot am I?

"How is Walli?" he said worriedly.

"He's had a hit of dope, just enough to get him through the gig. He'll shoot up when he comes offstage. He's all right to play."

"Thank God."

She was wearing satin hot pants and a sequined bra top.

She had put on a little weight since the recording sessions, Dave saw: her bust seemed bigger and she even had a cute tummy bulge. He offered her a drink. She asked for a Coke. "Help yourself to a cigarette," he said.

"I quit."

"That's why you've put on weight."

"No, it's not."

"That wasn't a put-down. You look fabulous."

"I'm leaving Walli."

That shocked him. He turned from the bar and stared at her. "Wow," he said. "Does he know yet?"

"I'm going to tell him after tonight's show."

"That's a relief. But what about all that stuff you told me about being a less selfish person and saving Walli's life?"

"I have a more important life to save."

"Your own?"

"My baby's."

"Christ." Dave sat down. "You're pregnant."

"Three months."

"That's why your shape has changed."

"And smoking makes me puke. I don't even use pot anymore."

The dressing room PA crackled, and a voice said: "Five minutes to showtime, everybody. All stage technicians should now be in performance positions."

Dave said: "If you're pregnant, why are you leaving Walli?"

"I'm not bringing up a child in that environment. It's one thing to sacrifice myself, something else to do it to a kid. This child is going to have a normal life."

"Where will you go?"

"I'm moving back in with my mom and dad." She shook her head in a gesture of wonder. "It's incredible. For ten years I've done everything I could to piss them off, but when I needed their help they just said yes. Fucking amazing."

The PA said: "One minute, everybody. The band is kindly invited to move to the wings whenever they're ready."

Dave was struck by a thought. "Three months . . ."

"I don't know whose baby it is," Beep said. "I conceived while you were making the album. I was on the pill, but sometimes I used to forget to take it, especially if I was stoned."

"But you told me that Walli and you seldom had sex."

"Seldom isn't never. I'd say there's a ten percent chance it's Walli's baby."

"So ninety percent mine."

Lew looked into Dave's tent. "Here we go," he said.

"I'm coming," Dave said.

Lew went, and Dave said to Beep: "Live with me."

She stared at him. "Do you mean it?"

"Yes."

"Even if it's not your baby?"

"I'm sure I'll love your baby. I love you. Hell, I love Walli. Live with me, please."

"Oh, God," she said, and she started to cry. "I was hoping and praying you'd say this."

"Does that mean you will?"

"Of course. It's what I'm longing for."

Dave felt as if the sun had risen. "Well, then, that's what we'll do," he said.

"What are we going to do about Walli? I don't want him to die."

"I have an idea about that," Dave said. "I'll tell you after the show."

"Go onstage, they're waiting for you."

"I know." He kissed her mouth softly. She put her arms around him and hugged him. "I love you," he said.

"I love you, too, and I was crazy to ever let you go."

"Don't do it again."

"Never."

Dave went out. He ran across the grass and up the steps to where the rest of the band was waiting in the wings. Then he was struck by a thought. "I forgot something," he said.

Buzz said irritably: "What? The guitars are onstage."

Dave did not answer. He ran back to his dressing room. Beep was still there, sitting down, wiping her eyes.

Dave said: "Shall we get married?"

"Okay," she said.

"Good."

He ran back to the scaffold.

"Everyone okay?" he said.

Everyone was okay.

Dave led the band onto the stage.

. . .

Claus Krohn asked Rebecca to have a drink after a meeting of the Hamburg parliament.

She was taken aback. It was four years since she had ended their love affair. For the past twelve months, she knew, Claus had been seeing an attractive woman who was the membership officer of a trade union. Claus meanwhile was an increasingly powerful figure in the Free Democratic Party, to which Rebecca also belonged. Claus and his girl-friend were a good match. In fact, Rebecca had heard they were planning to get married.

So she gave him a discouraging look.

"Not at the Yacht Bar," Claus added hastily. "Somewhere less furtive."

She laughed, reassured.

They went to a bar in the town center not far from the city hall. For old times' sake, Rebecca asked for a glass of Sekt. "I'll come right to the point," Claus said as soon as they had their drinks. "We want you to stand for election to the national parliament."

"Oh!" she said. "I would have been less surprised if you'd made a pass at me."

He smiled. "Don't be surprised. You're intelligent and attractive, you speak well, and people like you. You're re-spected by men of all parties here in Hamburg. You have almost a decade of experience in politics. You'd be an asset."

"But it's so sudden."

"Elections always seem sudden."

The chancellor, Willy Brandt, had engineered a snap elec-tion, to be held in eight weeks' time. If Rebecca agreed, she could be a member of parliament before Christmas.

When she got over the surprise, Rebecca felt eager. Her passionate desire was for the reunification of Germany, so that she and thousands more Germans could be reunited with their families. She would never achieve that in local politics—but as a member of the national parliament she might have some influence.

Her party, the FDP, was in a coalition government with the Social Democrats led by Willy Brandt. Rebecca agreed with Brandt's "Ostpolitik," trying to have contact with the

East despite the Wall. She believed this was the quickest way to undermine the East German regime.

"I'll have to talk to my husband," she said.

"I knew you'd say that. Women always do."

"It will mean leaving him alone a lot."

"This happens to all spouses of members of parliament."

"But my husband is special."

"Indeed."

"I'll talk to him this evening." Rebecca stood up.

Claus stood too. "On a personal note . . ."

"What?"

"We know each other quite well."

"Yes . . ."

"This is your destiny." He was serious. "You were meant to be a national politician. Anything less would be a waste of your talents. A criminal waste. I mean it."

She was surprised by his intensity. "Thank you," she said.

She felt both elated and dazed as she drove home. A new future had suddenly opened up. She had thought about national politics, but had feared it would be too difficult, as a woman and as the wife of a disabled husband. But now that the prospect was more than a fantasy she felt eager.

On the other hand, what would Bernd do?

She parked the car and hurried into their apartment. Bernd was at the kitchen table in his wheelchair, marking school essays with a sharp red pencil. He was undressed and wearing a bathrobe, which he could manage to put on himself. The most difficult garment, for him, was a pair of trousers.

She told him immediately about Claus's proposition. "Before you speak, let me say one more thing," she said. "If you don't want me to do this, I won't. No argument, no regrets, no recriminations. We're a partnership, and that means neither of us has the right to change our life unilaterally."

"Thank you," he said. "But let's talk about the details."

"The Bundestag sits from Monday to Friday about twenty weeks of the year, and attendance is compulsory."

"So you'd spend about eighty nights away in an average year. I can cope with that, especially if we get a nurse to come in and help me in the mornings."

"Would you mind?"

"Of course. But no doubt your nights at home would be all the sweeter."

"Bernd, you're so good."

"You have to do this," he said. "It's your destiny."

She gave a little laugh. "That's what Claus said."

"I'm not surprised."

Her husband and her ex-lover both thought that this was what she should do. She thought so too. She felt apprehensive: she believed she could do it, but it would be a challenge. National politics was tougher and nastier than local government. The press could be vicious.

Her mother would be proud, she thought. Carla ought to have been a leader, and probably would have been if she had not got trapped in the prison of East Germany. She would be thrilled that her daughter was fulfilling her defeated aspiration.

They talked it over for the next three evenings, then, on the fourth, Dave Williams arrived.

They were not expecting him. Rebecca was astonished to see him on the doorstep, wearing a brown suede coat and carrying a small suitcase with a Hamburg airport tag. "You could have called!" she said in English.

"I lost your number," he replied in German.

She kissed his cheek. "What a wonderful surprise!" She had liked Dave back in the days when Plum Nellie was playing on the Reeperbahn, and the boys had come to this apartment for their only square meal of the week. Dave had been good for Walli, whose talent had flowered in the partnership.

Dave came into the kitchen, set down his suitcase, and shook hands with Bernd. "Have you just flown in from London?" Bernd asked.

"From San Francisco. I've been traveling twenty-four hours." They spoke their usual mixture of English and German.

Rebecca put coffee on. As she got over her surprise, it occurred to her that Dave must have some special reason for this visit, and she felt anxious. Dave was explaining to Bernd about his recording studio, but Rebecca interrupted him. "Why are you here, Dave? Is something wrong?"

"Yes," said Dave. "It's Walli."

Rebecca's heart missed a beat. "What's the matter? Tell me! He's not dead . . ."

"No, he's alive. But he's a heroin addict."

"Oh, no." Rebecca sat down heavily. "Oh, no." She buried her face in her hands.

"There's more," said Dave. "Beep is leaving him. She's pregnant, and she doesn't want to raise a child in the drug scene."

"Oh, my poor little brother."

Bernd said: "What is Beep going to do?"

"She's moving into Daisy Farm with me."

"Oh." Rebecca saw that Dave looked embarrassed. He had resumed his romance with Beep, she guessed. That could only make things worse for her brother. "What can we do about Walli?"

"He needs to give up heroin, obviously."

"Do you think he can?"

"With the right kind of help. There are programs, in the States and here in Europe, that combine therapy with a chemical substitute, usually methadone. But Walli lives in Haight-Ashbury. There's a dealer on every corner, and if he doesn't go out and score, one of them will knock on his door. It's just too easy for him to lapse."

"So he has to move?"

"I think he has to move here."

"Oh, my goodness."

"Living with you, I think he could kick the habit."

Rebecca looked at Bernd.

"I'm concerned about you," Bernd said to her. "You have a job and a political career. I'm fond of Walli, not least because you love him. But I don't want you to sacrifice your life to him."

"It's not forever," Dave put in quickly. "But if you could keep him clean and sober for a year . . ."

Rebecca was still looking at Bernd. "I won't sacrifice my life. But I might have to put it on hold for a year."

"If you turn down a Bundestag seat now, the offer might never be renewed."

"I know."

Dave said to Rebecca: "I want you to come with me back to San Francisco and persuade Walli."

"When?"

"Tomorrow would be good. I've already made flight reservations."

"Tomorrow!"

But there was really no choice, Rebecca thought. Walli's life was at stake. Nothing compared with that. She would put him first; of course she would. She hardly needed to think about it.

All the same, she felt sad about turning down the thrilling prospect that had been so briefly held out to her.

Dave said: "What did you say, a moment ago, about the Bundestag?"

"Nothing," Rebecca said. "Just something else I was thinking of doing. But I'll come with you to San Francisco. Of course I will."

"Tomorrow?"

"Yes."

"Thank you."

Rebecca stood up. "I'll pack a bag," she said.

CHAPTER FIFTY

Jasper Murray was depressed. President Nixon—liar, cheat, and crook—was reelected by a huge majority. He won forty-nine states. George McGovern, one of the most unsuccessful candidates in American history, got only Massachusetts and the District of Columbia.

Worse, as new revelations about Watergate scandalized the liberal intelligentsia, Nixon's popularity remained strong. Five months after the election, in April 1973, the president's approval rating stood at 60–33.

"What do we have to do?" Jasper said frustratedly to anyone who would listen. The media, led by *The Washington Post,* revealed one presidential crime after another as Nixon scrambled desperately to cover up his involvement in a break-in. One of the Watergate burglars had written a letter, which the judge read out in court, complaining that the defendants had been subjected to political pressure to plead guilty and remain silent. If this was true, it meant the president was trying to pervert the course of justice. But voters seemed not to care.

Jasper was in the White House briefing room on Tuesday, April 17, when the tide turned.

The room had a slightly raised stage at one end. A lectern stood in front of a backdrop curtain that was colored a television-friendly shade of blue-gray. There were never enough chairs, and some reporters sat on the tan carpet while cameramen jostled for space.

The White House had announced that the president would

make a brief statement but take no questions. The reporters had assembled at three o'clock. It was now half past four and nothing had happened.

Nixon appeared at four forty-two. Jasper noticed that his hands seemed to be shaking. Nixon announced the resolution of a dispute between the White House and Sam Ervin, chair of the Senate committee that was investigating Watergate. White House staff would now be allowed to testify to the Ervin Committee, although they might refuse to answer any question. It was not much of a concession, Jasper thought. But surely an innocent president would not even be having this argument.

Then Nixon said: "No individual holding, in the past or present, a position of major importance in the administration should be given immunity from prosecution."

Jasper frowned. What did this mean? Someone must have been demanding immunity, someone close to Nixon. Now Nixon was publicly refusing it. He was hanging someone out to dry. But who?

"I condemn any attempts to cover up, no matter who is involved," said the president, who had tried to shut down the FBI investigation; and then he left the room.

Press secretary Ron Ziegler mounted the podium to a storm of questions. Jasper did not ask any. He was intrigued by the statement about immunity.

Ziegler now said that the announcement just made by the president was the "operative" statement. Jasper immediately recognized that as a weasel word, deliberately vague, intended to obscure the truth rather than to clarify it. The other journalists in the room saw it too.

It was Johnny Apple of *The New York Times* who asked whether that implied all previous statements were inoperative.

"Yes," said Ziegler.

The press corps were furious. This meant they had been lied to. For years they had been faithfully reporting Nixon's statements, giving them the credence due to the leader of the nation. They had been taken for fools.

They would never trust him again.

Jasper went back to the office of *This Day,* still wondering who had been the real target of Nixon's statement about immunity.

He got the answer two days later. He picked up the phone to hear a woman say, in a trembling voice, that she was secretary to White House counsel John Dean, and she was calling senior reporters in Washington to read a statement from him.

This in itself was bizarre. If the president's legal adviser wanted to say something to the press, he should have done so through Ron Ziegler. Clearly there was a rift.

"'Some may hope or think that I will become a scapegoat in the Watergate case,'" the secretary read. "'Anyone who believes that does not know me . . .'"

Ah, thought Jasper, the first rat abandons the sinking ship.

. . .

Maria was amazed by Nixon. He had no dignity. As more and more people realized what a fraud he was, he did not resign, but stayed in the White House, blustering and obfuscating and threatening and lying, lying, lying.

At the end of April, John Ehrlichman and Bob Haldeman resigned together. Both had been close to Nixon. Because of their German names they had been dubbed "the Berlin Wall" by those who felt shut out by them. They had organized criminal activities such as burglary and perjury for the president: could anyone possibly believe that they had done those things against his will and without telling him? The idea was laughable.

Next day, the Senate voted unanimously for a special prosecutor to be appointed, independent of the tainted Justice Department, to investigate whether the president should be charged with crimes.

Ten days later, Nixon's approval rating fell to 44–45 — the first time he had ever scored negative.

The special prosecutor went to work fast. He began to hire a team of lawyers. Maria knew one of them, a former Justice Department official called Antonia Capel. Antonia lived in Georgetown, not far from Maria's apartment, and one evening Maria rang her doorbell.

Antonia opened the door and looked surprised.

"Don't say my name," said Maria.

Antonia was puzzled, but she was quick-witted. "Okay," she said.

"Could we talk?"

"Of course—come in."

"Would you meet me at the coffee shop along the block?"

Antonia looked bewildered but said: "Sure. I'll ask my husband to bathe the kids . . . um, give me fifteen minutes?"

"You bet."

When Antonia arrived at the coffee shop she said: "Is my apartment bugged?"

"I don't know, but it might be, now that you're working for the special prosecutor."

"Wow."

"Here's the thing," said Maria. "I don't work for Dick Nixon. My loyalty is to the Justice Department and to the American people."

"Okay . . ."

"I don't have anything particular to tell you right now, but I want you to know that if there is any way I can help the special prosecutor, I will."

Antonia was smart enough to know that she was being offered a spy inside Justice. "That could be really important," she said. "But how will we stay in contact without giving the game away?"

"Call me from a pay phone. Don't give your name. Say anything about a cup of coffee. I'll meet you here the same day. Is this a good time?"

"Perfect."

"How are things going?"

"We're just getting started. We're looking for the right lawyers to join the team."

"On that subject, I have a suggestion: George Jakes."

"I think I've met him. Remind me who he is."

"He worked for Bobby Kennedy for seven years, first at Justice when Bobby was attorney general, then in the Senate. After Bobby was killed, George went to work at Fawcett Renshaw."

"He sounds ideal. I'll give him a call."

Maria stood up. "Let's leave separately. Reduces the chance of our being seen together."

"Isn't it terrible that we have to act so furtively when we're doing the right thing?"

"I know."

"Thank you for coming to see me, Maria. I really appreciate it."

"Good-bye," said Maria. "Don't tell your boss my name."

. . .

Cameron Dewar had a television set in his office. When the Ervin Committee hearings were being broadcast from the Senate, Cam's TV was on continuously—as was just about every other set in downtown Washington.

On the afternoon of Monday, July 16, Cam was working on a report for his new boss, Al Haig, who had replaced Bob Haldeman as White House chief of staff. Cam was not paying close attention to the televised testimony of Alexander Butterfield, a midlevel White House figure who had organized the president's daily schedule during Nixon's first term, then left to run the Federal Aviation Administration.

A committee lawyer called Fred Thompson was questioning Butterfield. "Were you aware of the installation of any listening devices in the Oval Office of the president?"

Cam looked up. That was unexpected. Listening devices—commonly called bugs—in the Oval Office? Surely not.

Butterfield was silent for a long time. The committee room went quiet. Cam whispered: "Jesus."

At last Butterfield said: "I was aware of listening devices, yes, sir."

Cam stood up. "Fuck, no!" he shouted.

On TV, Thompson said: "When were those devices placed in the Oval Office?"

Butterfield hesitated, sighed, swallowed, and said: "Approximately the summer of 1970."

"Christ almighty!" Cam yelled to his empty room. "How could this happen? How could the president be so stupid?"

Thompson said: "Tell us a little bit about how those devices worked—how they were activated, for example."

Cam yelled: "Shut up! Shut the fuck up!"

Butterfield went into a long explanation of the system, and eventually revealed that it was voice-activated.

Cam sat down again. This was a catastrophe. Nixon had secretly recorded everything that went on in the Oval Office. He had talked about burglaries and bribes and blackmail, all the time knowing that his incriminating words were being taped. "Stupid, stupid, stupid!" Cam said out loud.

Cam could guess what would happen next. Both the Ervin Committee and the special prosecutor would demand to hear the tapes. Almost certainly, they would succeed in forcing the president to hand them over: they were key evidence in several criminal investigations. Then the whole world would know the truth.

Nixon might succeed in keeping the tapes to himself, or perhaps destroying them; but that was almost as bad. For if he were innocent, the tapes would vindicate him, so why should he hide them? Destroying them would be seen as an admission of guilt—as well as one more in a lengthening list of crimes for which he could be prosecuted.

Nixon's presidency was over.

He would probably cling on. Cam knew him well by now. Nixon did not know when he was beaten—he never had. Once upon a time this had been a strength. Now it might lead him to suffer weeks, perhaps months of diminishing credibility and growing humiliation before he finally gave in.

Cam was not going to be part of that.

He picked up the phone and called Tim Tedder. They met an hour later at the Electric Diner, an old-fashioned luncheonette. "You're not worried about being seen with me?" said Tedder.

"It doesn't matter anymore. I'm leaving the White House."

"Why?"

"Haven't you been watching TV?"

"Not today."

"There's a voice-activated recording system in the Oval Office. It's taped everything that has been said in that room for the past three years. This is the end. Nixon is finished."

"Wait a minute. All the time he was arranging this stuff, he was bugging *himself*?"

"Yes."

"Incriminating himself."

"Yes."

"What kind of idiot does that?"

"I thought he was smart. I guess he had us all fooled. He sure had me fooled."

"What are you going to do?"

"That's why I called you. I'm making a new start in life.
I want a new job."

"You want to work for my security firm? I'm the only
employee—"

"No, no. Listen. I'm twenty-seven. I have five years' experience in the White House. I speak Russian."

"So you want to work for ... ?"

"The CIA. I'm well qualified."

"You are. You'd have to go through their basic training."

"No problem. Part of my new start."

"I'm happy to call my friends there, put in a good word."

"I appreciate that. And there's one other thing."

"What?"

"I don't want to make a big deal of this, but I do know
where the bodies are buried. The CIA has broken some
rules in this whole Watergate affair. I know all about the
CIA's involvement."

"I know."

"That last thing I want to do is blackmail anyone. You
know where my loyalties lie. But you might hint to your
friends in the Agency that, naturally, I wouldn't spill the
beans on my employer."

"I get it."

"So, what do you think?"

"I think you're a shoo-in."

.   .   .

George was happy and proud to be on the special prosecutor's team. He felt he was part of the group leading American politics, as he had been when working for Bobby
Kennedy. His only problem was that he did not know how
he could ever go back to the kind of penny-ante cases he
had been working at Fawcett Renshaw.

It took five months, but in the end Nixon was forced to
hand over to the special prosecutor three raw tapes from
the Oval Office recording system.

George Jakes was in the office with the rest of the team
when they listened to the tape from June 23, 1972, less than
a week after the Watergate burglary.

He heard the voice of Bob Haldeman. "The FBI is not
under control because Gray doesn't exactly know how to
control it."

The recording was echoey but Haldeman's cultured baritone was fairly clear.

Someone said: "Why would the president need to have the FBI under control?" It was a rhetorical question, George thought. The only reason was to stop the Bureau investigating the president's own crimes.

On the tape, Haldeman went on: "Their investigation is now leading into some productive areas because they have been able to trace the money."

George recalled that the Watergate burglars had had a lot of cash in new bills with sequential numbers. That meant that sooner or later the FBI would be able to find out who had given them the money.

Everyone now knew that this money came from CREEP. However, Nixon was still denying that he had known anything about it. Yet here he was talking about it six days after the burglary!

The gravelly bass voice of Nixon interrupted. "The people who donated money could just say they gave it to the Cubans."

George heard someone in the room say: "Holy crap!"

The special prosecutor stopped the tape.

George said: "Unless I'm mistaken, the president is proposing to ask his donors to perjure themselves."

The special prosecutor said dazedly: "Can you imagine that?"

He pressed the button and Haldeman resumed. "We don't want to be relying on too many people. The way to handle this now is for us to have Walters call Pat Gray and just say: 'Stay the hell out of this.'"

This was close to a story Jasper Murray had run based on a leak from Maria. General Vernon Walters was the deputy director of the CIA. The Agency had a long-standing agreement with the FBI: if an investigation by one threatened to expose secret operations of the other, that investigation could be halted by a simple request. Haldeman's idea seemed to be to get the CIA to pretend that the FBI's investigation into the Watergate burglars was somehow a threat to national security.

Which would be perversion of the course of justice.

On the tape, President Nixon said: "Right, fine."

The prosecutor stopped the tape again.

"Did you hear that?" George said incredulously. "Nixon said: 'Right, fine.'"

Nixon went on: "It's likely to blow the whole Bay of Pigs thing, which we think would be very unfortunate for the CIA and for the country and for American foreign policy." He seemed to be spinning a story that the CIA might tell the FBI, George thought.

"Yeah," said Haldeman. "That's the basis we'll do it on."

The prosecutor said: "The president of the United States sitting in his office telling his staff how to commit perjury!"

Everyone in the room was stunned. The president was a criminal, and they had the proof in their hands.

George said: "The lying bastard, we've got him."

On the tape, Nixon said: "I don't want them to get any ideas we're doing it because our concern is political."

Haldeman said: "Right."

In the room, gathered around the tape player, the assembled lawyers burst out laughing.

. . .

Maria was at her desk in the Justice Department when George called. "I just heard from our friend," he said. She knew he meant Jasper. He was speaking in code in case the phones were tapped. "The White House press office called the networks and booked air time for the president. Nine o'clock tonight."

It was Thursday, August 8, 1974.

Maria's heart leaped. Could this be the end at last? "Maybe he's going to resign," she said.

"Maybe."

"God, I hope so."

"It's either that or he'll just profess his innocence again."

Maria did not want to be alone when this happened. "Do you want to come over?" she said. "We'll watch it together."

"Yeah, okay."

"I'll make supper."

"Nothing too fattening."

"George Jakes, you're vain."

"Make a salad."

"Come at seven thirty."

"I'll bring the wine."

Maria went out to shop for dinner in the heat of Washington in August. She no longer cared much about her work. She had lost faith in the Justice Department. If Nixon resigned today, she would start looking for another job. She still wanted to be in government service: only the government had the muscle to make the world a better place. But she was sick of crime and the excuses of criminals. She wanted a change. She thought she might try for the State Department.

She bought salad, but she also got some pasta and Parmesan cheese and olives. George had refined tastes, and he was getting worse as he grew into middle age. But he certainly was not fat. Maria herself was not fat but, on the other hand, she was not thin. As she approached forty she was just getting, well, more like her mother, especially around the hips.

She left for the day a few minutes before five. A crowd had gathered outside the White House. They were chanting, "Jail to the Chief," a pun on the anthem "Hail to the Chief."

Maria caught the bus to Georgetown.

As her salary had improved over the years she had moved apartments, always to a larger place in the same neighborhood. She had got rid of all but one of the photos of President Kennedy during her last move. Her current place had a comfortable feel. Where George had always had rectilinear modern furniture and plain decor, Maria liked patterned fabrics and curved lines and lots of cushions.

Her gray cat Loopy came to greet her, as always, and rubbed her head against Maria's leg. Julius, the boy cat, was more aloof: he would show up later.

She set the table and washed the salad and grated the Parmesan cheese. Then she took a shower and put on a cotton summer dress in her favorite shade, turquoise. She thought about putting on lipstick and decided not to.

The evening news on TV was mostly speculation. Nixon had had a meeting with Vice President Gerald Ford, who might be president tomorrow. Press secretary Ziegler had announced to the White House reporters that the president would address the nation at nine, then had left the press briefing room without answering questions on what he would speak about.

George arrived at seven thirty, wearing slacks and loafers and a blue chambray shirt open at the neck. Maria tossed the salad and put the pasta in boiling water while he opened a bottle of Chianti.

Her bedroom door was open, and George looked inside. "No shrine," he said.

"I threw away most of the photographs."

They sat at her small dining table to eat.

They had been friends for thirteen years, and each had seen the other in the depths of despair. Each had had one overwhelming lover who had gone: Verena Marquand to the Black Panthers, President Kennedy into the hereafter. In different ways, both George and Maria had been left. They shared so much that they were comfortable together.

Maria said: "The heart is a map of the world, did you know that?"

"I don't even know what it means," he said.

"I saw a medieval map once. It showed the earth as a flat disc with Jerusalem in the center. Rome was bigger than Africa, and America was not even shown, of course. The heart is that kind of map. The self is in the middle and everything else is out of proportion. You draw the friends of your youth large, then later it's impossible to rescale them when other more important people need to be added. Anyone who has done you wrong is shown too big, and so is anyone you loved."

"Okay, I get it, but . . ."

"I've thrown out my photos of Jack Kennedy. But he will always be drawn too large on the map in my heart. That's all I mean."

After dinner they washed up, then sat on a large, soft couch in front of the TV with the last of the wine. The cats went to sleep on the rug.

Nixon came on at nine.

Please, Maria thought, let the torment end now.

Nixon was sitting in the Oval Office, a blue curtain behind him, the Stars and Stripes on his right and the president's flag on his left. The deep, gravelly voice began immediately. "This is the thirty-seventh time I have spoken to you from this office, where so many decisions have been made that shaped the history of this nation."

The camera began a slow zoom in. The president was wearing a familiar blue suit and tie. "Throughout the long and difficult period of Watergate, I have felt it was my duty to persevere, to make every possible effort to complete the term of office to which you elected me. In the past few days, however, it has become evident to me that I no longer have a strong enough political base in the Congress to justify continuing that effort."

George said excitedly: "That's it! He's resigning!"

Maria grabbed his arm in excitement.

The cameras pulled in for a close-up. "I have never been a quitter," Nixon said.

"Oh, shit," said George, "is he going back on it?"

"But, as president, I must put the interests of America first."

"No," said Maria, "he's not going back."

"Therefore I shall resign the presidency effective at noon tomorrow. Vice President Ford will be sworn in as president at that hour in this office."

"Yes!" George punched the air. "He's done it! He's gone!"

What Maria felt was not so much triumph as relief. She had woken up from a nightmare. In the dream, the highest officers in the land had been crooks, and no one could do anything to stop them.

But in real life they had been found out and shamed and deposed. She had a sense of safety, and realized that for two years now she had not felt that America was a secure place to be.

Nixon admitted no faults. He did not say that he had committed crimes, told lies, and tried to put the blame on other people. Turning the pages of his speech, he referred to his triumphs: China, arms limitation talks, Middle East diplomacy. He finished on a defiant note of pride.

"It's over," Maria said in a tone of incredulity.

"We won," said George, and he put his arms around her.

Then, without thinking about it, they were kissing.

It felt like the most natural thing in the world.

It was not a sudden burst of passion. They kissed playfully, exploring each other's lips and tongues. George tasted of wine. It was like discovering a fascinating topic of conversation they had previously overlooked. Maria found herself smiling and kissing at the same time.

However, their embrace soon turned passionate. Maria's pleasure became so intense it made her breathe hard. She unbuttoned George's blue shirt so that she could feel his chest. She had almost forgotten what it was like to have a man's bony frame in her arms. She relished his big hands touching the private places of her body, so different from her own small, soft fingers.

Out of the corner of her eye, she saw both cats leave the room.

George caressed her for a surprisingly long time. She had had only one previous lover, and he had not been so patient: by now he would have been on top of her. She was torn between pleasure in what George was doing and an almost panicky need to feel him inside her.

Then at last it happened. She had forgotten how good it felt. She crushed his chest to hers and lifted her legs to pull him farther in. She said his name again and again until she was overwhelmed by spasms of pleasure, and cried out. A moment later she felt him ejaculate inside her, and that made her convulse one more time.

They lay fused together, breathing hard. Maria could not touch him enough. She pressed one hand into his back, the other on his head, feeling his body, almost fearing that he might not be real, this could be a dream. She kissed his deformed ear. His panting breath was hot on her neck.

Slowly her breathing returned to normal. The world around became real again. The TV was still on, broadcasting reactions to the resignation. She heard a commentator say: "This has been a truly momentous day."

Maria sighed. "It sure has," she said.

.   .   .

George thought the ex-president should go to jail. Many people did. Nixon had committed more than enough crimes to justify a prison sentence. This was not medieval Europe, where kings were above the law: this was America, and justice was the same for everyone. The House Judiciary Committee had ruled that Nixon should be impeached, and Congress had endorsed the committee's report by a remarkable majority of 412 votes to 3. The public favored impeachment by 66 percent to 27. John Ehrlichman had already been sentenced to twenty months in prison for his crimes: it would be unfair if the man who had given him his orders were to escape punishment.

A month after the resignation, President Ford pardoned Nixon.

George was outraged, and so was just about everyone else. Ford's press secretary resigned. *The New York Times* said the pardon was "a profoundly unwise, divisive and unjust act" that had destroyed the new president's credibility at a stroke. Everyone assumed Nixon had cut a deal with Ford before handing power over to him.

"I can't take much more of this," said George to Maria in the kitchen of his apartment. He was mixing olive oil and red wine vinegar in a jug to make salad dressing. "Sitting behind a desk at Fawcett Renshaw while the country goes to hell."

"What are you going to do?"

"I've been thinking about it a lot. I want to go back into politics."

She turned to face him, and he was puzzled to see disapproval on her face. "What do you mean?" she said.

"The congressman for my mother's district, the Ninth Maryland, is retiring in two years. I think I can get nominated for the seat. In fact I know I can."

"So you've already talked to the Democratic Party there."

She was definitely angry with him, but he had no idea why. "Just exploratory discussions, yes," he said.

"Before you talked to me."

George was startled. Their romance was only a month old. Did he already have to clear everything with Maria? He almost said that, but bit back the words and tried something softer. "Maybe I should have talked to you first, but it didn't occur to me." He poured the dressing over the salad and started to toss it.

"You know I just applied for a really good job in the State Department."

"Of course."

"I think you know I want to go all the way to the top."

"And I bet you'll do it."

"Not with you, I won't."

"What are you talking about?"

"Senior State Department officials have to be nonpolitical. They must serve Democratic and Republican congressmen with equal diligence. If I'm known to be with a congressman I'll never get a promotion. They will always say: 'You can't really trust Maria Summers, she sleeps with Congressman Jakes.' They'd assume my loyalty was to you, not them."

George had not thought of that. "I'm really sorry," he said. "But what can I do?"

"How much does this relationship matter to you?" she said.

George thought her challenging words masked a plea. "Well," he said, "it's a little early to talk of marriage—"

"Early?" she said, getting angry. "I'm thirty-eight years old and you're only my second lover. Did you think I was looking for a casual fling?"

"I was going to say," he said patiently, "that if we do get married I assume we'll have children and you'll stay home and take care of them."

Her face was flushed with outrage. "Oh, is that what you assume? Not only do you plan to prevent me getting any further promotions, you actually expect me to give up my career altogether!"

"Well, that's what women usually do when they marry."

"The hell it is! Wake up, George. I realize that your mother devoted herself from the age of sixteen exclusively to caring for you, but you were born in 1936, for Christ's sake. We're in the seventies now. Feminism has arrived. Work is no longer something a woman does merely to pass the time until some man condescends to make her his domestic slave."

George was bewildered. This had come out of the blue. He had done something normal and reasonable, and she was spitting with rage. "I don't know why you're so goddamn ornery," he said. "I haven't ruined your career or made you a domestic slave, and I haven't actually asked you to marry me."

Her voice went quiet. "You asshole," she said. "You total asshole."

She left the room.

"Don't go," he said.

He heard the apartment door slam.

"Hell," he said.

He smelled smoke. The steaks were burning. He turned off the heat under the pan. The meat was charred black, inedible. He tipped the steaks into the garbage bin.

"Hell," he said again.

PART EIGHT

YARD

1976-1988

Grigori Peshkov was dying. The old warrior was eighty-seven, and his heart was failing.

Tanya had managed to get a message to his brother. Lev Peshkov was eighty-two but he had announced that he was coming to Moscow, in a private jet. Tanya had wondered if he would get permission to visit, but he had managed it. He had arrived yesterday and was due to visit Grigori today.

Grigori lay in bed in his apartment, pale and still. He was sensitive to pressure, and could not bear the weight of the bedclothes on his feet, so Tanya's mother, Anya, had placed two boxes in the bed, tenting the blankets so that they warmed without touching him.

Though he was weak, Tanya still felt the power of his presence. Even in repose his chin jutted pugnaciously. When he opened his eyes, he revealed that intense blue-eyed stare that had so often struck fear into the hearts of the enemies of the working class.

It was a Sunday, and family and friends came to visit. They were saying good-bye, though naturally they pretended otherwise. Tanya's twin, Dimka, and his wife, Natalya, brought Katya, their pretty seven-year-old. Dimka's ex-wife, Nina, turned up with the twelve-year-old Grisha, who had the beginnings of his great-grandfather's formidable intensity, despite his youth. Grigori smiled benignly on them all. "I fought in two revolutions and two world wars," he said. "It's a miracle I lasted this long."

He fell asleep, then, and most of the family went out, leaving Tanya and Dimka sitting at the bedside. Dimka's career had advanced: he was now an official of the State Planning Committee and a candidate member of the Politburo. He was still a close associate of Kosygin, but their attempts to reform the Soviet economy were always blocked by Kremlin conservatives. Dimka's wife, Natalya, was chair of the Analytical Department at the Foreign Ministry.

Tanya began to tell her brother about the latest feature she had written for TASS. At the suggestion of Vasili, who worked now in the Agriculture Ministry, she had flown to Stavropol, a fertile southern region where the collective farms were experimenting with a bonus system based on results. "Harvests are up," she told Dimka. "The reform is a big success."

"The Kremlin won't like bonuses," Dimka said. "They'll say the system smacks of revisionism."

"The system has been operating for years," she said. "The regional first secretary there is a real live wire. A man called Mikhail Gorbachev."

"He must have friends in high places."

"He knows Andropov, who goes to a spa in the region to take the waters." The KGB chief suffered from kidney stones, an agonizing ailment. If ever a man deserved such pain, Tanya thought, Yuri Andropov did.

Dimka was intrigued. "So this Gorbachev is a reformer who is friendly with Andropov?" he said. "That makes him an unusual man. I must keep an eye on him."

"I found him refreshingly commonsensical."

"We certainly need new ideas. Do you remember Khrushchev, back in 1961, forecasting that the USSR would overtake the USA in both production and military strength in twenty years?"

Tanya smiled. "At the time he was thought pessimistic."

"Now fifteen years have passed and we're farther behind than ever. And Natalya tells me the East European countries have also fallen behind their neighbors. They're kept quiet only by massive subsidies from us."

Tanya nodded. "It's a good thing we have huge exports of oil and other raw materials to help us pay the bills."

"But it's not enough. Look at East Germany. We have to have a damn wall to stop people escaping to capitalism."

Grigori stirred. Tanya felt guilty. She had been questioning her grandfather's fundamental beliefs while sitting at his deathbed.

The door opened and a stranger walked in. He was an old man, thin and bent but immaculately dressed. He had on a dark-gray suit that was molded to his body like something worn by the hero in a movie. His white shirt gleamed and his red tie glowed. Such clothes could only come from the West. Tanya had never met him, but all the same there was something familiar about him. This must be Lev.

He ignored Tanya and Dimka and looked at the man in the bed.

Grandfather Grigori gave him a look that said he knew the visitor but could not quite place him.

"Grigori," the newcomer said. "My brother. How did we get so old?" He spoke a queer old-fashioned dialect of Russian with the harsh accent of a Leningrad factory worker.

"Lev," said Grigori. "Is it really you? You used to be so handsome!"

Lev leaned over and kissed his brother on both cheeks, then they embraced.

Grigori said: "You got here just in time. I'm about done for."

A woman about eighty years old followed Lev in. She was dressed, Tanya thought, like a prostitute, in a stylish black dress and high heels, makeup and jewelry. Tanya wondered whether it was normal for old women to dress that way in America.

"I saw some of your grandchildren in the next room," Lev said. "They're a fine bunch."

Grigori smiled. "The joy of my life. How about you?"

"I have a daughter by Olga, the wife I never much liked, and a son by Marga here, who I preferred. I wasn't much of a father to either of my children. I never had your sense of responsibility."

"Any grandchildren?"

"Three," Lev said. "One's a movie star, one's a pop singer, and one's black."

"Black?" said Grigori. "How did that happen?"

"It happened the usual way, idiot. My son, Greg—named for his uncle, by the way—he fucked a black girl."

"Well, that's more than his uncle ever did," said Grigori, and the two old men chuckled.

Grigori said: "What a life I've had, Lev. I stormed the Winter Palace. We destroyed the tsars and built the first Communist country. I defended Moscow against the Nazis. I'm a general and Volodya is a general. I feel so guilty about you."

"Guilty about me?"

"You went to America and missed it all," Grigori said.

"I have no complaints," said Lev.

"I even got Katerina, though she preferred you."

Lev smiled. "And all I got was a hundred million dollars."

"Yes," said Grigori. "You got the worst of the deal. I'm sorry, Lev."

"It's okay," said Lev. "I forgive you." He was being ironic but, Tanya thought, Grigori did not seem to realize that.

Uncle Volodya came in. He was on his way to some army ceremony, wearing his general's uniform. Tanya realized with a sudden shock that this was the first time he had seen his real father. Lev stared at the son he had never met. "My God," Lev said. "He looks like you, Grigori."

"He's yours, though," said Grigori.

Father and son shook hands.

Volodya said nothing, seeming in the grip of an emotion so powerful that he could not speak.

Lev said: "When you lost me as a father, Volodya, you didn't lose much." Keeping hold of his son's hand, he looked him up and down: gleaming boots, Red Army uniform, combat medals, piercing blue eyes, iron gray hair. "I did, though," Lev said. "I guess I lost a lot."

. . .

As she left the apartment Tanya found herself wondering where the Bolsheviks had gone wrong, where Grandfather Grigori's idealism and energy had been perverted into tyranny. She went to the bus stop, heading for a rendezvous with Vasili. On the bus, thinking over the early years of the Russian Revolution, she wondered whether Lenin's decision to close all newspapers except the Bolshevik ones had been the key error. It meant that right from the start alternative ideas had had no circulation and the conventional wisdom could never be challenged. Gorbachev in Stavropol was exceptional in having been allowed to try something different. Such people were generally stifled. Tanya was a journalist, and suspected herself of egocentrically overrating the importance of a free press, but it seemed to her that the lack of critical newspapers made it much easier for other forms of oppression to flourish.

It was now four years since Vasili had been released. In that time he had shrewdly rehabilitated himself. At the Agriculture Ministry he had devised an educational radio serial set on a collective farm. As well as the dramas about unfaithful wives and disobedient children, the characters discussed agricultural techniques. Naturally the peasants who ignored advice from Moscow were lazy and shiftless, and the wayward teenagers who questioned the Communist Party's authority were the ones who were jilted by their boyfriends or failed their exams. The serial was a huge success. Vasili returned to Radio Moscow and was given an apartment in a block occupied by writers approved by the government.

Their meetings were clandestine, but Tanya also ran into him occasionally at union events or private parties. He was no longer the walking cadaver that had returned from Siberia in 1972. He had put on weight and regained some of his former presence. Now in his midforties, he would never again be movie-star handsome; but the lines of strain on his face somehow added to his allure. And he still had buckets of charm. Each time Tanya saw him he was with a different woman. They were not the nubile teenagers who had adored him in his thirties, though perhaps they were the middle-aged women those teenagers had become: smart females in chic clothes and high-heeled shoes who always seemed able to get hold of scarce nail varnish, hair dye, and stockings.

Tanya met him secretly once a month.

Each time he would bring her the latest installment of the book he was working on, written in the small, neat handwriting he had developed in Siberia to save paper. She would type it for him, correcting his spelling and punctuation where necessary. At their next meeting she would hand him the typescript for review and discuss it with him.

Millions of people around the world bought Vasili's books,

but he never met any of them. He could not even read the reviews, which were written in foreign languages and published in Western newspapers. So Tanya was the only person with whom he could discuss his work, and he listened hungrily to everything she had to say. She was his editor.

Tanya went to Leipzig every March to cover the book fair there, and each time she met with Anna Murray. She always came back with a present for Vasili from Anna—an electric typewriter, a cashmere overcoat—and news of even more money piling up in his London bank account. He would probably never get to spend any of it.

She still took careful precautions when meeting him. Today she got off the bus a mile from the rendezvous, and made sure she was not being followed while she walked to the café, called Josef's. Vasili was already there, sitting at a table with a vodka glass in front of him. On the chair beside him was a large buff envelope. Tanya waved casually, as if they were acquaintances meeting by chance. She got a beer from the bar, then sat opposite Vasili.

She was happy to see him looking so well. His face had a dignity he had not possessed fifteen years earlier. He still had soft brown eyes, but nowadays they were keenly perceptive as often as they twinkled with mischief. She realized there was no one, outside her family, whom she knew better. She knew his strengths: imagination, intelligence, charm, and the gritty determination that had enabled him to survive and keep writing for a decade in Siberia. She also knew his weaknesses, the main one of which was an irresistible urge to seduce.

"Thanks for the tip about Stavropol," she said. "I've done a nice piece."

"Good. Let's just hope the whole experiment doesn't get stamped on."

She handed Vasili the last episode, typed out, and nodded at the envelope. "Another chapter?"

"The last." He gave it to her.

"Anna Murray will be happy." Vasili's new novel was called *First Lady*. In it the American president's wife—as it might be, Pat Nixon—gets lost in Moscow for twenty-four hours. Tanya marveled at Vasili's power of invention. Seeing life in the USSR through the eyes of a well-meaning conservative American was a richly comic way to criticize

Soviet society. She slipped the envelope into her shoulder bag.

Vasili said: "When can you take the whole thing to the publisher?"

"As soon as I get a foreign trip. At the latest, next March, in Leipzig."

"March?" Vasili was disappointed. "That's six months away," he said in a tone of reproof.

"I'll try to get an assignment where I could meet her."

"Please do."

Tanya was offended. "Vasili, I risk my damn life to do this for you. Get someone else, if you can, or do the job yourself. Hell, I wouldn't mind."

"Of course." He was immediately contrite. "I'm sorry. I have so much invested in it—three years' work, all in the evenings after I come home from my job. But I have no right to be impatient with you." He reached across the table and put his hand over hers. "You've been my lifeline, more than once."

She nodded. It was true.

All the same, she still felt cross with him as she walked away from the café with the ending of his novel in her bag. What was bugging her? It was those women in high-heeled shoes, she decided. She felt that Vasili should have grown out of that phase. Promiscuity was adolescent. He demeaned himself by showing up at every literary party with a different date. By now he should have settled down in a serious relationship with a woman who was his equal. She could be younger, perhaps, but she should be able to match his intelligence and appreciate his work, perhaps even help him with it. He needed a partner, not a series of trophies.

She went to the TASS office. Before she reached her desk she was accosted by Pyotr Opotkin, the editor in chief for features, the department's political overseer. As always a cigarette dangled from his lips. "I've had a call from the Agriculture Ministry. Your piece on Stavropol can't go out," he said.

"What? Why not? The bonus system has been passed by the ministry. And it works."

"Wrong." Opotkin liked to tell people they were wrong. "It's been scrapped. There's a new approach, the Ipatovo Method. They send fleets of combine harvesters all over the region."

"Central control again, instead of individual responsibility."

"Exactly." He took the cigarette from his mouth. "You'll have to write a completely new article about the Ipatovo Method."

"What does the regional first secretary say?"

"Young Gorbachev? He's implementing the new system."

Of course he was, Tanya reflected. He was an intelligent man. He knew when to shut up and do as he was told. Otherwise he would not have become first secretary.

"All right," she said, stifling her anger. "I'll write a new piece."

Opotkin nodded and walked away.

It had been too good to be true, Tanya thought: a new idea, bonuses paid for good results, improved harvests in consequence, no input required from Moscow. It was a miracle the system had been permitted for a few years. In the long run, such a system was totally out of the question.

Of course it was.

CHAPTER FIFTY-TWO

George Jakes wore a new tuxedo. He looked pretty good in it, he thought. At forty-two he no longer had the wrestler's physique he had been so proud of in his youth, but he was still slim and straight, and the black-and-white wedding uniform flattered him.

He stood in Bethel Evangelical Church, which his mother had been attending for decades, in the Washington suburb he now represented as congressman. It was a low brick building, small and plain, and normally it was decorated only with a few framed quotations from the Bible: THE LORD IS MY SHEPHERD and IN THE BEGINNING WAS THE WORD. But today it was decked out for a celebration, with streamers and ribbons and masses of white flowers. The choir was belting out "Soon Come" while George waited for his bride.

In the front row, his mother wore a new dark blue suit and a matching pillbox hat with a little veil. "Well, I'm glad," Jacky had said when George told her he was getting married. "I'm fifty-eight years old, and I'm sorry you waited so gosh-darn long, but I'm happy you got here in the end." Her tongue was always sharp, but today she could not keep the proud smile from her face. Her son was getting married in her church, in front of all her friends and neighbors, and on top of that he was a congressman.

Next to her was George's father, Senator Greg Peshkov. Somehow he was able to make even a tuxedo look like creased pajamas. He had forgotten to put cuff links in his shirt, and his bow tie looked like a dead moth. No one minded.

Also in the front row were George's Russian grandparents, Lev and Marga, now in their eighties. Both looked frail, but they had flown from Buffalo for the wedding of their grandson.

By showing up at the wedding, and sitting in the front row, George's white father and grandparents were admitting the truth to the world; but no one cared. This was 1978, and what had once been a secret disgrace now hardly mattered.

The choir began to sing "You Are So Beautiful" and everyone turned and looked back toward the church door.

Verena came in on the arm of her father, Percy Marquand. George gasped when he saw her, and so did several people in the congregation. She wore a daring off-the-shoulder white dress that was tight to midthigh, then flared to a train. The caramel skin of her bare shoulders was as soft and smooth as the satin of her dress. She looked so wonderful it hurt. George felt tears sting his eyes.

The service passed in a blur. George managed to make the right responses, but all he could think was that Verena was his, now, forever.

The ceremony was folksy, but there was nothing modest about the wedding breakfast thrown afterward by the bride's father. Percy rented Pisces, a Georgetown nightclub that featured a twenty-foot waterfall at the entrance emptying into a giant goldfish pond on the floor below, and an aquarium in the middle of the dance floor.

George and Verena's first dance was to the Bee Gees' "Stayin' Alive." George was not much of a dancer, but it hardly mattered: everyone was looking at Verena, holding up her train with one hand while disco-dancing. George was so happy he wanted to hug everyone.

The second person to dance with the bride was Ted Kennedy, who had come without his wife, Joan: there were rumors that they had split. Jacky grabbed the handsome Percy Marquand. Verena's mother, Babe Lee, danced with Greg.

George's cousin Dave Williams, the pop star, was there with his sexy wife, Beep, and their five-year-old son, John Lee, named after the blues singer John Lee Hooker. The boy danced with his mother, and strutted so expertly that he made everyone laugh: he must have seen *Saturday Night Fever.*

Elizabeth Taylor danced with her latest husband, the millionaire would-be senator John Warner. Liz was wearing the famous square-cut thirty-three-carat Krupp diamond on the ring finger of her right hand. Seeing all this through a mist of euphoria, George realized dazedly that his wedding had turned into one of the outstanding social events of the year.

George had invited Maria Summers, but she had declined. After their brief love affair had ended in a quarrel, they had not spoken for a year. George had been hurt and bewildered. He did not know how he was supposed to live his life: the rules had changed. He also felt resentful. Women wanted a new deal, and they expected him to know, without being told, what the deal was, and to agree to it without negotiation.

Then Verena had emerged from seven years of obscurity. She had started her own lobbying company in Washington, specializing in civil rights and other equality issues. Her initial clients were small pressure groups who could not afford to employ their own full-time lobbyist. The rumor that Verena had once been a Black Panther seemed only to give her greater credibility. Before long she and George were an item again.

Verena seemed to have changed. One evening she said: "Dramatic gestures have their place in politics, but in the end advances are made by patient legwork: drafting legislation and talking to the media and winning votes." You've grown up, George thought, and he only just stopped himself from saying it.

The new Verena wanted marriage and children, and felt sure she could have both and a career too. Once burned, George did not again put his hand in the fire: if that was what she thought, it was not up to him to argue.

George had written a tactful letter to Maria, beginning: "I don't want you to hear this from someone else." He had told her that he and Verena were together again and talking about marriage. Maria had replied in tones of warm friendship, and their relationship had reverted to what it had been before Nixon resigned. But she remained single, and did not come to the wedding.

Taking a break from dancing, George sat down with his father and grandfather. Lev was downing champagne with relish and telling jokes. A Polish cardinal had been made Pope, and Lev had a fund of bad-taste Polish Pope jokes. "He did a miracle—made a blind man deaf!"

Greg said: "I think this is a highly aggressive political move by the Vatican."

George was surprised by that, but Greg usually had grounds for what he said. "How so?" said George.

"Catholicism is more popular in Poland than elsewhere in Eastern Europe, and the Communists aren't strong enough to repress religion there as they have in all other countries. There's a Polish religious press, a Catholic university, and various charities that get away with sheltering dissidents and noting human rights abuses."

George said: "So what is the Vatican up to?"

"Mischief. I believe they see Poland as the Soviet Union's weak spot. This Polish Pope will do more than wave at tourists from the balcony—you watch."

George was about to ask what the Pope *would* do when the room went quiet and he realized that President Carter had arrived.

Everyone applauded, even the Republicans. The president kissed the bride, shook hands with George, and accepted a glass of pink champagne, although he took only one sip.

While Carter was talking to Percy and Babe, who were long-term Democratic fund-raisers, one of the president's aides approached George. After a few pleasantries the man said: "Would you consider serving on the House Permanent Select Committee on Intelligence?"

George was flattered. Congressional committees were important. A seat on a committee was a source of power. "I've been in Congress only two years," he said.

The aide nodded. "The president is keen to advance black congressmen, and Tip O'Neill agrees." Tip O'Neill was the House majority leader, who had the prerogative of granting committee seats.

George said: "I'll be glad to serve the president any way I can—but intelligence?"

The CIA and other intelligence agencies reported to the president and the Pentagon, but they were authorized, funded, and in theory controlled by Congress. For security, control was delegated to two committees, one in the House and one in the Senate.

"I know what you're thinking," said the aide. "Intelligence committees are usually packed with conservative friends of the military. You're a liberal who has criticized the Pentagon over Vietnam and the CIA over Watergate. But that's why we want you. At present those committees don't oversee, they just applaud. And intelligence agencies that think they can get away with murder will commit murder. So we need someone in there asking tough questions."

"The intelligence community is going to be horrified."

"Good," said the aide. "After the way they behaved in the Nixon era, they need to be shaken up." He glanced across the dance floor. Following his gaze, George saw that President Carter was leaving. "I have to go," the aide said. "Do you want time to think?"

"Hell, no," said George. "I'll do it."

.   .   .

"Godmother? Me?" said Maria Summers. "Are you serious?"

George Jakes smiled. "I know you're not very religious. We're not, either, not really. I go to church to please my mother. Verena has been once in the last ten years, and that was for our wedding. But we like the idea of godparents."

They were having lunch in the Members' Dining Room of the House of Representatives, on the ground floor of the Capitol building, sitting in front of the famous fresco *Cornwallis Sues for Cessation of Hostilities*. Maria was eating meat loaf; George had a salad.

Maria said: "When's the baby due?"

"A month or so—early April."

"How is Verena feeling?"

"Terrible. Lethargic and impatient at the same time. And tired, always tired."

"It will soon be over."

George brought her back to the question. "Will you be godmother?"

She evaded it again. "Why have you asked me?"

He thought for a moment. "Because I trust you, I guess. I probably trust you more than anyone outside my family.

If Verena and I died in a plane crash, and our parents were too old or dead, I feel confident that you would make sure my children were cared for, somehow."

Maria was evidently moved. "It's kind of wonderful to be told that."

George thought, but did not say, that it was now unlikely Maria would have children of her own—she would be forty-four this year, he calculated—and that meant she had a lot of spare maternal affection to give to the children of her friends.

She was already like family. His friendship with her had lasted almost twenty years. She still went to see Jacky several times a year. Greg liked Maria, too, as did Lev and Marga. It was hard not to like her.

George did not give voice to any of these considerations, but instead said: "It would mean a lot to Verena and me if you would do it."

"Is it really what Verena wants?"

George smiled. "Yes. She knows that you and I had a relationship, but she's not the jealous type. Matter of fact, she admires you for what you've achieved in your career."

Maria looked at the men in the fresco, with their eighteenth-century coats and boots, and said: "Well, I guess I'll be like General Cornwallis, and surrender."

"Thank you!" said George. "I'm very happy. I'd order champagne, but I know you wouldn't drink it in the middle of a working day."

"Maybe when the baby is born."

The waitress picked up their plates and they asked for coffee. "How are things in the State Department?" George asked. Maria was now a big shot there. Her title was deputy assistant secretary, a post more influential than it sounded.

"We're trying to figure out what's happening in Poland," she said. "It's not easy. We think there's a lot of criticism of the government from inside the United Workers' Party, which is the Communist Party. Workers are poor, the elite are too privileged, and the 'propaganda of success' just calls attention to the reality of failure. National income actually fell last year."

"You know I'm on the House intelligence committee."

"Of course."

"Are you getting good information from the agencies?"

"It's good, as far as we know, but there's not enough of it."

"Would you like me to ask about that in the committee?"

"Yes, please."

"It may be that we need additional intelligence personnel in Warsaw."

"I think we do. Poland could be important."

George nodded. "That's what Greg said when the Vatican elected a Polish Pope. And he's usually right."

. . .

At the age of forty, Tanya became dissatisfied with her life.

She asked herself what she wanted to do with her next forty years, and found that she did not want to spend them as an acolyte to Vasili Yenkov. She had risked her freedom to share his genius with the world, but that had done nothing for her. It was time she focused on her own needs, she decided. What that meant, she did not know.

Her discontent came to a head at a party to celebrate the award of the Lenin Prize in literature to Leonid Brezhnev's memoirs. The award was risible: the three volumes of the Soviet leader's autobiography were not well written, not true, and not even by Brezhnev, having been ghostwritten. But the writers' union saw the prize as a useful pretext for a shindig.

Getting ready for the party, Tanya put her hair in a ponytail like Olivia Newton-John's in the movie *Grease*, which she had seen on an illicit videotape. The new hairstyle did not cheer her up as much as she had hoped.

As she was leaving the building, she ran into her brother in the lobby, and told him where she was going. "I see that your protégé, Gorbachev, made a fulsome speech in praise of Comrade Brezhnev's literary genius," she said.

"Mikhail knows when to kiss ass," Dimka said.

"You did well to get him onto the Central Committee."

"He already had the support of Andropov, who likes him," Dimka explained. "All I had to do was persuade Kosygin that Gorbachev is a genuine reformer." Andropov, the KGB chief, was increasingly the leader of the conservative faction in the Kremlin; Kosygin the champion of the reformers.

Tanya said: "Gaining the approval of both sides is unusual."

"He's an unusual man. Enjoy your party."

The do was held in the utilitarian offices of the writers' union, but they had managed to get hold of several cases of Bagrationi, the Georgian champagne. Under its influence, Tanya got into an argument with Pyotr Opotkin, from TASS. No one liked Opotkin, who was not a journalist but a political supervisor, but he had to be invited to social events because he was too powerful to offend. He buttonholed Tanya and said accusingly: "The Pope's visit to Warsaw is a catastrophe!"

Opotkin was right about that. No one had imagined how it would be. Pope John Paul II turned out to be a talented propagandist. When he got off the plane at Okecie military airport he fell to his knees and kissed the Polish ground. The picture was on the front pages of the Western press next morning, and Tanya knew—as the Pope must have known—that the image would find its way back into Poland by underground routes. Tanya secretly rejoiced.

Daniil, Tanya's boss, was listening, and he interjected: "Driving into Warsaw in an open car, the Pope was cheered by two million people."

Tanya said: "Two *million*?" She had not seen this statistic. "Is that possible? It must be something like five percent of the entire population—one in every twenty Poles!"

Opotkin said angrily: "What is the point of the party controlling television coverage when people can see the Pope for themselves?"

Control was everything for men such as Opotkin.

He was not done. "He celebrated mass in Victory Square in the presence of two hundred and fifty thousand people!"

Tanya knew that. It was a shocking figure, even to her, for it starkly revealed the extent to which Communism had failed to win the hearts of the Polish people. Thirty-five years of life under the Soviet system had converted nobody but the privileged elite. She made the point in appropriate Communist jargon. "The Polish working class reasserted their reactionary old loyalties at the first opportunity."

Poking Tanya's shoulder with an accusing forefinger, Opotkin said: "It was reformists like you who insisted on letting the Pope go there."

"Rubbish," said Tanya scornfully. Kremlin liberals such as Dimka had urged letting the Pope in, but they had lost the argument, and Moscow had told Warsaw to ban the

Pope—but the Polish Communists had disobeyed orders. In a display of independence unusual for a Soviet satellite, the Polish leader Edward Gierek had defied Brezhnev. "It was the Polish leadership that made the decision," Tanya said. "They feared there would be an uprising if they forbade the Pope's visit."

"We know how to deal with uprisings," said Opotkin.

Tanya knew she was only damaging her career by contradicting Opotkin, but she was forty and sick of kowtowing to idiots. "Financial pressures made the Polish decision inevitable," she said. "Poland gets huge subsidies from us, but it needs loans from the West as well. President Carter was very tough when he went to Warsaw. He made it clear that financial aid was linked to what they call human rights. If you want to blame someone for the Pope's triumph, Jimmy Carter is the culprit."

Opotkin must have known this was true, but he was not going to admit it. "I always said it was a mistake to let Communist countries borrow from Western banks."

Tanya should have left it there, and allowed Opotkin to save face, but she could not restrain herself. "Then you face a dilemma, don't you?" she said. "The alternative to Western finance is to liberalize Polish agriculture so that they can produce enough of their own food."

"More reforms!" Opotkin said angrily. "That is always your solution!"

"The Polish people have always had cheap food: that's what keeps them quiet. Whenever the government puts up prices, they riot."

"We know how to deal with riots," said Opotkin, and he walked away.

Daniil looked bemused. "Good for you," he said to Tanya. "Though he may make you pay."

Tanya said: "I want some more of that champagne."

At the bar she ran into Vasili. He was alone. Tanya realized that lately he had been showing up to events like this without a floozie on his arm, and she wondered why. But she was focused on herself tonight. "I can't do this much longer," she said.

Vasili handed her a glass. "Do what?"

"You know."

"I suppose I can guess."

"I'm forty. I have to live my own life."

"What do you want to do?"

"I don't know, that's the trouble."

"I'm forty-eight," he said. "And I feel something similar."

"What?"

"I don't chase girls anymore. Or women."

She was in a cynical mood. "Don't chase them—or just don't catch them?"

"I detect a note of skepticism."

"Perceptive of you."

"Listen," he said, "I've been thinking. I'm not sure we need to continue the pretense that we barely know one another."

"What makes you say that?"

He leaned closer and lowered his voice, so that she had to strain to hear him over the noise of the party. "Everyone knows that Anna Murray is the publisher of Ivan Kuznetsov, yet no one has ever connected her to you."

"That's because we're ultracautious. We never let anyone see us together."

"That being the case, there's no danger in people knowing that you and I are friends."

She was not sure. "Maybe. So what?"

Vasili tried a roguish smile. "You once told me you'd go to bed with me if I would give up the rest of my harem."

"I don't believe I ever said that."

"Perhaps you implied it."

"And anyway, that must have been eighteen years ago."

"Is it too late now to accept the offer?"

She stared at him, speechless.

He filled the silence. "You're the only woman who ever really mattered to me. Everyone else was just a conquest. Some I didn't even like. If I had never slept with her before, that was enough reason for me to seduce her."

"Is this supposed to make you more attractive to me?"

"When I got out of Siberia I tried to resume that life. It's taken me a long time, but I've realized the truth at last: it doesn't make me happy."

"Is that so?" Tanya was getting angrier.

Vasili did not notice. "You and I have been friends for a long time. We're soul mates. We belong together. When we sleep together, it will just be a natural progression."

"Oh, I see."

He was oblivious to her sarcasm. "You're single, I'm single. Why are we single? We should be together. We should be married."

"So, to sum up," Tanya said, "you've spent your life seducing women you never really cared for. Now you're pushing fifty and they don't really attract you—or perhaps you no longer attract them—so, at this point, you're condescending to offer me marriage."

"I may not have put this very well. I'm better at writing things down."

"You bet you haven't put it well. I'm the last resort of a fading Casanova!"

"Oh, hell, you're upset with me, aren't you?"

"*Upset* comes nowhere near it."

"This is the opposite of what I intended."

Over his shoulder, she caught the eye of Daniil. On impulse she left Vasili and crossed the room. "Daniil," she said. "I'd like to go abroad again. Is there any chance I could get a foreign posting?"

"Of course," he said. "You're my best writer. I'll do anything I can, within reason, to keep you happy."

"Thank you."

"And, coincidentally, I've been thinking that we need to strengthen our bureau in one particular foreign country."

"Which one?"

"Poland."

"You'd send me to Warsaw?"

"That's where it's all happening."

"All right," she said. "Poland it is."

. . . .

Cam Dewar was fed up with Jimmy Carter. He thought the Carter administration was timid, especially in its dealings with the USSR. Cam worked on the Moscow desk at CIA headquarters in Langley, nine miles from the White House. National Security Adviser Zbigniew Brzezinski was a tough anti-Communist, but Carter was cautious.

However, it was election year, and Cam hoped Ronald Reagan would get in. Reagan was aggressive on foreign policy, and promised to liberate intelligence agencies from Carter's milk-and-water ethical constraints. He would be more like Nixon, Cam hoped.

Early in 1980 Cam was surprised to be summoned by the deputy head of the Soviet bloc section, Florence Geary. She was an attractive woman a few years older than Cam: he was thirty-three, she was probably about thirty-eight. He knew her story. She had been hired as a trainee, used as a secretary for years, and given training only when she kicked up a stink. Now she was a highly competent intelligence officer, but she was still disliked by many of the men because of the trouble she had caused.

Today she was wearing a plaid skirt and a green sweater. She looked like a schoolteacher, Cam thought; a sexy schoolteacher, with good breasts.

"Sit down," she said. "The House intelligence committee thinks our information out of Poland is poor."

Cameron took a seat. He looked out of the window to avoid staring at her chest. "Then they know who to blame," he said.

"Who?"

"The director of the CIA, Admiral Turner, and the man who appointed him, President Carter."

"Why, exactly?"

"Because Turner doesn't believe in HUMINT." Human intelligence, or HUMINT, was what you got from spies. Turner preferred SIGINT, signals intelligence, obtained by monitoring communications.

"Do *you* believe in HUMINT?"

She had a nice mouth, he realized; pink lips, even teeth. He forced himself to concentrate on answering the question. "It's inherently unreliable, because all traitors are liars, by definition. If they're telling us the truth they must be lying to their own side. But that doesn't make HUMINT worthless, especially if it's assessed against data from other sources."

"I'm glad you think so. We need to beef up our HUMINT. How do you feel about working overseas?"

Cameron's hopes leaped. "Ever since I joined the Agency, six years ago, I've been asking for a foreign posting."

"Good."

"I speak Russian fluently. I'd love to go to Moscow."

"Well, life's a funny thing. You're going to Warsaw."

"No kidding."

"I don't kid."

"I don't speak Polish."

"You'll find your Russian useful. Polish schoolchildren have been learning Russian for thirty-five years. But you should learn some Polish too."

"Okay."

"That's all."

Cameron stood up. "Thanks." He went to the door. "Could we discuss this some more, Florence?" he said. "Maybe over dinner?"

"No," she said firmly. Then, just in case he had not got the message, she added: "Definitely not."

He went out and closed the door. Warsaw! On balance, he was pleased. It was a foreign posting. He felt optimistic. He was disappointed she had turned down his invitation to dinner, but he knew what to do about that.

He picked up his coat and went outside to his car, a silver Mercury Capri. He drove into Washington and threaded through the traffic to the Adams Morgan district. There he parked a block away from a storefront massage parlor called Silken Hands.

The woman at the reception desk said: "Hi, Christopher, how are you today?"

"Fine, thanks. Is Suzy free?"

"You're in luck, she is. Room Three."

"Great." Cam handed over a bill and went farther inside.

He pushed aside a curtain and entered a booth containing a narrow bed. Beside the bed, sitting on a plastic chair, was a heavyset woman in her twenties reading a magazine. She wore a bikini. "Hello, Chris," she said, putting down the magazine and standing up. "Would you like a hand job, as usual?"

Cam never had full intercourse with prostitutes. "Yes, please, Suzy." He gave her a bill and started taking off his clothes.

"It'll be my pleasure," she said, tucking the money away. She helped him undress, then said: "You just lie down and relax, baby."

Cam lay on the bed and closed his eyes while Suzy went to work. He pictured Florence Geary in her office. In his mind, she pulled the green sweater over her head and unzipped her plaid skirt. "Oh, Cam, I just can't resist you," she said in Cam's imagination. Wearing only her underwear, she came around her desk and embraced him. "Do anything you like to me, Cam," she said. "But please, do it hard."

In the massage parlor booth, Cam said aloud: "Yeah, baby."

. . .

Tanya looked in the mirror. She was holding a small container of blue eye shadow and a brush. Makeup was more easily available in Warsaw than in Moscow. Tanya did not have much experience with eye shadow, and she had noticed that some women applied it badly. On her dressing table was a magazine open at a photograph of Bianca Jagger. Glancing frequently at the picture, Tanya began to color her eyelids.

The effect was pretty good, she thought.

Stanislaw Pawlak sat on her bed in his uniform, with his boots on a newspaper to keep the covers clean, smoking and watching her. He was tall and handsome and intelligent, and she was crazy about him.

She had met him soon after arriving in Poland, on a tour of army headquarters. He was part of a group called the Gold Fund, able young officers selected by the defense minister, General Jaruzelski, for rapid advancement. They were frequently rotated to new assignments, to give them the breadth of experience necessary for the high command to which they were destined.

She had noticed Staz, as he was called, partly because he was so good-looking, and partly because he was obviously taken with her. He spoke Russian fluently. Having talked to her about his own unit, which handled liaison with the Red Army, he had then accompanied her on the rest of the tour, which was otherwise dull.

Next day he had turned up on her doorstep at six in the evening, having got her address from the SB, the Polish secret police. He had taken her to dinner at a hot new restaurant called the Duck. She quickly realized that he was as skeptical about Communism as she was. A week later she slept with him.

She still thought about Vasili, wondering how his writing was going, and whether he missed their monthly meetings. She was viscerally angry with him, though she was not sure why. He had been crass, but men *were* crass, especially the handsome ones. What she was really seething about was the years before his proposal. Somehow she felt that what she had done for him during that long time had been dishonored. Did he believe she had just been waiting, year after year, until he was ready to be her husband? That thought still infuriated her.

Staz was now spending two or three nights a week at her apartment. They never went to his place: he said it was little better than a barracks. But they were having a great time. And all along, in the back of her mind, she had been wondering if his anti-Communism might one day lead to action.

She turned to face him. "How do you like my eyes?"

"I adore them," he said. "They have enslaved me. Your eyes are like—"

"I mean my makeup, idiot."

"Are you wearing makeup?"

"Men are blind. How are you going to defend your country with such poor powers of observation?"

His mood became dark again. "We make no provision for defending our own country," he said. "The Polish army is totally subservient to the USSR. All our planning is about supporting the Red Army in an invasion of Western Europe."

Staz often talked like this, complaining about Soviet domination of the Polish military. It was a sign of how much he trusted her. In addition, Tanya had found that Poles spoke boldly about the failings of Communist governments. They felt entitled to complain in a way that other Soviet subjects did not. Most people in the Soviet bloc treated Communism as a religion that was a sin to question. The Poles tolerated Communism as long as it served them, and protested as soon as it fell short of their expectations.

All the same, Tanya now switched on her bedside radio. She did not think her apartment was bugged—the SB had their hands full spying on Western journalists, and probably left Soviet ones alone—but caution was an ingrained habit.

"We are all traitors," Staz finished.

Tanya frowned. He had never before called himself a traitor. This was serious. She said: "What on earth do you mean?"

"The Soviet Union has a contingency plan to invade

Western Europe with a force called the Second Strategic Echelon. Most of the Red Army tanks and personnel carriers headed for West Germany, France, Holland, and Belgium will pass through Poland on their way. The United States will use nuclear bombs to try to destroy those forces before they reach the West—that is, while they are still crossing Poland. We estimate that four hundred to six hundred nuclear weapons will be exploded in our country. There will be nothing left but a nuclear wasteland. Poland will have disappeared. If we cooperate in the planning of this event, how can we not be traitors?"

Tanya shuddered. It was a nightmare scenario—but terrifyingly logical.

"America is not the enemy of the Polish people," said Staz. "If the USSR and the USA go to war in Europe, we should side with the Americans, and liberate ourselves from the tyranny of Moscow."

Was he just blowing off steam, or something more? Tanya said carefully: "Is it just you who thinks like this, Staz?"

"Certainly not. Most officers my age feel the same. They pay lip service to Communism, but if you talk to them when they're drunk you'll hear another story."

"In that case, you have a problem," she said. "By the time the war begins, it will be too late for you to win the trust of the Americans."

"This is our dilemma."

"The solution is obvious. You have to open a channel of communication now."

He gave her a cool look. The thought crossed her mind that he might be an agent provocateur, assigned to provoke her into subversive remarks so that she could be arrested. But she could not imagine that a faker would be such a good lover.

Staz said: "Are we just talking, now, or are we having a serious discussion?"

Tanya took a breath. "I'm as serious as life and death," she said.

"Do you really think it could be done?"

"I know it," she said emphatically. She had been engaging in clandestine subversion for two decades. "It's the easiest thing in the world—but keeping it secret, and getting away with it, is more difficult. You would have to exercise the most extreme caution."

"Do you think I *should* do it?"

"Yes!" she said passionately. "I don't want another generation of Soviet children—or Polish children—to grow up under this stifling tyranny."

He nodded. "I can tell that you really mean it."

"I do."

"Will you help me?"

"Of course I will."

.   .   .

Cameron Dewar was not sure he would make a good spy. The undercover stuff he had done for President Nixon had been amateurish, and he was lucky not to have gone to jail with his boss, John Ehrlichman. When he joined the CIA he had been trained in the tradecraft of dead drops and brush passes, but he had never actually used such tricks. After six years at CIA headquarters in Langley he had at last been posted to a foreign capital, but he still had not done clandestine work.

The U.S. embassy in Warsaw was a proud white marble building on a street called Aleje Ujazdowskie. The CIA occupied a single office near the ambassador's suite of rooms. Off the office was a windowless storeroom that was used for developing photographic film. The staff was four spies and a secretary. It was a small operation because they had few informants.

Cam did not have much to do. He read the Warsaw newspapers, with the aid of a dictionary. He reported the graffiti he saw: LONG LIVE THE POPE and WE WANT GOD. He talked to men like himself who worked for the intelligence services of other countries in the North Atlantic Treaty Organization, NATO, especially those of West Germany, France, and Britain. He drove a used lime green Polski Fiat whose battery was so undersize that it had to be recharged every night or the car would not start in the morning. He tried to find a girlfriend among the embassy secretaries, and failed.

He felt a loser. His life had once seemed full of promise. He had been a star student at school and university, and his first job had been in the White House. Then it had all gone wrong. He was determined not to let his life be blighted by Nixon. But he needed a success. He wanted to be top of the class again.

Instead he went to parties.

Embassy staff who had wives and children were happy to go home in the evenings and watch American movies on videotape, so the single men got to go to all the less important receptions. Tonight Cam was heading to the Egyptian embassy for a gathering to welcome a new deputy ambassador.

When he started the Polski, the radio came on. He kept it tuned to the SB wavelength. Reception was often weak, but sometimes he could hear the secret police talking as they tailed people around the city.

Sometimes they were tailing him. The cars changed but it was usually the same two men, a swarthy one he called Mario and a fat guy he thought of as Ollie. There seemed to be no pattern to the surveillance, so he just assumed he was more or less always being watched. That was probably what they wanted. Maybe they deliberately randomized their surveillance precisely in order to keep him permanently on edge.

But he, too, had been trained. Surveillance should never be avoided in an obvious way, he had learned, for that is a signal, to the other side, that you are up to something. Form regular habits, he had been told: go to Restaurant A every Monday, Bar B every Tuesday. Lull them into a false sense of security. But look for gaps in their watchfulness, times when their attention lapses. That will be when you can do something unobserved.

As he drove away from the U.S. embassy he saw a blue Skoda 105 tuck into the traffic two cars behind him.

The Skoda trailed him across the city. He saw Mario at the wheel and Ollie in the front passenger seat.

Cam parked in Alzacka Street and saw the blue Skoda pull up a hundred yards past him.

He was sometimes tempted to talk to Mario and Ollie, as they were so much part of his life, but he had been warned never to do that, for then the SB would switch personnel and it would take him time to recognize the new people.

He entered the Egyptian embassy and took a cocktail

from a tray. It was so diluted he could hardly taste the gin. He talked to an Austrian diplomat about the difficulty of buying comfortable men's underwear in Warsaw. When the Austrian drifted away, Cam looked around and saw a blond woman in her twenties standing alone. She caught his eye and smiled, so he went to speak to her.

He swiftly found out that she was Polish, her name was Lidka, and she worked as a secretary in the Canadian embassy. She was wearing a tight pink sweater and a short black skirt that showed off her long legs. She spoke good English, and listened to Cam with an intensity of concentration that he found flattering.

Then a man in a pin-striped suit summoned her peremptorily, making Cam think he must be her boss, and the conversation broke up. Almost immediately Cam was approached by another attractive woman, and he began to think it was his lucky day. This one was older, about forty, but prettier, with short pale blond hair and bright blue eyes enhanced by blue eye shadow. She spoke to him in Russian. "I've met you before," she said. "Your name is Cameron Dewar. I'm Tanya Dvorkin."

"I remember," he said, glad of the chance to show off his fluency in Russian. "You're a reporter for TASS."

"And you're a CIA agent."

He certainly would not have told her that, so she must have guessed. Routinely, he denied it. "Nothing so glamorous," he said. "Just a humble cultural attaché."

"Cultural?" she said. "Then you can help me. What kind of painter is Jan Matejko?"

"I'm not sure," he said. "Impressionist, I think. Why?"

"Art really not your thing?"

"I'm more a music person," he said, feeling cornered.

"You probably love Szpilman, the Polish violinist."

"Absolutely. Such technique with the bow!"

"What do you think of the poet Wislawa Szymborska?"

"I haven't read much of his work, sadly. Is this a test?"

"Yes, and you failed. Szymborska is a woman. Szpilman is a pianist, not a violinist. Matejko was a conventional painter of court scenes and battles, not an impressionist. And you're no cultural attaché."

Cam was mortified to have been found out so easily. What a hopeless undercover agent he was! He tried to brush it off with humor. "I might just be a very bad cultural attaché."

She lowered her voice. "If a Polish army officer wanted to talk to a representative of the USA, you could arrange it, I guess."

Suddenly the conversation had taken a serious turn. Cam felt nervous. This could be some kind of trap.

Or it could be a genuine approach—in which case, it might represent a great opportunity for him.

He answered cautiously. "I can arrange for anyone to talk to the American government, naturally."

"In secret?"

What the hell was this? "Yes."

"Good," she said, and walked away.

Cam got another drink. What had that been about? Was it real, or had she been mocking him?

The party was coming to an end. He wondered what to do with the rest of the evening. He thought of going to the bar in the Australian embassy, where he sometimes played darts with amiable spooks from Oz. Then he saw Lidka standing nearby, again on her own. She really was very sexy. He said to her: "Do you have plans for dinner?"

She looked puzzled. "You mean recipes?"

He smiled. She had not come across the phrase *plans for dinner.* He said: "I meant, would you like to have dinner with me?"

"Oh, yes," she said immediately. "Could we go to the Duck?"

"Of course." It was an expensive restaurant, though not if you were paying in American dollars. He looked at his watch. "Shall we leave now?"

Lidka surveyed the room. There was no sign of the man in the pin-striped suit. "I'm free," she said.

They headed for the exit. As they were passing through the door the Soviet journalist, Tanya, reappeared and spoke to Lidka in bad Polish. "You dropped this," she said, holding out a red scarf.

"It's not mine," said Lidka.

"I saw it fall from your hand."

Someone touched Cam's elbow. He turned away from the confused conversation and saw a tall, good-looking man of about forty dressed in the uniform of a colonel in the

People's Army of Poland. In fluent Russian the man said: "I want to talk to you."

Cam replied in the same language. "All right."

"I will find a safe place."

Cam could do nothing but say: "Okay."

"Tanya will tell you where and when."

"Fine."

The man turned away.

Cameron turned his attention back to Lidka. Tanya was saying: "My mistake, how silly." She walked quickly away. Clearly she had wanted to distract Lidka for the few moments the soldier was talking to Cam.

Lidka was puzzled. "That was a bit strange," she said as they left the building.

Cam was excited, but he pretended to be equally mystified. "Peculiar," he said.

Lidka persisted. "Who was that Polish officer who spoke to you?"

"No idea," Cam said. "My car's this way."

"Oh!" she said. "You have a car?"

"Yes."

"Nice," said Lidka, looking pleased.

⋅ ⋅ ⋅

A week later, Cam woke up in bed in Lidka's apartment.

It was more of a studio: one room with a bed, a TV, and a kitchen sink. She shared the shower and toilet down the hall with three other people.

For Cam, it was paradise.

He sat upright. She was standing at the counter making coffee—with his beans: she could not afford real coffee. She was naked. She turned and walked to the bed, carrying a cup. She had wiry brown pubic hair and small pointed breasts with mulberry dark nipples.

At first he had been embarrassed about her walking around naked, because it made him want to stare, which was rude. When he confessed this she had said: "Look all you want, I like it." He still felt bashful, but not as much as before.

He had seen Lidka every night for a week.

He had had sex with her seven times, which was more than in his entire life up to that point, not counting hand jobs in massage parlors.

One day she had asked if he wanted to do it again in the morning.

He had said: "What are you, a sex maniac?"

She had been offended, but they had made it up.

While she brushed her hair, he sipped his coffee and thought about the day ahead. He had not yet heard from Tanya Dvorkin. He had reported the exchanges at the Egyptian embassy to his boss, Keith Dorset, and they had agreed there was nothing to do but wait and see.

He had a bigger issue on his mind. He knew the expression *honey trap*. Only a fool would fail to wonder whether Lidka had an ulterior motive in going to bed with him. He had to consider the possibility that she was working under orders from the SB. He sighed and said: "I have to tell my boss about you."

"Do you?" She did not seem alarmed. "Why?"

"American diplomats are supposed to date only nationals of NATO countries. We call it the 'fuck NATO rule.' They don't want us falling in love with Communists." He had not told her that he was a spy rather than a diplomat.

She sat on the bed beside him with a sad face. "Are you breaking up with me?"

"No, no!" The idea almost panicked him. "But I have to tell them, and they will check you out."

Now she looked worried. "What does that mean?"

"They'll investigate whether you could be an agent of the Polish secret police, or something."

She shrugged. "Oh, well, that's all right. They'll soon find out I'm nothing of the kind."

She seemed relaxed about it. "I'm sorry, but it has to be done," Cam said. "One-night stands don't matter, but we're obliged to report if it gets to be more than that, you know, a real loving relationship."

"Okay."

"We do have that, don't we?" Cam said nervously. "A real loving relationship?"

Lidka smiled. "Oh, yes," she said. "We do."

CHAPTER FIFTY-THREE

The Franck family traveled to Hungary in two Trabant cars. They were going on holiday. Hungary was a popular summer destination for East Germans who could afford the petrol.

As far as they could tell, they were not followed.

They had booked their holiday through the tourist office of the East German government. They had half-expected to be refused visas, even though Hungary was a Soviet bloc country; but they had been pleasantly surprised. Hans Hoffmann had missed an opportunity to persecute them: perhaps he was busy.

They needed two cars because they were taking Karolin and her family. Werner and Carla were madly fond of their granddaughter, Alice, now sixteen. Lili loved Karolin, but not Karolin's husband, Odo. He was a good man, and he had got Lili her present job, as administrator of a church orphanage; but there was something forced about his affection for Karolin and Alice, as if loving them was a good deed. Lili thought a man's love should be a helpless passion, not a moral duty.

Karolin felt the same. She and Lili were close enough to share secrets, and Karolin had confessed that her marriage had been a mistake. She was not miserable with Odo, but nor was she in love with him. He was kind and gentle, but not sexy: they made love about once a month.

So the holiday group was six people. Werner, Carla, and

Lili took the bronze car and Karolin, Odo, and Alice went in the white one.

It was a long drive, especially in a Trabi with a 600 cc two-stroke engine: six hundred miles all across Czechoslovakia. The first day took them to Prague, where they stayed overnight. When they left their hotel, on the morning of the second day, Werner said: "I'm pretty sure no one is following us. We seem to have got away with it."

They drove to Lake Balaton, fifty miles long, the largest lake in Central Europe. It was tantalizingly close to Austria, a free country. However, the entire border was fortified by one hundred fifty miles of electric fence, to prevent people escaping from the workers' paradise.

They pitched two tents side by side at a campsite on the southern shore.

They had a secret purpose: they were going to meet Rebecca.

It was Rebecca's idea. She had spent a year of her life looking after Walli, and he had succeeded in giving up drugs. He now had his own apartment near Rebecca's in Hamburg. In order to care for him, she had turned down a chance to stand for the Bundestag, the national parliament; but when he got well the offer had been renewed. Now she was an elected member, specializing in foreign policy. She had traveled to Hungary on an official trip, and seen that Hungary was deliberately attracting Western holidaymakers: tourism and cheap Riesling were the country's only means of earning foreign currency and reducing its massive trade deficit. The Westerners went to special, segregated holiday camps, but outside the camps there was nothing to stop fraternization.

So there was no law against what the Francks were doing. Their trip was permitted, and so was Rebecca's. Like them, she was coming to Hungary for a budget holiday. They would rendezvous as if by accident.

But the law was merely cosmetic in Communist countries. The Francks knew there would be terrible trouble if the secret police found out what they were up to. So Rebecca had arranged everything clandestinely, through Enok Andersen, the Danish accountant who still frequently crossed the border from West Berlin to East to see Werner. Nothing had been written down and there were no phone calls. Their greatest fear was that Rebecca would somehow be arrested—or even just kidnapped by the Stasi—and taken to a prison in East Germany. It would be a diplomatic incident, but the Stasi might do it anyway.

Rebecca's husband, Bernd, was not coming. His condition had deteriorated and his kidneys were malfunctioning. He was working only part-time, and could not travel far.

Werner straightened up from hammering in a tent peg to say quietly to Lili: "Take a look around. They didn't follow us here, but maybe they felt they didn't need to, because they had sent people on ahead."

Lili strolled around the site as if exploring. The campers at Lake Balaton were cheerful and friendly. As an attractive young woman, Lili was greeted and offered coffee or beer and snacks. Most tents were occupied by families, but there were some groups of men and a few of girls. No doubt the singles would find one another over the next few days.

Lili was single. She liked sex and had had several love affairs—including one with a woman, which her family did not know about. She had the same maternal instincts as other women, she supposed, and she adored Walli's child, Alice. But Lili was put off by the idea of having children of her own by the dismal prospect of raising them in East Germany.

She had been refused a place at university, because of her family's politics, so she had trained as a nursery nurse. She would never have been promoted if the authorities had had their way, but Odo had helped her get a job with the church, where hiring was not controlled by the Communist Party.

However, her real work was music. Along with Karolin, she continued to sing and play guitar in small bars and youth clubs, often in church halls. Their songs protested against industrial pollution, destruction of ancient buildings and monuments, clearing of natural forests, and ugly architecture. The government hated them, and they had both been arrested and cautioned for spreading propaganda. However, the Communists could not actually be *in favor* of poisoning rivers with factory effluent, so they found it difficult to take drastic action against environmentalists, and in fact usually tried to co-opt them into the toothless official Society for Nature and Environmental Protection.

In the USA, Lili's father said, conservatives accused environment campaigners of being antibusiness. It was more difficult for Soviet bloc conservatives to accuse them of being anti-Communist. After all, the whole point of Communism was to make industry work for the people rather than for the bosses.

One night Lili and Karolin had sneaked into a recording studio and made an album. It was not officially released, but cassette tapes of it in unmarked boxes had sold by the thousand.

Lili made a circuit of the campsite, which was occupied almost exclusively by East Germans: the camp for Westerners was a mile away. As she was returning to her family she noticed, outside a tent close to theirs, two men of about her own age drinking beer. One had receding fair hair, the other was dark with a Beatle haircut fifteen years out of date. The fair one met her eye and looked quickly away, which aroused her suspicion: young men did not generally avoid her eye. These two did not offer her a drink or ask her to join them. "Oh, no," she muttered.

Stasi men were not hard to spot. They were brutal, not smart. It was a career for people who craved prestige and power but had little intelligence and no talents. Rebecca's first husband, Hans, was typical. He was little more than a nasty bully, but he had risen steadily and now seemed to be one of their top commanders, driving around in a limousine and living in a large villa surrounded by a high wall.

Lili was reluctant to call attention to herself, but she decided she needed to verify her suspicion, so she had to be brazen. "Hello, guys!" she said amiably.

Both men grunted a perfunctory greeting.

Lili was not going to let them off easily. "Are you here with your wives?" she said. They could hardly fail to recognize that as a come-on.

The fair one shook his head and the other just said: "No." They were not clever enough to pretend.

"Really?" This was almost confirmation enough, she thought. What were two single men doing at a holiday camp if not looking for girls? And they were too badly dressed to be homosexual. "Tell me," said Lili, forcing a bright tone, "where do you go for a good time in the evenings here? Is there anywhere to dance?"

"I don't know."

That was enough. If these two are on holiday, I'm Mrs. Brezhnev, she thought. She walked away.

This was a problem. How could the Francks meet Rebecca without the Stasi men finding out?

Lili returned to her family. Both tents were now up. "Bad news," she told her father. "Two Stasi men. One row south and three tents east of us."

"I was afraid of that," said Werner.

. . .

They were to meet Rebecca two days later at a restaurant she had visited on her first trip. But before going there the Francks would have to shake off the secret police. Lili was worried, but her parents seemed unreasonably calm.

On the first day, Werner and Carla left early in the bronze Trabi, saying they were going to reconnoiter. The Stasi men followed them in a green Skoda. Werner and Carla were out all day and returned looking confident.

Next morning, Werner told Lili he was taking her for a hike. They stood outside the tent with rucksacks, helping each other adjust them. They put on stout boots and wide-brimmed hats. It was clear to anyone who looked that they were setting out for a long walk.

At the same time, Carla prepared to depart with shopping bags, making a list and saying loudly: "Ham, cheese, bread . . . anything else?"

Lili worried that they were being too obvious.

They were watched by the secret policemen, who were sitting outside their tent, smoking.

They set off in opposite directions, Carla heading for the car park, Lili and Werner for the beach. The Stasi agent with the Beatle haircut went after Carla, and the fair one followed Werner and Lili.

"So far, so good," said Werner. "We've split them."

When Lili and Werner got to the lake Werner turned west, following the shoreline. He had obviously scouted this the day before. The ground was intermittently rough. The fair-haired Stasi agent followed them at a distance, not without difficulty: he was not dressed for hiking. Sometimes they paused, pretending they needed a rest, to let him catch up.

They walked for two hours, then came to a long, deserted

beach. Partway along, a rough track emerged from the trees to dead-end at the high-tide mark.

Parked there was the bronze Trabant with Carla at the wheel.

There was no one else in sight.

Werner and Lili got into the car and Carla drove off, leaving the Stasi man stranded.

Lili resisted the temptation to wave good-bye.

Werner said to Carla: "You shook off the other guy."

"Yes," said Carla. "I created a diversion outside the grocery store by setting fire to a rubbish bin."

Werner grinned. "A trick you learned from me many years ago."

"Absolutely. Naturally he got out of his car and went to see what was happening."

"And then . . ."

"While he was distracted, I put a nail in his tire. Left him changing the wheel."

"Nice."

Lili said: "You two did this stuff in the war, didn't you?"

There was a pause. They never spoke much about the war. Eventually Carla said: "Yes, we did a little bit, nothing worth boasting about."

That was all they ever said.

They drove to a village and slowed down at a small house with a sign in English saying BAR. A man standing outside directed them to park in a field at the back, out of sight.

They went inside to a small bar too charming to be a government enterprise. Right away Lili saw her sister, Rebecca, and threw her arms around her. They had not been together for eighteen years. Lili tried to look at Rebecca's face but could not see for tears. Carla and Werner hugged Rebecca in turn.

When at last Lili's vision cleared she saw that Rebecca looked middle-aged, which was no surprise: she would be fifty next birthday. She was heavier than Lili remembered.

But the most striking thing was how smart she looked. She wore a blue summer dress with a pattern of small dots, and a matching jacket. Around her neck was a silver chain with a single large pearl, and she had a chunky silver bracelet on her arm. Her smart sandals had a cork heel. Slung over her shoulder was a navy blue leather bag. Politics was not notably well paid, as far as Lili knew. Could it be that *everyone* in West Germany was this well dressed?

Rebecca led them through the bar to a private room at the back where a long table was already laid with cold meat platters, bowls of salad, and bottles of wine. Standing by the table was a thin, handsome, wasted-looking man in a white T-shirt and skinny black jeans. He might have been in his forties, or perhaps younger if he had suffered an illness. Lili assumed he must be an employee of the bar.

Carla gasped, and Werner said, "Oh, my God."

Lili saw that the thin man was gazing expectantly at her. She suddenly noticed his almond-shaped eyes and realized that she was looking at her brother, Walli. She let out a small scream of shock: he looked so old!

Carla embraced Walli, saying: "My little boy! My poor little boy!"

Lili hugged and kissed him, crying all over again. "You look so different," she sobbed. "What happened to you?"

"Rock and roll," he replied with a laugh. "But I'm getting over it." He looked at his older sister. "Rebecca sacrificed a year of her life—and a great career opportunity—to save me."

"Of course I did," said Rebecca. "I'm your sister."

Lili felt sure Rebecca had not hesitated. For her, nothing came before family. Lili had a theory that it was because she was adopted that she felt so strongly.

Werner held Walli in his arms a long time. "We didn't know," he said, his voice thick with emotion. "We didn't know you were coming."

Rebecca said: "I decided to keep it a complete secret."

Carla said: "Isn't it dangerous?"

"It certainly is," said Rebecca. "But Walli wanted to take the risk."

Then Karolin walked in with her family. Like the others, she took a few moments to recognize Walli, then she gave a cry of shock.

"Hello, Karolin," he said. He took her hands and kissed her on both cheeks. "It's so good to see you again."

Odo said: "I'm Odo, Karolin's husband. I'm very glad to meet you at last."

Something flashed across Walli's face. It was gone in a split second, but Lili knew that Walli had seen and understood something about Odo that had shocked him, and had then covered up his shock instantly. The two men shook hands amiably.

Karolin said: "And this is Alice."

"Alice?" said Walli. He looked dazedly at the tall sixteen-year-old girl with long fair hair draping her face like curtains. "I wrote a song about you," he said. "When you were little."

"I know," she said, and kissed his cheek.

Odo said: "Alice knows her history. We told her everything, as soon as she was old enough to understand."

Lili wondered whether Walli heard the note of righteousness in Odo's voice. Or was she being oversensitive?

Walli said to Alice: "I love you, but Odo raised you. I'll never forget that, and I'm sure you won't either."

For a minute he choked up. Then he regained control and said: "Everybody, let's sit down and eat. This is a happy day." Lili realized that Walli had probably paid for everything.

They all sat around the table. For a few moments they were like strangers, feeling awkward, trying to think of something to say. Then several people spoke at once, all asking Walli questions. Everyone laughed. "One at a time!" Walli said, and they all relaxed.

Walli told them he had a penthouse in Hamburg. He was not married, though he had a girlfriend. About every eighteen months or two years he went to California, moved into Dave Williams's farmhouse for four months, and made a new album with Plum Nellie. "I'm an addict," he said. "But I've been clean for seven years, eight come September. When I do a gig with the band, I have a guard outside my dressing room to search people for drugs." He shrugged. "It seems extreme, I know, but there it is."

Walli had questions, too, especially for Alice. While she was answering them, Lili looked around the table. This was her family: her parents, her sister, her brother, her niece, and her oldest friend and singing partner. How lucky she was to have them all together in the same room, eating and talking and drinking wine.

The thought occurred to her that some families did this every week, and took it for granted.

Karolin was sitting next to Walli, and Lili watched them

together. They were having a good time. They still made one another laugh, she noticed. If things had been different—if the Berlin Wall had fallen—might their romance have been rekindled? They were still young: Walli was thirty-three, Karolin thirty-five. Lili pushed the thought away: it was an idle speculation, a foolish fantasy.

Walli retold the story of his escape from Berlin for Alice's benefit. When he got to the part where he sat all night waiting for Karolin, who did not show up, she interrupted him. "I was frightened," she said. "Frightened for myself, and for the baby inside me."

"I don't blame you," Walli said. "You did nothing wrong. I did nothing wrong. The only wrong was the Wall."

He described how he had driven through the checkpoint, busting the barrier. "I'll never forget that man I killed," he said.

Carla said: "It wasn't your fault—he was shooting at you!"

"I know," Walli said, and Lili knew from his tone of voice that at last he was at peace about this. "I feel sorry, but I don't feel guilty. I wasn't wrong to escape; he wasn't wrong to shoot at me."

"Like you said," Lili put in, "the only wrong is the Wall."

CHAPTER FIFTY-FOUR

Cam Dewar's boss, Keith Dorset, was a podgy man with sandy hair. Like a lot of CIA men, he dressed badly. Today he wore a brown tweed jacket, gray flannel trousers, a white shirt with brown pencil stripes, and a dull green tie. Seeing him walking down the street, the eye would slide over him while the brain dismissed him as a person of no account. Perhaps this was the effect he sought, Cameron thought. Or perhaps he just had bad taste.

"About your girlfriend, Lidka," Keith said, sitting behind a large desk in the American embassy.

Cam was pretty sure Lidka was free of any sinister associations, but he looked forward to having this confirmed.

Keith said: "Your request is denied."

Cam was astonished. "What are you talking about?"

"Your request is denied. Which of those four words are you having trouble understanding?"

CIA men sometimes behaved as if they were in the army, and able to bark orders at everyone below them in rank. But Cam was not that easily intimidated. He had worked at the White House. "Denied for what reason?" he said.

"I don't have to give reasons."

At the age of thirty-four, Cam had his first real girlfriend. After twenty years of rejection he was sleeping with a woman who seemed to want nothing but to make him happy. Panic at the prospect of losing her made him fool-hardy. "You don't *have* to be an asshole, either," he snapped.

"Don't you dare speak to me like that. One more smart-ass remark and you're on a plane home."

Cam did not want to be sent home. He backed off. "I apologize. But I'd still like to know the reasons for your denial, if I may."

"You have what we call 'close and continuing contact' with her, don't you?"

"Of course. I told you that myself. Why is it a problem?"

"Statistics. Most of the traitors we catch spying against the United States turn out to have relatives or close friends who are foreigners."

Cam had suspected something like this. "I'm not willing to give her up for statistical reasons. Do you have anything specific against her?"

"What makes you think you have the right to cross-examine me?"

"I'll take that as a no."

"I warned you about wisecracks."

They were interrupted by another agent, Tony Savino, who approached with a sheet of paper in his hand. "I'm just looking at the acceptance list for this morning's press conference," he said. "Tanya Dvorkin is coming for TASS." He looked at Cam. "She's the woman who spoke to you at the Egyptian embassy, isn't she?"

"She sure is," Cam said.

Keith said: "What's the subject of the press conference?"

"The launch of a new, streamlined protocol for Polish and American museums to loan each other works of art, it says here." Tony looked up from the paper. "Not the kind of thing to attract TASS's star writer, is it?"

Cam said: "She must be coming to see me."

.   .   .

Tanya spotted Cam Dewar as soon as she walked into the briefing room at the American embassy. A tall, thin figure, he was standing at the back like a lamppost. If he had not been here, she would have sought him out after the press conference, but this was better, less noticeable.

However, she did not want to look too purposeful when she approached him, so she decided to listen to the announcement first. She sat next to a Polish journalist whom she liked: Danuta Gorski, a feisty brunette with a big toothy grin. Danuta was a member of a semi-underground movement called the Defense Committee that produced pamphlets about workers' grievances and human rights violations. These illegal publications were called *bibula*. Danuta lived in the same building as Tanya.

While the American press officer was reading out the announcement he had already given them in printed form, Danuta murmured to Tanya: "You might want to take a trip to Gdańsk."

"Why?"

"There's going to be a strike at the Lenin Shipyard."

"There are strikes everywhere." Workers were demanding pay rises to compensate for a massive government increase in food prices. Tanya reported these as "work stoppages," for strikes happened only in capitalist countries.

"Believe me," said Danuta, "this one could be different."

The Polish government was dealing with each strike swiftly, granting pay rises and other concessions on a local basis, keen to shut down protests before they could spread like stains on a cloth. The nightmare of the ruling elite—and the dream of dissidents—was that the stains would join up until the cloth was entirely a new color.

"Different how?"

"They fired a crane operator who is a member of our committee—but they picked the wrong person to victimize. Anna Walentynowicz is a woman, a widow, and fifty-one years old."

"So she attracts a lot of sympathy from chivalrous Polish men."

"And she's a popular figure. They call her Pani Ania, Mrs. Annie."

"I might take a look." Dimka wanted to hear about any protest that promised to become serious, in case he might need to discourage a Kremlin crackdown.

As the press conference was breaking up, Tanya passed Cam Dewar and spoke to him quietly in Russian. "Go to the Cathedral of St. John on Friday at two and look at the Baryczkowski Crucifix."

"That's not a good place," the young man hissed.

"Take it or leave it," Tanya said.

"You have to tell me what this is about," Cam said firmly.

Tanya realized she had to risk talking to him for another

minute. "A line of communication in case the Soviet Union should invade Western Europe," she said. "The possibility of forming a group of Polish officers who would switch sides."

The American's jaw dropped. "Oh . . . Oh . . . ," he stuttered. "Right, yes."

She smiled at him. "Satisfied?"

"What's his name?"

Tanya hesitated.

Cam said: "He knows mine."

Tanya decided she had to trust this man. She had already placed her own life in his hands. "Stanislaw Pawlak," she said. "Known as Staz."

"Tell Staz that for security reasons he should never speak to anyone here at the embassy except me."

"Okay." Tanya walked quickly out of the building.

She gave Staz the message that evening. Next day she kissed him good-bye and drove two hundred miles north to the Baltic Sea. She had an old but reliable Mercedes-Benz 280S with vertically aligned twin headlamps. In the late afternoon she checked into a hotel in the old town of Gdańsk, directly across the river from the wharves and dry docks of the shipyard, which was on Ostrow Island.

On the following day it was one week exactly since the firing of Anna Walentynowicz.

Tanya got up early, put on canvas overalls, crossed the bridge to the island, reached the shipyard gate before sunrise, and strolled in with a group of young workers.

It was her lucky day.

The shipyard was plastered with newly pasted posters calling for Pani Ania to be given her job back. Small groups were gathering around the posters. A few people were handing out leaflets. Tanya took one and deciphered the Polish.

Anna Walentynowicz became an embarrassment because her example motivated others. She became an embarrassment because she stood up for others and was able to organize her coworkers. The authorities always try to isolate those who have leadership qualities. If we do not fight against this, then we will have no one to stand up for us when they raise work quotas, when health and safety reg-

ulations are broken, or when we are forced to work over-time.

Tanya was struck by that. This was not about more pay or shorter hours: it was about the right of Polish workers to organize for themselves, independently of the Communist hierarchy. She had a feeling this was a significant development. It started a small glow of hope in her belly.

She walked around the yard as the daylight strengthened. The sheer scale of shipbuilding was awesome: the thousands of workers, the kilotons of steel, the millions of rivets. The high sides of half-built ships rose far above her head, their mountainous weight perilously balanced by spiderweb scaffolding. Immense cranes bowed their heads over each ship, like adoring Magi around a giant manger.

Everywhere she went, workers were downing tools to read the leaflet and discuss the case.

A few men started a march, and Tanya followed them. They went in procession around the yard, carrying makeshift placards, handing out leaflets, calling on others to join them, growing in numbers. Eventually they came to the main gate, where they began telling arriving workers that they were on strike.

They closed the factory gate, sounded the siren, and flew the Polish national flag from the nearest building.

Then they elected a strike committee.

While that was going on they were interrupted. A man in a suit clambered up on an excavator and began to shout at the crowd. Tanya could not understand everything he said, but he seemed to be arguing against the formation of a strike committee—and the workers were listening to him. Tanya asked the nearest man who he was. "Klemens Gniech, the director of the shipyard," she was told. "Not a bad guy."

Tanya was aghast. How weak people were!

Gniech was offering negotiations if the strikers would first go back to work. To Tanya this seemed a transparent trick. Many people booed and jeered Gniech, but others nodded agreement, and a few drifted away, apparently headed for their workplaces. Surely it could not fall apart so fast?

Then someone jumped up on the excavator and tapped the director on the shoulder. The newcomer was a small, square-shouldered man with a bushy mustache. Although he seemed to Tanya an unimpressive figure, the crowd recognized him and cheered. They evidently knew who he was. "Remember me?" he yelled at the director in a voice loud enough for everyone to hear. "I worked here for ten years— then you fired me!"

"Who's that?" Tanya asked her neighbor.

"Lech Wałęsa. He's only an electrician, but everyone knows him."

The director tried to argue with Wałęsa in front of the crowd, but the little man with the big mustache gave him no leeway. "I declare an occupation strike!" he roared, and the crowd shouted their agreement.

Both the director and Wałęsa stepped down from the excavator. Wałęsa took command, something everyone seemed to accept without question. When he ordered the director's chauffeur to drive in his limousine and fetch Anna Walentynowicz, the chauffeur did as he was told and, even more astonishing, the director made no objection.

Wałęsa organized the election of a strike committee. The limousine returned with Anna, who was greeted by a storm of applause. She was a small woman with hair as short as a man's. She had round glasses and wore a blouse with bold horizontal stripes.

The strike committee and the director went in the Health and Safety Center to negotiate. Tanya was tempted to try to insinuate herself in there with them, but she decided not to push her luck: she was fortunate to have got inside the gates. The workers were welcoming the Western media, but Tanya's press card showed that she was a Soviet reporter for TASS, and if the strikers discovered that they would throw her out.

However, the negotiators must have had microphones on their tables, for their entire discussion was broadcast over loudspeakers to the crowd outside—which struck Tanya as democratic in the extreme. The strikers could instantly express their feelings about what was said by booing or cheering.

She figured out that the strikers now had several demands in addition to the reinstatement of Anna, including security from reprisals. The one that the director could not accept, surprisingly, was for a monument outside the factory gates to commemorate the massacre by police of shipyard workers protesting against food price rises in 1970.

Tanya wondered whether this strike would also end in a massacre. If it did, she realized with a chill, she was right in the firing line.

Gniech explained that the area in front of the gates had been designated for a hospital.

The strikers said they preferred a monument.

The director offered a commemorative plaque somewhere else in the shipyard.

They declined.

A worker said disgustedly into the microphone: "We're haggling over dead heroes like beggars under a lamppost!"

The people outside applauded.

Another negotiator appealed directly to the crowd: Did they want a monument?

They roared their answer.

The director retired to consult with his superiors.

There were now thousands of supporters outside the gates. People had been collecting donations of food for the strikers. Few Polish families could afford to give food away, but dozens of sacks of provisions were now passed through the gates for the men and women inside, and the strikers ate lunch.

The director came back in the afternoon and announced that the highest authorities had approved the monument in principle.

Wałęsa declared that the strike would go on until all the demands had been met.

And then, almost as an afterthought, he added that the strikers also wanted to discuss the formation of free independent trade unions.

Now, Tanya thought, this is getting *really* interesting.

. . .

On Friday after lunch Cam Dewar drove to the Old Town of Warsaw.

He was followed there by Mario and Ollie.

Most of Warsaw had been flattened in the war. The town had been reconstructed with straight roads and sidewalks and modern buildings. Such a cityscape was not suitable for clandestine meetings and furtive exchanges. However, the planners had striven to re-create the original Old Town with its cobbled streets and little alleys and irregular houses. It was done a little too well: the straight edges and regular patterns and fresh colors looked too new, like a movie set. Nevertheless, it provided a more congenial environment for secret agents than did the rest of the city.

Cam parked and walked to a high town house. There on the first floor was the Warsaw equivalent of Silken Hands. Cam had been a regular customer until he met Lidka.

In the main room of the apartment, the girls were sitting around in lingerie, watching television and smoking. A voluptuous blonde stood up immediately, letting her robe fall open briefly to give him a glimpse of plump thighs and lacy underwear. "Hello, Crystek, we haven't seen you for a couple of weeks!"

"Hi, Pela." Cam went to the window and looked down at the street. As usual, Mario and Ollie were sitting outside the bar opposite, drinking beer and watching the girls in summer dresses go by. They would expect him to remain inside for at least half an hour, maybe an hour.

So far, so good.

Pela said: "What's the matter, is your wife following you?" The other girls laughed.

Cam took out his money and gave Pela the usual fee for a hand job. "I need a favor today," he said. "Do you mind if I slip out the back door?"

"Is your wife going to come up here and make a fuss?"

"It's not my wife," he said. "It's my girlfriend's husband. If he makes trouble, offer him a free blow job. I'll pay."

Pela shrugged.

Cam went down the back stairs and out through the yard, feeling good. He had shaken off his followers—and they did not realize it. He would be back in under an hour, and he would go out by the front door. They would never know he had left the apartment.

He hurried across Old Town Market Square and along a street called Swietojanska to the Cathedral of St. John, a church devastated in the war and rebuilt since. The SB were no longer following him—but they might be following Stanislaw Pawlak.

The CIA station in Warsaw had held a long meeting to decide how to handle this contact. Every step had been planned.

Outside the church, Cam saw his boss, Keith Dorset. Today he had on a boxy gray suit from a Polish store, something he wore only for surveillance jobs. There was a cap stuffed into his jacket pocket. That was the all clear. If he had been wearing the hat, it would have meant that the SB were inside the church and the rendezvous should be aborted.

Cam entered by the Gothic main door in the west front. The awesome architecture and the atmosphere of sanctity amplified his feeling of portent. He was about to make contact with an enemy informant. It was a crucial moment.

If this went well, he would be firmly set on his career as a CIA agent. If not, he would be back behind a desk in Langley in no time.

Cam was pretending that Staz would not meet anyone but him. The purpose of this lie was to make it difficult for Keith to send Cam home. Keith was making trouble about Lidka, even though investigation had revealed that she had no connection with the SB and was not even a member of the Communist Party. However, if Cam could succeed in recruiting a Polish colonel as a spy for the CIA, such a triumph would put him in a strong position to defy Keith.

He looked around, scanning for secret policemen, but all he saw were tourists, worshippers, and priests.

He walked up the north aisle until he came to the chapel containing the famous sixteenth-century crucifix. The handsome Polish officer was standing in front of it, staring at the expression on the face of Christ. Cam stood beside him. They were alone.

Cam spoke in Russian. "This is the last time we'll talk."

Stanislaw replied in the same language. "Why?"

"Too dangerous."

"For you?"

"No, for you."

"How will we communicate? Through Tanya?"

"No. In fact, from now on please don't tell her anything about your relationship with me. Cut her out of the loop. You can still sleep with her, if that's what you're doing."

"Thank you," Stanislaw said ironically.

Cam ignored that. "What kind of car do you drive?"

"A green 1975 Saab 99." He recited the license plate number.

Cameron memorized it. "Where do you keep the car at night?"

"On Jana Olbrachta Street, near the apartment block where I live."

"When you park it, leave the window open a crack. We will slip an envelope through."

"Dangerous. What if someone else reads the note?"

"Don't worry. The envelope will contain a typed advertisement from someone who offers to wash your car at a low price. But when you pass a warm iron over the paper, a message will be revealed. It will tell you when and where to meet us. If you're not able to make the rendezvous, for any reason, it doesn't matter: we'll just send you another envelope."

"What will happen at these meetings?"

"I'll get to that." Cam had a list of things to say, agreed on by his colleagues at the planning meeting, and he needed to get through them as fast as possible. "About your group of friends."

"Yes?"

"Don't form a conspiracy."

"Why not?"

"You'll be found out. Conspirators always are. You have to wait until the last minute."

"So what can we do?"

"Two things. One, get ready. Make a list in your head of people you trust. Decide exactly how each one will turn against the Soviets if war breaks out. Make yourself known to dissident leaders such as Lech Wałęsa, but give them no hint of what you're up to. Reconnoiter the television station and plan how you'll take it over. But keep everything in your head."

"And the second thing?"

"Give us information." Cam tried not to show how tense he felt. This was the big ask, the one Stanislaw might refuse. "The order of battle of Soviet and other Warsaw Pact armies: numbers of men, tanks, aircraft—"

"I know what is meant by *order of battle.*"

"And their war plans in the event of a crisis."

There was a long pause, then at last Stanislaw said: "I can get those."

"Good," Cam said with feeling.

"And what do I get in return?"

"I'm going to give you a phone number and a code word. You must use it only in the event of a Soviet invasion of Western Europe. When you call the number you will be answered by a senior commander in the Pentagon who speaks Polish. He will treat you as the representative of the Polish resistance to the Soviet invasion. You will be, for all practical purposes, the leader of free Poland."

Stanislaw nodded thoughtfully, but Cam could tell he was attracted by the offer. After a few moments he said: "If I agree to this, I will be placing my life in your hands."

"You already have," said Cam.

. . .

The Gdańsk Shipyard strikers were careful to keep the international media fully briefed on their activities. Ironically, this was the best way to communicate with the Polish people. The Polish media were censored, but Western newspaper reports were picked up by the American-funded Radio Free Europe and broadcast right back into Poland. It was the main way Poles learned the truth about what was happening in their country.

Lili Franck followed events in Poland on the West German television news, which everyone in East Berlin could watch if they angled their aerials the right way.

The strike spread, to Lili's delight, despite all the government's efforts. The Gdynia shipyard came out, and public transport workers struck in sympathy. They formed the Interfactory Strike Committee (MKS), with its headquarters in the Lenin Shipyard. Its number one demand was the right to form free trade unions.

Like many others in East Germany, the Franck family discussed all this avidly, sitting in the upstairs drawing room of the town house in Berlin-Mitte, in front of their Franck television set. A rent was showing in the Iron Curtain, and they speculated eagerly about what it might lead to. If Poles could rebel, perhaps Germans could too.

The Polish government tried to negotiate factory by factory, offering generous raises to strikers who split from MKS and settled. The tactic failed.

Within a week, three hundred striking enterprises had joined the MKS.

The tottering Polish economy could not stand many days of this. The government at last accepted reality. The deputy prime minister was sent to Gdańsk.

A week later a deal was agreed on. The strikers were given the right to form free trade unions. It was a triumph that astonished the world.

If the Poles could win freedom, would the Germans be next?

. . .

Keith said to Cam: "You're still seeing that Polish girl."

Cam said nothing. Of course he was still seeing her. He was as happy as a kid in a candy store. Lidka was eager to have sex with him whenever he wanted it. Until now, few girls had wanted to have sex with him at all. "Do you like this?" she would say as she caressed him; and if he admitted he did, she would say: "But do you like it a little bit, do you like it a lot, or do you like it so much you want to die?"

Keith said: "I've told you that your request has been denied."

"But you haven't said why."

Keith looked angry. "I've made a decision."

"But is it the right decision?"

"Are you challenging my authority?"

"No, you're challenging my girlfriend."

Keith became angrier. "You think you have me over a barrel because Stanislaw won't speak to anyone else."

That was exactly what Cam thought, but he denied it. "It has nothing to do with Staz. I'm not willing to give her up for no reason."

"I may have to fire you."

"I still won't give her up. In fact—" Cam hesitated. The words that came into his mind were not what he had planned. But he said them anyway. "In fact, I'm hoping to marry her."

Keith changed his tone. "Cam," he said, "she may not be an agent of the SB, but she could still have an ulterior motive for sleeping with you."

Cam bristled. "If it's nothing to do with intelligence, it's nothing to do with you."

Keith persisted, speaking gently, as if trying not to hurt Cam's feelings. "A lot of Polish girls would like to go to America, you know that."

Cam did know that. The thought had occurred to him long ago. He felt embarrassed and humiliated that Keith should say it. He kept his face wooden. "I know," he said.

"Forgive me for saying it, but she could be deceiving you for that reason," Keith said. "Have you considered that possibility?"

"Yes, I've considered it," said Cam. "And I don't care."

. . .

In Moscow, the big question was whether to invade Poland.

The day before the Politburo debate, Dimka and Natalya clashed with Yevgeny Filipov at a preparatory meeting in the Nina Onilova Room. Filipov said: "Our Polish comrades require military assistance urgently, to resist the attacks of traitors in the employ of the capitalist-imperialist powers."

Natalya said: "You want an invasion, as in Czechoslovakia in 1968 and Hungary in 1956."

Filipov did not deny it. "The Soviet Union has the right to invade any country when the interests of Communism are under threat. That's the Brezhnev Doctrine."

Dimka said: "I'm against military action."

"There's a surprise," said Filipov sarcastically.

Dimka ignored that. "In both Hungary and Czechoslovakia, the counterrevolution was led by revisionist elements within the Communist Party ruling cadres," he said. "It was therefore possible to remove them, like chopping the head off a chicken. They had little popular support."

"Why should this crisis be different?"

"Because in Poland the counterrevolutionaries are working-class leaders with working-class backing. Lech Wałęsa is an electrician. Anna Walentynowicz is a crane driver. And hundreds of factories are on strike. We're dealing with a mass movement."

"We have to crush it all the same. Are you seriously suggesting that we abandon Polish Communism?"

"There's another problem," Natalya put in. "Money. Back in 1968 the Soviet bloc did not owe billions of dollars in foreign debt. Today we are totally dependent on loans from the West. You heard what President Carter said in Warsaw. Credit from the West is linked to human rights."

"So . . . ?"

"If we send the tanks into Poland, they will withdraw our line of credit. So, Comrade Filipov, your invasion will ruin the economy of the entire Soviet bloc."

There was a silence in the room.

Dimka said: "Does anyone have any other suggestions?"

.   .   .

To Cam it seemed an omen that a Polish officer had turned against the Red Army at the same time as Polish workers were rejecting Communist tyranny. Both events were signs of the same change. As he headed for his rendezvous with Stanislaw, he felt he might be part of a historic earthquake.

He left the embassy and got into his car. As he hoped, Mario and Ollie followed him. It was important that they had him under surveillance while he met with Stanislaw. If the interaction went as planned, Mario and Ollie would faithfully report that nothing suspicious had taken place.

Cam hoped Stanislaw had received and understood his instructions.

Cam parked in Old Town Market Square. Carrying a copy of today's *Trybuna Ludu,* the official government newspaper, he strolled across the square. Mario got out of his car and walked after him. Half a minute later, Ollie followed at a distance.

Cam headed down a side street with the two secret policemen in train.

He went into a bar, sat near the window, and asked for a beer. He could see his shadows loitering nearby. He paid for his drink as soon as it came, so that he would be able to leave quickly.

He checked his watch frequently while he drank his beer.

At one minute to three he went out.

He had practised this maneuver over and over at Camp Peary, the CIA's training center near Williamsburg, Virginia. He had been able to do it perfectly there. But this would be the first time he did it for real.

He quickened his pace a little as he approached the end

of the block. Turning the corner, he glanced back and saw that Mario was about thirty yards behind.

Just around the corner was a shop selling cigarettes and tobacco. Stanislaw was exactly where Cam expected him to be, standing outside the shop, looking in the window. Cam had about thirty seconds before Mario turned the corner—plenty of time to execute a simple brush pass.

All he had to do was exchange the newspaper he was carrying for the one in Stanislaw's hand, which was identical except that—all being well—it should contain the photocopies Stanislaw had made of documents in his safe at army headquarters.

There was only one snag.

Stanislaw was not carrying a newspaper.

Instead he had a large buff-colored envelope.

He had not followed his instructions to the letter. Either he had misunderstood, or he had imagined that the exact details did not matter.

Whatever the reason, things had gone wrong.

Panic froze Cam's brain. His step faltered. He did not know what to do. He wanted to scream abuse at Staz.

Then he controlled himself. He forced himself to be calm. He made a split-second decision. He would not abort the exchange. He would go through with it.

He walked straight toward Stanislaw.

As they brushed past one another, they exchanged the newspaper for the envelope.

Immediately, Stanislaw walked into the shop, carrying the newspaper, and disappeared from sight.

Cam walked on, carrying the envelope, which was an inch thick with the documents inside.

At the next corner he again glanced back and got a glimpse of Mario. The secret policeman was about twenty yards behind, apparently relaxed and confident. He had no notion of what had just happened. He had not even seen Stanislaw.

Would he notice that Cam was no longer carrying a newspaper, but held an envelope instead? If he did, he might arrest Cam and confiscate the envelope. That would be the end of Cam's triumph—and the end of Stanislaw's life.

It was summer. Cam had no coat under which to conceal the envelope. Besides, hiding it could be worse: Mario might be *more* likely to notice if Cam was suddenly empty-handed.

He passed a street newsstand, but realized he could not stop and buy a newspaper within Mario's sight, for that would draw attention to the fact that he no longer had his original paper.

He realized he had made a foolish mistake. He had been so mesmerized by the brush-past routine that he had not thought of the simplest way out. He should have taken the envelope and *kept* the newspaper.

Too late now.

He felt trapped. It was so frustrating he wanted to scream. Everything had gone perfectly but for one small detail!

He could step into a store and buy another newspaper. He looked for a newsagent's shop. But this was Poland, not America, and there was not a store on every block.

He turned another corner and sighted a rubbish bin. Hallelujah! He quickened his pace and looked inside. His luck was out: there were no newspapers. He spotted a magazine with a colorful cover. He snatched it up and walked on. As he walked, he surreptitiously folded the magazine so that the cover was inside and a page of plain black-and-white print was on the outside. He wrinkled his nose: there had been something disgusting in the bin, and the smell clung to the magazine. He tried not to breathe deeply as he slid the envelope between the pages.

He felt better. He now looked almost the same as he had before.

He returned to his car and took out his keys. This perhaps would be the moment they stopped him. He imagined Mario saying: "Just a minute, let me see that envelope you're trying to hide." As quickly as he could, he unlocked the door.

He saw Mario a few paces away.

Cam got into his car and placed the magazine in the footwell on the passenger side.

Glancing up, he saw Mario and Ollie getting into their car. It looked like he had got away with it.

For a moment, he felt too weak to move.

Then he started his engine and drove back to the embassy.

·   ·   ·

Cam Dewar sat in Lidka's bedsitting room, waiting for her to come home.

She had a photograph of him on her dressing table. Cam found that so pleasing that it almost made him cry. No girl had ever wanted a photo of him, let alone framed it and kept it by her mirror.

The room expressed her personality. Her favorite color was bright pink, and that was the shade of the bedcovers and the tablecloth and the cushions. The closet held few clothes, but they all flattered her: short skirts, V-necked dresses, pretty costume jewelry, prints with small flowers and bows and butterflies. Her bookshelf held all of Jane Austen in English and Tolstoy's *Anna Karenina* in Polish. In a box under the bed, like a secret stash of pornography, she had a collection of American magazines about home decoration, full of photographs of sunlit kitchens painted in bright colors.

Today Lidka had begun the tedious process of being vetted by the CIA as a potential wife. This was much more thorough than the investigation of a mere girlfriend. She had to write her life story, undergo days of interrogation, and take an extended lie-detector test. All this had been going on somewhere else in the embassy while Cam did his normal day's work. He was not allowed to see her until she came home.

It was going to be difficult for Keith Dorset to fire Cam now. The information Staz was producing was solid gold.

Cam had given Staz a compact thirty-five-millimeter camera, a Zorki, which was a Soviet-made copy of a Leica, so that he could photograph documents in his office with the door shut instead of feeding them through the photocopying machine in the secretaries' bullpen. He could pass Cam hundreds of pages of documents in a handful of rolls of film.

The latest question the Warsaw CIA station had asked Staz was: What would trigger a westward attack by the Red Army's Second Strategic Echelon? The files he had provided in answer had been so comprehensive that Keith Dorset had received a rare written compliment from Langley.

And still Mario and Ollie had never seen Staz.

So Cam was confident that he would not be fired, and his marriage would not be forbidden, unless Lidka turned out to be an actual agent of the KGB.

Meanwhile, Poland was lurching toward freedom. Ten million people had joined the first free trade union, called Solidarity. That was one in every three Polish workers. Poland's biggest problem now was not the Soviet Union but money. The strikes, and the consequent paralysis of Communist Party leadership, had crippled an already weak economy. The result was a shortage of everything. The government rationed meat, butter, and flour. Workers who had won generous pay rises found they could not buy anything with their money. The black market exchange rate for the dollar more than doubled, from one hundred twenty zlotys to two hundred fifty. First Secretary Gierek was succeeded by Kania, who was then replaced by General Jaruzelski, which made no difference.

Tantalizingly, Lech Wałęsa and Solidarity hesitated on the brink of overthrowing Communism. A general strike was prepared, then called off at the last minute, on the advice of the Pope and the new American president, Ronald Reagan, both of whom feared bloodshed. Cam was disappointed by Reagan's timidity.

He got off the bed and laid the table with cutlery and plates. He had brought home two steaks. Naturally diplomats were not subject to the shortages that afflicted the Poles. They were paying in desperately needed dollars: they could have anything they wanted. Lidka was probably eating better than even the Communist Party elite.

Cam wondered whether to make love to her before or after eating the steaks. Sometimes it was good to savor the anticipation. Other times he was in too much of a hurry. Lidka never minded either way.

At last she arrived home. She kissed his cheek, put down her bag, took off her coat, and went along the hall to the bathroom.

When she came back he showed her the steaks. "Very nice," she said. Still she did not look at him.

"Something's wrong, isn't it?" Cam said. He had never known her to be ill-tempered. This was unique.

"I don't think I can be a CIA wife," she said.

Cam fought down panic. "Tell me what's happened."

"I'm not going back tomorrow. I won't put up with it."

"What's the problem?"

"I feel like a criminal."

"Why, what did they do?"

At last she looked directly at him. "Do you believe I'm just using you to get to America?"

"No, I don't!"

"Then why did they ask me that?"

"I don't know."

"Does the question have anything to do with national security?"

"Nothing at all."

"They accused me of lying."

"Did you lie?"

She shrugged. "I didn't tell them everything. I'm not a nun, I've had lovers. I left one or two out—but your horrible CIA knew! They must have gone to my old school!"

"I know you've had lovers, I have too." Though not many, Cam thought, but he did not say it. "I don't mind."

"They made me feel like a prostitute."

"I'm sorry. But it really doesn't matter what they think of us, so long as they give you a security clearance."

"They're going to tell you a lot of nasty stories about me. Things they've been told by people who hate me—girls who are jealous, and boys I wouldn't sleep with."

"I won't believe them."

"Do you promise?"

"I promise."

She sat on his lap. "I'm sorry I was grouchy."

"I forgive you."

"I love you, Cam."

"I love you, too."

"I feel better now."

"Good."

"Do you want me to make *you* feel better?"

This kind of talk made Cam's mouth dry. "Yes, please."

"Okay." She stood up. "You just lie back and relax, baby," she said.

.   .   .

Dave Williams flew to Warsaw with his wife, Beep, and their son, John Lee, for the marriage of his brother-in-law, Cam Dewar.

John Lee could not read, although he was an intelligent eight-year-old and went to a fine school. Dave and Beep had taken him to an educational psychologist, and had learned that the boy suffered from a common condition called dyslexia, or word-blindness. John Lee would learn to read, but he would need special help and he would have to work extra hard at it. Dyslexia ran in families and afflicted boys more than girls.

That was when Dave realized what his own problem was.

"I believed I was dumb, all through school," he told Beep that evening, in the pine kitchen of Daisy Farm, after they had put John Lee to bed. "The teachers said the same. My parents knew I wasn't dumb, so they assumed I must be lazy."

"You're not lazy," she said. "You're the hardest-working person I know."

"Something was wrong with me, but we didn't know what it was. Now we do."

"And we'll be able to make sure John Lee doesn't suffer the way you did."

Dave's lifelong struggle with writing and reading was explained. It had not oppressed him for many years, not since he had become a songwriter whose lyrics were on the lips of millions. All the same he felt enormously relieved. A mystery had been unraveled, a cruel disability accounted for. Most important of all, he knew how to make sure it did not afflict the next generation.

"And you know what else?" Beep had said, pouring a glass of Daisy Farm cabernet sauvignon.

"Yeah," said Dave. "He's probably mine."

Beep had never been sure whether Dave or Walli was the father of John Lee. As the boy grew and changed and looked more and more like Dave, neither of them had known whether the likenesses were inherited or acquired: hand gestures, turns of phrase, enthusiasms, all could have been learned by a boy who adored his daddy. But dyslexia could not be learned. "It's not conclusive," Beep said. "But it's strong evidence."

"And anyway, we don't care," said Dave.

However, they had vowed never to speak of this doubt to anyone else, including John Lee himself.

Cam's wedding took place at a modern Catholic church in the small town of Otwock, on the outskirts of Warsaw. Cam had embraced Catholicism. Dave had no doubt the conversion was entirely cynical.

The bride wore a white dress that her mother had got married in: Polish people had to recycle clothing.

Lidka was slim and attractive, Dave thought, with long legs and a nice bust, but there was something about her mouth that suggested ruthlessness to him. Perhaps he was being harsh: fifteen years as a rock star had made him cynical about girls. They went to bed with men to seek some advantage for themselves more often than most people thought, in his experience.

The three bridesmaids had made themselves short summery dresses in bright pink cotton.

The reception was held at the American embassy. Woody Dewar paid for it, but the embassy was able to secure plentiful supplies of food, and something other than vodka to drink.

Lidka's father told a joke, half in Polish and half in English. A man walks into a government-owned butcher's shop and asks for a pound of beef.

"*Nie ma*—we don't have any."

"Pork, then."

"*Nie ma.*"

"Veal?"

"*Nie ma.*"

"Chicken."

"*Nie ma.*"

The customer leaves. The butcher's wife says: "The guy is crazy."

"Of course," says the butcher. "But what a memory!"

The Americans looked awkward, but the Poles laughed heartily.

Dave had asked Cam not to tell anyone that his brother-in-law was in Plum Nellie, but the news had got out, as it usually did, and Dave was besieged by Lidka's friends. The bridesmaids made a big fuss of him, and it was clear that Dave could go to bed with any of them, or even—one hinted—with all three at the same time, if he was so inclined.

"You should meet my bass player," Dave said.

While Cam and Lidka were doing their first dance, Beep said quietly to Dave: "I know he's a creep, but he's my brother, and I can't help feeling pleased he's found someone at last."

Dave said: "Are you sure Lidka isn't a gold digger who just wants an American passport?"

"That's what my parents are afraid of. But Cam's thirty-four and single."

"I guess you're right," Dave said. "What has he got to lose?"

• • •

Tanya Dvorkin was full of fear when she attended Solidarity's first national convention in September 1981.

The proceedings began in the cathedral at Oliwa, a northern suburb of Gdańsk. Two sharp stiletto towers menacingly flanked a low baroque portal through which the delegates entered the church. Tanya sat with Danuta Gorski, her Warsaw neighbor, the journalist and Solidarity organizer. Like Tanya, Danuta wrote blandly orthodox reports for the official press while privately pursuing her own agenda.

The archbishop gave a don't-make-trouble sermon about peace and love of the fatherland. Although the Pope was gung ho, the Polish clergy was conflicted about Solidarity. They hated Communism, but they were natural authoritarians, hostile to democracy. Some priests were heroically brave in defying the regime, but what the church hierarchy wanted was to replace a godless tyranny with a Christian tyranny.

However, it was not the church that bothered Tanya, nor any of the other forces tending to divide the movement. Much more ominous were the threatening maneuvers by the Soviet navy in the Gulf of Gdańsk, together with "land exercises" by one hundred thousand Red Army troops on Poland's eastern border. According to the article by Danuta in today's *Trybuna Ludu,* this military muscle-flexing was a response to increased American aggression. No one was fooled. The Soviet Union wanted to tell everyone that it was poised to invade if Solidarity made the wrong noises.

After the service the nine hundred delegates moved in buses to the campus of the University of Gdańsk, where the convention was to be held in the massive Olivia Sports Hall.

All this was highly provocative. The Kremlin hated Solidarity. Nothing so dangerous had happened in a Soviet bloc country in more than a decade. Democratically elected delegates from all over Poland were gathering to hold debates and pass resolutions by voting, and the Communist Party had no control whatsoever. It was a national parliament in all but name. It would have been called revolutionary, if that word had not been besmirched by the Bolsheviks. No wonder the Soviets were frantic.

The sports hall was equipped with an electronic scoreboard. As Lech Wałęsa stood to speak, it lit up with a cross and the Latin slogan POLONIA SEMPER FIDELIS, "Poland ever faithful."

Tanya went outside to her car and turned on the radio. Programs were normal all across the dial. The Soviets had not invaded yet.

The rest of Saturday passed without major drama. It was not until Tuesday that Tanya began to feel scared again.

The government had published a draft bill on workers' self-government that gave employees the right to be consulted about management appointments. Tanya reflected wryly that President Reagan would never for one minute consider giving such rights to Americans. Even so, the bill was not radical enough for Solidarity, for it stopped short of giving the workforce the power to hire and fire; so they proposed a national referendum on the issue.

Lenin must have turned in his mausoleum.

Worse, they added a clause saying that if the government refused a referendum, the union would organize one itself.

Tanya again felt the needle of fear. The union was beginning to play the leadership role normally reserved for the Communist Party. The atheists were taking over the church. The Soviet Union would never accept this.

The resolution was passed with only one vote against, and the delegates stood and applauded themselves.

But that was not all.

Someone proposed sending a message to workers in Czechoslovakia, Hungary, East Germany, and "all the nations of the Soviet Union." Among other things, it said: "We support those among you who have decided on the difficult road of struggle for free trade unions." It was passed by a show of hands.

They had gone too far, Tanya felt sure.

The Soviets' worst fear was that the Polish crusade for freedom would spread to other Iron Curtain countries—

and the delegates were rashly encouraging just that! The invasion now seemed inevitable.

Next day the press was full of Soviet outrage. Solidarity was interfering in the internal affairs of sovereign states, they screeched.

But still they did not invade.

. . .

Soviet leader Leonid Brezhnev did not want to invade Poland. He could not afford to lose credit with Western banks. He had a different plan. Cam Dewar found out from Staz what it was.

It always took a few days to process the raw material that Staz produced. Picking up his rolls of film in a dangerous clandestine brush pass was only the beginning. The film had to be developed in the darkroom at the American embassy, and the documents printed and photocopied. Then a translator with a high-level security clearance sat down and converted the material from Polish and Russian to English. If there were a hundred or more pages—as was frequent— it took days. The result had to be typed up and photocopied, again. Then at last Cam could see what kind of fish he had netted.

As the Warsaw winter freeze set in, Cam pored over the latest batch and found a well-worked-out and detailed scheme for a clampdown by the Polish government. Martial law would be declared, all freedoms would be suspended, and all agreements made with Solidarity would be reversed.

It was only a contingency plan. But Cam was astonished to learn that Jaruzelski had war-gamed it within a week of taking office. Clearly he had had this in mind right from the start.

And Brezhnev was relentlessly pressing him to go ahead.

Jaruzelski had resisted the pressure earlier in the year. Then, Solidarity had been well positioned to fight back, with workers occupying factories all over the country and preparations well advanced for a general strike.

At that time, Solidarity had prevailed, and the Communists had appeared to yield. But now the workers were off guard.

They were also hungry, tired, and cold. Everything was

scarce, inflation was rampant, and food distribution was sabotaged by Communist bureaucrats who wanted the old days back. Jaruzelski calculated that the people would take only so much hardship before they began to feel that the return of authoritarian government might be a blessing.

Jaruzelski *wanted* a Soviet invasion. He had sent a message to the Kremlin, asking bluntly: "Can we count on military assistance from Moscow?"

The reply he received had been equally blunt: "No troops will be sent."

This was good news for Poland, Cam reflected. The Soviets might bully and bluster, but they were not willing to take the ultimate step. Whatever happened, it would be done by Polish people.

However, Jaruzelski might yet clamp down, even without the backup of Soviet tanks. His plan was right there on Staz's film. Staz himself clearly feared that the plan would be carried out, for he had included a handwritten note. This was unusual enough for Cam to pay it serious attention. Staz had written: "Reagan can prevent this happening if he threatens to cut off financial aid."

Cam thought that was shrewd. Loans from Western governments and Western banks were keeping Poland afloat. The one thing worse than democracy would be bankruptcy.

Cam had voted for Reagan because he promised to be more aggressive in foreign policy. Now was his chance. If he acted quickly, Reagan could stop Poland taking a giant step backward.

· · ·

George and Verena had a pleasant suburban home in Prince George's County, Maryland, just outside the Washington city limits, in the suburb he represented as congressman. He had to go to church every week now, a different denomination each Sunday, to worship with his voters. His job involved a few such chores, but most of the time he was passionately engaged. Jimmy Carter was out and Ronald Reagan was in the White House, and George was able to fight for the poorest people in America, many of whom were black.

Every month or two Maria Summers came to see her godson, Jack, now eighteen months old and showing some of the feistiness of his grandmother Jacky. She usually brought him a book. After brunch George would wash the dishes and Maria would dry, and they would talk about intelligence and foreign policy.

Maria was still working at the State Department. Her boss was now Secretary of State Alexander Haig. George asked whether State was getting better information on Poland. "Much better," she said. "I don't know what you did, but the CIA really smartened up its act."

George passed her a bowl to dry. "So what's happening in Warsaw?"

"The Soviets will not invade. We know that. The Polish Communists asked them to, and they refused point-blank. But Brezhnev is pressing Jaruzelski to declare martial law and abolish Solidarity."

"That would be a shame."

"That's what the State Department thinks."

George hesitated. "I hear the word *but* coming along . . ."

"You know me too well." She smiled. "We have the power to stamp on the martial law plan. President Reagan would only have to say that future economic aid depends on human rights."

"Why doesn't he?"

"He and Al Haig don't really believe the Poles will impose martial law on themselves."

"Who knows? It might be smart to issue the warning anyway."

"That's what I think."

"So why don't they?"

"They don't want the other side to realize just how good our intelligence is."

"There's no point in having intelligence unless you use it."

"Maybe they will," said Maria. "But right now they're dithering."

.   .   .

Snow was falling in Warsaw two weekends before Christmas. Tanya spent Saturday night alone. Staz never explained why he was or was not free to stay at her apartment. She had never been to his place, though she knew where he lived. Since she had introduced him to Cam Dewar, Staz had been closemouthed about everything to do with the army. Tanya assumed this was because he was revealing secrets to the Americans. He was like a prisoner who is on good behavior all day while digging an escape tunnel at night.

But this was the second Saturday Tanya had spent without him. She was not sure why. Was he tiring of her? Men did. The only man who had remained a permanent part of her life was Vasili, and she had never slept with him.

She found she was missing Vasili. She had never allowed herself to fall in love with him, because he was promiscuous, but she felt drawn to him. What she liked in men, she was beginning to realize, was courage. The three most important men in her life had been Paz Oliva, Staz Pawlak, and Vasili. As it happened they were all terrifically handsome. But they were also brave. Paz had stood up to the might of the USA, Staz had betrayed the secrets of the Red Army, and Vasili had defied the power of the Kremlin. Of the three, Vasili was the one who most thrilled her imagination, for he had written devastating stories about the Soviet Union while starved and half-frozen in Siberia. She wondered how he was, and wished she knew what he was writing now. She wondered if he had gone back to his old Casanova ways, or had genuinely settled down.

She went to bed and read *Doctor Zhivago* in German—it still had not been published in Russian—until she felt sleepy and turned out the light.

She was awakened by banging. She sat upright and turned on the light. It was half past two in the morning. Someone was pounding on a door, though not her door.

She got up and looked out of the window. The cars parked on either side of the street were covered with a fresh layer of snow. In the middle of the road were two police cars and a BTR-60 armored personnel carrier, carelessly parked at random angles in the manner of cops who knew they could do anything they liked.

The noise from outside her apartment changed from banging to crashing. It sounded as if someone was trying to demolish the building with a sledgehammer.

Tanya put on a bathrobe and went to the hall. She picked up her TASS press card, which was lying on a hall table with her car keys and change. She opened her door and looked into the corridor. Nothing was happening, except that two of her neighbors were also nervously peeping out.

Tanya propped her door open with a chair and went out. The noise was coming from the next floor down. She looked over the banisters and saw a group of men in the military camouflage uniform of the ZOMO, the notorious security police. Wielding crowbars and hammers, they were breaking down the door of Tanya's friend Danuta Gorski.

Tanya yelled: "What are you doing? What's happening?"

Some of her neighbors also shouted questions. The police took no notice.

The door was opened from inside, and Danuta's husband stood there, a frightened man in pajamas and glasses. "What do you want?" he said. From within the apartment came the sound of children crying.

The cops strode in, shoving him out of the way.

Tanya ran down the stairs. "You can't do this!" she yelled. "You have to identify yourselves!"

Two big policemen came out of the apartment dragging Danuta, her abundant hair in disarray, wearing a nightdress and a white candlewick dressing gown.

Tanya stood in front of them, blocking the staircase. She held up her press card. "I am a Soviet reporter!" she shouted.

"Then get the fuck out of the way," one replied. He lashed out at her with a crowbar he held in his left hand. It was not a calculated blow, for he was striving to control the struggling Danuta with the other hand, but the iron bar caught Tanya across the face. She felt a blaze of pain and staggered back. The two police pushed past her and hauled Danuta down the stairs.

Tanya had blood in her right eye but she could see with her left. Another cop emerged from the apartment carrying a typewriter and a telephone answering device.

Danuta's husband reappeared with a child in his arms. "Where are you taking her?" he shouted. The police did not reply.

Tanya said to him: "I'm going to call the army right now and find out." Holding one hand to her injured face, she went back up the stairs.

She glanced in the hall mirror. She had a gash on her forehead and her cheek was red and already swelling with a bruise, but she thought the blow had not broken any bones.

She picked up the phone to call Staz.

It was dead.

She turned on the television and the radio. The TV was blank, the radio silent.

This was not just about Danuta, then.

A neighbor followed her in. "Let me call a doctor," the woman said.

"I don't have time." Tanya stepped into her little bathroom, held a towel under the tap, and washed her face gingerly. Then she returned to her bedroom and dressed quickly in thermal underwear, jeans and a heavy sweater, and a big, thick coat with a fur lining.

She ran down the stairs and got into her car. Snow was falling again but the main roads were clear, and she soon saw why. Tanks and army trucks were everywhere. With a growing apprehension of doom she realized that the arrest of Danuta was just a small part of something ominously massive.

The troops swarming into the center of Warsaw were not Russians, however. This was not like Prague in 1968. The vehicles had Polish army markings and the soldiers wore Polish uniforms. The Poles had invaded their own capital.

They were setting up roadblocks, but they had only just started, and for the moment it was possible to circumvent them. Tanya drove her Mercedes fast, pushing her luck on slippery bends, to Jana Olbrachta Street, in the west of the city. She parked outside Staz's building. She knew the address but she had never been here before: he always said it was little better than a barracks.

She ran inside. It took her a couple of minutes to find the right apartment. She banged on the door, praying he would be in, though she feared the overwhelming likelihood was that he was out on the streets with the rest of the army.

The door was opened by a woman.

Tanya was shocked into silence. Did Staz have another girlfriend?

The woman was blond and pleasant-looking, wearing a pink nylon nightdress. She stared at Tanya's face in consternation. "You've been hurt!" she said in Polish.

Tanya noticed, in the hallway behind the woman, a small

red tricycle. This woman was not his girlfriend, she was his wife, and they had a child.

Tanya felt a jolt of guilt like an electric shock. She had been taking Staz away from his family. And he had been lying to her.

With an effort, she wrenched her mind back to the present emergency. "I need to speak to Colonel Pawlak," she said. "It's urgent."

The woman heard her Russian accent, and her attitude changed in an instant. She glared angrily at Tanya. "So you're the Russian whore," she said.

Evidently Staz had not succeeded in keeping his love affair entirely secret from his wife. Tanya wanted to explain that she had not known he was married, but this was not the moment. "There's no time for that!" she said desperately. "They're taking over the city! Where is he?"

"He's not here."

"Will you help me find him?"

"No. Now fuck off and die." The woman slammed the door.

"Shit," said Tanya.

She stood outside the apartment door. She put her hand to her aching cheek: it seemed to be swelling grotesquely. She did not know what to do next.

The other person who might know what was going on was Cam Dewar. She probably could not phone him: she guessed all the civilian phones in the city had been cut off. However, Cam might go to the American embassy.

She ran outside, jumped back into her car, and headed for the south of the city. She cut across the outskirts, avoiding the city center, where there would be roadblocks.

So Staz had a wife. He had been deceiving both women. He was a smooth liar, Tanya thought bitterly: he was probably a good spy. Tanya was so angry that she felt like giving up on men. They were all the damn same.

She saw a group of soldiers putting up a placard on a lamppost. She stopped to look, though she did not risk getting out of her car. It was a decree issued by something called the Military Council for National Salvation. There was no such council: it had just been invented, no doubt by Jaruzelski. She read it with horror. Martial law was in force. Civil rights were suspended, the frontiers were closed, travel between cities was prohibited, all public gatherings were banned, there was a curfew from ten P.M. to six A.M., and the armed forces were authorized to use coercion to restore law and order.

This was the clampdown. And it had been carefully planned—that poster had been printed in advance. The plan was being carried out with ruthless efficiency. Was there any hope?

She drove off again. In a dark street two ZOMO men stepped into the light of her twin headlights, and one held up a hand to stop her. At that moment Tanya felt a stab of pain in her cheek, and made a split-second decision. She floored the accelerator pedal. She thanked the stars for her powerful German engine as the car leaped forward, startling the men, who jumped aside. She screeched around a corner and was out of their sight before they could deploy their guns.

A few minutes later she pulled up outside the white marble embassy. All the lights were on: they, too, would be trying to find out what was happening. She sprang out of her car and ran to the U.S. marine at the gate. "I have important information for Cam Dewar," she said in English.

The marine pointed behind her. "That looks like him now."

Tanya turned to see a lime green Polski Fiat pulling up. Cam was at the wheel. Tanya ran to the car, and Cam rolled down his window. He addressed her in Russian, as always. "My God, what did you do to your face?"

"I had a conversation with the ZOMO," she said. "Do you know what's happening?"

"The government has arrested just about every Solidarity leader and organizer—thousands of them," Cam said grimly. "All phone lines are dead. There are massive roadblocks on every major road in the country."

"But I see no Russians!"

"No. The Poles have done this to themselves."

"Did the American government know this was going to happen? Did Staz tell you?"

Cam said nothing.

Tanya took that for a yes. "Couldn't Reagan do something to stop it?"

Cam looked as perplexed and disappointed as Tanya felt. "I thought he could," he said.

Tanya could hear her own voice rising to a screech of frustration. "Then, for God's sake, why didn't he?"

"I don't know," said Cam. "I just don't know."

When Tanya got home to Moscow, there was a bunch of flowers from Vasili waiting for her in her mother's apartment. How had he found roses in Moscow in January?

The flowers were a spot of brightness in a desolate landscape. Tanya had suffered two shocks: Staz had deceived her, and General Jaruzelski had betrayed the Polish people. Staz was no better than Paz Oliva, and she had to wonder what was wrong with her judgment. Perhaps she was wrong about Communism, too. She had always believed it could not last. She had been a schoolgirl in 1956 when the Hungarian people's rebellion had been crushed. Twelve years later the same had happened to the Prague Spring, and after another thirteen years Solidarity had gone the same way. Maybe Communism really was the way of the future, as Grandfather Grigori had died believing. If so, a grim life was ahead for her nephew and niece, Dimka's children, Grisha and Katya.

Soon after Tanya arrived home, Vasili invited her to dinner.

They could be friends openly now, they agreed. He had been rehabilitated. His radio show was a long-running success, and he was a star of the writers' union. No one knew that he was also Ivan Kuznetsov, dissident author of *Frostbite* and other anti-Communist books that had been bestsellers in the West. It was remarkable, Tanya thought, that she and he had succeeded in keeping the secret so long.

She was getting ready to leave the office and go to Vasili's place when she was accosted by Pyotr Opotkin, screwing up his eyes against the smoke from the cigarette between his lips. "You've done it again," he said. "We're getting complaints at the highest level about your article on cows."

Tanya had visited the Vladimir Region, where Communist Party officials were so inefficient that cattle were dying on a huge scale while their feed rotted in barns. She had written an angry piece, and Daniil had sent it out. Now she said: "I suppose the corrupt and lazy bastards who let the cows die have complained to you."

"Never mind them," Opotkin said. "I've had a letter from the Central Committee secretary responsible for ideology!"

"He knows about cows, does he?"

Opotkin thrust a piece of paper at her. "We're going to have to publish a retraction."

Tanya took it from him but did not read it. "Why are you so concerned to defend people who are destroying our country?"

"We cannot undermine Communist Party cadres!"

The phone on Tanya's desk rang, and she picked it up. "Tanya Dvorkin."

A vaguely familiar voice said: "You wrote the article about cows dying in Vladimir."

Tanya sighed. "Yes, I did, and I have already been reprimanded. Who is this calling?"

"I am the secretary responsible for agriculture. My name is Mikhail Gorbachev. You interviewed me in 1976."

"So I did." Gorbachev was obviously going to add his condemnation to Opotkin's, Tanya assumed.

Gorbachev said: "I called to congratulate you on your excellent analysis."

Tanya was astonished. "I . . . uh, thank you, comrade!"

"It is desperately important that we eliminate such inefficiency on our farms."

"Uh, comrade Secretary, would you mind saying that to my editor in chief? We were just discussing the article, and he was talking of a retraction."

"Retraction? Rubbish. Put him on the phone."

Grinning, Tanya said to Opotkin: "Secretary Gorbachev would like to talk to you."

At first Opotkin did not believe her. He took the phone and said: "To whom am I speaking, please?"

From then on he was silent but for the occasional: "Yes, comrade."

At last he put down the phone. He walked away without speaking to Tanya.

It gave her profound satisfaction to crumple the retraction and toss it into the bin.

She went to Vasili's apartment not knowing what to expect. She hoped he was not going to ask her to join his harem. Just in case, she was wearing unsexy serge trousers and a drab gray sweater, to discourage him. All the same, she found herself looking forward to the evening.

He opened the door, wearing a blue sweater and a white shirt, both new-looking. She kissed his cheek, then studied him. His hair was gray, now, but still luxuriant and wavy. At fifty he was upright and slim.

He opened a bottle of Georgian champagne and put snacks on the table, squares of toast with egg salad and tomato, and fish roes on cucumber. Tanya wondered who had made them. It would not be beyond him to have one of his girlfriends do it.

The apartment was comfortable, full of books and pictures. Vasili had a tape deck that played cassettes. He was affluent now, even without the fortune in foreign royalties that he could not receive.

He wanted to know all about Poland. How had the Kremlin defeated Solidarity without an invasion? Why had Jaruzelski betrayed the Polish people? He did not think his apartment was bugged, but he played a Tchaikovsky cassette just in case.

Tanya told him that Solidarity was not dead. It had gone underground. Many of the men arrested under martial law were still in jail, but the sexist secret police had failed to appreciate the major role played by women. Almost all the female organizers were still at large, including Danuta, who had been arrested, then released. She was again working undercover, producing illegal newspapers and pamphlets, rebuilding lines of communication.

All the same, Tanya had no hope. If they rebelled again, they would be crushed again. Vasili was more optimistic. "It was a near thing," he said. "In half a century, no one has come so close to defeating Communism."

This was like the old days, Tanya thought, feeling comfortable as the champagne relaxed her. Back in the early sixties, before Vasili was jailed, they had often sat around like this, talking and arguing about politics and literature and art.

She told him about the phone call from Mikhail Gorbachev. "He's an odd one," Vasili said. "We in the agriculture ministry see a lot of him. He's Yuri Andropov's pet, and he seems to be a rock-solid Communist. His wife is even worse. Yet he backs reformist ideas, whenever he can do it without offending his superiors."

"My brother thinks highly of him."

"When Brezhnev dies—which can't be far distant now, please, God—Andropov will make a bid for the leadership, and Gorbachev will back him. If the bid fails, both men will be finished. They'll be sent to the provinces. But if Andropov succeeds, Gorbachev has a bright future."

"In any other country Gorbachev, at fifty, would be just the right age to become leader. Here, he's too young."

"The Kremlin is a geriatric ward."

Vasili served borsch, beetroot soup with beef. "This is good," Tanya said. She could not help asking: "Who made it?"

"I did, of course. Who else?"

"I don't know. Do you have a housekeeper?"

"Just a babushka who comes to clean the apartment and iron my shirts."

"One of your girlfriends, then?"

"I don't have a girlfriend at the moment."

Tanya was intrigued. She recalled the last conversation they had had before she went to Warsaw. He had claimed to have changed, and grown up. She had felt he needed to show that, not just say it. She had been sure it was just another line of chat intended to get her into bed. Could she have been wrong? She doubted it.

After they had eaten, she asked him how he felt about those royalties piling up in London.

"You should have the money," he said.

"Don't be silly. You wrote the books."

"I had little to lose—I was already in Siberia. They couldn't do much more to me, except kill me, and I would have been relieved to die. But you risked everything—your career, your freedom, your life. You deserve the money more than I do."

"Well, I wouldn't take it, even if you could give it to me."

"Then it will stay there until I die, probably."

"You wouldn't be tempted to escape to the West?"

"No."

"You sound sure."

"I am sure."

"Why? You'd be free to write whatever you like, all the time. No more radio serials."

"I wouldn't go . . . unless you went, too."

"You don't mean that."

He shrugged. "I don't expect you to believe me. Why should you? But you're the most important person in my life. You came to Siberia to find me—no one else did. You tried to get me released. You smuggled my work out to the free world. For twenty years, you've been the best friend a person could have."

She was moved. She had never looked at it that way. "Thank you for saying that," she said.

"It's no more than the truth. I'm not leaving." Then he added: "Unless, of course, you go with me."

She stared at him. Was he making a serious suggestion? She was frightened to ask. She looked out of the window at the snowflakes whirling in the lamplight.

Vasili said: "Twenty years, and we've never even kissed."

"True."

"Yet still you think I'm a heartless Casanova."

In truth she no longer knew what to think. Had he changed? Did people ever really change? She said: "After all this time, it would be a shame to spoil our record."

"And yet I want to, with all my heart."

She changed the subject. "Given the chance, would you defect to the West?"

"With you, yes. Not otherwise."

"I always wanted to make the Soviet Union a better place, not leave it. But after the defeat of Solidarity I find it difficult to believe in a better future. Communism could last a thousand years."

"It could last longer than me or you, at least."

Tanya hesitated on the brink. She was surprised by how much she wanted to kiss him. And more: she wanted to stay here, talking to him, on this couch in this warm apartment with those snowflakes falling outside the window, for a long, long time. What a strange feeling that was, she thought. Perhaps it was love.

So she kissed him.

After a while, they went into the bedroom.

. . .

Natalya was always first with the news. She came to Dimka's office in the Kremlin on Christmas Eve, looking anxious. "Andropov is not going to be at the Politburo meeting," she said. "He's too ill to leave the hospital."

The next Politburo meeting was scheduled for the day after Christmas.

"Damn," said Dimka. "That's dangerous."

Strangely, Yuri Andropov had turned out to be a good Soviet leader. For the previous fifteen years he had been the efficient head of a cruel and brutal secret service, the KGB. And now, as general secretary of the Communist Party of the Soviet Union, he continued to repress dissidents ruthlessly. But within the party he was astonishingly tolerant of new ideas and reforms. Like a medieval Pope who tortured heretics yet discussed with his cardinals arguments against the existence of God, Andropov talked freely to his inner circle — which included both Dimka and Natalya — about the shortcomings of the Soviet system. And the talk led to action. Gorbachev's brief was extended from agriculture to the entire economy, and he produced a program to decentralize the Soviet economy, taking some of the power of decision away from Moscow and giving it to managers closer to the problems.

Unfortunately Andropov fell ill shortly before Christmas 1983, having been leader for barely a year. This worried Dimka and Natalya. Andropov's stick-in-the-mud rival for the leadership had been Konstantin Chernenko, who was still number two in the hierarchy. Dimka feared that Chernenko would take advantage of Andropov's illness to regain the ascendancy.

Now Natalya said: "Andropov has written a speech to be read out."

Dimka shook his head. "That's not enough. In Andropov's absence, Chernenko will chair the meeting, and once that happens everyone will accept him as leader-in-waiting. And then the whole country will go backward." The prospect was too depressing to contemplate.

"Obviously we want Gorbachev to chair the meeting."

"But Chernenko is number two. I wish he'd go to hospital."

"He will soon — he's not a well man."

"But probably not soon enough. Is there any way we can bypass him?"

Natalya considered. "Well, the Politburo must do what Andropov tells it to do."

"So he could just issue an order saying Gorbachev will chair the meeting?"

"Yes, he could. He's still the boss."

"He could add a paragraph to his speech."

"Perfect. I'll call him and suggest it."

Later that afternoon Dimka got a message summoning him to Natalya's office. When he got there he saw that her eyes were gleaming with excitement and triumph. With her was Arkady Volsky, Andropov's personal aide. Andropov had summoned Volsky to the hospital and had given him a handwritten addendum to the speech. Volsky now gave it to Dimka.

The last paragraph read:

For reasons which you understand, I will not be able to chair meetings of the Politburo and Secretariat in the near future. I would therefore request members of the central committee to examine the question of entrusting the leadership of the Politburo and secretariat to Mikhail Sergeyevich Gorbachev.

It was expressed as a suggestion, but in the Kremlin a suggestion from the leader was the same thing as a direct order.

"This is dynamite," said Dimka. "They can't possibly disobey."

"What should I do with it?" said Volsky.

Dimka said: "First, make several photocopies, so that there's no point in anyone tearing it up. Then . . ." Dimka hesitated.

Natalya said: "Don't tell anyone. Just give it to Bogolyubov." Klavdii Bogolyubov was in charge of preparing the papers for Politburo meetings. "Be low-key. Just tell him to add the extra material to the red folder containing Andropov's speech."

They agreed that was the best plan.

Christmas Day was not a big festival. The Communists disliked its religious nature. They changed Santa Claus to Father Frost and the Virgin Mary to the Snow Maiden, and moved the celebration to New Year. That was when the children would get their gifts. Grisha, who was now twenty, was getting a cassette player, and Katya, fourteen, a new dress. Dimka and Natalya, as senior Communist politicians, did not dream of celebrating Christmas, regardless of their personal beliefs. Both went to work as usual.

The day after, Dimka went to the Presidium Room for the Politburo meeting. He was met at the door by Natalya, who had got there earlier. She looked distraught. She was holding open the red folder containing Andropov's speech. "They left it out!" she said. "They left out the last paragraph!"

Dimka sat down heavily. "I never imagined Chernenko would have the guts," he said.

There was nothing they could do, he realized. Andropov was in hospital. If he had stormed into the room and yelled at everyone, his authority would have been reasserted; but he could not. Chernenko had correctly estimated Andropov's weakness.

"They've won, haven't they?" said Natalya.

"Yes," said Dimka. "The Age of Stagnation begins again."

PART NINE

BOMB

1984-1987

George Jakes went to the opening of an exhibition of African American art in downtown Washington. He was not very interested in art, but a black congressman had to support such things. Most of his work as a congressman was more important.

President Reagan had enormously increased government spending on the military, but who was going to pay? Not the wealthy, who had received a big tax cut.

There was a joke that George often repeated. A reporter asked Reagan how he was going to reduce tax and increase spending at the same time. "I'm going to keep two sets of books," was the answer.

In reality Reagan's plan was to cut Social Security and Medicare. If he had his way, unemployed men and welfare mothers would lose out to finance the boom in the defense industry. The idea made George mad with rage. However, George and others in Congress were struggling to prevent this, and so far they had succeeded.

The upshot was a rise in government borrowing. Reagan had increased the deficit. All those shiny new weapons for the Pentagon would be paid for by future generations.

George took a glass of white wine from a tray held by a waiter and looked around the exhibits, then spoke briefly to a reporter. He did not have much time. Verena needed to go out tonight, to a Georgetown political dinner, so he would be in charge of their son, Jack, who was now four. They had a nanny — they had to, for they both had demanding jobs — but one of them was always on duty as backup in case the nanny should fail to show up.

He set his glass down untasted. Free wine was never

worth drinking. He put on his coat and left. A cold rain had started, and he held the exhibition catalogue over his head as he hurried to his car. His elegant old Mercedes was long gone: a politician had to drive an American vehicle. He now had a silver Lincoln Town Car.

He got in, switched on the windshield wipers, and set off for Prince George's County. He crossed the South Capitol Street Bridge and took Suitland Parkway east. He cursed when he saw how heavy the traffic was: he was going to be late.

When he got home, Verena's red Jaguar stood in the driveway, nose out, ready to go. The car had been a present from her father on her fortieth birthday. George parked next to it and walked into the house, carrying a briefcase full of papers, his evening's work.

Verena was in the hallway, looking spectacularly glamorous in a black cocktail dress and patent high-heeled pumps. She was as mad as a polecat. "You're late!" she yelled.

"I'm really sorry," George said. "The traffic on Suitland Parkway is crazy today."

"This dinner party is really important to me—three members of Reagan's cabinet will be there, and I'm going to be late!"

George understood her irritation. For a lobbyist, the chance to meet powerful people socially was priceless. "I'm here now," he said.

"I am not the maid! When we make an arrangement you have to keep it!"

This tirade was not unusual. She often got angry and screamed at him. He always tried to take it calmly. "Is Nanny Tiffany here?"

"No, she's not, she went home sick, that's why I had to wait for you."

"Where's Jack?"

"Watching TV in the den."

"Okay, I'll go and sit with him now. You go on out."

She made a furious noise and stalked off.

He kind of envied whoever was going to sit next to her at dinner. She was still the sexiest woman he had ever met. However, he now knew that being her long-distance lover, as he had for many years, was better than being her husband. In the old days they had had sex more times in a weekend than they did now in a month. Since they got married their frequent and furious rows, usually about child care, had eroded their affection for one another like a slow drip of strong vitriol. They lived together, they took care of their son, and they pursued their careers. Did they love one another? George no longer knew.

He went into the den. Jack was on the couch in front of the TV. The boy was George's great consolation. He sat next to him and put his arm around his small shoulders. Jack snuggled up.

The show featured a group of high school pupils involved in some kind of adventure. "What are you watching?" George asked.

"*Whiz Kids*. It's great."

"What's it about?"

"They catch crooks with their computers."

One of the child geniuses was black, George noticed, and he thought: How the world turns.

.   .   .

"We're really lucky to be invited to this dinner," said Cam Dewar to his wife, Lidka, as their cab pulled up outside a grand mansion on R Street near the Georgetown Library. "I want us both to make a good impression."

Lidka was scornful. "You are an important person in the secret police," she said. "I think *they* need to impress *you*."

Lidka did not understand how America worked. "The CIA is not the secret police," Cam said. "And I'm not a very important person by the standards of these people."

Cam was not exactly a nobody, all the same. Because of his past experience in the White House, he was now the CIA's liaison man with the Reagan administration. He was thrilled to have the job.

He had got over his disappointment with Reagan's failure in Poland. He put that down to inexperience. Reagan had been president for less than a year when Solidarity was crushed.

In the back of Cam's mind, a devil's advocate said that a president ought to be smart enough and knowledgeable enough to make confident decisions from the moment he takes office. He recalled Nixon saying: "Reagan is a nice guy, but he doesn't know what the Christ is going on in foreign policy."

But Reagan's heart was in the right place, that was the main thing. He was passionately anti-Communist.

Lidka said: "And your grandfather was a senator!"

That did not count for much either. Gus Dewar was in his nineties. After Grandmama died he had moved from Buffalo to San Francisco to be near Woody, Beep, and his great-grandson, John Lee. He was long retired from politics. Besides, he was a Democrat, and by Reaganite standards an extreme liberal.

Cam and Lidka walked up a short flight of steps to a red-brick house that looked like a small French château, with dormer windows in the slate roof and a white stone entrance topped by a small Greek pediment. This was the home of Frank and Marybell Lindeman, heavyweight donors to Reagan's campaign funds and multimillion-dollar beneficiaries of his tax cut. Marybell was one of half a dozen women who dominated Washington social life. She entertained the men who ran America. That was why Cam felt lucky to be here.

Although the Lindemans were Republicans, Marybell's dinners were cross-party affairs, and Cam was expecting to see senior men from both sides here tonight.

A butler took their coats. Looking around the grand hall, Lidka said: "Why do they have these terrible paintings?"

"It's called Western art," Cam said. "That's a Remington—very valuable."

"If I had all that money, I wouldn't buy pictures of cowboys and Indians."

"They're making a point. The impressionists were not necessarily the best painters ever. American artists are just as good."

"No, they're not—everyone knows that."

"Matter of opinion."

Lidka shrugged: another mystery of American life.

The butler showed them into a wide drawing room. It looked like an eighteenth-century salon, with a Chinese dragon carpet and a scatter of spindly chairs upholstered in yellow silk. Cam realized they were the first guests to arrive. A moment later, Marybell appeared through another door. She was a statuesque woman with a mass of red hair that might or might not have been its natural color. She was wearing a necklace of what looked, to Cam, like unusually large diamonds. "How kind of you to come early!" she said.

Cam knew this was a reproof, but Lidka was oblivious. "I couldn't wait to see your wonderful house," she gushed.

"And how do you like living in America?" Marybell asked her. "Tell me, what is the best thing about this country, in your opinion?"

Lidka thought for a moment. "You have all these black people," she said.

Cam suppressed a groan. What the hell was she saying?

Marybell was surprised into silence.

Lidka waved a hand to indicate the waiter holding a tray of champagne flutes, the maid bringing canapés, and the butler, all of whom were African American. "They do everything, like opening doors and serving drinks and sweeping the floor. In Poland we have no one to do that work—everyone has to do it themselves!"

Marybell looked a little frantic. Such talk was incorrect even in Reagan's Washington. Then she looked over Lidka's shoulder and saw another guest hovering. "Karim, darling!" she screeched. She embraced a handsome dark-skinned man in an immaculate pin-striped suit. "Meet Cam Dewar and his wife, Lidka. This is Karim Abdullah, from the Saudi embassy."

Karim shook hands. "I've heard of you, Cam," he said. "I work closely with some of your colleagues in Langley."

Karim was letting Cam know he was in Saudi intelligence.

Karim turned to Lidka. She was looking startled. Cam knew why. She had not expected to see someone as dark as Karim at Marybell's party.

However, Karim charmed her. "I have been told that Polish women are the most beautiful in the world," he said. "But I didn't believe it—until this moment." He kissed her hand.

Lidka could take any amount of that sort of bullshit.

"I heard what you were saying about black people," Karim said. "I agree with you. We have none in Saudi Arabia—so we have to import them from India!"

Cam could see that Lidka was bewildered by the fine distinctions of Karim's racism. To him, Indians were black but Arabs were not. Fortunately, Lidka knew when to shut up and listen to a man.

More guests came in. Karim lowered his voice. "However," he said conspiratorially, "we must be careful what we say—some of the guests may be liberals."

As if to illustrate his point, a tall, athletic-looking man with thick fair hair came in. He looked like a movie star. It was Jasper Murray.

Cam was not pleased. He had hated Jasper since they were teenagers. Then Jasper had become an investigative reporter and had helped to bring President Nixon down. His book about Nixon, *Tricky Dick,* had been a bestseller and a successful movie. He had been relatively quiet during the Carter administration, but had returned to the attack as soon as Reagan took over. He was now one of the most popular figures on television, up there with Peter Jennings and Barbara Walters. Only last night his show, *This Day,* had devoted half an hour to the American-backed military dictatorship in El Salvador. Murray had repeated claims by human rights groups that government death squads there had murdered thirty thousand people.

The network that broadcast *This Day* was owned by Frank Lindeman, Marybell's husband; so Jasper had probably felt unable to decline the invitation to dinner. The White House had put pressure on Frank to get rid of Jasper, but so far Frank had refused. Although he held a majority of shares, he had a board to answer to, and investors who could make trouble if he fired one of his biggest stars.

Marybell seemed to be anxiously waiting for something. Then one more guest arrived, rather late. She was a stunningly glamorous black woman lobbyist called Verena Marquand. Cam had not met her, but recognized her from photographs.

The butler announced dinner and they all moved through a double doorway to the dining room. The women made appreciative noises when they saw the long table decked with gleaming glassware and silver bowls of yellow hothouse roses. Cam saw that Lidka was wide-eyed. This outdid all the photographs in her home decorating magazines, he guessed. She had surely never seen or even imagined anything so lavish.

There were eighteen people around the table, but the conversation was immediately dominated by one person. She was Suzy Cannon, a vituperative gossip reporter. Half of what she wrote turned out to be untrue, but she had a jackal's nose for weakness. She was conservative, but more interested in scandal than politics. Nothing was private to her. Cam prayed that Lidka would keep her mouth shut. Anything said tonight might appear in tomorrow's newspaper.

But Suzy turned her gimlet eyes on Cam, to his surprise. "I believe you and Jasper know each other," she said.

"Not really," said Cam. "We met in London many years ago."

"But I hear that you both fell in love with the same girl."

How the hell did she know that? "I was fifteen, Suzy," Cam said. "I probably fell in love with half the girls in London."

Suzy turned to Jasper. "How about you? Do you remember this rivalry?"

Jasper had been deep in conversation with Verena Marquand, sitting next to him. Now he looked irritated. "If you're planning to write an article about teenage romances that took place more than twenty years ago, and call it news, Suzy, all I can say is you must be sleeping with your editor."

Everyone laughed: Suzy was in fact married to the news editor of her paper.

Cam noticed that Suzy's laugh was forced, and her eyes glared hatred at Jasper. He recalled that Suzy as a young journalist had been fired from *This Day* after a series of wildly inaccurate reports.

Now she said: "You must have been interested to watch Jasper's show on TV last night, Cam."

Cam said: "Not interested so much as dismayed. The president and the CIA are trying to support the anti-Communist government in El Salvador."

Suzy said: "And Jasper seems to be on the other side, doesn't he?"

Jasper said: "I'm on the side of truth, Suzy. I know this is hard for you to grasp." Cam noticed that no trace of his British accent remained.

Cam said: "I was sorry to see such propaganda on a major network."

Jasper snapped: "How would *you* report on a government that murders thirty thousand of its own citizens?"

"We don't accept that figure."

"Then how many citizens of El Salvador do *you* think have been murdered by their government? Give us the CIA estimate."

"You should have asked that before broadcasting your show."

"Oh, I did. I got no answer."

"No Central American government is perfect. You focus on the ones we support. I think you're simply anti-American."

Suzy smiled. "You're British, aren't you, Jasper?" she said with poisonous sweetness.

Jasper looked riled. "I became a U.S. citizen more than a decade ago. I'm so pro-American that I risked my damn life for this country. I spent two years in the United States Army—one of those in Vietnam. And I wasn't sitting on my ass behind a desk in Saigon, either. I saw action, and I killed people. You've never done that, Suzy. And how about you, Cam? What did you do in Vietnam?"

"I wasn't called up."

"Then maybe you should just shut the fuck up."

Marybell interrupted. "I think that's enough about Jasper and Cam." She turned to a congressman from New York sitting next to her. "I see that your city has banned discrimination against homosexuals. Are you in favor of that?"

The conversation turned to gay rights, and Cameron relaxed—too soon.

A question was asked about legislation in other countries, and Suzy said: "What's the law in Poland, Lidka?"

"Poland is a Catholic country," said Lidka. "We have no homosexuals there." A moment of silence ensued, and she added: "Thank God."

.   .   .

Jasper Murray left the Lindeman house at the same time as Verena Marquand. "Suzy Cannon is a real troublemaker," he said as they went down the steps.

Verena laughed, showing white teeth in the lamplight. "That's the truth."

They reached the sidewalk. The taxi Jasper had ordered was nowhere in sight. He walked with Verena to her car. "Suzy's got it in for me," he said.

"She can't do you much harm, can she? You're such a big shot now."

"On the contrary. There's a serious campaign against me in Washington right now. It's election year, and the administration doesn't want television programs like the one I did last night." He felt comfortable confiding in her. They had been thrown together the day they watched Martin Luther King die. That sense of intimacy had never really gone away.

Verena said: "I'm sure you can fight off a gossip attack."

"I don't know. My boss is an old rival called Sam Cakebread who has never liked me. And Frank Lindeman, who owns the network, would dearly love to get rid of me if he could find a pretext. Right now the board is afraid they'll be accused of biasing the news if they fire me. But one mistake and I'm out."

"You should be like Suzy, and marry the boss."

"I would if I could." He looked up and down the street. "I ordered a taxi for eleven o'clock, but I don't see it. The show won't pay for limousines."

"Do you want a ride?"

"That'd be great."

They got into her Jaguar.

She took off her high-heeled shoes and handed them to him. "Put these on the floor on your side, would you?" She drove in her stockings. Jasper felt a sexy frisson. He had always found Verena devastatingly alluring. He watched her as she pulled into the late-night traffic and accelerated down the street. She was a good driver, if a little too fast: no surprise there.

"There aren't many people I trust," he said. "I'm one of the most well-known people in America, and I feel more alone now than I ever have. But I trust you."

"I feel the same. I have since that awful day in Memphis. I've never felt more terrifyingly vulnerable than the moment I heard that shot. You covered my head with your arms. A person doesn't forget something like that."

"I wish I'd found you before George did."

She glanced over at him and smiled.

He was not sure what that meant.

They reached his building and she pulled up on the left side of the one-way street. "Thanks for the ride," Jasper said. He got out. Leaning back into the car, he picked up her shoes from the floor and placed them on the passenger seat. "Great shoes," he said. He slammed the door.

He walked around the car to the sidewalk and came to her window. She lowered the glass. "I forgot to kiss you good night," he said. He leaned into the car and kissed her lips. She opened her mouth immediately. The kiss became passionate in an instant. Verena reached behind his neck and pulled his head inside the car. They kissed with frantic eagerness. Jasper reached into the car and pushed his hand up inside the skirt of her cocktail dress until he could cup the soft cotton-covered triangle between her legs. She moaned and thrust her hips upward against his grasp.

Breathless, he broke the kiss. "Come inside."

"No." She moved his hand away from her groin.

"Meet me tomorrow."

She did not reply, but pushed him away until his head and shoulders were outside the car.

He said again: "Meet me tomorrow?"

She put the shift into gear. "Call me," she said. Then she put her foot down and roared away.

. . .

George Jakes was not sure whether to believe Jasper Murray's TV show. Even to George it seemed unlikely that President Reagan would support a government that murdered thousands of its own people. Then, four weeks later, *The New York Times* sensationally revealed that the head of El Salvador's death squad, Colonel Nicolás Carranza, was a CIA agent receiving $90,000 a year from American taxpayers.

Voters were furious. They had thought that after Watergate the CIA had been whipped into line. But it was clearly out of control, paying a monster to commit mass murder.

In his study at home, George finished the papers in his briefcase a few minutes before ten. He screwed the cap back onto his fountain pen, but sat there a few more minutes, reflecting.

No one on the House intelligence committee had known about Colonel Carranza, nor had any member of the equivalent Senate committee. Caught off guard, they were all embarrassed. They were supposed to supervise the CIA. People

thought this mess was their fault. But what could they do if
spooks lied to them?

He sighed and stood up. He left his study, turning out the
light, and stepped into Jack's room. The boy was fast asleep.
When he saw his child like this, so peaceful, George felt as
if his heart would burst. Jack's soft skin was surprisingly
dark, like Jacky's, even though he had two white grandparents. Light-skinned people were still favored in the African
American community, despite all the talk about black being
beautiful. But Jack was beautiful to George. His head lay on
his teddy bear at what looked like an uncomfortable angle.
George slipped a hand under the boy's head, feeling soft curls
just like his own. He lifted Jack's head a fraction, gently slid
the bear out, then carefully rested the head back on the
pillow. Jack slept on, oblivious.

George went to the kitchen and poured a glass of milk,
then carried it into the bedroom. Verena was already in bed,
wearing a nightdress, with a pile of magazines beside her,
reading and watching TV at the same time. George drank
the milk, then went into the bathroom and brushed his
teeth.

They seemed to be getting on a little better. They rarely
made love, these days, but Verena was more even-tempered.
In fact she had not erupted for a month or so. She was
working hard, often late into the evenings: perhaps she was
happier when her job was more demanding.

George took off his shirt and lifted the lid of the laundry
hamper. He was about to drop his shirt in when his eye was
caught by Verena's underwear. He saw a lacy black brassiere and matching panties. The set looked new, and he did
not recall seeing it on her. If she was buying sexy underwear, why was she not letting him view it? She sure as hell
was not shy about such things.

Looking more closely, he saw something even more
strange: a blond hair.

He was possessed by a terrible fear. His stomach cramped.
He picked the garments out of the hamper.

Carrying them into the bedroom, he said: "Tell me I'm
crazy."

"You're crazy," she said; then she saw what he had in his
hand. "Are you going to do my laundry?" she quipped, but
he could tell she was nervous.

"Nice underwear," he said.

"Lucky you."

"Except that I haven't seen it on you."

"Unlucky you."

"But someone has."

"Sure. Dr. Bernstein."

"Dr. Bernstein is bald. There's a blond hair in your underpants."

Her cappuccino skin went paler, but she remained defiant. "Well, Sherlock Holmes, what do you deduce from that?"

"That you had sex with a man with long blond hair."

"Why does it have to be a man?"

"Because you like men."

"I might like girls too. It's the fashion. Everyone is bisexual now."

George felt profoundly sad. "I note you're not denying that you're having an affair."

"Well, George, ya got me."

He shook his head incredulously. "Are you making light of this?"

"I guess I am."

"So you admit it. Who are you fucking?"

"I'm not going to tell you, so don't ask again."

George was having more and more difficulty suppressing his anger. "You act as if you've done nothing wrong!"

"I'm not going to pretend. Yes, I'm seeing someone I like. I'm sorry to hurt your feelings."

George was bewildered. "How did this happen so quickly?"

"It happened slowly. We've been married more than five years. The thrill is gone, like the song says."

"What did I do wrong?"

"You married me."

"When did you become so angry?"

"Am I angry? I thought I was just bored."

"What do you want to do?"

"I'm not giving him up for the sake of a marriage that hardly exists any longer."

"You know I can't accept that."

"So, leave. You're not a prisoner."

George sat down on her dressing table stool and buried his face in his hands. He was swamped by a wave of intense emotion, and found himself suddenly taken back to childhood. He recalled the embarrassment of being the only boy in the class who did not have a father. He felt again the agonies of envy he had suffered when he saw other boys with their fathers, throwing a ball, fixing a punctured bicycle tire, buying a baseball bat, trying on shoes. He boiled anew with rage at the man who had, in his eyes, abandoned his mother and him, caring nothing for the woman who had given herself to him, nor for the child that had been born of their love. He wanted to scream, he wanted to punch Verena, he wanted to weep.

He managed to speak at last. "I'm not leaving Jack," he said.

"Your choice," said Verena. She switched off the TV, threw her magazines to the floor, turned out the bedside light, and lay down, facing away from him.

"Is that it?" George said amazedly. "Is that all you have to say?"

"I'm going to sleep. I have a breakfast meeting."

He stared at her. Had he ever known her?

Of course he had. In his heart he had understood that there were two Verenas: one a dedicated activist for civil rights, the other a party girl. He loved them both, and he had believed that with his help they could become one happy, well-adjusted person. And he had been wrong.

He remained there for several minutes, looking at her in the dim light from the streetlamp on the corner. I waited so long for you, he thought; all those years of long-distance love. Then, at last, you married me, and we had Jack, and I thought everything would be all right, forever.

At last he stood up. He took off his clothes and put on pajamas.

He could not bring himself to get into bed beside her.

There was a bed in the guest room, but it was not made up. He went to the hall and got his warmest coat from the closet. He went to the guest room and lay down with the coat over him.

But he did not sleep.

. . .

George had noticed, some time ago, that Verena sometimes wore clothes that did not suit her. She had a pretty flower-print dress that she put on when she wanted to seem like an innocent girl, though in fact it made her look ridiculous. She had a brown suit that drained her face of color, but she had paid so much for it that she was not willing to admit it was a mistake. She had a mustard-colored sweater that made her wonderful green eyes go muddy and dull.

Everyone did the same, George reckoned. He himself had three cream-colored shirts that he wished would fray at the collars soon so that he could throw them away. For all sorts of reasons, people wore clothes they hated.

But never when meeting a lover.

When Verena put on the black Armani suit with the turquoise blouse and the black coral necklace, she looked like a movie star, and she knew it.

She had to be going to see her paramour.

George felt so humiliated that it was like a gnawing pain in his stomach. He could not subject himself to this much longer. It made him feel like jumping off a bridge.

Verena left early, and said she would be home early, so George figured they were going to meet for lunch. He had breakfast with Jack, then left him with Nanny Tiffany. He went to his rooms in the Cannon House Office Building, near the Capitol, and canceled his appointments for the day.

At twelve noon, Verena's red Jaguar was parked as usual in the lot near her downtown office. George waited down the block in his silver Lincoln, watching the exit. The red car appeared at half past twelve. He pulled into the traffic and followed her.

She crossed the Potomac and headed out into the Virginia countryside. As the traffic thinned he fell back. It would be embarrassing if she spotted him. He hoped she would not notice something as common as a silver Lincoln. He could not have done this in his distinctive old Mercedes.

A few minutes before one she pulled off the road at a country restaurant called the Worcester Sauce. George sped by, then U-turned a mile down the road and came back. He drove into the restaurant parking lot and took a slot from which he could see the Jaguar. Then he settled down to wait.

He brooded. He knew he was being stupid. He knew this could end in embarrassment or worse. He knew he should drive away.

But he had to know who his wife's lover was.

They came out at three.

He could tell by the way Verena walked that she had had a glass or two of wine with her lunch. They came across the lot hand in hand, she giggling at something the man said, and hot fury boiled inside George.

The man was tall and broad, with thick fair hair, quite long.

As they came closer, George recognized Jasper Murray. "You son of a bitch," he said aloud.

Jasper had always had a yen for Verena, right from the first time they had met, at the Willard Hotel on the day of Martin Luther King's "I have a dream" speech. But lots of men had a yen for Verena. George had never imagined that Jasper, of all of them, would be the betrayer.

They walked to the Jaguar and kissed.

George knew he should start his car and drive away. He had learned what he needed to know. There was nothing else to be done.

Verena's mouth was open, George could see. She leaned into Jasper with her hips. Both had their eyes closed.

George got out of his car.

Jasper grasped Verena's breast.

George slammed the car door and strode across the tarmac toward them.

Jasper was too absorbed in what he was doing but Verena heard the slam and opened her eyes. She saw George, pushed Jasper away, and screamed.

She was too late.

George reached back with his right arm then hit Jasper with a punch that had all the force of his back and shoulders in it. His fist connected with the left side of Jasper's face. George felt the deeply satisfying squish of soft flesh, then, a split second later, the hardness of teeth and bones. Then pain blazed in his hand.

Jasper staggered backward and fell to the ground.

Verena yelled: "George! What have you done?" She knelt beside Jasper, careless of her stockings.

Jasper lifted himself on one elbow and felt his face. "Fucking animal," he said to George.

George wanted Jasper to get up off the ground and hit back. He wanted more violence, more pain, more blood. He stared at Jasper for a long moment, seeing through a red mist. Then the fog cleared, and he realized Jasper was not going to get up and fight.

George turned around, went back to his car, and drove away.

When he got home, Jack was in his bedroom, playing with his collection of toy cars. George closed the door, so that Nanny Tiffany could not hear. He sat on the bed, which was covered by a counterpane that looked like a racing car. "I've got something very difficult to tell you," he said.

"What happened to your hand?" Jack said. "It's all red and puffed up."

"I banged it on something. You have to listen to me."

"Okay."

This was going to be hard for a four-year-old to understand. "You know I'll always love you," George said. "Just like Grandma Jacky loves me, even though I'm not a little boy anymore."

"Is Grandma coming today?"

"Maybe tomorrow."

"She brings cookies."

"Listen. Sometimes mommies and daddies stop loving each other. Did you know that?"

"Yeah. Pete Robbins's daddy doesn't love his mommy anymore." Jack's voice became solemn. "They got *divorced.*"

"I'm glad you understand that, because your mom and I don't love each other anymore."

George watched Jack's face, trying to see whether he understood or not. The boy looked bewildered, as if something apparently impossible seemed to be happening. The look on his face wrenched George's heart. He thought: How can I be doing something this cruel to the person I love most in the world?

How did I get here?

"You know I've been sleeping in the guest room."

"Yeah."

Here comes the hard part. "Well, I'm going to sleep at Grandma's house tonight."

"Why?"

"It's because Mom and I don't love each other."

"Okay, then, I'll see you tomorrow."

"I'm going to be sleeping at Grandma's a lot from now on."

Jack began to see that this would affect him. "Will you read my bedtime story?"

"Every night, if you like." George vowed to keep this promise.

Jack was still working out the implications. "Will you make my warm milk for breakfast?"

"Sometimes. Or Mom will. Or Nanny Tiffany."

Jack knew prevarication when he heard it. "I don't know," he said. "I think you better not sleep at Grandma's."

George ran out of courage. "Well, we'll see," he said. "Hey, how about some ice cream?"

"Yeah!"

It was the worst day of George's life.

. . .

Driving from the Capitol homeward to Prince George's County, George brooded on hostages. This year in Lebanon, four Americans and a Frenchman had been kidnapped. One of the Americans had been released, but the rest were languishing in some prison, unless they were already dead. George knew that one of the Americans was the CIA head of station in Beirut.

The kidnappers were almost certainly a militant Muslim group called Hezbollah, "the Party of God," founded in response to the Israeli invasion of Lebanon in 1982. They had been bankrolled by Iran and trained by Iranian Revolutionary Guards. The United States regarded Hezbollah as an arm of the Iranian government, and classified Iran as a sponsor of terrorism, therefore a country that should not be allowed to buy weapons. George found that ironic, given that President Reagan was sponsoring terrorism in Nicaragua by funding the Contras, a brutal antigovernment group that carried out assassinations and kidnappings.

All the same, George was angry about what was happening in Lebanon. He wanted to send the marines into Beirut with all guns blazing. People should be taught the cost of abducting American citizens!

He felt this strongly, but he knew it was an infantile response. Just as the Israeli invasion had bred Hezbollah, so a violent American attack on Hezbollah would spawn more terrorism. Another generation of young Middle Eastern men would grow up swearing revenge upon America, the great Satan. George and all thinking people realized, when the blood cooled, that revenge was self-defeating. The only answer was to break the chain.

Which was easier said than done.

George was also aware that he had personally failed that test. He had punched Jasper Murray. Jasper was no wimp, but he had sensibly resisted the temptation to fight back. As a result the damage had been limited—no credit to George.

George was living with his mother again—at the age of forty-eight! Verena was still in the family home with little Jack. George presumed that Jasper spent nights there, but he did not know for sure. He was struggling to find a way to live with divorce—just like millions of other men and women.

It was Friday night, and he turned his mind to the weekend. He was on his way to Verena's house. They had settled into a routine. George picked up Jack on Friday evening and took him to Grandma Jacky's house for the weekend, then brought him back home on Monday morning. It was not how George had wanted to raise his child, but it was the best he could manage.

He thought about what they would do. Tomorrow maybe they would go to the public library together and get some bedtime storybooks. Church on Sunday, of course.

He arrived at the ranch-style house that used to be his home. Verena's car was not in the driveway: she was not home yet. George parked and went to the front door. From politeness he rang the bell, then let himself in with his key.

The house was quiet. "It's only me," he called out. There was no one in the kitchen. He found Jack sitting in front of the TV, alone. "Hi, buddy," he said. He sat down and put his arm around Jack's shoulders. "Where's Nanny Tiffany?"

"She had to go home," Jack said. "Mommy's late."

George controlled his anger. "So you're on your own here?"

"Tiffany said it's a mergency."

"How long ago was that?"

"I don't know." Jack still could not reckon time.

George was furious. His son had been left alone in the house at the age of four. What was Verena thinking of?

He got up and looked around. Jack's weekend case stood in the hall. George checked inside and saw everything necessary: pajamas, clean clothes, teddy bear. Nanny Tiffany had done that before she left to deal with what Jack called her mergency.

He went into the kitchen and wrote a note: "I found Jack alone in the house. Call me."

Then he got Jack and went out to the car.

Jacky's house was less than a mile away. When they arrived, Jacky gave Jack a glass of milk and a homemade cookie. He told her all about the cat next door, which came to visit and got a saucer of milk. Then Jacky looked at George and said: "All right, what's eating you?"

"Step into the living room and I'll tell you." They moved to the next room, and George said: "Jack was on his own in the house."

"Oh, that should not happen."

"Damn right."

She overlooked the bad language for once. "Any idea why?"

"Verena didn't come home at the appointed time, and the nanny had to leave."

At that moment they heard a squeal of tires outside. They both looked out of the window and saw Verena getting out of her red Jaguar and running up the path to the door.

George said: "I'm going to kill her."

Jacky let her in. She ran to the kitchen and kissed Jack. "Oh, baby, are you okay?" she said tearfully.

"Yeah," said Jack nonchalantly. "I had a cookie."

"Grandma's cookies are great, aren't they?"

"You bet."

George said: "Verena, you'd better come in here and explain yourself."

She was panting and perspiring. For once she did not appear arrogantly in control. "I was only a few minutes late!" she cried. "I don't know why that goddamn nanny ran out on me!"

"You can't be late when you're looking after Jack," George said severely.

She resented that. "Oh, like you never were?"

"I never left him alone."

"It's very difficult on my own!"

"It's your damn fault you're on your own."

Jacky said: "George, you're in the wrong here."

"Stay out of this, Mom."

"No. It's my house and my grandson, and I won't stay out of anything."

"I can't overlook this, Mom! She did wrong."

"If I'd never done anything wrong, I wouldn't have you."

"That's nothing to do with it."

"I'm just saying we all make mistakes, and sometimes things turn out all right anyway. So stop beating Verena up. It won't do any good."

Reluctantly, George saw that she was right. "But what are we going to do?"

Verena said: "I'm sorry, George, but I just can't cope." She started to cry.

Jacky said: "Well, now that we've stopped yelling, maybe we can start thinking. This nanny of yours is no good."

Verena said: "You don't know how difficult it is to get a nanny! And it's worse for us than for most people. Everyone else hires illegal immigrants and pays them cash, but politicians have to have someone with a green card who pays taxes, so no one wants the job!"

"All right, calm down, I'm not blaming you," Jacky said to Verena. "Maybe I can help."

George and Verena stared at Jacky.

Jacky said: "I'm sixty-four, I'm about to retire, and I need something to do. I'll be your backup. If your nanny lets you down, just bring Jack here. Leave him here overnight when you need to."

"Boy," said George, "that sounds like a solution to me."

Verena said: "Jacky, that would be wonderful!"

"Don't thank me, honey, I'm being selfish. I'll get to see my grandson more."

George said: "Are you sure it won't be too much work, Mom?"

Jacky made a contemptuous noise. "When was the last time something was too much work for me?"

George smiled. "Never, I guess."

And that settled it.

CHAPTER FIFTY-SIX

Rebecca's tears were cold on her cheeks.

It was October, and a biting wind from the North Sea was blowing across Ohlsdorf Cemetery in Hamburg. This graveyard was one of the largest in the world, a thousand acres of sadness and mourning. It had a monument to victims of Nazi persecution, a walled grove for resistance fighters, and a mass grave for the thirty-eight thousand Hamburg men, women, and children killed in ten days by Operation Gomorrah, the Allied bombing campaign of summer 1943.

There was no special area for victims of the Wall.

Rebecca knelt down and picked up the dead leaves scattered over her husband's grave. Then she placed a single red rose on the earth.

She stood still, looking at the tombstone, remembering him.

Bernd had been dead a year. He had lived to sixty-two, which was good for a man with a spinal cord injury. In the end his kidneys had failed, a common cause of death in such cases.

Rebecca thought about his life. It had been blighted by the Wall, and by the injury he had received escaping from East Germany, but despite that he had lived well. He had been a good schoolteacher, perhaps a great one. He had defied the tyranny of East German Communism and escaped to freedom. His first marriage had ended in divorce, but he and Rebecca had loved each other passionately for twenty years.

She did not need to come here to remember him. She thought about him every day. His death was an amputation: she was constantly surprised to find he was not there. Alone in the flat they had shared for so long, she often talked to him, telling him about her day, commenting on the news, saying how she felt, hungry or tired or restless. She had not altered the place, and it still had the ropes and handles that had enabled him to move himself around. His wheelchair stood at the side of the bed as if ready for him to sit upright and haul himself into it. When she masturbated, she imagined him lying beside her, one arm around her, the warmth of his body, his lips on hers.

Fortunately her work was constantly absorbing and challenging. She was now a junior minister in the foreign affairs department of the West German government. Because she spoke Russian and had lived in East Germany she specialized in Eastern Europe. She had little free time.

Tragically, the reunification of Germany seemed ever farther away. Die-hard East German leader Erich Honecker appeared unassailable. People were still being killed trying to escape across the Wall. And in the Soviet Union the death of Andropov had only brought in yet another ailing septuagenarian leader, Konstantin Chernenko. From Berlin to Vladivostok, the Soviet empire was a bog in which its citizens struggled and often sank but never made progress.

Rebecca realized her mind had wandered from Bernd. It was time to go. "Good-bye, my love," she said softly, and she walked slowly away from the grave.

She pulled her heavy coat around her and folded her arms as she crossed the cold cemetery. She gratefully got into her vehicle and turned on the engine. She was still driving the van with the wheelchair hoist. It was time she traded it in for a normal car.

She drove to her apartment. Outside her building was a shiny black Mercedes S500, with a chauffeur in a cap standing beside it. Her spirits lifted. As she expected, she found that Walli had let himself into the apartment with his own key. He was sitting at the kitchen table with the radio on, tapping his foot to a pop song. On the table was a copy of Plum Nellie's latest album, *The Interpretation of Dreams.* "I'm glad I caught you," he said. "I'm on my way to the airport. I'm flying to San Francisco." He stood up to kiss her.

He would be forty in a couple of years, and he looked great. He still smoked, but he never took drugs or alcohol. He was wearing a tan leather jacket over a blue denim shirt. Some girl ought to snap him up, Rebecca thought; but although he had girlfriends he seemed in no hurry to settle down.

When she kissed him she touched his arm and noticed that the leather of his jacket was as soft as silk. It had probably cost a fortune. She said: "But you've only just finished your album."

"We're doing a tour of the States. I'm going to Daisy Farm for three weeks of rehearsal. We open in Philadelphia in a month."

"Give the boys my love."

"Sure will."

"It's a while since you toured."

"Three years. Hence the long rehearsal. But stadium gigs are where it's at now. It's not like the All-Star Touring Beat Revue, with twelve bands playing two or three songs each to a couple of thousand people in a theater or gymnasium. It's just fifty thousand people and us."

"Will you do some European dates?"

"Yes, but they haven't been fixed yet."

"Any in Germany?"

"Almost certainly."

"Let me know."

"Of course. I may be able to get you a free ticket."

Rebecca laughed. As Walli's sister she was treated like royalty whenever she went backstage at a Plum Nellie gig. The band had often talked in interviews about the old days in Hamburg, and how Walli's big sister used to give them their only good meal of the week. For that she was famous in the world of rock and roll.

"Have a great tour," she said.

"You're about to fly to Budapest, aren't you?"

"For a trade conference, yes."

"Will there be some East Germans there?"

"Yes, why?"

"Do you think one of them might be able to get an album to Alice?"

Rebecca grimaced. "I don't know. My relations with East German politicians are not warm. They think I'm a lackey of the capitalist-imperialists, and I think they are unelected thugs who rule by terror and keep their people imprisoned."

Walli smiled. "So, not much common ground, then."

"No. But I'll try."

"Thanks." He handed her the disc.

Rebecca looked at the photograph on the sleeve, of four middle-aged men with long hair and blue jeans. Buzz, the randy bass player, was overweight. The gay drummer, Lew, was losing his hair. Dave, the leader of the band, had a touch of gray in his hair. They were established, successful, and rich. She remembered the hungry kids who had come here to this apartment: thin, scruffy, witty, charming, and full of hopes and dreams. "You've done well," she said.

"Yeah," said Walli. "We have."

. . .

On the last evening of the Budapest conference, Rebecca and the other delegates were given a tasting of Tokaj wines. They were taken to a cellar owned by the Hungarian government bottling organization. It was in the Pest district, east of the Danube River. They were offered several different kinds of white wine: dry; strong; the lightly alcoholic nectar called *eszencia;* and the famous slow-fermented *aszú*.

All over the world, government officials were bad at throwing parties, and Rebecca feared this would be a dull occasion. However, the old cellar with its arched ceilings and stacked cases of booze had a cozy feel, and there were spicy Hungarian snacks of dumplings, stuffed mushrooms, and sausages.

Rebecca picked out one of the East German delegates and gave him her most engaging smile. "Our German wines are superior, don't you think?" she said.

She chatted flirtatiously with him for a few minutes, then asked him the question. "I have a niece in East Berlin, and I want to send her a pop record, but I'm afraid it might get damaged in the mail. Would you take it for me?"

"Yes, I suppose I could," he said dubiously.

"I'll give it to you tomorrow at breakfast, if I may. You're very kind."

"Okay." He looked troubled, and Rebecca thought there

was a chance he might hand over the disc to the Stasi. But all she could do was try.

When the wine had relaxed everyone, Rebecca was approached by Frederik Bíró, a Hungarian politician of her own age whom she liked. He specialized in foreign policy, as she did. "What's the truth about this country?" she asked him. "How is it doing, really?"

He looked at his watch. "We're about a mile from your hotel," he said. He spoke good German, like most educated Hungarians. "Would you like to walk back with me?"

They got their coats and left. Their route followed the broad, dark river. On the far bank, the lights of the medieval town of Buda rose romantically to a hilltop palace.

"The Communists promised prosperity, and the people are disappointed," Bíró said as they walked. "Even Communist Party members complain about the Kádár government." Rebecca guessed that he felt freer to talk out in the open air where they could not be bugged.

She said: "And the solution?"

"The strange thing is that everyone knows the answer. We need to decentralize decisions, introduce limited markets, and legitimize the semi-illegal gray economy so that it can grow."

"Who stands in the way of this?" She realized she was firing questions at him like a courtroom lawyer. "Forgive me," she said. "I don't mean to interrogate you."

"Not at all," he said with a smile. "I like people who speak in a direct way. It saves time."

"Men often resent being spoken to that way by a woman."

"Not me. You could say that I have a weakness for assertive women."

"Are you married to one?"

"I was. I'm divorced now."

Rebecca realized this was none of her business. "You were about to tell me who stands in the way of reform."

"About fifteen thousand bureaucrats who would lose their power and their jobs; fifty thousand top Communist Party officials who make almost all the decisions; and János Kádár, who has been our leader since 1956."

Rebecca raised her eyebrows. Bíró was being remarkably frank. The thought crossed her mind that Bíró's candid remarks may not have been totally spontaneous. Had this conversation perhaps been planned? She said: "Does Kádár have an alternative solution?"

"Yes," said Bíró. "To maintain the standard of living of Hungarian workers, he is borrowing more and more money from Western banks, including German ones."

"And how will you pay the interest on those loans?"

"What a good question," said Bíró.

They drew level with Rebecca's hotel, across the street from the river. She stopped and leaned on the embankment wall. "Is Kádár a permanent fixture?"

"Not necessarily. I'm close to a promising young man called Miklós Németh."

Ah, Rebecca thought, so this is the point of the conversation: to tell the German government, quietly and informally, that Németh is the reformist rival to Kádár.

"He's in his thirties, and very bright," Bíró continued. "But we fear a Hungarian repeat of the Soviet situation: Brezhnev replaced by Andropov and then Chernenko. It's like the queue for the toilet in a home for old men."

Rebecca laughed. She liked Bíró.

He bent his head and kissed her.

She was only half surprised. She had sensed that he was attracted to her. What surprised her was how excited she felt to be kissed. She kissed him back eagerly.

Then she drew back. She put her hands on his chest and pushed him away a little. She studied him in the lamplight. No man of fifty looked like Adonis, but Frederik had a face that suggested intelligence and compassion and the ability to smile wryly at life's ironies. He had gray hair cut short and blue eyes. He was wearing a dark blue coat and a bright red scarf, conservatism with a touch of gaiety.

She said: "Why did you get divorced?"

"I had an affair, and my wife left me. Feel free to condemn me."

"No," she said. "I've made mistakes."

"I regretted it, when it was too late."

"Children?"

"Two, grown up. They have forgiven me. Marta has remarried, but I'm still single. What's your story?"

"I divorced my first husband when I discovered he worked for the Stasi. My second husband was injured escaping over the Berlin Wall. He was in a wheelchair, but we were happy together for twenty years. He died a year ago."

"My word, you're about due for some good luck."

"Perhaps I am. Would you walk me to the hotel entrance, please?"

They crossed the road. On the corner of the block, where the streetlights were less glaring, she kissed him again. She enjoyed it even more this time, and pressed her body against his.

"Spend the night with me," he said.

She was sorely tempted. "No," she said. "It's too soon. I hardly know you."

"But you're going home tomorrow."

"I know."

"We may never meet again."

"I'm sure we will."

"We could go to my apartment. Or I'll come to your room."

"No, though I'm flattered by your persistence. Good night."

"Good night, then."

She turned away.

He said: "I travel often to Bonn. I'll be there in ten days' time."

She turned back, smiling.

He said: "Will you have dinner with me?"

"I'd love to," she said. "Call me."

"Okay."

She walked into the hotel lobby, smiling.

•

Lili was at home in Berlin-Mitte one afternoon when her niece, Alice, came, in a rainstorm, to borrow books. Alice had been refused admission to university, despite her outstanding grades, because of her mother's underground career as a protest singer. However, Alice was determined to educate herself, so she was studying English in the evenings after she finished her shift at the factory. Carla had a small collection of English-language novels inherited from Grandmother Maud. They went upstairs to the drawing room and looked through the books together while the rain drummed on the windows. They were old editions, prewar, Lili guessed.

Alice picked out a collection of Sherlock Holmes stories. She would be the fourth generation to read them, Lili calculated.

Alice said: "We've applied for permission to go to West Germany." She was all youthful eagerness.

"We?" Lili asked.

"Helmut and I."

Helmut Kappel was her boyfriend. He was a year older, twenty-two, and studying at university.

"Any special reason?"

"I've said we want to visit my father in Hamburg. Helmut's grandparents are in Frankfurt. But Plum Nellie is doing a world tour, and we really want to see my father onstage. Maybe we can time our visit to coincide with his German gig, if he does one."

"I'm sure he will."

"Do you think they'll let us go?"

"You may be lucky." Lili did not want to discourage youthful optimism, but she was doubtful. She herself had always been refused permission. Very few people were allowed to go. The authorities would suspect that people as young as Alice and Helmut did not intend to come back.

Lili suspected it herself. Alice had often talked wistfully of living in West Germany. Like most young people, she wanted to read uncensored books and newspapers, see new films and plays, and listen to music regardless of whether it was approved by the seventy-two-year-old Erich Honecker. If she managed to get out of East Germany, why would she come back?

Alice said: "You know, most of the things that got this family into bad odor with the authorities actually happened before I was born. They shouldn't be punishing me."

But her mother, Karolin, was still singing those songs, Lili thought.

The doorbell sounded, and a minute later they heard agitated voices in the hall. They went downstairs to investigate, and found Karolin standing there in a wet raincoat. Inexplicably, she was carrying a suitcase. She had been let in by Carla, who stood beside her in the hall, wearing an apron over her formal work clothes.

Karolin's face was red and puffy with crying.

Alice said: "Mother . . . ?"

Lili said: "Has something happened?"

Karolin said: "Alice, your stepfather has left me."

Lili was flabbergasted. Odo Vossler? It was surprising to her that mild Odo had the guts to leave his wife.

Alice put her arms around her mother, saying nothing.

Carla said: "When did this happen?"

Karolin wiped her nose with a handkerchief. "He told me three hours ago. He wants a divorce."

Lili thought: Poor Alice, left by two fathers.

Carla said indignantly: "But pastors are not supposed to get divorced."

"He's leaving the clergy, too."

"Good grief."

Lili realized that an earthquake had struck the family.

Carla became practical. "You'd better sit down. We'll go in the kitchen. Alice, take your mother's coat and hang it up to dry. Lili, make coffee."

Lili put water on to boil and took a cake out of the cupboard. Carla said: "Karolin, whatever has come over Odo?"

She looked down. "He is . . ." She obviously found this difficult to say. Averting her eyes, she said quietly: "Odo tells me he has realized that he is homosexual."

Alice gave a little scream.

Carla said: "What a terrible shock!"

Lili had a sudden flash of memory. Five years ago, when they had all met up in Hungary, and Walli had met Odo for the first time, she had seen a startled reaction pass over Walli's face, brief but vivid. Had Walli intuited the truth about Odo in that moment?

Lili herself had always suspected that Odo's love for Karolin was not a grand passion but more of a Christian mission. If a man should ever propose to Lili, she did not want him to do it out of the kindness of his heart. He should desire her so much he could hardly keep his hands off her: that was a good reason for a proposal of marriage.

Karolin looked up. Now that the awful truth was out, she was able to meet Carla's eye. "It's not a shock, really," she said quietly. "I sort of knew."

"How?"

"When we were first married, there was a young man called Paul, very good-looking. He was invited for supper a couple of times a week, and Bible study in the vestry, and on Saturday afternoons they would go for long, invigorating walks in Treptower Park. Perhaps they never did anything—Odo is not a deceiving man. But, when he made love to me, somehow I felt sure he was thinking about Paul."

"What happened? How did it end?"

Lili cut the cake into slices while she listened. She put the slices on a plate. No one ate any.

Karolin said: "I never knew the full story. Paul stopped coming to the house and to church. Odo never explained why. Perhaps they both pulled back from physical love."

Carla said: "Being a pastor, Odo must have suffered a terrible conflict."

"I know. I'm so sorry for him, when I'm not feeling angry."

"Poor Odo."

"But Paul was only the first of half a dozen boys, all very similar, terribly good-looking and sincere Christians."

"And now?"

"Now Odo has found real love. He is abjectly apologetic to me, but he has made up his mind to face what he truly is. He's moving in with a man called Eugen Freud."

"What will he do?"

"He wants to be a teacher in a theological college. He says it's his real vocation."

Lili poured boiling water on the ground coffee in the jug. Now that Odo and Karolin had split up, she wondered how Walli would feel. Of course he could not be reunited with Karolin and Alice because of the accursed Berlin Wall. But would he want to? He had not settled permanently with another woman. It seemed to Lili that Karolin really was the love of his life.

But all that was academic. The Communists had decreed that they could not be together.

Carla said: "If Odo has resigned as pastor, you'll have to leave your house."

"Yes. I'm homeless."

"Don't be silly. You'll always have a home here."

"I knew you'd say that," said Karolin, and she burst into tears.

The doorbell rang.

"I'll go," said Lili.

There were two men on the doorstep. One wore a chauffeur's uniform and held an umbrella over the other man, who was Hans Hoffmann.

"May I come in?" said Hans, but he walked into the hall without waiting for an answer. He was holding a package about a foot square.

His driver returned to the black ZIL limousine parked at the curb.

Lili spoke with distaste. "What do you want?"

"To speak to your niece, Alice."

"How did you know she was here?"

Hans smiled and did not bother to answer. The Stasi knew everything.

Lili went into the kitchen. "It's Hans Hoffmann. He wants Alice."

Alice stood up, pale with fear.

Carla said: "Take him upstairs, Lili. Stay with them."

Karolin half-rose out of her chair. "I should go with her."

Carla put a restraining hand on Karolin's arm. "You're in no state to deal with the Stasi."

Karolin accepted that and sat back down again. Lili held the door for Alice, who came out of the kitchen into the hall. The two women went upstairs, followed by Hans.

Lili almost offered Hans a cup of coffee, from automatic politeness, but she stopped herself. He could die of thirst first.

Hans picked up the Sherlock Holmes book Alice had left on the table. "English," he commented, as if that confirmed a suspicion. He sat down, tugging on the knees of his fine wool trousers to prevent creasing. He put the square packet on the floor beside his chair. He said: "So, young Alice, you wish to travel to West Germany. Why?"

He was a big shot now. Lili did not know what his exact title was, but he was more than just a secret policeman. He made speeches at national meetings and spoke to the press. However, he was not too important to persecute the Franck family.

"My father lives in Hamburg," Alice said in answer to his question. "So does my aunt Rebecca."

"Your father is a murderer."

"It happened before I was born. Are you punishing me for it? That isn't what you mean by Communist justice . . . is it?"

Hans gave that smug I-thought-so nod again. "A smart mouth, just like your grandmother. This family will never learn."

Lili said angrily: "We have learned that Communism means petty officials can take their revenge, without regard to justice or the law."

"Do you imagine that such talk is the way to persuade me to grant Alice permission to travel?"

"You've made up your mind already," Lili said wearily. "You're going to refuse. You wouldn't have come here to say yes to her. You just want to gloat."

Alice said: "Where in the writings of Karl Marx do we read that in the Communist state workers are not allowed to travel to other countries?"

"Restrictions are made necessary by the conditions prevailing."

"No, they're not. I want to see my father. You prevent me. Why? Just because you can! That has nothing to do with socialism and everything to do with tyranny."

Hans's mouth twisted. "You bourgeois people," he said in tones of disgust. "You can't bear it when others have power over you."

"Bourgeois?" said Lili. "I don't have a uniformed chauffeur to hold an umbrella over me while I walk from the car to the house. Nor does Alice. There's only one bourgeois in this room, Hans."

He picked up the package and handed it to Alice. "Open it," he said.

Alice took off the brown paper wrapping. Inside was a copy of Plum Nellie's latest album, *The Interpretation of Dreams*. Her face lit up.

Lili wondered what trick Hans was up to now.

"Why don't you play your father's record?" Hans said.

Alice withdrew the inner white envelope from the colored sleeve. Then with finger and thumb she took the black plastic disc from the envelope.

It came out in two pieces.

Hans said: "It seems to be broken. What a shame."

Alice began to cry.

Hans stood up. "I know the way out," he said, and he left.

. . .

Unter den Linden was the broad boulevard through East Berlin to the Brandenburg Gate. Under another name, the street continued into West Berlin through the park called the Tiergarten. Since 1961, though, Unter den Linden had dead-ended at the Brandenburg Gate, blocked by the Berlin Wall. From the park on the west side, the view of the Brandenburg Gate was disfigured by a high, ugly, gray-green fence covered with graffiti, and a sign in German that said:

WARNING
YOU ARE NOW LEAVING
WEST BERLIN

Beyond the fence was the killing field of the Wall.

Plum Nellie's road crew built a stage right up against the ugly fence and stacked a mighty wall of loudspeakers facing out into the park. On Walli's instructions, equally powerful speakers faced the other way, into East Berlin. He wanted Alice to hear him. A reporter had told him that the East German government objected to the speakers. "Tell them that if they take their wall down, I'll do the same with mine," Walli had said, and the quote was in all the papers.

Originally they had thought to do the German gig in Hamburg, but then Walli had heard about Hans Hoffmann breaking Alice's disc, and in retaliation he had asked Dave to reschedule in Berlin, so that a million East Germans would be able to hear the songs Hoffmann had attempted to deny to Alice. Dave had loved the idea.

Now they stood together, looking at the stage from the side as thousands of fans gathered in the park. "This is going to be the loudest we've ever been," said Dave.

"Good," said Walli. "I want them to hear my guitar all the way to fucking Leipzig."

"Remember the old days?" Dave said. "Those tinny little speakers they had in baseball stadiums?"

"No one could hear us—we couldn't hear ourselves!"

"Now a hundred thousand people can listen to music that sounds the way we intended."

"It's kind of a miracle."

When Walli returned to his dressing room, Rebecca was

there. "This is fantastic," she said. "There must be a hundred thousand people in the park!"

She was with a gray-haired man of about her own age. "This is my friend Fred Bíró," she said.

Walli shook his hand, and Fred said: "It's an honor to meet you." He spoke German with a Hungarian accent.

Walli was amused. So his sister was dating at the age of fifty-three! Well, good for her. The guy seemed to be her type, intellectual but not too solemn. And she looked younger, with a Princess Diana hairstyle and a purple dress.

They chatted for a while, then left him to get ready. Walli changed into clean blue jeans and a flame red shirt. Peering into the mirror, he put on eyeliner so that the crowd could read his expression better. He remembered with disgust the times when he had had to manage his drug intake so carefully: a small amount to keep him level during the performance, and a big hit afterward as his reward. He was not for one second tempted to return to those habits.

He was called to go onstage. He joined up with Dave, Buzz, and Lew. Dave's whole family was there to wish them well: his wife, Beep; their eleven-year-old son, John Lee; Dave's parents, Daisy and Lloyd; and even his sister, Evie; all looking proud of their Dave. Walli was glad to see them all, but their presence reminded him poignantly that he was not able to see his own family: Werner and Carla, Lili, Karolin and Alice.

But with any luck they would be listening on the other side of the Wall.

The band went onstage and the crowd roared their welcome.

.   .   .

Unter den Linden was jammed with thousands of Plum Nellie fans, old and young. Lili and her family, including Karolin, Alice, and Alice's boyfriend, Helmut, had been there since early morning. They had secured a position close to the barrier the police had set up to keep the crowd at a distance from the Wall. As the crowd had grown through the day, the street had developed a festival atmosphere, with people talking to strangers and sharing their picnics and playing Plum Nellie tapes on portable boom boxes. As darkness fell they opened bottles of beer and wine.

Then the band came on, and the crowd went wild.

East Berliners could see nothing but the four bronze horses pulling Victory's chariot atop the arch. But they could hear everything loud and clear: Lew's drumming; Buzz's thudding bass; Dave's rhythm guitar and high harmonies; and, best of all, Walli's perfect pop baritone and lyrical guitar lines. The familiar songs soared out of the speaker stacks and thrilled the moving, dancing crowd. That's my brother, Lili kept thinking; my big brother, singing to the world. Werner and Carla looked proud, Karolin was smiling, and Alice's eyes were shining.

Lili glanced up at a government office building nearby. Standing on a small balcony were half a dozen men in ties and dark coats, clearly visible by the streetlights. They were not dancing. One was taking photographs of the crowd. They must be Stasi, Lili realized. They were making a record of traitors disloyal to the Honecker regime — which was, nowadays, almost everyone.

Looking more closely, she thought she recognized one of the secret policemen. It was Hans Hoffmann, she was almost sure. He was tall and slightly stooped. He seemed to be speaking angrily, moving his right arm in a violent hammering gesture. Walli had said in an interview that the band wanted to play here because East Germans were not allowed to listen to their records. Hans must have known that his breaking Alice's disc was the reason for this concert and this crowd. No wonder he was angry.

She saw Hans throw up his hands in despair, turn, and leave the balcony, disappearing into the building. One song ended and another began. The crowd yelled their approval as they recognized the opening chords of one of Plum Nellie's biggest hits. Walli's voice came through the speakers: "This one is for my little girl."

Then he sang "I Miss Ya, Alicia."

Lili looked at Alice. Tears were streaming down her face, but she was smiling.

CHAPTER FIFTY-SEVEN

Illiam Buckley, the American kidnapped in Lebanon by Hezbollah on March 16, 1984, was officially described as a political officer at the U.S. embassy in Beirut. In fact he was the CIA head of station.

Cam Dewar knew Bill Buckley and thought he was a good guy. Bill was a slight figure in conservative Brooks Brothers suits. He had a head of thick graying hair and matinee-idol looks. A career soldier, he had fought in Korea and served with the Special Forces in Vietnam, ending with the rank of colonel. In the sixties he had joined the Special Activities Division of the CIA. That was the division that carried out assassinations.

Bill was single at fifty-seven. According to Langley gossip, he had a long-distance relationship with a woman called Candace in Farmer, North Carolina. She wrote him love letters and he telephoned her from all over the world. When he was in the USA, they were lovers. Or so people said.

Like everyone else at Langley, Cam was angry about the kidnapping and desperate to get Bill released. But all efforts failed.

And there was worse news. One by one, Bill's agents and informers in Beirut began to disappear. Hezbollah had to be getting their names from Bill. That meant he was being tortured.

The CIA knew Hezbollah's methods, and they could guess what was happening to Bill. He would be permanently blindfolded, chained at the ankles and wrists, and kept in a box like a coffin, day after day, week after week. After a few months of this he would be literally insane: drooling, gibbering, trembling, rolling his eyes, and letting out sudden random screams of terror.

So Cam was savagely pleased when at last someone came up with a plan of action against the kidnappers.

The plan originated not with the CIA, but with the president's national security adviser, Bud McFarlane. On his staff Bud had a gung-ho marine lieutenant colonel called Oliver North, known as Ollie. Among the men North had recruited to help him was Tim Tedder, and it was Tim who told Cam of McFarlane's plan.

Cam eagerly took Tim into the office of Florence Geary. Tim was a former CIA agent and an old acquaintance of Florence's. As always, he had his hair cut as if he were still in the army, and today he wore a safari suit that was as close to a military uniform as civilian dress could get.

"We're going to work with foreign nationals," Tim explained. "There will be three teams, each of five men. They won't be CIA employees and they won't even be Americans. But the Agency will train them, equip them, and arrange finance."

Florence nodded. "And what will these teams do?" she said neutrally.

"The idea is to get to the kidnappers before they strike," Tim said. "When we know that they're planning a kidnapping, or a bombing, or any other kind of terrorist act—we will direct one of the teams to go in and eliminate the perpetrators."

"Let me get this straight," said Florence. "These teams will kill terrorists *before* they commit crimes."

She was not as excited by the plan as Cam was, evidently, and he had a bad feeling.

"Exactly," said Tim.

"I have one question," said Florence. "Are you two out of your fucking minds?"

Cam was outraged. How could Florence be against this?

Tim said indignantly: "I know it's unconventional—"

"Unconventional?" Florence interrupted. "By the laws of every civilized country it's *murder*. There is no due process, there is no requirement of proof, and by your own admission the people you're targeting may have done nothing more than merely *think* about committing crimes."

Cam said: "Actually, it's not murder. We'd be acting like a cop who gets off an early shot at a criminal who is pointing a gun at him. It's called preemptive self-defense."

"So you're a lawyer, now, Cam."

"That's not my opinion, it's Sporkin's." Stanley Sporkin was the CIA general counsel.

"Well, Stan's wrong," said Florence. "Because we never see a pointed gun. We have no way of knowing who is about to commit a terrorist act. We don't have intelligence of that quality in Lebanon—we never have. So we'll end up killing people who we *think* might be planning terrorism."

"Perhaps we can improve the reliability of our information."

"What about the reliability of the foreign nationals? Who will be on these five-man teams? Local Beirut bad guys? Mercenaries? International-security-company Eurotrash? How can you trust them? How can you *control* them? Yet whatever they do will be our responsibility—especially if they kill innocent people!"

Tim said: "No, no—the whole operation will be arm's length and deniable."

"It doesn't sound very deniable to me. The CIA is going to train and equip them and finance their activities. And have you thought of the political consequences?"

"Fewer kidnappings and bombings."

"How can you be so naïve? If we strike at Hezbollah this way, you think they will sit back and say: 'Gosh, the Americans are tougher than we thought, maybe we'd better give up this whole terrorism idea.' No, no. They will be screaming for revenge! In the Middle East, violence always begets more violence—haven't you learned that yet? Hezbollah bombed the marine corps barracks in Beirut—why? According to Colonel Geraghty, who was the marine commander at the time, it was in response to the U.S. Sixth Fleet shelling innocent Muslims in the village of Suq al-Gharb. One atrocity brings another."

"So you're just going to give in and say nothing can be done?"

"Nothing *easy* can be done, just hard political work. We lower the temperature, we restrain both sides, and we bring them to the negotiating table, again and again, no matter how many times they walk out. We don't give up and, whatever happens, we don't escalate the violence."

"I think we can—"

But Florence was not yet done. "This plan is criminal, it's impractical, it has horrendous political consequences in the Middle East, and it endangers the reputations of the CIA, the president, and the USA. But that is not all. There is yet one more thing that completely rules it out."

She paused, and Cam was forced to say: "What?"

"We are forbidden *by the president* to carry out assassinations. 'No person employed by or acting on behalf of the United States Government shall engage in, or conspire to engage in, assassination.' Executive Order 12333. Ronald Reagan signed it in 1981."

"I think he's forgotten that," said Cam.

.　.　.

Maria met Florence Geary in downtown Washington at the Woodward and Lothrop department store, which everyone called Woodies. Their rendezvous was in the brassiere department. Most agents were men, and any man who followed them in here would be conspicuous. He might even get arrested.

"I used to be size thirty-four A," said Florence. "Now I'm thirty-six C. What happened?"

Maria chuckled. At forty-eight she was a little older than Florence. "Join the club of middle-aged women," she said. "I always had a big ass, but I used to have cute little boobs that stood up all on their own. Now I need serious support."

In two decades in Washington, Maria had assiduously cultivated contacts. She had learned early on how much was achieved—for good or ill—through personal acquaintance. Back in the days when the CIA had been using Florence as a secretary, instead of training her to be an agent as they had promised, Maria had sympathized with her plight, woman to woman. Maria's contacts were usually women, always liberal. She exchanged information with them, giving early warning of threatening moves by political opponents, and helped them discreetly, often by assigning higher priority to projects that might otherwise be sidelined by conservative men. The men did much the same.

They each picked out half a dozen bras and went to try them on. It was a Tuesday morning, and the changing room was empty. Nevertheless, Florence kept her voice low. "Bud McFarlane has come up with a plan that is complete madness," she said as she unbuttoned her blouse. "But Bill Casey committed the CIA." Casey, a crony of President Reagan's, was head of the CIA. "And the president said yes."

"What plan?"

"We're training assassination squads of foreign nationals to kill terrorists in Beirut. They call it preemptive counterterrorism."

Maria was shocked. "But that's a crime, by the laws of this country. If they succeed, McFarlane and Casey and Ronald Reagan will all be murderers."

"Exactly."

The two women took off the bras they were wearing and stood side by side in front of the mirror. "You see?" said Florence. "They've lost that sit-up-and-beg look."

"Mine, too."

There was a time, Maria reflected, when she would have been too embarrassed to do this with a white woman. Maybe things really were changing.

They started to try on the bras. Maria said: "Has Casey briefed the intelligence committees?"

"No. Reagan decided he could just inform the chair and vice chair of each committee, and the Republican and Democratic leaders of the House and Senate."

That explained why George Jakes had not heard about this, Maria deduced. Reagan had made a sly move. The intelligence committees had a quota of liberals, to ensure that at least some critical questions were asked. Reagan had found a way to sideline the critics and inform only those he knew would be supportive.

Florence said: "One of the teams is here in the States right now, on a two-week training course."

"So the whole thing is quite far advanced."

"Right." Florence looked at herself in a black bra. "My Frank is pleased that my bust has changed. He always wanted a wife with big tits. He claims he's going to church to thank God."

Maria laughed. "You have a nice husband. I hope he likes your new bras."

"And what about you? Who will appreciate your underwear?"

"You know me, I'm a career girl."

"Were you always?"

"There was a guy, a long time ago, but he died."

"I'm so sorry."

"Thank you."

"And no one else since?"

She hardly hesitated. "One near miss. You know, I like men, and I like sex, but I'm not prepared to give up my whole life and become an appendage to some guy. Your Frank obviously understands that, but not many men do."

Florence nodded. "Honey, you got that right."

Maria frowned. "What do you want me to do about these murder squads?" The thought occurred to her that Florence was a secret agent, after all, and she might have found out, or guessed, that Maria had leaked stories to Jasper Murray. Did she want Maria to leak this one?

But Florence said: "I don't want you to do anything, right now. The plan is still a stupid idea that may be nipped in the bud. I just want to be sure that someone outside the intelligence community knows about it. If the shit hits the fan, and Reagan starts lying about murder the way Nixon lied about burglary, at least you will know the truth."

"Meanwhile, we just pray that it never happens."

"Amen."

. . .

"We've selected our first target," said Tim Tedder to Cam. "We're going for the big guy."

"Fadlallah?"

"Himself."

Cam nodded. Muhammad Hussein Fadlallah was a leading Muslim scholar and a grand ayatollah. In his sermons he called for armed resistance to the Israeli occupation of Lebanon. Hezbollah said he was their inspiration, no more, but the CIA was convinced he was the mastermind behind the kidnapping campaign. Cam would be glad to see him dead.

Cam and Tim were sitting in Cam's office at Langley. On his desk was a framed photograph of himself with President Nixon, deep in conversation. Langley was one of the few places where a man could still be proud of having worked for Nixon. "Is Fadlallah planning more kidnappings?" Cam asked.

Tim said: "Is the Pope planning more baptisms?"

"What about the team? Are they trustworthy? Are they under control?" Florence Geary's objections had been overruled, but her misgivings had not been stupid, and Cam was now remembering what she had said.

Tim sighed. "Cam, if they were trustworthy, responsible people who respected legitimate authority, they wouldn't be available for hire as paid assassins. They are as reliable as such people ever are. And we have them more or less under control, for now."

"Well, at least we're not financing them. I got the money from the Saudis—three million dollars."

Tim raised his eyebrows. "That was well done."

"Thanks."

"We might consider putting the whole project techni- cally under the control of Saudi intelligence, to improve deniability."

"Good idea. But even then we'll need a cover story, after Fadlallah is killed."

Tim thought for a minute, then said: "Let's blame Israel."

"Yeah."

"Everyone will readily believe the Mossad did a thing like this."

Cam frowned uneasily. "I'm still worried. I wish I knew exactly how they were going to do it."

"Better if you don't know."

"I have to know. I might go to Lebanon. Get a closer look."

"If you do," said Tim, "go carefully."

•   •   •

Cam rented a white Toyota Corolla and drove south from the center of Beirut to the mostly Muslim suburb of Bir el- Abed. It was a jungle of ugly concrete apartment buildings interspersed with handsome mosques, each mosque on its broad lot, like a gracious specimen tree carefully cultivated in a clearing amid a crowded forest of rough pines. Poor though the country was, the traffic in the narrow streets was heavy, and the shops and street stalls were besieged by crowds. It was hot, and the Toyota had no air-conditioning, but Cam drove with the windows closed, fearful of contact with the unruly population.

He had visited the district once before, with a CIA guide, and he quickly found the street where Ayatollah Fadlallah lived. Cam drove slowly past the high-rise apartment building, then went all around the block and parked a hundred yards before the building on the opposite side of the road.

On the same street were several more apartment buildings, a cinema, and, most importantly, a mosque. Every afternoon at the same time, Fadlallah walked from his apartment building to the mosque for prayers.

That was when they would kill him.

No foul-ups, please, God, Cam prayed.

Along the short stretch of street Fadlallah would have to follow, cars were parked nose to tail at the curb. One of those cars contained a bomb. Cam did not know which.

Somewhere nearby the trigger man was concealed, watching the street like Cam, waiting for the ayatollah. Cam scanned the cars and the overlooking windows. He did not spot the trigger man. That was good. The assassin was well concealed, as he should be.

Cam had been assured by the Saudis that no innocent bystanders would be hurt. Fadlallah was always surrounded by bodyguards: some of them would undoubtedly suffer injury, but they always kept the general public well away from their leader.

Cam worried whether the bomb's effects could be predicted so accurately. But civilians were sometimes hurt in a war. Look at all the Japanese women and children killed at Hiroshima and Nagasaki. Of course, the United States had been at war with Japan, which it was not with Lebanon; but Cam told himself that the same principle applied. If a few passersby suffered cuts and bruises, the end surely justified the means.

Still, he was alarmed by the number of pedestrians. A car bomb was more suited to a lonely location. Here, a marksman with a high-powered rifle would have been a better choice.

Too late now.

He looked at his watch. Fadlallah was behind schedule. That was unnerving. Cam wished he would hurry.

There seemed to be a lot of women and girls on the

street, and Cam wondered why. A minute later he figured out that they were coming out of the mosque. There must have been some special event for females, the Muslim equivalent of a mothers' meeting. Unfortunately they were crowding the damn street. The squad might have to abort the explosion.

Now Cam hoped that Fadlallah would be even later.

He scanned the cityscape again, looking for an alert man concealing some kind of radio-operated triggering mechanism. This time he thought he spotted the man. Three hundred yards away, opposite the mosque, a first-floor window stood open in the side wall of a tenement. Cam would not have noticed the man but that the afternoon sun, moving down the western sky, had shifted the shadows to reveal the figure. Cam could not make out the man's features but recognized his body language: tense, poised, waiting, scared, two hands grasping something that might have been a transistor radio with a long retractable aerial, except that no one held on to a transistor radio for dear life.

More and more women came out of the mosque, some wearing only the hijab head scarf, others in the all-concealing burqa. They thronged the sidewalks in both directions. Soon, Cam hoped, the rush would be over.

He looked toward Fadlallah's building and saw, to his horror, that the ayatollah was coming out, surrounded by six or seven other men.

Fadlallah was a small old man with a long white beard. He wore a round black hat and white robes. His face had an alert, intelligent expression, and he was smiling slightly at something a companion was saying as they left the building and turned into the street.

"No," said Cam aloud. "Not now. Not now!"

He looked along the street. The sidewalks were still crowded with women and girls, talking, laughing, showing in their smiles and gestures the relief felt by people on leaving a holy place after a solemn service. Their duty was done, their souls were refreshed, and they were ready to resume the worldly life, looking forward to the evening ahead, to supper, conversation, amusement, family, and friends.

Except that some of them were going to die.

Cam jumped out of his car.

He waved frantically toward the tenement window where

the trigger man lurked, but there was no response. It was hardly surprising: Cam was too far away, and the man was concentrating on Fadlallah.

Cam looked across the street. Fadlallah was walking away from Cam, toward the mosque and the assassin's lair, at a brisk pace. The explosion had to be seconds away.

Cam ran along the street toward the tenement building, but his progress was slow because of the crowds of women. He drew curious and hostile looks, an obvious American running through a throng of Muslim women. He drew level with Fadlallah and saw one of the bodyguards point him out to another. Before many more seconds passed, someone would accost him.

He ran on, throwing caution to the winds. Fifty feet from the tenement he stopped, shouted, and waved at the assassin in the window. He could see the man clearly now, a young Arab with a wispy beard and a terrified expression. "Don't do it!" Cam yelled, knowing he was now hazarding his own life. "Abort, abort! For the love of God, abort!"

From behind, someone seized him by the shoulder and said something aggressive in harsh Arabic.

Then there was a tremendous bang.

Cam was thrown flat.

He was breathless, as if someone had hit him on the back with a plank. His head hurt. He could hear screams, men cursing, and the sliding sound of falling rubble. He rolled over, gasping, and struggled to his feet. He was alive, and as far as he could tell not seriously hurt. An Arab man lay motionless at his feet, probably the person who had grabbed him by the shoulder. The man had taken the full force of the blast, his body shielding Cam, it seemed.

He looked across the street.

"Oh, my Jesus," he said.

There were bodies everywhere, horribly twisted and bloodied and broken. Those not lying still were staggering, stanching wounds, screaming, and looking for their loved ones. Some people's loose Middle Eastern clothing had been blown away, and many of the women were half-naked in the true obscenity of violent death.

Two apartment buildings had their fronts destroyed, and masonry and household objects were still falling into the street, massive chunks of concrete alongside chairs and TV sets. Several buildings were burning. The road was littered with damaged cars, as if all the vehicles had been dropped from a height and had landed haphazard.

Cam knew immediately that the bomb had been too large, far too large.

On the other side of the street he saw the white beard and black hat of Fadlallah, who was being rushed back toward his building by his bodyguards. He appeared unhurt.

The mission had failed.

Cam stared at the carnage around him. How many had died? He guessed fifty, sixty, even seventy. And hundreds were injured.

He had to get out of there. In not many seconds people would start to think about who had done this. Even though his face was bruised and his suit was ripped, they would know he was American. He had to leave before it occurred to anyone that they had a chance of instant revenge.

He hurried back to his car. All the windows were smashed, but it looked as if it might go. He threw open the door. The seat was covered with broken glass. He pulled off his jacket and used it to sweep the seat free of shards. Then, in case he had missed any, he folded the jacket and placed it on the seat. He got in and turned the key.

The car started.

He pulled out, made a U-turn, and drove away.

He recalled Florence Geary's statement, which at the time he had thought hysterically exaggerated. "By the laws of every civilized country it's *murder*," she had said.

But it was not just murder. It was mass murder.

President Ronald Reagan was guilty.

And so was Cam Dewar.

.   .   .

On a small table in the living room, Jack was doing a jigsaw puzzle with his godmother, Maria, while his father, George, looked on. It was Sunday afternoon at Jacky Jakes's house in Prince George's County. They had all gone to Bethel Evangelical Church together, then had eaten Jacky's smothered pork chops—in onion gravy—with black-eyed peas. Then Maria had brought out the puzzle, carefully chosen to be neither too easy nor too hard for a five-year-old. Soon Maria would leave and George would drive Jack back to

Verena's house. Then George would sit down at the kitchen table with his files for a couple of hours and prepare for the week ahead in Congress.

But this was a moment of stillness, when no engagements pressed. The afternoon light fell on the two heads bent over the puzzle. Jack was going to be handsome, George thought. He had a high forehead, wide-apart eyes, a cute flat nose, a smiling mouth, a neat chin, all in proportion. Already his expressions showed his character. He was completely absorbed in the intellectual challenge of the puzzle, then when he or Maria placed a piece correctly he would smile with satisfaction, his small face lighting up. George had never known anything as fascinating and moving as this, the growth of his own child's mind, the daily dawning of new understanding, numbers and letters, mechanisms and people and social groups. Seeing Jack run and jump and throw a ball seemed a miracle, but George was even more heart-struck by this look of intense mental concentration. It brought to his eyes tears of pride and gratitude and awe.

He was grateful to Maria, too. She visited about once a month, always bringing a gift, always spending time with her godson, patiently reading with him or talking to him or playing games. Maria and Jacky had given Jack stability through the trauma of his parents' divorce. It was a year now since George had left the marital home. Jack was no longer waking up in the middle of the night and crying. He seemed to be settling into the new way of life—though George could not help feeling apprehensive about possible long-term effects.

They finished the jigsaw. Grandma Jacky was called in to admire the completed work, then she took Jack into the kitchen for a glass of milk and a cookie.

George said to Maria: "Thank you for all you do for Jack. You're the greatest godmother ever."

"It's no sacrifice," she said. "It's a joy to know him."

Maria was going to be fifty next year. She would never have a child of her own. She had nieces and nephews in Chicago, but the main object of her maternal love was Jack.

"I have something to tell you," Maria said. "Something important."

She got up and closed the living room door, and George wondered what was coming.

She sat down again and said: "That car bomb in Beirut the day before yesterday."

"That was awful," George said. "It killed eighty people and wounded two hundred, mostly women and girls."

"The bomb was not placed by the Israelis."

"Who did it, then?"

"We did."

"What the hell are you talking about?"

"It was a counterterrorism initiative by President Reagan. The perpetrators were Lebanese nationals, but they were trained, financed, and controlled by the CIA."

"Jesus. But the president is obliged by law to tell my committee about covert actions."

"I think you'll find he informed the chairman and vice chairman."

"This is horrible," George said. "But you sound pretty sure of it."

"I was told by a senior CIA person. A lot of Agency veterans were against this whole program. But the president wanted it and Bill Casey forced it through."

"What on earth got into them?" George wondered. "They committed mass murder!"

"They're desperate to put a stop to the kidnappings. They think Fadlallah is the mastermind. They were trying to take him out."

"And they fucked it up."

"But good."

"This has to come out."

"That's what I think."

Jacky came in. "Our young man is ready to go back to his mother."

"I'm coming." George stood up. "All right," he said to Maria. "I'll take care of it."

"Thanks."

George got into the car with Jack and drove slowly through the suburban streets to Verena's house. Jasper Murray's bronze Cadillac was in the driveway beside Verena's red Jaguar. That was opportune, if it meant Jasper was there.

Verena came to the door in a black T-shirt and faded blue jeans. George went inside and Verena took Jack away for his bath. Jasper came out of the kitchen, and George said: "A word with you, if I may."

Jasper looked wary, but said: "Sure."

"Shall we go into"—George almost said *my study,* but corrected himself—"the study?"

"Okay."

He saw with a pang that Jasper's typewriter was on his old desk, along with a stack of reference books a journalist might need: *Who's Who in America, Atlas of the World, Pears' Cyclopaedia, The Almanac of American Politics.*

The study was a small room with one armchair. Neither man wanted to take the chair behind the desk. After an awkward hesitation, Jasper pulled out the desk chair and placed it opposite the armchair, and they both sat down.

George told him what Maria had said, without naming her. As he talked, in the back of his mind he wondered why Verena preferred Jasper to him. Jasper had a hard edge of self-interested ruthlessness, in George's opinion. George had put this question to his mother, who had said: "Jasper's a TV star. Verena's father is a movie star. She spent seven years working for Martin Luther King, who was the star of the civil rights movement. Maybe she needs her man to be a star. But what do I know?"

"This is dynamite," Jasper said when George had told him the whole story. "Are you sure of your source?"

"It's the same as my source for the other stories I've given you. Completely trustworthy."

"This makes President Reagan a mass murderer."

"Yes," said George. "I know."

CHAPTER FIFTY-EIGHT

On that Sunday, while Jacky and George and Maria and little Jack were in church, singing "Shall We Gather at the River," Konstantin Chernenko died in Moscow.

It happened at twenty minutes past seven in the evening, Moscow time. Dimka and Natalya were at home, eating bean soup for supper with their daughter, Katya, a schoolgirl of fifteen, and Dimka's son, Grisha, a university student of twenty-one. The phone rang at seven thirty. Natalya picked it up. As soon as she said: "Hello, Andrei," Dimka guessed what had happened.

Chernenko had been dying ever since he became leader, a mere thirteen months ago. Now he was in the hospital with cirrhosis and emphysema. All Moscow was waiting impatiently for him to expire. Natalya had bribed Andrei, a nurse at the hospital, to call her as soon as Chernenko breathed his last. Now she hung up the phone and confirmed it. "He's dead," she said.

This was the moment of hope. For the third time in less than three years, a tired old conservative leader had died. Once again there was a chance for a new young man to step in and change the Soviet Union into the kind of country in which Dimka wanted Grisha and Katya to live and raise his grandchildren. But that hope had been disappointed twice before. Would the same happen again?

Dimka pushed his plate away. "We have to act now," he said. "The succession will be decided in the next few hours."

Natalya nodded agreement. "The only thing that matters is who chairs the next meeting of the Politburo," she said.

Dimka thought she was right. That was how things worked in the Soviet Union. As soon as one contender nosed ahead, no one would bet on any other horse in the race.

Mikhail Gorbachev was second secretary, and therefore officially deputy to the late leader. However, his appointment to that position had been hotly contested by the old guard, who had wanted Moscow party boss Viktor Grishin, seventy years old and no reformer. Gorbachev had won that race by only one vote.

Dimka and Natalya left the dining table and went into the bedroom, not wanting to discuss this in front of the children. Dimka stood at the window, looking out at the lights of Moscow, while Natalya sat on the edge of the bed. They did not have much time.

Dimka said: "With Chernenko dead, there are exactly ten full members of the Politburo, including Gorbachev and Grishin." The full members were the inner circle of Soviet power. "By my calculation, they divide right down the middle: Gorbachev has four supporters and Grishin has the same."

"But they aren't all in town," Natalya pointed out. "Two of Grishin's men are away: Shcherbitsky is in the United States, and Kunayev is at home in Kazakhstan, a five-hour flight away."

"And one of Gorbachev's men: Vorotnikov is in Yugoslavia."

"Still, that gives us a majority of three against two—for the next few hours."

"Gorbachev must call a meeting of full members tonight. I'll suggest he says it's to plan the funeral. Having called the meeting, he can chair it. And once he's chaired that meeting, it will seem automatic that he chairs all subsequent meetings and then becomes leader."

Natalya frowned. "You're right, but I'd like to nail it down. I don't want the absentees to fly in tomorrow and say everything has to be discussed all over again because they weren't here."

Dimka thought for a minute. "I don't know what else we can do," he said.

Dimka called Gorbachev on the bedroom phone. Gorbachev already knew that Chernenko was dead—he, too, had his spies. He agreed with Dimka that he should call the meeting immediately.

Dimka and Natalya put on their heavy winter coats and boots and drove to the Kremlin.

An hour later the most powerful men in the Soviet Union were gathering in the Presidium Room. Dimka was still worrying. Gorbachev's group needed a masterstroke that would make Gorbachev the leader irrevocably.

Just before the meeting, Gorbachev pulled a rabbit out of the hat. He approached his archrival, Viktor Grishin, and said formally: "Viktor Vasilyevich, would you like to chair this meeting?"

Dimka, standing close enough to hear, was astounded. What the hell was Gorbachev doing—conceding defeat?

But Natalya, right next to Dimka, was smiling triumphantly. "Brilliant!" she said with quiet elation. "If Grishin is proposed as chair the others will vote him down anyway. It's a false offer, an empty gift box."

Grishin thought for a moment and obviously came to the same conclusion. "No, comrade," he said. "You should chair this meeting."

And then Dimka realized, with growing jubilation, that Gorbachev had closed a trap. Now that Grishin had refused, it would be difficult for him to change his mind and demand the chairmanship tomorrow, when his supporters arrived. Any proposal to make Grishin chair would meet the argument that he had already turned down the position. And if he resisted that argument he would look like a ditherer anyway.

So, Dimka concluded, smiling broadly, Gorbachev would become the new leader of the Soviet Union.

And that was exactly what happened.

.   .   .

Tanya came home eager to tell Vasili her plan.

They had been more or less living together, unofficially, for two years. They were not married: once they became a legal couple they would never be allowed to leave the USSR together. And they were determined to get out of the Soviet bloc. Both felt trapped. Tanya continued to write reports for TASS that followed the party line slavishly. Vasili was now lead writer on a television show in which square-jawed KGB heroes outwitted stupid sadistic American spies. And both of them longed to tell the world that Vasili was the acclaimed novelist Ivan Kuznetsov, whose latest book, *The Geriatric Ward*—a savage satire on Brezhnev, Andropov, and Chernenko—was currently a bestseller in the West. Sometimes Vasili said all that mattered was that he had written the truth about the Soviet Union in stories that were read all over the world. But Tanya knew he wanted to take credit for his work, proudly, instead of fearfully concealing what he had done like a secret perversion.

But even though Tanya was bursting with enthusiasm, she took the trouble to turn on the radio in the kitchen before speaking. She did not really think their apartment was bugged, but it was an old habit, and there was no need to take chances.

A radio commentator was describing a visit by Gorbachev and his wife to a jeans factory in Leningrad. Tanya noted the significance. Previous Soviet leaders had visited steel mills and shipyards. Gorbachev celebrated consumer goods. Soviet manufactures ought to be as good as those of the West, he always said—something that had not even been a pipe dream for his predecessors.

And he took his wife with him. Unlike earlier leaders' wives, Raisa was not just an appendage. She was attractive and well-dressed, like an American first lady. She was intelligent, too: she had worked as a university lecturer until her husband became first secretary.

All this was hopeful but little more than symbolic, Tanya thought. Whether it came to anything would depend on the West. If the Germans and the Americans recognized liberalization in the USSR and worked to encourage change, Gorbachev might achieve something. But if the hawks in Bonn and Washington saw this as weakness, and made threatening or aggressive moves, the Soviet ruling elite would retreat back into its shell of orthodox Communism and military overkill. Then Gorbachev would join Kosygin and Khrushchev in the graveyard of failed Kremlin reformers.

"There's a conference of scriptwriters in Naples," Tanya said to Vasili, as the radio burbled in the background.

"Ah!" Vasili saw the significance immediately. The city of Naples had an elected Communist government.

They sat together on the couch. Tanya said: "They want to invite writers from the Soviet bloc, to prove that Hollywood is not the only place where television shows are made."

"Of course."

"You're the most successful writer of television drama in the USSR. You ought to go."

"The writers' union will decide who will be the lucky ones."

"With advice from the KGB, obviously."

"Do you think I have a chance?"

"Make an application, and I'll ask Dimka to put in a good word."

"Will you be able to come?"

"I'll ask Daniil to assign me to cover the conference for TASS."

"And then we'll both be in the free world."

"Yes."

"And then what?"

"I haven't worked out all the details, but that should be the easy part. From our hotel room we can phone Anna Murray in London. As soon as she finds out we're in Italy she'll catch the next plane. We'll give our KGB minders the slip and go with her to Rome. She will tell the world that Ivan Kuznetsov is really Vasili Yenkov, and he and his girlfriend are applying for political asylum in Great Britain."

Vasili was quiet. "Could it really happen, do you think?" he said, sounding almost like a child talking about a fairy tale.

Tanya took both his hands in hers. "I don't know," she said, "but I want to try."

⋅ ⋅ ⋅

Dimka had a big office in the Kremlin now. There was a large desk with two phones, a small conference table, and a couple of couches in front of a fireplace. On the wall was a full-size print of a famous Soviet painting, *The Mobilization Against Yudenich at the Putilov Machine Factory*.

His guest was Frederik Bíró, a Hungarian government minister with progressive ideas. He was two or three years older than Dimka, but he looked scared as he sat on the couch and asked Dimka's secretary for a glass of water. "Am I here to be reprimanded?" he said with a forced smile.

"Why do you ask that?"

"I'm one of a group of men who think Hungarian Communism has become stuck in a rut. That's no secret."

"I have no intention of reprimanding you for that or anything else."

"I'm to be praised, then?"

"Not that either. I assume you and your friends will form the new Hungarian regime as soon as János Kádár dies or resigns, and I wish you luck, but I didn't ask you here to tell you that."

Bíró put down his water without tasting it. "Now I'm really scared."

"Let me put you out of your misery. Gorbachev's priority is to improve the Soviet economy by reducing military expenditure and producing more consumer goods."

"A fine plan," Bíró said in a wary tone. "Many people would like to do the same in Hungary."

"Our only problem is that it isn't working. Or, to be exact, it isn't working fast enough, which comes to the same thing. The Soviet Union is bust, bankrupt, broke. The falling price of oil is the cause of the immediate crisis, but the long-term problem is the crippling underperformance of the planned economy. And it's too severe to be cured by canceling orders for missiles and making more blue jeans."

"What is the answer?"

"We're going to stop subsidizing you."

"Hungary?"

"All the East European states. You've never paid for your standard of living. We finance it, by selling you oil and other raw materials below market prices, and buying your crappy manufactures that no one else wants."

"It's true, of course," Bíró acknowledged. "But that's the only way to keep the population quiet and the Communist Party in power. If their standard of living falls, it won't be long before they start asking why they have to be Communists."

"I know."

"Then what are we supposed to do?"

Dimka shrugged deliberately. "That's not my problem, it's yours."

"It's our problem?" Bíró said incredulously. "What the fuck are you talking about?"

"It means you have to find the solution."

"And what if the Kremlin doesn't like the solution we find?"

"It doesn't matter," Dimka said. "You're on your own now."

Bíró was scornful. "Are you telling me that forty years of Soviet domination of Eastern Europe is coming to an end, and we are going to be independent countries?"

"Exactly."

Bíró looked at Dimka long and hard. Then he said: "I don't believe you."

.   .   .

Tanya and Vasili went to the hospital to visit Tanya's aunt Zoya, the physicist. Zoya was seventy-four and had breast cancer. As the wife of a general, she had a private room. Visitors were allowed in two at a time, so Tanya and Vasili waited outside with other family members.

After a while Uncle Volodya came out, holding the arm of his thirty-nine-year-old son, Kotya. A strong man with a heroic war record, Volodya was now as helpless as a child, following where he was led, sobbing uncontrollably into a handkerchief that was already sodden with tears. They had been married forty years.

Tanya went in with her cousin Galina, the daughter of Volodya and Zoya. She was shocked by her aunt's appearance. Zoya had been head-turningly beautiful, even into her sixties, but now she was cadaverously thin, almost bald, and clearly only days or perhaps hours from the end. However, she was drifting in and out of sleep, and did not seem to be in pain. Tanya guessed she was dosed with morphine.

"Volodya went to America after the war, to find out how they had made the Hiroshima bomb," Zoya said, contentedly indiscreet under the influence of the drug. Tanya thought of telling her to say no more, then reflected that these secrets no longer mattered to anyone. "He brought back a Sears Roebuck Catalogue," Zoya went on, smiling at the memory. "It was full of beautiful things that any American could buy: dresses, bicycles, records, warm coats for children, even tractors for farmers. I wouldn't have believed it—I would have taken it for propaganda—but Volodya had been there and knew it was true. Ever since then I've wanted to go to America, just to see it. Just to look at all that plenty. I don't think I'll make it now, though." She closed her eyes again. "Never mind," she murmured, and she seemed to sleep again.

After a few minutes, Tanya and Galina went out, and two of the grandchildren took their places at the bedside.

Dimka had arrived and joined the group waiting in the corridor. He took Tanya and Vasili aside and spoke to them in a low voice. "I recommended you for the conference in Naples," he said to Vasili.

"Thank you—"

"Don't thank me. I was unsuccessful. I had a conversation today with the unpleasant Yevgeny Filipov. He's in charge of this kind of thing now, and he knows that you were sent to Siberia for subversive activities back in 1961."

Tanya said: "But Vasili has been rehabilitated!"

"Filipov knows that. Rehabilitation is one thing, he said, and going abroad is another. It's out of the question." Dimka touched Tanya's arm. "I'm sorry, sister."

"We're stuck here, then," Tanya said.

Vasili said bitterly: "A leaflet at a poetry reading, a quarter of a century ago, and I'm still being punished. We keep thinking that our country is changing, but it never really does."

Tanya said: "Like Aunt Zoya, we're never going to see the world outside."

"Don't give up yet," said Dimka.

PART TEN

WALL

1988-1989

CHAPTER FIFTY-NINE

J asper Murray was fired in the fall of 1988.

He was not surprised. The atmosphere in Washington was different. President Reagan remained popular, despite having committed crimes far worse than those that had brought Nixon down: financing terrorism in Nicaragua, trading weapons for hostages with Iran, and turning women and girls into mangled corpses on the streets of Beirut. Reagan's collaborator Vice President George H. W. Bush looked likely to become the next president. Somehow—and Jasper could not figure out how this trick had been worked—people who challenged the president and caught him out cheating and lying were no longer heroes, as they had been in the seventies, but instead were considered disloyal and even anti-American.

So Jasper was not shocked, but he was deeply hurt. He had joined *This Day* twenty years ago, and he had helped make it a hugely respected news show. To be fired seemed like a negation of his life's work. His generous severance package did nothing to soothe the pain.

He probably should not have made a crack about Reagan at the end of his last broadcast. After telling the audience he was leaving, he had said: "And remember: if the president tells you it's raining, and he seems really, really sincere—take a look out of the window anyway . . . just to make sure." Frank Lindeman had been livid.

Jasper's colleagues threw a farewell party in the Old Ebbitt Grill that was attended by most of Washington's movers and shakers. Leaning against the bar, late in the evening, Jasper made a speech. Wounded, sad, and defiant, he said: "I love this country. I loved it the first time I came here, back in 1963. I love it because it's free. My mother escaped from Nazi Germany; the rest of her family never made it. The first thing Hitler did was take over the press and make it subservient to the government. Lenin did the same." Jasper had drunk a few glasses of wine, and as a result he was a shade more candid. "America is free because it has disrespectful newspapers and television shows to expose and shame presidents who fuck the Constitution up the ass." He raised his glass. "Here's to the free press. Here's to disrespect. And God bless America."

Next day Suzy Cannon, always eager to kick a man when he was down, published a long, vitriolic profile of Jasper. She managed to suggest that both his service in Vietnam and his naturalization as an American citizen were desperate attempts to conceal a virulent hatred of the United States. She also portrayed him as a ruthless sexual predator who had taken Verena away from George Jakes just as he had stolen Evie Williams from Cam Dewar back in the sixties.

The result was that he found it difficult to get another job. After several weeks of trying, at last another network offered him a position as European correspondent—based in Bonn.

"Surely you can do better than that," Verena said. She had no time for losers.

"No network will hire me as an anchor."

They were in the living room late in the evening, having just watched the news and about to get ready for bed.

"But Germany?" Verena said. "Isn't that a post for a kid on his way up the ladder?"

"Not necessarily. Eastern Europe is in turmoil. There could be some interesting stories coming out of that part of the world in the next year or two."

She was not going to let him make the best of it. "There are better jobs," she said. "Didn't *The Washington Post* offer you your own comment column?"

"I've worked in television all my life."

"You haven't applied to local TV," she said. "You could be a big fish in a small pond."

"No, I couldn't. I'd be a has-been on his way down." The prospect made Jasper shudder with humiliation. "I'm not going to do that."

Her face took on a defiant look. "Well, don't ask me to go to Germany with you."

He had been anticipating this, but he was taken aback by her blunt determination. "Why not?"

"You speak German, I don't."

Jasper did not speak very good German, but that was not his best argument. "It would be an adventure," he said.

"Get real," Verena said harshly. "I have a son."

"It would be an adventure for Jack, too. He'd grow up bilingual."

"George would go to court to stop me from taking Jack out of the country. We have joint custody. And I wouldn't do it anyway. Jack needs his father and his grandmother. And what about my work? I'm a big success, Jasper—I have twelve people working for me, all lobbying the government for liberal causes. You can't seriously ask me to give that up."

"Well, I guess I'll come home for the holidays."

"Are you serious? What kind of a relationship would we have? How long will it be before you're bouncing on a bed with a plump Rhinemaiden in blond plaits?"

It was true that Jasper had been promiscuous most of his life, but he had never cheated on Verena. The prospect of losing her suddenly seemed insupportable. "I can be faithful," he said desperately.

Verena saw his distress, and her tone softened. "Jasper, that's touching. I think you even mean it. But I know what you're like, and you know what I'm like. Neither of us can remain celibate for long."

"Listen," he pleaded. "Everyone in American television knows I'm looking for a job, and this is the only one I've been offered. Don't you understand? My back is up against the goddamn wall. I don't have an alternative!"

"I do understand, and I'm sorry. But we have to be realistic."

Jasper found her sympathy worse than her scorn. "Anyway, it won't be forever," he said defiantly.

"Won't it?"

"Oh, no. I'm going to make a comeback."

"In Bonn?"

"There will be more European stories leading the American television news than ever before. You just fucking watch me."

Verena's face turned sad. "Shit, you're really going, aren't you?"

"I told you, I have to."

"Well," she said regretfully, "don't expect me to be here when you come back."

. . .

Jasper had never been to Budapest. As a young man he had always looked west, toward America. Besides, all his life Hungary had been overcast by the gray clouds of Communism. But in November 1988, with the economy in ruins, something astonishing happened. A small group of young reform-minded Communists took control of the government and one of them, Miklós Németh, became prime minister. Among other changes, he opened a stock market.

Jasper thought this was astounding.

Only six months earlier Karoly Grosz, the thuggish chief of the Hungarian Communist Party, had told *Newsweek* magazine that multiparty democracy was "an historic impossibility" in Hungary. But Németh had enacted a new law allowing independent political "clubs."

This was a big story. But were the changes permanent? Or would Moscow soon clamp down?

Jasper flew into Budapest in a January blizzard. Beside the Danube, snow lay thick on the neo-Gothic turrets of the vast parliament building. It was in that building that Jasper met Miklós Németh.

Jasper had got the interview with the help of Rebecca Held. Although he had not previously met her, he knew about her from Dave Williams and Walli Franck. As soon as he got to Bonn he had looked her up: she was the nearest thing he had to a German contact. She was now an important figure in the German Foreign Office. Even better, she was a friend—perhaps a lover, Jasper guessed—of Frederik Bíró, aide to Miklós Németh. Bíró had fixed up the interview.

It was Bíró who now met Jasper in the lobby and escorted him through a maze of corridors and passageways to the office of the prime minister.

Németh was just forty-one. He was a short man with thick brown hair that fell over his forehead in a kiss curl. His face showed intelligence and determination, but also anxiety. For the interview he sat behind an oak table and nervously surrounded himself with aides. No doubt he was vividly aware that he was speaking not just to Jasper, but to the United States government—and that Moscow would be watching, too.

Like any prime minister, he talked mostly in predictable clichés. There would be hard times ahead, but the country would emerge stronger in the long run. And yadda yadda yadda, thought Jasper. He needed something better than this.

He asked whether the new political "clubs" could ever become free political parties.

Németh gave Jasper a hard, direct look, and said in a firm, clear voice: "That is one of our greatest ambitions."

Jasper concealed his astonishment. No Iron Curtain country had ever had independent political parties. Did Németh really mean it?

Jasper asked whether the Communist Party would ever give up its "leading role" in Hungarian society.

Németh gave him that look again. "In two years I could imagine that the head of government might not be a Politburo member," he said.

Jasper had to stop himself saying *Jesus Christ!*

He was on a roll, and it was time for the big one. "Might the Soviets intervene to stop these changes, as they did in 1956?"

Németh gave him the look for the third time. "Gorbachev has taken the lid off a boiling pot," he said, slowly and distinctly. Then he added: "The steam may be painful, but change is irreversible."

And Jasper knew he had his first great story from Europe.

. . .

A few days later he watched a videotape of his report as it had appeared on American television. Rebecca sat beside him, a poised, confident woman in her fifties, friendly but with an air of authority. "Yes, I think Németh means every word," she said in answer to Jasper's question.

Jasper had ended the report speaking to the camera in front of the parliament building, with snowflakes landing in his hair. "The ground is frozen hard here in this Eastern European country," he said on the screen. "But, as always, the seeds of spring are stirring underground. Clearly the Hungarian people want change. But will their Moscow overlords permit it? Miklós Németh believes there is a new mood of tolerance in the Kremlin. Only time will tell whether he is right."

That had been Jasper's sign-off, but now to his surprise he saw that another clip had been added to his piece. A spokesman for James Baker, secretary of state to newly inaugurated President George H. W. Bush, spoke to an invisible interviewer. "Signs of softening in Communist attitudes are not to be trusted," the spokesman said. "The Soviets are attempting to lull the United States into a false sense of security. There is no reason to doubt the Kremlin's willingness to intervene in Eastern Europe the minute they feel threatened. The urgent necessity now is to underscore the credibility of NATO's nuclear deterrent."

"Good God," said Rebecca. "What planet are they on?"

. . .

Tanya Dvorkin returned to Warsaw in February 1989.

She was sorry to leave Vasili on his own in Moscow, mainly because she would miss him, but also because she still nursed a faint anxiety that he would fill the apartment with nubile teenagers. She did not really believe it would happen. Those days were over. All the same the worry nagged at her a little.

However, Warsaw was a great assignment. Poland was in a ferment. Solidarity had somehow risen from its grave. Amazingly, General Jaruzelski—the dictator who had cracked down on freedom only seven years previously, breaking every promise and stamping on the independent trade union—had in desperation agreed to round-table talks with opposition groups.

In Tanya's opinion, Jaruzelski had not changed—the Kremlin had. Jaruzelski was the same old tyrant, but he was no longer confident of Soviet support. According to Dimka, Jaruzelski had been told that Poland must solve its own problems, without help from Moscow. When Mikhail Gorbachev first said this, Jaruzelski had not believed it. None of the East European leaders had. But that had been three years ago, and at last the message was beginning to sink in.

Tanya did not know what would happen. No one did. Never in her life had she heard so much talk of change, liberalization, and freedom. But the Communists were still in control in the Soviet bloc. Was the day coming nearer when she and Vasili could reveal their secret, and tell the world the true identity of the author Ivan Kuznetsov? In the past such hopes had always ended up crushed beneath the caterpillar tracks of Soviet tanks.

As soon as Tanya arrived in Warsaw, she was invited to dinner at the apartment of Danuta Gorski.

Standing at the door, ringing the bell, she remembered the last time she had seen Danuta, being dragged out of this very apartment by the brutish ZOMO security police in their camouflage uniforms, on the night seven years ago when Jaruzelski had declared martial law.

Now Danuta opened the door, grinning broadly, all teeth and hair. She hugged Tanya, then led her into the dining room of the small apartment. Her husband, Marek, was opening a bottle of Hungarian Riesling, and there was a plate of snack-size sausages on the table with a small dish of mustard.

"I was in jail for eighteen days," Danuta said. "I think they let me out because I was radicalizing the other inmates." She laughed, throwing back her head.

Tanya admired her guts. If I were a lesbian I could fall for Danuta, she thought. All the men Tanya had loved had been courageous.

"Now I'm part of this Round Table," Danuta went on. "Every day, all day."

"It is really a round table?"

"Yes, a huge one. The theory is that no one is in charge. But, in practice, Lech Wałęsa chairs the meetings."

Tanya marveled. An uneducated electrician was dominating the debate on the future of Poland. This kind of thing had been the dream of her grandfather the Bolshevik factory worker Grigori Peshkov. Yet Wałęsa was the anti-Communist. In a way she was glad Grandfather Grigori had not lived to see this irony. It might have broken his heart.

"Will anything come of the Round Table?" Tanya asked.

Before Danuta could answer, Marek said: "It's a trick. Jaruzelski wants to cripple the opposition by co-opting its leaders, making them part of the Communist government without changing the system. It's his strategy for staying in power."

Danuta said: "Marek is probably right. But the trick is not going to work. We're demanding independent trade unions, a free press, and real elections."

Tanya was shocked. "Jaruzelski is actually discussing free elections?" Poland already had phony elections, in which only Communist parties and their allies were allowed to field candidates.

"The talks keep breaking down. But he needs to stop the strikes, so he reconvenes the Round Table, and we demand elections again."

"What's behind the strikes?" Tanya said. "I mean, fundamentally?"

Marek interrupted again. "You know what people are saying? 'Forty-five years of Communism, and still there's no toilet paper.' We're poor! Communism doesn't work."

"Marek is right," said Danuta again. "A few weeks ago a store here in Warsaw announced that it would be accepting down payments for television sets on the following Monday. It didn't have any TVs, mind you, it was just hoping to get some. People started queuing on the Friday beforehand. By Monday morning there were fifteen thousand people in line—just to put their names on a list!"

Danuta stepped into the kitchen and returned with a fragrant bowl of *zupa ogórkowa,* the sour cucumber soup that Tanya loved. "So what will happen?" Tanya asked as she tucked in. "Will there be real elections?"

"No," said Marek.

"Maybe," said Danuta. "The latest proposal is that two-thirds of the seats in parliament should be reserved for the Communist Party, and there should be free elections for the remainder."

Marek said: "So we would still have phony elections!"

Danuta said: "But this would be better than what we have now! Don't you agree, Tanya?"

"I don't know," said Tanya.

The spring thaw had not arrived, and Moscow was still under its duvet of snow, when the new Hungarian prime minister came to see Mikhail Gorbachev.

Yevgeny Filipov knew that Miklós Németh was coming, and he buttonholed Dimka outside the leader's office a few minutes before the meeting. "This nonsense must be stopped!" he said.

These days, Filipov was looking increasingly frantic, Dimka observed. His gray hair was untidy, and he went everywhere in a rush. He was now in his early sixties, and his face was permanently set in the disapproving frown he had worn for so much of his life. His baggy suits and ultrashort haircut were back in fashion: kids in the West called the look retro.

Filipov hated Gorbachev. The Soviet leader stood for everything Filipov had been fighting against all his life: relaxation of rules instead of strict party discipline; individual initiative as opposed to central planning; friendship with the West rather than war against capitalist imperialism. Dimka could almost sympathize with a man who had wasted his days fighting a losing battle.

At least, Dimka hoped it had been a losing battle. The conflict was not over yet.

"What nonsense in particular are we talking about?" Dimka said wearily.

"Independent political parties!" Filipov said as if he were mentioning an atrocity. "The Hungarians have started a dangerous trend. Jaruzelski is now talking about the same thing in Poland. Jaruzelski!"

Dimka understood Filipov's incredulity. It was, indeed, astonishing that the Polish tyrant was now talking of making Solidarity a part of the nation's future, and of allowing political parties to compete in a Western-style election.

And Filipov did not know it all. Dimka's sister, in Warsaw for TASS, was sending him accurate information. Jaruzelski was up against the wall, and Solidarity was adamant. They were not just talking, they were planning an election.

This was what Filipov and the Kremlin conservatives were fighting to prevent.

"These developments are highly dangerous!" Filipov said. "They open the door to counterrevolutionary and revisionist tendencies. What is the point of that?"

"The point is that we no longer have the money to subsidize our satellites—"

"We have no satellites. We have allies."

"Whatever they are, they're not willing to do what we say if we can't pay for their obedience."

"We used to have an army to defend Communism—but not anymore."

There was some truth in that exaggeration. Gorbachev had announced the withdrawal from Eastern Europe of a quarter of a million troops and ten thousand tanks—an essential economy measure, but also a peace gesture. "We can't afford such an army," said Dimka.

Filipov was so indignant he looked as if he might burst. "Can't you see that you're talking about the end of everything we have worked for since 1917?"

"Khrushchev said it would take us twenty years to catch up with the Americans in wealth and military strength. It's now twenty-eight years, and we're farther behind than we were in 1961 when Khrushchev said it. Yevgeny, what are you fighting to preserve?"

"The Soviet Union! What do you imagine the Americans are thinking, as we run down our army and permit creeping revisionism among our allies? They're laughing up their sleeves! President Bush is a Cold Warrior, intent on overthrowing us. Don't fool yourself."

"I disagree," said Dimka. "The more we disarm, the less reason the Americans will have for building up their nuclear stockpile."

"I hope you're right," said Filipov. "For all our sakes." He walked away.

Dimka, too, hoped he was right. Filipov had put his finger on the flaw in Gorbachev's strategy. It relied upon President Bush being reasonable. If the Americans responded to disarmament with reciprocal measures, Gorbachev would be vindicated, and his Kremlin rivals would look foolish. But if Bush failed to respond—or, even worse, increased military spending—then it would be Gorbachev who looked a fool. He would be undermined, and his opponents might seize the opportunity to overthrow him and return to the good old days of superpower confrontation.

Dimka went to Gorbachev's suite of rooms. He was looking forward to meeting Németh. What was happening in Hungary was exciting. Dimka was also eager to find out what Gorbachev would say to Németh.

The Soviet leader was not predictable. He was a lifelong Communist who was nevertheless unwilling to impose Communism on other countries. His strategy was clear: glasnost and perestroika, openness and restructuring. His tactics were less obvious, and on any particular issue it was hard to know which way he would jump. He kept Dimka on his toes.

Gorbachev was not warm toward Németh. The Hungarian prime minister had asked for an hour and had been offered twenty minutes. It could be a difficult meeting.

Németh arrived with Frederik Bíró, whom Dimka already knew. Gorbachev's secretary immediately took the three of them into the grand office. It was a vast high-ceilinged room with paneled walls painted a creamy yellow. Gorbachev was behind a contemporary black-stained wood desk that stood in a corner. There was nothing on the desk but a phone and a lamp. The visitors sat down on stylish black leather chairs. Everything symbolized modernity.

Németh got down to business with few courtesies. He was about to announce free elections, he said. Free meant free: the result could be a non-Communist government. How would Moscow feel about that?

Gorbachev flushed, and the purple birthmark on his bald dome darkened. "The proper path is to return to the roots of Leninism," he said.

This did not mean much. Everyone who tried to change the Soviet Union claimed to be returning to the roots of Leninism.

Gorbachev went on: "Communism can find its way again, by going back to the time before Stalin."

"No, it can't," said Németh bluntly.

"Only the party can create a just society! This cannot be left to chance."

"We disagree." Németh was beginning to look ill. His face was pale and his voice was shaky. He was a cardinal challenging the authority of the Pope. "I must ask you one question very directly," he said. "If we hold an election and the Communist Party is voted out of power, will the Soviet Union intervene with military force as it did in 1956?"

The room went dead silent. Even Dimka did not know how Gorbachev would respond.

Then Gorbachev said one Russian word: "*Nyet.*" No.

Németh looked like a man whose death sentence had been repealed.

Gorbachev added: "At least, not as long as I'm sitting in this chair."

Németh laughed. He did not think Gorbachev was in danger of being deposed.

He was wrong. The Kremlin always presented a united front to the world, but it was never as harmonious as it pretended. People had no idea how shaky was Gorbachev's grip. Németh was satisfied to know what Gorbachev's own intentions were, but Dimka knew better.

However, Németh was not finished. He had won from Gorbachev a huge concession—a promise that the USSR would not intervene to prevent the overthrow of Communism in Hungary! Yet now, with surprising audacity, Németh pressed for a further guarantee. "The fence is dilapidated," he said. "It has to be either renewed or abandoned."

Dimka knew what Németh was talking about. The border between Communist Hungary and capitalist Austria was secured by a stainless steel electric fence one hundred and fifty miles long. It was naturally very expensive to maintain. To renew the whole thing would cost millions.

Gorbachev said: "If it needs renewing, then renew it."

"No," said Németh. He might have been nervous, but he was determined. Dimka admired his guts. "I don't have the money, and I don't need the fence," Németh went on. "It's a Warsaw Pact installation. If you want it, you should renew it."

"That isn't going to happen," said Gorbachev. "The Soviet Union no longer has that kind of money. A decade ago, oil was forty dollars a barrel and we could do anything. Now it's what, nine dollars? We're broke."

"Let me make sure we understand one another," said Németh. He was perspiring, and he wiped his face with a handkerchief. "If you do not pay, we will not renew the fence, and it will cease to operate as an effective barrier. People will be able to go to Austria, and we will not stop them."

There was another pregnant silence. Then at last Gorbachev sighed and said: "So be it."

That was the end of the meeting. The farewell courtesies were perfunctory. The Hungarians could not get away quickly enough. They had got everything they asked for. They shook hands with Gorbachev and left the room at a fast walk. It was as if they wanted to get back on the plane before Gorbachev had time to change his mind.

Dimka returned to his own office in a reflective mood. Gorbachev had surprised him twice: first by being unexpectedly hostile to Németh's reforms, and second by offering no real resistance to them.

Would the Hungarians abandon the fence? It was an essential part of the Iron Curtain. If suddenly people were allowed to walk over the border and into the West, that could be a change even more momentous than free elections.

But Filipov and the conservatives had not yet surrendered. They were on the alert for the least sign of weakness in Gorbachev. Dimka did not doubt that they had contingency plans for a coup.

He was looking thoughtfully at the large revolutionary picture on his office wall when Natalya called. "You know what a Lance missile is, don't you?" she said without preamble.

"A short-range surface-to-surface tactical nuclear weapon," he replied. "The Americans have about seven hundred in Germany. Fortunately their range is only about seventy-five miles."

"Not any longer," she said. "President Bush wants to upgrade them. The new ones will fly two hundred eighty miles."

"Hell." This was what Dimka feared and Filipov had predicted. "But this is illogical. It's not that long ago that Reagan and Gorbachev *withdrew* intermediate-range ballistic missiles."

"Bush thinks Reagan went too far with disarmament."

"How definite is this plan?"

"Bush has surrounded himself with Cold War hawks, according to the KGB station in Washington. Defense Secretary Cheney is gung ho. So is Scowcroft." Brent Scowcroft was the national security adviser. "And there's a woman called Condoleezza Rice, who is just as bad."

Dimka despaired. "Filipov is going to say: 'I told you so.'"

"Filipov and others. It's a dangerous development for Gorbachev."

"What's the Americans' timetable?"

"They're going to put pressure on the West Europeans at the NATO meeting in May."

"Shit," said Dimka. "Now we're in trouble."

. . .

Rebecca Held was at her apartment in Hamburg, late in the evening, working, with papers spread over the round table in the kitchen. On the counter were a dirty coffee cup and a plate with the crumbs of the ham sandwich she had eaten for supper. She had taken off her smart working clothes, removed her makeup, showered, and put on baggy old underwear and an ancient silk wrap.

She was preparing for her first visit to the United States. She was going with her boss, Hans-Dietrich Genscher, who was vice chancellor of Germany, foreign minister, and head of the Free Democratic Party, to which she belonged. Their mission was to explain to the Americans why they did not want any more nuclear weapons. The Soviet Union was becoming less threatening under Gorbachev. Upgraded nukes were not merely unnecessary: they might actually be counterproductive, undermining Gorbachev's peace moves and strengthening the hand of hawks in Moscow.

She was reading a German intelligence appraisal of the power struggle in the Kremlin when the doorbell rang.

She looked at her watch. It was half past nine. She was not expecting a visitor and she certainly was not dressed to receive one. However, it was probably a neighbor in the same building on some trivial errand, needing to borrow a carton of milk.

She did not merit a full-time bodyguard: she was not important enough to attract terrorists, thank God. All the same her door had a peephole so that she could check before opening up.

She was surprised to see Frederik Bíró outside.

She had mixed feelings. A surprise visit from her lover was a delight—but she looked a perfect fright. At the age of fifty-seven any woman wanted time to prepare before she showed herself to her man.

But she could hardly ask him to wait in the hall while she made up her face and changed her underwear.

She opened the door.

"My darling," he said, and kissed her.

"I'm pleased to see you, but you've caught me unawares," she said. "I'm a mess."

He stepped inside and she closed the door. He held her at arm's length and studied her. "Tousled hair, glasses, dressing gown, bare feet," he said. "You look adorable."

She laughed and led him into the kitchen. "Have you had dinner?" she said. "Shall I make you an omelette?"

"Just some coffee, please. I ate on the plane."

"What are you doing in Hamburg?"

"My boss sent me." Fred sat at the table. "Prime Minister Németh is coming to Germany next week to see Chancellor Kohl. He's going to ask Kohl a question. Like all politicians, he wants to know the answer before he asks it."

"What question?"

"I need to explain."

She put a cup of coffee in front of Fred. "Go ahead, I've got all night."

"I'm hoping it won't take that long." He ran a hand up her leg inside her robe. "I have other plans." He reached her underwear. "Oh!" he said. "Roomy panties."

She blushed. "I wasn't expecting you!"

He grinned. "I could get both hands inside there—both arms, maybe."

She pushed his hands away and moved to the other side of the table. "Tomorrow I'm going to throw out all my old underwear." She sat opposite him. "Stop embarrassing me and tell me why you're here."

"Hungary is going to open its border with Austria."

Rebecca did not think she had heard him right. "What are you talking about?"

"We're going to open our border. Let the fence fall into disrepair. Free our people to go where they want."

"You can't be serious."

"It's an economic decision as much as a political one. The fence is collapsing and we can't afford to rebuild it."

Rebecca was beginning to understand. "But if the Hungarians can get out, so can everyone else. How will you stop Czechs, Yugoslavs, Poles . . ."

"We won't."

". . . and East Germans. Oh, my goodness, my family will be able to leave!"

"Yes."

"It can't happen. The Soviets won't allow it."

"Németh went to Moscow and told Gorbachev."

"What did Gorbi say?"

"Nothing. He's not happy, but he won't intervene. He can't afford to renew the fence either."

"But . . ."

"I was there, at the meeting in the Kremlin. Németh asked him straight out, would the Soviets invade as they did in 1956? His answer was *nyet.*"

"Do you believe him?"

"Yes."

This was world-changing news. Rebecca had been working for this all her political life, but she could not believe it was really going to happen: her family, able to travel from East to West Germany! Freedom!

Then Fred said: "There is one possible snag."

"I was afraid of that."

"Gorbachev promised no military intervention, but he did not rule out economic sanctions."

Rebecca thought that was the least of their problems. "Hungary's economy will become west-facing, and it will grow."

"That's what we want. But it will take time. People may face hardship. The Kremlin may hope to push us into an economic collapse before the economy has time to adjust. Then there could be a counterrevolution."

He was right, Rebecca saw. This was a serious danger. "I knew it was too good to be true," she said despondently.

"Don't despair. We have a solution. That's why I'm here."

"What's your plan?"

"We need support from the richest country in Europe. If we can have a big line of credit from German banks, we can resist Soviet pressure. Next week, Németh will ask Kohl for a loan. I know you can't authorize such a thing on your own, but I was hoping you could give me a steer. What will Kohl say?"

"I can't imagine he'll say no, if the reward is open borders. Apart from the political gain, think what this could mean to the German economy."

"We may need a lot of money."

"How much?"

"Possibly a billion deutschmarks."

"Don't worry," Rebecca said. "You've got it."

. . . .

The Soviet economy was getting worse and worse, according to the CIA report in front of Congressman George Jakes. Gorbachev's reforms—decentralization, more consumer goods, fewer weapons—were not enough.

There was pressure on the East European satellites to follow the USSR by liberalizing their own economies, but any changes would be minor and gradual, the Agency forecast. If any country rejected Communism outright, then Gorbachev would send in the tanks.

That did not sound right to George, sitting in a meeting of the House intelligence oversight committee. Poland, Hungary, and Czechoslovakia were running ahead of the USSR, moving toward free enterprise and democracy, and Gorbachev was doing nothing to hold them back.

But President Bush and Defense Secretary Cheney believed passionately in the Soviet menace, and as always the CIA was under pressure to tell the president what he wanted to hear.

The meeting left George feeling dissatisfied and anxious. He took the dinky Capitol subway train back to the Cannon House Office Building, where he had a suite of three crowded rooms. The lobby had a reception desk, a couch for waiting visitors, and a round table for meetings. To one side was the administration office, crammed with staff desks and bookshelves and filing cabinets. On the opposite side was George's own room, with a desk and a conference table and a picture of Bobby Kennedy.

He was intrigued to see, on his list of afternoon appointments, a clergyman from Anniston, Alabama, the Reverend Clarence Bowyer, who wanted to talk to him about civil rights.

George would never forget Anniston. It was the town where the Freedom Riders had been attacked by a mob and their bus firebombed. It was the only time someone had tried seriously to kill George.

He must have said yes to the man's request for a meeting, though he could not now remember why. He assumed that a preacher from Alabama who wanted to see him would be African American, and he was startled when his assistant ushered in a white man. The Reverend Bowyer was about George's age, dressed in a gray suit with a white shirt and a dark tie, but wearing trainers, perhaps because he had to do a lot of walking in Washington. He had large front teeth and a receding chin, and salt-and-pepper hair that accentuated the resemblance to a red squirrel. There was something vaguely familiar about him. With him was a teenage boy who looked just like him.

"I try to bring the gospel of Jesus Christ to soldiers and others working at the Anniston army depot," Bowyer said, introducing himself. "Many of my congregation are African Americans."

Bowyer was sincere, George thought; and he had a mixed-race church, which was unusual. "What's your interest in civil rights, Reverend?"

"Well, sir, I was a segregationist as a young man."

"Many people were," George said. "We've all learned a lot."

"I've done more than learn," said Bowyer. "I have spent decades in deep repentance."

That seemed a little strong. Some of the people who asked for meetings with congressmen were more or less crazy. George's staff did their best to filter out the lunatics, but now and again one would slip through the net. However, Bowyer struck George as pretty sane. "Repentance," George repeated, playing for time.

"Congressman Jakes," said Bowyer solemnly, "I have come here to apologize to you."

"What for, exactly?"

"In 1961 I hit you with a crowbar. I believe I broke your arm."

In a flash George understood why the man looked familiar. He had been in the mob at Anniston. He had tried to hit Maria, but George had put his arm in the way. It still hurt in cold weather. George stared in astonishment at this earnest clergyman. "So that was you," he said.

"Yes, sir. I don't have any excuses to offer. I knew what I was doing, and I did wrong. But I have never forgotten you. I just would like you to know how sorry I am, and I wanted my son, Clam, to witness my confession of evildoing."

George was nonplussed. Nothing like this had ever happened to him. "So you became a preacher," he said.

"At first I became a drinker. Because of whisky, I lost my job and my home and my car. Then one Sunday the Lord led my footsteps to a little mission in a shack in a poor neighborhood. The preacher, who happened to be black, took as his text the twenty-fifth chapter of Matthew's gospel, especially verse forty: 'Inasmuch as ye have done it unto one of these the least of my brethren, ye have done it unto me.'"

George had heard more than one sermon on that verse. Its message was that a wrong done to anyone was a wrong done to Jesus. African Americans, who had more wrongs done to them than most citizens, gained strong consolation from that notion. The verse was even quoted on the Wales Window at the Sixteenth Street Baptist Church in Birmingham.

Bowyer said: "I went into that church to mock, and I came out saved."

George said: "I'm glad to hear of your change of heart, Reverend."

"I do not deserve your forgiveness, Congressman, but I hope for God's." Bowyer stood up. "I will not take up any more of your valuable time. Thank you."

George stood too. He felt that he had not responded adequately to a man in the grip of powerful emotion. "Before you go," he said, "let us shake hands." He took Bowyer's hand in both of his. "If God can forgive you, Clarence, I guess I should too."

Bowyer choked up. Tears came to his eyes as he shook George's hand.

On impulse, George embraced him. The man was shaking with sobs.

After a minute, George broke the hug and stepped back. Bowyer tried to speak but was unable to. Weeping, he turned and left the room.

His son shook George's hand. "Thank you, Congressman," the boy said in a shaky voice. "I can't express how much your forgiveness means to my father. You are a great man, sir." He followed Bowyer out of the room.

George sat back down, feeling dazed. Well, he thought, how about that?

.   .   .

He told Maria about it that evening.

Her reaction was unsympathetic. "I guess you're entitled to forgive them, it was your arm that got broken," she said. "Me, I'm not big on mercy for segregationists. I'd like to see Reverend Bowyer serve a couple of years in jail, or maybe on a chain gang. *Then* perhaps I'd accept his apology. All those corrupt judges and brutal cops and bomb makers are still walking around free, you know. They've never been brought to justice for what they did. Some are probably drawing their damn pensions. And they want forgiveness, too? I'm not going to help them feel comfortable. If their guilt makes them miserable, I'm glad. It's the least they deserve."

George smiled. Maria was getting feistier in her fifties. She was one of the most senior people in the State Department, respected by Republicans and Democrats alike. She carried herself with confidence and authority.

They were in her apartment, and she was making dinner, sea bass stuffed with herbs, while George laid the table. A delicate aroma filled the room, making George's mouth water. Maria topped up his glass of Lynmar Chardonnay, then put broccoli into a steamer. She was a little heavier than she used to be, and she was trying to adopt George's lean cuisine tastes.

After dinner they took their coffee to the couch. Maria was in a mellow mood. "I want to be able to look back and say that the world was a safer place when I left the State Department than when I arrived," she said. "I want my nephews and nieces, and my godson, Jack, to raise their children without the threat of a superpower holocaust hanging over them. Then I'll be able to say that my life was well spent."

"I understand how you feel," said George. "But it seems like a pipe dream. Is it possible?"

"Maybe. The Soviet bloc is nearer to collapse than at any time since the Second World War. Our ambassador to Moscow believes that the Brezhnev Doctrine is dead."

The Brezhnev Doctrine said that the Soviet Union controlled Eastern Europe, just as the Monroe Doctrine gave the same rights to the USA in South America.

George nodded. "If Gorbachev no longer wants to boss the Communist empire, that's a huge geopolitical gain for the USA."

"And we should be doing everything we can to help Gorbachev stay in power. But we're not, because President Bush believes the whole thing is a confidence trick by Gorbachev. So he's actually planning to *increase* our nuclear weapons in Europe."

"Which is guaranteed to undermine Gorbachev and encourage the hawks in the Kremlin."

"Exactly. Anyway, I have a bunch of Germans coming tomorrow to try and set him straight."

"Good luck with that," George said skeptically.

"Yeah."

George finished his coffee but he did not want to go. He felt comfortable, full of good food and wine, and he always enjoyed talking to Maria. "You know something?" he said. "Aside from my son and my mother, I like you better than anyone else in the world."

"How is Verena?" Maria said sharply.

George smiled. "She's seeing your old boyfriend Lee Montgomery. He's a *Washington Post* editor now. I think it's serious."

"Good."

"Do you remember . . ." He probably should not say this, but he had drunk half a bottle of wine, and he thought, What the hell? "Do you remember the time we had sex on this couch?"

"George," she said, "I don't do it often enough to forget."

"Unfortunately, neither do I."

She laughed, but said: "I'm glad."

He felt nostalgic. "How long ago was that?"

"It was the night Nixon resigned, fifteen years ago. You were young and handsome."

"And you were almost as beautiful as you are today."

"Why, you smooth talker."

"It was nice, wasn't it? The sex, I mean."

"Nice?" She pretended to be offended. "Is that all?"

"It was great."

"Yeah."

He was possessed by a feeling of regret for missed opportunities. "What happened to us?"

"We had separate paths to follow."

"I guess." There was a silence, then George said: "Do you want to do it again?"

"I thought you'd never ask."

They kissed, and immediately he remembered how it had been the first time: so relaxed, so natural, so right.

Her body had changed. It was softer, less taut, the skin dryer to his touch. He guessed the same was true of his own body: the wrestling muscles had gone long ago. But it made no difference. Her lips and tongue were fervently busy on his, and he felt the same eager pleasure at being drawn into the arms of a sensual and loving woman.

She unbuttoned his shirt. While he was taking it off, she stood up and quickly slipped out of her dress.

George said: "Before we go any farther . . ."

"What?" She sat down again. "Are you having second thoughts?"

"On the contrary. That's a pretty bra, by the way."

"Thank you. You can take it off me in a minute." She unbuckled his belt.

"But there's something I want to say. At the risk of spoiling everything . . ."

"Go ahead," she said. "Take a chance."

"I'm realizing something. I guess I should have figured it out before."

She watched him, smiling a little, saying nothing, and he had the strangest feeling that she knew exactly what was coming.

"I'm realizing that I love you," he said.

"Do you, really?"

"Yes. Do you mind? Is it okay? Have I ruined the atmosphere?"

"You fool," she said. "I've been in love with you for years."

.   .   .

Rebecca arrived at the State Department in Washington on a warm spring day. There were daffodils in the flower beds, and she was full of hope. The Soviet empire was weakening, perhaps fatally. Germany had the chance to become united and free. The Americans just needed a nudge in the right direction.

Rebecca reflected that it was because of Carla, her adoptive mother, that she was here in Washington, representing her country, negotiating with the most powerful men in the world. Carla had taken a terrified thirteen-year-old Jewish girl in wartime Berlin and had given her the confidence to become an international stateswoman. I must get a photograph to send her, Rebecca thought.

With her boss, Hans-Dietrich Genscher, and a handful of aides, she went into the art-moderne State Department building. The two-story lobby featured a huge mural called *The Defense of Human Freedoms,* which showed the five freedoms being protected by the American military.

The Germans were greeted by a woman whom Rebecca had known, until now, only as a warm, intelligent voice on the phone: Maria Summers. Rebecca was surprised to see that Maria was African American. Then she felt guilty at being surprised: there was no reason why an African American should not hold a high post in the State Department. Finally, Rebecca realized there were very few other dark faces in the building. Maria was unusual and Rebecca's surprise was, after all, justified.

Maria was friendly and welcoming, but it soon became clear that Secretary of State James Baker did not feel the same. The Germans waited outside his office for five minutes, then ten. Maria was clearly mortified. Rebecca began to worry. This could not be an accident. To keep the German vice chancellor waiting was a calculated insult. Baker must be hostile.

Rebecca had heard before of the Americans doing this kind of thing. Afterward they would tell the media that the visitors had been snubbed because of their views, and embarrassing stories would appear in the press back home. Ronald Reagan had done the same to the British opposition leader, Neil Kinnock, because he, too, was a disarmer.

Rebecca hardly cared about the insult as such. Male politicians postured a lot. It was just boys waving their dicks around. But it meant the meeting was likely to be unproductive, and that was bad news for detente.

After fifteen minutes they were shown in. Baker was a

lanky, athletic man with a Texas accent, but there was nothing of the country bumpkin about him: he was immaculately barbered and tailored. He gave Hans-Dietrich Genscher a notably brief handshake and said: "We are deeply disappointed in your attitude."

Fortunately, Genscher was no pussycat. He had been vice chancellor of Germany and foreign minister for fifteen years, and he knew how to ignore bad manners. A balding man in glasses, he had a fleshy, pugnacious face. "We feel that your policy is out-of-date," he said calmly. "The situation in Europe has changed, and you need to take that into account."

"We have to maintain the strength of the NATO nuclear deterrent," Baker said as if repeating a mantra.

Genscher controlled his impatience with a visible effort. "We disagree—and so do our people. Four out of five Germans want all nuclear weapons withdrawn from Europe."

"They are being duped by Kremlin propaganda!"

"We live in a democracy. In the end, the people decide."

Dick Cheney, the American secretary of defense, was also in the room. "One of the Kremlin's primary goals is to denuclearize Europe," he said. "We must not fall into their trap!"

Genscher was clearly irritated to be lectured on European politics by men who knew a good deal less about the subject than he did. He looked like a schoolteacher trying in vain to explain something to pupils who were deliberately being obtuse. "The Cold War is over," he said.

Rebecca was aghast to see that the discussion was going to be completely profitless. No one was listening: they had all made up their minds beforehand.

She was right. The two sides traded irritable remarks for a few more minutes, then the meeting broke up.

There was no photo opportunity.

As the Germans were leaving, Rebecca racked her brains for some way to rescue this, but came up with nothing.

In the lobby, Maria Summers said to Rebecca: "That didn't go the way I expected."

It was not an apology, but it was as near to one as Maria was permitted, by her position, to offer. "That's okay," said Rebecca. "I'm sorry there wasn't more dialogue and less point-scoring."

"Is there anything we can do to move the senior people closer together on this issue?"

Rebecca was about to say that she did not know, then she was struck by a thought. "Maybe there is," she said. "Why don't you bring President Bush to Europe? Let him see for himself. Have him talk to the Poles and the Hungarians. I believe he might change his mind."

"You're right," said Maria. "I'm going to suggest it. Thank you."

"Good luck," said Rebecca.

CHAPTER SIXTY

Lili Franck and her family were astonished.

They were watching the news on West German television. Everyone in East Germany watched West German television, even the Communist Party apparatchiks: you could tell by the angle of the aerials on their roofs.

Lili's parents were there, Carla and Werner, plus Karolin and Alice, and Alice's fiancé, Helmut.

Today, May 2, the Hungarians had opened their border with Austria.

They did not do it discreetly. The government held a press conference at Hegyeshalom, the place where the road from Budapest to Vienna crossed the border. They might almost have been *trying* to provoke the Soviets into a reaction. With great ceremony, in front of hundreds of foreign cameras, the electronic alarm and surveillance system were switched off along the entire frontier.

The Franck family stared in incredulity.

Border guards with giant wire cutters began to slice up the fence, pick up great rectangles of barbed wire, carry them away, and throw them carelessly into a pile.

Lili said: "My God, that's the Iron Curtain coming down."

Werner said: "The Soviets won't stand for this."

Lili was not so sure. She was not certain of anything these days. "Surely the Hungarians wouldn't have done this unless they expected the Soviets to accept it, would they?"

Her father shook his head. "They may *think* they can get away with it . . ."

Alice was bright-eyed with hope. "But this means Helmut and I can leave!" she said. She and her fiancé were desperate to get out of East Germany. "We can just drive to Hungary, as if we're going on holiday, then walk across the border!"

Lili sympathized: she yearned for Alice to have the opportunities in life that she herself had missed. But it could not possibly be that easy.

Helmut said: "Can we? Really?"

"No, you cannot," said Werner firmly. He pointed at the television set. "First of all, I don't see anyone actually walking across the border yet. Let's see if it really happens. Second, the Hungarian government could change its mind at any time and start arresting people. Third, if the Hungarians really do start to let people leave, the Soviets will send in the tanks and put a stop to it."

Lili thought her father might be too pessimistic. Now seventy, he was becoming timid in his old age. She had noticed it in business. He had scorned the idea of remote controls for television sets, and when they rapidly became indispensable his factory had had to scramble to catch up. "We'll see," Lili said. "In the next few days, some people are bound to try to escape. Then we'll find out whether anyone stops them."

Alice said excitedly: "What if Grandfather Werner is wrong? We can't just ignore a chance like this! What should we do?"

Her mother, Karolin, said anxiously: "It sounds dangerous."

Werner said to Lili: "What makes you think the East German government will continue to allow us to go to Hungary?"

"They'll have to," Lili argued. "If they canceled the summer holidays of thousands of families, there really would be a revolution."

"Even if it turns out to be safe for others, it may be different for us."

"Why?"

"Because we're the Franck family," Werner said in a tone of exasperation. "Your mother was a Social Democrat city councilor, your sister humiliated Hans Hoffmann, Walli killed a border guard, and you and Karolin sing protest songs. And our family business is in West Berlin, so they can't confiscate it. We've always been an irritant to the Communists. In consequence, unfortunately, we get special treatment."

Lili said: "So we have to take special precautions, that's all. Alice and Helmut will be extra cautious."

"I want to go, whatever the danger," Alice said emphatically. "I understand the risk, and I'm prepared to take it." She looked accusingly at her grandfather. "You've raised two generations under Communism. It's mean, it's brutal, it's stupid, and it's broke—yet it's still here. I want to live in the West. So does Helmut. We want our children to grow up in freedom and prosperity." She turned to her fiancé. "Don't we?"

"Yes," he said, though Lili sensed he was more wary than Alice.

"It's mad," said Werner.

Carla spoke for the first time. "It's not mad, my darling," she said forcefully to Werner. "It's dangerous, yes. But remember the things we did, the risks we took for freedom."

"Some of our number died."

Carla would not let up. "But we thought it was worth the risk."

"There was a war on. We had to defeat the Nazis."

"This is Alice and Helmut's war—the Cold War."

Werner hesitated, then sighed. "Perhaps you're right," he said reluctantly.

"Okay," said Carla. "In that case, let's make a plan."

Lili looked at the TV again. In Hungary, they were still dismantling the fence.

. . .

On election day in Poland, Tanya went to church with Danuta, who was a candidate.

It was a sunny Sunday, June 4, with a few puffy clouds in a blue sky. Danuta dressed her two children in their best clothes and brushed their hair. Marek put on a tie in the red and white colors of Solidarity, which were also the colors of the Polish flag. Danuta wore a hat, a white straw bowler with a red feather.

Tanya was in an agony of doubt. Was all this really happening? An election, in Poland? The fence coming down in Hungary? Disarmament in Europe? Did Gorbachev really mean it about openness and restructuring?

Tanya dreamed of freedom with Vasili. The two of them would tour the world: Paris, New York, Rio de Janeiro, Delhi. Vasili would be interviewed on television and talk about his work and the long years of secrecy. Tanya would write travel articles, maybe a book of her own.

But when she woke up from her daydream she waited, hour by hour, for the bad news: the roadblocks, the tanks, the arrests, the curfew, and the bald men in bad suits coming on television to announce that they had foiled a counter-revolutionary plot financed by the capitalist-imperialists.

The priest told his congregation to vote for the most godly candidates. As all Communists were in principle athe-ists, that was a clear steer. The authoritarian Polish clergy did not much like the liberal Solidarity movement, but they knew who their real enemies were.

The election had come sooner than Solidarity expected. The union had rushed to raise money, rent offices, hire staff, and mount a national election campaign, all in a few weeks. Jaruzelski had done this deliberately, to wrong-foot Solidar-ity, knowing that the government had an organization firmly in place and ready to go.

However, that was the last smart thing Jaruzelski had done. Since then the Communists had been lethargic, as if they were so sure of winning that they could hardly be both-ered to campaign. Their slogan was "With us it's safer," which sounded like a condom ad. Tanya had put that joke in her report for TASS, and to her surprise the editors had not taken it out.

In the people's minds this was a contest between Gen-eral Jaruzelski, the country's brutal leader for almost a de-cade, and the troublemaking electrician Lech Wałęsa. Danuta had her photograph taken with Wałęsa, as did every other Solidarity candidate, and the photographs had been put up everywhere. Throughout the campaign the union published a daily newspaper, written mostly by Danuta and her women friends. Solidarity's most popular poster showed Gary Coo-per as Marshal Will Kane, holding a ballot paper instead of a gun, with the slogan HIGH NOON, 4 JUNE 1989.

Perhaps the incompetence of the Communist campaign

was to be expected, Tanya thought. After all, the idea of going cap in hand to the people and saying "Please vote for me" was totally alien to the Polish ruling elite.

The new upper chamber, called the senate, had one hundred seats, and the Communists expected to win most of those. The Polish people had their backs to the wall, economically, and they would probably vote for the familiar Jaruzelski rather than the maverick Wałęsa, Tanya expected. In the lower chamber, called the Sejm, the Communists could not lose, because 65 percent of the seats were reserved for them and their allies.

Solidarity's aspirations were modest. They figured that if they won a substantial minority of votes, the Communists would be forced to give them a voice in the government.

Tanya hoped they were right.

After mass, Danuta shook hands with everyone in the church.

Then Tanya and the Gorski family went to the polling station. The ballot paper was long and complicated, so Solidarity had set up a stall outside to show people how to vote. Instead of marking their preferred candidates, they had to put a line through the ones they did not like. The Solidarity campaigners gleefully showed model ballot papers with all the Communists crossed out.

Tanya watched people voting. For most this was their first experience of a free election. She observed a shabbily dressed woman moving her pencil down the list, giving a little grunt of fulfillment each time she identified a Communist, and running her pencil through the name with a smile of pleasure. Tanya suspected the government might have been unwise to choose a system of marking the paper in which rejection could feel so physically satisfying.

She talked to some of the voters, asking what was on their minds when they made their choices. "I voted Communist," said a woman in an expensive coat. "They made this election possible." But most seemed to have picked Solidarity candidates. Tanya's sample was of course completely unscientific.

She went to Danuta's place for lunch, then the two women left Marek in charge of the children and drove in Tanya's car to Solidarity headquarters, which was upstairs at the Café Surprise, in the city center.

The mood there was up. The opinion polls gave Solidarity a lead, but no one relied on that because almost 50 percent were don't-knows. However, reports coming in from all over the country said morale was high. Tanya herself felt cheerful and optimistic. Whatever the result, a real election seemed to be taking place in a Soviet bloc country, and that alone was reason to be glad.

After the polls closed that evening Tanya went with Danuta to see her votes being counted. This was a tense moment. If the authorities decided to cheat, there were a hundred ways they could fix the result. Solidarity scrutineers watched closely, but no one saw any serious irregularity. This in itself was amazing.

And Danuta won by a landslide.

She had not really been expecting it, Tanya could tell from her look of pale shock. "I'm a deputy," she said unbelievingly. "Elected by the people." Then her face broke into that huge toothy grin, and she began to accept everyone's congratulations. So many people kissed her that Tanya began to worry about hygiene.

As soon as they could get away they drove through the lamplit streets back to the Café Surprise, where everyone was gathered around the television sets. Danuta's result was not the only landslide: Solidarity candidates were doing better than anyone expected, by far. "This is wonderful!" said Tanya.

"No, it's not," said Danuta gloomily.

Tanya realized that the Solidarity people were subdued. She was baffled by this glum reaction to triumphant news. "What on earth is wrong?"

"We're doing too well," Danuta said. "The Communists can't accept this. There will be a reaction."

Tanya had not thought of that.

"So far the government hasn't won anything," Danuta went on. "Even where they're unopposed, some Communist candidates haven't even gained the minimum fifty percent. It's too degrading. Jaruzelski will have to disallow the result."

"I'm going to speak to my brother," Tanya said.

She had a special number that enabled her to get through to the Kremlin quickly. It was late, but Dimka was still at the office. "Yes, Jaruzelski just called here," he told her. "I gather the Communists are being humiliated."

"What did Jaruzelski say?"

"He wants to impose martial law again, exactly as he did eight years ago."

Tanya's heart sank. "Shit." She remembered Danuta being dragged off to jail by the ZOMO thugs while her children cried. "Not again."

"He proposes to declare the election null and void. 'We still hold the levers of power in our hands,' he said."

"It's true," Tanya said dismally. "They have all the guns."

"But Jaruzelski is scared of doing this on his own. He wants Gorbachev's support."

Tanya was heartened. "What did Gorbi say?"

"He hasn't responded yet. Someone's waking him up right now."

"What do you think he'll do?"

"He'll probably tell Jaruzelski to solve his own problems. That's what he's been saying for the last four years. But I can't be sure. To see the party rejected so completely in a free election . . . that could be too much even for Gorbachev."

"When will you know?"

"Gorbachev is just going to say yes or no, then go back to sleep. Call me in an hour."

Tanya hung up. She did not know what to think. Clearly Jaruzelski was ready to clamp down, arrest all the Solidarity activists, throw civil liberties out the window, and reimpose his dictatorship, just as he had in 1981. It was what always happened when Communist countries got the smell of freedom in their nostrils. But Gorbachev said the old days were over. Was it true?

Poland was about to find out.

Tanya stared at the phone in an agony of suspense. What should she tell Danuta? She did not want to panic everyone. But maybe they should be warned of Jaruzelski's intentions.

Danuta said to her: "Now you're looking glum, too. What did your brother say?"

Tanya hesitated, then decided to say that nothing had been decided, which was the simple truth. "Jaruzelski called Gorbachev but hasn't reached him yet."

They continued to watch the screens. Solidarity was winning everything. So far, the Communists had not won a single contested seat. More results just confirmed the early signs. *Landslide* was hardly a strong enough word: it was more like a tsunami.

In the room over the café, euphoria mingled with fear. The gradual shift in power for which they had hoped was now out of the question. One of two things would happen in the next twenty-four hours. The Communists might again seize power by force. Or, if they did not, they were finished forever.

Tanya forced herself to wait a full hour before calling Moscow again.

"They talked," Dimka said. "Gorbachev refused to back a crackdown."

"Thank heaven," said Tanya. "So what is Jaruzelski going to do?"

"Backpedal just as fast as he can."

"Really?" Tanya could hardly believe such good news.

"He's out of options."

"I suppose he is."

"Enjoy the celebration."

Tanya hung up and spoke to Danuta. "There will be no violence," she said. "Gorbachev has ruled it out."

"Oh, my God," said Danuta in a voice that mingled incredulity with jubilation. "We really have won, haven't we?"

"Yes," said Tanya, with a feeling of satisfaction and hope that went all the way to the bottom of her heart. "This is the beginning of the end."

. . .

It was high summer and sweltering hot in Bucharest on July 7. Dimka and Natalya were there with Gorbachev for a Warsaw Pact summit. Their host was Nicolae Ceauşescu, the mad dictator of Romania.

The most important item on the agenda was "the Hungary problem." Dimka knew it had been put on the list by the East German leader, Erich Honecker. Hungary's liberalization threatened all the other Warsaw Pact countries, by calling attention to the repressive nature of their unreformed regimes, but it was worst for East Germany. Hundreds of East Germans on holiday in Hungary were leaving their tents and walking into the woods and through holes in the old fence to Austria and freedom. The roads leading from Lake Balaton to the frontier were littered with their tinny Trabant and Wartburg cars, abandoned without regret. Most had no passports, but that did not matter: they were transported to West Germany, where they were automatically given citizenship and helped to settle. No doubt they soon replaced their old cars with more reliable and comfortable Volkswagens.

The Warsaw Pact leaders met in a large room with flag-draped tables arranged in a rectangle. As always, aides such as Dimka and Natalya sat around the edges of the room. Honecker was the driving force, but Ceauşescu led the charge. He stood up from his seat next to Gorbachev and began to attack the reformist policies of the Hungarian government. He was a small, bent man with bushy eyebrows and wild eyes. Although he was talking to a few dozen people in a conference room, he shouted and gesticulated as if addressing thousands in a stadium. His twisted lips spat as he ranted. He made no bones about what he wanted: a repeat of 1956. He called for a Warsaw Pact invasion of Hungary to oust Miklós Németh and return the country to orthodox Communist Party rule.

Dimka looked around the room. Honecker was nodding. Czech hard man Miloš Jakeš wore an expression of approval. Bulgaria's Todor Zhivkov clearly agreed. Only Poland's leader, General Jaruzelski, sat unmoving and expressionless, perhaps humbled by his election defeat.

All these men were brutal tyrants, torturers, and mass murderers. Stalin had not been exceptional, he had been typical of Communist leaders. Any political system that allowed such people to rule was evil, Dimka reflected. Why did it take us all so long to figure that out?

But Dimka, like most of the people in the room, was watching Gorbachev.

The rhetoric no longer mattered. It was of no consequence who was right and who was wrong. No one in the room had the power to do anything without the consent of the man with the port-wine stain on his bald head.

Dimka thought he knew what Gorbachev was going to do. But he could never be sure. Gorbachev was divided, like the empire he ruled, between conservative and reformist tendencies. No speeches were likely to change his mind. Most of the time he just looked bored.

Ceauşescu's voice rose almost to a scream. At that moment Gorbachev caught the eye of Miklós Németh. The Russian gave the Hungarian a slight smile as Ceauşescu sputtered saliva and vituperation.

Then, to Dimka's utter astonishment, Gorbachev winked.

Gorbachev held the smile a second longer, then looked away and resumed his bored expression.

.   .   .

Maria managed to avoid Jasper Murray almost until the end of President Bush's European visit.

She had never met Jasper. She knew what he looked like: she had seen him on television, as everyone had. He was taller in real life, that was all. Over the years she had been the secret source of some of his best stories, but he did not know that. He only met George Jakes, the intermediary. They were careful. It was why they had never been found out.

She knew the whole story of Jasper's being fired from *This Day*. The White House had put pressure on Frank Lindeman, the owner of the network. That was how a star reporter came to be exiled. Although with the turmoil in Eastern Europe, plus Jasper's nose for a good story, the assignment had turned out to be a hot one.

Bush and his entourage, including Maria, ended up in Paris. Maria was standing in the Champs-Élysées with the press corps on Bastille Day, July 14, watching an interminable parade of military might, and looking forward to going home and making love to George again, when Jasper spoke to her. He pointed to a huge poster of Evie Williams advertising face cream. "She had a crush on me when she was fifteen years old," he said.

Maria looked at the picture. Evie Williams had been blacklisted by Hollywood for her politics, but she was a big star in Europe, and Maria recalled reading that her personal line of organic beauty products was making her more money than movies ever had.

"You and I have never met," Jasper said. "But I got to know your godson, Jack Jakes, when I was living with Verena Marquand."

Maria shook his hand warily. Talking to reporters was always dangerous. No matter what you said, the mere fact that you had had a conversation put you in a weak position, for then there could always be an argument about what you had actually said. "I'm glad to meet you at last," she said.

"I admire you for your achievements," he said. "Your career would be remarkable for a white man. For an African American woman, it's astonishing."

Maria smiled. Of course Jasper was charming—that was how he got people to talk. He was also completely untrustworthy, and would betray his mother for the sake of a story. She said neutrally: "How are you enjoying Europe?"

"Right now it's the most exciting place in the world," he said. "Lucky me."

"That's great."

"By contrast," Jasper said, "this trip has not been a success for President Bush."

Here it comes, Maria thought. She was in a difficult position. She had to defend the president and the policies of the State Department, even though she agreed with Jasper's assessment. Bush had failed to take leadership of the freedom movement in Eastern Europe: he was too timid. But she said: "We think it's been something of a triumph."

"Well, you have to say that. But, off the record, was it right for Bush to urge Jaruzelski—a Communist tyrant of the old school—to run for president in Poland?"

"Jaruzelski may well be the best candidate to oversee gradual reform," Maria said, though she did not believe it.

"Bush infuriated Lech Wałęsa by offering a paltry aid package of a hundred million dollars, when Solidarity had asked for ten billion."

"President Bush believes in caution," Maria argued. "He thinks the Poles need to reform their economy first, then get aid. Otherwise the money will be wasted. The president is a conservative. You may not like that, Jasper, but the American people do. That's why they elected him."

Jasper smiled, acknowledging a point scored, but he pressed on. "In Hungary, Bush praised the Communist government for removing the fence, not the opposition who put the pressure on. He kept telling the Hungarians not to go too far, too fast! What kind of advice is that from the leader of the free world?"

Maria did not contradict Jasper. He was one hundred percent correct. She decided to deflect him. To give herself a moment to think, she watched a low-loader go by bearing a long missile with a French flag painted on its side. Then she said: "You're missing a better story."

He raised a skeptical eyebrow. That accusation was not often leveled at Jasper Murray. "Go on," he said in a tone of mild amusement.

"I can't talk to you on the record."

"Off it, then."

She gave him a hard look. "So long as we're clear on that."

"We are."

"Okay. You probably know that some of the advice the president has been getting suggests that Gorbachev is a fraud, glasnost and perestroika are Communist flummery, and the whole charade is no more than a way to trick the West into dropping its guard and disarming prematurely."

"Who gives him this advice?"

The answer was the CIA, the national security adviser, and the secretary of defense, but Maria was not going to run them down when talking to a journalist, even off the record, so she said: "Jasper, if you don't know that already, you're not the reporter we all think you are."

He grinned. "Okay. So what's the big story?"

"President Bush was inclined to accept that advice—before he came on this trip. The story is that he has seen the reality on the ground here in Europe, and has altered his view accordingly. In Poland he said: 'I have this heady feeling that I'm witnessing history being made on the spot.'"

"Can I use that quote?"

"You may. He said it to me."

"Thanks."

"The president now believes that change in the Communist world is real and permanent, and we need to give it guarded encouragement, instead of kidding ourselves that it isn't really happening."

Jasper gave Maria a long look that, she thought, had in it

a measure of surprised respect. "You're right," he said at last. "That is a better story. Back in Washington the Cold Warriors, like Dick Cheney and Brent Scowcroft, are going to be mad as hell."

"You said that," Maria said. "I didn't."

. . .

Lili, Karolin, Alice, and Helmut drove from Berlin to Lake Balaton, in Hungary, in Lili's white Trabant. As usual, it took two days. On the way Lili and Karolin sang every song they knew.

They were singing to cover their fear. Alice and Helmut were going to try to escape to the West. No one knew what would happen.

Lili and Karolin would stay behind. Both were single but, all the same, their lives were in East Germany. They hated the regime, but they wanted to oppose it, not flee from it. It was different for Alice and Helmut, who had their lives in front of them.

Lili knew only two people who had tried to leave: Rebecca, and Walli. Rebecca's fiancé had fallen from a roof and been crippled for life. Walli had run over a border guard and killed him, a trauma that had haunted him for years. They were not happy precedents. But the situation had changed now—hadn't it?

On the first evening at the holiday camp they came across a middle-aged man called Berthold, sitting outside his tent, holding forth to half a dozen young people drinking beer from cans. "It's obvious, isn't it?" he said in a voice that was confidential but carrying. "The whole thing is a trap set by the Stasi. It's their new way of catching subversives."

A young man sitting on the ground, smoking a cigarette, seemed skeptical. "How does that work, then?"

"As soon as you cross the border, you're arrested by the Austrians. They hand you over to the Hungarian police, who send you back to East Germany in handcuffs. Then you go straight to the interrogation rooms in Stasi headquarters in Lichtenberg."

A girl standing nearby said: "How would you know a thing like that?"

"My cousin tried to cross the border here," said Berthold. "Last thing he said to me was: 'I'll send you a postcard from Vienna.' Now he's in a prison camp near Dresden, working in a uranium mine. It's the only way our government can get people to work in those mines, no one else will do it—the radiation gives you lung cancer."

The family discussed Berthold's theory in low voices before going to bed. Alice said scornfully: "Berthold is one of those men who know it all. How would he find out that his cousin is working in a uranium mine? The government doesn't admit to using prisoners that way."

But Helmut was worried. "He may be an idiot, but what if his story is true? The border could be a trap."

Alice said: "Why would the Austrians send escapers back? They have no love of Communism."

"They may not want the trouble and expense of dealing with them. Why should the Austrians care about East Germans?"

They argued for an hour and came to no conclusion. Lili lay awake for a long time, worrying.

Next morning in the communal dining room Lili spotted Berthold regaling a different group of young people with his theories, a large plate of ham and cheese in front of him. Was he genuine, or a Stasi faker? She felt she had to know. He looked as if he would be there some time. On impulse, she decided to search his tent. She left the room.

Tents were not secured: holidaymakers were simply advised not to leave money or valuables behind. All the same, Berthold's entrance was tightly laced.

Lili began to untie the strings, trying to appear relaxed, as if she had every right to do it. Her heart was like a drumbeat in her chest. She made an effort not to glance guiltily at people walking by. She was used to sneaking around—the gigs she played with Karolin were always semi-illegal—but she had never done anything quite like this. If Berthold should for some reason abandon his breakfast early and come back sooner than she expected, what would she say? "Oops, wrong tent, sorry!" The tents were all alike. He might not believe her—but what would he do, go to the police?

She opened the flap and stepped inside.

Berthold was neat, for a man. His clothes were folded in a suitcase, and there was a drawstring bag full of laundry. He had a sponge bag containing a safety razor and shaving soap. His bed was made of canvas stretched across metal tubing. Beside the bed was a small pile of magazines in German. It all looked innocent.

Don't rush, she told herself. Look carefully for clues. Who is this man and what is he doing here?

A sleeping bag was folded on top of the camp bed. When Lili picked it up she felt something heavy. She unzipped the bag and rummaged inside. She found a book of pornographic photos—and a gun.

It was a small black pistol with a short barrel. She did not know much about firearms, and she could not identify the make, but she thought it was what they called a nine-millimeter. It looked designed to be concealed.

She stuffed it into the pocket of her jeans.

She had the answer to her question. Berthold was not a know-all braggart. He was a Stasi agent, sent here to spread scare stories and discourage escapers.

Lili refolded the sleeping bag and stepped out of the tent. Berthold was not in sight. She quickly laced up the tent flap with trembling fingers. Another few seconds and she would be safe. As soon as Berthold looked for his gun, he would know that someone had been there, but if she could get away now he would never know who. Lili guessed he would not even report the theft to the Hungarian police, for they would surely disapprove of a German secret agent bringing a pistol to one of their holiday camps.

She walked briskly away.

Karolin was in Helmut and Alice's tent, and they were talking in low voices, still arguing about whether the border crossing might be a trap. Lili interrupted the discussion. "Berthold is a Stasi agent," she said. "I searched his tent." She drew the gun from her pocket.

"That's a Makarov," said Helmut, who had served in the army. "A Soviet-made semiautomatic pistol, standard issue for the Stasi."

Lili said: "If the border really were a trap, the Stasi would be keeping the fact secret. The way Berthold is telling everyone pretty much proves it's not true."

Helmut nodded. "That's good enough for me. We're going."

They all stood up. Helmut said to Lili: "Would you like me to get rid of the gun?"

"Yes, please." She handed it over, relieved to be rid of it.

"I'll find a secluded spot on the beach and throw it in the lake."

While Helmut was doing that, the women put towels and swimsuits and bottles of sun lotion into the trunk of the Trabi as if they were going off for a day's outing, maintaining the fiction of a family holiday. When Helmut came back, they drove to the grocery and bought cheese, bread, and wine for a picnic.

Then they headed west.

Lili kept looking behind, but as far as she could tell no one was following them.

They drove fifty miles and turned off the main road when they were close to the border. Alice had a map and a magnetic compass. As they wound around country roads, pretending to look for a picnic spot in the forest, they saw several cars with East German plates abandoned at the roadside, and knew they were in the right area.

There was no sign of officialdom, but Lili worried all the same. Clearly the East German secret police had an interest in escapers, but there was probably nothing they could do.

They were passing a small lake when Alice said: "I calculate we're less than a mile from the fence here."

A few seconds later Helmut, who was at the wheel, turned off the road onto an unpaved track through the trees. He stopped the car in a clearing a few steps from the water.

He turned off the engine. "Well," he said into the silence. "Are we going to pretend to have lunch?"

"No," said Alice, her voice high-pitched with tension. "I want to go, now."

They all got out of the car.

Alice led the way, checking the compass. The going was easy, with little undergrowth to slow their steps. Tall pines filtered the sunshine, throwing patches of gold onto the carpet of needles underfoot. The forest was quiet. Lili heard the cry of some kind of waterfowl, and occasionally the distant roar of a tractor.

They passed a yellow Wartburg Knight, half-hidden by low-hanging branches, its windows broken and its fenders already rusting. A bird flew out of its open trunk, and Lili wondered whether it had nested there.

She scanned the surroundings constantly, looking for

the patch of green or gray wool that would betray a uniform, but she saw no one. Helmut was equally alert, she noticed.

They climbed a rise, then the forest ran out abruptly. They emerged onto a strip of cleared land and saw, a hundred yards away, the fence.

It was not impressive. The posts were of rough-hewn wood. There were several rows of wire, which presumably had once been electrified. The top row, at a height of six feet, was plain barbed wire. On the far side was a field of yellow grain ripening in the August sun.

They crossed the cleared strip and came to the fence.

Alice said: "We can climb over the fence right here."

Helmut said: "They have definitely switched off the electricity . . . ?"

"Yes," said Alice.

Impatiently, Karolin reached out and touched the wire. She touched all the wires, grasping each firmly in her hand. "Off," she said.

Alice kissed and hugged her mother and Lili. Helmut shook hands.

A hundred yards away, from over a rise, two soldiers appeared in the gray tunics and tall peaked caps of the Hungarian Border Guard Service.

Lili said: "Oh, no!"

Both men leveled their rifles.

"Stand still, everyone," said Helmut.

Alice said: "I can't believe we got this close!" She began to cry.

"Don't despair," said Helmut. "It's not over yet."

Coming closer, the guards lowered their rifles and spoke in German. No doubt they knew exactly what was going on. "What are you doing here?" one said.

"We came to picnic in the woods," Lili said.

"A picnic? Really?"

"We meant no harm!"

"You are not allowed here."

Lili was desperately afraid the soldiers would arrest them. "All right, all right," she said. "We'll go back!"

She feared that Helmut might put up a fight. They might be killed, all four of them. She felt shaky and her legs were weak.

The second guard spoke. "Be careful," he said. He pointed along the fence in the direction from which he had come. "A quarter of a mile from here is a gap in the fence. You might accidentally cross the border."

The two guards looked at one another and laughed heartily. Then they went on their way.

Lili stared in astonishment at their retreating backs. They kept on walking, not looking back. Lili and the others watched them until they were out of sight in silence.

Then Lili said: "They seemed to be telling us . . ."

"To find the gap in the fence!" Helmut said. "Let's do it, quick!"

They hurried in the direction in which the guard had pointed. They kept close to the edge of the forest, in case they needed to hide. Sure enough, after a quarter of a mile they came to a place where the fence was broken. The wooden posts had been uprooted and the wires, snapped in places, lay flat on the ground. It looked as if a heavy truck had driven through it. The earth all around was heavily trodden, the grass brown and sparse. Beyond the gap, a path between two fields led to a distant clump of trees with a few roofs showing: a village, or perhaps just a hamlet.

Freedom.

A small pine tree nearby was hung with key rings, thirty, forty, maybe fifty of them. People had left behind the keys to their apartments and cars, a defiant gesture to show that they were never coming back. As the branches were moved by a light breeze, the metal glittered in the sunlight. It looked like a Christmas tree.

"Don't hesitate," Lili said. "We said good-bye ten minutes ago. Just go."

Alice said: "I love you, Mother, and Lili."

"Go," said Karolin.

Alice took Helmut's hand.

Lili looked up and down the cleared strip alongside the fence. There was no one in sight.

The two young people walked through the gap, stepping carefully over the fallen fence.

On the other side, they stopped and waved, even though they were only ten feet away. "We're free!" Alice said.

Lili said: "Give my love to Walli."

"And mine," said Karolin.

Alice and Helmut walked on, hand in hand, up the path between the fields of grain.

At the far end they waved again.

Then they entered the little village and disappeared from sight.

Karolin's face was wet with tears. "I wonder if we'll ever see them again," she said.

CHAPTER SIXTY-ONE

West Berlin made Walli nostalgic. He remembered being a teenager with a guitar, playing Everly Brothers hits in the Minnesänger folk club just off the Ku'damm, and dreaming of going to America to be a pop star. I got what I wanted, he thought—and a lot that I didn't.

While he was checking into his hotel he ran into Jasper Murray. "I heard you were over here," said Walli. "I guess what's happening in Germany is exciting to cover."

"It is," said Jasper. "Americans aren't normally interested in European news, but this is special."

"Your show, *This Day,* isn't the same without you. I hear its ratings are down."

"I probably ought to pretend to be sorry. What are you up to these days?"

"Making a new album. I left Dave mixing it in California. He'll probably fuck it up with strings and a glockenspiel."

"What brings you to Berlin?"

"I'm meeting my daughter, Alice. She escaped from East Germany."

"Are your parents still there?"

"Yes, and my sister Lili." And Karolin, Walli thought, but he did not mention her. He longed for her to escape, too. Deep in his heart he still missed her, despite all the years that had passed. "Rebecca's here in the West," he added. "She's a big shot in the Foreign Office now."

"I know. She's been helpful to me. Maybe we could do a

piece on a family divided by the Wall. It would show the human suffering caused by the Cold War."

"No," said Walli firmly. He had not forgotten the interview Jasper had done back in the sixties, which had caused so much trouble for the Francks in the East. "My family would be made to suffer by the East German government."

"Too bad. Good to see you, anyhow."

Walli checked into the Presidential Suite. He turned on the TV in the living room. The set was a Franck, made in his father's factory. The news was all about people fleeing East Germany via Hungary and, now, via Czechoslovakia too. He left the set on with the sound low. It was his habit to have the TV on when he was doing other things. He had been thrilled to learn that Elvis did the same.

He took a shower and put on fresh clothes. Then the desk called to say that Alice and Helmut were downstairs. "Send them up," Walli said.

He felt nervous, which was silly. This was his daughter. But he had seen her only once in her twenty-five years. At that time she had been a skinny teenager with long fair hair, reminding him of Karolin when he had first met her, back in the sixties.

A minute later the bell rang and he opened the door. Alice was now a young woman, with no teenage gawkiness. Her fair hair was cut in a bob, so she no longer looked so strikingly like the young Karolin, though she had Karolin's thousand-candlepower smile. She was dressed in shabby East German clothes and down-at-heel shoes, and Walli made a mental note to take her shopping.

He kissed her awkwardly on both cheeks and shook hands with Helmut.

Alice looked around the suite and said: "Wow, nice room."

It was nothing by comparison with hotels in Los Angeles, but Walli did not tell her that. She had a lot to learn, but there was plenty of time.

He ordered coffee and cakes from room service. They sat around the table in the living room. "This is weird," Walli said candidly. "You're my kid, but we're strangers."

"I know your songs, though," Alice said. "Every one. You weren't there, but you've been singing to me all my life."

"That's kind of awesome."

"Yeah."

They told him the story of their escape in detail. "Looking back, it was easy," Alice said. "But at the time I was scared to death."

They were living temporarily in an apartment rented for them by the Franck factory accountant, Enok Andersen. "What are you going to do, long term?" Walli asked.

Helmut said: "I'm an electrical engineer, but I'd like to learn about business. Next week I'm going on the road with one of the salesmen for Franck televisions. Your father, Werner, says that's the way to begin."

Alice said: "In the East I was working in a pharmacy. At first I'll probably do the same here, but one day I'd like to have my own shop."

Walli was pleased they were thinking about work. He had nursed a secret anxiety that they might want to live on his money, which would have been bad for them. He smiled and said: "I'm glad neither of you wants to be in the music business."

Alice said: "But the main thing we want to do is have children."

"I'm so glad. I can't wait to be a granddad rock star. Are you going to get married?"

"We've been talking about that," she said. "We never cared about it, living in the East, but now we kind of want to. How would you feel about that?"

"Marriage itself is not a big issue for me, but I'd be kind of thrilled if you decided to do it."

"Good. Daddy, would you sing at my wedding?"

That came from behind and knocked Walli over. It was all he could do not to cry. "Sure, honey," he managed to say. "I'd be glad to." To cover his emotion he turned to the television.

The screen was showing a demonstration the previous evening in Leipzig, in East Germany. Protesters carrying candles marched in silence from a church. They were peaceful, but police vans drove into the crowd, running over several people, then the cops jumped out and started arresting marchers.

Helmut said: "Those bastards."

Walli said: "What is the demonstration about?"

"The right to travel," said Helmut. "We've escaped, but we can't go back. Alice has you, now, but she can't visit her mother. And I'm separated from both my parents. We don't know if we'll ever see them again."

Alice said angrily: "People are demonstrating because there's no reason why we should live like this. I should be able to see my mother as well as my father. We should be allowed to go to and fro between East and West. Germany is one country. We should get rid of that Wall."

"Amen to that," said Walli.

. . .

Dimka liked his boss. Gorbachev in his deepest soul believed in the truth. Since Lenin died, every Soviet leader had been a liar. They had all glossed over what was wrong and declined to acknowledge reality. The most striking characteristic of Soviet leadership for the last sixty-five years was the refusal to face facts. Gorbachev was different. As he struggled to navigate through the storm that was battering the Soviet Union, he held on to that one guiding principle, that the truth must be told. Dimka was full of admiration.

Both Dimka and Gorbachev were pleased when Erich Honecker was deposed as leader of East Germany. Honecker had lost control of the country and the party. But they were disappointed by his successor. To Dimka's annoyance, Honecker's loyal deputy, Egon Krenz, took over. It was like replacing Tweedledum with Tweedledee.

All the same, Dimka thought Gorbachev would have to give Krenz a helping hand. The Soviet Union could not permit the collapse of East Germany. Perhaps the USSR could live with democratic elections in Poland and market forces in Hungary, but Germany was different. It was divided, like Europe, into East and West, Communist and capitalist; and if West Germany were to triumph that would signal the ascendancy of capitalism, and the end of the dream of Marx and Lenin. Even Gorbachev could not allow that—could he?

Krenz made the usual pilgrimage to Moscow two weeks later. Dimka shook the hand of a fleshy-faced man with thick gray hair and a look of smug satisfaction. He might have been a heartthrob in his youth.

In the grand office with the yellow-paneled walls, Gorbachev greeted him with cool courtesy.

Krenz brought with him a report by his chief economic

planner saying that East Germany was bankrupt. The report had been suppressed by Honecker, Krenz claimed. Dimka knew that the truth about East Germany's economy had been hidden for decades. All the propaganda about economic growth had been lies. Productivity in factories and mines was as low as 50 percent of that in the West.

"We have kept going by borrowing," Krenz told Gorbachev, sitting on a black leather chair in the grand Kremlin room. "Ten billion deutschmarks a year."

Even Gorbachev was shocked. "Ten *billion*?"

"We have been taking out short-term loans to pay the interest on long-term loans."

Dimka put in: "Which is illegal. If the banks find out . . ."

"The interest on our debt is now four and a half billion dollars a year, which is two-thirds of our entire foreign currency earnings. We must have your help to deal with this crisis."

Gorbachev bristled. He hated it when East European leaders begged for money.

Krenz wheedled. "East Germany is in a sense the child of the Soviet Union." He tried a masculine joke. "One should acknowledge the paternity of one's children."

Gorbachev did not even smile. "We are in no position to offer you assistance," he said bluntly. "Not in the present condition of the USSR."

Dimka was surprised. He had not expected Gorbachev to be this tough.

Krenz was baffled. "Then what am I to do?"

"You must be honest with your people, and tell them that they cannot continue to live in the manner they have become used to."

"There will be trouble," Krenz said. "A state of emergency would have to be declared. Measures must be taken to prevent a mass breakthrough across the Wall."

Dimka thought this was approaching political blackmail. Gorbachev did, too, and he stiffened. "In that case, do not expect to be rescued by the Red Army," Gorbachev said. "You have to solve these problems yourself."

Did he really mean it? Was the USSR really going to wash its hands of East Germany? Dimka's excitement mounted with his astonishment. Was Gorbachev willing to go all the way?

Krenz looked like a priest who has realized there is no God. East Germany had been created by the Soviet Union, subsidized from the Kremlin's coffers, and protected by the strength of the Soviet military. He could not take in the idea that that was all over. He clearly had absolutely no idea what to do next.

When he had gone, Gorbachev said to Dimka: "Issue a reminder to commanders of our forces in East Germany. They must not *under any circumstances* get involved in conflicts between the government there and its citizens. This is an absolute priority."

My God, Dimka thought, is this really the end?

. . .

By November there were demonstrations every week in major towns in East Germany. The numbers grew larger and the crowds grew bolder. They could not be crushed by brutal police baton charges.

Lili and Karolin were invited to play at a rally in the Alexander Platz, not far from their home. Several hundred thousand people showed up. Someone had painted a huge placard with the slogan WIR SIND DAS VOLK, "We are the people." All around the edges of the square were police in riot gear, waiting for the order to wade into the crowd with their truncheons. But the cops looked more frightened than the demonstrators.

Speaker after speaker denounced the Communist regime, and the police did nothing.

The organizers permitted pro-Communist speakers, too, and to Lili's astonishment the government's chosen defender was Hans Hoffmann. From her position in the wings, where she and Karolin were waiting for their turn onstage, she stared at the familiar, stooped figure of the man who had persecuted her family for a quarter of a century. Despite his expensive blue coat he was shivering from the cold—or perhaps it was fear.

When Hans tried to smile amiably, he succeeded only in looking like a vampire. "Comrades," he said, "the party has listened to the voices of the people, and new measures are on the way."

The crowd knew this was bullshit, and they began to hiss.

"But we must proceed in an orderly fashion, acknowledging the leading role of the party in developing Communism."

The hissing turned to booing.

Lili watched Hans closely. His expression showed rage and frustration. A year ago, one word from him could have destroyed any of the people in the crowd; but now, suddenly, they seemed to have the power. He could not even shut them up. He had to raise his voice to a shout in order to be heard, even with the help of the microphone. "In particular, we must not make every member of the state security organizations into scapegoats for whatever mistakes may have been made by the former leadership."

This was no less than a plea for sympathy on behalf of the bullies and sadists who had been oppressing the people for decades, and the crowd was outraged. They jeered and yelled: "*Stasi raus,*" "Stasi out."

Hans yelled at the top of his voice: "After all, they were only obeying orders!"

That brought a roar of incredulous laughter.

For Hans, to be laughed at was the worst fate. He flushed with rage. Suddenly Lili recalled the scene, twenty-eight years ago, when Rebecca had thrown Hans's shoes at him from the upstairs window. It had been the scornful laughter of the women neighbors that had driven Hans into a fury.

Now Hans remained at the microphone, unable to speak over the noise, but unwilling to give in. It was a battle of wills between him and the crowd, and he lost. His arrogant expression crumpled, and he seemed close to tears. At last he turned from the microphone and stepped away from the lectern.

He cast one more look at the crowd, laughing and jeering at him, and gave up. As he walked off, he saw Lili and recognized her. Their eyes met as she walked onstage with Karolin, both carrying guitars. In that instant he looked like a beaten dog, so tragic that Lili almost felt sorry for him.

Then she passed him and moved to center stage. Some of the crowd recognized Lili and Karolin, others knew their names, and they roared a welcome. Lili and Karolin went up to the microphones. They strummed a major chord, then together they launched into "This Land Is Your Land."

And the crowd went wild.

Bonn was a provincial town on the banks of the Rhine River. It was an unlikely choice for a national capital, and had been picked for precisely that reason, to symbolize its temporary nature, and the faith of the German people that one day Berlin would again be the capital of a reunited Germany. But that had been forty years ago, and Bonn was still the capital.

It was a boring place, but that suited Rebecca, for she worked too hard to have a social life, except when Fred Bíró was in town.

She was busy. Her area of expertise was Eastern Europe, which was in the throes of a revolution whose end no one could see. Most days she had working lunches, but today she took a break. She left the Foreign Office and walked on her own to an inexpensive restaurant where she ordered her favorite dish, *Himmel und Erde,* heaven and earth, made of potatoes and apples with bacon.

While she was eating, Hans Hoffmann appeared.

Rebecca pushed back her chair and stood up. Her first thought was that he had come to kill her. She was on the point of screaming for help when she noticed the expression on his face. He looked defeated and sad. Her fear vanished: he was no longer dangerous.

"Please don't be afraid, I mean no harm," he said.

She remained standing. "What do you want?"

"A few words. A minute or two, no more."

For a moment she wondered how he had managed to come from East to West Germany, then she realized that travel restrictions did not apply to senior officers in the secret police. They could do anything they liked. He had probably told his colleagues that he had an intelligence mission in Bonn. Perhaps he did.

The restaurant proprietor came over and said: "Is everything all right, Frau Held?"

Rebecca stared at Hans a moment longer. Then she said: "Yes, thank you, Günther, I think it's okay." She sat down again and Hans sat opposite.

She picked up her fork and put it down again. She had lost her appetite. "A minute or two, then."

"Help me," he said.

She could hardly believe her ears. "What?" she said. "Help *you*?"

"It's all falling apart. I have to get out. The crowds laugh at me. I'm afraid they'll kill me."

"What on earth do you imagine I might do for you?"

"I need a place to stay, money, papers."

"Are you out of your mind? After all you've done to me and my family?"

"Don't you understand why I did those things?"

"Because you hate us!"

"Because I love you."

"Don't be ridiculous."

"I was assigned to spy on you and your family, yes. I dated you in order to get inside the house. But then something happened. I fell in love with you."

He had said this once before, on the day she escaped over the Wall. He really meant it. He *was* out of his mind, she decided. She began to feel scared again.

"I told no one of my feelings," he said, smiling nostalgically, as if he were recalling an innocent youthful romance rather than a wicked deception. "I pretended to be exploiting you and manipulating your feelings. But I really loved you. Then you said we should get married. I was in heaven! I had the perfect excuse to give my superiors."

He was living in a dreamworld, but was that not true of the entire East German ruling elite?

"That year that we spent together, as man and wife, was the best time of my life," Hans said. "And your rejection broke my heart."

"How can you say that?"

"Why do you think I haven't remarried?"

She was stupefied. "I don't know," she said.

"I have no interest in other women. Rebecca, you are the love of my life."

She stared at him. She realized that this was not just a stupid story, a hopeless attempt to gain sympathy. Hans was sincere. He meant every word.

"Take me back," he pleaded.

"No."

"Please."

"The answer is no," she said. "It will always be no. Nothing you could say would change my mind. Please don't force me to use harsh words to make you understand." I don't know why I'm reluctant to hurt him, she thought; he never hesitated to be cruel to me. "Just accept what I have said to you and leave."

"All right," he said sadly. "I knew you'd say this, but I had to try." He stood up. "Thank you, Rebecca. Thank you for that year of happiness. I will always love you." He turned away and walked out of the restaurant.

Rebecca stared after him, still deep in shock. God in heaven, she thought; I wasn't expecting that.

CHAPTER SIXTY-TWO

I t was a cold November day in Berlin, with an obscuring mist and a brimstone smell of sulfur in the air from the smoky factories in the infernal East. Tanya, hastily transferred here from Warsaw to help cover the mounting crisis, felt that East Germany was about to have a heart attack. Everything was breaking down. In a remarkable repeat of what had happened in 1961 before the Wall went up, so many people had fled to the West that schools were closing for lack of teachers and hospitals were running on skeleton staffing. Those who remained behind became more and more angry and frustrated.

The new leader, Egon Krenz, was focusing on travel. He hoped that if he could satisfy people on that issue, other grievances would fade away. Tanya thought he was wrong: demanding more freedom was likely to become a habit with East Germans. Krenz had published new travel regulations on November 6 that would permit people to go abroad, with permission from the Interior Ministry, taking with them fifteen deutschmarks, about enough for a plate of sausages and a stein of beer in West Germany. This concession was scorned by the public. Today, November 9, the increasingly desperate leader had called a press conference to reveal yet another new travel law.

Tanya sympathized with the yearning of East Germans to be free to go where they wished. She longed for the same liberty for herself and Vasili. He was world famous, but he had to hide behind a pseudonym. He had never left the

Soviet Union, where his books were not published. He should be able to go and accept in person the prizes his alter ego had won, and bask a little in the sunshine of acclaim—and she wanted to go with him.

Unfortunately she did not see how East Germany could ever set its people free. It could hardly exist as an independent state: that was why they had built the Wall in the first place. If they let their citizens travel, millions would leave permanently. West Germany might be a prissily conservative country, with old-fashioned attitudes on women's rights, but it was a paradise by comparison with the East. No country could survive the exodus of its most enterprising young people. Therefore Krenz would never willingly give East Germans the one thing they wanted above all else.

So it was with low expectations that Tanya went to the International Press Center on Mohren Strasse a few minutes before six in the evening. The room was packed with journalists, photographers, and television cameras. The rows of red seats were full, and Tanya had to join the crowd around the sides of the room. The international press corps was here in force: they could smell blood.

Krenz's press officer, Günter Schabowski, came into the room with three other officials at six sharp and sat at the table on the platform. He had gray hair and wore a gray suit and a gray tie. He was a competent bureaucrat whom Tanya liked and trusted. For an hour he announced ministerial changes and administrative reforms.

Tanya marveled at the sight of a Communist government scrambling to satisfy a public demand for change. It was almost unknown. And on the rare occasions when it had happened, the tanks had rolled in soon afterward. She recalled the agonizing disappointments of the Prague Spring in 1968 and Solidarity in 1981. But, according to her brother, the Soviet Union no longer had the power or the will to crush dissent. She hardly dared to hope it was true. She pictured a life in which she and Vasili could write the truth without fear. Freedom. It was hard to imagine.

At seven Schabowski announced the new travel law. "It will be possible for every citizen of East Germany to leave the country using border crossing points," he said. That was not very illuminating, and several journalists asked for clarification.

Schabowski himself seemed uncertain. He put on a pair of half-moon spectacles and read the decree aloud. "Private travel to foreign countries can be applied for without presentation of existing visa requirements or proving the need to travel or familial relationships."

It was all written in obfuscatory bureaucratic language, but it sounded good. Someone said: "When does this new regulation come into effect?"

Schabowski clearly did not know. Tanya noticed that he was perspiring. She guessed that the new law had been drafted in a rush. He shuffled the papers in front of him, looking for the answer. "As far as I know," he said, "immediately, without delay."

Tanya was bewildered. Something was effective immediately—but what? Could anyone just drive up to a checkpoint and cross? But the press conference came to an end without any further information.

Tanya wondered what to write as she walked the short distance back to the Hotel Metropol on Friedrich Strasse. In the grubby grandiosity of the marble lobby, Stasi agents in their customary leather jackets and blue jeans lounged around, smoking and watching a television set with a bad picture. It was showing film from the press conference. As Tanya got her room key, she heard one receptionist say to another: "What does that mean? Can we just go?"

No one knew.

. . . .

Walli was in his West Berlin hotel suite, watching the news with Rebecca, who had flown in to see Alice and Helmut. They were all planning to have dinner together.

Walli and Rebecca puzzled over a low-key report on ZDF's seven o'clock *Today* program. There were new travel regulations for East Germans, but it was not clear what they meant. Walli could not figure out whether his family would be allowed to visit him in West Germany or not. "I wonder if I might even see Karolin again soon," he mused.

Alice and Helmut arrived a few minutes later, pulling off their cold-weather coats and scarves.

At eight Walli switched over to ARD's *Day Show,* but did not learn much more.

It seemed impossible that the Wall that had blighted

Walli's life could be opened. In a flash of memory that was all too familiar, he relived those few traumatic seconds at the wheel of Joe Henry's old black Framo van. He recalled his terror as he saw the border guard kneel down and aim the submachine gun, his panic as he swung the wheel and drove at the guard, his confusion as bullets shattered his windscreen. He was sickened as he felt the sensation of his wheels bumping over a human being. Then he crashed through the barrier to freedom.

The Wall had taken his innocence. It had also taken Karolin from him. And his daughter's childhood.

That daughter, now a few days from her twenty-sixth birthday, was saying: "Is the Wall still the Wall, or not?"

Rebecca said: "I can't make it out. It's almost as if they've opened the border by mistake."

Walli said: "Shall we go out and see what's happening on the streets?"

. . .

Lili, Karolin, Werner, and Carla regularly watched ARD's *Day Show,* as did millions of people in East Germany. They thought it told the truth, unlike their own state-controlled news shows, which depicted a fantasy world no one believed in. All the same, they were puzzled by the ambiguous eight o'clock news. Carla said: "Is the border open or not?"

Werner said: "It can't be."

Lili stood up. "Well, I'm going to have a look."

In the end all four of them went.

As soon as they stepped out of the house and breathed the cold night air, they felt the emotional charge in the atmosphere. The streets of East Berlin, dimly lit by yellow lamps, were unusually busy with people and cars. Everyone was headed the same way, toward the Wall, mostly in groups. Some young men were trying to thumb a ride, a crime that would have got them arrested a week ago. People were talking to strangers, asking what they knew, whether it was really true that they could go to West Berlin now.

Karolin said to Lili: "Walli is in West Berlin. I heard it on the radio. He must have come to see Alice." She looked thoughtful. "I hope they like each other."

The Franck family walked south on Friedrich Strasse until they saw, in the distance, the powerful floodlights of

Checkpoint Charlie, a compound that occupied the street for an entire block, from Zimmer Strasse on the near, Communist side, to Koch Strasse, which was free.

Coming closer, they saw people pouring out of the Stadtmitte subway station, swelling the crowd. There was also a line of cars, their drivers clearly unsure whether to approach the checkpoint or not. Lili sensed the feeling of celebration, but she was not sure they had anything to celebrate. As far as she could see, the gates were not open.

Many people held back, just out of range of the floodlights, afraid to show their faces; but the bolder ones approached nearer, committing the criminal offense of "unwarrantable intrusion into a border area," despite the risk of arrest and a sentence of three years in a labor camp.

The street narrowed as it approached the checkpoint, and the crowd thickened. Lili and her family pushed through to the front. Before them, under lights as bright as day, they could see the red-and-white gates for pedestrians and cars, the lounging border guards with their guns, the customs buildings, and the watchtowers rising over it all. Inside a glass-walled command post, an officer was talking on the telephone, making large, frustrated arm-waving gestures as he spoke.

To the left and right of the checkpoint, stretching away along Koch Strasse in both directions, was the hated Wall. Lili felt a sickening lurch in her stomach. This was the edifice that for most of her life had split her family into two halves that almost never met. She hated the Wall even more than she hated Hans Hoffmann.

Lili said aloud: "Has anyone tried to walk through?"

A woman next to her said angrily: "They turn you away. They say you need a visa from a police station. But I went to the police station and they didn't know anything about it."

A month ago, the woman would have shrugged her shoulders at this typical bureaucratic foul-up and gone home, but tonight things were different. She was still here, unsatisfied, protesting. No one was going home.

The people around Lili broke into a rhythmic chant: "Open up! Open up!"

When they trailed off, Lili thought she could hear chanting from the far side. She strained her ears. What were they saying? Eventually she made it out: "Come over! Come over!" She realized that West Berliners, too, must be gathering at checkpoints.

What was going to happen? How would this end?

A line of half a dozen vans came along Zimmer Strasse to the checkpoint, and fifty or sixty armed border guards got out.

Standing beside Lili, Werner said grimly: "Reinforcements."

. . .

Dimka and Natalya sat on the black leather chairs in Gorbachev's office feeling excited and tense. Gorbachev's strategy, of letting the Eastern European satellites go their own way, had led to a crisis that seemed about to boil over. This could be either dangerous or hopeful. Perhaps it was both.

For Dimka the issue was, as always, the sort of world his grandchildren would grow up in. Grigor, his son with Nina, was already married; Dimka and Natalya's daughter, Katya, was at university; both would probably have children in the next few years. What did the future hold for those kids? Was old-fashioned Communism really finished? Dimka still did not know.

Dimka said to Gorbachev: "Thousands of people are gathering at the Berlin Wall checkpoints. If the East German government does not open the gates, there will be riots."

"That's not our problem," said Gorbachev. It was a litany. He always said it. "I want to speak to Chancellor Kohl of West Germany," he went on.

Natalya said: "He's in Poland tonight."

"Get him on the phone as soon as you can—not later than tomorrow. I don't want him to start talking about German reunification. That would escalate the crisis. The opening of the Wall is probably all the destabilization that East Germany can deal with right now."

He was dead right, Dimka thought. If the border was opened, a united Germany could not be far in the future; but it was better not to raise such an inflammatory issue right now.

"I'll get on to the West Germans right away," said Natalya. "Anything else?"

"No, thank you."

Natalya and Dimka stood up. Gorbachev still had not

told them what to do about the immediate crisis. Dimka said: "What if Egon Krenz calls from East Berlin?"

"Don't wake me up."

Dimka and Natalya left the room.

Outside, Dimka said: "If he doesn't do something soon, it will be too late."

"Too late for what?" Natalya asked.

"Too late to save Communism."

.   .   .

Maria Summers was at Jacky Jakes's home in Prince George's County, having early supper with her godson, Jack. The TV was on, and she saw Jasper Murray, in a coat and scarf, reporting from Berlin. He was on the western, free side of Checkpoint Charlie, standing in a crowd near the little Allied guard post that had been built in the middle of Friedrich Strasse, beside a sign that said YOU ARE LEAVING THE AMERICAN SECTOR in four languages. Behind him she could see floodlights and watchtowers.

Jasper said: "The crisis of Communism is reaching a new peak of tension here tonight. After weeks of demonstrations, the East German government today announced the opening of the border with the West—but it seems no one has told the border guards or the passport police. So thousands of Berliners are gathering on both sides of the infamous Wall, demanding to exercise their brand-new right to cross over, while the government does nothing—and the armed guards grow increasingly nervous."

Jack finished his sandwich and went off for his bath. "He's nine years old, and newly shy," Jacky said with a wry smile. "He tells me he's too old to be bathed by his grandmother."

Maria was fascinated by the news from Berlin. She was remembering her lover, President Kennedy, saying to the world: "*Ich bin ein Berliner.*"

"I've spent my life working for the American government," she said to Jacky. "All that time, our aim has been to defeat Communism. But, in the end, Communism defeated itself."

"Why is it happening?" said Jacky. "I can't make it out."

"A new generation of leaders came to power, most importantly Gorbachev. When they opened the books and looked at the numbers, they said: 'If this is the best we can do, what's the point of Communism?' I feel as if I might as well never have joined the State Department—me and hundreds of other people."

"What else would you have done?"

Without thinking, Maria said: "Got married."

Jacky sat down. "George never told me your secrets," she said. "But I thought you must be in love with a married man, back in the sixties."

Maria nodded. "I've loved two men in my life," she said. "Him, and George."

Jacky said: "What happened? Did he go back to his wife? They usually do."

"No," said Maria. "He died."

"Oh, my goodness!" said Jacky. "Was it President Kennedy?"

Maria stared at her in astonishment. "How did you figure that out?"

"I didn't, I guessed."

"Please don't tell anyone! George knows, but no one else does."

"I can keep secrets." Jacky smiled. "Greg didn't know he was a father until George was six."

"Thank you. If it ever gets out I'll be all over those trashy supermarket newspapers. Goodness knows how much damage that would do to my career."

"Don't worry. But listen. George will be home soon. You two are practically living together now. You're so well matched." She lowered her voice. "I like you much better than Verena."

Maria laughed. "And my folks would have preferred George to President Kennedy, if they had known, you can bet on that."

"Do you think you and George might get married?"

"The problem is that I couldn't do my job if I were married to a congressman. I have to be bipartisan, or at least appear so."

"You'll retire one day."

"Another seven years and I'll be sixty."

"Will you marry him then?"

"If he asks me—yes."

. . .

Rebecca was at Checkpoint Charlie, on the western side, with Walli, plus Alice and Helmut. Rebecca was being careful to avoid Jasper Murray and his television cameras. She felt that joining a street mob was not the right thing for a Bundestag deputy, let alone a government minister. But she was not going to miss this. It was the greatest ever demonstration against the Wall—the Wall that had crippled the man she loved and blighted her life. The East German government could not possibly survive it—could they?

The air was cold, but she was warmed by the crowd. There were several thousand people in the stretch of Friedrich Strasse leading to the checkpoint. Rebecca and the others were near the front. Just past the Allied hut, a white line was painted across the road where Friedrich Strasse intersected Koch Strasse. The line showed where West Berlin ended and East Berlin began. On the corner, the Café Adler was doing a roaring trade.

The Wall ran along the cross street, Koch Strasse. There were in fact two walls, both made of tall concrete panels, separated by a strip of cleared land. On the Western side, the concrete was covered with colorful graffiti. Opposite where Rebecca stood was a gap beyond which were several armed guards standing in front of three red-and-white gates, two for vehicles and one for pedestrians. Behind the gates were three watchtowers. Rebecca could see soldiers behind the glass windows, scanning the crowd malevolently through binoculars.

Some of the people near Rebecca were talking to the guards, imploring them to let the people through from the East. The guards did not respond. An officer came up to the crowd and tried to explain that there were as yet no new regulations about travel from the East. No one believed him: they had seen it on TV!

The press of the crowd was irresistible, and gradually Rebecca was forced forward until she crossed the white line and found herself technically in East Berlin. The guards looked on helplessly.

After a while the guards retreated behind the gates. Rebecca was astounded. East German soldiers did not normally withdraw from a crowd: they controlled it, using whatever brutality was necessary.

Now the crossroads was clear of guards, and the crowd continued to edge forward. Either side of them, the double wall dead-ended in a short cross-wall linking inner and outer barriers and blocking access to the cleared strip. To Rebecca's amazement, two bold protesters climbed the wall and sat on the rounded upper edges of the concrete panels.

Guards approached them and said: "Please come down."

The climbers politely refused.

Rebecca's heart was thudding. The climbers were in East Berlin—as was she—and so could be shot by the guards for transgressing the Wall, as so many others had been in the last twenty-eight years.

But there was no shooting. Instead, several other people climbed the Wall in different places and sat on top, dangling their legs either side, defying the guards to do something about it.

The guards returned to their positions behind the gates.

This was amazing. By Communist standards it was lawlessness, anarchy. But no one was doing anything to stop it.

Rebecca remembered that Sunday in August 1961, when she was thirty, and she had left home to walk to West Berlin and found all the crossing points blocked by barbed wire. The barrier had now been there for half her lifetime. Could that era be coming to an end at last? She longed for it with all her heart.

The crowd was now in open defiance of the Wall, the guards, and the East German regime. And the mood of the guards was changing, Rebecca saw. Some talked to the protesters, which was forbidden. One protester reached out and snatched a guard's cap, putting it on his own head. The guard said: "Please may I have it back? I need it or I'll be in trouble." The protester good-naturedly handed it back.

Rebecca looked at her wristwatch. It was almost midnight.

• • •

On the eastern side, the people around Lili were chanting: "Let us go! Let us go!"

From the west side of the checkpoint came an answering chant: "Come! Come! Come!"

The crowd had inched closer to the guards, minute by minute, until now they were within touching distance of the gates, and the guards had retreated inside the compound.

Behind Lili a throng of tens of thousands, and a line of cars, stretched along Friedrich Strasse farther than she could see.

Everyone knew the situation was dangerously unstable. Lili feared the guards would just start firing into the crowd. They did not have enough ammunition to protect themselves from ten thousand angry people. But what else could they do?

In the next instant, Lili found out.

Suddenly an officer appeared and shouted: "*Alles auf!*"

All the gates swung open at once.

A roar went up from the waiting crowd, and they surged forward. Lili struggled to stay near her family as everyone flooded through the pedestrian and vehicle gateways. Running, stumbling, shouting and screaming for joy, they passed through the compound. The gates on the far side were also open. They surged through, and East met West.

People were weeping, hugging, and kissing. The waiting crowd had bunches of flowers and bottles of champagne. The noise of rejoicing was deafening.

Lili looked around. Her parents were close behind her. Karolin was just in front. She said: "I wonder where Walli and Rebecca are?"

.   .   .

Evie Williams's return to America was a triumph. She got a standing ovation on the first night of *A Doll's House* on Broadway. Ibsen's bleak, introspective drama was perfect for the brooding intensity of her best acting.

When at last the audience tired of applauding and left the theater Dave, Beep, and their sixteen-year-old son, John Lee, made their way backstage to join the crowd of admirers. Evie's dressing room was full of people and flowers, and there were several bottles of champagne on ice. But, strangely, the people were silent and the champagne was unopened.

There was a TV set in one corner, and most of the cast was crowded around it, silent, watching the news from Berlin.

Dave said: "What is it? What's happening?"

. . .

Cam was in his office at Langley with Tim Tedder, watching television and drinking Scotch. Jasper Murray was on the screen, live from Berlin, yelling excitedly: "The gates are open and the East Germans are coming! They're flooding through in their hundreds, in their thousands! This is a historic day! The Berlin Wall has fallen down!"

Cam muted the sound. "Would you believe it?"

Tedder held up his glass in a toast. "The end of Communism."

"It's what we've been working toward all these years," said Cam.

Tedder shook his head skeptically. "Everything we did was completely ineffective. Despite all our efforts Vietnam, Cuba, and Nicaragua became Communist countries. Look at other places where we tried to prevent Communism: Iran, Guatemala, Chile, Cambodia, Laos . . . None of them does us much credit. And now Eastern Europe is abandoning Communism with no help from us."

"All the same we should think of a way to take the credit. Or let the president take it, at least."

"Bush has been in office less than a year, and he's been behind the curve all along," Tim said. "He can't claim to have caused this: if anything, he tried to slow it down."

"Reagan, maybe?" Cam mused.

"Be sensible," said Tedder. "Reagan didn't do this. Gorbachev did it. Him and the price of oil. And the fact that Communism never really worked anyway."

"What about Star Wars?"

"A weapons system that was never going to get beyond the science fiction stage, as everyone knew, including the Soviets."

"Reagan made that speech, though. 'Mr. Gorbachev, tear down this wall.' Remember?"

"I remember. Are you going to tell people that Communism collapsed because Reagan made a speech? They'll never believe that."

"Sure they will," said Cam.

. . .

The first person Rebecca saw was her father, a tall man with thinning fair hair, a neatly knotted tie visible in the V of his coat. He looked older. "Look!" she screamed at Walli. "It's Father!"

Walli's face broke into a wide grin. "So it is," he said. "I didn't think we'd find them in this multitude." He put his arm around Rebecca's shoulders and together they pushed through the crush. Helmut and Alice followed close behind.

Movement was frustratingly difficult. The crowd was thick, and everyone was dancing, jumping for joy, and embracing strangers.

Rebecca saw her mother next to her father, then Lili and Karolin. "They haven't seen us yet," she said to Walli. "Wave!"

There was no point in shouting. Everyone was shouting. Walli said: "This is the biggest street party in the world."

A woman with her hair in curlers cannoned into Rebecca, and she would have fallen but that Walli's arm supported her.

Then the two groups at last reached one another. Rebecca threw herself into her father's arms. She felt his lips on her forehead. The familiar kiss, the touch of his slightly bristly chin, the faint fragrance of his aftershave, filled her heart to bursting.

Walli hugged their mother. Then they swapped. Rebecca could not see for tears. They embraced Lili and Karolin. Karolin kissed Alice, saying: "I didn't think I'd see you again so soon. I didn't know if I'd see you again ever."

Rebecca looked at Walli as he greeted Karolin. He took both of her hands, and they smiled at one another. Walli said simply: "I'm so happy to see you again, Karolin. So happy."

"Me, too," she said.

They formed a ring, arms around each other, there in the middle of the street, in the middle of the night, in the middle of Europe. "Here we are," said Carla, looking around the circle at her family, smiling broadly, happy. "Together again, at last. After all that." She paused, then said it again. "After all that."

EPILOGUE

November 4, 2008

They were a strange family group, Maria reflected, looking around the living room of Jacky Jakes's house at a few seconds before midnight.

There was Jacky herself, Maria's mother-in-law, eighty-nine years old and feistier than ever.

There was George, Maria's husband for the last twelve years, now white-haired at seventy-two. Maria had been a bride for the first time at the age of sixty, which would have embarrassed her if she had not been so happy.

There was George's ex-wife, Verena, undoubtedly the most beautiful sixty-nine-year-old woman in America. She was with her second husband, Lee Montgomery.

Then there was George's son with Verena: Jack, a lawyer, age twenty-eight, with his wife and their pretty five-year-old daughter, Marga.

They were watching TV. The broadcast was coming from a park in Chicago where two hundred forty thousand ecstatically happy people had gathered.

Onstage was an African American family: a handsome father, a beautiful mother, and two sweet little girls. It was election night, and Barack Obama had won.

Michelle Obama and the girls left the stage, and the president-elect went to the microphone and said: "Hello, Chicago."

Jacky, the matriarch of the Jakes family, said: "Hush, now, everybody. Listen up." She turned up the volume.

Obama wore a dark gray suit and a burgundy tie. Behind

him, rippling in a gentle breeze, were more American flags than Maria could count.

Speaking slowly, pausing after each phrase, Obama said: "If there is anyone out there who still doubts that America is a place where all things are possible, who still wonders if the dream of our founders is alive in our time, who still questions the power of our democracy—tonight is your answer."

Little Marga came up to Maria where she sat on the couch. "Granny Maria," she said.

Maria lifted the child onto her lap and said: "Hush, now, baby, everyone wants to listen to the new president."

Obama said: "It's the answer spoken by young and old, rich and poor, Democrat and Republican, black, white, Hispanic, Asian, Native American, gay, straight, disabled and not disabled—Americans who sent a message to the world that we have never been just a collection of individuals, or a collection of red states and blue states: we are, and always will be, the *United* States of America."

"Granny Maria," Marga whispered again. "Look at Granddad."

Maria looked at her husband, George. He was watching the television, but his lined brown face was streaming with tears. He was wiping them away with a big white handkerchief, but as soon as he dried his eyes the tears came again.

Marga said: "Why is Granddad crying?"

Maria knew why. He was crying for Bobby, and Martin, and Jack. For four Sunday school girls. For Medgar Evers. For all the freedom fighters, dead and alive.

"Why?" Marga said again.

"Honey," said Maria, "it's a long story."

Time's glory is to calm contending kings
To unmask falsehood and bring truth to light
To stamp the seal of time in aged things
To wake the morn and sentinel the night
To wrong the wronger till he render right

To ruinate proud buildings with thy hours
And smear with dust their glittering golden towers

—Shakespeare, *The Rape of Lucrece*

AVAILABLE FROM PENGUIN BOOKS

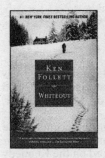  

PENGUIN BOOKS

Acknowledgments

My principal history adviser for The Century Trilogy has been Richard Overy. Other academic historians who helped with this volume were Clayborne Carson, Mary Fulbrook, Claire McCallum, and Matthias Reiss.

Numerous people who lived through the events of the era also helped me, either by checking my first draft or giving me interviews, especially: Mimi Alford on the Kennedy White House; Peter Asher on being a pop star; Jay Coburn and Howard Stringer on Vietnam; Frank Gannon on the Nixon White House, along with his colleagues Jim Cavanaugh, Tod Hullin, and Geoff Shephard; Congressman John Lewis on civil rights; and Angela Spizig and Annemarie Behnke on life in Germany. As always, Dan Starer of Research for Writers in New York City helped me find my advisers.

On my research trip to the American South my guides were: Barry McNealy in Birmingham, Alabama; Ron Flood in Atlanta, Georgia; and Ismail Naskai in Washington, DC. Ray Young at Fredericksburg's Greyhound station kindly dug out photographs from the sixties.

My friends Johnny Clare and Chris Manners read the first draft and made many useful criticisms. Charlotte Quelch corrected numerous errors.

My family helped me in immeasurable ways. Dr. Kim Turner advised me on many matters, especially medical. Jann Turner and Barbara Follett read the first draft and made perceptive and helpful comments.

Editors and agents who read the draft included Amy Berkower, Cherise Fisher, Leslie Gelbman, Phyllis Grann, Neil Nyren, Susan Opie, Jeremy Trevathan, and, as ever, Al Zuckerman.